詞性×例句×萬用延伸句型，
輕鬆學習零負擔

User's Guide 使用說明

滿分攻略 ① **把握時間快速投入學習**

　　面對滿滿的 7000 單字襲捲而來、毫無頭緒的你請別擔心，本書特別依照難易度將所有單字劃分成六個等級，學習者只要稍微翻找書頁，就能立刻找出適合自己的程度，迅速埋首書堆、潛心學習！

滿分攻略 ② **一字多用就可事半功倍**

　　看到密密麻麻文字就會兩眼昏花、慌張害怕？別擔心，本書按照字母排序，詳細列出每個單字的常用詞義與詞性，且根據不同詞性，給予專屬例句示範用法，甚至補充了同、反義字，常用片語，運用聯想法就能一次帶走、相當方便！

滿分攻略 ③ **紅色膠片幫助快速背誦**

　　手寫單字卡寫到手軟頭痛嗎？本書貼心附贈紅膠片，套用在頁面上，只會顯示出英文單字與例句、閱讀與背誦的過程中，先看英文、回想中文意思，對單字意思不熟悉、或不懂例句意思時，再移開紅色膠片看中文解釋，貼心設計，幫學習者事半功倍！

滿分攻略❹ 抓住重點就能運用自如

閱讀文章總是很順利，但碰到寫作就鬼打牆的你請別擔心，只要筆記眾多精心挑選的萬用例句，透過反覆閱讀，將他們的梗概熟記腦中，勤加練習，在考場上，即能下筆如有神助，發揮超乎想像的寫作實力！

滿分攻略❺ 延伸說法**擴充實用知識**

「怎麼單字加個介系詞就看不懂了」、「如何學到日常生活用語」，充滿好奇心的你請別擔心，「實用片語用語」讓你可以跳脫課本的範疇，更補充了許多生活和網路用語，隨時隨地都可以看懂英文、運用英文！

滿分攻略❻ 多聽多說**克服心理障礙**

發現外國人迎面而來就想避開、學了英文卻不敢開口的你請別擔心，單字旁標出了自然發音的重音節點，KK 音標的發音標示，還收錄了外師親錄的單字 MP3，只要用手機一掃 QR code，就能無時無刻置身在英語環境中！

Preface 前言

各位讀者大家好！

不論是英文初學者，或是接觸英文已有一段時間的人，大家應該都知道單字的重要性，一個單字可以有很多意思、很多詞性，也可以組成各式各樣的片語，或是用單字書寫千變萬化的句型。但是，正因為單字無所不在、範圍又多又廣，所以難以統整、歸納出一套清楚、有效的學習方法。

由教育部公布的升大學必備七千單字，替國、高中生訂定了一個範圍，因此學習英文單字不再是無邊無際、難以掌握的。然而，「七千」如此龐大的數字，反而讓孩子們聽了十分卻步，為了應付大考，許多人只好開始拿著單字本硬記死背，好不容易記下全部單字的所有意思，卻被它的詞性和字義弄得頭昏腦脹；學會了字義跟詞性，卻因為不懂文法、句型結構，所以還是寫不出完整的句子；或者是在閱讀測驗中，看到似曾相識的單字，組成片語、慣用語後卻猜不透意思，因此備感挫折。

為了讓眾多找不到方法來有效學習的人，能在背單字時，也能同時將文法和句型融會貫通，每個單字都會透過有條理的例句示範和重點提示，幫助學習者更清楚 了解用法。本書將 7000 單字依難易度分為六個 level，讀者可以依照自己的程度選擇 level，快速進入學習。內容方面，每個單字不只

標上音節點、音標輔助發音，還有外籍老師親錄的音檔，發音正確且道地，讀者可以隨時聽、隨時培養語感。並且，所有的單字都按照詞性，羅列出最常使用的字義，還搭配上同、反義字，兩相比較，更能清楚用法，更能利用連想法來充實字彙量。

　　如果一個單字只有一個例句，那有三種詞性的話，又要從何得知另外兩種詞性的用法呢？每個單字不同詞性的例句都分開撰寫，學習者可以一目瞭然，每個單字 在不同詞性時所擺放的位置、搭配何種介系詞、藉以辨別它們的使用時機。除此之外，只背單字是絕對不夠的。懂得如何在句子中、文章裡、對話時靈活 運用，才是真正的學會一個單字。因此，絕不能把文法、句型、片語和單字拆開來、當作四個不同的領域看，必須同時並進、同步學習，才能完整理解英文的語言結構。例句中的文法和句型特別抓出，補充相關的解說，無論是時態、動詞變化、字詞解析、特殊句型、延伸的片語用語，都在這個部分有精細的說明，並且透過適時地重複提點同樣的觀念，讓學習者可以一再複習、掌握技巧、並運用自如。學習語言若只是坐在桌前苦讀，那一定十分枯燥乏味，如果可以多方蒐集資訊，多看報章雜誌、書籍電影、多聽廣播或音樂，想必能替艱苦的學習之路增添不少趣味，這也是為什麼本書補充許多現代社會常會用到的生活片語、用語的原因，畢竟，語言絕不只是考試的內容，更是人與人之間溝通的媒介。

　　期許這本書能開始輕鬆無負擔地學習 7000 英文單字，開啟學習英文、與世界接軌的另一扇大門！

Contents 目錄

Level 3
駕輕就熟、更上一層樓——
累積實力3200單字

Level 4
自我勉勵、越背越上手——
提升程度4200單字

Level 1

輕鬆學習、入門無負擔——
掌握基礎1000單字

Level 1

輕鬆學習、入門無負擔——

掌握基礎1000單字

[Aa]

a/an [ə/æn]　🔊 Track 0001

冠 一、一個

▶There is a box of green apples on the floor for you to eat.
地板上有一箱青蘋果是要給你吃的。

a·ble [ˈebl]　🔊 Track 0002

形 能幹的、有能力的　同 capable 有能力的

▶She is able to speak German fluently（流利地）.
她能夠很流利地講德文。

a·bout [əˈbaʊt]　🔊 Track 0003

副 大約　介 關於　同 concerning 關於

▶副 Would you like to come to our party at about five p.m.
tomorrow? 你明天下午大約五點的時候願意來參加我們的
派對嗎？

▶介 I talked to him about the contract.
我和他談論關於合約的事情。

a·bove [əˈbʌv]　🔊 Track 0004

形 上面的　副 在上面　介 在……上面　名 上面

▶形 You can write to us at the above address.
你可以寫信到上面的地址給我們。

▶副 There are several bags of biscuits（餅乾）on the shelf（架
子）above. 上面的架子有幾袋餅乾。

▶介 There are many white birds flying above the blue sea.
藍色海面上有許多白色的鳥兒飛翔著。

▶名 In addition（附加）to all of the above, there is something
else I want to talk about.
除了上述事情之外，我還想說點別的事情。

ac·cord·ing [əˈkɔrdɪŋ]　🔊 Track 0005

介 根據……

▶According to the weather report, it will rain today. So, let's
bring the umbrella with us. 天氣預報說今天會下雨，所以我們
還是隨身帶著雨傘吧！

a·cross [əˈkrɔs]　🔊 Track 0006

副 橫過　介 穿過、橫過　同 cross 越過

▶副 The gap is too wide; I can't jump across.
這條溝太寬了，我跳不過去。

▶介 It is too dangerous（危險的）for a kid to walk across the
street by himself. 要一個小孩獨自過馬路太危險了。

文法字詞解析
a box of 意思是「一箱」，可以做為單位
量詞用在可數或不可數名詞之前。

萬用延伸句型
There is / are... 可放在句首，指出「某地
點有某物」。

文法字詞解析
副詞「fluently（流利地）」由形容詞
fluent 加上副詞字尾 ly 組成，用來修飾動
詞 speak。

文法字詞解析
above、on、over 都可用來表示「某物
在某物上面」，但 above 通常是指兩物
沒有接觸，而 on 則是兩物有接觸，例如
「在桌上 on the table」，over 則可以用
在某物越過或覆蓋在另一物上。

文法字詞解析
will 加上原形動詞用來表示未來發生的事
件、動作。

act [ækt] 　　🔊 Track 0007

名 行為、行動、法案　動 行動、扮演、下判決

▶名 An act asks us to not kill the animals in danger.
有一項法令要求人們不要殘殺瀕臨絕種的動物。

▶動 He is very good at acting. 他很擅長演戲。

ac·tion [`ækʃən] 　　🔊 Track 0008

名 行動、活動　同 behavior 行為、舉止

▶Many young people enjoy watching action films very much.
很多年輕人非常喜歡看動作片。

ac·tor [`æktə] 　　🔊 Track 0009

名 男演員　同 performer 演出者

▶He has become an excellent（優秀的）public speaker.
他成為了一名優秀的演說者。

ac·tress [`æktrɪs] 　　🔊 Track 0010

名 女演員　同 performer 演出者

▶The actress won the academy award for her latest movie.
女演員因為最新作品贏得奧斯卡獎。

add [æd] 　　🔊 Track 0011

動 增加　反 subtract 減去

▶Would you like to add some pepper in the soup?
你要不要在湯裡加些胡椒呢？

add·ress [ə`drɛs] 　　🔊 Track 0012

名 住址、致詞、講話　動 發表演說、對……說話
同 speech 演說

▶名 It will be too difficult for me to find you if you do not tell me your address.
如果你不告訴我你的地址，那麼我就很難找到你了。

▶動 It is too early for the president（總統）to announce his position on this matter now. 總統現在對民眾公開他對這件事情的立場還為時過早。

a·dult [ə`dʌlt] 　　🔊 Track 0013

形 成年的、成熟的　名 成年人　反 child 小孩

▶形 Don't let him watch that adult movie! He's only six!
別讓他看那部成人片，他才六歲耶！

▶名 We're all adults here; we have to be responsible for our own behaviors. 我們都是成年人了，要為了自己的行為負責。

a·fraid [ə`fred] 　　🔊 Track 0014

形 害怕的、擔心的　反 brave 勇敢的

▶Let's get on the bus right away. I am so afraid of being late.
我們快上公車吧，我很怕會遲到。

af·ter [`æftə] 　　🔊 Track 0015

形 以後的　副 以後、後來　連 在……以後　介 在……之後
反 before 在……之前

▶形 I never saw him again in the years after.
在之後的幾年我再也沒見過他了。

文法字詞解析
enjoy 後面若要接動詞，形式必須是動名詞（V-ing）。

文法字詞解析
此處使用現在完成式 has become，說明從過去就已經開始的動作，持續到現在才完成。現在完成式的形式是助動詞 have / has + 過去分詞 p.p.。

萬用延伸句型
What do you think about / of...? 此句型為固定用法，用於徵詢他人的意見。

萬用延伸句型
Would you like to... 的句型用於有禮貌的請示他人意見。

萬用延伸句型
用現在代替未來的條件句型：S. + V.（未來式）If + S. + V.

萬用延伸句型
There's nothing to... 沒有什麼好……的

Level **1** 輕鬆學習、入門無負擔——掌握基礎1000單字

Level **2**

Level **3**

Level **4**

Level **5**

Level **6**

▶ 副 He arrived shortly（不久）after.
不久後他就抵達了。

▶ 連 I'll call you after I get home.
我到家以後會打給你。

▶ 介 He showed up after dinner.
他在晚餐後出現了。

af·ter·noon [ˈæftəˈnun]　◀℈ *Track 0016*
名 下午　反 morning 上午
▶ He won't be here in the afternoon. 他下午不會在這裡。

a·gain [əˈgɛn]　◀℈ *Track 0017*
副 又、再
▶ Could you visit me again this evening and tell me more details about this matter? 晚上你能再與我碰面，告訴我細節嗎？

a·gainst [əˈgɛnst]　◀℈ *Track 0018*
介 反對、不同意　同 versus 對抗
▶ Many people are against his plan.
很多人都反對他的計畫。

age [edʒ]　◀℈ *Track 0019*
名 年齡　動 使變老　同 mature 使成熟
▶ 名 Can you tell me your age? 你可以告訴我你的年齡嗎？
▶ 動 How she's aged these years! 她這幾年變老了不少啊！

a·go [əˈgo]　◀℈ *Track 0020*
副 以前　同 since 以前
▶ How did she look when you met her in the library a week ago?
一星期前你在圖書館遇見她的時候，她看起來怎麼樣啊？

a·gree [əˈgri]　◀℈ *Track 0021*
動 同意、贊成　反 disagree 不同意
▶ The boss agreed to let him go home early.
老闆同意讓他早點回家。

a·gree·ment [əˈgrimənt]　◀℈ *Track 0022*
名 同意、一致、協議　反 disagreement 意見不一
▶ We all nodded in agreement at his suggestion.
對於他的提議，我們都很同意地點頭。

a·head [əˈhɛd]　◀℈ *Track 0023*
副 向前的、在……前面　反 behind 在……後面
▶ If you are interested in this English learning program, go ahead and sign up for it.
如果你對這個英語學習課程有興趣，就去登記吧。

air [ɛr]　◀℈ *Track 0024*
名 空氣、氣氛　同 atmosphere 氣氛
▶ The air quality in the city is bad.
這城市的空氣品質很糟。

文法字詞解析
若要說精確的「某一天的下午」，介係詞要用 on，例如：on the afternoon of 12th June（六月十二日的下午），若沒有精確的時間，則介係詞用 in。

萬用延伸句型
「How + adj. / adv. S. + V.！」為感嘆句句型，用來表示說話者驚訝、驚嘆。

文法字詞解析
let 所引導的祈使語氣，有「讓某人做某事」的意思。後面需要接受格，再接原形動詞，並且動詞前不加不定詞 to。

文法字詞解析
air quality = 空氣品質
air pollution = 空氣汙染

air·mail [ˈɛr͵mel] 🔊 *Track 0025*

名 航空郵件
▶How long will it take if you send it by airmail?
　如果你用航空郵件寄它的話，要花費多久時間呢？

萬用延伸句型
How long will / does it take... ……要多久？

air·plane/plane 🔊 *Track 0026*
[ˈɛr͵plen]/[plen]

名 飛機
▶We don't have enough money to go there by plane.
　我們沒有足夠的錢搭飛機去那裡。

文法字詞解析
搭乘交通工具的介係詞要用 by。若要表示「用走的」的話，可以說 on foot 或 by walking。

air·port [ˈɛr͵port] 🔊 *Track 0027*

名 機場
▶There is a large airport in the area where I live.
　在我住的地區有一個很大的機場。

Level
1
掌握基礎1000單字——
輕鬆學習、入門無負擔

all [ɔl] 🔊 *Track 0028*

形 所有的、全部的 副 全部、全然 名 全部 同 whole 全部
▶形 All my relatives came to visit me in the hospital.
　我所有的親戚都來醫院探望我。
▶副 I've been waiting all day for your call.
　我等你打來等了一整天。
▶名 All agree that he's probably lying.
　全部人都同意他大概在說謊。

文法字詞解析
have / has been V-ing 是現在完成進行式的用法，說明過去開始的某一個動作，一直持續到現在，而且還在進行中。

al·low [əˈlaʊ] 🔊 *Track 0029*

動 允許、准許 同 permit 允許
▶Her mom won't allow her to keep a cat.
　她媽媽不准她養貓。

al·most [ˈɔl͵most] 🔊 *Track 0030*

副 幾乎、差不多 同 nearly 幾乎、差不多
▶It's almost dark now. 天幾乎要黑了。

a·lone [əˈlon] 🔊 *Track 0031*

形 單獨的 副 單獨地
▶形 He is always alone. 他總是一個人。
▶副 I don't mind going to a movie alone.
　我不介意單獨一人去看電影。

Level
2

Level
3

Level
4

a·long [əˈlɔŋ] 🔊 *Track 0032*

副 向前 介 沿著 同 forward 向前
▶副 The staff asked people in the line to move along.
　工作人員要求隊伍中的人往前進。
▶介 My girlfriend came along with me last night.
　昨晚我女友跟我一起來。

Level
5

Level
6

al·ready [ɔlˈrɛdɪ] 🔊 *Track 0033*

副 已經 反 yet 還（沒）
▶Everyone has already left the office at seven.
　七點時大家都已經離開辦公室了。

文法字詞解析
at 若要作為時間介係詞，後面必須要加精確的時刻。

al·so [ˈɔlso] 🔊 *Track 0034*

副 也 同 too 也
▶You can also just buy the book from the store.
　你也可以就在商店買這本書。

al·ways [ˈɔlwez] 🔊 *Track 0035*

副 總是 反 seldom 不常、很少
▶He is always changing his mind.
　他總是反覆無常。

am [æm] 🔊 *Track 0036*

動 是
▶I am so tired after a long day of work.
　工作這麼長的一天，我已經很累了。

a·mong [əˈmʌŋ] 🔊 *Track 0037*

介 在……之中 同 amid 在……之間
▶She's my favorite among all my cousins.
　在我的表兄弟姊妹中，她是我最喜歡的一個。

and [ænd] 🔊 *Track 0038*

連 和
▶Both the English teacher and the Chinese teacher agree to this plan. 英文和國文老師都同意這個計畫。

an·ger [ˈæŋɡɚ] 🔊 *Track 0039*

名 憤怒 動 激怒 同 irritation 激怒
▶名 She could barely control（控制）her anger when she heard the news.
　她聽到消息時，幾乎控制不了憤怒。
▶動 Don't try to anger the boars. They'll attack you.
　別惹那些野豬，牠們會攻擊你。

an·gry [ˈæŋɡrɪ] 🔊 *Track 0040*

形 生氣的 同 furious 狂怒的
▶I think he will be very angry with you.
　我想他會對你很生氣。

an·i·mal [ˈænəml] 🔊 *Track 0041*

形 動物的 名 動物 同 beast 動物、野獸
▶形 It's not healthy to cook with animal fats every day. 每天都用動物脂肪來烹調並不健康。
▶名 What's your favorite animal in the zoo?
　你最喜歡動物園的哪一種動物？

an·oth·er [əˈnʌðɚ] 🔊 *Track 0042*

形 另一的、再一的 代 另一、再一
▶形 Let's take another way to the airport, shall we?
　我們從另外一條路去機場，好嗎？
▶代 I don't like this one. Let's choose（選擇）another one.
　我不是很喜歡這一個，我們選擇另外一個吧。

an·swer [ˈænsɚ] 🔊 Track 0043

名 答案、回答 動 回答、回報 同 response 回答

▶名 Would you like to know the answer to this question?
你想不想知道這個問題的答案呢？

▶動 Would you like me to answer the door for you?
你要我幫你去應門嗎？

萬用延伸句型
answer the phone call 接電話；
make a phone call 打電話

ant [ænt] 🔊 Track 0044

名 螞蟻

▶Killing ants is his favorite hobby. 殺螞蟻是他最喜歡的嗜好。

an·y [ˈɛnɪ] 🔊 Track 0045

形 任何的 代 任何一個

▶形 Do you have any pets? 你有任何寵物嗎？

▶代 I looked for a grocery store in the small village, but didn't find any. 我在小鎮裡找雜貨店，但一間都沒找到。

an·y·thing [ˈɛnɪˌθɪŋ] 🔊 Track 0046

代 任何事物

▶Is there anything important you want to tell me?
你是不是有什麼重要的事要告訴我？

ape [ep] 🔊 Track 0047

名 猿

▶How often do you go to the zoo to see the cute apes?
你多久去動物園看一次可愛的猿猴呢？

萬用延伸句型
How often do you...? 你有多常／多久一次……？

ap·pear [əˈpɪr] 🔊 Track 0048

動 出現、顯得 反 disappear 消失

▶My friend has not appeared at the award ceremony yet.
我的朋友還沒有出現在頒獎典禮上。

文法字詞解析
not...yet 還沒，通常與完成式連用。

ap·ple [ˈæp!] 🔊 Track 0049

名 蘋果

▶There are many apples on the big trees in our garden.
我家花園裡的大樹上長滿了蘋果。

A·pril/Apr. [ˈeprəl] 🔊 Track 0050

名 四月

▶My birthday is in April. 我的生日在四月。

文法字詞解析
年份、季節、月份前面要加介係詞 in。

are [ɑr] 🔊 Track 0051

動 是

▶There are a lot of good teachers in our school.
我們學校有很多優秀的老師。

文法字詞解析
a lot of + 可數／不可數名詞，表示「很多」。

ar·e·a [ˈɛrɪə] 🔊 Track 0052

名 地區、領域、面積、方面 同 region 地區

▶How long will it take for us to clean up the garbage all around this area? 我們要清理這個地區的垃圾要花費多久時間？

Level 1 輕鬆學習、入門無負擔——掌握基礎1000單字

Level 2
Level 3
Level 4
Level 5
Level 6

arm [ɑrm] 🔊 *Track 0053*

名 手臂 動 武裝、裝備

▶名 His arms are much longer than mine.
他的手臂比我的長多了。

▶動 You need to arm yourself before heading out into battle（戰鬥）. 你出發去戰鬥前得先把自己武裝好。

ar·my [ˈɑrmɪ] 🔊 *Track 0054*

名 軍隊、陸軍 同 military 軍隊

▶Would you like to join the army? 你要不要加入軍隊啊？

a·round [əˈraʊnd] 🔊 *Track 0055*

副 大約、在周圍 介 在……周圍

▶副 I'm just looking around the area.
我只是在這一區到處看看而已。

▶介 We have to take the road around the building.
我們得走繞過這棟大樓的那條路。

art [ɑrt] 🔊 *Track 0056*

名 藝術

▶My sister takes art classes here. 我姐姐在這裡上美術課。

as [æz] 🔊 *Track 0057*

副 像……一樣、如同 連 當……時候 介 作為
代 與……相同的人事物

▶副 Let's move on to the next topic as quickly as possible.
我們盡快換到下個主題吧。

▶連 The phone rang just as I was leaving.
當我正要離開時電話正好響了。

▶介 He works here as a clerk. 他作為職員在這裡工作。

▶代 My son did as I said. 我兒子照著我說的去做了。

文法字詞解析
1. as soon as possible 越快越好，儘快
2. as...as 用來比較兩個事物，表示同等、一樣。使用在句中的形式是：S1. V. as adj. / adv. as S2.

ask [æsk] 🔊 *Track 0058*

動 問、要求 同 question 問

▶There are many kinds of questions for the students to ask.
學生們有各式各樣的問題要問。

at [æt] 🔊 *Track 0059*

介 在

▶Would you like to see her at the end of the meeting?
你想在會議結束時見見她嗎？

Au·gust/Aug. [ˈɔgʌst] 🔊 *Track 0060*

名 八月

▶An important leader will take part in the meeting in August.
將有一名重要元首參加八月份的會議。

文法字詞解析
take part in... 參加……活動

aunt/aunt·ie/aunt·y 🔊 *Track 0061*

[ænt]/[ˈænti]/[ˈæntɪ]

名 伯母、姑、嬸、姨

▶How long will you stay at your aunt's home in the country?
你會在你鄉下姑媽的家住多久？

au·tumn [ˋɔtəm]
🔊 *Track 0062*

名 秋季、秋天
▶We like to appreciate the maple leaves in autumn.
我們喜歡在秋天賞楓。

文法字詞解析
autumn 和 fall 都表示秋天。

a·way [əˋwe]
🔊 *Track 0063*

副 遠離、離開
▶She comes from a land far, far away.
她來自一個很遠很遠的國度。

[Bb]

ba·by [ˋbebɪ]
🔊 *Track 0064*

形 嬰兒的　名 嬰兒　同 infant 嬰兒
▶形 What does the baby carriage（嬰兒車）you bought yesterday look like? 你昨天買的那輛嬰兒車長什麼樣子？
▶名 Have you ever seen her new baby girl?
你有見過她剛出生的小女兒嗎？

萬用延伸句型
What does sth. / sb. look like? 某物／某人長什麼樣子？

back [bæk]
🔊 *Track 0065*

形 後面的　副 向後地　名 後背、背脊　動 後退
反 front 前面、正面
▶形 There is a map of the world on the back wall.
後面的牆上有一幅世界地圖。
▶副 Let's walk back home together after school!
放學後我們一起走路回家吧！
▶名 We wrote our names on the back of the tickets so that we can distinguish（區分）them. 我們在票的背後寫上名字，這樣我們才能把它們區分開來。
▶動 He backed away as he saw the armed force.
他看到武裝軍隊便退縮了。

萬用延伸句型
...so that... ……以便……

bad [bæd]
🔊 *Track 0066*

形 壞的　反 good 好的
▶The apples have gone bad. Please throw them away.
蘋果都壞掉了，請把它們丟掉吧。

bag [bæg]
🔊 *Track 0067*

名 袋子　動 把……裝入袋中　同 pocket 口袋
▶名 Could you help me carry this bag? It's too heavy for me!
你能幫我拿這個袋子嗎？對我來說太重了。
▶動 She bagged all the leftovers（剩菜）to bring home to her dog. 她把剩菜都裝進袋子裡，以帶回家給她的狗。

萬用延伸句型
Could you help me...? 可以請你幫我……嗎？ 此句型可用在有禮貌的請求他人協助。

ball [bɔl]
🔊 *Track 0068*

名 舞會、球　同 sphere 球
▶He threw the ball at his dog. 他把球丟向他的狗。

Level 1 輕鬆學習、入門無負擔 掌握基礎1000單字

Level 2

Level 3

Level 4

Level 5

Level 6

bal·loon [bə'lun] 🔊 *Track 0069*

名 氣球 動 如氣球般膨脹

▶ 名 Many tourists came to Taitung for the International Balloon festival.
許多觀光客來台東看國際熱氣球節。

▶ 動 Trade deficits（赤字）have ballooned in recent years.
貿易逆差在近年來已經急速增大。

文法字詞解析

in recent years 近年（習慣與現在完成式連用）。

ba·nan·a [bə'nænə] 🔊 *Track 0070*

名 香蕉

▶ Would you like to buy bananas, pears（梨）or apples?
你想買香蕉、梨子、還是蘋果呢？

band [bænd] 🔊 *Track 0071*

名 帶子、隊、樂隊 動 聯合、結合 同 tie 帶子

▶ 名 There's a poster of my favorite band on the wall.
牆上有張我最喜歡的樂團的海報。

▶ 動 The settlers（移民者）banded together for protection（保護）.
移民者們聯合起來保護自己。

bank [bæŋk] 🔊 *Track 0072*

名 銀行、堤、岸

▶ Could you walk me to the nearest bank?
您可以陪我走到最近的銀行嗎？

萬用延伸句型

Could you walk me to...? 你可以陪我走去……嗎？
等同於 Could you walk with me to...?

bar [bɑr] 🔊 *Track 0073*

名 條、棒、橫木、酒吧 動 禁止、阻撓 同 block 阻擋、限制

▶ 名 Let's go to that little bar after work.
下班後我們去那個小酒吧吧。

▶ 動 The herd of about 500 ducks are barring the street.
大約有500隻的一大群鴨擋在街上。

文法字詞解析

bar 的動詞變化 bar, barred, barred

bar·ber ['bɑrbɚ] 🔊 *Track 0074*

名 理髮師 同 hairdresser 美髮師

▶ Not everyone can be a good barber.
並不是每個人都能成為一位優秀的理髮師。

base [bes] 🔊 *Track 0075*

名 基底、壘 動 以……作基礎 同 bottom 底部

▶ 名 Welcome to our secret base.
歡迎來到我們的秘密基地。

▶ 動 The movie was based on a true story.
那部電影是根據真實故事改編的。

base·ball ['bes,bɔl] 🔊 *Track 0076*

名 棒球

▶ We play baseball only on weekends.
我們只在週末打棒球。

文法字詞解析

on 後面加上時間詞的複數（例如：weekends、Thursdays）就有「每逢……」的意思，等同於 every + 時間。

bas·ic [ˋbesɪk]
◀≣ Track 0077
名 基本、要素 形 基本的 同 essential 基本的
▶名 There are some basics that you should know before you sign up. 在你報名之前，你應該瞭解一些基本事項。
▶形 After taking the course for a semester, she has some basic ideas about computer science.
修了一學期的課程之後，她對電腦科學有了基本認識。

bas·ket [ˋbæskɪt]
◀≣ Track 0078
名 籃子、籃網、得分
▶I took some eggs out of the basket. 我從籃子裡拿出一些蛋。

bas·ket·ball [ˋbæskɪtˌbɔl]
◀≣ Track 0079
名 籃球
▶How about playing basketball with us after school?
放學之後跟我們一起去打籃球怎麼樣？

萬用延伸句型
How about...? ……如何？

bat [bæt]
◀≣ Track 0080
名 蝙蝠、球棒
▶He smashed（打碎）the window with a bat.
他用球棒打碎了那扇窗戶。

bath [bæθ]
◀≣ Track 0081
名 洗澡 動 給……洗澡
▶名 Taking a warm bath before going to bed at night feels great.
晚上睡覺前洗個熱水澡感覺太棒了。
▶動 She bathed in the tub（澡盆）every night.
她每天都在澡盆裡泡澡。

bathe [beð]
◀≣ Track 0082
動 沐浴、用水洗 同 wash 洗
▶The video shows pet owners how to bathe a puppy dog without hurting their skin.
影片教導寵物飼主如何幫小狗洗澡才不會傷到牠們的皮膚。

bath·room [ˋbæθˌrum]
◀≣ Track 0083
名 浴室
▶How long does it take for you to clean the bathroom?
你打掃一次浴室要花多久時間？

be [bi]
◀≣ Track 0084
動 是、存在
▶I am only too pleased to be able to help you.
我非常高興能夠幫助你。

文法字詞解析
be 的動詞變化：
am, was, been（搭配第一人稱名詞）；
are, were, been（搭配第二人稱或複數名詞）；
is, was, been（搭配第三人稱名詞）

beach [bitʃ]
◀≣ Track 0085
名 海灘 動 拖（船）上岸 同 strand 海濱
▶名 There are a great number of people lying on the beach.
有很多人躺在海灘上。
▶動 They beached the ship on the island.
他們將船拖到島上。

Level 1 輕鬆學習、入門無負擔── 掌握基礎1000單字

Level 2

Level 3

Level 4

Level 5

Level 6

bear [bɛr] 🔊 *Track 0086*

名 熊 動 忍受、負荷、結果實、生子女 同 withstand 禁得起

▶ 名 Would you like a teddy bear or a toy dog as a birthday gift?
　你想要一隻玩具熊還是玩具狗作為生日禮物？

▶ 動 I can't bear to watch this terrible scene.
　我忍受不了看這糟糕的畫面。

文法字詞解析
bear 的動詞變化：bear, bore, born

beat [bit] 🔊 *Track 0087*

名 打、敲打聲、拍子 動 打敗、連續打擊、跳動 同 hit 打

▶ 名 Can you hear the beat of the drum（鼓）?
　你有聽到擊鼓聲嗎？

▶ 動 It's too hard for us to beat that strong team.
　要打敗那麼強的隊伍對我們來說太難了。

beau·ti·ful [ˈbjutəfəl] 🔊 *Track 0088*

形 美麗的、漂亮的 反 ugly 醜陋的

▶ There are always lots of beautiful girls and handsome（英俊的）boys in art school.
　藝術學院裡通常都有好多帥哥美女。

beau·ty [ˈbjutɪ] 🔊 *Track 0089*

名 美、美人、美的東西

▶ My mother is a natural beauty.
　我媽是個天生的美人。

be·cause [bɪˈkɔz] 🔊 *Track 0090*

連 因為 同 for 為了

▶ He was late for work because his car broke down this morning.
　他因為今早車子拋錨而上班遲到了。

文法字詞解析
because 是連接詞，後面可以直接加子句，because of 是介係詞片語，後面必須接名詞或動名詞。

be·come [bɪˈkʌm] 🔊 *Track 0091*

動 變得、變成

▶ When you become a parent in the future, you will understand how your parents feel.
　一旦你以後為人父母，就會理解你爸媽的感覺了。

文法字詞解析
become 的動詞變化：become, became, become

bed [bɛd] 🔊 *Track 0092*

名 床 動 睡、臥

▶ 名 My bed is my favorite thing in the room.
　我的床是我在房間裡最喜歡的東西。

▶ 動 I usually bed down at around eleven p.m.
　我通常都會在晚上十一點去睡覺。

文法字詞解析
bed 的動詞變化：bed, bedded, bedded

bee [bi] 🔊 *Track 0093*

名 蜜蜂

▶ My grandmother is always as busy as a bee.
　我奶奶和總是和蜜蜂一樣忙碌。

be·fore [bɪˈfor] 🔊 *Track 0094*

副 以前 介 早於、在……以前 連 在……以前
反 after 在……之後

▶ 副 I've never been here before. 我從來沒來過這裡。

▶ 介 I started studying three days before the exam.
　　我在考前開始唸書。

▶ 連 We ate dinner before going to the movie.
　　我們在去看電影前先吃了晚餐。

be·gin [bɪˋgɪn]　🔊 *Track 0095*

動 開始、著手　反 finish 結束、完成

▶ It's never too late for you to begin learning.
　無論何時開始學習都為時不晚。

be·hind [bɪˋhaɪnd]　🔊 *Track 0096*

副 在後、在原處　介 在……之後　反 ahead 在前

▶ 副 Students who were physically stronger ran toward the goal, while the weaker ones were left behind.
　　比較強壯的學生都衝向終點，而比較體弱的學生被留在原地。

▶ 介 She's the one in red sitting behind Joey.
　　她是坐在喬伊後面，穿紅色的那個。

be·lieve [bɪˋliv]　🔊 *Track 0097*

動 認為、相信　同 trust 信賴

▶ You shouldn't believe others so easily.
　你不該這麼輕易相信他人。

bell [bɛl]　🔊 *Track 0098*

名 鐘、鈴　同 ring 鈴聲、鐘聲

▶ Did the bell ring yet? 鐘響了沒？

be·long [bəˋlɔŋ]　🔊 *Track 0099*

動 屬於

▶ Put the bowl back where it belongs. 請把碗放回該放的地方。

be·low [bəˋlo]　🔊 *Track 0100*

介 在……下面、比……低　副 在下方、往下
同 under 在……下面

▶ 介 I live on the floor below his. 我住在他樓下那一層。

▶ 副 The lady who works below is our boss's daughter.
　　在樓下工作的那個小姐是我們老闆的女兒。

be·side [bɪˋsaɪd]　🔊 *Track 0101*

介 在……旁邊
同 by 在……旁邊

▶ She stood beside me when we took a photo of the whole class.
　我們拍全班合照時，她站在我旁邊。

best [bɛst]　🔊 *Track 0102*

形 最好的　副 最好地　反 worst 最壞的

▶ 形 Not everyone can buy the best goods at the best price.
　　不是每個人都能以最優惠的價格買到最好的東西。

▶ 副 Listen to your mom; she knows best.
　　聽媽媽的話，她最懂。

Level
1
輕鬆學習、入門無負擔——
掌握基礎1000單字

Level
2

Level
3

Level
4

Level
5

Level
6

bet·ter [ˈbɛtɚ]　　◀€ *Track 0103*

形 較好的、更好的 副 更好地 反 worse 更壞的

▶形 This pen is hard to use. I need a better one.
這筆真難用，我需要一支更好的。

▶副 Are you feeling better now? 你感覺有好一點嗎？

文法字詞解析
better 是 good 的比較級；best 是 good 的最高級。

be·tween [brˈtwin]　　◀€ *Track 0104*

副 在中間 介 在……之間

▶副 We have a meeting and a lecture（講座）today. Would you like to have a cup of coffee between? 我們今天要參加會議和講座，在這中間你想不想去喝杯咖啡？

▶介 I heard that there was a misunderstanding between them.
我聽說他們之間有誤會。

bi·cy·cle/bike [ˈbaɪsɪk!]/[baɪk]　　◀€ *Track 0105*

名 自行車 同 cycle 腳踏車

▶How long does it take for you to go to work by bike?
你騎自行車上班要多久時間？

big [bɪg]　　◀€ *Track 0106*

形 大的 反 little 小的

▶The room isn't big enough to fit us all.
這房間不夠大，裝不下我們全部人。

bird [bɝd]　　◀€ *Track 0107*

名 鳥 同 fowl 禽

▶Some birds flew over our heads just now.
剛才有些鳥飛過我們的頭頂上。

birth [bɝθ]　　◀€ *Track 0108*

名 出生、血統 反 death 死亡

▶Kevin hasn't left the small town since birth.
凱文從出生就不曾離開過這小鎮。

bit [bɪt]　　◀€ *Track 0109*

名 一點

▶The soup is a bit too hot. 這個湯有點太燙了。

bite [baɪt]　　◀€ *Track 0110*

名 咬、一口 動 咬 同 chew 咬

▶名 This chocolate tastes great. Want a bite?
這巧克力好好吃。要來一口嗎？

▶動 A snake bit him yesterday. 昨天一隻蛇咬了他。

文法字詞解析
bite 的動詞變化：bite, bit, bitten

black [blæk]　　◀€ *Track 0111*

形 黑色的 名 黑人、黑色 動（使）變黑 反 white 白色

▶形 Her black dress is the loveliest thing I've ever seen.
她的黑洋裝是我見過最美的東西。

▶名 My favorite color to wear is black.
我最喜歡穿的顏色是黑色。

▶動 The gentleman blacks his shoes every day.
那名紳士每天都把鞋子擦黑。

block [blɑk] 🔊 *Track 0112*

名 街區、木塊、石塊 動 阻塞 反 advance 前進

▶名 How long will it take me to get to that block by bus?
我坐公車到那個街區要多久？

▶動 The truck is blocking the road. 那台卡車阻擋在路上。

blood [blʌd] 🔊 *Track 0113*

名 血液、血統

▶The intern doctor passed out as she saw the blood on the patient's hands. 實習醫生看到病人手上的血就昏倒了。

blow [blo] 🔊 *Track 0114*

名 吹、打擊 動 吹、風吹 同 breeze 吹著微風

▶名 His leaving was a terrible（可怕的）blow to her.
他的離去對她是個可怕的打擊。

▶動 He blew the horn to warn（警告）the people in the neighboring（鄰近的）town. 他吹號角警告鄰近小城的居民。

blue [blu] 🔊 *Track 0115*

形 藍色的、憂鬱的 名 藍色

▶形 Would you like to buy this blue shirt or that red one?
你想買這件藍襯衫，還是那件紅襯衫？

▶名 Her favorite color used to be blue.
她以前最喜歡的顏色是藍色。

文法字詞解析
used to +v. 用來表示以前的習慣。

boat [bot] 🔊 *Track 0116*

名 船 動 划船 同 ship 船

▶名 How long does it take for us to get there by boat?
我們坐船去那裡要多久？

▶動 Can you tell me how often you go boating on the lake?
能不能告訴我你們多久去湖上划一次船？

bo·dy [ˋbɑdɪ] 🔊 *Track 0117*

名 身體 反 soul 靈魂

▶Not everyone is as good at using body language as you are.
不是每個人都像你一樣擅長使用肢體語言。

文法字詞解析
情緒動詞轉成形容詞時，如果是以過去分詞的形式表現，就是「感到……的」的意思，例如 excite（使……興奮）就可以變成 excited（感到興奮的）。

bone [bon] 🔊 *Track 0118*

名 骨 同 skeleton 骨骼

▶The dog was excited when I gave it a bone.
當我給那隻狗一根骨頭時，牠很興奮。

book [bʊk] 🔊 *Track 0119*

名 書 動 登記、預訂 同 reserve 預訂

▶名 I'm afraid it's too difficult for me to finish writing that book alone. 恐怕我獨自一個人來寫完這本書太難了。

▶動 I booked a hotel room for my trip in Hualian this summer.
我為了夏天的花蓮旅行預訂了旅館房間。

文法字詞解析
finish + N. / V-ing 完成

born [bɔrn] 🔊 *Track 0120*

形 天生的 同 natural 天生的

▶She was born in Germany（德國）. 她是在德國出生的。

Level 1 輕鬆學習、入門無負擔──掌握基礎1000單字

Level 2

Level 3

Level 4

Level 5

Level 6

both [boθ] 🔊 *Track 0121*

形 兩、雙 代 兩者、雙方 反 neither 兩者都不

▶ 形 Both sides were wounded（傷害）during the war.
戰爭過程中雙方都受傷了。

▶ 代 The two hats look so beautiful; why not buy both?
這兩頂帽子都很漂亮，為什麼不把它們都買下呢？

bot·tom [ˋbɑtəm] 🔊 *Track 0122*

名 底部、臀部 形 底部的 反 top 頂部

▶ 名 The chef put some custard on the bottom layer of the cake.
廚師在蛋糕底層放了一些卡士達醬。

▶ 形 If you dig deeper, you will find that the bottom layer（層）
is all sand.
如果你再挖深一點，你就會發現最下面的一層全是沙子。

bowl [bol] 🔊 *Track 0123*

名 碗 動 滾動

▶ 名 Let's go buy some more bowls because there are not
enough for so many guests. 我們再去買幾個碗吧，因為我
們有這麼多客人，碗不夠用了。

▶ 動 He bowled the ball into the gutter（溝）.
他把球滾進了溝裡。

box [bɑks] 🔊 *Track 0124*

名 盒子、箱 動 把……裝入盒中、裝箱 同 container 容器

▶ 名 I brought home a box of chocolates.
我帶了一盒巧克力回家。

▶ 動 They boxed the apples before shipping them to market.
他們把蘋果裝箱後再運往市場出售。

文法字詞解析
ship 是動詞，意思是「運送」；名詞為
shipment，意思是「貨物」。

boy [bɔɪ] 🔊 *Track 0125*

名 男孩 反 girl 女孩

▶ Would you like to have a boy or a girl in the future?
將來你是想要生個男孩還是女孩呢？

brave [brev] 🔊 *Track 0126*

形 勇敢的 同 valiant 勇敢的

▶ The brave girl raised her hand and pointed out the speaker's
mistake. 勇敢的女孩舉起手指出講者犯的錯誤。

bread [brɛd] 🔊 *Track 0127*

名 麵包

▶ How about some bread and a cup of coffee for you?
給你拿點麵包和一杯咖啡怎麼樣？

萬用延伸句型
How about sth for you?
你想要一點（某物）嗎？
How about some cookies for you?
你想要一點餅乾嗎？

break [brek] 🔊 *Track 0128*

名 休息、中斷、破裂 動 打破、弄破、弄壞 反 repair 修補

▶ 名 Let's have a break; I'm too tired.
我們休息一下吧，我太累了。

▶ 動 I broke my mother's favorite vase.
我打破了我媽媽最喜歡的花瓶。

文法字詞解析
break 的動詞變化：break, broke, broken

break·fast [ˋbrɛkfəst]　◀€ *Track 0129*

名 早餐　反 dinner 晚餐
▶Have you had breakfast yet? 你吃早餐了嗎？

文法字詞解析
yet 用在疑問句時，放在句尾，是「已經」的意思。

bridge [brɪdʒ]　◀€ *Track 0130*

名 橋
▶I have to cross a bridge to get to school every day.
　我每天都要過一條橋去上課。

文法字詞解析
cross 是動詞，意思是「渡過」；across 是介係詞，有「橫越」的意思。
例如：They walked across the street without looking at the traffic light.
他們不看紅綠燈就過馬路。

bright [braɪt]　◀€ *Track 0131*

形 明亮的、開朗的　同 light 明亮的
▶Mandy loves wear clothes of bright colors.
　曼蒂喜歡穿著亮色的衣服。

bring [brɪŋ]　◀€ *Track 0132*

動 帶來　同 carry 攜帶
▶Can you bring me a sandwich? 你可以幫我帶個三明治嗎？

文法字詞解析
bring 的動詞變化：bring, brought, brought

broth·er [ˋbrʌðɚ]　◀€ *Track 0133*

名 兄弟　反 sister 姊妹
▶My brother and I look the same. 我和我哥哥長得一模一樣。

brown [braʊn]　◀€ *Track 0134*

形 褐色的、棕色的　名 褐色、棕色
▶形 I left my brown jacket on the bus.
　我把棕色的夾克丟在公車上了。
▶名 Some people can't wear brown because it makes them look old. 有些人不能穿棕色，因為會讓他們看起來很老。

bug [bʌg]　◀€ *Track 0135*

名 小蟲、毛病　同 insect 昆蟲
▶Those bugs are actually quite cute if you look closely（近的）.
　靠近看的話，那些小蟲其實還蠻可愛的。

build [bɪld]　◀€ *Track 0136*

動 建立、建築　同 construct 建造
▶The museum was built by the local people in honor of a philanthropist.
　這間博物館是由當地人民為了紀念一位慈善家而建造的。

文法字詞解析
build 的動詞變化：build, built, built

build·ing [ˋbɪldɪŋ]　◀€ *Track 0137*

名 建築物
▶I don't think the building is big enough to hold so many people.
　我覺得這個建築物不足以容納那麼多的人。

bus [bʌs]　◀€ *Track 0138*

名 公車
▶Can you tell me how long it will take for me to get to your company（公司）by bus?
　你能告訴我坐公車到你們公司要多久嗎？

bus·y [ˋbɪzɪ]　　🔊 *Track 0139*

形 忙的、繁忙的　反 free 空閒的

▶Not all people are as busy as you always are.
不是所有人都像你一樣總是忙個不停。

but [bʌt]　　🔊 *Track 0140*

副 僅僅、只　連 但是　介 除了……以外　同 however 可是、然而

▶副 It took her but a few days to learn to play the song.
她只不過幾天的時間就學會彈那首歌了。

▶連 He was sick, but he still went to work.
他生病了，但他還是去上班了。

▶介 No one saw it happen but me.
除了我以外沒有人看到那件事發生。

but·ter [ˋbʌtɚ]　　🔊 *Track 0141*

名 奶油

▶Flour and butter are the basic ingredients for making bread.
麵粉和奶油是做麵包的基本原料。

文法字詞解析
That's my bread and butter.
= 那是我的謀生之道。

but·ter·fly [ˋbʌtɚ͵flaɪ]　　🔊 *Track 0142*

名 蝴蝶

▶I found a butterfly that got hurt when I was walking in the park.
我在公園散步的時候，發現一隻受傷的蝴蝶。

buy [baɪ]　　🔊 *Track 0143*

名 購買、買　動 買　同 purchase 買

▶名 That pot was a really good buy. 買那個鍋子很划算。

▶動 Would you like to go buy some decorations（裝飾）with me this weekend?
這個週末你跟我去買些裝飾用品好嗎？

文法字詞解析
buy 的動詞變化：buy, bought, bought

by [baɪ]　　🔊 *Track 0144*

介 被、藉由、在……之前、在……旁邊

▶I want to know how long it will take for us to get to Tokyo by air.
我想知道我們搭飛機飛往東京要多久。

[Cc]

cage [kedʒ]　　🔊 *Track 0145*

名 籠子、獸籠、鳥籠　動 關入籠中

▶名 Let's put the bird in the cage so that it won't fly away.
讓我們把鳥兒關在鳥籠裡吧，以防止牠飛走。

▶動 They caged the guinea pig lest it should run around the house. 他們把天竺鼠關起來，以防牠在屋子裡跑。

cake [kek]　　🔊 *Track 0146*

名 蛋糕

▶I'm really terrible at cutting cakes. 我超不會切蛋糕。

call [kɔl] ◀€ Track 0147

名 呼叫、打電話 動 呼叫、打電話

▶ 名 I was woken up by a strange call last night.
　 我昨晚被一通奇怪的電話吵醒。

▶ 動 Can you call Jenny for me? 你可以幫我打電話給珍妮嗎？

cam·el [ˋkæml̩] ◀€ Track 0148

名 駱駝

▶ Camels can live a month without water.
　 駱駝可以不喝水活一個月。

文法字詞解析
介係詞 without 的意思是「沒有……」，
後面要接名詞或動名詞。

ca·me·ra [ˋkæmərə] ◀€ Track 0149

名 照相機

▶ My camera broke for the third time this month.
　 我的相機光是這個月就已經壞掉三次了。

camp [kæmp] ◀€ Track 0150

名 露營 動 露營、紮營

▶ 名 The soldiers camped by the river after a long day of hiking.
　 軍人爬了一整天的山，在河邊紮營。

▶ 動 Should we invite him to go camping with us?
　 我們應該邀他跟我們一起去露營嗎？

文法字詞解析
should 在這裡表示「應該、應當」。

can [kæn] ◀€ Track 0151

動 裝罐 助動 能、可以 名 罐頭

▶ 動 I like eating canned food for dinner. 我喜歡吃罐裝食品當晚餐。

▶ 助動 Can you speak English? 你會講英語嗎？

▶ 名 My cat enjoys hearing the sound of me opening a can.
　 我的貓最喜歡聽我開罐頭的聲音。

文法字詞解析
can 的動詞變化：can, canned, canned

can·dy/sweet [ˋkændɪ]/[swit] ◀€ Track 0152

名 糖果 同 sugar 糖

▶ I brought some candy for the little girl next door.
　 我帶了一些糖果給住隔壁的小女孩。

cap [kæp] ◀€ Track 0153

名 帽子、蓋子 動 給……戴帽、覆蓋於……的頂端 同 hat 帽子

▶ 名 My cap was blown away when I was on the boat.
　 我在搭船的時候，帽子被吹走了。

▶ 動 The snow-capped mountain was a famous view to many foreign visitors.
　 由雪覆蓋的山在許多外國觀光客眼裡是個著名的景色。

文法字詞解析
cap 的動詞變化 cap, capped, capped

car [kɑr] ◀€ Track 0154

名 汽車

▶ There is a big white car in front of Jack's home.
　 有一輛白色的大車停在傑克家門前。

card [kɑrd] ◀€ Track 0155

名 卡片

▶ How long will it take for the card to reach his mother?
　 這張卡片寄達他母親那裡要花多久時間？

Level 1
掌握基礎1000單字 ── 輕鬆學習、入門無負擔

Level 2

Level 3

Level 4

Level 5

Level 6

care [kɛr]　🔊 *Track 0156*
名 小心、照料、憂慮 動 關心、照顧、喜愛、介意
同 concern 使關心
▶名 Please handle this box with care. 請小心搬運這個箱子。
▶動 I don't care what he says; I'm still angry.
　　我不管他說什麼，我還是很生氣。

care·ful [ˈkɛrfəl]　🔊 *Track 0157*
形 小心的、仔細的 同 cautious 十分小心的
▶He is not careful enough to find all the mistakes in the papers.
　　他不夠仔細，沒能找出文件裡的所有錯誤。

萬用延伸句型
not... enough to... 不夠……去達成……

car·ry [ˈkærɪ]　🔊 *Track 0158*
動 攜帶、搬運、拿 同 take 拿、取
▶The woman asked the concierge to carry her luggage to her room. 女士要求門房服務人員幫她把行李拿到房間。

case [kes]　🔊 *Track 0159*
名 情形、情況、箱、案例 同 condition 情況
▶There is a case full of clothes in my mother's bedroom, but the case is not ours. 在我媽媽的臥室裡有個箱子裡滿是衣服，但這箱子卻不是我們的。

cat [kæt]　🔊 *Track 0160*
名 貓、貓科動物 同 kitten 小貓
▶My cat thinks she is the most beautiful animal in the world.
　　我的貓覺得自己是全世界最美的動物。

catch [kætʃ]　🔊 *Track 0161*
名 捕捉、捕獲物 動 抓住、趕上 同 capture 捕獲
▶名 What a good catch! You could sell it for a lot of money.
　　這捕獲物真棒！你可以賣很多錢。
▶動 My cat is not interested in catching mice.
　　我的貓對抓老鼠沒有興趣。

文法字詞解析
catch 的動詞變化：catch, caught, caught

cause [kɔz]　🔊 *Track 0162*
動 引起 名 原因 同 make 引起、產生
▶動 The heavy rain and flood caused great damage to the villagers' properties. 豪雨和淹水對本地居民造成嚴重財產損失。
▶名 They're holding the concert for a good cause.
　　他們為了慈善的原因辦這場音樂會。

cent [sɛnt]　🔊 *Track 0163*
名 分（貨幣單位）
▶These cents are not enough for us to buy even a piece of cake.
　　這幾分錢還不夠我們買塊蛋糕呢！

cen·ter [ˈsɛntɚ]　🔊 *Track 0164*
名 中心、中央 反 edge 邊緣
▶Have you been to the new shopping center yet?
　　你去過那家新的購物中心了沒？

萬用延伸句型
Have you been to... yet? 你去過……了沒？

cer·tain [ˈsɝtən]　🔊 *Track 0165*

形 一定的　代 某幾個、某些　反 doubtful 不明確的

▶形 For a certain reason, no one likes going to that market.
因為某種特定原因，沒人喜歡去那家市場。

▶代 Certain of the people are new. 這之中的某些人是新來的。

chair [tʃɛr]　🔊 *Track 0166*

名 椅子、主席席位　同 seat 座位

▶He's so fat he broke the chair he sat on.
他胖到連他坐的椅子都壞了。

chance [tʃæns]　🔊 *Track 0167*

名 機會、意外　同 opportunity 機會

▶There is a high chance that he will win the Academy award.
他很有機會得奧斯卡獎。

chart [tʃɑrt]　🔊 *Track 0168*

名 圖表　動 製成圖表　同 diagram 圖表

▶名 The chart he drew is hard to understand.
他畫的那張圖表很難懂。

▶動 Do you know how to chart the course of the ship?
你知道怎麼把船的航線標出來嗎？

chase [tʃes]　🔊 *Track 0169*

名 追求、追逐　動 追捕、追逐　同 follow 追逐

▶名 The car chasing scene was my favorite.
我最喜歡飛車追逐那段劇情。

▶動 A kitten is chasing after a mouse on the street.
有隻小貓正在大街上追趕一隻老鼠。

check [tʃɛk]　🔊 *Track 0170*

名 檢查、支票　動 檢查、核對

▶名 I usually pay my rent by check. 我通常用支票付房租。

▶動 Can you check the numbers for me?
你可以幫我檢查一下這些數字嗎？

chick [tʃɪk]　🔊 *Track 0171*

名 小雞

▶The chick is so tiny I can hold it in my hand.
這隻小雞小到我可以拿在手中。

chick·en [ˈtʃɪkɪn]　🔊 *Track 0172*

名 雞、雞肉

▶Would you like a bit more salt in your chicken soup?
你要不要在雞湯裡多加些鹽呢？

chief [tʃif]　🔊 *Track 0173*

形 主要的、首席的　名 首領　同 leader 首領

▶形 My uncle is the chief executive office in this company.
我叔叔是這家公司的首席執行長。

▶名 The police chief is a tall, unhappy man.
這位警察局長是個高而憂鬱的男人。

萬用延伸句型
so... that... 如此……以致於……

文法字詞解析
rent 動詞的意思為「租借」；也可做為名詞，意思是「租金」

Level **1**
輕鬆學習、入門無負擔

掌握基礎1000單字

Level **2**

Level **3**

Level **4**

Level **5**

Level **6**

child [tʃaɪld]
🔊 *Track 0174*

名 小孩 同 kid 小孩

▶Why won't my child play with other kids?
為什麼我的孩子都不跟其他小孩玩？

Christ·mas/Xmas [ˈkrɪsməs]
🔊 *Track 0175*

名 聖誕節

▶A big party will be held in the company on Christmas this year.
今年公司將在聖誕節那天舉行一個盛大的派對。

church [tʃɜtʃ]
🔊 *Track 0176*

名 教堂

▶I go to church with my parents sometimes.
我有時候會和父母一起去教堂。

ci·ty [ˈsɪtɪ]
🔊 *Track 0177*

名 城市

▶Not all the people like to live in a big city.
並不是所有的人都喜歡居住在大城市。

class [klæs]
🔊 *Track 0178*

名 班級、階級、種類 同 grade 階級

▶There are very few boys in my class.
我們班上沒幾個男生。

clean [klin]
🔊 *Track 0179*

形 乾淨的 動 打掃 反 dirty 髒的

▶形 That restaurant isn't clean; I don't want to eat there.
那家餐廳不乾淨，我不想在那裡吃。

▶動 A group of volunteers helped the solitary old man to clean his house. 有一群志工幫獨居老人清理他的房子。

clear [klɪr]
🔊 *Track 0180*

形 清楚的、明確的、澄清的 動 澄清、清除障礙、放晴
反 ambiguous 含糊不清的

▶形 I just love the clear weather today.
我真愛今天晴朗的天氣。

▶動 He spent a whole day clearing the snow from the road.
他花了一整天清除路上的雪。

climb [klaɪm]
🔊 *Track 0181*

動 攀登、上升、爬

▶The boy is not old enough to climb up this mountain with his parents.
這個男孩還不夠大，不能跟著他的爸爸媽媽一起爬山。

clock [klɑk]
🔊 *Track 0182*

名 時鐘、計時器

▶It's not polite to give a clock to another as a present here.
在這裡送別人鐘當禮物是不禮貌的。

文法字詞解析
1. 要注意 child 的複數是 children。
2. play 是「玩耍」的意思，因為我們是「跟某個人玩」，不是「玩」某人，所以要 play 後面要接介係詞 with。

文法字詞解析
這裡的 just 作為強調的意思。

文法字詞解析
這裡的 as 有「作為」之意。

close [klos]/[kloz] 🔊 *Track 0183*

形 靠近的、親近的 動 關、結束、靠近 反 open（打）開
- ▶形 In this small village, all close relatives live next to each other.
  在這小村子裡，所有近親住在附近。
- ▶動 How about closing the window for a while?
  把窗戶關起來一會兒怎麼樣？

cloud [klaʊd] 🔊 *Track 0184*

名 雲 動（以雲）遮蔽
- ▶名 The shape of the clouds today is pretty strange.
  今天雲的形狀超奇怪的。
- ▶動 The fog clouds the road ahead. 大霧籠罩著前面的路。

文法字詞解析
這裡的 pretty 有「非常」的意思。

coast [kost] 🔊 *Track 0185*

名 海岸、沿岸
- ▶I'm visiting the west coast this summer vacation.
  這個暑假我要去西岸玩。

coat [kot] 🔊 *Track 0186*

名 外套 同 jacket 外套
- ▶There are lots of holes in the coat. 這外套有很多洞。

co·coa [ˈkoko] 🔊 *Track 0187*

名 可可粉、可可飲料、可可色
- ▶Would you like to have a cup of cocoa in our store when you come by next time?
  下次你路過的時候，要不要到我們店裡來喝杯可可呢？

文法字詞解析
come by 是動詞，意思是「順道路過」；跟 drop by 同樣意思。

cof·fee [ˈkɔfɪ] 🔊 *Track 0188*

名 咖啡
- ▶Sir, would you like black coffee today?
  先生，請問您今天想要黑咖啡嗎？

co·la/Coke [ˈkolə]/[kok] 🔊 *Track 0189*

名 可樂
- ▶I can't tell between Coke and Pepsi.
  我分不清楚可口可樂和百事可樂。

萬用延伸句型
tell between...and... 分辨……與……的差異

cold [kold] 🔊 *Track 0190*

形 冷的 名 感冒 反 warm 暖的
- ▶形 The dishes were cold, so I heated then with the microwave oven. 菜已經冷了，所以我用微波爐加熱。
- ▶名 He caught a cold after playing basketball in the rain.
  他在雨中打藍球後就感冒了。

co·lor [ˈkʌlɚ] 🔊 *Track 0191*

名 顏色 動 把……塗上顏色
- ▶名 My daughter's favorite color is pink.
  我女兒最喜歡的顏色是粉紅色。
- ▶動 There are many crayons（蠟筆）in the box for the children to color their pictures with.
  盒子裡有很多蠟筆供孩子們為他們的畫塗上顏色。

Level 1
輕鬆學習、入門無負擔——掌握基礎1000單字

Level 2

Level 3

Level 4

Level 5

Level 6

come [kʌm]
◀€ Track 0192

動 來 反 leave 離開

▶Can you come over after you finish your homework?
你功課做完後可以過來我這裡嗎？

com·mon [ˈkɑmən]
◀€ Track 0193

形 共同的、平常的、普通的 名 平民、普通 反 special 特別的

▶形 It's common to see people walk their dogs along the riverbank.
在這河邊很常看到有人在遛狗。

▶名 Many commons died in this attack（襲擊）while some were injured（受傷）.
在這次襲擊中有很多平民死亡和一些平民受傷。

文法字詞解析
have something in common = 有共同處

con·tin·ue [kənˈtɪnju]
◀€ Track 0194

動 繼續、連續 同 persist 持續

▶Let's continue to work and try to finish before sunset.
我們繼續工作吧，努力在太陽下山前完成。

cook [kʊk]
◀€ Track 0195

動 烹調、煮、燒 名 廚師

▶動 I can't cook at all. 我完全不會煮菜。

▶名 I'm the most horrible cook on earth. 我是全球最糟糕的廚師。

cook·ie/cook·y [ˈkʊkɪ]
◀€ Track 0196

名 餅乾

▶The little boys are fighting over a cookie.
那些小男孩為了一塊餅乾在打架。

cool [kul]
◀€ Track 0197

形 涼的、涼快的、酷的 動 使變涼 反 hot 熱的

▶形 Don't you just love the cool weather?
你不覺得很喜歡這涼快的天氣嗎？

▶動 Mary tried to cool down her brother for fear that he would start a fight. 瑪莉想叫她哥哥冷靜，以免他去跟人打架。

corn [kɔrn]
◀€ Track 0198

名 玉米

▶We feed corn to our chickens. 我們都用玉米來餵小雞。

cor·rect [kəˈrɛkt]
◀€ Track 0199

形 正確的 動 改正、糾正 同 right 正確的

▶形 I don't know the correct answer, either.
我也不知道正確答案。

▶動 I had to correct all his mistakes. 我得改正他所有的錯誤。

文法字詞解析
either 用在否定句句尾，表示「也」；如果是肯定句的「也」則是 too。

萬用延伸句型
All present and correct. 全員到齊。

cost [kɔst]
◀€ Track 0200

名 代價、價值、費用 動 花費、值 反 income 收入、收益

▶名 I bought this necklace（項鏈）at one thousand dollars; the cost sounds reasonable（合理的）.
我用一千美元買下了這條項鏈，這個價錢聽起來很合理。

▶動 This house cost me a lot. 這房子花了我很多錢。

文法字詞解析
cost 的動詞變化：cost, cost, cost

count [kaʊnt]

Track 0201

動 計數 **名** 計數

▶**動** She is seventeen yet still can't count.
她都十七歲了還是不會算數。

▶**名** Would you like another piece of cake? By my count you've had only two.
你要再來一塊蛋糕嗎？按我的計算，你只吃了兩塊。

萬用延伸句型
Count me in. 算我一份。

Level 1
輕鬆學習、入門無負擔——
掌握基礎1000單字

coun·try [ˈkʌntrɪ]

Track 0202

形 國家的、鄉村的 **名** 國家、鄉村 **同** nation 國家

▶**形** My grandmother prefers live in the country to life in the city.
我祖母喜歡鄉下生活勝過城市生活。

▶**名** Some people love their country way too much.
有些人實在太過愛國了。

course [kors]

Track 0203

名 課程、講座、過程、路線 **同** process 過程

▶What will we be learning in this course?
我們在這個課程中會學到什麼？

文法字詞解析
will be + v-ing 是未來進行式，用來表示未來某一個時間點正在進行的事情。

cov·er [ˈkʌvɚ]

Track 0204

名 封面、表面 **動** 覆蓋、掩飾、包含 **反** uncover 揭露、發現

▶**名** A good cover is important for a book.
一個好的封面對一本書來說很重要。

▶**動** The table is covered with dust（灰塵）.
這張桌子覆蓋滿了灰塵。

文法字詞解析
cover A with B 用 B 蓋住 A

cow [kaʊ]

Track 0205

名 母牛、乳牛

▶How often do you feed these cows per（每）day?
你一天餵這些牛幾次？

cow·boy [ˈkaʊˌbɔɪ]

Track 0206

名 牛仔

▶The cowboy walks into the bar（酒吧）and orders（點餐）a beer. 那名牛仔走進酒吧，點了一杯啤酒。

crow [kro]

Track 0207

名 啼叫、烏鴉 **動** 啼叫、報曉

▶**名** In the past few decades, the crow population in Japan exploded.
過去幾十年來，日本的烏鴉數量大幅增加。

▶**動** Our rooster crows at nine a.m. Isn't that a bit late?
我們的公雞都早上九點報曉，這不會有點太晚了嗎？

文法字詞解析
crow的動詞變化：crow, crowed, crowed或crow, crew, crowed

cry [kraɪ]

Track 0208

名 叫聲、哭聲、大叫 **動** 哭、叫、喊 **同** wail 慟哭

▶**名** She felt much better after a good cry.
好好哭一場後，她感覺好多了。

▶**動** "Are you crazy?" he cries.
「你瘋了喔？」他大叫。

Level 2

Level 3

Level 4

Level 5

Level 6

cub [kʌb] ◀≼ *Track 0209*

名 幼獸、年輕人
▶The cute little bear cubs are sleeping on their mother.
那些可愛的小熊睡在牠們的媽媽身上。

cup [kʌp] ◀≼ *Track 0210*

名 杯子 同 glass 玻璃杯
▶Would you like a cup of milk and a piece of bread for your breakfast this morning?
今天的早餐你要不要一杯牛奶加片麵包呢？

cut [kʌt] ◀≼ *Track 0211*

動 切、割、剪、砍、削、刪 名 切口、傷口 同 split 切開
▶動 He cut the rope with a knife. 他用刀子切斷了繩子。
▶名 When the chef had a cut in his hand, he was not allowed to handle the ingredients.
當廚師手上有傷口時，他是不能處理食材的。

文法字詞解析
cut 的動詞變化：cut, cut, cut

cute [kjut] ◀≼ *Track 0212*

形 可愛的、聰明伶俐的 同 pretty 可愛的
▶They start arguing（爭吵）over whose baby is the cutest.
他們為了誰的寶寶最可愛而爭吵。

[Dd]

dad·dy/dad/pa·pa/pa/pop ◀≼ *Track 0213*
[ˋdædɪ]/[dæd]/[ˋpɑpə]/[pɑ]/[pɑp]

名 爸爸
▶Have you ever seen her daddy? What does he look like?
你見過她爸爸嗎？他長什麼樣子？

萬用延伸句型
Have you ever... 你是否曾經……？

dance [dæns] ◀≼ *Track 0214*

名 舞蹈 動 跳舞
▶名 My friend in the dance department is always practicing.
我舞蹈系的朋友總是在練舞。
▶動 Would you like to dance with me?
你願意跟我跳支舞嗎？

danc·er [ˋdænsə] ◀≼ *Track 0215*

名 舞者
▶Most of the dancers I know are very pretty.
我認識的舞者幾乎都長得很漂亮。

dan·ger [ˋdendʒə] ◀≼ *Track 0216*

名 危險 反 safety 安全
▶The woman who was trapped in the mountain was in grave danger. 受困山區的婦女情況危急。

dark [dɑrk] ◀ Track 0217

名 黑暗、暗處 形 黑暗的 反 light 明亮的
▶名 We can't see a thing in the dark.
我們在黑暗中什麼也看不見。
▶形 The streets here are too dark. 這裡的街道太黑了。

date [det] ◀ Track 0218

名 日期、約會 動 約會、定日期 同 appointment 約會
▶名 Please fill in your ID number and your birth date in the blanks. 請在空格中填寫身分證字號和出生日期。
▶動 They've been dating for two years.
他們已經在一起兩年了。

文法字詞解析
1. 在第二個例句中，因為是從兩年前一直到現在都在交往，而且現在還持續在交往中，所以是用現在完成進行式。

萬用延伸句型
第二個例句也可以寫成：They've been dating since two years ago.

daugh·ter [ˋdɔtɚ] ◀ Track 0219

名 女兒 反 son 兒子
▶Every mother thinks her own daughter is the prettiest.
每個媽媽都覺得自己的女兒最漂亮。

day [de] ◀ Track 0220

名 白天、日 反 night 晚上
▶This is my first day at work. 這是我第一天工作。

dead [dɛd] ◀ Track 0221

名 死者 形 死的 反 live 活的
▶名 There are twenty dead in the big fire last night.
昨夜發生的這場大火中有二十名死者。
▶形 There were tens of thousands of dead bodies left on the battlefield（戰場）after war.
戰爭過後，成千上萬的屍體被遺留在戰場上。

deal [dil] ◀ Track 0222

動 處理、應付、做買賣、經營 名 買賣、交易 同 trade 交易
▶動 I can't deal with this alone. 這我沒辦法一個人應付。
▶名 I made a deal with my classmate that I would do the science report for her. 我和同學約定要替她寫自然科的報告。

文法字詞解析
deal 的動詞變化：deal, dealt, dealt

dear [dɪr] ◀ Track 0223

形 昂貴的、親愛的 副 昂貴地
感 阿！唉呀！（表示傷心、焦慮、驚奇等）
同 expensive 昂貴的
▶形 Dear John, I'm breaking up with you.
親愛的約翰，我要和你分手。
▶副 The jewels（珠寶）cost us too dear.
這些珠寶花費我們太高價了。
▶感 Oh dear, I've forgotten to put on pants.
哎呀，我忘記穿褲子了。

death [dɛθ] ◀ Track 0224

名 死、死亡 反 life 生命、活的東西
▶Everyone is afraid of death in one way or another.
大家或多或少都有點怕死。

Level 1
輕鬆學習、入門無負擔——掌握基礎1000單字

Level 2

Level 3

Level 4

Level 5

Level 6

De·cem·ber/Dec. [dɪˋsɛmbɚ] ◀╱ *Track 0225*

名 十二月
▶Do you want to go skiing（滑雪）with us in December?
你十二月份想跟我們出去滑雪嗎？

de·cide [dɪˋsaɪd] ◀╱ *Track 0226*

動 決定 同 determine 決定
▶She decided to quit smoking for the sake of her baby's health.
她決定為了寶寶的健康而戒菸。

文法字詞解析
decide 後面如果要接動詞，一定要用 to V. 的形式。

deep [dip] ◀╱ *Track 0227*

形 深的 副 深深地 反 shallow 淺的
▶形 I don't like swimming in deep pools.
我不喜歡在太深的游泳池游泳。
▶副 Her emotions（情緒）run deep, it's hard to tell what she's thinking. 她的情緒總是藏得很深，很難知道她在想什麼。

deer [dɪr] ◀╱ *Track 0228*

名 鹿
▶She is a sweet girl that looks like a baby deer.
她是個甜美的女孩，看起來像隻小鹿似的。

desk [dɛsk] ◀╱ *Track 0229*

名 書桌
▶I left my homework on the desk.
我把功課放在書桌上了。

die [daɪ] ◀╱ *Track 0230*

動 死 同 perish 死去
▶My uncle died last week. 我叔叔上禮拜過世了。

文法字詞解析
die 的動詞變化： die, died, died
萬用延伸句型
Never say die. 永不放棄。

dif·fer·ent [ˋdɪfərənt] ◀╱ *Track 0231*

形 不同的 反 identical 同一的
▶After having sandwiches for five days in a row, she decided to have something different for breakfast today.
連續五天早餐吃三明治之後，她決定今天要吃點不一樣的。

difficult [ˋdɪfəˌkʌlt] ◀╱ *Track 0232*

形 困難的 反 easy 簡單的
▶The test was too difficult for me.
這考試對我來說太難了。

dig [dɪg] ◀╱ *Track 0233*

動 挖、挖掘 反 bury 埋
▶I am so embarrassed I want to dig a hole and jump into it.
我丟臉到真想挖個洞跳下去。

文法字詞解析
dig 的動詞變化： dig, dug, dug

din·ner [ˋdɪnɚ] ◀╱ *Track 0234*

名 晚餐、晚宴 同 supper 晚餐
▶Would you like to have dinner with me?
你想跟我一起吃晚餐嗎？

dir·ect [dəˋrɛkt]
◀€ Track 0235

形 筆直的、直接的 動 指示、命令 同 order 命令、指示
- ▶形 She made the composition direct and clear with sentences that are easy to understand. 她用一些簡單易懂的句子,使她的作文變得直接且清楚。
- ▶動 The nice lady directs us to the department store. 那個好心的太太指示我們去百貨公司的路。

dirt·y [ˋdɝtɪ]
◀€ Track 0236

形 髒的 動 弄髒 反 clean 清潔的
- ▶形 I can't stand living in a dirty room. 我受不了住在髒的房間裡。
- ▶動 The children dirtied the floor. Let's clean it up. 孩子們把地板弄髒了,我們打掃一下吧。

dis·cov·er [dɪˋskʌvɚ]
◀€ Track 0237

動 發現 同 find 發現
- ▶He discovered a new insect. 他發現了一種新的昆蟲。

dish [dɪʃ]
◀€ Track 0238

名 (盛食物的)盤、碟 同 plate 盤、碟
- ▶Can you wash the dishes tonight? 你今天晚上可以洗盤子嗎?

do [du]
◀€ Track 0239

助動 (無詞意) 動 做 同 perform 做
- 助動 Do you want some coffee? 你想來點咖啡嗎?
- ▶動 Could you help me get it done before this Friday? It's urgent (緊急的). 你能在本週五前幫我把它做完嗎?這件事很緊急。

文法字詞解析
do 的動詞變化:do, did, done

doc·tor/doc [ˋdɑktɚ]
◀€ Track 0240

名 醫生、博士 同 physician 醫師
- ▶The doctor is famous for his patience and conscientiousness. 這位醫師以他的耐心和嚴謹自律聞名。

dog [dɔg]
◀€ Track 0241

動 尾隨、跟蹤 名 狗
- ▶動 He likes her so much he dogs her everywhere. 他太喜歡她了,以致她去哪他都跟蹤她。
- ▶名 There are three dogs and five cats in their house. 他們家有三條狗和五隻貓。

文法字詞解析
dog 的動詞變化:dog, dogged, dogged

doll [dɑl]
◀€ Track 0242

名 玩具娃娃 同 toy 玩具
- ▶Would you like a beautiful doll as your seventh birthday (生日) gift? 你想不想要一個漂亮的玩具娃娃作為七歲生日的禮物?

dol·lar/buck [ˋdɑlɚ]/[bʌk]
◀€ Track 0243

名 美元、錢
- ▶I spent two dollars on this cheap dress. 我花了兩美元買這件便宜的洋裝。

萬用延伸句型
sb. spend + (time) + V-ing / N.

Level
1
輕鬆學習、入門無負擔
掌握基礎1000單字

Level
2

Level
3

Level
4

Level
5

Level
6

door [dor]
◀ **Track 0244**

名 門 同 gate 大門

▶ Would you close the door? I feel a little cold.
你願不願意關上門？我覺得有點冷。

dove [dʌv]
◀ **Track 0245**

名 鴿子

▶ Do you know how many doves there are on the center square
（廣場）？你知道中央廣場上有多少隻鴿子嗎？

文法字詞解析
這個例句是由一個問句併入另一個問句所構成，可以拆成主要子句「Do you know?」和附屬子句「How many doves are there on the center square?」當附屬子句併入主要子句時，要將動詞放回主詞後面，不可倒裝。

down [daʊn]
◀ **Track 0246**

形 向下的 副 向下 介 沿著……而下 反 up 在上面

▶ 形 Dick is feeling a bit down today. Let's go comfort（安慰）him. 迪克今天情緒有點低落，我們去安慰他一下吧。

▶ 副 The boy climbed down the tree. 男孩爬下了樹。

▶ 介 Their house is halfway down the hill.
他們的房子坐落在半山腰。

down·stairs [ˌdaʊnˈstɛrz]
◀ **Track 0247**

形 樓下的 副 在樓下 名 樓下 反 upstairs 在樓上

▶ 形 The bathroom is downstairs. You can find it following the sign on the wall. 洗手間在樓下。跟隨牆上指標就能找到了。

▶ 副 Could you go downstairs to get some bread for me in the kitchen? 你可以下樓到廚房幫我拿點麵包嗎？

▶ 名 The downstairs consisted of（包含）three large rooms.
樓下有三間大房間。

doz·en [ˈdʌzn]
◀ **Track 0248**

名 （一）打、十二個

▶ It is reported that dozens of people died in the big fire.
據報導，有很多人在那場大火中喪命。

draw [drɔ]
◀ **Track 0249**

動 拉、拖、提取、畫、繪製 同 drag 拉、拖

▶ The little girl drew a picture of a horse.
小女孩畫了一幅馬的圖。

文法字詞解析
draw 的動詞變化 draw, drew, drawn

dream [drim]
◀ **Track 0250**

名 夢 動 做夢 反 reality 現實

▶ 名 I had such a strange dream last night.
我昨晚做了一個好奇怪的夢。

▶ 動 He dreamed about making lots of money.
他的夢想是賺很多錢。

文法字詞解析
dream 的動詞變化 dream, dreamed, dreamed 或是 dream, dreamt, dreamt

drink [drɪŋk]
◀ **Track 0251**

名 飲料 動 喝、喝酒

▶ 名 How about getting some drinks? I am a little thirsty（口渴的）. 我們去弄點飲料怎麼樣？我有點渴了。

▶ 動 It is against the law to drive after drinking wine.
喝酒後駕車是違法的。

文法字詞解析
drink 的動詞變化：drank, drank, drunk

drive [draɪv]　◀≣ *Track 0252*

名 駕車、車道 **動** 開車、驅使、操縱（機器等）

同 move 推動、促使

▶**名** It's too cold for us to go for a drive.
現在開車出去兜風實在太冷了。

▶**動** He drove the truck into a ditch（水溝）.
他把卡車開進水溝去了。

文法字詞解析
drive 的動詞變化：drive, drove, driven

driv·er [ˋdraɪvɚ]　◀≣ *Track 0253*

名 駕駛員、司機

▶David's driver's license was suspended for he drove under the influence of alcohol.
大衛的駕照，在他酒駕之後遭吊銷。

萬用延伸句型
Drink and drive 酒駕

dry [draɪ]　◀≣ *Track 0254*

形 乾的、枯燥無味的 **動** 把……弄乾、乾掉

同 thirsty 乾的、口渴的

▶**形** The paint on the chair is not yet dry.
椅子上的油漆還沒乾呢。

▶**動** The clothes are taking forever to dry.
衣服一直乾不了。

文法字詞解析
dry 的動詞變化：dry, dried, dried

duck [dʌk]　◀≣ *Track 0255*

名 鴨子

▶Could you help me count how many ducks there are in the river?
你能幫我數數看河裡一共有多少隻鴨子嗎？

duck·ling [ˋdʌklɪŋ]　◀≣ *Track 0256*

名 小鴨子

▶The ugly duckling grew up to be a beautiful swan（天鵝）.
那隻醜小鴨長大變成了美麗的天鵝。

dur·ing [ˋdjʊrɪŋ]　◀≣ *Track 0257*

介 在……期間

▶My neighbor will keep an eye on my garden during my business trip.
我出差期間，我的鄰居會替我照顧我的庭院。

[Ee]

each [itʃ]　◀≣ *Track 0258*

形 各、每 **代** 每個、各自 **副** 各、每個

▶**形** There are new houses on each side of the street.
街道兩邊都有新房子。

▶**代** How long will it take for each of them to finish our job?
要多久他們各人才能做完自己的那份工作？

▶**副** They said the oranges there are forty cents each.
他們說那裡的橘子每個售價四十分錢。

Level
1

輕鬆學習、入門無負擔 ——

掌握基礎1000單字

Level
2

Level
3

Level
4

Level
5

Level
6

ea·gle [`igl]
🔊 *Track 0259*

名 鷹

▶We sat there all afternoon watching the eagles.
我們在那裡坐了一整個下午觀賞老鷹。

ear [ɪr]
🔊 *Track 0260*

名 耳朵

▶His ears turn red when he is angry.
他生氣的時候耳朵會變紅。

萬用延伸句型
I'm all ears 我洗耳恭聽

ear·ly [`ɝlɪ]
🔊 *Track 0261*

形 早的、早期的、及早的 副 早、在初期 反 late 晚的

▶形 Some elderly people gathered in the park in the early morning to practice Tai Chi.
有些年長者早晨聚集在公園裡練習太極拳。

▶副 You'll have to get up early tomorrow.
你明天得早起。

萬用延伸句型
early bird discount 早鳥優惠

earth [ɝθ]
🔊 *Track 0262*

名 地球、陸地、地面 同 globe 地球

▶We have only one earth and we should protect it.
我們只有一個地球，應該要保護它。

ease [iz]
🔊 *Track 0263*

動 緩和、減輕、使舒適 名 容易、舒適、悠閒

同 relieve 緩和、減輕

▶動 Give me some medicine to ease the pain（疼痛）.
給我一點藥減輕疼痛吧。

▶名 He can always solve（解決）math problems with ease.
他總是能很輕鬆地解決數學難題。

east [ist]
🔊 *Track 0264*

形 東方的 副 向東方 名 東、東方 反 west 西方

▶形 Have you listened to the weather report? How long will the east wind last?
你聽了天氣預報嗎？這陣東風會持續多久呢？

▶副 The train heads east. You are going to the town in the north, so you can' take this train.
這班火車往東走。你要到北邊的城市，所以不能搭這班車。

▶名 Some of my classmates come from the east.
我有些同學是從東方來的。

eas·y [`izɪ]
🔊 *Track 0265*

形 容易的、不費力的 反 difficult 困難的

▶Playing the violin is easy for him. 拉小提琴對他來說很容易。

eat [it]
🔊 *Track 0266*

動 吃 同 dine 用餐

▶There was no time for me to eat my breakfast because I got up too late this morning.
我今天早上沒有時間吃早餐，因為起得太晚了。

文法字詞解析
eat 的動詞變化：eat, ate, eaten

edge [ɛdʒ]　　　🔊 Track 0267

名 邊、邊緣　同 border 邊緣
▶An adventurous young man stood by the edge of the cliff and took a selfie. 愛冒險的年輕人站在懸崖邊緣自拍。

egg [ɛg]　　　🔊 Track 0268

名 蛋
▶They threw eggs at the man's house. 他們拿蛋砸那個男人的家。

eight [et]　　　🔊 Track 0269

名 八
▶He was eight years old when the accident happened.
意外發生時，他八歲。

eigh·teen [ˈeˈtin]　　　🔊 Track 0270

名 十八
▶You are eighteen, old enough to take care of yourself.
你十八歲了，可以自己照顧自己了。

eight·y [ˈeti]　　　🔊 Track 0271

名 八十
▶The old man is eighty years old. 這個老人八十歲了。

ei·ther [ˈiðɚ]　　　🔊 Track 0272

形 （兩者之中）任一的　代 （兩者之中）任一　副 也（不）
▶形 I'm okay with either of these two restaurants.
去這兩家餐廳之中任一家我都沒問題。
▶代 Which restaurant do you prefer, the Chinese or the Mexican one? I am fine with either. 你喜歡中國餐廳還是墨西哥餐廳？
我去任何一家都可以。
▶副 If you're not going, I'm not either. 你不去的話我也不去。

e·le·phant [ˈɛləfənt]　　　🔊 Track 0273

名 大象
▶There are two elephants in our zoo. 我們動物園裡有兩頭大象。

e·le·ven [ɪˈlɛvn̩]　　　🔊 Track 0274

名 十一
▶There are eleven players in a football team.
一個足球隊裡有十一個球員。

else [ɛls]　　　🔊 Track 0275

副 其他、另外
▶We must hurry, or else we'll be late.
我們得快點，不然就要遲到了。

end [ɛnd]　　　🔊 Track 0276

名 結束、終點　動 結束、終止　反 origin 起源
▶名 The end of the movie is very sad. 這部電影的結局很悲傷。
▶動 I think it's time to end our relationship（關係）.
我想該是結束我們之間關係的時候了。

文法字詞解析

adventurous 是形容詞，意思是「喜好冒險的」；名詞為 adventure，意思是「冒險」。

Level
1
輕鬆學習、入門無負擔──
掌握基礎1000單字

Level
2

Level
3

萬用延伸句型

elephant in the room 明顯卻被忽視的事實

Level
4

Level
5

Level
6

Eng·lish [ˈɪŋglɪʃ]　　◀⁞ *Track 0277*

形 英國的、英國人的 名 英語

▶形 Could you introduce（介紹）me to your English friend?
你願意把我介紹給你的英國朋友嗎？

▶名 The little boy speaks English, Chinese and Japanese.
那個小男孩會說英文、中文和日文。

e·nough [əˈnʌf]　　◀⁞ *Track 0278*

形 充足的、足夠的 名 足夠 副 夠、充足 同 sufficient 足夠的

▶形 I don't think a hundred dollars is enough.
我覺得一百美元不夠。

▶名 He said he had enough money to buy a new house.
他說他的錢足夠買一幢新房子。

▶副 She is not old enough to travel to a foreign country by herself.
她年紀還不夠大，不能自己去旅行。

> **萬用延伸句型**
> adj/adv enough to + V. 足夠做⋯⋯ 或者
> 也可以用：so adj/adv as to V.

en·ter [ˈɛntɚ]　　◀⁞ *Track 0279*

動 加入、參加 反 exit 退出

▶Everyone shut up when the boss entered the room.
老闆一走進房間，大家都閉嘴了。

e·qual [ˈikwəl]　　◀⁞ *Track 0280*

名 對手 形 相等的、平等的 動 等於、比得上 同 parallel 相同的

▶名 Don't even try; you are not his equal in strength（力氣）.
還是別嘗試吧，力氣上你不是他的對手。

▶形 Women and men should have equal rights.
女人與男人應該要有平等的權利。

▶動 Ten plus（加上）five equals fifteen.
十加五等於十五。

> **文法字詞解析**
> equal 的動詞變化：equal, equaled,
> equaled 或 equal, equaled, equalled

e·ven [ˈivən]　　◀⁞ *Track 0281*

形 平坦的、偶數的、相等的 副 甚至 同 smooth 平坦的

▶形 I can't ride a bike if not on even ground.
如果不是平地，我就不會騎腳踏車。

▶副 Even John, who is always happy, cried at the news.
就連總是很開心的約翰聽到這個消息也哭了。

eve·ning [ˈivnɪŋ]　　◀⁞ *Track 0282*

名 傍晚、晚上

▶I'll visit him tomorrow evening. 我明天傍晚會去拜訪他。

ev·er [ˈɛvɚ]　　◀⁞ *Track 0283*

副 曾經、永遠 反 never 不曾

▶Have you ever seen a double rainbow?
你看過雙層彩虹嗎？

> **文法字詞解析**
> ever since 自從過去以來，必須搭配現在
> 完成式使用。

ev·er·y [ˈɛvrɪ]　　◀⁞ *Track 0284*

形 每、每個 反 none 一個也沒

▶How often do you and your family go back to your hometown
（家鄉）every year? 你和你的家人每年回老家幾次啊？

ex·am·i·na·tion/ ex·am [ɪɡ͵zæmə`neʃən]/[ɪɡ`zæm]
🔊 Track 0285

名 考試

▶There are plenty（大量）of students taking this exam.
有很多學生參加這場考試。

ex·am·ine [ɪɡ`zæmɪn]
🔊 Track 0286

動 檢查、考試 同 test 考試

▶He had a stomachache, and he went to the hospital and had his abdomen examined.
他覺得胃痛，所以他去醫院檢查腹部。

ex·am·ple [ɪɡ`zæmpl̩]
🔊 Track 0287

名 榜樣、例子 同 instance 例子

▶For example, a dog is a kind of animal.
舉例來說，狗是一種動物。

ex·cept/ex·cept·ing [ɪk`sɛpt]/[ɪk`sɛptɪŋ]
🔊 Track 0288

介 除了……之外 同 besides 除……之外

▶The whole class is going on the trip except for him.
除了他，全班都要參加這場旅行。

eye [aɪ]
🔊 Track 0289

名 眼睛

▶My eyes are tired after studying.
唸完書後我的眼睛很累。

[Ff]

face [fes]
🔊 Track 0290

名 臉、臉部 動 面對 同 look 外表

▶名 There's something strange on your face.
你臉上有怪怪的東西。

▶動 Can you turn around and face me? It's too hard to talk like this.
你可以轉過來面對我嗎？不然這樣超難講話的。

fact [fækt]
🔊 Track 0291

名 事實 反 fiction 虛構

▶Being a reporter, you should be able to tell between a story and a fact. 作為一個記者，你應該要能夠辨別故事和事實。

fac·to·ry [`fæktərɪ]
🔊 Track 0292

名 工廠 同 plant 工廠

▶My parents work in the factory over there.
我父母在那邊的工廠工作。

文法字詞解析

1. except for 是為介係詞片語，後面只能加名詞。

2. 不只是 except for，「excepting」、「other than」、「but」也是「除了……之外」的意思。

萬用延伸句型

In fact, S. + V. 事實上，……

例如：In fact, I'm not allowed to go out at night.
事實上，我不被允許在晚上出門。

Level 1
輕鬆學習、入門無負擔
掌握基礎1000單字

Level 2

Level 3

Level 4

Level 5

Level 6

fall [fɔl]
🔊 Track 0293

名 秋天、落下 動 倒下、落下 同 drop 落下、降下

▶名 During the afternoon, there was a sudden heavy fall of snow.
下午突然下起了大雪。

▶動 Many trees and houses fell down in that big rainstorm（暴風雨）. 在那場暴風雨中有許多樹和房子都倒了。

文法字詞解析
fall 的動詞變化：fall, fell, fallen

false [fɔls]
🔊 Track 0294

形 錯誤的、假的、虛偽的 反 correct 正確的

▶The dentist told her to clean her false tooth with a special solution. 牙醫告訴她要用特別的溶劑清理她的假牙。

fa·mi·ly [ˈfæməlɪ]
🔊 Track 0295

名 家庭 同 relative 親戚、親屬

▶Her family is poor but happy.
她的家庭很窮，但很快樂。

fan [fæn]
🔊 Track 0296

名 風扇、狂熱者 動 搧、搧動

▶名 Would you like me to turn on the fan? It's so hot in the room.
你要我把風扇打開嗎？房間裡太熱了。

▶動 Grandma is always sitting there fanning herself.
奶奶總是坐在那裡幫自己搧風。

文法字詞解析
fan 的動詞變化：fan, fanned, fanned

fa·nat·ic [fəˈnætɪk]
🔊 Track 0297

名 狂熱者 形 狂熱的

▶名 He's the only religious（宗教的） fanatic I know.
他是我認識的唯一一個宗教狂熱分子。

▶形 The fanatic fans screamed and shouted as they saw the Korean pop stars. 狂熱的歌迷看到韓國明星時就興奮地尖叫。

far [fɑr]
🔊 Track 0298

形 遙遠的、遠（方）的 副 遠方、朝遠處 同 distant 遠的

▶形 The store is too far away to reach by walking.
那家店用走的去太遠了。

▶副 Don't go far; you might get lost.
不要走遠，你可能會迷路。

farm [fɑrm]
🔊 Track 0299

名 農場、農田 動 耕種 同 ranch 大農場

▶名 Would you like to work on a farm?
你願意在農場工作嗎？

▶動 My grandparents used to farm.
我祖父母以前是種田的。

farm·er [ˈfɑrmɚ]
🔊 Track 0300

名 農夫

▶There are still a great many poor（貧窮的） farmers in China at present.
目前，在中國仍然有許多貧困的農民。

fast [fæst] 🔊 *Track 0301*

形 快速的 副 很快地 反 slow 緩慢的

▶形 I took a fast train to Taipei. 我搭很快的火車去台北。

▶副 He can translate the manuscript faster than I can.
他翻譯文稿比我快。

文法字詞解析
比較級的用法：比較級形容詞／副詞 + than + 比較的對象

fat [fæt] 🔊 *Track 0302*

形 肥胖的 名 脂肪 反 thin 瘦的

▶形 The dog is fatter than his owner（主人）.
那隻狗比牠的主人還胖。

▶名 If you eat too much food cooked in deep fat, you will put on weight soon. 如果你吃太多油炸食品，你就會很快增肥的。

fa·ther [ˈfɑðɚ] 🔊 *Track 0303*

名 父親 反 mother 母親

▶My father is my favorite man. 我爸爸是我最愛的男人。

fear [fɪr] 🔊 *Track 0304*

名 恐怖、害怕 動 害怕、恐懼 同 fright 恐怖

▶名 He has a huge fear of water. 他對水充滿恐懼。

▶動 I fear that he won't arrive in time. 我怕他無法及時趕到。

Feb·ru·ar·y/Feb. [ˈfɛbruˌɛrɪ] 🔊 *Track 0305*

名 二月

▶Would you like to go to Europe with us next February?
明年二月你願意跟我們一起去歐洲嗎？

feed [fid] 🔊 *Track 0306*

動 餵 同 nourish 滋養

▶The cat gets angry when we don't feed her.
我們如果沒餵貓，牠就會生氣。

文法字詞解析
feed 的動詞變化：feed, fed, fed

feel [fil] 🔊 *Track 0307*

動 感覺、覺得 同 experience 經歷、感受

▶I feel numbness in my legs after standing still for over an hour.
站著不動一個小時之後，我覺得雙腳麻痺。

文法字詞解析
1. feel 的動詞變化：feel, felt, felt
2. feel 是連綴動詞，後面可接形容詞補充說明主詞。

feel·ing [ˈfilɪŋ] 🔊 *Track 0308*

名 感覺、感受 同 sensation 感受

▶I have a feeling that this won't work.
我有種感覺，覺得這不會成功。

feel·ings [ˈfilɪŋz] 🔊 *Track 0309*

名 感情、敏感

▶You have to think more about other people's feelings.
你要多想想別人的感受。

few [fju] 🔊 *Track 0310*

形 少的 名 （前面與a連用）少數、幾乎 反 many 許多

▶形 He has very few friends. 他的朋友很少。

▶名 There are a few students in the room. 房間裡有幾個學生。

文法字詞解析
few 是否定用字，後面接可數名詞。

Level **1**

輕鬆學習、入門無負擔
掌握基礎1000單字

Level **2**

Level **3**

Level **4**

Level **5**

Level **6**

fif·teen [ˈfɪfˈtin]
🔊 *Track 0311*

名 十五

▶ Did you order fifteen books from our store?
您從我們書店訂購了十五本書是嗎？

fif·ty [ˈfɪftɪ]
🔊 *Track 0312*

名 五十

▶ Fifty dollars is enough for me to live for a month.
五十美元夠我生活一個月了。

fight [faɪt]
🔊 *Track 0313*

名 打仗、爭論 動 打仗、爭論 同 quarrel 爭吵

▶ 名 The boys got into a fight at school again.
那些男孩們又在學校和人家打架了。

▶ 動 The students started a campaign to fight for freedom of speech. 學生發起一個運動爭取言論自由。

文法字詞解析
fight 的動詞變化：fight, fought, fought

fill [fɪl]
🔊 *Track 0314*

動 填空、填滿 反 empty 倒空

▶ I filled the glass with water. 我用水填滿了玻璃杯。

fi·nal [ˈfaɪnl]
🔊 *Track 0315*

形 最後的、最終的 反 initial 最初的

▶ Is this your final decision（決定）？
這是你最終的決定嗎？

find [faɪnd]
🔊 *Track 0316*

動 找到、發現

▶ I can't find my glasses. 我找不到我的眼鏡。

fine [faɪn]
🔊 *Track 0317*

形 美好的 副 很好地 名 罰款 動 處以罰金 同 nice 好的

▶ 形 It's such a fine day today, isn't it? Let's go out for a walk!
今天天氣真好，對不對？我們出去散步吧！

▶ 副 The coach said that all the athletes did fine in the tournament.
教練說所有的選手在這次比賽中表現都不錯。

▶ 名 You have to pay the fine before this weekend.
這週末前，你必須繳罰款。

▶ 動 I heard that the judge（法官）fined him heavily.
我聽說法官重罰了他。

文法字詞解析
「such a (an) + 形容詞 + 單數可數名詞」
用來表示「這樣的、這等的」，有加強語氣的功能。

fin·ger [ˈfɪŋɚ]
🔊 *Track 0318*

名 手指 反 toe 腳趾

▶ The man gave us the middle finger. 那個男人對我們比了中指。

fin·ish [ˈfɪnɪʃ]
🔊 *Track 0319*

名 完成、結束 動 完成、結束 同 complete 完成

▶ 名 He was lazy from start to finish.
從開始到結束他都是個懶人。

▶ 動 About how long will it take you to finish all your summer homework? 你大概要多久才能完成你所有的暑假作業？

文法字詞解析
from start to finish 從頭到尾

fire [faɪr] 🔊 *Track 0320*

名 火 動 射擊、解雇、燃燒 同 dismiss 解雇

▶名 If your kid gets too close to the fire, he will get burnt（燃燒） easily. 如果你的孩子離火太近的話，他很容易會被燒傷的。

▶動 The employee got fired because he has been late for more than ten days in a raw. 這位員工因為連續十天都遲到而被解雇了。

first [fɜst] 🔊 *Track 0321*

名 第一、最初 形 第一的 副 首先、最初、最一 反 last 最後的

▶名 I'd never met a firefighter before; he's the first. 我之前都沒遇過消防員，他是第一個。

▶形 He's the first person to arrive every day. 他每天都第一個抵達。

▶副 Let's finish our homework first, shall we? 我們先來把功課做完好嗎？

fish [fɪʃ] 🔊 *Track 0322*

名 魚、魚類 動 捕魚、釣魚

▶名 The fish are swimming around happily. 魚兒們快樂地游來游去。

▶動 Would you like to go fishing with us next Saturday or Sunday? 你想不想下週六或週日跟我們一起去釣魚呢？

文法字詞解析
這裡的介系詞 around 有四處、到處的意思。

five [faɪv] 🔊 *Track 0323*

名 五

▶There are five members in her family. 她家有五個人。

floor [flor] 🔊 *Track 0324*

名 地板、樓層 反 ceiling 天花板

▶Would you like me to sweep（打掃）the floor again? It's still very dirty. 你要我再掃一遍地板嗎？它看起來還是很髒。

flow·er [ˈflaʊɚ] 🔊 *Track 0325*

名 花

▶I brought my mom some flowers. 我帶了一些花給我媽媽。

fly [flaɪ] 🔊 *Track 0326*

名 蒼蠅、飛行 動 飛行、飛翔

▶名 The whole office is trying to kill the fly. 整間辦公室的人都在試著殺蒼蠅。

▶動 Birds are born to fly. 鳥兒們生來就是要飛行。

文法字詞解析
fly 的動詞變化：fly, flew, flown

fog [fɑg] 🔊 *Track 0327*

名 霧

▶The fog is so heavy today. 今天的霧好濃。

fol·low [ˈfɑlo] 🔊 *Track 0328*

動 跟隨、遵循、聽得懂 同 trace 跟蹤

▶Mandy followed her father's step and became a lawyer. 曼蒂跟隨她父親的腳步成為律師。

Level
1

輕鬆學習、入門無負擔——
掌握基礎1000單字

Level
2

Level
3

Level
4

Level
5

Level
6

food [fud]
 Track 0329

名 食物

▶Would you like some food? You haven't had anything for the whole day. 你要吃點東西嗎？你已經一整天都沒吃東西了。

foot [fʊt]
 Track 0330

名 腳

▶There is a small temple（廟宇）at the foot of that big mountain. 在那座大山的山腳下有一個小寺廟。

文法字詞解析
foot 的複數是 feet。

for [fɔr]
 Track 0331

介 為、因為、對於 連 因為 同 as 因為

▶介 An apology is not enough for the hurt you made me feel. 你對我造成的傷害，僅僅道歉是不夠的。

▶連 She couldn't afford the brand-name handbag, for she had spent all her wages on her new laptop. 她現在買不起這個名牌手提包，因為她把工資都花在買手提電腦上了。

force [fors]
 Track 0332

名 力量、武力 動 強迫、施壓 同 compel 強迫

▶名 May the force always be with you. 願力量永與你同在。

▶動 I forced my brother to come with me. 我逼我弟弟跟我一起來。

for·eign [ˈfɔrɪn]
 Track 0333

形 外國的 反 native 本土的

▶I would love to visit a foreign country someday. 我總有一天想要去國外。

for·est [ˈfɔrɪst]
 Track 0334

名 森林 同 wood 森林

▶There are all kinds of animals in the forest. 森林裡有各種動物。

for·get [fɚˈgɛt]
 Track 0335

動 忘記 反 remember 記得

▶Don't forget to submit your application before Friday. 別忘了要在週五前提交申請書。

文法字詞解析
forget 後若接 to v，表示「忘記做……」，forget 加 V-ing 則表示「忘記已經做過……」。

fork [fɔrk]
 Track 0336

名 叉

▶He got so mad he threw a fork at her. 他氣到拿叉子丟她。

for·ty [ˈfɔrtɪ]
 Track 0337

名 四十

▶There are forty students in my class. 我們班上有四十個學生。

four [for]
 Track 0338

名 四

▶My four sisters all work in the same company. 我的四個姊妹都在同一家公司工作。

four·teen [ˈforˈtin]
🔊 *Track 0339*

名 十四

▶There are fourteen staff（員工）members in our store now, but I still think we need some more.
我們店裡現在有十四名員工了，但是我覺得我們還需要幾個。

---

free [fri]
🔊 *Track 0340*

形 自由的、免費的 動 釋放、解放 同 release 解放

▶形 All the beer will be on the house. You can have it for free.
今天啤酒都由老闆請客。你可以免費飲用。

▶動 They freed the bird and watched it fly away.
他們釋放了那隻鳥，看著牠飛走。

---

fresh [frɛʃ]
🔊 *Track 0341*

形 新鮮的、無經驗的、淡（水）的 反 stale 不新鮮的

▶Those vegetables aren't fresh.
那些蔬菜不新鮮。

Fri·day/Fri. [ˈfraɪˌde]
🔊 *Track 0342*

名 星期五

▶Let's go to visit the Browns on Friday night. They have moved to a new house.
這週五晚上我們去拜訪布朗一家吧，他們已經搬到新房子了。

---

friend [frɛnd]
🔊 *Track 0343*

名 朋友 反 enemy 敵人

▶My friends are all really easily excited people.
我的朋友們都是非常容易興奮的人。

---

frog [frɑg]
🔊 *Track 0344*

名 蛙

▶The small frog is my brother's pet.
那隻小青蛙是我弟弟的寵物。

---

from [frɑm]
🔊 *Track 0345*

介 從、由於

▶I come from the south.
我從南部來的。

---

front [frʌnt]
🔊 *Track 0346*

名 前面 形 前面的 反 rear 後面、背後

▶名 Mary tends to have motion sickness, so the teacher asked her to sit in the front of the bus.
瑪莉容易暈車，所以老師安排她坐在公車前面。

▶形 The people who sit in the front row are all short.
坐前排的人都很矮。

---

fruit [frut]
🔊 *Track 0347*

名 水果

▶Watermelon is my favorite fruit.
西瓜是我最喜歡的水果。

文法字詞解析
some 在這裡做代名詞使用。

萬用延伸句型
Feel free to... 此用法用來告知對方不需要猶豫、有需要就可以盡量請求幫助。
例如：If you have any questions, feel free to send an email to this address.
如果你有任何問題，歡迎寫電子郵件到這個信箱。

文法字詞解析
姓氏前加 the、後面再加上 s 可以表示一個家族。

文法字詞解析
第二個例句中，who 所引導的形容詞子句用來修飾先行詞 the people。

Level 1
輕鬆學習、入門無負擔──
掌握基礎1000單字

Level 2

Level 3

Level 4

Level 5

Level 6

full [fʊl]
形 滿的、充滿的 反 empty 空的　◀≋ *Track 0348*
▶The room is full of people. 房間裡滿滿都是人。

fun [fʌn]
名 樂趣、玩笑 同 amusement 樂趣　◀≋ *Track 0349*
▶The zoo is such a fun place to visit.
動物園真是個有趣的地方。

fun·ny [ˈfʌnɪ]
形 滑稽的、有趣的 同 humorous 滑稽的　◀≋ *Track 0350*
▶My uncle thinks himself very funny. 我舅舅覺得自己很有趣。

[Gg]

game [gem]
名 遊戲、比賽 同 contest 比賽　◀≋ *Track 0351*
▶I'm sad because my favorite team lost the game.
我難過，因為我最喜歡的球隊輸了比賽。

gar·den [ˈgɑrdn̩]
名 花園　◀≋ *Track 0352*
▶Peter studies garden designing in the community college.
彼得在社區大學裡學習園藝設計。

> **文法字詞解析**
> gardening 指的是「園藝」。

gas [gæs]
名 汽油、瓦斯　◀≋ *Track 0353*
▶I'll wait for you at the gas station by my house.
我在我家旁邊的加油站等你。

gen·er·al [ˈdʒɛnərəl]
形 大體的、一般的 名 將軍　◀≋ *Track 0354*
反 specific 特定的
▶形 The confidential information can not be revealed to the general public.
機密資料不能洩漏給一般大眾。
▶名 The old general is always talking about his dead friends.
那位老將軍總是在講他已死的朋友們的事。

get [gɛt]
動 獲得、成為、到達 同 obtain 獲得　◀≋ *Track 0355*
▶How about getting some advice（建議）from our teachers?
我們從老師那裡請教一些建議怎麼樣？

> **文法字詞解析**
> get 的動詞變化：get, got, gotten 或 get, got, got

ghost [gost]
名 鬼、靈魂 同 soul 靈魂　◀≋ *Track 0356*
▶Have you ever seen a ghost before? 你見過鬼嗎？

gift [gɪft] ◀ Track 0357
名 禮物、天賦 同 present 禮物
▶Nancy has a gift in music, and she has been taking piano lessons since she was six.
南茜有音樂天分，她從六歲就開始學鋼琴。

girl [gɝl] ◀ Track 0358
名 女孩 反 boy 男孩
▶The girls in my class are always talking about clothes.
我們班的女生總是在討論衣服的事。

give [gɪv] ◀ Track 0359
動 給、提供、捐助 反 receive 接受
▶Did you give her anything for Christmas?
你聖誕節有買什麼送她嗎？

glad [glæd] ◀ Track 0360
形 高興的 同 joyous 高興的
▶I'm so glad to see you today. 很高興今天見到你。

glass [ˋglæs] ◀ Track 0361
名 玻璃、玻璃杯 同 pane 窗戶玻璃片
▶Would you like a large glass of beer（啤酒）？
你要不要來一大杯啤酒呢？

glass·es [ˋglæsɪz] ◀ Track 0362
名 眼鏡
▶Did you notice her new glasses? 你有注意到她的新眼鏡嗎？

go [go] ◀ Track 0363
動 去、走 反 stay 留下
▶I'm sorry, but I can't go to your party.
我很抱歉，但我不能去你的派對。

god/god·dess [gɑd]/[ˋgɑdɪs] ◀ Track 0364
名 神／女神
▶There are lots of gods and goddesses in ancient（古代的）tales. 古代故事中有很多神和女神。

gold [gold] ◀ Track 0365
形 金的 名 金子
▶形 These gold coins（硬幣）are not enough for him to buy a house. 這幾枚金幣還不夠他買棟房子。
▶名 In the past, people used gold to buy food and other things from the market.
在過去，人們用金子從市場裡購買食物和其他物品。

good [gʊd] ◀ Track 0366
形 好的、優良的 名 善、善行 同 fine 好的
▶形 Pay attention to your diet. It's all for your own good.
注意飲食。這都是為了你自己好。
▶名 His only dream is to do good. 他唯一的夢想就是做善事。

文法字詞解析
give 的動詞變化：give, gave, given

文法字詞解析
go 動詞變化：go, went, gone

萬用延伸句型
so far so good 目前為止一切良好。
例 如：A: How's your work going？B: Well, so far so good.
甲：你的工作進展如何？乙：嗯，目前為止都還好。

Level 1 輕鬆學習、入門無負擔——掌握基礎1000單字
Level 2
Level 3
Level 4
Level 5
Level 6

good-bye/good·bye/good-by/good·by/bye·bye/bye

🔊 *Track 0367*

[gʊdˋbaɪ]/[gʊdˋbaɪ]/[gʊdˋbaɪ]/[ˋbaɪˌbaɪ]/[baɪ]

名 再見
▶We said goodbye to our friends at the airport.
　我們在機場和朋友們道別。

goose [gus]

🔊 *Track 0368*

名 鵝
▶The goose on my aunt's farm is bigger than a dog.
　我阿姨農場上的鵝比狗還大隻。

grand [grænd]

🔊 *Track 0369*

形 宏偉的、大的、豪華的　同 large 大的
▶We appreciate the grand palaces when we visited the European counties. 去歐洲國家旅遊時，我們欣賞一些宏偉的宮殿。

grand·child [ˋgrændˌtʃaɪld]

🔊 *Track 0370*

名 孫子
▶How often do you take your grandchild to the park?
　您多常帶您的孫子去公園啊？

grand·daugh·ter [ˋgrændˌdɔtɚ]

🔊 *Track 0371*

名 孫女、外孫女
▶His granddaughter is not old enough to find the way to the kindergarten（幼稚園）.
　他的孫女不夠大，還找不到去幼稚園的路。

grand·fath·er/grand·pa

🔊 *Track 0372*

[ˋgrændˌfɑðɚ]/[ˋgrændpɑ]

名 祖父、外祖父
▶My grandfather died a happy man.
　我祖父直到過世都很快樂。

grand·moth·er/grand·ma [ˋgrændˌmʌðɚ]/[ˋgrændmʌ]

🔊 *Track 0373*

名 祖母、外祖母
▶My grandmother is always angry about something or another.
　我祖母總是為某些大小事生氣。

grand·son [ˋgrændˌsʌn]

🔊 *Track 0374*

名 孫子、外孫
▶Fiona adores her grandson so much that she would buy anything for him. 費歐娜很疼她孫子，什麼都買給她。

grass [græs]

🔊 *Track 0375*

名 草　同 lawn 草坪
▶Don't step on the grass; they're sleeping.
　別踩草地，小草在睡覺呢。

gray/grey [gre]/[gre]
🔊 Track 0376

名 灰色 形 灰色的、陰沉的
▶名 The color grey has become popular because of a movie.
因為一部電影的關係，灰色變得受歡迎了。
▶形 I have so many grey hairs, it's sad. 我有好多根灰髮，真是悲慘。

great [gret]
🔊 Track 0377

形 大量的、很好的、偉大的、重要的 同 outstanding 突出的、傑出的
▶I think your idea is great. 我覺得你的點子很棒啊。

green [grin]
🔊 Track 0378

形 綠色的 名 綠色
▶形 Follow the green sign and you'll get there.
跟著綠色的牌子走就會到了。
▶名 I always wear green on Thursdays. 我星期四都穿綠色。

ground [graʊnd]
🔊 Track 0379

名 地面、土地 同 surface 表面
▶The starving vagabond picked up the bread on the ground and
put it in his mouth. 飢餓的流浪漢把地上的麵包撿起來放進嘴裡。

group [grup]
🔊 Track 0380

名 團體、組、群 動 聚合、成群 同 gather 收集
▶名 This game is supposed to be played in groups.
這個遊戲應該要分組玩。
▶動 She grouped all the flowers of the same color together.
她把同樣顏色的花聚集在一起。

文法字詞解析
be supposed to 和 should 有同樣的意思，都是「應該」，後面要加原形動詞。

grow [gro]
🔊 Track 0381

動 種植、生長 同 mature 變成熟、長成
▶The puppy had grown into a giant dog.
那隻小狗已經長成了一隻大狗。

文法字詞解析
grow 的動詞變化：grow, grew, grown

guess [gɛs]
🔊 Track 0382

名 猜測、猜想 動 猜測、猜想 同 suppose 猜測、認為
▶名 I'll give you three guesses as to what my dog's name is.
我讓你猜三次我的狗叫什麼名字。
▶動 I guess the answer is probably B. 我猜答案大概是B。

萬用延伸句型
Guess what? 你知道嗎？ 這個句子可以用在開頭，吸引他人的注意。
例如：Guess what? He just proposed to me! 你知道嗎？他剛剛跟我求婚了！

guest [gɛst]
🔊 Track 0383

名 客人 反 host 主人、東道主
▶Be my guest. Help yourself to the desserts and beverages on
the table. 請別客氣。自己取用桌上的點心和飲料。

guide [gaɪd]
🔊 Track 0384

名 引導者、指南 動 引導、引領 同 lead 引導
▶名 He is the most famous（有名的）guide here, so you won't
get lost in the forest.
他是這兒最有名的嚮導，所以你是不會在森林裡迷路的。
▶動 I am familiar with this place, so I'll guide you around.
我對這個地方很熟悉，讓我來帶你到處玩。

Level **1**
輕鬆學習、入門無負擔——
掌握基礎1000單字

Level **2**

Level **3**

Level **4**

Level **5**

Level **6**

gun [gʌn]
🔊 *Track 0385*
名 槍、砲
▶I've never fired a gun before. 我從來沒開過槍。

[Hh]

hair [hɛr]
🔊 *Track 0386*
名 頭髮
▶My mom cut my hair yesterday. 我媽媽昨天幫我剪了頭髮。

hair·cut [`hɛr⸴kʌt]
🔊 *Track 0387*
名 理髮
▶You really should get a haircut. 你真的該剪頭髮了。

文法字詞解析
「get a haircut」也可以說成「get sb.'s hair cut」，這個用法使用到「get + 主詞 + 主詞補語」的形式，如果是主動語態的話，主詞補語就用 to + V.，如果是被動語態就用 V. p.p.。

half [hæf]
🔊 *Track 0388*
形 一半的 副 一半地 名 半、一半
▶形 I'll have half an apple, thanks. 我吃半個蘋果好了，謝謝。
▶副 The little boy is almost half dead from hunger.
那小男孩幾乎餓得半死了。
▶名 Half of the students in the class are taking a part-time job.
這班上有半數的學生都有在打工。

ham [hæm]
🔊 *Track 0389*
名 火腿
▶Would you like a slice of ham? It's so yummy（美味的）!
要不要來一片火腿？它太美味了！

hand [hænd]
🔊 *Track 0390*
名 手 動 遞交 反 foot 腳
▶名 Could you give me a hand with the baggage（行李）?
你能幫我拿一下行李嗎？
▶動 I handed my dad a glass of beer. 我遞給我爸一杯啤酒。

hap·pen [`hæpən]
🔊 *Track 0391*
動 發生、碰巧 同 occur 發生
▶What happened? Why do you look so mad?
發生什麼事了？你怎麼看起來這麼火大？

萬用延伸句型
What happened? 怎麼了？
因為是已經發生的事情，所以 happen 用過去式。

hap·py [`hæpɪ]
🔊 *Track 0392*
形 快樂的、幸福的 反 sad 悲傷的
▶I'm so happy to see that my brother has won the race.
看到我弟弟贏了賽跑，我真是高興。

hard [hɑrd]
🔊 *Track 0393*
形 硬的、難的 副 努力地 同 stiff 硬的
▶形 It was hard for me to understand the foreign speakers' the speech. 對我來說，了解外國人的演說很困難。
▶副 My grandparents worked hard every day.
我的祖父母每天都努力工作。

hat [hæt]　　　🔊 Track 0394
名 帽子　同 cap 帽子
▶Would you like to go shopping with me? I want to buy a hat.
　你想跟我去逛街嗎？我想去買頂帽子。

hate [het]　　　🔊 Track 0395
名 憎恨、厭惡　動 憎恨、不喜歡　反 love 愛、愛情
▶名 He felt hate toward his enemies（敵人）．
　　他對他的敵人感到憎恨。
▶動 I don't want any spinach in the dish. I hate vegetables.
　　我不想要這道菜裡有任何菠菜。我討厭蔬菜。

have [hæv]　　　🔊 Track 0396
助動 已經　動 吃、有
▶助動 Have you tried their famous burger（漢堡）yet?
　　你已經試過了他們家超有名的漢堡了嗎？
▶動 I had the cake but still felt hungry.
　　我吃了蛋糕，可是還是很餓。

文法字詞解析
1. have 的動詞變化：have, had, had
2. 第一個例句中，是詢問對方「從以前到現在這整段時間內」有沒有吃過那家店的漢堡，所以是用現在完成式。

he [hi]　　　🔊 Track 0397
代 他
▶How often does he come to see you? Once a week or twice a month? 他多久來看你一次？一週一次還是一個月兩次？

head [hɛd]　　　🔊 Track 0398
名 頭、領袖　動 率領、朝某方向行進　同 lead 引導
▶名 The head of our group is a strong woman.
　　我們組織的領袖是個強壯的女人。
▶動 Where are you headed? We'll be going to Kaohsiung.
　　你們要往哪去？我們會去高雄。

health [hɛlθ]　　　🔊 Track 0399
名 健康
▶He had to take a day off because of health reasons.
　他因為健康理由必須請一天假。

hear [hɪr]　　　🔊 Track 0400
動 聽到、聽說　同 listen 聽
▶Have you heard that the new principal is a old-fashioned woman? 你聽說新來的校長是一位古板的女士嗎？

文法字詞解析
hear 的動詞變化：hear, heard, heard
萬用延伸句型
I heard that... 我聽說……

heart [hɑrt]　　　🔊 Track 0401
名 心、中心、核心　同 nucleus 核心
▶I gave you my heart, but you just didn't care.
　我把心都給你了，你卻不在乎。

heat [hit]　　　🔊 Track 0402
名 熱、熱度　動 加熱　反 chill 寒氣
▶名 The heat wave in Europe have causes dozens of deaths.
　　歐洲的熱浪已經造成數十人死亡。
▶動 Sit down and I'll heat the soup. 你坐下來，我來把湯加熱。

Level 1
輕鬆學習、入門無負擔──
掌握基礎1000單字

Level 2

Level 3

Level 4

Level 5

Level 6

heav·y [ˈhɛvɪ]
🔊 *Track 0403*

形 重的、猛烈的、厚的 反 light 輕的

▶The refrigerator was too heavy for the porter to carry on his own. 冰箱太重了，搬家師傅一個人扛不起來。

hel·lo [həˈlo]
🔊 *Track 0404*

感 哈囉（問候語）、喂（電話應答語）

▶How about saying hello to our new neighbors?
去向我們的新鄰居打個招呼怎麼樣？

help [hɛlp]
🔊 *Track 0405*

名 幫助 動 幫助 同 aid 幫助

▶名 Don't worry, you've already been of great help.
別擔心，你已經幫了大忙了。

▶動 Not every person likes to help others.
並不是每個人都樂於助人。

her [hɝ]
🔊 *Track 0406*

代 她的

▶Her kids are always very polite. 她的孩子總是很有禮貌。

hers [hɝz]
🔊 *Track 0407*

代 她的東西

▶This book is mine, and that book is hers.
這本書是我的，那本書是她的。

文法字詞解析
hers 作為所有格代名詞使用，代替所有格和所有格所修飾的名詞。

here [hɪr]
🔊 *Track 0408*

名 這裡 副 在這裡、到這裡 反 there 那裡

▶名 There is a mall 100 miles away from here.
離這裡一百英里處有一家購物中心。

▶副 There are a few mistakes（錯誤）here and there, but it's still a good essay（文章）.
雖然這裡那裡有一些錯誤，但這還是篇很好的文章。

high [haɪ]
🔊 *Track 0409*

形 高的 副 高度地 反 low 低的

▶形 My hat is too high for me to reach.
我的帽子放太高了，我拿不到。

▶副 There's a plane flying high up there.
有架飛機飛得很高。

hill [hɪl]
🔊 *Track 0410*

名 小山 同 mound 小丘

▶Many tourists admired the magnificent castle on the hill.
許多觀光客來瞻仰這山丘上宏偉的城堡。

him [hɪm]
🔊 *Track 0411*

代 他

▶Have you ever talked to him before?
你有跟他講過話嗎？

萬用延伸句型
Have you ever...?
你是否曾經……？

his [hɪz]
Track 0412

代 他的、他的東西

▶He is very tall and fat but his wife is small and short.
他又高又胖，但他的妻子很矮小。

his·to·ry ['hɪstərɪ]
Track 0413

名 歷史

▶The fire in the museum has caused great loss in the history record of Brazil. 博物館發生大火，造成巴西歷史文物紀錄的重大損失。

hit [hɪt]
Track 0414

名 打、打擊 動 打、打擊 同 strike 打、打擊

▶名 The website（網站）tracks（追蹤）how many hits it gets each day. 這個網站會記錄每天的點閱數。

▶動 The man is always hitting his dog.
那個男人老是在打自己的狗。

文法字詞解析
1. hit 的動詞變化：hit, hit, hit
2. hit 也有風行、賣座的意思，例如：Have you listened to the greatest hits album of that band? 你有聽過那個樂團的精選輯嗎？

hold [hold]
Track 0415

動 握住、拿著、持有 名 把握、控制 同 grasp 抓緊、緊握

▶動 Would you like me to hold your baby while you pay for the tickets? 你買票時要不要我幫你抱小孩？

▶名 I can never get a steady（穩定）hold on the heavy camera.
我總是無法把這個重重的相機握穩。

文法字詞解析
hold 的動詞變化：hold, held, held
萬用延伸句型
Hold on.（電話用語）請稍等。

hole [hol]
Track 0416

名 孔、洞 同 gap 裂口

▶There are so many holes in my jeans. 我的牛仔褲破了好多洞。

hol·i·day ['hɑlə͵de]
Track 0417

名 假期、假日 反 weekday 工作日、平常日

▶Christmas is an important holiday season in the western world.
耶誕節在西方世界是個重大的節日。

home [hom]
Track 0418

名 家、家鄉 形 家的、家鄉的 副 在家、回家 同 dwelling 住處

▶名 This is a beautiful place, but it's not my home.
這地方好美，但畢竟不是我的家鄉。

▶形 Don't give strangers your home phone number.
別把你家電話給陌生人。

▶副 I don't think he's home now. 我覺得他現在應該不在家。

萬用延伸句型
Make yourself at home. 請別拘束。
此句用在招呼客人時，告訴對方不用客氣。

home·work ['hom͵wɝk]
Track 0419

名 家庭作業 同 task 工作、作業

▶There is so much homework to do today; I have to start right now. 今天有好多功課要做，我得馬上開始做了。

hope [hop]
Track 0420

名 希望、期望 動 希望、期望 反 despair 絕望

▶名 He has no hope of being accepted（接受）.
他絕對沒希望被接受的。

▶動 I hope that the money I earn（賺取）is enough for me to support my family. 希望我賺的錢能足夠我養家

文法字詞解析
第二句 I hope 後面的 that 也可以省略不寫。

Level 1

Level 2

Level 3

Level 4

Level 5

Level 6

輕鬆學習、入門無負擔

掌握基礎1000單字

horse [hɔrs] 🔊 *Track 0421*
名 馬
▶My favorite horse is the brown one over there.
我最喜歡的馬是那邊棕色那匹。

hot [hɑt] 🔊 *Track 0422*
形 熱的、熱情的、辣的 反 icy 冰冷的
▶Do you like to wash your face with hot water or cold water?
你喜歡用熱水還是冷水洗臉？

hour [aʊr] 🔊 *Track 0423*
名 小時
▶It is said that the successful businessman spent one hour reading every day. 據說那位成功商人每天花一小時讀書。

house [haʊs] 🔊 *Track 0424*
名 房子、住宅 同 residence 房子、住宅
▶Your house is a lot bigger than mine. 你的房子比我的大好多。

how [haʊ] 🔊 *Track 0425*
副 怎樣、如何
▶How do I open this bottle? 我要怎麼開這個瓶子啊？

文法字詞解析
疑問副詞 how 用來詢問某事如何進行、對某事的意見等。

萬用延伸句型
How do you do? 你過得怎麼樣？
用於和對方第一次見面時，較正式的問候。

huge [hjudʒ] 🔊 *Track 0426*
形 龐大的、巨大的 反 tiny 微小的
▶That dog is really huge! It's bigger than me!
那狗也太巨大了吧！比我還要大欸！

hu·man [ˈhjumən] 🔊 *Track 0427*
形 人的、人類的 名 人 同 man 人
▶形 The criminal doesn't seem human to me because of his cruel deeds.
這名罪犯的殘酷行徑，使我覺得他不像個人。
▶名 Sometimes I really don't think my grandma is human.
有時候我真覺得我奶奶不是人。

hun·dred [ˈhʌndrəd] 🔊 *Track 0428*
名 百、許多 形 百的、許多的
▶名 She has hundreds of dresses. 她有數百件洋裝。
▶形 I've got a hundred things to do. 我有好多事情要做。

hun·gry [ˈhʌngrɪ] 🔊 *Track 0429*
形 饑餓的
▶You must be hungry. Would you like something to eat?
你一定覺得餓了。想要吃點東西嗎？

hurt [hɜt] 🔊 *Track 0430*
形 受傷的 動 疼痛 名 傷害
▶形 There is a hurt look on her face; let's ask her what happened.
她的表情看起來很受傷，我們去問問她出什麼事了。
▶動 Does your head still hurt? 你的頭還痛嗎？

文法字詞解析
hurt 的動詞變化：hurt, hurt, hurt

▶名 I can't bear to see the hurt in her eyes.
我真不忍看她那受傷的眼神。

hus·band [ˈhʌzbənd]　◀⧸ Track 0431

名 丈夫　反 wife 妻子
▶Even though Mary's husband has an out-of-wedlock affair, she still loves him. 即使瑪莉的丈夫有外遇，她還是愛他。

[Ii]

I [aɪ]　◀⧸ Track 0432

代 我
▶I don't like insects at all. 我一點都不喜歡昆蟲。

ice [aɪs]　◀⧸ Track 0433

名 冰 動 結冰　同 freeze 結冰
▶名 Do you want ice in your drink? 你的飲料裡要加冰嗎？
▶動 Is the beer iced? You know your uncle likes it best that way.
這啤酒有加冰嗎？你知道你舅舅最喜歡冰的。

i·de·a [aɪˈdiə]　◀⧸ Track 0434

名 主意、想法、觀念　同 notion 主意
▶Your idea sounds great.
你的主意聽起來很棒。

if [ɪf]　◀⧸ Track 0435

連 如果、是否
▶If you talk to him more, you'll see that he's not that bad.
如果你多跟他講點話，你就會發現他也沒那麼糟。

im·por·tant [ɪmˈpɔrtn̩t]　◀⧸ Track 0436

形 重要的　同 principal 重要的
▶It is important that you watch your diet in order to stay healthy.
如果想保持健康，很重要的是要注意飲食。

in [ɪn]　◀⧸ Track 0437

介 在……裡面、在……之內　反 out 在……外面
▶Are you looking for mom? She's in the house.
你在找我媽喔？她在房子裡。

inch [ɪntʃ]　◀⧸ Track 0438

名 英吋
▶How many inches have you grown since last summer?
你去年夏天以來長了幾吋？

in·side [ˈɪnˌsaɪd]　◀⧸ Track 0439

介 在……裡面 名 裡面、內部 形 裡面的 副 在裡面
反 outside 在……外面

文法字詞解析
此句型用於表達未來可能發生的事情，if 所引導的子句用現在式，主要子句則用未來式。

文法字詞解析
look for 尋找

Level 1 輕鬆學習、入門無負擔 掌握基礎1000單字

Level 2

Level 3

Level 4

Level 5

Level 6

▶介 Can we eat inside the car?
我們可以在車裡吃東西嗎？

▶名 There was a label（標籤）on the inside of the box.
盒子內側有個標籤。

▶形 He told me some inside news about the meeting（會議）.
他告訴我一些會議的內幕新聞。

▶副 He knows the city inside out.
他徹底瞭解這座城市。

in·ter·est [ˈɪntərɪst]   🔊 Track 0440

名 興趣、嗜好 動 使……感興趣 同 hobby 嗜好

▶名 The students showed no interest in this documentary.
學生對這部紀錄片沒有興趣。

▶動 You never talk, so I still don't know what interests you.
你都不講話，所以我還是不知道什麼事會讓你感興趣。

文法字詞解析
interest 除了興趣、嗜好之外，在商業用語上還有「利息」的意思，是不可數名詞。

in·to [ˈɪntu]   🔊 Track 0441

介 到……裡面

▶Let's go into the house before it starts raining.
我們在開始下雨前進房子裡去吧。

i·ron [ˈaɪən]   🔊 Track 0442

名 鐵、熨斗 形 鐵的、剛強的 動 熨、燙平 同 steel 鋼鐵

▶名 Would you like me to go to my aunt's and borrow an iron?
你要我去我姑姑家借個熨斗來嗎？

▶形 Dr. Strange has an iron will to fight against the evil power invading the Earth.
奇異博士有剛強的意志要對抗入侵地球的邪惡勢力。

▶動 Your clothes look terrible. Go iron them, okay?
你的衣服看起來超糟的，去燙一下好不好？

萬用延伸句型
Would you like me to...? 你要我去做……嗎？用在詢問他人是否需要協助。

is [ɪz]   🔊 Track 0443

動 是

▶This is an apple. 這是一個蘋果。

it [ɪt]   🔊 Track 0444

代 它

▶It is hot today. 今天好熱。

its [ɪts]   🔊 Track 0445

代 它的

▶Do you know its price? 你知道它的價格嗎？

[Jj]

jam [dʒæm]   🔊 Track 0446

名 果醬、堵塞

▶I like strawberry jam the best. 我最喜歡草莓果醬了。

萬用延伸句型
Stuck in a traffic jam 塞在車陣中

Jan·u·ar·y/Jan. [ˈdʒænjʊˌɛrɪ] 🔊 *Track 0447*
名 一月
▶I really wonder（想知道）what Australia looks like in January.
我真的很想知道澳洲在一月份的時候看起來是什麼樣子。

job [dʒɑb] 🔊 *Track 0448*
名 工作 同 work 工作
▶The employment agency helped the man find a job.
職業介紹所幫助這個人找到工作。

join [dʒɔɪn] 🔊 *Track 0449*
動 參加、加入 同 attend 參加
▶Would you like to join in our discussion（討論）？
你願意參與我們的討論嗎？

joke [dʒok] 🔊 *Track 0450*
名 笑話、玩笑 動 開玩笑 同 kid 開玩笑
▶名 The bully made a joke, but the other students in his class didn't find it funny. 霸凌者開了一個玩笑，但是班上的同學都不覺得有趣。
▶動 My friends are always joking around.
我的朋友們總是在開玩笑。

joy [dʒɔɪ] 🔊 *Track 0451*
名 歡樂、喜悅 反 sorrow 悲傷
▶It is too difficult for me to describe（描述）my joy in words.
我的喜悅難以用語言來形容。

juice [dʒus] 🔊 *Track 0452*
名 果汁
▶Would you like to have some orange juice or a cup of coffee?
你是想喝點柳橙汁，還是來杯咖啡呢？

July/Jul. [dʒuˈlaɪ] 🔊 *Track 0453*
名 七月
▶The summer holiday starts in early July.
暑假是從七月初開始放的。

jump [dʒʌmp] 🔊 *Track 0454*
名 跳躍、跳動 動 跳越、躍過
▶名 I took a small jump over the dog poop（大便）.
我小小跳躍了一下以越過狗屎。
▶動 Don't jump to conclusion when you don't see the whole picture of the event.
在還沒有看清事件全盤面貌之前，別妄下結論。

June/Jun. [dʒun] 🔊 *Track 0455*
名 六月、瓊（女子名） 反 spring 跳、躍
▶It's always so hot in June. 六月總是很熱。

萬用延伸句型
Would you like to join us?
你要加入我們嗎？

文法字詞解析
jump to conclusion = 妄下結論
jump on the bandwagon = 趕上潮流

Level 1
輕鬆學習、入門無負擔
掌握基礎1000單字

Level 2

Level 3

Level 4

Level 5

Level 6

just [dʒʌst] ◀ Track 0456

形 公正的、公平的 副 正好、恰好、剛才 同 fair 公平的

▶形 The principal（校長）is a just, wise（有智慧的）man.
校長是個公正、有智慧的男人。

▶副 I'm just a little older than you are. 我只比你大一點點。

[Kk]

keep [kip] ◀ Track 0457

名 保持、維持 動 保持、維持 同 maintain 維持

▶ You'd better get a job and start earning your keep.
你最好現在就去找份工作，負擔自己的生活費吧。

▶動 I want to keep jogging, but I have a class to go to.
我想要繼續慢跑，但我還得去上課。

文法字詞解析
1. keep 的動詞變化：keep, kept, kept
2. 第一句的 you'd better 是 you had better 的縮寫，表示「最好」，有命令的語氣。

keep·er [ˈkipɚ] ◀ Track 0458

名 看守人

▶ The zoo keepers took care of the leopard cubs around the clock.
動物園管理員24小時照顧這些新生的幼豹。

key [ki] ◀ Track 0459

形 主要的、關鍵的 名 鑰匙 動 鍵入

▶形 Which key word should I search with?
我該用哪個關鍵字搜尋？

▶名 I left my keys inside the house. 我把鑰匙留在房子裡了。

▶動 Can you key in these numbers for me?
可以幫我把數字打進去嗎？

kick [kɪk] ◀ Track 0460

名 踢 動 踢

▶名 The horse's kick made him fall to the ground.
那匹馬一踢他就倒地了。

▶動 Stop kicking your brother! That's not funny!
不要一直踢你哥哥，這一點都不有趣！

kid [kɪd] ◀ Track 0461

名 小孩 動 開玩笑、嘲弄 同 tease 嘲弄

▶名 The man can't get along with kids. He isn't patient enough.
這個人無法和小孩相處。他不夠有耐心。

▶動 You're a vampire（吸血鬼）? Are you kidding?
你是吸血鬼？你在開玩笑吧？

文法字詞解析
kid 的動詞變化：kid, kidded, kidded

kill [kɪl] ◀ Track 0462

名 殺、獵物 動 殺、破壞 同 slay 殺

▶名 The lion looks proud as he sits beside his kill.
那頭獅子看起來很驕傲地坐在牠的獵物旁。

▶動 Did you kill your sister or did you not?
你到底有沒有殺你姐姐？

kind [kaɪnd]　🔊 *Track 0463*

形 仁慈的 名 種類 反 cruel 殘酷的
- ▶形 The prime minister appeals to the citizens to be kind to the refugees. 首相呼籲人民要對難民友善。
- ▶名 They sell all kinds of fruit here. 他們這裡各種水果都有賣。

king [kɪŋ]　🔊 *Track 0464*

名 國王 同 ruler 統治者
- ▶The king treated（對待）his people badly all the time.
  這個國王一直對百姓很不好。

文法字詞解析
all the time 和 always 的意思相同。

kiss [kɪs]　🔊 *Track 0465*

名 吻 動 吻
- ▶名 He gave her a kiss on the lips. 他親吻了她的嘴唇。
- ▶動 The woman says she has never been kissed.
  那位女子說她從來沒被親過。

kitch·en [ˋkɪtʃɪn]　🔊 *Track 0466*

名 廚房
- ▶Where's your dad? Is he in the kitchen? 你爸呢？在廚房嗎？

kite [kaɪt]　🔊 *Track 0467*

名 風箏
- ▶There are a few people flying kites on the beach.
  有一些人在海灘放風箏。

kit·ten/kit·ty [ˋkɪtn̩]/[ˋkɪtɪ]　🔊 *Track 0468*

名 小貓
- ▶The kitten often scratches people who touch it.
  那隻貓常常抓那些摸牠的人。

knee [ni]　🔊 *Track 0469*

名 膝、膝蓋
- ▶The nurse told the athlete how to take care of the scratched knee. 護士教運動員如何照顧膝蓋上的傷口。

knife [naɪf]　🔊 *Track 0470*

名 刀 同 blade 刀片
- ▶Would you like to use chopsticks or a fork and knife?
  您想用筷子還是刀叉？

know [no]　🔊 *Track 0471*

動 知道、瞭解、認識 同 understand 瞭解
- ▶Linda and I have known each other for more than ten years.
  琳達和我已經認識彼此超過十年了。

文法字詞解析
know 的動詞變化：know, knew, known

萬用延伸句型
Trust me, you don't want to know.
此句用於告知對方可能會被接下來要說
的內容嚇到或不高興。

Level 1

輕鬆學習、入門無負擔——
掌握基礎1000單字

Level 2

Level 3

Level 4

Level 5

Level 6

[Ll]

lack [læk] 🔊 *Track 0472*

名 缺乏 動 缺乏 同 absence 缺乏

▶名 I can't do much because of the lack of money.
因為缺錢,所以我沒辦法做什麼事。

▶動 If you lack confidence, it'd be hard to do anything well.
如果你缺乏信心,那什麼事情都會很難做好。

文法字詞解析
注意 lack 在名詞和動詞裡的用法,許多人會在 lack 是動詞時加上 of,這種用法是錯誤的。

la·dy [ˈledɪ] 🔊 *Track 0473*

名 女士、淑女 反 gentleman 紳士

▶Would you like to know that young lady? I can introduce you to her. 你想不想認識那位年輕的小姐?我可以把你介紹給她。

lake [lek] 🔊 *Track 0474*

名 湖 同 pond 池塘

▶There are lots of white swans（天鵝）in the middle of the lake in the park. 公園的湖中央有很多隻白天鵝。

lamb [læm] 🔊 *Track 0475*

名 羔羊、小羊

▶My grandma loves eating lamb, but I really don't.
我奶奶喜歡吃羊,但我真的不喜歡。

lamp [læmp] 🔊 *Track 0476*

名 燈 同 lantern 燈籠、提燈

▶A car accident happened last night because the road lamp was broken. 昨晚發生一場車禍,因為路燈故障。

land [lænd] 🔊 *Track 0477*

名 陸地、土地 動 登陸、登岸 反 sea 海

▶名 Would you like to send your goods（貨物）by sea or by land? 您的貨物要透過海路運輸還是陸路運輸?

▶動 We landed in Hawaii two hours ago.
我們兩個小時前在夏威夷降落了。

large [lɑrdʒ] 🔊 *Track 0478*

形 大的、大量的 反 little 小的

▶The man was found to carry a large amount of illegal drug.
這名男子被發現夾帶大量非法藥品。

last [læst] 🔊 *Track 0479*

形 最後的 副 最後 名 最後 動 持續 同 final 最後的

▶形 The last train has already gone.
最後一班火車已經開走了。

▶副 I saw him last in New York.
我最後一次見到他是在紐約。

▶名 He's the last to arrive, as always.
他一如往常最後一個到。

▶動 How long does the show last? 這個節目持續多久?

文法字詞解析
last word = 結論、決定權
last straw = 導致失敗的最後一擊
to the last = 堅持到底、直到最後一刻
at last = 最後、終於

late [let]
🔊 Track 0480

形 遲的、晚的 副 很遲、很晚 反 early 早的

▶形 Why are you late again? 你怎麼又遲到了？

▶副 He always comes to work late. 他每次上班都遲到。

laugh [læf]
🔊 Track 0481

動 笑 名 笑、笑聲 反 weep 哭泣

▶動 He is laughing so hard he's on the floor.
他笑得太厲害，都摔到地上了。

▶名 Mike's classmates laughed at him for he attended the class in his pajamas. 麥可因為穿著睡衣去上課被同學笑。

law [lɔ]
🔊 Track 0482

名 法律 同 rule 規定、章程

▶My sister studies law in school. 我姐姐在學校讀法律。

lay [le]
🔊 Track 0483

動 放置、產卵 同 put 放置

▶That's a rooster（公雞）; it's not going to lay eggs.
那是隻公雞，牠不會生蛋的。

la·zy [ˈlezɪ]
🔊 Track 0484

形 懶惰的 反 diligent 勤奮的

▶My daughter is too lazy to help me with the housework（家事）.
我的女兒太懶了，不願意幫我做家事。

lead [lid]
🔊 Track 0485

名 領導、榜樣 動 領導、引領 反 follow 跟隨

▶名 We followed his lead, wishing to win the champion in the tournament. 我們追隨他的領導，希望在比賽中得到冠軍。

▶動 He leads his team well. 他把他的團隊領導得很好。

lead·er [ˈlidɚ]
🔊 Track 0486

名 領袖、領導者 同 chief 首領

▶The leader of the group is an old man.
那個團隊的領袖是個老男人。

leaf [lif]
🔊 Track 0487

名 葉

▶Help me clean up those leaves. 幫我清一下這些葉子。

learn [lɝn]
🔊 Track 0488

動 學習、知悉、瞭解 反 teach 教導

▶How long have you learned Spanish（西班牙語）?
你學西班牙文多久了？

least [list]
🔊 Track 0489

名 最少、最小 形 最少的、最小的 副 最少、最小
同 minimum 最少、最小

▶名 I can buy some daily necessities for the orphans. That is the least I could do. 我些日用品給這些孤兒。這是我最起碼能做的事了。

▶形 He has the least money out of all of us. 我們之中他的錢最少。

文法字詞解析
lay 的動詞變化：lay, laid, laid

文法字詞解析
lead 的動詞變化：lead, led, led

文法字詞解析
learn 的動詞變化：learn, learned, learned
萬用延伸句型
I learned from sb. that...
我從某人那裡聽說……
例如：I learned from his brother that he's going to study abroad.
我從他哥哥那裡聽說他要去留學了。

萬用延伸句型
Last but not least,... 最後，但同樣重要的。通常放在文章最後一段的開頭。

Level 1
輕鬆學習、入門無負擔——掌握基礎1000單字

Level 2

Level 3

Level 4

Level 5

Level 6

▶副 She's the least tall in her family. 她是全家個子最小的。

leave [liv] 🔊 Track 0490

動 離開 名 准假 同 depart 離開

▶動 Please don't leave us here. 請別把我們丟在這裡。

▶名 If you ask for leave, you will not be given the bonus（獎金）this month. 一旦你請假，你就得不到這個月的獎金了。

left [lɛft] 🔊 Track 0491

形 左邊的 名 左邊 反 right 右邊

▶形 The kid can use his left hand to use scissors.
這個孩子可以用左手使用剪刀。

▶名 Let's count from left to right.
我們從左到右數吧。

leg [lɛg] 🔊 Track 0492

名 腿 反 arm 手臂

▶I'd love to have her long legs. 真想擁有像她那麼長的腿。

less [lɛs] 🔊 Track 0493

形 更少的、更小的 副 更少、更小 反 more 更多

▶形 I have less money than you. 我的錢比你更少。

▶副 My book is less expensive than yours.
我的書比你的更便宜。

less·on [ˈlɛsn̩] 🔊 Track 0494

名 課

▶Peter had learned a less from his mistake.
彼得從這次犯錯經驗中學到教訓。

let [lɛt] 🔊 Track 0495

動 讓 同 allow 准許

▶She lets her children eat fast food every day.
她每天都讓小孩吃速食。

let·ter [ˈlɛtɚ] 🔊 Track 0496

名 字母、信

▶I got a letter from a fan! 我收到粉絲寄來的信了！

lev·el [ˈlɛvl̩] 🔊 Track 0497

名 水準、標準 形 水平的 同 horizontal 水準的

▶名 Her level of reading in English is very high.
她的英語閱讀程度很高。

▶形 You need to keep a level head in this situation（狀況）.
面對這種狀況，你必須保持平穩冷靜的心態。

lie [laɪ] 🔊 Track 0498

名 謊言 動 說謊、位於、躺著 反 truth 實話

▶名 There are lots of lies in the newspapers.
報紙上充滿了謊言。

▶動 He lies better than I ever can. 他比我更會撒謊。

life [laɪf] 🔊 *Track 0499*

名 生活、生命 同 existence 生命
▶I have never met this man in my life.
我這一生還沒見過這男人。

lift [lɪft] 🔊 *Track 0500*

名 舉起 動 升高、舉起 同 raise 舉起
▶名 Could you give me a lift to the train station?
　能讓我搭個便車去火車站嗎？
▶動 Would you like me to lift the box for you?
　你要我幫你舉起這個箱子嗎？

light [laɪt] 🔊 *Track 0501*

名 光、燈 形 輕的、光亮的 動 點燃、變亮 反 dark 黑暗
▶名 Turn on the lights, please. 請開個燈吧，謝謝。
▶形 The smartphone is light and efficient, which made it
　popular among teenagers.
　這款智慧型手機很輕且效率高，非常受青少年歡迎。
▶動 Her face lights up when she hears the good news.
　她聽到這個好消息，整張臉都亮了起來。

like [laɪk] 🔊 *Track 0502*

動 喜歡 介 像、如 反 dislike 不喜歡
▶動 You know I'll always like you the best.
　你知道我永遠最喜歡你了。
▶介 He's like my little brother. 他就像我弟弟似的。

like·ly [ˈlaɪklɪ] 🔊 *Track 0503*

形 可能的 副 可能地 同 probable 可能的
▶形 It is likely that Mike will get a promotion this year.
　今年麥可很有機會升遷。
▶副 He may be at home as likely as not. 他說不定在家呢。

lil·y [ˈlɪlɪ] 🔊 *Track 0504*

名 百合花
▶The lady is as beautiful as a lily. 這個女子像百合一樣漂亮。

line [laɪn] 🔊 *Track 0505*

名 線、線條 動 排隊、排成 同 string 繩、線
▶名 The line is too long. 這個隊伍太長了。
▶動 The streets were lined on both sides with people.
　街道兩旁都站著人。

li·on [ˈlaɪən] 🔊 *Track 0506*

名 獅子
▶The captain is as brave as a lion.
　這位上尉有如獅子一般地勇敢。

lip [lɪp] 🔊 *Track 0507*

名 嘴唇
▶She has really thick lips. 她的嘴唇很厚。

萬用延伸句型
How do you like...? 你覺得……如何？
例如：How do you like your English
class? 你覺得英文課如何？

文法字詞解析
likely 前面可以加 most、more 等副詞來加
強程度。

Level 1 輕鬆學習、入門無負擔 掌握基礎1000單字

Level 2

Level 3

Level 4

Level 5

Level 6

list [lɪst] 🔊 *Track 0508*

名 清單、目錄、列表 動 列表、編目

▶名 Betty always makes a shopping list before she goes to the grocery store.
貝蒂每次去超商，都會列好購物清單。

▶動 Is your name listed here? 你的名字有列在這裡嗎？

lis·ten [ˈlɪsn̩] 🔊 *Track 0509*

動 聽 同 hear 聽

▶Are you even listening to me? 你到底有沒有在聽我講話？

文法字詞解析
listen 和 hear 雖然都是聽，但用法不太一樣。llisten 是專注的聽，hear 則是不經意的聽到。

lit·tle [ˈlɪtl̩] 🔊 *Track 0510*

形 小的 名 少許、一點 副 很少地 反 large 大的

▶形 I feel tired; let's rest a little while, shall we?
我覺得累了，我們稍微休息一下好嗎？

▶名 He had little to tell us. Let's go ask another person.
他沒有什麼可以告訴我們，我們去問另一個人吧。

▶副 His health is improving（改善）little by little.
他的健康狀況正逐漸好轉。

live [laɪv]/[lɪv] 🔊 *Track 0511*

形 有生命的、活的 動 活、生存、居住 反 die 死

▶形 Don't touch the live wire（電線）!
不要碰那個帶電的電線！

▶動 It's too expensive for me to rent（租）a house alone, so I have to live with others.
我獨自一人租房子太貴了，我只能和別人合住。

long [lɔŋ] 🔊 *Track 0512*

形 長（久）的 副 長期地 名 長時間 動 渴望 反 short 短的

▶形 Because of the principal's long speech, students got impatient and distracted. 因為校長演講太冗長，學生們變得沒耐性且分心了。

▶副 They have worked hard all day long. 他們工作了一整天了。

▶名 Before long, all the children had left the room.
過不了多久，孩子們全都離開房間了。

▶動 He longs for a chance to visit Shanghai.
他渴望有機會去上海。

look [lʊk] 🔊 *Track 0513*

名 看、樣子、臉色 動 看、注視 同 watch 看

▶名 The look on his face after he heard the news was heartbreaking（令人心碎的）.
他聽到新聞之後臉上的表情令人心碎。

▶動 Stop looking at me, it makes me uncomfortable.
不要一直看我啦，很不舒服耶。

文法字詞解析
make + 受詞 + adj. / V. / V. p.p. / N.
使……變得……

lot [lɑt] 🔊 *Track 0514*

名 很多 同 plenty 很多

▶A lot of kids in my class love the zoo.
我們班上很多小朋友都很喜歡動物園。

loud [laʊd] 🔊 *Track 0515*

形 大聲的、響亮的 反 silent 安靜的
▶The man lost his temper and became loud in the conversation.
　對話中，那位男性發脾氣，講話大聲起來。

love [lʌv] 🔊 *Track 0516*

動 愛、熱愛 名 愛 同 adore 熱愛
▶動 She loves rock music. 她很喜愛搖滾樂。
▶名 I fell in love with him at first sight.
　　我第一眼看到他就墜入情網了。

low [lo] 🔊 *Track 0517*

形 低聲的、低的 副 向下、在下面 同 inferior 下方的
▶形 My low grades made my parents mad.
　　我很低的成績讓我的父母很生氣。
▶副 The apple is hanging（懸掛）low and is easy to pick.
　　那個蘋果掛得很低，很容易採到。

luck·y [ˈlʌkɪ] 🔊 *Track 0518*

形 有好運的
▶I was lucky enough to hit the jackpot.
　我太幸運了，中了彩券頭獎。

lunch/lunch·eon 🔊 *Track 0519*
[lʌntʃ]/[ˈlʌntʃən]

名 午餐
▶How about going out for lunch? I don't want to cook today.
　我們去外面吃午餐好不好？我今天不想煮飯了。

[Mm]

ma·chine [məˈʃin] 🔊 *Track 0520*

名 機器、機械
▶We know nothing about the machine, so it's too difficult for us to operate（操作）it.
　我們一點都不瞭解這台機器，因此我們很難操縱它。

mad [mæd] 🔊 *Track 0521*

形 神經錯亂的、發瘋的 同 crazy 瘋狂的
▶Why are you mad at me? 你為什麼對我生氣呢？

mail [mel] 🔊 *Track 0522*

名 郵件 動 郵寄 同 send 發送、寄
▶名 We've got so much mail today.
　　我們今天收到好多郵件喔。
▶動 Can you mail this letter for me?
　　可以幫我寄一下這封信嗎？

萬用延伸句型
Keep a low profile 低調行事

萬用延伸句型
be mad about... 對……很著迷

Level 1
輕鬆學習、入門無負擔 ── 掌握基礎1000單字

Level 2

Level 3

Level 4

Level 5

Level 6

make [mek]
動 做、製造　**同** manufacture 製造
▶I've made a cake just for you. 我專為你做了一個蛋糕。

Track 0523

man [mæn]
名 成年男人　**名** 人類（不分男女）　**反** woman 女人
▶**名** There are lots of men but few women in our company（公司）. 我們公司男多女少。
▶**名** Climate has changed a lot during the history of man.
氣候在人類歷史上產生了很大的變化。

Track 0524

man·y [`mɛnɪ]
形 許多　**同** numerous 很多
▶I heard many rumors about that candidate.
我聽了很多關於那位候選人的傳言。

Track 0525

map [mæp]
名 地圖　**動** 用地圖表示、繪製地圖
▶**名** I can't read maps, which is kind of a problem.
我看不懂地圖，這可真是個問題。
▶**動** This newly discovered island hasn't been mapped yet.
這座新發現的島嶼還沒有被繪製在地圖上。

Track 0526

文法字詞解析
map 的動詞變化：map, mapped, mapped

March/Mar. [mɑrtʃ]
名 三月
▶The weather is still a little bit cold in early March.
三月初的天氣還是有點冷。

Track 0527

mar·ket [`mɑrkɪt]
名 市場
▶I mother is used to buying groceries in the traditional market.
我母親習慣在統市場購物。

Track 0528

mar·ry [`mærɪ]
動 使結為夫妻、結婚　**反** divorce 離婚
▶They were married twenty years ago. 他們是二十年前結婚的。

Track 0529

mas·ter [`mæstɚ]
名 主人、大師、碩士　**動** 精通
▶**名** The dog likes sleeping on his master.
那隻狗喜歡睡在主人身上。
▶**動** I practiced and practiced but still couldn't master the art of playing the piano.
我一直練習，但還是沒辦法精通彈鋼琴的藝術。

Track 0530

文法字詞解析
be one's own master = 做自己的主人
be the master of situation = 控制局勢
master of ceremonies = 節目主持人

match [mætʃ]
名 比賽　**動** 相配　**同** contest 比賽
▶**名** Jack defeated his opponent by 3 to 0 in the tennis match.
傑克在網球賽中以三比零擊敗對手。
▶**動** The color of the shirt does not match that of the tie.
那件襯衫的顏色和領帶不配。

Track 0531

mat·ter [ˈmætɚ]
Track 0532

名 事情、問題 動 要緊 同 affair 事情、事件

▶ 名 What's the matter? Are you all right?
發生什麼事了？你還好嗎？

▶ 動 It doesn't matter whether she is here or not.
她是否在這裡一點都不要緊。

萬用延伸句型
No matter S1 + V1, S2 + V2… 不管……
例如：No matter where you are, I will try
my best to find you.
不管你在哪，我都會盡全力找到你。

May [me]
Track 0533

名 五月

▶ I was born in late May, which means that I'm a Gemini（雙子座）. 我是五月底出生的，所以我是雙子座。

may [me]
Track 0534

助 可以、可能

▶ It may rain in the afternoon, so let's just stay at home.
下午可能要下雨了吧，因此我們就待在家裡好了。

文法字詞解析
may 的時態變化：may, might

may·be [ˈmebɪ]
Track 0535

副 或許、大概

▶ Don't worry. Maybe your son is just lost, not missing.
別擔心。也許你兒子不是失蹤，只是迷路。

me [mi]
Track 0536

代 我

▶ Could you tell me how long I can keep these books and when I have to return them?
您能告訴我這些書我可以保留多久還有何時該歸還嗎？

mean [min]
Track 0537

動 意指、意謂 形 惡劣的 同 indicate 指出、顯示

▶ 動 Huh? I don't know what you mean.
啊？我不懂你的意思耶。

▶ 形 The boy is really mean to his sister.
那個男孩對他妹妹超壞的。

文法字詞解析
mean 的動詞變化：mean, meant, meant

萬用延伸句型
I didn't mean to... 我不是故意要……。
例如：Sorry, I didn't mean to break your
glasses.
抱歉，我不是故意弄壞你的眼鏡的。

meat [mit]
Track 0538

名 （食用）肉 反 vegetable 蔬菜

▶ Jane is a vegetarian. She doesn't include any meat in her diet.
珍是素食者。她不吃肉。

meet [mit]
Track 0539

動 碰見、遇到、舉行集會、開會 同 encounter 碰見

▶ Would you like to meet my family? 你想見見我家人嗎？

文法字詞解析
meet 的動詞變化：meet, met, met

mid·dle [ˈmɪdl̩]
Track 0540

名 中部、中間、在……中間 形 居中的

▶ 名 It is rude to stand up and walk around in the theater in the middle of the performance.
表演中在戲院中走動是很不禮貌的。

▶ 形 Let's sit in the middle row; it's the best place to watch a movie. 我們就坐在中間排吧，那是看電影的最佳地點。

文法字詞解析
center 是指在一個空間的中心點，
middle 則是大略在一個空間的中間位置。

mile [maɪl]　🔊 *Track 0541*

名 英里（＝1.6 公里）

▶There are still a few miles before we get to Taichung.
要到台中還有幾英里。

milk [mɪlk]　🔊 *Track 0542*

名 牛奶

▶Not everyone likes to drink milk.
並非每個人都喜歡喝牛奶。

mind [maɪnd]　🔊 *Track 0543*

名 頭腦、思想 動 介意 反 body 身體

▶名 You look troubled（煩惱的）. What's on your mind?
你看起來很煩惱，在想什麼呢？

▶動 Would you mind turning down the volume of the music?
你介意調低音樂音量嗎？

萬用延伸句型
if you don't mind... 如果你不介意的
話……。用在禮貌的請示他人。

min·ute [ˋmɪnɪt]　🔊 *Track 0544*

名 分、片刻 同 moment 片刻

▶He can hold his breath for three minutes. 他可以憋氣三分鐘。

Miss/miss [mɪs]　🔊 *Track 0545*

名 小姐 反 Mr./Mister 先生

▶Miss Smith is a tall young lady.
史密斯小姐是個高挑的年輕女性。

miss [mɪs]　🔊 *Track 0546*

動 想念、懷念 名 失誤、未擊中 反 hit 擊中

▶動 They are bound（必定的）to miss the train.
他們一定會錯過這班火車。

▶名 It is too hard to hit the target（目標）without（沒有）a
single（單一的）miss. 打靶要百發百中很難。

文法字詞解析
miss out（口語）＝ 損失大了
hit-and-miss（口語）＝ 時好時壞的、碰
運氣

mis·take [mɪˋstek]　🔊 *Track 0547*

名 錯誤、過失 同 error 錯誤

▶The careless mistake made Frank lose his credibility.
粗心的錯誤讓法蘭克失去信用。

mo·ment [ˋmomənt]　🔊 *Track 0548*

名 一會兒、片刻 同 instant 頃刻、一剎那

▶At the moment, only three people are in the room.
這一刻只有三個人在房間裡。

mom·my/mom·ma/ mom/ma·ma/ma/mum·my　🔊 *Track 0549*

[ˋmamɪ]/[mama]/[mam]/[ˋmamə]/[ma]/[ˋmʌmɪ]

名 媽咪

▶What did my mom look like when she was a little girl?
媽媽還是個小女孩的時候長什麼樣子呢？

Mon·day/Mon. [ˈmʌnde]
🔊 *Track 0550*

名 星期一

▶I was planning to visit him on Monday.
我本來打算週一去拜訪他的。

mon·ey [ˈmʌnɪ]
🔊 *Track 0551*

名 錢、貨幣 同 cash 現金

▶Gary wants to make money by selling his reproduction oil paintings.
蓋瑞想靠賣複製的油畫賺錢。

mon·key [ˈmʌŋkɪ]
🔊 *Track 0552*

名 猴、猿

▶This monkey is six years old. 這猴子六歲了。

month [mʌnθ]
🔊 *Track 0553*

名 月

▶I have to pay rent（租金）every month.
我每個月都要繳房租。

moon [mun]
🔊 *Track 0554*

名 月亮 反 sun 太陽

▶A full moon could cause a big flood tide. 滿月會造成漲潮。

more [mor]
🔊 *Track 0555*

形 更多的、更大的 反 less 更少的、更小的

▶There are more math majors than philosophy majors in the university. 這所大學裡，主修數學的學生比主修哲學的多。

morn·ing [ˈmɔrnɪŋ]
🔊 *Track 0556*

名 早上、上午

反 evening 傍晚、晚上

▶I go jogging every morning. 我每天早上都去慢跑。

most [most]
🔊 *Track 0557*

形 最多的、大部分的 名 最大多數、大部分 反 least 最少的

▶形 Most students in my class are really nice.
我們班大部分的學生人都很好。

▶名 I don't know about everyone else, but I think most would agree. 我是不知道其他人怎樣啦，但我覺得大部分的人都會同意吧。

moth·er [ˈmʌðɚ]
🔊 *Track 0558*

名 母親、媽媽 反 father 爸爸

▶My mother is always singing in the garden.
我媽媽總是在花園裡唱歌。

moun·tain [ˈmaʊntn̩]
🔊 *Track 0559*

名 高山

▶Richard likes to go mountain climbing in his free time.
理查有空時會去爬山。

文法字詞解析
most 的後面不能跟定冠詞、指示代名詞或所有格代名詞，若遇到這些情況，需改寫成 most of。

Level 1 輕鬆學習、入門無負擔——掌握基礎1000單字

Level 2

Level 3

Level 4

Level 5

Level 6

mouse [maʊs] 　　🔊 *Track 0560*
名 老鼠 同 rat 鼠
▶Guess what? I caught a mouse yesterday!
　猜猜發生了什麼事？我昨天抓到一隻老鼠耶！

mouth [maʊθ] 　　🔊 *Track 0561*
名 嘴、口、口腔
▶Shut your big mouth. This has nothing to do with you.
　閉上你的大嘴。這和你無關。

move [muv] 　　🔊 *Track 0562*
動 移動、行動 反 stop 停
▶The family next door is moving away. 隔壁的家庭要搬走了。

move·ment [ˋmuvmənt] 　　🔊 *Track 0563*
名 運動、活動、移動 同 motion 運動、活動
▶The hunters could sense any movement of their prey.
　獵人能感覺到獵物的一舉一動。

mov·ie/mo·tion
pic·ture/film/cin·e·ma 　🔊 *Track 0564*
[ˋmuvɪ]/[ˋmoʃən ˏpɪktʃɚ]/[fɪlm]/[ˋsɪnəmə]
名 （一部）電影
▶Would you like to go see a movie with me?
　你願意陪我去看場電影嗎？

Mr./Mis·ter [ˋmɪstɚ] 　　🔊 *Track 0565*
名 對男士的稱呼、先生
▶Mr. Lee is our English teacher. 李先生是我們的英文老師。

Mrs. [ˋmɪsɪz] 　　🔊 *Track 0566*
名 夫人
▶What does Mrs. Smith look like? We haven't met yet.
　史密斯夫人長什麼樣子呢？我們還沒有見過面。

Ms. [mɪz] 　　🔊 *Track 0567*
名 女士（代替Miss或Mrs.的字，不指明對方的婚姻狀況）
▶Ms. White, would you like to wait a moment? Our manager
　（經理）is having a meeting now.
　懷特小姐，您可以稍等片刻嗎？我們經理正在開會。

much [mʌtʃ] 　　🔊 *Track 0568*
名 許多 副 很、十分 形 許多的（修飾不可數名詞）
反 little 少、不多的
▶名 Stop wasting clean water. We don't have much left.
　　不要浪費乾淨的水。我們沒剩多少了。
▶副 I don't like it much. I think it's ugly.
　　我不太喜歡，我覺得好醜。
▶形 You've eaten too much again! 你又吃太多了。

文法字詞解析
「開會中」也可以用「at a meeting」來
表示。

mud [mʌd] 　🔊 *Track 0569*

名 爛泥、稀泥　同 dirt 爛泥

▶It's too hard for us to walk in the mud, so let's take another road. 在淤泥中走路太難了，我們換條路走吧！

mug [mʌg] 　🔊 *Track 0570*

名 帶柄的大杯子、馬克杯

▶I like to drink hot chocolate with a big mug on a cold winter day. 我喜歡在冬天用大馬克杯喝熱可可。

mu·sic [ˈmjuzɪk] 　🔊 *Track 0571*

名 音樂

▶Let's put on some music. It's too quiet in the room. 讓我們放聽點音樂吧，房間裡太安靜了。

must [mʌst] 　🔊 *Track 0572*

助動 必須、必定

▶You must be here at seven or we'll leave without you. 你一定要七點前到，不然我們會丟下你先離開喔。

my [maɪ] 　🔊 *Track 0573*

代 我的

▶Don't worry; he is my good friend as well as my doctor. 別擔心，他既是我的醫生也是我的好朋友。

[Nn]

name [nem] 　🔊 *Track 0574*

名 名字、姓名、名稱、名義　同 label 名字、稱號

▶What's your dog's name? 你的狗叫什麼名字？

na·tion [ˈneʃən] 　🔊 *Track 0575*

名 國家　同 country 國家

▶Would you like to take part in the nation-wide singing competition（比賽）？ 你想參加這個全國性的歌唱比賽嗎？

na·ture [ˈnetʃɚ] 　🔊 *Track 0576*

名 自然界、大自然

▶Meng Tzu's dogmatic teaching pointed that human beings are all kind in nature. 孟子的教條指出人性本善。

near [nɪr] 　🔊 *Track 0577*

形 近的、接近的、近親的、親密的　反 far 遠的

▶His house is near mine. 他家離我家很近。

文法字詞解析

hot chocolate 不可數，所以用 a mug of 來修飾。

文法字詞解析

name 做動詞使用有「替……命名」的意思。

文法字詞解析

形容詞字尾「-wide」表示「擴及某個領域的」。

Level 1 輕鬆學習、入門無負擔——掌握基礎1000單字

Level 2

Level 3

Level 4

Level 5

Level 6

neck [nɛk]
◀ *Track 0578*

名 頸、脖子

▶The cute little baby has no neck.
那個可愛的小寶寶沒脖子。

need [nid]
◀ *Track 0579*

名 需要、必要 動 需要 同 demand 需要、需求

▶名 Kevin is so kind that he always helps those in need.
凱文很善良，總是幫助需要的人。

▶動 I don't need your help. 我不需要你幫忙。

nev·er [`nɛvɚ]
◀ *Track 0580*

副 從來沒有、決不、永不 反 ever 始終、曾經

▶I'll never make such a mistake again.
我再也不會犯同樣的錯誤了。

new [nju]
◀ *Track 0581*

形 新的 反 old 老舊的

▶Would you like to try something new?
您要不要嘗試新鮮的東西？

news [njuz]
◀ *Track 0582*

名 新聞、消息（不可數名詞） 同 information 消息、報導

▶Have you heard the news yet? 你有聽到那個消息了嗎？

news·pa·per [`njuzˌpepɚ]
◀ *Track 0583*

名 報紙

▶He sells newspapers at the subway. 他在捷運賣報紙。

next [nɛkst]
◀ *Track 0584*

副 其次、然後 形 其次的 同 subsequent 後來的

▶副 I like this blue dress best and that white one next. What about you?
我最喜歡這條藍色的裙子，再來是那條白色的，你呢？

▶形 The train had departed before we arrived at the station. We had to wait for the next one. 我們到達車站時，火車已離站。我們得等下一班。

nice [naɪs]
◀ *Track 0585*

形 和藹的、善良的、好的 反 nasty 惡意的

▶If you are nice to the kid, he will also be friendly（友好的）to you. 只要你對那個孩子親切一點，他也同樣會對你很友好的。

night [naɪt]
◀ *Track 0586*

名 晚上 反 day 白天

▶What do you usually do at night? 你平常晚上都做什麼？

nine [naɪn]
◀ *Track 0587*

名 九個

▶You have nine brothers? You've got to be kidding!
你有九個兄弟喔？開玩笑的吧？

萬用延伸句型

A friend in need is a friend indeed 患難之交才是真朋友

nine·teen [ˈnaɪnˌtin]
Track 0588

名 十九

▶There are nineteen students in her class, including（包括）ten boys and nine girls.
她的班上有十九個學生，包括十個男生和九個女生。

文法字詞解析
including 和 included 都有包括的意思，但 including 是介係詞，要用在名詞或代名詞前，而 included 則是形容詞，用在名詞或代名詞的後方。

nine·ty [ˈnaɪntɪ]
Track 0589

名 九十

▶My grandma is ninety and still so healthy.
我奶奶都九十了依然非常健康。

no/nope [no]/[nop]
Track 0590

形 沒有、不、無

▶Why did you say no to his proposal（求婚）?
妳為什麼對他的求婚說不啊？

noise [nɔɪz]
Track 0591

名 喧鬧聲、噪音、聲音 反 silence 安靜

▶We spent a sleepless night being disturbed by the noise on the street. 我們因為街道上的噪音打擾，整夜睡不好。

nois·y [ˈnɔɪzɪ]
Track 0592

形 嘈雜的、喧鬧的、熙熙攘攘的 反 silent 安靜的

▶It's too noisy for me to concentrate（專心）on my studying.
太吵了，害得我都不能專心唸書。

noon [nun]
Track 0593

名 正午、中午

▶We'll have lunch together at noon. 我們中午會一起吃午餐。

nor [nɔr]
Track 0594

連 既不……也不、（兩者）都不 反 or 或是

▶He can neither（兩者都不）read nor write.
他既不會讀也不會寫。

文法字詞解析
使用「neither... nor...」的句型時，兩個子句的主詞和動詞要倒裝，變成「Neither V. + S. , nor V. + S.」。
例如：Neither could I hear what he said, nor could I tell where he is. 我既不能聽到他說的話，也找不到他在哪。

north [nɔrθ]
Track 0595

名 北、北方 形 北方的 反 south 南方、南方的

▶名 The airport is in the north of the country, but famous scenic spots are mostly in the south. 機場在該國的北方，但大多數知名景點都在南部。

▶形 The north branch（分支）of the shop is bigger.
這家店的北區分店比較大間。

nose [noz]
Track 0596

名 鼻子

▶There is something wrong with my nose. 我的鼻子有點怪怪的。

萬用延伸句型
There's something wrong with...（某人／事／物）有點問題。

not [nɑt]
Track 0597

副 不（表示否定）

▶You should not talk to your sister like that.
你不應該這樣對你妹妹講話。

Level 1 輕鬆學習、入門無負擔──掌握基礎1000單字

Level 2

Level 3

Level 4

Level 5

Level 6

note [not]
🔊 *Track 0598*

名 筆記、便條 動 記錄、注釋 同 write 寫下

▶名 Don't pass notes in class. 上課不要傳紙條。

▶動 Please note down every word that the teacher said in class.
請把老師在課堂上所說的每一個字都記下來。

noth·ing [ˋnʌθɪŋ]
🔊 *Track 0599*

副 決不、毫不 名 無關緊要的人、事、物

▶副 Don't be stupid, it was nothing like that.
別蠢了,根本就不是那樣。

▶名 Nothing can change my determination to study abroad.
沒有任何事可以動搖我出國讀書的決心。

no·tice [ˋnotɪs]
🔊 *Track 0600*

動 注意 名 佈告、公告、啟事 反 ignore 忽略

▶動 She didn't notice that I had entered the room.
她沒有看到我走進房間裡。

▶名 There was a notice on the board. 公布板上有張公告。

◁ 文法字詞解析
在第一個例句裡,「enter the room(進入房間)」是先發生的動作,「notice(注意)」則在它之後發生,但兩者都是過去發生的事,所以後者用過去式,前者則用過去完成式。

No·vem·ber/Nov. [noˋvɛmbɚ]
🔊 *Track 0601*

名 十一月

▶The next meeting (會議) will be in November.
下次會議將於十一月份舉行。

now [naʊ]
🔊 *Track 0602*

副 現在、此刻 名 如今、目前 反 then 那時、當時

▶副 Mom asked me to finish my homework now.
我媽叫我現在立刻把功課做完。

▶名 From now on, I promise (保證) I'll never be late again.
從現在起,我保證不會再遲到了。

num·ber [ˋnʌmbɚ]
🔊 *Track 0603*

名 數、數字

▶I am afraid you have dialed (撥) the wrong number.
恐怕您打錯號碼了。

◁ 萬用延伸句型
I am afraid (that)... 恐怕……

nurse [nɝs]
🔊 *Track 0604*

名 護士

▶When David saw the male nurse, he was kind of surprised.
大衛看到男性護士時,有點驚訝。

[Oo]

O.K./OK/okay [ˋoˌke]
🔊 *Track 0605*

名 好、沒問題

▶Are you sure you're okay? Do you need to sit down?
你確定你還好嗎?要不要坐下來?

o·cean [ˋoʃən]
◀ *Track 0606*

名 海洋 同 sea 海洋

▶It is said that there are lots of creatures in the ocean unknown to human. 據說海洋裡還有很多不為人類所知的生物。

o'clock [əˋklɑk]
◀ *Track 0607*

副 ……點鐘

▶Would you like to come to the party at 8 o'clock tonight? 您願意來參加今晚八點的派對嗎？

Oc·to·ber/Oct. [ɑkˋtobə]
◀ *Track 0608*

名 十月

▶Would you like to take your holiday in October? You can choose（選擇）any time you want. 你願意在十月份休假嗎？你可以選擇任何你想要的時間來休。

of [əv]
◀ *Track 0609*

介 含有、由……製成、關於、從、來自

▶I'm afraid of snakes. 我很怕蛇。

off [ɔf]
◀ *Track 0610*

介 從……下來、離開……、不在……之上 副 脫開、去掉

▶介 I used a special detergent to get the dirt off my jacket. 我用一個特別的清潔劑將髒污從我的外套上移除。

▶副 Would you like me to take your coat off, sir? 先生，要我幫你把外套脫下來嗎？

文法字詞解析
Take sth. off 意思是脫下 sth.，也可以寫成 take off sth.，不過 sth. 前面都要加上所有格或是冠詞。

of·fice [ˋɔfɪs]
◀ *Track 0611*

名 辦公室

▶There are few people in the office today. 今天辦公室裡人很少。

of·fi·cer [ˋɔfəsə]
◀ *Track 0612*

名 官員 同 official 官員

▶He is a good military（軍事的）officer. 他是名優秀的軍官。

of·ten [ˋɔfən]
◀ *Track 0613*

副 常常、經常

▶I often watch International news on this cable TV channel. 我常在這個有線電視頻道上觀看國際新聞。

oil [ɔɪl]
◀ *Track 0614*

名 油 同 petroleum 石油

▶All those countries are fighting over oil. 這些國家都在爭著搶油。

old [old]
◀ *Track 0615*

形 年老的、舊的 反 young 年輕的

▶You are never too old to learn. 活到老，學到老。

萬用延伸句型
Never too old to V. 做……永遠不嫌遲

Level
1
輕鬆學習、入門無負擔——
掌握基礎1000單字

Level 2

Level 3

Level 4

Level 5

Level 6

on [ɑn]
🔊 **Track 0616**

介 （表示地點）在……上、在……的時候、在……狀態中
副 在上

▶**介** There's a puppy on the car.
車上有一隻小狗。

▶**副** Put your coat on, now.
現在把大衣穿上吧。

once [wʌns]
🔊 **Track 0617**

副 一次、曾經 **連** 一旦 **名** 一次 **反** again 再一次

▶**副** Once upon a time, an innocent girl stumbled into an untrodden path in the forest.
從前，有個無知的女孩子闖進沒人走過的森林步道。

▶**連** Call me once you arrive.
你一旦到了，就打給我。

▶**名** Don't say it so many times; once is enough.
別說那麼多次了，一次就夠了。

one [wʌn]
🔊 **Track 0618**

形 一的、一個的 **名** 一、一個

▶**形** There is only space（空間）for one person in the bathroom.
廁所裡的空間只容得下一個人。

▶**名** I have two daughters; one is a teacher and the other is still a student.
我有兩個女兒，一個是老師，一個還是學生。

文法字詞解析
one..., another..., and the other表示「一個……，一個……，另一個」；
one,... another..., and others則表示「一個……，另一個……，其他剩下的」

on·ly [ˈonlɪ]
🔊 **Track 0619**

形 唯一的、僅有的 **副** 只、僅僅 **同** simply 僅僅、只不過

▶**形** Sara is an only child. She doesn't have any siblings.
莎拉是一個獨子。她沒有任何兄弟姊妹。

▶**副** I can finish only one part before next week.
下週前我只能完成其中一部分。

o·pen [ˈopən]
🔊 **Track 0620**

形 開的、公開的 **動** 打開 **反** close 關

▶**形** Can you keep the door open? It's a little hot in the office.
要不要讓門一直開著？辦公室有點熱。

▶**動** Open the gift! I got you something you'd like.
打開禮物啊！我幫你買了個你會喜歡的東西。

or [ɔr]
🔊 **Track 0621**

連 或者、否則

▶Would you like some ice cream（冰淇淋）or a Coke?
你會想要冰淇淋還是一杯可樂嗎？

文法字詞解析
or 作為「否則」時，可以這樣使用：
You'd better get up right now, or you will be late for school. 你最好現在起床，否則你上學會遲到。

or·ange [ˈɔrɪndʒ]
🔊 **Track 0622**

名 柳丁、柑橘 **形** 橘色的

▶**名** Jenny is always eating oranges.
珍妮老是在吃橘子。

▶**形** Maggie has a notebook with orange covers.
梅姬有一本橘色封面的筆記簿。

or·der [ˈɔrdɚ]　🔊 *Track 0623*

名 次序、順序、命令 動 命令、訂購 同 command 指揮、命令

▶ 名 The intern was told to put the files in alphabetic order.
實習生被要求要把檔案依字母順序排好。

▶ 動 We have no time to go to the train station, so let's just order the tickets by telephone（電話）.
我們沒時間去火車站，那麼就讓我們打電話訂票吧。

文法字詞解析
注意不要把「in order」跟表目的用法「in order to...（為了……）」搞混了。
in order to 可以擺在句首或句中，後面加原型動詞
例如：In order to lose weight, she does exercise every day.
為了減重，她每天都運動。

oth·er [ˈʌðɚ]　🔊 *Track 0624*

形 其他的、另外的 同 additional 其他的

▶ If you have any other questions, please let us know as soon as possible. 如果你有任何其他的問題，請儘快通知我們。

our(s) [ˈaʊr(z)]　🔊 *Track 0625*

代 我們的（東西）

▶ Do you know where our friends are waiting?
你知道我們的朋友們在哪裡等嗎？

文法字詞解析
請注意 our 和 ours 的用法，our 是所有格，ours 則是所有格代名詞。

out [aʊt]　🔊 *Track 0626*

副 離開、向外 形 外面的、在外的 反 in 在裡面的

▶ 副 After Nancy broke up with her boyfriend, she asked him to move out her apartment.
南茜和男友分手之後，就要求他搬出她的公寓。

▶ 形 The baseball player is already out, so he went to sit at the side. 那個棒球選手已經出局了，所以他就去旁邊坐著。

out·side [ˈaʊtˌsaɪd]　🔊 *Track 0627*

介 在……外面 形 外面的 名 外部、外面 反 inside 裡面的

▶ 介 Who's that outside the door? 門外那個是誰？

▶ 形 When the outside walls of the house is painted white, it looks like a palace（宮殿）.
當房子外部的牆壁都被漆成白色時，它看起來就像座宮殿。

▶ 名 The outside of the car looks old but inside it's brand new.
這部車的外部看起來舊舊的，但裡面很新。

o·ver [ˈovɚ]　🔊 *Track 0628*

介 在……上方、遍及、超過 副 翻轉過來 形 結束的、過度的

▶ 介 My aunt lives just over the hill. 我阿姨就住在山坡上方。

▶ 副 I knocked the vase over last night.
昨晚我把花瓶撞倒了。

▶ 形 Leaves will turn red when summer is over.
夏天結束後，樹葉就會變紅了。

own [on]　🔊 *Track 0629*

形 自己的 代 屬於某人之物 動 擁有 同 possess 擁有

▶ 形 I live in a small cottage with my five brothers, so I could not have my own room. 我和我的五個兄弟住在一個小屋裡，所以我沒有自己的房間。

▶ 代 Why are you eating my ice cream? Why don't you get your own? 你為什麼吃我的冰淇淋？幹嘛不自己去買一支？

▶ 動 Let's find out who owns the old house in the country.
我們把這棟鄉村老房子的主人查出來吧。

Level 1
輕鬆學習、入門無負擔——掌握基礎1000單字

Level 2

Level 3

Level 4

Level 5

Level 6

[Pp]

page [pedʒ] ◀ Track 0630

名 （書上的）頁
▶There are 670 pages in total; I need at least a week to finish reading it all.
一共有 670 頁，我至少需要一週的時間才能讀完。

paint [pent] ◀ Track 0631

名 顏料、油漆 動 粉刷、油漆、（用顏料）繪畫
同 draw 畫、描繪
▶名 How long will it take for the paint on the chair to dry?
椅子上的油漆多久才會乾啊？
▶動 Tom Sawyer tricked his friend into painting the fence for him.
湯姆騙他朋友來幫他粉刷牆面。

pair [pɛr] ◀ Track 0632

名 一雙、一對 動 配成對 同 couple 一對、一雙
▶名 Would you like to go to the mall （購物中心）with me? I want to buy a pair of shoes.
跟我去一趟那個購物中心好嗎？我想買雙鞋。
▶動 The students are all paired up two by two.
學生們都分組成一對一對的。

pants/trou·sers ◀ Track 0633
[pænts]/['trauzəz]

名 褲子
▶Don't take your pants off in front of the children, man!
這位先生，別在孩子面前脫褲子啊！

pa·pa/pop ['pɑpə]/[pɑp] ◀ Track 0634

名 爸爸
▶What does her papa look like? 她爸爸長什麼樣子呢？

pa·per ['pepə] ◀ Track 0635

名 紙、報紙
▶I'm so good at making paper airplanes. 我超會摺紙飛機。

par·ent(s) ['pɛrənt(s)] ◀ Track 0636

名 雙親、家長 反 child 小孩
▶At the school anniversary, Mr. Wang met several parents of his students. 校慶時，王老師遇到幾位學生的家長。

park [pɑrk] ◀ Track 0637

名 公園 動 停放（汽車等）
▶名 How often do you go to the park with your kids?
你多久帶你的孩子去一次公園？
▶動 I parked the car in front of your house.
我把車停在你家前面了。

文法字詞解析

跟鞋子、襪子等不同，即使只有一條褲子，pants 跟 trousers 的量詞還是會用 a pair of。

part [pɑrt] 🔊 *Track 0638*

名 部分 動 分離、使分開
▶ 名 Students were asked to divide their reports into three parts: introduction, body, conclusion.
學生被要求將報告分為三個部分：引言、主文、結論。
▶ 動 I can't bear to part with you. 我真的不想跟你分開。

par·ty [ˈpɑrtɪ] 🔊 *Track 0639*

名 聚會、黨派
▶ There will be hundreds of guests coming to our party.
將有上百位客人參加我們的派對。

pass [pæs] 🔊 *Track 0640*

名 （考試）及格、通行證 動 經過、消逝、通過 反 fail 不及格
▶ 名 I forgot my bus pass at home.
我把公車月票丟在家了。
▶ 動 Did you pass the exam?
你考試有通過嗎？

past [pæst] 🔊 *Track 0641*

形 過去的、從前的 名 過去、從前 介 在……之後
反 future 未來的
▶ 形 Maru hasn't contacted with her parents for the past three years. 瑪莉過去三年都沒有和父母親聯絡。
▶ 名 In the past, he used to be a really quiet dog.
過去牠曾是一隻很安靜的狗。
▶ 介 The boys walked past our house just now.
男孩們剛剛經過我們的房子。

pay [pe] 🔊 *Track 0642*

名 工資、薪水 動 付錢
▶ 名 Not every college （大學）student can get a good job with high pay now.
現在不是每個大學生都能找到一份薪水高的好工作。
▶ 動 Not all people with high education （教育）levels are paid well now. 如今並不是所有學歷高的人薪水都很高。

文法字詞解析
pay 的動詞變化：pay, paid, paid

pay·ment [ˈpemənt] 🔊 *Track 0643*

名 支付、付款
▶ Mandy saved enough money for the down payment for purchasing a house. 曼蒂存夠了買房子頭期款的前。

pen [pɛn] 🔊 *Track 0644*

名 鋼筆、原子筆
▶ My pen won't write. It makes me so mad.
我的筆都寫不出來，讓我很火大。

文法字詞解析
won't 是 will 的否定，在這裡有表達「不能」的意思。

pen·cil [ˈpɛnsl] 🔊 *Track 0645*

名 鉛筆
▶ How about buying our daughter a beautiful pencil box as her gift? 給我們的女兒買一個漂亮的鉛筆盒作為禮物如何？

Level 1 輕鬆學習、入門無負擔──掌握基礎1000單字

Level 2

Level 3

Level 4

Level 5

Level 6

peo·ple [ˈpipl̩]

◀€ *Track 0646*

名 人、人們、人民、民族
▶ How many people are there on the plane?
飛機上有幾個人？

per·haps [pɚˈhæps]

◀€ *Track 0647*

副 也許、可能　同 maybe 也許
▶ Perhaps you could think twice before you make the purchase.
也許你在下訂單購買前，可以再考慮一下。

per·son [ˈpɝsn̩]

◀€ *Track 0648*

名 人
▶ Who's that person standing at the back?
站在後面那個人是誰？

pet [pɛt]

◀€ *Track 0649*

名 寵物、令人愛慕之物　形 寵愛的、得意的
▶ 名 How about going to the pet shop to look at the cats? 要不要去一下寵物店看看貓？
▶ 形 This store sells pet food.
這間店有賣寵物食品。

pi·an·o [pɪˈæno]

◀€ *Track 0650*

名 鋼琴
▶ The little girl plays the piano all day, so her parents can't sleep.
那個小女孩整天在彈鋼琴，所以她父母都沒辦法睡覺。

pic·ture [ˈpɪktʃɚ]

◀€ *Track 0651*

名 圖片、相片　動 畫　同 image 圖像
▶ 名 Would you mind taking a picture for us?
你介意幫我們拍張照嗎？
▶ 動 I picture him with long hair and realize（發覺）it would look great. 我想像他留長髮會是什麼樣子，發覺會超好看的。

pie [paɪ]

◀€ *Track 0652*

名 派、餡餅
▶ The apple pies she bakes are the best.
她烤的蘋果派最棒了。

piece [pis]

◀€ *Track 0653*

名 一塊、一片　同 fragment 碎片
▶ To professor Richardson, modifying a thesis for his students is a piece of cake. 對理查森教授而言，幫學生修改論文只是小菜一碟，非常容易。

pig [pɪg]

◀€ *Track 0654*

名 豬
▶ Stop the car! A pig is crossing the street.
停車一下！有豬在過馬路。

place [ples]　◀€ Track 0655

名 地方、地區、地位 動 放置 反 displace 移開
▶名 My bedroom is my favorite place.
　　我的臥室是我最喜歡的地方。
▶動 I placed all the cups on the table.
　　我把杯子都放到桌上了。

plan [plæn]　◀€ Track 0656

動 計畫、規劃 名 計畫、安排 同 project 計劃
▶動 I plan to visit her next weekend. 我計畫下週末去拜訪她。
▶名 Do you have any plan for the Chinese New Year holidays?
　　你農曆過年放假有何計畫嗎？

plant [plænt]　◀€ Track 0657

名 植物、工廠 動 栽種 反 animal 動物
▶名 Tropical plants are really beautiful. 熱帶植物真的很漂亮。
▶動 How about planting some trees in our garden in spring?
　　春天的時候，我們在花園裡種幾棵樹如何？

play [ple]　◀€ Track 0658

名 遊戲、玩耍 動 玩、做遊戲、扮演、演奏 同 game 遊戲
▶名 All work and no play is no fun. 只工作不玩很無趣耶。
▶動 The children are playing with the dog. 孩子們正在跟狗玩。

play·er [ˋpleɚ]　◀€ Track 0659

名 運動員、演奏者、玩家 同 sportsman 運動員
▶The tennis player has won several gold medals（獎牌）.
　那名網球員獲得了不少金牌。

play·ground [ˋpleˏgraʊnd]　◀€ Track 0660

名 運動場、遊戲場
▶Some students were running on the playground, while others
　were taking a rest in the shade.
　有些學生在操場上跑步，有些學生在陰涼處休息。

please [pliz]　◀€ Track 0661

動 請、使高興、取悅 反 displease 得罪、觸怒
▶I heard that your dad is hard to please.
　我聽說你爸爸很難被取悅。

pock·et [ˋpɑkɪt]　◀€ Track 0662

名 口袋 形 小型的、袖珍的
▶名 I can't find my pen. I thought it was in my pocket.
　　我找不到我的筆。我還以為在口袋。
▶形 A pocket edition（版本）of the book will come out soon.
　　那本書的袖珍版即將問世。

po·et·ry [ˋpoˏɪtrɪ]　◀€ Track 0663

名 詩、詩集 同 verse 詩
▶Betty majors in literature, and she specializes in Virginia Woolf's
　poetry. 貝蒂主修文學，她專攻研究維吉尼亞‧吳爾芙的詩作。

文法字詞解析
plan 的動詞變化：plan, planned, planned

Level 1　輕鬆學習、入門無負擔──掌握基礎1000單字

Level 2

Level 3

Level 4

Level 5

Level 6

point [pɔɪnt] 🔊 *Track 0664*

名 尖端、點、要點、（比賽中所得的）分數 動 瞄準、指向
同 dot 點

▶ 名 There are many points I don't understand.
我有很多地方不懂。

▶ 動 Let me point you to the teacher's office.
我來指給你看去老師辦公室的路。

po·lice [pəˋlis] 🔊 *Track 0665*

名 警察

▶ The police officers asked the demonstrators who gathered illegally to disperse and leave.
警察要求非法聚集的抗議者分散開、離開。

po·lice·man/cop 🔊 *Track 0666*

[pəˋlismən]/[kɑp]
名 警察

▶ The policeman over there is very handsome.
那邊那個警察好帥。

pond [pɑnd] 🔊 *Track 0667*

名 池塘

▶ There are a great many ducks（鴨子）in the pond.
池塘裡有很多鴨子。

pool [pul] 🔊 *Track 0668*

名 水池

▶ A licensed lifeguard should be watching the swimmers by the pool. 有執照的救生員應該要在泳池旁邊看顧著游泳者。

poor [pʊr] 🔊 *Track 0669*

形 貧窮的、可憐的、差的、壞的 名 窮人 反 rich 富有的

▶ 形 The poor boy was sick for a whole month.
那個可憐的男孩病了一個月。

▶ 名 He gave his money to the poor.
他把錢給了窮人。

pop·corn [ˋpɑp͵kɔrn] 🔊 *Track 0670*

名 爆米花

▶ What's a movie without popcorn? 看電影沒有爆米花怎麼行？

po·si·tion [pəˋzɪʃən] 🔊 *Track 0671*

名 位置、工作職位、形勢 同 location 位置

▶ As far as I know, Rita is the best candidate to take over this position. 就我所知，瑞塔是接手這個職位的最佳人選。

pos·si·ble [ˋpɑsəbl] 🔊 *Track 0672*

形 可能的 同 likely 可能的

▶ I don't think what you said is possible.
我覺得你講的事是不可能的。

文法字詞解析

point 作為「點」，有些常用的片語：
turning point 轉捩點，如：It's the turning point of his life.
point of view 觀點，如：I can see things from your point of view.
make a point 強調，如：She made a point of thanking the host of the party.

文法字詞解析

pool table = 撞球桌

pow·er [ˋpaʊɚ]
🔊 *Track 0673*

名 力量、權力、動力 同 strength 力量
▶I don't have any power over my children.
　我完全沒辦法管得動我的孩子。

prac·tice [ˋpræktɪs]
🔊 *Track 0674*

名 實踐、練習、熟練 動 練習 同 exercise 練習
▶名 Kevin put lots of efforts to put this project into practice.
　凱文很努力將這個計畫付諸實行。
▶動 My daughter practices the violin（小提琴）every day.
　我女兒每天都練習拉小提琴。

pre·pare [priˋpɛr]
🔊 *Track 0675*

動 預備、準備
▶How long have you prepared for the exam?
　你為了考試已經準備多久了？

pret·ty [ˋprɪtɪ]
🔊 *Track 0676*

形 漂亮的、美好的 同 lovely 可愛的
▶My mom is a very pretty lady.
　我媽媽是個非常漂亮的女子。

price [praɪs]
🔊 *Track 0677*

名 價格、代價 同 value 價格、價值
▶I love this dress but the price is too high.
　我真喜歡這件洋裝，但價格太高了。

print [prɪnt]
🔊 *Track 0678*

名 印跡、印刷字體、版 動 印刷
▶名 The book is so classic that it is still in print after three decades.
　這本書如此經典，以至於三十年後還有在印刷。
▶動 Can you print these documents（文件）for me?
　可以幫我把這些文件印出來嗎？

prob·lem [ˋprɑbləm]
🔊 *Track 0679*

名 問題 反 solution 解答
▶He never tells other people his problems.
　他從來不把自己的問題告訴別人。

prove [pruv]
🔊 *Track 0680*

動 證明、證實 同 confirm 證實
▶The lawyer had enough evidence to prove the innocence of his client.
　律師有足夠證據證明他的當事人無罪。

pub·lic [ˋpʌblɪk]
🔊 *Track 0681*

形 公眾的 名 民眾 反 private 私人的
▶形 The public phone is not working. 那台公共電話壞了。
▶名 I hate speaking in public. 我不喜歡當眾演講。

文法字詞解析
price 可以作為「價格」，也可以作「代價」解釋。如：
Will they set a price on it?
（他們會訂出價格嗎？）
His success came at the price of losing his family.
（他的成功，代價就是失去了家庭。）

文法字詞解析
prove 的動詞變化：prove, proved, proven

Level
1
輕鬆學習、入門無負擔——掌握基礎1000單字

Level
2

Level
3

Level
4

Level
5

Level
6

pull [pʊl]
🔊 *Track 0682*

動 拉、拖　反 push 推
▶Don't pull your classmate's hair! 不要拔你同學的頭髮！

pur·ple [ˈpɝpḷ]
🔊 *Track 0683*

形 紫色的　名 紫色
▶形 This purple bag is mine. 這個紫色的袋子是我的。
▶名 I can't wear purple; it makes me look old.
　我不能穿紫色，會讓我看起來很老。

pur·pose [ˈpɝpəs]
🔊 *Track 0684*

名 目的、意圖　同 aim 目的
▶I think he spread the fake news on purpose.
　我想他是故意在散布假新聞。

push [pʊʃ]
🔊 *Track 0685*

動 推、壓、按、促進　名 推、推動　反 pull 拉、拖
▶動 He pushed his sister off the bed.
　他把妹妹推下床了。
▶名 We opened the door with one push.
　我們一推就把門打開了。

put [pʊt]
🔊 *Track 0686*

動 放置　同 place 放置
▶Alice asked her son to put away the toys before going to bed.
　艾莉絲要求她兒子睡前把玩具收好。

文法字詞解析
put 的動詞變化：put, put, put

[Qq]

queen [ˈkwin]
🔊 *Track 0687*

名 女王、皇后　反 king 國王
▶The queen told the soldiers（士兵）to cut his head off.
　皇后命令士兵們把他的頭砍掉。

ques·tion [ˈkwɛstʃən]
🔊 *Track 0688*

名 疑問、詢問　動 質疑、懷疑　反 answer 答案
▶名 To eat or not to eat, that is the question.
　到底要吃還是不吃呢？這就是問題所在。
▶動 Some people questioned the politician's motivation in visiting the veteran soldiers before the election.
　有些人質疑政客在選舉前拜訪老兵的動機。

文法字詞解析
out of the question = 不可能，如：
A trip to Australia is out of the question this year.（今年不可能去澳洲旅行了。）
out of question = 無庸置疑，如：
It's out of question that he will win.（他會贏，這是無庸置疑的。）

quick [kwɪk]
🔊 *Track 0689*

形 快的　副 快　同 fast 快
▶形 He has a quick mind, so it's easy for him to solve this problem.
　他思維敏捷，因此他來解決這個問題可說是輕而易舉。
▶副 Come quick! Your favorite song is on.
　快來啊！在播你最喜歡的歌喔。

qui·et [ˈkwaɪət] 🔊 *Track 0690*

形 安靜的 名 安靜 動 使平靜 同 still 寂靜的

▶形 Be quiet, for someone is sleeping in the room.
安靜點，因為有人在房間裡睡覺呢。

▶名 It's like the quiet before a storm.
感覺好像暴風雨前的寧靜一樣。

▶動 The teacher doesn't know how to quiet the students in the class. 這老師不知道如何讓班上的學生安靜下來。

quite [kwaɪt] 🔊 *Track 0691*

副 完全地、相當、頗

▶There are quite a few people in the concert hall for the pianist's performance. 音樂廳中有許多人聚集來看鋼琴手的表演。

[Rr]

race [res] 🔊 *Track 0692*

動 賽跑 名 種族、比賽 同 folk （某一民族的）廣大成員

▶動 I'll race you to the restaurant. 我跟你比賽誰先跑到餐廳。

▶名 My class won the relay（接力）race.
我們班贏了接力賽。

ra·di·o [ˈredɪo] 🔊 *Track 0693*

名 收音機

▶Would you like me to turn down the radio?
你要我把收音機的聲音調小一點嗎？

rail·road [ˈrelˌrod] 🔊 *Track 0694*

名 鐵路

▶The railroad was under repair, so several trains were canceled. 鐵路在維修中，所以一些火車班次取消了。

rain [ren] 🔊 *Track 0695*

名 雨、雨水 動 下雨 同 shower 雨、降雨

▶名 We need to get out of the rain or we'll catch a cold.
我們快去躲雨吧，不然就要感冒了。

▶動 I think it's going to rain. Do you have an umbrella?
我想快要下雨了，你有傘嗎？

rain·bow [ˈrenˌbo] 🔊 *Track 0696*

名 彩虹

▶Did you see the rainbow this morning?
你有看到今天早上的彩虹嗎？

raise [rez] 🔊 *Track 0697*

動 舉起、抬起、提高、養育 反 lower 下降

▶Tina is a widow. She raised up her two children by herself.
緹娜失去丈夫。她獨力扶養兩個小孩長大。

文法字詞解析

quite 表示相當，常見的搭配詞有：
quite a few 相當多，如：He made quite a few friends in college.
quite a bit 相當多，如：He knows quite a bit about human history.
quite a while 相當長的時間，如：We waited quite a while before the bus came.

文法字詞解析

raise 除了「舉起」，像是 "raise your hand" 之外，也有抽象的意思。
例如：
「提出一個問題」：raise a question；
「提起一個話題」：raise a topic / subject

Level **1**

Level **2**

Level **3**

Level **4**

Level **5**

Level **6**

輕鬆學習、入門無負擔──
掌握基礎1000單字

rat [ræt]　　🔊 *Track 0698*
名 老鼠　同 mouse 老鼠
▶The rat we caught was really fat.
我們抓到的那隻老鼠超胖的。

reach [ritʃ]　　🔊 *Track 0699*
動 伸手拿東西、到達　同 approach 接近
▶I can't reach the top of the shelf. Can you help me?
我拿不到書櫃頂部的東西。你可以幫我嗎？

萬用延伸句型
這裡也可以套用「too...to...（太……以至於不能……）」的句型，寫成：I'm too short to reach the book on the shelf.

read [rid]　　🔊 *Track 0700*
動 讀、看（書、報等）、朗讀
▶She learned to read at the age of three.
她三歲就學會閱讀了。

文法字詞解析
read 的動詞變化：read, read, read

read·y [ˋrɛdɪ]　　🔊 *Track 0701*
形 作好準備的
▶Are you ready to leave yet? 你準備好要走了嗎？

re·al [ˋriəl]　　🔊 *Track 0702*
形 真的、真實的　副 真正的　同 actual 真的、真正的
▶形 The scene in the horror movie looked so real to me.
恐怖片裡的場景看起來相當逼真。
▶副 My younger brother is real tall. 我弟弟真的很高。

文法字詞解析
once 在這裡是連接詞「一旦……就……」，意同於 as soon as。once 後面接的時間子句要用現在式代替未來式。

rea·son [ˋrizn]　　🔊 *Track 0703*
名 理由　同 cause 理由、原因
▶Not all people know the reason for her absence（缺席）.
不是所有人都知道她缺席的原因。

re·ceive [rɪˋsiv]　　🔊 *Track 0704*
動 收到　反 send 發送、寄
▶Have you received my email? 你有收到我的電子郵件嗎？

red [rɛd]　　🔊 *Track 0705*
名 紅色　形 紅色的
▶名 The girl in red is his sister. 那個穿紅衣服的女孩是他妹妹。
▶形 My brother believes that wearing red underwear（內衣褲）
means good luck. 我哥哥相信穿紅內衣會帶來好運。

re·mem·ber [rɪˋmɛmbɚ]　　🔊 *Track 0706*
動 記得　同 remind 使記起
▶My grandmother suffers from dementia. She can't remember
our names. 我祖母患有失智症。她記不得我們的名字。

re·port [rɪˋport]　　🔊 *Track 0707*
動 報告、報導　名 報導、報告
▶動 Would you like me to report on the whole event to you?
你要我把整件事向你報告嗎？
▶名 He finished his report late last night.
他昨晚到很晚終於把他的報告寫完了。

rest [rɛst]
🔊 *Track 0708*

動 休息 名 睡眠、休息 同 relaxation 休息
- ▶動 Let's go home and rest. 我們回家休息一下吧。
- ▶名 Do you want to take a rest? 要不要休息一下？

re·turn [rɪˋtɝn]
🔊 *Track 0709*

動 歸還、送回 名 返回、復發 形 返回的 反 depart 出發
- ▶動 Could you help me return the book to the library?
  你願意幫我把書還給圖書館嗎？
- ▶名 Gary helped me a lot, so I should offer him assistance in return. 蓋瑞幫我很多，所以作為回報，我也該協助他。
- ▶形 Did you get a return trip ticket? 你有買回程的票嗎？

rice [raɪs]
🔊 *Track 0710*

名 稻米、米飯
- ▶Not all people of the country live on rice.
  那個國家的人並非都以米為主食。

rich [rɪtʃ]
🔊 *Track 0711*

形 富裕的 同 wealthy 富裕的
- ▶Once you see the big villa（別墅）and expensive car, you will understand how rich he is. 一旦你看到他的大別墅和昂貴的車子，你就會明白他有多有錢了。

ride [raɪd]
🔊 *Track 0712*

動 騎、乘 名 騎馬、騎車或乘車旅行
- ▶動 What about going riding with me?
  要不要和我一起去騎馬？
- ▶名 Tom offered to give me a ride on the way back to the university. 湯姆願意在回大學時載我一程。

文法字詞解析
ride 的動詞變化：ride, rode, ridden

right [raɪt]
🔊 *Track 0713*

形 正確的、右邊的 名 正確、右方、權利 同 correct 正確的
- ▶形 He is the right person for the position（職位）.
  他是那個職位的合適人選。
- ▶名 I have every right to vote（投票）.
  我完全有投票的權利。

ring [rɪŋ]
🔊 *Track 0714*

動 按鈴、打電話 名 戒指、鈴聲
- ▶動 Your phone is ringing. Do you want me to get it for you?
  你的電話在響耶，要我幫你接嗎？
- ▶名 My boyfriend gave me this expensive ring.
  我男朋友給了我這個昂貴的戒指。

文法字詞解析
ring 的動詞變化：ring, rang, rung

rise [raɪz]
🔊 *Track 0715*

動 上升、增長 名 上升 同 ascend 升起
- ▶動 Get up, kids! Rise and shine!
  孩子們，該起床囉！
- ▶名 He was more surprised at his rise to fame than we were.
  對於他的名氣竄升，他比我們還驚訝。

文法字詞解析
rise 的動詞變化：rise, rose, risen

Level
1
輕鬆學習、入門無負擔
掌握基礎1000單字

Level
2

Level
3

Level
4

Level
5

Level
6

riv·er [ˈrɪvɚ]
◀ᴇ *Track 0716*

名 江、河 同 stream 小河

▶My parents live just across the river.
我父母就住在河對面而已。

road [rod]
◀ᴇ *Track 0717*

名 路、道路、街道、路線 同 path 路、道路

▶It's time for us to hit the road. 我們該上路了！

ro·bot [ˈrobət]
◀ᴇ *Track 0718*

名 機器人

▶Can robots be smarter than humans?
機器人有可能比人類更聰明嗎？

rock [rɑk]
◀ᴇ *Track 0719*

動 搖晃 名 岩石 同 stone 石頭

▶動 I rocked the baby until she fell asleep.
我搖晃著寶寶，直到她睡著為止。

▶名 Let's go rock-climbing next week.
我們下禮拜去攀岩吧。

roll [rol]
◀ᴇ *Track 0720*

動 滾動、捲 名 名冊、卷 同 wheel 滾動、打滾

▶動 Let's roll the scroll and put it in the closet.
我們把卷軸捲好收進櫃子裡吧。

▶名 Would you like me to buy a roll of film（底片）for you？
你要我幫你買一卷底片嗎？

roof [ruf]
◀ᴇ *Track 0721*

名 屋頂、車頂 反 floor 地板

▶Not all young people like to live under the same roof with their parents now. 現在不是所有年輕人都喜歡跟父母住在一起。

room [rum]
◀ᴇ *Track 0722*

名 房間、室 同 chamber 房間

▶I can't find my cat. She's not in my room.
我找不到我的貓，牠不在我房間。

文法字詞解析

room 在口語中也可當作動詞使用，表達「住在（某個房間）」的意思。
例如：Do they want to room together next year?
他們明年要不要住同一間寢室？

roost·er [ˈrustɚ]
◀ᴇ *Track 0723*

名 雄雞、好鬥者 同 cock 公雞

▶There are many hens（母雞）but only one rooster living in our coop（雞舍）.
我們雞舍裡有很多隻母雞，但是只有一隻公雞。

root [rut]
◀ᴇ *Track 0724*

名 根源、根 動 生根 同 origin 起源

▶名 He pulled the plant up from its roots.
他把那個植物連根拔起。

▶動 He was so astonished by the scene of the accident that he got rooted to the spot.
他因為車禍場景太過震驚，站在原地不動。

rope [rop] ◄€ *Track 0725*

名 繩、索 動 用繩拴住 同 cord 繩索

▶名 The rock climber tied a rope around his waist.
攀岩者把繩子綁在腰際。

▶動 I roped these sticks（木棍）together.
我把這些木棍用繩子拴在一起。

rose [roz] ◄€ *Track 0726*

名 玫瑰花、薔薇花 形 玫瑰色的

▶名 Not all women like roses.
不是所有女人都喜歡玫瑰。

▶形 Her face is a lovely rose color.
她的臉是漂亮的玫瑰色。

萬用延伸句型

「not every...」和「not all...」都有部分否定的含意，只是使用上要注意，如果是前者的話，後面要接單數名詞，後者的後面則要接複數名詞。

round [raʊnd] ◄€ *Track 0727*

形 圓的、球形的 名 圓形物、一回合 動 使旋轉 介 在……四周

▶形 The cusromerized namecard comes in a round shape.
這種特製的名片是圓形的。

▶名 We've all eaten already, but we can still go for a second round.
我們都吃過了，但再來吃一回也行。

▶動 As soon as I rounded the corner I saw the car.
我一轉過轉角，就看到那台車。

▶介 All the kids round the block（街區）are my age.
街區四周的所有孩子們都跟我差不多大。

文法字詞解析
當 round 作介係詞時，表達在……周圍時，可以和 around 互換使用。

row [ro] ◄€ *Track 0728*

名 排、行、列 動 划船 同 paddle 划船

▶名 There are eleven football players standing in a row.
有十一名足球運動員站成一排。

▶動 I'm too tired to row across the lake.
我太累了，無法划船到湖的另一邊。

rub [rʌb] ◄€ *Track 0729*

動 磨擦

▶I rubbed my lipstick（口紅）off.
我把口紅擦掉了。

文法字詞解析
rub 的動詞變化：rub, rubbed, rubbed

rub·ber [ˈrʌbɚ] ◄€ *Track 0730*

名 橡膠、橡皮 形 橡膠做的

▶名 The gloves（手套）are made of rubber.
這些手套是橡膠做的。

▶形 I killed the fly with a rubber band.
我用橡皮筋殺死了那隻蒼蠅。

rule [rul] ◄€ *Track 0731*

名 規則 動 統治 同 govern 統治、管理

▶名 Are there any rules I need to know?
有什麼我一定要知道的規則嗎？

▶動 It's said that Charles I ruled England for 11 years.
據說查理一世統治了英國十一年。

Level 1
輕鬆學習、入門無負擔──掌握基礎1000單字

Level 2

Level 3

Level 4

Level 5

Level 6

run [rʌn] ◀ Track 0732

動 跑、運轉 名 跑
- ▶動 Would you like to run your own business（生意）？
  你想不想經營自己的生意？
- ▶名 Tina likes to go for a run by the river at dusk.
  緹娜喜歡在黃昏時去河邊跑步。

文法字詞解析
run 的動詞變化：run, ran, run

[Ss]

sad [sæd] ◀ Track 0733

形 令人難過的、悲傷的 同 sorrowful 悲哀的
- ▶She must be very sad at this news; let's go and console（安慰）her. 聽到這個消息她一定很傷心，我們去安慰一下她吧！

safe [sef] ◀ Track 0734

形 安全的 反 dangerous 危險的
- ▶Are you sure this boat is safe? 你確定這船安全嗎？

sail [sel] ◀ Track 0735

名 帆、篷、航行、船隻 動 航行
- ▶名 He got hit by the sail and fell into the sea.
  他被船帆打中，摔進了海裡。
- ▶動 My uncle is always out sailing. 我叔叔總是在航海。

sale [sel] ◀ Track 0736

名 賣、出售 反 purchase 購買
- ▶The sign in front of the store says its having a sale for shoes.
  店門口的標語說，他們鞋子在特價中。

salt [sɔlt] ◀ Track 0737

名 鹽 形 鹽的 反 sugar 糖
- ▶名 You eat too much salt. That's unhealthy.
  你吃太多鹽了，不健康喔。
- ▶形 There is a lot of salt water on earth, but we can't drink it.
  地球上有大量的鹽水，可是我們卻不能飲用。

文法字詞解析
salt 是不可數名詞，可用 a pinch of salt（一撮鹽）來修飾。

same [sem] ◀ Track 0738

形 同樣的 副 同樣地 代 同樣的人或事 反 different 不同的
- ▶形 We work in the same company. Would you like me to introduce（介紹）him to you?
  我和他在同一家公司工作，要我幫你介紹一下嗎？
- ▶副 The two dresses look the same to me. Can you tell the difference between them?
  這兩件洋裝在我看來是一樣的。你分的出它們的不同嗎？
- ▶代 Your birthday's on August 31st? Mine's the same.
  你的生日是八月三十一日喔？我的也是一樣。

sand [sænd] ◀ Track 0739

名 沙、沙子
- ▶The children are playing in the sand. 孩子們在玩沙。

Sat·ur·day/Sat. [ˋsætɚde]　　🔊 *Track 0740*
名 星期六
▶I always sleep late on Saturdays. 我每週六都睡很晚。

save [sev]　　🔊 *Track 0741*
動 救、搭救、挽救、儲蓄 反 waste 浪費、消耗
▶The fireman sacrificed his life to save the little girl.
　消防員犧牲自己的生命救小女孩。

saw [sɔ]　　🔊 *Track 0742*
名 鋸 動 用鋸子鋸
▶名 The man left his saw by the tree.
　那男人把他的鋸子留在樹旁邊了。
▶動 Dad is busy sawing through the tree. 爸爸正忙著鋸那棵大樹。

文法字詞解析
saw 的動詞變化：saw, sawed, sawed 或 saw, sawed, sawn

say [se]　　🔊 *Track 0743*
動 說、講
▶"I think you're really cool," he said. 「我覺得你很酷耶，」他說。

文法字詞解析
say 的動詞變化：say, said, said

scare [skɛr]　　🔊 *Track 0744*
動 驚嚇、使害怕 名 害怕 同 frighten 使害怕
▶動 The eagle scared the chicks on the ground away.
　這隻老鷹把地上的小雞嚇跑了。
▶名 The sound is loud enough to give me a scare.
　那個聲音大得把我嚇了一跳。

文法字詞解析
若要表達自己很害怕，要用形容詞 scared，要說明某個東西很可怕，則是用形容詞 scary。

scene [sin]　　🔊 *Track 0745*
名 戲劇的一場、風景 同 view 景色
▶Jane is a drama queen. She is always trying to make a scene. 珍是一位戲精。她總是鬧大場面引人注意。

school [skul]　　🔊 *Track 0746*
名 學校
▶Is John home from school yet? 約翰從學校回到家了嗎？

sea [si]　　🔊 *Track 0747*
名 海 同 ocean 海洋
▶Let's go to the sea next weekend. 我們下週末去海邊吧。

sea·son [ˋsizn̩]　　🔊 *Track 0748*
名 季節
▶Autumn is my favorite（最喜歡的）season, because the weather is always fine.
　秋季是我最喜歡的季節，因為天氣總是很好。

文法字詞解析
從屬連接詞 because（因為）用來連接有因果關係的兩個句子。

seat [sit]　　🔊 *Track 0749*
名 座位 動 坐下 同 chair 椅子
▶名 There are enough seats for all attendees in the conference hall. 會議室裡有足夠的座位讓與會者坐。
▶動 The little girl seated on the horse is my sister.
　坐在馬上的那個小女孩是我的妹妹。

Level **1**
輕鬆學習、入門無負擔——
掌握基礎1000單字

Level **2**

Level **3**

Level **4**

Level **5**

Level **6**

sec·ond [ˈsɛkənd]
🔊 *Track 0750*

形 第二的 名 秒

▶形 He was still hungry after one pizza so he ate the second one. 他吃了一個披薩還是很餓，所以又吃了第二個。

▶名 The traffic light is counting down thirty seconds for the pedestrians to cross the street. 交通號誌倒數30秒讓行人通過馬路。

see [si]
🔊 *Track 0751*

動 看、理解 同 watch 看

▶The thief（小偷）broke into this old man's house last night, but no one saw him.
小偷昨晚闖入了老人的家，但是卻沒有人看見。

文法字詞解析
see 的動詞變化：see, saw, seen
萬用延伸句型
I'll be seeing you. 再見。 這句話和「See you soon.」的意思是一樣的。

seed [sid]
🔊 *Track 0752*

名 種子 動 播種於

▶名 My pet mouse loves eating seeds.
我的寵物老鼠就愛吃種子。

▶動 The lawn（草坪）is newly seeded.
這草坪才剛播過種。

seem [sim]
🔊 *Track 0753*

動 似乎

▶He seems to know many secrets of the wealthy man.
他似乎知道富人的許多秘密。

see·saw [ˈsiˌsɔ]
🔊 *Track 0754*

名 蹺蹺板

▶There are many children in the park. They are waiting for playing on the seesaw.
公園裡有很多小孩在等著玩蹺蹺板。

self [sɛlf]
🔊 *Track 0755*

名 自己、自我

▶I'm not my usual self today.
我今天實在太不像自己了。

self·ish [ˈsɛlfɪʃ]
🔊 *Track 0756*

形 自私的、不顧別人的

▶She's the most selfish old lady I've ever met.
她是我遇過最自私的老太太。

sell [sɛl]
🔊 *Track 0757*

動 賣、出售、銷售 反 buy 買

▶Are you sure you want to sell this beautiful car?
你確定你真的要賣掉這台美麗的車？

文法字詞解析
sell 的動詞變化：sell, sold, sold

send [sɛnd]
🔊 *Track 0758*

動 派遣、寄出 同 mail 寄信

▶The soldier sent the youngest soldiers to the frontline.
將軍把最年輕的士兵送上前線。

文法字詞解析
send 的動詞變化：send, sent, sent

sense [sɛns]
Track 0759

名 感覺、意義

▶He has a terrible sense of direction（方向）and always gets lost. 他的方向感超差，每次都迷路。

sen·tence [ˈsɛntəns]
Track 0760

名 句子、判決 動 判決 同 judge 判決

▶名 He wrote only three sentences in the letter.
他在信裡面只寫了三個句子。

▶動 The man who murdered his parents in law was sentenced to death.
謀殺岳父岳母的男人，被判了死刑。

Sep·tem·ber/Sept.
Track 0761

[sɛpˈtɛmbɚ]

名 九月

▶A new football（足球）season will begin in September.
新的足球賽季將於九月份開始。

serve [sɝv]
Track 0762

動 服務、招待

▶I've been waiting for twenty minutes but no one has come over to serve me. 我等二十分鐘了，都沒人過來服務我。

serv·ice [ˈsɝvɪs]
Track 0763

名 服務

▶The service fee of this hotel is included in the bill.
這家飯店的服務費有包含在帳單裡。

set [sɛt]
Track 0764

名（一）套、（一）副 動 放、擱置 同 place 放置

▶名 I bought a set of lovely teacups（茶杯）from her.
我從她那裡買了一組可愛的茶杯。

▶動 I helped my mom to set the table before the housewarming party. 入厝派對前，我幫我媽把餐桌擺設好。

sev·en [ˈsɛvən]
Track 0765

名 七

▶My dog just had seven puppies.
我的狗剛生了七隻小狗。

sev·en·teen [ˌsɛvənˈtin]
Track 0766

名 十七

▶We walked seventeen miles on foot.
我們走了十七英里的路。

sev·en·ty [ˈsɛvəntɪ]
Track 0767

名 七十

▶Seventy dollars? That's too much.
七十美元喔？太貴了。

萬用延伸句型

It doesn't make sense. 這不合理。
「make sense」的意思是「有道理、合理的」，如果覺得某事不可能發生但是卻發生了，就可以用這句話表達自己的訝異。

文法字詞解析

set 的動詞變化：set, set, set

萬用延伸句型

On your mark, get set, go! 各就各位，預備，開始！
這句話裡，set是形容詞，表示「準備好的」。我們常會在比賽開始前聽到裁判說這句話，和「ready, steady, go!」是同樣的意思。

萬用延伸句型

It costs too much 太貴了。或者也可以說：「It's too expensive.」

Level
1
輕鬆學習、入門無負擔──
掌握基礎1000單字

Level
2

Level
3

Level
4

Level
5

Level
6

sev·er·al [ˈsɛvərəl]
🔊 *Track 0768*

形 幾個的 代 幾個

▶形 I had dinner with her several times this week.
我這週和她一起吃過幾次晚餐。

▶代 Several of the windows were broken, but we don't know who did it.
有幾扇玻璃窗被砸破了，但不知道是誰幹的。

shake [ʃek]
🔊 *Track 0769*

動 搖、發抖 名 搖動、震動

▶動 Mr. Trump shaked the bottle before he drank the juice.
川普先生先搖了搖瓶子才喝果汁。

▶名 I gave the bottle several shakes before I drank the juice.
我搖了瓶子幾下，然後才喝果汁。

> **文法字詞解析**
> shake 的動詞變化：shake, shook, shaken

shall [ʃæl]
🔊 *Track 0770*

連 將

▶We shall be there in a few minutes.
我們幾分鐘內將會到。

> **文法字詞解析**
> 1. shall 的動詞變化：shall, should, should
> 2. shall 可用在表示未來將發生的事，也可用在徵求他人的意見，例如：Shall we go to the movies tonight?

shape [ʃep]
🔊 *Track 0771*

動 使成形 名 形狀 同 form 使成形

▶動 My parents are the ones who shaped my personality（個性）. 我的父母是塑造我的人格的人。

▶名 Mandy cut the paper into the shape of a cat.
曼蒂把紙剪成一隻貓的形狀。

shark [ʃɑrk]
🔊 *Track 0772*

名 鯊魚

▶Everyone screamed when the shark appeared（出現）.
鯊魚一出現，每個人都尖叫了。

sharp [ʃɑrp]
🔊 *Track 0773*

形 鋒利的、刺耳的、尖銳的、嚴厲的 同 blunt 嚴厲的

▶Her eyes are sharp for an old lady.
對一個老太太來說，她的眼睛超銳利的。

she [ʃi]
🔊 *Track 0774*

代 她

▶She is always talking to her sister and never looks at anyone else. 她總是在跟她姊姊講話，都不理別人。

sheep [ʃip]
🔊 *Track 0775*

名 羊、綿羊

▶I've never seen so many sheep at once before.
我從沒一次見過這麼多羊。

> **文法字詞解析**
> sheep 是不可數的名詞，即使有很多隻還是要說 sheep 而不是 sheeps。

sheet [ʃit]
🔊 *Track 0776*

名 床單

▶The maid was taught how to fold the sheet on her first day of work. 女僕上班第一天就先學習如何折疊床單。

shine [ʃaɪn]　◀Track 0777
動 照耀、發光、發亮　名 光亮　同 glow 發光
▶ 動 The kid polished the window, and the glass shines bright.
　小孩擦拭過窗戶後，玻璃乾淨地發亮。
▶ 名 The old car has lost its shine.
　那台舊車已經失去光亮了。

文法字詞解析
shine 的動詞變化有兩種，
解釋成「擦亮」時：shine, shined, shined
解釋成「發亮」時：shine, shone, shone

ship [ʃɪp]　◀Track 0778
名 大船、海船　同 boat 船
▶ The ship is departing in fifteen minutes.
　船十五分鐘之後就要開了。

文法字詞解析
ship 作為動詞則有「用船運送」的意思，
例如：I'd like to ship this package to
Japan. 我想把這個包裹用船運寄到日本。

shirt [ʃɜt]　◀Track 0779
名 襯衫
▶ Which shirt would you like? This one or that one?
　你要哪一件襯衫，這件還是那件？

shoe(s) [ʃu(z)]　◀Track 0780
名 鞋
▶ There are too many shoes in this store; I don't even know which pair to buy.
　這家店的鞋子太多了，我都不知道該買哪雙了。

文法字詞解析
除非是特別要講一隻鞋子，否則大部分
的情況下是都用複數 shoes。

shop/store [ʃɑp]/[stor]　◀Track 0781
名 商店、店鋪
▶ There's a new shop around the corner. 轉角有一家新開的店。

shore [ʃor]　◀Track 0782
名 岸、濱　同 bank 岸
▶ Brian went fishing at the shore of the lake.
　布萊恩到湖邊釣魚。

short [ʃɔrt]　◀Track 0783
形 矮的、短的、不足的　副 突然地　反 long 長的；遠的
▶ 形 This ruler is too short to measure the box; let's find another one. 這把尺太短了，量不了這個箱子的長度，我們再找另一把尺吧！
▶ 副 He stopped short when he saw that no one was following him.
　他發現沒人跟著他時，就突然停了下來。

shot [ʃɑt]　◀Track 0784
名 子彈、射擊　同 bullet 子彈
▶ He used only two shots to kill the bird.
　他只用了兩顆子彈就殺死了那隻鳥。

shoul·der [ˈʃoldə]　◀Track 0785
名 肩、肩膀
▶ Mike carried his two-year-old son on his shoulder.
　麥可把兩歲的兒子背在肩膀上。

Level
1
輕鬆學習、入門無負擔──
掌握基礎1000單字

Level
2

Level
3

Level
4

Level
5

Level
6

shout [ʃaʊt] ◀ Track 0786

動 呼喊、喊叫 名 叫喊、呼喊 同 yell 叫喊

▶動 Nick's father was drunk and shouted at him for no reason.
尼克的爸爸喝醉了，無緣無故對她大吼。

▶名 I heard a shout for help; someone must be in trouble.
我聽到了呼救聲，肯定有人遇上麻煩了。

show [ʃo] ◀ Track 0787

動 出示、表明 名 展覽、表演 同 display 陳列、展出

▶動 Let me show you some pictures of my boyfriend.
我來給你展示一些我男朋友的照片。

▶名 I'm going to a stage show tomorrow.
我明天要去看劇場表演。

shut [ʃʌt] ◀ Track 0788

動 關上、閉上

▶I wish she would shut her mouth sometimes.
我真希望她偶爾可以閉嘴。

文法字詞解析
shut 的動詞變化：shut, shut, shut

shy [ʃaɪ] ◀ Track 0789

形 害羞的、靦腆的 反 bold 大膽的

▶The toddler was not shy at all; she could perform in front of a large audience.
這個小孩一點都不害羞；她可以在一大群觀眾面前表演。

sick [sɪk] ◀ Track 0790

形 有病的、患病的、想吐的、厭倦的

▶He was very sick all day and didn't wake up.
他整天都在生病，一直沒有起來。

萬用延伸句型
be sick of sth. 受不了（某事）
例如：I'm sick of the neighbors' loud noises every night.
我受不了鄰居每晚都那麼吵了。

side [saɪd] ◀ Track 0791

名 邊、旁邊、側面 形 旁邊的、側面的 同 ill 生病的

▶名 Whose side are you on, mine or Jay's?
你站哪一邊，我這一邊還是阿傑這一邊？

▶形 Let's go through the side door; it's closer.
我們走側門好了，比較近。

sight [saɪt] ◀ Track 0792

名 視力、情景、景象

▶At the sight of the police officers, the thieves ran away.
一看到警察，小偷就跑走了。

sil·ly [ˈsɪlɪ] ◀ Track 0793

形 傻的、愚蠢的 同 foolish 愚蠢的

▶My uncle gets really silly when he's drunk.
我叔叔一喝醉就變得很蠢。

sil·ver [ˈsɪlvɚ] ◀ Track 0794

名 銀 形 銀色的

▶名 The necklace is made of silver. 這項鍊是銀製的。

▶形 The silver dress is very hard to wash. 這銀色洋裝好難洗。

sim·ple [ˈsɪmpl̩]

Track 0795

形 簡單的、簡易的 反 complex 複雜的

▶The operation procedure of the machine was quite simple.
這台機器的操作方式相當簡單。

Level

1

輕鬆學習、入門無負擔

掌握基礎1000單字

since [sɪns]

Track 0796

副 從……以來 介 自從 連 從……以來、因為、既然

▶副 He went to Canada（加拿大）ten years ago and has stayed there ever since.
他十年前去了加拿大，從那時以來就一直待在那裡了。

▶介 She has been teaching music in this private school since last September. 她從去年九月開始就在這間私立學校教音樂。

萬用延伸句型
since 用在現在完成式中：S. + have/has V p.p. since S. + Ved.

▶連 I can't go to your party since my sister is having a baby.
我無法去參加你的派對，因為我姊姊在生孩子。

sing [sɪŋ]

Track 0797

動 唱

▶She's always singing this same song.
她每次都唱這同一首歌。

文法字詞解析
sing 的動詞變化 sing, sang, sung

sing·er [ˈsɪŋɚ]

Track 0798

名 歌唱家、歌手、唱歌的人

▶I like that popular singer's sweet voice very much.
我很喜歡那位流行歌手甜美的嗓音。

sir [sɝ]

Track 0799

名 先生 反 madam 小姐

▶Would you like to order some wine with your meal（餐）, sir?
先生，您要不要叫些酒來配你的餐點呢？

sis·ter [ˈsɪstɚ]

Track 0800

名 姐妹、姐、妹 反 brother 兄弟

▶Which one is your sister, the one on the left or the one on the right?
哪個是你姊姊，左邊的那個還是右邊的？

Level

2

Level

3

Level

4

sit [sɪt]

Track 0801

動 坐 反 stand 站

▶The white woman was a discriminant; she refused to sit beside black men.
這名白人女性是位種族歧視者；她拒絕坐在黑人男性旁邊。

文法字詞解析
sit 的動詞變化 sit, sat, sat

Level

5

six [sɪks]

Track 0802

名 六

▶I slept about six hours last night.
我昨天晚上大概睡了六小時。

Level

6

six·teen [sɪksˈtin]

Track 0803

名 十六

▶My cat is already sixteen. Hard to believe, isn't it?
我的貓已經十六歲了呢，真難相信對不對？

six·ty [ˈsɪkstɪ]
Track 0804

名 六十

▶This room is big enough to hold sixty people at least, so please don't worry about it.
這個房間很大,至少能夠容納下六十個人,因此請不要擔心。

size [saɪz]
Track 0805

名 大小、尺寸

▶This shirt comes in three different sizes: small, medium, large.
這件襯衫有三種尺寸:小、中、大。

skill [skɪl]
Track 0806

名 技能 同 capability 技能

▶His dancing skills are great. 他的舞蹈技巧很好。

skin [skɪn]
Track 0807

名 皮、皮膚

▶Staying in the sun for too long is bad for your skin.
曬太陽太久對皮膚不好。

sky [skaɪ]
Track 0808

名 天、天空

▶There are a number of stars shining in the night sky.
夜空中群星閃爍。

sleep [slip]
Track 0809

動 睡 名 睡眠、睡眠期 反 wake 醒來

▶動 How long do you usually sleep every night?
你每晚大概睡多久?

▶名 Tom often works late during the week; he doesn't have enough sleep on weekdays.
湯姆總是加班到很晚,他週一到週五都睡眠不足。

slow [slo]
Track 0810

形 慢的、緩慢的 副 慢 動 (使)慢下來 反 fast 快的

▶形 The slower train is cheaper. 比較慢的火車也比較便宜。

▶副 The girl runs slower than her sister.
那個女孩跑得比她妹妹慢。

▶動 Slow down please, the kids can't catch up.
請慢一點,孩子們跟不上了。

small [smɔl]
Track 0811

形 小的、少的 反 large 大的

▶My sister looks very small by the side of her friend.
我妹妹和她朋友站在一起時顯得很矮小。

smart [smɑrt]
Track 0812

形 聰明的 同 intelligent 聰明的

▶His son is smart enough to solve these difficult mathematical (數學的)problems.
他兒子很聰明,能夠解答出這些數學難題。

文法字詞解析

1. sleep 的動詞變化:sleep, slept, slept
2. 在第二個例句中,sleep 是名詞,所以用 How much 來詢問睡眠時間的多寡,如果換作使用動詞的 sleep,就可以說:How long have you slept?
要注意,疑問詞「how long」是問時間長短,要問距離的長短(遠近)則要用「how far」。

smell [smɛl] 　　🔊 *Track 0813*

動 嗅、聞到 名 氣味、香味 同 scent 氣味、香味
▶動 I can't smell anything strange. 我沒聞到什麼奇怪的味道啊。
▶名 I don't like the smell of durian, but I enjoy the taste of it.
　　我不喜歡榴槤的氣味，但我喜歡它的味道。

文法字詞解析
smell的動詞變化：smell, smelled, smelled
或smell, smelt, smelt

smile [smaɪl] 　　🔊 *Track 0814*

動 微笑 名 微笑 反 frown 皺眉
▶動 Remember to smile even if you are tired.
　　就算累了也要記得微笑一下。
▶名 Why is there a smile on your face? Did something funny
　　happen? 你臉上為什麼帶著微笑？有發生什麼好笑的事嗎？

萬用延伸句型
Did something (adj.) happen?
發生了什麼（……的）事嗎？

smoke [smok] 　　🔊 *Track 0815*

名 煙、煙塵 動 抽菸 同 fume 煙、氣
▶名 I see smoke. Is something on fire?
　　我看到煙耶，有什麼東西著火了嗎？
▶動 Many free health programs in public hospital are helping
　　people who want to quit smoking.
　　許多公立醫院的健康計劃都有幫助人戒菸。

snake [snek] 　　🔊 *Track 0816*

名 蛇
▶He was taken to the hospital（醫院）because of a snake bite.
　　他因為遭蛇咬而被送到醫院去了。

snow [sno] 　　🔊 *Track 0817*

名 雪 動 下雪
▶名 There was heavy snow fall in the afternoon.
　　今天下午有場大雪。
▶動 It is always snowing here in December. 這裡十二月老是下雪。

文法字詞解析
現在進行式 be 動詞後放頻率副詞 always
用來表示經常發生的事。

so [so] 　　🔊 *Track 0818*

副 這樣、如此地 連 所以
▶副 I am so glad that you came to see me. 很高興你來看我。
▶連 My colleague（同事）is ill today, so I have to go to the meeting
　　alone. 我的同事今天生病了，所以我要一個人去開會了。

文法字詞解析
so 作為對等連接詞「所以」時，不可和
because 連用。

soap [sop] 　　🔊 *Track 0819*

名 肥皂
▶Some people prefer soap to shower gel.
　　有些人喜歡肥皂勝過沐浴乳。

so·da [ˋsodə] 　　🔊 *Track 0820*

名 汽水、蘇打
▶After drinking too much soda, I felt kind of sick.
　　喝了這麼多汽水，我感覺有點想吐。

so·fa [ˋsofə] 　　🔊 *Track 0821*

名 沙發 同 couch 沙發
▶The sofa my grandma bought is made of leather.
　　我奶奶買的沙發是皮製的。

Level 1
Level 2
Level 3
Level 4
Level 5
Level 6

輕鬆學習、入門無負擔
掌握基礎1000單字

soft [sɔft] 🔊 *Track 0822*
形 軟的、柔和的 反 hard 硬的
▶Her voice is very soft, like a cat walking across a piano.
她的聲音很柔和，有如貓走過鋼琴的聲音一般。

soil [sɔɪl] 🔊 *Track 0823*
名 土壤 動 弄髒、弄汙 同 dirt 泥、土
▶名 The soldier became homesick as soon as he stepped onto the foreign soil. 軍人一踏上外國的土地就開始想家。
▶動 I soiled my hands repairing（修理）the machine.
我修理機器的時候弄髒了手。

文法字詞解析
as soon as 表示「一……就……」。

some [sʌm] 🔊 *Track 0824*
形 一些的、若干的 代 若干、一些 同 certain 某些、某幾個
▶形 Could you buy some books for me when you go downtown（市區）? 你去城裡的時候能幫我買些書回來嗎？
▶代 Some dogs are friendly, but some are scary.
有些狗很友善，但有些很可怕。

some·one [ˈsʌmˌwʌn] 🔊 *Track 0825*
代 一個人、某一個人 同 somebody 某一個人
▶There is someone sitting in my seat, so I have to find another one. 有人坐在我的座位上了，所以我不得不再找另外一個座位。

some·thing [ˈsʌmθɪŋ] 🔊 *Track 0826*
代 某物、某事
▶It's really hot! I want to drink something cold.
天氣很熱！我想喝點涼的。

some·times [ˈsʌmˌtaɪmz] 🔊 *Track 0827*
副 有時
▶I go to school by bus sometimes. 我有時候會搭公車去上學。

文法字詞解析
sometimes 是頻率副詞，表示動作發生的頻率多寡。
頻率副詞還有以下幾個（依頻繁程度由高至低）：usually（常常）, often（通常）, never（從不）。

son [sʌn] 🔊 *Track 0828*
名 兒子 反 daughter 女兒
▶My son is always playing basketball outside.
我的兒子總是在外面打籃球。

song [sɔŋ] 🔊 *Track 0829*
名 歌曲
▶What's this song called? I can't remember.
這首歌叫什麼？我不記得了。

文法字詞解析
此處用到被動語態 be +V p.p.。意思是「這首歌被稱做什麼」，但中文不會這樣使用。

soon [sun] 🔊 *Track 0830*
副 很快地、不久 同 shortly 不久
▶With global warming effect, the ice cap in the north pole may vanish soon. 因為溫室效應，北極的冰帽可能會很快消失。

sorry [ˈsɔrɪ] 🔊 *Track 0831*
形 難過的、惋惜的、抱歉的 反 glad 開心的
▶I'm sorry for saying those words. 我很抱歉我說了那些話。

soul [sol]
🔊 *Track 0832*

名 靈魂、心靈 反 body 身體
▶ Food is good for the soul. 食物對心靈很有益處。

sound [saʊnd]
🔊 *Track 0833*

名 聲音、聲響 動 發出聲音、聽起來像 同 voice 聲音
▶ 名 The toddlers was imitating the hippo on TV, making a strange sound. 這個小孩在模仿電視上的河馬，一邊發出怪聲。
▶ 動 Your idea sounds good. Good job!
你的點子聽起來真不錯。幹得好！

萬用延伸句型

It sounds like + 子句 聽起來似乎⋯⋯。
例如：It sounds like we have no choice but to do that. 聽起來我們好像不得不做那件事了。

soup [sup]
🔊 *Track 0834*

名 湯 同 broth 湯
▶ This soup is too bland（淡而無味的）. We should have ordered（點餐）another kind.
這湯喝起來好淡，早知道就點另一種了。

文法字詞解析

should have + p.p.
當時／原本應該⋯⋯，表示過去應該做卻沒做的事。

sour [ˈsaʊr]
🔊 *Track 0835*

形 酸的 動 變酸 名 酸的東西
▶ 形 This candy tastes really sour.
這糖吃起來好酸啊。
▶ 動 The milk will sour in warm weather.
牛奶在暖和的天氣會發酸。
▶ 名 I like the sweeter candies, and he likes the sour.
我喜歡甜的糖果，他喜歡酸的。

south [saʊθ]
🔊 *Track 0836*

名 南、南方 形 南的、南方的 副 向南方、在南方 反 north 北方
▶ 名 There are mountains in the south of the country, so we enter it from the north.
這個國家南邊有山脈，所以我們從北邊入境。
▶ 形 There is a pet shop on the south side of the street.
這條街的南邊有家寵物店。
▶ 副 The birds fly south for the winter.
鳥兒們南飛過冬。

space [spes]
🔊 *Track 0837*

名 空間、太空 動 隔開、分隔
▶ 名 Give him some space. Talking to him now might make him angry. 給他一點空間吧，現在跟他講話他說不定會生氣。
▶ 動 You should space the chairs further from each other.
你應該把那些椅子隔開一點。

speak [spik]
🔊 *Track 0838*

動 說話、講話 同 talk 講話
▶ I can't speak Japanese at all. 我完全不會講日文。

文法字詞解析

speak 的動詞變化：speak, spoke, spoken

spe·cial [ˈspɛʃəl]
🔊 *Track 0839*

形 專門的、特別的 反 usual 平常的
▶ There is a special program in memory of the great senate representativeon TV.
有個為了紀念已故的偉大參議員的特別節目今天會播出。

Level 1 輕鬆學習、入門無負擔——掌握基礎1000單字

Level 2

Level 3

Level 4

Level 5

Level 6

speech [spitʃ]
🔊 *Track 0840*

名 言談、說話
▶The student was assigned to give a speech on the graduation ceremony. 這名學生被指派要在畢業典禮時演講。

spell [spɛl]
🔊 *Track 0841*

動 用字母拼、拼寫
▶How do you spell "tongue"（舌頭）？
「tongue」這個單字怎麼拼？

文法字詞解析
spell 的動詞變化：spell, spelled, spelled 或 spell, spelt, spelt

spend [spɛnd]
🔊 *Track 0842*

動 花費、付錢 同 consume 花費
▶Where should we spend our holiday? How about Hong Kong（香港）？我們該去哪裡度假呢？香港怎麼樣？

文法字詞解析
spend 的動詞變化 spend, spent, spent

spoon [spun]
🔊 *Track 0843*

名 湯匙、調羹
▶There is a small spoon in the cup; you can use it to eat pudding（布丁）. 杯子裡有個小湯匙，你可以用來吃布丁。

sport [sport]
🔊 *Track 0844*

名 運動 同 exercise 運動
▶Tennis is my favorite sport. 網球是我最喜歡的運動。

spring [sprɪŋ]
🔊 *Track 0845*

名 跳躍、彈回、春天、泉水 動 跳、躍、彈跳 同 jump 跳
▶名 Many tourists came to this area for bathing in the hot spring. 許多觀光客來這個區域泡溫泉。
▶動 The cat sprang onto the sink. 那隻貓跳到了洗手台上。

文法字詞解析
spring 的動詞變化 spring, sprang, sprung

stair [stɛr]
🔊 *Track 0846*

名 樓梯
▶Climbing the stairs is good for your health but not your knees. 爬樓梯對身體好，但對膝蓋不好。

stand [stænd]
🔊 *Track 0847*

動 站起、立起 名 立場、觀點 反 sit 坐
▶動 Will Marie please stand up? 瑪麗，可以請妳站起來嗎？
▶名 His stand toward the matter has not changed. 他對這個問題的立場沒有改變。

文法字詞解析
stand 的動詞變化 stand, stood, stood
在第二個例句中，介係詞 toward 用在表達對某事的看法。

star [stɑr]
🔊 *Track 0848*

名 星、恆星 形 著名的、卓越的 動 扮演主角
▶名 There are countless stars in the sky, just like many small but bright eyes. 天空中佈滿無數顆星星，就像很多明亮的小眼睛。
▶形 As the star football players entered the stadium, the crowd cheered for them. 明星足球員進到足球場時，許多人都為他們歡呼。
▶動 Audrey Hepburn starred in this film. 奧黛麗·赫本主演了這部電影。

start [stɑrt]

名 開始、起點 動 開始、著手 同 begin 開始

▶名 We'd better make an early start to avoid（避開）the traffic.
我們最好早點出發以避開塞車。

▶動 Where should we start? Do you have a plan?
我們要從哪裡開始著手？你有計畫嗎？

state [stet]

名 狀態、狀況、情形；州 動 陳述、說明、闡明
同 declare 聲明、表示

▶名 The case is still in an unclear state; we shall not draw a conclusion now.
這個案子狀態還不明；所以我們現在還不能下結論。

▶動 He stated his view at the meeting.
他在會議上陳述了他的觀點。

state·ment [ˈstetmənt]

名 陳述、聲明、宣佈

▶His statement is very confusing.
他的陳述很令人困惑。

sta·tion [ˈsteʃən]

名 車站

▶The train station is always full of people. 火車站總是滿滿多人。

stay [ste]

名 逗留、停留 動 停留 同 remain 留下

▶名 I was assigned to accompany the delegation from Russia during their stay.
我被指派俄國代表團留駐期間要陪同他們。

▶動 How long do you plan to stay here?
你打算在此停留多久

step [stɛp]

名 腳步、步驟 動 踏 同 pace 步

▶名 I'll teach you how to do it step by step.
讓我一步一步教你做吧。

▶動 As soon as she stepped out of the room he walked in.
她一踏出房間，他就走了進來。

still [stɪl]

形 無聲的、不動的 副 仍然

▶形 The nights here are so quiet and still.
這裡的夜晚總是安靜無聲。

▶副 I still think we should try again.
我還是覺得我們應該再試一次。

stone [ston]

名 石、石頭 同 rock 石頭

▶The witch cast a spell on the boy and turned him into stone.
巫婆對小男孩施咒語，把他變成石頭了。

文法字詞解析

How long 有「多久、多長時間」的意思，使用時須注意要搭配 stay, live 等含有「延續」含意的動詞。

萬用延伸句型

As soon as... 一……就……

Level 1 輕鬆學習、入門無負擔──掌握基礎1000單字

Level 2

Level 3

Level 4

Level 5

Level 6

stop [stɑp] ◀€ *Track 0857*
名 停止 動 停止、結束 同 halt 停止
▶名 I got off at the wrong stop this morning.
我今天早上下錯車站了。
▶動 The rain has already stopped. 雨已經停了。

文法字詞解析
stop 的動詞變化：stop, stopped, stopped

sto·ry [ˋstorɪ] ◀€ *Track 0858*
名 故事 同 tale 故事
▶My mom always had some interesting bedtime stories for me.
我媽媽以前都會跟我說些有趣的床邊故事。

strange [strendʒ] ◀€ *Track 0859*
形 陌生的、奇怪的、不熟悉的 反 familiar 熟悉的
▶It's strange enough to see a penguin（企鵝）appearing in our city. 居然在我們的城市看到了一隻企鵝，這真夠奇怪的。

street [strit] ◀€ *Track 0860*
名 街、街道
▶There is a very long street in this old town.
這個古鎮有條很長的街道。

strong [strɔŋ] ◀€ *Track 0861*
形 強壯的、強健的 副 健壯地 反 weak 虛弱的
▶形 Though he looked strong, he actually didn't have much strength. 雖然他看起來強壯，卻沒有什麼力氣。
▶副 He is now well over sixty, but is still going strong.
他已經六十多歲了，可是還強壯得很。

stu·dent [ˋstjudn̩t] ◀€ *Track 0862*
名 學生 反 teacher 老師
▶Not every student could understand what the teacher said in class. 並非每個學生都能明白老師在課堂上說過的話。

stud·y [ˋstʌdɪ] ◀€ *Track 0863*
名 學習 動 學習、研究
▶名 My dad devotes（奉獻）himself to the study of birds.
我的父親致力於研究鳥類。
▶動 I don't have time to study after work.
我工作完就沒空唸書了。

stu·pid [ˋstjupɪd] ◀€ *Track 0864*
形 愚蠢的、笨的 反 wise 聰明的
▶This may sound like a stupid question, but he really doesn't understand it.
這個問題聽起來可能很愚蠢，但是他確實不明白。

文法字詞解析
助動詞 may 後面的動詞要改為原形動詞。

such [sʌtʃ] ◀€ *Track 0865*
形 這樣的、如此的 代 這樣的人或物
▶形 He is such an easygoing person that he doesn't seem to get upset with anything.
他脾氣如此好，好像不會因為任何事生氣。

▶代 He thought I wanted to make him angry, but such was not my intention（意圖）.
他以為我想惹他生氣，但那不是我的本意。

sug·ar [ˈʃʊgɚ]　◀€ *Track 0866*
名 糖　反 salt 鹽
▶It is said the cutting down sugar consumption is good for your health. 據說減少糖的攝取對健康很好。

sum·mer [ˈsʌmɚ]　◀€ *Track 0867*
名 夏天、夏季
▶What's the weather like in summer here? I know nothing about this place.
這裡的夏季天氣如何呢？我一點也不瞭解這個地方。

sun [sʌn]　◀€ *Track 0868*
名 太陽、日 動 曬
▶名 I like it when the sun is up. 我喜歡太陽掛在空中的日子。
▶動 My parents are outside sunning themselves.
我父母在外面曬太陽。

文法字詞解析
sun 的動詞變化 sun, sunned, sunned

Sun·day/Sun. [ˈsʌnde]　◀€ *Track 0869*
名 星期日
▶Would you like to have a picnic on Sunday?
你想星期天去野餐嗎？

文法字詞解析
「星期」前方的介係詞必須用 on

su·per [ˈsupɚ]　◀€ *Track 0870*
形 很棒的、超級的
▶The astronomers predicted that there would be a super planet crash due to gravity.
天文學家預測因為引力的關係將會產生大行星相撞的現象。

sup·per [ˈsʌpɚ]　◀€ *Track 0871*
名 晚餐、晚飯　反 breakfast 早餐
▶I had a wonderful（極好的）supper yesterday. What about you? 昨天我吃了一頓很棒的晚飯，你呢？

文法字詞解析
「用餐」的「用」動詞要用 have。

sure [ʃʊr]　◀€ *Track 0872*
形 一定的、確信的 副 確定 反 doubtful 懷疑的
▶形 I am sure he lied about this matter.
我確定他在這件事上撒了謊。
▶副 It sure is cold outside. Let's just stay at home today.
外面實在很冷。我們今天就待在家裡吧。

萬用延伸句型
在對話中，"Sure."可以表達「yes（好）」或是「you're welcome（不客氣）」的意思，例如："Do you want me to get you a drink?" "Sure. Please." 「要我幫你拿點喝的嗎？」 「好啊，麻煩了。」

sur·prise [sɚˈpraɪz]　◀€ *Track 0873*
名 驚喜、詫異 動 使驚喜、使詫異 同 amaze 使大為驚奇
▶名 To our surprise, the long-term allies broke their diplomatic tie with each other. 令我們驚訝的是，長期結盟的兩國切斷彼此的外交關係了。
▶動 He surprised us all by bringing his wife.
他帶了太太來，把我們都嚇了一跳。

Level
1
輕鬆學習、入門無負擔——
掌握基礎1000單字

Level
2

Level
3

Level
4

Level
5

Level
6

sweet [swit]
🔊 *Track 0874*

形 甜的、甜味的 名 糖果

▶形 The drink is too sweet. 這飲料太甜了。

▶名 I gave the little girl some sweets. 我給了小女孩一些糖果。

swim [swɪm]
🔊 *Track 0875*

動 游、游泳 名 游泳

▶動 Let's go swimming in the river.
我們一起去河裡游泳吧。

▶名 It has been hot for days. Let's go for a swim on Saturday.
天氣炎熱了好幾天了。我們週六去游泳吧。

> **文法字詞解析**
> swim 的動詞變化：swim, swam, swum

[Tt]

ta·ble [ˈtebl̩]
🔊 *Track 0876*

名 桌子 同 desk 桌子

▶Mr. Hank did not admit to have any agreement with his opponent under the table.
漢克先生不承認有和對手私下達成任何協定。

> **萬用延伸句型**
> There is / are... 可放在句首，指出「某地點有某物」。

tail [tel]
🔊 *Track 0877*

名 尾巴、尾部 動 尾隨、追蹤 反 head 率領

▶名 We are at the tail of the bus queue（長隊）.
我們在公車候車隊伍的末尾。

▶動 I tailed him all the way to this little bar（酒吧）.
我一路跟蹤他到這個小酒吧。

take [tek]
🔊 *Track 0878*

動 抓住、拾起、量出、吸引

▶Can you take me to the train station?
你可以帶我去火車站嗎？

> **文法字詞解析**
> take 的動詞變化：take, took, taken

tale [tel]
🔊 *Track 0879*

名 故事 同 story 故事

▶Ben likes to tell tall tales to his kids.
班喜歡對他的孩子說些誇大的故事。

talk [tɔk]
🔊 *Track 0880*

名 談話、聊天 動 說話、對人講話 同 converse 談話

▶名 We made small talk as we waited for the bus.
我們邊等公車邊瞎聊。

▶動 I am too shy to talk to her.
我太害羞了，不敢跟她說話。

tall [tɔl]
🔊 *Track 0881*

形 高的 反 short 矮的

▶Not every girl is tall enough to become a stewardess（空姐）.
並不是每個女孩身高都足以成為空姐。

taste [test]
名 味覺 **動** 品嘗、辨味
▶**名** This dish is not to my taste. 這道菜不合我的口味。
▶**動** The host of the traveling program had to taste the strange local food. 旅行節目的主持人會嘗試一些奇怪的當地食物。

🔊 *Track 0882*

tax·i·cab/tax·i/cab
['tæksɪ.kæb]/['tæksɪ]/[kæb]
名 計程車
▶You're drunk. I'll call a taxi for you.
你醉了，我幫你叫台計程車吧。

🔊 *Track 0883*

tea [ti]
名 茶水、茶
▶Would you like a cup of tea, a glass of water or a cup of coffee?
你是想要一杯茶、一杯水還是一杯咖啡呢？

🔊 *Track 0884*

> **文法字詞解析**
> tea 是不可數名詞，前方可以加上單位量詞修飾。

teach [titʃ]
動 教、教書、教導
▶She teaches math in a cram school.
她在補習班教數學。

🔊 *Track 0885*

> **文法字詞解析**
> teach 的動詞變化：teach, taught, taught

teach·er ['titʃɚ]
名 教師、老師
▶All the teachers are in the office over there.
所有的老師都在那邊的辦公室裡。

🔊 *Track 0886*

tell [tɛl]
動 告訴、說明、分辨 **同** inform 告知
▶Did you tell him about what happened?
你跟他講發生了什麼事了嗎？

🔊 *Track 0887*

> **文法字詞解析**
> tell 的動詞變化：tell, told, told

ten [tɛn]
名 十
▶There are still ten pictures left in my camera（照相機）after I deleted（刪除）most of the others.
我刪除了很多照片後，相機裡還有十張照片。

🔊 *Track 0888*

than [ðæn]
連 比 **介** 與……比較
▶**連** I'd rather go by bus than by train.
比起搭火車我寧願搭公車。
▶**介** She looks younger than I am, but she's actually a lot older.
她看起來比我年輕，但她的年紀其實大我很多。

🔊 *Track 0889*

thank [θæŋk]
動 感謝、謝謝 **名** 表示感激
同 appreciate 感謝
▶**動** I can't thank you enough. 我對您真是感激不盡。
▶**名** I sent Mrs. Williams a gift as a token of thanks.
我送威廉太太一個禮物表達感謝。

🔊 *Track 0890*

Level 1
掌握基礎1000單字 輕鬆學習、入門無負擔

Level 2

Level 3

Level 4

Level 5

Level 6

that [ðæt]

Track 0891

形 那、那個 副 那麼、那樣

▶形 Is that book yours or is it Charlie's?
那本書是你的還是查理的？

▶副 She's not that bad! She just talks a lot.
她也沒那麼糟嘛！只是話有點多而已。

the [ðə]

Track 0892

冠 用於知道的人或物之前、指特定的人或物

▶The cake is really good. 這個蛋糕真是好吃。

their(s) [ðɛr(z)]

Track 0893

代 他們的（東西）、她們的（東西）、它們的（東西）

▶My class is generally friendly with each other, but theirs is a mess（混亂）.
我們班大致上都還算互相很友善，但他們班則是一片混亂。

文法字詞解析
each other 是代名詞，可以代表兩兩互相，如果是多人之間的互相，就用 one another。

them [ðɛm]

Track 0894

代 他們

▶Can you tell them about this for me?
你可以幫我跟他們講這件事嗎？

then [ðɛn]

Track 0895

副 當時、那時、然後

▶I didn't hear you at that time; I was wearing my earphones then. 我當時沒聽見你說話；我那時候戴著耳機。

there [ðɛr]

Track 0896

副 在那兒、往那兒 反 here 在這兒

▶The girl there is my sister. Pretty, right?
那裡的那個女孩是我妹妹。她很漂亮吧？

these [ðiz]

Track 0897

代 這些、這些的（this的複數） 反 those 那些

▶Would you like to help me wash up all these bowls and plates（盤子）? 你願意幫我洗洗這些碗和盤子嗎？

they [ðe]

Track 0898

代 他們

▶Have you heard that they got married secretly（秘密地）last month? 你聽說了嗎？他們上個月秘密地結婚了。

thing [θɪŋ]

Track 0899

名 東西、物體 同 object 物體

▶The woman likes hoarding things in her house.
這個女士喜歡在家中堆放雜物。

think [θɪŋk]

Track 0900

動 想、思考 同 consider 考慮

▶Do you think she will get mad at me? 你想她會生我的氣嗎？

文法字詞解析
think 的動詞變化 think, thought, thought

third [θɝd] 🔊 *Track 0901*

名 第三 形 第三的

▶形 There is an interval（間隔）between the third and (the) fourth acts. 第三和第四幕之間有一次休息。

▶名 The badminton player entered the semifinal and won the third in the tournament.
羽球選手進入準決賽，在比賽中贏得第三名。

文法字詞解析
between（用於兩者）之間；among（用於三者以上）之間

thir·teen [ˋθɝtin] 🔊 *Track 0902*

名 十三

▶This math problem seems to be too difficult to work out for a thirteen-year-old. 這道數學題對於一個十三歲的人來說太難了。

thir·ty [ˋθɝtɪ] 🔊 *Track 0903*

名 三十

▶It's almost seven thirty! Let's hurry up or we may miss our flight（航班）.
快七點半了，我們趕快吧，否則就可能錯過我們的航班了。

this [ðɪs] 🔊 *Track 0904*

形 這、這個 代 這個 反 that 那個

▶形 Which hat do you like better? What about this light blue one?
你比較喜歡哪頂帽子呢？這個淺藍色的怎麼樣？

▶代 How about buying this? I think it's the most beautiful one.
買這個怎麼樣？我覺得這是最漂亮的一個了。

those [ðoz] 🔊 *Track 0905*

代 那些、那些的（that的複數）

▶Would you like to help me put aside（在一邊）all those useless （沒用的）things?
你願意幫我把那些沒有用的東西全部放到一旁嗎？

though [ðo] 🔊 *Track 0906*

副 但是、然而 連 雖然、儘管 同 nevertheless 雖然

▶副 The price of the product is rather high; many people still bought it though. 這個產品價格相當高；許多人還是買了。

▶連 He does not lead a happy life though he is rich.
他的生活並不開心，雖然他很有錢。

文法字詞解析
從屬連接詞 though /although 所引導的子句可以放在主要子句之前或之後，做副詞子句。

thought [θɔt] 🔊 *Track 0907*

名 思考、思維

▶My first thought when I saw him was "what big ears"!
我見到他時，第一個想法是「他耳朵好大啊！」

thou·sand [ˋθaʊzn̩d] 🔊 *Track 0908*

名 一千、多數、成千

▶There are thousands of people in this shopping center now.
這購物中心現在有上千人。

three [θri] 🔊 *Track 0909*

名 三

▶Are you sure you can finish in three days? 你確定三天做得完？

文法字詞解析
這個句子是在詢問未來的情況，因此 in three days 表示「三天後」。

throw [θro]
🔊 *Track 0910*

動 投、擲、扔

▶I threw away all the clothes I don't wear.
我把我不穿的衣服全丟了。

Thurs·day/Thurs./Thur. [ˈθɝzde]
🔊 *Track 0911*

名 星期四

▶How about having dinner together on Thursday?
我們週四一起吃晚飯怎麼樣？

thus [ðʌs]
🔊 *Track 0912*

副 因此、所以 同 therefore 因此

▶The tuition of the private university was not affordable to her, thus she deferred the admission.
她無法負擔私立學校的學費，所以她決定延後入學。

tick·et [ˈtɪkɪt]
🔊 *Track 0913*

名 車票、入場券

▶Could you buy a movie ticket for me?
你能幫我買張電影票嗎？

tie [taɪ]
🔊 *Track 0914*

名 領帶、領結 動 打結

▶名 I don't know how to put on a tie. 我不知道怎麼打領帶。

▶動 I tied my shoelaces（鞋帶）just now but they've come apart（分開）again.
我才剛綁好了鞋帶，結果鞋帶又掉了。

ti·ger [ˈtaɪɡɚ]
🔊 *Track 0915*

名 老虎

▶The tiger in the zoo has gotten out of the cage（籠子）.
動物園的老虎跑出籠子了。

time [taɪm]
🔊 *Track 0916*

名 時間

▶Successful people only spend time on things that could benefit them in life or in work. 成功人士只花時間在對工作或人生有益的事情上。

ti·ny [ˈtaɪnɪ]
🔊 *Track 0917*

形 極小的 反 giant 巨大的

▶Her eyes are tiny and cute. 她的眼睛又小又可愛。

tire [taɪr]
🔊 *Track 0918*

動 使疲倦 名 輪胎

▶動 Long walks tire me out easily.
走很長一段路很容易就會讓我很累。

▶名 We have a flat tire. Good thing we have a spare（備用的）.
我們爆胎了，幸好還有備用的。

to [tu]　　🔊 *Track 0919*

介 到、向、往
▶Are you going to the post office later? 你待會要去郵局嗎？

to·day [tə`de]　　🔊 *Track 0920*

名 今天 副 在今天、本日 反 tomorrow 明天
▶名 Today is Mother's birthday. 今天是媽媽的生日。
▶副 Let's go to visit the Williams today.
　　我們今天就去拜訪威廉斯一家吧。

to·geth·er [tə`gɛðɚ]　　🔊 *Track 0921*

副 在一起、緊密地 同 alone 單獨地
▶To me, the most important thing is to stay together with my
family when they need me. 對我來說，最重要的是在家人需要
我時和他們待在一起。

to·mor·row [tə`mɔro]　　🔊 *Track 0922*

名 明天 副 在明天
▶名 Tomorrow is my birthday. 明天是我生日。
▶副 How about going out for dinner tomorrow?
　　我們明天出去吃晚飯怎麼樣？

tone [ton]　　🔊 *Track 0923*

名 風格、音調
▶The clerk spoke to the customers in an indifferent tone.
員工用冷漠的語調和客人說話。

to·night [tə`naɪt]　　🔊 *Track 0924*

名 今天晚上 副 今晚
▶名 Tonight is John's birthday party.
　　今晚是約翰的生日派對。
▶副 Let's go out for a drink tonight. 今晚我們出去喝一杯吧。

too [tu]　　🔊 *Track 0925*

副 也
▶Where are you going? Can I come too?
你要去哪裡？我可以一起來嗎？

tool [tul]　　🔊 *Track 0926*

名 工具、用具 同 device 設備、儀器
▶I need some tools to fix the lamp with.
我需要一些工具來修這個燈。

top [tɑp]　　🔊 *Track 0927*

形 頂端的 名 頂端 動 勝過、高於 反 bottom 底部
▶形 The manager put maintaining company's reputation in top
　　priority. 經理把維護公司名譽這件事看成最重要的。
▶名 There is a national（國家的）flag（旗幟）on top of the
　　building. 在大樓的頂端有一面國旗。
▶動 I've seen a lot of strange things but nothing can top that.
　　我看過很多怪事，但沒什麼能比這個更怪了。

Level 1
輕鬆學習、入門無負擔——
掌握基礎1000單字

Level 2

Level 3

Level 4

Level 5

Level 6

文法字詞解析
「too」和「either」都有「也」的意思，
也都放在句尾，但「too」是放在肯定句
句尾，「either」則是放在否定句句尾。

to·tal [ˈtotl̩]
🔊 Track 0928

形 全部的 名 總數、全部 動 總計 同 entire 全部
▶形 His project ended in total failure. 他的計劃徹底失敗。
▶名 There are 4500 employees in this company in total.
這家公司總共有4500名員工。
▶動 His spending last week totaled 100 dollars.
他上禮拜的花費總計一百美元。

touch [tʌtʃ]
🔊 Track 0929

名 接觸、碰、觸摸 同 contact 接觸
▶Please keep in touch. 請保持聯絡。

to·ward(s) [təˈwɔrd(z)]
🔊 Track 0930

介 對……、向……、對於
▶We walked together towards the department store.
我們一起走向百貨公司。

town [taʊn]
🔊 Track 0931

名 城鎮、鎮
▶She will be out of town for the weekend. 她這周末會出城去。

toy [tɔɪ]
🔊 Track 0932

名 玩具
▶How about giving our daughter a toy dog as her birthday gift?
送我們的女兒一隻玩具狗作為生日禮物怎麼樣？

文法字詞解析
as 介係詞在這裡的有「當作」之意。

train [tren]
🔊 Track 0933

名 火車 動 教育、訓練 同 educate 教育
▶名 How long does it take for you to go to London by train?
你坐火車去倫敦要多長時間？
▶動 She is training to become a nurse.
她在經過訓練成為一名護士。

tree [tri]
🔊 Track 0934

名 樹
▶Would you like me to climb up the tree and get the ball for you?
你要我爬到樹上幫你把球拿回來嗎？

trip [trɪp]
🔊 Track 0935

名 旅行 動 絆倒 同 journey 旅行
▶名 Taking a trip to the hometown of Shakespeare has always
been my dream. 到莎士比亞的故鄉旅行一直是我的夢想。
▶動 I tripped on a tree root（根）and fell.
我被一個樹根絆倒了。

文法字詞解析
trip 的動詞變化：trip, tripped, tripped

trou·ble [ˈtrʌbl̩]
🔊 Track 0936

名 憂慮 動 使煩惱、折磨 同 disturb 使心神不寧
▶名 What's the trouble? You look really tired.
有什麼問題嗎？你看起來好累。
▶動 Don't trouble yourself over such stupid things.
別因這種蠢事煩惱了。

文法字詞解析
look 是感官動詞，屬於連綴動詞的一種，因此後方可直接接主詞補語。

true [tru]
形 真的、對的 反 false 假的、錯的　　🔊 *Track 0937*
▶Is it true that Joey and Linda broke up?
喬依和琳達分手是真的嗎？

萬用延伸句型
Is it true that... ? ……是真的嗎？

try [traɪ]
名 試驗、嘗試 動 嘗試 同 attempt 企圖、嘗試　　🔊 *Track 0938*
▶名 What's that new flavor? I'll have a try.
那個新口味是什麼？我來試試看吧。
▶動 Before taking the wedding photos, Betty tried on several gowns.
拍婚紗之前，貝蒂試穿了幾件禮服。

文法字詞解析
try 的動詞變化：try, tried, tried

T-shirt [ˋtiʃɝt]
名 T恤　　🔊 *Track 0939*
▶I bought a T-shirt for my mother. 我幫我媽買了件T恤。

Tues·day/Tues./Tue. [ˋtjuzde]
名 星期二　　🔊 *Track 0940*
▶I will be visiting Mr. Smith on Tuesday; do you want to come with me? 我星期二要去拜訪史密斯先生，跟我一起去怎麼樣？

文法字詞解析
例句中使用未來進行式，暗示「拜訪史密斯先生」是已經安排好要做的事情。

tum·my [ˋtʌmɪ]
名 （口語）肚子　　🔊 *Track 0941*
▶Johnny, would you like the doctor to examine your tummy?
強尼，要不要醫生幫你檢查一下你的肚子？

turn [tɝn]
名 旋轉、轉動 動 旋轉、轉動 同 rotate 旋轉　　🔊 *Track 0942*
▶名 Take a right turn at the intersection, and you will see the museum. 在路口左轉，你就會看到博物館了。
▶動 Could you turn on the TV? It's time for the news.
打開電視好嗎？播新聞的時間到了。

twelve [twɛlv]
名 十二　　🔊 *Track 0943*
▶How about buying a dozen（一打）of cups? You know we have twelve guests in all.
買一打茶杯怎麼樣？你知道我們一共有十二位客人。

twen·ty [ˋtwɛntɪ]
名 二十　　🔊 *Track 0944*
▶There are around twenty cows and ten bulls（公牛）in that farm. 那個農場裡大約有二十頭乳牛和十頭公牛。

twice [twaɪs]
副 兩次、兩倍　　🔊 *Track 0945*
▶How often do you get a physical（身體的）examination? Twice a year? 你多久做一次身體檢查？一年做兩次嗎？

Level 1
輕鬆學習、入門無負擔——掌握基礎1000單字

Level 2

Level 3

Level 4

Level 5

Level 6

two [tu] 🔊 Track 0946

名 二

▶Two hours is too short for me to clean up the house.
兩個小時讓我打掃整個房子太短了。

[Uu]

un·cle [ˋʌŋkl̩] 🔊 Track 0947

名 叔叔、伯伯、舅舅、姑父、姨父

▶Hamlet was wondering whether he should revenge on his uncle. 哈姆雷特在想要不要像叔叔報仇。

un·der [ˋʌndɚ] 🔊 Track 0948

介 小於、少於、低於 副 在下、在下面、往下面
反 over 在……上方

▶介 Let's sit under the tree for a while.
我們在樹下坐一下吧。

▶副 The submarine（潛水艇）went under an hour ago.
那艘潛水艇一小時前潛下去了。

un·der·stand [ˏʌndɚˋstænd] 🔊 Track 0949

動 瞭解、明白 同 comprehend 理解

▶I don't understand why you're always so angry.
我不懂你為什麼總是在生氣。

> **萬用延伸句型**
> I don't understand... 我不明白……
> understand 後面可以依情況接 how / why / where 等疑問詞。

u·nit [ˋjunɪt] 🔊 Track 0950

名 單位、單元

▶I was in the same unit with my cousin when I entered the company. 我在剛進公司時，和我的表姊在同一個單位工作。

un·til/till [ənˋtɪl]/[tɪl] 🔊 Track 0951

連 直到……為止 介 直到……為止

▶連 I didn't know how long he had been waiting in the office until he called me.
直到他打電話給我的時候我才知道他在辦公室等了多久。

▶介 I'll wait for you until seven. If you're still not here, I'll leave.
我會等你到七點，如果你還沒來，我可要走了。

> **萬用延伸句型**
> Not until..., V + S... 直到……才……。
> not until 置於句首時，主要子句要用倒裝句。例如：Not until now did he realize the importance of his wife. 直到現在他才意識到他妻子的重要性。

up [ʌp] 🔊 Track 0952

副 向上地 介 在高處、向（在）上面 反 down 向下地

▶副 It's too early for me to get up. Please let me sleep for a few more minutes. 現在起床還太早，請讓我再睡幾分鐘吧。

▶介 There's a little house up the hill. 山丘上有間小房子。

up·stairs [ˋʌpˏstɛrz] 🔊 Track 0953

副 往（在）樓上 形 樓上的 名 樓上

▶副 Can you go upstairs and get my bag for me?
你到樓上幫我拿包包好不好？

▶形 I like watching birds from the upstairs window.
　我喜歡從樓上的窗戶賞鳥。

▶名 The house has no upstairs.
　這房子沒有樓上（只有一層）。

us [ʌs] ◀€ Track 0954

代 我們

▶Let's go and ask her if she could give us some help.
　我們去問問她是否能給我們一些幫助。

文法字詞解析
在這個例句中，使用了 if 所引導的名詞子句做為受詞補語。

use [juz] ◀€ Track 0955

動 使用、消耗 名 使用

▶動 I don't know how to use this machine.
　我不知道如何使用這台機器。

▶名 The conference is in use; you shall not enter it now.
　會議室在使用中；現在不能進去。

文法字詞解析
在第一個例句中，使用了含疑問詞 how 的間接問句。原本的句子應該是：I don't know how I can use this machine. 此句將主詞和情狀助動詞 I can 用 to 代替。

use·ful [ˈjusfəl] ◀€ Track 0956

形 有用的、有益的、有幫助的

▶These tools are not very useful.
　這些工具不是很有用。

[Vv]

veg·e·ta·ble [ˈvɛdʒətəbl] ◀€ Track 0957

名 蔬菜 反 meat 肉類

▶Would you like to go to the market to buy some vegetables with me? 想不想跟我去市場買些蔬菜？

文法字詞解析
vegetable 是可數名詞，因此在泛指蔬菜時要用複數 vegetables。

ver·y [ˈvɛrɪ] ◀€ Track 0958

副 很、非常

▶She's a very tall girl.
　她是個很高的女孩。

view [vju] ◀€ Track 0959

名 看見、景觀 動 觀看、視察 同 sight 看見、景象

▶名 I enjoyed the view from the villa.
　我很喜歡度假小屋的視野。

▶動 I view him as my friend and enemy（敵人）.
　我把他視為我的朋友與敵人。

vis·it [ˈvɪzɪt] ◀€ Track 0960

動 訪問 名 訪問

▶動 Let's go visit the new neighbor（鄰居）this afternoon.
　我們今天下午去拜訪新鄰居吧。

▶名 We will visit to the retired professor next weekend.
　我們下周末會去拜訪退休的教授。

Level 1
掌握基礎 1000 單字
輕鬆學習、入門無負擔

Level 2
Level 3
Level 4
Level 5
Level 6

voice [vɔɪs]
🔊 *Track 0961*

名 聲音、發言
▶ The singer has a lovely voice.
那名歌手有很甜美的聲音。

[Ww]

wait [wet]
🔊 *Track 0962*

動 等待 名 等待、等待的時間
▶ 動 I've been waiting for two hours and the bus still won't come.
我等了兩小時公車還不來。
▶ 名 Despite the long wait for dining in the Japanese restaurant, we still enjoyed the ramen noodles.
儘管為了去日本餐廳用餐等很久,我們還是很享受拉麵。

walk [wɔk]
🔊 *Track 0963*

動 走、步行 名 步行、走、散步
▶ 動 How long will it take for you to walk home?
你走回家要多長時間?
▶ 名 Let's take a walk after dinner.
我們吃完晚餐來散個步吧。

wall [wɔl]
🔊 *Track 0964*

名 牆壁
▶ There are lots of posters(海報)on my wall.
我牆上有很多海報。

want [wɑnt]
🔊 *Track 0965*

動 想要、要 名 需要 同 desire 想要
▶ 動 I want to go abroad when I grow up. 我長大後想出國。
▶ 名 Our company(公司)is in want of an engineer(工程師).
我們公司需要一名工程師。

war [wɔr]
🔊 *Track 0966*

名 戰爭 反 peace 和平
▶ Many families were torn apart due to the war.
因為戰爭,許多家庭被拆散。

warm [wɔrm]
🔊 *Track 0967*

形 暖和的、溫暖的 動 使暖和
▶ 形 This jacket is warmer than it looks. 這外套比看起來更暖。
▶ 動 They warmed themselves by the fire. 他們在火旁邊取暖。

wash [wɑʃ]
🔊 *Track 0968*

動 洗、洗滌 名 洗、沖洗 同 clean 弄乾淨
▶ 動 Wash your hands before you eat. 吃東西前請先洗手。
▶ 名 This car really needs a wash. 這車真的需要洗了。

萬用延伸句型
drive sb. up the wall 把(某人)逼瘋
例如:The cat keeps eating my hair. It's driving me up the wall.
貓一直吃我頭髮,快把我逼瘋了。

waste [west]　🔊 *Track 0969*

動 浪費、濫用 名 浪費 形 廢棄的、無用的 反 save 節省

▶動 He wasted too much money when he was young.
他年輕的時候浪費了太多的錢。

▶名 It is a waste of time playing the games on the mobile phone.
玩手機遊戲時很浪費時間的事情。

▶形 The waste products（產品）are taken away by the garbage truck. 那些廢棄產品被垃圾車帶走了。

watch [wɑtʃ]　🔊 *Track 0970*

動 注視、觀看、注意 名 手錶 反 ignore 忽略

▶動 Do you like watching baseball games?
你喜歡看棒球賽嗎？

▶名 This watch was inherited from my grandfather, so I cherished it very much.
這支手錶是我祖父傳下來給我的，所以我很珍惜它。

萬用延伸句型
Watch out! 小心！

wa·ter [wɔtɚ]　🔊 *Track 0971*

名 水 動 澆水、灑水

▶名 Drink lots of water to stay healthy. 要多喝點水，才會健康。

▶動 Can you water my flowers for me when I'm gone?
我不在的時候你可以幫我的花澆水嗎？

way [we]　🔊 *Track 0972*

名 路、道路

▶Can you show me the way to the zoo?
你可以告訴我走哪條路去動物園嗎？

we [wi]　🔊 *Track 0973*

代 我們

▶We'll be arriving at around ten. 我們大概十點會到。

weak [wik]　🔊 *Track 0974*

形 無力的、虛弱的 同 feeble 虛弱的

▶The kid was weak after he underwent the chemo therapy.
小孩接受化療之後就變得很虛弱。

wear [wɛr]　🔊 *Track 0975*

動 穿、戴、耐久

▶She looks very beautiful when she wears this blue skirt（裙子）. 她穿這件藍裙子的時候看起來很漂亮。

文法字詞解析
wear 的動詞變化：wear, wore, worn

weath·er [wɛðɚ]　🔊 *Track 0976*

名 天氣

▶If you don't know what to say, you can just talk about the weather. 不知道說什麼的話，那就聊天氣吧。

wed·ding [wɛdɪŋ]　🔊 *Track 0977*

名 婚禮、結婚 同 marriage 婚禮、結婚

▶Would you like to come to our wedding?
你願意來參加我們的婚禮嗎？

Level **1**

輕鬆學習、入門無負擔
掌握基礎1000單字

Level **2**

Level **3**

Level **4**

Level **5**

Level **6**

Wedne·sday/Wed./ Weds. [ˈwɛnzde]

🔊 *Track 0978*

名 星期三
▶ Can you finish your work by Wednesday?
你星期三前可以完成工作嗎？

文法字詞解析
在這個例句中，by 有「在……之前、不遲於」的意思。

week [wik]

🔊 *Track 0979*

名 星期、工作日
▶ How many times do you play tennis（網球）per week?
你一星期打幾次網球啊？

week·end [ˈwikˌɛnd]

🔊 *Track 0980*

名 週末（星期六和星期日）
▶ Tina works as a volunteer in the nursery home on weekends.
蒂娜週末會在育幼院當義工。

weigh [we]

🔊 *Track 0981*

動 稱重
▶ He weighs sixty kilos. 他有六十公斤重。

weight [wet]

🔊 *Track 0982*

名 重、重量
▶ Kevin tried to lose weight before the taekwondo contest.
凱文試圖在跆拳道比賽之前減重。

wel·come [ˈwɛlkəm]

🔊 *Track 0983*

動 歡迎 名 親切的接待 形 受歡迎的 感 （親切的招呼）歡迎
▶ 動 Let's welcome the most popular（受歡迎的）movie star in our country. 讓我們一起歡迎全國最受歡迎的電影明星。
▶ 名 Let's give the professor（教授）a warm welcome.
讓我們熱烈歡迎教授。
▶ 形 You're always welcome here at our home.
隨時歡迎你來我們家。
▶ 感 Welcome! I hope you enjoy our party.
歡迎！希望你很享受這次派對。

well [wɛl]

🔊 *Track 0984*

形 健康的 副 好、令人滿意地 反 badly 壞、拙劣地
▶ 形 I am not well today, so it's too hard for me to concentrate （專心於）on my work.
我今天不舒服，因此難以集中精神工作。
▶ 副 We have been working together for decades; I know him quite well. 我們已經一起工作幾十年了；我跟他很熟。

文法字詞解析
serve sb. well = 對某人有益
well off = 富裕的、幸運的
as well = 同樣地

west [wɛst]

🔊 *Track 0985*

名 西方 形 西部的、西方的 副 向西方 反 east 東方
▶ 名 Do you know which country lies to the west of Egypt?
你知道埃及以西是哪個國家嗎？
▶ 形 The west wind is too strong for the ship to sail.
西風刮得太猛了，那艘船都沒辦法航行了。

▶ 副 I can't tell whether I am driving west or not.
我不會判斷我到底是不是在向西行駛。

what [hwɑt]　◀≣ *Track 0986*

形 什麼　代 （疑問代詞）什麼
▶ 形 What day is today? 今天星期幾？
▶ 代 I couldn't hear what he said. 我聽不到他說什麼。

when [hwɛn]　◀≣ *Track 0987*

副 什麼時候、何時　連 當……時　代 （關係代詞）那時
▶ 副 Not all the people know when to work hard and when to have a good rest.
並非所有的人都知道何時該努力工作，何時該好好休息。
▶ 連 I'll call you when I get there. 當我到那裡時會打給你。
▶ 代 Since when has he been living here?
他從什麼時候開始住這裡的？

萬用延伸句型
Since when...? 從什麼時候開始……？
使用這個句型的話，後面要接現在完成式。

where [hwɛr]　◀≣ *Track 0988*

副 在哪裡　代 在哪裡　名 地點
▶ 副 Where did you park the car? 你把車停在哪？
▶ 代 My supervisor wanted to know where the blackmail was from. 我的主管想知道這封威脅信函是來自哪裡。
▶ 名 I've been to where he's talking about.
我去過他在講的那個地方。

文法字詞解析
blackmail 黑函，指的是「威脅信函」

wheth·er ['hwɛðɚ]　◀≣ *Track 0989*

連 是否、無論如何　同 if 是否
▶ I don't know whether he's gone yet.
我不知道他走了沒。

which [hwɪtʃ]　◀≣ *Track 0990*

形 哪一個　代 哪一個
▶ 形 Not every student knows which university （大學）he or she should enter.
不是每個學生都知道他（她）該上哪個大學。
▶ 代 Blue? White? Which color looks better?
藍色？白色？哪個顏色比較好看？

while [hwaɪl]　◀≣ *Track 0991*

名 時間　連 當……的時候、另一方面
▶ 名 I haven't seen him for a long while.
我已經很久沒見到他了。
▶ 連 After corresponding with my pen pal for a while, I decided to meet him in person.
在與筆友通信一陣子之後，我決定和他本人見面。

white [hwaɪt]　◀≣ *Track 0992*

形 白色的　名 白色　反 black 黑色
▶ 形 The white car over there is mine.
那邊那輛白色的車是我的。
▶ 名 I don't look good when wearing white.
我穿白色不好看。

Level 1　輕鬆學習、入門無負擔──掌握基礎1000單字

Level 2

Level 3

Level 4

Level 5

Level 6

who [hu]
◄⟨ *Track 0993*

代 誰

▶Who's the lady in red? 穿紅色的那位小姐是誰？

whole [hol]
◄⟨ *Track 0994*

形 全部的、整個的 名 全體、整體 反 partial 部分的

▶形 I don't know the whole story; I just heard some gossips about this matter.
我不知道整個故事；我只聽說了一些關於這件事的八卦。

▶名 What do you think about the plan as a whole?
你對這個計畫整體而言感覺如何？

whom [hum]
◄⟨ *Track 0995*

代 誰

▶That is the man whom they were talking about.
這就是他們一直在談論的那個男人。

whose [huz]
◄⟨ *Track 0996*

代 誰的

▶Whose cup is this? 這杯子是誰的？

why [hwaɪ]
◄⟨ *Track 0997*

副 為什麼

▶Why were you late yesterday? 你昨天怎麼遲到了？

wide [waɪd]
◄⟨ *Track 0998*

形 寬廣的 副 寬廣地 同 broad 寬的、闊的

▶形 The road was not wide enough for the truck to pass through. 這條路不夠寬，卡車無法通過。

▶副 I've travelled far and wide but there's no place I like as much as home. 我到處旅遊過，但沒有一個地方比家鄉更讓我喜愛。

wife [waɪf]
◄⟨ *Track 0999*

名 妻子 反 husband 丈夫

▶His wife is very pretty and cooks well.
他太太又漂亮又會煮菜。

will [wɪl]
◄⟨ *Track 1000*

名 意志、意志力 助動 將、會

▶名 You shouldn't force people to do things against their will.
你不該要人家做違背他們意志的事啊。

▶助動 Will you be at the meeting tomorrow? 你明天會去開會嗎？

win [wɪn]
◄⟨ *Track 1001*

動 獲勝、贏 反 lose 輸

▶He won the championship in the tournament. 他贏得比賽的冠軍。

wind [wɪnd]
◄⟨ *Track 1002*

名 風 同 breeze 微風

▶The wind is so strong today. 今天風好強喔。

萬用延伸句型
To whom it may concern,... 敬啟者。常用在書信的開頭，如果收信人是不特定或不確定的人，就可以用這種說法。

文法字詞解析
win 的動詞變化：win, won, won

win·dow [ˈwɪndo]
🔊 *Track 1003*

名 窗戶

▶Help me shut the windows before it starts raining.
在下雨前幫我把窗戶關好吧。

文法字詞解析
help sb. (to) do sth. 幫某人做某事

wine [waɪn]
🔊 *Track 1004*

名 葡萄酒

▶Bordeaux is a city famous for its wine.
波爾多是個以紅酒出名的城市。

win·ter [ˈwɪntɚ]
🔊 *Track 1005*

名 冬季 反 summer 夏天

▶I don't like winters because I'm afraid of the cold.
我不喜歡冬天，因為我怕冷。

wish [wɪʃ]
🔊 *Track 1006*

動 願望、希望 名 願望、希望

▶動 I wish I could travel（旅行）to the space one day.
我希望有一天我能遨遊太空。

▶名 It's your birthday! Make a wish!
今天是你的生日！許個願吧！

文法字詞解析
I wish(that)... / I hope(that)... 我希望……。
雖然「wish」和「hope」在中文都有「希望」的意思，但兩者後面接子句的用法卻不同。wish 多半接的是不太可能成真、無法改變、與事實相反的事情，而「hope」後面則會接可能發生的事，因此 wish 後常接假設語氣，hope 則接現在式、未來式、完成式等一般時態。

with [wɪð]
🔊 *Track 1007*

介 具有、帶有、和……一起、用 反 without 沒有

▶The woman with blond hair was said to be a body double for a superstar. 金髮女士據說是巨星的替身。

wom·an [ˈwʊmən]
🔊 *Track 1008*

名 成年女人、婦女 反 man 成年男人

▶The woman is looking for her son. 那個女人在找她的兒子。

wood(s) [wʊd(z)]
🔊 *Track 1009*

名 木材、樹林

▶The boys got lost in the woods. 那些男孩在樹林裡迷路了。

word [wɜd]
🔊 *Track 1010*

名 字、單字、話

▶How many words are there in this article（文章）?
這篇文章有幾個字？

work [wɜk]
🔊 *Track 1011*

名 工作、勞動 動 操作、工作、做 同 labor 工作、勞動

▶名 The employees were not allowed to take recess before the work was done. 員工在完成工作以前不能休息。

▶動 I can't work out this difficult problem. 我解不了這道難題。

文法字詞解析
work 的動詞變化 work, worked, worked

work·er [ˈwɜkɚ]
🔊 *Track 1012*

名 工作者、工人

▶We don't have enough skilled workers to finish this project（工程）. 我們沒有足夠有經驗的工人來完成這項工程。

Level **1**
輕鬆學習、入門無負擔
掌握基礎1000單字

Level **2**

Level **3**

Level **4**

Level **5**

Level **6**

world [wɜld] ◀€ *Track 1013*
名 地球、世界
▶Who's your favorite singer in the world?
你全世界最喜歡的歌手是誰？

worm [wɜm] ◀€ *Track 1014*
名 蚯蚓或其他類似的小蟲 動 蠕行 同 crawl 蠕行
▶名 The worm was used as a bait by the fisher. 釣客用蟲當作誘餌。
▶動 The children wormed their way over to us through the crowd（人群）. 孩子們緩慢地從人群中擠到我們身旁。

wor·ry [ˈwɜɪ] ◀€ *Track 1015*
名 憂慮、擔心 動 煩惱、擔心、發愁
▶名 The little girl has no worry in her life.
這個小女孩人生中完全無憂無慮。
▶動 I can't help worrying about the old man's health.
我忍不住為這名老人的健康擔憂。

萬用延伸句型
can't help V-ing 忍不住……

worse [wɜs] ◀€ *Track 1016*
形 更壞的、更差的 副 更壞、更糟 名 更壞的事 反 better 更好的
▶形 I'm bad at math, but he's even worse.
我數學很爛，但他還比我更差。
▶副 His illness（病況）keeps getting worse.
他的病況越來越惡化了。
▶名 What's worse, they didn't survive the avalanche and were buried alive. 更糟的是，他們沒能逃過雪崩而被活埋。

worst [wɜst] ◀€ *Track 1017*
形 最壞的、最差的 副 最差地、最壞地
名 最壞的情況（結果、行為） 反 best 最好的
▶形 It was said to be the worst storm（暴風雨）in years.
這場暴風雨據說是幾年來最厲害的一次。
▶副 He did the worst out of us all. 他是我們之中做得最差的。
▶名 Hope for the best, but prepare for the worst.
抱最好的願望，作最壞的準備。

文法字詞解析
1.「in + 時間」代表的是「在（一段時間）內……」可和過去式或未來式連用。
2. out of 從數個之中

write [raɪt] ◀€ *Track 1018*
動 書寫、寫下、寫字
▶Can you write your name here? 你可以把名字寫在這裡嗎？

文法字詞解析
write 的動詞變化：write, wrote, written

writ·er [ˈraɪtɚ] ◀€ *Track 1019*
名 作者、作家 同 author 作者
▶Not all people know this writer, though they know his books well.
儘管大家都聽過這位作家的書，卻不一定知道作者本人是誰。

wrong [rɔŋ] ◀€ *Track 1020*
形 壞的、錯的 副 錯誤地、不適當地 名 錯誤、壞事
同 false 錯的
▶形 I got one wrong answer in the test, so I didn't get full marks.
我考試中錯了一題，所以我沒能得滿分。
▶副 He guessed wrong three times in a row. 他一連猜錯了三次。

▶ 名 Lots of people can't tell right from wrong.
很多人不會分辨善惡。

[Yy]

yam/sweet po·ta·to
🔊 Track 1021

[jæm]/[swit pəˈteto]

名 山藥、甘薯

▶ My grandma loves eating yam all day. 我奶奶最愛整天吃蕃薯。

year [jɪr]
🔊 Track 1022

名 年、年歲

▶ Amis have the harvest festival every year, which is a great feature of their culture.
阿美族每年辦豐年祭,是他們文化的特色。

yel·low [ˈjɛlo]
🔊 Track 1023

形 黃色的 名 黃色

▶ 形 The yellow dress suits you better. 黃色那件洋裝比較適合妳。

▶ 名 How long will it take for you to paint all the walls yellow?
你把所有的牆壁都粉刷成黃色的話要花多長時間?

yes/yeah [jɛs]/[jɛə]
🔊 Track 1024

副 是的 名 是、好

▶ 副 Yes, not all people I met like to talk about the weather.
是的,不是我遇到的所有人都喜歡談論天氣。

▶ 名 Can I go with you? Please say yes!
我可以跟你去嗎?說好嘛!

yes·ter·day [ˈjɛstɚde]
🔊 Track 1025

名 昨天、昨日

▶ Where were you yesterday? I couldn't find you anywhere.
你昨天去哪了?我到哪都找不到你。

yet [jɛt]
🔊 Track 1026

副 直到此時、還(沒) 連 但是、而又 反 already 已經

▶ 副 I sent a questionnaire to Nick, but he hasn't replied yet.
我寄了一份問卷給尼克,但他還沒有回覆。

▶ 連 He tried hard, yet he couldn't succeed(成功).
他努力試過,但沒有成功。

you [ju]
🔊 Track 1027

代 你、你們

▶ Are you all right? 你還好嗎?

young [jʌŋ]
🔊 Track 1028

形 年輕的、年幼的 名 青年 反 old 老的

▶ 形 Those young men are really good at dancing.
那些年輕人很會跳舞。

▶图 The adult animals take good care of their young.
那些成年動物都將幼獸照顧得很好。

your(s) [jʊr(z)]
◀⋷ *Track 1029*

形 你的（東西）、你們的（東西）

▶It's your turn to clean the classroom after school.
放學後輪到你們打掃教室了。

yuck·y [ˈjʌkɪ]
◀⋷ *Track 1030*

形 令人厭惡的、令人不快的

▶The mixed juice looked yucky, so I dared not drink it.
混合果汁看來很噁心，所以我沒敢喝它。

yum·my [ˈjʌmɪ]
◀⋷ *Track 1031*

形 舒適的、愉快的、美味的

▶Where did you buy this cake? It's so yummy!
你這蛋糕是在哪裡買的啊？真好吃！

[Zz]

ze·ro [ˈzɪro]
◀⋷ *Track 1032*

图 零

▶The minister of education said there is zero tolerance for bully on campus.
教育部長說對校園霸凌零容忍。

文法字詞解析
Zero hour = 關鍵時刻

zoo [zu]
◀⋷ *Track 1033*

图 動物園

▶There are a great many kinds of animals in the zoo.
動物園裡有很多種動物。

NOTE

下面有兩篇文章，全是根據 Level1 的單字寫出來的，文章中超出 level1 的單字，有註記在一旁。

請先不要看全文的中文翻譯，試著讀讀看這兩篇文章，若能全盤了解意思，代表你對 Level1 單字已經駕輕就熟，可以升級到 Level2 囉！快來自我挑戰看看吧！

Reading Practice 1

If you cannot live without your car, Zurich might be the last city you would like to visit. In Zurich, people don't welcome cars! Over the past 20 years, this city has been using smart ways to make traffic lighter. One method is to limit the total number of parking spaces. Some people complain that there are never enough parking spaces. This is just what the city expected: if people find parking more difficult, they will drive less.

Also, the total number of cars in the city is counted. Over 3500 computers are used to check the cars that enter the city. If the number is higher than the city can deal with, the traffic lights on the roads that lead to the city will be kept red. Now, you may wonder why Zurich is doing this. The answer is simple: the city wants to make more space for its people.

Reading Practice 2

What does the word "family" mean to you? An American study showed that people today have different ideas about what makes a family. Most people who were interviewed（訪談）agreed that a husband, a wife, and a child are a family. On the other hand, 81% think a man and a woman, with a child, but not married, are a family, too.

The study found that whether people have a child or not is very important in the modern thinking of a family. Though many people think whether a couple is married or not, as long as they have a child, they are a family. Yet, the precentage drops to 40% if the couple don't have a child.

Another finding of the study showed that 30% of the interviewed people have no problem seeing pets as part of one's family, but they do not think a same-sex couple is a family.

Level
1
輕鬆學習、入門無負擔——
掌握基礎1000單字

Level
2

Level
3

Level
4

Level
5

Level
6

Reading Practice1 中譯

如果你生活中缺少不了車子，蘇黎世可能不是你會想去參觀的地方。在蘇黎世，人們不歡迎汽車！過去二十多年來，這個城市用了聰明的方式避免交通壅塞。其中一個方法是限制停車位的總數。有些人抱怨停車位總是不夠用。這就是城市所期待的：如果人們發現停車很困難，他們就會比較少開車。

此外，城市裡的汽車數字也被精密計算。超過 3500 台電腦被用來檢視進入城市的車輛。如果車輛數目超過城市所能負荷，進入城市的道路上交通號誌就會都是紅燈。現在，你可能會想，蘇黎世為什麼要這樣做呢？答案很簡單：這個城市想要多留一些空間給行人。

Reading Practice2 中譯

「家庭」這個字對你來說意義為何？有一項美國研究指出，現代人對於組成一個家庭的元素有不同的想法。大部分受訪的人都同意，丈夫、妻子，和孩子組成一個家庭。另一方面，百分之81受訪者認為一個男人、一個女人，雖然沒有結婚，但有小孩，也是一個家庭。

這個研究發現，在現代人思想中，是否有小孩，是取決是否為一個家庭的重要因素。雖然許多人認為，不管是已婚夫妻或未婚情侶，帶著孩子，就算是家庭，但沒有孩子的話，就只有百分之 40 的人會認為這對夫妻或情侶是一個家庭。

這項調查另一個發現是，百分之 30 的受訪者能接受將寵物視為家庭的一員，但他們不認為一對同性伴侶能組成一個家庭。

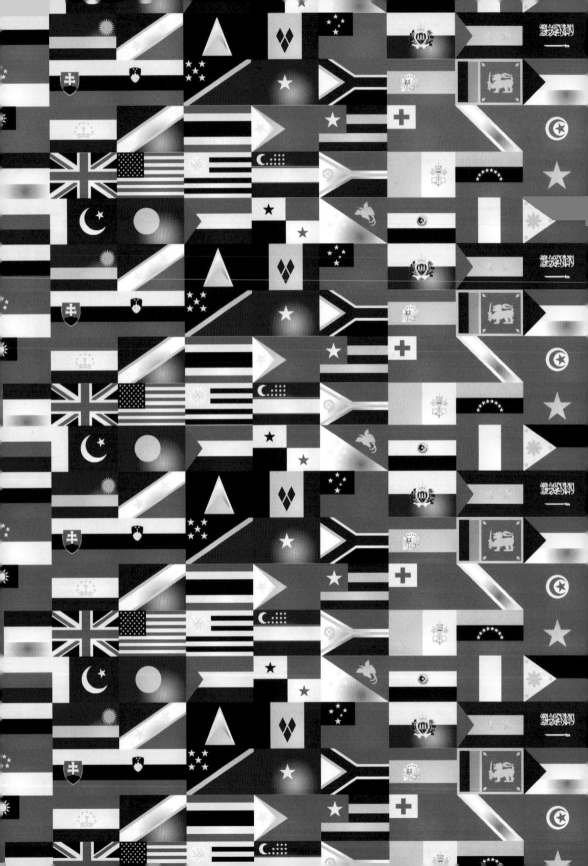

Level 2

漸入佳境、學習零壓力——
邁向常用2200單字

Level 2

漸入佳境、學習零壓力——
邁向常用1000單字

[Aa]

a·bil·i·ty [əˋbɪlətɪ]　🔊 *Track 1034*
名 能力　同 capacity 能力
▶Good ability in communication is required for this position.
好的溝通能力是這個職位所必須的。

a·broad [əˋbrɔd]　🔊 *Track 1035*
副 在國外、到國外　同 overseas 在國外
▶It won't be too long before I come back from abroad.
沒多久之後我就會從國外回來的。

ab·sence [ˋæbsn̩s]　🔊 *Track 1036*
名 缺席、缺乏　反 presence 出席
▶Don't speak ill of Mary in her absence.
別在瑪莉不在的時候說她的壞話。

ab·sent [ˋæbsn̩t]　🔊 *Track 1037*
形 缺席的
▶He is always absent on Thursdays. 他每星期四都會缺席。

ac·cept [əkˋsɛpt]　🔊 *Track 1038*
動 接受　反 refuse 拒絕
▶The manager（經理）accepted my suggestion as soon as I proposed（提出）it at the meeting.
在會議上我一提出建議，經理就馬上接受了。

ac·tive [ˋæktɪv]　🔊 *Track 1039*
形 活躍的　同 dynamic 充滿活力的
▶She is always very active at school. 她在學校總是很活躍。

ad·dition [əˋdɪʃən]　🔊 *Track 1040*
名 加、加法　同 supplement 增補
▶In addition to savory foods, the restaurant also provides sweets like doughnuts. 除了鹹食，這間餐廳也提供甜甜圈等甜食。

ad·vance [ədˋvæns]　🔊 *Track 1041*
名 前進　動 使前進　同 progress 前進
▶名 It would be great if you could finish the work in advance.
你能提前完成工作的話就太好了。
▶動 It is no wonder that he has soon advanced to the manager（經理）position. He is born to be a leader.
怪不得不久他就被提升為經理。他有當領導者的天賦。

文法字詞解析
星期的前面必須加介係詞 on

萬用延伸句型
As soon as S + V, S + V. 一……就……。
這個句型用於表達幾乎同時發生的兩個動作，如果是說明過去發生的事，則從屬連接詞片語 As soon as 所引導的副詞子句和主要子句都用過去式，如果是要說明未來發生的事，As soon as 所引導的副詞子句要用現在式，主要子句則要用未來式。

文法字詞解析
副詞 in addition 和介係詞 in addition to 意思相同，但兩者的用法不同。In addition 放句首時，後面必須加上逗號，再接主詞、動詞組成的完整句；in addition to 則是直接加上名詞或動名詞。

萬用延伸句型
(It is) no wonder... 難怪……

af·fair [əˈfɛr]
🔊 *Track 1042*

名 事件 同 matter 事件

▶What do you think of the love affair between the president（總統）and his secretary（秘書）？
你覺得總統和他秘書之間的戀愛事件如何？

aid [ed]
🔊 *Track 1043*

名 援助 動 援助

▶名 It doesn't matter whether he offers aid to me or not.
他要不要幫我的忙，對我來說沒有影響。

▶動 Can you aid me in doing this job?
你可以幫我處理這個工作嗎？

aim [em]
🔊 *Track 1044*

名 瞄準、目標 動 企圖、瞄準 同 target 目標

▶名 Our aim is to increase the sales number by 20 percent.
我們的目標是要增加百分之20的銷售量。

▶動 We aim to become the best team ever.
我們的目標是成為史上最棒的團隊。

air·craft [ˈɛrˌkræft]
🔊 *Track 1045*

名 飛機、飛行器 同 jet 噴射飛機

▶I learnt from the newspaper that the aircraft crashed（墜毀）as soon as it took off.
我從報紙上獲悉，那架飛機剛一起飛就墜毀了。

air·line [ˈɛrˌlaɪn]
🔊 *Track 1046*

名 （飛機）航線、航空公司

▶We chose the low-cost airline when we traveled to Japan.
我們去日本旅行時，選擇搭廉價航空。

a·larm [əˈlɑrm]
🔊 *Track 1047*

名 恐懼、警報器 動 使驚慌

▶名 Why did the alarm go off? Is there a fire?
警報器怎麼響了呢？火災了嗎？

▶動 I don't want to alarm you, but there's a bee on your head.
我不是要使你驚慌喔，可是你頭上有一隻蜜蜂。

al·bum [ˈælbəm]
🔊 *Track 1048*

名 相簿、專輯

▶Would you please buy me Mayday's new album?
你能買五月天的新專輯給我嗎？

a·like [əˈlaɪk]
🔊 *Track 1049*

形 相似的、相同的 副 相似地、相同地 反 different 不一樣的

▶形 The two painting look so alike. Are they replicas?
這兩幅畫看起來很像。它們是複製品嗎？

▶副 They talk alike and even think alike.
他們說話很像、連想法都很像。

文法字詞解析
fire 若是指具體的「一場」火災時，是可數名詞，如果是講抽象的概念，就是不可數名詞。

文法字詞解析
副詞 even（甚至）應放在被修飾語的前方，否則會改變強調的事物，造成語意的不同。

Level 1

Level 2

漸入佳境、學習零壓力——
邁向常用2200單字

Level 3

Level 4

Level 5

Level 6

a·live [ə'laɪv]
◀ Track 1050

形 活的 反 dead 死的
▶The victims of the air crash tried everything to stay alive.
空難的受難者進一切努力活下去。

al·mond ['ɑmənd]
◀ Track 1051

名 杏仁、杏樹
▶Can you make some almond cakes for the guests?
你可以做些杏仁餅來招待客人嗎？

a·loud [ə'laʊd]
◀ Track 1052

副 高聲地、大聲地
▶She told the student to read the book aloud.
她要那名學生大聲地把書唸出來。

al·pha·bet ['ælfəˌbɛt]
◀ Track 1053

名 字母、字母表
▶How long did it take for you to remember the English alphabet?
你花了多長時間背誦英語字母表？

al·though [ɔl'ðo]
◀ Track 1054

連 雖然、縱然 同 though 雖然
▶Although she's tall, she actually weighs quite little.
她雖然高，但其實體重很輕。

文法字詞解析
表達「雖然……，但是……」時，不可
用「Although S +V, but S + V」的句型，
因為 Although 和 but 都屬於連接詞。

al·to·geth·er [ˌɔltə'gɛðɚ]
◀ Track 1055

副 完全地、總共 反 partly 部分地
▶I counted; there were a hundred tickets altogether.
我算過了，共有一百張票。

a·mount [ə'maʊnt]
◀ Track 1056

名 總數、合計 動 總計 同 sum 總計
▶名 Teenagers spend a large amount of time on socializing with friends. 青少年花大量時間在社交活動上。
▶動 The total cost of repairs amounts to US$100.
修理費用總計要一百美元。

文法字詞解析
amount to 表示「總計為……」。

an·cient ['enʃənt]
◀ Track 1057

形 古老的、古代的 同 antique 古老的
▶The ancient people used primitive utensils.
古代人用原始的器具。

an·kle ['æŋkl]
◀ Track 1058

名 腳踝
▶What? Have you broken your ankle again?
什麼？你又弄傷腳踝了嗎？

an·y·bod·y/an·y·one
◀ Track 1059

['ɛnɪˌbɑdɪ]/['ɛnɪˌwʌn]

代 任何人
▶It doesn't matter whether you tell anyone else or not.
你要不要告訴別人都沒差。

an·y·how [ˈɛnɪˌhaʊ] 🔊 *Track 1060*

副 隨便、無論如何 **同** however 無論如何

▶The accident was terrible, right? Anyhow, at least we're all okay now.
那次意外太慘了，對吧？總之，至少我們現在都沒事了。

an·y·time [ˈɛnɪˌtaɪm] 🔊 *Track 1061*

副 任何時候 **同** whenever 無論何時

▶If you want to order from us, you can call me anytime.
如果您想從我們這裡訂貨，請隨時給我打電話。

萬用延伸句型
例句中用的是「if S + V, S shall / will / can / may + V」的條件句型，用來描述不變的事實。

an·y·way [ˈɛnɪˌwe] 🔊 *Track 1062*

副 無論如何

▶It doesn't matter whether you can afford the car; you wouldn't need it anyway.
你能不能買得起車子並不重要；你也不會用到它。

an·y·where/an·y·place 🔊 *Track 1063*
[ˈɛnɪˌhwɛr]/[ˈɛnɪˌples]

副 任何地方

▶Eating anywhere is fine with me. 在哪吃我都沒問題。

萬用延伸句型
That's fine by me / That's fine with me.
我都可以。用來表達自己不介意做某事。

ap·art·ment [əˈpɑrtmənt] 🔊 *Track 1064*

名 公寓 **同** flat 公寓

▶Tom had a housewarming party after he moved into his new apartment. 湯姆搬進新公寓後辦了一個慶祝派對。

ap·pear·ance [əˈpɪrəns] 🔊 *Track 1065*

名 出現、露面 **同** look 外表

▶We all judge people by their appearance to some degree (程度). 我們某個程度上都會由外表評判他人。

ap·pe·tite [ˈæpəˌtaɪt] 🔊 *Track 1066*

名 食慾、胃口

▶The kid had no appetite for vegetables; he longed for some desserts. 小孩沒有胃口吃蔬菜；他想要吃點心。

ap·ply [əˈplaɪ] 🔊 *Track 1067*

動 請求、應用 **同** request 請求

▶Why don't you apply for the scholarship (獎學金)?
你何不申請獎學金呢？

a·pron [ˈeprən] 🔊 *Track 1068*

名 圍裙 **同** flap 圍裙

▶She is the lady in the pink apron. 她是穿著粉紅圍裙那個小姐。

ar·gue [ˈɑrgju] 🔊 *Track 1069*

動 爭辯、辯論

▶If you two want to argue, why don't you do it privately (私下地)? 如果你們倆想要爭論，為什麼不私下解決呢？

Level **1**

Level **2**

Level **3**

Level **4**

Level **5**

Level **6**

漸入佳境、學習零壓力──
邁向常用2200單字

ar·gu·ment [ˈɑrgjəmənt]　🔊 Track 1070

名 爭論、議論 同 dispute 爭論

▶She's always getting into arguments with people.
她總是在和人發生爭論。

arm [ɑrm]　🔊 Track 1071

名 手臂 動 武裝、備戰

▶名 The kidnapper grabbed the kid by her arm and wouldn't let her go. 綁架犯抓住小孩的手臂不放。

▶動 Arm yourselves; the enemy is coming.
做好武裝準備吧，敵人要來了。

萬用延伸句型
cost an arm and a leg 非常貴
例如：The drone cost me an arm and a leg.
這無人機貴死我了。

arm·chair [ˈɑrmˌtʃɛr]　🔊 Track 1072

名 扶椅

▶I bought an armchair for my grandma.
我買了一張有扶手的椅子給我奶奶。

ar·range [əˈrendʒ]　🔊 Track 1073

動 安排、籌備

▶I arranged a meeting with my client at 11 o'clock this morning.
我今早11點安排了和客戶的會議。

ar·range·ment [əˈrendʒmənt]　🔊 Track 1074

名 佈置、準備 反 disturb 擾亂

▶Would you please make arrangements for our accommodations（膳宿）? 您能為我們安排好住宿嗎？

ar·rest [əˈrɛst]　🔊 Track 1075

動 逮捕、拘捕 名 阻止、扣留 反 release 釋放

▶動 The thief was arrested by the police.
小偷被警察逮捕了。

▶名 The police put the man under arrest.
警察扣押了那個男人。

文法字詞解析
第一個例句中，小偷是被警察逮捕，所以 arrest 要以被動語態表示。

ar·rive [əˈraɪv]　🔊 Track 1076

動 到達、來臨 反 leave 離開

▶Have our guests arrived yet? 我們的客人抵達了沒？

ar·row [ˈæro]　🔊 Track 1077

名 箭 同 quarrel 箭

▶He fired an arrow at the deer（鹿）. 他對那頭鹿射了一箭。

ar·ti·cle/es·say [ˈɑrtɪkl̩]/[ˈɛse]　🔊 Track 1078

名 文章、論文

▶I submitted an article to the editor of the magazine.
我繳交了一篇文章給雜誌的編輯。

art·ist [ˈɑrtɪst]　🔊 Track 1079

名 藝術家、大師

▶That artist is the greatest in the era（時代）.
那名藝術家是那個時代最偉大的一位。

a·sleep [əˋslip]
🔊 *Track 1080*

形 睡著的　反 awake 醒著的

▶It was almost two hours before I fell asleep last night.
昨晚我差不多躺了兩個小時才睡著。

as·sis·tant [əˋsɪstənt]
🔊 *Track 1081*

名 助手、助理　同 aid 助手

▶The professor had her assistant prepare the tools for this experiment. 教授上助理準備實驗要用的工具。

at·tack [əˋtæk]
🔊 *Track 1082*

動 攻擊　名 攻擊　同 assault 攻擊

▶動 The cat attacked the dog when it was sleeping.
那隻貓趁著那隻狗在睡覺的時候攻擊牠。

▶名 There has been many attacks on the president this past month.
過去一個月以來總統被攻擊了好幾次。

文法字詞解析
心臟病就是心臟被攻擊了，因此可用 heart attack 來表示。

at·tend [əˋtɛnd]
🔊 *Track 1083*

動 出席

▶Tom's supervisor was angry because he didn't attend the important meeting.
湯姆的主管很生氣，因為他沒出席這個重要的會議。

at·ten·tion [əˋtɛnʃən]
🔊 *Track 1084*

名 注意、專心　同 concern 注意

▶Would you please pay attention when I'm talking?
我在講話時拜託你專心聽好嗎？

a·void [əˋvɔɪd]
🔊 *Track 1085*

動 避開、避免　反 face 面對

▶Once you've learned a lesson from a mistake, you will avoid making the same mistake next time.
一旦你從一次錯誤中吸取了教訓，你就會避免再次犯同樣的錯誤。

[Bb]

ba·by·sit [ˋbebɪˌsɪt]
🔊 *Track 1086*

動 （臨時）照顧嬰孩

▶In order to earn enough money for her tuition, Pearl had to babysit for her neighbor.
為了賺錢付學費，寶兒必須幫鄰居做保母。

ba·by·sit·ter [ˋbebɪsɪtɚ]
🔊 *Track 1087*

名 保姆

▶Why don't you hire a babysitter to look after your baby?
為什麼不請一位保姆來替你照顧寶寶呢？

Level 1

Level 2

漸入佳境、學習零壓力——
邁向常用2200單字

Level 3

Level 4

Level 5

Level 6

back·ward [ˈbækwəd]   🔊 Track 1088
形 向後方的、面對後方的 反 forward 向前方的
▶The village is considered（被認為是）backward because of how dirty it is.
那個村莊因為太髒亂了，而被認為是個落後的地方。

back·wards [ˈbækwədz]   🔊 Track 1089
副 向後地 反 forwards 向前方地
▶The crowd moved backward to make way for the superstar.
群眾往後退，讓路給巨星走。

bake [bek]   🔊 Track 1090
動 烘、烤 同 toast 烘、烤
▶We have to bake as much bread as possible, because we have so many guests.
我們必須儘量多烤些麵包，因為我們有很多位客人。

bak·er·y [ˈbekərɪ]   🔊 Track 1091
名 麵包坊、麵包店
▶What do you think about opening a bakery near the school?
你覺得在學校附近開一家麵包店怎麼樣？

萬用延伸句型
What do you think of / about sb / sth?
你覺得……怎麼樣？

bal·co·ny [ˈbælkənɪ]   🔊 Track 1092
名 陽臺 同 porch 陽臺
▶Vicky stood on the balcony to see her son off.
維琪站在陽台上面為她兒子送別。

bam·boo [bæmˈbu]   🔊 Track 1093
名 竹子
▶The bamboo forest behind our house is home to thousands of fireflies（螢火蟲）.
我們家後面的竹林有很多螢火蟲。

bank·er [ˈbæŋkə]   🔊 Track 1094
名 銀行家
▶My brother got a job as a banker.
我弟弟得到了銀行家的工作。

bar·be·cue/BBQ [ˈbɑrbɪkju]   🔊 Track 1095
名 烤肉 同 roast 烤肉
▶What about inviting the Smiths to have a barbecue with us this weekend?
週末請史密斯一家過來和我們一起烤肉怎麼樣？

bark [bɑrk]   🔊 Track 1096
動（狗）吠叫 名 吠聲 同 roar 吼叫（獅子）
▶動 The puppy kept barking at the stranger.
小狗一直對著陌生人吠叫。
▶名 I heard barks outside all night.
我整晚都聽見外面有狗叫聲。

萬用延伸句型
all bark and no bite 直譯就是「只會吠叫，不會咬人」，即光會說大話恐嚇人，卻不做什麼實際上的行動。
例如：You don't need to be afraid of Mr. Kim. He's all bark and no bite.
不用怕金先生，他光會裝腔作勢，不會真的對你怎樣。

base·ment [ˋbesmənt]
🔊 Track 1097
名 地下室、地窖　同 cellar 地窖
▶ Mr. Wang stored some wine in the basement.
王先生貯存一些酒在地下室裡。

basics [ˋbesɪks]
🔊 Track 1098
名 基礎、原理　反 trivial 瑣碎的
▶ In this class, Mr. Brown will introduce some basics about computer science. 在這堂課裡，布朗先生會介紹一些電腦科學的基礎概念。

ba·sis [ˋbesɪs]
🔊 Track 1099
名 根據、基礎　同 bottom 底部
名詞複數 bases
▶ They have arguments on a daily basis. 他們天天都吵架。

bat·tle [ˋbætl]
🔊 Track 1100
名 戰役　動 作戰　同 combat 戰鬥
▶ 名 What do you think of his inspiring（鼓舞的）speech before the battle?
你覺得他在戰前所做的那場鼓舞人心的演講怎麼樣？
▶ 動 The two sides battled all night. 兩軍徹夜戰鬥。

bead [bid]
🔊 Track 1101
名 珠子、串珠　動 穿成一串　同 pearl 珠子
▶ 名 The nun held her prayer beads and mumbled some prayers.
修女拿著念珠，小聲說著她的祈禱。
▶ 動 Tears are beaded on her cheeks（臉頰）.
她雙頰掛著成串的淚珠。

bean [bin]
🔊 Track 1102
名 豆子、沒有價值的東西　同 straw 沒有價值的東西
▶ Would you like me to cook some beans for supper?
你想不想要我晚餐煮點豆子？

bear [bɛr]
🔊 Track 1103
名 熊　動 忍受　同 endure 忍受
▶ 名 I've never seen a real bear before.
我都沒看過真正的熊。
▶ 動 I can't bear the noises on the street.
我無法忍受街道上的噪音。

beard [bɪrd]
🔊 Track 1104
名 鬍子
▶ I like how your beard looks. 我喜歡你鬍子的樣子。

bed·room [ˋbɛdˏrum]
🔊 Track 1105
名 臥房
▶ I think you should open the window to air your bedroom as soon as you get up.
我覺得你應該每天一起床就把窗子打開給臥室通風。

文法字詞解析
bear 的動詞變化：bear, bore, born

文法字詞解析
look 用複數 looks 時常表示「容貌、外貌」。

萬用延伸句型
I think (that)... 我認為……

Level 1
Level 2
漸入佳境、學習零壓力—邁向常用2200單字
Level 3
Level 4
Level 5
Level 6

141

beef [bif]
🔊 *Track 1106*

名 牛肉

名詞複數 beeves, beefs

▶It will take me an hour to cook the beef thoroughly（徹底地）.
把牛肉煮熟要花我一個小時的時間。

beep [bip]
🔊 *Track 1107*

名 警笛聲 動 發出嗶嗶聲

▶名 My watch makes a beeping sound.
我的手錶會發出嗶嗶的聲音。

▶動 WMy watch beeps every hour on the hour.
我的手錶每個整點會發出嗶聲響。

beer [bɪr]
🔊 *Track 1108*

名 啤酒 同 bitter 苦

▶Would you like some beer or wine for your dinner?
晚餐您要喝啤酒或葡萄酒嗎？

bee·tle [ˋbitl]
🔊 *Track 1109*

名 甲蟲 動 急走

▶名 I am really afraid of beetles. 我非常害怕甲蟲。

▶動 How about beetling off for a drink at that bar during the break? 趁休息時間，我們趕快去那間酒吧喝幾杯怎麼樣？

beg [bɛg]
🔊 *Track 1110*

動 乞討、懇求 同 appeal 懇求

▶I beg you a pardon? I didn't hear you.
可以請你再說一次嗎？我剛才沒聽見。

be·gin·ner [bɪˋgɪnɚ]
🔊 *Track 1111*

名 初學者 同 freshman 新手

▶It will take a beginner quite a long time to learn all this.
一名初學者會需要花費相當長的一段時間來學會這些東西。

be·lief [bɪˋlif]
🔊 *Track 1112*

名 相信、信念 同 faith 信念

▶His belief that he's always right will cause huge problems.
他「自己永遠是對的」的信念將會造成很大的問題。

be·liev·a·ble [bɪˋlivəbl]
🔊 *Track 1113*

形 可信任的 同 credible 可信的

▶I think what he said is believable.
我認為他說的是可信的。

belt [bɛlt]
🔊 *Track 1114*

名 皮帶 動 圍繞 同 strap 皮帶；seat belt 安全帶

▶名 Please fasten your seat belt as soon as you get in the car.
請上車就繫好安全帶。

▶動 If you don't belt your jeans, they're going to fall down.
你不把牛仔褲繫上皮帶的話，褲子可要掉下來了。

萬用延伸句型

說到啤酒，大家應該常會想到一票人拿著啤酒喧嘩看熱鬧的場景。因此有個慣用說法，在當你發現有人正在出風頭，但你覺得自己可以做得更好時，就可以對旁邊的人說 Hold my beer!（幫我拿一下我的啤酒！）然後自己衝上去挑戰對方。

舉例來說，如果打籃球的時候敵方灌籃後還來個後空翻，一副很挑釁的樣子，但你覺得你可以翻得比他好，Hold my beer! 這句就派上用場了。即使手上沒有啤酒也可以用。

bench [bɛntʃ]
◀ *Track 1115*

名 長凳 同 settle 長椅

▶The old man sat on the bench, reading his newspaper quietly.
老人坐在長椅上，安靜地讀報紙。

bend [bɛnd]
◀ *Track 1116*

動 使彎曲 名 彎曲 反 stretch 伸直

▶動 He bent down to pick up the soap. 他彎下腰來撿肥皂。

▶名 You'd better slow down. There is a sharp bend ahead in the road. 你最好減速，前方路上有急轉彎。

文法字詞解析
bend 的動詞變化 bend, bent, bent

be·sides [bɪˋsaɪdz]
◀ *Track 1117*

介 除了……之外 副 並且 同 otherwise 除此之外

▶介 Is there any other way for us to go to the airport besides a taxi? 除了坐計程車外，還有別的方式能去機場嗎？

▶副 I don't have enough money to travel. Besides, I haven't time to do it, either.
我沒有足夠的錢去旅行。再說，我也沒時間去旅行。

bet [bɛt]
◀ *Track 1118*

動 下賭注 名 打賭 同 gamble 打賭

▶動 I bet with my friends that our national team will win in the baseball game.
我和朋友們打賭，我國的代表隊會贏得這場棒球比賽。

▶名 I'll treat you to dinner if I lose the bet.
如果我賭輸了，我請你吃晚餐。

文法字詞解析
bet 的動詞變化：bet, bet, bet

be·yond [bɪˋjɑnd]
◀ *Track 1119*

介 在遠處、超過 副 此外 反 within 不超過

▶介 What do you think of this picture? I think it's beautiful beyond description（形容）.
你覺得這幅畫怎麼樣？我覺得它美得讓人無法形容。

▶副 I can't see anything as far as the house and beyond.
我在這棟房子及更遠處實在看不到什麼東西。

bill [bɪl]
◀ *Track 1120*

名 帳單 同 check 帳單

▶I will pay the bill. It's my treat today. 我來付帳單。今天我請客。

萬用延伸句型
Bill, please. 不好意思，我要結帳。

bind [baɪnd]
◀ *Track 1121*

動 綁、包紮 反 release 鬆開

▶Women in the Qing Dynasty used to bind their feet.
清朝的女人總是裹著小腳。

文法字詞解析
1. bind 的動詞變化：bind, bound, bound
2. used to 用來表示過去常做的行為、過去的習慣。

bit·ter [ˋbɪtɚ]
◀ *Track 1122*

形 苦的、嚴厲的 反 sweet 甜的

▶Why does medicine always taste bitter? 為什麼藥總是這麼苦呢？

black·board [ˋblæk͵bord]
◀ *Track 1123*

名 黑板

▶He wrote down the answer on the blackboard.
他在黑板上寫下答案。

Level 1

Level 2

漸入佳境、學習零壓力——邁向常用2200單字

Level 3

Level 4

Level 5

Level 6

blank [blæŋk]　🔊 *Track 1124*

形 空白的　名 空白　同 empty 空的

▶形 He gave me a blank look when I asked him a question.
我問他問題時，他的表情一片空白。

▶名 We have to fill in the blank questions in the test.
這次考試有填空題。

blind [blaɪnd]　🔊 *Track 1125*

形 瞎的

▶The blind old man is very sensitive to sounds.
眼盲的老人對聲音非常敏感。

blood·y [ˋblʌdɪ]　🔊 *Track 1126*

形 流血的

▶Not everyone knows how the bloody incident（事件）was brought about.
並非人人都知道這起流血事件是如何引起的。

文法字詞解析

在英國 bloody 這個單字視使用情境也可當作髒話用，是不想說出 f 開頭的單字時可替換使用的好選擇。

board [bord]　🔊 *Track 1127*

名 板、佈告欄　同 wood 木板

▶I can't see the words on the board from here.
我從這邊看不到板子上的字。

boil [bɔɪl]　🔊 *Track 1128*

動 （水）沸騰、使發怒　名 煮　同 rage 發怒

▶動 Put the dumplings into the boiling water and wait until they float. 把水餃放進滾水裡，並且等到它們浮起來。

▶名 The fire is not big enough to bring the milk to a boil.
火不夠大，沒辦法把牛奶煮沸。

bomb [bɑm]　🔊 *Track 1129*

名 炸彈　動 轟炸

▶名 After the bomb hit, few houses were left standing.
空襲之後，房子所剩無幾。

▶動 Terrorists（恐怖分子）bombed several police stations.
恐怖分子炸毀了幾所警察局。

bon·y [ˋbonɪ]　🔊 *Track 1130*

形 多骨的、骨瘦如柴的　同 skinny 骨瘦如柴的

▶It is more important to be healthy than bony slim.
健康總比只剩皮包骨好。

book·case [ˋbʊk͵kes]　🔊 *Track 1131*

名 書櫃、書架

▶Helen removed all the books from the bookcase before she moved out the apartment.
海倫搬出公寓前，把書都從書架上清空。

bor·row [ˋbaro]　🔊 *Track 1132*

動 借來、採用　反 loan 借出

▶Can I borrow your pencil? 我可以借一下你的鉛筆嗎？

boss [bɔs]
🔊 *Track 1133*

名 老闆、主人 動 指揮、監督 同 manager 負責人、經理

▶名 The boss called me to his office and asked about this matter.
老闆叫我去他的辦公室並詢問我這件事情。

▶動 She enjoys bossing her husband around.
她喜歡對她丈夫頤指氣使。

文法字詞解析
enjoy 後面的動詞必須加 ing

both·er [ˈbɑðɚ]
🔊 *Track 1134*

動 打擾 同 annoy 打擾

▶I don't want to bother you, but could you tell me the password to access the database?
我不想打擾你，但可以告訴我資料庫的密碼嗎？

bot·tle [ˈbɑtl̩]
🔊 *Track 1135*

名 瓶 動 用瓶裝 同 container

▶名 The bottle broke into pieces on the floor.
瓶子在地板上摔成了碎片。

▶動 He didn't know when this wine was bottled.
他不知道這酒是何時裝瓶的。

bow [baʊ]
🔊 *Track 1136*

名 彎腰、鞠躬 動 向下彎

▶名 The actors and actresses bowed to the audience after the show. 表演結束後，演員對觀眾鞠躬。

▶動 They all bowed down in front of the emperor（皇帝）.
他們都在皇帝面前跪拜了。

bowl·ing [ˈbolɪŋ]
🔊 *Track 1137*

名 保齡球

▶Do you want to go bowling this Saturday?
你這星期六要不要去打保齡球？

文法字詞解析
go 後面要加字尾有 ing 的運動或戶外活動，像是 go bowling, go golfing, go swimming 等。

brain [bren]
🔊 *Track 1138*

名 腦、智力 同 intelligence 智力

▶Use your brain! This isn't such a hard question.
用用腦吧！這不是什麼困難的問題啊。

branch [bræntʃ]
🔊 *Track 1139*

名 枝狀物、分店、分公司 動 分支 反 trunk 樹幹

▶名 The bank has many branches in the north of the country.
這家銀行在該國北部有很多分部。

▶動 The store has branched out all over the city.
這家店在整個城市發展出很多家分支。

brand [brænd]
🔊 *Track 1140*

名 品牌 動 打烙印 同 mark 做記號

▶名 Which brand of computer do you prefer?
你喜歡哪個牌子的電腦？

▶動 The terrible scene is branded in my mind.
那個可怕的畫面已經烙印在我的心中。

Level 1

Level 2

漸入佳境、學習零壓力——邁向常用2200單字

Level 3

Level 4

Level 5

Level 6

brick [brɪk]
◀≋ *Track 1141*
名 磚頭、磚塊
▶He broke the window with a brick. 他用一個磚塊打碎了窗戶。

brief [brif]
◀≋ *Track 1142*
形 短暫的 名 摘要、短文 反 long 長的
▶形 There was a brief pause（停頓）in the conversation between the two leaders.
兩位領導人之間的談話出現了一個短暫的停頓。
▶名 We made a brief introduction of our products to our potential clients. 我們對可能的顧客簡短介紹了新的產品。

broad [brɔd]
◀≋ *Track 1143*
形 寬闊的 反 narrow 窄的
▶My friend is very broad-minded. He wouldn't be mad at trivial things. 我朋友很心胸寬大。他不會為小事生氣。

broad·cast [ˈbrɔdˌkæst]
◀≋ *Track 1144*
動 廣播、播出 名 廣播節目 同 announce 播報
▶動 Would you broadcast this news as quickly（很快地）as possible? 您能儘快播送這條新聞嗎？
▶名 We listened to the broadcast this morning.
我們今天早上聽了廣播。

brunch [brʌntʃ]
◀≋ *Track 1145*
名 早午餐
▶Do you want to meet up for brunch tomorrow?
你明天要不要一起來吃個早午餐？

文法字詞解析
brunch 就是 breakfast（早餐）和 lunch（午餐）兩個字的結合。

brush [brʌʃ]
◀≋ *Track 1146*
名 刷子 動 刷、擦掉 同 wipe 擦去
▶名 I used a brush to clean my shoe.
我使用刷子清了清我的鞋子。
▶動 The cat likes it when I brush her. 我的貓喜歡我用梳子刷牠。

bun/roll [bʌn]/[rol]
◀≋ *Track 1147*
名 小圓麵包、麵包捲 同 roll 麵包捲
▶I had a cup of tea and a bun in the afternoon.
我下午的時候喝了一杯茶，吃了個小圓麵包。

bun·dle [ˈbʌndl]
◀≋ *Track 1148*
名 捆、包裹 同 package 包裹
▶Would you please give this bundle of old clothes to the poor people on the street? 請你拿這包舊衣服給街上的窮人們好嗎？

burn [bɝn]
◀≋ *Track 1149*
動 燃燒 名 烙印 同 fire 燃燒
▶動 The cook said he didn't burn the toast; it was caramelized.
廚師說他沒有把土司烤焦；那是焦糖化現象。
▶名 The burns on his body look terrible.
他身上的燒傷看起來很慘。

文法字詞解析
burn 的動詞變化：burn, burned, burnt

burst [bɝst] 🔊 Track 1150

動 破裂、爆炸 名 猝發、爆發 同 explode 爆炸

▶動 She burst into tears and then ran out without saying anything.
她突然大哭，然後什麼也沒說就跑出去了。

▶名 The car disappeared in a sudden burst of speed.
那輛車忽然速度全開，很快地消失了。

busi·ness [ˈbɪznɪs] 🔊 Track 1151

名 商業、買賣 同 commerce 商業

▶How's business going these days?
最近生意如何啊？

but·ton [ˈbʌtṇ] 🔊 Track 1152

名 扣子 動 用扣子扣住 同 clasp 扣住

▶名 The button fell off the cuff.
扣子從袖口掉落了。

▶動 Why don't you button up your coat? It is so cold outside.
你為什麼不扣上大衣的鈕扣呢？外頭很冷耶。

[Cc]

cab·bage [ˈkæbɪdʒ] 🔊 Track 1153

名 包心菜

▶Would you please get me some cabbages?
你幫我買些包心菜回來好嗎？

ca·ble [ˈkebḷ] 🔊 Track 1154

名 纜繩、電纜 同 wire 電線

▶We don't have cable TV, so we usually watch movies and news on the Internet.
我們沒安裝有線電視台，所以通常是看網路上的電影和新聞。

café/cafe [kəˈfe] 🔊 Track 1155

名 咖啡館

▶I am a little thirsty; let's go to the café to have some coffee.
我有點口渴了，我們去咖啡館喝杯咖啡吧。

caf·e·te·ri·a [ˌkæfəˈtɪrɪə] 🔊 Track 1156

名 自助餐館 同 restaurant 餐廳

▶I often hang out with my friends at the school cafeteria.
我常常和朋友聚在學校的餐廳裡。

cal·en·dar [ˈkæləndɚ] 🔊 Track 1157

名 日曆

▶I got a new calendar for this year.
我為了今年買了一個新的日曆。

Level 1
Level 2
Level 3
Level 4
Level 5
Level 6

漸入佳境、學習零壓力——
邁向常用2200單字

calm [kɑm]　🔊 Track 1158

形 平靜的 名 平靜 動 使平靜 同 peaceful 平靜的

▶ 形 He's always calm no matter what happens.
無論發生什麼事，他總是很平靜。

▶ 名 The boss is quiet after receiving the call. I guess it's the calm before the storm.
老闆接到電話後很安靜，我想是暴風雨前的寧靜吧。

▶ 動 Would you please try to calm down and tell me where you are? 請冷靜下來，告訴我你在哪裡好嗎？

萬用延伸句型
I guess (that)… 我想……

can·cel [ˋkænsl̩]　🔊 Track 1159

動 取消 同 erase 清除

▶ Several flights were cancelled because of the sever weather condition. 因為天氣狀況不好，有些航班被取消了。

文法字詞解析
cancel 的動詞變化：cancel, canceled, canceled 或 cancel, cancelled, cancelled

can·cer [ˋkænsɚ]　🔊 Track 1160

名 癌、腫瘤

▶ I hope we find a cure for cancer soon.
希望我們能盡早找到治療癌症的方式。

can·dle [ˋkændl̩]　🔊 Track 1161

名 蠟燭、燭光 同 torch 光芒

▶ These candles not only look cute but also smell good.
這些蠟燭不但看起來可愛，而且聞起來也很香。

萬用延伸句型
not only...but also... 不只……而且……

cap·tain [ˋkæptɪn]　🔊 Track 1162

名 船長、艦長 同 chief 首領、長官

▶ The captain asked the sailors to abandon the ship because it was sinking. 船長要水手棄船，因為它要沉了。

car·pet [ˋkɑrpɪt]　🔊 Track 1163

名 地毯 動 鋪地毯 同 mat 地席

▶ 名 Which carpet do you like best? 你最喜歡哪條地毯？
▶ 動 The stairs were carpeted so that the children won't get hurt when they fall down.
樓梯上鋪著地毯，孩子們跌倒時就不會受傷。

萬用延伸句型
Which one do you like best?
哪一個是你最喜歡的？
也可以說：Which one is your favorite?

car·rot [ˋkærət]　🔊 Track 1164

名 胡蘿蔔

▶ Would you please get me some carrots on the way home?
回家路上順便幫我買點胡蘿蔔好嗎？

cart [kɑrt]　🔊 Track 1165

名 手拉車

▶ The kid put all the toys in the cart, but his father wouldn't pay for them. 小孩把玩具都放進購物車中，但他爸爸沒有要付錢買這些玩具。

car·toon [kɑrˋtun]　🔊 Track 1166

名 卡通

▶ The kids are in the living room watching a cartoon.
孩子們正在客廳看卡通。

cash [kæʃ]
🔊 Track 1167

名 現金 動 付現 同 currency 貨幣

▶名 Young people seldom use cash to pay for their purchases; they use online payment.
年輕人很少用現金付錢；他們用線上支付。

▶動 Would you please cash this check for me?
請幫我兌現這張支票好嗎？

cas·sette [kæˈsɛt]
🔊 Track 1168

名 卡帶、盒子

▶There is a little window in the cassette case so that you can see the tape.
錄音帶上有個小窗，能看見裡面的磁帶。

cast·le [ˈkæsl]
🔊 Track 1169

名 城堡 同 palace 皇宮

▶How long did it take you to finish this sand castle?
你建完這個沙堡花了多長時間啊？

cave [kev]
🔊 Track 1170

名 洞穴 動 挖掘 同 hole 洞

▶名 His hobby is exploring caves.
他的嗜好是探索洞穴。

▶動 Many cellars caved in during the earthquake.
地震中有很多地窖都塌陷了。

ceil·ing [ˈsilɪŋ]
🔊 Track 1171

名 天花板 反 floor 地板

▶There is a beautiful fresco on the ceiling of the church.
教堂的天花板上有美麗的壁畫。

cell [sɛl]
🔊 Track 1172

名 細胞

▶You can see the red blood cells with this microscope（顯微鏡）. 你可以用顯微鏡看到這些紅血球細胞。

cen·tral [ˈsɛntrəl]
🔊 Track 1173

形 中央的

▶I plan to go to Central Park this weekend; would you like to go with me?
我打算這個週末去中央公園，你願意跟我一起去嗎？

cen·tu·ry [ˈsɛntʃərɪ]
🔊 Track 1174

名 世紀

▶Alfred Adler is one of the greatest psychologists in the twentieth century. 阿德勒是二十世紀最偉大的心理學家之一。

ce·re·al [ˈsɪrɪəl]
🔊 Track 1175

名 穀類作物

▶Do you want cereal for breakfast?
你要吃營養穀片當早餐嗎？

文法字詞解析
監獄中的房間經常也像是細胞一樣隔成多個一模一樣的小格子，因此也可稱作 cell。

Level 1

Level 2

漸入佳境、學習零壓力——
邁向常用2200單字

Level 3

Level 4

Level 5

Level 6

chalk [tʃɔk]　　🔊 *Track 1176*
名 粉筆
▶Would you please bring two boxes of chalk for our teacher?
你能幫我們的老師拿兩盒粉筆來嗎？

萬用延伸句型
Would you please (help me)...?
請你 (幫忙我)……好嗎？

change [tʃendʒ]　　🔊 *Track 1177*
動 改變、兌換 名 零錢、變化 同 coin 硬幣
▶動 I need several minutes to change; would you like to wait downstairs?
我需要幾分鐘來換衣服，你能在樓下等我嗎？
▶名 The wealthy man gave me a one-thousand-dollar bill and asked me to keep the change.
有錢人拿了千元大鈔給我，叫我留著零錢。

char·ac·ter [ˈkærɪktɚ]　　🔊 *Track 1178*
名 個性
▶The main characters in the stage play will be acted by my friends. 這部戲的主角將由我的朋友飾演。

charge [tʃɑrdʒ]　　🔊 *Track 1179*
動 索價、命令 名 費用、職責 同 rate 費用
▶動 How much do you charge by the hour?
你每小時怎麼收費？
▶名 Would you please tell me who is in charge here?
您能告訴我這裡是誰負責管理嗎？

文法字詞解析
在這個人手一機的年代，charge 還有個經常用到的意思，就是當作「充電」的動詞來使用。例如要說「替我的手機充電」，就是「charge my phone」。

cheap [tʃip]　　🔊 *Track 1180*
形 低價的、易取得的 副 低價地 反 expensive 昂貴的
▶形 Your dress is cheaper than mine.
你的洋裝比我的更便宜。
▶副 I got the book for cheap at the bookstore.
我在書局以低價買到這本書。

cheat [tʃit]　　🔊 *Track 1181*
動 欺騙 名 詐欺、騙子 同 liar 騙子
▶動 He always cheats on exams.
他考試每次都作弊。
▶名 That young man is such a cheat.
那個年輕男子真是個騙子。

chem·i·cal [ˈkɛmɪkl̩]　　🔊 *Track 1182*
形 化學的 名 化學
▶形 If you put hydrogen and helium together, there will be a chemical reaction.
如果你把氫和氦放在一起，會產生化學反應。
▶名 I don't think you should touch those chemicals.
我覺得那些化學製品你還是不要摸吧。

chess [tʃɛs]　　🔊 *Track 1183*
名 西洋棋
▶Would you like to play chess with me? 你想不想陪我下西洋棋？

child·ish [ˈtʃaɪdɪʃ] 🔊 Track 1184

形 孩子氣的；幼稚的 同 naive 天真的
▶Speaking ill of other people is a childish behavior.
在背後說人壞話是幼稚的行為。

文法字詞解析
在例句中，how childish she is 是名詞子句當作受詞使用。

child·like [ˈtʃaɪldlaɪk] 🔊 Track 1185

形 純真的 反 mature 成熟的
▶She is nearly fifty, yet still retains a childlike innocence（天真無邪）.
她年近半百了，卻還是維持著孩童般的天真無邪。

文法字詞解析
yet 在這裡是對等連接詞，連接兩個意思相反的句子。

chin [tʃɪn] 🔊 Track 1186

名 下巴
▶She always complains about having a sharp chin.
她總是抱怨自己下巴太尖。

choc·o·late [ˈtʃɔkəlɪt] 🔊 Track 1187

名 巧克力
▶Would you please bring me a box of chocolates?
你能幫我帶一盒巧克力嗎？

choice [tʃɔɪs] 🔊 Track 1188

名 選擇 形 精選的 同 selection 選擇
▶名 I have no choice but to give up the job offer.
我別無選擇，只能放棄這個工作機會。
▶形 The shop sells choice apples.
那個商店在賣精選蘋果。

choose [tʃuz] 🔊 Track 1189

動 選擇 同 select 選擇
▶There are many colors for you to choose from.
我們有非常多種顏色可供您選擇。

文法字詞解析
choose 的動詞變化：choose, chose, chosen

chop·stick(s) [ˈtʃɑpˌstɪk(s)] 🔊 Track 1190

名 筷子
▶Not everyone likes using chopsticks to eat.
不是每個人都喜歡用筷子吃飯。

cir·cle [ˈsɝkl̩] 🔊 Track 1191

名 圓形 動 圍繞 同 round 環繞
▶名 Would you please sit in a circle on the floor?
你們能不能在地板上坐成一圈啊？
▶動 Mandy tried hard to get into the social circle of the wealthy people.
曼蒂很努力想躋身於有錢人的社交圈之中。

cit·i·zen [ˈsɪtəzn̩] 🔊 Track 1192

名 公民、居民 同 inhabitant 居民
▶The government's purpose is to serve citizens.
政府的存在目的本來就是要服務人民。

Level 1

Level 2

漸入佳境、學習零壓力──
邁向常用2200單字

Level 3

Level 4

Level 5

Level 6

claim [klem]　　　🔊 Track 1193

動 主張 名 要求、權利 同 right 權利

▶動 He claimed that he wasn't involved in the bribery case.
他宣稱他沒有涉入此賄賂案件。

▶名 Do you believe his claim? I don't.
你相信他的主張嗎？我可不信。

clap [klæp]　　　🔊 Track 1194

動 鼓（掌）、拍擊 名 拍擊聲

▶動 We clapped really hard when the famous pianist appeared.
當那位著名的鋼琴家出現時，我們大力地鼓掌。

▶名 A clap of thunder reverberated（迴響）through the house.
一聲雷鳴在屋子裡迴響。

clas·sic [ˈklæsɪk]　　　🔊 Track 1195

形 古典的 名 經典作品 同 ancient 古代的

▶形 I prefer classic music to pop music.
我喜歡古典樂勝過流行音樂。

▶名 Would you like to read this novel? It's a classic.
你想不想讀這本小說？它可是經典作品哦。

萬用延伸句型
Would you like to...？你想不想……？

claw [klɔ]　　　🔊 Track 1196

名 爪 動 抓 同 grip 抓、緊握

▶名 The eagle has sharp claws.
那隻老鷹的腳爪非常鋒利。

▶動 The kitten clawed at me when I touched her.
那隻貓在我摸牠時抓了我一把。

clay [kle]　　　🔊 Track 1197

名 黏土 同 mud 土

▶The pot is made of clay. 這個壺是黏土做的。

clean·er [ˈklinɚ]　　　🔊 Track 1198

名 清潔工、清潔劑 同 detergent 清潔劑

▶The cleaners usually come in the afternoon.
那些清潔工通常都是下午來。

clerk [klɝk]　　　🔊 Track 1199

名 職員

▶There are only four clerks in our company. What about yours?
我們公司只有四個職員，你們呢？

clev·er [ˈklɛvɚ]　　　🔊 Track 1200

形 聰明的、伶俐的 反 stupid 愚蠢的

▶I don't think my son is clever enough to work out the math problem. 我覺得我的兒子還沒聰明到能解出這道數學難題。

cli·mate [ˈklaɪmɪt]　　　🔊 Track 1201

名 氣候 同 weather 天氣

▶Extreme climate has caused great damage to agriculture in our country. 極端氣候現象已經對我國的農業造成重大的損失。

文法字詞解析
季節前面的介係詞要加 in。

Level
1

Level
2

Level
3

Level
4

Level
5

Level
6

漸入佳境、學習零壓力──
邁向常用2200單字

clos·et [ˈklɑzɪt]
Track 1202

名 櫥櫃 同 cabinet 櫥櫃
▶I forgot to clean up the closet last week.
上星期我忘記清理櫥櫃了。

cloth [klɔθ]
Track 1203

名 布料 同 textile 紡織品
▶Would you please find another piece of cloth to match this one for me?
麻煩你幫我找到和這塊布相配的布料好嗎？

clothe [kloð]
Track 1204

動 穿衣、給……穿衣
▶What do you think of the girl that is clothed in a red dress over there?
你覺得那邊穿著紅洋裝的那個女孩怎麼樣？

文法字詞解析
clothe 的動詞變化：clothe, clothed, clothed

clothes [kloz]
Track 1205

名 衣服 同 clothing 衣服
▶Linda wears different clothes to work every day; she must has a very large closet.
琳達每天穿不同的衣服去上班；她一定有個超大的衣櫃。

cloth·ing [ˈkloðɪŋ]
Track 1206

名 衣服 同 clothes 衣服
▶My favorite kind of clothing is the kind that's easy to wash.
我最喜歡好洗的那種衣服。

cloud·y [ˈklaʊdɪ]
Track 1207

形 烏雲密佈的、多雲的 反 bright 晴朗的
▶It's cloudy outside now. My favorite weather!
現在外面烏雲密佈的，我最喜歡這種天氣了！

clown [klaʊn]
Track 1208

名 小丑、丑角 動 扮丑角 同 comic 滑稽人物
▶名 In the U.S., some people associate clowns with murderers.
美國，有些人會把小丑跟謀殺犯聯想在一起。
▶動 He was just clowning. Don't take it seriously.
他只是在搞笑而已，別太正經看待。

club [klʌb]
Track 1209

名 俱樂部、社團 同 association 協會、社團
▶Did you belong to any clubs in high school?
你高中的時候有參加社團嗎？

coach [kotʃ]
Track 1210

名 教練、顧問 動 訓練 同 counselor 顧問、參事
▶名 TOur couch reminded us of the strategies before the game started. 教練在比賽開始前提醒我們策略。
▶動 She'll be coaching the football team kids all summer.
她整個夏天都要輔導足球隊的小朋友。

文法字詞解析
第二個例句中，用未來進行式表達計畫要在將來做的事。

coal [kol]
Track 1211

名 煤　同 fuel 燃料

▶There are a great many coal mines in that part of the town.
那座小鎮那裡有很多煤礦。

cock [kɑk]
Track 1212

名 公雞　同 rooster 公雞

▶The cocks that live by my house crow very early.
我家旁邊的那些公雞都很早叫。

cock·roach/roach
Track 1213

['kɑkˌrotʃ]/[rotʃ]

名 蟑螂

▶I hate cockroaches, especially when they fly.
我討厭蟑螂，尤其是會飛的那種。

coin [kɔɪn]
Track 1214

名 硬幣　動 鑄造　同 money 錢幣

▶名 Edward tossed a coin to decide whether he should take the job. 愛德華用擲硬幣的方式決定要不要接受這份工作機會。
▶動 He's always coining new phrases.
他總是在創造新的流行語。

col·lect [kə'lɛkt]
Track 1215

動 收集　同 gather 收集

▶Gary likes to collect baseball cards when he was a kid.
戴瑞還小時，喜歡收集棒球卡片。

col·or·ful ['kʌlɚfəl]
Track 1216

形 富有色彩的

▶There are many colorful balloons in her baby's room.
她寶寶的房間裡有許多五彩繽紛的氣球。

comb [kom]
Track 1217

名 梳子　動 梳、刷　同 brush 梳子、刷

▶名 I got a new comb because my old one fell into the toilet.
我買了一把新的梳子，因為舊的掉進馬桶裡了。
▶動 My daughter likes to comb her own hair.
我女兒最愛梳自己的頭髮。

com·fort·a·ble ['kʌmfɚtəbl]
Track 1218

形 舒服的　同 content 滿意的

▶The bed feels so soft and comfortable.
這張床好軟好舒服。

com·pa·ny ['kʌmpənɪ]
Track 1219

名 公司、同伴　同 enterprise 公司

▶Our company is located in a business district.
我們公司位在一個商業區中。

comp·are [kəm`pɛr]　　🔊 *Track 1220*

動 比較　同 contrast 對比
▶You can't compare apples with oranges.
　你不能拿蘋果和橘子來比較啊。

com·plain [kəm`plen]　　🔊 *Track 1221*

動 抱怨　同 grumble 抱怨
▶Would you please stop complaining about the weather?
　請不要再抱怨天氣了好嗎？

com·plete [kəm`plit]　　🔊 *Track 1222*

形 完整的　動 完成　同 conclude 結束
▶形 Would you please give me a complete report by next
　Friday?
　麻煩下週五之前給我一份完整的報告好嗎？
▶動 It took me ten days to complete the jigsaw puzzle.
　我花了十天才完成拼圖。

萬用延伸句型
Do you mind...? 你介意……嗎？

com·put·er [kəm`pjutɚ]　　🔊 *Track 1223*

名 電腦
▶I got a new computer for my brother.
　我為我弟買了一台新電腦。

con·firm [kən`fɝm]　　🔊 *Track 1224*

動 證實　同 establish 證實
▶I confirmed my reservation of the hotel room through Internet.
　我透過網路確認訂房。

萬用延伸句型
confirm that + 子句 確認

con·flict [`kɑnflɪkt]　　🔊 *Track 1225*

名 衝突、爭鬥　動 衝突　同 clash 衝突
▶名 She always does her best to avoid（避免）conflict.
　她總是盡全力避免衝突。
▶動 These two points conflict each other.
　這兩點互相衝突了。

Con·fu·cius [kən`fjuʃəs]　　🔊 *Track 1226*

名 孔子
▶Confucius is considered the greatest of the ancient Chinese
　sages（聖人）. 孔子被認為是中國古代最偉大的聖賢。

文法字詞解析
在這個例句中，孔子是「被人們認為」，
所以 consider 用了被動語態。

con·grat·u·la·tions [kən͵grætʃəˋleʃənz]　　🔊 *Track 1227*

名 祝賀、恭喜　同 blessing 祝福
▶Congratulations on your graduation（畢業）!
　恭喜你畢業了！

文法字詞解析
congratulation 作為祝賀詞，常以複數型
態表示。

con·sid·er [kən`sɪdɚ]　　🔊 *Track 1228*

動 考慮、把……視為　同 deliberate 仔細考慮
▶I consider taking public transportation to work a good way to
　do our part for the earth.
　我認為搭乘大眾交通工具去上班是為地球盡一份心力的方式。

Level 1

Level 2

漸入佳境、學習零壓力──
邁向常用2200單字

Level 3

Level 4

Level 5

Level 6

con·tact [ˋkɑntækt]
◀€ *Track 1229*

名 接觸、親近 動 接觸 同 approach 接近
▶名 I don't have a lot of contacts listed in my phone.
　　我的手機裡沒有列出很多聯絡人。
▶動 Let's keep in contact after graduation.
　　我們畢業後要保持聯絡。

con·tain [kənˋten]
◀€ *Track 1230*

動 包含、含有 反 exclude 不包括
▶There are other laws that contain provisions（條款）that
　provide personal protection（保護）to citizens.
　還有一些法律包含了對公民人身保護的條款。

con·trol [kənˋtrol]
◀€ *Track 1231*

名 管理、控制 動 支配、控制 同 command 控制、指揮
▶名 The weather is out of our control. 天氣不是我們能控制的。
▶動 He's not good at controlling his temper. 他不太會控制脾氣。

文法字詞解析
control 的動詞變化：control, controlled, controlled

con·trol·ler [kənˋtrolə]
◀€ *Track 1232*

名 管理員 同 administrator 管理人
▶The controller is responsible for many things.
　管理者必須對許多事情負責。

con·ve·nient [kənˋvinjənt]
◀€ *Track 1233*

形 方便的、合宜的 同 suitable 適當的
▶Let's come up with a convenient excuse for not going.
　我們來想一個不去的適當藉口吧。

con·ver·sa·tion [kɑnvəˋseʃən]
◀€ *Track 1234*

名 交談、談話 同 dialogue 交談
▶Betty has a pleasant conversation with her date.
　貝蒂和約會對象有很愉快的對話。

cook·er [kʊkə]
◀€ *Track 1235*

名 炊具
▶I bought a slow cooker today. 我今天買了一個慢炊鍋。

cop·y/Xe·rox/xe·rox [ˋkɑpɪ]/[ˋzɪrɑks]
◀€ *Track 1236*

名 拷貝 同 imitate 仿製
▶I made a copy of the document（文件）. 我拷貝了這份文件。

cor·ner [ˋkɔrnə]
◀€ *Track 1237*

名 角落 同 angle 角
▶The bakery at the corner is famous for its croissant.
　轉角那家烘焙坊的可頌麵包很有名。

文法字詞解析
the corner 前擺的介係詞會影響到語意的變化。如果是 in the corner 的話，就是在「房屋內」的角落；如果是 at the corner，則是「在屋外」，像街角等的角落。

cost·ly [ˋkɔstlɪ]
◀€ *Track 1238*

形 價格高的 同 expensive 昂貴的
▶The apartment is too costly for me to buy.
　這個公寓太貴了，我根本買不起。

cot·ton [ˈkɑtn̩]
🔊 *Track 1239*

名 棉花

▶I like clothes that are made of cotton. 我喜歡棉花做的衣服。

cough [kɔf]
🔊 *Track 1240*

動 咳出 名 咳嗽

▶動 I had a runny nose and couldn't stop coughing.
我鼻塞而且不停地咳嗽。

▶名 You have a bad cough. I think you need to see a doctor.
你咳嗽得很厲害，我覺得你該去看個醫生。

coun·try·side [ˈkʌntrɪˌsaɪd]
🔊 *Track 1241*

名 鄉間

▶What do you think about moving to the countryside after we
both retire? 你覺得我們都退休之後搬到鄉下怎麼樣？

coun·ty [ˈkaʊntɪ]
🔊 *Track 1242*

名 郡、縣

▶It will take you about two hours to reach the county I live in by
bus. 你坐公車到我住的郡大概要花兩個小時的時間。

cou·ple [ˈkʌpl̩]
🔊 *Track 1243*

名 配偶、一對 動 結合

▶名 In Arabian culture, married couples don't usually hold
hands on the street.
阿拉伯文化中，已婚的夫妻不常在大街上牽手。

▶動 The two train cars were coupled together, and then the
passengers were allowed to board.
火車的兩節車廂連結在一起後，乘客就可以上車了。

> **文法字詞解析**
> a couple of 可以用來修飾「一對」東西，
> 也可以說是「少許、少量」的東西。

cour·age [ˈkɝɪdʒ]
🔊 *Track 1244*

名 勇氣 反 fear 恐懼

▶Not everyone has the courage to speak their mind.
不是每個人都有勇氣實話實說。

court [kort]
🔊 *Track 1245*

名 法院

▶The lawyer was very eloquent on the court.
律師在法庭上辯才無礙。

> **文法字詞解析**
> take sb. to court 對某人提出告訴

cou·sin [ˈkʌzn̩]
🔊 *Track 1246*

名 堂（表）兄弟姊妹

▶I don't even know how many cousins I have; there're too many.
我自己都不知道我有幾個堂（表）兄弟姊妹了，實在太多了。

crab [kræb]
🔊 *Track 1247*

名 蟹

▶We have two kinds of crabs. Would you like to buy hairy（多
毛的）or green crabs?
我們有兩種蟹，您是想買毛蟹還是要買青蟹呢？

Level **1**

Level **2**

漸入佳境、學習零壓力──
邁向常用2200單字

Level **3**

Level **4**

Level **5**

Level **6**

crane [kren] ◀€ Track 1248

名 起重機、鶴
▶We got a crane to move this machine.
我們弄了一台起重機來移動這個機器。

cray·on [ˈkreən] ◀€ Track 1249

名 蠟筆
▶The toddlers draw their parents with crayons on the paper.
小朋友用蠟筆在紙上畫出他們的父母。

cra·zy [ˈkrezɪ] ◀€ Track 1250

形 發狂的、瘋顛的 同 mad 發狂的
▶The idea sounds crazy, but I like it.
這主意聽起來很瘋狂，但我就喜歡。

萬用延伸句型
(It) Sounds + adj. 聽起來很……。

cream [krim] ◀€ Track 1251

名 乳酪、乳製品
▶Can you get me some cream to add into the coffee?
你可以給我一點奶精讓我放在咖啡裡嗎？

cre·ate [krɪˋet] ◀€ Track 1252

動 創造 同 design 設計
▶Human beings have created various gadgets to make life more convenient.
人類創造許多小工具來使生活更便利。

crime [kraɪm] ◀€ Track 1253

名 罪、犯罪行為 同 sin 罪
▶I can't come up with any way to control the rising crime rate（犯罪率）.
我想不出什麼方法來控制不斷上升的犯罪率。

cri·sis [ˈkraɪsɪs] ◀€ Track 1254

名 危機 同 emergency 緊急關頭
名詞複數 crises
▶The financial crisis（金融危機）is affecting the whole world.
這次金融危機影響了整個世界。

文法字詞解析
affect 是及物動詞，後面直接接受詞。

crop [krɑp] ◀€ Track 1255

名 農作物 同 growth 產物
▶Wheat and corn are both common crops in the United States.
小麥和玉米在美國是常見的作物。

文法字詞解析
crop rotation＝輪耕制度

cross [krɔs] ◀€ Track 1256

名 十字形、交叉 動 使交叉、橫過、反對 同 oppose 反對
▶名 Jane wears a small golden（金色的）cross.
珍戴著一隻小小的金十字架。
▶動 Are you going to cross the street now or are you going to just stand here forever?
你到底要過馬路還是要一輩子站在這裡啊？

crow [kro] 🔊 *Track 1257*

名 烏鴉 動 啼叫

▶名 The little girl is making friends with the crow.
那個小女孩正在和烏鴉交朋友。

▶動 This rooster crows at 3 a.m. every day, so we ended up cooking him. 這隻公雞每天都凌晨三點啼叫，我們後來就乾脆把牠煮來吃了。

crowd [kraʊd] 🔊 *Track 1258*

名 人群、群眾 動 擁擠 同 group 群眾

▶名 The crowd gathered in the plaza for the firework show tonight. 人群聚集在廣場，準備看今晚的煙火秀。

▶動 Stop crowding the street and let us pass.
不要擠在路上，讓我們過嘛。

cru·el [ˈkruəl] 🔊 *Track 1259*

形 殘忍的、無情的 同 mean 殘忍的

▶He is really cruel to his wife. 他對他妻子很殘忍。

cul·ture [ˈkʌltʃɚ] 🔊 *Track 1260*

名 文化

▶If you understand the culture of a country, you will not make silly（愚蠢的）mistakes.
一旦你瞭解了一國的文化，你就不會再犯愚蠢的錯誤了。

cure [kjʊr] 🔊 *Track 1261*

動 治療 名 治療 同 heal 治療

▶動 With the advancement of medicine, more diseases can be cured.
隨著醫藥的發展，更多疾病能被治癒。

▶名 Doctors are searching for a cure that will wipe out cancer.
醫生們正在尋找治療癌症的醫療方法。

cu·ri·ous [ˈkjʊrɪəs] 🔊 *Track 1262*

形 求知的、好奇的

▶I am very curious about what his new girlfriend looks like.
對於他的新女朋友長什麼樣子我非常好奇。

萬用延伸句型
What does sb / sth. look like? 某人／某物長什麼樣子？

cur·tain/drape [ˈkɝtn̩]/[drep] 🔊 *Track 1263*

名 窗簾 動 掩蔽

▶名 Would you please draw the curtains? I can hardly open my eyes.
你把窗簾拉上好嗎？我幾乎睜不開眼睛了。

▶動 Would you please buy some material to curtain the house?
你能不能買一些布料來幫房子裝上窗簾？

cus·tom [ˈkʌstəm] 🔊 *Track 1264*

名 習俗、習慣 同 tradition 習俗、傳統

▶It is a custom to give red envelopes with lucky money inside during Chinese New Year.
新年時給紅包是個習俗。

文法字詞解析
With luck money inside 是 "with + O + O.C." 的結構。

萬用延伸句型
It is +N 片語 /adj. + to+ V. 用虛主詞代替後面的真主詞。

Level 1

Level 2

漸入佳境、學習零壓力──
邁向常用2200單字

Level 3

Level 4

Level 5

Level 6

cus·tom·er [ˈkʌstəmə]

◀€ *Track 1265*

名 顧客、客戶 同 client 客戶

▶What do you think about sending some beautiful vases（花瓶）to our customers as Christmas presents?
你覺得送客戶一些漂亮的花瓶作為聖誕禮物怎麼樣？

[Dd]

dai·ly [ˈdelɪ]

◀€ *Track 1266*

形 每日的 名 日報

▶形 It takes him two hours to read the daily newspaper.
他要花上兩小時來閱讀日報。

▶名 Has the new daily arrived in the mail yet?
新的日報寄來了沒有？

dam·age [ˈdæmɪdʒ]

◀€ *Track 1267*

名 損害、損失 動 毀損

▶名 The typhoon has done great damage to the county in the south.
颱風對南部的鄉鎮造成嚴重損失。

▶動 The goods are damaged on the way.
貨品在路上毀損了。

dan·ger·ous [ˈdendʒərəs]

◀€ *Track 1268*

形 危險的 反 secure 安全的

▶Crossing the street without looking both sides is dangerous.
沒有先往兩邊看就直接過馬路是很危險的。

da·ta [ˈdetə]

◀€ *Track 1269*

名 資料、事實、材料 同 information 資料

▶We backed up the data in the hard disk drive.
我們將資料備份在硬碟裡。

dawn [dɔn]

◀€ *Track 1270*

名 黎明、破曉 動 開始出現、頓悟 反 dusk 黃昏

▶名 He always sets out for work at dawn.
他每次都一破曉就出門去上班。

▶動 It dawned on him that all his grandma really wanted was attention.
他終於頓悟，原來他的奶奶只是想要人家注意她。

deaf [dɛf]

◀€ *Track 1271*

形 耳聾

▶Tom turned a deaf ear to his mother's advice.
湯姆裝作沒聽見他母親的勸告。

de·bate [dɪˈbet]

◀€ *Track 1272*

名 討論、辯論 動 討論、辯論 同 discuss 討論

文法字詞解析
使用手機下載東西時，常會出現提醒，告訴你這次下載會「consume data」，也就是會消耗你的手機網路流量的意思。如果不是使用吃到飽的方案，遇到這種情況時就盡量等到有無線網路的地方再下載吧！

文法字詞解析
turn a deaf ear to = 對……充耳不聞
fall on deaf ears = 被別人忽視

▶ 名 It took the students a month to prepare for this debate.
這些學生花了一個月的時間來準備這次的辯論賽。

▶ 動 They've been debating this for an hour and still haven't arrived at an agreement.
他們花了一個小時來討論這個問題，還沒有達成一致意見。

debt [dɛt]　　🔊 Track 1273

名 債、欠款 同 obligation 債、欠款

▶ I bought a lot of luxuries and ended up in debt this month.
我這個月買很多奢侈品，結果負債了。

de·ci·sion [dɪ'sɪʒən]　　🔊 Track 1274

名 決定、決斷力 同 determination 決定

▶ It's too hard for me to make a decision.
要我做出決定實在太難了。

dec·o·rate [ˈdɛkəˌret]　　🔊 Track 1275

動 裝飾、佈置 同 beautify 裝飾

▶ He decorated the house with many colored lights.
他用彩燈裝飾房子。

de·gree [dɪ'gri]　　🔊 Track 1276

名 學位、程度 同 extent 程度

▶ Kevin is the only one who has a master's degree in his family.
凱文是他家族中唯一擁有碩士學位的人。

de·lay [dɪ'le]　　🔊 Track 1277

動 延緩 名 耽擱

▶ 動 The plane was delayed because of the weather.
因為天氣關係，飛機延遲起飛了。

▶ 名 There was a delay in the schedule.
時程表有點耽擱。

de·li·cious [dɪ'lɪʃəs]　　🔊 Track 1278

形 美味的 同 yummy 美味的

▶ This dish is very delicious. Would you like some more?
這盤菜味道鮮美，你要不要再吃一些？

de·liv·er [dɪ'lɪvɚ]　　🔊 Track 1279

動 傳送、遞送、發表（演說） 同 transfer 傳送

▶ Nick Vujicic delivered a speech to a group of drug-abusing teenagers.
力克·胡哲對一群吸毒的青少年發表演說。

den·tist [ˈdɛntɪst]　　🔊 Track 1280

名 牙醫、牙科醫生

▶ He went to the dentist last week.
他上禮拜去看了牙醫。

萬用延伸句型
It takes + (time) + to do sth.
某人花了（多少時間）做某事

文法字詞解析
deliver a speech to = 對⋯⋯發表演說

Level
1

Level
2

漸入佳境、學習零壓力——
邁向常用2200單字

Level
3

Level
4

Level
5

Level
6

de·ny [dɪˋnaɪ]
🔊 *Track 1281*

動 否認、拒絕 同 reject 拒絕

▶The businessman denied that he had harassed the female employee in his company.
商人否認有騷擾公司的女員工。

de·part·ment [dɪˋpɑrtmənt]
🔊 *Track 1282*

名 部門、處、局 同 section 部門

▶The accounting（會計）department is just next door.
會計部門就在隔壁而已。

de·pend [dɪˋpɛnd]
🔊 *Track 1283*

動 依賴、依靠 同 rely 依賴

▶I have no one but you to depend on.
我只有你一個人可以依靠了。

depth [dɛpθ]
🔊 *Track 1284*

名 深度、深淵 同 gravity 深遠

▶She's a shallow（淺的）girl. She has no depth.
她是個膚淺的女孩，毫無深度。

de·scribe [dɪˋskraɪb]
🔊 *Track 1285*

動 敘述、描述 同 define 解釋

▶The host of the program describes the beautiful village as Shangri-La in reality.
節目的主持人將這個小鎮迷描述成現實中的香格里拉。

de·sert [ˋdɛzət]/[dɪˋzɝt]
🔊 *Track 1286*

名 沙漠、荒地 動 拋棄、丟開 形 荒蕪的 反 fertile 肥沃的

▶名 It's hard to imagine what living in a desert is like unless you've actually lived there.
除非真的在沙漠住過，很難想像住在那裡是什麼感覺。

▶動 All his friends have deserted him, and no one is willing to help him anymore.
他所有的朋友都拋棄了他，也沒人再願意幫他了。

▶形 I used to live in a desert region. It wasn't that bad.
我以前住在沙漠地區，也沒那麼糟啦。

de·sign [dɪˋzaɪn]
🔊 *Track 1287*

名 設計 動 設計 同 sketch 設計、構思

▶名 The smartphone is specially designed for the elderly citizens.
這款智慧型手機是特別設計給老年人使用的。

▶動 The machine is designed by a master.
這機器可是大師設計的。

de·sire [dɪˋzaɪr]
🔊 *Track 1288*

名 渴望、期望 同 fancy 渴望

▶There is no one who doesn't desire happiness（幸福）and health.
沒有人不渴望幸福和健康。

文法字詞解析

中文有「美食沙漠」的說法，用來描述某處實在沒什麼好吃的，而在英文中也有 food desert 這個用法，但意思稍稍有點不同，說的是某處缺乏超級市場等能夠提供生鮮食品的來源，通常是指較為窮困的區域。

des·sert [dɪˈzɝt]
◀◢ Track 1289

名 餐後點心、甜點
▶Macaron is a popular French dessert.
馬卡龍是受歡迎的法式點心。

de·tect [dɪˈtɛkt]
◀◢ Track 1290

動 查出、探出、發現 同 discover 發現
▶It's easy for the radar（雷達）to detect planes.
雷達很容易偵測到飛機。

de·vel·op [dɪˈvɛləp]
◀◢ Track 1291

動 發展、開發
▶We need to develop a way to finish the job faster.
我們得開發一個方式來快點完成工作。

文法字詞解析
a developing country = 開發中國家
a developed country = 已開發國家

de·vel·op·ment [dɪˈvɛləpmənt]
◀◢ Track 1292

名 發展、開發
▶Product development is the key to success.
產品研發才是成功的關鍵。

dew [dju]
◀◢ Track 1293

名 露水、露
▶My shoes are wet with dew.
我的鞋子被露水弄濕了。

di·al [ˈdaɪəl]
◀◢ Track 1294

名 刻度盤 動 撥（電話） 同 call 打電話
▶名 I looked at the dial to check my speed.
我看了一下儀表板以確認行駛的速度。
▶動 Please dial zero and the receptionist will connect the line for you.
請撥零，總機會為您轉接。

dia·mond [ˈdaɪmənd]
◀◢ Track 1295

名 鑽石
▶It took him a long time to earn enough money to buy a diamond ring for his wife.
他花了很長一段時間才賺到足夠的錢來給他的妻子買一枚鑽石戒指。

萬用延伸句型
diamond in the rough 即「未經琢磨的鑽石」，可以拿來描述外表看起來似乎不怎麼厲害，但實際上能力非常好的人。

di·a·ry [ˈdaɪərɪ]
◀◢ Track 1296

名 日誌、日記本 同 journal 日誌
▶There is a diary on this old man's desk.
這個老人的書桌上放著一本日記。

dic·tion·ar·y [ˈdɪkʃənˌɛrɪ]
◀◢ Track 1297

名 字典、辭典
▶Sarah is very knowledgeable. We call her "a walking dictionary."
莎拉很博學。我們叫她「行動字典」。

Level 1

Level 2

漸入佳境、學習零壓力——
邁向常用2200單字

Level 3

Level 4

Level 5

Level 6

dif·fer·ence [ˈdɪfərəns] ◀€ *Track 1298*

名 差異、差別 反 similarity 相似處
▶There is no great difference between the two objects; they are the same in nature.
這兩樣物體沒有太大的差別，它們本質上都是一樣的。

dif·fi·cul·ty [ˈdɪfəˌkʌltɪ] ◀€ *Track 1299*

名 困難 反 ease 簡單
▶We had difficult identifying the direction in the dense fog.
在濃霧中，我們無法辨別方向。

di·no·saur [ˈdaɪnəˌsɔr] ◀€ *Track 1300*

名 恐龍
▶The dinosaurs disappeared from the Earth in the ancient times.
恐龍在遠古時代就從地球上消失了。

di·rec·tion [dəˈrɛkʃən] ◀€ *Track 1301*

名 指導、方向 同 way 方向
▶Would you take me to the hotel? I have a poor sense of direction, and I am afraid I will get lost.
您能帶我到那個旅館去嗎？我的方向感很差，我擔心我會迷路。

di·rec·tor [dəˈrɛktɚ] ◀€ *Track 1302*

名 指揮者、導演
▶The director has won several awards for his latest movie.
這位導演因為最新一部電影作品贏得好幾個獎項。

dis·agree [ˌdɪsəˈgri] ◀€ *Track 1303*

動 不符合、不同意 反 agree 同意
▶I take it from your silence that you disagree.
從你的沉默中我知道你不同意。

dis·agree·ment [ˌdɪsəˈgrimənt] ◀€ *Track 1304*

名 意見不合、不同意 反 agreement 同意
▶They are in disagreement on this issue（問題）; I hope it can be solved as soon as possible.
他們在這個問題上意見不一致，我希望能儘快解決。

dis·ap·pear [ˌdɪsəˈpɪr] ◀€ *Track 1305*

動 消失、不見 反 appear 出現
▶The words were written with a special ink, and they would disappear in ten minutes.
這些字是用特別的墨水寫的，它們過十分鐘就會消失。

dis·cuss [dɪˈskʌs] ◀€ *Track 1306*

動 討論、商議 同 consult 商議
▶It took them very little time to discuss this matter.
他們只花了一點點時間來討論這件事情。

文法字詞解析
玩遊戲時經常會遇到 difficulty 這個單字，在這種情境下是「難度」的意思。

萬用延伸句型
I hope (that) + S.+ V. 我希望……

萬用延伸句型
be written with 用……寫成的，被動語態。
write 的動詞三態：write, wrote, written

dis·cus·sion [dɪˋskʌʃən] 🔊 *Track 1307*

名 討論、商議 同 consultation 商議
▶The current discussion topic is Jane's new boyfriend.
現在大家正在討論的主題是珍妮的新男友。

dis·hon·est [dɪsˋɑnɪst] 🔊 *Track 1308*

形 不誠實的 反 honest 誠實的
▶The boss dismissed the dishonest employee.
老闆把不誠實的員工解僱了。

dis·play [dɪˋsple] 🔊 *Track 1309*

動 展出 名 展示、展覽 同 show 展示
▶動 They displayed their products（產品）in the windows.
他們把產品陳列在櫥窗裡。
▶名 There are many fancy cars on display now.
現在有很多豪華汽車展出。

dis·tance [ˋdɪstəns] 🔊 *Track 1310*

名 距離 同 length 距離、長度
▶He is nearsighted, so it's hard for him to see the mountain in
the distance. 他有近視，所以想要看見遠山太難了。

dis·tant [ˋdɪstənt] 🔊 *Track 1311*

形 疏遠的、有距離的
▶She's been distant ever since we had the fight last week.
我們上禮拜吵架後她就對我很疏遠。

di·vide [dəˋvaɪd] 🔊 *Track 1312*

動 分開 同 separate 分開
▶We divided the cake into four portions.
我們把蛋糕分成四份。

di·vi·sion [dəˋvɪʒən] 🔊 *Track 1313*

名 分割、除去
▶They agreed upon a division of the book into ten units.
他們同意將這本書分成十個單元。

diz·zy [ˋdɪzɪ] 🔊 *Track 1314*

形 暈眩的、被弄糊塗的
▶After we had a ride on the roller coaster, I felt quite dizzy.
玩過雲霄飛車之後，我感到頭暈。

dol·phin [ˋdɑlfɪn] 🔊 *Track 1315*

名 海豚
▶No wonder people like dolphins. They are so cute.
怪不得大家都喜歡海豚。牠們好可愛。

don·key [ˋdɑŋkɪ] 🔊 *Track 1316*

名 驢子、傻瓜 同 mule 驢，騾子
▶There is a donkey eating grass on the field over there.
有頭驢子正在那邊的田野上吃草。

文法字詞解析
和 dizzy 同樣表示「頭暈」的單字還有
很多，如 light-headed（輕微的暈眩）、
dazed（較為嚴重，例如被電到的人會出
現這樣的情形）、groggy（因為很累所
以有點暈）、wobbly（腳軟而沒辦法好
好走）、woozy（感覺像喝醉一般的暈
眩），畢竟頭暈的方式也有很多種呢。

Level 1
Level 2

漸入佳境、學習零壓力——
邁向常用2200單字

Level 3
Level 4
Level 5
Level 6

dot [dɑt]
 Track 1317

名 圓點 動 以點表示

▶名 He likes wearing ties with dots on them.
他喜歡打有點點的領帶。

▶動 The lake is dotted with little boats.
湖面上佈滿了小船。

dou·ble [ˋdʌbl]
 Track 1318

形 雙倍的 副 雙倍地 名 二倍 動 加倍 反 single 單一的

▶形 It won't be long before the total output（產量）is double that of last year.
不久之後總產量就會是去年的兩倍了。

▶副 You should be double careful when you cross the street.
你過馬路時要加倍小心。

▶名 Your pay is the double of mine.
你的薪資是我的兩倍。

▶動 The number of racoons in the city has doubled in the past decade. 這個城市的浣熊數量在過去十年倍增。

> **萬用延伸句型**
> It won't be long before... 不久後就會……

doubt [daʊt]
 Track 1319

名 疑問 動 懷疑 反 believe 相信

▶名 There is no room for doubt, because the police have found enough evidence（證據）.
沒有懷疑的餘地了，因為警察已經找到了足夠的證據。

▶動 I doubt that he really killed his sister.
我不相信他真殺了他的妹妹。

dough·nut [ˋdoˏnʌt]
 Track 1320

名 油炸圈餅、甜甜圈

▶My mother is good at making doughnuts.
我媽媽很會做甜甜圈。

down·town [ˋdaʊnˋtaʊn]
 Track 1321

副 鬧區的 名 鬧區、商業區

▶副 We went downtown yesterday, but there was nothing we wanted to buy.
我們昨天到市區去，卻沒有什麼東西要買的。

▶名 Living in the downtown of New York, he need a high salary to cover his expenses.
因為住在紐約市中心，他需要高薪才能支付生活花費。

Dr. [ˋdɑktɚ]
 Track 1322

名 醫生、博士 同 doctor 醫生

▶Would you please tell me how I can find Dr. Wilson? It's urgent（急迫的）.
能請你告訴我如何才能找到威爾遜醫生嗎？我有急事。

drag [dræg]
 Track 1323

動 拖曳 同 pull 拖、拉

▶Tina dragged the unused carpet out of the house on her own.
蒂娜自己一個人把沒用到的地毯拖到房子外面。

> **文法字詞解析**
> 在口語中，drag 也有變裝成異性的意思。例如 Drag Queen 就是大家所說的變裝皇后。

drag·on [ˋdrægən]　🔊 *Track 1324*

名 龍
▶The Chinese consider the dragon a lucky animal.
中國人認為龍是一種吉祥的動物。

drag·on·fly [ˋdrægənˏflaɪ]　🔊 *Track 1325*

名 蜻蜓
▶It looks like a blue dragonfly, but actually it's just a blue flower.
它看上去像隻藍色蜻蜓，但是事實上它只是一朵藍色的花。

文法字詞解析
in fact 和 actually 都有「事實上」的意思，但 in fact 是用在補充前面所說的話，actually 卻是要修正前面所說的話。

dra·ma [ˋdræmə]　🔊 *Track 1326*

名 劇本、戲劇 同 theater 戲劇
▶Helen likes binge-watching Korean dramas on the weekend.
海倫喜歡在週末時追韓劇。

draw·er [ˋdrɔɚ]　🔊 *Track 1327*

名 抽屜、製圖員
▶Would you please open the drawer and get me the files（文件）？請你打開抽屜，把文件拿給我好嗎？

draw·ing [ˋdrɔɪŋ]　🔊 *Track 1328*

名 繪圖 同 illustration 圖表
▶The counselor could tell the mental state of their clients from their drawings
諮商師可以由個案畫的圖判斷他們的心理狀態。

dress [drɛs]　🔊 *Track 1329*

名 洋裝 動 穿衣服 同 clothe 穿衣服
▶名 Let's go shopping together and buy some new dresses.
我們一起去逛逛商店並買些新洋裝吧。
▶動 She dressed her kids very casually（隨性的）.
她替孩子穿上隨性的服裝。

drop [drɑp]　🔊 *Track 1330*

動 （使）滴下、滴
▶The rain dropped to the ground. 雨滴落在地。

drug [drʌg]　🔊 *Track 1331*

名 藥、藥物 同 medicine 藥
▶The man was sentenced ten years in prison for peddling drugs to people. 這名男子因為兜售毒品而被判十年刑期。

drug·store [ˋdrʌgˏstor]　🔊 *Track 1332*

名 藥房 同 pharmacy 藥房
▶Would you tell me how I can get to the nearest drugstore?
你能告訴我最近的藥房怎麼去嗎？

drum [drʌm]　🔊 *Track 1333*

名 鼓
▶Can you stop playing drums at midnight?
你可以不要半夜打鼓嗎？

文法字詞解析
stop 後面接動名詞表示「停止做某事」，接不定詞表示「停下來去做某事」。

Level
1

Level
2

漸入佳境、學習零壓力——邁向常用2200單字

Level
3

Level
4

Level
5

Level
6

dry·er [draɪɚ]
🔊 Track 1334

名 烘乾機、吹風機

▶Would you pass the dryer to me? I just had a shower and my hair is totally（完全地）wet.
你能把吹風機遞給我一下嗎？我剛洗了個澡，頭髮全濕了。

dull [dʌl]
🔊 Track 1335

形 遲鈍的、單調的 同 flat 單調的

▶The work in this office is always dull.
這個辦公室的工作總是很單調。

dumb [dʌm]
🔊 Track 1336

形 啞的、笨的 反 smart 聰明的

▶The dumb girl could only express her feelings through hand gestures. 喑啞的女孩只能透過手勢表達她的感受。

dump·ling [ˈdʌmplɪŋ]
🔊 Track 1337

名 麵團、餃子

▶It took my mom thirty minutes to make these dumplings on the table. 媽媽花了半小時做了桌子上的這些餃子。

du·ty [ˈdjutɪ]
🔊 Track 1338

名 責任、義務 同 responsibility 責任

▶The soldier took his duty very seriously.
這名軍人認真看待他的職責。

[Ee]

earn [ɝn]
🔊 Track 1339

動 賺取、得到 同 obtain 得到

▶It's time you start earning a living. 你是時候該自己謀生了。

earth·quake [ˈɝθˌkwek]
🔊 Track 1340

名 地震 同 tremor 地震

▶It was reported that the earthquake left thousands of people homeless. 據報導，地震使數千人無家可歸。

east·ern [ˈistɚn]
🔊 Track 1341

形 東方的、東方人 反 western 西方的

▶This eastern country is quite beautiful.
這個東方的國家非常美麗。

ed·u·ca·tion [ˌɛdʒəˈkeʃən]
🔊 Track 1342

名 教育 同 instruction 教育

▶Not every child in the poor area has the opportunity（機會）to receive good education.
不是每個貧困地區的孩子都有機會接受良好的教育。

萬用延伸句型
It is sb.'s duty to do sth.
做某事是某人的職責。

文法字詞解析
主詞 child 是單數，因此前面的修飾語是用 not every 而非 not all，且搭配的動詞要加 s。

ef·fect [əˈfɛkt] ◀ _Track 1343_

名 影響、效果 動 引起、招致 同 produce 引起

▶名 His words have no effect on her.
他說的話對她完全沒有影響。

▶動 You should try to effect an intermediation（調解）to solve the problem.
你們應該要試著透過調解來解決這個問題。

ef·fec·tive [əˈfɛktɪv] ◀ _Track 1344_

形 有效的 反 vain 無效的

▶Scientists are look for a more effective way to generate electricity.
科學家還在尋找更有效的發電方式。

ef·fort [ˈɛfət] ◀ _Track 1345_

名 努力 同 attempt 努力嘗試

▶He barely ever makes an effort in anything.
無論是什麼事情，他幾乎從來不付出一點努力。

el·der [ˈɛldə] ◀ _Track 1346_

形 年長的 名 長輩 反 junior 晚輩

▶形 I have never seen your elder brother. What does he look like?
我從來沒見過你的哥哥，他長什麼樣子啊？

▶名 I hear that she is the elder of the two sisters.
我聽說她是兩姐妹之中的姐姐。

e·lect [ɪˈlɛkt] ◀ _Track 1347_

動 挑選、選舉 形 挑選的 同 select 挑選

▶動 We elected Rita as the president of the student association.
我們選瑞塔為學生會的會長。

▶形 An elect group of specialists（專家）are chosen to carry out the plan.
一群精挑細選的專家將要負責執行這個計畫。

el·e·ment [ˈɛləmənt] ◀ _Track 1348_

名 基本要素 同 component 構成要素

▶What are the crucial（必要的）elements to a successful company? 一個成功的公司需要哪些元素呢？

el·e·va·tor [ˈɛləˌvetə] ◀ _Track 1349_

名 升降機、電梯 同 escalator 電扶梯

▶The elevator is under repair, so we had to take the stairs.
電梯在維修中，所以我們得走樓梯。

e·mot·ion [ɪˈmoʃən] ◀ _Track 1350_

名 情感 同 feeling 情感

▶He smiled, but there was some other emotion just below the surface.
他笑了笑，但在他的微笑中隱藏著一種難以捉摸的情感。

萬用延伸句型
spare no effort to + 原 V：盡全力做某事
例如：They spared no effort to make sure we felt at home in their Airbnb.
他們盡全力讓我們在他們的 Airbnb 住得有回到家的感覺。

文法字詞解析
element 也有「元素」的意思，因此大家上化學課都要會的元素週期表全名就叫做 periodic table of elements（通常簡稱 periodic table）。

Level
1

Level
2

漸入佳境、學習零壓力——
邁向常用2200單字

Level
3

Level
4

Level
5

Level
6

en·cour·age [ɪnˈkɝɪdʒ]
🔊 Track 1351

動 鼓勵 同 inspire 激勵
▶ Fiona encouraged her students to register for the singing competition. 費歐娜鼓勵學生參加歌唱比賽。

en·cour·age·ment [ɪnˈkɝɪdʒmənt]
🔊 Track 1352

名 鼓勵 同 incentive 鼓勵
▶ Your encouragement will make her more confident. 你的鼓勵會使她更加有信心的。

end·ing [ˈɛndɪŋ]
🔊 Track 1353

名 結局、結束 同 terminal 終點
▶ Not all lovers have happy endings like that in the fairy tales（童話故事）. 並不是每對戀人都能像童話故事中一樣有個美好的結局。

en·e·my [ˈɛnəmɪ]
🔊 Track 1354

名 敵人 同 opponent 敵手
▶ The best way to destroy your enemies is to make them your friends. 擊潰敵人最好的方法，就是使他們成為你的朋友。

en·er·gy [ˈɛnədʒɪ]
🔊 Track 1355

名 能量、精力 同 strength 力量
▶ I don't have enough energy to go hiking. 我沒有足夠的體力去爬山。

en·joy [ɪnˈdʒɔɪ]
🔊 Track 1356

動 享受、欣賞 同 appreciate 欣賞
▶ We all enjoyed the movie a lot. 我們都非常喜歡那部電影。

en·joy·ment [ɪnˈdʒɔɪmənt]
🔊 Track 1357

名 享受、愉快 同 pleasure 愉快
▶ He recorded the song for his own enjoyment. 他為了自己的享受而錄了這首歌。

en·tire [ɪnˈtaɪr]
🔊 Track 1358

形 全部的 反 partial 部分的
▶ The entire office is surprised to hear the news. 整個辦公室的人聽到這個消息都很驚訝。

en·trance [ˈɛntrəns]
🔊 Track 1359

名 入口 同 exit 出口
▶ Two mascots are greeting shoppers by the entrance of the department store. 兩個吉祥物人偶在百貨公司入口歡迎購物者。

en·ve·lope [ˈɛnvəˌlop]
🔊 Track 1360

名 信封
▶ Will you please put the photo in the envelope and send it for me? 您能幫我把這張照片放在信封裡，並把它寄出去嗎？

文法字詞解析

ending 解釋作「結局」時是可數名詞。

萬用延伸句型

make an entrance 有「入場」的意思。
例如：They're all dressed up and ready to make an entrance.
他們已經打扮完畢，準備浩浩蕩蕩地入場。

en·vi·ron·ment [ɪnˋvaɪrənmənt] ◀≦ *Track 1361*

名 環境
▶We need to protect our environment for a better future.
我們得為了一個更好的未來而保護環境。

e·ras·er [ɪˋresɚ] ◀≦ *Track 1362*

名 橡皮擦
▶Would you please lend me your eraser? 你能借我橡皮擦嗎？

er·ror [ˋɛrɚ] ◀≦ *Track 1363*

名 錯誤 同 mistake 錯誤
▶The online grammar checker can pick out the errors in your article. 線上文法檢查軟體可以幫你找到文章中的錯誤。

es·pe·cial·ly [əˋspɛʃəlɪ] ◀≦ *Track 1364*

副 特別地 反 mostly 一般地
▶Let's pay more attention to the structure（結構）of the article, especially the latter（後面的）part.
我們要多注意這篇文章的結構，特別是後半部分。

e·vent [ɪˋvɛnt] ◀≦ *Track 1365*

名 事件 同 episode 事件
▶She spent all night planning the event.
她一整個晚上都在計畫這次活動。

ex·act [ɪgˋzækt] ◀≦ *Track 1366*

形 正確的 同 precise 準確的
▶I don't know the exact number of students in the school this semester. 我不曉得新學期中學校裡學生的準確人數是多少。

ex·cel·lent [ˋɛkslənt] ◀≦ *Track 1367*

形 最好的 同 admirable 極好的
▶Would you like to tell me where you picked up your excellent English? 你能告訴我你是在哪裡學會這樣一口流利的英語嗎？

ex·cite [ɪkˋsaɪt] ◀≦ *Track 1368*

動 刺激、鼓舞 反 calm 使鎮定
▶The night before the wedding, Aaron was too excited to fall asleep. 婚禮的前一晚，艾倫興奮得睡不著。

ex·cite·ment [ɪkˋsaɪtmənt] ◀≦ *Track 1369*

名 興奮、激動 同 turmoil 騷動
▶I'm accustomed（習慣的）to working in an environment full of noise and excitement. 我習慣在喧鬧的房間裡工作。

ex·cuse [ɪkˋskjuz] ◀≦ *Track 1370*

名 藉口 動 原諒 反 blame 責備
▶名 Finding excuses for the mistake is not a good strategy.
如為錯誤找藉口並不是最好的策略。
▶動 There's no way we can excuse this behavior（表現）.
我們絕不能原諒這樣的表現。

萬用延伸句型
in the event of 若發生了（某事）……
例如：In the event of an emergency, please leave the building from this door. 若發生緊急事件，請從這扇門離開大樓。

萬用延伸句型
There's no way + S. + V. 絕對不可能……。
和「It is impossible to...」同義。

Level 1

Level 2

漸入佳境、學習零壓力──
邁向常用2200單字

Level 3

Level 4

Level 5

Level 6

ex·er·cise [ˈɛksəˌsaɪz] ◀≣ *Track 1371*

名 練習 動 運動 同 practice 練習

▶名 Have you done the exercise in the book yet?
書上的練習題你做了沒？

▶動 We should exercise every day; it's good for our health.
我們每天做運動吧，這對我們的身體健康有好處。

ex·ist [ɪgˈzɪst] ◀≣ *Track 1372*

動 存在 同 be 存在

▶The mysterious species no longer exist on earth; we can only find the fossils.
這種神祕生物已不存在世界上；我們只找得到化石。

ex·pect [ɪkˈspɛkt] ◀≣ *Track 1373*

動 期望 同 suppose 期望

▶How long do you expect to stay here? 你打算在這裡待多久？

ex·pen·sive [ɪkˈspɛnsɪv] ◀≣ *Track 1374*

形 昂貴的 反 cheap 便宜的

▶I think this car is too expensive. 我覺得這部車太貴了。

ex·pe·ri·ence [ɪkˈspɪrɪəns] ◀≣ *Track 1375*

名 經驗 動 體驗 同 occurrence 經歷、事件

▶名 My experience is that people don't like it when others point out their mistakes.
我的經驗是，人們不喜歡別人指出他們的錯誤。

▶動 The people who had experienced famine would cherish food.
經歷過飢荒的人會珍惜食物。

ex·pert [ˈɛkspɝt] ◀≣ *Track 1376*

形 熟練的 名 專家 反 amateur 業餘、外行

▶形 She is an expert language teacher. 她是個熟練的語言教師。

▶名 He is an expert on computers; why don't we go and ask him?
他是電腦方面的專家，為什麼不去問他呢？

ex·plain [ɪkˈsplen] ◀≣ *Track 1377*

動 解釋

▶Would you please explain the math problem to me again? I still don't understand.
您能再為我解釋一下這道數學題嗎？我還是不明白。

ex·press [ɪkˈsprɛs] ◀≣ *Track 1378*

動 表達、說明 同 indicate 表明

▶Ryan used some diagrams on his slides to express his ideas clearly. 雷恩在投影片上用一些圖表來表達自己的想法。

ex·tra [ˈɛkstrə] ◀≣ *Track 1379*

形 額外的 副 特別地 同 additional 額外的

▶形 Would you like to give yourself an extra day off?
你願意再給自己一天額外的假期嗎？

▶副 They charge extra for wine. 喝酒要額外收費。

文法字詞解析
因為懷孕的人通常都會「期待」孩子出生，因此可以用 expecting 來描述「懷孕的」。

文法字詞解析
這個字當作名詞使用時，有「特快車」的意思。例如〈東方快車謀殺案〉中的火車就叫做 Orient Express。

eye·brow/brow [ˈaɪˌbraʊ]/[braʊ] ◀≣ *Track 1380*

名 眉毛
▶I don't think I'm pretty, but I really like my eyebrows.
　我不覺得我漂亮，但我挺喜歡自己的眉毛。

[Ff]

fail [fel] ◀≣ *Track 1381*

動 失敗、不及格 反 achieve 實現、達到
▶David failed to complete the triathlon competition.
　大衛沒能夠完成鐵人三項競賽。

fail·ure [ˈfeljɚ] ◀≣ *Track 1382*

名 失敗、失策 反 success 成功
▶There might be a power failure tonight.
　今天晚上可能會停電。

fair [fɛr] ◀≣ *Track 1383*

形 公平的、合理的 副 光明正大地 同 just 公正的
▶形 It's not fair to make him do all the work.
　讓他一個人做所有的事情太不公平了。
▶副 Their team never plays fair.
　他們那隊從來不堂堂正正地比賽。

fa·mous [ˈfeməs] ◀≣ *Track 1384*

形 有名的、出名的
▶This 100-year-old bakery is famous for its pineapple cake.
　這間百年烘焙坊的鳳梨酥很有名。

fault [fɔlt] ◀≣ *Track 1385*

名 責任、過失 動 犯錯 同 error 過失
▶名 There is a fault in this machine; please find someone to fix it soon.
　這台機器故障了。請儘快找人來修一下。
▶動 No one could fault his performance（演出）.
　他的演出無懈可擊。

fa·vor [ˈfevɚ] ◀≣ *Track 1386*

名 喜好 動 贊成
▶名 The situation is in their favor.
　情勢對他們有利。
▶動 Can you tell me how many people favor the proposal（提議）？你能告訴我有多少人贊同這項提議嗎？

fa·vor·ite [ˈfevərɪt] ◀≣ *Track 1387*

形 最喜歡的 同 precious 珍愛的
▶This is my favorite song ever.
　這是我最愛的一首歌。

文法字詞解析
try to 後面加原形動詞時，它有「試著達到某個目的」的意思，當 try 用過去式時，則暗示了嘗試的事情沒有成功。

萬用延伸句型
do sb. a favor 幫（某人）一個忙
例如：Do me a favor and close the door, okay?
幫個忙，把門關起來好不好？

Level
1

Level
2

漸入佳境、學習零壓力——
邁向常用2200單字

Level
3

Level
4

Level
5

Level
6

fear·ful [ˈfɪrfəl]
🔊 Track 1388

形 可怕的、嚇人的　同 afraid 害怕的

▶I am fearful that she would get lost in the mountain.
我擔心她會在山裡迷路。

fee [fi]
🔊 Track 1389

名 費用　同 fare 費用

▶Is there anything like a management（管理）fee or parking fee in this place? 在這個地方有沒有管理費和停車費？

fe·male [ˈfimel]
🔊 Track 1390

形 女性的　名 女性　同 feminine 女性的

▶形 Is your cat male or female?
你的貓是公的還母的？

▶名 It doesn't matter whether you are a male or female; you can all join the club.
是男是女都沒關係，所有人都可以參加這個俱樂部。

fence [fɛns]
🔊 Track 1391

名 籬笆、圍牆　動 防衛、防護

▶名 Frank built a fence the front yard to prevent his puppies from running out. 法蘭克在前院四周建起圍牆來防止小狗跑掉。

▶動 We fenced the house to keep thieves out.
我們把房子圍起來，這樣小偷才不會進來。

萬用延伸句型

on the fence 無法在兩個選項中做出選擇
例如：I'm still on the fence about whether to go to this wedding or that one. Why do they have to be on the same day?
到底要去哪場婚禮，我還是無法做出選擇。為什麼要選在同一天辦呢？

fes·ti·val [ˈfɛstəvḷ]
🔊 Track 1392

名 節日　同 holiday 節日

▶She's all dressed up for the festival.
她為了這個節慶好好打扮了一番。

fe·ver [ˈfivɚ]
🔊 Track 1393

名 發燒、熱、入迷

▶I have a slight（輕微的）fever. 我有點輕微的發燒。

field [fild]
🔊 Track 1394

名 田野、領域

▶The children are running around in the field.
孩子們在田野奔跑。

fight·er [ˈfaɪtɚ]
🔊 Track 1395

名 戰士

▶He's one of our best fighters.
他是我們最優秀的戰士之一。

fig·ure [ˈfɪgjɚ]
🔊 Track 1396

名 人影、畫像、數字　動 演算　同 symbol 數字、符號

▶名 The figures on the wall of the ancient tomb were considered special codes. 古代墳墓牆上的符號被認為是特別的密碼。

▶動 Can you please figure the total? I'll pay it with a check.
請你把總價算出來好嗎？我將用支票支付。

film [fɪlm]
名 電影、膠捲 同 cinema 電影

🔊 *Track 1397*

▶My friend told me that a new action film is on.
朋友說有一部新的動作片正在上映。

fire·man/fire·wom·an
[ˈfaɪrmən]/[ˈfaɪrwʊmən]

🔊 *Track 1398*

名 消防員 / 女消防員

▶The firemen are not able to put out the fire.
這些消防人員無法滅火。

firm [fɝm]
形 堅固的 副 牢固地 同 enterprise 公司

🔊 *Track 1399*

▶形 His grip is too firm and I can't run away.
他抓得太緊了，我都逃不了。

▶副 The protestors stood firm as the police tried to disperse them.
抗議者在警察試圖驅離他們時仍站著不動。

fish·er·man [ˈfɪʃəmən]
名 漁夫

🔊 *Track 1400*

▶The fishermen here are very friendly. 這裡的漁夫們都很友善。

fit [fɪt]
形 適合的 動 適合 名 適合 同 suit 適合

🔊 *Track 1401*

▶形 The manager（經理）thinks he is fit for this job.
經理覺得他很適合這份工作。

▶動 I don't think this tuxedo fits you. 我不認為這件燕尾服適合你。

▶名 The shoes are a perfect fit for me.
這雙鞋子對我來說剛剛好。

fix [fɪks]
動 使穩固、修理 同 repair 修理

🔊 *Track 1402*

▶Would you help me fix this machine?
你能幫我修一下這台機器嗎？

flag [flæg]
名 旗、旗幟 同 banner 旗、橫幅

🔊 *Track 1403*

▶This country had the national flag designed by its people.
這個國家的國旗是自己的人民設計的。

flash [flæʃ]
動 閃亮 名 一瞬間 同 flame 照亮

🔊 *Track 1404*

▶動 That driver keeps flashing his lights at me.
那個司機一直用車燈閃我。

▶名 Seeing the police officers, the vendors ran away in a flash.
一看到警察，攤販一下子就跑走了。

flash·light/flash
[ˈflæʃˌlaɪt]/[flæʃ]

🔊 *Track 1405*

名 手電筒、閃光 同 lantern 燈籠

▶Did you bring a flashlight? It's dark down here.
你有帶手電筒嗎？這下面好暗喔。

文法字詞解析
如果覺得還要分男女太麻煩了，或穿著消防人員服裝根本也看不出性別，可以直接說 fire fighter 也一樣是消防員的意思。

文法字詞解析
white flag 是「白旗」，表示投降的意思。而 red flag（紅旗）則和投降完全無關，是用來表達警告、危險的意思。例如若你在相親時發現對方服務態度無禮、還會兇自己的媽媽，這就是個很大的 red flag，在警告你最好快逃為上策。

Level 1
Level 2
漸入佳境、學習零壓力——邁向常用2200單字
Level 3
Level 4
Level 5
Level 6

flat [flæt] 　　　　　🔊 *Track 1406*

名 平的東西、公寓 形 平坦的

▶名 He decided to move to a new flat because his house was too old. 他決定搬到新公寓去住，因為他的家太老舊了。

▶形 Our ancestors（祖先）thought the earth was flat, not round. 我們的祖先認為地球是平的，而不是圓的。

flight [flaɪt] 　　　　　🔊 *Track 1407*

名 飛行

▶Some business travelers expect comfort during a long flight. 有些商務旅行者期望有舒適的長途旅行。

flood [flʌd] 　　　　　🔊 *Track 1408*

名 洪水、水災 動 淹沒 反 drought 旱災

▶名 No wonder they said that this is the most terrible flood in this country. All crops were destroyed. 難怪他們說這是該國最嚴重的一次水災。所有作物都死光了。

▶動 The rice fields were flooded. 稻田被淹沒了。

flour [flaʊr] 　　　　　🔊 *Track 1409*

名 麵粉 動 撒粉於

▶名 The flour in the kitchen is not enough to make bread. 廚房的麵粉不夠用來做麵包。

▶動 The board is not dry enough to make pastry（糕餅）; please flour it first. 砧板不夠乾，做不成糕餅。請先在上面撒上麵粉。

flow [flo] 　　　　　🔊 *Track 1410*

動 流出、流動 名 流程、流量 同 stream 流動

▶動 Most rivers on the earth flow into the sea. 地球上的河流大部分都流入了海洋。

▶名 People who don't go with the flow are sometimes called mavericks. 不會隨波逐流的人，有時候被稱作是特立獨行者。

flu [flu] 　　　　　🔊 *Track 1411*

名 流行性感冒

▶I have the flu, so I won't be able to make it to class today. 我得了流感，所以今天沒辦法去上課了。

flute [flut] 　　　　　🔊 *Track 1412*

名 橫笛、用笛吹奏

▶It doesn't matter if you don't play the flute well. 你長笛吹不好不要緊。

fo·cus [ˋfokəs] 　　　　　🔊 *Track 1413*

名 焦點、焦距 動 使集中在焦點、集中 同 concentrate 集中

▶名 The peeress showed up and became the focus of the occasion. 貴婦出現後就成為這個場合的焦點。

▶動 It makes me so sad that no one focuses on the serious problem. 沒有一個人關注這個嚴重的問題，這讓我很傷心。

文法字詞解析

flight 也有「樓梯」的意思。從一層樓要去下一層樓時，會經過的那一段樓梯就叫「a flight of stairs」。

文法字詞解析

flu 其實是 influenza（流行性感冒）的簡稱。

fog·gy [ˈfɑgɪ]

🔊 *Track 1414*

形 多霧的、朦朧的

▶It's very foggy today; would you please drive the car as slowly（緩慢地）as possible?
今天霧很大，能請你儘量把車開慢一點嗎？

文法字詞解析

foggy 除了可以是說霧多、視線不清以外，也可以用「foggy memory」來形容記憶模糊。

fol·low·ing [ˈfɑloɪŋ]

🔊 *Track 1415*

名 下一個 形 接著的 同 next 下一個

▶名 Will the following please come to the front as soon as possible?
能請下列人員儘快到前面來嗎？

▶形 The following three paragraphs are about the origin of this custom.
接下來的三段會講到這項習俗的來源。

fool [ful]

🔊 *Track 1416*

名 傻子 動 愚弄、欺騙 同 trick 戲弄

▶名 You made me look like a fool.
你害我出醜。

▶動 When I knew he has been fooling me all the time, I was very sad.
當我知道了他一直都在欺騙我時，我感到很傷心。

fool·ish [ˈfulɪʃ]

🔊 *Track 1417*

形 愚笨的、愚蠢的 反 wise 聰明的

▶That's the most foolish thing I've ever heard.
這是我聽過最蠢的事。

foot·ball [ˈfʊtˌbɔl]

🔊 *Track 1418*

名 足球、橄欖球

▶My son is bored because no one wants to play football with him.
沒人想跟我兒子踢足球，所以他覺得很無聊。

文法字詞解析

表示某人感受如何的形容詞字尾常常以「-ed」表示，表示某物令人覺得如何的形容詞得用「-ing」表示。所以如果說某人 boring 的話，就代表那個人很無趣、沒有意思。

for·eign·er [ˈfɔrɪnɚ]

🔊 *Track 1419*

名 外國人

▶Xenophobia has made the local people very unfriendly to foreigners.
仇外心理讓本地人對外國相當不友善。

for·give [fɚˈgɪv]

🔊 *Track 1420*

動 原諒、寬恕 反 punish 處罰

▶I can't forgive what you did to my mom.
我無法原諒你對我媽做的事。

文法字詞解析

forgive 的動詞變化：forgive, forgave, forgiven

form [fɔrm]

🔊 *Track 1421*

名 形式、表格 動 形成 同 construct 構成

▶名 We filled out the application form for the visa.
我們填寫了簽證的申請表。

▶動 We formed a group quickly to discuss the problem.
我們很快地組成了小組以討論這個問題。

Level 1
Level 2
邁向常用2200單字——漸入佳境、學習零壓力
Level 3
Level 4
Level 5
Level 6

for·mal [ˈfɔrml̩] 🔊 *Track 1422*
形 正式的、有禮的
▶The letter is too formal in its wording（措辭）; let's rewrite（重寫）it.
這封信在措辭上太正式了，我們重寫一封吧。

for·mer [ˈfɔrmɚ] 🔊 *Track 1423*
形 以前的、先前的 反 present 現在的
▶He always speaks ill of his former friends. He hates them.
他老是說他之前朋友的壞話。他很討厭他們。

for·ward [ˈfɔrwɚd] 🔊 *Track 1424*
形 向前的 名 前鋒 動 發送 同 send 發送
▶形 She's a really forward kind of girl.
她是很前衛大膽的那種女孩。
▶名 Can you tell me who the best forward of the football team is? 你能告訴我這個球隊最好的前鋒是誰嗎？
▶動 We forwarded the email to all registered member of our association.
我們把電子郵件轉寄給所有協會的註冊成員。

文法字詞解析
在電子郵件的標題中有時會看到 Fwd: 的字樣，其實就是 forward 的縮寫，表示這封郵件是轉寄的。

for·wards [ˈfɔrwɚdz] 🔊 *Track 1425*
副 今後、將來、向前
▶Susan leaned（倚靠）forwards against the table without saying anything.
蘇珊欠身向前靠著桌子，一言不發。

fox [fɑks] 🔊 *Track 1426*
名 狐狸、狡猾的人
▶It took the hunter a long time to find the fox and its cubs（幼獸）. 獵人花了很長時間才找到狐狸和牠的小孩。

frank [fræŋk] 🔊 *Track 1427*
形 率直的、坦白的 同 sincere 真誠的
▶To be frank, I prefer sticking with the old system.
老實說，我比較喜歡維持舊的系統。

free·dom [ˈfridəm] 🔊 *Track 1428*
名 自由、解放、解脫 同 liberty 自由
▶The martyr's sacrifice for our freedom will always be remembered.
我們會永遠記得烈士們為了爭取自由的犧牲。

free·zer [ˈfrizɚ] 🔊 *Track 1429*
名 冰庫、冷凍庫 同 refrigerator 冰箱
▶There is always food in the freezer. Take whatever you want.
冰箱裡總是有食物。你想吃什麼就拿什麼。

friend·ly [ˈfrɛndlɪ] 🔊 *Track 1430*
形 友善的、親切的 同 kind 親切的
▶We are taught to be friendly to strangers.
我們被教導要對陌生人友善。

文法字詞解析
雖然最後以 -ly 結尾，但 friendly 並不是副詞。它是形容詞喔！要注意！

fright [fraɪt]　　　◀≲ *Track 1431*

名 驚駭、恐怖、驚嚇　同 panic 驚恐

▶The cat gave me quite a fright. 那隻貓嚇了我一跳。

fright·en [ˈfraɪtn̩]　　　◀≲ *Track 1432*

動 震驚、使害怕　同 scare 使恐懼

▶The ghost frightened the kids away from the house.
那隻鬼把孩子們從房子嚇走了。

func·tion [ˈfʌŋkʃən]　　　◀≲ *Track 1433*

名 功能、作用

▶According to the manual, the machine has many different functions.
根據使用手冊，這個機器有很多不同的功能。

萬用延伸句型
According to... 表示「根據…」。

fur·ther [ˈfɝðə]　　　◀≲ *Track 1434*

副 更進一步地　形 較遠的　動 助長

▶副 She refused to further talk about what happened.
她拒絕進一步說出到底發生了什麼事。

▶形 It is my dream to go abroad for further studies.
出國進修是我的夢想。

▶動 We'll do all we can to further your plans.
我們將盡力促成你們的計畫。

fu·ture [ˈfjutʃə]　　　◀≲ *Track 1435*

名 未來、將來　反 past 過往

▶The boy wants to be an astronaut（太空人）in the future and travel in space.
男孩想將來成為一名太空人，在太空中旅行。

文法字詞解析
future 如果要表示「將來」時，前面一定要加定冠詞，如果寫成「in future」的話，意思就不一樣了，會變成「從今以後、日後」的意思。

[Gg]

gain [gen]　　　◀≲ *Track 1436*

動 得到、獲得　名 得到、獲得　同 obtain 得到

▶名 "No pain, no gain" is quite a famous saying.
「一分耕耘，一分收穫」是句很有名的諺語。

▶動 He is still trying to gain her trust.
他仍然在試著得到她的信任。

ga·rage [gəˈrɑdʒ]　　　◀≲ *Track 1437*

名 車庫

▶Would you please drive my car to the garage?
你能幫我把車開到車庫去嗎？

gar·bage [ˈgɑrbɪdʒ]　　　◀≲ *Track 1438*

名 垃圾

▶It's my turn to take out the garbage this week.
這個星期該我把垃圾拿出去丢。

Level 1

Level 2

漸入佳境、學習零壓力——
邁向常用2200單字

Level 3

Level 4

Level 5

Level 6

gar·den·er [ˈgɑrdn̩ɚ]　　🔊 *Track 1439*

名 園丁、花匠
▶There is a gardener trimming（修剪）up the trees in the garden now.
花園裡有個園丁正在修剪花園裡的樹木。

gate [get]　　🔊 *Track 1440*

名 門、閘門
▶Could you wait for me at the gate of the park?
你能在那個公園的門口等我嗎？

gath·er [ˈgæðɚ]　　🔊 *Track 1441*

動 集合、聚集　同 collect 收集
▶Students gathered in the auditorium for the commencement.
學生們聚集在禮堂參加畢業典禮。

gen·er·al [ˈdʒɛnərəl]　　🔊 *Track 1442*

名 將領、將軍 形 普遍的、一般的
▶名 The general is an old but good-looking man.
那名將軍雖老但非常帥氣。
▶形 There is a general feeling of anxiety in the room tonight.
今晚這房裡的人普遍都很焦慮。

> **文法字詞解析**
> in general = 通常

gen·er·ous [ˈdʒɛnərəs]　　🔊 *Track 1443*

形 慷慨的、大方的、寬厚的　反 harsh 嚴厲的
▶Not all people are able to be so generous to their enemies.
不是所有的人都能對他們的敵人如此寬容。

gen·tle [ˈdʒɛntl̩]　　🔊 *Track 1444*

形 溫和的、上流的　同 soft 柔和的
▶People often expect nurses to be gentle and patient.
人們通常期望護士是溫柔且有耐心的。

gen·tle·man [ˈdʒɛntl̩mən]　　🔊 *Track 1445*

名 紳士、家世好的男人
▶Would you please bring this gentleman a glass of beer?
請給這位先生來杯啤酒好嗎？

ge·og·ra·phy [dʒiˈɑgrəfɪ]　　🔊 *Track 1446*

名 地理（學）
▶Geography used to be a required course for primary school students.
地理以前是小學生的必修課程。

gi·ant [ˈdʒaɪənt]　　🔊 *Track 1447*

名 巨人 形 巨大的、龐大的　同 huge 巨大的
▶名 Shakespeare is a giant among playwrights（劇作家）.
莎士比亞可是劇作家中的巨擘。
▶形 The giant poster（海報）of the actor hangs in the theater.
那位演員的大型海報掛在劇場裡。

gi·raffe [dʒəˈræf]
Track 1448

名 長頸鹿
▶You'll never believe this. There's a giraffe in our yard!
你絕對無法相信，我們院子裡有一隻長頸鹿耶！

glove(s) [glʌv(z)]
Track 1449

名 手套
▶It's getting cold; let's take out the woolen（羊毛的）gloves.
天氣變冷了，我們把羊毛手套拿出來吧。

glue [glu]
Track 1450

名 膠水、黏膠 動 黏、固著
▶名 Would you please buy a bottle of glue for me on the way?
你能不能順便幫我買瓶膠水回來？
▶動 I tried to glue up the broken mirror but in vain.
我想把破掉的鏡子黏回去但是失敗了。

goal [gol]
Track 1451

名 目標、終點 同 destination 終點
▶Once you establish a goal in your heart, you have to try your best to reach it.
一旦你心中確立了一個目標，就要竭盡全力去達到它。

goat [got]
Track 1452

名 山羊
▶Would you please tell me the difference between a goat and a sheep? 你能告訴我山羊和綿羊之間的區別嗎？

gold·en [ˈgoldn]
Track 1453

形 金色的、黃金的
▶Speech is silver（銀）, silence is golden. At least that's what some people think.
雄辯是銀，沉默是金。至少有些人是這樣想啦。

golf [gɔlf]
Track 1454

名 高爾夫球 動 打高爾夫球
▶名 I heard that you like playing golf very much.
我聽說你非常喜歡打高爾夫球。
▶動 Do you have time this weekend? Let's go golfing, shall we?
你這個週末有空嗎？我們去打高爾夫球好嗎？

文法字詞解析
「高爾夫球員」則稱為 golfer。

gov·ern [ˈgʌvən]
Track 1455

動 統治、治理 同 regulate 管理
▶He is just a politician who has no idea how to govern a country.
他只是個政客，沒有治理國家的理念。

gov·ern·ment [ˈgʌvənmənt]
Track 1456

名 政府 同 administration 政府
▶Don't you think the government isn't doing enough for us?
你不覺得政府為我們做的還不夠多嗎？

Level 1

Level 2

漸入佳境、學習零壓力——邁向常用2200單字

Level 3

Level 4

Level 5

Level 6

grade [gred]　　　🔊 Track 1457
名 年級、等級
▶He is in third grade in the elementary school.
他現在念小學三年級。

grape [grep]　　　🔊 Track 1458
名 葡萄、葡萄樹
▶Will you please buy some fruit such as apples or grapes and bring them back to me?
你能買些水果回來嗎？例如蘋果或者葡萄。

grass·y [ˈgræsɪ]　　　🔊 Track 1459
形 多草的
▶Let's slide down this grassy slope（斜坡）. It looks fun.
我們順著這草坡滑下去吧，看起來好像很好玩。

greed·y [ˈgridɪ]　　　🔊 Track 1460
形 貪婪的
▶Don't be so greedy. Leave some food for the rest of us.
別那麼貪心，留一點食物給我們其他人吃嘛。

greet [grit]　　　🔊 Track 1461
動 迎接、問候　同 hail 招呼
▶When the prime minister had a meeting with the mayor, the men greeted each other warmly.
首相與市長見面時，兩人熱情地互相打招呼。

growth [groθ]　　　🔊 Track 1462
名 成長、發育　同 progress 進步
▶He had a growth spurt（衝刺）when he was fifteen.
他十五歲的時候忽然長高了很多。

guard [gɑrd]　　　🔊 Track 1463
名 警衛　動 防護、守衛
▶名 The guard looks mean, but he's actually a nice man.
那個警衛看起來很兇，但他其實人很好。
▶動 The soldier was assigned to guard the camp at night.
這名軍人被指派在夜間守衛營地。

gua·va [ˈgwɑvə]　　　🔊 Track 1464
名 芭樂
▶Do you like guava juice or grapefruit（葡萄柚）juice better?
你比較喜歡芭樂汁還是葡萄柚汁？

gui·tar [gɪˈtɑr]　　　🔊 Track 1465
名 吉他
▶He is really great at playing the guitar. 他吉他彈得好極了。

guy [gaɪ]　　　🔊 Track 1466
名 傢伙
▶What do you think of that guy wearing a blue T-shirt over there?
你覺得那邊那個穿著藍色 T 恤的傢伙怎麼樣？

文法字詞解析
老師在為學生打分數時，其實就是在劃分學生成績的「等級」，因此打分數的這個動作也叫做「grade」。聽到老師說「I have to grade some reports」，就知道有些報告正等著他改囉！

萬用延伸句型
除了例句中的問法外，也可以換個說法，例如：Which one do you like better, guava juice or grapefruit juice?

[Hh]

hab·it ['hæbɪt]
🔊 *Track 1467*

名 習慣

▶I made it a habit to read newspaper in the morning.
我習慣在早晨閱讀報紙。

hall [hɔl]
🔊 *Track 1468*

名 廳、堂

▶There will be a celebration（慶祝）in the hall. Will you attend it? 大廳裡將有個慶祝活動，你會參加嗎？

ham·burg·er/burg·er
['hæmbɝɡɚ]/['bɝɡɚ]
🔊 *Track 1469*

名 漢堡

▶Not every person likes to eat hamburgers.
並不是每個人都喜歡吃漢堡。

ham·mer ['hæmɚ]
🔊 *Track 1470*

名 鐵鎚 動 鎚打

▶名 Would you please find me some nails and a hammer?
請你幫我找一些釘子和一把鎚子來好嗎？

▶動 My heart hammered hard as I ran.
我一邊跑，心臟一邊像被槌子敲一樣猛跳。

hand·ker·chief ['hæŋkɚtʃɪf]
🔊 *Track 1471*

名 手帕

▶Would you please lend me a handkerchief? I forgot mine at home. 請你借給我一條手帕好嗎？我把自己的放在家裡了。

han·dle ['hændl]
🔊 *Track 1472*

名 把手 動 觸、手執、管理、對付 同 manage 管理

▶名 I turned the handle and opened the door, then it took me ten minutes to carry that big box in.
我轉了轉把手，把門打開。然後我花了十分鐘才把那個大箱子搬進屋裡。

▶動 I have to handle the order, so let's postpone the meeting.
我必須要處理訂單，所以把會議延後吧。

hand·some ['hænsəm]
🔊 *Track 1473*

形 英俊的 同 attractive 吸引人的

▶Everyone who sees him says he is very handsome. What do you think? 每個見過他的人都說他很帥，你覺得呢？

hang [hæŋ]
🔊 *Track 1474*

動 吊、掛 同 suspend 吊、掛

▶We hung an oil painting on the wall of the living as decoration.
我們掛了一幅油畫在客廳牆上當作裝飾。

文法字詞解析
如果要說「忘記做某事」時要注意，因為忘記是在想起來之前就發生的事，所以要用過去式。如果使用現在式「Don't forget to ...」的話，是用來提醒、告知「不要忘記做某事」。

文法字詞解析
雖然 everyone 給人有種「所有人、大家」的錯覺，但要記得 everyone 是單數名詞，動詞現在式要加 s 喔。

Level
1

Level
2

漸入佳境、學習零壓力—
邁向常用2200單字

Level
3

Level
4

Level
5

Level
6

hard·ly [ˈhɑrdlɪ]　🔊 *Track 1475*

副 勉強地、僅僅　同 barely 僅僅

▶He could hardly see anything clearly（清楚地）in this room. It is too dark. 他在這個房間裡幾乎什麼也看不清楚。太暗了。

hate·ful [ˈhetfəl]　🔊 *Track 1476*

形 可恨的、很討厭的　同 hostile 不友善的

▶He is such a hateful person; it's no wonder that people around him dislike（厭惡）him so much.
他是如此可惡的一個人，難怪他周圍的人都很厭惡他。

heal·thy [ˈhɛlθɪ]　🔊 *Track 1477*

形 健康的

▶In order to stay healthy, you had better keep regular hours.
為了保持健康，你做好要有規律作息。

heat·er [ˈhitɚ]　🔊 *Track 1478*

名 加熱器

▶There is no gas heater in the house, so we can't cook meals here. 房子裡沒有瓦斯爐，因此我們無法在這裡煮飯。

> **文法字詞解析**
> heater 也可以是電暖爐的意思，而一般嵌在牆壁上的壁爐則叫做 fireplace。

height [haɪt]　🔊 *Track 1479*

名 高度

▶I dare not to cross the suspension bridge for I am afraid of height. 我不敢過這個吊橋，因為我怕高。

help·ful [ˈhɛlpfəl]　🔊 *Track 1480*

形 有用的　同 useful 有用的

▶Why don't we bring them some books? They might（也許）be helpful to them.
為什麼不帶些書給他們呢？也許對他們會有點用。

hen [hɛn]　🔊 *Track 1481*

名 母雞

▶How often does the hen lay（生蛋）eggs a month?
這隻母雞一個月生幾次蛋？

> **文法字詞解析**
> lay「生蛋」這個字可能會和躺下的動詞「lie」的過去式搞混，而 lie 做為「說謊」時的過去式則是「lied」，閱讀和使用的時候要特別注意。

he·ro/her·o·ine [ˈhɪro]/[ˈhɛroɪn]　🔊 *Track 1482*

名 英雄、勇士 / 女傑、女英雄

▶I don't want to be a hero. All I want is to live my life in peace.
我不想成為英雄，只想要過著平靜的生活。

hide [haɪd]　🔊 *Track 1483*

動 隱藏　同 conceal 隱藏

▶The fugitive hid one million dollars under the bridge.
這名逃犯在橋下藏了一百萬現金。

> **文法字詞解析**
> hide 的動詞變化：hide, hid, hidden

high·way [ˈhaɪˌwe]　🔊 *Track 1484*

名 公路、大路　同 road 路

▶Should we take the highway? It might be faster.
我們要不要走公路？可能會快一點

> **文法字詞解析**
> take 後面加上交通工具、道路、路線可以用來表示「利用某交通工具、某條路到達某個地方」。

hip [hɪp] ◀≶ *Track 1485*

名 臀部、屁股

▶I couldn't help crying out as soon as the needle went into my hip. 針一插進我的臀部，我就忍不住叫了出來。

hip·po·pot·a·mus/ ◀≶ *Track 1486*
hip·po [ˌhɪpəˈpɑtəməs]/[ˈhɪpo]

名 河馬

▶There are a lot of hippopotamuses in this river. Have you seen them? 這條河裡有很多河馬，你有看過嗎？

hire [haɪr] ◀≶ *Track 1487*

動 雇用、租用 名 雇用、租金 同 employ 雇用

▶動 We hired a maid to deal with the house chores.
我們雇用一個幫傭處理家中雜務。

▶名 We have several bicycles for hire.
我們這裡有一些腳踏車供出租。

文法字詞解析
hire 和 rent 在某些情況下可以替換使用，像是在租用汽車、腳踏車、電器用品時。

hob·by [ˈhɑbɪ] ◀≶ *Track 1488*

名 興趣、嗜好 同 pastime 娛樂

▶My hobby is collecting（收集）stamps; what about yours?
我的嗜好是集郵，你呢？

hold·er [ˈholdɚ] ◀≶ *Track 1489*

名 持有者、所有人

▶He is the holder of the world record of eating the most hotdogs in a minute. 他是「一分鐘吃最多熱狗」世界紀錄的保持人。

home·sick [ˈhomˌsɪk] ◀≶ *Track 1490*

形 想家的、思鄉的

▶The homesick boy made a call to his parents.
想家的少年打了電話給他的父母。

hon·est [ˈɑnɪst] ◀≶ *Track 1491*

形 誠實的、耿直的 同 truthful 誠實的

▶You need to be honest with your feelings and tell him what you really think.
你應該誠實面對自己的感受，告訴他你真正的想法。

hon·ey [ˈhʌnɪ] ◀≶ *Track 1492*

名 蜂蜜、花蜜

▶She drinks honey lemon tea every day.
她每天都喝蜂蜜檸檬茶。

hop [hɑp] ◀≶ *Track 1493*

動 跳過、單腳跳 名 單腳跳、跳舞 同 jump 跳

▶動 The kangaroo hopped away after it attacked the visitor in the park. 袋鼠在公園裡攻擊遊客之後就跳走了。

▶名 The bird crossed the lawn（草坪）in a series（系列）of hops. 那隻鳥兒一蹦一跳地穿過草坪。

文法字詞解析
hop 用作名詞時是可數的，要特別注意。

Level 1

Level 2

Level 3

Level 4

Level 5

Level 6

漸入佳境、學習零壓力──
邁向常用2200單字

hos·pi·tal [ˈhɑspɪtl̩]　◀€ *Track 1494*

名 醫院　同 clinic 診所

▶Would you please take him to hospital? 請你帶他去醫院好嗎？

文法字詞解析

「去醫院」是一個概念，並沒有特定去哪一家醫院，所以 hospital 的前面不用加定冠詞。

host/host·ess [host]/[ˈhostɪs]　◀€ *Track 1495*

名 主人、女主人

▶The host of the talk show can always think of a fun way to interact with his guest. 這個脫口秀節目的主持人總是可以想出有趣的方式和來賓互動。

ho·tel [hoˈtɛl]　◀€ *Track 1496*

名 旅館　同 hostel 青年旅舍

▶It took me almost half an hour to get to the hotel. 我花了差不多快半小時才到達那間旅館。

how·ev·er [hauˈɛvɚ]　◀€ *Track 1497*

副 無論如何　連 然而

▶副 However tired you may be, you must finish the work as soon as possible.
不管你有多累，你都必須儘快完成這份工作。

▶連 She's a lovely girl. However, her brother has no manners.
她是個可愛的女孩，然而她哥哥卻一點禮貌都沒有。

hum [hʌm]　◀€ *Track 1498*

名 嗡嗡聲　動 作嗡嗡聲

▶名 I can hear the hum of bees as I walk out of my room.
我走出房間的時候聽見了蜜蜂的嗡嗡聲。

▶動 The boy hummed so much his mother got mad.
那個男孩太愛哼歌，他媽都生氣了。

hum·ble [ˈhʌmbl̩]　◀€ *Track 1499*

形 身份卑微的、謙虛的　同 modest 謙虛的

▶Despite his humble background, he strived to become a successful entrepreneur.
儘管出身卑微，他還是努力成為一位成功創業家。

hu·mid [ˈhjumɪd]　◀€ *Track 1500*

形 潮濕的　同 moist 潮濕的

▶It won't be long before the air here becomes humid. 過不了多久這邊的空氣就會變得潮濕起來。

hu·mor [ˈhjumɚ]　◀€ *Track 1501*

名 詼諧、幽默　同 comedy 喜劇

▶There's a lot of humor in the works he writes.
他寫的作品都非常幽默。

文法字詞解析

humor 是美式的拼法，英式的拼法則是 humour。

hun·ger [ˈhʌngɚ]　◀€ *Track 1502*

名 餓、饑餓

▶The philanthropist experienced hunger that the victims of the famine felt for empathy.
慈善家體驗飢荒受害者的飢餓感受，才能有同理心。

hunt [hʌnt] 🔊 *Track 1503*

動 獵取 名 打獵 同 chase 追捕

▶動 In ancient times, both men and women used to hunt.
在古代，男人與女人都曾狩獵。

▶名 The villagers（村民）asked him to take part in the tiger hunt. 村民們叫他去參加獵虎行動。

hunt·er ['hʌntɚ] 🔊 *Track 1504*

名 獵人

▶They made a law to forbid（禁止）the hunters to enter this area. 他們立法禁止獵人們進入這個區域。

hur·ry ['hɝɪ] 🔊 *Track 1505*

動 （使）趕緊 名 倉促 同 rush 倉促

▶動 Let's hurry a bit, or else we can't catch the bus and get to school on time. 我們得快點，要不然我們就沒辦法趕上公車準時到學校了。

▶名 He was in such a hurry that he left his passport behind.
他時間太趕了，以致忘了帶護照。

[Ii]

ig·nore [ɪg'nor] 🔊 *Track 1506*

動 忽視、不理睬 同 neglect 忽視

▶This is just a minor glitch, so you can just ignore it.
這只是一個小失誤，所以你可以忽略它。

ill [ɪl] 🔊 *Track 1507*

名 疾病、壞事 形 生病的 副 壞地 同 sick 生病的

▶名 It's a doctor's job to cure the ill. 醫生的工作就是治好病人。

▶形 I've felt ill all day. 我整天都覺得病懨懨的。

▶副 He always speaks ill of others behind their backs.
他總是在別人背後說他們壞話。

i·mag·ine [ɪ'mædʒɪn] 🔊 *Track 1508*

動 想像、設想 同 suppose 設想

▶I imagine him to be a tall, angry-looking man.
我想像他是一個高高的、看起來很不爽的男人。

im·por·tance [ɪm'pɔrtn̩s] 🔊 *Track 1509*

名 重要性

▶Not everyone knows the importance of being honest.
並不是每個人都懂得誠實的重要性。

im·prove [ɪm'pruv] 🔊 *Track 1510*

動 改善、促進

▶The mayor wants to improve the social welfare system.
市長想要改善社會福利制度。

萬用延伸句型

S. + V. , or else S. + V.
……，要不然……。

or else 和 otherwise 同義，但從用法上來看，otherwise 除了可以放在句中之外，也可以放在句首，如果放在句首的話，前後句的中間要有分號隔開。

Level **1**

Level **2**

Level **3**

Level **4**

Level **5**

Level **6**

漸入佳境、學習零壓力──邁向常用2200單字

im·prove·ment [ɪmˈpruvmənt] ◀€ *Track 1511*

名 改善
▶The house feels much bigger after we redecorated（重新裝潢）. What an improvement!
房子在重新裝潢後感覺大多了。真是一大進步啊！

in·clude [ɪnˈklud] ◀€ *Track 1512*

動 包含、包括、含有 同 contain 包含
▶The chorus includes thirteen girls and fifteen boys.
這個合唱團裡包含13個女孩和15個男孩。

in·come [ˈɪnˌkʌm] ◀€ *Track 1513*

名 所得、收入 同 earnings 收入
▶Most of his income went into his wife's pockets.
他大部分的所得都被他太太拿走了。

in·crease [ˈɪnkris]/[ɪnˈkris] ◀€ *Track 1514*

名 增加 動 增加 反 reduce 減少
▶名 The number of Chinese drama fans is on the increase.
喜歡中國戲劇的影迷在增加中。
▶動 I can't believe that the number of people who agree actually increased.
真難相信，同意的人數居然增加了。

in·de·pen·dence [ˌɪndɪˈpɛndəns] ◀€ *Track 1515*

名 自立、獨立
▶Today, let us celebrate our Independence Day!
今天讓我們來慶祝獨立紀念日吧！

in·de·pend·ent [ˌɪndɪˈpɛndənt] ◀€ *Track 1516*

形 獨立的
▶Not all children are able to be independent of their parents.
不是所有的孩子都能夠離開父母獨立生活。

in·di·cate [ˈɪndəˌket] ◀€ *Track 1517*

動 指出、指示 同 imply 暗示
▶Will you please indicate your expected salary（薪水）in your resume（履歷）? 請你在履歷中註明你所期望的薪水好嗎？

in·dus·try [ˈɪndəstrɪ] ◀€ *Track 1518*

名 工業
▶It is said that tourist industry may boost the economy of the region. 據說旅遊業可以促進這個地區的經濟發展。

in·flu·ence [ˈɪnfluəns] ◀€ *Track 1519*

名 影響 動 影響
▶名 Her advice has no influence on Peter.
她的勸告對彼得毫無影響。
▶動 I don't want to influence your decision.
我不想影響你做決定。

萬用延伸句型
用來表達強烈情緒的感嘆句有兩種寫法，一種是「What a + N.！」，另一種則是「How + adj. + S. + V.！」。

萬用延伸句型
under the influence 酒醉的
例　如：He was driving under the influence and nearly hit a lamp post.
他酒醉駕車，差點撞到路燈。

ink [ɪŋk]
◄€ Track 1520

名 墨水、墨汁 動 塗上墨水

▶名 I marked the sentences to be modified in red ink.
　我將待修改的句子用紅筆標記出來。

▶動 Would you please ink my pen for me?
　你能不能幫我把筆多加些墨水？

in·sect [ˈɪnsɛkt]
◄€ Track 1521

名 昆蟲 同 bug 蟲子

▶Not all insects in nature are harmful（有害的）to human
beings. 自然界中不是所有的昆蟲都對人類有害。

in·sist [ɪnˈsɪst]
◄€ Track 1522

動 堅持、強調

▶I insist that you stay for dinner.
　我堅持要你留下來吃晚餐。

in·stance [ˈɪnsɪstəns]
◄€ Track 1523

名 實例 動 舉證 同 example 例子

▶名 There are jobs more dangerous than truck driving; for
instance, training lions.
　有些工作比開卡車還要危險，例如馴獅就是。

▶動 There are many dirty insects you can instance, such as
flies. 你可以列舉出很多骯髒的昆蟲，比如蒼蠅。

in·stant [ˈɪnsɪstənt]
◄€ Track 1524

形 立即的、瞬間的 名 立即 同 immediate 立即的

▶形 Would you like to have a cup of instant coffee?
　想不想喝杯即溶咖啡？

▶名 He finished reading the note in an instant.
　他一下子就讀完這張紙條了。

in·stru·ment [ˈɪnstrəmənt]
◄€ Track 1525

名 樂器、器具

▶The only instrument I can play is the guitar.
　我唯一會彈的一種樂器就是吉他。

in·ter·nat·ion·al [ˌɪntɚˈnæʃənl]
◄€ Track 1526

形 國際的 同 universal 全世界的

▶There are neither international rules nor any international
standards here.
　這裡不存在任何國際規章或國際準則。

in·ter·view [ˈɪntɚˌvju]
◄€ Track 1527

名 面談 動 面談、會面

▶名 Would you please give me a chance? I really hope to have
an interview with you.
　您能給我一次機會嗎？我真的非常希望有機會與你面談。

▶動 The director of the personnel department wants to
interview the applicant in person.
　人事部的主任想要親自面試求職者。

文法字詞解析
因為泡麵的特色就是泡下去便可以馬上
吃，因此在英文中可用 instant noodles
來稱呼。此外，杯裝的泡麵也可叫 cup
noodles，也有人用日文的「拉麵」發音
稱為 cup ramen，或韓文的「拉麵」發
音稱為 cup ramyeon。

Level 1

Level 2

漸入佳境、學習零壓力──
邁向常用2200單字

Level 3

Level 4

Level 5

Level 6

in·tro·duce [ˌɪntrəˈdjus]　　🔊 *Track 1528*
動 介紹、引進
▶Would you like to introduce him to me?
　你能不能把他介紹給我認識呢？

in·vent [ɪnˈvɛnt]　　🔊 *Track 1529*
動 發明、創造
▶To invent something, you need curiosity and creativity.
　發明新東西需要好奇心和創造力。

in·vi·ta·tion [ˌɪnvəˈteʃən]　　🔊 *Track 1530*
名 請帖、邀請
▶I did send you an invitation. It might have got blocked by your mailbox.
　我有送出邀請函給你啊，可能被你的電子郵件信箱擋掉了。

文法字詞解析
在例句中，如果只用「I sent you an invitation」就會比較像在陳述「我寄邀請函給你了」這件事，但寫成「did send」就會變成強調「我『確實』有寄邀請函給你」。

in·vite [ɪnˈvaɪt]　　🔊 *Track 1531*
動 邀請、招待
▶Who do you want to invite to your wedding?
　你要請誰參加你的婚禮？

is·land [ˈaɪlənd]　　🔊 *Track 1532*
名 島、安全島
▶He used to live on a small island off the shore（海岸）.
　他過去住在離海邊不遠的一個小島上。

i·tem [ˈaɪtəm]　　🔊 *Track 1533*
名 項目、條款　**同** segment 項目
▶We listed the items to purchase before heading off to the shopping mall. 出發前往購物中心前，我們會列好要購買的物品項目。

[Jj]

jack·et [ˈdʒækɪt]　　🔊 *Track 1534*
名 夾克　**同** coat 外套
▶Would you please get me my jacket? My wallet is in it.
　請你幫我把外套拿過來一下好嗎？我的錢包在裡面。

jam [dʒæm]　　🔊 *Track 1535*
動 阻塞　**名** 果醬
▶**動** The door was jammed, and we had to aske a locksmith for help. 門卡住了，我們只好請鎖匠幫忙。
▶**名** Strawberry jam is my favorite kind of jam.
　草莓果醬是我最喜歡的一種果醬。

文法字詞解析
jam... into... = 把……塞進……裡
a traffic jam = 塞車

jazz [dʒæz]　　🔊 *Track 1536*
名 爵士樂
▶It doesn't matter whether you like jazz or not.
　你喜不喜歡爵士樂都不要緊。

jeans [dʒinz] 🔊 *Track 1537*

名 牛仔褲 同 pants 褲子

▶Mom, would you buy me a pair of jeans? My old pair is torn.
媽媽，妳能買條牛仔褲給我嗎？我舊的那條破了。

文法字詞解析
因為 jeans 通常都用複數，如果以 pair
來修飾可以更清楚表示牛仔褲的數量。

jeep [dʒip] 🔊 *Track 1538*

名 吉普車

▶What's the matter with my jeep? I can't get it to start.
我的吉普車出了什麼毛病？我都發動不了。

jog [dʒɑg] 🔊 *Track 1539*

動 慢跑

▶We often jog along the river in the early morning when the
weather is fine. 我們常在天氣好時在早晨沿河邊慢跑。

joint [dʒɔɪnt] 🔊 *Track 1540*

名 接合處 形 共同的

▶名 He suffered（遭受）from arthritis（關節炎）in his leg joints.
他的腿得了關節炎。

▶形 It was not long before they completed the project by their
joint efforts. 沒過多久他們就透過共同努力完成了這個專案。

judge [dʒʌdʒ] 🔊 *Track 1541*

名 法官、裁判 動 裁決 同 umpire 裁判

▶名 The judge sentenced him to death in court.
法官在法庭上判他死刑。

▶動 We should not judge people by their appearance.
我們不應該用外表去評斷別人。

judge·ment/judg·ment 🔊 *Track 1542*

[ˈdʒʌdʒmənt]

名 判斷力

▶It's too early to make a judgment on what the result will be.
現在就對結果下判斷還為時過早。

juic·y [ˈdʒusɪ] 🔊 *Track 1543*

形 多汁的

▶There are some fresh juicy oranges in this store.
這家店裡有些新鮮多汁的柳丁。

文法字詞解析
除了用來描述水果多汁以外，juicy 也可
以拿來搭配「八卦」、「祕密」使用，
例如 juicy gossip 即是指非常勁爆的八
卦。

[Kk]

ketch·up [ˈkɛtʃəp] 🔊 *Track 1544*

名 番茄醬

▶You can choose to have the fish chips with ketchup, gravy, or
curry sauce.
吃炸魚柳時，可以沾番茄醬、肉醬，或者咖哩醬。

Level **1**

Level **2**

漸入佳境、學習零壓力──
邁向常用2200單字

Level **3**

Level **4**

Level **5**

Level **6**

kin·der·gar·ten [ˈkɪndəˌɡɑrtn̩] 🔊 *Track 1545*

名 幼稚園

▶Could you tell me why there are so many children in that kindergarten?
你能告訴我為什麼那個幼稚園有那麼多的孩子嗎？

king·dom [ˈkɪndəm] 🔊 *Track 1546*

名 王國

▶The Persian Kingdom was a great kingdom in history.
波斯帝國是歷史上重要的帝國時期。

文法字詞解析
字尾「-dom」在這裡的意思是「某個特別受到管轄的區域」；另外，用在 freedom、boredom 等字裡時，則表示「某種狀態」

knock [nɑk] 🔊 *Track 1547*

動 敲、擊 名 敲打聲 同 hit 打擊

▶動 You should knock on the door before you come in.
你進來之前應該要敲門啊。

▶名 Was there a knock on the door just now, or was it my imagination?
剛剛有敲門聲嗎？還是我自己想像的？

knowl·edge [ˈnɑlɪdʒ] 🔊 *Track 1548*

名 知識 同 scholarship 學問

▶We learned some important knowledge from this educational TV program.
我們由這個教育性質電視節目中學到一些重要的知識。

ko·a·la [kəˈɑlə] 🔊 *Track 1549*

名 無尾熊

▶Have you ever hugged a koala?
你抱過無尾熊嗎？

[Ll]

la·dy·bug/la·dy·bird 🔊 *Track 1550*
[ˈledɪˌbʌg]/[ˈledɪˌbɝd]

名 瓢蟲

▶What does a ladybug look like? I have never seen one.
瓢蟲長什麼樣子呢？我從來沒看過。

lane [len] 🔊 *Track 1551*

名 小路、巷 同 path 小路

▶There are many small lanes in the village.
在這個村莊裡有很多小巷。

文法字詞解析
我們開車時開的「車道」也叫做「lane」。因此有個說法「stay in your own lane」，直譯就是叫你待在自己的車道，不要開進別人的車道，延伸為「不要多管別人閒事」的意思。

lan·guage [ˈlæŋɡwɪdʒ] 🔊 *Track 1552*

名 語言

▶She is keen in learning different languages.
她很積極地學習各種語言。

lan·tern [ˈlæntən]
🔊 Track 1553

名 燈籠　同 lamp 燈
▶ The lantern festival is an important Chinese holiday.
元宵燈籠節是一個重要的中國節日。

lap [læp]
🔊 Track 1554

名 膝部　動 舐、輕拍
▶ 名 She has her cat rest on her lap.
她讓她的貓睡在她大腿上。
▶ 動 The puppy is lapping up the milk. 那隻小狗在舔牛奶。

lat·est [ˈletɪst]
🔊 Track 1555

形 最後的
▶ I don't want to be the latest person to arrive for the meeting.
我可不想成為最後一個到場開會的人。

law·yer [ˈlɔjɚ]
🔊 Track 1556

名 律師
▶ I want to study law and become a lawyer in the future.
我想學法律，將來當一名律師。

lead·er·ship [ˈlidɚʃɪp]
🔊 Track 1557

名 領導力　同 guidance 領導
▶ The people in the company owe（歸功於）the success to his leadership.
對於這次的成功，公司的人必須感謝他的領導能力。

le·gal [ˈlig!]
🔊 Track 1558

形 合法的　同 lawful 合法的
▶ They signed a legal agreement on this matter.
他們就這件事情簽署了一項法律合約。

lem·on [ˈlɛmən]
🔊 Track 1559

名 檸檬
▶ I like oranges more than lemons. What about you?
比起檸檬我更喜歡橘子。你呢？

lem·on·ade [ˌlɛmənˈed]
🔊 Track 1560

名 檸檬水
▶ The kids are selling lemonade by the street.
孩子們在路邊賣檸檬汁。

lend [lɛnd]
🔊 Track 1561

動 借出　反 borrow 借來
▶ I regretted lending him so much money.
我後悔借他這麼多錢。

length [lɛŋkθ]
🔊 Track 1562

名 長度
▶ The movie at its full length is three hours long.
這部電影完整的長度是三小時。

文法字詞解析
laptop 就是從 lap 這個字衍生而來，lap 有「膝部」的意思，top 則是「上面」的意思，「放在在膝上的電腦」就成了單字「筆記型電腦」的由來了。

文法字詞解析
lend 的動詞變化：lend, lent, lent

Level **1**

Level **2**
邁向常用2200單字── 漸入佳境、學習零壓力

Level **3**

Level **4**

Level **5**

Level **6**

leop·ard [ˈlɛpəd] 🔊 *Track 1563*

名 豹

▶The snow leopard is a beautiful but rare animal.
雪豹是一種美麗但不常見的動物。

let·tuce [ˈlɛtɪs] 🔊 *Track 1564*

名 萵苣

▶I bought some lettuce for making salad.
我買了一些萵苣生菜來做沙拉。

li·bra·ry [ˈlaɪˌbrɛrɪ] 🔊 *Track 1565*

名 圖書館

▶Would you please take him to the library?
請你帶他到圖書館去好嗎？

lick [lɪk] 🔊 *Track 1566*

名 / 動 舔食、舔

▶名 The dog gave me a huge lick.
這隻狗狠狠舔了我一下。

▶動 My cat licks herself all day.
我的貓整天在舔自己。

lid [lɪd] 🔊 *Track 1567*

名 蓋子

▶I lifted the lid of the jar to take out the pickles.
我把罐子的蓋子打開，拿出裡面的醬菜。

light·ning [ˈlaɪtnɪŋ] 🔊 *Track 1568*

名 閃電

▶There were many flashes of lightning during the storm last night. 昨晚下暴雨的時候出現了好多次閃電。

lim·it [ˈlɪmɪt] 🔊 *Track 1569*

名 限度、極限 動 限制 同 extreme 極限

▶名 I am a very patient person, but there's a limit to everything.
我算是很有耐心的人，可是凡事都有個限度吧。

▶動 We must limit ourselves to one cake each.
我們必須限定每人只吃一塊蛋糕。

link [lɪŋk] 🔊 *Track 1570*

名 關聯 動 連結 同 connect 連結

▶名 Click the link and you will reach the official website of out company.
點這個連結，就可以連到我們公司的官方網站。

▶動 Can you link me to your blog（部落格）？
你可以給我你部落格的連結嗎？

liq·uid [ˈlɪkwɪd] 🔊 *Track 1571*

名 液體

▶What's this strange green liquid on the bathroom floor?
廁所地上這綠綠的奇怪液體是什麼？

文法字詞解析
和 lightning 長得非常像的一個單字是 lightening，它的意思是「變淡、變亮」，兩者完全不同喔！

lis·ten·er [ˈlɪsnɚ]

Track 1572

名 聽眾、聽者

▶She rarely speaks, but is a good listener.
她不太講話，但是個很好的聆聽者。

loaf [lof]

Track 1573

名 一塊
名詞複數 loaves

▶Would you please give me a loaf of bread? I feel a little bit hungry now.
請你給我一條麵包好嗎？我現在感覺有點餓了。

文法字詞解析
bread 是不可數名詞，可以接上 a loaf of（一條）、a slice of（一片）、a piece of（一小塊）來描述得更精確。

lo·cal [ˈlokl]

Track 1574

形 當地的 名 當地居民 同 regional 地區的

▶形 The local ecological system may be threatened by foreign species. 本地的生態系統可能會因為外來物種而遭到威脅。

▶名 The locals here are always very kind to strangers.
這裡的居民對於陌生人都很親切。

lo·cate [ˈloket]

Track 1575

動 設置、居住

▶The building you're looking for is located at the edge of the town.
你在找的那棟大樓位於城鎮邊緣。

lock [lɑk]

Track 1576

名 鎖 動 鎖上

▶名 WThe safe comes with an electronic lock, which may level up its security.
保險箱用電子鎖，可以提升安全性。

▶動 Why didn't you lock the door? No wonder your stuff got stolen.
你怎麼沒鎖門呢？難怪你的東西會被偷。

log [lɔg]

Track 1577

名 圓木 動 伐木、把……記入航海日誌 同 wood 木頭

▶名 He got hit by a log when working in the forest.
他在森林裡工作時被一根圓木打到。

▶動 The captain logged the happenings of the day in his journal.
這名船長把當天發生的事記在日誌裡。

lone [lon]

Track 1578

形 孤單的

▶He is a lone wolf kind of person; he'll never join us.
他是喜歡單打獨鬥的那種人，他不會加入我們的。

文法字詞解析
lone wolf 在這裡變成了形容詞修飾 kind，表示「喜歡孤獨的那種人」。

lone·ly [ˈlonlɪ]

Track 1579

形 孤單的、寂寞的 同 solitary 寂寞的

▶The old man was so lonely that he became sick.
這個老人寂寞到生病了。

Level
1

Level
2

漸入佳境、學習零壓力——
邁向常用2200單字

Level
3

Level
4

Level
5

Level
6

lose [luz]
🔊 *Track 1580*

動 遺失、失去、輸 同 fail 失敗、失去
▶It doesn't matter if you lose the game, you'll still be champion (冠軍). 就算你輸了這次比賽也沒差，你一樣會是冠軍。

los·er [ˈluzɚ]
🔊 *Track 1581*

名 失敗者 反 winner 勝利者
▶I feel like such a loser when I see my friends being rich and famous. 看到我的朋友們又有錢又有名，我就覺得自己很失敗。

loss [lɔs]
🔊 *Track 1582*

名 損失
▶You have to compensate for the loss.
你需要賠償損失。

love·ly [ˈlʌvlɪ]
🔊 *Track 1583*

形 美麗的、可愛的
▶What a lovely little daughter you have! 你的小女兒多可愛啊！

lov·er [ˈlʌvɚ]
🔊 *Track 1584*

名 愛人
▶Have you seen his lover? What does she look like?
你見過他的情人嗎？她長什麼樣子呢？

low·er [ˈloɚ]
🔊 *Track 1585*

動 降低
▶The producer wants to increase the sales by lowering the price.
製造商想透過降價來增加銷售量。

luck [lʌk]
🔊 *Track 1586*

名 幸運 同 fortune 幸運
▶Let's go to the casino (賭場) to try our luck.
我們去賭場碰碰運氣吧。

[Mm]

mag·a·zine [ˌmægəˈzin]
🔊 *Track 1587*

名 雜誌
▶Would you please allow me to bring this magazine home?
您允許我把這本雜誌帶回家嗎？

ma·gic [ˈmædʒɪk]
🔊 *Track 1588*

名 魔術 形 魔術的
▶名 He sometimes performs magic for his colleagues on special occasions.
他有時候會在特別場合上表演魔術給同事看。
▶形 The magic show we saw last night was great.
我們昨天晚上看的魔術表演真棒。

文法字詞解析
feel like 接名詞的時候，解釋成「感覺像某東西」。
feel like 也可以接 V-ing，表示「想要……」

萬用延伸句型
Who cares? 那又怎樣？誰在乎？
用來表達某事或某人一點都不重要、用不著擔心。

文法字詞解析
magazine 另有個較少見的意思，指「彈匣」。在玩戰鬥遊戲時可能會經常看見。

ma·gi·cian [mə`dʒɪʃən] 🔊 *Track 1589*
名 魔術師
▶I don't think I could ever become a magician.
　我覺得我應該永遠不可能當得了魔術師。

main [men] 🔊 *Track 1590*
形 主要的 名 要點 同 principal 主要的
▶形 What do you think of the main idea of the article（文章）?
　你覺得這篇文章的中心思想怎麼樣？
▶名 His ideas are impractical（不切實際的）but very exciting.
　他的概念很不實際，但很刺激。

main·tain [men`ten] 🔊 *Track 1591*
動 維持 同 keep 維持
▶I always try to maintain good relationship with my parents in law. 我總是努力要和岳父岳母維持好的關係。

male [mel] 🔊 *Track 1592*
形 男性的 名 男性 反 female 女性的
▶形 The male nurse standing at the door looks really bored.
　站在門口那個男護士看起來覺得很無聊的樣子。
▶名 Males are usually physically（身體上地）stronger than females.
　男性在身體上通常要比女性強壯。

man·da·rin [`mændərɪn] 🔊 *Track 1593*
名 國語、中文
▶I speak English, French and Mandarin; what about you?
　我會講英語、法語和國語，你呢？

man·go [`mæŋgo] 🔊 *Track 1594*
名 芒果
▶Not all people like eating mangoes.
　不是所有的人都喜歡吃芒果。

man·ner [`mænɚ] 🔊 *Track 1595*
名 方法、禮貌 同 form 方法
▶She expects her kids to have good table manners.
　她希望她的小孩可以有好的餐桌禮儀。

mark [mɑrk] 🔊 *Track 1596*
動 標記 名 記號 同 sign 記號
▶動 Let me mark the correct answers for you.
　讓我幫你標出正確答案吧。
▶名 Why is there a mark on the sheep's back? What does it mean? 為什麼那隻綿羊背上有記號？是什麼意思？

mar·riage [`mærɪdʒ] 🔊 *Track 1597*
名 婚姻
▶Marriage is an important aspect of an individual's life.
　婚姻在一個人生活中是相當重要的面向。

文法字詞解析
字根「main」的意思是「手」，「tain」是「握著」的意思，兩者合在一起「手一直握著」就成了「維持某個水平、狀態」；如果要表達「維持生命、生活」的話，則要用 sustain，字首「sus-」表示「下面、向下」。

文法字詞解析
「physic」是身體的意思，加上形容詞字尾「-al」就變成「身體上的」，在加上附詞字尾「-ly」就成了「身體上地」。

文法字詞解析
要注意 mango 的複數是加 es 而不是 s，同樣的情況還有「hero(es) 英雄」、「potato(es) 馬鈴薯」。

Level 1

Level 2

邁向常用2200單字──漸入佳境、學習零壓力

Level 3

Level 4

Level 5

Level 6

mask [mæsk] ◀ Track 1598

名 面具 動 遮蓋

▶名 We are supposed to wear masks to the ball（舞會）.
我們應該要戴面具去舞會。

▶動 She always masks her sadness（悲傷）with a smile.
她總是用微笑掩飾自己的悲傷。

mass [mæs] ◀ Track 1599

名 大量 同 quantity 大量

▶Social media has become a popular way to promote an idea to the mass. 社群網站是個推廣想法給大眾的常用方式。

mat [mæt] ◀ Track 1600

名 墊子、蓆子 同 rug 毯子

▶It is no wonder that she asked for a mat to sit on; the floor is too cold. 怪不得她要墊子來坐，這地板太冷了。

match [mætʃ] ◀ Track 1601

名 火柴、比賽 動 相配

▶名 Will you wear that gray（灰色的）tie? It's a good match with your blue shirt.
你要戴那條灰色的領帶嗎？它跟你的藍襯衫很相配哦。

▶動 Can you recommend（推薦）a blouse（短上衣）to match my new trousers? 您能推薦一款短上衣來配我的新褲子嗎？

mate [met] ◀ Track 1602

名 配偶 動 配對

▶名 I thought I found my soul mate, but it was just infatuation.
我以為我找到靈魂伴侶了，但其實那只是一時意亂情迷。

▶動 It's mating season and the dogs in my house are all getting anxious（焦慮的）.
現在是交配的季節，所以我家的狗都很焦慮。

ma·te·ri·al [məˋtɪrɪəl] ◀ Track 1603

名 物質 同 composition 物質

▶Could you tell me what material this is made of?
你能不能告訴我這是用什麼材料做成的？

meal [mil] ◀ Track 1604

名 一餐、餐

▶We had a quick meal and hurried to the meeting.
我們迅速吃了一餐，然後趕去開會了。

mean·ing [ˋminɪŋ] ◀ Track 1605

名 意義 同 implication 含意

▶Will you explain the meanings of these foreign words?
你能解釋這些外文單字的意思嗎？

means [minz] ◀ Track 1606

名 方法

▶I will persuade him to accept my proposal by all means.
我會用盡各種方式使他接受我的提案。

文法字詞解析

be supposed to 如果用現在式，指的是預定要做的計劃；如果用過去式，指的是「預期會發生、實際卻沒發生的事」，也可以用 should have + Vp.p. 表示。
另外，「should」在中文也譯做「應該」，只是和 be supposed to 的意思並不一樣，它指的是「做某件事情是正確的、是對的」。例如：You should dry your hair before you go to bed. 你睡前應該把頭髮吹乾。

文法字詞解析

像是麥當勞的兒童餐就稱為「Happy Meal」。

mea·sur·a·ble [ˈmɛʒərəbl̩]
◀< *Track 1607*
形 可測量的
▶There has been a measurable improvement in his work.
他的工作已經有了很大的改進。

mea·sure [ˈmɛʒɚ]
◀< *Track 1608*
動 測量
▶I used the measuring tape to measure the length of the book case. 我用一個皮尺來測量書櫃的長度。

mea·sur·ement [ˈmɛʒəmənt]
◀< *Track 1609*
名 測量 同 estimate 估計
▶It's not polite to ask someone about their measurements.
問人家三圍數字是不禮貌的。

med·i·cine [ˈmɛdəsn̩]
◀< *Track 1610*
名 醫學、藥物 同 drug 藥物
▶You have a cold. You should take some medicine.
你感冒了，該吃點藥了。

meet·ing [ˈmitɪŋ]
◀< *Track 1611*
名 會議
▶If we're late for the meeting, we'll be in huge trouble.
如果我們開會遲到，我們就慘了。

mel·o·dy [ˈmɛlədɪ]
◀< *Track 1612*
名 旋律 同 tune 旋律
▶The melody of the folk song made me recall my childhood years.
民俗歌謠的旋律讓我想起我的童年。

mel·on [ˈmɛlən]
◀< *Track 1613*
名 瓜、甜瓜
▶I bought some melons from the market just now.
我剛剛從市場買了一些瓜。

mem·ber [ˈmɛmbɚ]
◀< *Track 1614*
名 成員
▶Are you a member of the club?
你是那個社團的社員嗎？

mem·o·ry [ˈmɛmərɪ]
◀< *Track 1615*
名 記憶、回憶
▶That was a terrible memory that I'd rather forget.
那個回憶超糟糕的，我還寧可忘記。

me·nu [ˈmɛnju]
◀< *Track 1616*
名 菜單
▶The menu is printed in Japanese, English, and Mandarin.
菜單有印日文、英文、以及中文版。

文法字詞解析
去超市買東西時，常常會被問要不要加入會員，這裡的「會員」就是叫做 member。而「會員卡」的説法是「loyalty card」。

Level 1

Level 2

漸入佳境、學習零壓力——
邁向常用2200單字

Level 3

Level 4

Level 5

Level 6

mes·sage [ˈmɛsɪdʒ]　🔊 Track 1617

名 訊息
▶Since he is not in, would you like to leave a message for him?
既然他不在，您要不要留個訊息給他？

文法字詞解析
in 在例句中是形容詞，表示「在某個空間內」。

met·al [ˈmɛtl̩]　🔊 Track 1618

名 金屬 形 金屬的
▶名 The utensils are made of special metal so they can last longer. 這些器具是用特殊金屬做成的，可以用比較久。
▶形 There are lots of metal cooking utensils（器具）in our kitchen.
我們的廚房裡有很多金屬的廚具。

me·ter [ˈmitɚ]　🔊 Track 1619

名 公尺
▶The parking meter isn't working.
停車收費器壞了。

文法字詞解析
isn't working 和 doesn't work 雖然都有「壞掉、不能運作」的意思，但 isn't working 表示「在這個當下是壞的，但之前可能還可以運作」，doesn't work 表示「完全不能用」。

meth·od [ˈmɛθəd]　🔊 Track 1620

名 方法 同 style 方式
▶The math problem can be solved in different methods.
這個數學題可以用不同的方法解答。

mil·i·tar·y [ˈmɪləˌtɛrɪ]　🔊 Track 1621

形 軍事的 名 軍事 同 army 軍隊
▶形 I heard that he did a year's military service.
我聽說他服過一年兵役。
▶名 The military has taken over the government.
軍方已經接管政府了。

mil·lion [ˈmɪljən]　🔊 Track 1622

名 百萬
▶There are millions of American veterans（老兵）from the Second World War.
參加過第二次世界大戰的美國退伍軍人有數百萬人。

mine [maɪn]　🔊 Track 1623

名 礦、礦坑 代 我的東西
▶名 The children went to explore the old mine.
孩子們跑去探索那個老礦坑了。
▶代 She is a great friend of mine.
她是我很好的朋友。

萬用延伸句型
Your guess is good as mine. 意為「我也不知道」。
例如：
A: Where's your mom?
B: Your guess is good as mine.
A：你媽人呢？
B：我也不知道啊。

mi·nus [ˈmaɪnəs]　🔊 Track 1624

介 減、減去 形 減的 名 負數 反 plus 加的
▶介 Ten minus three is seven. 十減三是七。
▶形 The temperature will be minus 10 degrees tomorrow. 明天氣溫為零下十度。
▶名 We have to weigh the pluses and minuses of the project.
我們必須權衡這個計畫的利弊。

mir·ror [ˈmɪrɚ]
🔊 *Track 1625*

名 鏡子 動 反映

▶ 名 Look in the mirror and you'll see why everyone is staring at you. 照個鏡子吧，你就會知道大家為什麼一直盯著你看了。

▶ 動 His confused（疑惑的）expression（表情）mirrors mine. 他臉上露出和我一模一樣的困惑神情。

萬用延伸句型
1. you'll see (that) ... 你會瞭解到……
2. stare at sb. 盯著某人看

mix [mɪks]
🔊 *Track 1626*

動 混合 名 混合物 同 combine 結合

▶ 動 We mixed the Chinese music and Western pop music in this song.
我們將中式音樂和西式流行音樂結合。

▶ 名 It's a mix of guava juice and orange juice.
那是芭樂汁和柳橙汁的混合物。

mod·el [ˈmɑdl̩]
🔊 *Track 1627*

名 模型、模特兒 動 模仿

▶ 名 Not every girl is tall enough to be a model.
不是每個女孩都有足夠的身高能去當模特兒。

▶ 動 The kids model themselves after their mother.
那些孩子們以媽媽為榜樣。

mo·dern [ˈmɑdɚn]
🔊 *Track 1628*

形 現代的 反 ancient 古代的

▶ In modern society, people are more dependent on mobile gadget. 現代社會中，人們更加依賴行動裝置。

mon·ster [ˈmɑnstɚ]
🔊 *Track 1629*

名 怪物

▶ When I was a child, I was worried that there were monsters under my bed. 我還是個孩子時，總擔心床下有怪物。

mos·qui·to [məˈskito]
🔊 *Track 1630*

名 蚊子

▶ There are so many annoying（討厭的）mosquitoes in summer, especially in the wet areas.
夏天總是有那麼多討厭的蚊子，尤其是在潮濕的地方。

文法字詞解析
especially 用做「尤其、特別是」時，後面接名詞、介系詞片語、副詞片語等。要注意的是，especially 絕對不能用在句首。

moth [mɔθ]
🔊 *Track 1631*

名 蛾、蛀蟲

▶ Is that a butterfly or a moth? 那是隻蝴蝶還是飛蛾？

mo·tion [ˈmoʃən]
🔊 *Track 1632*

名 運動、動作 同 movement 運動

▶ Jenny suffered from motion sickness during the long trip on the train. 珍妮在長途旅行移動中暈車了。

mo·tor·cy·cle [ˈmotɚˌsaɪkl̩]
🔊 *Track 1633*

名 摩托車

▶ Will you please let me use your motorcycle tomorrow?
你明天可以借我用你的摩托車嗎？

Level 1
Level 2
漸入佳境、學習零壓力——邁向常用2200單字
Level 3
Level 4
Level 5
Level 6

mov·a·ble [ˋmuvəbl]　🔊 *Track 1634*

形 可移動的　同 mobile 移動式的
▶This dresser（化妝台）is movable.
這個梳妝檯是可移動的。

MRT/mass rapid transit/sub·way/un·der·ground/me·tro　🔊 *Track 1635*

[mæsˋræpɪdˋtrænsɪt]/[ˋsʌbˏwe]/[ˋʌndɚˏgraʊnd]/[ˋmɛtro]
名 地下道、地下鐵
▶How long does it take for you to go to work by MRT?
你搭乘捷運去上班要多久時間？

mule [mjul]　🔊 *Track 1636*

名 騾
▶He is as stubborn as a mule. Don't try to convince him.
他和驢子一樣頑固。不用嘗試說服他了。

mul·ti·ply [ˋmʌltəplaɪ]　🔊 *Track 1637*

動 增加、繁殖、相乘
▶Let's multiply the height by the width to determine（確定）the area. 我們用寬乘以高來確定面積。

mu·se·um [mjuˋziəm]　🔊 *Track 1638*

名 博物館
▶We visited the National Historical Museum on our school trip.
我們校外教學去參觀國家歷史博物館。

mu·si·cian [mjuˋzɪʃən]　🔊 *Track 1639*

名 音樂家
▶He's a talented musician, but he gave up music to work as a lawyer.
他是個天才音樂家，但他卻放棄了音樂，跑去當律師。

萬用延伸句型
要表達某人很有天分，可以說：He / She has talent. 或是 He / She is talented.

[Nn]

nail [nel]　🔊 *Track 1640*

名 指甲、釘子 動 敲
▶名 She's painting my nails right now so can't come to the phone. 她現在不能接電話，因為她正在幫我擦指甲油。
▶動 We should nail these boards together.
我們應該要把這些木板釘在一起。

na·ked [ˋnekɪd]　🔊 *Track 1641*

形 裸露的、赤裸的
▶We cannot observe the solar eclipse with naked eyes.
我們不能用肉眼觀察日蝕。

nap·kin [ˈnæpkɪn] 🔊 *Track 1642*

名 餐巾紙 同 towel 紙巾

▶Would you please pass me some napkins? I need to wipe（擦）my mouth.
請你遞給我一些餐巾紙好嗎？我要擦一下嘴巴。

nar·row [ˈnæro] 🔊 *Track 1643*

形 窄的、狹長的 動 變窄 同 tight 緊的

▶形 The bridge is too narrow for two trucks to pass.
這座橋太窄，兩輛卡車無法並排通過。

▶動 The road narrows here, so you need to drive carefully.
路在這裡變窄了，你要小心點開車。

文法字詞解析
第二個例句也可以用 because 來寫，變成：
You need to drive carefully because the road narrows here.
要注意 because、so 不能同時出現。

na·tion·al [ˈnæʃənl] 🔊 *Track 1644*

形 國家的

▶We saluted to the national anthem.
我們對國歌表示尊敬。

nat·u·ral [ˈnætʃərəl] 🔊 *Track 1645*

形 天然生成的

▶Many natural disasters（自然災害）happened this year.
今年發生了不少自然災害。

naugh·ty [ˈnɔtɪ] 🔊 *Track 1646*

形 不服從的、淘氣的

▶The boy is quite naughty both at home and at school.
這個小男孩在家或在學校都很頑皮。

near·by [ˈnɪrˈbaɪ] 🔊 *Track 1647*

形 短距離內的 副 不遠地 同 around 附近

▶形 We planned to dine at a nearby restaurant this evening.
我們計劃今晚在附近的餐館吃飯。

▶副 Will you stop nearby for lunch with us, Bob?
鮑伯，你願意在附近停下來跟我們吃頓飯嗎？

萬用延伸句型
Will you / Would you...?
你是否願意……？

near·ly [ˈnɪrlɪ] 🔊 *Track 1648*

副 幾乎 同 almost 幾乎

▶He is nearly as tall as my brother. 他幾乎和我的哥哥一樣高。

neat [nit] 🔊 *Track 1649*

形 整潔的 反 dirty 髒的

▶One who is organized always keeps his/her desk clean and neat.
很有規劃的人總是保持桌面整潔。

文法字詞解析
寫作的時候要注意，中文裡面非特定的性別時可以用「他」來一以代之，但英文則要將「his / her」都寫出來才行。

nec·es·sa·ry [ˈnɛsəˌsɛrɪ] 🔊 *Track 1650*

形 必要的、不可缺少的

▶It took me a whole month to prepare all the necessary materials.
我花了整整一個月的時間才準備好所有必需的資料。

Level 1
Level 2
Level 3
Level 4
Level 5
Level 6

漸入佳境、學習零壓力——
邁向常用2200單字

neck·lace [`nɛklɪs]
◀€ *Track 1651*

名 項圈、項鍊

▶She doesn't like wearing necklaces. 她不喜歡戴項鍊。

nee·dle [`nidl̩]
◀€ *Track 1652*

名 針、縫衣針 動 用針縫

▶名 I am afraid of the needle.
我害怕針頭。

▶動 She needled the blisters（水泡）on his feet.
她刺破了他腳上的水泡。

文法字詞解析
You are trying to find a needle in a haystack.
你這是在大海撈針。

neg·a·tive [`nɛgətɪv]
◀€ *Track 1653*

形 否定的、消極的 名 反駁、否認、陰性

▶形 It is no wonder that he has a negative opinion on this matter. 難怪他對這件事持反對意見。

▶名 I ran a test on his blood, but the result was negative.
我驗了一下他的血，不過結果是陰性的。

neigh·bor [`nebɚ]
◀€ *Track 1654*

動 靠近於…… 名 鄰居

▶動 Our school neighbors a giant park.
我們學校靠近一個很大的公園。

▶名 I don't like leaving our child in the care of a neighbor.
我不喜歡把孩子留給鄰居照顧。

nei·ther [`niðɚ]
◀€ *Track 1655*

副 兩者都不 代 也非、也不 連 兩者都不 反 both 兩者都

▶副 If you're not going, then neither am I.
如果你不去的話，那我也不去。

▶代 Neither of us would take the alternative course.
我們兩人都沒要修這堂選修課。

▶連 Neither Mike nor I have seen this film.
麥克和我都沒有看過這部電影。

文法字詞解析
either 和 neither 都有否定的意思，但 either 表示「也」，neither 則表示「也不」。所以兩者用法並不相同。
例如：I'm not clever. My brother is not, either.
如果要用 neither 說明同一件事的話，則必須這樣寫：I'm not clever. Neither is my brother.

neph·ew [`nɛfju]
◀€ *Track 1656*

名 姪子、外甥

▶My nephew is a member of the school basketball team.
我姪子是籃球校隊的一名隊員。

nest [nɛst]
◀€ *Track 1657*

名 鳥巢 動 築巢

▶名 There were several swallows living in the nest under the roof of our house. 我們家屋簷下的鳥窩中住著幾隻燕子。

▶動 There are several birds nesting in the oak（橡樹）tree.
有幾隻鳥在橡樹上築巢。

net [nɛt]
◀€ *Track 1658*

名 網 動 用網捕捉、結網

▶名 Some small fishes escaped through the meshes.
有些小於從魚網隙縫逃走了。

▶動 The little boy netted a butterfly easily.
小男孩輕易地就用網子捕捉到蝴蝶。

niece [nis]
Track 1659

名 姪女、外甥女

▶My niece is a beautiful young lady.
我的姪女是個美麗的年輕女性。

no·bod·y ['noˌbɑdɪ]
Track 1660

代 無人 名 無名小卒

▶代 Nobody cares where you're going. 沒人管你要去哪裡啦。
▶名 He's just a nobody in the industry（業界）.
他在業界只不過是個無名小卒。

nod [nɑd]
Track 1661

動 點、彎曲 名 點頭

▶動 In India, people may nod to show disagreement.
印度人點頭可能是表示不同意。
▶名 He gave me a nod as he walked by.
他走過的時候對我點了個頭。

none [nʌn]
Track 1662

代 沒有人

▶If you want a tutor（家庭教師）, there is none better than my sister.
如果你想找一個家教的話，那我妹妹再適合不過了。

noo·dle ['nudḷ]
Track 1663

名 麵條

▶Instant noodles in Japan are know for their variety of flavors.
日本泡麵以多種口味而著名。

north·ern ['nɔrðɚn]
Track 1664

形 北方的

▶It took me fifteen minutes to reach the park in the northern part of the city.
我花了十五分鐘才到達了城市北部的那個公園。

note·book ['notˌbʊk]
Track 1665

名 筆記本

▶I need a new notebook; my current one isn't big enough.
我需要一本新的筆記本，我現在這本不夠大。

nov·el ['nɑvḷ]
Track 1666

形 新穎的、新奇的 名 長篇小說 同 original 新穎的

▶形 Everyone thinks that the design is very novel.
大家都認為這個設計很新穎。
▶名 He likes to sit in bed and read novels.
他喜歡坐在床上看小說。

nut [nʌt]
Track 1667

名 堅果、螺帽

▶Experts say that nuts are good for our health.
專家們都說堅果有益於身體健康。

文法字詞解析
當 none 做為一個句子的主詞，並且牽涉到一個群體裡的人時，動詞可以用單數或複數的形態表示。
例如：None of them are interested in this film.
他們之中沒有一個人對這部電影有興趣。

文法字詞解析
在第二個例句中，因為床是軟的，坐在床上時會陷進床墊中，所以介係詞用 sit「in」bed。

Level 1
Level 2
漸入佳境、學習零壓力──邁向常用2200單字
Level 3
Level 4
Level 5
Level 6

[Oo]

o·bey [ə`be]
◀ *Track 1668*

動 遵行、服從 同 submit 服從

▶If you don't obey the rules, you may fail the professional test.
如果你不遵守規則，你可能無法通過這項專業考試。

ob·ject [əb`dʒɛkt]
◀ *Track 1669*

名 物體 動 抗議、反對 同 thing 物、東西 反 agree 同意

▶名 No one knows the names of the objects in this lab（實驗室）.沒人知道這個實驗室裡這些物體的名稱。

▶動 I object to his suggestion.
我反對他的提議。

oc·cur [ə`kɝ]
◀ *Track 1670*

動 發生、存在、出現 同 happen 發生

▶Did anything strange occur when I was gone?
我不在的時候有發生什麼奇怪的事嗎？

of·fer [`ɔfɚ]
◀ *Track 1671*

名 提供 動 建議、提供

▶名 Would you please give me a special offer?
請你給我一個特別優惠價好嗎？

▶動 He offered me a glass of wine.
他問我要不要一杯葡萄酒。

of·fi·cial [ə`fɪʃəl]
◀ *Track 1672*

形 官方的、法定的 名 官員、公務員 同 authorize 公認

▶形 This is the group's official website.
這是個團體的官方網站。

▶名 In my opinion, he is a pompous（傲慢自大的）official.
在我看來，他是個傲慢自大的官員。

萬用延伸句型
In my opinion,... 依我看來，……。這個句型可以用來闡述自己的看法、意見。其他類似的開頭語還有 To me, In my (point of) view, As for me 等。

o·mit [o`mɪt]
◀ *Track 1673*

動 遺漏、省略、忽略 同 neglect 忽略

▶We omitted some superfluous sentences in the article.
我們將文章中多餘的句子刪除掉。

on·ion [`ʌnjən]
◀ *Track 1674*

名 洋蔥

▶My son hates eating onions.
我兒子討厭吃洋蔥。

op·er·ate [`ɑpəˌret]
◀ *Track 1675*

動 運轉、操作

▶Follow the manual and you will know how to operate the machine.
跟著操作手冊指示，你就會知道如何操作機器。

文法字詞解析
這個單字也有「進行手術」的意思，而「為（某人）進行手術」即是「operate on (somebody)」。因此手術室常稱為 operating room / operating theater。

o·pin·ion [ə`pɪnjən]　◀€ Track 1676

名 觀點、意見　同 view 觀點

▶In my opinion, he is not capable（有能力的）enough to cope（對付）with such a difficult affair.
在我看來，他處理這件如此棘手的事情能力還不夠。

or·di·nar·y [`ɔrdn͵ɛrɪ]　◀€ Track 1677

形 普通的　同 usual 平常的

▶I'm just an ordinary girl with ordinary dreams.
我只是個普通的女孩，有著普通的夢想。

文法字詞解析
在 ordinary 前面加上字首 extra-（特別地、超乎一般地）就變成了 extraordinary「異常的、非凡的」。

or·gan [`ɔrgən]　◀€ Track 1678

名 器官

▶It is said 3D printing techniques can be used to manufacture human organs.
據說3D列印技術可以製造出人類的器官。

or·gan·i·za·tion [͵ɔrgənə`zeʃən]　◀€ Track 1679

名 組織、機構　同 institution 機構

▶I'm not clever enough to be the brains of the organization.
我不夠聰明，沒有資格成為這個組織的軍師。

文法字詞解析
brain 如果用複數時，代表某個非常有智慧、有能力的人

or·gan·ize [`ɔrgən͵aɪz]　◀€ Track 1680

動 組織、系統化

▶Organizing a conference would take a lot of time.
籌辦研討會要花很多時間。

ov·en [`ʌvən]　◀€ Track 1681

名 爐子、烤箱　同 stove 爐子

▶I hope I didn't leave the oven on.
希望我沒忘記關烤箱。

o·ver·pass [͵ovə`pæs]　◀€ Track 1682

名 天橋、高架橋

▶Traffic has become smoother after they constructed（建造）the overpass.
他們建了那個高架橋後交通就變得比較順暢了。

over·seas [͵ovə`siz]　◀€ Track 1683

形 國外的、在國外的　副 在海外、在國外　同 abroad 在國外

▶形 Over the years, hundreds of overseas students have studied at that university（大學）.
幾年來，有幾百個留學生在那所大學裡唸過書。

▶副 Some of my colleagues were sent overseas to expand our market.
我有一些同事被派駐海外拓展市場。

owl [aʊl]　◀€ Track 1684

名 貓頭鷹

▶My pet owl is always sleeping. 我的寵物貓頭鷹總是在睡覺。

Level 1

Level 2

漸入佳境、學習零壓力──
邁向常用2200單字

Level 3

Level 4

Level 5

Level 6

own·er [ˈonɚ]
Track 1685

名 物主、所有者 同 holder 持有者

▶The owner of the dog didn't use a leash when waking it.
這隻狗的主人遛狗時沒有用牽繩。

ox [ɑks]
Track 1686

名 公牛

名詞複數 oxen

▶The ox was mad and started chasing after us.
那頭公牛生氣了，在我們後面跑。

[Pp]

pack [pæk]
Track 1687

名 一包 動 打包

▶名 Will you buy three packs of gum（口香糖）for my kid on your way home?
你能在回家的路上幫我家小孩買三盒口香糖回來嗎？

▶動 How will you pack the goods we ordered?
你們將如何包裝我們訂購的貨物？

pac·kage [ˈpækɪdʒ]
Track 1688

名 包裹 動 包裝

▶名 A package was sent to you this morning.
今早有個包裹寄來給你。

▶動 Products（產品）packaged in beautiful wrappers（包裝紙）sell well. 包著漂亮包裝紙的產品銷量很好。

pain [pen]
Track 1689

名 疼痛 動 傷害

▶名 The pain was too much and he fainted（昏倒）.
實在太疼痛了，於是他昏了過去。

▶動 It pains me to hear you cry. 聽到你哭，我就覺得心痛。

pain·ful [ˈpenfəl]
Track 1690

形 痛苦的

▶Would you please not discuss this painful subject anymore?
請不要再談論這件痛苦的事情了，好嗎？

paint·er [ˈpentɚ]
Track 1691

名 畫家

▶I saw the painter being interviewed on TV last night.
我昨晚在電視上看到這名畫家在受訪。

paint·ing [ˈpentɪŋ]
Track 1692

名 繪畫

▶There are three paintings on the wall; which one do you like best? 牆上有三幅畫，你最喜歡哪一幅呢？

文法字詞解析

這句也可以改寫成：Do you know to whom the dog belongs? 在這個句子中，使用到片語「belongs to sb.」，其中 sb. 是受詞，所以句子裡的代名詞要用 whom 而不是 who。

文法字詞解析

第一個例句中，pain 是名詞，所以要用限定詞 much 來修飾；如果說：「It was so painful that he fainted.」的話，painful 是形容詞，所以可以直接用副詞 so 來修飾。

pa·ja·mas [pə`dʒæməz]
◄≡ Track 1693

名 睡衣

名詞複數 pajamas

▶The man was sleepwalking in his pajamas on the street.
這個人穿著睡衣夢遊走在街上。

palm [pɑm]
◄≡ Track 1694

名 手掌

▶Do you believe in palm reading? 你相信掌紋算命嗎？

pan [pæn]
◄≡ Track 1695

名 平底鍋

▶She hit the thief with a frying pan. 她用平底鍋打了那個小偷。

pan·da [`pændə]
◄≡ Track 1696

名 貓熊

▶Pandas are very rare animals. 貓熊是很稀有的動物。

pa·pa·ya [pə`paɪə]
◄≡ Track 1697

名 木瓜

▶I can't stand the smell of papaya.
我受不了木瓜聞起來的味道。

par·don [`pɑrdṇ]
◄≡ Track 1698

名 原諒 動 寬恕 同 forgive 原諒

▶名 I beg your pardon; It is too noisy for me to hear clearly（清楚地）.
麻煩再說一次好嗎？這裡太吵了，我聽不太清楚。

▶動 We can't pardon this kind of rudeness（無禮）.
我們不能原諒這種無禮行為。

萬用延伸句型
I beg your pardon. 麻煩再說一次。或者也可以很簡潔地說「Pardon?」。

par·rot [`pærət]
◄≡ Track 1699

名 鸚鵡

▶Why do parrots like to repeat what people say?
為什麼鸚鵡喜歡學人說話？

par·tic·u·lar [pə`tɪkjələ]
◄≡ Track 1700

形 特別的 同 special 特別的

▶This is a particular case that should be looked at carefully.
這是一種特殊情況，必須仔細研究。

part·ner [`pɑrtnə]
◄≡ Track 1701

名 夥伴

▶We used to be business partners, but we are no longer business partners.
我們以前是生意的夥伴，但不再合作了。

pas·sen·ger [`pæsṇdʒə]
◄≡ Track 1702

名 旅客

▶There are plenty of passengers on the plane flying to New York. 飛往紐約的飛機上有相當多的乘客。

Level 1

Level 2

漸入佳境、學習零壓力——
邁向常用2200單字

Level 3

Level 4

Level 5

Level 6

paste [pest]　🔊 *Track 1703*

名 漿糊 動 黏貼 同 glue 黏著劑、膠水

▶名 The boy glued the paper together with paste.
那個男孩用漿糊把紙黏在一起。

▶動 Paste this note on the board, please.
請把這張紙條貼在板子上。

pat [pæt]　🔊 *Track 1704*

動 輕拍 名 拍 同 tap 輕拍

▶動 To comfort the crying girl, I patted her on the shoulder.
為了安慰這個哭泣的女孩，我拍了拍她的肩膀。

▶名 He gave me a pat on the back as he left the room.
他離開房間時輕拍了一下我的背。

path [pæθ]　🔊 *Track 1705*

名 路徑 同 route 路程

▶Would you tell me which path leads to the village?
你能告訴我哪條路通往那個小村莊嗎？

pa·tient [ˈpeʃənt]　🔊 *Track 1706*

形 忍耐的 名 病人

▶形 He was not patient enough to listen to what I said.
他沒有耐心來聽完我的話。

▶名 The doctor must make sure that the patient has enough time to rest.
醫生必須保證病人有足夠的時間休息。

pat·tern [ˈpætən]　🔊 *Track 1707*

名 模型、圖樣 動 仿照

▶名 The pattern on the cloth looks very fashionable.
這塊布上的圖樣看起來很有時尚感。

▶動 We patterned the plan after his old one.
我們這次的計畫是仿照他之前的那個訂的。

peace [pis]　🔊 *Track 1708*

名 和平 反 war 戰爭

▶He likes his peace and quiet. 他喜歡過著和平安靜的生活。

peace·ful [ˈpisfəl]　🔊 *Track 1709*

形 和平的 同 quiet 平靜的

▶The peaceful atmosphere in the church made me feel calm.
教堂裡和平的氣氛使我很平靜。

peach [pitʃ]　🔊 *Track 1710*

名 桃子

▶Wash the peach before you eat it.
吃桃子前要先洗一下。

pea·nut [ˈpiˌnʌt]　🔊 *Track 1711*

名 花生

▶I'm allergic to peanuts. 我對花生過敏。

萬用延伸句型

be off the beaten path 位置偏僻、位於較少人知道的地方
例 如：This restaurant is off the beaten path and gets fewer customers.
這家餐廳位置鮮為人知，因此顧客較少。

萬用延伸句型

hold one's peace 描述「雖然有話想說，但還是忍住，硬吞了下去」的情境。
例如：I knew my mom would get mad if I complained, so I held my peace.
我知道如果我抱怨的話我媽一定會生氣，所以我還是忍住了。

pear [pɛr] ◀≦ *Track 1712*

名 梨子

▶The pears he gave us were very juicy.
他給我們的梨子很多汁。

pen·guin [ˈpɛngwɪn] ◀≦ *Track 1713*

名 企鵝

▶Penguins like cold environments.
企鵝喜歡寒冷的環境。

pep·per [ˈpɛpɚ] ◀≦ *Track 1714*

名 胡椒

▶I added some pepper to the corn soup to increase flavor.
我加了胡椒在湯裡以增添風味。

per [pɚ] ◀≦ *Track 1715*

介 每、經由 同 through 經由

▶Would you like to send these goods per rail, or per plane?
你是想通過鐵路來送這些貨物,還是飛機呢?

per·fect [ˈpɝfɪkt] ◀≦ *Track 1716*

形 完美的 同 ideal 完美的、理想的

▶She's perfect in my eyes.
在我的眼中她是最完美的。

pe·ri·od [ˈpɪrɪəd] ◀≦ *Track 1717*

名 期間、時代 同 era 時代

▶During the period, people would know their neighbors quite well.
在這個時期,人們和鄰居都互相熟識。

per·son·al [ˈpɝsn̩l] ◀≦ *Track 1718*

形 個人的 同 private 私人的

▶Would you like to open a personal account in our bank?
你想在我們銀行開一個個人帳戶嗎?

pho·to·graph/pho·to ◀≦ *Track 1719*

[ˈfotəˌgræf]/[ˈfoto]

名 照片 動 照相

▶名 Look at this cute photo of my baby!
快看看我寶寶這張可愛的照片!

▶動 He's trying to photograph the foxes but they keep moving around.
他正在試著拍下那些狐狸,可是牠們一直動來動去的。

pho·tog·ra·pher [fəˈtɑgrəfɚ] ◀≦ *Track 1720*

名 攝影師

▶The photographer explained how to make good composition for a photo.
攝影師解釋如何為相片做出好的構圖。

文法字詞解析
environment 既是可數也是不可數名詞,不可數的時候代表「自然環境」,可數的時候表示特定地區、有特定的氣溫和特定動植物生存的地方。

文法字詞解析
英文之中的「句號」也稱為 period。

Level
1

Level
2

漸入佳境、學習零壓力——
邁向常用2200單字

Level
3

Level
4

Level
5

Level
6

phrase [frez] 🔊 *Track 1721*

名 片語 動 表意

▶名 We tried to avoid colloquial phrases in the PowerPoint slides. 我們試著避免在投影片上使用過於口語的詞彙。

▶動 I'm not sure how to phrase it, so let me just show you in a picture.
我不知道怎麼講才能表達我的意思，所以讓我直接用圖解的跟你說明好了。

pick [pɪk] 🔊 *Track 1722*

動 摘、選擇 名 選擇

▶動 Would you please pick up the yellow wallet for me?
請你幫我把那個黃色錢包撿起來好嗎？

▶名 Here are twenty books. Take your pick!
這裡有二十本書，你隨意挑吧！

pic·nic [ˈpɪknɪk] 🔊 *Track 1723*

名 野餐 動 去野餐

▶名 We always have picnics when the weather is fine.
天氣好的時候我們總是會去野餐。

▶動 This is a nice park to picnic in.
這個公園很適合野餐。

pi·geon [ˈpɪdʒən] 🔊 *Track 1724*

名 鴿子 同 dove 鴿子

▶It is no wonder that people like pigeons. They are a symbol of peace. 難怪人們喜愛鴿子。牠們是和平的象徵。

pile [paɪl] 🔊 *Track 1725*

名 堆 動 堆積 同 heap 堆積

▶名 I had a pile of test sheets in my locker.
我的置物櫃裡有一大疊考卷。

▶動 Can you pile the files （文件） over there?
你可以把文件在那邊堆成一疊嗎？

pil·low [ˈpɪlo] 🔊 *Track 1726*

名 枕頭 動 以……為枕 同 cushion 靠墊

▶名 Not everyone likes to sleep on a pillow, but some can't sleep without it.
不是每個人都喜歡枕著枕頭睡覺，但是有些人沒有枕頭睡不著覺。

▶動 The child pillowed his head on his mother's lap.
那個孩子把頭枕在媽媽的大腿上。

pin [pɪn] 🔊 *Track 1727*

名 針 動 釘住 同 clip 夾住

▶名 I used a pin to fix the notice on the bulletin board.
我用大頭針把這張通知固定在布告欄上。

▶動 She pinned a rose in her hair.
她在頭上別了一朵玫瑰。

萬用延伸句型

pick sb.'s nose 挖鼻孔
例　如：Stop picking your nose while eating!
不要一邊吃飯一邊挖鼻孔！

萬用延伸句型

be on pins and needles 非常焦慮
例如：I have been on pins and needles all day, waiting for news from the police station.
我整天都焦慮無比，等著警察局的消息。

pine·ap·ple [ˈpaɪnˌæpl] ◀≝ *Track 1728*

名 鳳梨
▶I like to eat pineapples very much. 我很喜歡吃鳳梨。

ping-pong/ta·ble ten·nis ◀≝ *Track 1729*
[ˈpɪŋˌpɑŋ]/[ˈtebḷˈtɛnɪs]

名 乒乓球
▶Ping-pong is the one sport I can play.
乒乓球是我唯一會的運動。

pink [pɪŋk] ◀≝ *Track 1730*

形 粉紅的 名 粉紅色
▶形 Do you like this pink skirt? I think it looks great on you.
你喜歡這件粉紅色的裙子嗎？我覺得它很適合你。
▶名 Why do so many girls like pink?
為什麼這麼多女生喜歡粉紅色？

文法字詞解析
衣服穿在某人身上的時候，介係詞要用
on，人穿著某件衣服時，介係詞要用 in。
例如：the T-shirt on her 她身上的 T 恤；
the girl in the blue T-shirt 穿著藍色 T 恤
的女孩。

pipe [paɪp] ◀≝ *Track 1731*

名 管子 動 以管傳送 同 tube 管子
▶名 It won't be long before the village gets water through pipes.
過不了多久那個村子就能透過水管獲得供水了。
▶動 The music is piped into the restaurant.
音樂透過纜線在餐廳內播送。

pitch [pɪtʃ] ◀≝ *Track 1732*

動 投擲、間距 同 throw 投、擲
▶I pitched the ball so far that the catcher wouldn't reach it.
我把球投太遠，捕手接不到。

piz·za [ˈpitsə] ◀≝ *Track 1733*

名 比薩
▶There was a traffic jam so my pizza was late.
因為塞車的關係，我的比薩很晚才送到。

plain [plen] ◀≝ *Track 1734*

形 平坦的 名 平原
▶形 It is quite plain that there are some mistakes in his test.
顯然他的試卷中有一些錯誤。
▶名 There is a road that goes straight across the plain.
有一條路筆直地穿過平原。

萬用延伸句型
It's quite plain that... 很顯然地。也可以
用 obviously 來表示。使用時，obviously
可以放在句首，或是放在動詞後面。

plan·et [ˈplænɪt] ◀≝ *Track 1735*

名 行星
▶Astronomers believe that there is live on other planets.
天文學家相信別的星球上是有生物的。

plate [plet] ◀≝ *Track 1736*

名 盤子 同 dish 盤子
▶My mom asked me to finish the food on the plate as soon as possible. 媽媽叫我快點把盤子裡的食物吃完。

Level 1

Level 2

漸入佳境、學習零壓力——
邁向常用2200單字

Level 3

Level 4

Level 5

Level 6

plat·form [ˈplætˌfɔrm]
◀€ *Track 1737*

名 平臺、月臺 同 stage 平臺

▶Rita saw her son off on the platform.
瑞塔在月台上為她兒子送別。

play·ful [ˈplefəl]
◀€ *Track 1738*

形 愛玩的

▶Is he always this playful? 他平常一直都這麼愛玩嗎？

pleas·ant [ˈplɛznt]
◀€ *Track 1739*

形 愉快的

▶The weather is really pleasant. 天氣很舒服。

pleas·ure [ˈplɛʒɚ]
◀€ *Track 1740*

名 愉悅 反 misery 悲慘

▶It's been a pleasure meeting you. 很高興認識你。

plus [plʌs]
◀€ *Track 1741*

介 加 名 加號 形 加的 同 additional 附加的

▶介 I want a burger plus large fries. 我要一個漢堡加大薯。

▶名 Positive attitude is always a plus on an interview.
正向的態度可以在面試中產生加分效果。

▶形 It's plus five degrees outside, not minus.
外面溫度是正五度，不是負五度。

po·em [ˈpoɪm]
◀€ *Track 1742*

名 詩

▶I don't really care for poems. 我實在對詩沒興趣。

po·et [ˈpoɪt]
◀€ *Track 1743*

名 詩人

▶It is no wonder that so many people like this poet and his
poems a lot. He is good at describing people's mood. 難怪這
麼多人都很喜歡這位詩人和他的詩。他很擅長描寫人的心情。

poi·son [ˈpɔɪzn]
◀€ *Track 1744*

名 毒藥 動 下毒

▶名 He put poison in his mother's tea.
他在他媽媽的茶裡放了毒藥。

▶動 He tried to poison the rats but the rats were too smart for
him. 他試著毒死老鼠，但老鼠都太聰明了。

pol·i·cy [ˈpɑləsɪ]
◀€ *Track 1745*

名 政策

▶The citizens hope the government can enforce（施行）the
new policy as soon as possible.
市民們希望政府能儘快施行這個新政策。

po·lite [pəˈlaɪt]
◀€ *Track 1746*

形 有禮貌的

▶Not every clerk in this bank is polite enough to the customers.
不是銀行的每位員工都對顧客夠禮貌。

文法字詞解析
形容詞字尾「-ful」表示「充滿……的」。

文法字詞解析
相反地，「沒禮貌的」則是「impolite」。

pop·u·lar [`pɑpjələ`]

Track 1747

形 流行的

▶K-pop is increasingly popular in Asia.
韓國流行音樂在亞洲越來越受歡迎。

pop·u·la·tion [ˌpɑpjəˋleʃən]

Track 1748

名 人口

▶Would you tell me what the population of the city is?
你能告訴我這個城市有多少人口嗎？

pork [pork]

Track 1749

名 豬肉

▶She doesn't eat pork. 她不吃豬肉。

文法字詞解析
肉類通常都是不可數名詞，例如：beef（牛肉）、pork（豬肉）、lamb（羊肉）。

port [port]

Track 1750

名 港口　同 harbor 海港

▶The port is not far from my home. 港口離我家不遠。

pose [poz]

Track 1751

動 擺出　名 姿勢　同 posture 姿勢

▶動 You should really pose this issue at the meeting.
你真的應該在會議上提出這個問題。

▶名 Teenagers like to have certain poses for their selfies.
青少年喜歡用特定一些姿態自拍。

pos·i·tive [`pɑzətɪv]

Track 1752

形 確信的、積極的、正的　同 certain 確信的

▶There is positive proof（證據）that the man next to me did it.
有確切的證據證明是我身旁的那個男人幹的。

pos·si·bil·i·ty [ˌpɑsəˋbɪlətɪ]

Track 1753

名 可能性

▶The possibility that he would accept our proposal is quite low.
他接受我們提案的可能性很低。

post [post]

Track 1754

名 郵件　動 郵寄、公佈、快速地

▶名 Would you please tell me where the nearest post office is?
請告訴我最近的郵局在哪好嗎？

▶動 Will you help me post this notice on the wall?
請你幫我把這個通知貼在牆上好嗎？

文法字詞解析
post 也可以用在「在網路上發表文章」，例如；She posted an article on Facebook. 她在臉書上發表了一篇文章。

post·card [`post.kard]

Track 1755

名 明信片

▶I sent my aunt a postcard while traveling in England.
我在英國旅行時，寄了明信片給我的阿姨。

pot [pɑt]

Track 1756

名 鍋、壺　同 vessel 器皿

▶Will you help me wash up those pots and plates in the kitchen?
幫忙我洗廚房裡的那些鍋碗瓢盆好嗎？

Level 1

Level 2

Level 3

Level 4

Level 5

Level 6

漸入佳境、學習零壓力——
邁向常用2200單字

po·ta·to [pə'teto] 　◀≣ *Track 1757*

名 馬鈴薯
▶Would you like a salad or a baked potato? Both of them are delicious.
你想要一份沙拉還是烤馬鈴薯？它們都很美味。

萬用延伸句型
Would you like A or B？你比較想要 A 還是 B？也可以説：Do you prefer A or B?

pound [paʊnd] 　◀≣ *Track 1758*

名 磅、英磅 動 重擊
▶名 Not all the people are willing to buy potatoes at the price of five dollars per pound.
不是所有人都願意買五美元一磅的馬鈴薯。
▶動 Gary was so angry that he pounded the wall, which scared his kids.
蓋瑞生氣到用手捶牆壁，嚇到他小孩。

pow·er·ful [`paʊɚfəl] 　◀≣ *Track 1759*

形 有力的
▶The bomb is powerful enough to destroy this whole village.
這枚炸彈威力很大，足以毀滅整個村莊。

praise [prez] 　◀≣ *Track 1760*

動 稱讚 名 榮耀 同 compliment 稱讚
▶動 He praised his children a lot.
他經常稱讚自己的孩子。
▶名 Don't be so humble! You deserve（值得）the praise.
不用這麼謙虛，你本來就很值得被稱讚啊。

文法字詞解析
第二個例句使用了省略主詞的祈使句句型，祈使句的否定形式是在動詞的前面加上 don't 或 never。此外因為使用祈使句時，説話的對象通常都在説話者的身邊，主詞不是「你」就是「我們」，所以不會有「doesn't」的情況出現。

pray [pre] 　◀≣ *Track 1761*

動 祈禱 同 beg 祈求
▶The Prime minister prayed for peace in the country in the shrine.
首相在寺廟裡祈求國內和平。

pre·fer [prɪ'fɝ] 　◀≣ *Track 1762*

動 偏愛、較喜歡 同 favor 偏愛
▶Would you tell me which flavor（口味）you prefer?
你能告訴我你比較喜歡哪一種口味嗎？

pres·ence [`prɛzn̩s] 　◀≣ *Track 1763*

名 出席 同 attendance 出席
▶We have to talk about the issue at his presence.
必須要他在場，我們才能談這個議題。

pres·ent [`prɛzn̩t] 　◀≣ *Track 1764*

形 目前的 名 片刻、禮物 動 呈現 同 gift 禮物
▶形 How many of the group are present today?
今天這組有多少人出席？
▶名 Are you sure you want to get her a chicken for present?
你確定你真的要送她一隻雞當禮物嗎？
▶動 The situation（情勢）presents a serious problem.
這個事態引起了嚴重的問題。

pres·i·dent [ˈprɛzədənt]
◀ Track 1765

名 總統
▶She is elected as the president of the student association.
她被選為學生會會長。

press [prɛs]
◀ Track 1766

名 印刷機、新聞界 動 壓下、強迫 同 force 強迫
▶名 The press got really excited over this scandal（醜聞）.
新聞界因為這件醜聞非常興奮。
▶動 If you press the button, terrible things will happen.
如果按下這個按鈕會發生很可怕的事喔。

pride [praɪd]
◀ Track 1767

名 自豪 動 使自豪
▶名 I take pride in being your friend.
能和你作朋友，我很自豪。
▶動 She prided herself on her cooking.
她因自己善於烹飪而自豪。

prince [prɪns]
◀ Track 1768

名 王子
▶Have you ever seen Prince William? What does he look like?
你見過威廉王子嗎？他長什麼樣子呢？

prin·cess [ˈprɪnsɪs]
◀ Track 1769

名 公主
▶Not all people know well of the princess and her family.
不是所有人都很瞭解這位公主和她的家庭。

prin·ci·pal [ˈprɪnsəpl̩]
◀ Track 1770

形 首要的 名 校長、首長
▶形 Our principal problem is that we lack money.
我們的主要問題是缺錢。
▶名 Our principal encourages us to join more extracurricular activities.
校長鼓勵我們多參加課外活動。

文法字詞解析
要注意 lack 的詞性，才能確定後面要不要放介係詞。如果是動詞的話，後面要直接接受詞，如果是名詞的話，後面則要加上介係詞 of 才能再接受詞。

prin·ci·ple [ˈprɪnsəpl̩]
◀ Track 1771

名 原則 同 standard 規範
▶He's a man with no principles.
他是個沒原則的男人。

print·er [ˈprɪntɚ]
◀ Track 1772

名 印刷工、印表機
▶What's the matter with this printer? 這台印表機怎麼了？

pris·on [ˈprɪzn̩]
◀ Track 1773

名 監獄 同 jail 監獄
▶He was put into prison for robbing the bank.
他因為搶了銀行而被關進監獄了。

Level 1
Level 2
Level 3
Level 4
Level 5
Level 6

漸入佳境、學習零壓力──
邁向常用2200單字

pris·on·er [ˈprɪznɚ]　◀€ *Track 1774*

名 囚犯

▶The prisoners are planning to escape from the jail.
囚犯在計畫越獄。

pri·vate [ˈpraɪvɪt]　◀€ *Track 1775*

形 私密的

▶Did you have a private talk with the man who came to your office yesterday?
你有跟昨天到你辦公室來的那個人私下談談嗎？

prize [praɪz]　◀€ *Track 1776*

名 獎品 動 獎賞、撬開 同 reward 獎品

▶名 He hurt his foot and didn't get the first prize in this race（賽跑）.他的腳受傷了，所以在這次賽跑中沒能獲得第一名。

▶動 He prized the box open with an iron bar.
他用一根鐵棒把那箱子撬開。

> **文法字詞解析**
> prize 解釋做「撬開」時是及物動詞，但受詞的後方一定要加上副詞或介係詞。

pro·duce [prəˈdjus]/[ˈpradjus]　◀€ *Track 1777*

動 生產 名 產品 同 make 生產

▶動 The writer could produce more than three novels within a year. 這位作者一年可以產出三本小說。

▶名 The place is known for its dairy（乳製品的）produce.
這地方因生產乳製品而出名。

> **文法字詞解析**
> be known 後面加上不同的介係詞會產生不同的用法，因此常常會讓人混淆。除了 be known for（因……而著名）之外，還有「be known as（以做為……而著名」，以及「be known to（為……所知）」。

pro·duc·er [prəˈdjusɚ]　◀€ *Track 1778*

名 製造者

▶This company is the best car producer in this area.
這家公司是該地區最好的汽車製造者。

pro·gress [ˈpragrɛs]/[prəˈgrɛs]　◀€ *Track 1779*

名 進展 動 進行 同 proceed 進行

▶名 It took us a month to make some progress.
我們花了一個月的時間才取得了一點進展。

▶動 They had to revise（修改）the plan so as to progress their project smoothly（順利地）.
為了使工程能順利進行，他們必須修改方案。

proj·ect [ˈpradʒɛkt]/[prəˈdʒɛkt]　◀€ *Track 1780*

名 計畫 動 推出、投射

▶名 We are determined（堅決的）to finish the project.
我們決心完成這項計畫。

▶動 Don't project your own evil thoughts onto other people.
別把自己邪惡的想法投射在其他人身上。

prom·ise [ˈpramɪs]　◀€ *Track 1781*

名 諾言 動 約定 同 swear 承諾

▶名 He never keeps his promises. 他從來不信守諾言。

▶動 I am sorry that I can't promise anything.
很抱歉我無法承諾什麼。

pro·nounce [prəˈnaʊns] ◀≋ Track 1782
動 發音
▶I had difficulty pronouncing the French word.
發音這個法文字，對我來說很難。

pro·pose [prəˈpoz] ◀≋ Track 1783
動 提議、求婚 同 offer 提議
▶Why don't you propose to her? 你為什麼不向她求婚呢？

pro·tect [prəˈtɛkt] ◀≋ Track 1784
動 保護
▶He is always working on protecting endangered（瀕臨絕種的）animals. 他總是致力於保護瀕臨絕種的動物。

proud [praʊd] ◀≋ Track 1785
形 驕傲的 同 arrogant 傲慢的
▶The mother is so proud of her son.
這位母親對兒子非常引以為傲。

pro·vide [prəˈvaɪd] ◀≋ Track 1786
動 提供 同 supply 提供
▶The Korean restaurant provides free side dishes.
這家韓式餐廳提供免費小菜。

pud·ding [ˈpʊdɪŋ] ◀≋ Track 1787
名 布丁
▶He ate up all the pudding. 他把所有的布丁都吃光了。

pump [pʌmp] ◀≋ Track 1788
名 抽水機 動 抽水、汲取
▶名 We need a new pump but I don't know where to get one.
我們需要新的抽水機，但我不知道去哪裡買。
▶動 He's helping us pump water out of the flooded house.
他正在幫我們將水從被淹沒的房子裡抽出去。

pump·kin [ˈpʌmpkɪn] ◀≋ Track 1789
名 南瓜
▶Would you like some pumpkin pie for a snack?
你要不要來點南瓜派當點心吃？

pun·ish [ˈpʌnɪʃ] ◀≋ Track 1790
動 處罰
▶To punish the cheating child, the teacher asked him to copy the while textbook.
為了懲罰作弊的小孩，老師要求他抄寫整本教科書。

pun·ish·ment [ˈpʌnɪʃmənt] ◀≋ Track 1791
名 處罰
▶Not all people believe that punishment is the only way to solve a problem.
不是所有人都認為懲罰是解決問題的唯一方法。

萬用延伸句型
do sb. proud 意為「讓某人感到驕傲」。也可以用反身代名詞表示「讓自己感到驕傲」。
例如：My son really did me proud by winning the race.
我兒子贏得比賽，真是太讓我感到驕傲了。
What an amazing cake! You really did yourself proud this time!
你這蛋糕烤得太棒了！你真應該為自己感到驕傲！

文法字詞解析
some 可以用來修飾可數或不可數名詞

Level 1
Level 2
Level 3
Level 4
Level 5
Level 6

漸入佳境、學習零壓力—邁向常用2200單字

pu·pil [ˈpjupl̩] ◀ Track 1792
名 學生、瞳孔 同 student 學生
▶The pupils are asked to search for information related to aborigines.
學生被要求檢索有關原住民的資料。

pup·pet [ˈpʌpɪt] ◀ Track 1793
名 木偶、傀儡 同 doll 玩偶
▶Would you like to take your little son to see a puppet show?
你要不要帶你的小兒子去看場木偶戲呢？

pup·py [ˈpʌpɪ] ◀ Track 1794
名 小狗
▶Why don't we buy a cute little puppy as her birthday present?
為什麼我們不買隻可愛的小狗給她當生日禮物呢？

purse [pɝs] ◀ Track 1795
名 錢包 同 wallet 錢包
▶Is this black purse yours?
這個黑色的錢包是你的嗎？

puz·zle [ˈpʌzl̩] ◀ Track 1796
名 難題、謎 動 迷惑 同 mystery 謎
▶名 The puzzle is too hard for me.
這謎題對我來說太難了。
▶動 We puzzled over the question for the whole afternoon.
我們整個下午都在苦思這個問題。

文法字詞解析
pupil 通常指的是中小學的學生，student 則可以是小學生、中學生、大學生。另外，如果要說某學生「就讀於某學校」的話，要說 a student at + (school)。

文法字詞解析
puzzle over sth. 花長時間苦思

[Qq]

qual·i·ty [ˈkwɑlətɪ] ◀ Track 1797
名 品質
▶The quality of service in this restaurant has improved a lot.
那個飯店的服務品質已經有了很大的改善。

quan·ti·ty [ˈkwɑntətɪ] ◀ Track 1798
名 數量
▶A large quantity of scarce metal was found in this area.
大量的稀有金屬在這一區被發現。

quar·ter [ˈkwɔrtɚ] ◀ Track 1799
名 四分之一 動 分為四等分
▶名 We pay our rent（租金）at the end of each quarter.
我們是在每個季末付房租的。
▶動 There are four people here; how about quartering the pizza?
這裡有四個人，我們把披薩餅分成四等份怎麼樣？

文法字詞解析
quarter 可以用來講時間和金錢，例如：a quarter to nine 表示「還有四分之一個小時就到九點」，也就是八點四十五分；a quarter past eight 表示「過了八點鐘之後的四分之一個鐘頭」，也就是八點十五分。用在金錢上，a quarter dollar 就是25分錢。

quit [kwɪt]
◀ *Track 1800*

動 離去、解除
▶You had better quit smoking. 你最好要戒菸。

文法字詞解析
quit 的動詞變化：quit, quit, quit

quiz [kwɪz]
◀ *Track 1801*

名 測驗 動 對……進行測驗 同 test 測驗
名詞複數 quizzes
▶名 We will have a quiz tomorrow morning.
我們明天早晨有一個小測驗。
▶動 The teacher quizzed us on the last chapter.
老師考了我們上一章的內容。

[Rr]

rab·bit [ˋræbɪt]
◀ *Track 1802*

名 兔子
▶My pet rabbit smells really bad. 我的寵物兔子真的很臭。

rain·y [ˋrenɪ]
◀ *Track 1803*

形 多雨的
▶It's often rainy in winter in this city.
這個城市冬天常下雨。

range [rendʒ]
◀ *Track 1804*

名 範圍 動 排列 同 limit 範圍
▶名 Will you provide us with products（產品）within the price range? 你能提供我們這種價格範圍內的產品嗎？
▶動 The price ranges from two thousand to five thousand.
價格的範圍在兩千到五千之間。

rap·id [ˋræpɪd]
◀ *Track 1805*

形 迅速的 同 quick 迅速的
▶The rapid development of Internet has made our life more convenient. 網路快速發展，使我們的生活更便利。

rare [rɛr]
◀ *Track 1806*

形 稀有的
▶This is a very rare kind of insect. 這是很稀有的一種昆蟲。

rath·er [ˋræðɚ]
◀ *Track 1807*

副 寧願
▶I would rather you choose this expensive one.
我寧願你選這個貴的。

real·i·ty [rɪˋælətɪ]
◀ *Track 1808*

名 真實 同 truth 真實
▶Virtual reality has been used in games and military training.
虛擬實境被應用在遊戲與軍事訓練上。

文法字詞解析
電視上常播的真人實境秀就稱為 reality TV。

Level 1

Level 2

漸入佳境、學習零壓力──
邁向常用2200單字

Level 3

Level 4

Level 5

Level 6

real·ize [ˋrɪəˌlaɪz]
◀€ *Track 1809*

動 實現、瞭解

▶To realize his dream, Hank sacrificed a lot.
為了實現夢想，他犧牲了很多。

re·cent [risn̩t]
◀€ *Track 1810*

形 最近的

▶Would you tell me what you have been busy doing in recent years? 你能告訴我你近幾年都在忙些什麼嗎？

re·cord [ˋrɛkəd]/[rɪˋkɔrd]
◀€ *Track 1811*

名 紀錄、唱片 動 記錄

▶名 She broke the world record set by herself.
她打破了自己所創的世界紀錄。

▶動 The song was recorded in our studio（工作室）.
這首歌是我們工作室裡錄的。

rec·tan·gle [ˋrɛktæŋgl̩]
◀€ *Track 1812*

名 長方形

▶The garden is shaped like a rectangle.
這個院子是長方形的。

re·frig·er·a·tor/ fridge/ice·box [rɪˋfrɪdʒəˌretə]/[frɪdʒ]/[ˋaɪsˌbɑks]
◀€ *Track 1813*

名 冰箱

▶Why don't you put the soup in the refrigerator?
你為什麼不把湯放到冰箱裡呢？。

re·fuse [rɪˋfjuz]
◀€ *Track 1814*

動 拒絕 同 reject 拒絕

▶Brian refused to admit his mistakes.
布萊恩拒絕承認他的錯誤。

re·gard [rɪˋgɑrd]
◀€ *Track 1815*

動 注視、認為 名 注視 同 judge 認為

▶動 It is no wonder that people in China regard pandas as their national treasure.
怪不得中國人把熊貓視為國寶。

▶名 She said you had no regard for her feelings.
她說你沒有考慮到她的心情。

re·gion [ˋridʒən]
◀€ *Track 1816*

名 區域 同 zone 區域

▶There aren't many houses in this region.
這個區域的房子不多

reg·u·lar [ˋrɛgjələ]
◀€ *Track 1817*

形 平常的、定期的、規律的 同 usual 平常的

▶We should keep regular hours to stay healthy.
我們應該作息規律以保持健康。

文法字詞解析
方形則是 square，而三角形稱作 triangle。

萬用延伸句型
hold sb. in high regard 非常尊敬某人
例如：The students have always held this professor in high regard.
學生們一直非常敬重這位教授。

re·ject [rɪˋdʒɛkt]
◀ Track 1818

動 拒絕
▶He asked her to be his girlfriend but was rejected.
他請她做他的女朋友，但被拒絕了。

re·la·tion [rɪˋleʃən]
◀ Track 1819

名 關係
▶What's the relation between these two matters?
這兩件是之間有何關聯呢？

re·la·tion·ship [rɪˋleʃənˏʃɪp]
◀ Track 1820

名 關係
▶We're all interested in the two actors' relationship.
我們都對那兩位演員的關係很感興趣。

萬用延伸句型
be in a relationship 正在交往中
例如：I can't believe you two have been in a relationship for two years and never told me.
真不敢相信你們已經交往兩年了，居然沒有告訴我。

re·peat [rɪˋpit]
◀ Track 1821

動 重複 名 重複
▶動 The pupils repeated the teachers' words.
學生重述了老師的話。
▶名 I'm tired of seeing all these repeats on TV.
電視上那些重複的節目我都看膩了。

re·ply [rɪˋplaɪ]
◀ Track 1822

名 回答、答覆 同 respond 回答
▶Please reply as soon as possible.
請儘快回覆。

re·port·er [rɪˋportɚ]
◀ Track 1823

名 記者 同 journalist 記者
▶The reporter is very tired after a long night at the scene of the accident.
那名記者在意外現場待了漫長的一晚後非常疲累。

re·quire [rɪˋkwaɪr]
◀ Track 1824

動 需要 同 need 需要
▶This position requires a good ability in organizing things.
要擔任這個職務，需要有好的組織籌畫能力。

re·quire·ment [rɪˋkwaɪrmənt]
◀ Track 1825

名 需要
▶Would you tell us what your company's requirements are?
能告訴我們，貴公司有哪些要求嗎？

re·spect [rɪˋspɛkt]
◀ Track 1826

名 尊重 動 尊重、尊敬 同 adore 尊敬
▶名 Let's show some respect to the elderly citizens.
我們要對年長者有一些尊敬。
▶動 You need to respect yourself before others can respect you.
在得到別人尊重前，你必須先尊重自己。

萬用延伸句型
pay sb. respect 對某人表現尊重
例如：You should pay your parents respect instead of being rude at them all the time.
你應該對你雙親尊重些，而不是老是對他們這麼無禮。

Level 1
Level 2
Level 3
Level 4
Level 5
Level 6

漸入佳境、學習零壓力──邁向常用2200單字

re·spon·si·ble [rɪ`spɑnsəbl] 🔊 *Track 1827*

形 負責任的

▶ I am responsible to take care of my pet.
我有責任要照顧我的寵物。

res·tau·rant [`rɛstərənt] 🔊 *Track 1828*

名 餐廳

▶ How about we find a restaurant and sit down?
我們找家餐廳坐下來好嗎？

rest·room [`rɛstrum] 🔊 *Track 1829*

名 洗手間、廁所

▶ Could you tell me where the restroom is? I can't find it in this building.
能告訴我洗手間在哪嗎？我在這棟樓裡找不到洗手間。

re·sult [rɪ`zʌlt] 🔊 *Track 1830*

名 結果 動 導致 同 consequence 結果

▶ 名 Would you tell me the final result of the poll（投票）?
能告訴我這次投票最後的結果嗎？

▶ 動 The accident resulted in many deaths.
這次意外造成不少人死亡。

萬用延伸句型

As a result, S. +V. 結果……
例如：She did exercise every morning since last winter. As a result, she has lost twenty pounds. 她從去年冬天就每天早上都做運動，結果她減了二十磅。

re·view [rɪ`vju] 🔊 *Track 1831*

名 複習 動 回顧、檢查 同 recall 回憶

▶ 名 It took us several weeks to have a review of the term's work. 我們花了幾週的時間來複習一學期的功課。

▶ 動 I jotted down some key points when reviewing the lesson.
我複習這一課時，寫下了一些重點。

rich·es [`rɪtʃɪz] 🔊 *Track 1832*

名 財產 同 wealth 財產

▶ Riches do not always bring contentment. 財富並不總使人滿足。

rock [rɑk] 🔊 *Track 1833*

動 搖動 名 岩石

▶ 動 She rocked the baby until he fell asleep.
她搖晃著寶寶直到他睡著為止。

▶ 名 You shouldn't let the kids climb those huge rocks.
你不應該讓孩子在那些大岩石上面爬。

rock·y [`rɑkɪ] 🔊 *Track 1834*

形 岩石的、搖擺的

▶ The landscape（地表）is really rocky there.
那裡的地形充滿了岩石。

文法字詞解析

形容詞字尾「-y」表示「某物有……的質地」。

role [rol] 🔊 *Track 1835*

名 角色

▶ Patience plays an important role when getting along with kids.
和小孩相處，耐心扮演重要的角色。

roy·al [ˋrɔɪəl] ◀╎ *Track 1836*

形 皇家的 同 noble 貴族的
▶The scandal of the royal family was a shocking news.
皇室家族的醜聞是個令人震驚的消息。

rude [rud] ◀╎ *Track 1837*

形 野蠻的、粗魯的
▶The boy is always so rude to his parents.
那個男孩總是對自己的父母很沒禮貌。

rul·er [ˋrulɚ] ◀╎ *Track 1838*

名 統治者 同 sovereign 統治者
▶The ruler of the country is quite stupid.
這個國家的統治者挺笨的。

run·ner [ˋrʌnɚ] ◀╎ *Track 1839*

名 跑者
▶Would you tell me which runner won the first place in this race?
你能告訴我哪位跑者在這次的比賽中獲得了第一嗎？

rush [rʌʃ] ◀╎ *Track 1840*

動 突擊 名 急忙、突進
▶動 Gary rushed to the airport for fear that he would miss his flight. 蓋瑞趕路到機場，怕錯過了他的班機。
▶名 It's a bit of a rush, but we'll still try to be there on time.
是有點趕啦，但我們會盡量準時到。

[Ss]

safe·ty [ˋseftɪ] ◀╎ *Track 1841*

名 安全 同 security 安全
▶Safety is what you should consider when traveling abroad.
去國外旅行，要注意安全。

sail·or [ˋselɚ] ◀╎ *Track 1842*

名 船員、海員
▶He has always dreamed of being a sailor.
他一直夢想著當一名船員。

sal·ad [ˋsæləd] ◀╎ *Track 1843*

名 生菜食品、沙拉
▶What do you want to eat? How about some fruit salad?
你想吃什麼？來點蘋果沙拉怎麼樣？

salt·y [ˋsɔltɪ] ◀╎ *Track 1844*

形 鹹的
▶The dish is too salty; I can't swallow it.
這道菜太鹹了；我吃不下去。

文法字詞解析

字尾「-er」表示「做……的人」，因此 ruler 就是「負責統治的人」，employer 就是「雇用他人的人」，也就是「雇主」。不過「-er」還有「用來做……的物品」之意，「rule」則有「畫線」的意思，所以「ruler」也可以是「用來畫線的工具」，也就是「尺」。

萬用延伸句型

「Right in front of my salad」是個口語説法，用於抱怨其他人竟當場在你面前做一些你不想看到的事時。例如你的朋友們突然在你面前激烈擁吻，你就可以説：Really? Right in front of my salad?（無論事情發生時你有沒有在吃沙拉，都可以這麼説。）

Level 1

Level 2

Level 3

Level 4

Level 5

Level 6

漸入佳境、學習零壓力——
邁向常用2200單字

sam·ple [ˈsæmpl̩]
🔊 Track 1845

名 樣本
▶We brought some samples for our client.
　我們拿了一些樣品給顧客。

sand·wich [ˈsændwɪtʃ]
🔊 Track 1846

名 三明治
▶The sandwich I got today tasted terrible.
　我今天買的那個三明治超難吃的。

sat·is·fy [ˈsætɪsˌfaɪ]
🔊 Track 1847

動 使滿足 同 please 使滿意
▶I guess not all people are satisfied with their jobs.
　我猜並不是所有的人都對他們的工作感到滿意。

sauce [sɔs]
🔊 Track 1848

名 調味醬 動 加調味醬於……
▶名 The chef used herbs to add flavor to the sauce.
　主廚用香草來替醬汁增加風味。
▶動 Would you like me to sauce the beef with pepper?
　你想不想要我用胡椒粉給牛肉調味？

sci·ence [ˈsɔsə]
🔊 Track 1849

名 科學
▶50 students graduated from the science department last year.
　去年有五十名理科畢業生。

萬用延伸句型
當有人覺得某事很難懂，可是你覺得根本簡單到不行時，就可以對他說：「It's not rocket science!」即「這又不是什麼太空科學之類的東西！」

sci·en·tist [ˈsaɪəntɪst]
🔊 Track 1850

名 科學家
▶Both his parents are distinguished scientists.
　他的父母都是卓越的科學家。

scis·sors [ˈsɪzɚz]
🔊 Track 1851

名 剪刀
名詞複數 scissors
▶Will you please pass me the scissors?
　請遞給我剪刀好嗎？

score [skor]
🔊 Track 1852

名 分數 動 得分、評分
▶名 I can never get a high score in math examinations.
　我總是無法在數學考試中獲得高分。
▶動 He scored a zero on the test.
　他在這次考試得了零分。

screen [skrin]
🔊 Track 1853

名 螢幕
▶We like to watch movies on the big screen.
　我們喜歡用大螢幕看電影。

文法字詞解析
the silver screen = 銀光幕、大銀幕

search [sɝtʃ] 🔊 *Track 1854*

動 搜索、搜尋 名 調查、檢索 同 seek 尋找

▶動 We searched for collocations in the English articles.
我們在這些英文文章中尋找常用的字詞搭配。

▶名 The police are off on a search for the lost child.
警察們正在尋找那個失蹤的孩子。

se·cret [`sikrɪt] 🔊 *Track 1855*

名 秘密

▶What do you think about arranging（安排）to let them meet in secret?
你覺得安排他們秘密會面怎麼樣？

sec·re·ta·ry [`sɛkrəˌtɛrɪ] 🔊 *Track 1856*

名 秘書

▶Not everyone can be an efficient（效率高的）secretary.
不是每個人都能成為一個高效率的秘書。

sec·tion [`sɛkʃən] 🔊 *Track 1857*

名 部分

▶Please don't smoke here. Go to the smoking section instead.
請不要在這裡吸菸，去吸菸區吧。

se·lect [sə`lɛkt] 🔊 *Track 1858*

動 挑選 同 pick 挑選

▶We selected the green scarf instead of the yellow one.
我們選擇綠色的、而不是黃色的圍巾。

se·lec·tion [sə`lɛkʃən] 🔊 *Track 1859*

名 選擇、選定

▶We have a selection of new and cheap skirts.
我們這裡有精選新且便宜的裙子。

se·mes·ter [sə`mɛstə] 🔊 *Track 1860*

名 半學年、一學期

▶George failed history last semester.
喬治上學期歷史被當了。

sep·a·rate [`sɛpəˌret] 🔊 *Track 1861*

形 分開的 動 分開

▶形 Would you please give us separate bedrooms?
請你為我們各自安排一個臥室好嗎？

▶動 Can you separate the apples from the peaches for me?
你可以幫我把蘋果和桃子分開放嗎？

se·ri·ous [`sɪrɪəs] 🔊 *Track 1862*

形 嚴肅的

▶Take it easy. It's nothing serious.
放輕鬆。這不是什麼嚴重的事。

ser·vant [ˈsɝvənt]
◀€ Track 1863

名 僕人、傭人
▶The cat thinks we're all her servants.
這隻貓覺得我們都是牠的僕人。

set·tle [ˈsɛtl̩]
◀€ Track 1864

動 安排、解決
▶After fighting with each other for ten days, we finally settled on this case. 吵架十天之後，我們終於和好了。

set·tle·ment [ˈsɛtl̩mənt]
◀€ Track 1865

名 解決、安排
▶I think there is no chance of a settlement for the dispute（糾紛）. 我認為這場糾紛根本無法解決。

share [ʃɛr]
◀€ Track 1866

名 份、佔有 動 共用
▶名 He gave his son a minor（較小的）share of his wealth（財產）. 他把小部分的財產分給了兒子。
▶動 Would you like to share your experience with us?
你願意跟我們分享你的經驗嗎？

shelf [ʃɛlf]
◀€ Track 1867

名 棚架、架子
▶There are many Russian（俄國的）romance（浪漫）novels on her shelves. 她的書架上有很多俄國愛情小說。

文法字詞解析
保存期限也可稱為「shelf life」，即某個食品能擺放在貨架上賣的期限。例如你可以說：Milk has a very short shelf life.
（牛奶的保存期限非常短。）

shell [ʃɛl]
◀€ Track 1868

名 貝殼 動 剝
▶名 The building was an empty（空的）shell after the fire.
這場大火過後，這座建築剩下的只是一個空殼。
▶動 It is no wonder that she shells peas（豌豆）so fast.
怪不得她剝豌豆剝得那麼快。

shock [ʃɑk]
◀€ Track 1869

名 衝擊 動 震撼、震驚 同 frighten 驚恐
▶名 His sudden death shocked us. 他驟逝的消息令我們震驚。
▶動 I was shocked to hear that she was actually forty. She looks eighteen!
聽到她居然四十歲，真是嚇死我了。她看起來像十八耶！

shoot [ʃut]
◀€ Track 1870

動 射傷、射擊 名 射擊、嫩芽
▶動 There was a man with a gun shooting at the crowds.
有一名持槍男子向人群射擊。
▶名 There are several deer eating the young shoots on the trees.
有幾頭鹿正在吃樹上的嫩枝。

文法字詞解析
shoot 的動詞變化：shoot, shot, shot

shorts [ʃɔrts]
◀€ Track 1871

名 短褲
▶I want to buy a pair of shorts. Would you like to go with me?
我想去買條短褲。你能陪我去嗎？

show·er [ˈʃaʊɚ]

🔊 Track 1872

名 陣雨、淋浴 動 淋浴、澆水

▶名 You should really go take a shower.
　你真的該去沖個澡了。

▶動 I already showered. It's your turn now.
　我已經淋浴過了，換你了。

shrimp [ʃrɪmp]

🔊 Track 1873

名 蝦子

▶I can't eat shrimps for I am allergic to seafood.
　我不能吃蝦子，我對海鮮過敏。

side·walk [ˈsaɪdˌwɔk]

🔊 Track 1874

名 人行道 同 pavement 人行道

▶There is a big crack（裂縫）in the sidewalk, so be careful.
　人行道上有一條大裂縫，所以你要小心。

sign [saɪn]

🔊 Track 1875

名 記號、標誌 動 簽署

▶名 What does this sign mean?
　這個標誌是什麼意思？

▶動 I hesitated when I had to sign on the contract.
　我簽署合約時猶豫了。

文法字詞解析
手語稱為 sign language，而「打手語」
這個動詞也稱為 sign。

si·lence [ˈsaɪləns]

🔊 Track 1876

名 沉默 動 使……靜下來

▶名 She needs complete silence to sleep.
　她需要完全的安靜才能睡覺。

▶動 The teacher tried to silence the pupils.
　那個老師試著要讓學生們安靜下來。

si·lent [ˈsaɪlənt]

🔊 Track 1877

形 沉默的

▶Would you please be silent? My baby is sleeping now.
　請您保持安靜好嗎？我的寶寶正在睡覺呢。

silk [sɪlk]

🔊 Track 1878

名 絲、綢

▶Not every woman's skin is as smooth as silk.
　不是每個女人的皮膚都像絲綢一樣光滑。

萬用延伸句型
as smooth as silk 形容如絲一般滑順
例　如：Wow! Your hair is as smooth as silk!
哇！你的頭髮真絲滑！

sim·i·lar [ˈsɪmələ]

🔊 Track 1879

形 相似的、類似的 同 alike 相似的

▶The boys look really similar to each other.
　那些男孩實在長得很像。

sim·ply [ˈsɪmplɪ]

🔊 Track 1880

副 簡單地、樸實地、僅僅

▶It takes simply a press on the button to start the machine.
　只要輕輕一按就可以啟動機器了。

Level 1

Level 2

漸入佳境、學習零壓力──
邁向常用2200單字

Level 3

Level 4

Level 5

Level 6

sin·gle [ˈsɪŋgl̩]　　◀≣ Track 1881

形 單一的 名 單一
▶形 Whether she is single or married remined a mystery.
　　她到底單身還是已婚，還是沒人知道。
▶名 Have you listened to her new single yet?
　　你聽了她的新單曲了沒？

sink [sɪŋk]　　◀≣ Track 1882

動 沉沒、沉 名 水槽
▶動 My feet sank into the mud. 我的雙腳陷到泥裡去了。
▶名 The housewife（家庭主婦）always keeps the sink as
　　clean as possible.
　　那個主婦總是儘量保持洗手台的清潔。

文法字詞解析
sink 的動詞變化：sink, sank, sunk (sunken)

skill·ful/skilled [ˈskɪlfəl]/[skɪld]　　◀≣ Track 1883

形 熟練的、靈巧的
▶She is very skilled in music. 她非常擅長音樂。

skin·ny [ˈskɪnɪ]　　◀≣ Track 1884

形 皮包骨的
▶He looks much too skinny to be a weightlifter（舉重運動員）.
　　他看起來太瘦了，不可能是舉重運動員。

文法字詞解析
much too 後面要接形容詞，比 too + adj.
要來得強度更強。

skirt [skɝt]　　◀≣ Track 1885

名 裙子
▶What do you think of my new skirt? It cost me two hundred
　　dollars. 你覺得我的新裙子怎麼樣？它可花了我兩百美元。

sleep·y [ˈslipɪ]　　◀≣ Track 1886

形 想睡的、睏的
▶You look so sleepy. Are you sure you don't need a rest?
　　你看起來昏昏欲睡的，你確定你不用休息一下嗎？

slen·der [ˈslɛndɚ]　　◀≣ Track 1887

形 苗條的 同 slim 苗條的
▶The model watches her diet to remain slender.
　　模特兒很注意飲食，以維持苗條。

slide [slaɪd]　　◀≣ Track 1888

動 滑動 名 滑梯
▶動 The rock slide down the slope.
　　大石塊滑下山坡。
▶名 I bought a slide for your little daughter.
　　我為你的小女兒買了一個滑梯。

slim [slɪm]　　◀≣ Track 1889

形 苗條的 動 變細
▶形 She looks slim, but she's actually surprisingly heavy.
　　她看起來很苗條，但體重意外地重。
▶動 She hopes to slim down in a few months.
　　她希望幾個月內可以變苗條。

slip [slɪp] ◀≋ *Track 1890*
動 滑倒
▶She slipped on a banana peel（皮）. 她踩到香蕉皮滑倒了。

slip·per(s) [ˋslɪpɚ(z)] ◀≋ *Track 1891*
名 拖鞋
▶Your slippers are all worn out. 你的拖鞋都已經穿壞了。

snack [snæk] ◀≋ *Track 1892*
名 小吃、點心 **動** 吃點心
▶**名** The kids had some snacks during the recess.
小朋友休息時間吃了點心。
▶**動** The little boy is snacking on donuts.
那個男孩正在吃甜甜圈當點心。

snail [snel] ◀≋ *Track 1893*
名 蝸牛
▶I picked up the snail and put it down at the side of the street.
我把那隻蝸牛撿起來，放在街道的旁邊。

snow·y [ˋsnoɪ] ◀≋ *Track 1894*
形 多雪的、積雪的
▶The snowy forest was beautiful. 那座積雪的森林非常美麗。

soc·cer [ˋsɑkɚ] ◀≋ *Track 1895*
名 足球
▶Would you like to play soccer with us next weekend?
下個週末你願意跟我們一起踢足球嗎？

so·cial [ˋsoʃəl] ◀≋ *Track 1896*
形 社會的
▶The stateman devoted himself to fighting for social justice.
政治家致力於爭取社會正義。

文法字詞解析
social networking = 社群網路
social event = 社交場合
social worker = 社會福利工作者

so·ci·e·ty [səˋsaɪətɪ] ◀≋ *Track 1897*
名 社會 **同** community 社區、社會
▶It is no wonder that this event had a bad influence on society.
難怪這件事情對社會造成了壞影響。

sock(s) [sɑk(s)] ◀≋ *Track 1898*
名 短襪
▶There is a hole in one of my socks. 我有隻襪子上有個洞。

sol·dier [ˋsoldʒɚ] ◀≋ *Track 1899*
名 軍人
▶Do you know how long your brother has been a soldier for?
你知道你兄弟當了多久的兵了嗎？

so·lu·tion [səˋluʃən] ◀≋ *Track 1900*
名 溶解、解決、解釋 **同** explanation 解釋
▶We spend three days to find the solution to the problem.
我們花了三天找到這個問題的解決方式。

Level
1

Level
2

漸入佳境、學習零壓力──
邁向常用2200單字

Level
3

Level
4

Level
5

Level
6

solve [sɑlv]
🔊 *Track 1901*

動 解決
▶Would you please help us find a method to solve this problem?
請您幫我們想個辦法來解決這個難題好嗎？

some·bod·y [ˈsʌmˌbɑdɪ]
🔊 *Track 1902*

代 某人、有人 名 重要人物 同 someone 某人
▶代 Why don't you ask somebody else to help you?
為什麼不請別人幫助你呢？
▶名 He thinks he's somebody, but he actually isn't that famous.
他覺得自己是重要人物，但他其實也沒那麼有名。

some·where [ˈsʌmˌhwɛr]
🔊 *Track 1903*

副 在某處
▶Your phone must be somewhere in this room.
你的手機應該在這房間裡某處。

sort [sɔrt]
🔊 *Track 1904*

名 種 動 一致、調和
▶名 What sort of person is he? 他是哪種人？
▶動 We have to sort the document before we could call it a day.
今天下班前我們必須將文件分類好。

source [sors]
🔊 *Track 1905*

名 來源、水源地 同 origin 起源
▶My wages（薪水）are the principal source of my income.
薪資是我收入的主要來源。

south·ern [ˈsʌðən]
🔊 *Track 1906*

形 南方的
▶Not all students in this school are from the southern part of the country.
這個學校不是所有的學生都是來自那個國家的南部。

soy·bean/soy·a/ soy [ˈsɔɪˌbin]/[ˈsɔɪə]/[sɔɪ]
🔊 *Track 1907*

名 大豆、黃豆
▶This drink is made from soybeans.
這個飲料是黃豆做的。

speak·er [ˈspikə]
🔊 *Track 1908*

名 演說者
▶There are a crowd of people gathered around the speaker.
有一大群人在演說者周圍聚集起來。

speed [spid]
🔊 *Track 1909*

名 速度、急速 動 加速 同 haste 急速
▶名 The train moves at a high speed.
火車以高速前進。
▶動 Would you please speed up? We want to get there in time.
您能加快速度嗎？我們想準時到達那裡。

文法字詞解析

要注意的是，somewhere 不能用於否定，所以如果已經預期答案是肯定的話，疑問句才能用 somewhere，否則的話要用 anywhere。
例如：Are you going somewhere next weekend?
你下個周末有要去哪嗎？
Is there a spare seat anywhere for my little girl?
哪裡有座位可以讓我的小女兒坐？

文法字詞解析

「be made from」和「be made of」都是「用……製成」的意思。但用法卻截然不同。be made of 表示物質在製作過程中的本質不會改變，為物理變化；而 be made from 則是物質的本質在製作過程中會經過徹底的改變，為化學變化。

文法字詞解析

speed 的動詞變化：speed, sped, sped

spell·ing [ˈspɛlɪŋ]　　🔊 Track 1910

名 拼讀、拼法
▶There are some spelling mistakes in the essay.
　這篇文章中有些拼字的錯誤。

spi·der [ˈspaɪdɚ]　　🔊 Track 1911

名 蜘蛛
▶I can't stand spiders. 我完全受不了蜘蛛。

spin·ach [ˈspɪnɪtʃ]　　🔊 Track 1912

名 菠菜
▶Would you like cabbage or spinach? 你要甘藍菜還是菠菜？

spir·it [ˈspɪrɪt]　　🔊 Track 1913

名 精神 同 soul 精神、靈魂
▶This necklace will protect you from evil spirits.
　這條項鍊會保護你免受惡靈傷害。

spot [spɑt]　　🔊 Track 1914

動 弄髒、認出 名 點 同 stain 弄髒
▶動 I spot my sister over there. 我認出我妹妹在那裡。
▶名 The shoplifter was caught on the spot.
　在商店的小偷當場被抓到。

spread [sprɛd]　　🔊 Track 1915

動 展開、傳佈 名 寬度、桌布 同 extend 擴展
▶動 She tried to spread rumors about her opponent.
　她試圖散步關於對手的謠言。
▶名 The spread of pests（害蟲）damaged countless（無數
　的）fruit trees.
　蟲害的蔓延損害了無數的果樹。

spring [sprɪŋ]　　🔊 Track 1916

動 彈開、突然提出 名 泉水、春天
▶動 They sprung a surprise attack on the enemy.
　我們對敵人發動了一次突擊。
▶名 I will graduate next spring. What about you?
　我明年春天畢業，你呢？

文法字詞解析
spning 的動詞變化：spring, sprang, sprung

square [skwɛr]　　🔊 Track 1917

形 公正的、方正的 名 正方形、廣場
▶形 Do you prefer a square table or a round one?
　你比較想要方形的桌子還是圓的？
▶名 There is a stage in the center of the square.
　在廣場中央有一個舞台。

squir·rel [ˈskwɝəl]　　🔊 Track 1918

名 松鼠
名詞複數 squirrels
▶Have you ever touched a squirrel? 你摸過松鼠嗎？

Level 1

Level 2

漸入佳境、學習零壓力——
邁向常用2200單字

Level 3

Level 4

Level 5

Level 6

stage [stedʒ]　　🔊 *Track 1919*

名 舞臺、階段 動 上演

▶ 名 The disease is still in its primary（初期的） stage.
這個疾病仍然在初發階段。

▶ 動 They're staging a play in this theater next month.
他們下個月將在這座戲院上演一齣戲。

stamp [stæmp]　　🔊 *Track 1920*

動 壓印 名 郵票、印章

▶ 動 He stamped her card passport quickly.
他很快地在她的護照上蓋了印章。

▶ 名 I used to collect stamps when I was young.
我小時候會收集郵票。

stan·dard [ˈstændəd]　　🔊 *Track 1921*

名 標準 形 標準的 同 model 標準

▶ 名 She is still single because she has high standards.
她的標準很高，所以還是單身。

▶ 形 This is a standard process, nothing to worry about.
這是標準程序，沒什麼好擔心的。

steak [stek]　　🔊 *Track 1922*

名 牛排

▶ Can you give me some steak and bread?
您能給我一些牛排和麵包嗎？

steal [stil]　　🔊 *Track 1923*

動 偷、騙取

▶ Don't try to steal ideas from your classmates.
不要偷用你同學的點子。

文法字詞解析
steal 的動詞變化：steal, stole, stolen

steam [stim]　　🔊 *Track 1924*

名 蒸汽 動 蒸、使蒸發、以蒸汽開動

▶ 名 That ship runs on steam. 那艘船是靠著蒸汽行駛的。

▶ 動 Lots of ships are steaming into the harbor（港口）.
有很多輪船正駛抵港口。

steel [stil]　　🔊 *Track 1925*

名 鋼、鋼鐵

▶ How about installing（安裝） a steel door?
我們裝一扇鋼製的門怎麼樣？

stick [stɪk]　　🔊 *Track 1926*

名 棍、棒 動 黏 同 attach 貼上

▶ 名 It doesn't matter whether the stick is strong or not.
這條木棍結不結實都沒什麼關係。

▶ 動 The note won't stick to the wall.
這字條都沒辦法好好黏在牆上。

文法字詞解析
stick 的動詞變化：stick, stuck, stuck

stom·ach [ˈstʌmək]　　🔊 *Track 1927*

名 胃 同 belly 胃

▶ Tina felt butterflies in her stomach. 蒂娜緊張到胃裡像有蝴蝶在飛。

storm [stɔrm] ◀€ *Track 1928*

名 風暴 動 襲擊
- ▶名 The weather man says there will be a storm soon.
  天氣預報員說很快會有暴風雨。
- ▶動 The storm hit Japan and caused great damage.
  暴風雨襲擊日本造成嚴重損害。

stove [stov] ◀€ *Track 1929*

名 火爐、爐子 同 oven 爐子
- ▶The room is as hot as a stove. 這屋子熱得像火爐一樣。

straight [stret] ◀€ *Track 1930*

形 筆直的、正直的
- ▶She walked straight up to him and slapped（打巴掌）him.
  她筆直地走向他，賞了他一巴掌。

strang·er [ˈstrendʒɚ] ◀€ *Track 1931*

名 陌生人
- ▶The kid is afraid of talking to strangers.
  這個小孩害怕跟陌生人講話。

straw [strɔ] ◀€ *Track 1932*

名 稻草
- ▶Her hair looks like straw. 她的頭髮像稻草似的。

straw·ber·ry [ˈstrɔˌbɛrɪ] ◀€ *Track 1933*

名 草莓
- ▶Why don't you try some strawberry jam?
  為什麼不試試看草莓果醬呢？

萬用延伸句型
Why don't you ...? 你為什麼不……呢？
這個句型可以用來提供他人建議。

stream [strim] ◀€ *Track 1934*

名 小溪 動 流動
- ▶名 The stream behind my house flows（流動）quite fast.
  我家後面的小溪流得很快。
- ▶動 Tears are streaming down her face. 淚水沿著她的臉流下。

stress [strɛs] ◀€ *Track 1935*

名 壓力 動 強調、著重 同 emphasis 強調
- ▶名 Would you please tell me how you handle your stress?
  請您告訴我您是如何處理壓力的嗎？
- ▶動 You need to stress the second syllable（音節）of this word.
  這個單字第二個音節應該要念重音。

stretch [strɛtʃ] ◀€ *Track 1936*

動 / 名 伸展
- ▶動 I stretched in my seat because I felt so tired.
  我在位子上伸展了一下，因為我覺得好累。
- ▶名 Our coach instructed us to stretch before swimming.
  我們教練教我們游泳前要先伸展。

Level 1
Level 2
漸入佳境、學習零壓力——
邁向常用2200單字
Level 3
Level 4
Level 5
Level 6

strict [strɪkt]　🔊 *Track 1937*

形 嚴格的　同 harsh 嚴厲的
▶ The professor is very strict about the format of the report.
　 教授嚴格規定報告的格式。

strike [straɪk]　🔊 *Track 1938*

動 打擊、達成(協議) 名 罷工
▶ 動 It took them half a month to strike a bargain（交易）.
　 經過了半個月的時間，他們雙方才達成了交易。
▶ 名 It was three months before the strike ended.
　 過了三個月的時間，罷工才結束。

文法字詞解析
strike 的動詞變化：
strike, struck, stricken

string [strɪŋ]　🔊 *Track 1939*

名 弦、繩子、一串
▶ The kitten loves playing with string. 那隻小貓最愛玩繩子。

strug·gle [ˋstrʌgl̩]　🔊 *Track 1940*

動 努力、奮鬥 名 掙扎、奮鬥
▶ 動 Not all people have to struggle every day for their survival
　 （生存）. 不是所有的人都必須為了生存而每天奮鬥。
▶ 名 He got wounded in the struggle. 他在搏鬥中受了傷。

sub·ject [ˋsʌbdʒɪkt]　🔊 *Track 1941*

名 主題、科目 形 服從的、易受……的　同 topic 主題
▶ 名 What's your favorite subject at school?
　 你在學校最喜歡哪個科目？
▶ 形 If there is a heavy snow, the trains are subject to delay.
　 如果下大雪，火車往往就會延誤。

sub·tract [səbˋtrækt]　🔊 *Track 1942*

動 扣除、移走
▶ The kids are learning add and subtract at primary school.
　 孩子們在小學時期學習加法與減法。

sub·way [ˋsʌbˏwe]　🔊 *Track 1943*

名 地下鐵
▶ How long will it take for you to get there by subway?
　 你搭乘地鐵去那裡要花多長時間啊？

suc·ceed [səkˋsid]　🔊 *Track 1944*

動 成功
▶ The book proposed there major principals to succeed.
　 這本書提出三項成功的法則。

萬用延伸句型
succeed sb. as sth. 繼承（某人）的（某個職位）
例如：He succeeded his father as CEO of the company.
他繼承了他爸的職位，成為這家公司的CEO。

suc·cess [səkˋsɛs]　🔊 *Track 1945*

名 成功
▶ It is no wonder that his new book was a great success.
　 難怪他的新書十分成功。

suc·cess·ful [səkˋsɛsfəl]　🔊 *Track 1946*

形 成功的
▶ He is a successful businessman. 他是個成功的商人。

sud‧den [ˋsʌdn̩]　🔊 *Track 1947*

形 突然的 名 意外、突然

▶形 We were scared by the sudden blackout.
　突然停電，我們都嚇了一跳。

▶名 All of a sudden, everything went quiet.
　突然一切都安靜了下來。

suit [sut]　🔊 *Track 1948*

名 套 動 適合 同 fit 適合

▶名 Can you help me pick out a black suit?
　你可以幫我挑一套黑色西裝嗎？

▶動 Would you like to make an appointment in advance?
　Would Friday morning suit you?
　您想不想提前預約呢？星期五早上對你來說合適嗎？

文法字詞解析
撲克牌的「花色」（黑桃、梅花等）也稱為 suit。

sun‧ny [ˋsʌnɪ]　🔊 *Track 1949*

形 充滿陽光的 同 bright 晴朗的

▶It's such a sunny day. Why don't we go out for a walk?
　今天的天氣真好，為什麼我們不出去散散步呢？

su‧per‧mar‧ket [ˋsupɚ͵mɑrkɪt]　🔊 *Track 1950*

名 超級市場

▶Let's head to the supermarket to buy some groceries.
　我們到超級市場買些東西吧。

sup‧ply [səˋplaɪ]　🔊 *Track 1951*

動 供給 名 供應品 同 furnish 供給

▶動 Plenty of food was supplied from the other states.
　從其他各州來了不少充足的食品供給。

▶名 Who's responsible for the supplies? 是誰負責供貨？

sup‧port [səˋport]　🔊 *Track 1952*

動 支持 名 支持者、支撐物 同 uphold 支持

▶動 Can you give some examples to support your argument
　（論點）？你能舉幾個例子來證實你的論點嗎？

▶名 Without your support, I can't accomplish the task.
　沒有你的支持，我無法完成這個任務。

文法字詞解析
在許多網站或應用程式頁面上都能看到 support 這一項。需要幫助、支援時即可點此與客服人員聯絡。

sur‧face [ˋsɝfɪs]　🔊 *Track 1953*

名 表面 動 使形成表面 同 exterior 表面

▶名 On the surface everything looks fine, but actually there are
　a lot of problems.
　表面上看起來一切安好，但其實有很多的問題。

▶動 The divers swam toward the surface of the water.
　潛水者游向水面。

sur‧vive [sɚˋvaɪv]　🔊 *Track 1954*

動 倖存、殘存

▶The little boy survived the earthquake.
　那個小男孩從地震中倖存下來。

Level 1

Level 2

漸入佳境、學習零壓力──
邁向常用2200單字

Level 3

Level 4

Level 5

Level 6

swal·low [ˈswɑlo] 🔊 *Track 1955*

名 燕子 動 吞咽

▶名 There are swallows flying in the sky.
有一群燕子在天空中飛。

▶動 The old lady has difficulty swallowing biscuit.
老太太沒辦法吞下這個餅乾。

swan [swɑn] 🔊 *Track 1956*

名 天鵝

▶Do you see the swans? They're so beautiful!
你有看到天鵝嗎？牠們很漂亮吧！

sweat·er [ˈswɛtɚ] 🔊 *Track 1957*

名 毛衣、厚運動衫

▶It is cold outside. Why don't you put on a sweater?
外面很冷，你為什麼不套上一件毛衣呢？

sweep [swip] 🔊 *Track 1958*

動 掃、打掃 名 掃除、掠過

▶動 Grandma is always sweeping the house.
奶奶總是在打掃房子。

▶名 Let's give our room a good sweep.
讓我們把房間好好掃一下吧。

文法字詞解析
sweep 的動詞變化：
swept, swept, swept

swing [swɪŋ] 🔊 *Track 1959*

動 搖動

▶The monkey is swinging from branch to branch.
那隻猴子從這根樹枝晃到另一根樹枝。

文法字詞解析
swing 的動詞變化：
swing, swung, swung

sym·bol [ˈsɪmbḷ] 🔊 *Track 1960*

名 象徵、標誌 同 sign 標誌

▶Roses are a symbol of romance and passion.
玫瑰是浪漫和熱情的象徵。

[Tt]

tal·ent [ˈtælənt] 🔊 *Track 1961*

名 天分、天賦

▶He has a lot of talent in acting. 他很有演戲天分。

talk·a·tive [ˈtɔkətɪv] 🔊 *Track 1962*

形 健談的 反 mute 沉默的

▶The talkative man kept telling tall tales. 多話的男人一直在吹牛。

文法字詞解析
形容詞字尾「-ative」表示「喜歡做某事的、傾向於做某事的、有某種特質的」，所以 talkative 就是「喜歡講話的、健談的」；competitive 就是「競爭性的、好競爭的」。

tan·ge·rine [ˈtændʒərɪn] 🔊 *Track 1963*

名 柑、桔

▶Would you like some tangerines? I got some from my granny
（奶奶）. 你要不要吃些橘子？是我從我奶奶那拿來的。

tank [tæŋk]
🔊 *Track 1964*

名 水槽、坦克

▶Don't pour the sour milk into the water tank.
不要把壞掉的牛奶倒進水槽裡。

tape [tep]
🔊 *Track 1965*

名 帶、捲尺、磁帶 動 用捲尺測量 同 record 磁帶、唱片

▶名 Would you lend me your tape? I want to do some listening practice on the weekends.
能借用你的錄音帶嗎？我想在週末做些聽力練習。

▶動 Would you please help me tape up the envelope?
能請你幫我把信封用膠帶貼起來嗎？

tar·get [ˈtɑrgɪt]
🔊 *Track 1966*

名 目標、靶子 同 goal 目標

▶The company didn't meet its target this year.
這個公司今年沒有實現目標。

task [tæsk]
🔊 *Track 1967*

名 任務 同 work 任務

▶The task requires a thorough plan to accomplish.
這個任務需要周延計畫才能完成。

tast·y [ˈtestɪ]
🔊 *Track 1968*

形 好吃的 同 delicious 好吃的

▶The food here is very tasty. 這裡的食物很美味。

team [tim]
🔊 *Track 1969*

名 隊 同 group 組、隊

▶Would you tell me which team won this game in the end?
你能告訴我最後是哪一隊贏了這場比賽嗎？

tear [tɪr]/[tɛr]
🔊 *Track 1970*

名 眼淚 動 撕、撕破

▶名 His sad story moved me to tears.
他那悲傷的故事讓我感動得流下了眼淚。

▶動 She tore his letter up and walked away.
她把他的信撕了，然後揚長而去。

文法字詞解析
tear 的動詞變化：tear, tore, torn

teen(s) [tin(z)]
🔊 *Track 1971*

名 十多歲

▶What did he look like when he was in his teens?
當他還是十幾歲的時候，他長什麼樣子呢？

teen·age [ˈtinˌedʒ]
🔊 *Track 1972*

形 十幾歲的

▶Teenage girls tend to imitate their idles.
青少年喜歡模仿他們的偶像。

Level 1
Level 2
漸入佳境、學習零壓力——邁向常用2200單字
Level 3
Level 4
Level 5
Level 6

teen·ag·er [ˈtinˌedʒɚ]
Track 1973

名 青少年

▶His family is really poor, so he has been earning money since he was a teenager.
他的家很窮，所以他十幾歲的時候就開始賺錢了。

tel·e·phone/phone
Track 1974

[ˈtɛləˌfon]/[fon]

名 電話 動 打電話

▶名 There is a telephone on my desk, but I seldom（很少）use it. 我的書桌上有台電話，但是我卻很少用它。

▶動 More people are willing to telephone than to write.
比起寫信來，有更多人願意打電話。

文法字詞解析
大家常拿的手機可稱 smartphone、cell phone 或 mobile phone 等，不過因為現在拿手機的人似乎比拿電話的人多了，因此 phone 也普遍可以代稱手機了。

tel·e·vi·sion/TV [ˈtɛləˌvɪʒən]
Track 1975

名 電視

▶How often do you watch television at home every week?
你每週在家看幾次電視？

tem·ple [ˈtɛmpl]
Track 1976

名 寺院、神殿

▶We were required to remain solemn in the temple.
我們被要求在寺廟裏要保持肅靜。

ten·nis [ˈtɛnɪs]
Track 1977

名 網球

▶Would you like to play tennis with us tomorrow?
你願意明天和我們一起去打網球嗎？

tent [tɛnt]
Track 1978

名 帳篷

▶There are several tents in the camping base.
在營裡有一些帳篷。

term [tɝm]
Track 1979

名 條件、期限、術語 動 稱呼

▶名 Why not agree to these terms? They are beneficial（有利的）for us at least.
為什麼不同意這些條件呢？它們至少對我們是有利的啊。

▶動 They termed the play a tragedy.
他們把這齣戲稱為一齣悲劇。

萬用延伸句型
be on friendly terms with sb. 與某人感情不錯
例如：I had no idea she's still on friendly terms with her ex-husband.
我都不知道她和她前夫依舊維持不錯的關係。

ter·ri·ble [ˈtɛrəbl]
Track 1980

形 可怕的、駭人的 同 horrible 可怕的

▶It will be a terrible blow to him. 這對他將是一個可怕的打擊。

ter·rif·ic [təˈrɪfɪk]
Track 1981

形 驚人的

▶They did a terrific job in this project.
他們在這個計畫中表現極佳。

test [tɛst] 　　🔊 *Track 1982*
名 考試 動 試驗、檢驗
▶名 Can you tell me what I should bring for this test?
　你可以告訴我這次考試我要帶什麼東西嗎？
▶動 Let's test this theory（理論）and see if it works.
　我們來試驗看看這個理論是不是真的有用。

text·book [ˈtɛkstˌbʊk] 　　🔊 *Track 1983*
名 教科書
▶The teacher underlines the important points in the textbook.
　老師畫下在教科書中的重點。

the·a·ter [ˈθiətɚ] 　　🔊 *Track 1984*
名 戲院、劇場 反 stadium 劇場
▶Would you tell me what play is on at your theater now?
　你能告訴我你們戲院現在正在上演什麼戲嗎？

there·fore [ˈðɛrˌfor] 　　🔊 *Track 1985*
副 因此、所以 同 hence 因此
▶She got sick and therefore didn't got to school.
　她生病了，所以就沒去學校。

thick [θɪk] 　　🔊 *Track 1986*
形 厚的、密的
▶The book was so thick that it took me three months to finish it.
　這本書太厚了，我花了三個月才讀完。

thief [θif] 　　🔊 *Track 1987*
名 小偷、盜賊
名詞複數 thieves
▶The thief couldn't find anything valuable（有價值的）in the
　man's house. 這個小偷在那個人家中找不到任何有價值的東西。

thin [θɪn] 　　🔊 *Track 1988*
形 瘦的、薄的、稀疏的 同 slender 薄的
▶Why don't you wear a thinner shirt today? It is so hot outside.
　今天你為什麼不穿件較薄的襯衫呢？外面很熱哦。

thirs·ty [ˈθɝstɪ] 　　🔊 *Track 1989*
形 口渴的
▶I'm thirsty. Can we get a drink please?
　我很渴，拜託我們去喝個飲料好不好？

throat [θrot] 　　🔊 *Track 1990*
名 喉嚨
▶I have this strange feeling in my throat.
　我的喉嚨裡有種怪怪的感覺。

through [θru] 　　🔊 *Track 1991*
介 經過、通過 副 全部、到最後

文法字詞解析
除了 therefore 之外，so、thus、as a result 等也都是表達因果關係的詞語。

文法字詞解析
形容詞字尾「-able」有「具備某種特質或條件」的意思，所以像是 valuable 就是「有價值的」、comfortable 就是「舒服的」。

Level 1

Level 2

漸入佳境、學習零壓力──
邁向常用2200單字

Level 3

Level 4

Level 5

Level 6

▶介 Modern people tend to obtain information through Internet.
現代人常透過網路獲取資訊。

▶副 There was an awful（可怕的）storm last night but the baby slept right through it.
昨夜風雨很大，但這個寶寶卻一直睡著沒醒。

through·out [θruˈaʊt]
🔊 *Track 1992*

介 遍佈、遍及 副 徹頭徹尾

▶介 You can find this plant throughout this region.
你能在這個地區到處發現這種植物的存在。

▶副 The material was flawed（使有缺陷）throughout.
那個材料處處有瑕疵。

thumb [θʌm]
🔊 *Track 1993*

名 拇指 動 用拇指翻

▶名 The baby enjoys sucking（吸）his thumb.
那個寶寶喜歡吸大拇指。

▶動 He thumbed through the book and decided that it was boring. 他迅速翻過這本書，然後判斷這本書應該很無聊。

thun·der [ˈθʌndɚ]
🔊 *Track 1994*

名 雷、打雷 動 打雷

▶名 The sound of the thunder last night was loud enough to wake me up. 昨晚的雷聲很大，把我吵醒了。

▶動 It thundered all night and the cat was horrified.
整晚一直在打雷，那隻貓嚇死了。

tip [tɪp]
🔊 *Track 1995*

名 小費、暗示 動 付小費

▶名 How much should I give the porter as a tip?
我該給行李搬運工多少小費？

▶動 Will you tip the waiter later? 你等一下會給服務生小費嗎？

ti·tle [ˈtaɪtl]
🔊 *Track 1996*

名 稱號、標題 動 加標題 同 headline 標題

▶名 In my opinion, the title of this book is very beautiful.
在我看來，這本書的書名真是取得漂亮。

▶動 I haven't yet titled my novel. Any suggestions?
我還沒有給我的小說設定標題，你有什麼建議嗎？

toast [tost]
🔊 *Track 1997*

名 土司麵包 動 烤、烤麵包

▶名 Toast for breakfast again? Come on, let's get something else! 早餐又吃土司喔？唉唷，我們吃點別的嘛！

▶動 We toasted the host halfway through the luncheon.
我們在餐會進行到一半時向主人敬酒。

toe [to]
🔊 *Track 1998*

名 腳趾

▶She is dressed in white from head to toe.
她從頭到腳穿得一身白。

文法字詞解析
thumb 最後面的 b 是不發音的，要注意喔！

萬用延伸句型
from head to toe 從頭到腳
例 如：You need to make sure that you look good from head to toe for the audition.
這次試鏡你得注意全身上下都要打扮得漂漂亮亮。

tofu/bean curd [ˈtofu]/[bin kɝd] 🔊 *Track 1999*

名 豆腐
▶Tofu is very popular in this area. 在這個地區豆腐很受歡迎。

toi·let [ˈtɔɪlɪt] 🔊 *Track 2000*

名 洗手間
▶The maid was asked to clean the toilet.
女僕被要求去打掃廁所。

to·ma·to [təˈmeto] 🔊 *Track 2001*

名 番茄
▶Is a tomato a kind of vegetable or a kind of fruit?
番茄到底是蔬菜還是水果？

tongue [tʌŋ] 🔊 *Track 2002*

名 舌、舌頭
▶I bit my tongue and it hurt a lot. 我咬到自己的舌頭，好痛喔。

tooth [tuθ] 🔊 *Track 2003*

名 牙齒、齒
名詞複數 teeth
▶Tom had his wisdom tooth pulled off.
湯姆拔掉了他智齒。

top·ic [ˈtɑpɪk] 🔊 *Track 2004*

名 主題、談論 同 theme 主題
▶Politics is not a proper topic for the conversation.
政治不太適合做談話的主題。

tour [tur] 🔊 *Track 2005*

名 旅行 動 遊覽 同 travel 旅行
▶名 Are you coming on this tour too? 你也要參加這次旅行嗎？
▶動 The two brothers plan to tour the world.
這兄弟倆計畫環遊世界。

tow·el [taʊl] 🔊 *Track 2006*

名 毛巾
▶Would you pass me a towel? I had a shower just now and my
hair is still wet.
能遞給我一條毛巾嗎？我剛洗了個澡，頭髮還是濕的。

tow·er [ˈtaʊɚ] 🔊 *Track 2007*

名 塔 動 高聳
▶名 There is a tower on the top of the hill. Can you see it?
山丘上有座塔，你看見了嗎？
▶動 An old castle towers over the bustling（熙攘的）city.
有座古老的城堡高聳於這個繁華的城市之上。

track [træk] 🔊 *Track 2008*

名 路線 動 追蹤

萬用延伸句型

as red as a tomato 紅得跟番茄一樣
例如：When he saw his crush, his face
became as red as a tomato.
他看到他暗戀的對象時，臉紅得跟番茄
一樣。

文法字詞解析

歌手辦巡迴演唱會時，因為也得旅行到
世界各地，就稱為「be on tour」。

Level
1

Level
2

漸入佳境、學習零壓力──
邁向常用2200單字

Level
3

Level
4

Level
5

Level
6

▶名 The activity was so much fun that we lost track of time.
這個活動如此有趣，以至於我們忘記了時間。

▶動 The hunter tracked the wolf late into the night.
獵人追蹤狼直到深夜。

trade [tred]　◀╡ Track 2009
名 商業、貿易 動 交易

▶名 Women's clothing has become a trade of its own.
女性服飾業已經成了自成一格的行業了。

▶動 This company trades with many foreign companies.
這個公司跟多個外國公司有貿易往來。

tra·di·tion [trə`dɪʃən]　◀╡ Track 2010
名 傳統 同 custom 習俗

▶Not all people like to follow traditions; some like new things.
不是所有人都喜歡遵循傳統，有些人喜歡新事物。

tra·di·tion·al [trə`dɪʃənl]　◀╡ Track 2011
形 傳統的

▶This is a really traditional kind of wedding.
這是很傳統的那種婚禮。

traf·fic [`træfɪk]　◀╡ Track 2012
名 交通

▶We have to follow the traffic signals for safety.
我們要遵守交通號誌以策安全。

trap [træp]　◀╡ Track 2013
名 圈套、陷阱 動 誘捕 同 snare 誘捕

▶名 The mouse trap didn't catch any mice.
這個捕鼠器沒抓到半隻老鼠。

▶動 The cat trapped the mouse in the corner.
那隻貓把老鼠擋在角落不讓牠離開。

trav·el [`trævl]　◀╡ Track 2014
動 旅行 名 旅行

▶動 He has traveled to a lot of places. 他到過很多地方旅行。

▶名 More and more people are going abroad for travel.
有越來越多的人出國旅遊。

trea·sure [`trɛʒɚ]　◀╡ Track 2015
名 寶物、財寶 動 收藏、珍藏

▶名 The merchant saw the rare metal in this area as a treasure.
商人將這個區域的稀有金屬視為寶物。

▶動 You should treasure your friendships all your life.
你應該一生都珍惜友誼。

treat [trit]　◀╡ Track 2016
動 處理、對待

▶You should just treat this matter lightly; it's not a big deal.
你應該將這件事輕輕帶過就好，這不是什麼大不了的事。

文法字詞解析
網站的訪客數、點擊流量也可稱為 traffic。

萬用延伸句型
it's not a big deal. 這沒什麼大不了的。

treat·ment [ˈtritmənt]
🔊 *Track 2017*

名 款待
▶The patient will undergo a series of medical treatments.
病人將接受一系列的治療。

tri·al [ˈtraɪəl]
🔊 *Track 2018*

名 審問、試驗 同 experiment 實驗
▶The case is still under trial. I will let you know as soon as I get the news. 案子還在審訊當中。我一得到消息就會讓你知道。

tri·an·gle [ˈtraɪˏæŋgl̩]
🔊 *Track 2019*

名 三角形
▶What does this triangle sign mean?
這個三角形牌子是什麼意思？

trick [trɪk]
🔊 *Track 2020*

名 詭計 動 欺騙、欺詐
▶名 The tricks of the magician amazed the audience.
魔術師的把戲令觀眾驚訝。
▶動 I was tricked into handing him my money.
我被他騙了，把我的錢給了他。

文法字詞解析
萬聖節常說的「不給糖就搗蛋」就使用了這個字，叫做 trick or treat。

trou·sers [ˈtraʊzəz]
🔊 *Track 2021*

名 褲、褲子 同 pants 褲子
▶How do you like this pair of trousers? It looks terrific on you.
你喜歡這條褲子嗎？穿在你身上好看極了。

truck [trʌk]
🔊 *Track 2022*

名 卡車 同 van 貨車
▶Would you lend me your truck? I have some goods to transport（運送）. 能把你的卡車借給我用嗎？我有一些貨要運。

trum·pet [ˈtrʌmpɪt]
🔊 *Track 2023*

名 喇叭、小號 動 吹喇叭
▶名 My dad plays the trumpet and I play the guitar.
我爸爸會吹小號，而我會彈吉他。
▶動 Will you teach me how to trumpet? I would like to learn.
你能教我吹喇叭嗎？我想學。

trust [trʌst]
🔊 *Track 2024*

名 信任 動 信任 同 believe 相信
▶名 A good marriage is based on trust.
美滿的婚姻建立在互相信任的基礎上。
▶動 You shouldn't trust him. He's a good liar.
你不該相信他，他非常擅長說謊。

truth [truθ]
🔊 *Track 2025*

名 真相、真理 同 reality 事實
▶The criminal confessed and told the truth.
這名罪犯坦承犯行。

文法字詞解析
truth be told = 老實說
in truth = 事實上

Level
1

Level
2

漸入佳境、學習零壓力──
邁向常用2200單字

Level
3

Level
4

Level
5

Level
6

tube [tjub] 🔊 *Track 2026*
名 管、管子 同 pipe 管子
▶Let's heat the glass tube before we start our experiment（實驗）. 開始實驗之前，我們先把玻璃管熱一下。

tun·nel [ˈtʌnl̩] 🔊 *Track 2027*
名 隧道、地道
▶We drove through the tunnel. 我們開車經過隧道。

tur·key [ˈtɝkɪ] 🔊 *Track 2028*
名 火雞
▶They roasted（烤）a turkey for dinner.
他們烤了一隻火雞當晚餐。

tur·tle [ˈtɝtl̩] 🔊 *Track 2029*
名 龜、海龜
▶The turtles' eggs on the beach are eaten up by many large birds. 海龜在沙灘上的蛋被很多大鳥們吃光了。

type [taɪp] 🔊 *Track 2030*
名 類型 動 打字
▶名 I don't like this type of skirt. 我不喜歡這種裙子。
▶動 Would you type up this form for me?
幫我打一下這份表格好嗎？

ty·phoon [taɪˈfun] 🔊 *Track 2031*
名 颱風
▶IA typhoon is similar to a cyclone.
颱風跟颶風是相似的。

[Uu]

ug·ly [ˈʌglɪ] 🔊 *Track 2032*
形 醜的、難看的
▶Even though she is pretty, she considers herself ugly.
雖然她很漂亮，但她還是覺得自己很醜。

um·brel·la [ʌmˈbrɛlə] 🔊 *Track 2033*
名 雨傘
▶We brought the umbrella with us in case it would rain.
我們帶著傘，以防下雨。

un·der·wear [ˈʌndɚˌwɛr] 🔊 *Track 2034*
名 內衣
▶When nobody is home I don't bother dressing up and walk around in my underwear.
沒人在家的時候，我就懶得穿衣服，直接穿著內衣走來走去。

u·ni·form [ˈjunəˌfɔrm]
🔊 *Track 2035*

名 制服、校服、使一致 同 outfit 全套服裝
▶Staff in the post office would wear uniform on duty.
郵局的員工上班時穿著制服。

up·on [əˈpɑn]
🔊 *Track 2036*

介 在……上面
▶The cat is sitting upon the chair. 那隻貓坐在椅子上。

文法字詞解析
upon 的意思等同於 on 或 onto，不過是比較正式的用法。

up·per [ˈʌpɚ]
🔊 *Track 2037*

副 在上位 同 superior 上級的
▶What rooms are there on the upper level?
上面那層有哪些房間？

used [juzd]
🔊 *Track 2038*

形 用過的、二手的
▶The new car usually cost more than a used one.
新車通常比二手車貴。

used to [just tu]
🔊 *Track 2039*

副 習慣的
▶I'm used to having a bath in the morning when I get up.
我習慣每天早上起來洗澡。

us·er [ˈjuzɚ]
🔊 *Track 2040*

名 使用者 同 consumer 消費者
▶Some users have complained that the website （網站）is too confusing （令人困惑的）. 有些使用者抱怨這個網站太難懂了。

文法字詞解析
大家常用的「使用者說明」可稱為 user guide、user manual、user guidebook 等。

u·su·al [ˈjuʒʊəl]
🔊 *Track 2041*

副 通常的、平常的 同 ordinary 平常的
▶Would you like to meet me at the usual place?
我們在老地方見面好嗎？

[Vv]

va·ca·tion [veˈkeʃən]
🔊 *Track 2042*

名 假期 動 度假 同 holiday 假期
▶名 Do you have any plans for this winter vacation?
這個寒假你有什麼打算？
▶動 They will vacation in Switzerland during Christmas.
他們耶誕節期間將到瑞士度假。

val·ley [ˈvælɪ]
🔊 *Track 2043*

名 溪谷、山谷
▶We enjoyed the beautiful view in the valley.
我們欣賞山谷中的美景。

Level 1
Level 2

漸入佳境、學習零壓力——邁向常用2200單字

Level 3
Level 4
Level 5
Level 6

val·ue [ˈvælju]
◀ *Track 2044*

名 價值 動 重視、評價

▶名 What's of the greatest value is usually invisible.
最有價值的事物通常是肉眼看不見的。

▶動 I value our friendship a lot. 我非常重視我們之間的友誼。

vic·to·ry [ˈvɪktərɪ]
◀ *Track 2045*

名 勝利 同 success 勝利、成功

▶ Let's hold a party to celebrate （慶祝）the victory.
我們辦個派對來慶祝一下這次勝利吧。

vid·e·o [ˈvɪdɪo]
◀ *Track 2046*

名 電視、錄影

▶ Video games are good for the brain. 電動玩具對腦部有幫助喔。

vil·lage [ˈvɪlɪdʒ]
◀ *Track 2047*

名 村莊

▶ It is no wonder that many people living in the cities want to
move to villages. 難怪很多在城市居住的人想搬到村莊裡去住。

vi·o·lin [ˌvaɪəˈlɪn]
◀ *Track 2048*

名 小提琴 同 fiddle 小提琴

▶ I think you play the violin quite well.
我覺得你的小提琴拉得很好。

vis·i·tor [ˈvɪzɪtɚ]
◀ *Track 2049*

名 訪客、觀光客

▶ There is a strange old lady standing in front of your house.
你的房子前面站著一個怪怪的老太太。

vo·cab·u·lar·y [vəˈkæbjəˌlɛrɪ]
◀ *Track 2050*

名 單字、字彙

▶ He has a wide vocabulary. It's no wonder that he can read
very difficult articles.
他的辭彙量很大，難怪連很難的文章都能讀懂。

vol·ley·ball [ˈvɑlɪˌbɔl]
◀ *Track 2051*

名 排球

▶ I am fond （喜歡）of playing volleyball. 我很喜歡打排球。

vote [vot]
◀ *Track 2052*

名 選票 動 投票 同 ballot 選票

▶名 He got less votes than last time. 他這次獲得的選票比上次少。

▶動 Most women voted for this candidate （候選人）.
大部分婦女都投票給這名候選人。

vot·er [ˈvotɚ]
◀ *Track 2053*

名 投票者

▶ The voters lined up to cast their ballot in the case.
投票者將選票投入箱子裡。

文法字詞解析

play 後面加球類運動的話，兩者之間不用加定冠詞，如果後面加樂器的話，中間就要加上定冠詞來限定後面的名詞。

[Ww]

waist [west] 🔊 *Track 2054*
名 腰部
▶The skirt is too loose at the waist.
這件裙子腰身太鬆。

wait·er/wait·ress 🔊 *Track 2055*
[ˈwetɚ]/[ˈwetrɪs]
名 服務生 / 女服務生
▶There are ten waiters and fifteen waitresses in that restaurant.
那個餐廳有十個男服務生和十五個女服務生。

wake [wek] 🔊 *Track 2056*
動 喚醒、醒
▶Will you please wake me up at five a.m. tomorrow morning?
請你明天早上五點鐘叫我起床好嗎？

文法字詞解析
in the wake of... = 繼……之後，如：
Problems followed in the wake of the earthquake.
地震後，許多問題接踵而來。

wal·let [ˈwɑlɪt] 🔊 *Track 2057*
名 錢包、錢袋
▶I had some name cards in my wallet.
我放一些名片在皮夾裡。

wa·ter·fall [ˈwɔtɚˌfɔl] 🔊 *Track 2058*
名 瀑布
▶I heard that you took many pictures of the waterfall yesterday.
我聽說昨天你拍了許多瀑布的照片。

wa·ter·mel·on [ˈwɔtɚˌmɛlən] 🔊 *Track 2059*
名 西瓜
▶Which flavor do you want, watermelon or mango?
你要哪種口味，西瓜還是芒果？

wave [wev] 🔊 *Track 2060*
名 浪、波 動 搖動、波動 同 sway 搖動
▶名 Be careful of the bigger waves. 要小心比較大的浪。
▶動 He waved goodbye and got on the bus.
他揮手告別，上了公車。

文法字詞解析
中文會說突然來了波「熱浪」，英文同樣也有「heat wave」的說法。

weap·on [ˈwɛpən] 🔊 *Track 2061*
名 武器、兵器
▶The police didn't have any weapon at hand when encountering the villain.
警察遇到惡混時，沒有帶任何武器。

wed [wɛd] 🔊 *Track 2062*
動 嫁、娶、結婚 同 marry 結婚
▶He thinks that I am too poor to wed his sister.
他認為我太窮，不配娶他的妹妹。

Level
1

Level
2

漸入佳境、學習零壓力──
邁向常用2200單字

Level
3

Level
4

Level
5

Level
6

week·day [ˋwik͵de]　◀€ *Track 2063*

名 平日、工作日

▶Not all the offices are open from 9:00 a.m. to 5:00 p.m. on weekdays.
不是所有的辦公室在工作日都是從上午九點到下午五點辦公。

west·ern [ˋwɛstən]　◀€ *Track 2064*

形 西方的、西方國家的

▶Western values brought cultural shock to me.
西方價值觀讓我有文化衝擊的感受。

wet [wɛt]　◀€ *Track 2065*

形 潮濕的 動 弄濕

▶形 Your socks are totally wet. 你的襪子都濕透了。
▶動 The dog has wet the floor. 那隻狗把地板都弄濕了。

whale [hwel]　◀€ *Track 2066*

名 鯨魚

▶A whale is no less a mammal（哺乳動物）than a horse is.
鯨魚和馬一樣都是哺乳動物。

what·ev·er [hwɑtˋɛvɚ]　◀€ *Track 2067*

形 任何的 代 任何

▶形 Whatever flavor ice cream is fine with me.
任何一種冰淇淋口味對我來說都很好。
▶代 Would you like to have something to eat? You can take whatever you want.
你想不想吃點東西呢？你想要什麼就拿什麼。

wheel [hwil]　◀€ *Track 2068*

名 輪子、輪 動 滾動

▶名 Generally（一般地）speaking, a car has four wheels, but some cars have more. 一般來講，一輛汽車有四個輪子，但是有的車會多一些輪子。
▶動 He wheeled round and ran away. 他一轉身便跑掉了。

when·ev·er [hwɛnˋɛvɚ]　◀€ *Track 2069*

副 無論何時 連 無論何時 同 anytime 任何時候

▶副 Whenever I have free time, I would read electronic books.
任何時間，只要我有空，我就會讀電子書。
▶連 You can visit us whenever you want to.
你無論何時想拜訪我們都可以。

wher·ev·er [hwɛrˋɛvɚ]　◀€ *Track 2070*

副 無論何處 連 無論何處

▶副 Would you please tell me wherever you found this book?
你能告訴我到底是在什麼地方找到這本書的嗎？
▶連 Would you please leave me alone? You can go wherever you like. 別來吵我好嗎？你愛去哪就去哪吧。

whis·per [ˈhwɪspɚ] 🔊 *Track 2071*
動 耳語 名 輕聲細語 同 murmur 低語聲
▶動 There are some girls whispering in the corner of the room.
房間的角落處有幾個女孩子在竊竊私語。
▶名 Some students are debating the problem in whispers.
有幾個學生在低聲辯論這個問題。

who·ev·er [huˈɛvɚ] 🔊 *Track 2072*
代 任何人、無論誰
▶Whoever applies for this job vacancy has to take a computer test.
任何想要應徵這個職務的人都要經過電腦測驗。

wid·en [ˈwaɪdn̩] 🔊 *Track 2073*
動 使……變寬、增廣
▶Her eyes widened when she heard the news.
聽到那個消息，她的雙眼睜得老大。

width [wɪdθ] 🔊 *Track 2074*
名 寬、廣 同 breadth 寬度
▶I don't know the width of the road.
我不知道這條路有多寬。

wild [waɪld] 🔊 *Track 2075*
形 野生的、野性的
▶We learned how to survive in the wild.
我們學習如何在野外求生。

文法字詞解析
be wild about = 對……很熱心
rumors run wild = 謠言滿天飛

will·ing [ˈwɪlɪŋ] 🔊 *Track 2076*
形 心甘情願的
▶Not everyone is willing to share the sorrows（悲傷）of others.
不是每個人都樂於分擔別人的悲傷。

wind·y [ˈwɪndɪ] 🔊 *Track 2077*
形 多風的
▶It's so windy outside. My umbrella got blown away.
外面風那麼大，我的傘都被吹走了。

wing [wɪŋ] 🔊 *Track 2078*
名 翅膀、翼 動 飛
▶名 The little bird's wing was injured（受傷的）.
這隻小鳥的翅膀受傷了。
▶動 The plane winged over the Alps.
這架飛機飛越了阿爾卑斯山。

win·ner [ˈwɪnɚ] 🔊 *Track 2079*
名 勝利者、優勝者 同 victor 勝利者
▶The winner of the competition can have a large sum of prize money.
這個競賽的贏家可以贏得大筆獎金。

Level 1
Level 2
漸入佳境、學習零壓力——邁向常用2200單字
Level 3
Level 4
Level 5
Level 6

251

wire [waɪr]
◀≋ *Track 2080*

名 金屬絲、電線

▶The rope is not strong enough. Let's use a wire instead.
這根繩子不夠結實,我們改用金屬線吧。

wise [waɪz]
◀≋ *Track 2081*

形 智慧的、睿智的 同 smart 聰明的

▶It's a wise decision to quit smoking.
戒菸是明智的決定。

with·in [wɪðˋɪn]
◀≋ *Track 2082*

介 在……之內 同 inside 在……之內

▶We'll arrive within two hours.
我們兩個小時內就會到了。

文法字詞解析

within 和 in 在用法上很容易弄混,in 搭配上未來式時,它的意思是「經過某一段時間以後」,而 within 則是「在那段時間以內」。所以,如果把例句改成「We'll arrive in two hours.」的話,這句話的意思就會變成:「我們過兩小時後回來。」

with·out [wɪðˋaʊt]
◀≋ *Track 2083*

介 沒有、不

▶You guys have to go without me.
你們去吧,我不一起去了。

wolf [wʊlf]
◀≋ *Track 2084*

名 狼

▶The wolf looks a lot like a dog.
這隻狼看起來真像狗啊。

wond·er [ˋwʌndɚ]
◀≋ *Track 2085*

名 奇蹟、驚奇 動 對……感到疑惑

▶名 No wonder he ended up marrying her.
難怪他最後娶了她。

▶動 He wondered why she was always so unhappy.
他實在不懂她為什麼總是這麼不開心。

文法字詞解析

wonder 後面可以加 wh 開頭的疑問詞作為間接問句,表示「想知道……」。

won·der·ful [ˋwʌndɚfəl]
◀≋ *Track 2086*

形 令人驚奇的、奇妙的 同 marvelous 令人驚奇的

▶The weather has been wonderful. 近來天氣好極了。

wood·en [ˋwʊdn̩]
◀≋ *Track 2087*

形 木製的

▶The wooden casket was passed down from my grandfather.
這個木箱是我祖父傳下來的。

文法字詞解析

有字尾「-en」的字可以是形容詞也可以是動詞,如果作為形容詞,意思是「由某種材質所製成」,像是「wooden box(木箱)」、「golden ring(金戒指)」。

wool [wʊl]
◀≋ *Track 2088*

名 羊毛

▶This wool suit is too expensive for me to buy.
這套毛料套裝太貴了,我買不起。

worth [wɝθ]
◀≋ *Track 2089*

名 價值

▶Whatever is worth doing at all is worth doing well.
凡是值得做的事就值得把它做好。

wound [wund]

Track 2090

名 傷口 動 傷害 同 harm 傷害

▶名 The soldier put some medicine on his wound.
軍人在他的傷口上塗藥。

▶動 There were many soldiers wounded in the Second World War. 有很多士兵在第二次世界大戰中負傷。

[Yy]

yard [jɑrd]

Track 2091

名 庭院、院子

▶There are three apple trees and two pear trees in our yard.
我們家院子有三棵蘋果樹和兩棵梨樹。

youth [juθ]

Track 2092

名 青年

▶The writer used to be rebellious in his youth.
這位作者以前年輕時很叛逆。

[Zz]

ze·bra [ˈzibrə]

Track 2093

名 斑馬

名詞複數 zebras, zebra

▶The kids smiled are the sight of the cute zebra cubs.
小朋友看到可愛的新生小斑馬就微笑。

文法字詞解析

除了用來描述真正的傷口，wound 也可用來表示心理上受傷。例如當朋友開你玩笑時，就可以假裝受傷地說一句：You wound me!（你這樣說我好受傷！）

Level 1

Level 2

漸入佳境、學習零壓力——
邁向常用2200單字

Level 3

Level 4

Level 5

Level 6

下面有兩篇文章，全是根據 Level2 的單字寫出來的，文章中超出 level2 的單字，有註記在一旁。

請先不要看全文的中文翻譯，試著讀讀看這兩篇文章，若能全盤了解意思，代表你對 Level2 單字已經駕輕就熟，可以升級到 Level3 囉！快來自我挑戰看看吧！

Reading Practice 1

The modern pizza was first invented in Naples, Italy but the word pizza is Greek in origin（來源）, which is changed from the Greek word pikte, meaning solid（固體的）or clotted（阻塞的）.

The ancient Greeks covered their bread with oils, herbs and cheese. The first major change that led to flat bread pizza was the use of tomato as topping. It was common for the poor of the area around Naples to add tomato to their yeast-based flat bread, and so the pizza began. While it is difficult to say for sure who invented the pizza, it is believed that modern pizza was first made by baker Raffaele Esposito of Naples.

A story was passed down that that the famous flavor of pizza, Pizza Margherita, was invented in 1889, when the Royal Palace of Capodimonte asked the Neapolitan pizzaiolo Raffaele Esposito to create a pizza in honor（致敬）of the visiting Queen Margherita.

Of the three different pizzas he created, the Queen strongly preferred a pie swathed in the colors of the Italian flag: red（tomato）, green（basil）, and white（mozzarella）. Supposedly, this kind of pizza was then named after the Queen as Pizza Margherita. Later, the dish has become popular in many parts of the world.

The first Pizza Hut, the chain of pizza restaurants know to many people nowadays, appeared in the United States during the 1930s. In the modern time, there are many flavors of pizza worldwide, along with several dish based upon pizza.

Reading Practice 2

Football or soccer, which is considered to be the most popular sport in the world, is a team sport playedbetween two teams of eleven players using a spherical ball.

The object of the game, which is played on a wide rectangular field with a goal on each end of the field, is to score by putting the ball into the adversary goal. The goal is kept by a goalkeeper, who is allowed, at the exception（例外） of other players, to use his / her hands in the game. The winners are those who score the most goals.

If the football（or soccer）match ends in a draw the two teams may be redirected to playextra time and / or penalty（罰）shootouts（each team taking turns to have a set number of kicks at the goal.）

The way football is played now was first codified in England. Nowadays, it is governed by the FIFA, "Fédération Internationale de Football Association" （International Federation（聯邦）of Association Football.）

The game is played now all over the world and competitions are organized nationally, continentally and internationally. The most prestigious of football competitions is the World Cup, which is held every four years.

Level 1

Level 2

Level 3

Level 4

Level 5

Level 6

邁向常用2200單字——漸入佳境、學習零壓力

　　現代的披薩最早是在義大利的那普勒司發明的，但 pizza 這個字是原自希臘文裡 pikte 這個表示「固體」或「阻塞」的單字。

　　古代希臘人會放油，香草和起司在麵包上。最早讓這種扁平麵包變成披薩樣子的改變是使用番茄作為佐料。那不勒斯附近地區的窮人會烘烤這種發酵扁平麵包，於是披薩就產生了。

　　雖然很難確切地指出是誰發明出披薩的，但據說，現代的披薩最早是由那不勒斯的烘焙師傅拉費爾．艾波西托做出來的。

　　有個傳說是，現在很受著名的瑪格麗特披薩，是在 1889 年由卡波堤蒙特皇宮委託披薩師傅拉費爾．艾波西托創造出一款要獻給來訪的馬格麗特皇后的披薩。在師傅創造的三種披薩中，皇后最中意的披薩餅，上面有義大利國旗上的三種顏色：紅色的蕃茄，綠色的羅勒，以及白色的馬札瑞拉起司。之後，這種披薩就以馬格麗特皇后命名。之後，這道菜餚在世界各地變的很受歡迎。

　　現在許多人知道的連鎖披薩店必勝客，是在 1930 年代在美國開第一家店。現在，披薩在世界各地有許多不同的口味，也有以披薩為基礎發展出的不同菜餚。

　　被認為是全球最受歡迎運動的足球，是由兩隊各由十一名球員組成隊伍競賽的團隊運動。

　　足球比賽是在兩端各有一個球門的長方型球場上舉行，目標是要把球射進對手的球門裡。球場上，只有守門員可以用手碰球。進球次數較多的一隊贏得比賽。

　　如果比賽終了，兩隊平手，就會進行延長賽，或者罰球（兩隊輪流射門。）

　　現代足球賽進行方式，最早是在英格蘭確立的。現在，足球規則是由國際足球總會制定的。

　　目前，全球各地有國家、各大洲，以及國際的足球賽。最著名的是每四年舉辦一次的世界盃足球賽。

Level 3

駕輕就熟、更上一層樓——
累積實力3200單字

Level 3

駕輕就熟、更上一層樓——
累積實力3200單字

[Aa]

a·board [əˋbord]　🔊 *Track 2094*

副 / 介 在船（飛機、火車）上

▶副 A crew of eight flight attendant will take care of the passengers onboard. 八位空服員要照顧機上所有乘客。

▶介 We are the last two to go aboard the ship.
我們是最後上船的兩個人。

---

ac·cept·a·ble [əkˋsɛptəbl̩]　🔊 *Track 2095*

形 可接受的

▶I don't think your price terms are acceptable, so we won't consider your company. 我們覺得你們的價格條件不可接受，因此不打算考慮貴公司了。

---

ac·ci·dent [ˋæksədənt]　🔊 *Track 2096*

名 事故、偶發事件 同 casualty 事故

▶He had a terrible accident and almost died.
他遭遇了一場可怕的事故，差點就死了。

---

ac·count [əˋkaʊnt]　🔊 *Track 2097*

名 帳目、記錄 動 視為、負責

▶名 I forgot my account and password to this website.
我忘記我在這個網站的帳號和密碼。

▶動 Can you account for his actions? 你能為他的行為負責嗎？

---

ac·cu·rate [ˋækjərɪt]　🔊 *Track 2098*

形 正確的、準確的 同 correct 正確的

▶Would you mind sending the accurate data to our company this afternoon?
您介意今天下午把準確資料送到我們公司來嗎？

---

ache [ek]　🔊 *Track 2099*

名 疼痛 同 pain 疼痛

▶My grandparents both feel aches in their backs.
我的祖父母都覺得背在隱隱作痛。

---

a·chieve·(ment) [əˋtʃiv(mənt)]　🔊 *Track 2100*

動 實現、完成 名 成績、成就

▶動 I paid a lot of effort to achieve my goal.
我付出很多努力達成我的目標。

▶名 He made a great achievement in the field of business.
他在商業領域做出了一番成就。

文法字詞解析

「aboard」（在船、飛機、火車上）這個單字和「abroad」（在國外）長得實在很像，又常在旅行時用到，因此很容易搞混。那該怎麼分辨呢？很簡單，我們「登機」、「上火車」的動作叫做「board」，上飛機前需要的「登機證」叫「boarding pass」。因此，後面是「board」的「aboard」就是兩者之中表示「在船、飛機、火車上」的單字了。

萬用延伸句型

Would you mind V-ing... 您介意……嗎？

ac·tiv·i·ty [æk`tɪvətɪ]　◀ᴇ *Track 2101*

名 活動、活躍

▶Do you mind if we invite a foreign guest to take part in this activity? 您介意我們邀請一位外賓參加這次活動嗎？

ac·tu·al [`æktʃʊəl]　◀ᴇ *Track 2102*

形 實際的、真實的

▶I can't tell her actual age from her appearance.
　我無法從她的外表看出她的真實年齡。

ad·di·tion·al [ə`dɪʃən!]　◀ᴇ *Track 2103*

形 額外的、附加的　同 extra 額外的

▶We might have to ask an additional charge for your items.
　我們可能要向您的物品進行額外收費。

ad·mire [əd`maɪr]　◀ᴇ *Track 2104*

動 欽佩、讚賞

▶How do I know whether she admires you or not? You'll have to ask her yourself.
　我怎麼會知道她欣不欣賞你啊？你應該自己去問她啊。

ad·mit [əd`mɪt]　◀ᴇ *Track 2105*

動 容許……進入、承認　反 forbid 禁止

▶I was admitted into the prestigious university.
　我獲准進入那間著名大學就讀。

adopt [ə`dɑpt]　◀ᴇ *Track 2106*

動 收養

▶Why don't you adopt a child if you are so fond of kids?
　既然你很喜歡小孩子，那為什麼不去領養一個呢？

ad·vanced [əd`vænst]　◀ᴇ *Track 2107*

形 在前面的、先進的　同 forward 前面的

▶I don't think this poor country can catch up with the advanced countries（先進國家）.
　我覺得這個貧窮的國家趕不上先進的國家。

ad·van·tage [əd`væntɪdʒ]　◀ᴇ *Track 2108*

名 利益、優勢　同 benefit 利益

▶We should take advantage of this chance.
　我們應該要好好利用這次機會。

ad·ven·ture [əd`vɛntʃə]　◀ᴇ *Track 2109*

名 冒險

▶I love listening to stories about her adventures.
　我喜歡聽關於她各種冒險的故事。

ad·ver·tise(ment)/

ad [ˌædvə`taɪz(mənt)]/[æd]　◀ᴇ *Track 2110*

動 登廣告　名 廣告、宣傳

文法字詞解析

這裡的「parties」指的不是我們平常「開趴」的「派對」，而是指「各方相關人士」。

Level 1

Level 2

Level 3

累積實力3200單字

駕輕就熟、更上一層樓——

Level 4

Level 5

Level 6

萬用延伸句型

Do you mind if I... 你介意我……
這個句型和「Do you mind V-ing」雖然長得很像，但兩個句型的主角是不同人喔！舉例來說，如果你問：「Do you mind opening the door?」，那麼你是要請對方去關門。如果你問：「Do you mind if I open the door?」，那麼要去關門的人是你自己，對方不用移動。

▶動 We advertised for our campaign by sending emails to potential participants.
我們透過寄電子郵件給可能參加的人,來為活動打廣告。

▶名 I suggest putting an advertisement in the newspaper.
我建議在報紙上登廣告。

ad·vice [əd'vaɪs]　◀€ *Track 2111*

名 忠告

▶Don't follow the man's advice for he is just an amateur.
那個人只是業餘的,不用聽他的建議。

ad·vise [əd'vaɪz]　◀€ *Track 2112*

動 勸告

▶It was the second time that she had advised me to take part in this plan. 這是她第二次來勸我參與這次計畫了。

ad·vi·ser/ad·vi·sor　◀€ *Track 2113*
[əd'vaɪzə]

名 顧問

▶By the time you find the adviser, we will have solved all the problems. 等你找到顧問,我們都已經解決完所有問題了。

萬用延伸句型
By the time... 到了……的時候(後面可接各種時態的動詞)

af·fect [ə'fɛkt]　◀€ *Track 2114*

動 影響　同 influence 影響

▶Only a few people were affected by the lack of produce.
農產品短缺,只有影響到少數人。

af·ford [ə'ford]　◀€ *Track 2115*

動 給予、供給、能負擔

▶Can you really afford to buy a car? 你真的買得起車嗎?

af·ter·ward(s) [ˈæftəwəd(z)]　◀€ *Track 2116*

副 以後

▶Paul has an appointment with his boss, so he ate dinner and went out soon afterwards.
保羅跟他的老闆有約,所以他吃過晚飯不久以後就出去了。

ag·ri·cul·ture [ˈægrɪˌkʌltʃə]　◀€ *Track 2117*

名 農業、農藝、農學

▶My sister studies agriculture in university. 我姊姊在大學念農業。

文法字詞解析
要説「某人在大學念的是……」的時候,可以用「study + 某科目」這個説法。如果要説「主修是……」,則可以説「major in + 科目」。例如,若這位姊姊主修的就是農業學,就可以説她「majors in agriculture」。

air-con·di·tion·er　◀€ *Track 2118*
[ˈɛrˌkənˈdɪʃənə]

名 空調

▶Do you mind if I turn off the air-conditioner?
你介意我關掉空調嗎?

文法字詞解析
把冷氣打開則是説「turn on」。雖然「open」也是「打開」的意思,但一般不説「open the air conditioner」,可能會讓人誤會你是真的要把冷氣拆開來看。

al·ley [ˈælɪ]　◀€ *Track 2119*

名 巷、小徑

▶The alley is so narrow that the fire truck couldn't pass through it. 這條巷道太窄了,消防車無法通過。

a·maze·(ment) [ə'mez(mənt)] 🔊 *Track 2120*

動 使……吃驚 名 吃驚

▶動 It amazed me that he was actually younger than me.
他居然比我還年輕，真是太讓我震驚了。

▶名 The students all looked at me in amazement when I told them the test was cancelled.
我跟學生們說考試取消時，他們都很驚愕地看著我。

am·bas·sa·dor [æm'bæsədɚ] 🔊 *Track 2121*

名 大使、使節

同 diplomat 外交官

▶The ambassador's responsibility is to maintain the diplomatic tie with our ally.
大使的責任就是要維持和我們友邦的外交關係。

am·bi·tion [æm'bɪʃən] 🔊 *Track 2122*

名 雄心壯志、志向

▶His daughter wants to be an astronaut（太空人）in the future; what a great ambition!
他女兒長大後想成為一名太空人，多麼遠大的抱負啊！

> **萬用延伸句型**
> What + a + adj. + N! 多麼……的……啊！
> （強調、讚嘆的句型）

Level 1

Level 2

Level 3

Level 4

Level 5

Level 6

駕輕就熟、更上一層樓——累積實力3200單字

an·gel ['endʒəl] 🔊 *Track 2123*

名 天使

▶The kind-hearted girl is like an angel to me.
那好心的女孩對我來說就像個天使。

an·gle ['æŋgl] 🔊 *Track 2124*

名 角度、立場

▶You should look at this problem from a different angle.
你應該從另外一個角度來看待這件事情。

an·nounce·(ment) [ə'naʊns(mənt)] 🔊 *Track 2125*

動 宣告、公佈、通知 名 宣佈、宣告 同 declare 宣佈

▶動 It would be so kind of you to announce the guests when they come in.
你能在客人來的時候通報一聲的話就太好了。

▶名 Have you heard the boss's announcement?
你聽到老闆宣布的事了沒？

a·part [ə'pɑrt] 🔊 *Track 2126*

副 分散地、遠離地 反 together 一起地

▶We were separated far apart after graduation.
我們畢業之後分隔兩地。

> **文法字詞解析**
> apart 的意思是「分散地、遠離地」，它和「a part」（一部分）兩字長得很像，因此連母語人士都常會不小心寫錯。但它們的意思和用法可是大不同，要小心喔！

ap·par·ent [ə'pærənt] 🔊 *Track 2127*

形 明顯的、外表的 同 obvious 明顯的

▶It's apparent that she is unwilling（不願意）to go with us.
很明顯，她不願意跟我們出去。

ap·peal [ə`pil]　🔊 *Track 2128*

名 吸引力、懇求　動 引起……的興趣

▶名 I really don't see the appeal of this product.
我真看不出這個產品的吸引力在哪。

▶動 I was appealed by the advertisement.
我被這廣告吸引。

ap·pre·ci·ate [ə`priʃɪˌet]　🔊 *Track 2129*

動 欣賞、鑑賞、感激

▶We can't fully（完全地）appreciate foreign works unless we can understand their cultures.
除非我們能了解其他文化，要不然我們無法完全欣賞到外國作品的精髓。

ap·proach [ə`protʃ]　🔊 *Track 2130*

動 接近

▶I don't think the driver slowed down when the car approached the intersection（十字路口）.
我認為車子向十字口靠近的時候，司機沒有減速。

ap·prove [ə`pruv]　🔊 *Track 2131*

動 批准、認可

▶Our supervisor didn't approve our proposal.
我們的主管沒有同意我們的提案。

a·quar·i·um [ə`kwɛrɪəm]　🔊 *Track 2132*

名 水族館

▶Would you like to go to the aquarium with me?
你要不要和我一起去水族館？

a·rith·me·tic [ə`rɪθməˌtɪk]　🔊 *Track 2133*

名 算術　形 算術的

▶名 My little brother is not good at arithmetic.
我弟弟數學不好。

▶形 Maybe you should get your brother to help you work out the arithmetic problem.
你或許應該叫哥哥來幫你解答這道算術題。

ar·riv·al [ə`raɪvl]　🔊 *Track 2134*

名 到達

▶At the arrival of the Korean star, many fans in the lobby began to cheer. 韓國明星一到達，許多影迷就開始歡呼。

ash [æʃ]　🔊 *Track 2135*

名 灰燼、灰

▶His ashes were placed in a pot. 他的骨灰被放進一個壺裡。

a·side [ə`saɪd]　🔊 *Track 2136*

副 在旁邊

▶Tom took me aside and talked to me about this matter.
湯姆把我拉到一邊來談這件事。

文法字詞解析

在這一句中的「works」不是我們常見的「工作、職業」的意思喔！它代表的是「作品」，例如藝術作品、音樂作品、文學作品等，都包含在這個範圍內。

萬用延伸句型

all joking aside... 即「先把玩笑話放到一邊」，也就是「好，不說笑了，說點正經的」的意思。

例如：I bet you all want to kill me for calling a meeting right now! Okay, all joking aside, I need some suggestions for the next project.

我這個時間叫大家來開會，你們一定很想殺了我吧！好，不說笑了，關於下個案子，我需要一些建議。

as·sist [ə`sɪst]
動 說明、援助 同 help 說明
▶I assisted my uncle to move out the cabinet.
我協助我的叔叔把櫃子搬出屋外。

ath·lete [`æθlit]
Track 2138
名 運動員
▶I don't think he is the most experienced athlete in the team.
我認為他並不是隊上最有經驗的運動員。

at·tempt [ə`tɛmpt]
Track 2139
動／名 嘗試、企圖
▶動 It was the first time that he had attempted to get in touch with his mom after the quarrel.
這還是他吵架後第一次試圖聯繫母親。
▶名 It is the first time that the shy boy has made an attempt at a joke in front of us.
這是這個害羞的男孩子第一次試圖在我們面前開玩笑。

at·ti·tude [`ætə͵tjud]
Track 2140
名 態度、心態、看法
▶Gary always holds a positive attitude toward his work.
蓋瑞總是對工作抱持正面態度。

at·tract [ə`trækt]
Track 2141
動 吸引
▶The park in that city is very famous and attracts many people.
這公園在這個城市非常有名，吸引了很多人。

at·trac·tive [ə`træktɪv]
Track 2142
形 吸引人的、動人的
▶The scenic spot is so attractive because of the beautiful lake.
這個景點因為美麗的湖很具吸引力。

| 文法字詞解析 |
attractive 經常用來形容人的「長相」或其他事物的「外型」吸引人，不過也可以用在說一個點子聽起來很吸引人喔！

au·di·ence [`ɔdɪəns]
Track 2143
名 聽眾 同 spectator 觀眾
▶I feel nervous speaking in front of such a large audience.
在這麼多觀眾面前說話，讓我感覺很緊張。

au·thor [`ɔθɚ]
Track 2144
名 作家、作者 同 writer 作者
▶He is my favorite author. I've read every single one of his books.
他是我最喜愛的作家，他的每本書我都讀過了。

au·to·mat·ic [͵ɔtə`mætɪk]
Track 2145
形 自動的
▶There is an automatic telling machine in the convenience store.
在便利商店裡有一台自動提款機。

Level 1

Level 2

Level 3

駕輕就熟、更上一層樓——累積實力3200單字

Level 4

Level 5

Level 6

au·to·mo·bile/au·to

Track 2146

[ˋɔtəməˏbil]/[ˋɔto]

名 汽車 同 car 汽車

▶There is no one who can design an automobile which pleases every driver.

沒有人能設計出能讓每個司機都滿意的車。

---

a·vail·a·ble [əˋveləbl]

Track 2147

形 可利用的、可取得的

▶The latest version of I-phone will be available on the market next month.

I-phone最新的版本，下個月將可以在市場上買到。

---

av·e·nue [ˋævəˏnju]

Track 2148

名 大道、大街

▶Can you tell me where Second Avenue is?

你能告訴我第二大街在哪裡嗎？

---

av·er·age [ˋævərɪdʒ]

Track 2149

名 平均數

▶It's not easy for him to spend one hour a day on average on English.

每天平均花一個小時來唸英語對他來說並不容易。

---

a·wake [əˋwek]

Track 2150

動 喚醒、提醒

▶Why are you still awake at 2:00 AM?

妳為什們凌晨兩點還醒著？

---

a·wak·en [əˋwekən]

Track 2151

動 使……覺悟

▶There must be something which can awaken him to a sense of duty.

肯定有什麼事情能夠喚起他的責任感。

---

a·ward [əˋwɔrd]

Track 2152

名 獎品、獎賞 動 授與、頒獎

▶名 The novel earned the writer a literary（文學的）award.

這部長篇小說為作家贏得了文學獎。

▶動 He was awarded the top prize by the committee.

他被委員會授予了頭獎。

---

a·ware [əˋwɛr]

Track 2153

形 注意到的、覺察的

▶It will be a long time before people are aware of this consequence（後果）.

人們要過很久才會意識到這個後果。

---

aw·ful [ˋɔful]

Track 2154

形 可怕的、嚇人的 同 horrible 可怕的

▶To buy a used car was an awful decision.

買一台二手車真是個糟糕的決定。

文法字詞解析

大家常常用的「please」（請）也可以當作動詞喔！在這句中的 please 就是動詞，它是「討好」、「使開心」的意思。

文法字詞解析

雖然英文中大部分的形容詞都是放在名詞前面，但也有一些會放在後面，這些形容詞就叫做「後置形容詞」，像 available 這種以「able」結尾的形容詞就幾乎都是如此。

萬用延伸句型

It will be a long time before...
要很久以後才會……

ax/axe [æks] ◀≋ Track 2155

名 斧 動 劈、砍

▶名 People in the ancient times used stone axes.
以前古人使用石斧。

▶動 The man felt very tired after axing the tree.
那個男人在砍了那棵樹後覺得很累。

[Bb]

back·ground [ˋbækˏɡraʊnd] ◀≋ Track 2156

名 背景

▶The background of the slide should be changed.
這個投影片的背景需要被換掉。

文法字詞解析
這一句的 might 後面其實省略了「mind his impoverished back-ground」，也就是說整個句子的完整意思是「我不介意他貧困的背景，但我父母可能會介意他貧困的背景」。同樣的事情重複兩次不是很奇怪嗎？在英文中也很討厭重複，因此才把 might 後面的內容都乾脆省略了。

ba·con [ˋbekən] ◀≋ Track 2157

名 培根、燻肉

▶I love having bacon for breakfast.
我最愛早餐吃培根。

bac·te·ri·a [bækˋtɪrɪə] ◀≋ Track 2158

名 細菌

▶It is possible for lab（實驗室）assistants（助手）to multiply bacteria in the laboratory（實驗室）.
實驗助手能夠在實驗室繁殖細菌。

文法字詞解析
這一句中出現了 lab 和 laboratory，但其實它們的意思根本是一樣的，lab 是 laboratory 的縮寫。此外，lab 還可以當作拉布拉多狗（labrador retriever）的縮寫。所以當有人告訴你他有 lab 時，不見得代表他很有錢、擁有一座實驗室。

bad·ly [ˋbædlɪ] ◀≋ Track 2159

副 非常地、惡劣地

▶I don't believe that Tom would speak badly of Bill.
我不相信湯姆會說比爾的壞話。

bad·min·ton [ˋbædmɪntən] ◀≋ Track 2160

名 羽毛球

▶Ms. Dai won the championship in the international badminton tournament.
戴女士贏得國際羽球比賽的冠軍。

bag·gage [ˋbæɡɪdʒ] ◀≋ Track 2161

名 行李

同 lugguge 行李

▶Jane, hurry up! It's time for us to check in our baggage.
珍妮，快點啦！我們該去托運行李了。

文法字詞解析
baggage 和 luggage 同樣都能當作「行李」的意思，不過 baggage 能夠拿來暗示人「心理上的」包袱，例如「emotional baggage」指的就是「情緒上的負擔」，luggage 則沒有這層意思。

bait [bet] ◀≋ Track 2162

名 誘餌 動 誘惑

▶名 A fish rose to the bait soon after I set up my fishing equipment.
我裝設好設備沒多久，就有魚來吃餌了。

▶動 He baited me into giving him my password.
他引誘我給他我的密碼。

Level 1
Level 2
Level 3
駕輕就熟、更上一層樓——
累積實力3200單字
Level 4
Level 5
Level 6

ba·lance [`bæləns] ◀ Track 2163

名 平衡 動 使平衡

▶名 Not every woman is able to keep balance between her family and career.

不是每個女人都能在自己的家庭和事業上維持平衡。

▶動 Not everyone can balance the advantages of living in a big city against the disadvantages（不利）.

不是每個人都能權衡住在大城市的利與弊。

ban·dage [`bændɪdʒ] ◀ Track 2164

名 繃帶

▶The bandage on his would was covered with dirt, so he changed it.

傷口上的繃帶有灰塵，所以他把繃帶換掉。

bang [bæŋ] ◀ Track 2165

動 重擊、雷擊

▶He banged the door in anger.

他怒得大聲甩上門。

bare [bɛr] ◀ Track 2166

形 暴露的、僅有的 同 naked 暴露的

▶He is bare to the waist because it's so hot.

他光著上身，因為實在太熱了。

bare·ly [`bɛrlɪ] ◀ Track 2167

副 簡直沒有、幾乎不能

▶I barely know him at all, so can't tell you what he's like.

我幾乎不太認識他，所以無法跟你說他到底是怎樣的人。

barn [bɑrn] ◀ Track 2168

名 穀倉

▶We took shelter in the barn during the thunderstorm.

暴風雨期間，我們在穀倉躲雨。

bar·rel [`bærəl] ◀ Track 2169

名 大桶

▶Would you please draw me a glass of beer from the barrel?

請你從大桶子裡裝一杯啤酒給我好嗎？

bay [be] ◀ Track 2170

名 海灣

▶Let's go to the bay later and have a swim.

我們待會去海灣游泳吧。

beam [bin] ◀ Track 2171

動 放射、發光、眉開眼笑

▶She beamed at the joke that the host of the talk show told.

她被脫口秀主持人的笑話逗得眉開眼笑。

文法字詞解析

這裡說 bang 是「雷擊」的意思，那大聲甩上門為什麼也可以用 bang 呢？因為大聲甩上門不是也會發出如雷聲般大的聲音嗎？因此，像是用力捶門、槍響等等這類如雷貫耳的聲音，也可以用 bang 來表示。

beast [bist]
🔊 Track 2172
名 野獸
▶Long long ago, there was war between the birds and the beasts.
很久很久以前，鳥類與獸類之間發生了一場戰爭。

beg·gar [ˈbɛgɚ]
🔊 Track 2173
名 乞丐
▶The beggar could not walk by himself for his was amputated below his left knee.
這個乞丐無法自己走路，因為他左腳膝蓋以下都被截肢。

be·have [bɪˈhev]
🔊 Track 2174
動 行動、舉止 同 act 行動
▶It's very hard for parents to train their children to behave well at the table. 父母要訓練自己的孩子用餐時舉止得體是很困難的。

be·ing [ˈbiɪŋ]
🔊 Track 2175
名 生命、存在
▶I don't believe that there are strange beings from outer space.
我不相信有來自外太空的奇特生物。

bel·ly/stom·ach/tum·my [ˈbɛlɪ]/[ˈstʌmək]/[ˈtʌmɪ]
🔊 Track 2176
名 腹、胃
▶His belly is huge, probably because he eats so much.
他的肚子超大的，大概是因為他吃很多吧。

be·neath [bɪˈniθ]
🔊 Track 2177
介 在……下
▶The bandit his its treasure beneath the tree.
土匪把他的寶物藏在樹下。

ben·e·fit [ˈbɛnəfɪt]
🔊 Track 2178
名 益處、利益 同 advantage 利益
▶名 This project is of great benefit to everyone.
這項工程對每個人都大有好處。

ber·ry [ˈbɛrɪ]
🔊 Track 2179
名 漿果、莓
▶The girls have gone picking berries. 女孩子們採莓果去了。

bi·ble [ˈbaɪbḷ]
🔊 Track 2180
名 聖經
▶She reads the bible every day before going to sleep.
她每天睡覺前都會讀聖經。

bil·lion [ˈbɪljən]
🔊 Track 2181
名 十億、一兆、無數
▶It cost billions of dollars to build the sewage system.
建造污水系統要花幾十億。

文法字詞解析
beast 指的是「野獸」的意思，聽起來很可怕。但大家想到野獸，常會想到他們擁有強大的蠻力，也就是說野獸多半都「很強」。因此近年來口語中可以用 beast 來描述某人「很強」，例如若你朋友籃球打得很好，就可以說「My friend is a beast at basketball」。

萬用延伸句型
I don't believe that... 我不相信……

文法字詞解析
有些自認高高在上的人，會覺得一些其他的人、事、物都在自己「之下」，這時就可以用 beneath 這個字。例如若叫一位自認高高在上的人去掃地，他可能會說：「Things like that are beneath me!」（這種事在我「之下」，我怎麼可能去做呢！）

Level 1
Level 2
Level 3
Level 4
Level 5
Level 6

駕輕就熟、更上一層樓——累積實力3200單字

bin·go [ˈbɪngo]
🔊 *Track 2182*

名 賓果遊戲

▶They play bingo to kill time before their mom comes home.
他們玩賓果以消磨時間、等媽媽回家。

bis·cuit [ˈbɪskɪt]
🔊 *Track 2183*

名 餅乾、小甜麵包

▶Put the biscuits in the box over there.
請把餅乾放到那邊的盒子裡。

blame [blem]
🔊 *Track 2184*

動 責備 同 accuse

▶The residents in this neighborhood blamed the officials for the surge of water.
居民把淹水這件事怪罪到當地官員頭上。

blan·ket [ˈblæŋkɪt]
🔊 *Track 2185*

名 氈、毛毯

▶It's a little cold tonight. Would you like me to bring you a blanket?
今晚有點冷，我幫您拿條毯子好嗎？

bleed [blid]
🔊 *Track 2186*

動 流血、放血

▶You're bleeding! What happened?
你在流血耶！怎麼了？

bless [blɛs]
🔊 *Track 2187*

動 祝福

▶He was blessed with great talent.
他天資非常聰穎。

blouse [blaʊs]
🔊 *Track 2188*

名 短衫

▶My sister wears blouse and trousers to work.
我姐姐穿著襯衫和長褲去上班。

bold [bold]
🔊 *Track 2189*

形 大膽的 同 brave 勇敢的

▶He is a very bold man. 他是個非常大膽的男子。

boot [but]
🔊 *Track 2190*

名 長靴

▶My boots are too small. They're giving me blisters（水泡）.
我的靴子太小了，我都長水泡了。

bor·der [ˈbɔrdə]
🔊 *Track 2191*

名 邊 同 edge 邊

▶When we passed the border, the guard asked to see our visa.
越過邊界時，守衛要求看我們的簽證。

文法字詞解析

blame 這個單字的用法常會有人搞錯，認為只要是「罵人」（例如吵架的時候互相謾罵）都可以用這個字。其實 blame 並不是「罵」的意思，它含有「責怪」的意思，而人們在責怪別人時常會順口罵出來，才會因此讓許多人誤以為 blame 就是「罵」。事實上，如果你在罵人的時候並沒有要責怪對方，純粹只是想罵他而已，那是不能用 blame 這個字來表示的。

文法字詞解析

bleed 的動詞變化：bleed、bled、bled

bore [bor]
🔊 *Track 2192*

動 鑽孔 名 無聊的人 同 drill 鑽孔

▶動 I don't think that they need to bore for water.
　我認為他們不需要鑿井取水。

▶名 My grandma is a dreadful（可怕的）bore.
　我奶奶是個超級無趣的人。

brake [brek]
🔊 *Track 2193*

名 / 動 煞車

▶名 The brakes on this bike aren't working.
　這腳踏車上的煞車壞了。

▶動 The driver didn't brake when he saw the girl.
　駕駛看到女孩時沒有踩煞車。

brass [bræs]
🔊 *Track 2194*

名 黃銅、銅器

▶Not everyone knows that brass is an alloy（合金）of copper（銅）and zinc（鋅）.
　不是每個人都知道黃銅是銅和鋅的合金。

brav·er·y [ˈbrevərɪ]
🔊 *Track 2195*

名 大膽、勇敢 同 courage 勇氣

▶It's hard to show bravery in the face of danger.
　面臨危險時，很難表現出大無畏的精神。

breast [brɛst]
🔊 *Track 2196*

名 胸膛、胸部

▶How about having chicken breast today for dinner?
　今天我們晚餐吃雞胸肉怎麼樣？

breath [brɛθ]
🔊 *Track 2197*

名 呼吸、氣息

▶I couldn't catch my breath after running for such a long distance.
　我跑了很長距離之後有點喘不過氣。

breathe [brið]
🔊 *Track 2198*

動 呼吸、生存

▶You're hugging me too tightly. I can't breathe!
　你抱太緊了，我都不能呼吸了！

breeze [briz]
🔊 *Track 2199*

名 微風 動 微風輕吹、輕鬆通過

▶名 We sit here enjoying the cool breeze from the lake.
　我們坐在這裡享受湖面上吹來的涼爽微風。

▶動 He breezed through the test without even trying.
　他毫無努力就輕輕鬆鬆地通過了這次考試。

bride [braɪd]
🔊 *Track 2200*

名 新娘

▶The bride toasted to the quest at the banquet.
　新娘在晚宴中間向賓客敬酒。

文法字詞解析

bore是現在式，但它同時也是「bear」（忍受、承擔）的過去式，我們來大致整理一下：
bear的動詞變化：bear, bore, born
或bear, bore, borne
bore的動詞變化：bore, bored, bored
另外也要注意，不要把bored的過去式跟形容詞bored（感到厭倦的）搞混了喔。

萬用延伸句型

hold sb.'s breath 憋氣
例如：You can hold your breath for two minutes? That's amazing!
你能憋氣兩分鐘，真不簡單。

Level 1
Level 2
Level 3
Level 4
Level 5
Level 6

駕輕就熟、更上一層樓——累積實力3200單字

bril·liant [ˈbrɪljənt]
Track 2201

形 有才氣的、出色的

▶He is a brilliant scholar（學者）in physics.
他是個出色的物理學者。

brook [brʊk]
Track 2202

名 川、小河、溪流

▶There are small fishes in the brook.
小河裡有魚。

broom [brum]
Track 2203

名 掃帚、長柄刷

▶Witches ride brooms. 女巫都騎掃帚。

brow(s) [braʊ(z)]
Track 2204

名 眉毛

▶Her brow is wrinkled in outrage（憤怒）. 她憤怒得皺起了眉頭。

bub·ble [ˈbʌbl̩]
Track 2205

名 泡沫、氣泡

▶The dog is having fun playing with the bubble when taking a shower. 小狗洗澡時玩泡泡玩得很開心。

buck·et/pail [ˈbʌkɪt]/[pel]
Track 2206

名 水桶、提桶

▶Would you please go and fill this bucket with water for me?
請你去替我裝滿一桶水來好嗎？

bud [bʌd]
Track 2207

名 芽 動 萌芽 同 flourish 茂盛

▶名 The branches in the garden are in full bud.
花園裡的枝頭都長滿了花蕾。

▶動 Unless you water the seeds regularly（定期地）, they will not bud in spring. 如果你不定期給那些種子澆水，它們在春天是不會發芽的。

budg·et [ˈbʌdʒɪt]
Track 2208

名 預算

▶Our school cut the budget on renovation of the dormitory.
我們學校刪減了整修宿舍的預算。

buf·fa·lo [ˈbʌfl̩o]
Track 2209

名 水牛、野牛

▶There were lots of buffaloes in North America 100 years ago.
一百年前，北美有大量的野牛。

buf·fet [ˈbʌfɪt]
Track 2210

名 自助餐

▶We had buffet at the luxurious restaurant.
我們在奢華的餐廳享用自助餐。

文法字詞解析

句中的 outrage（憤怒）還有一個伙伴叫「outrageous」，是形容詞。既然 outrage 是「憤怒」，outrageous 就是「令人憤怒的」囉！同時，outrageous 還能用來表示「很難以置信的」，例如若你的鄰居把他家的汽車停進了你家的游泳池，你不但憤怒，同時又覺得這難以置信，就可以説：That's outrageous!

文法字詞解析

和 bud 相關的形容詞 budding 即「萌芽的」、「新崛起的」的意思。像是剛出道的歌手如同剛冒出來的嫩芽一般還有很大的成長空間以及無限可能性，就可以稱為 budding singer。

bulb [bʌlb]
◀ *Track 2211*

名 電燈泡

▶The bulb has burned out. Can we get someone to replace（取代）it? 燈泡燒壞了，我們可不可以找人來換一個啊？

bull [bʊl]
◀ *Track 2212*

名 公牛

▶The bull rushed at the man in a fit of madness.
那頭公牛憤怒地朝著那個男子奔去。

bul·let [`bʊlɪt]
◀ *Track 2213*

名 子彈、彈頭

▶He got hit by a bullet; luckily, didn't die.
他被子彈射中了，但幸好沒死。

bump [bʌmp]
◀ *Track 2214*

動 碰、撞

▶The drunk driver drove recklessly and bumped into the road lamp. 酒醉駕駛亂開車，撞到路燈。

bunch [bʌntʃ]
◀ *Track 2215*

名 束、串、捆

▶Miss White received a bunch of flowers from her admirer（愛慕者）.
懷特小姐收到愛慕者所送的一束花。

bur·den [`bɝdn̩]
◀ *Track 2216*

名 負荷、負擔

▶I was overwhelmed by the financial burden for my family.
我被家裡的經濟負擔擊垮。

bur·glar [`bɝglɚ]
◀ *Track 2217*

名 夜盜、竊賊

▶As soon as I came downstairs, the burglar ran away.
我一下樓，竊賊便狂奔而逃。

bur·y [`bɛrɪ]
◀ *Track 2218*

動 埋

▶The dog buried the bone in the yard.
那隻狗把骨頭埋在院子裡。

bush [bʊʃ]
◀ *Track 2219*

名 灌木叢

▶Who is there hiding behind the bush?
灌木叢後面躲著的那個人是誰？

buzz [bʌz]
◀ *Track 2220*

名 嗡嗡聲

▶The buzz sound of the machine was really annoying.
機器的嗡嗡聲很令人心煩。

文法字詞解析

bump 可當名詞表示「突起」的含意，例如路上可能會有凸出的部份就稱為 bump，孕婦突出的肚子也可稱為 bump。還有雞皮疙瘩也是突起的，所以叫做 goosebumps。

萬用延伸句型

beat around the bush 給了很多若有似無的暗示，就是不直說重點
例如：
A: I think this is written well, it's just that I wouldn't have written it this way, you know what I mean? Like, it's probably just a personal preference and—
B: Stop beating around the bush. If you hate it just say so.
A：我覺得這寫得很好，只是如果是我就不會這樣寫，你懂我意思吧？就是，大概只是個人偏好啦—
B：不要在那邊廢話了。你不喜歡的話就直接說出來。

Level 1
Level 2
Level 3
Level 4
Level 5
Level 6

駕輕就熟、更上一層樓——
累積實力3200單字

[Cc]

cabin [ˈkæbɪn] ◀ *Track 2221*
名 小屋、茅屋
▶There is a small cabin in the woods, but no one lives in it.
樹林裡有個小屋，但是沒人住。

cam·pus [ˈkæmpəs] ◀ *Track 2222*
名 校區、校園
▶Would you tell me something about your campus life?
能告訴我有關你校園生活的一些事嗎？

cane [ken] ◀ *Track 2223*
名 手杖、棒
▶The old lady held a cane in her hand to walk.
老太太手裡拿著拐杖走路。

ca·noe [kəˈnu] ◀ *Track 2224*
名 獨木舟 動 划獨木舟
▶名 Do you know the man in the canoe?
你認識在獨木舟裡的那個男人嗎？
▶動 I don't think they can canoe across the river in such weather.
我不認為他們能在這樣的天氣划著小舟過河。

can·yon [ˈkænjən] ◀ *Track 2225*
名 峽谷 同 valley 山谷
▶I've never been to the Grand Canyon.
我從來沒去過大峽谷。

ca·pa·ble [ˈkepəbl̩] ◀ *Track 2226*
形 有能力的 同 able 有能力的
▶He is capable of many things, but not including playing the erhu. 他能夠做很多事，但不包含演奏二胡。

cap·i·tal [ˈkæpətl̩] ◀ *Track 2227*
名 首都、資本 形 主要的
▶名 The capital city of our city is not the most populated area in our country.
首都不是我國人口最密集的地區。
▶形 What you suggested was quite a capital idea.
你的建議是個非常好的主意。

cap·ture [ˈkæptʃɚ] ◀ *Track 2228*
動 捉住、吸引 名 擄獲、戰利品
▶動 The villagers（村民）hope they can capture the tiger as soon as possible.
村民們希望他們能儘快抓住那隻老虎。
▶名 He had to play dead to avoid（避免）capture by the enemy.
他不得不裝死，以免被敵人俘虜。

文法字詞解析

說「校園裡」時，我們比較少說「inside the campus」，而是說「on campus」。而「校外」則可以說「off campus」。

萬用延伸句型

There is no doubt that...毫無疑問地，……

car·pen·ter [ˈkɑrpəntɚ] 　🔊 *Track 2229*

名 木匠

▶How long have you been a carpenter here?
你在這個地方做了幾年木匠了啊？

car·riage [ˈkærɪdʒ] 　🔊 *Track 2230*

名 車輛、車、馬車

▶We took a carriage for cars were not allowed in the town.
小鎮裡禁行汽車，所以我們搭馬車。

cast [kæst] 　🔊 *Track 2231*

動 用力擲、選角 名 投、演員班底 同 throw 投、擲

▶動 I won't cast a glance at her unless she apologizes（道歉）to me.
除非她向我道歉，否則我看都不會看她一眼。

▶名 No one will know who is in the cast until Friday.
週五前沒人知道演員陣容裡會有誰。

ca·su·al [ˈkæʒʊəl] 　🔊 *Track 2232*

形 偶然的、臨時的、隨意的

▶The casual attitude of the novice worker irritated the manager.
新進員工隨便的態度惹惱了經理。

cat·er·pil·lar [ˈkætɚˌpɪlɚ] 　🔊 *Track 2233*

名 毛毛蟲

▶The caterpillar has turned into a butterfly.
那隻毛毛蟲長成了一隻蝴蝶。

cat·tle [ˈkætl̩] 　🔊 *Track 2234*

名 小牛

▶It doesn't matter whether the cattle are in the shed or not.
牛在不在圍欄裡都不要緊。

萬用延伸句型
It doesn't matter whether...
無論是否……都沒有關係

cel·e·brate [ˈsɛləˌbret] 　🔊 *Track 2235*

動 慶祝、慶賀

▶I heard that you won the first place in the contest（比賽）. Let's go celebrate!
聽說你比賽得了第一名，我們去慶祝吧！

cen·ti·me·ter [ˈsɛntəˌmitɚ] 　🔊 *Track 2236*

名 公分、釐米

▶My brother is six centimeters taller than me.
我弟弟比我高六公分。

文法字詞解析
centimeter 是美式的用法，在英式英文中則是拼成 centimetre。

ce·ram·ic [səˈræmɪk] 　🔊 *Track 2237*

形 陶瓷的 名 陶瓷品

▶形 The ceramic works of the artist were sold in the exhibition.
藝術家的瓷器作品在展覽中被賣出。

▶名 I'm good at designing ceramics.
我很擅長設計陶瓷品。

Level 1
Level 2
Level 3
累積實力3200單字 駕輕就熟、更上一層樓
Level 4
Level 5
Level 6

chain [tʃen]

🔊 *Track 2238*

名 鏈子 動 鏈住

▶ 名 Why is there a chain on the door? 你的門上為什麼裝鏈子？

▶ 動 Do you mind if I chain the dog to a post?
你介意我把狗拴在柱子上嗎？

chal·lenge [ˈtʃælɪndʒ]

🔊 *Track 2239*

名 挑戰 動 向⋯⋯挑戰

▶ 名 I took the challenge to achieve the sales goal set by my
supervisor.
我接受挑戰，試著完成主管訂下的銷售目標。

▶ 動 I don't think he will challenge us anytime soon.
我不覺得他最近會向我們發出挑戰。

萬用延伸句型
challenge sb. to sth. 向（某人）發起挑戰（做
某事）
例如：He challenged me to a hotdog-eating
contest.
他向我發起挑戰，要跟我比賽吃熱狗。

cham·pi·on [ˈtʃæmpɪən]

🔊 *Track 2240*

名 冠軍 同 victor 勝利者

▶ He is the world champion of swimming this year.
他是今年的游泳世界冠軍。

change·a·ble [ˈtʃendʒəbḷ]

🔊 *Track 2241*

形 可變的

▶ I think these terms are changeable.
我認為這些條件是可變的。

chan·nel [ˈtʃænḷ]

🔊 *Track 2242*

名 通道、頻道 動 傳輸

▶ 名 A good marketing channel is more important than the
quality of a product itself.
良好的銷售管道比產品品質本身更重要。

▶ 動 I don't believe that he will channel the information（消息）
to me. 我不相信他會傳遞消息給我。

chap·ter [ˈtʃæptɚ]

🔊 *Track 2243*

名 章、章節

▶ It took me two and a half hours to finish one chapter of this
novel. 看完這本小說的一章花了我兩個半小時。

charm [tʃɑrm]

🔊 *Track 2244*

名 魅力

▶ I think she is a woman of great charm.
我覺得她是一個很迷人的女人。

chat [tʃæt]

🔊 *Track 2245*

動 聊天、閒談

▶ Do you mind if I chat with him for a couple of minutes?
你介意我跟他聊幾分鐘嗎？

文法字詞解析
隨著網路的發達，chat 也延伸出了名
詞的用法。傳訊息聊天時的「對話」也
稱作 chat，而整個群組的對話則可稱為
group chat。

cheek [tʃik]

🔊 *Track 2246*

名 臉頰

▶ Her daughter kissed her on the cheek.
她的女兒親她的臉頰。

cheer [tʃɪr]
🔊 *Track 2247*

名 歡呼 動 喝采、振奮

▶名 You can hear the cheers of the crowd.
　　你可以聽到群眾們的歡呼聲。

▶動 We cheered for our national basketball team during the game.
　　我們比賽期間為國家代表隊加油。

cheer·ful ['tʃɪrfəl]
🔊 *Track 2248*

形 愉快的、興高采烈的

▶He is a cheerful old man in his nineties.
　他是個九十幾歲的樂觀老人。

cheese [tʃiz]
🔊 *Track 2249*

名 乾酪、乳酪

▶Try this cheese! My mom made it herself.
　試試看這個乳酪吧！這可是我媽媽親手做的哦。

cher·ry ['tʃɛrɪ]
🔊 *Track 2250*

名 櫻桃、櫻木

▶Who's the one who cut down the cherry tree?
　砍櫻桃樹的人是誰？

chest [tʃɛst]
🔊 *Track 2251*

名 胸、箱子 同 box 箱子

▶Helen felt pain in her chest and had a hard time breathing.
　海倫胸口疼痛、呼吸困難。

chew [tʃu]
🔊 *Track 2252*

動 咀嚼

▶You must chew your food well so that you can digest（消化）it easier.
　你必須把食物嚼碎，這樣你才能很容易就消化它。

child·hood ['tʃaɪld‚hʊd]
🔊 *Track 2253*

名 童年、幼年時代

▶Whether happy or sad, childhood memories can follow you throughout your whole life.
　不管是喜是悲，童年的記憶可能會跟著你一輩子。

chill [tʃɪl]
🔊 *Track 2254*

動 使變冷、名 寒冷

▶動 It's easy for us to catch a chill in such weather.
　　我們在這種天氣裡很容易著涼。

▶名 Don't stand outside in the chill.
　　別站在外面的冷天中。

chill·y ['tʃɪlɪ]
🔊 *Track 2255*

形 寒冷的

▶It's a little bit chilly out here. Did you bring a coat?
　外面這裡有點冷，你有帶外套嗎？

文法字詞解析

這裡出現了一個連母語人士都常用錯的字：Who's。Who's 是 Who is 的縮寫，它念起來和 whose（誰的）一模一樣，所以常有人把它們兩個搞混。我們來看看例句：

Who's the owner of this cat? = Who is the owner of this cat? 誰是這貓的主人？
Whose cat is this? 這貓是誰的？

Level 1

Level 2

Level 3

Level 4

Level 5

Level 6

駕輕就熟、更上一層樓——累積實力3200單字

chim·ney [ˈtʃɪmnɪ]

🔊 *Track 2256*

名 煙囪

▶ The little boy believes that Santa Clause would come down the chimney.
小男孩相信聖誕老公公會從煙囪下來。

chip [tʃɪp]

🔊 *Track 2257*

名 碎片 動 切

▶ 名 The ground is littered with chips of wood.
地上滿是木屑。

▶ 動 Put in some water after chipping the potatoes.
把馬鈴薯切成片後往裡面多加點水吧。

choke [tʃok]

🔊 *Track 2258*

動 使窒息

▶ The old lady choked on some water.
那位老太太被水嗆到了。

chop [tʃɑp]

🔊 *Track 2259*

動 砍、劈

▶ We don't have much wood in the house; let's go chop some more.
屋裡柴火不多了，我們再去砍些柴吧。

> **文法字詞解析**
> chop 多半用於「砍樹」、「劈柴」、「切菜」等方面，一般不會用在人身上，因為感覺很危險。但空手道中不是也會有「劈」的動作嗎？這個動作就可以稱做 karate chop。

cig·a·rette [ˈsɪgəˌrɛt]

🔊 *Track 2260*

名 香菸 同 smoke 香菸

▶ Nicotine in cigarette is said to be harmful to human health.
香菸中的尼古丁，據說對人的健康有害。

cir·cus [ˈsɝkəs]

🔊 *Track 2261*

名 馬戲團

▶ Would you like to go to the circus with me?
你要不要跟我一起去看馬戲表演啊？

civ·il [ˈsɪvl]

🔊 *Track 2262*

形 國家的、公民的

▶ You can't deprive（剝奪）us of our basic civil rights.
你不能剝奪我們基本的公民權利。

clas·si·cal [ˈklæsɪkl]

🔊 *Track 2263*

形 古典的

▶ Do you mind if I play some classical music in the office?
你介意我在辦公室放些古典音樂嗎？

click [klɪk]

🔊 *Track 2264*

名 滴答聲

▶ Now, you can pay for your purchase on the Internet by a click.
現在，你可以按一下滑鼠，就在網路上付清購物款項。

> **文法字詞解析**
> 我們在按滑鼠的時候也會發出類似時鐘在走的那種「滴答聲」，因此按滑鼠的這個動作也叫做 click。在這個人手一電腦的時代，這可是個很重要的單字喔！

cli·ent [ˈklaɪənt]
🔊 Track 2265

名 委託人、客戶 同 customer 客戶
▶Our client has complained about the flaws in the product.
我們的顧客抱怨產品的瑕疵。

clin·ic [ˈklɪnɪk]
🔊 Track 2266

名 診所
▶By the time he arrived at the clinic, he found that it was closed.
等到了診所，他才發現診所關門了。

clip [klɪp]
🔊 Track 2267

名 夾子、紙夾
▶Would you fasten these forms with a paper clip?
你能用迴紋針把這些表格夾起來嗎？

clue [klu]
🔊 Track 2268

名 線索
▶I have no clue how to solve the math problem.
要怎麼解這個數學題，我一點線索也沒有。

cock·tail [ˈkɑkˌtel]
🔊 Track 2269

名 雞尾酒
▶Would you like to come to our cocktail party tomorrow?
你願意來參加我們明天的雞尾酒會嗎？

co·co·nut [ˈkokəˌnət]
🔊 Track 2270

名 椰子
▶I like to drink coconut juice when I feel thirsty.
我口渴的時候喜歡喝椰子汁。

col·lar [ˈkɑlɚ]
🔊 Track 2271

名 衣領
▶He seized the man by the collar and yelled some words unfit for children's ears.
他抓住那個男人的衣領，嚷嚷一些兒童不宜的字眼。

col·le·ction [kəˈlɛkʃən]
🔊 Track 2272

名 聚集、收集 同 analects 選集
▶He has a large collection of CDs of this singer.
他收集了很多這個歌手的唱片。

col·lege [ˈkɑlɪdʒ]
🔊 Track 2273

名 學院、大學
▶Tina left home to study in college.
緹娜離家去讀大學。

col·o·ny [ˈkɑlənɪ]
🔊 Track 2274

名 殖民地
▶Some African countries used to be the colony of Britain.
有些非洲國家曾是英國的殖民地。

文法字詞解析

clip 可表示各式各樣的「夾子」，從夾紙的迴紋針到夾頭髮的髮夾都可以簡單稱作 clip。此外，從較長的影片中截取出來的較短的一段影片也可稱作 clip。

Level 1
Level 2
Level 3
Level 4
Level 5
Level 6

駕輕就熟、更上一層樓 — 累積實力3200單字

col·umn [ˋkɑləm] 🔊 *Track 2275*

名 圓柱、專欄、欄

▶There are hundreds of white marble columns in the temple.
神廟裡有上百根白色的大理石柱。

com·bine [kəmˋbaɪn] 🔊 *Track 2276*

動 聯合、結合 同 join 連結

▶We combined the two report and created a new essay.
我們將兩篇報告結合成一個新的研究論文。

com·fort [ˋkʌmfət] 🔊 *Track 2277*

名 舒適 動 安慰

▶名 I prefer a life of safety and comfort.
我比較想要一個充滿安全感與舒適感的人生。

▶動 It's really hard to comfort crying girls. 安慰在哭的女生超難的。

com·ma [ˋkɑmə] 🔊 *Track 2278*

名 逗號

▶You should put a comma here instead of a period.
你應該在這裡放個逗號，而不是句號。

com·mand [kəˋmænd] 🔊 *Track 2279*

動 命令、指揮 名 命令、指令

▶動 He commanded several troops（軍隊）when he was young. 他年輕的時候指揮了好幾個軍隊。

▶名 The soldiers took actions at the command of the general.
士兵在將軍一聲令下，就開始行動。

com·mer·cial [kəˋmɝʃəl] 🔊 *Track 2280*

形 商業的 名 商業廣告 同 business 商業

▶形 Would you tell me how I can get to the commercial bank nearby? 你能告訴我如何才能到這附近的商業銀行嗎？

▶名 Some people considered the commercial discriminating to women. 有些人認為這個廣告是歧視女性。

com·mit·tee [kəˋmɪtɪ] 🔊 *Track 2281*

名 委員會、會議

▶What do you think of the committee's decision? Do you agree with it? 你是怎麼看待委員會的決定的？你同意這個決定嗎？

com·mu·ni·cate [kəˋmjunəˌket] 🔊 *Track 2282*

動 溝通、交流

▶Not all people know how to communicate with their boss and colleagues（同事）.
不是所有人都知道如何與他們的上司和同事溝通。

com·par·i·son [kəmˋpærəsn̩] 🔊 *Track 2283*

名 對照、比較 同 contrast 對照

▶In comparison with the old version, the new smart phone is more energy efficient.
跟舊版本比較，新的智慧型手機更省電。

文法字詞解析

是否有時會覺得「行」跟「列」誰是直的、誰是橫的很難分呢？英文的「column」跟「row」就比較不會有這種煩惱。「column」既然有「柱子」的意思，那它當然是直的，剩下的「row」就是橫的了。

萬用延伸句型

What do you think of...? 你對……有什麼想法？

com·pete [kəmˋpit] ◀€ *Track 2284*
動 競爭
▶This contract is very valuable; it is no wonder that several companies are competing for it. 這份合約非常值錢，難怪好幾家公司正在為這一份合約而競爭。

com·plaint [kəmˋplent] ◀€ *Track 2285*
名 抱怨、訴苦
▶Would you tell me how you will handle our customers' complaints?
能告訴我你將如何處理顧客的投訴嗎？

萬用延伸句型
Would you tell me...? 你能告訴我……嗎？

com·plex [ˋkɑmplɛks] ◀€ *Track 2286*
形 複雜的、合成的 名 複合物、綜合設施
▶形 Don't write too many complex sentences unless it's necessary.
除非必要，否則不要寫太多的複雜句。
▶名 Too many complex sentences may make the article difficult to read.
太多複雜句會讓這篇文章變得難讀。

萬用延伸句型
Unless it is necessary,...
除非必要，否則……

con·cern [kənˋsɝn] ◀€ *Track 2287*
動 關心、涉及
▶Don't mess with what doesn't concern you; let's just stand aside. 不要插手與自己無關的事，我們還是置身事外的好。

con·cert [ˋkɑnsɝt] ◀€ *Track 2288*
名 音樂會、演奏會
▶He'll be giving a concert in our city.
他會在我們的城市開演唱會。

con·clude [kənˋklud] ◀€ *Track 2289*
動 締結、結束、得到結論 同 end 結束
▶The reporter concluded his presentation with a chart that summarizes the content.
報告者用一個摘要內容的圖表來總結他的演講。

con·clu·sion [kənˋkluʒən] ◀€ *Track 2290*
名 結論、終了
▶I don't think we can draw any conclusion from the evidence （證據）at hand.
我們從手頭上的這些證據還無法得出任何結論。

con·di·tion [kənˋdɪʃən] ◀€ *Track 2291*
名 條件、情況 動 以……為條件
▶名 The doctor watched the condition the patient.
醫生在觀察病人的狀況。
▶動 Jessica just got promoted recently; no wonder that they say ability and effort condition success.
潔西卡最近升官了，怪不得他們會說才幹和努力是成功的條件。

Level 1
Level 2
Level 3
Level 4
Level 5
Level 6

累積實力3200單字 駕輕就熟、更上一層樓

cone [kon]
Track 2292

名 圓錐

▶Do you mind if I buy some ice cream cones with my pocket money, Mom? 媽媽，你介意我用零用錢買幾個冰淇淋甜筒嗎？

con·fi·dent [ˈkɑnfədənt]
Track 2293

形 有信心的 同 certain 有把握的

▶Rita was confident that she could win the champion in the speech contest. 瑞塔有自信可以贏得演講比賽的冠軍。

con·fuse [kənˈfjuz]
Track 2294

動 使迷惑

▶He confused the meanings of the two words. 他把這兩個字的意思弄混了。

con·nect [kəˈnɛkt]
Track 2295

動 連接、連結 同 link 連接

▶The bridge connects both sides of the river. 這座橋將河的兩岸連結起來。

con·nec·tion [kəˈnɛkʃən]
Track 2296

名 連接、連結

▶It's difficult for me to figure out the connection between these two things. 指出這兩個事物間的關聯對我而言太難了。

con·scious [ˈkɑnʃəs]
Track 2297

形 意識到的 同 aware 意識到的

▶Tina wasn't conscious about her spelling mistake in her autobiography. 緹娜沒意識到她自傳中有拼字錯誤。

con·sid·er·a·ble [kənˈsɪdərəbl]
Track 2298

形 應考慮的、相當多的

▶There is a considerable sum of money in the wallet. 錢包裡有一筆可觀的錢。

con·sid·er·a·tion
Track 2299

[kənˌsɪdəˈreʃən]

名 考慮

▶What a good plan! We must give it our fullest consideration. 多好的計畫啊！我們必須認真地考慮一下它。

con·stant [ˈkɑnstənt]
Track 2300

形 不變的、不斷的

▶The constant rain had left many areas in the city flooded with water. 持續降雨讓許多地區遭到淹水。

con·ti·nent [ˈkɑntənənt]
Track 2301

名 大陸、陸地

▶There are seven continents in the world. 世界上有七大洲。

文法字詞解析

除了大家常吃的冰淇淋甜筒叫做「cone」以外，還有一種常見的 cone，也就是我們在街上可能會看到的那種橘色的交通用圓錐。它可以稱為 traffic cone。

文法字詞解析

bother 作為動詞是「打擾」的意思，因此加上形容詞字尾「-some」就變成了「擾人的、煩人的」的意思。

con·tract [ˈkɑntrækt]/[kənˈtrækt]
🔊 *Track 2302*

名 契約、合約 動 訂契約 同 pact 契約

▶名 We stated the right and obligations of both parties in the contract. 我們在合約中載明雙方的權利與義務。

▶動 I wonder if he will contract an agreement with them.
真好奇他會不會跟他們締結協議。

couch [kaʊtʃ]
🔊 *Track 2303*

名 長沙發、睡椅

▶He just got off work and headed straight to the couch to take a nap.
他才剛下班，馬上就走去長沙發上小睡了。

count·a·ble [kaʊntəbḷ]
🔊 *Track 2304*

形 可數的

▶Will you tell me what the function of this countable noun（名詞）in this sentence is?
你能告訴我在這個句子中的這個可數名詞作用是什麼嗎？

cow·ard [ˈkaʊəd]
🔊 *Track 2305*

名 懦夫、膽子小的人

▶I don't think he is a coward, though others laugh at him.
儘管別人都嘲笑他，但是我認為他不是一個懦夫。

cra·dle [ˈkredḷ]
🔊 *Track 2306*

名 搖籃 動 放在搖籃裡

▶名 The baby fell asleep in the cradle.
小寶寶在搖籃裡睡著了。。

▶動 I don't think you need to cradle the baby in your arms all day.
我認為你不用整天都把嬰兒抱在懷裡搖晃著。

crash [kræʃ]
🔊 *Track 2307*

名 撞擊 動 摔下、撞毀

▶名 When he heard the news about the plane crash, he couldn't help bursting into tears.
聽到空難消息的時候，他忍不住放聲哭了起來。

▶動 She knocked into a customer and the dishes crashed to the floor.
她撞到一名顧客，盤子都摔到地板上了。

文法字詞解析
電腦當機或程式當掉時，也都可以用 crash 來描述。

crawl [krɔl]
🔊 *Track 2308*

動 爬

▶You have to crawl before you can walk.
人要學走，先得學爬。

cre·a·tive [krɪˈetɪv]
🔊 *Track 2309*

形 有創造力的 同 imaginative 有創造力的

▶The creative teaching method was adopted in many schools.
創意教學法在許多學校中被採用。

Level 1

Level 2

Level 3

駕輕就熟、更上一層樓——
累積實力3200單字

Level 4

Level 5

Level 6

cre·a·tor [krɪˋetɚ]
🔊 Track 2310

名 創造者、創作家

▶Who's the creator of this brilliant music piece?
這首極好的樂曲的創造者是誰？

crea·ture [ˋkritʃɚ]
🔊 Track 2311

名 生物、動物

▶This creature lives in the depths of the sea.
這種生物生活在海洋深處。

cred·it [ˋkrɛdɪt]
🔊 Track 2312

名 信用、信託 動 相信、信賴 同 faith 信任

▶名 She didn't took the credit for the success of the campaign.
她沒因為這個活動成功而居功。

▶動 They credited her for this new invention.
他們把此新發明歸功於她。

creep [krip]
🔊 Track 2313

動 爬、戰慄

▶The tortoise（烏龜）is creeping along quite slowly.
那隻烏龜爬得很慢。

crew [kru]
🔊 Track 2314

名 夥伴們、全體船員

▶The crew on this ship is mostly from Malaysia（馬來西亞）.
這艘船上的船員幾乎都是馬來西亞來的。

crick·et [ˋkrɪkɪt]
🔊 Track 2315

名 蟋蟀

▶We can only find this kind of cricket in North America.
我們只能在北美洲找到這種蟋蟀。

crim·i·nal [ˋkrɪmən!]
🔊 Track 2316

形 犯罪的 名 罪犯

▶形 Robbery is a criminal act and should be condemned.
搶劫是犯罪行為，應該要譴責。

▶名 The police should catch the criminal as soon as possible.
警察應該儘快抓到罪犯。

crisp/crisp·y [krɪsp]/[ˋkrɪspɪ]
🔊 Track 2317

形 脆的、清楚的

▶There are some crisp apples on the table; would you like one? 桌上有些脆蘋果，你要不要來一個？

crown [kraʊn]
🔊 Track 2318

名 王冠 動 加冕、報酬 同 reward 酬報

▶名 The little girl wore a gown and a crown to the costume party.
小女孩穿著禮服戴著皇冠去參加扮裝舞會。

▶動 The king crowned his son in 1456.
國王在 1456 年為他的兒子加冕。

萬用延伸句型

give sb. some credit 給（某人）一點肯定
例 如：Don't be so down on yourself. You worked very hard, right? Give yourself some credit!
不要這麼自怨自艾的。你已經很努力了不是嗎？給自己一點肯定吧！

萬用延伸句型

crowning glory 可用來表示某人最驕傲的一個成就、或某物品最出色的一個部份。
例如：
Out of all of his paintings, the one of the night sky is his crowning glory.
他所有的畫作中，夜空的那幅畫是最讓他驕傲的作品。
Dinner was delicious! The soup was lovely and so was the salad. However, the steak really was the crowning glory.
這晚餐實在太好吃了！湯跟沙拉都很不賴，不過還是牛排最出色了。

crun·chy [ˈkrʌntʃɪ] 🔊 *Track 2319*

名 鬆脆的、易裂的

▶How about buying some crunchy fresh vegetables today?
今天去買點又脆又新鮮的蔬菜怎麼樣？

crutch [krʌtʃ] 🔊 *Track 2320*

名 支架、拐杖

▶The crippled man needed a pair of crutches to walk.
跛腳的男人需要拐杖才能走路。

cul·tu·ral [ˈkʌltʃərəl] 🔊 *Track 2321*

形 文化的

▶It's no wonder that this city has become the cultural center of this country.
難怪這個城市會成為這個國家的文化中心。

cup·board [ˈkʌbəd] 🔊 *Track 2322*

名 食櫥、餐具櫥

▶Do you need some sugar? I will get some from the cupboard for you.
你要一點些糖嗎？我幫你到櫥櫃裡去拿一些來。

cur·rent [ˈkɝənt] 🔊 *Track 2323*

形 流通的、目前的 名 電流、水流 同 present 目前的

▶形 She's our current advisor so you should go talk to her.
她是我們目前的諮詢人，所以你應該去跟她談。

▶名 The current events shown on the Internet are often presented with bias.
網路上的時事新聞常常是帶著偏見的。

cy·cle [ˈsaɪkl̩] 🔊 *Track 2324*

名 週期、循環 動 循環、騎腳踏車

▶名 That can be a dangerous cycle unless someone can prevent it.
除非有人能阻止，否則這有可能成為一個惡性循環。

▶動 My dad cycles to work every day.
我爸爸每天騎腳踏車去上班。

[Dd]

dair·y [ˈdɛrɪ] 🔊 *Track 2325*

名 酪農場 形 酪農的

▶名 Would you like to work in a dairy?
你覺得在一個酪農場工作怎麼樣？

▶形 The girl is allergic to dairy product.
女孩對乳製品過敏。

Level 1
Level 2
Level 3
駕輕就熟、更上一層樓——
累積實力3200單字
Level 4
Level 5
Level 6

dam [dæm]
🔊 *Track 2326*

名 水壩 動 堵住、阻塞

▶名 The river otter built a dam with twitches and small stone.
水獺用小樹枝和小石子建造水壩。

▶動 The man tried to dam his sadness in front of others.
那名男子試著在別人面前制住自己的悲傷。

dare [dɛr]
🔊 *Track 2327*

動 敢、挑戰 同 brave 勇敢的面對

▶Don't you dare touch me again! I will call the police at once!
你敢再碰我，我會立刻報警！

darl·ing [ˈdɑrlɪŋ]
🔊 *Track 2328*

名 親愛的人 形 可愛的 同 lovely 可愛的

▶名 Good morning, darling! What a beautiful day today!
早安，親愛的！今天天氣多好啊！

▶形 We should hold a party for our darling son.
我們應該幫親愛的兒子開一個派對。

dash [dæʃ]
🔊 *Track 2329*

動 碰撞、投擲

▶Congratulations on winning first place in the 100-meter dash!
恭喜你獲得百米賽跑第一名！

deaf·en [ˈdɛfən]
🔊 *Track 2330*

動 使耳聾

▶The loud explosion almost deafened her.
那個巨大的爆炸聲幾乎把她弄聾了。

文法字詞解析
動詞字尾「-en」具有「讓⋯⋯有某種特質」的意思，因此這個單字 deaf 是「耳聾的」，加了字尾 -en 中就變成了「讓⋯⋯耳聾」。

deal·er [ˈdilɚ]
🔊 *Track 2331*

名 商人 同 merchant 商人

▶The illegal drug dealer was arrested by the police this morning.
非法的毒品商今早被警察逮捕。

文法字詞解析
在玩撲克牌的時候，「發牌」的動作可以稱為 deal。因此，發牌的人也可以稱為 dealer。

dec·ade [ˈdɛked]
🔊 *Track 2332*

名 十年、十個一組

▶It's the first time I've been back to my college since a decade ago.
這是十年來我第一次回到我的母校。

deck [dɛk]
🔊 *Track 2333*

名 甲板

▶There are some passengers sitting on the deck chatting.
有些旅客正坐在甲板上聊天。

文法字詞解析
說起來，deck 這個字也和撲克牌有關，我們平常玩的「一疊」牌組，也可以稱為 a deck of cards。不只撲克牌，其他的紙牌也適用。

deed [did]
🔊 *Track 2334*

名 行為、行動

▶He will someday suffer from his wrong deeds.
他有一天一定會因為他的惡行遭到報應。

deep·en [ˋdipən] ◀ *Track 2335*
動 加深、變深
▶We need to deepen our understanding of the subject before we can make a decision.
我們在下決定前，需要先加深對這個主題的瞭解。

de·fine [dɪˋfaɪn] ◀ *Track 2336*
動 下定義
▶People have different ways to define "beauty."
人們有不同定義「美」的方式。

def·i·ni·tion [ˌdɛfəˋnɪʃən] ◀ *Track 2337*
名 定義
▶It's difficult for me to give a definition of happiness（幸福）.
對我來說為幸福下個定義很難。

萬用延伸句型
It's difficult for sb. to... 要某人（做某事）很難

de·liv·er·y [dɪˋlɪvərɪ] ◀ *Track 2338*
名 傳送、傳遞 同 distribution 分配、分發
▶Would you please tell me when you will make a delivery?
能請您告訴我你們什麼時候可以送貨嗎？

de·moc·ra·cy [dəˋmɑkrəsɪ] ◀ *Track 2339*
名 民主制度
▶People in the communist society may not approve the benefits of democracy.
共產國家可能不認同民主的好處。

de·moc·ra·tic [ˌdɛməˋkrætɪk] ◀ *Track 2340*
形 民主的
▶The laws really reflect the democratic spirit of the country.
這些法律確實反映了這個國家的民主精神。

de·pos·it [dɪˋpɑzɪt] ◀ *Track 2341*
名 押金、存款 動 存入、放入
▶名 I don't think I need a deposit account.
我覺得我不需要開個定期存款帳戶。
▶動 You'll have to deposit your bags at the counter（櫃檯）.
你必須把皮包寄放在櫃檯。

de·scrip·tion [dɪˋskrɪpʃən] ◀ *Track 2342*
名 敘述、說明 同 portrait 描寫
▶It's hard for me to give a description of her beauty in words.
她的美我難以用語言來形容。

de·sign·er [dɪˋzaɪnɚ] ◀ *Track 2343*
名 設計師
▶The fashion designer has her own taste in outfits.
時尚設計師對服裝有自己的品味。

萬用延伸句型
beyond description 言語無法描述
例如：His room was a mess. It was beyond description. I couldn't even tell where the floor was.
他的房間太亂了，根本是言語無法描述的。我連地板在哪都看不出來了。

Level 1
Level 2
Level 3
駕輕就熟、更上一層樓
累積實力3200單字
Level 4
Level 5
Level 6

de·sir·a·ble [dɪˋzaɪrəbl̩]
Track 2344

形 值得的、稱心如意的
▶She is searching high and low for a desirable job.
她正在到處找一份好工作。

de·stroy [dɪˋstrɔɪ]
Track 2345

動 損毀、毀壞 反 create 創造
▶The whole structure was destroyed in the earthquake.
整棟建築在地震中被摧毀。

de·tail [ˋditel]
Track 2346

名 細節、條款
▶Would you tell me what happened in detail?
您能詳細地告訴我發生了什麼事嗎？

de·ter·mine [dɪˋtɝmɪn]
Track 2347

動 決定 同 decide 決定
▶The exam results could determine your future.
考試成績可能會決定你的前途。

dev·il [ˋdɛvl̩]
Track 2348

名 魔鬼、惡魔
▶Faust made a deal with the devil. He exchanged wealth with his soul.
浮士德與惡魔交易，用他的靈魂換取財富。

di·a·logue [ˋdaɪəlɔg]
Track 2349

名 對話 同 conversation 對話
▶Not every writer is very good at writing dialogues.
不是每個作家都非常擅長寫對白。

diet [ˋdaɪət]
Track 2350

名 飲食 動 節食
▶名 A healthy diet creates a body resistant （有抵抗力的）to disease.
保健飲食有助於增強體內對疾病的抵抗力。
▶動 Susan is dieting to lose weight, isn't she?
蘇珊正在節食減肥，不是嗎？

dil·i·gent [ˋdɪlədʒənt]
Track 2351

形 勤勉的、勤奮的
▶The little girl is not only clever but also diligent.
那個小女孩不但聰明而且還很勤奮。

dim [dɪm]
Track 2352

形 微暗的 動 變模糊
▶形 The light in the room is too dim for me to read.
這個房間裡的光線太暗了，我沒辦法看書。
▶動 The lights dimmed as the performance was about to begin.
表演即將開始時，燈光暗下來。

萬用延伸句型

go into detail 詳細說明
例如：I don't have time to go into detail right now. Just follow me and I'll explain later.
我現在沒時間詳細說明，你先跟我來就對了，我晚點跟你解釋。

萬用延伸句型

on a diet 正在減重
例如：Please stop sending me cakes. I'm on a diet.
拜託不要一直送我蛋糕了，我正在減重中。

dime [daɪm]
Track 2353

名 一角的硬幣

▶Can you give me a dime for two nickels（五分硬幣）？
你能不能用兩個五分硬幣換一個一角的硬幣給我？

dine [daɪn]
Track 2354

動 款待、用膳

▶How about dining with us tonight? I'll pay.
今晚和我們一起吃飯怎麼樣？我請客。

dip [dɪp]
Track 2355

動 浸、沾 名 浸泡、(價格)下跌

▶動 He dipped the sashimi in the soy sauce.
他用生魚片沾醬油。

▶名 I heard that the price of grain has taken a dip.
我聽說穀物價格下跌了。

dirt [dɝt]
Track 2356

名 泥土、塵埃

▶The dog enjoys digging around in the dirt.
那隻狗喜歡在泥土裡亂挖。

dis·ap·point [ˌdɪsəˋpɔɪnt]
Track 2357

動 使失望

▶I worked hard in order not to disappoint my parents.
我努力工作，為了不讓父母失望。

dis·ap·point·ment
[ˌdɪsəˋpɔɪntmənt]
Track 2358

名 令人失望的舉止

▶The singer won't be performing? What a disappointment!
那個歌手不會來表演嗎？真是令人失望！

disco/dis·co·theque
[ˋdɪsko]/[ˌdɪskəˋtɛk]
Track 2359

名 迪斯可、酒吧、小舞廳

▶Why don't you come to the disco with me tonight?
你晚上何不和我一起去迪斯可？

dis·count [ˋdɪskaʊnt]
Track 2360

名 折扣 動 減價

▶名 Shoppers can get a huge discount during the anniversary.
週年慶時，人們可以享有很好的折扣。

▶動 That store is discounting all its slow-selling goods.
那家商店正在削價出售所有滯銷貨。

dis·cov·er·y [dɪˋskʌvərɪ]
Track 2361

名 發現

▶It is no wonder that the discovery caused a big sensation（轟動）in the scientific world.
毫無意外地，那項發現在科學界引起了巨大轟動。

萬用延伸句型

Why don't you...? 你何不……？

文法字詞解析

slow-selling goods 是「賣不好的商品、滯銷品」，那「供不應求的商品」又是什麼呢？就是「hot commodity」囉！而如果要說某個東西賣得很好、炙手可熱，就可以說「sth. sells like hotcakes」。

Level 1

Level 2

Level 3

駕輕就熟、更上一層樓──

累積實力3200單字

Level 4

Level 5

Level 6

dis·ease [dɪˋziz] 🔊 *Track 2362*

名 疾病、病症

▶ The incurable disease has become a nightmare for people in the impoverished area.
無法治癒的疾病變成這個貧窮區域居民的噩夢。

disk/disc [dɪsk] 🔊 *Track 2363*

名 唱片、碟片、圓盤狀的東西

▶ Would you please help me save the data on a disc?
請您幫我把那些資料儲存到磁片上好嗎？

dis·like [dɪsˋlaɪk] 🔊 *Track 2364*

動 討厭、不喜歡 名 反感

▶ 動 I dislike getting up early in the morning.
我不喜歡早上早起，你呢？

▶ 名 I took an instant dislike to him.
我一見他就不喜歡。

ditch [dɪtʃ] 🔊 *Track 2365*

名 排水溝、水道 動 挖溝、拋棄

同 trench 溝、溝渠

▶ 名 He nodded off when driving and ended up driving into the ditch. 他邊開車邊打盹，結果把車開進排水溝了。

▶ 動 She ditched her boyfriend to hang out with her friends.
她丟下她的男朋友，和朋友們出去玩了。

dive [daɪv] 🔊 *Track 2366*

動 跳水 名 垂直降落 同 take a dive 一落千丈

▶ 動 The fugitive dived into the river to run away from the police officers. 逃犯為了逃避警察追捕跳入河裡。

▶ 名 What a beautiful dive! Don't you think so?
多麼優美的跳水！你不覺得嗎？

dock [dɑk] 🔊 *Track 2367*

名 船塢、碼頭 動 裁減、停泊 同 anchor 停泊

▶ 名 Would you please give me a lift? I'm afraid my car is still in dock. 請讓我搭個便車好嗎？我的汽車還在修理中。

▶ 動 Would you please not dock my wages? I swear this will never happen again.
請您不要扣我的工資好嗎？我發誓這件事再也不會發生了。

dodge [dɑdʒ] 🔊 *Track 2368*

動 閃開、躲開 同 avoid 躲開

▶ She is fast enough to dodge the attack.
她的速度夠快，能夠避開別人的攻擊。

do·mes·tic [dəˋmɛstɪk] 🔊 *Track 2369*

形 國內的、家務的

▶ The woman who suffered from domestic violence finally divorced her husband.
受到家暴的那位女士最終和丈夫離婚了。

文法字詞解析
大家所熟知的 DJ 其實就是 disk/disc jockey 的簡稱。

文法字詞解析
大家小時候玩的「躲避球」，英文就叫做「dodgeball」。

dose [dos]

◀ Track 2370

名 一劑（藥）、藥量 動 服藥

▶名 Take a dose of the medicine three times a day.
這種要每天要服用三劑。

▶動 It's time to dose up the children with cough syrup（糖漿）.
該給孩子們喝止咳糖漿了。

doubt·ful [ˈdautfəl]

◀ Track 2371

形 有疑問的、可疑的

▶I'm doubtful that he's really going to come to the meeting.
我懷疑他不會真的來開會。

drain [dren]

◀ Track 2372

動 排出、流出、喝乾 名 排水管 同 dry 乾

▶動 Can you pull out the plug（塞子）and drain the bathtub?
你把塞子拔出來，讓浴缸的水排乾好不好？

▶名 It is no wonder that the drains overflowed（溢出）after the heavy rain.
雨下得很大，難怪下水道會溢出水來。

dra·mat·ic [drəˈmætɪk]

◀ Track 2373

形 戲劇性的 同 theatrical 戲劇性的

▶She always speaks in such a dramatic way.
她講話總是很戲劇性的樣子。

drip [drɪp]

◀ Track 2374

動 滴下 名 滴、水滴 同 drop 水滴

▶動 The popes on the wall is dripping. We should try to fix it.
牆上的水管漏水，我們應該要修理它。

▶名 There is an increasing switch to drip irrigation（灌溉）in all areas.
所有地區轉換成滴灌的趨勢正在增加。

drown [draʊn]

◀ Track 2375

動 淹沒、淹死

▶The boy drowned in the river behind his school.
那個男孩在他學校後面的河裡淹死了。

drowsy [ˈdraʊzɪ]

◀ Track 2376

形 沉寂的、懶洋洋的、睏的 同 sleepy 睏的

▶I felt drowsy in my philosophy（哲學）and math classes.
哲學課和數學課讓我感到昏昏欲睡。

drunk [drʌŋk]

◀ Track 2377

形 酒醉的、著迷的 名 醉漢

▶形 The drunk driver was fined for driving under the influence of alcohol.
酒醉駕駛因為受到酒精影響狀態下開車而遭到罰款。

▶名 The drunk got hurt because he bumped into a pole yesterday.
那個醉漢受傷了，因為昨天他撞到柱子了。

文法字詞解析

dramatic 這個單字還有個伙伴「melodramatic」。雖然兩個都是「戲劇化的」的意思，但 melodramatic 帶有貶意，暗示「太過誇張地戲劇化」、「不需要很戲劇化的事還搞得很戲劇化」。

文法字詞解析

除了 drunk 以外還有一個類似的形容詞 drunken，它們有什麼差別呢？原來，drunk 純粹是指喝醉的狀態，喝醉一次不代表就會一直喝醉。而 drunken 則指長期酗酒的、經常喝醉的。

Level
1

Level
2

Level
3

Level
4

Level
5

Level
6

駕輕就熟、更上一層樓——
累積實力3200單字

due [dju]

形 預定的 名 應付款、應得的東西　　◀ *Track 2378*

▶形 The final report is due next Monday.
期末報告下週一截止。

▶名 She asked no more than her due. 她並沒有提出非分的要求。

dump [dʌmp]

動 拋下 名 垃圾場　　◀ *Track 2379*

▶動 You shouldn't dump your stuff in front of other people's house. 你不該在人家家門口亂倒東西啊。

▶名 There is a very big dump out of the town.
鎮外有個很大的垃圾場。

dust [dʌst]

名 灰塵、灰 動 打掃、拂去灰塵 同 dirt 灰塵　　◀ *Track 2380*

▶名 The bookshelves are coated in dust. 書架上積了一層灰塵。

▶動 Why don't you dust the room every day?
你為什麼不每天都打掃房間呢？

[Ee]

ea·ger [ˈigɚ]

形 渴望的　　◀ *Track 2381*

▶She is eager to have you meet her friends.
她很渴望你見見她的朋友。

earn·ings [ˈɝnɪŋz]

名 收入 同 salary 薪水　　◀ *Track 2382*

▶He can lead a comfortable life with his yearly earnings from this job. 他可以用目前工作的年薪過著舒適的生活。

ech·o [ˈɛko]

名 回音 動 發出回聲　　◀ *Track 2383*

▶名 The room is so large you can hear echoes in it.
這房間大到你在裡面可以聽到回聲。

▶動 His cries echoed through the tunnel.
他的大叫聲在山洞中迴盪。

ed·it [ˈɛdɪt]

動 編輯、發行　　◀ *Track 2384*

▶He had to edit the book before it can be published（出版）.
在這本書能出版前，他得先編輯一下。

e·di·tion [əˈdɪʃən]

名 版本　　◀ *Track 2385*

▶The second edition of the book will be released next month.
這本書的第二版下個月會發行。

萬用延伸句型
It's impolite of you to...（＋原形動詞）你（做某事）很不禮貌

ed·i·tor [ˈɛdɪtə]
🔊 *Track 2386*

名 編輯者

▶Will you have a talk with our chief editor in the office?
你能到辦公室去跟我們的總編輯談談嗎？

ed·u·cate [ˈɛdʒəˌket]
🔊 *Track 2387*

動 教育 同 teach 教導

▶Mr. Thompson has his own principal in educating his children.
湯普森先生有自己一套教育小孩的原則。

ed·u·ca·tion·al [ˌɛdʒəˈkeʃənl]
🔊 *Track 2388*

形 教育性的

▶What do you think of the recent educational policy? Does it really work?
你怎麼看待最近的教育政策？它真的有效嗎？

ef·fi·cient [ɪˈfɪʃənt]
🔊 *Track 2389*

形 有效率的

▶Isn't she an efficient secretary? I don't think anyone can deny that.
難道她不是一個很有能力的秘書嗎？我想沒人可以否認這一點吧。

el·bow [ˈɛlˌbo]
🔊 *Track 2390*

名 手肘

▶The woman pushed other away with her elbow to get on the crowded bus.
這個女士用手肘把別人推開，好搭上擁擠的公車。

eld·er·ly [ˈɛldəlɪ]
🔊 *Track 2391*

形 上了年紀的 同 old 老的

▶When the elderly get on the bus, the young are expected to give them their seats.
老人上車來的時候，年輕人被認為應該讓座給他們。

election [ɪˈlɛkʃən]
🔊 *Track 2392*

名 選舉

▶I don't think he will take part in the election this year.
我覺得他今年不會參加競選。

e·lec·tric/e·lec·tri·cal [ɪˈlɛktrɪk]/[ɪˈlɛktrɪkl]
🔊 *Track 2393*

形 電的

▶Would you help me turn off the electric power?
能幫我把電源關掉嗎？

e·lec·tric·i·ty [ɪˌlɛkˈtrɪsətɪ]
🔊 *Track 2394*

名 電

▶About a million households could not have electricity after the earthquake. 大約一百萬戶在地震之後無電可用。

文法字詞解析

have sb. Vp.p. 讓某人（接受）……
這裡用到了使役動詞的被動用法，表示受詞並不是主動去做某事，而是被動的接受某事。

萬用延伸句型

Not many people can... 很少人可以……

Level
1

Level
2

Level
3

駕輕就熟、更上一層樓 ── 累積實力3200單字

Level
4

Level
5

Level
6

e·lec·tron·ic [ɪˌlɛkˋtrɑnɪk]

Track 2395

形 電子的

▶Nothing will change unless you buy some new electronic instruments.
除非你購買一些新的電子儀器，不然什麼也不會改變。

e·mer·gen·cy [ɪˋmɝdʒənsɪ]

Track 2396

名 緊急情況 同 crisis 危機

▶We had a first aid kit in case of emergency.
我們保留急救箱以防有緊急事件。

em·per·or [ˋɛmpərɚ]

Track 2397

名 皇帝 同 sovereign 君主、元首

▶This emperor is considered stupid by most historians.
大部分的歷史學家都認為這個皇帝很蠢。

文法字詞解析
可愛的皇帝企鵝就是 emperor penguin。

em·pha·size [ˋɛmfəˌsaɪz]

Track 2398

動 強調 同 stress 強調

▶Please emphasize this matter and its importance so that they know what to do next.
請強調一下這件事及其重要性，好讓他們知道下一步該做什麼。

em·ploy [ɪmˋplɔɪ]

Track 2399

動 從事、雇用 同 hire 雇用

▶The company would not employ inexperienced workers.
公司不會雇用沒有經驗的員工。

em·ploy·ment [ɪmˋplɔɪmənt]

Track 2400

名 職業

▶He has been out of employment for two years.
他已經失業兩年了。

em·ploy·ee [ˌɛmplɔɪˋi]

Track 2401

名 從業人員、職員 同 worker 工作人員

▶The loyal（忠實的）employees hang on to their boss's every word. 那些忠誠的員工專注地聽老闆講話。

em·ploy·er [ɪmˋplɔɪɚ]

Track 2402

名 老闆、雇主 同 boss 老闆

▶What do you think of our new employer? Do you think he is kind enough?
你覺得我們的新老闆怎麼樣？你覺得他是否夠親切呢？

文法字詞解析
從以上幾個單字可以看出字尾的妙用喔！字尾「-er」有「……者」之意，而字尾「-ee」則是「被……者」之意。employ（雇用）加上字尾「-ee」就是「被雇用者」，也就是員工；而加上字尾「-er」就是「雇用者」，也就是老闆。

emp·ty [ˋɛmptɪ]

Track 2403

形 空的 動 倒空 同 vacant 空的

▶形 The envelope was empty. The letter had been taken away.
信封是空的。信件被拿走了。

▶動 I emptied the box and threw it away.
我把箱子倒空，然後拿去丟。

en·a·ble [ɪnˋebḷ]
◀≶ Track 2404

動 使能夠
▶The Internet enables people to access more information.
網路使人能夠接觸到更多資訊。

實用片語用語
enable sb. to... 讓某人能……

en·er·ge·tic [ɛnəˋdʒɛtɪk]
◀≶ Track 2405

形 有精力的 同 vigrous 精力旺盛的
▶Exercise makes you feel more energetic.
運動會讓你感覺更精力充沛。

en·gage [ɪnˋgedʒ]
◀≶ Track 2406

動 僱用、允諾、訂婚
▶My sister is engaged with her boyfriend of ten years.
姊姊和她交往十年的男友訂婚了。

en·gage·ment [ɪnˋgedʒmənt]
◀≶ Track 2407

名 預約、訂婚
▶Her engagement ring was not as expensive as her wedding ring.
她的訂婚戒指沒有結婚戒指那麼貴。

en·gine [ˋɛndʒən]
◀≶ Track 2408

名 引擎
▶As soon as the driver started the engine of the car, it exploded.
駕駛一啟動引擎，車子就爆炸了。

en·gi·neer [ɛndʒəˋnɪr]
◀≶ Track 2409

名 工程師
▶I want to be a civil engineer in the future; what about you?
我將來想成為一名土木工程師，你呢？

en·joy·a·ble [ɪnˋdʒɔɪəbḷ]
◀≶ Track 2410

形 愉快的
同 delighyful 愉快的
▶I think the movie last night was very enjoyable.
我覺得昨晚的電影很有趣。

en·try [ˋɛntrɪ]
◀≶ Track 2411

名 入口
▶I registered for the entry level course of French.
我註冊參加初階的法文課。

文法字詞解析
entry-level = 畢業後剛進入職場工作

en·vi·ron·men·tal [ɪnˋvaɪrənmɛntḷ]
◀≶ Track 2412

形 環境的
▶People should pay attention to not only environmental protection but also to animal protection.
人們應該同時關注環境保護和動物保護這兩方面。

Level 1
Level 2
Level 3
Level 4
Level 5
Level 6

駕輕就熟、更上一層樓──
累積實力3200單字

en·vy [ˈɛnvɪ] 🔊 *Track 2413*

名 羨慕、嫉妒 動 對……羨慕

▶ 名 I said something negative about my opponent out of envy.
我出於嫉妒說了關於對手的負面言論。

▶ 動 I really envy her for getting to go abroad all the time.
她可以常常出國，我好羨慕啊。

e·rase [ɪˈres] 🔊 *Track 2414*

動 擦掉

▶ It is hard for him to erase that painful experience from his mind.
要忘掉那段痛苦的經歷對他來說很難。

es·cape [əˈskep] 🔊 *Track 2415*

動 逃走 名 逃脫 同 flee 逃走

▶ 動 The prisoners escaped from the jail with the help of their accomplice.
囚犯在同夥的幫助下逃出監獄。

▶ 名 We planned our escape ten days beforehand.
我們十天前就計畫了如何逃脫。

e·vil [ˈivḷ] 🔊 *Track 2416*

形 邪惡的 名 邪惡

▶ 形 The evil man kills his wives and hides them in a room.
那名邪惡的男人殺掉自己的妻子們，把屍體藏在房間裡。

▶ 名 Some say that the love of money is the root of all evil.
有人說貪財是萬惡之源。

ex·cel·lence [ˈɛksḷəns] 🔊 *Track 2417*

名 優點、傑出

▶ There is no shortcut（捷徑）to excellence.
成功沒有捷徑。

ex·change [ɪksˈtʃendʒ] 🔊 *Track 2418*

名 交換 動 兌換

▶ 名 The book exchange our department held was a success.
我們系上辦的書籍交換會很成功。

▶ 動 Can we exchange money in this bank?
可以在這家銀行換錢嗎？

ex·hi·bi·tion [ˌɛksəˈbɪʃən] 🔊 *Track 2419*

名 展覽

▶ They went to the photo exhibition this afternoon.
他們今天下午去了攝影展。

ex·is·tence [ɪgˈzɪstəns] 🔊 *Track 2420*

名 存在

▶ Many scientists believe in the existence of extraterrestrials.
許多科學家相信外星人的存在。

文法字詞解析

大家是否也玩過密室逃脫遊戲呢？這樣的遊戲就叫做 escape room game / escape the room game。

萬用延伸句型

be the bane of sb.'s existence 是（某人）的剋星、造成（某人）很大麻煩的人、事、物。

例如：I normally like cats, but my neighbor's cat really is the bane of my existence.
我通常是喜歡貓的，但我鄰居的貓簡直是想害死我。

ex·it [ˈɛgzɪt]
◀ Track 2421

名 出口 動 離開 反 entrance 入口

▶名 Will you tell me where the exit is? I can't find it.
你能告訴我出口在哪嗎？我找不到。

▶動 He exited the room as soon as he picked up the phone.
他一接起電話就走出房間。

ex·pec·ta·tion [ˌɛkspɛkˈteʃən]
◀ Track 2422

名 期望

▶His son exceeded（超越）everyone's expectations by getting into a good school.
他的兒子超越了每個人的期望，進入了一所好學校。

ex·pense [ɪkˈspɛns]
◀ Track 2423

名 費用 同 payment 付款

▶I'll get back to you after I add up this month's expenses.
我把這個月的費用加一加再回覆你。

ex·per·i·ment [ɪkˈspɛrəmənt]
◀ Track 2424

名 / 動 實驗

▶名 What do you think of this experiment with the foreign experts?
你覺得和外國專家進行的這次實驗如何？

▶動 They plan to experiment on animals. 他們打算在動物身上做實驗。

ex·plode [ɪkˈsplod]
◀ Track 2425

動 爆炸、推翻

▶We have to find the bomb before it explodes.
我們得在炸彈爆炸前找到它。

ex·port [ˈɛksport]
◀ Track 2426

動 輸出 名 出口貨、輸出

▶動 Due to the high tariff of the U.S., our company stopped exporting our product to the country.
因為美國關稅很高，我們公司就不將產品出口到美國了。

▶名 The country's exports are mostly agriculture products.
那個國家的出口貨大部分是農產品。

文法字詞解析
相反地，「進口」則是「import」。export 與 import 不只可以用在商務的進出口上，也可以拿來表示數位檔案的匯入、匯出等功能。

ex·pres·sion [ɪkˈsprɛʃən]
◀ Track 2427

名 表達

▶The picture was beautiful beyond expression. 這張圖美得無法形容。

ex·pres·sive [ɪkˈsprɛsɪv]
◀ Track 2428

形 表達的

▶I like expressive pieces of music. 我喜歡很有表現力的樂曲。

ex·treme [ɪkˈstrim]
◀ Track 2429

形 極度的 名 極端的事

▶形 Extreme weather conditions has caused damage to many countries around the world.
極端氣候狀況已經對世界各地許多國家造成損失。

▶名 I don't think it's the time to resort to（依靠、求助於）extremes yet. 我覺得現在還沒必要一定要用極端的方式來解決。

文法字詞解析
extreme 加上「-ly」後就變成副詞「extremely」（非常）。如果厭倦了在對話中不斷地使用「very」，不妨換成「extremely」試試看吧！更能夠以誇張的方式表達強調之意喔。

Level 1

Level 2

Level 3

駕輕就熟、更上一層樓——累積實力3200單字

Level 4

Level 5

Level 6

[Ff]

fa·ble [ˈfebl̩] ◀€ Track 2430
名 寓言 同 legend 傳說
▶I heard that fable when I was little. 我小時候就聽過那個寓言了。

fac·tor [ˈfæktɚ] ◀€ Track 2431
名 因素、要素 同 cause 原因
▶There are many factors behind this phenomenon.
這個現象背後有許多因素。

fade [fed] ◀€ Track 2432
動 凋謝、變淡
▶The jacket faded after the wash.
那件夾克在洗過後顏色就變淡了。

faint [fent] ◀€ Track 2433
名 昏厥 形 暗淡的
▶名 The girl went into a faint at the sight of the corpse of a dog.
女孩子一看到狗的屍體就暈倒。
▶形 Our chances of victory are very faint now.
現在我們獲勝的機會已經微乎其微了。

fair·ly [ˈfɛrlɪ] ◀€ Track 2434
副 相當地、公平地
▶It's a fairly good book. You really should read it.
這是一本相當不錯的書，你真的應該讀一讀。

fair·y [ˈfɛrɪ] ◀€ Track 2435
名 仙子 形 神仙的
▶名 When I was little, I wanted to be a fairy. 我小時候想當仙女。
▶形 Her fairy godmother（教母）appeared as soon as she
started crying. 她一哭起來，仙女教母就出現了。

faith [feθ] ◀€ Track 2436
名 信任 同 trust 信任
▶Have faith! He's stronger than you think.
有信心點吧！他比你想的更堅強。

fake [fek] ◀€ Track 2437
形 冒充的 動 仿造
▶形 He sold fake paintings to earn money. 他賣假畫來賺錢。
▶動 He faked his mother handwriting in this letter.
他假冒母親的筆跡寫這封信。

fa·mil·iar [fəˈmɪljɚ] ◀€ Track 2438
形 熟悉的、親密的
▶Not all people are familiar with the local laws.
不是所有的人都熟悉當地的法律。

萬用延伸句型
be not for the faint-hearted 不適合膽小的人
This ride is not for the faint hearted. I don't recommend going on it.
這遊樂設施不適合膽小的人，我不推薦你玩。

文法字詞解析
有些人會買一串可愛的小燈來裝飾房間，這種一整串的小燈泡稱為 fairy lights。

fan/fa·nat·ic [fæn]/[fəˋnætɪk] 🔊 *Track 2439*
名 狂熱者、迷（粉絲） 同 follower 跟隨者
▶The Internet（網路）is a great way to meet fellow fans.
要認識其他的粉絲，網路是個很好的管道。

fan·cy [ˋfænsɪ] 🔊 *Track 2440*
名 想像力、愛好
▶It would cost you a lot to dine at the fancy restaurant.
要在這間豪華餐廳吃飯，會花妳很多錢。

fare [fɛr] 🔊 *Track 2441*
名 費用、運費 同 fee 費用
▶Let us split the taxi fare. 我們來分攤計程車費吧。

far·ther [ˋfɑrðɚ] 🔊 *Track 2442*
副 更遠地 形 更遠的 同 further 更遠的
▶副 We can't go any farther. Why don't we take a break?
我們走不動了，為什麼不歇一會兒呢？
▶形 The farther hill is five kilometers away.
那座更遠的小山在五公里以外。

fash·ion [ˋfæʃən] 🔊 *Track 2443*
名 時髦、流行 同 style 時髦
▶Fashion and travel are the most popular TV show genres.
流行和旅行是最受歡迎的電視節目類型。

文法字詞解析
in fashion = 合於時尚、正在流行
out of fashion = 過時了

fash·ion·a·ble [ˋfæʃənəbl̩] 🔊 *Track 2444*
形 流行的、時髦的
▶There is a small store selling fashionable dresses in that street. 那條街有一家賣流行服飾的小店。

fas·ten [ˋfæsn̩et] 🔊 *Track 2445*
動 緊固、繫緊
▶Fasten your seatbelt（安全帶）or you might get fined.
把安全帶繫好，不然你可能會被罰喔。

fate [fet] 🔊 *Track 2446*
名 命運、宿命
▶Who knows what fate has in store for us?
誰知道接下來有什麼樣的命運在等待我們呢？

萬用延伸句型
Who knows... 誰知道……

fau·cet/tap [ˋfɔsɪt]/[tæp] 🔊 *Track 2447*
名 水龍頭
▶To save water, we should turn off the faucet when brushing teeth. 為了省水，我們刷牙時要關掉水龍頭。

fax [fæks] 🔊 *Track 2448*
名 傳真
▶Would you like to tell me your telephone number or fax number?
請告訴我你的電話號碼或者傳真號碼好嗎？

Level 1
Level 2
Level 3
Level 4
Level 5
Level 6

駕輕就熟、更上一層樓——
累積實力3200單字

feath·er [ˈfɛðɚ]
🔊 Track 2449

名 羽毛、裝飾

▶ Her coat is made of fake feathers.
她的外套是假羽毛做的。

fea·ture [ˈfitʃɚ]
🔊 Track 2450

名 特徵、特色

▶ The key feature of the cellphone is the voice input function.
這種手機的重要功能是語音輸入。

file [faɪl]
🔊 Track 2451

名 檔案 動 存檔、歸檔

▶ 名 Would you please collect the files for me?
請你幫我把這些檔案收集一下好嗎？

▶ 動 I filed the letters carefully.
我小心地把這些信件歸檔了。

fire·work [ˈfaɪrˌwɝk]
🔊 Track 2452

名 煙火

▶ Would you like to see the firework display with us?
你想不想跟我們一起去看煙火秀？

fist [fɪst]
🔊 Track 2453

名 拳頭、拳打、緊握

▶ He punched the wall and hurt his fist.
他搥了牆壁一拳，結果傷了拳頭。

flame [flem]
🔊 Track 2454

名 火焰 動 燃燒

▶ 名 The flame consumed more than half of the forest.
火焰已經吞噬這座森林的一半。

▶ 動 Her anger flamed up in an instant.
她的怒火一瞬間就燃燒了起來。

fla·vor [ˈflevɚ]
🔊 Track 2455

名 味道、風味 動 添情趣、添風味

▶ 名 I don't like the flavor of this soup.
我不喜歡這湯的味道。

▶ 動 How about flavoring the fish with sugar and vinegar（醋）？
我們用糖和醋給魚調味怎麼樣？

flea [fli]
🔊 Track 2456

名 跳蚤

▶ Let's go to the flea market later.
我們待會去個跳蚤市場吧。

flesh [flɛʃ]
🔊 Track 2457

名 肉體、軀殼

▶ The sorrow is more than flesh and blood can bear.
這種悲傷已超過血肉之軀的人所能承受的。

文法字詞解析

我們聽音樂、看 MV 的時候，常會看到歌名後面寫著「ft.（某個人的名字）」，其中「ft.」表示「featuring」，也是從「feature」這個字衍生出來的，有「客串、特別出演」的意思。

萬用延伸句型

Would you like to...? 你想不想要……？

文法字詞解析

punch 的意思是「用力一擊」，而「punchline」就是一個笑話中的「笑點、梗」。所以如果有人把某件好笑的事情「破梗」了，就可以說他「screw up the punchline」。

文法字詞解析

如果想要說某個東西是「某某口味」，該怎麼說呢？很簡單，用「（口味名稱）-flavored」就可以了。例如草莓口味的冰淇淋就是 strawberry-flavored ice cream。

float [flot]
 Track 2458

動 使漂浮

▶There is a log floating in the middle of the river.
河中央漂浮著一根圓木。

flock [flɑk]
 Track 2459

名 禽群、人群

▶Crowds of visitors flock to the zoo to see the animals.
大批遊客湧向動物園去看動物。

fold [fold]
 Track 2460

動 折疊

▶You can fold the new type of cell phone.
這種新型手機是可以摺疊的。

folk [fok]
 Track 2461

名 人們 形 民間的

▶名 They are the best folks on earth, for they are not only kind but also diligent.
他們是世上最好的人,因為他們不但善良而且勤勞。

▶形 He is not only a very popular folk singer but also a famous writer. 他不但是一位很受歡迎的民歌手,而且還是一位著名的作家。

fol·low·er [ˋfɑloˇ]
 Track 2462

名 跟隨者、屬下

▶Many ancient Greeks were followers of Socrates(蘇格拉底).
許多古希臘人都是蘇格拉底的追隨者。

文法字詞解析

follower 這個字即是大家都知道的 follow(跟隨)加上字尾「-er」(……者)所組成的,變成「跟隨者」的意思。

fond [fɑnd]
 Track 2463

形 喜歡的

▶Our new manager is very fond of the decoration in the office.
我們的經理很喜歡辦公室的裝飾。

fore·head/brow
 Track 2464

[ˋfɔrˏhɛd]/[braʊ]

名 前額、額頭

▶I don't like my foreheard very much. It's too wide.
我不怎麼喜歡自己的額頭,太寬了。

for·ev·er [fəˋɛvˇ]
 Track 2465

副 永遠 同 always 永遠

▶Pharaohs(法老)in ancient Egypt believed they could live forever.
古埃及的法老相信自己有個不死之軀。

forth [forθ]
 Track 2466

副 向外、向前、在前方

▶Our director came forth and pointed out the glitches in the system. 我們的組長挺身而出,指出系統的缺陷。

Level 1

Level 2

Level 3

駕輕就熟、更上一層樓──累積實力3200單字

Level 4

Level 5

Level 6

for·tune [ˈfɔrtʃən]
◀ Track 2467
名 運氣、財富　同 luck 幸運
▶If I get rich, I'll be sure to share my fortune with you.
如果我變有錢，我一定會跟你分享我的財富。

found [faʊnd]
◀ Track 2468
動 建立、打基礎　同 establish 建立
▶They founded the company together.
他們一起建立了那個公司。

foun·tain [ˈfaʊntn̩]
◀ Track 2469
名 噴泉、噴水池
▶Some children were playing water by the fountain in the plaza.
有些小孩在廣場中央的噴泉玩水。

freeze [friz]
◀ Track 2470
動 凍結
▶All the water in the river was frozen. 河裡的水都結冰了。

fre·quent [ˈfrikwənt]
◀ Track 2471
形 常有的、頻繁的　同 regular 經常的
▶Not everyone in my family enjoys his frequent visits.
我們家不是每個人都喜歡他經常來訪。

friend·ship [ˈfrɛndʃɪp]
◀ Track 2472
名 友誼、友情
▶Our friendship has lasted for more than two decades.
我們的友誼已經持續超過二十年了。

frus·trate [ˈfrʌstret]
◀ Track 2473
動 使受挫、擊敗　同 defeat 擊敗
▶The terrible weather frustrated our hopes of going out.
惡劣的天氣使我們外出的願望無法實現了。

fry [fraɪ]
◀ Track 2474
動 油炸、炸
▶What do you think of frying the fish for our dinner?
你覺得炸魚來作為我們的晚飯怎麼樣？

fund [fʌnd]
◀ Track 2475
名 資金、財源　動 投資、儲蓄
▶名 We are raising funds for setting up a new laboratory.
我們在募款來建造新的實驗室。
▶動 Can you tell me who is funding the project?
您能告訴我是誰為這個計畫提供資金嗎？

fur [fɝ]
◀ Track 2476
名 毛皮、軟皮
▶Would you please let me know for whom you have bought this fur coat? 請問您能告訴我這件皮大衣是買給誰的嗎？

文法字詞解析
found 是動詞原形，意為「建立、打基礎」，但它同時也是動詞 find（找到）的過去式形式，因此很容易搞混。我們來把兩者比較看看：
find 的動詞變化：find, found, found
found 的動詞變化：found, founded, founded

文法字詞解析
fry 的動詞變化：fry、fried、fried

fur·ni·ture [ˈfɝnɪtʃɚ] 🔊 *Track 2477*

名 傢俱、設備
▶We purchased some used furniture for the new apartment.
我們購買一些二手家具放在新公寓。

[Gg]

gal·lon [ˈgælən] 🔊 *Track 2478*

名 加侖
▶How many miles can you drive with a gallon of gas?
你一加侖汽油能開多少英里？

gam·ble [ˈgæmbl̩] 🔊 *Track 2479*

動 賭博 名 賭博、投機 同 bet 打賭
▶動 It was so foolish of the old man to gamble away all his money.
這個老人賭博輸掉了自己所有的錢，真是太愚蠢了。
▶名 All of us think it is a gamble.
我們都認為這是一場豪賭。

gang [gæŋ] 🔊 *Track 2480*

名 一隊（工人）、一群（囚犯）
▶The gang is planning a robbery.
那幫罪犯正在計畫搶劫。

文法字詞解析
口語中稱呼自己的一幫朋友也可用 gang 這個字，不代表你們是幫派、工人或囚犯。

gap [gæp] 🔊 *Track 2481*

名 差距、缺口
▶My grandfather tired his best to bridge the generation gap.
我的祖父努力減少代溝。

gar·lic [ˈgɑrlɪk] 🔊 *Track 2482*

名 蒜
▶Would you like to try this garlic flavored rice?
你要不要試試這種蒜味的飯？

gas·o·line/gas·o·lene/
gas [ˈgæsl̩ˌin]/[ˌgæsˈlˈin]/[gæs] 🔊 *Track 2483*

名 汽油 同 petroleum 石油
▶An automobile can consume a lot of gasoline.
一輛汽車能消耗很多的汽油。

ges·ture [ˈdʒɛstʃɚ] 🔊 *Track 2484*

名 手勢、姿勢 動 打手勢
▶名 The gesture means "okay" in the U.S. but it means money in Japan.
在美國代表 "ok" 的手勢在日本代表「錢」。
▶動 I gestured to the waiter to come over.
我打手勢要服務生過來。

Level 1
Level 2
Level 3
Level 4
Level 5
Level 6

駕輕就熟、更上一層樓──累積實力3200單字

glance [glæns]
Track 2485

動 瞥視、看一下 名 一瞥 同 glimpse 瞥見
- ▶動 Will you stop glancing left and right in a meeting? It's not polite. 請不要在會議上左顧右盼好嗎？這不禮貌。
- ▶名 They exchanged glances and walked out.
  他們互使眼色，然後走了出去。

glob·al [ˈglobl]
Track 2486

形 球狀的、全球的
- ▶Global warming effect has caused great impact on our life.
  全球暖化對我們的生活有很大影響。。

glo·ry [ˈglorɪ]
Track 2487

名 榮耀、光榮 動 洋洋得意
- ▶名 His good deeds had brought glory to our family.
  他的善行為我們家帶來了光榮。
- ▶動 The team gloried in their eventual（最終的）victory.
  這支球隊因最後獲勝而洋洋得意。

glow [glo]
Track 2488

動 熾熱、發光 名 白熱光 同 blaze 光輝
- ▶動 The wolf's eyes glowed in the darkness（黑暗）.
  狼的眼睛在黑暗中發亮。
- ▶名 Do you see the glow of the sunset over there?
  你看到那邊落日的光輝了嗎？

gos·sip [ˈgɑsəp]
Track 2489

名 閒聊 動 說閒話 同 chat 閒聊
- ▶名 Kate likes to talk about gossips in the office.
  凱特喜歡在辦公室聊八卦。
- ▶動 She likes to gossip with her friends. 她喜歡跟朋友們講閒話。

gov·er·nor [ˈgʌvɚnɚ]
Track 2490

名 統治者 同 president 總統
- ▶Do you mind if I invite the governor of the state to our banquet（宴會）? 你不介意我請州長來參加宴會吧？

gown [gaʊn]
Track 2491

名 長袍、長上衣
- ▶Would you like this wedding gown or that one?
  你是喜歡這件結婚禮服呢，還是那件？

grab [græb]
Track 2492

動 急抓、逮捕 同 snatch 抓住
- ▶He grabbed her hand before she could walk away.
  在她能走遠前，他抓住了她的手。

grad·u·al [ˈgrædʒʊəl]
Track 2493

形 逐漸的、漸進的 反 sudden 突然的
- ▶Rita is making gradual improvement in her English proficiency.
  瑞塔的英文能力漸漸進步中。

萬用延伸句型
Do you mind if...? 你介意……嗎？
例如：Do you mind if I turn off the music?
你介意我關掉音樂嗎？

grad·u·ate [ˈgrædʒuˌet] 🔊 Track 2494

名 畢業生 動 授予學位、畢業
▶名 Isn't he a college graduate?
　他不是大學畢業生嗎？
▶動 He has been working in this famous company before he even graduated from university（大學）.
　他大學還沒畢業就已經在這家知名企業工作了。

grain [gren] 🔊 Track 2495

名 穀類、穀粒
▶Grain and pork are the staple food of residents in this area.
　穀物和豬肉是這一區居民的主要食物。

gram [græm] 🔊 Track 2496

名 公克
▶Would you tell me how much per gram your silver is?
　你能告訴我你的銀製品每克多少錢嗎？

grasp [græsp] 🔊 Track 2497

動 掌握、領悟、抓牢 同 grab 抓住
▶It's hard to grasp the meaning of his words.
　他講的話的意思實在很難懂。

grass·hop·per [ˈgræsˌhɑpɚ] 🔊 Track 2498

名 蚱蜢
▶That grasshopper is as big as my hand!
　那隻蚱蜢跟我的手一樣大耶！

green·house [ˈgrinˌhaʊs] 🔊 Track 2499

名 溫室
▶He couldn't care less about the greenhouse effect.
　他對溫室效應的議題毫無興趣。

萬用延伸句型
can't care less about... 完全不關心

grin [grɪn] 🔊 Track 2500

動 / 名 露齒而笑
▶動 The villain grinned when seeing his hostage suffer.
　壞人看到被他綁架的人受苦就露齒微笑。
▶名 She walks in with a huge grin.
　她帶著大大的笑容走進來。

gro·cer·y [ˈgrosərɪ] 🔊 Track 2501

名 雜貨店
▶I don't think you can buy everything you want in this grocery store.
　我認為你在這個雜貨店買不到你想要的所有東西。

文法字詞解析
一般而言，會在 grocery store（生鮮雜貨店）或超市買到的東西可以通稱為 groceries，注意要用複數形式喔！不能說「我去超市買了『一個 grocery』」。

guard·i·an [ˈgɑrdɪən] 🔊 Track 2502

名 保護者、守護者
▶The police are supposed to be guardians of law and order.
　警察應該要是法律和秩序的護衛者才對。

Level 1
Level 2
Level 3
駕輕就熟、更上一層樓——
累積實力3200單字
Level 4
Level 5
Level 6

guid·ance [ˈgaɪdn̩s] ◄ Track 2503

名 引導、指導

▶The little girl looked to her mother for guidance.
那個小女孩看向她的母親等她指示。

gum [gʌm] ◄ Track 2504

名 膠、口香糖

▶The kids were admonished not to leave gum on the table.
小朋友被告誡不能把口香糖留在桌上。

gymnasium [dʒɪmˈnezɪəm] ◄ Track 2505

名 體育館、健身房

▶How often do you go to the gymnasium nearby?
你多常去附近的健身房？

文法字詞解析
gymnasium 也可以簡稱 gym，是比較常用的用法。

[Hh]

hair·dres·ser [ˈhɛrˌdrɛsɚ] ◄ Track 2506

名 理髮師

▶Why don't you ask the hairdresser to trim（修剪）your beard?
為什麼不讓理髮師幫你修剪一下鬍髯呢？

hall·way [ˈhɔlˌwe] ◄ Track 2507

名 玄關、門廳

▶Would you please not leave your garbage in the hallway? It's attracting flies here.
請您別把垃圾放在玄關裡好嗎？這樣會引來蒼蠅。

hand·ful [ˈhændˌfəl] ◄ Track 2508

形 少量、少數

▶Only a handful of students joined this campaign.
只有一些學生參加了這個活動。

handy [ˈhændɪ] ◄ Track 2509

形 手巧的、手邊的 同 convenient 方便的、隨手可得的

▶You should bring a flashlight. It might come in handy.
你帶個手電筒吧，可能會派上用場。

har·bor [ˈhɑrbɚ] ◄ Track 2510

名 港灣 同 port 港口

▶The harbor smells like fish. 港口聞起來有魚的味道。

文法字詞解析
港口是船隻停泊的地方，給人安心的感覺，於是 harbor 也延伸出了動詞用法，表示「暗藏（某些情感）」的意思。例如對某人暗藏著厭惡的情緒，可說 harbor ill feelings towards sb.，而暗藏著暗戀的情緒則可以說 harbor a crush on sb.。

harm [hɑrm] ◄ Track 2511

名 損傷、損害 動 傷害、損害 同 damage 損害

▶名 If we interfere（干涉）, we will cause more harm than good. 倘若我們進行干預，造成的問題會比帶來的好處多。

▶動 I didn't mean to harm your reputation.
我無意敗壞你的名聲。

harm·ful [ˋhɑrmfəl] 🔊 Track 2512

形 引起傷害的、有害的 同 destructive 破壞的

▶It is harmful for you to drink too much wine.
過量喝酒對你的身體有害。

文法字詞解析
是不是覺得「harmful」和「harm」長得很像，似乎有關係呢？確實，harmful 就是 harm 加上形容詞字尾「-ful」，變成表示「有害的」的形容詞。

har·vest [ˋhɑrvɪst] 🔊 Track 2513

名 收穫 動 收穫、收割穀物

▶名 The villagers gathered at the plaza to pray for a good harvest this year. 村民聚集在廣場祈求今年豐收。

▶動 We will harvest the fruit before first frost（霜）.
我們會在初霜之前採摘這些水果。

hast·y [ˋhestɪ] 🔊 Track 2514

形 快速的

▶I don't think that it's right to make such a hasty decision.
我認為如此倉促地做出決定是不正確的。

hatch [hætʃ] 🔊 Track 2515

動 計畫、孵化

▶Would you tell me when the eggs will hatch?
您能告訴我蛋什麼時候孵化嗎？

萬用延伸句型
Would you tell me when...
你可不可以告訴我什麼時候……

hawk [hɔk] 🔊 Track 2516

名 鷹

▶We watched the hawk with binoculars（望遠鏡）.
我們用望遠鏡觀賞那隻鷹。

文法字詞解析
binoculars 和 telescope 都是望遠鏡的意思，那他們之間有什麼不同呢？從字首可以看出，前者的「bi-」代表有兩個鏡片的「雙筒望遠鏡」，多半是在距離沒有那麼遠的活動中使用，像是賞鳥、看演唱會等；而「tele-」則有「在遠方」的意思，所以後者就是可以看很遠的大型望遠鏡，例如天文望遠鏡。

hay [he] 🔊 Track 2517

名 乾草

▶Looking for the missing child is like seeking a needle in the hay. 尋找這個失蹤的小孩就像是在草堆裡找一根針。

head·line [ˋhɛdͺlaɪn] 🔊 Track 2518

名 標題、寫標題 同 title 標題

▶Would you please give this article a headline?
請您為這篇文章擬一個大標題好嗎？

文法字詞解析
headline 這個單字經常以複數形式出現。例如報紙上的頭條我們常會稱為「the headlines on the newspaper」，而「上頭條」則可以說成「make the headlines」。

head·quar·ters [ˋhɛdͺkwɔrtɚz] 🔊 Track 2519

名 總部、大本營

▶Where are your company's headquarters? 你公司的總部在哪？

heal [hil] 🔊 Track 2520

動 治癒、復原 同 cure 治癒

▶Has your wound healed yet? 你的傷癒合了沒？

heap [hip] 🔊 Track 2521

名 積累 動 堆積

▶名 There are a lot of books lying in a heap on the floor.
有很多書堆放在地板上。

▶動 He heaped his old magazine in the living room.
他把舊雜誌堆在客廳裡。

Level 1
Level 2
Level 3
Level 4
Level 5
Level 6

累積實力3200單字 駕輕就熟、更上一層樓——

heav·en [ˈhɛvən]　　🔊 *Track 2522*
名 天堂
▶They are a match made in heaven.
　他們是天造地設的一對。

heel [hil]　　🔊 *Track 2523*
名 腳後跟
▶Wearing high heels may be harmful to your ankle.
　穿高跟鞋可能會傷害你的腳踝。

文法字詞解析
高跟鞋「high heels」也可以簡稱為「heels」。
相對地，平底的鞋則可以簡稱「flats」。

hell [hɛl]　　🔊 *Track 2524*
名 地獄、悲慘處境　同 misery 悲慘、苦難
▶They believe that evil people will go to hell.
　他們相信邪惡的人會下地獄。

hel·met [ˈhɛlmɪt]　　🔊 *Track 2525*
名 頭盔、安全帽
▶If you wear a safety helmet, you won't get hurt.
　如果你戴安全帽就不會受傷了。

hes·i·tate [ˈhɛzəˌtet]　　🔊 *Track 2526*
動 遲疑、躊躇
▶He hesitated before he signed the contract.
　他簽合約之前猶豫了。

hike [haɪk]　　🔊 *Track 2527*
名 徒步旅行、健行
▶I am going hiking next month; would you like to go with me?
　下個月我要去健行，你想不想跟我一起去呢？

hint [hɪnt]　　🔊 *Track 2528*
名 暗示　同 imply 暗示
▶Didn't you pick up the subtle hints in his letter?
　你難道沒有發現他信中的微妙暗示嗎？

萬用延伸句型
take the hint 接收到暗示、領會
例　如：After she ignored him for two
hours, he finally took the hint and left.
她忽視他兩個小時後，他終於領會了她的
意思，離開了。

his·to·ri·an [hɪsˈtoriən]　　🔊 *Track 2529*
名 歷史學家
▶Evans is not only a writer but also a historian.
　伊文斯不但是個作家，還是位歷史學家。

his·tor·ic [hɪsˈtɔrɪk]　　🔊 *Track 2530*
形 歷史性的
▶The historic value of the old statue was approved by the historians.
　這個雕像的歷史價值被歷史學家認可。

his·tor·i·cal [hɪsˈtɔrɪk]　　🔊 *Track 2531*
形 歷史的
▶We should look at all of this from a historical standpoint（觀點）. 我們應該從歷史的觀點來看待這一切。

hive [haɪv]
🔊 *Track 2532*
名 蜂巢、鬧區
▶Can you tell me how many bees there are in the hive?
你能否告訴我這個蜂巢裡有多少蜜蜂？

hol·low [ˈhɑlo]
🔊 *Track 2533*
形 中空的、空的 同 empty 空的
▶These chocolate eggs are hollow. 這些巧克力蛋是中空的。

ho·ly [ˈholɪ]
🔊 *Track 2534*
形 神聖的、聖潔的
▶Saints are holy people. 所謂聖人就是神聖的人。

home·town [ˈhomˌtaʊn]
🔊 *Track 2535*
名 家鄉
▶Would you like to tell me what your hometown is like?
你能告訴我你的家鄉是什麼樣子嗎？

hon·es·ty [ˈɑnɪstɪ]
🔊 *Track 2536*
名 正直、誠實
▶I value honesty above all else.
我把誠實看得比什麼都重要。

hon·or [ˈɑnɚ]
🔊 *Track 2537*
名 榮耀、尊敬 同 respect 尊敬
▶Would you honor me by dining with me tonight?
今晚你能賞光與我共進晚餐嗎？

horn [hɔrn]
🔊 *Track 2538*
名 喇叭
▶The impatient drivers pushed horns at each other.
不耐煩的司機們對彼此鳴喇叭。

hor·ri·ble [ˈhɑrəbl̩]
🔊 *Track 2539*
形 可怕的
▶The accident was horrible, as I'm sure all who witnessed（見證）it could tell you.
這次意外超慘的，我相信所有看到它發生的人都會這麼說。

horror [ˈhɑrɚ]
🔊 *Track 2540*
名 恐怖、畏懼 同 panic 恐慌
▶Some people like to watch horror movies.
有些人喜歡看空恐怖片。

hour·ly [ˈaʊrlɪ]
🔊 *Track 2541*
形 每小時的 副 每小時地
▶形 I'm paid on an hourly basis; what about you?
我的工資是以小時計算的，你呢？
▶副 This medicine is to be taken hourly.
這個藥是每小時服一次。

萬用延伸句型
Can you tell me...? 你可不可以告訴我……？

文法字詞解析
除了車子的喇叭，一些像喇叭一樣會發出響聲的樂器也可以稱為 horn。例如法國號 French horn、英國管 English horn 等等。

Level **1**

Level **2**

Level **3**

駕輕就熟、更上一層樓──
累積實力3200單字

Level **4**

Level **5**

Level **6**

house·keep·er [ˈhaʊsˌkipɚ]   🔊 Track 2542

名 主婦、管家
▶Our housekeeper is already very old but still quite efficient.
　我們的管家年紀很大了，但做事還是很有效率。

文法字詞解析
我們都知道 house 指的是房子，keep 有維持的意思，再加上意思是「……者」的字尾「-er」，可知 house-keeper 就是「維持房子的人」，也就是管家了。

hug [hʌg]   🔊 Track 2543

動 抱、緊抱 名 緊抱、擁抱 同 embrace 擁抱
▶動 They hugged each other before saying goodbye.
　他們在說再見前擁抱了一下。
▶名 I give my children a hug every day. 我每天都抱抱孩子一下。

hu·mor·ous [ˈhjumərəs]   🔊 Track 2544

形 幽默的、滑稽的 同 funny 好笑的
▶The story was more humorous than romantic.
　那個故事不是很浪漫，但很好笑。

萬用延伸句型
be more... than... 比起……更……

hush [hʌʃ]   🔊 Track 2545

動 使寂靜 名 寂靜 同 silence 寂靜
▶動 Can you hush the baby for me? 可以幫我讓寶寶安靜一下嗎？
▶名 His words brought a hush of embarrassment in the room.
　他的話讓房間陷入尷尬的寂靜。

hut [hʌt]   🔊 Track 2546

名 小屋、茅舍
▶Let's go to visit the old man living in the little wooden hut.
　我們去探望一下那個住在一間小木屋裡的老人吧。

[Ii]

ic·y [ˈaɪsɪ]   🔊 Track 2547

形 冰的
▶It was stupid of him to walk on the icy road at night.
　他晚上在結冰的路上走真是太笨了。

萬用延伸句型
It was stupid of sb. to... （某人）這樣做很笨

i·de·al [aɪˈdiəl]   🔊 Track 2548

形 理想的、完美的 同 perfect 完美的
▶That was not an ideal time to bring up a serious topic.
　那不是一個談到嚴肅話題的理想時機。

i·den·ti·ty [aɪˈdɛntətɪ]   🔊 Track 2549

名 身分
▶Would you please show me your identity card?
　你能出示一下你的身分證嗎？

萬用延伸句型
Would you please...? 可不可以請您……？

ig·no·rance [ˈɪgnərəns]   🔊 Track 2550

名 無知、不學無術 反 knowledge 學識
▶Some people's ignorance makes me really mad.
　有些人的無知讓我實在不太開心。

im·age [ˈɪmɪdʒ]

Track 2551

名 影像、形象

▶The idle has a positive image in the fans' mind.
這名偶像在影迷心目中有正面的形象。

i·mag·i·na·tion [ɪˌmædʒəˈneʃən]

Track 2552

名 想像力、創作力

▶The little girl has a really active imagination.
這個小女孩的想像力非常豐富。

im·me·di·ate [ɪˈmidɪɪt]

Track 2553

形 直接的、立即的

▶We need your immediate reply.
我們需要你立即回覆。

文法字詞解析
immediate 的 副 詞 形 式 immediately 比
immediate 還更常見，尤其在要求別人盡快
為你完成某個工作、或馬上跟你聯絡時，
經常用到這個字。

im·port [ɪmˈport]/[ˈɪmport]

Track 2554

動 進口、輸入 名 輸入品、進口 反 export 出口

▶動 Most of the wheat products were imported from Europe.
大部分的小麥製品是由歐洲進口。

▶名 The import of tea has gone up sharply（急劇地）these years.
近年來茶葉的進口大大增加了。

im·press [ɪmˈprɛs]

Track 2555

動 留下深刻印象、使感動

▶The audience was impressed by her performance.
她的表演給所有的觀眾都留下了深刻的印象。

im·pres·sive [ɪmˈprɛsɪv]

Track 2556

形 印象深刻的

▶Don't you think the film was quite impressive?
你不覺得那部電影很令人印象深刻嗎？

萬用延伸句型
Don't you think...? 你不覺得……？
Don't you think 和 Do you think 的意思
差不多，但就像中文的「你不覺得……」
與「你覺得......」之間也有微妙差異一
樣，「Don't you think...」多了一點反問
的味道。

in·deed [ɪnˈdid]

Track 2557

副 實在地、的確

▶After I met him, I realized that he was indeed a very strange man.
見過他後，我發現他的確是個怪人。

in·di·vid·u·al [ˌɪndəˈvɪdʒuəl]

Track 2558

形 個別的 名 個人

▶形 It is difficult for a teacher to give individual attention to his or her students. 老師很難照顧到每一個學生。

▶名 The nurse tries to give individual attention to each patient in the ward.
護士嘗試要給病房裡每位病人個別的照顧。

in·door [ˈɪnˌdor]

Track 2559

形 屋內的、室內的 反 outdoor 戶外的

▶Are you interested in indoor sports?
你對室內運動感興趣嗎？

萬用延伸句型
Are you interested in...? 你對……有興趣嗎？

Level 1
Level 2
Level 3
Level 4
Level 5
Level 6

駕輕就熟、更上一層樓——
累積實力3200單字

in·doors [ɪn`dorz]
🔊 *Track 2560*

副 在室內 反 outdoors 在戶外

▶On rainy days, we often stay indoors all day long.
在下雨天，我們常常整天待在室內。

in·dus·tri·al [ɪn`dʌstrɪəl]
🔊 *Track 2561*

形 工業的

▶Industrial pollution is becoming a huge problem.
工業污染現在成為了很嚴重的問題。

in·fe·ri·or [ɪn`fɪrɪɚ]
🔊 *Track 2562*

形 較低的、較劣的 同 worse 較差的

▶The food in this restaurant was inferior to that of the one next
to it. 這家餐廳的菜比隔壁那家更難吃。

文法字詞解析
inferior 有「比較差的」的意思，那麼「比較好的」呢？可以說 superior。

in·form [ɪn`fɔrm]
🔊 *Track 2563*

動 通知、報告

▶Do you mind if I inform him about the bad news now?
你介意我現在就把壞消息告訴他嗎？

in·jure [`ɪndʒɚ]
🔊 *Track 2564*

動 傷害、使受傷 同 hurt 傷害

▶I heard he got injured in this accident. How is he now?
聽說他在事故中受傷，那他現在怎麼樣了？

in·ju·ry [`ɪndʒərɪ]
🔊 *Track 2565*

名 傷害、損害

▶He has suffered serious injuries. 他受了很嚴重的傷。

inn [ɪn]
🔊 *Track 2566*

名 旅社、小酒館

▶There are some taverns and inns in this small town.
這個小鎮裡有一些酒館和旅社。

in·ner [`ɪnɚ]
🔊 *Track 2567*

形 內部的、心靈的 同 outer 外部的

▶It is hard for anyone to know what others' inner thoughts
might be. 我們很難知道別人內心的想法。

文法字詞解析
inner circle = (組織、政黨內的) 核心集團
inner peace = 內心的平靜
inner voice = 內心的聲音

in·no·cent [`ɪnəsn̩t]
🔊 *Track 2568*

形 無辜的、純潔的 反 guilty 罪惡的

▶There is still no hard evidence（證據）to prove that he is
innocent.
還沒有確切的證據可以證明他是無辜的。

in·spect [ɪn`spɛkt]
🔊 *Track 2569*

動 調查、檢查

▶Our responsibility is to inspect the products to make sure they
are flawless.
我們的責任就是檢查產品，確定它們沒有瑕疵。

in·spec·tor [ɪnˈspɛktɚ]
🔊 *Track 2570*

名 視察員、檢查者
▶The inspector is asking for details of the missing cars.
視察員正要求提供遺失汽車的細節。

in·stead [ɪnˈstɛd]
🔊 *Track 2571*

副 替代
▶I think we should go right instead of left.
我覺得我們應該走右邊而不是走左邊。

instruction [ɪnˈstrʌkʃən]
🔊 *Track 2572*

名 指令、教導
▶Why don't you give your staff some detailed instructions about this matter?
為何不給你的下屬有關此事的詳細指令呢？

in·ter·nal [ɪnˈtɝnl̩]
🔊 *Track 2573*

形 內部的、國內的
▶The internal conflict within the company was not initiated by our department.
公司內部的衝突不是源自於我們的部門。

in·ter·rupt [ˌɪntəˈrʌpt]
🔊 *Track 2574*

動 干擾、打斷 同 intrude 打擾
▶Sorry to interrupt you, but would you please send me the documents（文件）this afternoon?
對不起，打擾了，您能在今天下午就把檔案寄送給我嗎？

萬用延伸句型
Sorry to interrupt you, but...
很抱歉打擾你，但……（可接上需要對方幫忙的事物）

in·tro·duc·tion [ˌɪntrəˈdʌkʃən]
🔊 *Track 2575*

名 引進、介紹
▶Do you mind if I give a brief introduction about our product first?
你介意我先簡短介紹一些我們的產品嗎？

in·ven·tor [ɪnˈvɛntɚ]
🔊 *Track 2576*

名 發明家
▶I don't think this inventor is as talented as they say.
我覺得這名發明家不如大家所說的那麼有才華。

萬用延伸句型
as... as they say 如人們所說的一樣……

in·ves·ti·gate [ɪnˈvɛstəˌget]
🔊 *Track 2577*

動 研究、調查 同 inspect 調查
▶If the police won't investigate this matter, let's just do it ourselves.
如果警察不調查這件事，那我們就自己來調查。

i·vo·ry [ˈaɪvərɪ]
🔊 *Track 2578*

名 象牙 形 象牙製的
▶名 Ivory is costly and hard to obtain（取得）.
象牙很寶貴，很難取得。
▶形 People with limited life experience are said to be living in an ivory tower.
生活經驗有限的人被形容為生活在象牙塔中。

Level 1

Level 2

Level 3

Level 4

Level 5

Level 6

駕輕就熟、更上一層樓──累積實力3200單字

[Jj]

jail [dʒel]　　　　　🔊 *Track 2579*

名 監獄　同 prison 監獄
▶Not all neighbors knew that he had been in jail for two years.
　不是所有的鄰居都知道他曾在監獄被關了兩年。

jar [dʒɑr]　　　　　🔊 *Track 2580*

名 刺耳的聲音、廣口瓶
▶The book offers some tips for removing the stubborn jar lid.
　這本書提供一打開罐子蓋子的秘訣。

jaw [dʒɔ]　　　　　🔊 *Track 2581*

名 顎、下巴
▶Her jaw looks like a man's.
　她的下顎看起來像個男人的下巴似的。

jeal·ous [ˈdʒɛləs]　　🔊 *Track 2582*

形 嫉妒的　同 envious 嫉妒的、羨慕的
▶I don't think he is jealous of his colleague's success.
　我認為他並不是嫉妒他同事的成功。

jel·ly [ˈdʒɛlɪ]　　　　🔊 *Track 2583*

名 果凍
▶Would you like to put some jelly on the bread?
　你想不想在麵包上塗些果醬呢？

jet [dʒɛt]　　　　　🔊 *Track 2584*

名 噴射機、噴嘴　動 噴出
▶名 When the jet passes overhead, we can hear the sound.
　飛機飛過頭頂時，我們可以聽見聲音。
▶動 Water is jetting out from the broken pipe.
　水正從破裂的水管裡噴出來。

jew·el [ˈdʒuəl]　　　　🔊 *Track 2585*

名 珠寶
▶My mother doesn't really care about jewels.
　我媽媽對珠寶沒什麼興趣。

jew·el·ry [ˈdʒuəlrɪ]　　🔊 *Track 2586*

名 珠寶
▶The jewelry I own is mostly cheap.
　我擁有的珠寶大部分很便宜。

jour·nal [ˈdʒɝnl̩]　　　🔊 *Track 2587*

名 期刊　同 magazine 雜誌
▶Kevin keeps a learning journal to track his studies.
　凱文有做學習日記，記錄他唸書的進度。

文法字詞解析
人在遇到驚人的事情時總會把嘴巴張得很大，而嘴巴張很大的話下巴就會掉下來，因此 jaw-dropping 這個形容詞便用來描述某件事很令人吃驚。

文法字詞解析
jewelry 和前一個 jewel 都是「珠寶」的意思，那麼差別在哪裡呢？原來，jewelry 通常用於表示「珠寶的通稱」，所以你的項鍊手環耳環墜子擺在一起，就可以統稱 jewelry。jewel 的複數 jewels 也可以通稱珠寶，但單數時則可以單個單個的算「一件珠寶」。

jour·ney [ˈdʒɝnɪ]　🔊 *Track 2588*

名 旅程 動 旅遊

▶名 He gave a very descriptive（描述的）account of his journey. 他對他這次旅行做出十分生動的敘述。

▶動 He used to journey to that small town a lot.
他常常旅行到那個小鎮。

---

joy·ful [ˈdʒɔɪfəl]　🔊 *Track 2589*

形 愉快的、喜悅的 同 glad 高興的

▶The joyful atmosphere at the party cheered me up.
派對歡樂的氣氛使我心情變好。

jun·gle [ˈdʒʌŋgl̩]　🔊 *Track 2590*

名 叢林

▶Can you tell me what you saw in the jungle?
你能不能告訴我在叢林中你看到了什麼？

junk [dʒʌŋk]　🔊 *Track 2591*

名 垃圾 同 trash 垃圾

▶Why did you buy such a piece of junk?
你買這垃圾幹嘛？

文法字詞解析
junk 後面常常會再接一些其他的名詞，例如 junk mail 就是我們電子信箱裡常會收到的垃圾郵件，也可以說是「spam」；junk call 則是推銷電話、廣告電話的意思；或者小時候我們一定學過 junk food 這個字，意指不健康的垃圾食物。

jus·tice [ˈdʒʌstɪs]　🔊 *Track 2592*

名 公平、公正

▶People consider the legal court the last ditch for justice.
人們認為法庭式正義的最後一道防線。

[Kk]

kan·ga·roo [ˌkæŋgəˈru]　🔊 *Track 2593*

名 袋鼠

▶Have you ever seen a kangaroo? What does it look like?
你有看過袋鼠嗎？牠長什麼樣子呢？

ket·tle [ˈkɛtl̩]　🔊 *Track 2594*

名 水壺

▶Be careful when you pour out hot water from the kettle.
從水壺倒出熱水時請小心。

key·board [ˈkiˌbord]　🔊 *Track 2595*

名 鍵盤

▶The computer set comes with a key-board and a mouse.
這個電腦組有附鍵盤和滑鼠。

---

kid·ney [ˈkɪdnɪ]　🔊 *Track 2596*

名 腎臟

▶Would you like some pig kidney soup?
你要不要喝豬腎湯？

Level 1
Level 2
Level 3
Level 4
Level 5
Level 6

累積實力3200單字 — 駕輕就熟、更上一層樓 —

ki·lo·gram/kg [ˈkɪləˌgræm] ◀≡ *Track 2597*

名 公斤

▶ Will you tell me how much I should pay for the two kilograms of pork?

能告訴我這兩公斤豬肉要多少錢嗎？

ki·lo·me·ter/km [ˈkɪləˌmitɚ] ◀≡ *Track 2598*

名 公里

▶ How many kilometers can this car go in an hour?

這輛車一個小時可以開多少公里？

kit [kɪt] ◀≡ *Track 2599*

名 工具箱

▶ The tool kit was kept in the warehouse.

工具箱放在倉庫裡。

kneel [nil] ◀≡ *Track 2600*

動 下跪

▶ He said he wouldn't forgive you even if you kneeled down before him.

他說他不會原諒你的，就算你在他面前下跪也一樣。

> **文法字詞解析**
> kneel 的動詞變化：kneel, kneeled, kneeled 或 kneel, knelt, knelt

knight [naɪt] ◀≡ *Track 2601*

名 騎士、武士 動 封……為爵士

▶ 名 Have you heard stories about the Knights of the Round Table?

你有聽過圓桌武士的故事嗎？

▶ 動 He wasn't knighted by the Queen at that time.

他當時沒被女王封為爵士。

knit [nɪt] ◀≡ *Track 2602*

動 編織 名 編織物

▶ 動 My aunt knitted a sweater for me.

我阿姨為我織了一件毛衣。

▶ 名 My sister bought some winter knits for me.

我姐姐買了幾件冬天穿的針織衫給我。

knob [nɑb] ◀≡ *Track 2603*

名 圓形把手、球塊

▶ Why don't you replace the old knobs on the doors?

為什麼不把門上的舊把手都換掉呢？

knot [nɑt] ◀≡ *Track 2604*

名 結 動 打結

▶ 名 The couple finally tied the knot.

這對情侶終於結為連理。

▶ 動 He knotted the ends of the rope together.

他把繩頭結在一起。

> **文法字詞解析**
> tie the knot = 結為連理

[Ll]

la·bel [ˈlebl̩]
🔊 *Track 2605*

名 標籤 動 標明
- ▶名 I removed the label from the jar.
  我把標籤從罐子上移除。
- ▶動 The boy was labeled a troublemaker（鬧事者）.
  這男孩被人稱作搗蛋鬼。

lace [les]
🔊 *Track 2606*

名 花邊、緞帶 動 用帶子打結
- ▶名 I like the cushion with the lace better.
  我比較喜歡有花邊的那個抱枕。
- ▶動 Her dress was laced with gold.
  她的洋裝鑲有金色飾帶。

lad·der [ˈlædɚ]
🔊 *Track 2607*

名 梯子
- ▶It's a superstition that walking under a ladder brings bad luck.
  從梯子底下走過會帶來壞運，是個迷信的想法。

lat·ter [ˈlætɚ]
🔊 *Track 2608*

形 後者的
- ▶I think the latter idea is better. What do you think?
  我覺得後面這個主意更好，你覺得呢？

laugh·ter [ˈlæftɚ]
🔊 *Track 2609*

名 笑聲
- ▶The clown brought a lot of laughter to the elderly citizens.
  小丑為老年人帶來歡笑。

laun·dry [ˈlɔndrɪ]
🔊 *Track 2610*

名 洗衣店、送洗的衣服
- ▶When does the wash come back from the laundry?
  洗衣店的衣服什麼時候能取回來？

lawn [lɔn]
🔊 *Track 2611*

名 草地
- ▶I'd much rather lie down on the lawn than work in the office.
  比起在辦公室工作，我更想躺在草坪上。

leak [lik]
🔊 *Track 2612*

動 洩漏、滲漏 名 漏洞
- ▶動 The official leaked confidential information to the enemy.
  這名官員洩漏機密資訊給敵國。
- ▶名 Would you please come over to my place and mend a leak in my hot water tank?
  你能不能到我家修補一下熱水箱上的洞？

萬用延伸句型
mow the lawn 割草
例如：She paid Tommy to mow the lawn for her.
她付錢給湯米要他幫她割草。

Level 1
Level 2
Level 3 累積實力3200單字 駕輕就熟、更上一層樓
Level 4
Level 5
Level 6

leap [lip]
🔊 *Track 2613*

動 使跳過 名 跳躍

▶動 A lot of fish leapt out of water and landed on the shore.
有很多條魚躍出水面落到岸上。

▶名 You had better watch before you leap.
你最好看清楚再跳過去(要三思而後行)。

leath·er [ˈlɛðɚ]
🔊 *Track 2614*

名 皮革

▶This wallet feels to me like leather.
我覺得這錢包像是皮革製的。

lei·sure [ˈliʒɚ]
🔊 *Track 2615*

名 空閒

▶Watching Youtube videos is my favorite leisure time activity.
看Youtube頻道是我最喜歡的消遣活動。

length·en [ˈlɛŋθən]
🔊 *Track 2616*

動 加長

▶Some people say that to save time is to lengthen life.
有人說節約時間就等於延長壽命。

文法字詞解析
在 lengthen 的後面加上表示「……者」的字尾「-er」，就變成 lengthener，是「加長器」的意思。加長器要用來加長什麼？那就看前面加上什麼字而定了。例如加長睫毛的就是 eyelash lengthener，加長裙子的就是 skirt lengthener，還有鉛筆削一削變得太短、很難拿，也可以靠 pencil lengthener 來解決。

lens [lɛns]
🔊 *Track 2617*

名 透鏡

▶Would you please bring me that pair of glasses with plastic lenses?
你能把那副塑膠鏡片的眼鏡拿給我嗎？

li·ar [ˈlaɪɚ]
🔊 *Track 2618*

名 說謊者

▶Are you simple enough to believe what that liar told you?
你會蠢到相信那騙子說的話嗎？

lib·er·al [ˈlɪbərəl]
🔊 *Track 2619*

形 自由主義的、開明的、慷慨的 同 generous 慷慨的

▶There are many educators（教育家）advocating（提倡）a liberal education.
有很多教育家提倡開明教育。

lib·er·ty [ˈlɪbətɪ]
🔊 *Track 2620*

名 自由 同 freedom 自由

▶We admired the magnificent Statue of Liberty from a ferry.
我們在郵輪上瞻仰宏偉的自由女神像。

文法字詞解析
take the liberty of + V-ing = 自作主張做某事

li·brar·i·an [laɪˈbrɛrɪən]
🔊 *Track 2621*

名 圖書館員

▶My father is the librarian of our school.
我父親是我們學校的圖書館館員。

life·boat [ˈlaɪfˌbot]
名 救生艇
▶Passengers gathered on the deck, waiting to get on the lifeboat. 乘客擠在甲板上等待搭乘救生艇。

life·guard [ˈlaɪfˌgɑrd]
名 救生員
▶It is best for you to swim only in places where there is a lifeguard. 你最好只在有救生員的地方游泳。

> **萬用延伸句型**
> It is best for you to... 對你來說⋯⋯最好

life·time [ˈlaɪfˌtaɪm]
名 一生
▶It's the chance of a lifetime. 這是一生中難得再遇到的機會。

light·house [ˈlaɪtˌhaʊs]
名 燈塔
▶There is a lighthouse flashing in the distance.
有一座燈塔在遠處發出閃爍的光。

limb [lɪm]
名 枝幹
▶The little girl likes sitting on the limb of this tree.
這個小女孩喜歡坐在這棵樹的枝幹上。

lin·en [ˈlɪnɪn]
名 亞麻製品
▶I spent all weekend washing dirty linen.
我花了一個週末洗髒的亞麻床單。

lip·stick [ˈlɪpˌstɪk]
名 口紅、唇膏
▶Emily bought a fuchsia lipstick.
艾蜜莉買了桃紅色的唇膏。

> **文法字詞解析**
> lip 是「嘴唇」的意思，而 stick 則是指棒狀物。其他類似也是棒狀的東西有口紅膠、護唇膏等。前者可以稱為 glue stick，後者可稱為 chapstick。

lit·ter [ˈlɪtɚ]
名 雜物、一窩（小豬或小狗）、廢物 動 散置
同 rubbish 廢物、垃圾
▶名 Don't throw litter about. Put it in the trash can.
不要亂丟紙屑，請把它丟到垃圾桶吧。
▶動 You should not litter in the classroom.
你不應該在教室亂丟垃圾。

live·ly [ˈlaɪvlɪ]
形 有生氣的 同 bright 有生氣的
▶She is usually more lively in front of her friends.
她在朋友面前通常表現得比較活躍。

liv·er [ˈlɪvɚ]
名 肝臟
▶Staying up constantly may cause harm to the liver.
長期熬夜對肝不好。

Level 1
Level 2
Level 3
Level 4
Level 5
Level 6

駕輕就熟、更上一層樓——
累積實力3200單字

load [lod] ◀⟩ *Track 2632*
名 負載 動 裝載
- ▶名 The financial problem of her family is a heavy load for her.
  家中的財務問題對她來說是很重的負擔。
- ▶動 Let's load these goods（貨物）into the truck together.
  我們一起把這些貨物裝到卡車上吧。

lob·by [ˈlɑbɪ] ◀⟩ *Track 2633*
名 休息室、大廳 同 entrance 入口
- ▶Wait for me in the lobby at three p.m. 下午三點在大廳等我。

lob·ster [ˈlɑbstɚ] ◀⟩ *Track 2634*
名 龍蝦
- ▶Would you like to have a lobster for dinner?
  你晚餐想不想吃龍蝦？

lol·li·pop [ˈlɑlɪˌpɑp] ◀⟩ *Track 2635*
名 棒棒糖
- ▶The little boy is eating a purple lollipop.
  那個小男孩在吃一根紫色的棒棒糖。

loose [lus] ◀⟩ *Track 2636*
形 寬鬆的
- ▶The shirt is too loose for me. 這襯衫對我來說太寬鬆了。

loos·en [ˈlusn̩] ◀⟩ *Track 2637*
動 鬆開、放鬆 同 relax 放鬆
- ▶We helped the intimidated boy to loosen up and involve in social
  activities. 我們幫助害羞的小男孩放輕鬆並參與社交活動。

lord [lɔrd] ◀⟩ *Track 2638*
名 領主 同 owner 物主
- ▶He used to be a lord, but not anymore.
  他以前是個君主，但現在不是了。

loud·speak·er [ˈlaʊdˌspikɚ] ◀⟩ *Track 2639*
名 擴音器
- ▶They announced the news over the loudspeaker.
  他們透過擴音器宣布消息。

lug·gage [ˈlʌgɪdʒ] ◀⟩ *Track 2640*
名 行李 同 baggage 行李
- ▶I lost my luggage, and the airline staff helped me the retrieve
  it. 我行李弄丟了，航空公司的員工幫我找回它。

lull·a·by [ˈlʌləˌbaɪ] ◀⟩ *Track 2641*
名 搖籃曲
- ▶名 The baby fell asleep as soon as his mother began singing
  a lullaby.
  小嬰兒的媽媽一哼搖籃曲，這個小嬰兒就很快睡著了。

文法字詞解析
loose 和 lose（輸）的發音一樣，長得也很像，即使母語人士也非常容易搞錯，要注意喔！

萬用延伸句型
Can you help me...? 可以幫我……嗎？
例如：Can you help me open this bottle?
可以幫我打開這個瓶子嗎？

lung [lʌŋ]

◀️ *Track 2642*

名 肺臟

▶There is a close connection between smoking and lung cancer.
吸煙跟肺癌之間有密切的關係。

[Mm]

mag·i·cal [ˋmædʒɪkl̩]

◀️ *Track 2643*

形 魔術的、神奇的

▶The magical effect of herbal medicine amazed some foreigners.
草藥的神奇效果使一些外國人感到驚訝。

mag·net [ˋmægnɪt]

◀️ *Track 2644*

名 磁鐵

▶New York is a great magnet for many foreigners.
紐約對於外國人來說是一個具有極大吸引力的地方。

maid [med]

◀️ *Track 2645*

名 女僕、少女

▶Why don't you ask your house maid to clean your room today?
為什麼不叫你的女傭今天把你的房間打掃一下呢？

萬用延伸句型
Why don't you...? 你何不⋯⋯？

ma·jor [ˋmedʒɚ]

◀️ *Track 2646*

形 較大的、主要的 動 主修

▶形 What's the major industry of your nation?
你們國家的主要行業是什麼？

▶動 I major in English in university.
我在大學主修英語。

ma·jor·i·ty [məˋdʒɔrətɪ]

◀️ *Track 2647*

名 多數 反 minority 少數

▶The majority of students in my class have cellphones.
班上大部分學生都有手機。

mall [mɔl]

◀️ *Track 2648*

名 購物中心

▶Would you like to go to the shopping mall with me? I want to buy some clothes there.
你想不想跟我一起去購物中心呢？我想到那裡買些衣服。

man·age [ˋmænɪdʒ]

◀️ *Track 2649*

動 管理、處理

▶He who manages his time well can have an affluent life.
能將時間管理好的人能有富裕的生活。

Level 1

Level 2

Level 3

Level 4

Level 5

Level 6

駕輕就熟、更上一層樓——
累積實力3200單字

man·age·ment [ˈmænɪdʒmənt] 🔊 *Track 2650*

名 處理、管理

▶What do you think of the management of the hotel? Good or bad?
你覺得這間旅館經營得如何？是好還是壞呢？

man·age·a·ble [ˈmænɪdʒəbl̩] 🔊 *Track 2651*

形 可管理的、易處理的

▶Dividing a huge task into small and manageable would be helpful.
將大的任務分成細項、易於管理的工作，會有幫助。

man·ag·er [ˈmænɪdʒɚ] 🔊 *Track 2652*

名 經理

▶What do you think of the new manager?
你覺得新來的經理怎麼樣？

man·kind/hum·an·kind 🔊 *Track 2653*
[mænˈkaɪnd]/[ˈhjumənˌkaɪnd]

名 人類 同 humanity 人類

▶Do you think that mankind has made the world a better place?
你覺得人類有讓世界成為一個更好的地方嗎？

man·ners [ˈmænɚz] 🔊 *Track 2654*

名 禮貌、風俗 同 custom 風俗

▶Old people like to lecture kids on their manners.
老人喜歡教訓小孩要有禮貌。

mar·ble [ˈmɑrbl̩] 🔊 *Track 2655*

名 大理石

▶There is a huge marble statue at the square.
廣場上有座巨大的大理石雕塑。

march [mɑrtʃ] 🔊 *Track 2656*

動 前進、行軍 名 行軍、長途跋涉 同 hike 健行

▶動 A crowd of people marched on the street to express their proposal. 一群人上街遊行表示他們的訴求。
▶名 These shoes are good for long marches.
這雙鞋子很適合長途跋涉時穿著。

mar·vel·ous [ˈmɑrvələs] 🔊 *Track 2657*

形 令人驚訝的

▶That was a marvelous ballet performance.
那是一場精采的芭蕾表演。

math·e·mat·i·cal 🔊 *Track 2658*
[ˌmæθəˈmætɪkl̩]

形 數學的

▶The teacher showed us how to solve the mathematical problem.
老師算這道數學題給我們看。

文法字詞解析
從以上四個單字中，可以看出字尾的重要性喔！字根 manage（管理、處理）加上名詞字尾「-ment」變成了名詞形式「management」，加上意為「能夠」的形容詞字尾「-able」變成了意為「可管理的」的「manageable」，加上意為「……者」的名詞字尾「-er」變成了意為「管理者」（也就是經理）的 manager。

文法字詞解析
manners 當作「禮貌、風俗」時，那個「s」是必要的。如果是單數 manner，意思則是「方式、樣子」，例如「in a friendly manner」就是「以友善的方式……」。

文法字詞解析
「marvel」是「令……感到驚奇」的意思，加上形容詞字尾「-ous（帶有某種特質的）」就變成了「marvelous（令人驚奇的）」。

math·e·mat·ics/ math [ˌmæθəˈmætɪks]/[mæθ]
🔊 Track 2659

名 數學

▶My brother does well in mathematics at school.
哥哥在學校的數學成績很好。

ma·ture [məˈtjʊr]
🔊 Track 2660

形 成熟的 同 adult 成熟的、成年的

▶He is not mature enough to be given such an important task.
他還不夠成熟，還無法勝任如此重大的任務。

may·or [ˈmeɚ]
🔊 Track 2661

名 市長

▶The mayor called for people to minimize the waste of energy and clean water. 市長呼籲市民節約使用電和水。

mead·ow [ˈmɛdo]
🔊 Track 2662

名 草地

▶There are many herds（獸群）of cattle on the meadow.
草地上有許多牛群。

mean·ing·ful [ˈminɪŋfəl]
🔊 Track 2663

形 有意義的 同 significant 有意義的

▶The ancient words were not meaningful to us; we have to decipher them.
這個古文字對我們來說沒有意義；我們得要進行解碼。

mean·while [ˈminˌhwaɪl]
🔊 Track 2664

副 同時 名 期間 同 meantime 同時

▶副 John is washing dishes. Meanwhile, his sister is eating cake. 約翰在洗盤子。同時，他姊姊正在吃蛋糕。

▶名 We have a one-hour break between the two exams. In the meanwhile, what about getting something to eat? 在兩場考試的中間我們有一個小時可以休息。在這期間吃點東西如何？

med·al [ˈmɛdl̩]
🔊 Track 2665

名 獎章

▶It doesn't matter whether you win the gold medal or not. You are still the best in my heart.
你能不能獲得金牌都不重要，在我心中你是最棒的。

med·i·cal [ˈmɛdɪkl̩]
🔊 Track 2666

形 醫學的

▶He received the most advanced medical treatment.
他接受最進步的醫藥治療。

me·di·um/me·di·a [ˈmidɪəm]/[ˈmidɪə]
🔊 Track 2667

名 媒體

▶Don't believe everything that is reported by the media.
不要相信媒體報導的所有事情。

萬用延伸句型
It doesn't matter whether...
無論是否……都無所謂

Level 1

Level 2

Level 3
駕輕就熟、更上一層樓——
累積實力3200單字

Level 4

Level 5

Level 6

mem·ber·ship [ˈmɛmbɚˌʃɪp] 🔊 *Track 2668*
名 會員
▶You have to pay an annual fee to renew your membership.
你必須繳年費才能更新你的會員資格。

mem·o·rize [ˈmɛməˌraɪz] 🔊 *Track 2669*
動 記憶
▶It is hard for him to memorize all the words in the book.
要他記住這本書的所有單字很難。

mend [mɛnd] 🔊 *Track 2670*
動 修補、修改 同 repair 修理
▶Will you please mend the sleeves of this shirt?
請你把這件襯衫的袖子補一下好嗎？

men·tal [ˈmɛntl̩] 🔊 *Track 2671*
形 心理的、心智的
▶We should take care of not only our physical（身體的）health but also our mental health.
我們不僅要照顧身體健康，還要照顧心理健康。

men·tion [ˈmɛnʃən] 🔊 *Track 2672*
動 提起 名 提及
▶動 Do you mind if I mention this matter at the meeting?
你介意我在會議中提及這件事嗎？
▶名 He made no mention of your request.
他沒有提到你的要求。

mer·chant [ˈmɝtʃənt] 🔊 *Track 2673*
名 商人
▶The merchant cheated the consumers for his own profit.
這名商人為了自己利益而欺騙消費者。

mer·ry [ˈmɛrɪ] 🔊 *Track 2674*
形 快樂的
▶Let's eat, drink, and be merry.
我們來大吃大喝、好好享樂吧！

mess [mɛs] 🔊 *Track 2675*
名 雜亂 動 弄亂
▶名 The dog made a mess in the house.
這隻狗把房子裡弄得一團亂。
▶動 The monkey messed the yard and ran away.
這隻猴子把庭院弄亂後就逃跑了。

mi·cro·phone/ mike [ˈmaɪkrəˌfon]/[maɪk] 🔊 *Track 2676*
名 麥克風
▶Your microphone isn't working. We can't hear you.
你的麥克風壞了，我們聽不到你的聲音。

萬用延伸句型
It is hard for sb. to... 對某人來説，（做某事）很難

文法字詞解析
由於有個片語 talk about（説到關於某事），許多人也會使用「mention about」這個説法。但 mention 這個單字本身就包含了「關於」的意思，所以 about 是多餘的，mention about 的説法是不對的喔！

mi·cro·wave [ˈmaɪkrəˌwev]　　🔊 *Track 2677*

名 微波爐　動 微波

▶ 名 We used the microwave to heat the instant packaged food.
我們用微波爐來加熱包裝食物。

▶ 動 Please don't microwave the eggs. It's not safe.
不要把雞蛋放到微波爐去微波，不安全。

might [maɪt]　　🔊 *Track 2678*

名 權力、力氣　同 power 權力

▶ I pushed with all my might but still can't get the car to move.
我用全身的力氣推，但車子還是不會動。

might·y [ˈmaɪtɪ]　　🔊 *Track 2679*

形 強大的、有力的

▶ There is no doubt that this country has become a mighty nation. 毫無疑問，這個國家已經成為了一個強國。

mill [mɪl]　　🔊 *Track 2680*

名 磨坊、工廠　動 研磨

▶ 名 He worked part-time in his uncle's mill.
他在他叔叔的工廠兼差。

▶ 動 I need to mill flour today; would you like to help me?
我今天需要研磨麵粉，你願意幫我嗎？

mil·lion·aire [ˌmɪljənˈɛr]　　🔊 *Track 2681*

名 百萬富翁

▶ The millionaire lives a very quiet life.
這個百萬富翁過著非常平靜的生活。

min·er [ˈmaɪnə]　　🔊 *Track 2682*

名 礦夫

▶ Not all of us can understand how hard the coal miners' life is.
並不是所有人都能理解煤礦工人的生活有多艱辛。

mi·nor [ˈmaɪnə]　　🔊 *Track 2683*

形 較小的、次要的　名 未成年者

▶ 形 She's always making a fuss（大驚小怪）over minor things.
她總是大驚小怪的。

▶ 名 The pub doesn't allow minors inside.
這個酒吧不允許未成年人進來。

mi·nor·i·ty [maɪˈnɔrətɪ]　　🔊 *Track 2684*

名 少數　反 majority 多數

▶ The minority groups fought for their own welfare.
弱勢團體為自己爭取權益。

mir·a·cle [ˈmɪrəkḷ]　　🔊 *Track 2685*

名 奇蹟　同 marvel 令人驚奇的事物

▶ Don't you think the computer is a miracle of modern science and technology? 難道你不認為電腦是當代科學技術的奇蹟嗎？

文法字詞解析

miner 就是「礦坑」（mine）加上表示「……者」的字尾「-(e)r」。

Level 1

Level 2

Level 3
駕輕就熟、更上一層樓——累積實力3200單字

Level 4

Level 5

Level 6

mis·er·y [ˈmɪzərɪ]　◀€ Track 2686
名 悲慘　同 distress 悲痛
▶ The documentary showed the misery of the elderly loners.
這個紀錄片呈現獨居老人的悲慘生活。

mis·sile [ˈmɪsḷ]　◀€ Track 2687
名 發射物、飛彈
▶ Many countries are trying to develop all kinds of missiles.
許多國家都在研發各種導彈。

miss·ing [ˈmɪsɪŋ]　◀€ Track 2688
形 失蹤的、缺少的
▶ The missing child was finally safely home.
那個失蹤的孩子終於安全到家了。

mis·sion [ˈmɪʃən]　◀€ Track 2689
名 任務
▶ Our mission is to make sure that children in our country receive good education.
我們的任務是確認我國的孩子們得到好的教育。

文法字詞解析
大家熟知的電影《不可能的任務》即為 Mission Impossible。

mist [mɪst]　◀€ Track 2690
名 霧　動 被霧籠罩　同 fog 霧
▶ 名 The mist in the mountain disoriented the climbers.
山裡的霧讓登山者找不到方向。
▶ 動 The hills mist over in the morning.
早上小山丘籠罩在薄霧之中。

mix·ture [ˈmɪkstʃɚ]　◀€ Track 2691
名 混合物
▶ Will you tell me the constituents（成分）of the mixture?
你能告訴我這種混合物的成分是什麼嗎？

mob [mɑb]　◀€ Track 2692
名 民眾　動 群集
▶ 名 Would you tell me why this man is surrounded by the mob?
你能告訴我為什麼這個人被民眾包圍起來了嗎？
▶ 動 I don't want to be mobbed by reporters tomorrow.
我可不想明天被記者包圍。

mo·bile [ˈmobɪl]　◀€ Track 2693
形 可動的　同 movable 可動的
▶ It is so nice of you to lend me your mobile phone.
你借手機給我用，你人真好。

moist [mɔɪst]　◀€ Track 2694
形 潮濕的　同 damp 潮濕的
▶ It took her a year to get used to the moist climate here.
她花了一年的時間才適應這裡的潮濕氣候。

文法字詞解析
雖說「潮濕」聽起來似乎不是很舒服的事，但 moist 很多時候其實是個正面的字喔！像是鎖水保濕的化妝品，功能就是讓你的臉部肌膚變得 moist。

mois·ture [ˈmɔɪstʃɚ]
Track 2695

名 溼氣

▶The moisture in the air may make people feel hotter.
濕氣會使人們覺得更悶熱。

monk [mʌŋk]
Track 2696

名 僧侶、修道士

▶The monks who live in that temple are usually dressed in
grey. 那個寺廟裡的僧侶通常都穿著灰色。

mood [mud]
Track 2697

名 心情 同 feeling 感覺

▶Will you tell me why you are in no mood to study today?
你能告訴我為什麼你今天沒心情唸書嗎？

mop [mɑp]
Track 2698

名 拖把 動 擦拭 同 wipe 擦

▶名 Why don't you buy a new mop? 為什麼不去買支新拖把？
▶動 He mopped the floor quickly and then washed the dishes.
他很快地擦了地板，然後洗了盤子。

mor·al [ˈmɔrəl]
Track 2699

形 道德上的 名 寓意

▶形 Do you think euthanasia（安樂死）is moral?
你覺得安樂死符合道德標準嗎？
▶名 Each fable would include a moral of the story.
每個預言都有道德的意義在。

mo·tel [moˈtɛl]
Track 2700

名 汽車旅館

▶Will you tell me where the nearest motel is?
你能告訴我最近的汽車旅館在哪裡嗎？

mo·tor [ˈmotɚ]
Track 2701

名 馬達、發電機

▶I don't think the salesman（銷售員）knows which company
produces this kind of electric motor.
我認為那個銷售員並不知道這種電動馬達是哪家公司生產的。

mur·der [ˈmɝdɚ]
Track 2702

名 謀殺 動 謀殺、殘害 同 assassinate 暗殺

▶名 The suspect of the murder case was convicted yesterday.
謀殺案的嫌疑犯昨天被判決定罪。
▶動 The man murdered the singer and tried to escape.
那個男人謀殺了那位歌手並試圖逃跑。

mus·cle [ˈmʌsl]
Track 2703

名 肌肉

▶Exercising can not only develop your muscles but also help
you keep fit. 運動不僅能鍛練肌肉更有助於保持身體健康。

萬用延伸句型
scream bloody murder 可不是大喊「殺人
啦」的意思，而是純粹指叫得很大聲。
例如：She screamed bloody murder when
she saw a cockroach.
她看到蟑螂的時候叫得很大聲。

Level
1

Level
2

Level
3

Level
4

Level
5

Level
6

駕輕就熟、更上一層樓──
累積實力3200單字

mush·room [`mʌʃrum] 🔊 *Track 2704*

名 蘑菇 動 急速生長

▶名 The mushroom with bright color may be poisonous.
有鮮艷顏色的菇類可能有毒。

▶動 New flats and offices have mushroomed all over the city.
這座城市到處如雨後春筍般地出現了許多新公寓和辦公大樓。

mu·si·cal [`mjuzɪkl̩] 🔊 *Track 2705*

形 音樂的 名 音樂劇

▶形 Don't you know that he is from a great musical family?
難道你不知道嗎？他出身於一個偉大的音樂世家。

▶名 He hates watching musicals.
他討厭觀賞音樂劇。

mys·ter·y [`mɪstərɪ] 🔊 *Track 2706*

名 神秘

▶The origin of the Stonehenge remains mystery.
英國巨石陣的來源還是個謎。

[Nn]

nan·ny [`nænɪ] 🔊 *Track 2707*

名 奶媽

▶You should hire a nanny to look after your child.
你應該請個保姆來照顧你們的孩子。

nap [næp] 🔊 *Track 2708*

名 小睡、打盹

▶It's my habit to take a nap at noon.
我有睡午覺的習慣。

萬用延伸句型
It's sb.'s habit to... ……是某人的習慣

na·tive [`netɪv] 🔊 *Track 2709*

形 本國的、天生的

▶I wish I could go back to my native homeland.
我真希望能回到我生長的故鄉。

na·vy [`nevɪ] 🔊 *Track 2710*

名 海軍、艦隊

▶My brother is in the navy.
我弟弟是海軍。

文法字詞解析
因為海軍的制服多半都會配有類似寶藍色、深海藍的顏色，所以 navy 也可以作為顏色，用中文說就是「海軍藍」。

ne·ces·si·ty [nə`sɛsətɪ] 🔊 *Track 2711*

名 必需品

▶Mobile phones are a necessity for modern people.
手機對現代人來說是必需品。

neck·tie [ˈnɛkˌtaɪ]
🔊 Track 2712

名 領帶

▶How about buying a necktie for your boyfriend（男朋友）as his birthday（生日）gift?
幫你男朋友買條領帶當作生日禮物怎麼樣？

文法字詞解析
領帶也可以直接說 tie。而蝴蝶結形狀的那種領結，則可以稱為 bow tie。

neigh·bor·hood [ˈnebɚˌhʊd]
🔊 Track 2713

名 社區

▶Why don't you move to another neighborhood?
你何不搬到別的社區呢？

nerve [nɝv]
🔊 Track 2714

名 神經

▶The noise in the urban area really gets nerves.
城市裡的噪音讓人很緊張。

nerv·ous [ˈnɝvəs]
🔊 Track 2715

形 神經質的、膽怯的

▶The merest（微小的）little thing makes him nervous.
連微不足道的小事也會使他緊張。

net·work [ˈnɛtˌwɝk]
🔊 Track 2716

名 網路

▶There is a network of caves under the mountain.
這座山裡面有許多相通的洞穴。

nick·name [ˈnɪkˌnem]
🔊 Track 2717

名 綽號 動 取綽號

▶名 What was your nickname in high school?
你高中時的綽號是什麼？

▶動 They nicknamed the boy "shorty".
他們幫那個男孩取了「矮子」的綽號。

no·ble [ˈnobl̩]
🔊 Track 2718

形 高貴的 名 貴族

▶形 Despite his noble background, his reckless behaviors ruined his life.
儘管他出身高貴，他的無理行為還是毀了他的生活。

▶名 The nobles in the area are mostly very old now.
這一帶的貴族現在大部分都很老了。

nor·mal [ˈnɔrml̩]
🔊 Track 2719

形 標準的、正常的 同 regular 正常的、規律的

▶She doesn't like wearing normal clothes.
她不喜歡穿正常的衣服。

文法字詞解析
normal 意為「正常的」，那麼「不正常的」呢？可以在前面加上字首「ab-」，變成「abnormal」，就是不正常的意思了。

nov·el·ist [ˈnɑvl̩ɪst]
🔊 Track 2720

名 小說家

▶The novelist can produce three novels a year.
這名小說家一年可以寫出三本小說。

Level 1
Level 2
Level 3
駕輕就熟、更上一層樓——累積實力3200單字
Level 4
Level 5
Level 6

nun [nʌn]　　　　　　　　　🔊 *Track 2721*

名 修女、尼姑

▶I was so surprised at the news that she became a nun in the end. 得知她最終當了修女的消息，我感到很震驚。

[Oo]

oak [ok]　　　　　　　　　🔊 *Track 2722*

名 橡樹、橡葉

▶We often took shade by the oak tree beside our house. 我們常在我們家旁邊的橡樹下乘涼。

ob·serve [əbˋzɝv]　　　　　🔊 *Track 2723*

動 觀察、評論

▶We sit here observing the people who walk by. 我們坐在這裡觀察行人。

文法字詞解析
observe 去掉 e 加上形容詞字尾「-ant」就變成了形容詞 observant，它的意思是「富有觀察力的」。

ob·vi·ous [ˋɑbvɪəs]　　　　🔊 *Track 2724*

形 顯然的、明顯的　同 evident 明顯的

▶It's really obvious that they're twins. They look so alike! 他們很顯然是雙胞胎，長那麼像！

oc·ca·sion [əˋkeʒən]　　　　🔊 *Track 2725*

名 事件、場合 動 引起

▶名 Tomorrow is your stepfather's birthday. Why not take this occasion to thank him? 明天是你繼父的生日。何不藉此機會感謝一下你的繼父呢？

▶動 His remarks（話語）are going to occasion a quarrel（爭吵）sooner or later. 他講的話遲早有一天會引起爭吵。

odd [ɑd]　　　　　　　　　🔊 *Track 2726*

形 單數的、怪異的

▶It would be odd if you asked about her age. 你問她年紀的話，會很奇怪。

文法字詞解析
「odd number」指奇數（即 1、3、5……等不能被 2 整除的數字），那偶數呢？則叫做 even number。

on·to [ˋɑntu]　　　　　　　　🔊 *Track 2727*

介 在……之上

▶I don't think you can jump onto the bus while it's moving. 我認為你不能在公車移動的時候跳上車。

op·er·a·tor [ˋɑpəˏretə]　　　🔊 *Track 2728*

名 操作者

▶The operator of the machine was injured in the accident. 這個機器的操作者在意外中受傷了。

op·por·tu·ni·ty [ˌɑpəˈtjunətɪ] 🔊 Track 2729
名 機遇、機會
▶It's a great opportunity for us to tell him what we really think.
這是個好機會，讓我們能跟他說出我們的真正想法。

op·po·site [ˈɑpəsɪt] 🔊 Track 2730
形 相對的、對立的 同 contrary 對立的
▶He holds opposite views to mine in this matter.
他和我在這件事上，抱持相反看法。

op·ti·mis·tic [ˌɑptəˈmɪstɪk] 🔊 Track 2731
形 樂觀（主義）的 反 pessimistic 悲觀的
▶It is hard for him to keep optimistic about the whole thing.
他很難對這整件事情保持樂觀的態度。

or·i·gin [ˈɔrədʒɪn] 🔊 Track 2732
名 起源
▶Don't you think it's fun to study the origin of life?
難道你不認為研究生命的起源很有趣嗎？

o·rig·i·nal [əˈrɪdʒənl] 🔊 Track 2733
形 起初的 名 原作
▶形 It doesn't matter whether you give me the original copy or not. 你是不是給我正本都沒關係。
▶名 I don't care whether this is a duplicate（複製品）or the original. 這是複製品還是原作我都無所謂。

or·phan [ˈɔrfən] 🔊 Track 2734
名 孤兒 動 使（孩童）成為孤兒
▶名 An orphan as he is, he worked hard and finally succeeded.
雖然他是孤兒，但他努力工作而且成功了。
▶動 The orphaned child is sent to an asylum（院）.
那個成為孤兒的孩子被送到孤兒院了。

ought to [ɔt tu] 🔊 Track 2735
助 應該
▶Don't you think you ought to be more careful?
難道你不覺得你應該要更小心點嗎？

out·door [ˈaʊtˌdor] 🔊 Track 2736
形 戶外的 反 indoor 室內的
▶I think we should have more outdoor activities like this.
我覺得我們應該有更多像這樣的戶外活動。

out·doors [ˈaʊtˈdorz] 🔊 Track 2737
副 在戶外、在屋外
▶How about giving a party outdoors? 在戶外舉行一個派對如何？

out·er [ˈaʊtɚ] 🔊 Track 2738
形 外部的、外面的
▶Some tiles on the outer wall of the building fell off.
這棟大樓外牆上的一些磁磚剝落了。

文法字詞解析
此句也可以使用表達「站在對立一方」、「反對」的動詞 oppose，寫成 He always opposes her views.。

文法字詞解析
句中的 asylum 是「院」的意思，除了孤兒院以外，老人院、精神病院等等的「院」都可以用這個字。另外，孤兒院也可以稱為「orphanage」。

Level 1
Level 2
Level 3
Level 4
Level 5
Level 6

駕輕就熟、更上一層樓──
累積實力3200單字

out·line [ˈaʊtˌlaɪn]　　🔊 Track 2739

名 外形、輪廓　動 畫出輪廓　同 sketch 畫草圖、草擬

▶名 It is hard to see the outline of these buildings clearly（清楚地）in the heavy fog.
很難在大霧中看清楚建築物的輪廓。

▶動 He outlined the plan for her quickly.
他很快地為她大概草擬出計畫的內容。

o·ver·coat [ˈovɚˌkot]　　🔊 Track 2740

名 大衣、外套

▶You had better put on an overcoat for it is freezing outside.
你最好穿上大衣，因為外面非常冷。

owe [o]　　🔊 Track 2741

動 虧欠、欠債

▶The bank asked him to pay back what he owed as soon as possible.
銀行要求他盡快償還所欠的款項。

own·er·ship [ˈonɚˌʃɪp]　　🔊 Track 2742

名 主權、所有權　同 possession 所有物

▶The coffee shop is under new ownership.
這間咖啡店已經換新主人了。

文法字詞解析
其實從單字中的「over-」就可以知道，overcoat 指的是將所有衣服包住、穿在最外層的大衣，通常會是長度及膝、嚴冬才會穿的厚重大衣；如果只是要說一般的大衣，就可以說「topcoat」。

[Pp]

pad [pæd]　　🔊 Track 2743

名 墊子、印臺　動 填塞　同 cushion 墊子

▶名 The mouse pad is designed very nicely.
這個滑鼠墊設計得很好。

▶動 The cat padded softly into the room.
那隻貓輕輕地走進了房間。

pail [pel]　　🔊 Track 2744

名 桶

▶We used a pail to collect the rain for flushing toilet.
我們用一個桶子收集雨水，用來沖馬桶。

pal [pæl]　　🔊 Track 2745

名 夥伴　同 companion 同伴

▶My dog is my best pal.
我的狗是我最好的朋友。

文法字詞解析
pal 的意思是很親密的朋友，例如要說自己見了一位老友就可以說「meet up with an old pal」；或是曾經風行過一段時間的交「筆友」就是「pen pal」。

pal·ace [ˈpælɪs]　　🔊 Track 2746

名 宮殿

▶Buckingham palace is a famous scenic spot.
白金漢宮是一個知名的景點。

pale [pel]
Track 2747

形 蒼白的

▶The woman looked pale when she was about the deliver her baby. 這女士臨盆之前看起來臉色慘白。

pan·cake [ˈpænˌkek]
Track 2748

名 薄煎餅

▶The pancakes made by my mother are really tasty; would you like to have a try?
我媽媽做的煎餅非常好吃,你想不想吃吃看?

pan·ic [ˈpænɪk]
Track 2749

名 驚恐 動 恐慌 同 scare 驚嚇

▶名 The fire alarm caused a panic in the building.
火災警報響起,造成大樓裡一片恐慌。

▶動 Don't panic, boys. There is no danger here.
不要慌,孩子們,這裡沒有危險。

pa·rade [pəˈred]
Track 2750

名 遊行 動 參加遊行、閱兵

▶名 The parade of mascots attracted many viewers.
吉祥物的遊行吸引許多觀眾。

▶動 The peacock (孔雀) paraded the street showing off its feathers. 那隻孔雀招搖地在街上走,炫耀牠的羽毛。

par·a·dise [ˈpærəˌdaɪs]
Track 2751

名 天堂

▶To a book lover, the library is like a paradise.
對一個愛書的人來說,圖書館就是天堂。

par·cel [ˈpɑrsl]
Track 2752

名 包裹 動 捆成

▶名 Would you please tell me what this parcel contains?
能請您告訴我這個包裹裡面有什麼嗎?

▶動 Can you parcel some food for the boys to carry to their picnic? 麻煩你包一些食品讓孩子們帶去野餐好嗎?

par·tic·i·pate [pɑrˈtɪsəˌpet]
Track 2753

動 參與

▶I don't know whether you or I should participate in the important meeting. 我不知道你還是我應該參加這次重要的會議。

pas·sage [ˈpæsɪdʒ]
Track 2754

名 通道

▶There's a secret passage in the house.
這間房子有個秘密通道。

pas·sion [ˈpæʃən]
Track 2755

名 熱情 同 emotion 情感

▶Pearl shows passion for her favorite sport—soccer.
寶兒對最喜愛的運動——足球展現出極大的熱情。

萬用延伸句型

rain on sb.'s parade 毀掉(某人)的計畫,或毀掉(某人)的興致。畢竟要是遊行的時候下雨肯定是很掃興的吧。
例如:I hate to rain on your parade, but I don't think our parents will agree to let us travel so far.
我是沒有很想掃你的興啦,但我還是覺得我們的家長肯定不會讓我們去那麼遠的地方旅行。

Level 1

Level 2

Level 3

累積實力3200單字
駕輕就熟、更上一層樓

Level 4

Level 5

Level 6

pass·port [ˈpæsˌport]
◀ Track 2756

名 護照
▶Would you please show me your passport, Miss?
小姐，請出示您的護照好嗎？

pass·word [ˈpæsˌwɜd]
◀ Track 2757

名 口令、密碼
▶A secured password should include numbers and letters.
安全的密碼應該要含有字母和數字。

pa·tience [ˈpeʃəns]
◀ Track 2758

名 耐心
▶I can tell that his patience is wearing thin.
我看得出來，他快沒耐心了。

萬用延伸句型
try sb.'s patience 造成（某人）不耐煩
例 如：Stop trying my patience. I don't have time to answer your questions.
不要一直煩我，我沒時間回答你的問題。

pause [pɔz]
◀ Track 2759

名 暫停、中止 同 cease 停止
▶There was a pause before she answered my question.
她停頓了一下才回答我的問題。

pave [pev]
◀ Track 2760

動 鋪築
▶I don't believe this treaty（條約）will pave the way for peace.
我不相信這個條約將為和平鋪路。

pave·ment [ˈpevmənt]
◀ Track 2761

名 人行道
▶Don't ride your bike onto the pavement. You might hit someone.
不要把車騎到人行道上，可能會撞到人。

paw [pɔ]
◀ Track 2762

名 腳掌 動 以掌拍擊
▶名 The puppy stepped on the broken glass and hurt its paw.
小狗採到碎玻璃，傷了他的腳掌。
▶動 He pawed at the air trying to grab at the rope.
他在空中亂抓，試著抓住繩子。

pay/sal·a·ry/wage
◀ Track 2763
[pe]/[ˈsælərɪ]/[wedʒ]

名 薪水
▶In my opinion, the pay of this company isn't that bad.
在我看來，這間公司的薪水還不錯。

pea [pi]
◀ Track 2764

名 豌豆
▶What do you want to eat, beans or peas?
你要吃哪個，蠶豆還是豌豆？

文法字詞解析
大家聽過「豌豆公主」的故事嗎？這個故事在英文中就是叫做 The Princess and the Pea。

peak [pik]
Track 2765

名 山頂 動 豎起
同 top 頂端
▶名 By the time of the end of the month, the sales will have reached a new peak.
到月底的時候，銷售額將會達到新的高峰。
▶動 The unemployment（失業）rate peaked at 7.3% last week.
上禮拜失業率已達到百分之七點三的高峰。

pearl [pɝl]
Track 2766

名 珍珠
▶Not all these necklaces（項鍊）are made of real pearls.
這些項鍊不是全部都用真正的珍珠做成的。

文法字詞解析
描述某人的牙齒有如珍珠一樣白皙好看，就可稱之為 pearly whites（加複數 s 是因為牙齒通常不會只有一顆）。

peel [pil]
Track 2767

名 果皮 動 剝皮
▶名 Edward stepped on the banana peel and slipped.
愛德華踩到香蕉皮、滑倒了。
▶動 I can't peel all these potatoes by myself.
我沒辦法一個人幫這麼多馬鈴薯削皮。

peep [pip]
Track 2768

動 窺視、偷看
▶He peeped through to keyhole into the room.
他透過鑰匙孔窺視房間。

文法字詞解析
偷窺狂有個較為口語的說法叫做「peeping Tom」。

pen·ny [ˈpɛnɪ]
Track 2769

名 便士、分
▶The refugees came to our country without a penny.
難民身無分文地來到我們國家。

per·form [pɚˈfɔrm]
Track 2770

動 執行、表演
▶The students will perform an opera next Friday. Would you like to see it?
這些學生下星期五將表演歌劇。你想不想去看？

per·form·ance [pɚˈfɔrməns]
Track 2771

名 演出
▶This musical is considered a brilliant（出色的）performance.
這齣音樂劇是公認的出色演出。

per·mis·sion [pɚˈmɪʃən]
Track 2772

名 許可
同 approval 許可
▶Without my parents' permission, I can not use their computer.
沒有我父母親的允許，我不能使用他們的電腦。

Level 1
Level 2
Level 3
Level 4
Level 5
Level 6

駕輕就熟、更上一層樓——
累積實力3200單字

per·mit [pə`mɪt]/[`pɜmɪt] 　🔊 *Track 2773*

動 容許、許可　名 批准　同 allow 允許

▶動 We won't discuss both questions unless time permits.
除非時間許可，否則我們不會兩個問題都討論。

▶名 Unless you have a work permit, you cannot work here.
除非你有許可證，否則就不能在這裡工作。

文法字詞解析
「-sion」或類似的「-tion」是將字根轉換成名詞的字尾。因此，permit 加上了字尾「-sion」，變成了 permission，也就是 permit 的名詞形式。

per·son·al·i·ty [ˌpɜsṇˈælətɪ] 　🔊 *Track 2774*

名 個性、人格

▶She has a pleasant personality, so everybody likes to get along with her.
她個性討喜，所以大家都喜歡和她相處。

per·suade [pə`swed] 　🔊 *Track 2775*

動 說服　同 convince 說服

▶Would you please persuade her out of her foolish plans?
請你勸她放棄她那些愚蠢的計畫好嗎？

pest [pɛst] 　🔊 *Track 2776*

名 害蟲、令人討厭的人

▶The grains are often attacked by pests.
這些穀物經常受到害蟲的破壞。

文法字詞解析
有個相關的實用單字 pesticide（殺蟲劑），就是用來殺害「害蟲」的。

pick·le [`pɪkḷ] 　🔊 *Track 2777*

名 醃菜　動 醃製

▶名 She was good at making jams and pickles.
她很擅長做果醬和泡菜。

▶動 By the time I came back, Grandmother had already pickled many cucumbers（小黃瓜）for us.
等到我回來的時候，奶奶已經為我們醃好許多小黃瓜了。

pill [pɪl] 　🔊 *Track 2778*

名 藥丸

▶It is not good for you to take sleeping pills every night.
每天晚上都服用安眠藥的話對你是不好的。

pi·lot [`paɪlət] 　🔊 *Track 2779*

名 飛行員、領航員

▶Not everyone can meet all the requirements（要求）of being a pilot.
不是每個人都能達到成為一名飛行員的所有要求。

pine [paɪn] 　🔊 *Track 2780*

名 松樹

▶We went into the pine forest for adventure.
我們進到松樹林裡冒險。

pint [paɪnt] 　🔊 *Track 2781*

名 品脫

▶Tim loves milk very much. No wonder he drank a pint in one go. 提姆很喜歡牛奶。難怪他一口氣喝了一品脫。

pit [pɪt] 🔊 *Track 2782*

名 坑洞 動 挖坑

▶名 Be careful, or you might fall into the pit.
小心點，不然你可能會掉到洞裡。

▶動 His face is pitted with chicken pox（水痘）.
他的臉上都是水痘疤。

pit·y [ˈpɪtɪ] 🔊 *Track 2783*

名 同情 動 憐憫 同 compassion 同情

▶名 It was a pity that you missed the stage performance.
很可惜你錯過了這場舞台表演。

▶動 I really pity her for having to live with such a crazy mother-in-law.
我真同情她，要跟一個瘋瘋癲癲的婆婆一起住。

plas·tic [ˈplæstɪk] 🔊 *Track 2784*

名 塑膠 形 塑膠的

▶名 Plastics don't rust like metal.
塑膠不像金屬一樣會生銹。

▶形 Can you leave the trash in a plastic bag?
請你把垃圾放在塑膠袋好不好？

plen·ty [ˈplɛntɪ] 🔊 *Track 2785*

名 豐富 形 充足的

▶名 There is plenty of time, so we don't have to rush.
時間還很多呢，所以我們不用急。

▶形 Cars didn't use to be so plenty in this area back then.
以前這一區沒有那麼多車子。

plug [plʌg] 🔊 *Track 2786*

名 插頭 動 接插頭

▶名 The plug of your charger is incompatible with my cell phone.
你充電器的插頭和我的手機不能互通使用。

▶動 He plugged his ears so he didn't have to hear his sister scream. 他把耳朵塞住，就不用聽他妹妹大吼大叫了。

plum [plʌm] 🔊 *Track 2787*

名 李子

▶I bought some plums to eat after dinner.
我買了一些李子晚餐後吃。

plumb·er [ˈplʌmɚ] 🔊 *Track 2788*

名 水管工

▶Let's get a plumber in to mend that burst pipe.
我們請個水管工來修理那根爆裂的管子吧。

pole [pol] 🔊 *Track 2789*

名 杆

▶He's the guy standing under the flag pole.
他就是站在旗桿下那個傢伙。

文法字詞解析
plum 在英文中也可以用來表示一種「顏色」。因此你可以說你想要一件 plum-colored dress（李子色的洋裝）。

Level 1

Level 2

Level 3

Level 4

Level 5

Level 6

駕輕就熟、更上一層樓——
累積實力3200單字

pol·i·ti·cal [pəˋlɪtɪkl̩] ◀ *Track 2790*

形 政治的
▶The political party has been established for more than three decades. 這個政黨已經成立三十年了。

文法字詞解析
political asylum = 政治庇護

pol·i·ti·cian [ˌpɑləˋtɪʃən] ◀ *Track 2791*

名 政治家
▶I can't stand politicians. Most of them are liars.
我受不了政治人物，他們幾乎都是騙子。

pol·i·tics [ˋpɑləˌtɪks] ◀ *Track 2792*

名 政治學
▶He has a serious aspiration（抱負）to a career in politics.
他有從政的雄心壯志。

poll [pol] ◀ *Track 2793*

名 投票、民調 動 得票、投票 同 vote 投票
▶名 What do you think about conducting（實施）a public opinion poll? 你覺得實施一項民意調查如何？
▶動 What do you think of polling all the members about the change in rules?
你覺得我們就規則的變化請全體成員投票怎麼樣？

pol·lute [pəˋlut] ◀ *Track 2794*

動 污染
▶The waste emitted from the factory may pollute the river.
工廠排放的廢水汙染了河流。

文法字詞解析
pollute 加上名詞字尾「-tion」則會變成 pollution，也就是「污染」的名詞說法。

po·ny [ˋponɪ] ◀ *Track 2795*

名 小馬
▶I want a pony for my birthday. 我想要一匹小馬當生日禮物。

pop/pop·u·lar [pɑp]/[ˋpɑpjələ] ◀ *Track 2796*

形 流行的 名 流行
▶形 He is very interested in popular songs and wants to become a song writer in the future.
他對流行歌曲很感興趣，將來想當個作曲家。
▶名 I love pop. It's my favorite kind of music.
我最愛流行音樂了，那是我最喜歡的一種音樂。

porce·lain/chi·na ◀ *Track 2797*

[ˋpɔrslɪn]/[ˋtʃaɪnə]

名 瓷器
▶I don't know enough about porcelain to be able to tell the value of these plates. 我不太懂瓷器，所以估不出這些盤子的價錢。

por·tion [ˋporʃən] ◀ *Track 2798*

名 部分 動 分配
▶名 The wealthy man donated a large portion of his property to the orphanage.
有錢人將他財產的一大部分捐給這間孤兒院。

▶動 She portioned out the cake so that everyone had a piece.
她把蛋糕切成很多塊，讓每人都有一份。

por·trait [ˋportret]
◀€ *Track 2799*

名 肖像
▶The portrait of her mother was her most prized possession （所有物）.
她母親的這張肖像是她最珍愛的物品。

post·age [ˋpostɪdʒ]
◀€ *Track 2800*

名 郵資
▶The postage was paid by the company.
公司會支付郵資。

post·er [ˋpostɚ]
◀€ *Track 2801*

名 海報
▶I took all the posters off the wall. 我把牆上的海報都拿下來了。

post·pone [postˋpon]
◀€ *Track 2802*

動 延緩、延遲 同 delay 延遲
▶If we postpone the release of the new product, our financial （財政的）situation will be precarious（危險的）.
如果我們延遲發佈新產品的話，我們的財務將岌岌可危。

post·pone·ment [postˋponmənt]
◀€ *Track 2803*

名 延後
▶The postponement of the meeting made several people mad.
會議延後的事情讓許多人很生氣。

pot·ter·y/ce·ram·ics
◀€ *Track 2804*

[ˋpɑtɚɪ]/[sɚˋræmɪks]

名 陶器
▶There is going to be a pottery exhibition at the art gallery（美術館）. 美術館將舉辦一次陶瓷展。

pour [por]
◀€ *Track 2805*

動 澆、倒
▶It never rains but it pours.
屋漏偏逢連夜雨。

文法字詞解析
pour out = 傾訴
pour down = (雨水) 傾瀉而下

pov·er·ty [ˋpɑvɚtɪ]
◀€ *Track 2806*

名 貧窮
▶The poor children lived their lives in poverty.
那些可憐的孩子一生過著貧窮的生活。

pow·der [ˋpaʊdɚ]
◀€ *Track 2807*

名 粉 動 灑粉
▶名 The powder can serve as detergent.
這種粉末可以當作清潔劑使用。
▶動 She spends hours powdering her face.
她花好幾個小時在臉上灑粉。

Level
1

Level
2

Level
3

Level
4

Level
5

Level
6

駕輕就熟、更上一層樓——
累積實力3200單字

prac·ti·cal [ˈpræktɪkḷ]

🔊 *Track 2808*

形 實用的 同 useful 有用的
▶The plans sounded practical.
這些計畫聽起來可行。

prayer [prɛr]

🔊 *Track 2809*

名 禱告
▶Not everyone says his or her prayers every night before going to bed. 不是每個人每晚睡覺前都會禱告。

pre·cious [ˈprɛʃəs]

🔊 *Track 2810*

形 珍貴的 同 valuable 珍貴的
▶He makes good use of every precious minute to study.
他好好利用寶貴的每一分鐘來唸書。

prep·a·ra·tion [ˌprɛpəˈreʃən]

🔊 *Track 2811*

名 準備
▶It's time to make some preparations for the dinner party.
是時候為晚宴做點準備了。

pres·sure [ˈprɛʃər]

🔊 *Track 2812*

名 壓力 動 施壓
▶名 Not everyone can work under high pressure.
不是每個人都能承受龐大的工作壓力，
▶動 He was pressured into signing the contract.
他被施壓強迫簽這個合約。

pre·tend [prɪˈtɛnd]

🔊 *Track 2813*

動 假裝
▶The thief pretended to be a normal customer in the store.
小偷假裝成店裡的顧客。

pre·vent [prɪˈvɛnt]

🔊 *Track 2814*

動 預防、阻止
▶Vitamin C is supposed to prevent colds.
維生素 C 被認為能預防感冒。

pre·vi·ous [ˈprivɪəs]

🔊 *Track 2815*

形 先前的 同 prior 先前的
▶The transfer student had some bad experience in the previous school. 轉學生在前一間學校有些不好的經驗。

priest [prist]

🔊 *Track 2816*

名 神父
▶The priest in this church is a very old man.
這座教堂的神父是個非常老的男人。

pri·mar·y [ˈpraɪˌmɛrɪ]

🔊 *Track 2817*

形 主要的
▶Tom's primary defect（缺點）is laziness.
湯姆最主要的缺點就是懶惰。

文法字詞解析
字首「pre-」有「在……之前」的意思，而字根「vent」是「來」的意思，所以 prevent 就是「在來之前預防、阻止」。如果後面再加上形容詞字尾「-ive」，就變成「預防的、防止的」。

prob·a·ble [ˈprɑbəbl̩]
◄ Track 2818

形 可能的
▶I don't think the probable outcome（結果）would be in our favor. 我認為最可能的結果大概不會對我們有利。

proc·ess [ˈprɑsɛs]
◄ Track 2819

名 過程 動 處理
▶名 A lot of goods were damaged in the shipping（運送）process.
在運送過程中，有許多貨物都損壞了。
▶動 The food is processed on the production line.
食物在這條生產線上被加工。

prod·uct [ˈprɑdəkt]
◄ Track 2820

名 產品
▶Their product has become the undisputed（無可置疑的）market leader.
他們的產品在市場上無可匹敵。

prof·it [ˈprɑfɪt]
◄ Track 2821

名 利潤 動 獲利
▶名 There is very little profit in selling newspapers at present.
現在賣報紙所能獲得的利潤很少。
▶動 A lot of people profit from the activity.
有很多人在這項活動中獲益。

pro·gram [ˈprogræm]
◄ Track 2822

名 節目
▶The TV program has a large crowd of viewers in this country.
這個電視節目在這個國家有很大一群觀眾。

pro·mote [prəˈmot]
◄ Track 2823

動 提倡
▶What do you think of the government's decision to promote public welfare（福利）？
你如何看待政府發展公共福利的決定？

proof [pruf]
◄ Track 2824

名 證據 同 evidence 證據
▶I don't think there is enough proof to support the case.
我認為還沒有足夠的證據來證明這個案件。

prop·er [ˈprɑpɚ]
◄ Track 2825

形 適當的
▶Not all the rich are able to make proper use of their money.
不是所有的有錢人都會適度地花錢。

prop·er·ty [ˈprɑpɚtɪ]
◄ Track 2826

名 財產
▶Your invention is your intellectual property.
這塊地是我的財產。

萬用延伸句型
process of elimination 刪去法
例如：I didn't know what Jenny looked like, but I still figured out which one in the picture was her by process of elimination.
我不知道珍妮長什麼樣子，但我還是透過刪去法推斷出她是照片中的哪一個人。

文法字詞解析
-proof 當作字尾時有「防……」的含意，如 waterproof（防水的）、bulletproof（防彈的）。

Level 1
Level 2
Level 3
Level 4
Level 5
Level 6

駕輕就熟、更上一層樓——
累積實力3200單字

pro·pos·al [prə`pozl]　🔊 *Track 2827*

名 提議、求婚
► His proposal to her was rejected.
　他對她求婚，卻被拒絕了。

pro·tec·tion [prə`tɛkʃən]　🔊 *Track 2828*

名 保護
► There will be a seminar（研討會）on environmental protection held in London.
　倫敦將要舉行一個關於環境保護問題的討論會。

pro·tec·tive [prə`tɛktɪv]　🔊 *Track 2829*

形 保護的
► Henry holds a protective attitude when educating his children.
　亨利對小孩採取保護型的教育方式。

pub [pʌb]　🔊 *Track 2830*

名 酒館
► How about going down to the pub and drinking some beer?
　我們去酒館喝幾杯啤酒怎麼樣？

punch [pʌntʃ]　🔊 *Track 2831*

動 以拳頭重擊 名 打、擊
► 動 I want to punch his face every time I see him.
　我每次看到他就想揍他的臉。
► 名 He landed a punch in his brother's stomach.
　他往他弟弟的肚子打了一拳。

pure [pjʊr]　🔊 *Track 2832*

形 純粹的
► The businessmen always pursue the greatest profit.
　商人總是追求最大的利益。

pur·sue [pə`su]　🔊 *Track 2833*

動 追捕、追求
► It is necessary for us to pursue success with the utmost（最大的）effort.
　我們有必要以最大的努力來追求成功。

[Qq]

quar·rel [`kwɔrəl]　🔊 *Track 2834*

名 / 動 爭吵
► 名 What's the matter with him? Did he have a quarrel with his girlfriend? 他怎麼了？他和他女朋友吵架了嗎？
► 動 What's wrong with them? Why do they quarrel with each other all the time? 他們怎麼了？為什麼老是吵架啊？

文法字詞解析
如果這位媽媽對自己的孩子不但保護，還太過保護呢？這樣的人也不是沒有，我們可以加上表示「太過、超過」的字首「over-」，描述這樣的人為「overprotective」（保護過度的、保護慾過強的）。

queer [kwɪr]

形 違背常理的、奇怪的
▶The villagers tried to avoid contacting with the queer young man. 多麼離奇的一個故事啊！我從來沒聽過像這樣的事。

quote [kwot]
Track 2836

動 引用、引證
▶What do you think of these sentences quoted from this book? 你覺得這些從這本書裡引用的句子如何？

文法字詞解析
大家寫文章時，如果要引用某人的話就會使用到「quotation mark」，也就是「引號」。

[Rr]

ra·cial [ˈreʃəl]
Track 2837

形 種族的
▶Racial prejudice（偏見）is still a problem in the world now. 現在的世界上，種族偏見還是個問題。

ra·dar [ˈredɑr]
Track 2838

名 雷達
▶I see an enemy aircraft（飛機）on the radar screen. 我在雷達螢幕上看到了敵人的飛機。

rag [ræg]
Track 2839

名 破布、碎片
▶The rags were used to mop the floor. 破布被用來擦地板。

rai·sin [ˈrezn̩]
Track 2840

名 葡萄乾
▶Would you please bring me some raisins when you return from the supermarket? 你從超級市場回來時能幫我帶一些葡萄乾嗎？

rank [ræŋk]
Track 2841

名 行列、等級、社會地位
▶His rank was third in the contest（比賽）. 他在這個比賽中得了第三名。

rate [ret]
Track 2842

名 比率 動 估價
▶名 At this rate we're going to be late. 照這個速率下去，我們要遲到了。
▶動 I rated the app five stars. 我給了這個應用程式評價五顆星。

文法字詞解析
rate 這個單字在這個重視消費者回饋的年代已經越來越常見了。例如在下載 app 的時候，就常會出現請你「rate」這個 app 之類的文字。而你想找些新的 app 來用用時，也可以參考它的「rating」（也就是 rate + 字尾 ing），即它的「評價」。

raw [rɔ]
Track 2843

形 生的、原始的
▶The rising price of the raw material may affect the market. 原物料的價格上漲會影響市場。

Level 1

Level 2

Level 3

駕輕就熟、更上一層樓——累積實力3200單字

Level 4

Level 5

Level 6

ray [re]   🔊 *Track 2844*
名 光線
▶It's very hard for me to see clearly under direct rays of light.
在光線的直射下，我很難看清楚東西。

ra·zor [ˋrezɚ]   🔊 *Track 2845*
名 剃刀、刮鬍刀
▶Sarcasm is like a razor. It hurt people's feelings.
諷刺言語就像刀。它會傷害人的感受。

re·act [rɪˋækt]   🔊 *Track 2846*
動 反應、反抗 同 respond 回應
▶I didn't expect him to react so violently.
我沒想到他會有這麼激烈的反應。

萬用延伸句型
I didn't expect sb. to... 我沒預期到（某人）會……

re·ac·tion [rɪˋækʃən]   🔊 *Track 2847*
名 反應
▶His reaction to the surprise was really funny to watch.
對於這次驚喜，他的反應超好笑。

rea·son·a·ble [ˋriznəbl]   🔊 *Track 2848*
形 合理的
▶I don't think it's a reasonable thing to do.
我不覺得這是合理的事情。

re·ceipt [rɪˋsit]   🔊 *Track 2849*
名 收據
▶Would you please give me a receipt for this dress?
請您幫我為這件洋裝開張收據好嗎？

re·ceiv·er [rɪˋsivɚ]   🔊 *Track 2850*
名 收受者
▶You have to put the receiver back after using the phone.
你打完電話後應該要把話筒放回原位啊。

文法字詞解析
receiver 是「接受者」的意思，那麼為什麼在例句中也可以延伸當作「電話的話筒」的意思呢？因為電話的話筒，本來就是用來接收其他人說的話的「接受者」嘛！

rec·og·nize [ˋrɛkəgˏnaɪz]   🔊 *Track 2851*
動 認知 同 know 知道
▶Do you recognize the man standing there?
你認得那個站在那裡的男人嗎？

re·cord·er [rɪˋkɔrdɚ]   🔊 *Track 2852*
名 紀錄員
▶Where did you get the recorder?
你這台錄音機是從哪裡買來的？

re·cov·er [rɪˋkʌvɚ]   🔊 *Track 2853*
動 恢復、重新獲得
▶It took him three months to recover from the illness.
他花了三個月才從疾病中康復。

re·duce [rɪˋdjus]　🔊 *Track 2854*
動 減輕
▶The cancer patient was reduced to skin and bones.
那個癌症患者瘦得皮包骨。

萬用延伸句型
reduce sb. to tears 讓（某人）落淚
例如：Watching videos of dogs being adopted always reduces me to tears.
每次看狗被領養的影片，我就哭到不行。

re·gion·al [ˋridʒənl̩]　🔊 *Track 2855*
形 區域性的
▶The regional singing contest will be held at the school auditorium.
這個地區歌唱大賽會在學校的禮堂舉行。

re·gret [rɪˋgrɛt]　🔊 *Track 2856*
動 後悔、遺憾 名 悔意
▶動 I don't believe that I will regret leaving him.
我相信我不會因為離開他而後悔。
▶名 There's a lot of regret in his voice.
他的聲音充滿了悔意。

re·late [rɪˋlet]　🔊 *Track 2857*
動 敘述、有關係
▶It's easy for me to relate to the characters in the story.
我很容易可以體會這個故事中的角色。

re·lax [rɪˋlæks]　🔊 *Track 2858*
動 放鬆
▶I usually relax myself by listening to classical music.
我常聽古典音樂來放鬆。

re·lease [rɪˋlis]　🔊 *Track 2859*
動 解放 名 釋放
▶動 Unless he releases the hostage first, we can't shoot him.
除非他先釋放人質，否則我們是不能向他開槍的。
▶名 The release of the prisoners is impossible until the war comes to an end.
除非戰爭結束，否則戰俘是不可能得到釋放的。

文法字詞解析
歌手出專輯時，他們的新專輯就叫做 new release，因為專輯也是從原先保密的狀態下「釋放」出來，不是嗎？

re·li·a·ble [rɪˋlaɪəbl̩]　🔊 *Track 2860*
形 可靠的 同 dependable 可靠的
▶I don't think it's a reliable brand of washing machine.
我覺得這不是一個可靠的洗衣機品牌。

re·lief [rɪˋlif]　🔊 *Track 2861*
名 解除、減輕
▶He breathed a sigh of relief on hearing that she was back.
他一聽到她回來的消息，就如釋重負地鬆了口氣。

re·li·gion [rɪˋlɪdʒən]　🔊 *Track 2862*
名 宗教
▶Buddhism is an important religion in Asia.
佛教是在亞洲很重要的宗教。

Level
1

Level
2

Level
3
駕輕就熟、更上一層樓──
累積實力3200單字

Level
4

Level
5

Level
6

343

re·li·gious [rɪˋlɪdʒəs] 🔊 *Track 2863*
形 宗教的
▶Many religious believers（信教者）go to Mecca（麥加）.
許多虔誠的教徒都會去麥加。

re·ly [rɪˋlaɪ] 🔊 *Track 2864*
動 依賴
▶Now that you are a grown-up, you should not rely on your parents. 既然你長大了，就不應該依靠你的父母。

re·main [rɪˋmen] 🔊 *Track 2865*
動 殘留、仍然、繼續
▶The writer remained poor all his life.
那個作家終生貧窮。

re·mind [rɪˋmaɪnd] 🔊 *Track 2866*
動 提醒
▶This song reminds me of the good old days.
這首歌使我想起以前美好的時光。

re·mote [rɪˋmot] 🔊 *Track 2867*
形 遙遠的
▶I haven't the remotest idea what she meant.
我一點都不明白她是什麼意思。

re·move [rɪˋmuv] 🔊 *Track 2868*
動 移動
▶We removed the boxes from the room.
我們把箱子從房間裡移出去。

re·new [rɪˋnju] 🔊 *Track 2869*
動 更新、恢復、補充
▶I have to renew the computer system constantly.
我必須持續更新電腦系統。

rent [rɛnt] 🔊 *Track 2870*
名 租金 動 租借
▶名 The rent of the house is too expensive for me to afford. 這個房子的租金太貴了，我負擔不起。
▶動 I rent an apartment downtown. 我在市區租一間公寓。

re·pair [rɪˋpɛr] 🔊 *Track 2871*
動 修理 名 修理
▶動 My dad is trying to repair the car. 我爸正在試著修車。
▶名 The toilet is out of repair. 這馬桶需要修理了。

re·place [rɪˋples] 🔊 *Track 2872*
動 代替
▶I replaced the broken bulb with a new one.
我把壞掉的燈泡換成新的。

文法字詞解析
描述某人總是固定進行某事，即使和宗教無關，也可以用 religious 的副詞 religiously 來表示。
例 如：She goes to the park every day at 7 o'clock religiously.
她每天七點都準時前往公園。

萬用延伸句型
beyond repair 修不了了，沒救了
例 如：The car is beyond repair. We have to get a new one.
這車已經沒辦法修了。我們得買一台新的。

re·place·ment [rɪˋplesmənt]　🔊 *Track 2873*

名 取代

▶We need a replacement for the secretary who left.
我們需要一個人代替已離職的秘書。

rep·re·sent [ˌrɛprɪˋzɛnt]　🔊 *Track 2874*

動 代表、象徵

▶David represented our department to make a presentation.
大衛代表我們的部門做報告。

rep·re·sent·a·tive [rɛprɪˋzɛntətɪv]　🔊 *Track 2875*

形 典型的、代表的 名 典型、代表人員

▶形 The symbol（符號）is representative of peace.
這個符號代表了和平。

▶名 They sent a representative to take part in the meeting.
他們派了個代表參加會議。

re·pub·lic [rɪˋpʌblɪk]　🔊 *Track 2876*

名 共和國

▶I come from the Republic of China. What about you?
我來自中華民國，你呢？

re·quest [rɪˋkwɛst]　🔊 *Track 2877*

名 要求 動 請求 同 beg 乞求

▶名 Would you please allow me to make a small request?
請您允許我提出一個小小的要求好嗎？

▶動 Can you request him to come before ten a.m. tomorrow?
請你告訴他在明天上午十點以前來好嗎？

re·serve [rɪˋzɝv]　🔊 *Track 2878*

動 保留 名 貯藏、保留

▶動 He reserved a table at the restaurant.
他在那家餐廳預訂了一個位子。

▶名 They keep a large reserve of firewood（木柴）for cold weather. 他們貯存大量的木柴，以備天冷時使用。

re·sist [rɪˋzɪst]　🔊 *Track 2879*

動 抵抗

▶Once you see her beauty, you will know that no man could resist her charm. 一旦你看到她的美貌，你就會知道沒有男人能夠抵擋住她的魅力。

re·source [rɪˋsors]　🔊 *Track 2880*

名 資源

▶Resources management is an important business skill.
資源管理是一項重要的經營技能。

re·spond [rɪˋspɑnd]　🔊 *Track 2881*

動 回答

▶The boy remained silent and would not respond to my question.
這個男孩保持沉默、不回答我的問題。

文法字詞解析

要描述一個人講話「語帶保留」、或個性上比較不喜歡把很多事說出來，則可以用與 reserve 長得很像的形容詞 reserved 來表示。

Level 1

Level 2

Level 3

駕輕就熟、更上一層樓——累積實力3200單字

Level 4

Level 5

Level 6

re·sponse [rɪ'spɑns]
◀€ *Track 2882*

名 回應、答覆
▶I'm still waiting for her response. 我還在等待她的答覆。

re·spon·si·bil·i·ty
◀€ *Track 2883*

[rɪˌspɑnsə'bɪlətɪ]

名 責任
▶Who should take responsibility to this mistake?
誰應該為這個錯誤負責？

re·strict [rɪ'strɪkt]
◀€ *Track 2884*

動 限制
▶Would you like to tell me why the membership of the club is
restricted to men only?
你能不能告訴我為什麼這個俱樂部的成員僅限於男士？

re·veal [rɪ'vil]
◀€ *Track 2885*

動 顯示
▶These plans reveal a complete failure of imagination.
這些計畫顯得毫無想像力。

rib·bon [ˈrɪbən]
◀€ *Track 2886*

名 絲帶、破碎條狀物
▶There was a white ribbon in her black hair.
她的黑髮中繫了一條白色的緞帶。

文法字詞解析
因為緞帶經常被綁成蝴蝶結的形狀，因此 ribbon 這個字也可以引申用來表示「蝴蝶結」的意思。

rid [rɪd]
◀€ *Track 2887*

動 使擺脫、除去
▶Let's get rid of the bad habits!
我們擺脫這個壞習慣吧！

rid·dle [ˈrɪdl̩]
◀€ *Track 2888*

名 謎語
▶The children love solving riddles. 這些孩子們很愛解謎語。

ripe [raɪp]
◀€ *Track 2889*

形 成熟的
▶Are the bananas ripe yet? 香蕉成熟了嗎？

risk [rɪsk]
◀€ *Track 2890*

名 危險 動 冒險
▶名 There's a huge risk, but it's worth it. 風險很大，但很值得。
▶動 I don't think I want to risk losing my job over this.
我不覺得我想冒著失去工作的風險做這件事。

roar [ror]
◀€ *Track 2891*

名 吼叫 動 怒吼
▶名 The little girl was frightened by the lion's roars.
小女孩被這獅子的吼叫聲嚇壞了。
▶動 The lion roared for it was scared by the visitor.
獅子被遊客嚇到，吼了一聲。

roast [rost]
🔊 *Track 2892*

動 烘烤 形 烘烤的 名 烘烤的肉

▶動 The beef is roasting in the oven.
烤箱裡正烤著牛肉呢。

▶形 The roast lamb is only served in high-class restaurants.
烤羊肉只有在高級餐廳才有賣。

▶名 How about having a hot dog roast next Sunday?
我們下個星期天來烤熱狗怎麼樣？

rob [rɑb]
🔊 *Track 2893*

動 搶劫

▶He robbed a bank back when he was young.
他以前年輕的時候搶過銀行。

rob·ber ['rɑbə]
🔊 *Track 2894*

名 強盜

▶The robber grabbed the purse and ran.
那名強盜抓了皮包就跑。

rob·ber·y ['rɑbərɪ]
🔊 *Track 2895*

名 搶案

▶The robbery which happened last week was committed by a retired banker. 上週發生的搶案是一名退休銀行員犯下的。

robe [rob]
🔊 *Track 2896*

名 長袍 動 穿長袍

▶名 The wise old wizard（巫師）wears a robe.
那個有智慧的老巫師披著長袍。

▶動 The serious old lady is robed in black.
那個正經的老太太穿著黑色的袍子。

rock·et ['rɑkɪt]
🔊 *Track 2897*

名 火箭 動 發射火箭

▶名 We sent an unmanned（無人操縱的）rocket into earth orbit（軌道）. 我們把一個無人駕駛的火箭送入了地球軌道。

▶動 Our profits rocketed recently. 我們最近的利潤劇增。

ro·man·tic [ro`mæntɪk]
🔊 *Track 2898*

形 浪漫的 名 浪漫主義者

▶形 It is said that Frenchmen are among the most romantic people in the world.
據說法國人是世界上最浪漫的民族之一。

▶名 I heard that he was a romantic. Do you think so?
我聽說他是個浪漫主義者，你覺得他是嗎？

rot [rɑt]
🔊 *Track 2899*

動 腐敗 名 腐壞

▶動 Some people think that too much television rots your brain.
有些人認為看太多電視會使你的頭腦退化。

▶名 He's always talking rot. I wish he would shut up.
他老是在講一些廢話，真希望他閉嘴。

文法字詞解析

這個字當動詞時，也可用來表示「將某人嘲弄、批評得體無完膚」的意思。例如若 Peter 說 John 衣服難看、鞋子醜、沒品味，就可以說 Peter roasted John。

萬用延伸句型

hopeless romantic 無可救藥的浪漫主義者
例如：Jamie cries tears of joy when he sees old couples holding hands. He's a hopeless romantic.
傑米只要看到年邁的愛侶牽手就會立刻流下喜悅的淚水。他就是這樣一個無可救藥的浪漫主義者。

Level 1
Level 2
Level 3
駕輕就熟、更上一層樓──累積實力3200單字
Level 4
Level 5
Level 6

rot·ten [ˈrɑtn̩] 🔊 Track 2900

形 腐化的

▶The rotten meat gives out bad smell.
腐敗的肉發出惡臭。

rough [rʌf] 🔊 Track 2901

形 粗糙的 名 粗暴的人、草圖

▶形 I only have a rough idea what the movie is about.
我對這部電影的內容只有大約的概念。

▶名 Would you please pass me the pencil near the pile of roughs?
請你把那疊草圖旁的那支鉛筆遞給我好嗎？

文法字詞解析
a rough ride = 崎嶇艱難的路途

rou·tine [ruˈtin] 🔊 Track 2902

名 慣例 形 例行的

▶名 As soon as she learns the office routine, she will be an excellent assistant.
她一旦熟悉了辦公室的日常事務，就會成為一名優秀的助手。

▶形 I'm having a routine medical（醫學的）examination next week.
我下禮拜要做例行的健康檢查。

rug [rʌg] 🔊 Track 2903

名 地毯

同 carpet 地毯

▶There is a big hole in the rug.
這塊地毯上有一個大洞。

ru·mor [ˈrumɚ] 🔊 Track 2904

名 謠言 動 謠傳

▶名 Nobody with common sense（見識）will believe such a rumor.
沒有哪個有常識的人會相信這樣的謠言。

▶動 Rumor has it that a professional killer was hired to assassinate the former president.
有謠傳說有位職業殺手受雇要刺殺前總統。

萬用延伸句型
It is rumored that... 傳聞説……

rust [rʌst] 🔊 Track 2905

名 鐵銹 動 生鏽

▶名 She reads extensively（廣泛地）so that she can keep her mind from rust.
她廣泛閱讀以防止腦筋遲鈍。

▶動 You must practice more so that your skills will not rust.
你必須多多練習以防止技術荒廢。

rust·y [ˈrʌstɪ] 🔊 Track 2906

形 生鏽的、生疏的

▶The medal stairs were rusty, so they were torn down.
金屬樓梯聲生鏽了，即將被拆除。

[Ss]

sack [sæk] ◀≋ *Track 2907*
名 大包、袋子
▶We put all the clothes in a sack when we moved to the new apartment. 我們搬家到新公寓時,把衣服都裝在布袋裡。

sake [sek] ◀≋ *Track 2908*
名 緣故、理由
▶It doesn't matter whether you do this for your own sake or not. 你做這件事是不是為了自身利益都無關緊要。

sat·is·fac·to·ry [ˌsætɪsˈfæktərɪ] ◀≋ *Track 2909*
形 令人滿意的
▶I don't think his performance is satisfactory. 我不覺得他的表現令人滿意。

sau·cer [ˈsɔsɚ] ◀≋ *Track 2910*
名 托盤、茶碟
▶I can't find cups and saucers that match. 我找不到相配的茶杯和茶托。

sau·sage [ˈsɔsɪdʒ] ◀≋ *Track 2911*
名 臘腸、香腸
▶Help yourself to the roasted pork sausage. 請自己取用烤豬肉香腸。

sav·ing(s) [ˈsevɪŋ(z)] ◀≋ *Track 2912*
名 拯救、救助、存款
▶Don't put all your savings into a deposit account. 別把你所有的積蓄都存入帳戶。

scale(s) [skel(z)] ◀≋ *Track 2913*
名 刻度、尺度、天秤
▶Lots of lands have become deserts on a large scale. 許多田地大面積地變成了沙漠。

scarce [skɛrs] ◀≋ *Track 2914*
形 稀少的 同 rare 稀有的
▶Medicine was scarce in this remote area. 藥物在這偏遠地區非常短缺。

scare·crow [ˈskɛrˌkro] ◀≋ *Track 2915*
名 稻草人
▶Scarecrows are supposed to scare away birds. 稻草人的功能應該是幫忙嚇走小鳥。

scarf [skɑrf] ◀≋ *Track 2916*
名 圍巾、頸巾
▶Would you like this blue scarf? 你想要這條藍色的圍巾嗎?

文法字詞解析
描述某人的眼睛張得無比地大時,可以說 sb.'s eyes are as big as saucers。不過 saucer 在盤子界還算是長得比較小的,因此這個誇飾法勉強可以接受,要是說 sb.'s eyes are as big as plates,那就有點太大了。

文法字詞解析
scarf 的複數形式可以說成 scarves 或 scarfs。

Level 1

Level 2

Level 3

駕輕就熟、更上一層樓——累積實力3200單字

Level 4

Level 5

Level 6

scar·y [ˈskɛrɪ]
Track 2917

形 駭人的

▶Let's tell scary stories at night. 我們晚上來講可怕的故事吧。

scat·ter [ˈskætɚ]
Track 2918

動 散佈

▶It's time for the farmers to scatter the seeds in the fields.
到了農民播種的時節了。

sched·ule [ˈskɛdʒʊl]
Track 2919

名 時刻表 動 將……列表 同 list 列表

▶名 We worked hard in order not to fall behind the schedule.
我們努力工作，為了不要使進度落後。

▶動 My boss told me to schedule a meeting for her.
我老闆要我幫她訂好會議時程。

schol·ar [ˈskɑlɚ]
Track 2920

名 有學問的人、學者

▶The scholar is always burying himself in books.
這名學者總是埋首於書堆中。

schol·ar·ship [ˈskɑlɚʃɪp]
Track 2921

名 獎學金

▶It is difficult for a student to win the scholarship in this
university（大學）. 學生要在這所大學裡獲得獎學金很難。

sci·en·tif·ic [ˌsaɪənˈtɪfɪk]
Track 2922

形 科學的、有關科學的

▶The scientific advancement has brought convenience to out
life. 科學進步為生活帶來便利。

scoop [skup]
Track 2923

名 舀取的器具 動 挖、掘、舀取

▶名 Do you want another scoop of ice cream?
你要再一球冰淇淋嗎？

▶動 I scooped out a handful of peanuts to eat.
我挖了一把花生出來吃。

文法字詞解析
由於小道消息、獨家新聞都是需要去「挖掘」的，就樣挖冰淇淋一樣要挖得很深才挖得到，因此小道消息、獨家新聞也可以稱為「scoop」（名詞）。

scout [skaʊt]
Track 2924

名 斥候、偵查 動 斥候、偵查

▶名 It took him several hours to have a scout around to see
what he could find.
他花了好幾個小時四處搜尋，看看能找到些什麼。

▶動 I volunteer to go over and scout the enemy grounds.
我自願過去偵察敵營。

scream [skrim]
Track 2925

動 大聲尖叫、作出尖叫聲 名 大聲尖叫

▶動 The little girl screamed at the sight of a cockroach.
小女孩一看到蟑螂就尖叫。

▶名 I heard a terrible scream from the next room.
我聽到隔壁房間傳來可怕的尖叫聲。

screw [skru] ◀≀ *Track 2926*

名 螺絲 動 旋緊、轉動

▶名 Where did the screw go? Did it roll under the sofa?
那個螺絲去哪了？是滾到沙發下面了嗎？

▶動 Let's screw the two pipes together so that the water won't leak out.
我們把這兩根管子接起來旋緊，這樣水就不會漏出來了。

scrub [skrʌb] ◀≀ *Track 2927*

動 擦拭、擦洗 名 刷子

▶動 I scrubbed the pot to remove the stain from it.
我刷鍋子，想把上面的髒污清掉。

▶名 We should really give the floor a good scrub.
我們真的應該好好擦洗一下地板了。

seal [sil] ◀≀ *Track 2928*

名 海豹、印章 動 獵海豹、蓋章、密封

▶名 The cute seal is good at performing tricks.
這隻可愛的海豹很擅長表演。

▶動 He forgot to seal his letter.
他忘了把信封起來。

sec·ond·a·r·y [ˈsɛkənˌdɛrɪ] ◀≀ *Track 2929*

形 第二的

▶Women's careers shouldn't be secondary to men's.
婦女的職業生涯不該次於男人們的職業生涯。

se·cu·ri·ty [sɪˈkjʊrətɪ] ◀≀ *Track 2930*

名 安全 同 safety 安全

▶The manager put emphasis on the digital security.
經理很重視數位安全。

seek [sik] ◀≀ *Track 2931*

動 尋找

▶Money does not always bring you the happiness you seek.
金錢不見得能帶給你你在找尋的幸福。

seize [siz] ◀≀ *Track 2932*

動 抓、抓住

▶Why don't you seize this rare opportunity? It's now or never.
為什麼不抓住這個難得的機會呢？機不可失啊。

sel·dom [ˈsɛldəm] ◀≀ *Track 2933*

副 不常地、難得地

▶He seldom mentions his family. 他很少提及他的家庭背景。

sen·si·ble [ˈsɛnsəbl] ◀≀ *Track 2934*

形 可感覺的、理性的

▶The quake of the earth was not sensible to the residents in the city. 這次地震對居民是無感的。

萬用延伸句型

sb.'s lips are sealed 直譯為「某人的嘴唇密封起來了」，也就是「絕對不會說出去」、「會保守祕密」的意思。

例如：I promise not to tell your parents! My lips are sealed! But can I tell your brother?

我保證不會跟你父母說，我口風很緊的。不過我可不可以告訴你哥啊？

文法字詞解析

seek 的動詞變化：seek, sought, sought

Level 1
Level 2
Level 3
Level 4
Level 5
Level 6

駕輕就熟、更上一層樓──累積實力3200單字

sen·si·tive [ˈsɛnsətɪv]

🔊 *Track 2935*

形 敏感的

▶ Women are sensitive to many things.
女人們對很多事都很敏感。

sep·a·ra·tion [ˌsɛpəˈreʃən]

🔊 *Track 2936*

名 分離、隔離

▶ The dog infected with rabies was kept in separation.
這隻感染狂犬病的狗被隔離。

sew [so]

🔊 *Track 2937*

動 縫、縫上

▶ Would you sew the button on for me?
你能幫我把扣子縫上嗎？

sex [sɛks]

🔊 *Track 2938*

名 性、性別

▶ Can you tell me what sex your cat is? I can't tell.
你能告訴我你的貓的性別嗎？我分不出來。

sex·u·al [ˈsɛkʃʊəl]

🔊 *Track 2939*

形 性的

▶ Not all the people know that the disease is passed on by sexual contact.
不是所有人都知道這種病會透過性接觸而傳染。

sex·y [ˈsɛksɪ]

🔊 *Track 2940*

形 性感的

▶ What do you think of the heroine（女主角）in this film? Don't you think she is sexy?
你覺得這部影片裡的女主角如何？你不覺得她很性感嗎？

shade [ʃed]

🔊 *Track 2941*

名 陰涼處、樹蔭 動 遮住、使陰暗

▶ 名 We rested in the shade of the tree halfway through the marathon.
馬拉松跑到一半，我們就在樹蔭下休息。

▶ 動 I shaded my eyes from the sun.
我遮著眼睛擋住陽光。

shad·ow [ˈʃædo]

🔊 *Track 2942*

名 陰暗之處、影子 動 使有陰影

▶ 名 Our shadows follow us everywhere.
我們的影子到哪裡都跟著我們。

▶ 動 The mountain is shadowed by clouds.
那座山被雲遮住了。

shad·y [ˈʃedɪ]

🔊 *Track 2943*

形 多蔭的、成蔭的

▶ Let's take a walk on the shady avenue.
到林蔭大道上去散散步吧。

文法字詞解析

相反地，「不敏感的」可説 insensitive。通常這是個負面用語，用來形容某人很不會看人臉色，説出冒犯的話、不體貼。

萬用延伸句型

be afraid of sb.'s own shadow 連自己的影子都怕，即非常容易受驚的意思。
例如：Harry is afraid of his own shadow, so I don't think you should show him the snake. He might have a heart attack.
哈利連自己的影子都怕，所以我覺得你還是不要拿蛇給他看吧。他可能會心臟病發。

shal·low [ˈʃælo]
Track 2944

形 淺的、膚淺的
▶The tray is very shallow.
這個托盤很淺。

shame [ʃem]
Track 2945

名 羞恥、羞愧 動 使羞愧
▶名 Don't you feel any shame after making her cry?
把她弄哭，你一點都不羞愧嗎？
▶動 Their team shamed ours by winning by thirty points.
他們隊大贏我們隊三十分，讓我們羞愧極了。

It's a shame that... 真可惜……
例如：It's a shame that we lost the game because of the absence of the team leader.
真可惜，我們因為隊長的缺席而輸了這場比賽。

sham·poo [ʃæmˈpu]
Track 2946

名 洗髮精 動 清洗
▶名 What brand of shampoo do you like best?
你最喜歡哪種牌子的洗髮精？
▶動 He shampooed his dog every week.
他每個禮拜都會洗他的狗。

shave [ʃev]
Track 2947

動 刮鬍子、剃
▶It will be a long time before he shaves off his beard.
他要過很久才會去刮鬍子。

shep·herd [ˈʃɛpəd]
Track 2948

名 牧羊人、牧師
▶The shepherd can count his sheep within seconds.
牧羊人能在幾秒內數出他的羊群數量。

shin·y [ˈʃaɪnɪ]
Track 2949

形 發光的、晴朗的
▶Why is this coin shinier than the others?
為什麼這個錢幣比其他的更亮？

文法字詞解析

shiny 和另一個長得很像的形容詞 shining 都有「發光」的意思，那麼它們之間有什麼差別呢？原來，shining 用來描述「自己本身就會發光」的東西，例如太陽（the sun is shining）；而 shiny 則是用來描述「反射光線、自己本身不會發光」的東西，例如錢幣、擦得很亮的皮鞋等等。

short·en [ˈʃɔrtn̩]
Track 2950

動 縮短、使變短
▶Daytime shortens in the winter.
冬天時白天會變短。

short·ly [ˈʃɔrtlɪ]
Track 2951

副 不久、馬上 同 soon 不久
▶I'll be with you shortly.
我馬上就過來你這裡。

shov·el [ˈʃʌvl̩]
Track 2952

名 鏟子 動 剷除
▶名 The kid has a toy shovel when he plays with the sand.
小孩用玩具鏟子玩沙。
▶動 It is not easy for him to shovel all the coal into the truck.
把所有的煤都鏟入卡車對他來說並不容易。

Level 1

Level 2

Level 3

累積實力3200單字 駕輕就熟、更上一層樓

Level 4

Level 5

Level 6

shrink [ʃrɪŋk]

🔊 *Track 2953*

動 收縮、退縮
▶ My dress shrunk after I washed it.
我的洋裝洗過後就縮水了。

sigh [saɪ]

🔊 *Track 2954*

動 / 名 嘆息
▶ 動 The old lady sighed when she realized that the charity campaign was a sham.
老太太知道這個慈善活動只是詐騙時，嘆了一口氣。
▶ 名 He heaved a sigh and put down the newspaper.
他嘆了口氣，放下報紙。

sig·nal [ˈsɪgnl]

🔊 *Track 2955*

名 信號、號誌 動 打信號
▶ 名 Can you get a signal on your phone?
你的手機收得到訊嗎？
▶ 動 He signaled the message with little flags.
他用幾支小旗子打了信號。

sig·nif·i·cant [sɪgˈnɪfəkənt]

🔊 *Track 2956*

形 有意義的
▶ I don't think this proposal they put forward is significant.
我認為他們提出的這個提議沒有什麼意義。

sim·i·lar·i·ty [ˌsɪməˈlærətɪ]

🔊 *Track 2957*

名 類似、相似 同 resemblance 相似
▶ I listed the similarity and difference between the two products.
我列出了這兩項產品的相似處與相異處。

sin [sɪn]

🔊 *Track 2958*

名 罪、罪惡 動 犯罪
▶ 名 Lying is not always a sin.
說謊不見得一定是種罪。
▶ 動 I believe that it's human to sin.
我覺得犯錯是人之常情。

sin·cere [sɪnˈsɪr]

🔊 *Track 2959*

形 真實的、誠摯的 同 genuine 真誠的
▶ He sounds sincere, but I'm still not sure if I should believe him.
他聽起來很真誠，但我還是不知道是否要相信他。

sip [sɪp]

🔊 *Track 2960*

動 啜飲、小口地喝 同 drink 喝
▶ He sipped the wine slowly.
他慢慢地喝這個葡萄酒。

sit·u·a·tion [ˌsɪtʃʊˈeʃən]

🔊 *Track 2961*

名 情勢 同 condition 情況
▶ The economic situation of the country is deteriorating.
這個國家的經濟狀況正在惡化。

skate [sket]
Track 2962

動 溜冰、滑冰

▶A large number of people like to skate here.
很多人都喜歡來這個地方溜冰。

ski [ski]
Track 2963

名 滑雪板 動 滑雪

▶名 Can you rent skis for us?
可不可以幫我們租滑雪板？

▶動 We went skiing in the mountain.
我們到山裡去滑雪。

skip [skɪp]
Track 2964

動 略過、跳過 名 略過、跳過 同 omit 省略

▶動 It doesn't matter if you skip some descriptions in the novel.
你跳過小說裡的幾個描述不看也沒有關係。

▶名 The cute little girl walked with a skip.
那個小女孩邊走邊跳。

文法字詞解析
跳繩可稱為 skip rope 或 jump rope。

sky·scrap·er [ˈskaɪˌskrepɚ]
Track 2965

名 摩天大樓

▶There are lots of skyscrapers in New York.
紐約有許多摩天大樓。

slave [slev]
Track 2966

名 奴隸 動 做苦工

▶名 The government treated the slaves badly.
政府對奴隸們很不好。

▶動 People have to slave away to get their own houses.
人們為了能買到屬於自己的房子而得拚死拚活地工作。

sleeve [sliv]
Track 2967

名 衣袖、袖子

▶Let's roll up our sleeves and get down to work now.
讓我們捲起衣袖，現在開始工作吧。

萬用延伸句型
wear sb.'s heart on sb.'s sleeve 描述（某人）總是毫不掩藏自己的情緒。
例如：You can easily tell that he's upset. He wears his heart on his sleeve.
你很容易就能看出他不開心。他從來不會掩藏自己的情緒。

slice [slaɪs]
Track 2968

名 片、薄的切片 動 切成薄片

▶名 I had a slice of pizza for lunch.
我午餐吃了一片披薩。

▶動 Can you please help me wash these potatoes and then slice them?
請你幫我先把馬鈴薯洗乾淨，然後再把它們切成薄片好嗎？

slip·per·y [ˈslɪpərɪ]
Track 2969

形 滑溜的

▶Watch your steps. The ground is slippery.
小心腳步。地面濕滑。

Level
1

Level
2

Level
3

駕輕就熟、更上一層樓──
累積實力3200單字

Level
4

Level
5

Level
6

slope [slop]
◀€ *Track 2970*

名 坡度、斜面

▶Do you know any skiing slopes with a nice view?
你知道哪裡有景色不錯的滑雪斜坡嗎？

smooth [smuð]
◀€ *Track 2971*

形 平滑的 動 使平滑、使平和

▶形 The movie star's skin is as smooth as silk.
這位電影明星的皮膚如絲綢般光滑。

▶動 I'm sure the conflicts will smooth out soon.
我相信這些衝突會很快平息下來的。

snap [snæp]
◀€ *Track 2972*

動 折斷、迅速抓住

▶The branch snapped as soon as the boy stood on it.
這個男孩一站上去，樹枝就折斷了。

sol·id [`sɑlɪd]
◀€ *Track 2973*

形 固體的

▶The solid food is difficult to swallow for the elderly people.
這個固體的食物對老年人來說很難吞嚥。

some·day [`sʌmˌde]
◀€ *Track 2974*

副 將來有一天、來日

▶I hope I can go to Mars（火星）someday.
我希望有一天能去火星。

some·how [`sʌmˌhaʊ]
◀€ *Track 2975*

副 不知何故

▶Somehow, he thinks I hate him.
不知道為什麼，他覺得我討厭他。

some·time [`sʌmˌtaɪm]
◀€ *Track 2976*

副 某些時候、來日

▶I will visit London sometime in the future.
我未來有一天一定會去倫敦旅遊。

some·what [`sʌmˌhwɑt]
◀€ *Track 2977*

副 多少、幾分

▶I think his report is somewhat exaggerated（誇張）.
我覺得他的報告有點誇張。

sore [sor]
◀€ *Track 2978*

形 疼痛的 名 痛處 同 painful 疼痛的

▶形 I don't think he will get sore about this matter.
我不認為他會為此事而大動肝火。

▶名 I don't think it's necessary for us to reopen（重新打開、重新開放）those old sores.
我認為我們沒必要再提以前那些傷心事了。

文法字詞解析

要「折斷」或「迅速抓住」某個東西，需要非常快速、力道大且乾淨俐落的動作才能辦到。在罵人時常常也需要罵得很快、很凶、很狠才能達到效果，因此 snap 這個字也可以用來描述「突然破口大罵」的動作。
例如："Mind your own business," he snapped.
「少多管閒事」，他大罵道。

文法字詞解析

sometime（some 與 time 中間沒有空格）指「某些時候、來日」的意思。而如果 some 與 time 中間有空格（some time）則是「一些時間」的意思。
例如：Give me some time to think it over.
給我一點時間讓我想一下。

sor·row [ˋsɑro] Track 2979

名 悲傷、感到哀傷 同 grief 悲傷

▶The old man was all in sorrow after he lost his son.
老人失去兒子之後，悲傷不已。

spade [sped] Track 2980

名 鏟子

▶What's that spade for? I didn't know you're into gardening.
那個鏟子是幹嘛的？我還真不知道你對園藝有興趣。

spa·ghet·ti [spəˋgɛtɪ] Track 2981

名 義大利麵

▶Would you like spaghetti for dinner?
你晚餐想吃義大利麵嗎？

文法字詞解析
義大利麵依麵的形狀有好幾種說法，以下就來介紹幾種最常見的：
spaghetti 是我們常常在家自己煮的細圓麵；fettuccine 是寬扁麵；而小時候常吃到的、跟三色蔬菜一起煮的螺旋麵就是 rotini；最後，可以放在湯裡也可以加醬料食用的通心粉則是 macaroni。而所有義大利麵的統稱則是 pasta。

spe·cif·ic [spɪˋsɪfɪk] Track 2982

形 具體的、特殊的、明確的 同 precise 明確的

▶Can you give me some specific details?
你能告訴我一些具體細節嗎？

spice [spaɪs] Track 2983

名 香料

▶Did you add spice to this cake, Mom? It tastes great.
媽媽，妳有在蛋糕裡加香料嗎？它好吃極了。

spill [spɪl] Track 2984

動 使溢流 名 溢出

▶動 The waitress kept pouring water into the glass until it spilled over. 女服務生一直倒水到杯子裡，直到滿出來。

▶名 The oil spill is really bad for the environment.
溢出的石油對環境很不好。

文法字詞解析
spill 的動詞變化：spill, spilled, spilled 或 spill, spilt, spilt

spin [spɪn] Track 2985

動 旋轉、紡織 名 旋轉

▶動 The top has been spinning for a long time.
那個陀螺轉很久了。

▶名 The ballet dancer did several spins.
那位芭蕾舞者轉了好幾圈。

spit [spɪt] Track 2986

動 吐、吐口水 名 唾液

▶動 I don't think you can spit wherever you like.
我覺得你不能隨地吐痰。

▶名 Susan's spit flew as she shouted.
蘇珊大叫時口水濺得到處都是。

spite [spaɪt] Track 2987

名 惡意

▶The villain said something mean out of spite.
壞人出於惡意，說了惡劣的話。

splash [splæʃ]
🔊 Track 2988

動 濺起來 名 飛濺聲
▶動 The kids are splashing around in the pool.
孩子們在池裡潑水。
▶名 The rain is coming down in a splash. 大雨飛濺下來。

spoil [spɔɪl]
🔊 Track 2989

動 寵壞、損壞
▶Some people think that they would spoil the kid when they spare the rod. 有些人認為，省了棍子、就會寵壞小孩。

sprain [spren]
🔊 Track 2990

動 / 名 扭傷
▶動 No one knows how he sprained his wrist.
沒有人知道他是怎麼扭傷自己手腕的。
▶名 What's the difference between a sprain and a strain（拉傷）? 扭傷和拉傷之間有什麼差別？

spray [spre]
🔊 Track 2991

名 噴霧器 動 噴、濺
▶名 Is the water spray system ready for use?
水霧噴射系統是不是已經可以用了？
▶動 They sprayed paint on the wall. 他們在牆上噴上油漆。

sprin·kle [ˈsprɪŋkḷ]
🔊 Track 2992

動 灑、噴淋
▶How about sprinkling some sugar on the top of this birthday cake? 在這個生日蛋糕上撒點糖如何？

spy [spaɪ]
🔊 Track 2993

名 間諜
▶The country sent a spy to Russia last year.
這個國家去年派了一名間諜前往俄羅斯。

squeeze [skwiz]
🔊 Track 2994

動 壓擠、擠壓 名 緊抱、擁擠 同 crush 壓、榨
▶動 I don't think we can squeeze our way through the crowd.
我覺得我們沒辦法從人群裡擠過去。
▶名 He gave my hand a squeeze. 他捏了一下我的手。

stab [stæb]
🔊 Track 2995

動 刺、戳 名 刺傷
▶動 A villain stabbed the politician in the back.
有個惡混從背後捅了這名政客一刀。
▶名 He killed the woman with a stab to the heart.
他向這個女人的心臟刺了一刀，殺死了她。

sta·ble [ˈstebḷ]
🔊 Track 2996

形 穩定的 同 steady 穩定的
▶It won't be long before a stable government is formed in this nation. 不久，這個國家就會形成一個穩定的政府了。

文法字詞解析
食物放太久腐壞了也稱為 spoil，例如過期的牛奶就叫做 spoiled milk / spoilt milk。

萬用延伸句型
squeeze into sth. 擠進……裡面
例如：The lady squeezed into the narrow seat.
那位女士擠進窄小的座位裡。

sta·di·um [ˈstedɪəm] 　🔊 *Track 2997*
名 室外運動場
▶The regional baseball game was held at the school stadium.
　區域棒球賽在學校的體育場中舉行。

staff [stæf] 　🔊 *Track 2998*
名 棒、竿子、全體人員
▶I don't think this welfare（福利）policy is fair to all the staff in the company.
　我認為這項福利政策並不是對公司所有員工都公平。

文法字詞解析
如果想要說一家店的「人員不足」，可以加上表示「不足、太少」的字首「under-」以及形容詞字尾「-ed」變成「understaffed」。

stale [stel] 　🔊 *Track 2999*
形 不新鮮的、陳舊的　同 old 老舊的
▶There was only a piece of stale cake left in the refrigerator.
　冰箱裡只剩下一塊不新鮮的蛋糕了。

stare [stɛr] 　🔊 *Track 3000*
名 / 動 盯、凝視
▶名 He gave us a rude stare and walked away.
　他很不禮貌地瞪了我們一眼，走掉了。
▶動 It is not polite of you to stare at strangers on the street.
　在街上盯著陌生人看很不禮貌。

starve [stɑrv] 　🔊 *Track 3001*
動 餓死、饑餓
▶I don't think they will starve to death if they continue to work hard.
　我認為如果他們繼續努力工作，他們就不會餓死。

stat·ue [ˈstætʃʊ] 　🔊 *Track 3002*
名 鑄像、雕像
▶A statue of the martyr was erected in this park.
　殉道者的雕像矗立在公園裡。

stead·y [ˈstɛdɪ] 　🔊 *Track 3003*
形 穩固的　副 穩固地
▶形 Will you hold the ladder steady for me, Mike?
　麥克，請幫我把梯子扶穩好嗎？
▶副 The young couple is going steady.
　那對年輕情侶正在穩定交往中。

文法字詞解析
就像我們賽跑前會喊「預備，起」一樣，在英國起跑前也常會喊「ready, steady, go」。

steep [stip] 　🔊 *Track 3004*
形 險峻的
▶The mountain slope is too steep for the visitors to climb.
　這個山坡太陡，遊客們爬不上去。

step·child [ˈstɛpˌtʃɪld] 　🔊 *Track 3005*
名 前夫（妻）所生的孩子
▶Linda married an old man, and now she has three step children. 琳達嫁給一個老先生，現在她有三個小孩。

step·father [ˈstɛpˌfɑðɚ]

🔊 *Track 3006*

名 繼父、後父
▶The stepfather doesn't love this child.
這個繼父不愛這個孩子。

step·mother [ˈstɛpˌmʌðɚ]

🔊 *Track 3007*

名 繼母、後母
▶I've heard that he has a new stepmother. What does she look like? 聽說他有一個新後母了，那她長什麼樣子呢？

ster·e·o [ˈstɛrɪo]

🔊 *Track 3008*

名 立體音響
▶I spent thirty thousand dollars on this stereo.
我花了三萬元買這台音響。

stick·y [ˈstɪkɪ]

🔊 *Track 3009*

形 黏的、棘手的
▶Will you tell me what the sticky stuff in the box is?
你能告訴我這盒子裡黏黏的東西是什麼嗎？

stiff [stɪf]

🔊 *Track 3010*

形 僵硬的
▶The old man's back is very stiff. 那個老男人的背很僵硬。

sting [stɪŋ]

🔊 *Track 3011*

動 刺、叮
▶She was stung by bees. 她被蜜蜂叮了。

stir [stɝ]

🔊 *Track 3012*

動 攪拌
▶Stir the paste until the milk and flour are fully mixed.
攪拌麵糊，直到牛奶和麵粉完全混合。

stitch [stɪtʃ]

🔊 *Track 3013*

名 編織、一針 動 縫、繡
▶名 The would was so deep that the doctor had to stitch it.
這個傷口很深，以至於醫生必須要把它縫合。
▶動 You should stitch the buttons on this shirt by yourself.
你應該自己幫這件襯衫縫上鈕扣了。

stock·ing(s) [ˈstɑkɪŋ(z)]

🔊 *Track 3014*

名 長襪
▶Won't your children ask who put gifts in their stockings on Christmas（耶誕節）？難道你的孩子不會問耶誕節的時候是誰把禮物放在他們的長襪裡嗎？

stool [stul]

🔊 *Track 3015*

名 凳子
▶Cindy stood on the stool to reach books on the top of the shelf.
辛蒂站在小凳子上，才能夠拿到書架頂層的書。

文法字詞解析

繼父稱為 stepfather，繼母稱為 stepmother，那孩子呢？很簡單，我們留下「step-」這個字首，改成 stepchild、stepson、stepdaughter 就可以指「並非自己親生，再婚後跟著新的老公或老婆過來的孩子」了。而如果是跟著繼父或繼母過來的「非親生兄弟姊妹」則可以稱為 stepbrother、stepsister。

萬用延伸句型

stitch A on B 將 A 縫到 B 上

storm·y [ˈstɔrmɪ] ◀Track 3016

形 暴風雨的、多風暴的

▶I don't think ships are allowed to go to sea in such stormy weather. 我覺得這種天氣沒有船會被允許出海的。

---

strat·e·gy [ˈstrætədʒɪ] ◀Track 3017

名 戰略、策略

▶I think you should change your marketing strategy.
我覺得你們應該改變你們的行銷策略。

---

strength [strɛnθ] ◀Track 3018

名 力量、強度

▶His strength is superior to mine. 他的力氣比我大。

---

strip [strɪp] ◀Track 3019

名 條、臨時跑道 動 剝、剝除

▶名 He took a strip of paper and fold it into a star.
他拿了一個長形紙條，把它折成星星狀。

▶動 Can you tell me what stripped the trees of its leaves?
你能告訴我是什麼把樹葉全部都颳走了嗎？

---

struc·ture [ˈstrʌktʃɚ] ◀Track 3020

名 構造、結構 動 建立組織

▶名 It is hard for me to figure out the structure of the long sentence. 我很難明白這個長句的結構。

▶動 It is not so easy for them to structure a strong defensive (防禦的) line. 他們想要構成一條堅固的防線並不容易。

---

stub·born [ˈstʌbɚn] ◀Track 3021

形 頑固的 同 obstinate 頑固的

▶My grandpa is quite stubborn. 我的爺爺相當頑固。

---

stu·di·o [ˈstjudɪˌo] ◀Track 3022

名 工作室、播音室

▶I take classes in the dance studio. 我在舞蹈工作室上課。

---

stuff [stʌf] ◀Track 3023

名 東西、材料 動 填塞、裝填

▶名 I've got lots of stuff in my drawer. 我抽屜裡有很多東西。

▶動 He stuffed himself with food. 他用食物塞滿肚子。

---

style [staɪl] ◀Track 3024

名 風格、時尚

▶Not all people like his writing style, though he is a famous writer. 儘管他是一個很有名的作家，但卻不是所有人都喜歡他的寫作風格。

---

sub·stance [ˈsʌbstəns] ◀Track 3025

名 物質、物體、實質

▶The unknown substance in the jar caused panic to the local people. 罐子裡不知名的物質引起當地人恐慌。

文法字詞解析

也可以用 stormy 這個字描述一個人的表情、五官像暴風雨一樣乖戾不平靜。
例如：His stormy features made him hard to approach.
他的外表看起來脾氣不太好的樣子，讓他顯得很難親近。

文法字詞解析

「髮型」稱為 hairstyle，「生活型態」稱為 lifestyle，「服裝風格」則是 clothing style / outfit style。

Level **1**

Level **2**

Level **3**

駕輕就熟、更上一層樓──
累積實力3200單字

Level **4**

Level **5**

Level **6**

sub·urb [ˋsʌbɝb]
Track 3026

名 市郊、郊區

▶I don't think my neighbors will move out to the suburbs this year. 我覺得我的鄰居今年不會搬到郊區去住。

suck [sʌk]
Track 3027

動 吸、吸取、吸收

▶動 The mosquitoes live on sucking blood.
蚊子們都靠著吸血維生。

suf·fer [ˋsʌfɚ]
Track 3028

動 受苦、遭受 同 endure 忍受

▶He suffers from lung cancer. 他受肺癌之害。

sufficient [səˋfɪʃənt]
Track 3029

形 充足的 同 enough 充足的

▶I don't believe that they have sufficient food and water on the ship. 我相信他們在船上沒有充足的食物和水。

sug·gest [səˋdʒɛst]
Track 3030

動 提議、建議 同 hint 建議

▶I suggest him to ask help from the employment agency.
我建議他向職事務所求助。

su·i·cide [ˋsuəˌsaɪd]
Track 3031

名 自殺、自滅

▶The number of suicides has increased these years.
最近幾年自殺案件的數量增加了。

suit·a·ble [ˋsutəbḷ]
Track 3032

形 適合的 同 fit 適合的

▶I don't think this man is suitable for this job.
我不覺得這個男人適合這個工作。

sum [sʌm]
Track 3033

名 總數 動 合計

▶名 Not even the manager knows the sum required.
經理也不知道所需要的總額是多少。

▶動 The total costs last month sum up to ten thousand dollars.
上月的總花費高達一萬美元。

sum·ma·ry [ˋsʌmərɪ]
Track 3034

名 摘要

▶Can you give me a summary of the movie?
你可以跟我說一下這部電影的摘要嗎？

sum·mit [ˋsʌmɪt]
Track 3035

名 頂點、高峰

▶The presidents of Russia, the U.S., and some European countries attended the summit.
俄國、美國，以及一些歐洲國家的總統有出席這次高峰會。

萬用延伸句型

suck it up 用於勸人自認倒楣、接受事實。
例如：
A: Why am I being punished for something I didn't do?
B: If you can't prove you didn't do it, just suck it up.
A：事情又不是我幹的，為什麼我要被處罰？
B：如果你沒辦法證明不是你幹的，那你還是自認倒楣乖乖受罰吧。

萬用延伸句型

sum up 總結
例如：To sum up, I believe our company is in good shape right now.
總而言之，我認為我們公司現在狀況不錯。

su·pe·ri·or [sə`pɪrɪɚ] 🔊 Track 3036

形 上級的　名 長官

▶形 According to the latest report, the enemy forces are superior in numbers. 最新報導說敵軍在數量上佔有優勢。

▶名 John has become our direct superior.
約翰成了我們的頂頭上司。

sup·pose [sə`poz] 🔊 Track 3037

動 假定

▶You were supposed to turn in the report by this Friday.
你應該要在這週五前繳交報告。

萬用延伸句型
Do you suppose...? 你猜……嗎？
這個句型可以用來引導他人說出他們的意見。

sur·round [sə`raʊnd] 🔊 Track 3038

動 圍繞

▶Let's listen to the sounds of the summer night that surround us. 讓我們仔細聽一聽環繞我們的夏夜之聲吧。

sur·vey [`sɝve] 🔊 Track 3039

動／名 考察、測量、實地調查

▶動 The marketing research team surveyed the consumers' preference. 市場調查團隊調查了消費者的偏好。

▶名 Would you like to tell me what findings you have got from the market survey?
你能告訴我你在市場調查中有什麼發現嗎？

sur·viv·al [sə`vaɪvl] 🔊 Track 3040

名 殘存、倖存

▶Survival is our first imperative（必要的事）, don't you think so?
我們的當務之急是設法生存下來，你不這樣認為嗎？

萬用延伸句型
Don't you think so? 你不覺得是如此嗎？

sur·vi·vor [sə`vaɪvɚ] 🔊 Track 3041

名 生還者

▶There was only one survivor from the plane crash.
這次飛機失事只有一名倖存者。

sus·pect [`sʌspɛkt] 🔊 Track 3042

動 懷疑　名 嫌疑犯

▶動 I suspect that he killed his parents.
我懷疑是他殺了他的父母。

▶名 There are seven suspects for this murder.
這起謀殺案有七個嫌疑犯。

sus·pi·cion [sə`spɪʃəs] 🔊 Track 3043

名 懷疑

▶I have a strong suspicion that John is the killer.
我強烈懷疑約翰就是殺手。

swear [swɛr] 🔊 Track 3044

動 發誓、宣誓

▶I swear that I didn't steal your idea.
我發誓我沒有偷用你的想法。

文法字詞解析
swear 的動詞變化：swear, swore, sworn

sweat [swɛt] 　　　　🔊 *Track 3045*

名 汗水 動 出汗

▶ 名 I guess he must be very nervous; there is sweat on his forehead. 我猜他一定很緊張，他額頭直冒汗。

▶ 動 I am sweating all over; is there any place here for me to take a shower?
我渾身上下汗水淋漓，這裡有地方可以洗澡嗎？

swell [swɛl] 　　　　🔊 *Track 3046*

動 膨脹

▶ The kid's forehead swelled with the bite of the unknown insect.
小孩的額頭因為被不知名的昆蟲叮咬，腫起來了。

swift [swɪft] 　　　　🔊 *Track 3047*

形 迅速的

▶ I think the river is too swift for you to swim here.
我覺得這河水流得太急了，你不能在這裡游泳。

switch [swɪtʃ] 　　　　🔊 *Track 3048*

名 開關 動 轉換

▶ 名 Will you help me turn off the switch in my room?
請你幫我把我房間裡的開關關掉好嗎？

▶ 動 He walked in and switched on th light.
他走了進來，把燈打了開來。

sword [sord] 　　　　🔊 *Track 3049*

名 劍、刀

▶ I've always wanted to hold a real sword.
我一直想要拿拿看一把真的劍。

sys·tem [ˈsɪstəm] 　　　　🔊 *Track 3050*

名 系統

▶ The human resource department made some changes in the hiring system. 人事資源部門對雇用系統做了一些調整。

[Tt]

tab·let [ˈtæblɪt] 　　　　🔊 *Track 3051*

名 塊、片、碑、牌

▶ If you take the tablet, your headache will go away.
吃一顆藥，你的頭就不會痛了。

tack [tæk] 　　　　🔊 *Track 3052*

名 大頭釘 動 釘住

▶ 名 He got hurt because he stepped on a tack.
他因踩到圖釘而受傷了。

▶ 動 Let's tack some posters to the wall, shall we?
我們把一些海報釘在牆上好嗎？

萬用延伸句型

Don't sweat it！別擔心！這句話常用在口語中，告訴他人沒什麼好憂心的。
例如：Don't sweat it! You still have two days to finish your thesis.
別擔心！你還有兩天可以完成你的論文。

文法字詞解析

由於 tablet 能夠拿來描述各種「片狀」、「塊狀」等物品，因此使用範圍很廣泛，從小小的片狀藥丸到我們常用的平板電腦都可以稱為 tablet。

tag [tæg]
🔊 *Track 3053*

名 標籤 動 加標籤、尾隨

同 label 標籤

▶名 The stray cat has a name tag on its collar.
流浪貓的項圈上有一個名牌。

▶動 He tagged us in the picture.
他把我們標記在相片上了。

tai·lor ['telɚ]
🔊 *Track 3054*

名 裁縫師 動 裁製

▶名 This tailor is famous for making good suits.
這位裁縫以做高級西裝而出名。

▶動 The clinic tailors its treatment to individual needs.
那個診所的治療方法適合個別需要。

tame [tem]
🔊 *Track 3055*

形 馴服的、單調的 動 馴服

▶形 The pet dog was very tame.
這隻寵物狗看起來很溫順。

▶動 I wouldn't know how to tame a lion.
我可不知道怎麼馴服獅子。

tap [tæp]
🔊 *Track 3056*

名 輕拍聲 動 輕打

▶名 Did you hear a tap on the window?
你有聽到有人有人輕叩窗戶嗎？

▶動 The girl taps her fingers on the desk impatiently（不耐煩地）. 那個女孩不耐煩地用手指輕扣桌面。

tax [tæks]
🔊 *Track 3057*

名 稅

▶Can you tell me how much the airport tax is?
您能不能告訴我機場稅是多少錢？

tease [tiz]
🔊 *Track 3058*

動 嘲弄、揶揄 名 揶揄

▶動 Don't tease the girl! She might cry.
不要逗那個女孩了！她會哭喔！

▶名 She is a big tease and really fun to be with.
她很愛戲弄人，跟她在一起很有趣。

tech·ni·cal ['tɛknɪkl̩]
🔊 *Track 3059*

形 技術上的、技能的

▶I don't know anything about technical matters.
我完全不懂技術問題。

tech·nique [tɛk'nik]
🔊 *Track 3060*

名 技術、技巧

▶We went abroad to learn the latest manufacturing technique.
我們去國外學習最新的製造技術。

文法字詞解析
在社群網站上經常用到的「標記」功能，就是用 tag 這個字喔！所以我們可以請別人把自己「tag」在相片中。

萬用延伸句型
I don't know anything about... 我不知道任何和……有關的事。

Level 1

Level 2

Level 3

駕輕就熟、更上一層樓——累積實力3200單字

Level 4

Level 5

Level 6

tech·nol·o·gy [tɛkˋnɑlədʒɪ] 🔊 *Track 3061*
名 技術學、工藝學
▶Technology is advancing so fast these days.
最近技術真的進步得好快啊。

tem·per [ˋtɛmpɚ] 🔊 *Track 3062*
名 脾氣
▶I lost my temper when the kid said something rude.
我聽到小孩說粗魯的話，就發脾氣了。

tem·per·a·ture [ˋtɛmprətʃɚ] 🔊 *Track 3063*
名 溫度、氣溫
▶How about asking a nurse to take his temperature?
請一位護士幫他量量體溫怎麼樣？

tem·po·ra·ry [ˋtɛmpəˏrɛrɪ] 🔊 *Track 3064*
形 暫時的
▶The temporary worker will leave tomorrow.
那名臨時工明天就會離開了。

tend [tɛnd] 🔊 *Track 3065*
動 傾向、照顧 同 incline 傾向
▶British people tend to be rather conservative（保守的）.
英國人一般相當保守。

ten·der [ˋtɛndɚ] 🔊 *Track 3066*
形 溫柔的、脆弱的、幼稚的 同 soft 輕柔的
▶The man was tender and gentle to his daughter.
這人對女兒相當溫柔又紳士。

ter·ri·to·ry [ˋtɛrəˏtorɪ] 🔊 *Track 3067*
名 領土、版圖
▶That's unfamiliar（不熟悉的）territory to me.
對我來說那是不熟悉的領域。

text [tɛkst] 🔊 *Track 3068*
名 課文、本文
▶I am reading a text on Chinese philosophy（哲學）.
我正在讀中國哲學的課文。

thank·ful [ˋθæŋkfəl] 🔊 *Track 3069*
形 欣慰的、感謝的 同 grateful 感謝的
▶I am so thankful that she feels better today.
她今天感覺好多了，我真欣慰。

the·o·ry [ˋθiərɪ] 🔊 *Track 3070*
名 理論、推論 同 inference 推論
▶The professor has no idea how he should connect the theory and practice.
教授不知道要如何連結理論與實務。

文法字詞解析
雖然 tender 有「溫柔的」的意思，但一般是用來描述「動作、事情」，而不是描述「人」。如果你想說自己「很溫柔」，說「I'm tender」，會令人覺得你在說自己的肉「很柔軟、好好吃」喔。這當然是不行的。

thirst [θɜst]　🔊 *Track 3071*

名 口渴、渴望

▶Many boys have a thirst for adventure.
有許多男孩子都渴望冒險。

thread [θrɛd]　🔊 *Track 3072*

名 線 動 穿線

▶名 WI brought my fishing rod and my fishing thread with me.
我把釣魚竿和釣魚線帶在身上。

▶動 I'm not good at threading needles.
我超不會穿針的。

threat [θrɛt]　🔊 *Track 3073*

名 威脅、恐嚇

▶Some foods present（引起）a threat to people's health.
有些食物會威脅人體健康。

threat·en [ˈθrɛtn̩]　🔊 *Track 3074*

動 威脅

▶The strikers were threatened with dismissal（解雇）unless they returned to work.
罷工者受到威脅，說如果他們不復工就會被解雇。

tick·le [ˈtɪkl̩]　🔊 *Track 3075*

動 搔癢、呵癢

▶He tickled my feet. 他搔了我的腳癢。

tide [taɪd]　🔊 *Track 3076*

名 潮、趨勢

▶The tide is low right now, so we can see the island.
現在退潮，所以我們可以看到那座島。

ti·dy [ˈtaɪdɪ]　🔊 *Track 3077*

形 整潔的 動 整頓

▶形 Jenny always keeps her room tidy and put her files in order.
珍妮總是保持房間整潔、把資料夾按照順序放好。

▶動 You must tidy up your room before going out.
出門之前一定要收拾一下房間。

tight [taɪt]　🔊 *Track 3078*

形 緊的、緊密的 副 緊緊地、安穩地

▶形 This pair of trousers is too tight for me to wear.
這條褲子太緊了，我穿不下。

▶副 The bandage was tied very tight. 繃帶綁得很緊。

tight·en [ˈtaɪtn̩]　🔊 *Track 3079*

動 勒緊、使堅固

▶I have to tighten my belt for I have little money at hand.
我沒剩多少錢，所以我得勒緊褲帶、節儉一點。

萬用延伸句型

萬用延伸句型
empty threat 指雖然口口聲聲威脅人家，卻不做出實際上的行動。
例如：He said he'd get his revenge, but it was all empty threats.
他說他會報仇，不過那都是空談。

文法字詞解析

除了表示「衣物很緊」等等「空間方面」的「緊」之外，tight 也可以用來說人與人之間的關係很「緊密」。

Level 1

Level 2

Level 3

駕輕就熟、更上一層樓──累積實力3200單字

Level 4

Level 5

Level 6

tim·ber [ˈtɪmbɚ]　🔊 Track 3080
名 木材、樹林　同 wood 木材、樹林
▶A lot of timber was destroyed in the forest fire.
　有許多木材在這次森林大火中燒毀了。

tis·sue [ˈtɪʃʊ]　🔊 Track 3081
名 面紙
▶The kid blew his nose with his tissue. 小孩拿衛生紙擤鼻涕。

to·bac·co [təˈbæko]　🔊 Track 3082
名 煙草
▶It's forbidden to sell tobacco to children under the age of 16.
　禁止人們向十六歲以下的兒童出售煙草。

萬用延伸句型
It's forbidden to... ⋯⋯是被禁止的

ton [tʌn]　🔊 Track 3083
名 噸
▶How many tons of water is there in the pool?
　這個池子裡有多少噸水？

tor·toise [ˈtɔrtəs]　🔊 Track 3084
名 烏龜
▶I can't tell if the tortoise is awake or asleep.
　我看不出這隻烏龜到底是睡著還是醒著。

toss [tɔs]　🔊 Track 3085
動 投擲　名 投、擲　同 throw 投、丟
▶動 He tossed a coin into the wishing pond. 他把硬幣投倒許願池裡。
▶名 A toss of a coin decides who should play first.
　丟擲錢幣決定誰先開球。

tour·ism [ˈtʊrɪzəm]　🔊 Track 3086
名 觀光、遊覽
▶The nation is famous for its tourism. 那個國家以旅遊業聞名。

萬用延伸句型
be famous for... 因⋯⋯而出名

tour·ist [ˈtʊrɪst]　🔊 Track 3087
名 觀光客
▶The tourist complained that the room was too dirty for him to
stay in. 那名遊客抱怨說房間太髒了，沒辦法入住。

tow [to]　🔊 Track 3088
動 拖曳　名 拖曳　同 pull 拖、拉
▶動 Would you please help me tow my car to the nearest garage?
　請你幫我把我的車拖到最近的汽車修理廠好嗎？
▶名 My car's broken down; would you please give me a tow?
　我的車拋錨了，能用您的車幫我拖車嗎？

trace [tres]　🔊 Track 3089
動 追溯　名 蹤跡
▶動 The dog can trace the missing child with it sensibility to scent.
　這隻狗對氣味很敏感，可以追蹤失蹤的小孩。
▶名 There was barely（幾乎）a trace of salt in the soup.
　湯裡幾乎一點鹽也沒有。

trad·er [ˈtredɚ]

🔊 *Track 3090*

名 商人

▶The trader was good at finding bargains.
這個商人很擅長找到好的交易機會。

trail [trel]

🔊 *Track 3091*

名 痕跡、小徑 動 拖著、拖著走

▶名 We took a walk along the trail.
我們沿著小徑散步。

▶動 The dog trailed after me. 那隻狗尾隨著我。

trans·port [ˈtrænsport]

🔊 *Track 3092*

動 輸送、運輸 名 輸送

▶動 They transported the goods very quickly.
他們很快地運送了貨物。

▶名 They chose another means of transport because it was cheaper.
他們選擇了另一個運輸方法，因為這樣會便宜很多。

trash [træʃ]

🔊 *Track 3093*

名 垃圾

▶Can you take out the trash please?
可以請你把垃圾拿出去丟嗎？

trav·el·er [ˈtrævlɚ]

🔊 *Track 3094*

名 旅行者、旅客

▶The man claimed that he was a time traveler.
這人聲稱他是時空旅行者。

tray [tre]

🔊 *Track 3095*

名 托盤

▶Would you mind putting the tray over there?
你介不介意把托盤放到那邊去呢？

trem·ble [ˈtrɛmbl]

🔊 *Track 3096*

名 顫抖、發抖 動 顫慄

▶名 There was a tremble in her voice.
她的嗓音有些顫抖。

▶動 The whole house trembled when the train went by.
火車經過時，整座房子都在震動。

trend [trɛnd]

🔊 *Track 3097*

名 趨勢、傾向

▶Being skinny is a trend nowadays（現今）.
保持骨感是現今的時尚。

tribe [traɪb]

🔊 *Track 3098*

名 部落、種族

▶The anthropologist studied the social hierarchy in the tribe.
人類學家研究這個部落的社會階級。

文法字詞解析

垃圾桶可稱為 trash can、trash bin、garbage can、garbage bin、rubbish bin 等。

Level 1

Level 2

Level 3

Level 4

Level 5

Level 6

駕輕就熟、更上一層樓──

累積實力3200單字

trick·y [ˈtrɪkɪ]　🔊 Track 3099
形 狡猾的、狡詐的
▶I'm in a rather tricky position; could you help me out?
我的處境很棘手，你願意幫幫我嗎？

troop [trup]　🔊 Track 3100
名 軍隊
▶The troop was sent to defeat the rebels. 部隊被派去擊退叛軍。

trop·i·cal [ˈtrɑpɪkl̩]　🔊 Track 3101
形 熱帶的
▶There is luxuriant（繁茂的）tropical vegetation（植物）in our country. 我們國家有很多繁茂的熱帶植物。

trunk [trʌŋk]　🔊 Track 3102
名 樹幹、大行李箱、象鼻
▶Would you please help me open the trunk?
請你幫我打開這個行李箱好嗎？

truth·ful [ˈtruθfəl]　🔊 Track 3103
形 誠實的 同 honest 誠實的
▶Don't believe him, not all the news he told you is truthful.
別信他，他告訴你的所有消息未必都是真實的。

tub [tʌb]　🔊 Track 3104
名 桶、盤
▶I bought a tub and put it in the bathroom.
我買了一個盆子，放在浴室。

tug [tʌg]　🔊 Track 3105
動 用力拉 名 拖拉 同 pull 拖、拉
▶動 The little girl tugged at her mother's sleeve.
那個小女孩扯扯她媽媽的衣角。
▶名 I felt a tug at my sleeve and turned around.
我感覺到有人拉了一下我的袖子，便轉過身來。

tulip [ˈtjuləp]　🔊 Track 3106
名 鬱金香
▶Would you like to see our tulip fields sometime next week?
下個禮拜你們想不想找時間去看看我們那片鬱金香花田？

tum·ble [ˈtʌmbl̩]　🔊 Track 3107
動 摔跤、跌落
▶She tumbled down the hill. 她一路翻滾下山坡。

tune [tjun]　🔊 Track 3108
名 調子、曲調 動 調整音調
▶名 She likes to sing, but she is always out of tune.
她喜歡唱歌，但她總是走音。
▶動 Do you mind if I tune the television set to Channel 7?
你介不介意我把電視機調到第七頻道？

文法字詞解析
scout troop = 童子軍

文法字詞解析
為樂器調音的動作也稱為 tune。

tutor [ˈtjutɚ] 🔊 *Track 3109*

名 家庭教師、導師 動 輔導

▶名 My tutor is a learned（有學問的）scholar.
我的家教是一位學識淵博的學者。

▶動 How about tutoring your child by yourself?
你要不要自己來輔導你的孩子？

twig [twɪg] 🔊 *Track 3110*

名 小枝、嫩枝

▶The bird built its nest with twigs and hay.
小鳥用小樹枝和乾草築巢。

twin [twɪn] 🔊 *Track 3111*

名 雙胞胎

▶The twin brothers are alike not only in appearance but also in personality. 那對雙胞兄弟不但外表相似，而且性格也很像。

twist [twɪst] 🔊 *Track 3112*

動 扭曲

▶He twisted his arm in a fight. 他在打架的時候扭到手臂了。

type·writ·er [ˈtaɪpˌraɪtɚ] 🔊 *Track 3113*

名 打字機

▶I still use my old typewriter. 我還是用我的老式打字機。

typ·i·cal [ˈtɪpɪkl̩] 🔊 *Track 3114*

形 典型的

▶He is a typical Virgo; he is meticulous with everything.
他是典型處女座。他對每件事都很謹慎小心。

[Uu]

un·ion [ˈjunjən] 🔊 *Track 3115*

名 聯合、組織

▶He was elected the leader of the union.
他被選為工會的領導人。

u·nite [juˈnaɪt] 🔊 *Track 3116*

動 聯合、合併

▶We united to achieve our shared goal.
我們團結追求共同的目標。

u·ni·ty [ˈjunətɪ] 🔊 *Track 3117*

名 聯合、統一

▶There is little unity of purpose among the members.
成員之間缺乏共同的目標。

文法字詞解析

一次提到雙胞胎之中的兩個人時使用複數稱為「twins」，而如果要說雙胞胎中的其中一個則使用單數「a twin」。
例如：I'm a twin. My brother and I are twins.
我是雙胞胎的其中一個。我哥和我是雙胞胎。

實用片語用語

unite against sb. / sth. 聯合起來對抗某人／某事物
例如：All citizens united against corruption.
所有的國民都聯合起來反貪污。

Level 1
Level 2
Level 3
Level 4
Level 5
Level 6

駕輕就熟、更上一層樓——累積實力3200單字

u·ni·verse [ˈjunəˌvɝs]
🔊 Track 3118

名 宇宙、天地萬物
▶The universe is much bigger than we can imagine.
宇宙比我想像中的大多了。

un·less [ənˈlɛs]
🔊 Track 3119

連 除非
▶You should not give up the chance unless you have something more important to do.
你應該不要放棄這個機會，除非你有重要的事情可以做。

up·set [ʌpˈsɛt]
🔊 Track 3120

動 顛覆、使心煩 名 顛覆、煩惱 同 overturn 顛覆
▶動 The news upset him emotionally（感情上）.
這個消息使他心煩意亂。
▶名 No one expected two upsets in three games.
大家都沒想到，三場球賽中就有兩場是弱隊獲勝。

[Vv]

va·cant [ˈvekənt]
🔊 Track 3121

形 空閒的、空虛的
▶There are some vacant offices on the third floor.
三樓有幾間空著的辦公室。

val·u·a·ble [ˈvæljuəbl]
🔊 Track 3122

形 貴重的
▶Real friendship（友誼）is more valuable than money; don't you think so? 真正的友誼比金錢更寶貴，你不這樣認為嗎？

van [væn]
🔊 Track 3123

名 貨車
▶My dad is the man in the van. 貨車裡那個男人就是我爸。

van·ish [ˈvænɪʃ]
🔊 Track 3124

動 消失、消逝
▶Many types of animals have vanished from the Earth.
已經有很多種類的動物從地球上絕跡了。

va·ri·e·ty [vəˈraɪətɪ]
🔊 Track 3125

名 多樣化
▶I have a variety of books in my study.
在我的書房有各式各樣的書。

var·i·ous [ˈvɛrɪəs]
🔊 Track 3126

形 多種的
▶There are various dishes in this banquet.
這場晚宴有很多不同菜餚。

var·y [ˈvɛrɪ]
Track 3127

動 使變化、改變

▶The quality of fruits varies from season to season.
水果的品質隨季節變化而有所不同。

vase [ves]
Track 3128

名 花瓶

▶Would you please help me glue the broken vase together?
請你幫我把破碎的花瓶黏合起來好嗎？

ve·hi·cle [ˈviɪkḷ]
Track 3129

名 交通工具、車輛

▶The company has developed several types of eco-friendly vehicles. 這家公司發展好幾種環保的車輛形號。

verse [vɝs]
Track 3130

名 詩、詩句

▶She could quote any chapter and verse in this book easily.
她能夠毫不費力地引用這本書的任何章節和句子。

> **文法字詞解析**
> 除了詩句外，在提到歌曲時也可以用 verse 來表示歌曲的某一段。

vest [vɛst]
Track 3131

名 背心、馬甲 **動** 授給

▶**名** Put on the life vest before you get on the jet-ski.
玩水上摩托車之前請穿上救生背心。

▶**動** The executive（行政的）power is usually vested in the president. 行政權通常會被賦予總統。

vice-pres·i·dent [vaɪs ˈprɛzədənt]
Track 3132

名 副總統

▶Once the president of the company retired, the vice-president took over. 該公司的總經理一退休，公司就變成副總管理了。

vic·tim [ˈvɪktɪm]
Track 3133

名 受害者

▶The victims of the flood still don't have a home.
水災的受害者還是沒有家。

vi·o·lence [ˈvaɪələns]
Track 3134

名 暴力 **同** force 暴力

▶Nothing good ever comes out of violence.
暴力從來沒有帶來過什麼好東西。

vi·o·lent [ˈvaɪələnt]
Track 3135

形 猛烈的

▶The man is violent and often beats his wife.
這個男人很暴力，常打自己的太太。

vi·o·let [ˈvaɪəlɪt]
Track 3136

名 紫羅蘭 **形** 紫羅蘭色的

▶**名** I bought a bouquet（花束）of violets. 我買了一束紫羅蘭。

▶**形** The violet curtain created an elegant atmosphere in the living room. 紫羅蘭色的窗簾為客廳創造出高雅的氣氛。

Level 1
Level 2
Level 3
Level 4
Level 5
Level 6

駕輕就熟、更上一層樓——
累積實力3200單字

vis·i·ble [ˈvɪzəbḷ]

🔊 *Track 3137*

形 可看見的

▶Police regulations prescribe（規定）that an officer's number must be clearly visible.
警察條例要求執行職務者的號碼標誌必須清楚易見。

文法字詞解析
加上代表「不、沒有」的字首「in-」，變成「invisible」，就成了 visible 的相反詞「看不見的、隱形的」。

vi·sion [ˈvɪʒən]

🔊 *Track 3138*

名 視力、視覺、洞察力

▶The old man's teeth were shaking, and his vision was blurred.
老人的牙齒動搖、眼睛視力模糊。

vi·ta·min [ˈvaɪtəmɪn]

🔊 *Track 3139*

名 維他命

▶Lemons are rich in vitamin C. 檸檬含豐富的維生素 C。

viv·id [ˈvɪvɪd]

🔊 *Track 3140*

形 閃亮的、生動的

▶My daughter is a child with vivid imagination.
我女兒是一個想像力活躍的孩子。

vol·ume [ˈvɑljəm]

🔊 *Track 3141*

名 卷、冊、音量、容積

▶Would you turn down the volume of the music?
你可以將音樂音量轉小嗎？

[Ww]

wag [wæg]

🔊 *Track 3142*

動 搖擺 名 搖擺、搖動

▶動 Dogs wag their tails when they are pleased.
狗一高興就搖尾巴。

▶名 The puppy greeted his master with a wag of his tail.
那隻小狗搖了一下尾巴迎接主人。

wage [wedʒ]

🔊 *Track 3143*

名 週薪、工資

▶Peter can get a high wage from his full-time job.
彼得的全職工作薪水很高。

文法字詞解析
這個字也經常使用複數型態 wages 來代表整體的工資。

wag·on [ˈwægən]

🔊 *Track 3144*

名 四輪馬車、貨車

▶Who's the man on the back of the wagon?
貨車後面那個男人是誰？

wak·en [ˈwekən]

🔊 *Track 3145*

動 喚醒、醒來

▶I feel as if I had wakened from a nightmare（噩夢）.
我覺得好像剛從噩夢中醒來。

wan·der [ˈwɑndɚ] 🔊 *Track 3146*
動 徘徊、漫步
▶Would you please not wander off the point? 請你不要離題好嗎？

warmth [wɔrmθ] 🔊 *Track 3147*
名 暖和、溫暖、熱忱 同 zeal 熱忱
▶I can feel the hospitality and warmth of the local people.
　我可以感覺到當地人的好客心和溫暖。

warn [wɔrn] 🔊 *Track 3148*
動 警告、提醒
▶Let me warn you: he's really hard to please.
　我警告你一下：他超難取悅的。

wax [wæks] 🔊 *Track 3149*
名 蠟、蜂蠟、月盈
▶The doll is made of wax. 這個娃娃是蠟做的。

weak·en [ˈwikən] 🔊 *Track 3150*
動 使變弱、減弱
▶Nothing can weaken his resolve（決心）to become a lawyer.
　什麼也動搖不了他要當律師的決心。

wealth [wɛlθ] 🔊 *Track 3151*
名 財富、財產
▶Health is better than wealth. 健康勝於財富。

wealth·y [ˈwɛlθɪ] 🔊 *Track 3152*
形 富裕的、富有的
▶Richard is born with a silver spoon in mouth; he was born to a wealthy family. 理查出生在有錢家庭，他含著銀湯匙出生。

weave [wiv] 🔊 *Track 3153*
名 織法、編法
▶I observed how a spider weave its net.
　我觀察蜘蛛如何編織牠的網。

文法字詞解析
weave 的動詞變化：weave, wove, woven

web [wɛb] 🔊 *Track 3154*
名 網、蜘蛛網
▶I walked straight into a spider web. 我直接撞上了蜘蛛網。

weed [wid] 🔊 *Track 3155*
名 野草、雜草
▶You have to clear up the weed before your plants can grow.
　你要先把雜草除掉，你的植物才會生長。

weep [wip] 🔊 *Track 3156*
動 哭泣，哭 同 cry 哭
▶The mother wept over her dead child.
　那個媽媽因孩子死去而哭泣。

文法字詞解析
weep 的動詞變化：weep, wept, wept

Level 1
Level 2
Level 3
累積實力3200單字
駕輕就熟、更上一層樓
Level 4
Level 5
Level 6

wheat [hwit]　🔊 *Track 3157*

名 小麥、麥子

▶This old man is a leading authority on wheat diseases.
這位老人是小麥病蟲害方面的權威。

whip [hwɪp]　🔊 *Track 3158*

名 鞭子 動 鞭打

▶名 It's cruel of you to use your whip on your horse.
你用鞭子抽你的馬是很殘忍的。

▶動 You really shouldn't whip your kids.
你真的不應該拿鞭子抽你的孩子。

whis·tle [ˈhwɪsḷ]　🔊 *Track 3159*

名 口哨、汽笛 動 吹口哨

▶名 The life guard blew the whistle to warn people of danger in the water. 救生員吹哨子警告遊客注意危險的水域。

▶動 A man cannot whistle and drink at the same time.
沒人可以邊吹口哨邊喝水吧。

wick·ed [ˈwɪkɪd]　🔊 *Track 3160*

形 邪惡的、壞的

▶People thought him dangerous and wicked.
人們認為他是危險且邪惡的。

wil·low [ˈwɪlo]　🔊 *Track 3161*

名 柳樹

▶They're sitting under the willow tree. 他們坐在柳樹下面。

wink [wɪŋk]　🔊 *Track 3162*

動 眨眼、使眼色 名 眨眼、使眼色

▶動 Why did he wink at me? 他幹嘛對我眨眼睛？

▶名 She turned around and gave me a wink.
她轉過身，對我眨眼。

wipe [waɪp]　🔊 *Track 3163*

動 擦拭 名 擦拭、擦

▶動 I wiped the table with tissues.
我用衛生紙擦桌子。

▶名 He gave the table mats a quick wipe.
他把桌上的碗盤墊快速擦了一下。

wis·dom [ˈwɪzdəm]　🔊 *Track 3164*

名 智慧

▶The old man is full of wisdom. 這個老男人充滿了智慧。

wrap [ræp]　🔊 *Track 3165*

動 包裝 名 包裝紙

▶動 The souvenir was wrapped with beautiful cloth.
紀念品被用漂亮的布包裝。

▶名 Why don't you buy a woolen（羊毛製的）wrap for yourself?
為什麼不為你自己買條羊毛圍巾呢？

萬用延伸句型
at the same time 同時……

文法字詞解析
wink 和 blink 兩個字都是「眨眼」的意思，那兩者有什麼差別呢？原來，blink 就是普通的眨眼睛，沒什麼特別意思，而 wink 則是帶有暗示或特殊涵意，不是單純地眨眼睛。因此，若有人 wink at you，表示他想暗示你一些事或對你放電。若有人 blink at you，表示他只是呆滯地在那邊眨眼睛而已，那是人類正常的生理運作。

wrist [rɪst]
◀ Track 3166
名 腕關節、手腕
▶She sprained her wrist when playing billiard.
她打撞球時扭傷了手腕。

[Yy]

yawn [jɔn]
◀ Track 3167
動 打呵欠 名 打呵欠
▶動 Jason yawned halfway through Mr. Benson's speech.
傑森在班森先生演講到一半時，打了哈欠。
▶名 He stretched hard with a yawn. 他大力伸懶腰、打了個呵欠。

萬用延伸句型
It's impolite of you to... 你（做某事）很不禮貌

yell [jɛl]
◀ Track 3168
動 大叫、呼喊
▶I don't think you should yell at that old man like that.
我認為你不該對那位老人那樣大吼大叫。

yolk [jok]
◀ Track 3169
名 蛋黃、卵黃
▶You have yolk on your chin. Rub it off!
你的下巴沾著蛋黃，擦掉吧！

[Zz]

zip·per [ˋzɪpɚ]
◀ Track 3170
名 拉鏈
▶The zipper of my backpack was broken.
我背包的拉鍊壞了。

zone [zon]
◀ Track 3171
名 地區、地帶、劃分地區
▶Would you please tell me what time zone you are in?
請您告訴我你在哪個時區好嗎？

萬用延伸句型
zone out 注意力不集中、不專心
例如：You have to stop zoning out in class.
你不能老是在上課的時候不專心。

Level 1
Level 2
Level 3
駕輕就熟、更上一層樓——累積實力3200單字
Level 4
Level 5
Level 6

377

下面有四篇文章，全是根據 Level1-3 的單字寫出來的，文章中超出 level3 的單字，有註記在一旁。

請先不要看全文的中文翻譯，試著讀讀看這四篇文章，若能全盤了解意思，代表你對 Level3 單字已經駕輕就熟，可以升級到 Level4 囉！快來自我挑戰看看吧！

Reading Practice 1

A group of researchers have shown that pleasure and positive states of mind are better for our health. This new approach to health is not only more powerful, but also has no side effects.

Central to this claim are recent findings that even getting an education may add as much as ten years to you lifespan（壽命）. National Geographic featured John de Rosen in the book *The Incredible Medicine*, which discussed old age. De Rosen, an artist, continued to paint until the week he passed away at age 91. The book notes: "Some scientists believe that retirement（退休）to an inactive life man cause or worsen medical problems, thus shortening life. According to a study of retired people, adults over 65 can learn a creative skill, like oil painting, as rapidly as younger students." So, retiring form a job in a sense means retiring from life unless one adds some new and interesting activities to his life.

Reading Practice 2

Stonehenge is an ancient monument situated about ten miles north of Salisbury（索爾茲柏里）in England. It was built about 4500 years ago, but by whom and for what purpose remains a mystery. The builders must have known geometry（幾何學）. They may have been influenced by the Mycenaeans（邁錫尼文明）, whose building techniques was similar. Some of the stone must have been brought from West Wales, over 135 miles away. These stones weigh more than fifty tons. They may have been brought on rafts and rollers. Experts say that it must have taken more than one thousand workers more than five years to transport them.

Stonehenge was probably built in three stages. First, new comers from Europe built a temple for showing respect to the sun. Later, the "Beaker" people （貝爾陶器文化）added the stone circles. Finally, people of the Wessex Culture changed Stonehenge into an observatory. They could observe exact time of Midsummer and Midwinter.

Reading Practice 3

Stress means pressure, or an intense state of mind. It is one of the most common cause of health problem in modern life.

There are a number of physical effects of stress. Stress can affect the heart. It can increase the pulse rate, make the heart miss beats, and can cause high blood pressure. Stress can affect the respiratory （呼吸）system. It can lead to asthma （氣喘症）. It can cause a person to breathe too fast. Also, it can affect the stomach. It can cause stomach aches and lead to problem in digesting food.

Emotions are also easily affected by stress. People suffering from stress often feel worried. They may have panic attacks. They often overact to little problems. Long-term stress can lead to a variety of serious mental illnesses. Extreme feeling of sadness and hopelessness can be the result of continued and increasing stress. It may put one's mental health at risk.

So, in order to avoid mental illness, we have to reduce stress, which may affect out life. Try to relax a little, and the effect may be obvious.

Reading Practice 4

There are a lot of benefits to using renewable energy. First, naturally generated energy resources are found over wide geographical areas. On the other hand, non-renewable resources, such as crude oil and coal, only exist in a limited number of countries. In addition to that, mass deployment （應用）of renewable energy and increased energy efficiency may result in significant energy security, climate change mitigation （減緩）, and economic benefits. Recent studies concluded that as carbon dioxide emitters begin to be considered responsible for damages resulting from greenhouse gas emission, people are more motivated to develop renewable energy technologies.

Level 1

Level 2

Level 3

累積實力3200單字 駕輕就熟、更上一層樓──

Level 4

Level 5

Level 6

Eco-friendly energy systems are rapidly becoming more efficient and cheaper. Their share of total energy consumption（消耗）is increasing. Growth in consumption of coal and oil could end by 2020 due to increased uptake of solar power and wind power.

Reading Practice1 中譯

　　有一群研究者指出，樂趣與正向的心態較有益於我們的健康。這種新健康秘訣不僅很有效，而且無副作用。

　　在這項聲明中很重要的一點是，即使是受教育也可以使你壽命延長十年。國家地理雜誌在《神奇之藥》這本書中特別提到約翰・胡笙，一位持續作畫到他在 92 歲過世當週的藝術家。這本書提到：「有些科學家相信，退休後缺少活動的生活，會導致或者惡化一些疾病狀況，導致壽命簡短」。根據一項針對退休人員的研究，65 歲以上的人，學習油畫這類的創意技巧，可以和年輕學生一樣快。所以，工作退休後，就像人生也玩完了一樣—除非有增加新的有趣事來調劑生活。

Reading Practice2 中譯

　　巨石陣是一個古代的紀念碑，位於英格蘭的索爾伯里茲郡北方十英里處。它建造於 4500 年前，但是由誰、為何而建仍然是個謎。建造者應該是熟知幾何學。他們可能是受到邁錫尼文化的影響，因為建築的技術很相似。這些石頭重量超過五十噸。它們可能是利用木筏或滾輪運送到這裡的。專家說至少需要一千五百名勞工、花超過五年時間，才能搬運這些石頭。

　　巨石陣可能經過三個階段。首先，歐洲的外來者建造像太陽神致敬的廟。後來，貝爾陶器文化時期的人增加了石圈。最後，威賽克斯文化把巨石陣改造成觀測台。他們可以觀察仲夏和冬至的確切時間。

Level
1

Level
2

Level
3

Level
4

Level
5

Level
6

Reading Practice3 中譯

壓力代表一種心理緊繃的狀態。它是現代社會中最常見的一種壓力來源。壓力會影響心臟。它會增加脈搏的速度，使心律不整，也會造成高血壓。壓力會影響呼吸系統。它可能引發氣喘症，導致一個人呼吸過快。此外，它可能會影響胃。它可能會導致胃痛，引起消化的問題。

情緒也容易受到壓力影響。有壓力的人可能會時常感到擔心。他們可能會恐慌發作。他們常對小問題過度反應。長期壓力可能會導致各種嚴重的心理疾病。持續的壓力可能帶來極端的感傷或者無助感。可能對心理健康造成風險。

因此，為了避免心理疾病，我們必須減少會影響生活的壓力。試著放鬆一點，效果會很明顯。

Reading Practice4 中譯

使用可更新能源有很多好處。首先，自然產生的能源在很多地理區域都可以找到。另一方面，像石油和煤炭這種非可更新資源，只存在特定的一些國家而已。此外，大量應用可更新資源、以及增加能量效率，可以帶來更好的資源效率，減緩氣候變遷、以及經濟的利益。最近研究指出，因為人們開始了解到二氧化碳排放者需要為溫室氣體排放造成的損失負責，會更有動力發展可更新資源的科技。

環保能源系統快速變得更有效且便宜。它們提供的能源，在總能源消耗量中的比例也越來越高。到 2020 年，煤炭和石油的消耗，就有希望會因為太陽能以及風力發電而停止成長了。

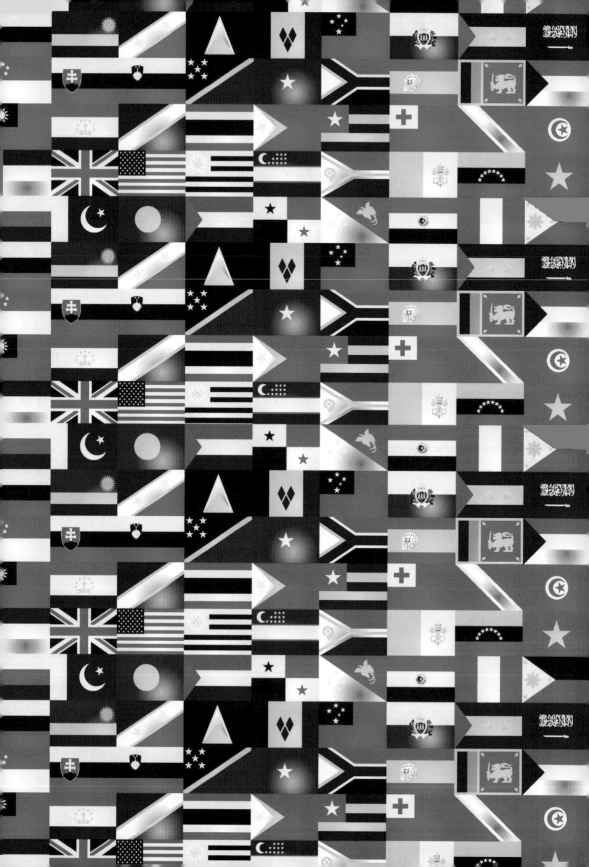

Level 4

自我勉勵、越背越上手——
提升程度4200單字

Level 4

自我勉勵、越背越上手——
提升程度4200單字

[Aa]

a·ban·don [ə`bændən]
🔊 Track 3172

動 放棄 同 desert 遺棄
▶He abandoned his family and joined the rebel army.
他拋棄家庭，加入了軍隊。

ab·do·men [`æbdəmən]
🔊 Track 3173

名 腹部
▶He felt a great deal of pain in his abdomen.
他感到腹部非常痛。

ab·so·lute [`æbsəlut]
🔊 Track 3174

形 絕對的 同 complete 絕對的
▶You should know that there is no absolute standard for it.
你應該知道這件事情沒有絕對的標準。

ab·sorb [əb`sɔrb]
🔊 Track 3175

動 吸收
▶The sponge can absorb most of the moisture in the container.
海綿可以吸收容器裡大部分的水分。

ab·stract [`æbstrækt]
🔊 Track 3176

形 抽象的 反 concrete 具體的
▶I wish I could understand such an abstract concept.
真希望我能理解如此抽象的概念。

> 萬用延伸句型
> I wish I could... 真希望我可以……

ac·a·dem·ic [ˏækə`dɛmɪk]
🔊 Track 3177

形 學院的、大學的
▶This professor put emphasis on the academic significance of the essays. 教授很重視報告的學術重要性。

ac·cent [`æksɛnt]
🔊 Track 3178

名 口音、腔調
▶It is obvious that she is Irish, because she speaks with an Irish accent.
顯然她是個愛爾蘭人，因為她說話帶有愛爾蘭口音。

> 萬用延伸句型
> It's obvious that... 很明顯地……

ac·cep·tance [ək`sɛptəns]
🔊 Track 3179

名 接受
▶This kind of view has not received wide acceptance yet.
這種觀點還沒有得到廣泛的認可。

ac·cess [ˈæksɛs]
🔊 Track 3180

名 接近、會面　動 接近、會面

▶名 I can't have access to the database.
我無法取用資料庫資訊。

▶動 Not everyone in the company has the right to access the secret file.
不是公司裡的每個人都有權利取出這個秘密檔案。

ac·ci·den·tal [ˌæksəˈdɛntl]
🔊 Track 3181

形 偶然的、意外的

▶Running into her in that coffee shop was purely（純粹地） accidental. 在那家咖啡店遇到她是純粹出於偶然。

萬用延伸句型
run into... 意外遇上（某人）

ac·com·pa·ny [əˈkʌmpənɪ]
🔊 Track 3182

動 隨行、陪伴、伴隨

▶Lightning usually accompanies thunder. 閃電通常伴隨著雷聲。

ac·com·plish [əˈkɑmplɪʃ]
🔊 Track 3183

動 達成、完成　同 finish 完成

▶I'm afraid that it's too difficult for me to accomplish the task alone. 要我獨自完成這項任務恐怕很難。

ac·com·plish·ment [əˈkɑmplɪmənt]
🔊 Track 3184

名 達成、成就

▶When you finish the oil painting, you can have great sense of achievement.
當你完成一幅油畫，你會有很大的成就感。

ac·coun·tant [əˈkaʊntənt]
🔊 Track 3185

名 會計師

▶Would you please help me find a good accountant?
你能幫我找個好的會計師嗎？

ac·cu·ra·cy [ˈækjərəsɪ]
🔊 Track 3186

名 正確、精密

▶It is impossible to say with any accuracy how many people are affected. 不可能準確說出到底有多少人受影響。

ac·cuse [əˈkjuz]
🔊 Track 3187

動 控告　同 denounce 控告

▶Once we have gathered enough proof, we can accuse him at the court.
一旦收集到足夠的證據，我們就可以在法庭上控告他了。

萬用延伸句型
accuse sb. of sth. 指控（某人）做了某事
例如：His neighbors accused him of theft.
他的鄰居指控他偷竊。

ac·id [ˈæsɪd]
🔊 Track 3188

名 酸性物質　形 酸的

▶名 The acid rain may cause harm to human health.
酸雨可能導致人類健康受損。

▶形 No one likes to hear your acid words.
沒有人喜歡聽你尖酸刻薄的話。

Level 1
Level 2
Level 3
Level 4
自我勉勵、越背越上手——提升程度4200單字
Level 5
Level 6

ac·quaint [ə`kwent]　🔊 *Track 3189*

動 使熟悉、告知
▶It will take you some time to acquaint yourself with a new job.
要熟悉一項新的工作是需要一些時間的。

ac·quain·tance [ə`kwentəns]　🔊 *Track 3190*

名 認識的人、熟人　同 companion 同伴
▶The woman was just a nodding acquaintance of mine.
那個女人士有見過面、認識的人而已。

ac·quire [ə`kwaɪr]　🔊 *Track 3191*

動 取得、獲得　同 obtain 獲得
▶Would you please tell me how he acquired his wealth?
請你告訴我他的財富是怎樣得來的?

a·cre [`ekə]　🔊 *Track 3192*

名 英畝
▶We own more than 100 acres of farmland. What about you?
我們擁有超過一百英畝的農田,你們呢?

a·dapt [ə`dæpt]　🔊 *Track 3193*

動 使適應
▶I'm afraid that she can't adapt herself quickly to the new climate.
恐怕她無法很快適應這種新氣候。

ad·e·quate [`ædəkwɪt]　🔊 *Track 3194*

形 適當的、足夠的　同 enough 足夠的
▶We don't have adequate information about the new project.
我們沒有關於新計畫的足夠資訊。

ad·jec·tive [`ædʒɪktɪv]　🔊 *Track 3195*

名 形容詞
▶An adjective is used to describe or add to the meaning of a noun. 形容詞的功能是用來描述或增加名詞的意思。

ad·just [ə`dʒʌst]　🔊 *Track 3196*

動 調節、對準
▶Not all people can adjust themselves to the busy modern life in big cities. 不是所有人都能適應大都市忙碌的現代生活。

ad·just·ment [ə`dʒʌstmənt]　🔊 *Track 3197*

名 調整、調節
▶The company made an adjustment in my salary.
公司對我的薪資作了調整。

ad·mi·ra·ble [`ædmərəbl̩]　🔊 *Track 3198*

形 令人欽佩的
▶The deeds of the admirable woman will always be remembered by the local people.
那位受尊敬女士的善行,會永遠被當地人記住。

文法字詞解析
a nodding acquaintance = 點頭之交

文法字詞解析
其實 admirable 這個字就是由 admire (欣賞)加上意為「可以、能夠」的字尾「-able」變成的。

ad·mi·ra·tion [ˌædməˈreʃən] ◀︎ Track 3199
名 欽佩、讚賞
▶He has a lot of admiration for his classmate.
他非常欣賞他的同學。

ad·mis·sion [ədˈmɪʃən] ◀︎ Track 3200
名 准許進入、入場費
▶We were granted the admission to meet the Queen.
我們獲准謁見皇后。

ad·verb [ˈædvɚb] ◀︎ Track 3201
名 副詞
▶Don't you know that adverbs are used to modify（修飾）
verbs and adjectives?
副詞是用來修飾動詞和形容詞的，難道你不知道嗎？

a·gen·cy [ˈedʒənsɪ] ◀︎ Track 3202
名 代理商
▶My company's got many agencies in major cities of the country.
我的公司在國內主要城市有很多家代理機構。

a·gent [ˈedʒənt] ◀︎ Track 3203
名 代理人
▶The real estate agent introduced the property for us.
房地產仲介向我們介紹這棟房產。

ag·gres·sive [əˈgrɛsɪv] ◀︎ Track 3204
形 侵略的、攻擊的
▶A good salesman must be aggressive if he wants to succeed.
要做個好推銷員一定要有衝勁才能成功。

a·gree·a·ble [əˈgriəbl] ◀︎ Track 3205
形 令人愉快的
▶She's a very agreeable girl so people like to talk to her.
她是個很好講話的女孩子，所以大家都喜歡跟她講話。

AIDS/ac·quired ◀︎ Track 3206
im·mune de·fi·ciensy syn·drome
[edz]/[əˈkwaɪrd ɪˈmjun dɪˈfɪʃənsɪ ˈsɪnˌdrom]
名 愛滋病
▶As of now, we still haven't found a cure to AIDS.
直到現在，我們還是沒有發現愛滋病的治療方式。

al·co·hol [ˈælkəˌhɔl] ◀︎ Track 3207
名 酒精
▶Those who are addicted to alcohol may suffer from liver
diseases.
酒精成癮的人可能會有肝臟的疾病。

萬用延伸句型
Don't you know that...? 你不知道……嗎？
這個句型頗有把對方當笨蛋的味道，所以如果你不想惹到人，最好避免使用。

Level 1

Level 2

Level 3

Level 4

自我勉勵、越背越上手——提升程度4200單字

Level 5

Level 6

a·lert [əˋlɝt]
Track 3208

名 警報 形 機警的

▶名 The dog sat in front of the house, on alert.
那隻狗機警地坐在房門口。

▶形 You left your door open again? You really need to be more alert. 你又忘記關門？你真的應該更機警一點。

al·low·ance/ pock·et mon·ey [əˋlaʊəns]/[ˋpakɪtˋmʌnɪ]
Track 3209

名 津貼、補助

▶The elderly citizens were worried that their retirement allowance may be canceled.
老年人擔心他們的退休零用金會被取消。

a·lu·mi·num [əˋlumɪnəm]
Track 3210

名 鋁

▶There are a great many cooking utensils（器具）made of aluminum now. 現在有相當多的炊具都是鋁製的。

a.m. [ˋeˋɛm]
Track 3211

副 上午

▶How about meeting at ten a.m. next Sunday?
我們下星期日早上十點見面好不好？

am·a·teur [ˋæmətʃʊr]
Track 3212

名 業餘愛好者 形 業餘的
反 professional 專業的

▶名 Julia is an amateur photographer, and she is specialized in taking photos of wild animals.
茱莉亞是一位業餘攝影師，她專門拍攝野生動物照片。

▶形 The pictures can be taken by not only professional photographers but also amateur photographers.
這些照片不但專業攝影師能拍，業餘攝影師也能拍得出來。

am·bi·tious [æmˋbɪʃəs]
Track 3213

形 有野心的

▶The ambitious man is always looking for ways to beat his opponents.
這個充滿野心的人總是在尋找擊敗對手的方法。

a·mid/a·midst [əˋmɪd]/[əˋmɪdst]
Track 3214

連 在……之中

▶Not all people can stand firm amid temptations（誘惑）.
不是所有人都能夠禁得住各種誘惑。

a·muse [əˋmjuz]
Track 3215

動 娛樂、消遣

▶It was too rainy to play outside, so she amused herself with a book.
雨太大不適合在外面玩，所以她看書消遣。

文法字詞解析

這個單字說成 aluminum（美式）和 aluminium（英式）都可以，兩者差一個 i。

a·muse·ment [ə`mjuzmənt] 🔊 *Track 3216*

名 娛樂、有趣
▶To our amusement, the toddler imitated his father in an exaggerated way.
　小朋友誇張方式模仿他爸爸講話，逗得我們很開心。

a·nal·y·sis [ə`næləsɪs] 🔊 *Track 3217*

名 分析
▶His analysis of the problem shows great insight（洞察力）.
　他對該問題的分析顯示出敏銳的洞察力。

an·a·lyze [`ænḷaɪz] 🔊 *Track 3218*

動 分析、解析
▶Would you analyze the structure of the sentence for me?
　你能幫我分析一下這個句子的結構嗎？

an·ces·tor [`ænsɛstɚ] 🔊 *Track 3219*

名 祖先、祖宗
▶It is said that our ancestor crossed the ocean and cultivated the new continent.
　據說我們的祖先橫渡海洋，開墾了新大陸。

文法字詞解析
ancestor 指的是單一的祖先（例如你的曾曾曾祖父就算是一個 ancestor），而要統稱全體的「家族史」則可以說 ancestry。

an·ni·ver·sa·ry [ˌænə`vɝsərɪ] 🔊 *Track 3220*

名 周年紀念日
▶Don't you remember that next Monday is the anniversary of when we first met?
　你還記得嗎？下週一是我們相遇的週年紀念日。

an·noy [ə`nɔɪ] 🔊 *Track 3221*

動 煩擾、使惱怒 同 irritate 使惱怒
▶He was annoyed by the mosquitoes（蚊子）.
　那些蚊子讓他覺得很煩。

an·nu·al [`ænjʊəl] 🔊 *Track 3222*

形 一年的、年度的
▶Jenny reminded her father to have the annual health checkup.
　珍妮提醒他的父親要去做年度健康檢查。

anx·i·e·ty [æŋ`zaɪətɪ] 🔊 *Track 3223*

名 憂慮、不安、渴望
▶She paced around the room in anxiety. 她焦慮地繞著房間走。

文法字詞解析
焦慮症發作叫做 anxiety attack。

anx·ious [`æŋkʃəs] 🔊 *Track 3224*

形 憂心的、擔憂的
▶We are anxious to ensure that there is no misunderstanding（誤解）between us. 我們急於確保我們之間沒有誤解。

a·pol·o·gize [ə`pɑləˌdʒaɪz] 🔊 *Track 3225*

動 道歉、認錯
▶It is too late to apologize for the mistake.
　現在為錯誤道歉太遲了。

Level 1

Level 2

Level 3

Level 4

自我勉勵、越背越上手——
提升程度4200單字

Level 5

Level 6

389

a·pol·o·gy [əˋpɑlədʒɪ]　　🔊 *Track 3226*

名 謝罪、道歉

▶ I owe you an apology for what I did last night; I hope you can forgive me.
我為昨天晚上的事向你道歉，希望你能夠原諒我。

ap·pli·ance [əˋplaɪəns]　　🔊 *Track 3227*

名 器具、家電用品

▶ There household appliances were displayed on the fourth floor.
家用電器在四樓展售。

ap·pli·cant [ˋæpləkənt]　　🔊 *Track 3228*

名 申請人、應徵者

▶ It is no wonder that there were few applicants for the job.
難怪沒有什麼人申請這份工作。

ap·pli·ca·tion [æpləˋkeʃən]　　🔊 *Track 3229*

名 應用、申請

▶ His application to the school was rejected.
他申請這所學校被拒。

文法字詞解析
大家常下載的「app」就是「application」的簡單說法，指的是「應用程式」。

ap·point [əˋpɔɪnt]　　🔊 *Track 3230*

動 任命、約定、指派、任用

▶ He appointed her as his doctor. 他指名她為他看病。

ap·point·ment [əˋpɔɪntmənt]　　🔊 *Track 3231*

名 指定、約定、指派、任用

▶ I was told that I can't meet the diplomat without an appointment. 我被告知說，沒有預約不能去見外交官。

ap·pre·ci·a·tion [əͺpriʃɪˋeʃən]　　🔊 *Track 3232*

名 賞識、鑑識

▶ I have a lot of appreciation for people who are considerate（體貼）. 我很欣賞待人體貼的人。

ap·pro·pri·ate [əˋproprɪɪt]　　🔊 *Track 3233*

形 適當的、適切的　同 proper 適當的

▶ Why don't you get a dress appropriate for the occasion?
為什麼不買一件適合該場合穿的洋裝呢？

文法字詞解析
appropriate 的相反詞是 inappropriate，即「不適當的」。

ap·prov·al [əˋpruvl]　　🔊 *Track 3234*

名 承認、同意

▶ Without his approval, I can not proceed to carry out the plan.
沒有他的同意，我無法繼續進行這項計畫。

arch [ɑrtʃ]　　🔊 *Track 3235*

名 拱門、拱形　動 變成弓形

▶ 名 It is a pity that I have never been to the Triumphal（凱旋的）Arch. 我從來沒去過凱旋門，真是遺憾。

▶ 動 He arched his eyebrows when he saw my report card.
他看到我的成績單時，挑了挑眉。

a·rise [əˈraɪz]
◀€ *Track 3236*

動 出現、發生

▶When obstacles arise, you may want to change your goals.
當障礙出現，你可能會想改變目標。

arms [ɑrmz]
◀€ *Track 3237*

名 武器、兵器

▶The company is a manufacturer（製造者）of arms.
那個公司是武器製造商。

a·rouse [əˈraʊz]
◀€ *Track 3238*

動 喚醒

▶The notice aroused anger among customers.
那個公告激起了消費者的公憤。

ar·ti·cle [ˈɑrtɪkl̩]
◀€ *Track 3239*

名 論文、物件

▶Could you tell me what do you think of the article?
你能不能告訴我，你認為這篇文章怎麼樣？

artificial [ˌɑrtəˈfɪʃəl]
◀€ *Track 3240*

形 人工的

▶There are some artificial flowers on the table; do you like them? 桌上放著一些假花，你喜歡它們嗎？

ar·tis·tic [ɑrˈtɪstɪk]
◀€ *Track 3241*

形 藝術的、美術的

▶The interior design of her room is very artistic.
她房間的室內設計非常有藝術水準。

a·shamed [əˈʃemd]
◀€ *Track 3242*

形 以……為恥

▶I am too ashamed to confess that I was involved in that scandal.
我覺得太丟臉，不敢承認我有涉及這樁醜聞。

as·pect [ˈæspɛkt]
◀€ *Track 3243*

名 方面、外貌、外觀

▶We can look at this problem from several aspects.
我們可以從幾個不同的面向探討這個問題。

as·pi·rin [ˈæspərɪn]
◀€ *Track 3244*

名 （藥）阿斯匹靈

▶If you have a headache, why don't you take an aspirin?
既然你頭疼，為什麼不吃一片阿斯匹靈呢？

as·sem·ble [əˈsɛmbl̩]
◀€ *Track 3245*

動 聚集、集合

▶More than a thousand people assembled in the plaza for the firework show.
超過一千人聚集在廣場看煙火秀。

文法字詞解析

arise 的動詞變化：arise, arose, arisen

萬用延伸句型

nothing to be ashamed of 沒什麼好丟臉的

例如：You forgot to wear a bra today? So what? That's nothing to be ashamed of.
你今天忘記穿胸罩喔？那又怎樣？沒什麼好丟臉的。

Level 1

Level 2

Level 3

Level 4

自我勉勵、越背越上手——提升程度4200單字

Level 5

Level 6

as·sem·bly [əˋsɛmblɪ] ◀€ *Track 3246*

名 集會、集合、會議
▶Not all citizens have the rights of assembly and expression in that country.
在那個國家不是所有公民都有集會和發表言論的權利。

as·sign [əˋsaɪn] ◀€ *Track 3247*

動 分派、指定
▶I was assigned to take care of the seriously-ill patient.
我被指派要去照顧重症病患。

as·sign·ment [əˋsaɪnmənt] ◀€ *Track 3248*

名 分派、任命
▶Would you like to tell me how you are going to finish the assignment?
能告訴我你將如何完成作業嗎？

as·sist·ance [əˋsɪstəns] ◀€ *Track 3249*

名 幫助、援助
▶It's too hard for me to move this piano without assistance.
沒有人幫忙的話，我很難挪動這架鋼琴。

as·so·ci·ate [əˋsoʃɪt]/[əˋsoʃɪ,et] ◀€ *Track 3250*

名 同事 動 聯合
▶名 Not every associate in our company is friendly to me.
在我們公司，不是每一位同事都對我很友善。
▶動 Not every woman associates happiness with having money.
不是每個女人都把幸福和有錢聯想在一起。

as·so·ci·a·tion [ə,sosɪˋeʃən] ◀€ *Track 3251*

名 協會、聯合會
▶Would you tell me what association you have with the color green? 能否告訴我綠色會使你產生什麼聯想？

as·sume [əˋsum] ◀€ *Track 3252*

動 假定、擔任
▶The prince assumed power when he was only fifteen.
那個王子在十五歲時就掌權了。

as·sur·ance [əˋʃurəns] ◀€ *Track 3253*

名 保證、保險 同 insurance 保險
▶His assurance that the program is effective was not trustworthy.
他保證的這個程式有用的話一點都不值得信任。

as·sure [əˋʃur] ◀€ *Track 3254*

動 向……保證、使確信 同 guarantee 向……保證
▶I can assure you that you will get the best bargain in our shop.
我向你保證在這間店買東西價錢是最划算的。

文法字詞解析

除了工作上的「任務」之外，assignment 也能指學生的「回家作業」。

萬用延伸句型

I assure you... 我向你保證……
例如：I assure you that everything is under control.
我向你保證，一切都在掌握之中。

ath·let·ic [æθˈlɛtɪk]
🔊 *Track 3255*

形 運動的、強健的

▶The athletic girl can play badminton, soccer, and basketball well. 這個擅長運動的女孩會打羽球、踢足球，還有打籃球。

ATM/au·to·mat·ic tell·er ma·chine [ˌɔtəˈmætɪk ˈtɛlə məˈʃin]
🔊 *Track 3256*

名 自動櫃員機

▶I'm surprised that you've never used an ATM before. 我很驚訝，你居然沒用過自動提款機。

at·mos·phere [ˈætməsˌfɪr]
🔊 *Track 3257*

名 大氣、氣氛

▶There is an atmosphere of peace and calm in the country. 在鄉間有一種和平寧靜的氣氛。

at·om [ˈætəm]
🔊 *Track 3258*

名 原子

▶I read that we're all made of atoms. 我在書上讀到，我們都是原子做的。

a·tom·ic [əˈtɑmɪk]
🔊 *Track 3259*

形 原子的

▶The Second World War was when the atomic bomb was first used. 在第二次世界大戰中，第一次使用了原子彈。

at·tach [əˈtætʃ]
🔊 *Track 3260*

動 連接、附屬、附加

▶You shouldn't attach all the blame to the taxi-driver. 你不應該把全部責任都歸咎於計程車司機。

at·tach·ment [əˈtætʃmənt]
🔊 *Track 3261*

名 連接、附著

▶Please find the attachment of the email for the detailed catalogue of our product. 請看電子郵件附件檔案，有我們產品的詳細目錄。

at·trac·tion [əˈtrækʃən]
🔊 *Track 3262*

名 魅力、吸引力

▶Would you like to tell me what the best attraction in New York is? 你能不能告訴我紐約最具吸引力的是什麼？

au·di·o [ˈɔdɪo]
🔊 *Track 3263*

名 聲音

▶First of all, let's have a look at our audio-visual classroom. 首先，讓我們看一下視聽教室吧。

au·thor·i·ty [əˈθɔrətɪ]
🔊 *Track 3264*

名 權威、當局

▶The authorities were expected to solve the problem of power shortage. 當局被期待要解決電力短缺的問題。

文法字詞解析

ATM這個縮寫除了拿來表示「自動櫃員機」，同時在網路用語中也可以當作「at the moment」（現在）的縮寫。通常只用於線上傳訊息、留言時，口語中不會出現。
例如：Give me a sec, I'm all tied up atm. 等一下，我現在超忙的。

文法字詞解析

除了表示郵件的「附件」等實際上的附加物，也可表示心理上的「依附感」。例如若你新養了一條狗，狗漸漸開始對你有好感，就可以說 The dog is forming an attachment with me.

Level 1

Level 2

Level 3

Level 4

提升程度4200單字 — 自我勉勵、越背越上手

Level 5

Level 6

393

au·to·bi·og·ra·phy
[ˌɔtəbaɪˋɑgrəfɪ]
Track 3265

名 自傳

▶The autobiography of Nelson Mandela was adapted into a movie. 曼德拉的自傳被改編成一部電影。

文法字詞解析
biography（傳記）加上代表了「自動、自己」的字首「auto-」，就變成了「自傳」的意思。

a·wait [əˋwet]
Track 3266

動 等待

▶Do you know what delights（快樂的事） await you there?
你知道那裡有什麼快樂的事在等著你嗎？

awk·ward [ˋɔkwəd]
Track 3267

形 笨拙的、不熟練的

▶I felt very awkward and out of place at the formal ball.
在那個正式的舞會上，我感到局促不安，很不自在。

[Bb]

back·pack [ˋbækˌpæk]
Track 3268

名 背包 動 背負簡便行李旅行

▶名 The backpack of the youngster was filled with souvenirs from the local people.
年輕人的背包裡裝滿了當地人送他的紀念品。

▶動 They backpacked through the countryside.
他們在鄉間當背包客。

文法字詞解析
「背包客（backpacker）」就是「backpack」這個字加上「-er」結尾而組成的。

bald [bɔld]
Track 3269

形 禿頭的、禿的

▶Don't you think the bald eagle looks scary?
你不覺得禿鷹看起來很可怕嗎？

bal·let [ˋbæle]
Track 3270

名 芭蕾

▶Can you tell me how long you have been learning ballet up to now? 你能告訴我你目前為止學了多久的芭蕾嗎？

bank·rupt [ˋbæŋkrʌpt]
Track 3271

名 破產者 形 破產的

▶名 His property was all confiscated, and he became a bankrupt.
他的財產都被沒收了，他宣告破產。

▶形 The factory in the village went bankrupt last month.
上個月村子裡的那間工廠倒閉了。

bar·gain [ˋbɑrgɪn]
Track 3272

名 協議、成交 動 討價還價

▶名 What a bargain! This beautiful dress cost me only two dollars.
真是太划算了！這件漂亮的洋裝只花了我兩美元。

▶動 We refuse to bargain over the price.
我們拒絕在價格上討價還價。

萬用延伸句型
What a bargain! 真便宜！

bar·ri·er [ˈbærɪɚ]
◀€ Track 3273

名 障礙
▶Language barrier was the major cause that caused the misunderstanding. 語言障礙是導致誤會的主要原因。

ba·sin [ˈbesṇ]
◀€ Track 3274

名 盆、水盆
▶The baby is sitting in the basin. 那個寶寶正坐在水盆裡。

bat·ter·y [ˈbætərɪ]
◀€ Track 3275

名 電池
▶Don't forget to charge the battery at night.
別忘了晚上要幫電池充電。

beak [bik]
◀€ Track 3276

名 鳥嘴
▶The bird on the balcony has a worm in its beak.
陽臺上的那隻鳥嘴裡叼著一隻蟲子。

beam [bim]
◀€ Track 3277

名 光線、容光煥發、樑 動 照耀、微笑
▶名 I can see a beam of light in the cave.
我能在洞穴裡看見一束光線。
▶動 She beamed with joy when she saw her son.
她看到她兒子時面露喜色。

be·hav·ior [bɪˈhevjɚ]
◀€ Track 3278

名 舉止、行為 同 action 行為
▶Shouldn't you be ashamed of your foolish behavior?
難道你不該對你自己的愚蠢行為感到羞恥嗎？

bi·og·ra·phy [baɪˈɑgrəfɪ]
◀€ Track 3279

名 傳記
▶The writer collected stories of Steve Jobs and compiled his biography. 作者收集賈伯斯的故事，撰寫他的傳記。

bi·ol·o·gy [baɪˈɑlədʒɪ]
◀€ Track 3280

名 生物學
▶Bob has been bad at biology in school all these years.
這些年鮑伯在學校生物一直都學得不好。

blade [bled]
◀€ Track 3281

名 刀鋒
▶The man licked the blood from the blade.
那個男人舔掉了刀刃上的血。

blend [blɛnd]
◀€ Track 3282

名 混合 動 使混合、使交融
▶名 I love this blend of strawberry and mango juice.
我喜歡這個草莓和芒果汁的混合飲料。
▶動 The new building does not blend in with its surroundings.
新的建築無法融合在周圍景物中。

文法字詞解析

不是所有的「光線」都可以稱為 beam 喔！beam 有「樑柱」的意思，因此當作「光線」時，指的就是像柱子這樣「一束」、「很集中」的光線。所以，在黑暗中用手電筒探照的「一束光」就可以稱 beam；走在無遮蔽的路上，太陽照下來，則不能稱為 beam（如果太陽集中成一束光照在你身上，應該會烤焦的）。

萬用延伸句型

...all these years 這些年來一直都……

Level 1
Level 2
Level 3
Level 4
提升程度4200單字
自我勉勵、越背越上手
Level 5
Level 6

bless·ing [ˈblɛsɪŋ]

◀≣ *Track 3283*

名 恩典、祝福

▶We sent her our blessings for her birthday.
我們為她的生日送上了祝福。

blink [blɪŋk]

◀≣ *Track 3284*

名 眨眼 動 使眨眼、閃爍

▶名 The pickpocket ran away and disappeared in the blink of an eye. 扒手跑走了，一眨眼的時間就消失。

▶動 She blinked when I opened the curtains.
我打開窗簾時她眨了眨眼睛。

文法字詞解析

blink-and-you-miss-it 形容只要一眨眼就會錯過，也就是出現的時間極為短暫，微不足道。
例如：He appeared in this commercial, but it was just a blink-and-you-miss-it role.
他有出演這個廣告，不過是個微不足道的小角色。

bloom [blum]

◀≣ *Track 3285*

名 開花期 動 開花

▶名 The daffodils（黃水仙花）are in full bloom now.
水仙花現在正盛開著。

▶動 Will you tell me when these plants bloom? In spring or summer? 你能告訴我這些植物什麼時候開花嗎？是在春天還是夏天？

blos·som [ˈblɑsəm]

◀≣ *Track 3286*

名 花、花簇 動 開花、生長茂盛

▶名 The daffodils on the hill were in full blossom.
山坡上的水仙花盛開中。

▶動 The flowers are blossoming in our garden.
我們花園裡的花都盛開了。

blush [blʌʃ]

◀≣ *Track 3287*

名 羞愧、慚愧 動 臉紅

▶名 The topic brought a blush to her cheeks.
這個話題讓她羞得兩頰通紅。

▶動 She blushed when she saw her crush（暗戀的人）.
她看到暗戀的人時臉就紅了。

boast [bost]

◀≣ *Track 3288*

名 / 動 自誇

▶名 Just ignore his boasts. 別聽他自誇。

▶動 The man loves to boast about his achievements.
這個男人很愛自誇自己的成就。

bond [bɑnd]

◀≣ *Track 3289*

名 契約、束縛、抵押

▶The bond between us is hard to break.
我們之間的羈絆是難以打破的。

bounce [baʊns]

◀≣ *Track 3290*

名 彈、跳 動 彈回

▶名 My little son can't catch the ball on its first bounce.
我的小兒子在球第一次反彈時接不住球。

▶動 The kids are bouncing on the trampoline.
小孩在彈簧床上彈跳。

萬用延伸句型

bounce back 在遇到重大挫折或疾病後康復、重新振作起來。
例如：After going bankrupt, he bounced back surprisingly quickly.
他破產後，以驚人的速度重新崛起。

brace·let [ˈbreslɪt]
Track 3291

名 手鐲

▶The woman wearing a jade bracelet is my aunt.
那位戴著玉手鐲的女士是我的阿姨。

bras·siere/bra [brəˈzɪr]/[brɑ]
Track 3292

名 胸罩、內衣

▶I need to go shopping for a new bra. 我得去買新胸罩了。

breed [brid]
Track 3293

動 生育、繁殖 名 品種

▶動 The couple's job is breeding dogs. 這對夫妻的工作是繁殖狗。

▶名 What breed of dog do you think I'm most like?
你覺得我最像哪種狗？

文法字詞解析
breed 的動詞變化：breed, bred, bred

bride·groom/groom [ˈbraɪdˌgrum]/[grum]
Track 3294

名 新郎

▶Have you seen the bridegroom in the car today? What does
he look like? 你今天在車上看見新郎了嗎？他長什麼樣子呢？

broil [brɔɪl]
Track 3295

動 烤、炙

▶The chef broiled the salmon on the coal stove.
廚師用煤爐烤鮭魚。

broke [brok]
Track 3296

形 一無所有的、破產的

▶I can't lend you any money. I'm broke myself.
我沒辦法借你錢，我自己都破產了。

bru·tal [ˈbrutl]
Track 3297

形 野蠻的、殘暴的

▶I guess it's time to face the brutal reality.
看來是面對殘酷現實的時候了。

bul·le·tin [ˈbʊlətɪn]
Track 3298

名 公告、告示

▶Mandy posted her wedding invitation card on the bulletin board.
曼蒂將她的婚禮邀請函張貼在公布欄上。

[Cc]

cab·i·net [ˈkæbənɪt]
Track 3299

名 小櫥櫃、內閣

▶Would you please tell me how many cabinet members there
are? 您能告訴我到底有多少內閣成員嗎？

Level 1

Level 2

Level 3

Level 4

提升程度4200單字

自我勉勵、越背越上手

Level 5

Level 6

cal·cu·late [ˈkælkjəˌlet]
🔊 *Track 3300*

動 計算

▶I calculated the number of laborers we will need on the construction site.

我估算了工地需要的勞工人數。

---

cal·cu·la·tion [ˌkælkjəˈleʃən]
🔊 *Track 3301*

名 計算

▶Why didn't they announce the results at each stage of the calculation?

為什麼他們沒有公佈每個階段的計算結果呢？

---

cal·cu·la·tor [ˈkælkjəˌletɚ]
🔊 *Track 3302*

名 計算機

▶I don't think it's proper for you to give him a calculator as a present.

我覺得你送他一個計算機作為禮物不合適。

---

cal·o·rie [ˈkælərɪ]
🔊 *Track 3303*

名 卡、卡路里

▶She always checks the calories before eating anything.

她每次吃東西前都先看一下有多少卡路里。

---

cam·paign [kæmˈpen]
🔊 *Track 3304*

名 戰役、活動 **動** 作戰、從事活動

▶**名** The campaign for the election ended up successful.

那次競選活動結果很成功。

▶**動** We decided to campaign for better working conditions.

我們決定積極爭取改善工作條件。

---

can·di·date [ˈkændəˌdet]
🔊 *Track 3305*

名 候選人

▶Three candidates were running for the election campaign.

有三位候選人要參與競選。

---

ca·pac·i·ty [kəˈpæsətɪ]
🔊 *Track 3306*

名 容積、能力 **同** size 容量

▶I believe that the theater has a seating capacity of more than 800.

我相信這個劇場可容納超過八百名觀眾。

---

cape [kep]
🔊 *Track 3307*

名 岬、海角

▶Have you been to the cape in Kenting?

你去過墾丁那個海岬嗎？

---

cap·i·tal·(ism)
🔊 *Track 3308*

[ˈkæpət!]/[ˌkæpət!ˌɪzəm]

名 資本（資本主義）、首都

▶Some people mistake Mumbai as the capital of India.

有些人會誤以為孟買是印度首都。

文法字詞解析

如果在 calculate 的前面加上意為「誤……」的字首「mis-」，則會變成表示「誤算、計算錯誤」的單字 miscalculate。

文法字詞解析

cape也有「披風」的意思（就是超級英雄會穿的那種）。

cap·i·tal·ist [ˈkæpətḷɪst]
◀€ *Track 3309*

名 資本家

▶There is no such thing as a good capitalist.
所謂善良的資本家是不存在的。

ca·reer [kəˈrɪr]
◀€ *Track 3310*

名（終身的）職業、生涯

▶Tina takes teaching as a life-long career.
緹娜以教書作為一生職志。

car·go [ˈkɑrgo]
◀€ *Track 3311*

名 貨物、船貨

▶Could you tell me how long it will take for the cargoes to arrive?
你能告訴我貨物抵達要多久嗎？

car·ri·er [ˈkærɪɚ]
◀€ *Track 3312*

名 運送者

▶He works as a mail carrier.
他的工作是郵差。

carve [ˈkɑrv]
◀€ *Track 3313*

動 切、切成薄片

▶The sculptor carved the piece of wood into a statue of a fairy.
雕刻家將這塊木頭刻成一個仙子的造型。

cat·a·logue/ cat·a·log [ˈkætəlɔg]
◀€ *Track 3314*

名 目錄 動 編輯目錄 同 list 目錄

▶名 Please send me your current catalogue as soon as possible.
請將你現有的目錄盡快寄給我。

▶動 Please ask someone to catalogue the new books as soon as possible.
請盡快請人把新書編成目錄吧。

cease [sis]
◀€ *Track 3315*

名 停息 動 終止、停止

▶名 I don't think that the temporary（暫時的）cease of war means permanent peace.
我認為暫時的停火並不意味著永久的和平。

▶動 TThe teenager was asked to cease spread rumors on the Internet.
青少年被要求停止在網路上散布謠言。

cel·e·bra·tion [ˌsɛləˈbreʃən]
◀€ *Track 3316*

名 慶祝、慶祝典禮

▶I suppose we shall be having some sort of celebration for the bride.
我想我們大概會為新娘慶賀一番吧。

文法字詞解析

carve 不只可以用在「切肉」、「切水果」等等美食方面，也可以在藝術方面用來表示「雕刻」，例如木雕就可以稱為 wood carving。

Level 1

Level 2

Level 3

Level 4

Level 5

Level 6

提升程度4200單字

自我勉勵、越背越上手

abcdefghijklmnopqrstuvwxyz

ce·ment [sə`mɛnt] ◀≲ *Track 3317*

名 水泥 動 用水泥砌合、強固

▶名 The cement was used to mend the cracks in the wall.
水泥被用來修補牆上的裂縫。

▶動 The broken bowl was cemented with glue.
這個破碗是用膠水黏合起來的。

CD/com·pac disk ◀≲ *Track 3318*

[`si`di]/[`kɑmpækt dɪsk]

名 光碟

▶Do you mind if I bring this CD home?
你介不介意我帶著這張 CD 回家？

cham·ber [`tʃembə] ◀≲ *Track 3319*

名 房間、寢室 同 room 房間

▶The prisoners were kept in a narrow chamber.
囚犯們都被關在一個狹小的房間裡。

cham·pion·ship [`tʃæmpiənʃɪp] ◀≲ *Track 3320*

名 冠軍賽

▶Zoe won the championship in the speech contest.
柔伊在演講比賽中贏得冠軍。

char·ac·ter·is·tic ◀≲ *Track 3321*

[ˌkærɪktə`rɪstɪk]

名 特徵 形 有特色的

▶名 The curly hair is a distinguishing（有區別的）characteristic
of this type of dog. 捲毛是這種狗與眾不同的一個特徵。

▶形 Indecision is characteristic of him. 優柔寡斷是他的特徵。

char·i·ty [`tʃærətɪ] ◀≲ *Track 3322*

名 慈悲、慈善、寬容 同 generosity 寬宏大量

▶There are many people regularly giving money to charity.
有很多人經常為慈善事業捐款。

chem·is·try [`kɛmɪstrɪ] ◀≲ *Track 3323*

名 化學

▶I prefer chemistry to physics; what about you?
我喜歡化學甚於物理，你呢？

cher·ish [`tʃɛrɪʃ] ◀≲ *Track 3324*

動 珍愛、珍惜

▶To save water is to cherish life. 節約用水就是珍惜生命。

chirp [tʃɝp] ◀≲ *Track 3325*

名 蟲鳴鳥叫聲 動 蟲鳴鳥叫

▶名 I heard the chirps of birds in the early morning.
我一大早就聽到鳥啁啾聲。

▶動 Do you hear the birds chirping in the trees?
你有聽到小鳥在樹上鳴叫嗎？

文法字詞解析
這個單字的念法要特別注意喔！cham
這個音節跟 ham、am 等看似押韻，但實
際上它是和 came、fame 押韻。注意看
看後面的音標吧！

文法字詞解析
chirpy (adj.) 要描述一個人總像小鳥一
樣嘰嘰喳喳、開朗健談，就可以說他很
chirpy。

chore [tʃor]
🔊 *Track 3326*

名 雜事、打雜

▶I spent the whole Saturday morning dealing with the household chores. 我花了一整個星期六早上做家事。

cho·rus [ˈkorəs]
🔊 *Track 3327*

名 合唱團、合唱

▶Let us take part in the church（教堂）chorus. 讓我們去參加教會的合唱團吧。

ci·gar [sɪˈgɑr]
🔊 *Track 3328*

名 雪茄

▶Would you like to tell me how much a cigar costs in Britain? 你能告訴我在英國一支雪茄多少錢嗎？

ci·ne·ma [ˈsɪnəmə]
🔊 *Track 3329*

名 電影院、電影

▶How often do you go to the cinema with your family? 你跟家人多久去看一次電影？

cir·cu·lar [ˈsɝkjələ]
🔊 *Track 3330*

形 圓形的

▶We took the circular route to get to the airport. 我們走環形道路去機場。

cir·cu·late [ˈsɝkjəˌlet]
🔊 *Track 3331*

動 傳佈、循環

▶Why not open a window to allow the air to circulate? 為什麼不打開窗子讓空氣流通呢？

cir·cu·la·tion [ˌsɝkjəˈleʃən]
🔊 *Track 3332*

名 通貨、循環、發行量

▶The book has had a big circulation since it was published. 此書一經問世，便大量發行。

cir·cum·stance [ˈsɝkəmˌstæns]
🔊 *Track 3333*

名 情況 同 condition 情況

▶Though the circumstance is harsh, the man managed to succeeded in business. 雖然環境艱困，這個人還是能夠經商成功。

ci·vil·ian [səˈvɪljən]
🔊 *Track 3334*

名 平民、一般人 形 平民的

▶名 The government is widely disliked by civilians. 這個政府現在深受平民厭惡。

▶形 He resigned his commission（軍職）to take up a civilian job. 他辭去軍職而從事了平民工作。

civ·i·li·za·tion [ˌsɪvl̩əˈzeʃən]
🔊 *Track 3335*

名 文明、開化 同 culture 文化

▶I'm so glad to return from grandma's Internet-less house to civilization. 能從奶奶沒有網路的家回到文明世界真是太開心了。

文法字詞解析
一首歌曲的「副歌」也叫作 chorus。畢竟副歌就是一首歌中出現最多次、大家也最容易記起來一起合唱的部分不是嗎？

Level 1

Level 2

Level 3

Level 4
提升程度4200單字
自我勉勵、越背越上手

Level 5

Level 6

文法字詞解析
字尾「-less」是「沒有、缺乏……」的意思，所以「Internet-less」就是「沒有網路的」。

clar·i·fy [ˈklærəˌfaɪ]
🔊 Track 3336

動 澄清、變得明晰
▶He clarified his stance on this issue.
他澄清了自己在這個議題上的立場。

clash [klæʃ]
🔊 Track 3337

名 衝突、猛撞 **動** 衝突、猛撞
▶**名** The demonstration ended in a violent clash with the police.
遊行示威以與警察的激烈衝突而告終。
▶**動** It's a pity that the two concerts clash; I wanted to go to both of them.
真可惜兩場音樂會時間上有衝突，我本來想兩場都去的。

萬用延伸句型
It's a pity that... 真可惜……。

clas·si·fi·ca·tion [ˈklæsəfəˈkeʃən]
🔊 Track 3338

名 分類
▶It's the job of a biologist to make classifications of animals.
把動物分類是生物學家的工作之一。

clas·si·fy [ˈklæsəˌfaɪ]
🔊 Track 3339

動 分類
▶Would you classify her novels as literature or something else?
你認為她的小說屬於文學類，還是其他類？

cliff [klɪf]
🔊 Track 3340

名 峭壁、斷崖
▶It takes courage and strength to climb these cliffs.
攀登這些懸崖需要勇氣和力量。

cli·max [ˈklaɪmæks]
🔊 Track 3341

名 頂點、高潮 **動** 達到頂點
▶**名** The climax of the movie occurred when the protagonist returned to his hometown.
電影的高潮出現在主角回到故鄉時。
▶**動** The play climaxed in the third act.
那齣戲在第三幕達到高潮。

clum·sy [ˈklʌmzɪ]
🔊 Track 3342

形 笨拙的
▶She's a clumsy person who trips over herself a lot.
她是個笨拙的人，常會不小心絆倒。

coarse [kors]
🔊 Track 3343

形 粗糙的 **同** rough 粗糙的
▶It doesn't matter if my clothes are made of coarse cloth.
我的衣服是用粗布製成的也沒什麼關係。

code [kod]
🔊 Track 3344

名 代號、編碼
▶You can put in the code of the produce when you want to place an order. 你下訂單時，可以輸入商品的代碼。

文法字詞解析
口語中有個叫 bro code 的說法，指男性好友之間不需言說的條約，例如不可以追自己兄弟的女友、不可以把家裡的啤酒都喝光等。

col·lapse [kəˋlæps]
🔊 *Track 3345*

動 崩潰、倒塌
▶There is fear of a US collapse.
有人擔心美國的經濟可能會崩潰。

com·bi·na·tion [ˌkɑmbəˋneʃən]
🔊 *Track 3346*

名 結合
▶We tried every conceivable（想得到的）combination but it still didn't work.
我們把所有能想到的各種組合都試了一遍，結果還是沒有用。

com·e·dy [ˋkɑmədɪ]
🔊 *Track 3347*

名 喜劇
▶The Taming of the Shrew is a comedy by William Shakespeare.
<馴悍記>是莎士比亞所作的一齣喜劇。

com·ic [ˋkɑmɪk]
🔊 *Track 3348*

形 滑稽的、喜劇的　名 漫畫
▶形 What do you think about the comic characters in this play?
你覺得這部劇中的喜劇人物怎麼樣？
▶名 I love reading comic books after school.
放學後我喜歡看漫畫。

com·mand·er [kəˋmændə]
🔊 *Track 3349*

名 指揮官
▶It's very foolish of the commander to expose his men to unnecessary（不必要的）risks.
這個指揮官讓士兵們冒不必要的危險真是太愚蠢了。

com·ment [ˋkɑmɛnt]
🔊 *Track 3350*

名 評語、評論　動 做註解、做評論
▶名 The sports analyst didn't have any comment on the athlete's performance.
運動播報員對這位運動員的表現沒有任何評論。
▶動 Would you please comment on the conclusion?
請您對這一個結論發表一下意見好嗎？

com·merce [ˋkɑmɝs]
🔊 *Track 3351*

名 商業、貿易　同 trade 貿易
▶How can we maximize（最大化）the benefits of electronic commerce? 我們該如何使電子商務的利益最大化？

com·mit [kəˋmɪt]
🔊 *Track 3352*

動 委任、承諾
▶He would not commit himself in any way. 他不願做出任何承諾。

com·mu·ni·ca·tion [kəˌmjunəˋkeʃən]
🔊 *Track 3353*

名 通信、溝通、交流
▶English is often considered an important tool of communication.
英文被認為是一個很重要的溝通工具。

文法字詞解析
我們都知道 comic books 是漫畫書，不過其實要注意的是不是所有的漫畫都可以叫 comic books 喔。對美國人而言，日本出品的漫畫叫作 manga，較不會叫作 comic books。說到 comic books，他們會想到的是像 Marvel 等公司出品的那種漫畫，例如蝙蝠俠、蜘蛛人等等。

文法字詞解析
communication skill 溝通技巧

自我勉勵、越背越上手——提升程度4200單字

Level 1　Level 2　Level 3　Level 4　Level 5　Level 6

com·mu·ni·ty [kə`mjunətɪ]
🔊 *Track 3354*

名 社區

▶ Not everyone is willing to invest some time in community service. 不是每個人都願意在社區服務上花時間。

com·pan·ion [kəm`pænjən]
🔊 *Track 3355*

名 同伴

▶ The dog is my intimate friend and good companion.
這隻狗是我的好朋友、好夥伴。

com·pe·ti·tion [ˌkɑmpə`tɪʃən]
🔊 *Track 3356*

名 競爭、競爭者 同 rival 對手

▶ Our company faced a keen competition trying to expand our product line. 我們的公司在拓展新產品線時，面臨激烈的競爭。

com·pet·i·tive [kəm`pɛtətɪv]
🔊 *Track 3357*

形 競爭的

▶ He is a very competitive person and never backs down from a challenge. 他非常愛競爭，遇到挑戰從不退縮。

com·pet·i·tor [kəm`pɛtətɚ]
🔊 *Track 3358*

名 競爭者

▶ Which competitor do you think will win?
你覺得哪個競爭者會贏？

com·pli·cate [`kɑmpləˌket]
🔊 *Track 3359*

動 使複雜

▶ If you use vague language in the negotiation, you will be complicating things.
如果你在談判中使用模糊的語言，就會使問題變複雜。

com·pose [kəm`poz]
🔊 *Track 3360*

動 組成、作曲

▶ Do you know how to compose music on the computer?
你知道如何在電腦上作曲嗎？

com·pos·er [kəm`pozɚ]
🔊 *Track 3361*

名 作曲家、設計者

▶ He is not only a composer but also a conductor, which made him very busy. 他不但是名作曲家而且還是位指揮家，雙重身份使他非常繁忙。

com·po·si·tion [ˌkɑmpə`zɪʃən]
🔊 *Track 3362*

名 組合、作文、混合物

▶ There are a lot of spelling mistakes in your composition.
你的作文中有很多拼字錯誤。

con·cen·trate [`kɑnsˌtret]
🔊 *Track 3363*

動 集中

▶ I can't concentrate when on my studies with the kids running around me. 小孩在我的周圍跑來跑去，我無法專心念書。

文法字詞解析

competitive 的意思很多，可以指「競爭力強的」、「喜歡競爭的」、「擅長競爭的」等等。

con·cen·tra·tion [ˌkɑnsˈtreʃən] ◀€ *Track 3364*

名 集中、專心
▶It's very hard for me to keep my concentration with such a loud noise.
吵鬧聲讓我很難保持精神集中。

con·cept [ˈkɑnsɛpt] ◀€ *Track 3365*

名 概念
▶The professor explained the abstract concept with charts and graphs.
教授用圖表來解釋這項抽象的概念。

con·cern·ing [kənˈsɝnɪŋ] ◀€ *Track 3366*

連 關於
▶Let us see all the official documents concerning the sale of this land.
讓我們看看買賣這塊土地的所有官方文件吧。

con·crete [ˈkɑnkrit] ◀€ *Track 3367*

名 水泥、混凝土 形 具體的、混凝土的 反 abstract 抽象的
▶名 The house is made from concrete.
這房子是混凝土做的。
▶形 Would you like to let me know if you got any concrete proposals?
你能不能告訴我你是否有具體的建議呢？

文法字詞解析
我們中文所說的「都市叢林」在英文中則叫做「水泥叢林」concrete jungle。

con·duc·tor [kənˈdʌktɚ] ◀€ *Track 3368*

名 指揮、指導者
▶The musicians of the orchestra can read the conductor's signals.
交響樂團的音樂家們可以理解指揮的手勢。

con·fer·ence [ˈkɑnfərəns] ◀€ *Track 3369*

名 招待會、會議 同 meeting 會議
▶There will be an international conference held in London next month. 有一個國際性的會議將於下個月在倫敦舉行。

con·fess [kənˈfɛs] ◀€ *Track 3370*

動 承認、供認
▶I think it's time for me to confess the whole thing.
我想現在是坦白整件事情的時候了。

萬用延伸句型
confess to V-ing 承認（做了某事）
例 如：She confessed to dying her dog green.
她承認自己把狗染成了綠色。

con·fi·dence [ˈkɑnfədəns] ◀€ *Track 3371*

名 信心、信賴
▶Too much confidence can hurt you. Don't you think so?
過分的自信會傷害到你，你不這樣認為嗎？

con·fine [kənˈfaɪn] ◀€ *Track 3372*

動 限制、侷限
▶I wish the speaker could confine himself to the subject.
我希望演說者不要離題。

Level 1
Level 2
Level 3
Level 4
提升程度4200單字
自我勉勵、越背越上手
Level 5
Level 6

con·fu·sion [kənˈfjuʒən] 🔊 *Track 3373*
名 迷惑、混亂
▶The ambiguous phrases in the essay caused confusion.
文章中模稜兩可的用語使人困惑。

con·grat·u·late [kənˈgrætʃəˌlet] 🔊 *Track 3374*
動 恭喜
▶He congratulated himself on his narrow escape.
他慶祝了自己能死裡逃生。

con·gress [ˈkɑŋgrəs] 🔊 *Track 3375*
名 國會
▶Several members of the congress attended the press
conference. 有些國會成員出席了這場記者會。

con·junc·tion [kənˈdʒʌŋkʃən] 🔊 *Track 3376*
名 連接、關聯
▶The novel should be read in conjunction with the author's
biography. 這本小說應該和作者傳記一起讀。

con·quer [ˌkɑŋkɚ] 🔊 *Track 3377*
動 征服
▶I don't believe man will conquer the weather in the near future.
我不相信人類在不久的將來會征服天氣。

con·science [ˈkɑnʃəns] 🔊 *Track 3378*
名 良心
▶It's surprising that he killed so many people without having a
guilty conscience.
他殺了這麼多人還不會良心不安，真是令人驚訝。

萬用延伸句型
It is surprising that... ……真是令人驚訝

con·se·quence [ˈkɑnsəˌkwɛns] 🔊 *Track 3379*
名 結果、影響
▶The man tried to avoid facing the consequences of his wrong
deeds. 這個人嘗試逃避錯誤造成的後果。

con·se·quent [ˈkɑnsəˌkwɛnt] 🔊 *Track 3380*
形 必然的、隨之引起的
▶I'm afraid the rise in price was consequent of the failure of the
crops. 恐怕物價上漲是因為收成不好所引起的。

con·ser·va·tive [kənˈsɚvətɪv] 🔊 *Track 3381*
名 保守主義者 形 保守的、保守黨的
▶名 The conservative old man is strongly against abortion.
保守的老人堅決反對墮胎。
▶形 My parents are kind of conservative. 我父母有點保守。

con·sist [kənˈsɪst] 🔊 *Track 3382*
動 組成、構成
▶I don't think that all people know that matters consist of atoms.
我覺得不是所有人都知道各種物質是由原子組成的。

con·sis·tent [kən'sɪstənt] 🔊 *Track 3383*

形 一致的、調和的

▶The usages of terms should be consistent throughout the whole essay.
整篇文章的用語應該要統一。

con·so·nant ['kɑnsənənt] 🔊 *Track 3384*

名 子音 形 和諧的 反 vowel 母音

▶名 What do you think of my pronunciation of this consonant?
你覺得我這個子音的發音怎麼樣？

▶形 Her style was consonant with her personality.
她的衣著風格很符合她的性格。

con·sti·tute ['kɑnstə/tjut] 🔊 *Track 3385*

動 構成、制定

▶A slight error in thought may constitute a life-long regret.
一念之差就可能變成終身的悔恨。

con·sti·tu·tion [/kɑnstə'tjuʃən] 🔊 *Track 3386*

名 憲法、構造

▶I don't know anything about the constitution of the United Nations Organization.
我完全不清楚聯合國組織的章程。

con·struct [kən'strʌkt] 🔊 *Track 3387*

動 建造、構築

▶It took them two years to construct the bridge.
他們用了兩年的時間建這座橋。

con·struc·tion [kən'strʌkʃən] 🔊 *Track 3388*

名 建築、結構

▶There was a great outcry（強烈抗議）about the construction of the new airport.
民眾強烈抗議修建新的機場。

con·struc·tive [kən'strʌktɪv] 🔊 *Track 3389*

形 有建設性的

▶Don't say anything unless your criticism is constructive.
如果你的批評沒有建設性，就別說出來。

con·sult [kən'sʌlt] 🔊 *Track 3390*

動 請教、諮詢 同 confer 協商

▶The pupils consulted the instructor about the format of the report. 學生請教講師有關於報告格式的問題。

con·sul·tant [kən'sʌltənt] 🔊 *Track 3391*

名 諮詢者

▶How often do you see the consultant who is in charge of your head treatment?
你多久去看一次負責處理你頭部傷勢的醫師？

Level 1

Level 2

Level 3

Level 4
自我勉勵、越背越上手──提升程度4200單字

Level 5

Level 6

con·sume [kən`sum] ◀€ *Track 3392*

動 消耗、耗費 **同** waste 耗費

▶The teenagers may consume a lot of calories for they very active. 青少年很好動，可能會消耗大量卡路里。

con·sum·er [kən`sumə] ◀€ *Track 3393*

名 消費者

▶We always ask consumers for their feedback.
我們總是會詢問消費者的回饋。

con·tain·er [kən`tenə] ◀€ *Track 3394*

名 容器

▶Would you please help me look for my soap container?
你能幫我找我的肥皂盒嗎？

con·tent [`kɑntɛnt]/[kən`tɛnt] ◀€ *Track 3395*

名 內容、滿足、目錄 **形** 滿足的、願意的

▶**名** The content of the confidential report could not be revealed to the public.
機密報告的內容不能透露給大眾。

▶**形** He seemed to be more content with his former job than this one.
與這份工作相比，他似乎對自己以前的那份工作更滿意。

> **文法字詞解析**
> 書籍的目錄可稱為 contents。

con·tent·ment [kən`tɛntmənt] ◀€ *Track 3396*

名 滿足

▶The man sighed in contentment as he sipped his beer.
那名男子一邊啜飲啤酒一邊滿足地嘆息。

con·test [`kɑntɛst]/[kən`tɛst] ◀€ *Track 3397*

名 比賽 **動** 與……競爭、爭奪

▶**名** The air guitar contest was held in Russia.
空氣吉他大賽在俄國舉行。

▶**動** There are three candidates contesting for the presidency （總統職位）.
有三個候選人在爭奪總統的位子。

con·text [`kɑntɛkst] ◀€ *Track 3398*

名 上下文、文章脈絡

▶You can use context to figure out what an unfamiliar word means. 你可以利用上下文來猜出一個陌生的單字是什麼意思。

> **萬用延伸句型**
> take sth. out of context 即把某段話單獨引出來使用，且不提供上下文，令聽者或讀者感到困惑或誤解。例如在和朋友談論電影劇情，說到「外星人從他的胸口竄了出來」，若是這句話被人take out of context，以為你說的是真的發生的事，那可就會上新聞了。

con·tin·u·al [kən`tɪnjʊəl] ◀€ *Track 3399*

形 連續的

▶I've had enough of her continual chatter; what about you?
我已厭煩了她的喋喋不休，你呢？

con·tin·u·ous [kən`tɪnjʊəs] ◀€ *Track 3400*

形 不斷的、連續的

▶Artificial intelligence is in continuous improvement.
人工智慧持續在進步中。

con·trar·y [ˈkɑntrɛrɪ]   Track 3401

名 矛盾 形 反對的

▶名 On the contrary to my expectation, he lost the game.
和我預期相反，他輸了比賽。

▶形 You should go with me unless your view is contrary to mine.
如果你的看法不是與我的相反，你就應該跟我去。

con·trast [ˈkɑn͵træst]/[kənˈtræst]   Track 3402

名 對比 動 對照

▶名 The black furnishings provide an interesting contrast to the white walls. Don't you think so?
黑色傢俱和白色牆壁形成很有趣的對比，你不覺得嗎？

▶動 Her behaviors in private contrasted sharply with what she appeared in public.
她私下的行為和她公開的的形象反差很大。

con·trib·ute [kənˈtrɪbjʊt]   Track 3403

動 貢獻

▶It was generous of her to contribute such a large sum.
她很大方，捐助了這麼一大筆錢。

con·tri·bu·tion [͵kɑntrəˈbjuʃən]   Track 3404

名 貢獻、捐獻

▶There was no mention of her contribution here. Do you know why?
這裡沒有提到她的貢獻，你知道為什麼嗎？

con·ve·nience [kənˈvinjəns]   Track 3405

名 便利

▶Would you please deliver the goods at your earliest convenience?
請您方便的話盡早送貨好嗎？

con·ven·tion [kənˈvɛnʃən]   Track 3406

名 會議、條約、傳統

▶It is convention that we have the dragon dance on New Year celebration. 新年時舞龍舞獅是一項習俗。

con·ven·tion·al [kənˈvɛnʃənl̩]   Track 3407

形 會議的、傳統的

▶I wish you weren't so conventional in the clothes you wear.
要是你的穿衣風格不要那麼保守就好了。

con·verse [kənˈvɝs]   Track 3408

動 談話

▶Would you give me half an hour to converse with you?
能跟您談談嗎？半小時就可以了。

con·vey [kənˈve]   Track 3409

動 傳達、運送

▶I found it very hard to convey my feelings in words.
我發現我很難用言語來表達我的感情。

Level 1
Level 2
Level 3
Level 4
Level 5
Level 6

提升程度4200單字

自我勉勵、越背越上手

con·vince [kən`vɪns] ◀€ *Track 3410*
動 說服、信服
▶I tried to convince him to quit playing the online games.
我試圖說服他不要再玩線上遊戲。

co·op·er·ate [ko`ɑpəˌret] ◀€ *Track 3411*
名 協力、合作
▶You need to cooperate or you'll never get anything done.
你們不合作點的話,什麼也做不完的。

co·op·er·a·tion [koˌɑpə`reʃən] ◀€ *Track 3412*
名 合作、協力
▶Thank you very much for your cooperation.
非常謝謝您的合作。

co·op·er·a·tive [ko`ɑpəˌretɪv] ◀€ *Track 3413*
名 合作社 形 合作的
▶名 The cooperative serves as a supply center for the villagers.
合作社對村民來說是一個中央補給站。
▶形 Not both sides are willing to take cooperative attitudes on this issue.
在這件事情上,並不是雙方都願意採取合作的態度。

文法字詞解析
cooperative 指的是「合作的」,但帶有一點被動的含意。也就是説,如果一個人很 cooperative,代表他願意乖乖配合、不會做出什麼反抗的行為。然而,他不見得會主動為目標做出任何貢獻、提供任何幫助,他只是「被動地配合」而已。因此,若你老闆叫你要「cooperative」,他的意思是要叫你不要亂來,配合公司計畫,而不是叫你「主動為公司某個案子貢獻力量」。

cope [kop] ◀€ *Track 3414*
動 處理、對付
▶I don't know how to cope with the problem of poor vision.
我不知道如何解決視力不好的問題。

cop·per [`kɑpɚ] ◀€ *Track 3415*
名 銅 形 銅製的
▶名 China's copper imports increased by 80% last year.
去年中國銅進口激增了百分之八十。
▶形 The copper kettles have higher quality.
銅製的水壺品質較高。

cord [kɔrd] ◀€ *Track 3416*
名 電線、繩
▶Why don't you tie up the package with a heavy cord?
為什麼不用粗繩將行李捆牢呢?

文法字詞解析
extension cord = 延長線
strike a cord = 引起共鳴

cork [kɔrk] ◀€ *Track 3417*
名 軟木塞 動 用軟木塞栓緊
▶名 The cork flew off with a pop.
瓶塞砰的一聲飛了出去。
▶動 Would you please cork up the bottle? It might leak.
請你用軟木塞塞住瓶子好嗎?它可能會漏水。

cor·re·spond [ˌkɔrə`spɑnd] ◀€ *Track 3418*
動 符合、相當
▶The features of the product do not correspond to the description on the catalogue. 產品的特色和目錄上的描述不相符。

cos·tume [ˈkɑstjum]

Track 3419

名 服裝、服飾、劇裝
▶Why would you wear a costume to work?
你為什麼要穿戲服去上班？

cot·tage [ˈkɑtɪdʒ]

Track 3420

名 小屋、別墅
▶The poor family lived in a cottage.
貧窮的家庭住在簡陋小屋裡。

coun·cil [ˈkaʊnsḷ]

Track 3421

名 議會、會議
▶What do you think about discussing the problem in the council?
你覺得在會議上討論這個問題如何？

count·er [ˈkaʊntɚ]

Track 3422

名 櫃檯、計算機 動 反對、反抗
▶名 There was an enormous cat crouching（蹲坐）on the counter.
櫃檯上蹲坐著一隻碩大的貓。
▶動 If no one counters the plan, we'll carry it out.
沒人反對這個計畫的話，我們就會執行了。

自我勉勵、越背越上手 提升程度4200單字

cou·ra·geous [kəˈredʒəs]

Track 3423

形 勇敢的
▶It was courageous of him to stand up to his boss.
他敢反對他的上司，真是勇敢。

cour·te·ous [ˈkɝtjəs]

Track 3424

形 有禮貌的
▶The lady appeared rather courteous at the presence of the officials. 官員們在場時，女士顯得相當有禮貌。

cour·te·sy [ˈkɝtəsɪ]

Track 3425

名 禮貌
▶Lack of courtesy is considered as a disease of modern society.
缺乏禮貌被認為是當今社會的一大弊病。

crack [kræk]

Track 3426

名 裂縫、瑕疵 動 使爆裂、使破裂
▶名 This house is an old building. It is no wonder that there are so many cracks in the wall.
這間房子是一間很老的建築物了，難怪這面牆上有那麼多裂縫。
▶動 Her voice cracked with grief.
她悲傷得語不成聲。

craft [kræft]

Track 3427

名 手工藝
▶The hotel lobby has a display of local crafts.
飯店的大廳裡有當地的工藝品展覽。

文法字詞解析
costume party = 化裝舞會

萬用延伸句型
crack under pressure 因壓力大而崩潰
例如：He cracked under pressure from work and had to see a doctor.
他因為工作壓力大而崩潰，只好去看醫生。

cram [kræm]
🔊 Track 3428

動 把……塞進、狼吞虎嚥地吃東西
▶I crammed a lot of tasks into my schedule.
我在行事曆裡塞滿很多要做的事。

cre·a·tion [krɪˋeʃən]
🔊 Track 3429

名 創造、創世
▶I think imagination is the source of creation; what do you think of that? 我認為想像是創作之源，你覺得呢？

cre·a·tiv·i·ty [ˌkrieˋtɪvətɪ]
🔊 Track 3430

名 創造力
▶As an artist, she has a lot of creativity.
身為藝術家，她很有創意。

crip·ple [ˋkrɪpl̩]
🔊 Track 3431

名 瘸子、殘疾人
▶It's disgraceful（可恥的）of you to make fun of a cripple.
你取笑瘸子是很可恥的。

crit·ic [ˋkrɪtɪk]
🔊 Track 3432

名 批評家、評論家
▶The critic uploaded a video to share his comment about the new movie. 評論家上傳了一個關於新電影的評論影片。

crit·i·cal [ˋkrɪtɪkl̩]
🔊 Track 3433

形 評論的
▶My boss is always critical of me. 我的老闆總愛挑我的毛病。

crit·i·cism [ˋkrɪtəˌsɪzəm]
🔊 Track 3434

名 評論、批評的論文
▶The superstar reacted calmly to the criticism to her on the Internet. 巨星平靜地回應了網路上的批評。

crit·i·cize [ˋkrɪtəˌsaɪz]
🔊 Track 3435

動 批評、批判
▶It's hard to criticize one's own work, don't you think so?
評價自己的工作並非容易的事，你不覺得嗎？

cru·el·ty [ˋkruəltɪ]
🔊 Track 3436

名 冷酷、殘忍
▶I don't believe she will willingly（甘願地）put up with his cruelty to her. 我相信她不會甘願忍受他的虐待的。

crush [krʌʃ]
🔊 Track 3437

名 毀壞、壓榨 動 壓碎、壓壞
▶名 There was such a crush of spectators that no one could move. 觀眾多到都擠在一起了，誰也無法動彈。
▶動 Don't crush this box; there are flowers inside.
別壓壞這個盒子，裡面有花。

文法字詞解析

和這個單字相關的形容詞是 crippled。這個單字可以指有殘疾的人，但也可以描述某人因為某種原因有劣勢、無法正常發揮。舉例來說，若有個擇角選手戴著眼罩去參加比賽，根本看不到，這個情況下就可以用 crippled 來描述他。

cube [kjub]
◀ Track 3438

名 立方體、正六面體

▶The girl chewed on the ice cubes in her juice, which shocked her date.
女孩拿果汁中的冰塊起來咬，嚇到她的約會對象。

cu·cum·ber [ˈkjukʌmbɚ]
◀ Track 3439

名 小黃瓜、黃瓜

▶The rabbit likes eating cucumbers. 那隻兔子很喜歡吃小黃瓜。

cue [kju]
◀ Track 3440

名 暗示

▶The actor missed his cue and came onto the stage late.
那個演員錯過了向他發出的暗示，所以太慢上場了。

cun·ning [ˈkʌnɪŋ]
◀ Track 3441

形 精明的、狡猾的

▶I think your new secretary is too cunning to trust.
我覺得你的新秘書太狡猾了，不能相信。

cu·ri·os·i·ty [ˌkjʊrɪˈɑsətɪ]
◀ Track 3442

名 好奇心

▶I peeked into the deserted houseout of curiosity.
我出於好奇心偷看了配器房屋裡面。

curl [kɝl]
◀ Track 3443

名 捲髮、捲曲 動 使捲曲

▶名 I prefer to have my hair in curls.
我比較喜歡保持捲頭髮。

▶動 I like to curl up with a story book.
我喜歡蜷曲而臥地看故事書。

curse [kɝs]
◀ Track 3444

動 詛咒、罵

▶He cursed when he stepped on his own foot.
他踩到自己的腳時大罵了一句。

curve [kɝv]
◀ Track 3445

名 曲線 動 使彎曲

▶名 The population curve of this city has slowed down.
這個城市的人口曲線已趨平緩。

▶動 The seacoast curved beautifully.
這海岸的海岸線彎曲得十分美麗。

cush·ion [ˈkʊʃən]
◀ Track 3446

名 墊子 動 緩和……衝擊

▶名 IThe pregnant woman placed a cushion under her waist.
懷孕的女士在腰部底下放了一個墊子。

▶動 I don't think that the training program helps to cushion the effect of unemployment（失業）.
我認為這項訓練計畫無益於緩衝失業造成的影響。

文法字詞解析

小黃瓜總是冰冰涼涼的（cool），因此有個比喻「as cool as a cucumber」，即是描述人非常冷靜沉著。

萬用延伸句型

put sb. under a curse 詛咒某人
例如：The witch put him under a curse because he stepped on her cat.
因為他踩到了巫婆的貓，於是巫婆對他下了咒。

Level 1
Level 2
Level 3
Level 4
Level 5
Level 6

提升程度4200單字 自我勉勵、越背越上手

[Dd]

damn [dæm]

🔊 *Track 3447*

動 指責、輕蔑

▶This play is awful. It is no wonder that it is damned by the reviewers（評論家）.
這部戲糟透了。難怪它被評論家們批評得一無是處。

damp [dæmp]

🔊 *Track 3448*

形 潮濕的　動 使潮濕　同 moist 潮濕的

▶形 The cookies went soft because of the damp weather.
因為天氣潮溼，餅乾變軟了。

▶動 How about damping your cloth before cleaning the windows?
擦窗戶前先把布弄濕怎麼樣？

dead·line [ˈdɛdˌlaɪn]

🔊 *Track 3449*

名 限期

▶It is impossible（不可能的）for us to meet the deadline because of the terrible weather.
由於天氣惡劣，因此我們無法如期完成任務。

de·clare [dɪˈklɛr]

🔊 *Track 3450*

動 宣告、公告

▶Our boss declared that everybody will have a pay raise this year. 我們的老闆宣布每個人今年都會加薪。

dec·o·ra·tion [ˌdɛkəˈreʃən]

🔊 *Track 3451*

名 裝飾

▶Will you tell me when you can finish the decoration of the living room? 你能告訴我你們什麼時候才能把客廳裝飾好嗎？

de·crease [dɪˈkris]

🔊 *Track 3452*

動 減少、減小　名 減少、減小　反 increase 增加

▶動 I am afraid the population here will decrease year by year.
我擔心這裡的人口會逐年減少。

▶名 I am afraid that there will be some decrease in exports.
恐怕出口貨物會有所減少。

de·feat [dɪˈfit]

🔊 *Track 3453*

名 挫敗、擊敗　動 擊敗、戰勝

▶名 He took the defeat well and put himself together soon.
他能夠接受失敗，並且很快振作。

▶動 I wish our basketball team could defeat their team next season. 但願我們的籃球隊能在下個賽季中打敗他們那隊。

de·fend [dɪˈfɛnd]

🔊 *Track 3454*

動 保衛、防禦

▶He tried to defend his friend from the bullies.
他試著保護他被霸凌的朋友。

文法字詞解析
damp-proof = 防潮的

文法字詞解析
admit defeat = 承認失敗
defeat the purpose = 使挫敗

de·fense [dɪ'fɛns]
◀ Track 3455

名 防禦

▶In a basketball game, attack is the best defense.
籃球比賽中，進攻就是最好的防禦。

de·fen·si·ble [dɪ'fɛnsəbl]
◀ Track 3456

形 可辯護的、可防禦的

▶I don't think the theory he put forward is defensible.
我覺得他提出的理論站不住腳。

de·fen·sive [dɪ'fɛnsɪv]
◀ Track 3457

形 防禦的、保衛的

▶He holds a defensive attitude when it comes to his literary work.
他談到自己的文學作品，就採取防禦的態度。

def·i·nite ['dɛfənɪt]
◀ Track 3458

形 確定的 同 precise 確切的

▶It is obvious that they are unwilling（不願意的）to give us a definite answer.
顯然他們不願意給我們一個明確的答覆。

del·i·cate ['dɛləkət]
◀ Track 3459

形 精細的、精巧的

▶We used some bubble wrap to protect the delicate statue.
我們用一些泡泡包裝紙來保護這個脆弱的雕像。

de·light [dɪ'laɪt]
◀ Track 3460

名 欣喜 動 使高興

▶名 The play was excellent and the audience roared in delight.
這部戲太棒了，觀眾們都興高采烈地歡呼起來了。

▶動 The circus show delights everyone present.
這馬戲團的表演讓每個在場的人都覺得很開心。

de·light·ful [dɪ'laɪtfəl]
◀ Track 3461

形 令人欣喜的

▶It was a delightful party. What a pity you couldn't attend!
這是一次愉快的聚會，你沒來真可惜啊。

de·mand [dɪ'mænd]
◀ Track 3462

名 要求 動 要求

▶名 All of them caved in to the boss's demand.
他們都屈從了老闆的要求。

▶動 They demanded that the all videos should come with subtitles.
他們要求所有的影片都要有字幕。

dem·on·strate ['dɛmən„stret]
◀ Track 3463

動 展現、表明

▶This election demonstrated democracy in action.
這次選舉是以實際行動體現了民主。

萬用延伸句型

In my defense... 不過，為我自己辯護一下……

例如：I thought that stranger was my friend. In my defense, they really looked alike.
我以為那個陌生人是我朋友。但要為我自己辯護一下，他們真的長得很像。

萬用延伸句型

in high demand極受歡迎、很多人搶著要

例如：This product is in high demand. It's literally flying off the shelves.
這產品非常受歡迎，每次一上架馬上就被搶光了。

Level 1

Level 2

Level 3

Level 4

自我勉勵、越背越上手——
提升程度4200單字

Level 5

Level 6

dem·on·stra·tion
🔊 *Track 3464*
[ˌdɛmənˈstreʃən]
名 證明、示範
▶The intern teacher made a demonstration of her teaching this morning.
實習老師今天早上作了教學演示。

dense [dɛns]
🔊 *Track 3465*
形 密集的、稠密的
▶There was dense fog, so the traffic slowed down.
因為有濃霧，大家都減速行駛。

de·part [dɪˈpɑrt]
🔊 *Track 3466*
動 離開、走開　同 leave 離開
▶He departed early in the morning so that he wouldn't miss the early train.
為了不錯過早班的火車，他一大早就離開了。

de·par·ture [dɪˈpɑrtʃɚ]
🔊 *Track 3467*
名 離去、出發
▶I don't think he knows the exact departure time of the flight.
我認為他不知道飛機起飛的準確時間。

de·pend·a·ble [dɪˈpɛndəbl]
🔊 *Track 3468*
形 可靠的
▶The veteran worker is dependable and trustworthy.
資深員工很可靠而且值得信任。

de·pend·ent [dɪˈpɛndənt]
🔊 *Track 3469*
名 從屬者　形 從屬的、依賴的
▶名 Please list all your dependents here on the form.
請把你所有的受撫養人列在這個表格上。
▶形 I am afraid that I can't be dependent on my old parents any more. 恐怕我再也不能依靠我那年邁的父母了。

de·press [dɪˈprɛs]
🔊 *Track 3470*
動 壓下、降低
▶Rainy weather always depresses me.
雨天總使我心情抑鬱。

de·pres·sion [dɪˈprɛʃən]
🔊 *Track 3471*
名 下陷、降低
▶Tina suffered from depression after she was dismissed by her former employer.
緹娜被前老闆解雇之後就患了憂鬱症。

de·serve [dɪˈzɝv]
🔊 *Track 3472*
動 值得、應得
▶Ms. Jolie deserves the honor of the best actress award.
裘莉女士值得最佳女演員的獎項。

文法字詞解析
當某人的腦袋已經「密度太高」、「很稠密」，可想而知若還要往裡面裝東西可是很困難的，因此當你覺得有人怎麼講都聽若罔聞、而且明明是簡單的小事卻無法理解時，也可以說他很 dense。

文法字詞解析
dependent 的相反詞即 independent，也就是「獨立的」、「自主的」。

des·per·ate [ˈdɛspərɪt]　🔊 *Track 3473*

形 絕望的

▶Don't you believe a desperate man will stop at nothing to get what he wants? 難道你不相信一個亡命之徒為了達到自己的目的什麼事都做得出來嗎？

de·spite [dɪˈspaɪt]　🔊 *Track 3474*

介 不管、不顧

▶Despite the economic depression, his company thrived. 儘管經濟不景氣，他的公司還是經營得很好。

de·struc·tion [dɪˈstrʌkʃən]　🔊 *Track 3475*

名 破壞、損壞

▶His desire for money will lead him to his destruction one day; I wish he could understand that soon. 對錢的慾望有一天終將導致他的毀滅，但願他能很快明白這一點。

de·tec·tive [dɪˈtɛktɪv]　🔊 *Track 3476*

名 偵探、探員　形 偵探的

▶名 I don't think the detective can reason out how the murderer has escaped.
我認為這名偵探無法弄明白兇手是如何逃脫的。

▶形 Are there any detective agencies here?
這裡有偵探事務所嗎？

de·ter·mi·na·tion　🔊 *Track 3477*
[dɪˌtɜməˈneʃən]

名 決心

▶His determination and perseverance led him to success.
他的決心和毅力使他能夠成功。

de·vice [dɪˈvaɪs]　🔊 *Track 3478*

名 裝置、設計

▶A computer is a device for processing information; the more you use it, the more you know.
電腦是用來處理資訊的。你用得越勤，瞭解的就越多。

de·vise [dɪˈvaɪz]　🔊 *Track 3479*

動 設計、想出

▶He is devising a new plan to get us out of here.
他正在設計一個能幫助我們逃出去的計畫。

de·vote [dɪˈvot]　🔊 *Track 3480*

動 貢獻、奉獻

▶The retired businessman devoted himself in education.
退休商人投入教育之中。

di·a·per [ˈdaɪəpɚ]　🔊 *Track 3481*

名 尿布

▶Will you change the baby's diaper? I am a bit busy now.
你能幫孩子換一片尿布嗎？我現在有點忙。

文法字詞解析
其實這個字非常微妙，描述的是「幾乎已經絕望但還沒有完全絕望（還是有一點渺小的希望）」的狀態。也就是說，如果有個人真的已經完全絕望了，每天行屍走肉，我們不能形容他是 desperate。如果有個人狀況悽慘但他至少還有做點動作想改善這個情形（例如快要掉下懸崖了但還是拚命抓住繩子），則可以用 desperate 來描述。

萬用延伸句型
leave sb. to sb.'s own devices 放任（某人）自生自滅
例如：Her kids are really independent. She can leave them to their own devices for the whole afternoon and they'll be just fine.
她的孩子很獨立。她可以放他們不管一整個下午，他們也都好好的。

Level 1
Level 2
Level 3
Level 4
提升程度4200單字 自我勉勵、越背越上手
Level 5
Level 6

417

dif·fer [ˋdɪfɚ]
🔊 *Track 3482*

動 不同、相異
▶The two scholars differ in their opinion on this issue.
這兩個學者對於這項議題的意見不同。

di·gest [daɪˋdʒɛst]/[ˋdaɪdʒɛst]
🔊 *Track 3483*

動 瞭解、消化 名 摘要、分類
▶動 It often takes them quite a long time to digest new ideas.
他們吸收新點子往往需要相當長的一段時間。
▶名 It took her ten minutes to read the digest of the week's news.
她花了十分鐘的時間來讀一週新聞摘要。

di·ges·tion [dəˋdʒɛstʃən]
🔊 *Track 3484*

名 領會、領悟、消化
▶This kind of tea acts as an aid to digestion.
這種茶可幫助消化。

dig·i·tal [ˋdɪdʒɪtl̩]
🔊 *Track 3485*

形 數字的、數位的
▶What do you think of this digital camera? It's the latest model this year.
你覺得這款數位相機如何？它可是今年的最新款哦。

dig·ni·ty [ˋdɪgnətɪ]
🔊 *Track 3486*

名 威嚴、尊嚴
▶In my opinion, only a truly（真正地）free person has dignity.
在我看來只有真正自由的人才具有尊嚴。

di·li·gence [ˋdɪlədʒəns]
🔊 *Track 3487*

名 勤勉、勤奮
▶The artist succeeded because of his talent and diligence.
藝術家因為才華和努力而成功。

di·plo·ma [dɪˋplomə]
🔊 *Track 3488*

名 文憑、畢業證書
▶I wish he could work hard enough to get his history diploma this year.
我希望他能夠勤奮，才能在今年獲得歷史學學位證書。

dip·lo·mat [ˋdɪpləmæt]
🔊 *Track 3489*

名 外交官
▶The diplomat was criticized for his faux pas in public.
外交官因為在公開場合失言而受到批評。

dis·ad·van·tage [ˌdɪsədˋvæntɪdʒ]
🔊 *Track 3490*

名 缺點、不利 反 advantage 優點
▶You will be put at a disadvantage unless you change your plan immediately（立即）.
除非你馬上改變你的計畫，否則你將處於不利的地位。

萬用延伸句型

I beg to differ. 請容我提出反對意見。
例如：You think that we should go with Plan A? I beg to differ.
你覺得我們應該進行 A 計畫嗎？請容我提出反對意見。

文法字詞解析

uphold the dignity of ... = 維護……的尊

dis·as·ter [dɪzˈæstɚ]
🔊 *Track 3491*

名 天災、災害

▶Natural disaster has caused great damage to this small town.
自然災害對這個小鎮造成嚴重損害。

dis·ci·pline [ˈdɪsəplɪn]
🔊 *Track 3492*

名 紀律、訓練 動 懲戒

▶名 The children lack discipline, and they are not old enough to understand the rules of the school.
孩子們很散漫，同時年齡也不夠大，還不懂學校的規定。

▶動 I've disciplined myself to do two hours of exercise each day. 我堅持每天運動兩個小時。

dis·con·nect [ˌdɪskəˈnɛkt]
🔊 *Track 3493*

動 斷絕、打斷

▶We forgot to pay the bill; it is no wonder that the electricity company has disconnected our electricity.
我們忘了付電費了，難怪會被電力公司斷電。

dis·cour·age [dɪsˈkɝɪdʒ]
🔊 *Track 3494*

動 阻止、妨礙

▶Peter's father discourages him from signing a contract with the pop-star agent company.
彼得的父親希望他不要和偶像經紀公司簽約。

dis·cour·age·ment
[dɪsˈkɝɪdʒmənt]
🔊 *Track 3495*

名 失望、氣餒

▶It is obvious that the failure was a great discouragement to him.很明顯地，那次失敗很令他失望。

dis·guise [dɪsˈgaɪz]
🔊 *Track 3496*

名 掩飾 動 喬裝、假扮

▶名 It was a surprise that no one recognized her when she was in disguise.
當她喬裝打扮的時候居然沒人認出她，這真令人吃驚。

▶動 I disguised myself as a tree.
我把自己裝扮成一棵樹。

dis·gust [dɪsˈgʌst]
🔊 *Track 3497*

名 厭惡 動 使厭惡

▶名 She turned away in disgust.
她厭惡地轉過頭去。

▶動 Some of his ideas really disgust me.
他有些點子讓我很反感。

dis·miss [dɪsˈmɪs]
🔊 *Track 3498*

動 摒除、解散

▶The meeting was dismissed after the manager finished his report. 會議在經理發表完報告之後就結束了。

文法字詞解析

大家最不希望看到的「網路斷線」也稱為 disconnect。若要停止連線至無線網路，就可以說 disconnect from wi-fi。

Level 1
Level 2
Level 3
Level 4
Level 5
Level 6

提升程度4200單字

自我勉勵、越背越上手

dis·or·der [dɪsˋɔrdəˋ] 🔊 *Track 3499*

名 無秩序 動 使混亂

▶名 The disorder in the meeting room made our manager upset.
會議室一片混亂，讓經理很不開心。

▶動 Anxiety may disorder the stomach.
憂慮可能會引起胃部不適。

> **文法字詞解析**
> 這個單字也可用來表示某些疾病造成的症狀，如 kidney disorder 即表示腎臟出了毛病。

dis·pute [dɪˋspjut] 🔊 *Track 3500*

名 爭論 動 爭論

▶名 His honesty is beyond dispute.
他的誠實是無可爭議的。

▶動 They disputed over the decision.
他們就這個決策吵了起來。

dis·tinct [dɪˋstɪŋkt] 🔊 *Track 3501*

形 個別的、獨特的

▶Don't you think these two ideas are quite distinct from each other?
難道你不覺得這兩種觀念截然不同嗎？

dis·tin·guish [dɪˋstɪŋgwɪʃ] 🔊 *Track 3502*

動 辨別、分辨

▶It is hard for me to distinguish him from his brother.
我很難區分他和他的哥哥。

dis·tin·guished [dɪˋstɪŋgwɪʃt] 🔊 *Track 3503*

形 卓越的

▶It won't be long before you find that he is distinguished in many different areas.
很快你就會發現他在眾多領域中都很出眾。

dis·trib·ute [dɪˋstrɪbjut] 🔊 *Track 3504*

動 分配、分發

▶My part time job was to distribute layers at the train station.
我的兼職工作是在車站發傳單。

dis·tri·bu·tion [ˌdɪstrəˋbjuʃən] 🔊 *Track 3505*

名 分配、配給

▶It is obvious that they don't agree with his opinion about the distribution of income and wealth.
顯然他們不同意他關於收入和財富分配問題的看法。

dis·trict [ˋdɪstrɪkt] 🔊 *Track 3506*

名 區域 同 region 區域

▶There are many famous restaurants in this district.
在這一區有許多餐廳。

dis·turb [dɪˋstɝb] 🔊 *Track 3507*

動 使騷動、使不安 同 annoy 惹惱、打擾

▶It is quite clear that he didn't want to disturb his father at night.
顯然他不想在晚上打擾他的父親。

> **文法字詞解析**
> 想好好做事卻一直被親友傳的訊息打擾嗎？這時 disturb 這個單字就派上用場了。找找看，你的手機或許有一個「請勿打擾」模式，開啟它後各式各樣的麻煩訊息就不會一直跳出來吵你了。這個東西在英文就叫作「Don't disturb mode」。

di·vine [dəˈvaɪn]
Track 3508

形 神的、神聖的

▶To err is human; to forgive is divine.
　犯錯是人之常情、原諒卻是神聖的。

di·vorce [dəˈvors]
Track 3509

名 離婚、解除婚約　動 使離婚、離婚

▶名 It took their daughter several years to understand the true cause of their divorce.
　他們的女兒花了好幾年的時間才明白他們離婚的真正原因。

▶動 It took my aunt a long time to decide to divorce her husband.
　嬸嬸花了很長時間才決定跟她的丈夫離婚。

dom·i·nant [ˈdɑmənənt]
Track 3510

形 支配的

▶They built the castle in the dominant position above the town.
　他們把這座城堡建在市鎮中的一個高處。

dom·i·nate [ˈdɑmə‚net]
Track 3511

動 支配、統治

▶It is inappropriate to dominate someone who is kind and sweet.
　操控善良的人很不應該。

文法字詞解析
除了真正支配、統治外，在比賽中佔有極大優勢、把對方壓著打，也可以說是「dominate」。

dor·mi·to·ry/dorm
Track 3512
[ˈdɔrmə‚torɪ]/[dɔrm]

名 宿舍

▶It takes me half an hour to get to my dormitory from the library.
　從圖書館到我的宿舍要花半個小時。

down·load [ˈdaʊn‚lod]
Track 3513

動 下載、往下傳送

▶I downloaded the electronic file of the thesis from the online database.
　我從線上資料庫下載這篇論文的電子檔。

doze [doz]
Track 3514

名 打瞌睡　動 打瞌睡

▶名 I has a quick doze on the train, so that I could continue working after the journey.
　我在火車上小睡了一會，這樣旅程結束後我就能繼續工作。

▶動 Several students dozed off during the old professor's lecture.
　有些學生在這位老教授演講期間打瞌睡。

Level 1

Level 2

Level 3

Level 4

自我勉勵、越背越上手——
提升程度4200單字

Level 5

Level 6

draft [dræft]　🔊 Track 3515

名 草稿 動 撰寫、草擬 同 sketch 草稿、草擬

▶名 There is no point in going over the draft when it hasn't been finished yet.
草稿還未完成時就拿來研讀，沒多大意義。

▶動 There is no point in drafting the contract now, because they haven't agreed to all the terms yet.
現在草擬合約毫無意義，因為他們還未同意全部的條件。

dread [drɛd]　🔊 Track 3516

名 非常害怕 動 敬畏、恐怖 同 fear 恐怖

▶名 It is quite clear that most people have a dread of snakes.
很顯然，大部分人都怕蛇。

▶動 I dread to talk with the authoritative scientist.
我不敢跟這位有威望的科學家交談。

drift [drɪft]　🔊 Track 3517

名 漂流物 動 漂移

▶名 A drift of logs just went past us on the river.
河上剛剛有一大堆的木頭漂了過去。

▶動 No one noticed a tiny fishing boat drifting slowly（緩慢地）along. 沒有人注意到有一隻小小的漁船正在緩緩地漂去。

> **文法字詞解析**
> 除了在水面上的漂移之外，開賽車時高難度的漂移（甩尾）也稱作 drift。

drill [drɪl]　🔊 Track 3518

名 鑽、錐、操練 動 鑽孔

▶名 During the earthquake drill, several kids fell off the stairs and got injured.
在地震演習期間，有些小孩跌下樓梯而受傷了。

▶動 Would you like me to ask some workmen（工人）to drill in the wall?
要不要我叫些工人在牆上鑽孔呢？

du·ra·ble [ˈdjʊrəb!]　🔊 Track 3519

形 耐穿的、耐磨的

▶You'd better buy some canvas（帆布）bags which are durable.
你最好買一些耐用的帆布袋子。

dust·y [ˈdʌstɪ]　🔊 Track 3520

形 覆著灰塵的

▶It's windy and dusty here in spring; I wish I could move to another city next year.
這裡的春天有風沙，但願我明年能搬到另外一個城市去住。

DVD/dig·it·al vid·e·o disk/dig·it·al ver·sa·tile disk　🔊 Track 3521

[ˈdɪdʒɪt! ˈvɪdɪo dɪsk]/[ˈdɪdʒɪt! ˈvɝsətɪl dɪsk]

名 影音光碟機

▶Can you recommend the best DVD player in the store?
你能推薦一下這家店裡最好的 DVD 機嗎？

dye [daɪ]
◀€ *Track 3522*

名 染料 動 染、著色

▶名 What dye did you use to get such lovely golden-red hair?
你到底是用什麼染料弄得這一頭金紅色的亮麗頭髮？

▶動 My mom has gray hair, and she dyed it black again.
我媽媽有白頭髮，她把它染黑。

dy·nam·ic [`daɪnəˌmaɪt]
◀€ *Track 3523*

形 動能的、動力的 同 energetic 有力的

▶It is the economic recession（衰退）that caused the dynamic market disappeared.
由於經濟衰退導致了活躍市場的消失。

dyn·as·ty [`daɪnəstɪ]
◀€ *Track 3524*

名 王朝、朝代

▶The treasure was passed down by an aristocrat of Qing dynasty.
這項寶物是由清朝的貴族傳下來的。

[Ee]

ear·nest [`ɝnɪst]
◀€ *Track 3525*

名 認真 形 認真的

▶名 I don't think he was apologizing in earnest.
我覺得他並不是真誠地道歉。

▶形 I don't think he was earnest when he said he would come.
我認為他說他會來並不是認真的。

ear·phone [`ɪrˌfon]
◀€ *Track 3526*

名 耳機

▶Why not put on your earphones and try the equipment?
為什麼不戴上耳機試一下設備呢？

ec·o·nom·ic [ˌikə`nɑmɪk]
◀€ *Track 3527*

形 經濟上的

▶Economics was not an easy field to major in.
經濟學不是一門很容易的主修科目

ec·o·nom·i·cal [ˌikə`nɑmɪkl]
◀€ *Track 3528*

形 節儉的

▶This car is economical to run because it doesn't use much fuel.開這輛車蠻省錢的，因為它耗油不多。

ec·o·nom·ics [ˌikə`nɑmɪks]
◀€ *Track 3529*

名 經濟學

▶I majored in economics in college; what about you?
我大學主修經濟學，你呢？

文法字詞解析
sad 不只有難過的意思，還有「糟透了、難以接受」的意思，使用時要注意。

文法字詞解析
economic 和 economical 雖然長得很像、都是形容詞、又都和經濟有關，但意思不完全一樣喔！ economic 指的是「和經濟學有關的、和經濟有關的」，而 economical 則有「經濟實惠的」、「節省的」的意思。

Level 1

Level 2

Level 3

Level 4

自我勉勵、越背越上手——
提升程度4200單字

Level 5

Level 6

e·con·o·mist [ɪˈkɑnəmɪst] 🔊 *Track 3530*
名 經濟學家
▶What do you think of inviting the famous economist to give us a speech? 你覺得我們邀請那位著名的經濟學家來為我們做一次演講怎麼樣？

e·con·o·my [ɪˈkɑnəmɪ] 🔊 *Track 3531*
名 經濟
▶I'm afraid that the economy has yet to improve. 恐怕經濟狀況還沒改善，你覺得呢？

efficiency [əˈfɪʃənsɪ] 🔊 *Track 3532*
名 效率
▶We employed a new technique to improve work efficiency. 我們採用新技術來改進工作效率。

e·las·tic [ɪˈlæstɪk] 🔊 *Track 3533*
名 橡皮筋 形 有彈性的
▶名 I used the elastic to shoot a mosquito. 我用橡皮筋射了蚊子。
▶形 The elastic suit is really stretchy. 這件有彈性的衣服超能伸展的。

e·lec·tri·cian [ˌɪlɛkˈtrɪʃən] 🔊 *Track 3534*
名 電機工程師
▶The electrician helped us to get rid of the glitches in the robotic production line. 電子工程師幫助我們解決生產線上的故障問題。

e·lec·tron·ics [ˌɪlɛkˈtrɑniks] 🔊 *Track 3535*
名 電機工程學
▶I work for a small electronics firm; what about you? 我在一家小型的電子公司工作，你呢？

el·e·gant [ˈɛləgənt] 🔊 *Track 3536*
形 優雅的
▶It is obvious that his elegant clothes contrasted with his rough speech. 顯然他優雅的服飾與粗俗的語言形成鮮明的對比。

el·e·men·ta·ry [ˌɛləˈmɛntərɪ] 🔊 *Track 3537*
形 基本的
▶Not everyone knows that the elementary school is affiliated（隸屬於）to that university. 不是每個人都知道這所小學附屬於那所大學。

e·lim·i·nate [ɪˈlɪməˌnet] 🔊 *Track 3538*
動 消除
▶Our team was eliminated from the semi-final in the tournament. 我們的隊伍在準決賽中被淘汰了。

文法字詞解析
這個單字也可以用來表示心理上的「彈性」，即遇到挫折後也能很快地「彈回來」。

else·where [ˈɛlsˌhwɛr]　🔊 *Track 3539*
副 在別處
▶Do you know if there is intelligent life elsewhere in the universe?
你知道宇宙中是否有其他地方有智慧生命嗎？

e-mail/email [ˈimel]　🔊 *Track 3540*
名 電子郵件　動 發電子郵件
▶名 I got an email yesterday that wasn't meant for me.
我昨天收到寄錯的電子郵件。
▶動 I think it's better for you to email us instead of sending a letter.
我認為相對於寄信來說，你們最好是寄電子郵件給我們。

em·bar·rass [ɪmˈbærəs]　🔊 *Track 3541*
動 使困窘
▶The ambiguous announcement embarrassed everyone attending the meeting.
這項模糊的宣言使參與會議的人相當尷尬。

em·bar·rass·ment　🔊 *Track 3542*
[ɪmˈbærəsmənt]
名 困窘
▶The embarrassment on his face was obvious when he realized that he had a hole in his pants.
他發現褲子上有破洞時，表情顯然超窘的。

em·bas·sy [ˈɛmbəsɪ]　🔊 *Track 3543*
名 大使館
▶The embassy has become an obvious target for terrorist（恐怖分子）attacks. 大使館已經成為恐怖分子攻擊的明顯目標。

e·merge [ɪˈmɝdʒ]　🔊 *Track 3544*
動 浮現
▶A young tennis player emerged victorious in the American open. 一位年輕的選手在美國網球公開賽中脫穎而出。

e·mo·tion·al [ɪˈmoʃənl]　🔊 *Track 3545*
形 情感的
▶Her mother is sick; it is no wonder that she had a major emotional breakdown.
她的母親生病了，怪不得她情緒上崩潰得很厲害。

em·pha·sis [ˈɛmfəsɪs]　🔊 *Track 3546*
名 重點、強調
▶The entrepreneur put emphasis on the social responsibility of the enterprise. 這位企業家強調企業的社會責任。

em·pire [ˈɛmpaɪr]　🔊 *Track 3547*
名 帝國
▶The Roman Empire existed for several centuries.
羅馬帝國存在了幾百年。

文法字詞解析
emotional 不只可以表示「情感上的」，也可以表示「情感豐富的」。例如當你的朋友看電影哭了四次、一直到出了電影院還停不下來，就可以勸他不要那麼 emotional。

Level 1

Level 2

Level 3

Level 4

提升程度4200單字
自我勉勵、越背越上手

Level 5

Level 6

en·close [ɪnˋkloz]
🔊 Track 3548

動 包圍

▶Would you please enclose an address proof dated within the latest three months?
請附上最近三個月內的地址證明書好嗎？

en·coun·ter [ɪnˋkaʊntɚ]
🔊 Track 3549

名 遭遇 **動** 遭遇

▶**名** It was a strange encounter that brought us together.
是一次奇妙的邂逅使我們在一起的。

▶**動** I'm afraid that you will encounter such problems in the future.
恐怕你將來會遇到這類問題。

en·dan·ger [ɪnˋdendʒɚ]
🔊 Track 3550

動 使陷入危險

▶A conservation area was set up to protect this species for it is endangered.
有一個保育區被建立起來，以保護這個瀕危物種。

en·dure [ɪnˋdjʊr]
🔊 Track 3551

動 忍受

▶They are deeply in love with each other and endured a lot together.
他們深愛彼此，一起經過許多考驗。

en·force [ɪnˋfors]
🔊 Track 3552

動 實施、強迫

▶The new tax law will be enforced next year.
新的稅法將會在明年實施。

文法字詞解析
enforce the law = 執法
enforce a contract = 履行合約

en·force·ment [ɪnˋforsmənt]
🔊 Track 3553

名 施行

▶I don't think that weak law enforcement is the main problem.
我認為執法不力不是問題的關鍵。

en·gi·neer·ing [ˌɛndʒəˋnɪrɪŋ]
🔊 Track 3554

名 工程學

▶He gave up engineering and took to medicine.
他放棄了工程學，開始從事醫學。

en·large [ɪnˋlardʒ]
🔊 Track 3555

動 擴大

▶I used a photo editing software to enlarge the picture.
我使用相片編輯軟體來放大這張相片。

en·large·ment [ɪnˋlardʒmənt]
🔊 Track 3556

名 擴張

▶What do you think of sending my mother an enlargement of our baby's photo?
你覺得寄張我們小寶寶的放大照片給我母親怎麼樣？

萬用延伸句型
What do you think of...? 你覺得……怎樣？

e·nor·mous [ɪˈnɔrməs]
🔊 *Track 3557*

形 巨大的 同 vast 巨大的

▶Parents' words often have enormous impact on the children's mental development.
父母親的話常常對小孩的心理狀態發展有很大的影響。

en·ter·tain [ˌɛntəˈten]
🔊 *Track 3558*

動 招待、娛樂

▶He is performing magic tricks to entertain the guests.
他正在表演魔術以娛樂客人們。

en·ter·tain·ment [ˌɛntəˈtenmənt]
🔊 *Track 3559*

名 款待、娛樂

▶Would you like to play the piano for our entertainment?
你願意為我們彈鋼琴助興嗎?

en·thu·si·asm [ɪnˈθjuzɪˌæzəm]
🔊 *Track 3560*

名 熱衷、熱情 同 zeal 熱心

▶The proposal was greeted with great enthusiasm.
這個建議得到了熱情的回應。

en·vi·ous [ˈɛnvɪəs]
🔊 *Track 3561*

形 羨慕的、妒忌的 同 jealous 妒忌的

▶She is envious of Mary's slim figure. 她嫉妒瑪麗的苗條身材。

e·qual·i·ty [ɪˈkwɑlətɪ]
🔊 *Track 3562*

名 平等

▶The sanitor fought for gender equality in workplace.
這位參議員致力爭取職場的兩性平權。

e·quip [ɪˈkwɪp]
🔊 *Track 3563*

動 裝備

▶You need to equip yourself with a sharp pencil and an eraser for the exam.
你必須準備一枝尖銳的鉛筆和一塊橡皮擦去參加考試。

e·quip·ment [ɪˈkwɪpmənt]
🔊 *Track 3564*

名 裝備、設備

▶The government has an interest in importing scientific equipment. 政府對引進科學設備很感興趣。

e·ra [ˈɪrə]
🔊 *Track 3565*

名 時代

▶He was a great emperor. It is no wonder that his death marked the end of an era.
他是個偉大的皇帝。難怪他的死象徵著一個時代的結束。

er·rand [ˈɛrənd]
🔊 *Track 3566*

名 任務

▶My supervisor sent me on errands this morning.
我的主管今天早上叫我去出差。

萬用延伸句型

entertain oneself with sth. (做某事)娛樂自己、打發時間
例如:He had nothing to do and entertained himself with a few movies.
他沒事好做,於是看了幾部電影作為娛樂。

文法字詞解析

除了實質上的設備,心理的素質也可稱作 equipment,例如要說某人心理上還沒準備好,不適任這個工作,即可說 he doesn't have the equipment to cope with this task。

Level 1

Level 2

Level 3

Level 4

自我勉勵、越背越上手——
提升程度4200單字

Level 5

Level 6

es·ca·la·tor [ˈɛskəˌletə]
◀ Track 3567

名 手扶梯
▶I don't want to walk anymore; let's take the escalator.
我不想再走路了，我們搭手扶梯吧。

es·say [ˈɛse]
◀ Track 3568

名 短文、隨筆
▶The essay was published in the international journal.
這篇論文被刊登在國際期刊上。

es·tab·lish [əˈstæblɪʃ]
◀ Track 3569

動 建立 同 found 建立
▶How do we establish a good credit policy? That's a problem.
如何才能建立好的信貸政策？這是個難題。

es·tab·lish·ment [əˈstæblɪʃmənt] ◀ Track 3570

名 組織、建立
▶It took us six years to finish the establishment of that school.
我們花了六年的時間才完成了那所學校的興建。

es·sen·tial [ɪˈsɛnʃəl]
◀ Track 3571

名 基本要素 形 本質的、必要的、基本的 同 basic 基本的
▶名 Creativity and good composition are the essentials of a good photo.
創意以及好的構圖是一張好相片最重要的元素。
▶形 The most essential thing you need to know about this course is that we won't have any exams.
這堂課你最需要知道的重點就是不會有考試。

es·ti·mate [ˈɛstəˌmet]
◀ Track 3572

名 評估 動 評估
▶名 His estimate of the situation is not so optimistic.
他對形勢的估計不那麼樂觀。
▶動 He is highly estimated among his colleagues.
他在同事之間獲得很高的評價。

e·val·u·ate [ɪˈvæljʊˌet]
◀ Track 3573

動 估計、評價
▶Would you let me know how you evaluate success?
您能否告訴我您是如何評價成功的嗎？

e·val·u·a·tion [ɪˌvæljʊˈeʃən]
◀ Track 3574

名 評價
▶Would you like to do a quick evaluation for me?
你能幫我迅速地估個價嗎？

e·ve [iv]
◀ Track 3575

名 前夕
▶On New Year's Eve, all family members reunited at my grandfather's place.
新年前夕，所有家族成員聚集在我外公家。

萬用延伸句型

establish oneself 為自己建立名聲
例如：After years of hard work, he established himself as the best teacher in the school.
經過多年的努力，他為自己打下了「全校最佳教師」的名聲。

e·ven·tu·al [ɪˋvɛntʃʊəl]　🔊 Track 3576
形 最後的　同 final 最後的
▶It was his foolish behavior that led to his eventual failure.
正是他的愚蠢行為導致了他最後的失敗。

ev·i·dence [ˋɛvədəns]　🔊 Track 3577
名 證據　動 證明
▶名 The prosecutor held the evidence that he was guilty.
檢察官手上有他犯罪的證據。
▶動 I don't think he has enough to evidence his innocence.
我認為他並不足以證明自己的無辜。

ev·i·dent [ˋɛvədənt]　🔊 Track 3578
形 明顯的
▶This truth seems to be self-evident, don't you think so?
這個真理似乎是不言而喻的，你不這樣認為嗎？

ex·ag·ger·ate [ɪgˋzædʒə͵ret]　🔊 Track 3579
動 誇大
▶If you always exaggerate, people will no longer believe you.
一旦你老是誇大事情，人們便不會相信你了。

ex·am·i·nee [ɪg͵zæməˋni]　🔊 Track 3580
名 應試者
▶The examinees lined up to have their ID checked.
應試者排隊拿出身分證件受檢。

ex·am·in·er [ɪgˋzæmɪnɚ]　🔊 Track 3581
名 主考官、審查員
▶It is my first time as an examiner.
這是我第一次擔任主考官。

ex·cep·tion [ɪkˋsɛpʃən]　🔊 Track 3582
名 反對、例外
▶There is always an exception to any rule.
任何規律總有例外。

ex·haust [ɪgˋzɔst]　🔊 Track 3583
名 排氣管　動 耗盡
▶名 They have taken measures to prevent exhaust pollution.
他們已經採取措施防止廢氣污染。
▶動 It is said that fossil fuel will be exhausted within decades.
據說化石燃料在數十年內會被用盡。

ex·hib·it [ɪgˋzɪbɪt]　🔊 Track 3584
名 展示品、展覽　動 展示
▶名 There's a painting exhibit at the art gallery this week.
這星期美術館有個畫展。
▶動 Why don't you exhibit your paintings? They are wonderful!
你為什麼不展出你的畫呢？它們太棒了！

萬用延伸句型
It is self-evident that... ……是不言而喻的。
例如：It is self-evident that parents affect their children's behavior.
家長對孩子的行為有所影響是不言而喻的。

文法字詞解析
exhausted 描述筋疲力盡、也就是所有的力量都已經「耗盡」了。

Level 1
Level 2
Level 3
Level 4
Level 5
Level 6

提升程度4200單字 自我勉勵、越背越上手

ex·pand [ɪk`spænd]
◀€ *Track 3585*

動 擴大、延長

▶He has an ambition to expand the company to an international enterprise.
他有野心將公司擴大成國際企業。

ex·pan·sion [ɪk`spænʃən]
◀€ *Track 3586*

名 擴張

▶It's time for the company to consolidate（整頓）after several years of rapid expansion.
公司經過幾年的迅速發展之後，該整頓一下了。

ex·per·i·men·tal [ɪkˌspɛrə`mɛntḷ]
◀€ *Track 3587*

形 實驗性的

▶The medicine is still in the experimental stage.
這種藥還在實驗階段。

ex·pla·na·tion [ˌɛksplə`neʃən]
◀€ *Track 3588*

名 說明、解釋

▶For all your explanation, I understand no better than before.
儘管你做了詳細解釋，我還是不懂。

ex·plore [ɪk`splor]
◀€ *Track 3589*

動 探查、探險

▶The adventurous man explored the untrodden area.
愛冒險的人去探索了無人到過的區域。

ex·plo·sion [ɪk`sploʒən]
◀€ *Track 3590*

名 爆炸

▶More than 40 people were wounded in the explosion.
超過四十人在爆炸事件中受傷。

ex·plo·sive [ɪk`splosɪv]
◀€ *Track 3591*

名 炸藥 形 爆炸的、(性情)暴躁的

▶名 Dynamite is a powerful explosive.
炸藥是一種強有力的爆炸物。

▶形 His explosive personality makes people either hate him or fear him.
他暴躁的個性令人不是討厭他就是怕他。

文法字詞解析
當作名詞時，explosive 經常以複數形式 explosives 出現，統稱「炸藥」。

ex·pose [ɪk`spoz]
◀€ *Track 3592*

動 暴露、揭發

▶You really shouldn't expose certain body parts in public.
在公眾場合不要暴露出某些身體部位比較好吧。

ex·po·sure [ɪk`spoʒɚ]
◀€ *Track 3593*

名 顯露

▶Long-term exposure to radioactive materials may cause harm to human health.
長期暴露在放射性物質，可能會危害人體健康。

ex·tend [ɪkˋstɛnd]
🔊 Track 3594

動 延長
▶Can you please extend your visit for a few days?
你們訪問的時間能不能延長幾天？

ex·tent [ɪkˋstɛnt]
🔊 Track 3595

名 範圍
▶To some extent, this note helped me to comprehend the article better.
某些程度來說，這個註記幫助我更加理解這篇文章。

[Ff]

fa·cial [ˋfeʃəl]
🔊 Track 3596

形 面部的、表面的
▶I can't really see his facial expression from here.
我從這裡看不清楚他的臉部表情。

文法字詞解析
facial是形容詞，但隨著美容風潮的興起，也可以當作名詞直接稱呼「面部保養」（即 facial treatment 的簡單說法）。
例如：I'm going to get a facial this weekend.
我這週末要去做臉。

fa·cil·i·ty [fəˋsɪlətɪ]
🔊 Track 3597

名 容易、靈巧
▶She has great facility in learning languages.
她很有學習語言的才能。

faith·ful [ˋfeθfəl]
🔊 Track 3598

形 忠實的、耿直的、可靠的 同 loyal 忠實的
▶The soldiers were faithful to the general.
軍人對於將軍很忠心。

fame [fem]
🔊 Track 3599

名 名聲、聲譽
▶He gained fame from posting videos of himself online.
他因為在網路上發佈自己的影片而出了名。

fan·tas·tic [fænˋtæstɪk]
🔊 Track 3600

形 想像中的、奇異古怪的
▶He often has lots of fantastic ideas.
他常常異想天開。

文法字詞解析
fantastic 在口語中也可以表示「很棒的」、「極好的」，和 great、wonderful、excellent 同義。

fan·ta·sy [ˋfæntəsɪ]
🔊 Track 3601

名 空想、異想
▶That's not a fantasy novel. It's sci-fi.
那本不是奇幻小說啦，是科幻才對。

fare·well [ˋfɛrˋwɛl]
🔊 Track 3602

名 告別、歡送會
▶The farewell party for the retired worker will begin at six.
退休人員的送別會將會在六點開始。

Level 1
Level 2
Level 3
Level 4
Level 5
Level 6

提升程度4200單字
自我勉勵、越背越上手

431

fa·tal [ˈfetl̩]　🔊 *Track 3603*

形 致命的、決定性的　同 mortal 致命的

▶Don't you think even a very small mistake would be fatal to our plan? 難道你不覺得即使是一個很小的錯誤，對我們的計畫都將是致命的嗎？

fa·vor·a·ble [ˈfevərəbl̩]　🔊 *Track 3604*

形 有利的、討人喜歡的

▶The condition was favorable for the host team. 情況對於地主隊有利。

feast [fist]　🔊 *Track 3605*

名 宴會、節日　動 宴請、使高興

▶名 Why don't we invite him to the feast? 我們為何不邀請他來參加宴會呢？

▶動 You'll have all the time in the world to feast your eyes on the beautiful scenery. 你會有很多時間可以享受這裡的美景。

fer·ry [ˈfɛrɪ]　🔊 *Track 3606*

名 渡口、渡船　動 以船運輸

▶名 They took a ferry to the island. 他們搭乘渡船到島上去。

▶動 Do you ferry people across the river every day? 你每天都會用渡船送人們過這條河嗎？

fer·tile [ˈfɝtl̩]　🔊 *Track 3607*

形 肥沃的、豐富的

▶It is hard for the farmers to get a harvest on these less fertile fields. 農民們很難在這些貧瘠的土地上獲得豐收。

fetch [fɛtʃ]　🔊 *Track 3608*

動 取得、接來

▶The dog was taught to fetch the slippers for its owner. 這隻狗被訓練幫牠的主人拿拖鞋來。

fic·tion [ˈfɪkʃən]　🔊 *Track 3609*

名 小說、虛構

▶I am fond of reading all kinds of fiction; what about you? 我很喜歡讀各種小說，你呢？

fierce [fɪrs]　🔊 *Track 3610*

形 猛烈的、粗暴的、兇猛的　同 violent 猛烈的

▶The lion is really fierce when hungry. 這獅子餓的時候都很兇暴。

fi·nance [faɪˈnæns]　🔊 *Track 3611*

名 財務　動 融資

▶名 The finance director of our company has a doctoral diploma. 我們公司的財務總監有博士的學位。

▶動 Can you tell me who financed this organization? 你可以告訴我是誰在為這個組織提供資金嗎？

文法字詞解析

有個俚語 Fact is stranger than fiction，描述有時真實世界發生的事情比虛構的文學作品情節還來得離奇。

fi·nan·cial [faɪˋnænʃəl]
🔊 *Track 3612*

形 金融的、財政的

▶What do you think of the financial crisis? Did it affect your country?
你如何看待這次的金融危機呢？它影響到你們的國家了嗎？

fire·crack·er [ˋfaɪrˏkrækəˋ]
🔊 *Track 3613*

名 鞭炮

▶Jack ran away immediately（立即）as soon as the firecracker was lit up. 鞭炮一被點燃，傑克就立刻跑開了。

fire·place [ˋfaɪrˏples]
🔊 *Track 3614*

名 壁爐、火爐

▶The illegal firecracker factory was shut down after being reported to the environmental bureau.
這家非法煙火工廠被舉報至環保局之後就關門了。

flat·ter [ˋflætəˋ]
🔊 *Track 3615*

動 諂媚、奉承

▶It is quite obvious that he is flattering you.
顯然他是在奉承你。

flee [fli]
🔊 *Track 3616*

動 逃走、逃避

▶The robber fled the scene really quickly.
這個強盜很快速地從現場逃掉了。

flex·i·ble [ˋflɛksəbḷ]
🔊 *Track 3617*

形 有彈性的、易曲的

▶What's your schedule tomorrow afternoon? I'm pretty flexible.
你明天下午的行程如何？我的時間很有彈性的。

flu·ent [ˋfluənt]
🔊 *Track 3618*

形 流暢的、流利的

▶Tom can speak fluent English.
湯姆能講一口流利的英語。

flunk [flʌŋk]
🔊 *Track 3619*

名 失敗、不及格 動 失敗、放棄 同 fail 失敗

▶名 His flunk in the exam made his parents so mad.
他考試不及格的事讓他父母很生氣。

▶動 Did he flunk in the final exam again this year?
他今年期末考試又不及格了嗎？

flush [flʌʃ]
🔊 *Track 3620*

名 紅光、繁茂 動 水淹、使興奮、用水沖洗

▶名 Tina told the embarrassing truth with a flush on her face.
蒂娜臉紅著講述這個令人尷尬的事實。

▶動 Did you forget to flush the toilet again?
你又忘記沖馬桶了喔？

文法字詞解析

firecrackers 通常是在地上點燃的那種鞭炮，而煙火則通常說 fireworks。兩者都常以複數出現，可能是因為像鞭炮、煙火這類東西通常都是大量大量地放，很少會有人去數有幾個。

文法字詞解析

flee 的動詞變化：flee, fled, fled

Level 1

Level 2

Level 3

Level 4

提升程度4200單字 ——自我勉勵、越背越上手

Level 5

Level 6

foam [fom]
Track 3621

名 泡沫 動 起泡沫

▶ 名 Why is the toilet full of foam?
馬桶裡怎麼一堆泡沫？

▶ 動 The sick dog is foaming at the mouth.
那隻病犬口吐白沫。

for·bid [fɚˋbɪd]
Track 3622

動 禁止、禁止入內

▶ Dogs are forbidden in this building.
狗被禁止進入這棟建築物。

fore·cast [forˋkæst]
Track 3623

動 預測、預報

▶ No one is able to forecast how long the war will last.
沒有人能預測出這場戰爭會持續多久。

for·ma·tion [fɔrˋmeʃən]
Track 3624

名 形成、成立

▶ What do you think of the formation of the new government?
你怎麼看待新政府的組成呢？

for·mu·la [ˋfɔrmjələ]
Track 3625

名 公式、法則

▶ The prodigydeduced the formula for his teacher.
這個神童幫他的老師推演出這個公式。

fort [fort]
Track 3626

名 堡壘、炮台

▶ I don't think the enemy can occupy this fort within a week.
我認為敵軍一週內佔領不了這個要塞。

for·tu·nate [ˋfɔrtʃənɪt]
Track 3627

形 幸運的、僥倖的 同 lucky 幸運的

▶ My sister is fortunate enough to win the first prize in the speech contest. 我妹妹在演講比賽中很幸運地獲得了一等獎。

文法字詞解析
fortunate 的相反詞則是加上表示「不、沒有」的字首「un-」，變成 unfortunate（不幸的）。

fos·sil [ˋfɑsl]
Track 3628

名 化石、舊事物 形 陳腐的

▶ 名 The kids admired the fossils of dinosaurs in the museum.
小朋友在博物館裡瞻仰恐龍的化石。

▶ 形 I wanted to find a fossil leaf on the mountain, but in the end I find nothing.
我本來想在山上找到一塊葉子化石，可是最後我什麼也沒找到。

foun·da·tion [faʊnˋdeʃən]
Track 3629

名 基礎、根基 同 base 基礎

▶ Will you tell me how you laid the foundation for your success?
你能告訴我你是如何為你的成功打下基礎的嗎？

文法字詞解析
化妝的時候，在臉上打下「基礎」用的粉底也可以稱為 foundation。

found·er [ˈfaʊndɚ]
Track 3630

名 創立者、捐出基金者

▶The former first lady is the founder of the charity organization.
前第一夫人是這個慈善機構的創辦人。

fra·grance [ˈfregrəns]
Track 3631

名 芬香、芬芳

▶Beauty without virtue is a rose without fragrance.
無德之美猶如沒有香味的玫瑰，徒有其表。

fra·grant [ˈfregrənt]
Track 3632

形 芳香的、愉快的

▶The air in the park is warm and fragrant in spring.
春天的時候，公園裡的空氣既溫暖又芬芳。

frame [frem]
Track 3633

名 骨架、體制 動 構築、框架

▶名 He is a tall man with a skinny frame.
他是個高且骨架窄的男子。

▶動 Will you frame the picture for me? It was painted by my daughter studying abroad.
請你為這幅畫加個框好嗎？它是我在國外留學的女兒畫的。

萬用延伸句型
frame of mind 心理狀態
例如：His frame of mind is low right now. I don't think you should bother him.
他現在心情低落，最好不要打擾他吧。

free·way [ˈfriˌwe]
Track 3634

名 高速公路

▶I didn't know what to do when my car broke down on the freeway yesterday.
昨天我的車在高速公路上拋錨的時候，我都不知道怎麼辦才好。

fre·quen·cy [ˈfrikwənsɪ]
Track 3635

名 時常發生、頻率

▶Don't you think accidents have been happening with increasing frequency these years?
難道你不覺得近幾年來事故的發生越來越頻繁了嗎？

fresh·man [ˈfrɛʃmən]
Track 3636

名 新生、大一生

▶I am afraid I have to live in the dormitory in my freshman year at college.
恐怕我大學一年級得住宿舍了。

frost [frɔst]
Track 3637

名 霜、冷淡 動 結霜

▶名 Snow and frost covered the roads and the fields.
雪和霜覆蓋在道路和田地上。

▶動 The cold frosted all the windows in the morning.
清晨，低溫使得所有的窗子都結了霜。

文法字詞解析
frostbite = 凍傷

Level 1
Level 2
Level 3
Level 4
提升程度4200單字 自我勉勵、越背越上手
Level 5
Level 6

frown [fraʊn] 🔊 *Track 3638*

名 不悅之色 動 皺眉、表示不滿

▶名 The victim's father answered the journalist's question with a frown. 這個受害者的父親皺著眉回答記者的問題。

▶動 She is always frowning for some reason.
她不知道為什麼總是皺著眉頭。

frus·tra·tion [ˌfrʌsˈtreʃən] 🔊 *Track 3639*

名 挫折、失敗

▶It is hard for the young man to understand the old man who has met so many frustrations in his life.
這個年輕人很難理解這位曾在生活中歷經無數挫折的老人。

fu·el [ˈfjuəl] 🔊 *Track 3640*

名 燃料 動 燃料補給

▶名 Let's find out what sort of fuel these new machines need.
我們一起來找出這些新機器需要哪種燃料吧。

▶動 I want to fuel my car later. 我待會想幫我的車加油。

ful·fill [fʊlˈfɪl] 🔊 *Track 3641*

動 實踐、實現、履行 同 finish 完成

▶Once you promise someone, you must fulfill your promise by all means.
一旦你許諾他人了，你就必須盡一切辦法履行你的諾言。

ful·fill·ment [fʊlˈfɪlmənt] 🔊 *Track 3642*

名 實現、符合條件

▶DI gained a sense of fulfillment from volunteering in the orphanage. 我在孤兒院做志工，獲得很大的成就感。

func·tion·al [ˈfʌŋkʃənl̩] 🔊 *Track 3643*

形 作用的、機能的

▶Is the machine fully functional?
這個機器有完全地在運作嗎？

fun·da·men·tal [ˌfʌndəˈmɛntl̩] 🔊 *Track 3644*

名 基礎、原則 形 基礎的、根本的

▶名 They know nothing about these fundamentals.
他們一點都不瞭解這些基本原理。

▶形 Fresh air is fundamental to good health.
新鮮空氣對健康是不可缺少的。

fu·ner·al [ˈfjunərəl] 🔊 *Track 3645*

名 葬禮、告別式

▶It is said that there were hardly any dry eyes at the funeral.
據說在那場葬禮上很少有人不落淚的。

fu·ri·ous [ˈfjʊrɪəs] 🔊 *Track 3646*

形 狂怒的、狂鬧的 同 angry 發怒的

▶The furious man threatened to explode the gas tank.
這個生氣的男人威脅要引爆瓦斯桶。

萬用延伸句型

add fuel to the flames 火上加油、讓事情變得更糟

例如：The rumors are already bad enough. Why did you have to add fuel to the flame?
那些傳言已經夠糟糕了，你為什麼還要火上加油呢？

fur·nish [ˈfɝnɪʃ]
Track 3647

動 供給、裝備

▶We have a budget to furnish our new apartment.
我們有一筆要買新公寓家具的預算。

fur·ther·more [ˈfɝðəˌmor]
Track 3648

副 再者、而且

▶I don't think I will go to the cinema with him; furthermore, I have no time to do so.
我想我不會跟他去看電影的，而且我也沒時間去。

[Gg]

gal·ler·y [ˈgælərɪ]
Track 3649

名 畫廊、美術館

▶The artist displayed his paintings in the gallery.
藝術家在畫廊展示他的畫作。

gang·ster [ˈgæŋstɚ]
Track 3650

名 歹徒、匪徒

▶There are quite a few people interested in movies about American police and gangsters.
有不少人都對看美國警匪片很感興趣。

gaze [gez]
Track 3651

名 注視、凝視 **動** 注視、凝視

▶**名** His gaze made me feel uneasy so I turned away.
他的目光讓我很不自在，所以我便轉頭了。

▶**動** She gazed lovingly at her cat.
她充滿愛意地凝視著她的貓。

gear [gɪr]
Track 3652

名 齒輪、裝具 **動** 開動、使適應

▶**名** Most cars have four forward gears.
大多數汽車有四個前進檔。

▶**動** The economic recovery would be geared with the efforts of all citizens. 經濟復甦需要靠所有人民的努來來促成。

gene [dʒin]
Track 3653

名 基因、遺傳因子

▶She eats a lot but never gets fat. It must be the genes.
她吃得很多，但都不會胖。大概是基因的關係吧。

gen·er·a·tion [ˌdʒɛnəˈreʃən]
Track 3654

名 世代

▶There are bound to be generation gaps no matter how hard people try to understand each other.
無論大家如何試著瞭解彼此，世代代溝還是免不了的。

文法字詞解析

與 furnish 相關的一個形容詞是 furnished（有家具的）。這可是相當重要的一個單字，尤其在租房子之前一定要看好是 furnished（有家具的）還是 unfurnished（沒有附家具的），差一點點就差很多。

文法字詞解析

gaze 和 stare 都有「一直盯著看」的意思，那麼兩者的差別在哪裡呢？原來，stare 通常不是很禮貌、甚至帶有比較兇的感覺，例如覺得路人長得很奇怪一直盯著看、或覺得你朋友講了很蠢的話讓你目瞪口呆，這種就是 stare。而 gaze 則通常帶有專注或喜愛的感情成分在其中，例如情侶之間含情脈脈地凝視著就可以用 gaze。

Level 1
Level 2
Level 3
Level 4

自我勉勵、越背越上手——提升程度4200單字

Level 5
Level 6

gen·er·os·i·ty [ˌdʒɛnəˈrɑsətɪ]　🔊 Track 3655

名 慷慨、寬宏大量　同 charity 寬容

▶Young as Rita is, she showed generosity to her younger brother.
雖然瑞塔很年輕，她卻懂得對弟弟大方。

gen·ius [ˈdʒinjəs]　🔊 Track 3656

名 天才、英才

▶I don't think that he is a math genius.
我認為他並不是個數學天才。

gen·u·ine [ˈdʒɛnjʊɪn]　🔊 Track 3657

形 真正的、非假冒的　同 real 真的

▶It is not easy for me to distinguish cultured pearls from genuine pearls.
辨別真正的珍珠和養殖珍珠對我來說真不容易。

germ [dʒɝm]　🔊 Track 3658

名 細菌、微生物、病菌

▶The sterilizing process can kill the germs in the packaged food.
衛生處理過程可以殺死包裝食物的細菌。

gift·ed [ˈɡɪftɪd]　🔊 Track 3659

形 有天賦的、有才能的

▶That scientist is very gifted and made many discoveries.
那位科學家非常有才華，有了許多大發現。

文法字詞解析
a gifted child 有天賦的小孩，也可以叫做 "a child prodigy"。

gi·gan·tic [dʒaɪˈɡæntɪk]　🔊 Track 3660

形 巨人般的

▶The gigantic monument stands in the center of the park.
這個巨大的紀念碑立在公園的中心。

gig·gle [ˈɡɪɡl̩]　🔊 Track 3661

名 咯咯笑　動 咯咯地笑

▶名 She let out a giggle when he tickled her.
他一搔她癢，她便咯咯笑。

▶動 Jenny giggled when she saw the handsome man.
珍妮看到那個帥哥時，咯咯地笑了起來。

gin·ger [ˈdʒɪndʒɚ]　🔊 Track 3662

名 薑　動 使有活力

▶名 I like having ginger milk tea during breakfast.
我喜歡在早餐時間喝薑母奶茶。

▶動 What do you think about gingering up the party by playing a song? 你覺得表演一首歌來活絡宴會的氣氛怎麼樣？

文法字詞解析
這個字也可以用來描述紅髮的人的髮色。

glide [ɡlaɪd]　🔊 Track 3663

名 滑動、滑走　動 滑行

▶名 The skater went by with a series of glides.
那位溜冰選手以一連串的滑步從旁邊經過。

▶動 The novice skier learned how to glide down the slope.
滑雪的初學者學習如何從坡道上往下滑。

glimpse [glɪmps]　🔊 *Track 3664*

名 瞥見、一瞥　動 瞥見、隱約看見　同 glance 瞥見

▶名 Despite the humble outfit of the celebrity, I recognized him at the first glimpse.
雖然這位名人穿著很樸素，我還是一眼就認出他。

▶動 I glimpsed him at the other side of the room but he was soon gone.
我有在房間另一邊瞥見他，但他很快就不見了。

globe [glob]　🔊 *Track 3665*

名 地球、球

▶My dream is to visit every corner of the globe; what about you? 我的夢想是遊遍世界各地，你呢？

glo·ri·ous [ˋglorɪəs]　🔊 *Track 3666*

形 著名的、榮耀的

▶The glorious victory was earned after much hard work.
這次輝煌的勝利是靠著許多努力累積而贏得的。

goods [gʊdz]　🔊 *Track 3667*

名 商品、貨物

▶The goods are now in transit（運輸）. You'll need to wait for a few more days.
這批貨物正在運輸途中，你還得再等幾天。

grace [gres]　🔊 *Track 3668*

名 優美、優雅

▶We admire the duchess for her grace and elegance.
我們景仰女公爵的高雅氣質。

grace·ful [ˋgresfəl]　🔊 *Track 3669*

形 優雅的、雅致的

▶She used to be a dancer; it is no wonder that all her motions are quite graceful.
她曾經當過舞者，難怪她的一舉一動都很優美。

gra·cious [ˋgreʃəs]　🔊 *Track 3670*

形 親切的、溫和有禮的

▶The gracious lady was well-liked by everyone in the neighborhood.
這名親切的太太很受全社區的人歡迎。

grad·u·a·tion [ˏgrædʒʊˋeʃən]　🔊 *Track 3671*

名 畢業

▶I wish I could get a good job after graduation.
但願我畢業後能找到一份好工作。

gram·mar [ˋgræmɚ]　🔊 *Track 3672*

名 文法

▶To me, Japanese grammar rules are quite complicated.
對我來說，日文文法規則相當複雜。

文法字詞解析

名詞 grace（優雅）加上意為「充滿」的形容詞字尾「-ful」，就會變成 graceful（優美的、優雅的）。

Level 1
Level 2
Level 3
Level 4
提升程度4200單字　自我勉勵、越背越上手
Level 5
Level 6

gram·mat·i·cal [grəˋmætɪkl̩] 🔊 *Track 3673*

形 文法上的
▶There are several grammatical mistakes in the composition.
這份作文中有幾處文法上的錯誤。

grape·fruit [ˋgrepˌfrut] 🔊 *Track 3674*

名 葡萄柚
▶It is a kind of very delicious grapefruit. Would you like to try?
這是一種非常好吃的葡萄柚。你想試試看嗎？

grate·ful [ˋgretfəl] 🔊 *Track 3675*

形 感激的、感謝的
▶I was grateful for your assistance. 我很感激你的協助。

grat·i·tude [ˋgrætəˌtjud] 🔊 *Track 3676*

名 感激、感謝
▶I don't know how to properly express my gratitude.
我真不知道如何適切地表現出我的感激。

grave [grev] 🔊 *Track 3677*

形 嚴重的、重大的 名 墓穴、墳墓
▶形 The economy of this country is in grave danger of collapsing.
這個國家的經濟有垮台的危機。
▶名 She put down flowers on his grave. 她在他的墳墓上放了花。

greas·y [ˋgrizɪ] 🔊 *Track 3678*

形 塗有油脂的、油膩的
▶Too much greasy food isn't good for you.
太油膩的食物對你的身體不好。

greet·ing(s) [ˋgritɪŋ(z)] 🔊 *Track 3679*

名 問候、問候語
▶He's in a good mood and gave us a cheery greeting this
morning. 他今天的心情很好，早上愉快地跟我們打招呼。

grief [grif] 🔊 *Track 3680*

名 悲傷、感傷
▶It is obvious that the poor woman was buried in grief after her
son's death.
顯然這個可憐的婦人在兒子死後一直沉浸在悲痛之中。

grieve [griv] 🔊 *Track 3681*

動 悲傷、使悲傷
▶Jessica's husband passed away. We grieved for her loss.
潔西卡的丈夫過世了。我們為她失去摯愛而哀悼。

grind [graɪnd] 🔊 *Track 3682*

動 研磨、碾
▶It took about four or five years for me to grind and polish it.
把它磨平擦亮就花了我四五年的工夫。

guar·an·tee [ˌgærənˋti]　◀≼ *Track 3683*

名 擔保品、保證人　動 擔保、作保　同 promise 保證

▶名 Can to offer us a life-time guarantee?
您願意為我們提供永久保固嗎？

▶動 We guaranteed to our customers that the products were flawless. 我們向顧客保證這些產品沒有瑕疵。

guilt [gɪlt]　◀≼ *Track 3684*

名 罪、內疚

▶He felt no guilt for stealing his mother's money.
他偷自己母親的錢，卻一點都不覺得內疚。

guilt·y [ˋgɪltɪ]　◀≼ *Track 3685*

形 有罪的、內疚的

▶Are you guilty of robbing the bank or no?
你到底有沒有犯下搶銀行的罪？

gulf [gʌlf]　◀≼ *Track 3686*

名 灣、海灣

▶I don't think there is a gulf between my daughter and me.
我認為我和我女兒之間沒有隔閡。

文法字詞解析

guilt trip 是一種心理戰術，即説一些話讓對方感到莫名內疚，因而不知不覺答應你的要求。例如明知對方不想來參加活動，卻一直跟他説「來嘛來嘛，你不來我好寂寞，我難過」，讓對方不得不勉強答應，這就是 guilt trip 的表現。

[Hh]

ha·bit·u·al [həˋbɪtʃʊəl]　◀≼ *Track 3687*

形 習慣性的

▶She's a habitual liar so I don't think you should believe her that easily.
她有說謊的習慣，所以我覺得你不該那麼輕易相信她。

halt [hɔlt]　◀≼ *Track 3688*

名 休止　動 停止、使停止

▶名 You've been working all day; why not call a halt?
你已經工作了一整天，為什麼不歇一歇呢？

▶動 Inputting this command will halt the computer.
輸入這個命令可以使這台電腦停止運行。

hand·writ·ing [ˋhændˌraɪtɪŋ]　◀≼ *Track 3689*

名 手寫

▶I mimicked Mary's handwriting and sent a letter to her teenage son.
我模仿瑪莉的筆跡寫信給她十幾歲的兒子。

hard·en [ˋhɑrdn̩]　◀≼ *Track 3690*

動 使硬化

▶The water hardened and ice was formed.
水變硬結成了冰。

Level 1

Level 2

Level 3

Level 4

自我勉勵、越背越上手──提升程度4200單字

Level 5

Level 6

hard·ship [ˈhardʃɪp]
◀€ *Track 3691*

名 艱難、辛苦

▶Despite the hardship, the single mother raised three children on her own.

儘管困難重重，這名單親媽媽還是獨力扶養三個孩子長大。

hard·ware [ˈhardˌwɛr]
◀€ *Track 3692*

名 五金用品

▶I don't think they are very interested in your hardware.

我覺得他們對你的五金用品不是很感興趣。

har·mon·i·ca [harˈmɑnɪkə]
◀€ *Track 3693*

名 口琴

▶How about buying our daughter a harmonica as her birthday（生日）gift? 買個口琴給我們的女兒當生日禮物怎麼樣？

har·mo·ny [ˈharmənɪ]
◀€ *Track 3694*

名 一致、和諧 同 accord 一致

▶There is perfect harmony between the husband and the wife.

這對夫妻之間的感情非常融洽。

harsh [harʃ]
◀€ *Track 3695*

形 粗魯的、令人不快的

▶Nancy was emotionally hurt by her son's harsh words.

南茜因她兒子嚴厲的語言而心裡受傷。

haste [hest]
◀€ *Track 3696*

名 急忙、急速

▶She forgot her glasses in her haste to leave.

她在匆忙離開時忘記拿眼鏡了。

萬用延伸句型

make haste 加快腳步、趕緊行動
例如：If we don't make haste, we're gonna be late.
我們再不快點就要遲到了。

has·ten [ˈhesn̩]
◀€ *Track 3697*

動 趕忙

▶We have to hasten to make a decision because there simply isn't time. 我們得趕緊下決定，因為真的沒時間了。

ha·tred [ˈhetrɪd]
◀€ *Track 3698*

名 怨恨、憎惡

▶Bias and hatred have led to conflicts between these racial groups. 偏見和仇恨使這兩個種族團體間的衝突加劇。

head·phone(s) [ˈhɛdˌfon(z)]
◀€ *Track 3699*

名 頭戴式耳機、聽筒

▶What's the matter with the headphones? I can't hear anything at all. 這個耳機怎麼了？我什麼也聽不到啊。

文法字詞解析

earphones 也是「耳機」的意思，差別在於，headphones 通常是頭戴式的耳機，而非插在耳朵裡的那種耳機。

health·ful [ˈhɛlθfəl]
◀€ *Track 3700*

形 有益健康的

▶Not all vegetables in the world are healthful foods.

並非世界上的各種蔬菜都是有益於健康的食物。

hel·i·cop·ter [ˈhɛlɪˌkɑptɚ] ◀€ Track 3701

名 直升機
▶I've never been on a helicopter before. 我都沒搭過直昇機呢。

herd [hɝd] ◀€ Track 3702

名 獸群、成群 動 放牧、使成群
▶名 I met a herd of cattle passing though the road on my way to the remote village.
我在前往這個偏遠村莊的途中遇到牛群橫越道路。
▶動 They herded the prisoners onto the train.
他們把這群囚犯驅趕上火車。

hes·i·ta·tion [ˌhɛzəˈteʃən] ◀€ Track 3703

名 遲疑、躊躇 反 determination 決心
▶I hope our manager could agree to this plan without any hesitation. 但願我們的經理能毫不猶豫地同意這項計畫。

high·ly [ˈhaɪlɪ] ◀€ Track 3704

副 大大地、高高地
▶The master spoke highly of his works in the exhibition.
在展覽會上大師對他的作品評價很高。

home·land [ˈhomˌlænd] ◀€ Track 3705

名 祖國、本國
▶Why don't you go back to your homeland if you miss it so much?
既然你這麼想念你的祖國，那為什麼不回國去呢？

hon·ey·moon [ˈhʌnɪˌmun] ◀€ Track 3706

名 蜜月 動 度蜜月
▶名 The couple went to Bali for their honeymoon.
這對夫妻到峇里島度蜜月。
▶動 We will honeymoon in Spain.
我們將去西班牙度蜜月。

文法字詞解析
要說兩人「在蜜月中」時，可以說 on honeymoon 或 on sb.'s honeymoon。
例如：We will be visiting Germany on our honeymoon.
我們蜜月時會去德國。

hon·or·a·ble [ˈɑnərəbl̩] ◀€ Track 3707

形 體面的、可敬的
▶I wish my son could become an honorable man.
我希望我兒子能當個正直的人。

hook [hʊk] ◀€ Track 3708

名 鉤、鉤子 動 鉤、用鉤子鉤住
▶名 Will you help me hang my coat on the hook, Susan?
蘇珊，你能幫我把外套掛在鉤上嗎？
▶動 Can you hook the window when you come in?
你能在進屋的時候把窗戶扣好嗎？

文法字詞解析
流行音樂中常常會有一段旋律非常讓人印象深刻、讓人會不自覺跟著哼唱，那一段旋律就叫做歌曲裡的「hook」。

hope·ful [ˈhopfəl] ◀€ Track 3709

形 有希望的
▶It is hopeful that he will advance to the final round of the professional Go tournament.
他有希望晉級到職業圍棋大賽的決賽。

Level 1

Level 2

Level 3

Level 4

自我勉勵、越背越上手——
提升程度4200單字

Level 5

Level 6

ho·ri·zon [həˋraɪz]

◀€ *Track 3710*

名 地平線、水平線

▶The sun is rising above the horizon.
太陽升到地平線上了。

hor·ri·fy [ˋhɔrəˌfaɪ]

◀€ *Track 3711*

動 使害怕、使恐怖

▶The terrible scene horrified me.
這恐怖的景象嚇到我了。

hose [hoz]

◀€ *Track 3712*

名 水管 動 用水管澆洗

▶名 We need enough hoses to put the big fire out.
我們需要足夠的水管以撲滅大火。

▶動 He hosed the bubbles off the car.
他用水管把車上的泡泡沖掉。

host [host]

◀€ *Track 3713*

動 主辦 名 主人、主持人、一大群 反 guest 客人

▶動 I don't think this country will host the Games this year.
我認為該國今年將不會主辦這屆運動會。

▶名 I don't think he will be the host for tonight's program.
我覺得他不會是今晚的節目主持人。

hos·tel [ˋhostl]

◀€ *Track 3714*

名 青年旅社

▶The owner of the hostel greeted us with warmth and hospitality.
青年旅館的老闆溫暖熱情地接待我們。

house·hold [ˋhaʊsˌhold]

◀€ *Track 3715*

形 家庭

▶This young girl often helps her mother with household chores.
這個年輕女孩常常幫她的媽媽做家事。

house·wife [ˋhaʊsˌwaɪf]

◀€ *Track 3716*

名 家庭主婦

▶Not every woman wants to be a housewife.
不是每個女人都想成為家庭主婦。

house·work [ˋhaʊsˌwɝk]

◀€ *Track 3717*

名 家事

▶It is essential that husband and wife should share the burden of housework.
丈夫和妻子應該要分擔家務，這是很重要的。

hu·man·i·ty [hjuˋmænətɪ]

◀€ *Track 3718*

名 人類、人道

▶We should treat animals with humanity.
我們應該以仁慈之心對待動物。

文法字詞解析

和 horizon 相關的一個形容詞是 horizontal，指的是「水平的」的意思。horizontal 經常和另一個字 vertical（垂直的）一起出現，一個是橫的一個是直的，依瞬間可能有點難判斷，但只要記得 horizon 是地平線，地平線是橫的，就能馬上知道誰是誰啦。

文法字詞解析

可用來概稱所有的人類。例如「能把全世界所有人類都殺光的災難」就是「a disaster that can wipe out humanity」。

hur·ri·cane [ˈhɝɪˌken]

◀≲ *Track 3719*

名 颶風

▶The hurricane razed the town to the ground.
颶風將這個村莊夷為平地。

hy·dro·gen [ˈhaɪdrədʒən]

◀≲ *Track 3720*

名 氫、氫氣

▶The scientists found that water is made up of oxygen and hydrogen.
科學家們發現水是由氫和氧構成的。

[Ii]

ice·berg [ˈaɪsˌbɝg]

◀≲ *Track 3721*

名 冰山

▶The Titanic sank after hitting an iceberg.
鐵達尼號在撞上冰山後就沉了。

i·den·ti·cal [aɪˈdɛntɪkl̩]

◀≲ *Track 3722*

形 相同的 同 same 相同的

▶The identical twins sometimes exchanged identities to trick their parents.
這對同卵雙胞胎有時候會交換身分，戲弄父母。

i·den·ti·fi·ca·tion/ ID [aɪˌdɛntəfəˈkeʃən]

◀≲ *Track 3723*

名 身分證

▶Will you please give me some forms of identification to prove yourself?
您能給我一些證明身份的文件來證明你自己嗎？

i·den·ti·fy [aɪˈdɛntəˌfaɪ]

◀≲ *Track 3724*

動 認出、鑑定

▶It took the police some time to identify the accident victims.
警察費了不少時間來驗明事故遇難者的身份。

id·i·om [ˈɪdɪəm]

◀≲ *Track 3725*

名 成語、慣用語

▶Some Chinese idioms are kind of funny.
有些中文諺語其實還蠻好笑的。

id·le [ˈaɪdl̩]

◀≲ *Track 3726*

形 閒置的 動 閒混

▶形 I want to just spend all day sitting there being idle.
我真想整天坐在那裡處度時光。

▶動 The kids idled around in the house, doing nothing meaningful.
小孩在屋子裡閒晃，不做正事。

萬用延伸句型

be the tip of the iceberg 只是冰山一角
例如：What we see now is the tip of the iceberg. Many problems lie underneath.
我們現在看到的只是冰山一角，還有很多隱藏的問題是我們看不見的。

Level 1

Level 2

Level 3

Level 4

自我勉勵、越背越上手──提升程度4200單字

Level 5

Level 6

i·dol [ˈaɪdl̩] ◀≝ Track 3727

名 偶像
▶The pop singer is the idol of young people.
這位流行歌手是年輕人崇拜的偶像。

ig·no·rant [ˈɪgnərənt] ◀≝ Track 3728

形 缺乏教育的、無知的
▶It is obvious that he is ignorant of what happened.
顯然他不知道發生了什麼事。

il·lus·trate [ˈɪləstret] ◀≝ Track 3729

動 舉例說明
▶The manager illustrated the concept with some graphs.
這位經理用圖表解釋這個概念。

il·lus·tra·tion [ˌɪlʌsˈtreʃən] ◀≝ Track 3730

名 說明、插圖
▶I like magazines full of illustrations.
我喜歡看插圖多的雜誌。

i·mag·in·able [ɪˈmædʒɪnəbl̩] ◀≝ Track 3731

形 可想像的
▶I don't think that he is the most suitable person imaginable.
我覺得他不是想得到的人選中最合適的一位。

i·mag·i·nar·y [ɪˈmædʒəˌnɛrɪ] ◀≝ Track 3732

形 想像的、不實在的
▶Unicorns are imaginary; they don't really exist.
獨角獸是想像出來的；牠們並不真的存在。

i·mag·i·na·tive [ɪˈmædʒəˌnetɪv] ◀≝ Track 3733

形 有想像力的
▶She is not only hardworking but also imaginative.
她不但勤奮而且富有想像力。

im·i·tate [ˈɪməˌtet] ◀≝ Track 3734

動 仿效、效法
▶He liked to imitate his brother and annoy him.
他喜歡模仿他哥哥，讓他哥哥很不高興。

im·i·ta·tion [ˌɪməˈteʃən] ◀≝ Track 3735

名 模仿、仿造品
▶The imitation of the oil painting looked identical to the genuine one.
油畫的仿製品看起來和原作完全一樣。

im·mi·grant [ˈɪməgrənt] ◀≝ Track 3736

名 移民者
▶I think there will be more and more immigrants in China.
我認為中國會有越來越多的移民者。

文法字詞解析

idol 可以指平常在電視可以看到、唱唱跳跳的「偶像」（一種職業）、任何你景仰的人、也可以拿來指神明或神像等「被人崇拜的對象」。

文法字詞解析

imaginary 與下面的單字 imaginative 都是和想像力有關的形容詞，兩者的差別是 imaginary 是「想像出來的、虛構的、並不是真實存在的」，而 imaginative 則是「有想像力的」。所以我們可以稱讚小孩子 imaginative（有想像力），但不能說他們 imaginary，那樣就變成不存在的孩子了。

im·mi·grate [ˈɪməˌgret]　◀ Track 3737

動 遷移、移入

▶ Soon after Richard immigrated in this country, he found a job and settled down.
理查移民到這個國家之後，就找到工作並且定居下來。

im·mi·gra·tion [ˌɪməˈgreʃən]　◀ Track 3738

名 （從外地）移居入境

▶ Would you like to tell me how to enquire about the immigration state?
你能告訴我如何查詢有關移居的情況嗎？

im·pact [ˈɪmpækt]/[ɪmˈpækt]　◀ Track 3739

名 碰撞、撞擊 動 衝擊、影響

▶ 名 The impact of the stone against the window shattered（打碎）the glass.
石頭撞擊窗戶，打碎了玻璃。

▶ 動 I don't think my suggestion would impact their decision.
我想我的建議大概不會影響他們做的決定吧。

im·ply [ɪmˈplaɪ]　◀ Track 3740

動 暗示、含有 同 hint 暗示

▶ He didn't outright say that he hated me, but he implied it.
他沒有直接說他討厭我，但他有暗示他討厭我。

im·pres·sion [ɪmˈprɛʃən]　◀ Track 3741

名 印象

▶ He tried very hard to make a good impression when meeting her for the first time.
他在第一次和她見面時，非常努力留下一個好印象。

萬用延伸句型

be under the impression that... 一直以為／認為……

例如：What? I was under the impression that he was your brother. So he's not?
什麼？我一直以為他是你弟。原來不是嗎？

---

in·ci·dent [ˈɪnsədənt]　◀ Track 3742

名 事件

▶ The political incident was covered by the police and never published. 政治事件被警察掩蓋，未被公開。

in·clud·ing [ɪnˈkludɪŋ]　◀ Track 3743

介 包含、包括

▶ Three others, including the gunman（槍手）, were killed.
另有三人死亡，包括那名槍手。

in·di·ca·tion [ˌɪndəˈkeʃən]　◀ Track 3744

名 指示、表示

▶ The manual gave clear indication about how to get rid of common glitches.
使用手冊有清楚指示要如何處理常見的故障問題。

in·dus·tri·al·ize [ɪnˈdʌstrɪəlˌaɪz]　◀ Track 3745

動 （使）工業、產業化

▶ Many towns in the coastal（沿海的）area have begun to industrialize. 沿海地區的許多鄉鎮已開始工業化。

Level 1
Level 2
Level 3
Level 4
Level 5
Level 6

自我勉勵、越背越上手——提升程度4200單字

in·fant [ˈɪnfənt] 🔊 Track 3746

名 嬰兒、未成年人

▶The infant deserted on the street and rescued by a social worker. 被遺棄在街上的嬰兒被社工救回。

in·fect [ɪnˈfɛkt] 🔊 Track 3747

動 使感染

▶The wound must be kept clean so that germs do not infect it. 傷口須保持清潔，才不會細菌感染。

in·fec·tion [ɪnˈfɛkʃən] 🔊 Track 3748

名 感染、傳染病

▶You need to keep the wound clean, or you might get an infection.
你應該要保持傷口乾淨，否則可能會感染的。

in·fla·tion [ɪnˈfleʃən] 🔊 Track 3749

名 膨脹、脹大

▶I don't think that the increase of wages can keep up with inflation.
我認為薪水漲幅跟不上通貨膨脹。

> **文法字詞解析**
> inflation 是通貨膨脹，而「通貨緊縮」只要將字首換成「de-」，變成「deflation」即是。

in·flu·en·tial [ˌɪnfluˈɛnʃəl] 🔊 Track 3750

形 有影響力的

▶The celebrity's words were influential to teenagers.
名人的話對青少年深具影響力。

in·for·ma·tion [ˌɪnfəˈmeʃən] 🔊 Track 3751

名 知識、見聞

▶Would you like to give me any information on this matter?
關於此事，你能提供什麼消息給我嗎？

in·for·ma·tive [ɪnˈfɔrmətɪv] 🔊 Track 3752

形 提供情報的

▶We need to design attractive and informative brochures（小冊子）.
我們必須設計吸引人又資訊豐富的小冊子。

> **文法字詞解析**
> 相反地，要抱怨說明書、課程提供的資訊根本毫無用途、或提供的資訊實在太少，可以說「uninformative」（沒有提供資訊的、提供太少資訊的）。

in·gre·di·ent [ɪnˈɡridɪənt] 🔊 Track 3753

名 成份、原料

▶Would you like to tell me what the ingredients of the cake are?
您能告訴我這個蛋糕是用什麼原料做成的嗎？

in·i·tial [ɪˈnɪʃəl] 🔊 Track 3754

形 開始的 名 姓名的首字母

▶形 My initial reaction when hearing the news was to smile.
我剛聽到這消息時，一開始的反應是微笑。

▶名 The initial plan was altered for several times.
起初的計畫，後來更改過好幾次。

in·no·cence [ˈɪnəsn̩s]
◀ Track 3755

名 清白、天真無邪

▶ I don't believe in his innocence; what about you?
我不相信他是清白的，你相信嗎？

in·put [ˈɪnˌpʊt]
◀ Track 3756

名 輸入 動 輸入

▶ 名 It is said that adequate input is essential for language learning. 據說足夠的接觸對於語言學習很重要。

▶ 動 Would you please input the data into the computer for me?
請你幫我把資料登錄到電腦中好嗎？

in·sert [ˈɪnsɚt]/[ɪnˈsɚt]
◀ Track 3757

名 插入物 動 插入

▶ 名 What do you think about the special insert in the magazine?
你覺得這本雜誌的那個特別插頁怎麼樣？

▶ 動 The book would be improved by inserting another chapter.
這本書如果再插入一個章節就更好了。

in·spec·tion [ɪnˈspɛkʃən]
◀ Track 3758

名 檢查、調查

▶ Would you please tell me where the customs inspection is?
您能告訴我海關檢查站在哪裡嗎？

in·spi·ra·tion [ɪnspəˈreʃən]
◀ Track 3759

名 鼓舞、激勵

▶ Her music was great inspiration to many.
她的音樂激勵了許多人。

in·spire [ɪnˈspaɪr]
◀ Track 3760

動 啓發、鼓舞

▶ His literary work inspired some of his contemporary novelists.
他的作品啓發了一些同時代的小說家。

in·stall [ɪnˈstɔl]
◀ Track 3761

動 安裝、裝置 同 establish 建立、安置

▶ How long will it take to install a telephone and connect it to the exchange?
安裝電話機並與總機接通要多久？

in·stinct [ˈɪnstɪŋkt]
◀ Track 3762

名 本能、直覺

▶ Why don't you trust your instinct and do what you think is right?
為什麼不相信你的直覺，並按你認為對的去做呢？

in·struct [ɪnˈstrʌkt]
◀ Track 3763

動 教導、指令

▶ The coach instructed the players to move up the field.
教練指導球員往場上移動。

文法字詞解析
句中的 many 代稱 many people，在這裡是當作名詞的功能使用。

Level 1

Level 2

Level 3

Level 4

自我勉勵、越背越上手——提升程度4200單字

Level 5

Level 6

in·struc·tor [ɪnˋstrʌktɚ] 🔊 *Track 3764*

名 教練、指導者
▶ The English instructor is very patient. 這位英語講師很有耐心。

in·sult [ɪnˋsʌlt]/[ˋɪnsʌlt] 🔊 *Track 3765*

動 侮辱 名 冒犯
▶ 動 I never meant to insult you; would you please forgive me?
　我不是有意要侮辱你的，請原諒我好嗎？
▶ 名 The foreigner's words were considered to be an insult to the local laborers.
　外國人的話被認為是對本地勞工的侮辱。

萬用延伸句型
I never meant to V. 我不是有意要（做某事）

in·sur·ance [ɪnˋʃʊrəns] 🔊 *Track 3766*

名 保險
▶ Once you join our company, we will make sure that you will get insurance. 一旦你加入我們公司，我們一定會幫你加保。

in·tel·lec·tu·al [ˏɪntlˋɛktʃʊəl] 🔊 *Track 3767*

名 知識份子 形 智力的
▶ 名 Mensa is an association which recruit intellectual people around the world.
　門薩是一個在國際上招募高智商人的協會。
▶ 形 Both his parents are extremely smart; it is no wonder that he is an intellectual person.
　他的父母親都非常聰明，難怪他也是個智力超高的人。

in·tel·li·gence [ɪnˋtɛlədʒəns] 🔊 *Track 3768*

名 智能
▶ It is obvious that he is a man of very high intelligence.
　顯然他是個非常聰明的人。

文法字詞解析
因為知道了很多情報就能夠做出比較聰明的反應，所以間諜們工作上用到的「情報」也可以稱為 intelligence。

in·tel·li·gent [ɪnˋtɛlədʒəjnt] 🔊 *Track 3769*

形 有智慧（才智）的
▶ She is not only very intelligent but also very modest.
　她不但很聰明，而且非常謙虛。

in·tend [ɪnˋtɛnd] 🔊 *Track 3770*

動 計畫、打算
▶ Let's ask her what she intends to do.
　我們問問她打算做什麼吧。

in·tense [ɪnˋtɛns] 🔊 *Track 3771*

形 極度的、緊張的
▶ The basketball game last night was really intense.
　昨晚的籃球賽超緊張的。

文法字詞解析
除了指「情勢」很緊張外，intense 也能拿來描述人的眼神非常有力、專注。

in·ten·si·fy [ɪnˋtɛnsəˏfaɪ] 🔊 *Track 3772*

動 加強、增強
▶ To intensity creativity in the company, the manager arranged some courses for us.
　為了促進公司員工的創意，經理幫我們安排一些課程。

in·ten·si·ty [ɪnˈtɛnsətɪ] ◀≼ *Track 3773*

名 強度、強烈
▶The poem showed great intensity of feeling.
這首詩表現出強烈的激情。

in·ten·sive [ɪnˈtɛnsɪv] ◀≼ *Track 3774*

形 強烈的、密集的
▶It took him four nights to finish the intensive course.
他花了四個晚上完成密集課程。

in·ten·tion [ɪnˈtɛnʃən] ◀≼ *Track 3775*

名 意向、意圖
▶I have no intention of coming to this terrible place again!
我再也不想到這個糟糕的地方來了！

in·ter·act [ˌɪntɚˈrækt] ◀≼ *Track 3776*

動 交互作用、互動
▶The exchange students were encouraged to interact with local students.
交換學生被鼓勵要和本地學生多交流。

in·ter·ac·tion [ˌɪntɚˈækʃən] ◀≼ *Track 3777*

名 交互影響、互動
▶There should be more interaction between the social services and local doctors.
社會公益服務機構和當地醫生應該加強互動。

in·ter·fere [ˌɪntɚˈfɪr] ◀≼ *Track 3778*

動 妨礙 同 interrupt 打斷
▶I hope you won't interfere with my plans.
我希望你不要干擾我的計畫。

in·ter·me·di·ate [ˌɪntɚˈmidɪt] ◀≼ *Track 3779*

名 調解 形 中間的
▶名 Not every intermediate is able to solve the dispute perfectly（完美地）each time.
不是每個調解人每次都能夠完美地解決爭端。
▶形 We enrolled in the intermediate level of Spanish course.
我們登記參加中級的西班牙文課程。

Internet [ˈɪntɚˌnɛt] ◀≼ *Track 3780*

名 網際網路
▶Let us search for the answers on the Internet, shall we?
我們上網找答案好嗎？

in·ter·pret [ɪnˈtɝprɪt] ◀≼ *Track 3781*

動 說明、解讀、翻譯
▶Would you please interpret for me? I don't understand what she is talking about.
請你為我翻譯一下好嗎？我聽不懂她在說什麼。

萬用延伸句型

have no intention of V-ing 完全沒有意願（做某事）

Level 1
Level 2
Level 3
Level 4
Level 5
Level 6

自我勉勵、越背越上手──
提升程度4200單字

451

in·ter·rup·tion
[ˌɪntəˈrʌpʃən] ◀€ *Track 3782*

名 中斷、妨礙

▶The speaker could not tolerate any interruption in the middle of her presentation.
講者無法忍受演講中間被人打斷。

in·ti·mate
[ˈɪntəmɪt] ◀€ *Track 3783*

名 知己 形 親密的

▶名 He is not only my teacher but also my intimate.
他不但是我的老師，還是我的密友。

▶形 They are not only business associates but also intimate friends.
他們不但是生意上的夥伴，而且還是親密的朋友。

in·to·na·tion
[ˌɪntoˈneʃən] ◀€ *Track 3784*

名 語調、吟詠

▶Would you be careful about your pronunciation and intonation?
請注意一下你的發音和語調好嗎？

in·vade
[ɪnˈved] ◀€ *Track 3785*

動 侵略、入侵

▶The Mongolia people invaded Europe and brought changes to the culture there.
蒙古人入侵歐洲，為當地文化帶來改變。

萬用延伸句型
invade sb.'s privacy 侵犯（某人）的隱私
例 如：You can't just go into her room like that. That's invading her privacy.
你不能就這樣進去她房間，會侵犯人家隱私的。

in·va·sion
[ɪnˈveʒən] ◀€ *Track 3786*

名 侵犯、侵害

▶The alien invasion in 2528 was predicted in ancient books.
古書中預測了2528年外星人侵襲地球的事。

in·ven·tion
[ɪnˈvɛnʃən] ◀€ *Track 3787*

名 發明、創造

▶The flying skateboard is my newest invention.
那個飛行滑板是我的最新發明。

in·vest
[ɪnˈvɛst] ◀€ *Track 3788*

動 投資

▶He invested a lot of time in trying to help poor children.
他把大量時間用在設法幫助貧窮兒童上。

in·vest·ment
[ɪnˈvɛstmənt] ◀€ *Track 3789*

名 投資額、投資

▶Education is a good investment. 教育是很好的投資。

in·ves·ti·ga·tion
[ɪnˌvɛstəˈgeʃən] ◀€ *Track 3790*

名 調查

▶The investigation of this murder case ceased after the time of legal memory passed.
這個謀殺案的調查，在法定追溯期過了之後就停止了。

萬用延伸句型
be under investigation 正在被調查中
例 如：The retired politician is under investigation right now.
這位已退休的政治人物正受到調查。

in·volve [ɪnˈvɑlv]
◀ Track 3791

動 牽涉、包括
▶You should involve yourself in school life more.
　你應該更融入學校生活。

in·volve·ment [ɪnˈvɑlvmənt]
◀ Track 3792

名 捲入、連累
▶He is convinced that Shirley's involvement will ruin their relationship.
　他確信雪莉的捲入會毀掉他們的關係。

i·so·late [ˈaɪsˌlet]
◀ Track 3793

動 孤立、隔離 同 separate 分開
▶The bullied child was isolated by his peers.
　這個被霸凌的小孩被同儕孤立。

i·so·la·tion [ˌaɪsˈleʃən]
◀ Track 3794

名 分離、孤獨
▶It is difficult for any country to develop in isolation.
　任何國家都難以在封閉的狀態下得到發展。

itch [ɪtʃ]
◀ Track 3795

名 癢 動 發癢
▶名 I had an itch on my back all of a sudden.
　我的後背突然很癢。
▶動 The allergy to seafood made me itch all over.
　對海鮮過敏，讓我全身發癢。

文法字詞解析
itch 是名詞，表示「癢」；也可以當作動詞，表示「發癢」。那如果要用形容詞表示「癢的」呢？可以説「itchy」。
例如：My back has been itchy all week.
我的背已經一整個禮拜都癢癢的了。

[Jj]

jeal·ous·y [ˈdʒɛləsɪ]
◀ Track 3796

名 嫉妒
▶A man driven by jealousy is capable of anything.
　嫉妒心可使人什麼都做得出來。

ju·nior [ˈdʒunjɚ]
◀ Track 3797

名 年少者 形 年少的
▶名 She is three years his junior. I hope they can become good friends.
　她比他小三歲，我希望他們能成為好朋友。
▶形 Alice became a junior assistant in the law firm after graduation.
　艾莉絲畢業後，去法律公司做初級助理。

Level 1
Level 2
Level 3
Level 4
自我勉勵、越背越上手──提升程度4200單字
Level 5
Level 6

[Kk]

keen [kin]　　　　🔊 Track 3798
形 熱衷的、敏銳的
▶He was keen to pursue a career path in politics.
　他很積極追求政治生涯。

knuck·le [ˈnʌkl̩]　　　🔊 Track 3799
名 關節　動 將指關節觸地
▶名 The man who's cracking his knuckles looks mean.
　那個把關節弄得喀喀作響的男人看起來很兇的樣子。
▶動 Let's stop chatting and knuckle down to work.
　別再聊了，我們開始認真工作吧。

[Ll]

la·bor [ˈlebɚ]　　　🔊 Track 3800
名 勞力　動 勞動
▶名 There is a clear division of labor in ants.
　螞蟻間有明確的分工。
▶動 She labored five years on that book.
　她寫那本書足足寫了五年。

lab·o·ra·to·ry/lab　🔊 Track 3801
[ˈlæbrəˌtorɪ]/[læb]
名 實驗室
▶The white rat is frequently（常常）used as a laboratory animal.
　白鼠常被用來做為實驗用動物。

lag [læg]　　　　🔊 Track 3802
名 落後　動 延緩
▶名 It is obvious that you will get jet lag after traveling overseas.
　顯然在出國旅遊之後你會出現時差反應。
▶動 Our son lags behind others in the class because of playing video games.
　我們兒子因為玩電動玩具而導致學習落後於班上其他同學。

land·mark [ˈlændˌmɑrk]　🔊 Track 3803
名 路標
▶The monument was a landmark in the city.
　紀念碑是城市裡的地標。

萬用延伸句型
go into labor 開始分娩
例如：She went into labor at midnight and the baby came out at three.
她半夜開始分娩，寶寶在三點的時候生出來了。

land·scape [ˈlænskep]

Track 3804

名 風景 動 進行造景工程

▶名 The landscape of the foreign country was very impressive to me.
外國的景色令我印象深刻。

▶動 We're having both places landscaped.
我們要在兩處地方都建造園林。

land·slide/mud·slide

Track 3805

[ˈlænd͵slaɪd]/[ˈmʌd͵slaɪd]

名 山崩

▶Not all the people think about the causes of landslides when they suffer from it. 不是所有人都會在遭遇土石流的同時，去思考土石流發生的原由。

文法字詞解析
描述一場比賽的贏家與輸家差距甚大，跟經歷了山崩的地帶和沒有經歷山崩的地帶之間的高度差一樣很大，即可說 win by a landslide（以極大的差距獲勝）。

large·ly [ˈlɑrdʒlɪ]

Track 3806

副 大部分地

▶His success is largely due to his hard work.
他的成功主要是靠自己的努力得來的。

late·ly [ˈletlɪ]

Track 3807

副 最近

▶He seems preoccupied lately; something must be bothering him.
他最近似乎心事重重；他一定是為某事煩心。

launch [lɔntʃ]

Track 3808

名 開始 動 發射

▶名 I don't think the launch of the new ship will start on time.
我覺得新船下水儀式不會按時進行了。

▶動 This country has already launched a spaceship（太空船）successfully.
這個國家已經成功地發射了太空船。

law·ful [ˈlɔfəl]

Track 3809

形 合法的 同 legal 合法的

▶I don't think he has reached the lawful age to drink in the bar.
我認為他還未達到法定年齡，不能進酒吧喝酒。

lead [lid]

Track 3810

名 / 動 領導

▶名 It doesn't matter whether their team will be in the lead or not at half time.
他們隊在前半場領先與否都沒什麼大不了的。

▶動 He led his team to victory.
他帶領著他的隊伍獲得勝利。

文法字詞解析
lead 的動詞變化：lead, led, led

lean [lin]

Track 3811

動 傾斜、倚靠

▶It's dangerous to lean against the door on the subway train.
在地鐵車輛上面靠著車門是很危險的。

Level
1

Level
2

Level
3

Level
4

Level
5

Level
6

提升程度4200單字

自我勉勵、越背越上手

learn·ed [ˈlɝnd]
🔊 *Track 3812*

形 學術性的、博學的

▶Many learned men are arguing with him on the Internet .
有很多學者在網路上跟他爭論。

learn·ing [ˈlɝnɪŋ]
🔊 *Track 3813*

名 學問

▶Not all the students know exactly what their purposes of learning are.
不是所有學生都很清楚自己學習的目的是什麼。

lec·ture [ˈlɛktʃɚ]
🔊 *Track 3814*

名 演講 動 對……演講

▶名 Will you attend the lecture given by Professor Wang tomorrow?
明天你會參加王教授的講座嗎？

▶動 The professor kept lecturing though he saw some students were dozing off.
教授看到有些學生打瞌睡，還是繼續講課。

lec·tur·er [ˈlɛktʃərɚ]
🔊 *Track 3815*

名 演講者

▶Will you tell me what the lecturer's topic is?
你能告訴我這位演講者的題目是什麼嗎？

leg·end [ˈlɛdʒənd]
🔊 *Track 3816*

名 傳奇

▶According to the old legends, it was Romulus who became the founder of Rome.
按照古老的傳說，羅穆盧斯成為了古羅馬的建國者。

lei·sure·ly [ˈliʒɚlɪ]
🔊 *Track 3817*

形 悠閒的 副 悠閒地

▶形 The leisurely atmosphere and slow pace in the town made me relax.
這個小鎮悠閒的氣氛和緩慢的步調讓我感覺放鬆。

▶副 Latin Americans stroll（漫步）leisurely through life.
拉丁美洲人的生活節奏很從容不迫。

li·cense/li·cence [ˈlaɪsn̩s]
🔊 *Track 3818*

名 執照 動 許可

▶名 It is easy for him to obtain a driver's license in this country.
他很容易就在這個國家考取了駕照。

▶動 It is impossible（不可能的）for the restaurant to sell spirits for it is not licensed for it.
這家飯店不可能賣烈酒，因為它沒有賣烈酒的許可證。

light·en [ˈlaɪtn̩]
🔊 *Track 3819*

動 變亮、減輕

▶The sky begins to lighten after the storm.
暴風雨後天空開始放晴。

文法字詞解析

由於父母「唸」孩子時有時也蠻像是老師在諄諄教誨、講大道理，因此父母「唸」孩子這件事也可以用 give a lecture 來描述。

lim·i·ta·tion [ˌlɪməˋteʃən] 🔊 *Track 3820*

名 限制

▶There are some limitation on medical research to protect subjects' human right.
為了保障受試者的人權，醫藥研究是有限制的。

liq·uor [ˋlɪkɚ] 🔊 *Track 3821*

名 烈酒

▶You must keep away from liquor and tobacco, or your illness will get worse.
你必須不沾菸酒，否則你的病情將會加重。

lit·er·ar·y [ˋlɪtəˌrɛrɪ] 🔊 *Track 3822*

形 文學的

▶I don't like to read this man's literary criticism.
我不喜歡讀這個人的文學評論。

lit·er·a·ture [ˋlɪtərətʃɚ] 🔊 *Track 3823*

名 文學

▶I major in English literature in university; what about you?
我大學主修英國文學，你呢？

loan [lon] 🔊 *Track 3824*

名 借貸 動 借、貸

▶名 How can I apply for a housing loan?
我要如何申請房屋貸款呢？

▶動 Will you loan me some money? I need to buy a pair of shoes for a job interview.
你能借我一些錢嗎？我需要買一雙面試穿的鞋。

lo·ca·tion [loˋkeʃən] 🔊 *Track 3825*

名 位置

▶It is obvious that he doesn't know the location of the World Trade Center.
他顯然不知道世貿中心在哪裡。

lock·er [ˋlɑkɚ] 🔊 *Track 3826*

名 有鎖的收納櫃、寄物櫃

▶I stuffed my backpack into the locker.
我把我的背包塞進了寄物櫃中。

log·ic [ˋlɑdʒɪk] 🔊 *Track 3827*

名 邏輯

▶There is no logic in spending money on clothes you don't wear.把錢花在你不穿的衣服上是沒有道理的。

log·i·cal [ˋlɑdʒɪk!] 🔊 *Track 3828*

形 邏輯上的

▶The logical reasoning in his thesis amazed other scholars in his field. 他論文的邏輯推論使同領域的學者感到驚艷。

萬用延伸句型

can't hold sb.'s liquor 酒量很差

例 如：Tom really can't hold his liquor. He falls asleep after one glass.
湯姆酒量很差，喝一杯就會睡著了。

文法字詞解析

有很多寄物櫃的房間（例如球隊隊員使用的）稱為 locker room。

Level 1
Level 2
Level 3

Level 4
提升程度4200單字
自我勉勵、越背越上手

Level 5
Level 6

lo·tion [ˈloʃən]　🔊 Track 3829

名 洗潔劑

▶Her lotion smells like candy and apples.
她的乳液聞起來像是糖果和蘋果的味道。

lousy [ˈlaʊzɪ]　🔊 Track 3830

形 卑鄙的

▶He was criticized for the lousy structure of his lesson plan.
他被批評說他的教案太過粗糙。

loy·al [ˈlɔɪəl]　🔊 Track 3831

形 忠實的

▶I don't think that there is any necessity to be loyal to a cruel ruler. 我覺得沒有必要為一個殘暴的國君效忠。

loy·al·ty [ˈlɔɪəltɪ]　🔊 Track 3832

名 忠誠

▶It is a surprise that you should doubt his loyalty to the company and the work.
你居然會懷疑他對公司和工作的忠誠，真令人驚訝。

lu·nar [ˈlunɚ]　🔊 Track 3833

形 月亮的、陰曆的

▶It is said that liquid water can not exist on the lunar surface.
據說液態水不可能出現在月球表面上。

lux·u·ri·ous [lʌgˈʒʊrɪəs]　🔊 Track 3834

形 奢侈的

▶Don't you think the furniture in the villa is too luxurious?
難道你不覺得這個別墅裡的傢俱都太奢華了嗎？

lux·u·ry [ˈlʌkʃərɪ]　🔊 Track 3835

名 奢侈品、奢侈

▶Clean water is a luxury for people in some regions.
對一些地區的人來說，乾淨的水是種奢侈品。

[Mm]

ma·chin·er·y [məˈʃinɚɪ]　🔊 Track 3836

名 機械

▶Some human labor was replaced by machinery in this factory.
這間工廠中，有些勞工被機器取代了。

mad·am/ma'am　🔊 Track 3837

[ˈmædəm]/[mæm]

名 夫人、女士

▶Would you like to see some other dresses, madam?
夫人，您想不想看看其他的洋裝呢？

文法字詞解析

lousy 可以拿來形容卑鄙的、差勁的，除了可以罵人、罵物品品質不好、罵某人表現很差外，也能拿來描述自己的心情或狀態。

萬用延伸句型

live in the lap of luxury 過著極為奢華的生活
例如：If given the choice, who wouldn't want to live in the lap of luxury?
如果可以，誰不想過極盡奢華的生活？

mag·net·ic [mæg`nɛtɪk]
◀€ *Track 3838*

形 磁性的

▶Once the switch is closed, the magnetic path has a lower reluctance（磁阻）.
一旦開關關閉，磁路就具有較低的磁阻。

mag·nif·i·cent
[mæg`nɪfəsənt]
◀€ *Track 3839*

形 壯觀的、華麗的

▶The magnificent scenery of Grand Canyon amazed all visitors.
遊客為大峽谷的壯麗景色感到震驚。

make·up [`mekˏʌp]
◀€ *Track 3840*

名 結構、化妝

▶She put on so much makeup for her wedding her mom didn't recognize her.
她在婚禮上化的妝太濃，以致連她媽都認不出她。

man·u·al [`mænjʊəl]
◀€ *Track 3841*

名 手冊 形 手工的

▶名 There are a lot of useful tips in this manual.
這本小冊子裡有很多實用的小建議。

▶形 There are a manual control system and an automatic one in this factory.
這間工廠有手控與自動控制系統。

man·u·fac·ture [ˏmænjə`fæktʃɚ] ◀€ *Track 3842*

名 製造業 動 大量製造

▶名 How about importing some foreign manufactures? Maybe we can learn from them.
進口一些外國製品怎麼樣？或許我們可以從這些產品學到什麼。

▶動 Before manufacturing the product, we spent a year testing on the prototype.
在大量生產這項產品之前，我們花了一年測試產品雛型。

man·u·fac·turer
[ˏmænjə`fæktʃərɚ]
◀€ *Track 3843*

名 製造者

▶The manufacturer has gotten several complaints from customers. 這家製造商從顧客那裡接到不少抱怨電話。

mar·a·thon [`mærəθɑn]
◀€ *Track 3844*

名 馬拉松

▶There are thousands of people taking part in this marathon.
參加此次馬拉松比賽的人有幾千人。

mar·gin [`mɑrdʒɪn]
◀€ *Track 3845*

名 邊緣 同 edge 邊

▶I jotted down some notes on the margin of the pages.
我在書頁空白處寫下一些筆記。

文法字詞解析
當我們想說一個人的個性非常有吸引力、能夠像磁鐵一般把大家都吸過去時，就可以說他擁有「a magnetic personality」。

文法字詞解析
想要來場 marathon，但又覺得懶惰嗎？沒關係，懶人也有懶人的馬拉松方式。
在英文中如果很長很長一段時間都坐在原地，連看好幾部電影或影集，也可以稱為 marathon。畢竟要一次從頭到晚看完每一季的《冰與火之歌》也是很令人疲憊的事。

Level 1

Level 2

Level 3

Level 4

提升程度4200單字 ｜ 自我勉勵、越背越上手

Level 5

Level 6

ma·tu·ri·ty [məˋtjʊrətɪ]   🔊 *Track 3846*

名 成熟期

▶This job calls for a person with a great deal of maturity.
這個工作需由成熟老練的人去做。

max·i·mum [ˋmæksəməm]   🔊 *Track 3847*

名 最大量 形 最大的

▶名 I can swim a maximum of two miles; what about you?
我游泳最遠能游兩英里，你呢？

▶形 The maximum capacity of the theater is three hundred people.
這個劇院最多可以容納三百人。

mea·sure(s) [ˋmɛʒɚ(z)]   🔊 *Track 3848*

動 度量單位、尺寸

▶Have you gotten your waist measured yet?
你量腰圍了沒？

me·chan·ic [məˋkænɪk]   🔊 *Track 3849*

名 機械工

▶There is not a mechanic who hasn't had such problems.
沒有一個技工不會碰到此類問題的。

me·chan·i·cal [məˋkænɪk!]   🔊 *Track 3850*

形 機械工、技工

▶They were using a mechanical shovel to clear up the streets.
他們在用機械鏟土機清理街道。

mem·o·ra·ble [ˋmɛmərəb!]   🔊 *Track 3851*

形 值得紀念的

▶I think graduation is a memorable event.
我認為畢業是一件難忘的事。

me·mo·ri·al [məˋmorɪəl]   🔊 *Track 3852*

名 紀念品 形 紀念的

▶名 The ruins of Twin Towers were built into a memorial for the victims.
雙子星大廈的遺跡被建立成一個受難者的紀念館。

▶形 He made an entry of the memorial events in his diary.
他把值得紀念的大事記入日記中。

mer·cy [ˋmɝsɪ]   🔊 *Track 3853*

名 慈悲

▶Don't you think that there is no use asking for his mercy?
你不覺得祈求他的同情是沒用的嗎？

mere [mɪr]   🔊 *Track 3854*

形 僅僅、不過

▶He is a mere child; don't blame him for the minor mistake.
他只是一個小孩；別為了小錯誤怪他。

文法字詞解析

知道了 maximum（最大值），當然就會想要知道「最小值」怎麼說。答案是 minimum，這個字同樣地也可以當作形容詞「最小的」。

文法字詞解析

大家可能學過 memory 是「記憶、回憶」的意思，而大家可能也學過 able 是「能夠」的意思。既然 memorable 是由「能夠回憶」所組成，也難怪它的意思是「值得紀念的」了。

mer·it [ˈmɛrɪt]
Track 3855

名 價值

▶If you focus on her merits instead of her shortcomings, you will find that she is very easy-going. 如果你注意她的優點，而不是她的缺點，你就會發現她很好相處。

mes·sen·ger [ˈmɛsn̩dʒɚ]
Track 3856

名 使者、信差

▶Can you act as a messenger for me?
你可以幫我帶個訊息嗎？

mess·y [ˈmɛsɪ]
Track 3857

形 髒亂的 同 dirty 髒的

▶Your bedroom is always so messy.
你的臥室老是這麼亂。

mi·cro·scope [ˈmaɪkrəˌskop]
Track 3858

名 顯微鏡

▶Germs can only be seen with the aid of a microscope because they are too small.
只有借助顯微鏡才能看得見細菌，因為它們太微小了。

mild [maɪld]
Track 3859

形 溫和的

▶The mild weather in the country made it one of the most livable areas in the world.
這個國家溫和的天氣使它成為世界最宜居住的城市之一。

min·er·al [ˈmɪnərəl]
Track 3860

名 礦物

▶Would you please give me a bottle of mineral water? I am thirsty. 請給我一瓶礦泉水好嗎？我渴了。

min·i·mum [ˈmɪnəməm]
Track 3861

名 最小量 形 最小的

▶名 Would you let me know if there is a minimum for the first deposit?
您能不能告訴我第一次儲蓄有沒有最低限額？

▶形 What's the minimum wage per hour if I work here?
如果我在這裡工作的話，最低薪水是每小時多少錢？

min·is·ter [ˈmɪnɪstɚ]
Track 3862

名 神職人員、部長

▶The minister has indicated that he may resign next year.
該部長已暗示他明年可能辭職。

min·is·try [ˈmɪnɪstrɪ]
Track 3863

名 牧師、部長、部

▶According to the Ministry of Education, the national college entrance exam will be innovated next year.
教育部表示，全國大學入學考試將會在明年改革。

文法字詞解析

除了表示髒亂外，messy 也可拿來形容很難搞、「一片混亂」的狀況。例如一宗牽涉到許多大企業內部醜聞的謀殺案，就能以 messy 來形容。

萬用延伸句型

Would you let me know if...?
你可以告訴我是否……嗎？

Level 1
Level 2
Level 3
Level 4
Level 5
Level 6

提升程度4200單字

自我勉勵、越背越上手——

mis·chief [ˈmɪstʃɪf] 🔊 *Track 3864*

名 胡鬧、危害

▶The mischief of the children really annoyed the old lady.
小孩的頑皮行為熱惱了老婦人。

mis·er·a·ble [ˈmɪzərəbl̩] 🔊 *Track 3865*

形 不幸的

▶There are still many people whose living conditions are miserable.
仍有許多人的生活條件是很艱苦的。

mis·for·tune [mɪsˈfɔrtʃən] 🔊 *Track 3866*

名 不幸

▶I'm really sorry for the poor girl who has the misfortune to get married to him.
我真同情那個不幸和他結婚的可憐女孩啊。

mis·lead [mɪsˈlid] 🔊 *Track 3867*

動 誤導

▶The advice of the aged will not mislead you.
不聽老人言，吃虧在眼前。

文法字詞解析
mislead 的動詞變化：mislead, misled, misled

mis·un·der·stand 🔊 *Track 3868*

[ˌmɪsʌndɚˈstænd]

動 誤解

▶He misunderstood my words and thought that I was trying to insult him.
他誤會我的話，以為我要污辱他。

文法字詞解析
misunderstand 的動詞變化：
misunderstand, misunderstood, misunderstood

mod·er·ate [ˈmɑdərɪt] 🔊 *Track 3869*

形 適度的、溫和的

▶Do you mind if the position requires moderate travel?
本職缺需要適度的出差，你介意嗎？

mod·est [ˈmɑdɪst] 🔊 *Track 3870*

形 謙虛的

▶He isn't very modest but sometimes geniuses are like that.
他不怎麼謙虛，不過天才有時候就是這樣嘛。

mod·es·ty [ˈmɑdəstɪ] 🔊 *Track 3871*

名 謙虛、有禮

▶Her fake modesty bugs her classmates a lot.
她假裝謙虛的態度讓她的同學們覺得有點煩。

mon·i·tor [ˈmɑnətɚ] 🔊 *Track 3872*

名 監視器 動 監視

▶名 Why don't we install a monitor in the meeting room?
何不在會議室安裝一個監視器呢？

▶動 My supervisor is always monitoring whether I can keep up with the schedule.
我的主管總是在監看我是否有跟上工作的進度。

month·ly [ˋmʌnθlɪ] 🔊 Track 3873

名 月刊 形 每月一次的

▶名 It is clear that the monthly has been popular since it came out. 顯然這個月刊自從出版以來就一直很受歡迎。

▶形 The rent for his apartment is his biggest monthly expense. 公寓的租金是他每月最大的一筆開支。

mon·u·ment [ˋmɑnjəmənt] 🔊 Track 3874

名 紀念碑

▶We admire the monument of Alexander Hamilton, one of the founding fathers of the U.S. 我們瞻仰美國開國元老，亞歷山大‧漢米爾頓的雕像。

more·o·ver [morˋovɚ] 🔊 Track 3875

副 並且、此外

▶The composition is not well written, and moreover, there are many spelling mistakes in it. 這篇作文寫得不好，而且，還有許多拼字錯誤。

文法字詞解析
moreover 是個比較正式的字，用來補充說明前面的資訊或是加強論點，多半用在書寫而非口語中。

most·ly [ˋmostlɪ] 🔊 Track 3876

副 多半、主要地

▶The audience consists mostly of women. 觀眾多數都是婦女。

mo·ti·vate [ˋmotəˌvet] 🔊 Track 3877

動 刺激、激發

▶To motivate the athletes, the coach set a clear goal and said some encouraging words. 為了提升運動員的動機，教練設立明確目標，並且說了些鼓勵的話。

mo·ti·va·tion [ˌmotəˋveʃən] 🔊 Track 3878

名 動機

▶You can do anything if you've got the motivation. 只要有了動力，什麼都可以做到。

moun·tain·ous [ˋmaʊntənəs] 🔊 Track 3879

形 多山的

▶He used to live in a mountainous district. 他過去住在山區。

mow [mo] 🔊 Track 3880

動 收割

▶We mowed the lawn in the yard on the weekend. 我們週末時在庭院除草。

文法字詞解析
「割草機」則可以稱為「lawn mower」。

MTV/mu·sic tel·e·vi·sion 🔊 Track 3881

[ˋmjuzɪk ˋtɛləˌvɪʒən]

名 音樂電視頻道

▶The MTV channels aren't as popular as they used to be. 這些音樂電視頻道沒有像以前那麼受歡迎了。

Level 1
Level 2
Level 3
Level 4
提升程度4200單字 自我勉勵、越背越上手
Level 5
Level 6

mud·dy [ˈmʌdɪ] 🔊 *Track 3882*

形 泥濘的

▶Would you please help me take off these muddy boots?
請幫我脫掉這滿是泥漿的靴子好嗎？

mul·ti·ple [ˈmʌltəpl] 🔊 *Track 3883*

形 複數的、多數的

▶The test included two parts: multiple choice questions and essay questions. 測驗包括兩部分：選擇題和問答題。

mur·der·er [ˈmɝdərɚ] 🔊 *Track 3884*

名 兇手

▶It's too hard for him to find the murderer without any help.
沒有任何協助的話，他一個人很難找到兇手。

mur·mur [ˈmɝmɚ] 🔊 *Track 3885*

名 低語 動 細語、抱怨

▶名 I heard a low murmur of conversation in the hall.
我聽到大廳裡有竊竊私語聲。

▶動 He murmured something, but I didn't catch what he said.
他嘀咕了一句什麼話，可是我沒聽清楚。

mus·tache [ˈmʌstæʃ] 🔊 *Track 3886*

名 髭

▶Why don't you shave off your mustache? It grows so fast.
為什麼不刮掉你的鬍子呢？它長得太快了。

mu·tu·al [ˈmjutʃʊəl] 🔊 *Track 3887*

形 相互的、共同的

▶To achieve mutual agreement, we negotiated for several hours.
為了達到雙方同意，我們協商好幾個小時。

mys·te·ri·ous [mɪsˈtɪrɪəs] 🔊 *Track 3888*

形 神祕的

▶There are many mysterious stories about the Egyptian（埃及的）pyramids（金字塔）. 關於埃及金字塔有許多神祕的故事。

文法字詞解析

在社群網站正夯的這個年代，mutual 這個單字還多了一個含意，就是「我有關注你，你也有關注我」，這種兩邊互相有關注、互相有加好友（而不是一方單方面追蹤）的狀況達成時，兩人的關係就可以稱為「mutuals」，當名詞使用。

[Nn]

name·ly [ˈnemlɪ] 🔊 *Track 3889*

副 即、就是

▶I think there is only one person good enough to do this job, namely you. 我覺得只有一個人足夠優秀能肩負此任，那就是你。

na·tion·al·i·ty [ˌnæʃənˈæləti] 🔊 *Track 3890*

名 國籍、國民

▶The fugitive faked his nationality when he tried to get the visa.
逃犯假造了護照上的國籍，以取得簽證。

near·sight·ed [ˈnɪrˈsaɪtɪd]
🔊 *Track 3891*

形 近視的

▶It is hard for a nearsighted person to see distant objects clearly.
一個近視的人很難看清楚遠處的物體。

need·y [ˈnidɪ]
🔊 *Track 3892*

形 貧窮的、貧困的 同 poor 貧窮的

▶We raised funds for the needy family in the impoverished area.
我們為貧窮地區中需要幫助的家庭募款。

ne·glect [nɪˈɡlɛkt]
🔊 *Track 3893*

名 不注意、不顧 動 疏忽

▶名 His neglect of his children caused them to drift away from him. 他對自己孩子不關心的態度，讓他們逐漸離他而去。

▶動 It is bad for us to pay attention to one side and neglect the other. 只顧一方面，不顧另一方面，對我們是不好的。

ne·go·ti·ate [nɪˈɡoʃɹet]
🔊 *Track 3894*

動 商議、談判

▶We negotiated about the terms in the contract during the meeting. 在會議中，我們協調合約中的條款。

nev·er·the·less/
none·the·less [ˌnɛvɚðəˈlɛs]/[ˌnʌnðəˈlɛs]
🔊 *Track 3895*

副 儘管如此、然而

▶She said she didn't want to go. Nevertheless, her parents still forced her to.
她說她不想去，儘管如此，她的父母還是強迫她去了。

提升程度4200單字

自我勉勵、越背越上手

night·mare [ˈnaɪtˌmɛr]
🔊 *Track 3896*

名 惡夢、夢魘

▶I had a nightmare about being knifed by a five-legged man last night.
我昨天晚上做了一個惡夢，夢到被一個五隻腳的男人拿刀砍。

non·sense [ˈnɑnsɛns]
🔊 *Track 3897*

名 廢話、無意義的話

▶In fact, I don't think what he said was total nonsense.
事實上，我覺得他說的話不全是一派胡言。

noun [naʊn]
🔊 *Track 3898*

名 名詞

▶There is no point in using so many nouns of the same meaning in an article. 在文章中使用太多同義名詞沒有多大意義。

now·a·days [ˈnaʊəˌdez]
🔊 *Track 3899*

副 當今、現在

▶Nowadays, more people use online messenger instead of making phone calls.
現代，許多人用線上通訊軟體，而不是打電話。

文法字詞解析

相反地，「遠視的」就可以說成 farsighted。此外，farsighted 還有「有遠見的」的意思，畢竟「遠視」也可以說成是「看得比較遠」吧。

文法字詞解析

描述一個人正經、認真，即可用 no-nonsense 來形容。

nu·cle·ar [ˈnjuklɪə]
🔊 Track 3900

形 核子的

▶North Korea has promised the international society to get rid of its nuclear weapons. 北韓向國際社會承諾要放棄核武。

nu·mer·ous [ˈnjumərəs]
🔊 Track 3901

形 為數眾多的

▶There are numerous stars shining in the sky.
天空中群星閃爍。

nurs·er·y [ˈnɝsərɪ]
🔊 Track 3902

名 托兒所

▶I am afraid that I have to resign my child to the care of the nursery. 恐怕我得把孩子交給托兒所照顧了。

ny·lon [ˈnaɪlɑn]
🔊 Track 3903

名 尼龍

▶Don't you think nylon really changed people's life at that time?
難道你不覺得尼龍確實改變了當時人們的生活嗎？

[Oo]

o·be·di·ence [əˈbidjəns]
🔊 Track 3904

名 服從、遵從

▶Some people consider obedience to parents a way to show filial piety. 有些人認為服從是表現孝道的方式。

萬用延伸句型
Some people believe that... 有些人相信……

o·be·di·ent [əˈbidɪənt]
🔊 Track 3905

形 服從的

▶The obedient students listened to their teacher's every word.
那些乖巧的學生非常聽老師的話。

ob·jec·tion [əbˈdʒɛkʃən]
🔊 Track 3906

名 反對

▶There is no objection to your opening the window.
你開窗並沒有什麼不可以的。

ob·jec·tive [əbˈdʒɛktɪv]
🔊 Track 3907

形 實體的、客觀的 名 目標 同 neutral 中立的 同 goal 目標

▶形 You should try to be more objective about it.
你應該儘量客觀地對待此事。
▶名 The objective of every game is to win.
任何遊戲的目標都是要贏。

文法字詞解析
objective 是「客觀的」，相反地「主觀的」則是 subjective。

ob·ser·va·tion [ˌɑbzɝˈveʃən]
🔊 Track 3908

名 觀察力

▶We compiled a report based on the observation of the wild animals. 我們根據觀察野生動物的結果來寫這份報告。

ob·sta·cle [ˈɑbstəkl̩]
🔊 *Track 3909*

名 障礙物、妨礙
▶Peter strived to overcome the obstacles.
彼得努力克服障礙。

ob·tain [əbˈten]
🔊 *Track 3910*

動 獲得
▶She failed to obtain a scholarship. 她沒有獲得獎學金。

oc·ca·sion·al [əˈkeʒənl̩]
🔊 *Track 3911*

形 應景的、偶爾的
▶I enjoy an occasional night out at the theater; what about you?
我偶爾晚上會出去看戲，你呢？

oc·cu·pa·tion [ˌɑkjəˈpeʃən]
🔊 *Track 3912*

名 職業
▶Would you please state your name, age and occupation?
請說明您的姓名、年齡和職業好嗎？

oc·cu·py [ˈɑkjəˌpaɪ]
🔊 *Track 3913*

動 佔有、花費（時間）
▶The old lady occupied several seats on the subway train for her grandchildren.
老太太在地下鐵車廂上幫她的孫子佔了好幾個位子。

of·fend [əˈfɛnd]
🔊 *Track 3914*

動 使不愉快、使憤怒、冒犯
▶He didn't mean to offend you by pointing out the mistake.
他指出錯誤，並不是為了冒犯你。

萬用延伸句型
try not to... 試著盡量不做某事

of·fense [əˈfɛns]
🔊 *Track 3915*

名 冒犯、進攻
▶Offense is the best defense when playing sports.
在運動場上，進攻是最好的防禦。

of·fen·sive [əˈfɛnsɪv]
🔊 *Track 3916*

形 令人不快的
▶He likes using offensive language with his brothers.
他喜歡和他的兄弟使用一些無禮的語言。

op·er·a [ˈɑpərə]
🔊 *Track 3917*

名 歌劇
▶We are planning to go to the opera this Sunday; would you like to go with us? 我們計畫這個星期天去看歌劇表演，你想不想跟我們一起去呢？

op·er·a·tion [ˌɑpəˈreʃən]
🔊 *Track 3918*

名 作用、操作
▶The physician has performed three operation within two days.
醫生在兩天內執行了三場手術。

Level 1
Level 2
Level 3
Level 4
自我勉勵、越背越上手——
提升程度4200單字
Level 5
Level 6

op·pose [ə`poz]   ◀⁞ *Track 3919*

動 和……起衝突、反對 反 agree 同意

▶The construction onincinerator was opposed by local people.
焚化爐的建造遭到本地人反對。

o·ral [`orəl]   ◀⁞ *Track 3920*

名 口試 形 口述的

▶名 Not everyone is able to pass the orals easily.
不是每個人都能毫不費力地通過口試。

▶形 Not every student has good written and oral English skills.
不是每個學生都有良好的英語寫作及口語能力。

文法字詞解析
因為口試是可以一場一場數出來的考試，所以它是可數名詞。

orbit [`ɔrbɪt]   ◀⁞ *Track 3921*

名 軌道 動 把……放入軌道

▶名 In recent years a number of communication satellites were put into orbit.
近年來，有很多通訊衛星被送上軌道。

▶動 The earth orbits the sun.
地球沿軌道繞著太陽運行。

or·ches·tra [`ɔrkɪstrə]   ◀⁞ *Track 3922*

名 樂隊、樂團

▶Not all people know that the orchestra was established under the patronage（贊助）of the government.
不是所有人都知道這個交響樂團是在政府贊助下成立的。

文法字詞解析
patron 是贊助者、資助者的意思，所以 patronage 就是「（金錢上的）贊助」。

or·gan·ic [ɔr`gænɪk]   ◀⁞ *Track 3923*

形 器官的、有機的

▶Do you know why organic foods are often more expensive?
你知道有機食品為什麼這麼貴嗎？

oth·er·wise [`ʌðə͂waɪz]   ◀⁞ *Track 3924*

副 否則、要不然

▶I've been sick these days; otherwise I would do it myself.
我最近不太舒服，否則這件事我就親自去做了。

out·come [`aʊt͵kʌm]   ◀⁞ *Track 3925*

名 結果、成果 同 result 結果

▶I think there can be but one outcome to this affair.
我認為這件事只可能有一種結局。

out·stand·ing [`aʊt`stændɪŋ]   ◀⁞ *Track 3926*

形 傲人的、傑出的

▶The outstanding achievement of the teenager was reported on TV. 這名青少年傑出的事蹟在電視上被報導。

文法字詞解析
與 outstanding 長得有點像的一個片語是「stand out」。它也有「特別的」的意思，但不見得一定是「特別傑出的」，也有可能純粹只是特別。
例　如：He stands out in the crowd because of his green hair.
因為他的頭髮是綠色的，所以在人群中特別顯眼。

o·val [`ovl]   ◀⁞ *Track 3927*

名 橢圓形 形 橢圓形的

▶名 The mirror is an oval shape. 那個鏡子是橢圓形的。

▶形 She has a lovely oval face. 她長著一張可愛的鵝蛋臉。

o·ver·come [ˌovɚˋkʌm]　🔊 *Track 3928*

動 擊敗、克服

▶As long as you work hard, you can overcome the difficulties.
只要你努力，就能克服困難。

文法字詞解析
overcome 的動詞變化：
overcome, overcame, overcome

o·ver·look [ˌovɚˋlʊk]　🔊 *Track 3929*

動 俯瞰、忽略

▶I'll overlook your mistake this time.
我這次就容忍你的錯誤吧。

o·ver·night [ˋovɚˋnaɪt]　🔊 *Track 3930*

形 徹夜的、過夜的　**副** 整夜地

▶**形** Not every actress can win overnight fame with her first film.不是每個女演員都能第一部電影就一舉成名。
▶**副** Not every person is lucky enough to became rich overnight.
不是每個人都能幸運地一夜致富。

o·ver·take [ˌovɚˋtek]　🔊 *Track 3931*

動 趕上、突擊

▶He had to drive very fast to overtake the opponent.
他必須開得很快，才能超過敵手。

文法字詞解析
overtake 的動詞變化：
overtake, overtook, overtaken

o·ver·throw [ˌovɚˋθro]　🔊 *Track 3932*

動 推翻、瓦解

▶The tyranny was overthrown by the long-suppressed people.
長期被壓抑的人民推翻了暴政。

文法字詞解析
overthrow 的動詞變化：
overthrow, overthrew,overthrown

ox·y·gen [ˋɑksədʒən]　🔊 *Track 3933*

名 氧（氧氣）

▶Put on the oxygen mask when the cabin pressure suddenly drops. 當艙壓降低時，要戴上氧氣面罩。

[Pp]

pa·ce [pes]　🔊 *Track 3934*

名 一步、步調　**動** 踱步

▶**名** It is hard for their country to keep pace with other developed countries.
他們國家很難趕上其他己開發國家。
▶**動** Why is he pacing around in the living room?
他在客廳裡走來走去幹嘛。

pan·el [ˋpænl̩]　🔊 *Track 3935*

名 方格、平板

▶The solar panel can transform the heat from the sun into energy.
太陽能板可以將太陽的熱能轉化成能源。

Level 1
Level 2
Level 3
Level 4
Level 5
Level 6

提升程度4200單字 — 自我勉勵、越背越上手

par·a·chute [ˈpærəˌʃut] Track 3936
名 降落傘 動 空投
▶名 The airman failed to deploy the parachute after he jumped out of the plane.
飛行軍官跳出飛機之後，無法打開跳傘。
▶動 I don't think he will parachute the supplies to them.
認為他不會空投補給品給他們。

par·a·graph [ˈpærəˌgræf] Track 3937
名 段落
▶It is hard for us to understand the whole paragraph given by our teacher.
我們很難讀懂老師給的那一整段文章。

par·tial [ˈpɑrʃəl] Track 3938
形 部分的
▶Do you mind if I only make a partial payment for these goods?
你介意我對這些貨物先付部分的錢嗎？

文法字詞解析
「partial to」可用來表示對某事物有特別的喜好。例如若你特別喜歡吃蛋，就可以說 I'm partial to eggs。

par·tic·i·pa·tion [pɑrˌtɪsəˈpeʃən] Track 3939
名 參加
▶His participation is not welcomed by the rest of us.
他的參與不受我們其他人的歡迎。

par·ti·ci·ple [ˈpɑrtəsəpḷ] Track 3940
名 分詞
▶The participle is used to describe the subject of the sentence.
分詞被用來形容這句話的主詞。

part·ner·ship [ˈpɑrtnɚˌʃɪp] Track 3941
名 合夥
▶I wish Mike could take me into partnership in his firm.
真希望麥克能讓我成為他公司的合夥人。

pas·sive [ˈpæsɪv] Track 3942
形 被動的
▶He is a very passive person, never talking unless talked to.
他很被動，別人不跟他講話，他就不講話。

文法字詞解析
有個說法叫做「passive-aggressive」，同時具有「被動」和「攻擊」兩項特質，到底是表示什麼樣的情況呢？其實這是用來描述某人不想光明正大地攻擊人，於是光講一些看似無害但暗藏玄機的話、或是做一些看似無害但懷有敵意的舉動。舉例來說，若 A 叫 B 幫他做事，B 滿口答應但心裡不爽，就故意做得很慢，讓 A 無法在期限內獲得需要的成果，B 這樣的舉動就是 passive-aggressive 的表現。

pas·ta [ˈpɑstə] Track 3943
名 麵團、義大利麵
▶What do you want to eat for lunch? How about pasta?
你午餐想吃什麼呢？義大利麵怎麼樣？

peb·ble [ˈpɛbḷ] Track 3944
名 小圓石
▶The pebbles by the river were moved away by the excavator.
怪手將河邊的小石頭挖走。

pe·cu·liar [pɪˈkjuljɚ] 🔊 *Track 3945*

形 獨特的 同 special 特別的
▶The tofu tastes peculiar, so I abandoned it.
豆腐味道怪怪的，所以我把它丟了。

ped·al [ˈpɛdl̩] 🔊 *Track 3946*

名 踏板 動 踩踏板
▶名 He didn't have enough time to put his foot down on the brake pedal. 他沒有足夠的時間把腳放到煞車踏板上。
▶動 You must pedal rapidly（迅速地）enough to make the machine run smoothly（平穩地）.
你必須快速地踩踏板，才能使機器運轉平穩。

peer [pɪr] 🔊 *Track 3947*

名 同輩 動 凝視
▶名 As peers, there are many interesting（有趣的）things we can talk about.
身為同輩，我們有很多有趣的事情可以談論。
▶動 There is no need to peer at them from behind the curtain.
沒必要從簾子後面偷看他們。

pen·al·ty [ˈpɛnl̩tɪ] 🔊 *Track 3948*

名 懲罰
▶Some humanitarian activists proposed that death penalty should be abandoned. 有些人道主義份子提議，死刑應該被廢除。

per·cent [pɚˈsɛnt] 🔊 *Track 3949*

名 百分比
▶I am afraid that we can give you only a five percent discount.
恐怕我們只能給你九五折優惠。

per·cent·age [pɚˈsɛntɪdʒ] 🔊 *Track 3950*

名 百分率
▶It is a surprise that the film should attract a large percentage of the people.
這部電影竟然吸引了大部分的觀眾，真令人驚訝。

per·fec·tion [pɚˈfɛkʃən] 🔊 *Track 3951*

名 完美
▶His performance was sheer（十足的）perfection, wasn't it?
他的表演十分完美，不是嗎？

per·fume [ˈpɝfjum] 🔊 *Track 3952*

名 香水、賦予香味
▶The young lady was told not to wear perfume to work.
年輕女士被要求上班不要噴香水。

per·ma·nent [ˈpɝmənənt] 🔊 *Track 3953*

形 永久的
▶Don't you want to get a permanent job?
難道你不想得到一份固定的工作嗎？

文法字詞解析
要說「某物的百分之多少」可以用「（數字）percent of……」來表示。
例如：Forty percent of the students take the bus to school.
40% 的學生搭乘公車上學。

Level 1
Level 2
Level 3
Level 4
Level 5
Level 6

自我勉勵、越背越上手——提升程度4200單字

471

per·sua·sion [pɚˋsweʒən]　◀ *Track 3954*

名 說服

▶Despite our persuasion, he was still unwilling to undergo the surgery.

儘管我們說服他，他還是不願意接受手術。

per·sua·sive [pɚˋswesɪv]　◀ *Track 3955*

形 有說服力的

▶ I don't think his argument is persuasive enough to convince everyone.

我認為他的論點說服力不強，無法說服大家。

文法字詞解析

persuasive 是 從 persuade 這 個 字 延伸而來的。要注意的是，persuade 和 convince 的意思並不一樣，前者是「說服、勸服某人去做某事」，後者則是「使某人相信某種說法是真的」。

pes·si·mis·tic [ˌpɛsəˋmɪstɪk]　◀ *Track 3956*

形 悲觀的　反 optimistic 樂觀的

▶There is no reason to be pessimistic about your future.

沒有理由對你的未來感到悲觀。

pet·al [ˋpɛtḷ]　◀ *Track 3957*

名 花瓣

▶She decorated the table with some petals.

她用花瓣裝飾桌子。

phe·nom·e·non [fəˋnɑməˌnɑn]　◀ *Track 3958*

名 現象

▶Don't you think it's a common phenomenon? It happens almost everywhere（到處）.

難道你不認為這是一個普遍的現象嗎？它幾乎到處都在發生。

phi·los·o·pher [fəˋlɑsəfɚ]　◀ *Track 3959*

名 哲學家

▶The philosopher enlightened the youngster with some useful mottos.

哲學家用以一些有用的座右銘來啟發這名年輕人。

文法字詞解析

古老傳說中的「賢者之石」就是 philosopher's stone。

phil·o·soph·i·cal [ˌfɪləˋsɑfɪkḷ]　◀ *Track 3960*

形 哲學的

▶It is difficult for the students to answer this philosophical problem.

對於學生而言這個哲學問題們很難回答。

phi·los·o·phy [fəˋlɑsəfɪ]　◀ *Track 3961*

名 哲學

▶Will you tell me what your philosophy on life is?

能告訴我你的生活哲學是什麼嗎？

pho·tog·ra·phy [fəˋtɑgrəfɪ]　◀ *Track 3962*

名 攝影學

▶It is not easy for you to learn photography by yourself.

要自學攝影並不是很容易。

phys·i·cal [ˈfɪzɪkl̩]
🔊 *Track 3963*

形 身體的

▶Participants of the triathlon have to watch their physical condition. 三項鐵人競賽的參賽者必須要注意他們的身體狀況。

文法字詞解析
大家都知道體育課叫做 PE，其實就是 Physical Education 的縮寫。

phy·si·cian/doc·tor
🔊 *Track 3964*

[fəˈzɪʃən]/[ˈdɑktɚ]

名 （內科）醫師

▶I hope the physician can save his life.
我希望醫生能挽救他的生命。

phys·i·cist [ˈfɪzɪsɪst]
🔊 *Track 3965*

名 物理學家

▶It is quite clear that what the physicist thinks about the world differs from others.
很明顯，這位物理學家對世界的看法與其他人不同。

phys·ics [ˈfɪzɪks]
🔊 *Track 3966*

名 物理學

▶I wish I could do well in physics.
我希望能把物理學得很好。

pi·an·ist [pɪˈænɪst]
🔊 *Track 3967*

名 鋼琴師

▶His dream was to become a pianist. 他的夢想是成為鋼琴師。

pick·poc·ket [ˈpɪkˌpɑkɪt]
🔊 *Track 3968*

名 扒手

▶When the pickpocket was about to leave, he was caught by the police. 扒手正要離開的時候被警察抓住了。

pi·o·neer [ˌpaɪəˈnɪr]
🔊 *Track 3969*

名 先鋒、開拓者 動 開拓

▶名 The old man was the pioneer in modern medicine study.
這位老人正是現代醫學研究的先驅。

▶動 It was this lady who pioneered the use of the drug.
正是這名女士最先使用這種藥品。

pi·rate [ˈpaɪrət]
🔊 *Track 3970*

名 海盜 動 掠奪

▶名 The children enjoy hearing stories about pirates.
這些孩子們很喜歡聽海盜的故事。

▶動 If you watch the pirated movies, you will be breaking the law. 觀看盜版的電影，就是犯法。

文法字詞解析
由於「盜版」版權不屬於自己的東西這樣的行為和海盜似乎也沒什麼兩樣，因此 pirate 這個字也可以拿來表示「盜版」的意思。

plen·ti·ful [ˈplɛntɪfəl]
🔊 *Track 3971*

形 豐富的

▶The weather has been very nice; it is no wonder that the farmers had a plentiful harvest this year.
天氣狀況一直都很好，難怪今年農民們獲得了大豐收。

Level 1
Level 2
Level 3
Level 4
Level 5
Level 6

提升程度4200單字 自我勉勵、越背越上手

plot [plɑt]   🔊 *Track 3972*

名 陰謀、情節 動 圖謀、分成小塊

▶名 The author made sure that the plots should be surprising to the readers. 作者確保故事情節是出乎讀者預料的。

▶動 The new factory's district is all plotted out.
新廠區的範圍都已劃定。

plu·ral [ˈplʊrəl]   🔊 *Track 3973*

名 複數 形 複數的

▶名 Does the student know the plural of this word?
這個學生知道這個單字的複數嗎？

▶形 Plural marriage still exists in the area.
這個地區還存在著一夫多妻制。

p.m./P.M. [ˈpiˈɛm]   🔊 *Track 3974*

副 下午

▶I am afraid that he is out of the office in the morning. How about meeting him at 3 p.m.?
恐怕他上午不在辦公室。下午三點見他怎麼樣？

poi·son·ous [ˈpɔɪzəs]   🔊 *Track 3975*

形 有毒的

▶He was bitten by a poisonous snake.
他被毒蛇咬到了。

pol·ish [ˈpɑlʃən]   🔊 *Track 3976*

名 磨光 動 擦亮

▶名 Will you give your shoes a polish? We will be going to a party tonight.
你能把你的鞋子擦一擦嗎？今晚我們要出席一場宴會。

▶動 The writer polished the article before she submits it to the editor.
這名寫手在把文章交給編輯之前，先將稿子潤飾過。

文法字詞解析
就像第二個例句裡的用法，「polish」不只表示具體的「擦亮」，還可以解釋成「修飾、潤飾」文章。

pol·lu·tion [ˈpɑlɪʃ]   🔊 *Track 3977*

名 污染

▶The air pollution can't be reduced unless the government can pass a new law.
除非國家能頒佈新法，否則空氣污染無法減輕。

pop·u·lar·i·ty [ˌpɑpjəˈlærətɪ]   🔊 *Track 3978*

名 名望、流行

▶Famous people have to pay a high price for popularity, but not all the people know that.
為了出名，名人要付出很高的代價，但不是所有人都知道這一點。

port·a·ble [ˈpɔrtəbḷ]   🔊 *Track 3979*

形 可攜帶的

▶The portable computer can work as efficiently as a desktop computer. 手提電腦的效率可以和桌上型電腦一樣好。

por·ter [ˈportɚ] ◀≲ *Track 3980*

名 搬運工
▶ Will you tell me how much I should give the porter as a tip?
你能告訴我應該給行李搬運工多少小費嗎？

por·tray [porˈtre] ◀≲ *Track 3981*

動 描繪 同 depict 描繪
▶ The novelist is good at portraying the characters in his work.
小說家善於在作品中描繪人物的個性。

pos·sess [pəˈzɛs] ◀≲ *Track 3982*

動 擁有
▶ The country possesses rich mineral deposits.
這個國家擁有豐富的礦藏。

> **文法字詞解析**
> 被鬼「附身」時，身體等於是被對方所「擁有」了，因此「附身」也可以用 possess 這個字來表示。

pos·ses·sion [pəˈzɛʃən] ◀≲ *Track 3983*

名 擁有物
▶ A true friend is the best possession.
真誠的朋友是最寶貴的財富。

pre·cise [prɪˈsaɪs] ◀≲ *Track 3984*

形 明確的 同 exact 確切的
▶ We were expected to be precise and brief for the presentation.
我們報告時，應該要精確且簡短。

pre·dict [prɪˈdɪkt] ◀≲ *Track 3985*

動 預測
▶ I can't predict when I'll meet her again.
我無法預測什麼時候會再見到她。

> **文法字詞解析**
> 在後面加上表示「能夠」的字尾「-able」，就能變成形容詞 predictable（能夠預測的）。再在前面加上表示「不、沒有」的字首「un-」，就能變成形容詞 unpredictable（無法預測的）。

pref·er·a·ble [ˈprɛfərəl] ◀≲ *Track 3986*

形 較好的
▶ Health without riches is preferable to riches without health.
有健康而無財富比有財富而無健康更好。

preg·nan·cy [ˈprɛgnənsɪ] ◀≲ *Track 3987*

名 懷孕
▶ Do you mind telling me what you ate during this pregnancy?
你能告訴我你這次懷孕期間都吃了些什麼嗎？

preg·nant [ˈprɛgnənt] ◀≲ *Track 3988*

形 懷孕的
▶ What? She's six months pregnant? I didn't even notice that.
什麼？她懷孕六個月了？我竟然都沒注意到。

> **文法字詞解析**
> 要說「懷了……」可以用「pregnant with...」來表示。例如「懷了雙胞胎」，就是「pregnant with twins」，「懷了兒子」可以說「pregnant with a boy」。

prep·o·si·tion [ˌprɛpəˈzɪʃən] ◀≲ *Track 3989*

名 介系詞
▶ The prepositions can be used for expressing time, position, methods, or reasons.
介係詞可以用來表達時間、地點、方式、或理由。

Level 1
Level 2
Level 3
Level 4
Level 5
Level 6

自我勉勵、越背越上手——
提升程度4200單字

pre·sen·ta·tion [ˌprɛznˈteʃən] ◀≤ Track 3990

名 贈送、呈現
▶He gave a presentation today in class.
他今天在課堂上做了報告。

pres·er·va·tion [ˌprɛzəˈveʃən] ◀≤ Track 3991

名 保存
▶Marinade was once used for food preservation.
醃漬是以前用來保存食物的方法。

pre·serve [prɪˈzɝv] ◀≤ Track 3992

動 保存、維護
▶Let's preserve our natural resources from now on, shall we?
讓我們從現在開始保護我們的自然資源好嗎？

pre·ven·tion [prɪˈvɛnʃən] ◀≤ Track 3993

名 預防
▶I am greatly convinced that prevention is better than a cure.
我深信預防重於治療。

prime [praɪm] ◀≤ Track 3994

名 初期 形 首要的 同 principal 首要的
▶名 The serial drama was on TV during the prime time—six to eight in the evening.
這個連續劇在電視的黃金時段一晚間六點到八點之間一播出。
▶形 This problem is a matter of prime importance.
這個問題是一個首要的問題。

prim·i·tive [ˈprɪmətɪv] ◀≤ Track 3995

形 原始的 同 original 原始的
▶Our modern society is more advanced than the primitive society.
現代社會比原始社會先進多了。

pri·va·cy [ˈpraɪvəsɪ] ◀≤ Track 3996

名 隱私
▶The paparazzi was accused of invading the celebrity's privacy.
狗仔隊被指控侵犯了名人的隱私。

priv·i·lege [ˈprɪvlɪdʒ] ◀≤ Track 3997

名 特權 動 優待
▶名 No one has the right to grant（賦予）him such privilege.
沒人擁有賦予他這種特權的權利。
▶動 I'm privileged to enter this room.
我被給予了進入這間房間的特權。

pro·ce·dure [prəˈsidʒɚ] ◀≤ Track 3998

名 手續、程序
▶The whole procedure of the lawsuit could take months.
整個法律訴訟的過程可能要耗時數月。

文法字詞解析
果醬即是水果得以「保存」下來的一個形式，因此果醬除了大家熟知的 jam 外也可稱為 preserves。

文法字詞解析
如要說「濫用特權」，可稱為 abuse of privileges。

pro·ceed [prə`sid]   ◀€ Track 3999

動 進行
▶The misunderstanding should be resolved before we can proceed with the negotiation.
我們必須澄清誤會才能繼續協商。

pro·duc·tion [prə`dʌkʃən]   ◀€ Track 4000

名 製造
▶We must reduce the production cost, or we won't be getting any profits.
我們必須降低生產成本，不然我們根本沒辦法獲利啊。

文法字詞解析
除了「製造過程」、「製造」外，production 有時也可以拿來說「製造的成果」，也就是「成品」。例如電影公司製造出來的「電影」，就可以說是 production。

pro·duc·tive [prə`dʌktɪv]   ◀€ Track 4001

形 生產的、多產的
▶I don't think it was a productive meeting.
我覺得這不是一次富有成效的會議。

pro·fes·sion [prə`fɛʃən]   ◀€ Track 4002

名 專業
▶My father is a high school teacher by profession; what about your father?
我爸爸是一名高中老師，你爸爸呢？

pro·fes·sion·al [prə`fɛʃənl]   ◀€ Track 4003

名 專家 形 專業的
▶名 He is a real professional. Why don't we ask him for some advice?
他是個真正的專家，為什麼不問問他的意見呢？
▶形 The professional terms in this article will be explained in the supplement.
這篇文章中專業的術語會在附件當中解釋。

pro·fes·sor [prə`fɛsə]   ◀€ Track 4004

名 教授
▶When he came to this university, he was the youngest professor there.
他來到這所大學的時候，就成為了那所大學裡最年輕的教授。

文法字詞解析
可簡稱為 prof。

prof·it·a·ble [`prɑfɪtəbl]   ◀€ Track 4005

形 有利的 同 beneficial 有利的
▶I don't think it's a deal that is profitable to all of the partners.
我認為這並不是一宗對所有合夥人都有利的買賣。

prom·i·nent [`prɑmənənt]   ◀€ Track 4006

形 突出的
▶He has a really prominent chin. 他的下巴很突出。

prom·is·ing [`prɑmɪsɪŋ]   ◀€ Track 4007

形 有可能的、有希望的
▶The talented young man has a promising career development.
有天賦的年輕人，事業發展相當被看好。

Level 1
Level 2
Level 3
Level 4
自我勉勵、越背越上手——
提升程度4200單字
Level 5
Level 6

pro·mo·tion [prəˋmoʃən] 🔊 Track 4008

名 增進、促銷、升遷
▶The promotion of the employee will take effect next month.
這名員工的晉升，將在下個月生效。

prompt [prɑmpt] 🔊 Track 4009

形 即時的 名 提詞
▶形 He was very prompt in dealing with the issue.
他非常即時地出面對應這項議題。
▶名 I think she needs to be given a prompt.
我覺得她需要人提詞。

文法字詞解析
寫作文時有時上面常會有一段文字「提示」你必須寫什麼樣的內容，這段文字也稱為 prompt。

pro·noun [ˋpronaʊn] 🔊 Track 4010

名 代名詞
▶"I", "you" and "he" are all personal pronouns.
I、you 和 he 都是人稱代名詞。

pro·nun·ci·a·tion 🔊 Track 4011
[prəˏnʌnsɪˋeʃən]

名 發音
▶It is hard for us to imitate the pronunciation of native speakers.
我們很難模仿母語人士的發音。

pros·per [ˋprɑspɚ] 🔊 Track 4012

動 興盛
▶The company prospered for it jumped on the bandwagon of e-commerce.
這家公司能發展的好，是因為搭上了電子商務的順風車。

pros·per·i·ty [prɑsˋpɛrətɪ] 🔊 Track 4013

名 繁盛
▶I wish all of your family happiness and prosperity.
祝福您全家過得快樂、事業繁盛。

pros·per·ous [ˋprɑspərəs] 🔊 Track 4014

形 繁榮的
▶The town used to be a very prosperous one.
這個城鎮過去很繁榮。

pro·tein [ˋprotiɪn] 🔊 Track 4015

名 蛋白質
▶A balanced diet should contain both starch and protein.
均衡的飲食需要含有澱粉和蛋白質。

文法字詞解析
許多人常喝的高蛋白飲品就稱為 protein shake。

pro·test [prəˋtɛst] 🔊 Track 4016

名 抗議 動 反對、抗議
▶名 It is wrong for the government to turn a deaf ear to people's protests.
政府對人們的抗議充耳不聞，這是不對的。
▶動 He protested that he didn't do it, but they still punished him. 雖然他抗議說自己明明沒做，但他們還是處罰了他。

prov·erb [ˈprɑvɝb] ◀ *Track 4017*

名 諺語
▶A proverb goes that "haste makes waste."
有個諺語說「欲速則不達」。

psy·cho·log·i·cal [ˌsaɪkəˈlɑdʒɪkl̩] ◀ *Track 4018*

形 心理學的
▶The doctor said he had some psychological problems.
醫生說他有心理問題。

psy·chol·o·gist [saɪˈkɑlədʒɪst] ◀ *Track 4019*

名 心理學家
▶It was the psychologist, Sigmund Freud, who put forward a theory and shocked the entire world.
心理學家西格蒙德・佛洛伊德提出了一個震驚全世界的理論。

psy·chol·o·gy [saɪˈkɑlədʒɪ] ◀ *Track 4020*

名 心理學
▶He obtained a degree in psychology this year; what about you?
他今年獲得了心理學學位，你呢？

pub·li·ca·tion [ˌpʌblɪˈkeʃən] ◀ *Track 4021*

名 發表、出版
▶The publication industry in the country thrived in the 21st century.
這個國家的出版業在二十一世紀裡發展興盛。

pub·lic·i·ty [pʌbˈlɪsətɪ] ◀ *Track 4022*

名 宣傳、出風頭
▶This incident was very famous at that time and got a lot of publicity.
這件事情在當時非常轟動，引起了公眾的極大關注。

pub·lish [ˈpʌblɪʃ] ◀ *Track 4023*

動 出版
▶I hope the writer can publish another book.
我希望作者能再出版一本書。

pub·lish·er [ˈpʌblɪʃɚ] ◀ *Track 4024*

名 出版者、出版社
▶Will you tell me why the publisher refused to publish this book?
你能告訴我出版社為什麼拒絕出版這本書嗎？

pur·suit [pɚˈsut] ◀ *Track 4025*

名 追求
▶The pursuit of happiness is a process that would probably last for a lifetime.
追求幸福是持續一生的過程。

文法字詞解析
上面所學的 publication 在學術界尤其常用，教授學者們若沒有 publication，是沒辦法獲得重視的。因此有個說法 publish or perish，即「不出版，就得死」。

Level 1

Level 2

Level 3

Level 4

自我勉勵、越背越上手——
提升程度4200單字

Level 5

Level 6

[Qq]

quake [kwek]　　　　🔊 Track 4026

名 地震、震動　動 搖動、震動

▶名 More than a thousand people were left in the quake.
超過一千人因為地震而無家可歸。

▶動 He stood there quaking with fear when the teacher scolded him. 老師責罵他的時候，他站在那兒嚇得直打哆嗦。

quilt [kwɪlt]　　　　🔊 Track 4027

名 棉被　動 把……製成被褥

▶名 I don't think the quilt is thick enough to protect him from the cold. 我覺得這條被子的厚度不足以為他禦寒。

▶動 Quilting the secret letters in his belt is still not safe enough.
把密信縫入他的腰帶還是不夠可靠。

quo·ta·tion [kwo'teʃən]　　🔊 Track 4028

名 引用

▶ I'm afraid that I can't give you our quotation right now. Sorry for the inconvenience.
恐怕現在不能給您我們的報價，帶來不便敬請諒解。

[Rr]

rage [redʒ]　　　　🔊 Track 4029

名 狂怒　動 暴怒　同 anger 憤怒

▶名 My father slammed the door in a rage.
我爸爸盛怒之下大力甩門。

▶動 She always rages against her husband over some household affairs.
她總是為一些家庭瑣事而對她的丈夫大發雷霆。

萬用延伸句型
in a fit of rage 在震怒之下
例　如：He threw several dishes at the wall in a fit of rage.
他在震怒之下朝牆壁扔了好幾個盤子。

rain·fall ['ren,fɔl]　　　🔊 Track 4030

名 降雨量

▶ There is too much rainfall in this area, isn't there?
這個地區的雨水太多了，不是嗎？

re·al·is·tic [rɪə'lɪstɪk]　　🔊 Track 4031

形 現實的

▶ I don't think this plan you put forward is realistic enough.
我覺得你提出的計畫還不夠切合實際。

re·bel (1) ['rɛbl]　　　🔊 Track 4032

名 造反者、叛亂、謀反　同 revolt 叛亂

▶ The rebels destroyed the small town in the south.
叛軍摧毀了這個南方的小鎮。

文法字詞解析
rebel troop = 反叛軍

re·bel (2) [rɪˋbɛl] ◀≣ *Track 4033*

動 叛亂、謀反

▶It is a surprise that these people should choose to rebel against their government.
這些人竟然會選擇反叛政府，真令人驚訝。

re·call [ˋrɪkɔl]/[rɪˋkɔl] ◀≣ *Track 4034*

名 取消、收回 動 回憶起、恢復

▶名 I believe that he has something to do with the temporary recall of embassy staff.
我想他跟這次大使館人員的臨時召回有關係。

▶動 I am afraid that we have to recall our diplomat in Russia.
恐怕我們得召回在俄羅斯的大使。

re·cep·tion [rɪˋsɛpʃən] ◀≣ *Track 4035*

名 接受

▶Their wedding reception will be held at the luxurious restaurant.
他們的婚宴將在這家奢華的餐廳舉行。

文法字詞解析
因為飯店的櫃臺就是「接待、接受」顧客的地方，因此飯店的接待櫃臺也可稱為 reception。

rec·i·pe [ˋrɛsəpɪ] ◀≣ *Track 4036*

名 食譜、秘訣

▶Why don't we try this new recipe introduced by the gourmet（美食家）?
為什麼不嘗試一下那位美食家所介紹的新食譜呢？

re·cite [rɪˋsaɪt] ◀≣ *Track 4037*

動 背誦

▶Can you recite the poem written by the famous poet, Williams Blake? 你背得出著名詩人威廉・布雷克寫的詩嗎？

rec·og·ni·tion [ˏrɛkəgˋnɪʃən] ◀≣ *Track 4038*

名 認知

萬用延伸句型
I wish I could... 真希望我可以……（用於事實上做不到的事）

▶I wish I could avoid recognition by wearing dark glasses.
真希望我戴上墨鏡就不會有人認出我來。

re·cov·er·y [rɪˋkʌvərɪ] ◀≣ *Track 4039*

名 恢復

▶The recovery from the injury may take months.
傷勢復原可能要花幾個月的時間。

rec·re·a·tion [ˏrɛkrɪˋeʃən] ◀≣ *Track 4040*

名 娛樂

▶Will you tell me what kind of recreation you like best?
你能告訴我你最喜歡的娛樂是什麼嗎？

re·cy·cle [riˋsaɪkḷ] ◀≣ *Track 4041*

動 循環利用

▶It is obvious that few people are aware of the importance of recycling at present.
很明顯，現在意識到資源回收的重要性的人並不多。

Level 1

Level 2

Level 3

Level 4

自我勉勵、越背越上手——提升程度4200單字

Level 5

Level 6

re·duc·tion [rɪˋdʌkʃən] ◀€ *Track 4042*

名 減少 同 decrease 減少
▶A 20% reduction in the housing price is expected within a decade. 預估在未來十年，房價會下跌百分之二十。

re·fer [rɪˋfɜ] ◀€ *Track 4043*

動 參考、提及
▶Don't you think his remark refers to all of us in the company? 難道你不覺得他的話是針對公司所有人的嗎？

ref·er·ence [ˋrɛfərəns] ◀€ *Track 4044*

名 參考
▶I don't think the reference book is of any use to us. 我覺得這本參考書對我們沒什麼用處。

re·flect [rɪˋflɛkt] ◀€ *Track 4045*

動 反射
▶I think you must reflect upon how to answer the question. 我認為你必須思考一下如何回答那個問題。

re·flec·tion [rɪˋflɛkʃən] ◀€ *Track 4046*

名 反射、反省
▶The baby was amused by his own reflection in the mirror. 小寶寶看到鏡子裡自己的倒影，感覺很開心。

re·form [rɪˋfɔrm] ◀€ *Track 4047*

動 改進
▶It is expected that the corrupting bureauratic system would be reformed soon. 腐敗的官僚體系應該要早點被改革。

re·fresh [rɪˋfrɛʃ] ◀€ *Track 4048*

動 使恢復精神
▶How about refreshing yourself with a cup of tea before you go out? 在你出門前，喝杯茶提提神怎麼樣？

re·fresh·ment [rɪˋfrɛʃmənt] ◀€ *Track 4049*

名 清爽、茶點
▶Would you like some refreshments while waiting? 在等待的時候，您要不要來點提神小點心呢？

ref·u·gee [ˌrɛfjʊˋdʒi] ◀€ *Track 4050*

名 難民
▶It is hard for us to handle the refugee problem properly. 我們很難適當地處理難民問題。

re·fus·al [rɪˋfjuzl] ◀€ *Track 4051*

名 拒絕 同 denial 拒絕、否認
▶Tom's proposal to his girlfriend was met with refusal. 湯姆向女友求婚被拒絕了。

萬用延伸句型

reflect in sth. 反射、倒映在（某物）上
例如：He saw his own face reflected in the mirror.
他在鏡子上看到了自己的臉。

文法字詞解析

電腦網頁跑不動，等得不耐煩時，不是都會按下「重新整理」嗎？這個動作就叫作 refresh the page。

re·gard·ing [rɪˋgɑrdɪŋ]
◀ Track 4052

介 關於

▶Do you mind telling me what you know regarding the case?
你介意告訴我關於這個案子你都知道些什麼嗎？

reg·is·ter [ˋrɛdʒɪstɚ]
◀ Track 4053

名 名單、註冊 動 登記、註冊

▶名 Have you filled out the hotel register? Can you tell me how to do it?
你已經填寫過了旅館登記簿嗎？你能告訴我如何填寫它嗎？

▶動 We registered to be the volunteer during the Olympic Games. 我們註冊報名當奧運期間的志工。

reg·is·tra·tion [ˏrɛdʒɪˋstreʃən]
◀ Track 4054

名 註冊

▶Would you mind telling me your registration fee?
請告知我你們的註冊費用是多少好嗎？

reg·u·late [ˋrɛgjəˏlet]
◀ Track 4055

動 調節、管理

▶This equipment helps to regulate the temperature of the room.
這種設備有助於調節室內溫度。

reg·u·la·tion [ˏrɛgjəˋleʃən]
◀ Track 4056

名 調整、法規

▶The legal assistant is familiar with regulations related to tax reporting.
法律事務所的助手對報稅的法規很熟悉。

re·jec·tion [rɪˋdʒɛkʃən]
◀ Track 4057

名 廢棄、拒絕

▶I was annoyed at her rejection of my proposal.
我為她拒絕我的提議而感到不快。

rel·a·tive [ˋrɛlətɪv]
◀ Track 4058

形 相對的、有關係的 名 親戚

▶形 It's time for us to discuss some facts relative to the problem.
我們該討論一下與這個問題相關的一些事實了。

▶名 I have too many relatives to count.
我的親戚太多了，都數不清了。

re·lax·a·tion [ˏrilæksˋeʃən]
◀ Track 4059

名 放鬆

▶It is hard for us to accept this routine that leaves no time for relaxation. 我們很難接受這種不留休息時間的規定。

re·lieve [rɪˋliv]
◀ Track 4060

動 減緩

▶The patient requested some medication to relieve his pain.
病人要求接受止痛治療。

Level 1

Level 2

Level 3

Level 4

自我勉勵、越背越上手──
提升程度4200單字

Level 5

Level 6

re·luc·tant [rɪˋlʌktənt]
🔊 Track 4061

形 不情願的

▶Gary was reluctant to apologize to his girlfriend.
蓋瑞很不願意向女友道歉。

---

re·mark [rɪˋmɑrk]
🔊 Track 4062

名 注意 動 注意、評論

▶名 This is nothing worthy（值得的）of remark, and not everyone will take it to heart.
這不是什麼值得注意的事，而且也不是每個人都會把它放在心上。

▶動 "Wow, you sure are dressed well today." he remarked.
「哇，你今天穿得真好看啊。」他評論道。

---

re·mark·a·ble [rɪˋmɑrkəbl̩]
🔊 Track 4063

形 值得注意的

▶He made remarkable progress in his studies very quickly.
他在學習上很快取得顯著進步。

---

rem·e·dy [ˋrɛmədɪ]
🔊 Track 4064

名 醫療 動 治療、補救

▶名 Is there any remedy to heartache?
有什麼方式能夠治療心痛呢？

▶動 Time is the best remedy for emotional wounds.
感情受傷，最好就是靠時間來治癒。

---

rep·e·ti·tion [ˌrɛpɪˋtɪʃən]
🔊 Track 4065

名 重複

▶Repetition is a good way to learn a language.
重複是學習語言一個不錯的方式。

---

rep·re·sen·ta·tion
[ˌrɛprɪzɛnˋteʃən]
🔊 Track 4066

名 代表、表示、表現

▶I don't think this painting is a representation of peace.
我認為這幅畫描繪的並不是和平。

---

rep·u·ta·tion [ˌrɛpjəˋteʃən]
🔊 Track 4067

名 名譽、聲望

▶He has a reputation for being a huge partygoer.
他以愛開趴而出名。

---

res·cue [ˋrɛskju]
🔊 Track 4068

名 搭救 動 援救

▶名 Seeing the rescue team, the boys trapped in the cave sighed with relief. 看到搜救隊伍的人時，被困在在洞穴裡的男孩全都鬆了一口氣。

▶動 The police don't know how to rescue the hostage（人質）yet.
警察目前還不知道如何營救人質。

文法字詞解析

reluctant 的名詞形式是 reluctance。

萬用延伸句型

come to sb.'s rescue 前來援救某人
例 如：Luckily the fire fighters came to his rescue in time.
幸好消防員即時前來救他。

re·search [`rɪsɝtʃ]
🔊 *Track 4069*

名 研究 動 調查

▶名 The latest research that vegan diet can help people lose weight.
最近的研究指出，吃素可以幫助人減肥。

▶動 How long have you been researching into the cause of cancer?
你研究癌症的起因多久了？

re·search·er [rɪ`sɝtʃɚ]
🔊 *Track 4070*

名 調查員

▶It is difficult for the researchers to prove how this happened.
研究員們很難證明為何此事會發生。

re·sem·ble [rɪ`zɛmbl]
🔊 *Track 4071*

動 類似

▶Hank resembles his father in looks.
漢克長得很像他爸爸。

res·er·va·tion [ˌrɛzɚ`veʃən]
🔊 *Track 4072*

名 保留

▶Would you make the reservations for our holiday this time?
這次能請你為我們度假做一下預訂安排嗎？

re·sign [rɪ`zaɪn]
🔊 *Track 4073*

動 辭職、使順從

▶He resigned last week, and doubtlessly it was a great loss to us.他上星期辭職了，這對我們來說無疑是一個巨大的損失。

res·ig·na·tion [ˌrɛzɪg`neʃən]
🔊 *Track 4074*

名 辭職、讓位

▶His resignation is accepted by the Board.
董事會接受了他的辭職。

re·sis·tance [rɪ`zɪstəns]
🔊 *Track 4075*

名 抵抗

▶There is a lot of resistance to this new law.
反對這項新法律的人很多。

res·o·lu·tion [ˌrɛzə`luʃən]
🔊 *Track 4076*

名 果斷、決心 同 determination 決心

▶He had a strong resolution to find his father's killer.
他有強烈的決心，要找到他的殺父仇人。

re·solve [rɪ`zɑlv]
🔊 *Track 4077*

名 決心 動 解決、分解

▶名 He has made a resolve to give up smoking.
他已經決定不吸菸了。

▶動 Jerry resolved to quit smoking in the coming year.
傑瑞下定決心，明年要戒菸。

文法字詞解析
辭職即「放棄」自己的職位，而 resign 也可以當作「放棄」抵抗、接受事實的意思。例如當某人本來非常不願意參加某個活動，後來勉強答應，完全不做任何抵抗，即是 resigned 的表現。

Level 1
Level 2
Level 3
Level 4
提升程度4200單字 自我勉勵、越背越上手──
Level 5
Level 6

re·spect·a·ble [rɪˋspɛktəbl̩]
◀≋ Track 4078

形 可尊敬的

▶I don't think it is respectable to be drunk in front of your in-laws.
我認為在岳父母面前喝醉實在不太體面。

文法字詞解析
岳父稱 father-in-law，岳母稱 mother-in-law，兩者合在一起就是你的 in-laws。

re·spect·ful [rɪˋspɛktfəl]
◀≋ Track 4079

形 有禮的

▶We greeted the authoritative author with a respectful manner.
我們帶著敬意向權威作者致意。

re·store [rɪˋstor]
◀≋ Track 4080

動 恢復

▶The doctors restored his eyesight.
醫生們恢復了他的視力。

re·stric·tion [rɪˋstrɪkʃən]
◀≋ Track 4081

名 限制

▶It is a surprise that they should say there is no restriction to how many apples we can take.
他們竟然說沒限制我們可以拿走幾顆蘋果，真是令人驚訝。

re·tain [rɪˋten]
◀≋ Track 4082

動 保持

▶She still retains a clear memory of the matter.
她仍很清晰地記得這件事。

文法字詞解析
矯正牙齒後，為了不讓牙齒又跑回去原來的地方，有時會使用「維持器」。這個東西就叫作 retainer。

re·tire [rɪˋtaɪr]
◀≋ Track 4083

動 隱退

▶Everyone thinks that it's time for the man to retire.
大家都覺得這個人該退休了。

re·tire·ment [rɪˋtaɪrmənt]
◀≋ Track 4084

名 退休

▶The couple lived on their retirement allowance in their seventies.
這對夫妻靠著退休金過活。

re·treat [rɪˋtrit]
◀≋ Track 4085

名 撤退 動 撤退

▶名 They made a hasty retreat when they realized that they were under-equipped.
他們發覺自己的武器帶太少時，就趕緊撤退了。

▶動 A good general knows when to attack and when to retreat.
一名優秀的將軍知道何時進攻，何時撤退。

文法字詞解析
除了從戰爭中撤退外，retreat 也可以表示從現實生活中「撤退」，也就是去找個地方躲起來度假啦！因此像是山中小屋、海邊度假村等，都是理想的 holiday retreat。

re·un·ion [riˋjunjən]
◀≋ Track 4086

名 重聚、團圓

▶The annual family reunion will take place on New Year's Eve.
年度家族聚會訂在新年前夕舉行。

re·venge [rɪˈvɛndʒ]

◀€ *Track 4087*

名 報復 動 報復 同 retaliate 報復

▶名 It is quite clear that he did this all out of revenge.
很顯然，他這樣做完全是出於報復。

▶動 He intended to revenge himself on the bully.
他企圖向霸凌他的人復仇。

re·vise [rɪˈvaɪz]

◀€ *Track 4088*

動 修正、校訂

▶It took him two hours to help her revise the article at night.
晚上他花了兩小時才幫她改好了文章。

re·vi·sion [rɪˈvɪʒən]

◀€ *Track 4089*

名 修訂

▶I don't think the law is in need of revision.
我覺得這項法律無需修訂。

rev·o·lu·tion [ˌrɛvəˈluʃən]

◀€ *Track 4090*

名 革命、改革

▶The Industrial revolution has brought great changes in the manufacturing method.
工業革命為製造方法帶來很大的變革。

rev·o·lu·tion·ar·y

◀€ *Track 4091*

[ˌrɛvəˈluʃənɛrɪ]

形 革命的

▶Don't you think it is a revolutionary new way of growing wheat?
難道你不認為這是一種全新的種植小麥的方法嗎？

re·ward [rɪˈwɔrd]

◀€ *Track 4092*

名 報酬 動 酬賞

▶名 They offered a reward for anyone who found their lost puppy.
他們提供報酬給找到他們走失小狗的人。

▶動 These villagers（村民）don't know how to reward him for all his help.
這些村民不知道如何報答他的種種幫助。

rhyme [raɪm]

◀€ *Track 4093*

名 韻、韻文 動 押韻

▶名 He knows nothing about rhyme and meter（格律）.
他對韻律一無所知，真是遺憾。

▶動 It is a pity that the last two lines of this poem don't rhyme properly.
真遺憾，這首詩的最後兩行沒有押好韻。

rhythm [ˈrɪðəm]

◀€ *Track 4094*

名 節奏、韻律

▶People danced to the rhythm of the song on the party.
人們在宴會上隨著歌曲韻律跳舞。

萬用延伸句型
no rhyme or reason 毫無邏輯、看不出頭緒
例如：Seems to me there's no rhyme or reason to his proposal.
我覺得他的提案看不出一點邏輯。

Level
1

Level
2

Level
3

Level
4

Level
5

Level
6

自我勉勵、越背越上手——
提升程度4200單字

ro·mance [ro`mæns] ◀≷ *Track 4095*
動 羅曼史
▶Mary kept secret about her summer romance in Italy.
瑪莉把在義大利的夏日羅曼史當作是心底的秘密。

rough·ly [`rʌflɪ] ◀≷ *Track 4096*
副 粗暴地、粗略地
▶The young man roughly pushed the old woman aside.
這個年輕人把這位老婦人粗暴地推到了一邊。

route [rut] ◀≷ *Track 4097*
名 路線
▶Don't you think it's the quickest route to America?
難道你不認為這是去美國的最快路線嗎？

ru·in [`rʊɪn] ◀≷ *Track 4098*
名 破壞 動 毀滅 同 destroy 破壞
▶名 I can't tell what led to the hero's ruin in the book.
我看不出是什麼導致了書中男主角的毀滅。
▶動 He ruined our surprise party for Susan by accidentally telling Susan about it.
他一不小心跟蘇珊講了要為她開驚喜派對的事，完全毀了這場驚喜。

文法字詞解析
ruin 使用複數形式 ruins 時，常可以用來表示（已經有點毀壞掉的）「遺跡」。例如古希臘、古羅馬等地留下來的一些不怎麼完好的古蹟，就可以稱為 ruins。

ru·ral [`rʊrəl] ◀≷ *Track 4099*
形 農村的
▶There are lots of people still living in poverty in rural areas.
在廣大的農村地區，仍有很多人生活在貧困之中。

[Ss]

sac·ri·fice [`sækrəˌfaɪs] ◀≷ *Track 4100*
名 獻祭 動 供奉、犧牲
▶名 She made sacrifice for her children, but they showed no gratitude to her.
她為小孩犧牲很多，但小孩都沒有感謝她。
▶動 He is willing to sacrifice a great deal for her.
他能夠為她做出巨大的犧牲。

sal·a·ry [`sælərɪ] ◀≷ *Track 4101*
名 薪水、薪俸、付薪水 同 wage 薪水
▶It's very difficult for a graduate to get a job with a good salary nowadays.
現在對於畢業生來說找一份薪水高的工作很難。

sales·per·son/ sales·man/sales·wom·an 🔊 *Track 4102*

[ˈselzˌpɚs]/[ˈselzmən]/[ˈselzˌwʊmən]

名 售貨員、推銷員

▶Should we ask a salesperson to demonstrate this new washing machine? 我們要不要請一位推銷員來示範一下如何使用這台新式洗衣機呢？

sat·el·lite [ˈsætlˌaɪt] 🔊 *Track 4103*

名 衛星

▶The debris of the deserted satellite became a pollution in the space. 廢棄人造衛星的殘骸成為太空中的汙染物。

sat·is·fac·tion [ˌsætɪsˈfækʃən] 🔊 *Track 4104*

名 滿足

▶It is obvious that the success brought him great satisfaction. 顯然成功為他帶來了極大的滿足。

scarce·ly [ˈskɛrslɪ] 🔊 *Track 4105*

副 勉強地、幾乎不　同 hardly 幾乎不

▶She scarcely earns enough money to make ends meet. 她幾乎沒有賺足夠的錢來平衡收支。

scen·ery [ˈsinərɪ] 🔊 *Track 4106*

名 風景、景色

▶The scenery was beautiful beyond description. Don't you think so? 那風景美麗得難以形容，你不這樣認為嗎？

scold [skold] 🔊 *Track 4107*

名 好罵人的人、潑婦　動 責罵

▶名 His father gave him a bad scold this morning. 他父親今天早上狠狠地罵了他一頓。

▶動 She has a bad temper and is always scolding her children. 她脾氣很壞，老是責備自己的子女。

文法字詞解析

scold 是「罵」的意思，但僅止於上對下的「責罵」，如果吵架時罵對方髒話之類的情境是不能稱為 scold 的。

scratch [skrætʃ] 🔊 *Track 4108*

動 抓

▶The cat is scratching herself again. 這貓又在抓自己了。

screw·driv·er [ˈskruˌdraɪvɚ] 🔊 *Track 4109*

名 螺絲刀

▶Will you go and fetch me a screwdriver, please? 請你去幫我拿把螺絲起子來好嗎？

sculp·ture [ˈskʌlptʃɚ] 🔊 *Track 4110*

名 雕刻、雕塑　動 以雕刻裝飾

▶名 The sculpture of Roldan is displayed in the national museum. 羅丹的雕像被陳列在國家博物館中。

▶動 There are two horses sculptured in bronze（青銅）at the gate. 在大門口有兩匹用青銅雕塑的馬。

Level 1

Level 2

Level 3

Level 4

自我勉勵、越背越上手──
提升程度4200單字

Level 5

Level 6

sea·gull/gull [ˈsigʌl]/[gʌl]　🔊 *Track 4111*

名 海鷗
▶The sound of seagulls crying brings her back to her childhood holidays by the sea.
她聽到海鷗的叫聲就回憶起童年時在海邊度假的情景。

sen·ior [ˈsinjɚ]　🔊 *Track 4112*

名 年長者　形 年長的　同 elder 年紀較大的
▶名 You need to talk to some seniors about the problem.
　你應該要去和一些年長者討論一下這個問題。
▶形 The senior members of the association were against the renovative project.
　協會中年長的成員反對這項改革計畫。

set·tler [ˈsɛtlɚ]　🔊 *Track 4113*

名 殖民者、居留者
▶The first settlers of this country were prisoners.
第一批到達這個國家的移民是囚犯。

se·vere [səˈvɪr]　🔊 *Track 4114*

形 嚴厲的
▶He is a severe critic when it comes to his own work.
對於自己的作品，他是個很嚴厲的批評者。

shame·ful [ˈʃemfəl]　🔊 *Track 4115*

形 恥辱的
▶There is nothing shameful about losing a game.
比賽輸了沒什麼好可恥的。

shav·er [ˈʃevɚ]　🔊 *Track 4116*

名 理髮師
▶I don't think that you should use the shaver while taking a bath.
我覺得你在洗澡的時候不應該使用電動刮鬍刀。

shel·ter [ˈʃɛltɚ]　🔊 *Track 4117*

名 避難所、庇護所　動 保護、掩護　同 protect 保護
▶名 Victims of the earthquake took shelter in the school auditorium.
　地震的受災戶在學校禮堂避難。
▶動 The hen sheltered her chicks from the rain.
　那隻母雞保護她的小雞免受雨淋。

shift [ʃɪft]　🔊 *Track 4118*

名 變換　動 變換
▶名 If you really like the job, would you like to work on the night shift?
　如果你真的喜歡這份工作，你願不願意上夜班呢？
▶動 Would you please tell me if I should shift gears before making a turn? 你能告訴我在轉彎之前該不該換檔嗎？

short·sight·ed [`ʃɔrt`saɪtɪd]　🔊 Track 4119
形 近視的
▶The shortsighted man could not see the long-term profit of the investment. 短視近利的人看不出這項投資的長期報酬。

文法字詞解析
近視也可稱為 nearsighted。

shrug [ʃrʌg]　🔊 Track 4120
動 聳肩
▶He never speaks, and mostly just shrugs.
他都不講話，通常只會聳聳肩而已。

shut·tle [`ʃʌtl]　🔊 Track 4121
名 縫紉機的滑梭　動 往返
▶名 There is a shuttle service between the city center and the airport. 在市中心和飛機場之間有往返的接駁班車。
▶動 I usually shuttle between these two cities for work.
我常會為了工作在這兩個城市間穿梭。

sight·see·ing [`saɪt͵siɪŋ]　🔊 Track 4122
名 觀光、遊覽
▶I spent most of my time on sightseeing. What about you?
我大部分時間都用在觀光遊覽上了。你呢？

sig·na·ture [`sɪgnətʃɚ]　🔊 Track 4123
名 簽名
▶The signature on the document was so vague that I couldn't recognize it.
這個文件上的簽名很模糊，我認不出這些字。

sig·nif·i·cance [sɪg`nɪfəkəns]　🔊 Track 4124
名 重要性
▶Nobody can achieve anything of real significance unless he works very hard. 一個人要是不努力，他就將一事無成。

sin·cer·i·ty [sɪn`sɛrətɪ]　🔊 Track 4125
名 誠懇、真摯
▶He finds it hard to speak with sincerity.
他覺得要誠懇地講話是很困難的事。

萬用延伸句型
find it hard to（＋原形動詞）覺得（做到某事）很難

sin·gu·lar [`sɪŋgjəlɚ]　🔊 Track 4126
名 單數　形 單一的、個別的
▶名 The singular of "mice" is "mouse".
「mice」的單數形是「mouse」。
▶形 I had a singular experience in Africa.
我在非洲時有過一次奇特的經歷。

site [saɪt]　🔊 Track 4127
名 地基、位置　動 設置　同 location 位置
▶名 We were trapped in the camping site in the mountain when the storm hit. 暴風雨來襲時，我們被困在露營的營地。
▶動 Do you think it is safe to site the power station here?
你覺得在這裡建造發電廠安全嗎？

Level 1
Level 2
Level 3
Level 4
自我勉勵、越背越上手——
提升程度4200單字
Level 5
Level 6

sketch [skɛtʃ]
🔊 Track 4128

名 素描、草圖 動 描述、素描

▶名 Will you please give me a sketch of your plan?
請你跟我談談你的計畫概略好嗎？

▶動 The kid sketched his mother with a pencil.
小孩用鉛筆素描他的母親。

sledge/sled [slɛdʒ]/[slɛd]
🔊 Track 4129

名 雪橇 動 用雪橇搬運

▶名 The kids are outside playing on the sledge.
孩子們在外面玩雪橇。

▶動 Do you want to go sledging with us later?
待會要不要跟我們一起去玩雪橇？

sleigh [sle]
🔊 Track 4130

名 有座雪橇、雪橇、乘坐雪橇

▶My feet were as cold as stone when I got out of the sleigh.
我從雪橇上下來時兩隻腳凍得像石頭一樣。

slight [slaɪt]
🔊 Track 4131

形 輕微的 動 輕視

▶形 The girl can detect any slight changes in the appearance of her friend.
這個女孩可以察覺到她朋友外貌上細微的變化。

▶動 Mr. Paul is highly respected because he never slights anyone.
保羅先生非常受人尊敬，因為他從不輕視任何人。

萬用延伸句型
not in the slightest 一點都不
例如：
A: Are you scared?
B: Not in the slightest.
A：你怕嗎？
B：一點都不怕。

slo·gan [ˈslogən]
🔊 Track 4132

名 標語、口號

▶Our slogan is "Time is money, efficiency is life".
我們的口號是「時間就是金錢，效率就是生命」。

smog [smɑg]
🔊 Track 4133

名 煙霧、煙

▶There are still some big cities with smog problems.
仍有些大城市有著煙霧排放的問題。

sneeze [sniz]
🔊 Track 4134

名 噴嚏 動 輕視、打噴嚏

▶名 I counted seven sneezes coming from the neighboring room. 我聽到隔壁房間有人打了七個噴嚏。

▶動 Sarah sneezed wheninhaling the pollen.
莎拉吸到花粉就打噴嚏。

sob [sɑb]
🔊 Track 4135

名 啜泣 動 哭訴、啜泣 同 cry 哭

▶名 A sob welled up in his throat when he saw his mother.
他看到媽媽時，喉嚨裡發出一聲嗚咽。

▶動 The poor little boy sobbed himself to sleep.
那個可憐的小男孩啜泣著入睡了。

文法字詞解析
刻意賺人熱淚的故事即稱為 sobstory（並非褒義）。

sock·et [ˈsɑkɪt]

Track 4136

名 凹處、插座
▶Ryan put a cover on the socket to keep it from dust.
雷恩將插座覆蓋住，以免灰塵跑進去。

soft·ware [ˈsɔftˌwɛr]

Track 4137

名 軟體
▶There are many kinds of software in my computer.
我的電腦裡有很多軟體。

文法字詞解析
和軟體相對的硬體則稱作 hardware。此外還有韌體（firmware）。

so·lar [ˈsolɚ]

Track 4138

形 太陽的 反 lunar 月球的
▶Don't you think that we can use solar energy to do many things today? 你不覺得如今我們可以利用太陽能做很多事情嗎？

soph·o·more [ˈsɑfmˌor]

Track 4139

名 二年級學生
▶As a sophomore, I really feel that time flies.
作為一名大二學生，我真的感覺時光飛逝。

sor·row·ful [ˈsɑrəfəl]

Track 4140

形 哀痛的、悲傷的
▶Why does the whole family look so sorrowful?
為什麼那一家人全都看起來很悲傷？

sou·ve·nir [ˌsuvəˈnɪr]

Track 4141

名 紀念品、特產
▶Would you please accept this as a souvenir for our friendship?
請接受這個作為我們友誼的紀念好嗎？

spare [spɛr]

Track 4142

形 剩餘的 動 節省、騰出
▶形 It is obvious that he has nothing to do in his spare time.
顯然他在休閒時間裡無事可做。
▶動 Take a chair, I have lots to spare anyway.
拿一張椅子去吧，反正我還有很多張可以騰出來。

spark [spɑrk]

Track 4143

名 火花、火星 動 冒火花、鼓舞
▶名 There is a wild spark in his eyes.
他的眼裡有著野性的火花。
▶動 It was this incident that sparked her interest in politics.
是這個事件激起了她對政治的興趣。

文法字詞解析
除了真的火花外，兩人相當來電擦出的「火花」也可稱為 spark。

spar·kle [ˈspɑrkl̩]

Track 4144

名 閃爍 動 使閃耀
▶名 His eyes always have sparkles in them when he's excited.
他在興奮時眼睛總是閃閃發亮。
▶動 The girl's eyes sparkled with passion when she talked about dancing. 小女孩講到跳舞，眼神裡充滿熱情的光輝。

Level 1
Level 2
Level 3
Level 4
提升程度4200單字
自我勉勵、越背越上手
Level 5
Level 6

spar·row [ˈspæro] ◀≋ Track 4145
名 麻雀
▶There is a worm in the sparrow's beak.
那隻麻雀的嘴裡叼著一隻蟲子。

spear [spɪr] ◀≋ Track 4146
名 矛、魚叉 動 用矛刺
▶名 People in the primitive tribe hunted with spears.
原始部落的人用茅來打獵。
▶動 Do you know how to spear fish? 你知道怎樣叉魚嗎？

spe·cies [ˈspiʃɪz] ◀≋ Track 4147
名 物種
▶There are millions of species of animals and plants on the earth. 地球上動物和植物種類有幾百萬種。

spic·y [ˈspaɪsɪ] ◀≋ Track 4148
形 辛辣的、加香料的
▶What about having some spicy food for a change?
嚐嚐辛辣的菜換一下口味如何？

spir·i·tu·al [ˈspɪrɪtʃʊəl] ◀≋ Track 4149
形 精神的、崇高的 反 material 物質的
▶The spiritual fulfillment can be gained through meditation.
冥想會帶來心靈的滿足。

splen·did [ˈsplɛndɪd] ◀≋ Track 4150
形 輝煌的、閃耀的
▶Have you seen her wedding dress? It's just splendid!
妳有看到她的結婚禮服嗎？超級美的！

split [splɪt] ◀≋ Track 4151
名 裂口 動 劈開、分化
▶名 The little girl did a split out of nowhere just to show off.
那個小女孩沒事就劈個腿以示炫耀。
▶動 I think it's better for us to split up so that the enemy can't track us.
我覺得我們還是分開走比較好，敵人就追蹤不到我們。

sports·man/ sports·wom·an [ˈsportsmən]/[ˈsportsˌwʊmən] ◀≋ Track 4152
名 男運動員／女運動員
▶I'm not a great sportsman, but I enjoy watching football matches. 我不是一名偉大的運動員，但我喜歡看足球比賽。

sports·man·ship [ˈsportsmənˌʃɪp] ◀≋ Track 4153
名 運動員精神
▶The players bowed to each other after the game to show sportsmanship.
選手在比賽結束時互相鞠躬致意，表現運動家精神。

文法字詞解析
瀕臨絕種的物種稱為 endangered species。

文法字詞解析
split 的動詞變化：split, split, split

sta·tus [ˈstetəs]

🔊 *Track 4154*

名 地位、身分

▶The social status of the aborigines has been raised a lot in the past decade.
過去十年來，原住民的社會地位大幅提升。

stem [stɛm]

🔊 *Track 4155*

名 杆柄、莖幹 動 起源、阻止

▶名 It is clear that the stem of the rose was broken by someone.
顯然這支玫瑰的莖是被人折斷的。

▶動 His error stemmed from carelessness.
顯然他的錯誤是由於粗心大意而造成的。

sting·y [ˈstɪndʒɪ]

🔊 *Track 4156*

形 有刺的、會刺的

▶It is no wonder that nobody is willing to talk to such a stingy man.
這樣小氣的人，難怪誰也不願意和他說話。

strength·en [ˈstrɛŋθən]

🔊 *Track 4157*

動 加強、增強

▶Listening to TED talks can help you strengthen your mind.
聽TED演講可以讓你的心智更強壯。

strive [straɪv]

🔊 *Track 4158*

動 苦幹、努力

▶Just wishing for peace is not enough. We must strive for it.
只希望和平是不夠的。我們一定要去爭取它。

文法字詞解析
strive 的動詞變化：strive, strove, striven

stroke [strok]

🔊 *Track 4159*

名 打擊、一撞 動 撫摸

▶名 I felt so bad when I heard that he had a stroke yesterday.
聽說他昨天中風了，我感到非常遺憾。

▶動 She stroked her child's hair as he slept.
她在孩子睡覺時輕撫他的頭髮。

sub·ma·rine [ˈsʌbməˌrin]

🔊 *Track 4160*

名 潛水艇 形 海底的

▶名 Would you please tell me why a submarine can float and sink?
你能告訴我為什麼潛水艇既能浮在水面，又能潛入水底嗎？

▶形 When were the submarine cables laid across the Atlantic?
橫越大西洋的海底電纜是什麼時候鋪設的？

sug·ges·tion [səgˈdʒɛstʃən]

🔊 *Track 4161*

名 建議

▶I followed the doctor's suggestion and started to watch my diet.
我聽從醫師的建議，開始注意飲食。

Level 1

Level 2

Level 3

Level 4

自我勉勵、越背越上手——提升程度4200單字

Level 5

Level 6

sum·ma·rize [`sʌmə.raɪz] 🔊 *Track 4162*

[動] 總結、概述

▶I summarize the main points in the last paragraph of the article.
我在文章的最後一段摘要了重點。

surf [sɝf] 🔊 *Track 4163*

[名] 湧上來的波 [動] 衝浪、乘浪

▶[名] They took off their clothes and ran into the surf.
他們脫掉衣服，奔向海浪。

▶[動] How about going surfing with us next weekend?
下週末跟我們去衝浪怎麼樣？

文法字詞解析
surf and turf = 海陸套餐

sur·geon [`sɝdʒən] 🔊 *Track 4164*

[名] 外科醫生

▶I'm afraid that you should go to see the surgeon first.
恐怕你應該先去看看外科醫生。

sur·ger·y [`sɝdʒərɪ] 🔊 *Track 4165*

[名] 外科醫學、外科手術

▶Would you tell her that the surgery is scheduled within two weeks? 請告訴她手術將在兩週內進行好嗎？

sur·ren·der [sə`rɛndə] 🔊 *Track 4166*

[名] 投降 [動] 屈服、投降

▶[名] The enemy were forced to make an unconditional（無條件的）surrender. 敵軍被迫無條件投降。

▶[動] He would rather die than surrender. 他寧死也不投降。

sur·round·ings [sə`raʊndɪŋz] 🔊 *Track 4167*

[名] 環境、周圍

▶The kid was told to watch changes in the surroundings to protect himself.
小孩被要求要注意四周的變化來保護自己。

sus·pi·cious [sə`spɪʃən] 🔊 *Track 4168*

[形] 可疑的

▶There were suspicious circumstances about his death.
關於他的死，有一些值得懷疑的情況。

sway [swe] 🔊 *Track 4169*

[名] 搖擺、支配 [動] 支配、搖擺

▶[名] It is clear that he is under the sway of his parents.
顯然他是受他父母控制的。

▶[動] No one could sway his stance on this issue.
沒有人能動搖他在這個議題上的立場。

萬用延伸句型
hold sway over sb./sth. 對（某人或某事）有極大影響
例 如：Even though he already retired, he still holds sway over our company's decisions.
雖然他已經退休了，他對我們公司做的所有決策還是影響甚大。

syl·la·ble [`sɪləbl̩] 🔊 *Track 4170*

[名] 音節

▶Would you please tell me which syllable the stress of this word falls on?
請你告訴我這個字的重音是在哪個音節上好嗎？

sym·pa·thet·ic [ˌsɪmpəˈθɛtɪk] ◀≣ *Track 4171*

形 表示同情的
▶My uncle is a very sympathetic person.
我叔叔是一個富有同情心的人。

sym·pa·thy [ˈsɪmpəθɪ] ◀≣ *Track 4172*

名 同情
▶You should show empathy rather than sympathy to your friend. 你應該要對朋友表示同理心，而不是同情心。

sym·pho·ny [ˈsɪmfənɪ] ◀≣ *Track 4173*

名 交響樂、交響曲
▶I don't think that the first movement of the symphony is beautiful.
我覺得這部交響樂的第一樂章沒有那麼優美。

文法字詞解析
movement 一般的意思是「運動」，但用在音樂術語中就表示一個「樂章」。

syr·up [ˈsɪrəp] ◀≣ *Track 4174*

名 糖漿
▶Would you like to have some bread with syrup?
你想不想吃一些配糖漿的麵包？

sys·tem·at·ic [ˌsɪstəˈmætɪk] ◀≣ *Track 4175*

形 有系統的、有組織的
▶We explained the problem in a systematic way.
我們以有系統的方式解釋了這個問題。

[Tt]

tap [tæp] ◀≣ *Track 4176*

名 輕拍聲 動 輕打
▶名 He gave the microphone a tap before speaking to make sure it works.
他在講話前先輕叩一下擴音器，以確定它能用。
▶動 He tapped his fingers to signal the waitress.
他彈了手指，示意女服務生過來。

tech·ni·cian [tɛkˈnɪʃən] ◀≣ *Track 4177*

名 技師、技術員
▶The company sent two technicians there to fix the machine.
公司派兩個技術員去那裡修理機器。

tech·no·log·i·cal ◀≣ *Track 4178*
[tɛknəˈlɑdʒɪkl]
形 工業技術的
▶We must further strengthen collaboration in technological fields so that we won't lag behind others.
我們必須進一步加強技術領域的合作，才不致於落後於他人。

Level 1
Level 2
Level 3
Level 4
Level 5
Level 6

提升程度4200單字 自我勉勵、越背越上手──

tel·e·gram [ˈtɛləˌɡræm]   🔊 *Track 4179*

名 電報

▶In the old days, information was transmitted through telegram.
早期，資訊會用電報來傳遞。

tel·e·graph [ˈtɛləˌɡræf]   🔊 *Track 4180*

名 電報機 動 打電報

▶名 The news came by telegraph.
消息以電報傳來。

▶動 Would you telegraph us if you are interested in our products?
如果你對我們的產品感興趣的話，能否以電報回覆？

tel·e·scope [ˈtɛləˌskop]   🔊 *Track 4181*

名 望遠鏡

▶I wish we could find another planet like Earth with the Hubble Space Telescope（哈伯太空望遠鏡）.
我希望我們能透過哈伯太空望遠鏡找到另外一個跟地球類似的星球。

ten·den·cy [ˈtɛndənsɪ]   🔊 *Track 4182*

名 傾向、趨向

▶The kid showed a tendency to be overactive while interacting with others.
這個小孩和人互動時，出現過動的傾向。

tense [tɛns]   🔊 *Track 4183*

動 緊張 形 拉緊的

▶動 She tensed when she noticed that there was a stranger outside. 當她發現外頭有個陌生人的時候她就緊張起來了。

▶形 There was a tense silence in the waiting crowd.
在等候的人群中有一種緊張的寂靜感。

ten·sion [ˈtɛnʃən]   🔊 *Track 4184*

名 拉緊

▶Didn't you feel the air of tension at the meeting?
你沒感覺到會議上的氣氛有點緊張嗎？

ter·ri·fy [ˈtɛrəˌfaɪ]   🔊 *Track 4185*

動 使恐懼、使驚嚇

▶I was terrified by the news that the plane was about to crash.
我聽說飛機即將墜毀的消息時，非常驚恐。

ter·ror [ˈtɛrɚ]   🔊 *Track 4186*

名 駭懼、恐怖 同 fear 恐懼

▶He fled in terror when he saw the murder happen.
他看到謀殺案發生時，害怕地逃開了。

theme [θim]   🔊 *Track 4187*

名 主題、題目

▶Do you mind telling me what the theme of your paper is?
你介意告訴我你的論文主題是什麼嗎？

萬用延伸句型

tense up 突然緊張起來

例 如：As soon as she heard he was coming too, she tensed up.
她一聽到他也要來，就突然緊張起來。

thor·ough [ˋθɝo]

◀€ *Track 4188*

形 徹底的
▶We had thorough examination of the production to find out what caused the flaws in the products. 我們必須詳細檢查生產線，才會知道造成產品瑕疵的原因為何。

thought·ful [ˋθɔtfəl]

◀€ *Track 4189*

形 深思的、思考的
▶He has a thoughtful look on his face all the time. 他臉上總是帶著沉思的表情。

文法字詞解析
這個單字也可用來形容某人「十分貼心」、「考慮周到」。

tim·id [ˋtɪmɪd]

◀€ *Track 4190*

形 羞怯的
▶He is too timid to talk to strangers. 他太膽小了，不敢跟陌生人講話。

tire·some [ˋtaɪrsəm]

◀€ *Track 4191*

形 無聊的、可厭的
▶Her nagging is so tiresome. 她一直念個不停，煩死了。

tol·er·a·ble [ˋtɑlərəbl]

◀€ *Track 4192*

形 可容忍的、可忍受的
▶The noise is loud, but tolerable. 那個雜音很吵，但還可忍受。

tol·er·ance [ˋtɑlərəns]

◀€ *Track 4193*

名 包容力
▶A wise man cannot only put forward his opinions but must also develop tolerance for others' opinions. 一個聰明的人不僅要能提出自己的意見，還要能包容他人的意見。

tol·er·ant [ˋtɑlərənt]

◀€ *Track 4194*

形 忍耐的
▶If you are tolerant of others, they will be tolerant in turn. 你對別人容忍，別人也會對你容忍。

tol·er·ate [ˋtɑləˏret]

◀€ *Track 4195*

動 寬容、容忍
▶Not many people would tolerate lateness. 沒有多少人能夠容忍別人遲到。

tomb [tum]

◀€ *Track 4196*

名 墳墓、塚 同 grave 墳墓
▶The old man placed a bouquet in front of the tomb. 老人在墓碑前面放了花束。

tough [tʌf]

◀€ *Track 4197*

形 困難的
▶The questions on the test were really tough. 考試題目超難的。

萬用延伸句型
tough it out 硬撐過去
例如：It's getting cold, but our heater is broken. Guess we have to tough it out. 天氣越來越冷，但我們的暖氣壞了。看來只能硬撐過去了。

Level 1
Level 2
Level 3
Level 4 提升程度4200單字 自我勉勵、越背越上手
Level 5
Level 6

trag·e·dy [ˈtrædʒədɪ] 🔊 *Track 4198*

名 悲劇
▶I prefer comedy to tragedy. What about you, Bob?
我喜歡喜劇甚於悲劇。鮑勃，你呢？

trag·ic [ˈtrædʒɪk] 🔊 *Track 4199*

形 悲劇的
▶The tragic accident of the plane crash killed more than 500 passengers onboard.
這場悲慘的墜機意外造成機上超過五百名乘客喪生。

trans·fer [trænsˈfɜ] 🔊 *Track 4200*

名 遷移、調職 動 轉移
▶名 I don't think I can get there without a transfer.
我不認為我到那裡不用轉車。
▶動 I don't believe he will transfer all his property to his daughter.
我不相信他會把他所有的財產都轉移給他的女兒。

trans·form [trænsˈfɔrm] 🔊 *Track 4201*

動 改變
▶How about transforming the garage into a guest house?
把車庫改成客房怎麼樣？

trans·late [trænsˈlet] 🔊 *Track 4202*

動 翻譯
▶Can you translate the article from English into Japanese?
你能把這篇文章由英文翻譯成日文嗎？

trans·la·tion [trænsˈleʃən] 🔊 *Track 4203*

名 譯文
▶I haven't read the translation of the article yet.
我還沒讀過那篇文章的翻譯。

trans·la·tor [trænsˈletɚ] 🔊 *Track 4204*

名 翻譯者、翻譯家
▶The translator was blamed for causing misunderstanding between the two national leaders.
這名譯者被責怪，說他造成兩國元首之間的誤會。

文法字詞解析
translator 指的是筆譯的譯者，如果要說「口譯員」的話則是 interpreter。

trans·por·ta·tion [ˌtrænspɚˈteʃən] 🔊 *Track 4205*

名 輸送、運輸工具
▶Will you tell me how much the transportation of these goods by train costs? 如果用火車裝運這批貨物的話要花多少錢呢？

tre·men·dous [trɪˈmɛndəs] 🔊 *Track 4206*

形 非常、巨大的 同 enormous 巨大的
▶The public speaker has tremendous amount of energy, so his speech touched many people. 這位公眾演說者展現極大的能量，所以他的演講能感動很多人。

trib·al [ˈtraɪbl̩]
◀ Track 4207

形 宗族的、部落的

▶Does anyone know this rare tribal language?
這裡有人懂這種罕見的部落語言嗎？

tri·umph [ˈtraɪəmf]
◀ Track 4208

名 勝利 動 獲得勝利

▶名 The excitement of triumph made him become conceited.
勝利的喜悅讓他變得自負。

▶動 Justice will triumph over evil, at least that's what people say.
正義必將戰勝不義，至少大家都是這樣說的。

trou·ble·some [ˈtrʌbl̩səm]
◀ Track 4209

形 麻煩的、困難的

▶It is a troublesome problem. Let's discuss it together.
這是一個棘手的問題。我們一起討論一下吧。

文法字詞解析
字根「-some」的意思是「有……性質的」，前面常常接名詞。

tug-of-war [tʌg əv wɔr]
◀ Track 4210

名 拔河

▶It doesn't matter which team will win the tug-of-war.
哪個隊贏得拔河比賽都不重要。

twin·kle [ˈtwɪŋkl̩]
◀ Track 4211

名 閃爍 動 閃爍、發光

▶名 The fog has vanished, and we can see the distant twinkle of the harbor light.
霧散了，我們能看見港灣的燈光在遠處閃爍。

▶動 There are few stars twinkling tonight.
今晚閃爍的星星寥寥無幾。

typ·ist [ˈtaɪpɪst]
◀ Track 4212

名 打字員

▶The typist could complete the tasks assigned to her accurately and efficiently.
打字員能夠準確且有效率地完成她的交辦任務。

[Uu]

un·der·pass [ˈʌndɚˌpæs]
◀ Track 4213

名 地下道

▶It's safer for us to take the underpass. Don't you think so?
我們走地下通道吧，這樣比較安全。你不這樣認為嗎？

文法字詞解析
相對於 underpass，從地上架空過去的「天橋」或「高架道路」則可以稱為 overpass。

u·nique [juˈnik]
◀ Track 4214

形 唯一的、獨特的

▶Her ideas are always strange and unique.
她的點子總是又奇怪又獨特。

u·ni·ver·sal [ˌjunəˈvɝsl̩]
🔊 *Track 4215*

形 普遍的、世界性的、宇宙的
▶ Smile is considered a universal language.
微笑被認為是全球共通的語言。

u·ni·ver·si·ty [ˌjunəˈvɝsətɪ]
🔊 *Track 4216*

名 大學
▶ How long will it take for us to get to that university by bus?
我們搭公車到那所大學要花多長時間？

up·load [ˌʌpˈlod]
🔊 *Track 4217*

動 上傳（檔案）
▶ What do you think about uploading these pictures onto the Internet? 你覺得把這些照片上傳到網路上怎麼樣？

文法字詞解析
相反地，要「下載」東西則是稱為 download。

ur·ban [ˈɝbən]
🔊 *Track 4218*

形 都市的
▶ People in the urban area are always in a rush.
都市裡的人們總是在趕時間。

urge [ɝdʒ]
🔊 *Track 4219*

動 驅策、勸告
▶ He strongly urged us to leave.
他強烈勸告我們趕快離開。

ur·gent [ˈɝdʒənt]
🔊 *Track 4220*

形 急迫的、緊急的
▶ I'm afraid something urgent has come up. Perhaps I won't be able to see you tonight. 我有些急事，恐怕今晚不能見你了。

us·age [ˈjusɪdʒ]
🔊 *Track 4221*

名 習慣、習俗、使用
▶ The conventional usage of each content word is introduced in the reference book. 每個重要單字的常見用法都有在這本參考書中被介紹。

[Vv]

vain [ven]
🔊 *Track 4222*

形 無意義的、徒然的
▶ All his efforts were in vain.
他所有的努力都是徒然。

文法字詞解析
描述某人有如孔雀一般非常重視自己的華美外表，也可使用 vain 這個字。

vast [væst]
🔊 *Track 4223*

形 巨大的、廣大的 同 enormous 巨大的
▶ There is a vast expanse（廣闊的區域）of desert in this poor country. 在這個貧窮的國家裡有著大片的沙漠。

veg·e·tar·ian [ˌvɛdʒəˋtɛrɪən] 🔊 Track 4224

名 素食主義者
▶The vegetarian enjoys sharing her recipe on her blog.
這位素食者在網誌上介紹食譜。

verb [vɝb] 🔊 Track 4225

名 動詞
▶Will you tell me how to use the verb in this sentence?
你能告訴我如何在句中運用這個動詞嗎？

ver·y [ˋvɛrɪ] 🔊 Track 4226

副 很、完全地
▶Don't you think they are very eager to go there with us?
難道你不覺得他們很想跟我們一起去那裡嗎？

ves·sel [ˋvɛsl] 🔊 Track 4227

名 容器、碗
▶What about putting some water into the vessel to see what will happen next?
要不要往容器裡倒入一些水，看看下一步會發生什麼樣的事情？

文法字詞解析
vessel 這個單字也常拿來表示「船」的意思，畢竟船也能容得下很多東西。

vin·eg·ar [ˋvɪnɪgɚ] 🔊 Track 4228

名 醋
▶The soup tasted strange because I added too much vinegar.
這湯喝起來怪怪的，因為我加太多醋了。

vi·o·late [ˋvaɪəˌlet] 🔊 Track 4229

動 妨害、違反
▶Didn't he violate the traffic regulations?
他不是違反交通規則了嗎？

vi·o·la·tion [ˌvaɪəˋleʃən] 🔊 Track 4230

名 違反、侵害
▶Violation of the traffic rules means heavy fines in this country.
在這個國家，觸犯交通法規可能會被罰很多錢。

vir·gin [ˋvɝdʒɪn] 🔊 Track 4231

名 處女 形 純淨的
▶名 There are some stories about the Virgin Mary. Have you heard them?
有一些關於聖母瑪利亞的故事。你有聽過嗎？
▶形 There are large stretches（連綿）of virgin forests in the northern part of the country.
在這個國家北部有大片的原始森林。

萬用延伸句型
virgin ears 尚未受到玷污的耳朵。用於心靈純潔的兒童或天真單純的人。
例 如：Don't talk about your sex life in front of my son! It's not something meant for virgin ears.
不要在我兒子前面談論你的性生活，玷污了他純潔的耳朵。

vir·tue [ˋvɝtʃu] 🔊 Track 4232

名 貞操、美德
▶It is a virtue to respect others' privacy.
尊重他人隱私是種美德。

Level 1
Level 2
Level 3
Level 4
自我勉勵、越背越上手──提升程度4200單字
Level 5
Level 6

vir·us [ˈvaɪrəs]
🔊 Track 4233

名 病毒

▶I wish we human beings could find ways to destroy all the viruses soon.
我希望我們人類能很快找到方法消滅所有的病毒。

vis·u·al [ˈvɪʒuəl]
🔊 Track 4234

形 視覺的

▶The presenter used a poster as his visual aid.
演講者用海報當作視覺的輔助品

vi·tal [ˈvaɪtl̩]
🔊 Track 4235

形 生命的、不可或缺的

▶We consider this discovery of vital importance.
我們認為這個發現非常重要。

文法字詞解析
「生命徵象」即可稱為 vital signs。

vol·ca·no [vɑlˈkeno]
🔊 Track 4236

名 火山

▶The volcano has become a popular tourist spot.
這座火山已成為一個受歡迎的觀光景點了。

vol·un·tar·y [ˈvɑlənˌtɛrɪ]
🔊 Track 4237

形 自願的、自發的

▶His decision to leave was voluntary.
他離開的決定是自願的。

vol·un·teer [ˌvɑlənˈtɪr]
🔊 Track 4238

名 自願者、義工 動 自願做……

▶名 How long have you been working in this community as a volunteer?
你在這個社區當義工多久了？

▶動 She volunteered to teach in the school, but I don't know how long she will stay there.
她自願到那個學校教書，但我不知道她會在那待多久。

vow·el [ˈvaʊəl]
🔊 Track 4239

名 母音 反 consonant 子音

▶Will you tell me the differences between vowels and consonants（子音）in English?
你能告訴我英語中母音和子音之間的區別嗎？

voy·age [ˈvɔɪɪdʒ]
🔊 Track 4240

名 旅行、航海 動 航行

▶名 During his voyage, the sailor oriented himself by observing the stars.
航行期間，水手透過觀察星象來判斷航行的方向。

▶動 It took the captain and his sailors five years to finish voyaging the world. 船長和他的船員們花了五年的時間才完成了航行世界的任務。

文法字詞解析
祝福別人旅途愉快時總會說上一句「bon voyage!」，但這句並不是英文喔！它是從法文來的。

[Ww]

wal·nut [ˈwɔlnət]
◀⟨ Track 4241
名 胡桃樹
▶How about we use walnuts to make a cake?
我們用胡桃來做蛋糕怎麼樣？

web·site [ˈwɛbˌsaɪt]
◀⟨ Track 4242
名 網站
▶The official website of the hospital was hacked yesterday.
這家醫院的官方網站昨天被駭客入侵。

week·ly [ˈwiklɪ]
◀⟨ Track 4243
名 週刊 形 每週的 副 每週地
▶名 I wish I could publish an article in this weekly one day.
要是有一天我能在這本週刊上發表文章就好了。
▶形 Her boyfriend writes weekly love letters to her.
她的男朋友每個星期都寫一封情書給她。
▶副 My parents and I go to the park weekly.
每個星期爸爸媽媽跟我都一起去公園。

wel·fare [ˈwɛlˌfɛr]
◀⟨ Track 4244
名 健康、幸福、福利 同 benefit 利益
▶Social welfare is the main concern of the local people.
社會福利是當地人最關心的議題。

wit [wɪt]
◀⟨ Track 4245
名 機智、賢人
▶Her articles are full of wit.
她的文章充滿了機智。

witch/wiz·ard [wɪtʃ]/[ˈwɪzəd]
◀⟨ Track 4246
名 女巫師 / 男巫師
▶The wedding was in full swing when the witch came in.
當女巫進來時婚禮正進行得熱鬧。

with·draw [wɪðˈdrɔ]
◀⟨ Track 4247
動 收回、撤出
▶The motion was withdrawn in the end.
那項動議最終被撤銷了。

wit·ness [ˈwɪtnɪs]
◀⟨ Track 4248
名 目擊者 動 目擊
▶名 I'm afraid that the witness needs to be investigated.
恐怕那名證人還需要調查一下。
▶動 Several people witnessed the car crash.
許多人目擊了車禍。

文法字詞解析
website 也可以簡稱 site。此外，還有一個相關的單字 webpage，指的是「網頁」的意思。

文法字詞解析
withdraw 的動詞變化：
withdraw, withdrew, withdrawn

Level 1
Level 2
Level 3
Level 4
Level 5
Level 6

自我勉勵、越背越上手——提升程度4200單字

wreck [rɛk]

Track 4249

名 （船隻）失事、殘骸 動 遇險、摧毀、毀壞

▶名 The wrecks of Titanic were found decades after it sank.
鐵達尼號的殘骸，在它沉沒幾十年後被發現。

▶動 They were looking for the person who set the fire and wrecked the hotel.
他們在調查到底是誰放火把飯店燒毀了。

文法字詞解析
描述人整個崩潰、有如船隻的殘骸般殘破，也可稱他為 wreck。

wrin·kle [ˈrɪŋkl̩]

Track 4250

名 皺紋 動 皺起

▶名 It is obvious that she is beginning to get wrinkles round her eyes.
顯然她的眼角開始有皺紋了。

▶動 The quality of this shirt is very good; it will not wrinkle.
這件襯衫的品質非常好，不會皺。

[Yy]

year·ly [ˈjɪrlɪ]

Track 4251

形 每年的 副 每年、年年

▶形 The rainfall this year exceeded the yearly average.
今年的雨量超過了年平均降雨量。

▶副 She can only go home yearly.
她每年只能回家一次。

yo·gurt [ˈjogɚt]

Track 4252

名 優酪乳

▶Would you like to have some low fat yogurt? It tastes very good.
你想不想喝點低脂的優酪乳？它味道很好哦。

文法字詞解析
yogurt 也可以拼成 yoghurt，唸起來一樣。

youth·ful [ˈjuθfəl]

Track 4253

形 年輕的

▶Being positive and eat healthy would be the key to remain youthful.
保持樂觀心態，並且吃得健康，是保持年輕的秘訣。

NOTE

Level
1

Level
2

Level
3

Level
4

Level
5

Level
6

自我勉勵、越背越上手──
提升程度4200單字

Level 4 程度檢測閱讀練習

下面有四篇文章，全是根據 Level1-4 的單字寫出來的，文章中超出 level4 的單字，有註記在一旁。

請先不要看全文的中文翻譯，試著讀讀看這四篇文章，若能全盤了解意思，代表你對 Level4 單字已經駕輕就熟，可以升級到 Level5 囉！快來自我挑戰看看吧！

Reading Practice 1

New York is often called the City of New York to distinguish it from the State of New York. It has also been called by many nicknames, such as the "City that Never Sleeps" and the "Center of the Universe."

A global power city, New York exerts (發　揮) a significant impact upon commerce, finance, media, art, fashion, research, technology, education, and entertainment. It is also an important center for international diplomacy as well as the cultural and financial capital of the world.

The famous Statue of Liberty is one of the most visited spots in New York. It is a sculpture on Liberty Island which greeted millions of immigrants as they came to America by ship in the late 19th and early 20th centuries. It is a globally recognized symbol of the United States and its democracy.

Reading Practice 2

Cloud computing(運算) means storing and accessing data and programs over the Internet instead of your computer's hard drive. It involves computing over a network, where a program or application may run on many connected computers at the same time. It typically uses connected hardware machines called servers(伺服器). Individual users can use the server's processing power to run an application, store date, or perform any other computing task.

Cloud computing could change the entire computer industry. However, there are still some concerns about the security of the data stored on the remote machines. The cloud service provider needs to establish clear and relevant policies that described how they encrypt (加密) data that is processed or stored within the cloud to prevent unauthorized (未經授權的) access.

Reading Practice 3

Apple Inc. is an American multinational corporation (企業) that designs and sells consumer electronics, computer software, and personal computers. The company was named Apple Computer, Inc. at first. The word "Computer" was removed from its name in 2007, as its traditional focus on personal computers shifted towards computer electronics.

The company's best-known hardware products are the Macintosh line of computers, the iPod, the iPhone X, and iOS operating system. Also, Apple is the third-largest mobile phone maker after Samsung and Nokia.

Fortune magazine named Apple the most admired company in the United States and in the world from 2008 to 2012. However, the company has received much criticism for the treatment of its contractor's (承包商) labor, and for its environmental and business practices.

Reading Practice 4

Scratchy throats, stuffy noses and body aches all spell misery, but being able to tell if the cause is a cold or flu may make a difference in how long the pain lasts. That's because the prescription (處方箋) drugs available for the flu need to be taken soon after the illness sets in although the symptoms (症狀) can be eased with over the counter medications (藥物). As for colds, the sooner a person stars taking over-the-counter remedy, the sooner relief will come. Cold symptoms such as stuffy nose, runny nose and scratchy throat typically develop gradually, and adults and teens often do not get a fever. On the other hand, fever is one of the characteristic features of the flu for all ages. Also, in general, flu symptoms including fever and chills, sore throat, and body aches come on suddenly and are severer than cold symptoms.

Level 1

Level 2

Level 3

Level 4

自我勉勵、越背越上手──提升程度4200單字

Level 5

Level 6

Reading Practice1 中譯

紐約常被稱為是紐約市，以和紐約州作區別。它有一些別名，像是「不夜城」、以及「世界的中心」。

作為全球知名的大城，紐約在商業、媒體、藝術、流行、研究、科技、教育、以及娛樂方面，都發揮很大的影響力。它也是重要的國際外交中心，以及全球文化與財務的中心都市。

自由女神像是紐約市最多人參觀的景點之一。它是在自由島上的雕像，在 19 世紀末、20 世紀初時，它迎接了數百萬名前來美國的移民。它也是全世界公認，代表美國民主精神的象徵。

Reading Practice2 中譯

雲端運算指的是透過網路、而不是在你自己的硬碟裡，儲存或者取用資料。它牽涉到透過網路運算，一個程式可以同時在許多互相連接的電腦上運作。通常這種硬碟機器被稱為是伺服器。個別用戶可以用伺服器的運算能力來運作一個應用程式、儲存資料，或者進行其他的運算工作。

雲端運算可能會改變整個電腦產業。然而，人們對於將資料儲存在遠端電腦中，還是有些安全上的疑慮。雲端運算服務提供者，需要建立清楚易懂的條款，說明他們會如何將在儲存在雲端、或者在雲端上處理的數據資料加密，以防止未經授權者來取用這些資料。

Reading Practice3 中譯

蘋果公司是位於美國的跨國企業，它設計與銷售電子用品、電腦軟體，以及個人電腦。這家公司最早叫做「蘋果電腦有限公司」。到了 2007 年，「電腦」這個字被拿掉，因為公司已不再只守住個人電腦的傳統，轉向製造電腦和電子產品。

這家公司最有名的硬體產品是麥金塔系列的電腦、iPod、iPhoneX、以及 iOS 作業系統。此外，蘋果公司是繼三星和 Nokia 之後，第三大手機製造商。

《財富》雜誌在 2008 年到 2012 年間，將蘋果公司譽為全美以及全球最值得讚賞的企業。然而，這家公司也因為承包商勞工待遇、環境議題、商業手段等而受過批評。

　　喉嚨發癢、鼻塞、全身痠痛，都讓人很難受，但是能不能判斷這是感冒引起、還是流感引起的，會讓對治療有大的影響。這就是為什麼得到流感的時候，儘管症狀可以用藥房買到的成藥緩解，還是得要在症狀出現後，盡快服用處方籤藥物才能治好。至於一般感冒，越早開始服用成藥，症狀就會越早舒緩。感冒的症狀，像是鼻塞、流鼻水、或者喉嚨癢，基本上都是慢慢變嚴重的，而且成人和青少年得到感冒時，不會發燒。然而，不管幾歲的人得到流感，幾乎都會發燒。此外，一般來說，流感症狀，包括發燒、發冷、喉嚨痛、以及全身痠痛，都會比感冒更嚴重。

Level
1

Level
2

Level
3

Level
4

自我勉勵、越背越上手──
提升程度4200單字

Level
5

Level
6

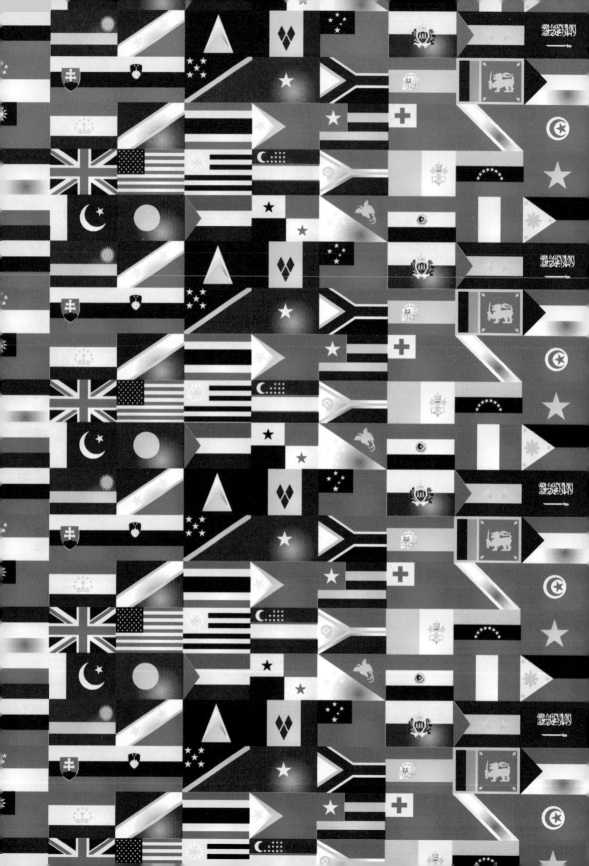

Level 5

突飛猛進、程度大進擊——
擴增實力5400單字

Level 5
突飛猛進、程度大進擊——
擴增實力5400單字

[Aa]

a·bide [ə`baɪd]
◀≋ *Track 4254*

動 容忍、忍耐 同 tolerate 容忍
▶We had to abide by the unreasonable school regulations on the outfit. 我們必須遵守學校對於服裝的不合理規定。

文法字詞解析
abide 的動詞變化:abide, abode, abode 或是 abide, abided, abided

a·bol·ish [ə`bɑlɪʃ]
◀≋ *Track 4255*

動 廢止、革除 反 establish 建立
▶People would continue to fight to abolish slavery（奴隸制度）. 人們會繼續為廢除奴隸制度而奮鬥。

a·bor·tion [ə`bɔrʃən]
◀≋ *Track 4256*

名 流產、墮胎
▶The reason why abortion is illegal（違法的）in some countries is that it is not allowed by their religions. 墮胎在一些國家屬於違法行為,原因是它不被他們的宗教信仰所允許。

a·brupt [ə`brʌpt]
◀≋ *Track 4257*

形 突然的 同 sudden 突然的
▶The abrupt thunderstorms caused water surge in the town. 突然發生的雷雨造成小鎮淹水。

文法字詞解析
abrupt change = 劇變

ab·surd [əb`sɝd]
◀≋ *Track 4258*

形 不合理的、荒謬的
▶What an absurd suggestion! 多麼荒唐的建議!

a·bun·dant [ə`bʌndənt]
◀≋ *Track 4259*

形 豐富的 反 scarce 稀少的
▶It is said that the area is abundant with mineral resources. 據說這個地區礦藏資源豐富。

a·cad·e·my [ə`kædəmɪ]
◀≋ *Track 4260*

名 學院、專科院校
▶This academy of music is so famous that many students are eager to enter it. 這所音樂學院非常有名,所以有很多學生都想進去就讀。

ac·cus·tom [ə`kʌstəm]
◀≋ *Track 4261*

動 使習慣於
▶The volunteer worker got accustomed to taking care of the elderly people. 志工漸漸習慣照顧老人。

ace [es]
◄€ Track 4262

名 傑出人才 形 一流的、熟練的

▶名 The coach did not send the ace on our team on the first round. 教練在第一回合沒有派出我們隊的王牌球員。

▶形 He is the ace mechanic here.
他是這裡第一流的機械師。

文法字詞解析
撲克牌中的「A」英文中就稱為 ace。

ac·knowl·edge [ək`nɑlɪdʒ]
◄€ Track 4263

動 承認、供認 反 deny 否認

▶People used to not acknowledge that the earth is round.
以前的人們不承認地球是圓的事實。

ac·knowl·edge·ment
[ək`nɑlɪdʒmənt]
◄€ Track 4264

名 承認、坦白、自白 反 denial 否認

▶Why don't you send him a small sum of money in acknowledgement of his help?
為何不寄一小筆錢給他以感謝他的幫助呢？

ac·ne [`æknɪ]
◄€ Track 4265

名 粉刺、面皰

▶It's impolite to pop the acne in public.
在公共場所擠痘痘很不禮貌。

ad·mi·ral [`ædmərəl]
◄€ Track 4266

名 海軍上將

▶My son wants to be an admiral when he grows up. What about yours? 我兒子長大後想當海軍上將。你兒子呢？

ad·o·les·cence [æd`ɛsns]
◄€ Track 4267

名 青春期

▶Some people show rebellious characters in their adolescence.
有些人在青少年時期會表現出反叛特性。

ad·o·les·cent [æd`ɛsnt]
◄€ Track 4268

形 青春期的、青少年的 同 teenage 青少年的

▶The adolescent life will influence the young people a lot in their later life.
青春期的生活會對年輕人之後的生活產生很大的影響。

a·dore [ə`dor]
◄€ Track 4269

動 崇拜、敬愛、崇敬

▶I adore my boss very much and so do other people who know him. 我很喜愛我的老闆，認識他的人也都很喜愛他。

文法字詞解析
現在這個字較少用於「尊敬」這方面，而較多用於表示「疼愛」、「喜愛」。例如看到可愛的小孩或小動物，就可以說自己 adore 他們。

adult·hood [ə`dʌlt͵hʊd]
◄€ Track 4270

名 成年期

▶Youngsters in Israel received military training before they reach adulthood.
以色列的青少年在成年以前就會接受軍事訓練。

Level 1
Level 2
Level 3
Level 4
Level 5
Level 6

擴增實力5400單字

突飛猛進、程度大進擊——

ad·ver·tis·er [ˈædvɚˌtaɪzɚ] 🔊 *Track 4271*

名 廣告客戶
▶The job of advertisers is to capture our attention.
　廣告商的工作就是要吸引我們的注意。

af·fec·tion [əˈfɛkʃən] 🔊 *Track 4272*

名 親情、情愛、愛慕 反 hate 仇恨
▶The mother showed great affection to her new-born baby.
　這名母親非常關愛地看著剛出生的寶寶。

a·gen·da [əˈdʒɛndə] 🔊 *Track 4273*

名 議程、節目單
▶Let's work out the agendas for the next two meetings.
　我們把下兩次會議的議程制定出來吧。

ag·o·ny [ˈægənɪ] 🔊 *Track 4274*

名 痛苦、折磨 同 torment 痛苦
▶The patient is writhing（翻滾）on the bed in agony.
　病人痛得在床上打滾。

萬用延伸句型
prolong the agony 延長痛苦的時間
例如：You should just finish your work
tonight instead of prolonging the agony.
你還是今天晚上就把工作做完吧，長痛
不如短痛。

ag·ri·cul·tur·al [ˌægrɪˈkʌltʃərəl] 🔊 *Track 4275*

名 農業的
▶Farmers in the underdeveloped country are developing effective agricultural technique.
　落後國家的農夫正在開發有效的農業技術。

AI/ar·ti·fi·cial in·tel·li·gence [ˌɑrtəˈfɪʃəl ɪnˈtɛlədʒəns] 🔊 *Track 4276*

名 人工智慧
▶I wish one day we could produce lots of AI robots to work for us.
　我希望有一天我們能製造出許多智慧型機器人來為我們工作。

air·tight [ˈɛrˌtaɪt] 🔊 *Track 4277*

形 密閉的、氣密的
▶Processed foods in airtight packages may be allowed in your check-in luggage.
　有真空包裝的加工食品可以放在托運行李中。

文法字詞解析
airtight container = 密封容器

air·way [ˈɛrˌwe] 🔊 *Track 4278*

名 空中航線
▶It is said that a royal airway will be built at this airport.
　據說這個機場將建造一條皇家專用的飛機跑道。

aisle [aɪl] 🔊 *Track 4279*

名 教堂的側廊、通道
▶The clerk of the grocery store told me that the flavoring agents are in the third aisle.
　超商店員告訴我調味料放在第三個走道。

al·ge·bra [ˈældʒəbrə] 🔊 *Track 4280*

名 代數

▶I was not good at algebra in middle school.
我中學時不怎麼擅長代數。

a·li·en [ˈeliən] 🔊 *Track 4281*

形 外國的、外星球的 名 外國人、外星人 同 foreign 外國人

▶形 It doesn't matter whether they are alien workers or not.
他們是不是外國工作人員都不要緊的。

▶名 Scientists believe that aliens somewhere in the universe may have advanced technology.
科學家相信宇宙中的外星人有更先進的科技。

al·ler·gic [əˈlɜdʒɪk] 🔊 *Track 4282*

形 過敏的、厭惡的

▶Will you tell me why some people are allergic to dust but some are not?
你能告訴我為何有些人會對粉塵過敏，而有些人卻不會嗎？

al·ler·gy [ˈælədʒɪ] 🔊 *Track 4283*

名 反感、食物過敏

▶The doctor diagnosed（診斷）him as having a pollen（花粉）allergy. 醫生診斷出他有花粉過敏症。

al·li·ga·tor [ˈæləˌgetə] 🔊 *Track 4284*

名 鱷魚

▶It is said that alligators usually（通常）live in the rivers and lakes in the hot wet parts.
據說鱷魚一般生活在濕熱地帶的河流和湖泊中。

al·ly [əˈlaɪ] 🔊 *Track 4285*

名 同盟者 動 使結盟 反 enemy 敵人

▶名 The country has many allies in terms of military, education, and economy.
該國有許多軍事、教育、以及經濟上的盟友。

▶動 The reason why the small country allied itself to the stronger power was that it could save itself from being destroyed.
小國和強國聯盟的原因是為了使自己免於滅亡。

al·ter [ˈɔltə] 🔊 *Track 4286*

動 更改、改變 同 vary 變更

▶I don't think there is any necessity to alter our plan at present.
我認為目前還沒有必要修改我們的計畫。

al·ter·nate [ˈɔltəˌnet]/[ˈɔltɜˌnɪt] 🔊 *Track 4287*

動 輪流、交替 形 交替的、間隔的

▶動 DYou have to inform your supervisor if you want to alternate you work shift. 你要變動值班時間，需要先跟主管報備。

▶形 There will be a week of alternate rain and sunshine（陽光）. 下禮拜將會有時雨天有時晴天。

萬用延伸句型
It is said that... 據說……

Level 1

Level 2

Level 3

Level 4

Level 5

Level 6

突飛猛進、程度大進擊——
擴增實力5400單字

al·ti·tude [ˈæltə͵tjud]　🔊 *Track 4288*

图 高度、海拔　回 height 高度

▶The altitude of the mountain was measured each year.
山的高度每年都會被測量。

am·ple [ˈæmpl̩]　🔊 *Track 4289*

形 充分的、廣闊的　回 enough 充足的

▶I wish I could find a room that provides ample sunlight（陽光）through windows.
我希望能找到一個有充足陽光透進窗戶來的房間。

an·chor [ˈæŋkɚ]　🔊 *Track 4290*

图 錨狀物　動 停泊、使穩固

▶图 I am afraid that we have to lie at anchor outside the harbor. There is no room for us in it.
恐怕我們得在港外拋錨停泊了。裡面沒有空位了。

▶動 We have to anchor the tent with pegs, or the wind will blow it away.
我們得用椿子來固定帳篷，要不然風會把它吹走的。

an·them [ˈænθəm]　🔊 *Track 4291*

图 讚美詩、聖歌

▶The football player knelt down to the national anthem at the beginning of the game.
足球員在比賽開始聽到國歌時便下跪。

an·tique [ænˈtik]　🔊 *Track 4292*

图 古玩、古董　形 古舊的、古董的　回 ancient 古代的

▶图 The King is fond of collecting curiosities. It is no wonder that the palace is full of priceless antiques.
國王熱愛收藏珍品。難怪宮殿裡到處都是無價的古玩。

▶形 This is an antique chair, so all those salespeople want to buy it.
這是一把古董椅，所以那些商人都想把它買下來。

文法字詞解析
curiosity 除了解釋成「好奇心」以外，在這個句子中的意思則是「珍玩、珍品」。

ap·plaud [əˈplɔd]　🔊 *Track 4293*

動 鼓掌、喝采、誇讚

▶It is a surprise that they all applauded him for his decision.
他們居然一致贊成他的決定，這真令人驚訝。

ap·plause [əˈplɔz]　🔊 *Track 4294*

图 喝采　回 praise 稱讚

▶The opera singer was met with a shower of applause.
觀眾位歌劇演唱者鼓掌。

apt [æpt]　🔊 *Track 4295*

形 貼切的、恰當的　回 suitable 適當的

▶A man apt to promise is apt to forget.
輕易承諾的人容易忘記承諾。

ar·chi·tect [ˈɑrkəˌtɛkt] 🔊 *Track 4296*
名 建築師
▶The architect visited the construction site with his blueprint.
建築師帶著藍圖到工地視察。

ar·chi·tec·ture [ˈɑrkəˌtɛktʃə] 🔊 *Track 4297*
名 建築、建築學、建築物 同 building 建築物
▶My sister studies architecture at the university. What about your sister?
我妹妹在大學裡學建築。你妹妹呢？

a·re·na [əˈrinə] 🔊 *Track 4298*
名 競技場 同 stadium 競技場
▶It is said that it is the remains of an arena from ancient Roman（古羅馬的）times.
據說這就是古羅馬時期的競技場遺跡。

ar·mor [ˈɑrmə] 🔊 *Track 4299*
名 盔甲 動 裝甲
▶名 The knight requested to know the real identity of the visitor under armor. 騎士要盔甲底下的訪客報上真實身分。
▶動 It was useful to armor the troops in ancient wars.
在古代戰爭中給軍隊裝備盔甲很有用。

文法字詞解析
armor 為美式拼法，英式拼法則為 armour。

as·cend [əˈsɛnd] 🔊 *Track 4300*
動 上升、登
▶We spent too much time ascending the mountain.
我們爬上山實在花太久了。

ass [æs] 🔊 *Track 4301*
名 驢子、笨蛋、傻瓜
▶The ass on our farm is always very quiet.
我們農場上的驢子總是很安靜。

as·sault [əˈsɔlt] 🔊 *Track 4302*
名 攻擊 動 攻擊 同 attack 攻擊
▶名 The soldiers made a strong assault on the town.
士兵們猛烈攻擊這座城。
▶動 It is impossible（不可能的）for us to assault the castle on all sides.
我們是不可能從四面八方向城堡發起突擊的。

文法字詞解析
除了戰爭方面的「攻擊」外，assault 也能指生活中可能遇到的侵犯、侵害事件。例如「性侵害」就可稱為 sexual assualt。

as·set [ˈæsɛt] 🔊 *Track 4303*
名 財產、資產 同 property 財產
▶Time is the most valuable asset of each individual.
時間是每個人最珍貴的資產。

as·ton·ish [əˈstɑnɪʃ] 🔊 *Track 4304*
動 使⋯⋯吃驚
▶He astonished us with wine he brewed（釀造）himself.
他拿出自己親手釀的酒，讓我們大吃一驚。

Level 1
Level 2
Level 3
Level 4
Level 5
Level 6

擴增實力5400單字 突飛猛進、程度大進擊

519

as·ton·ish·ment [əˋstɑnıʃmənt] ◀€ *Track 4305*

名 吃驚
▶To my astonishment, a stranger came up to me and claimed to be my brother.
令我驚訝的是，有個陌生人走向我，聲稱是我的哥哥。

a·stray [əˋstre] ◀€ *Track 4306*

副 迷途地、墮落地 形 迷途的、墮落的
▶副 If it weren't for the guide, they would have gone astray.
如果不是那個領隊的話，他們就迷路了。
▶形 The letter is astray; we didn't get it in the mail.
那封信遺失了，我們沒有收到。

as·tro·naut [ˋæstrənɔt] ◀€ *Track 4307*

名 太空人
▶Inspired by Neil Armstrong, the kid aspired to become an astronaut.
受到阿姆斯壯的啓發，這個小孩立志要成為太空人。

as·tron·o·my [əsˋtrɑnəmı] ◀€ *Track 4308*

名 天文學
▶Will you tell me the differences between astrology（占星術）and astronomy?
你能告訴我占星術和天文學之間的區別嗎？

at·ten·dance [əˋtɛndəns] ◀€ *Track 4309*

名 出席、參加 反 absence 缺席
▶The teacher takes attendance before classes.
這位老師在上課前都會記錄出席人數。

au·di·to·ri·um [ˏɔdəˋtorıəm] ◀€ *Track 4310*

名 禮堂、演講廳 同 hall 會堂
▶There are so many students in the auditorium that I can't find my friends. 禮堂裡人山人海，以致於我找不到我的朋友們。

aux·il·ia·ry [ɔgˋzıljərı] ◀€ *Track 4311*

形 輔助的
▶The auxiliary wheels were taken off after I learned how to ride a bike. 我學會騎腳踏車之後，輔助輪就被移除了。

awe [ɔ] ◀€ *Track 4312*

名 敬畏 動 使敬畏 同 respect 尊敬
▶名 His paintings filled people with awe and joy.
他的畫使人們心中充滿喜樂與敬畏。
▶動 She was awed by his amazing piano skills.
他驚人的鋼琴技巧讓她完全著迷了。

a·while [əˋhwaıl] ◀€ *Track 4313*

副 暫時、片刻 反 forever 永遠
▶Please stay awhile and have a rest.
請待在這裡休息一下吧。

萬用延伸句型
Up to now... 直到現在……

萬用延伸句型
in awe of sb. 非常敬畏（某人）
例如：Even though they live in the same house, he's in awe of his roommate.
雖然他們明明就住在同一間房子裡，他還是對自己的室友非常敬畏。

[Bb]

bach·e·lor [ˈbætʃələ] ◀€ Track 4314
名 單身漢、學士 同 single 單身男女
▶Kevin got his bachelor's degree in his thirties.
凱文在三十幾歲時拿到學士學位。

back·bone [ˈbækˌbon] ◀€ Track 4315
名 脊骨、脊柱 同 spine 脊柱
▶It is obvious that he is an Englishman to the backbone.
顯然他是一個道道地地的英國人。

badge [bædʒ] ◀€ Track 4316
名 徽章
▶The boy always forgets to wear the school badge.
這男孩總是忘記佩戴校徽。

bal·lot [ˈbælət] ◀€ Track 4317
名 選票 動 投票 同 vote 投票
▶名 Many people watched the live broadcast of ballot counting for the election.
許多人觀看選舉開票的實況轉播。
▶動 They balloted for a new chairman.
他們投票選出了新主席。

ban [bæn] ◀€ Track 4318
動 禁止 名 禁令、查禁
▶動 Swimming in this lake is banned.
規定禁止人們在這個湖裡游泳。
▶名 There is a ban on smoking in the theatre.
這個劇院裡禁止吸煙。

ban·dit [ˈbændɪt] ◀€ Track 4319
名 強盜、劫匪 同 robber 強盜
▶Most people hate bandits very much.
大部分人們都非常痛恨強盜。

ban·ner [ˈbænə] ◀€ Track 4320
名 旗幟、橫幅 同 flag 旗幟
▶I'm afraid that banner ads and photographs attract more attention than artwork.
恐怕旗幟廣告和照片比藝術品更能吸引注意力。

ban·quet [ˈbæŋkwɪt] ◀€ Track 4321
名 宴會 動 宴客 同 feast 宴會
▶名 We exchanged name cards during the banquet.
我們在晚宴時交換名片。
▶動 They banqueted all day and night.
他們沒日沒夜地在開宴會。

文法字詞解析

bandit 和同義詞 robber 都有強盜、搶匪的意思，那麼它們之間有沒有差別呢？硬要說的話，bandit 比較可能是集團犯案，也就是屬於一個強盜集團；而 robber 則不一定，就算只有一個人也可以當 robber。無論你的本業是什麼，如果一時興起想去搶劫，就可以稱為 robber，而 bandit 既然是集團的一部分就比較有系統一點，不是隨隨便便一個人就可以變成 bandit 的。

Level 1
Level 2
Level 3
Level 4
Level 5

擴增實力5400單字——突飛猛進、程度大進擊

Level 6

bar·bar·i·an [bɑrˋbɛrɪən] 🔊 *Track 4322*

名 野蠻人　形 野蠻的

▶ 名 The barbarians on the remote island are completely isolated from the outside world.
偏遠島嶼上的野蠻人完全與外界隔絕。

▶ 形 It's said that there is a barbarian tribe living in this forest.
據說有一個原始部落居住在這個林區。

bar·ber·shop [ˋbɑrbɚˌʃɑp] 🔊 *Track 4323*

名 理髮店

▶ The barbershop is an immense success.
那間理髮店的生意興隆。

bare·foot [ˋbɛrˌfʊt] 🔊 *Track 4324*

形 赤足的　副 赤足地

▶ 形 The barefoot boy began to cry because he stepped on glass.
那個赤腳的男孩因為踩到了玻璃而大哭。

▶ 副 You'd better not walk barefoot on the damp hard sand.
你最好不要赤著腳在既潮濕又硬梆梆的沙灘上行走。

bar·ren [ˋbærən] 🔊 *Track 4325*

形 不毛的、土地貧瘠的　反 fertile 肥沃的

▶ It is hard for us to plant any crop on this barren land.
我們要在貧瘠的土地上種植作物很難。

bass [bes] 🔊 *Track 4326*

名 低音樂器、男低音歌手　形 低音的

▶ 名 It is obvious that the opera star is a fine bass.
這位歌劇明星顯然是位優秀的男低音歌手。

▶ 形 The bass soloist（獨唱者）had an excellent voice.
這位男低音獨唱者的聲音非常棒。

文法字詞解析
bass 還有一個意思，是鱸魚的一種。

batch [bætʃ] 🔊 *Track 4327*

名 一批、一群、一組　同 cluster 群、組

▶ My grandma baked a batch of cookies.
我奶奶烤了一堆餅乾。

bat·ter [ˋbætɚ] 🔊 *Track 4328*

動 連擊、重擊　同 beat 打擊

▶ It is the second time that I heard someone battering at the door.
這是我第二次聽到有人在使勁敲門。

文法字詞解析
在 batter 後面加上字尾「-ed」即能變成形容詞 battered，意思是「受到打擊的、被打得狼狽不堪的」。

ba·zaar [bəˋzɑr] 🔊 *Track 4329*

名 市場、義賣會

▶ I bought a scarf with plaid pattern in the bazaar.
我在市集買了格子花紋的圍巾。

beau·ti·fy [ˋbjutəˌfaɪ] 🔊 *Track 4330*

動 美化

▶ We should spare no effort to beautify our environment.
我們應該不遺餘力地美化我們的環境。

before·hand [bɪ'for,hænd] 🔊 *Track 4331*
副 事前、預先 **反** afterward 之後、後來
▶I'm afraid that we should arrive at the meeting place beforehand.
我們恐怕應該提前到達碰面的地點。

---

be·half [bɪ'hæf] 🔊 *Track 4332*
名 代表
▶Peter negotiate with the employer on behalf of his colleagues.
彼得代表同事們跟雇主協商。

---

be·long·ings [bə'lɔŋɪnz] 🔊 *Track 4333*
名 所有物、財產 **同** possession 財產
▶We came home to find our belongings scattered about the room.
我們回到家裡，看到東西被扔得滿屋都是。

---

be·lov·ed [bɪ'lʌvd] 🔊 *Track 4334*
形 鍾愛的、心愛的 **同** darling 親愛的
▶He bought his beloved daughter a pony.
他買了一匹小馬給他心愛的女兒。

---

ben·e·fi·cial [,bɛnə'fɪʃəl] 🔊 *Track 4335*
形 有益的、有利的 **反** harmful 有害的
▶It's beneficial for us to exercise in the morning every day.
每天早晨做運動對我們是有益的。

---

be·ware [bɪ'wɛr] 🔊 *Track 4336*
動 當心、小心提防
▶Beware of the online frauds.
小心網路詐騙。

---

bid [bɪd] 🔊 *Track 4337*
名 投標價 **動** 投標、出價
▶**名** That small obscure（無名的）firm won the bid finally.
那個不起眼的小公司最終得了標。
▶**動** He bid $30000 on the oil painting.
他出價三萬美元來買下那幅油畫。

---

black·smith [`blæk,smɪθ] 🔊 *Track 4338*
名 鐵匠、鍛工
▶A blacksmith's job is not an easy one. What do you think?
鐵匠的工作很不容易。你覺得呢？

---

blast [blæst] 🔊 *Track 4339*
名 強風、風力 **動** 損害 **反** breeze 微風
▶**名** The blast of the gun frightened the pedestrians.
槍的爆破聲響嚇到路過行人。
▶**動** If he doesn't open the door, we'll have to blast it open.
他還是不開門的話，我們只好把門炸開了。

文法字詞解析
不是所有的事情都可以用「beware」這個字來提醒人家小心。beware 通常是用來警告人家要小心「還沒發生但有可能會發生」的事，例如若某處可能會有蛇出沒，就可以提醒人「beware of snakes」；若朋友已經快被蛇咬到了，要叫他小心，用「beware」就嫌太遲了。

文法字詞解析
bid 的動詞變化：bid, bidded , bidded 或是 bide, bade, bidden

Level 1
Level 2
Level 3
Level 4
Level 5
Level 6

突飛猛進、程度大進擊——擴增實力5400單字

blaze [blez]
Track 4340
動 火焰、爆發
▶Lights were blazing in every room yesterday.
昨天每個房間都燈火通明。

bleach [blitʃ]
Track 4341
名 漂白劑 動 漂白、脫色 反 dye 染色
▶名 You can get rid of the strain on the shirt by soaking it in the bleach. 你把襯衫泡在漂白水中，就可以去除污漬。
▶動 You should really bleach your white shirt.
你最好用漂白粉漂洗你的白襯衫。

bliz·zard [ˈblɪzəd]
Track 4342
名 暴風雪
▶It is very dangerous for you to attempt to drive during a blizzard.
你試圖在暴風雪中開車是很危險的。

blond/blonde [blɑnd]
Track 4343
名 金髮的人 形 金髮的
▶名 We would like a blond to appear in this advertisement.
我們想找一個金髮的人來拍這支廣告。
▶形 Would you tell me who that blond girl standing at the corner of the room is?
你能告訴我站在牆角的那個金髮女郎是誰嗎？

blot/stain [blɑt]/[sten]
Track 4344
名 污痕、污漬 動 弄髒、使蒙羞
▶名 Is there any way to remove the ink blot on my dress?
有什麼辦法能去掉我洋裝上的墨漬嗎？
▶動 Many names were blotted out from the list.
有很多人的名字從名單上被刪掉了。

blues [bluz]
Track 4345
名 憂鬱、藍調
▶Blues and Jazz are my favorite music genres.
藍調和爵士是我最喜歡的音樂類型。

blur [blɝ]
Track 4346
名 模糊、朦朧 動 變得模糊
▶名 We're traveling so fast that everything outside passed by in a blur.
我們前進很快，外面的一切景物都看不清楚了。
▶動 My sight was blurred because of tears.
我的視線因淚水變得模糊。

bod·i·ly [ˈbɑdɪlɪ]
Track 4347
形 身體上的 副 親自、親身 反 spiritual 精神的
▶形 He believed that the woman in white was a goddess in bodily form. 他相信穿白衣服的女士是女神的化身。
▶副 He carried the baby bodily into the car.
他把寶寶整個抱進車子裡。

萬用延伸句型
You'd better... 你最好……

文法字詞解析
大家熟知的 R&B 其實就是 Rhythm & Blues（節奏藍調）的縮寫。

body·guard [ˈbɑdɪˌgɑrd]
🔊 *Track 4348*

名 護衛隊、保鑣
▶The big guy standing at his side may be his bodyguard.
站在他身旁的那個大個子可能是他的保鑣。

bog [bɑg]
🔊 *Track 4349*

名 濕地、沼澤 動 陷於泥沼
▶名 Don't try to walk across that bog.
別試著去穿越那個沼澤。
▶動 The renovation bogged down because of a lack in funds.
整修因為缺乏資金而停擺。

bolt [bolt]
🔊 *Track 4350*

名 門閂 動 閂上、吞嚥
▶名 You can slide the bolt back and open the door.
你可以推開門閂，把門打開。
▶動 You'd better bolt all the doors and windows before you leave.
你出去前最好把所有門窗都閂上。

文法字詞解析
bolt 還能當作動詞表示快速行動、快速移動的意思。知名牙買加短跑運動員 Usain Bolt 的姓氏可以說是非常符合他在田徑場上的表現。

bo·nus [ˈbonəs]
🔊 *Track 4351*

名 分紅、紅利
▶As soon as the employees got the annual bonus, they went shopping together. 員工們一拿到年度獎金，就跑去購物。

boom [bum]
🔊 *Track 4352*

名 隆隆聲、繁榮 動 發出低沉的隆隆聲、急速發展
同 thunder 隆隆聲
▶名 It is said that he made a lot of money during the property boom.
據說他在房地產業繁榮的期間發了大財。
▶動 The economy boomed during the past two years.
前兩年，經濟快速地發展。

文法字詞解析
音樂常會發出很大的隆隆聲，因此可以隨身攜帶的音響就稱為 boombox。

booth [buθ]
🔊 *Track 4353*

名 棚子、攤子
▶Would you please watch over my booth? I have to do something urgent at once. 請您幫忙留意一下我的攤位好嗎？
我必須馬上去辦一些緊急的事。

bore·dom [ˈbordəm]
🔊 *Track 4354*

名 乏味、無聊
▶The hacker broke into the system of the government out of sheer boredom.
駭客入侵政府的系統，單純只是因為無聊。

bos·om [ˈbʊzəm]
🔊 *Track 4355*

名 胸懷、懷中 同 breast 胸部
▶She hugged the baby at her bosom.
她把孩子抱在胸口。

Level
1

Level
2

Level
3

Level
4

Level
5

突飛猛進、程度大進擊——擴增實力5400單字

Level
6

bot·a·ny [ˈbɑtənɪ] ◀€ *Track 4356*

名 植物學
▶Not everyone knows that zoology（動物學）and botany are the two main branches of biology.
不是每個人都知道動物學和植物學是生物學的兩大分支。

bou·le·vard [ˈbuləˌvɑrd] ◀€ *Track 4357*

名 林蔭大道 同 avenue （林蔭）大道
▶Protestors gathered on the boulevard in front of the presidential office building.
抗議者聚集在總統府前面的大道上。

bound [baʊnd] ◀€ *Track 4358*

名 彈跳 動 跳躍
▶名 His ability to sing improved in leaps and bounds.
他的歌唱能力簡直是大躍進了。
▶動 The children bounded all the way to the ice cream stand.
孩子們一路跳躍著到冰淇淋攤。

bound·a·ry [ˈbaʊndərɪ] ◀€ *Track 4359*

名 邊界 同 border 邊界
▶It is obvious that the river is the boundary between the two countries. 顯然這條河就是兩國的分界線。

bow·el [ˈbaʊəl] ◀€ *Track 4360*

名 腸子、惻隱之心
▶He has noticed some blood in his bowel movements.
他發現大便裡有點血。

box·er [ˈbɑksɚ] ◀€ *Track 4361*

名 拳擊手
▶The boxer had retired from the ring.
拳擊手退休了，不再上場。

box·ing [ˈbɑksɪŋ] ◀€ *Track 4362*

名 拳擊
▶I enjoy all the sports with the exception of boxing. What about you? 我喜歡拳擊之外的所有運動。你呢？

boy·hood [ˈbɔɪhʊd] ◀€ *Track 4363*

名 少年期、童年
▶Not everyone has a happy boyhood.
不是每個人都擁有一個幸福的童年。

brace [bres] ◀€ *Track 4364*

名 支架、鉗子 動 支撐、鼓起勇氣 同 prop 支撐物
▶名 The girl got teased for because she wore braces.
這位女孩因為戴牙套而被同學取笑。
▶動 Brace yourself, the boss is going to come in and yell at us.
你要做好心理準備喔，老闆要進來大罵我們了。

萬用延伸句型
be bound to + 原 V. 肯定會（做某事）
例如：Don't worry. He's bound to show up sooner or later.
不用擔心，他肯定遲早會出現的。

萬用延伸句型
with the exception of... 除 了 ……，和 except 同義。

braid [bred]
🔊 Track 4365

名 髮辮、辮子 動 編結辮帶或辮子

▶名 He likes pulling his classmates' braids.
他喜歡拉他同學的辮子。

▶動 It takes me about ten minutes in the morning to braid my hair. 每天早上我都要花大概十分鐘的時間綁我的辮子。

breadth [brɛdθ]
🔊 Track 4366

名 寬度、幅度 反 length 長度

▶The breadth of her knowledge won her respect from the colleagues. 她知識的廣度令同事相當尊敬。

bribe [braɪb]
🔊 Track 4367

名 賄賂 動 行賄

▶名 He is honest enough to reject bribe.
他夠忠誠老實,不會收受賄賂。

▶動 It is said that they tried to bribe the reporter into silence.
據說他們曾試圖收買該記者好堵住他的嘴。

brief·case ['brif,kes]
🔊 Track 4368

名 公事包、公文袋

▶Would you please open your briefcase? It's routine inspection.
請你打開公事包好嗎?這是例行檢查。

broad·en ['brɔdn]
🔊 Track 4369

動 加寬 同 widen 加寬

▶Education and experience had broadened his vision and understanding.
教育和經歷使他的眼界開闊。

bronze [branz]
🔊 Track 4370

名 青銅 形 青銅製的

▶名 Bronze was used in producing household utensils in ancient times.
在古代,銅被使用來製造家用器具。

▶形 It is said that this bronze bell dates from the 16th century.
據說這座青銅鐘是在十六世紀時製造的。

文法字詞解析
這個字也常用來形容人的膚色有如剛曬過太陽般、呈現健康的青銅色。

brooch [brotʃ]
🔊 Track 4371

名 別針、胸針

▶What do you think about buying a beautiful brooch as her present?
你覺得買一個漂亮的胸針當作送她的禮物怎麼樣?

brood [brud]
🔊 Track 4372

名 同一窩孵出的幼鳥 動 孵蛋、擔憂

▶名 I found a brood of little birds in my garden.
我在我家花園找到了一窩幼鳥。

▶動 There is no use brooding over one's failure.
老是擔憂失敗是沒有用的。

Level 1

Level 2

Level 3

Level 4

Level 5

擴增實力5400單字 突飛猛進、程度大進擊

Level 6

broth [brɔθ]
🔊 *Track 4373*

名 湯、清湯　同 soup 湯
▶ The chef has a secret recipe for this broth.
主廚有一個煮清湯的秘密食譜。

broth·er·hood [ˈbrʌðɚˏhʊd]
🔊 *Track 4374*

名 兄弟關係、手足之情
▶ Soldiers who fight together often have a strong feeling of brotherhood.
一起作戰的士兵之間常懷有深厚的兄弟情誼。

browse [braʊz]
🔊 *Track 4375*

名 瀏覽　動 瀏覽、翻閱
▶ 名 Are these books yours? Can I have a browse?
這些書是你的嗎？我可以瀏覽一下嗎？
▶ 動 I browsed through the magazine and marked the most interesting page.
我快速翻閱了雜誌，並把最有趣的那一頁做了記號。

文法字詞解析
大家上網常用的「瀏覽器」叫作 browser，就是從這個單字來的。

bruise [bruz]
🔊 *Track 4376*

名 青腫、瘀傷　動 使……青腫、使……瘀傷
▶ 名 I have a few cuts and bruises, would you please buy some band-aid（OK繃）for me?
我身上有幾處割傷和瘀傷，麻煩您幫我買幾個OK繃好嗎？
▶ 動 Would you tell me how you bruised your arm?
你能告訴我你是怎麼把手臂弄瘀青的嗎？

文法字詞解析
bruise 不只是身體上的受傷、瘀傷，也用來講讓某人在感情、心靈上受到傷害。

bulge [bʌldʒ]
🔊 *Track 4377*

名 腫脹　動 鼓脹、凸出　同 swell 腫脹
▶ 名 The bag of candy made a bulge in the child's pocket.
那袋糖果使得這孩子的口袋凸出一塊。
▶ 動 Can you see those muscles bulging under his shirt?
你有沒有看到他衣服下面凸出的肌肉？

bulk [bʌlk]
🔊 *Track 4378*

形 容量、龐然大物
▶ Would you let me know if there is a discount on bulk purchases?
請告訴我如果我大量購買的話是否能有些折扣呢？

bul·ly [ˈbʊlɪ]
🔊 *Track 4379*

名 暴徒　動 脅迫
▶ 名 The little boy kicked his bullies.
那個小男孩踢了霸凌他的人一腳。
▶ 動 You really shouldn't bully your classmates.
你真的不應該欺負同學。

bu·reau [ˈbjʊro]
🔊 *Track 4380*

名 政府機關、辦公處　同 agency 行政機關
▶ The environmental bureau called for people to recycle plastic bottles. 環保署呼籲人們要回收塑膠瓶。

butch·er [ˈbʊtʃə]

🔊 *Track 4381*

名 屠夫 動 屠殺、殘害 同 slaughter 屠殺

▶名 The butcher handed me the meat I bought happily.
那名屠夫開心地把我買的肉遞給我。

▶動 He butchered the pig with a small sharp knife.
他用一把鋒利的小刀殺豬。

[Cc]

cac·tus [ˈkæktəs]

🔊 *Track 4382*

名 仙人掌

▶The cactus is said to be able to absorb radiation.
據說仙人掌可以吸收輻射。

文法字詞解析
cactus 的複數可以說成 cactuses 或 cacti。

calf [kæf]

🔊 *Track 4383*

名 小牛

▶What happened to the cute little calf on your farm?
你們農場那頭可愛的小牛怎麼了？

cal·lig·ra·phy [kəˈlɪgrəfɪ]

🔊 *Track 4384*

名 筆跡、書法

▶Will you tell me whom you learned Chinese calligraphy from?
你能告訴我你是跟誰學書法的嗎？

ca·nal [kəˈnæl]

🔊 *Track 4385*

名 運河、人工渠道 同 ditch 管道

▶Groceries used to be transported into the town through the canal. 以前在這小鎮，日用品都是用運河運送的。

can·non [ˈkænən]

🔊 *Track 4386*

名 大砲

▶It was hard for them to win the fight without enough cannons.
沒有足夠的大炮，他們很難打贏這場仗。

文法字詞解析
從大砲裡面射出來的砲彈則稱為 cannonball。

car·bon [ˈkɑrbən]

🔊 *Track 4387*

名 碳、碳棒

▶The reason the temperature is rising is the large amount of carbon dioxide（二氧化碳）.
氣溫之所以會升高是因為大量的二氧化碳。

card·board [ˈkɑrdˌbɔrd]

🔊 *Track 4388*

名 卡紙、薄紙板

▶Mary used cardboard to make decorations for the party.
瑪麗用紙板做派對的裝飾。

care·free [ˈkɛrˌfri]

🔊 *Track 4389*

形 無憂無慮的 反 anxious 憂慮的

▶Once you graduate, there will be no carefree vacation anymore.
一旦你畢業了，就不會再有無憂無慮的假期了。

Level 1
Level 2
Level 3
Level 4
Level 5
Level 6

突飛猛進、程度大進擊—擴增實力5400單字

care·tak·er [ˈkɛrˌtekə] 🔊 *Track 4390*
名 看管人、照顧者
▶The caretaker at the orphanage was accused of abusing children.
孤兒院的照顧者被指控虐待兒童。

car·na·tion [karˈneʃən] 🔊 *Track 4391*
名 康乃馨
▶She bought a bouquet of carnations for her mother.
她為媽媽買了一束康乃馨。

car·ni·val [ˈkarnəvl̩] 🔊 *Track 4392*
名 狂歡節慶 同 festival 節日
▶Will you tell me what you plan to do at the carnival?
你能告訴我你去參加狂歡節的時候打算做什麼嗎？

carp [karp] 🔊 *Track 4393*
名 鯉魚 動 吹毛求疵
▶名 He caught a lot of carps in the lake.
他在湖中抓到了不少鯉魚。
▶動 She carped about the dishes served in this restaurant.
她對餐廳的菜吹毛求疵。

car·ton [ˈkartn̩] 🔊 *Track 4394*
名 紙板盒、紙板
▶The empty carton is big enough to store all the eggs you bought. 這空紙盒夠大，可以裝得下你買的所有雞蛋。

cat·e·go·ry [ˈkætəˌgori] 🔊 *Track 4395*
名 分類、種類 同 classification 分類
▶The video should belong to the category of Sci-fi movies.
這個影片應該是屬科幻電影類。

ca·the·dral [kəˈθidrəl] 🔊 *Track 4396*
名 主教的教堂 同 church 教堂
▶There is no other building older than this cathedral in the city.
這座教堂是城裡最古老的建築。

cau·tion [ˈkɔʃən] 🔊 *Track 4397*
名 謹慎 動 小心 同 warn 小心、警告
▶名 It is wise for you to exercise caution in crossing the street.
你過馬路時採取小心的態度是明智的。
▶動 I must caution you against the danger because it's difficult for you to fulfill this task. 我必須告誡你應該慎防危險，因為這次任務完成起來會很艱難。

cau·tious [ˈkɔʃəs] 🔊 *Track 4398*
形 謹慎的、小心的 同 wary 小心的
▶You can never be too cautious when purchasing a house.
買房子，再謹慎也不為過。

萬用延伸句型
a carton of sth. 一紙盒的（某物）
例 如：There's nothing but a carton of milk in the fridge.
冰箱裡除了一紙盒的牛奶什麼也沒有。

萬用延伸句型
throw caution to the wind 直譯就是「把所有的小心謹慎都丟到風裡」，表達「不顧風險、冒險一試」的意思。例如本來節衣縮食的人忽然開始瘋狂賭博，這樣的行為就是 throw caution to the wind。

ce·leb·ri·ty [sə`lɛbrətɪ]
🔊 *Track 4399*

名 名聲、名人
▶How are you getting along with the celebrity next door to you?
你和住在你隔壁的那個名人相處得怎麼樣？

cel·er·y [`sɛlərɪ]
🔊 *Track 4400*

名 芹菜
▶The celery tasted bitter, so the kid spitted it out.
芹菜吃起來苦苦的，所以小孩把它吐掉。

cel·lar [`sɛlɚ]
🔊 *Track 4401*

名 地窖、地下室 動 貯存於 同 basement 地下室
▶名 It is said that wine shall be stored in a cool cellar.
據說葡萄酒應該儲存在涼快的地下室裡。
▶動 It is said that the wine has been cellared for twenty years.
據說酒已經在地窖裡存了有二十年之久。

文法字詞解析
用來儲藏東西的地下室可以稱為 cellar 或 basement；相反地用來儲藏東西的閣樓則可以稱為 attic。

cel·lo [`tʃɛlo]
🔊 *Track 4402*

名 大提琴
▶My elder sister plays the cello in an orchestra.
我姐姐在管弦樂隊中演奏大提琴。

cell-phone/cell·phone/ cel·lu·lar phone/mo·bile phone
🔊 *Track 4403*
[sɛl fon]/[sɛl fon]/[`sɛljʊlɚ fon]/[`mobɪl fon]

名 行動電話
▶You'd better buy a new cell-phone so that we can contact you.
你最好買個新手機，好讓我們能聯繫上你。

Cel·si·us/Cen·ti·grade/ cen·ti·grade [`sɛlsɪəs]/[`sɛntəˌgred]/[`sɛntəˌgred]
🔊 *Track 4404*

形 攝氏的
▶The normal temperature of the human body is 37 degrees Celsius.
人體的正常溫度是攝氏三十七度。

文法字詞解析
雖然台灣是用攝氏做為衡量溫度的標準，但在美國則是用華氏作為溫標，而華式的英文是「Fahrenheit」。

cer·e·mo·ny [`sɛrəˌmonɪ]
🔊 *Track 4405*

名 慶典、儀式 同 celebration 慶祝
▶The opening ceremony of the monument will start at eight.
紀念館的開幕儀式將在八點開始。

cer·tif·i·cate [sɚ`tɪfəkɪt]
🔊 *Track 4406*

名 證書、憑證 動 發證書
▶名 I made photocopies of my certificated of professional skills and language proficiency.
我影印了專業技能和語文能力的證照。
▶動 Since you say his abilities are certificated, will you show it to me?
既然你說他的能力有文件為證，那你願意給我看一下嗎？

Level 1

Level 2

Level 3

Level 4

Level 5

突飛猛進、程度大進擊──擴增實力5400單字

Level 6

chair·per·son/chair/ chair·man [ˈtʃɛrˌpɜsn̩]/[tʃɛr]/[ˈtʃɛrmən]
🔊 *Track 4407*

名 主席

▶It won't be long before we know who the chairman of Senate（參議院）is.

很快我們就會知道誰是參議院的主席了。

chair·wom·an [ˈtʃɛrˌwʊmən]
🔊 *Track 4408*

名 女主席

▶Don't you think the new chairwoman is very well-spoken?

你不覺得新上任的女主席很會說話嗎？

chant [tʃænt]
🔊 *Track 4409*

名 讚美詩、歌 動 吟唱 同 hymn 讚美詩

▶名 There are several beautiful chants I want to teach you today.

今天我要教你們唱幾首十分美妙的歌。

▶動 Before the concert was over, the audience chanted "Encore."

演唱會結束前，觀眾齊聲喊「安可」。

chat·ter [ˈtʃætɚ]
🔊 *Track 4410*

動 喋喋不休

▶The teacher asked the children to stop chattering in class.

老師叫孩子們在課堂上不要一直嘰嘰喳喳地講話。

check·book [ˈtʃɛkˌbʊk]
🔊 *Track 4411*

名 支票簿

▶It's not possible for you to retrieve（找回）the lost checkbook.

指望你找回遺失的支票本是不可能的。

check-in [tʃɛkˌɪn]
🔊 *Track 4412*

名 報到、登記

▶Would you please tell me where the check-in desk is?

請你告訴我旅客登記櫃檯在哪？

check-out [ˈtʃɛkˌaʊt]
🔊 *Track 4413*

名 檢查、結帳離開

▶I am afraid that this check-out time is not so convenient for me.

恐怕這個退房時間對我來說不是很方便。

check·up [ˈtʃɛkˌʌp]
🔊 *Track 4414*

名 核對

▶The curator made a regular checkup at the museum before he went off duty.

館長下班前，在博物館中做例行的檢查和巡視。

chef [ʃɛf]
🔊 *Track 4415*

名 廚師 同 cook 廚師

▶Isn't he one of the top chefs in America?

他不是美國最好的廚師之一嗎？

chem·ist [ˈkɛmɪst]
🔊 Track 4416

名 化學家、藥商
▶The chemist analyzed the poison and looked for its antidote.
化學家分析毒藥,尋找解毒劑。

chest·nut [ˈtʃɛsnət]
🔊 Track 4417

名 栗子 形 紅棕栗色的
▶名 A man in the street is selling bags of hot chestnuts.
街上有個男人在賣一包包的熱栗子。
▶形 She got her long chestnut hair cut.
她把她栗色的長頭髮剪掉了。

chill [tʃɪl]
🔊 Track 4418

動 使變冷 名 寒冷 形 冷的 同 cold 冷
▶動 The night air chilled my bones. 夜間的氣候使我寒冷徹骨。
▶名 Mandy thinks the chill in winter is refreshing.
曼蒂認為冬天的寒冷令人有精神。
▶形 There was no one walking on the streets on that chill morning.
在那個寒冷的早晨,沒有人走在街道上。

chim·pan·zee [ˌtʃɪmpænˋzi]
🔊 Track 4419

名 黑猩猩
▶The chimpanzee loved eating bananas.
那隻猩猩很愛吃香蕉。

choir [kwaɪr]
🔊 Track 4420

名 唱詩班 同 chorus 合唱隊
▶Do you know that the church choir is to sing tonight?
你知道今晚教堂唱詩班要唱詩嗎?

chord [kɔrd]
🔊 Track 4421

名 琴弦
▶Her touching word struck the chord of my heart.
他的感人話語撥動我心弦。

chub·by [ˈtʃʌbɪ]
🔊 Track 4422

形 圓胖的、豐滿的
▶What a naughty chubby kid! Does anyone here know him?
好頑皮的一個胖小孩啊!這裡有人認識他嗎?

cir·cuit [ˈsɝkɪt]
🔊 Track 4423

名 電路、線路
▶He knows well of not only the circuit device itself but also its design principle.
他不僅很瞭解電路設備本身,還很瞭解它的設計原理。

cite [saɪt]
🔊 Track 4424

動 例證、引用 同 quote 引用
▶The research results cited in my thesis were listed in the reference section.
我論文中引用的研究結果都列在參考資料中。

文法字詞解析
注意這個字的發音,「ch」是發「k」的音喔。

文法字詞解析
彈吉他、鋼琴等都常會用到的「和弦」就是稱為 chord。因此當你要彈奏某首歌,抓不到和弦時,可以上網搜尋「歌名 + chords」,說不定會有好心人為你詳細地列出來。

Level 1
Level 2
Level 3
Level 4
Level 5
Level 6

突飛猛進、程度大進擊——擴增實力5400單字

civ·ic [ˋsɪvɪk]

🔊 Track 4425

形 城市的、公民的　同 urban 城市的

▶It is a civic duty for us to not throw garbage on the street.
不隨地丟垃圾是公民的義務。

文法字詞解析
在外國也有一些學校會上的「公民課」
可以稱為 civics。

clam [klæm]

🔊 Track 4426

名 蛤、蚌

▶Heavy metal was found in the oysters and clams by the seashore. 海邊的牡蠣和蛤蠣都被發現含有重金屬。

clan [klæn]

🔊 Track 4427

名 宗族、部落　同 tribe 部落

▶Will you tell me what the clan system is?
你能告訴我族譜系統是什麼嗎？

clasp [klæsp]

🔊 Track 4428

名 釦子、鉤子　動 緊抱、扣緊　同 buckle 釦子、扣緊

▶名 I think you'd better fasten it with a clasp, or it will come loose again.
我覺得你最好用鉤子把它扣住，要不然它又會變鬆的。

▶動 You'd better clasp the bracelet your mother gave you around your wrist. 你最好把你媽媽送給你的手鐲戴在手腕上。

clause [klɔz]

🔊 Track 4429

名 子句、條款

▶It is obvious that you misunderstood what the main clause was. 很顯然你誤解了主要子句應該是哪一個。

cling [klɪŋ]

🔊 Track 4430

動 抓牢、附著　同 grasp 抓牢

▶He clings to the last hope of getting a job at the prestigious company.
他抓住最後的希望，想進入那家名望很高的公司。

文法字詞解析
cling 的動詞變化 cling, clung, clung

clock·wise [ˋklɑk͵waɪz]

🔊 Track 4431

形 順時針方向的　副 順時針方向地

▶形 The P.E. teacher（體育老師）had his students running in a clockwise direction on the playground.
體育老師讓他的學生們在操場上按順時針方向跑步。

▶副 You must twist the knob clockwise, or you can't open it.
你必須按順時針方向轉動門把，否則你開不了門。

clo·ver [ˋklovɚ]

🔊 Track 4432

名 苜蓿、三葉草

▶Have you ever seen a four-leaf clover?
你有看過四葉草（幸運草）嗎？

clus·ter [ˋklʌstɚ]

🔊 Track 4433

名 簇、串　動 使生長、使成串　同 batch 組、群

▶名 The cluster of flowers were sent by the patients' family.
這束花是來自病人的家屬。

文法字詞解析
a cluster of = 一串
a galaxy cluster = 星系團

▶動 There are roses clustering round my window and I can see them in bloom every day.
有很多玫瑰花繞著我的窗戶生長，而且我能每天看到它們盛開。

clutch [klʌtʃ]

🔊 Track 4434

名 抓握 動 緊握、緊抓 同 hold 抓握

▶名 He made a clutch at the branch but still fell.
他伸手要抓那根樹枝，但還是摔下來了。

▶動 The mother clutched her baby in her arms.
媽媽緊緊地把嬰兒抱在手臂裡。

coast·line [ˈkostˌlaɪn]

🔊 Track 4435

名 海岸線

▶The ferry sailed along the coastline.
渡輪沿著海岸航行。

co·coon [kəˈkun]

🔊 Track 4436

名 繭 動 用防水布遮蓋

▶名 You can find many cocoons in the forest now.
你現在能在森林裡找到很多繭。

▶動 He cocooned the machine to keep it dry.
他把機器遮蓋起來，它才不會濕掉。

coil [kɔɪl]

🔊 Track 4437

名 線圈、捲 動 捲、盤繞 同 curl 捲

▶名 Would you please pass me a coil of thread, Tom? I need to sew these clothes.
湯姆，請你遞給我一捲線好嗎？我需要縫一下這些衣服。

▶動 The fisher coiled the fishing thread to pull up the fish.
漁夫捲起釣魚線把魚拉上來。

col·league [ˈkɑlig]

🔊 Track 4438

名 同僚、同事

▶What do you think of the new colleague in the marketing department?
你覺得行銷部門新來的那個同事怎麼樣？

文法字詞解析
同事也可稱為 coworker 或 co-worker。

colo·nel [ˈkɝn!]

🔊 Track 4439

名 陸軍上校

▶The white-haired colonel is always eating fried chicken.
那個白髮的上校總是在吃炸雞。

co·lo·ni·al [kəˈlonɪəl]

🔊 Track 4440

名 殖民地的居民 形 殖民地的

▶名 It is obvious that these men are colonials and have lived here for a long time.
顯然這些人都是殖民地的居民，並且已經在這生活了很久。

▶形 A new form of language was developed on the colonial area.
在殖民地區有種新式的語言發展出來。

Level 1
Level 2
Level 3
Level 4
Level 5
Level 6

突飛猛進、程度大進擊——擴增實力5400單字

com·bat [ˈkɑmbæt]
Track 4441

名 戰鬥、格鬥 動 戰鬥、抵抗 同 battle 戰鬥

▶名 There were plenty of people killed in the combat zone.
有很多人死在戰場上。

▶動 Linda was motivated to combat the disease with his parents' encouragement.
琳達在父母的鼓勵下，有動力對抗病魔。

co·me·di·an [kəˈmidɪən]
Track 4442

名 喜劇演員

▶The comedian's performance was very amusing（有趣的）.
這名喜劇演員的表演很有趣。

com·et [ˈkɑmɪt]
Track 4443

名 彗星

▶Will you tell me why the ancients regarded the comet as an evil omen?
你能告訴我為什麼古人認為彗星是一種不祥的預兆嗎？

com·men·ta·tor [ˈkɑmənˌtetɚ]
Track 4444

名 時事評論家 同 critic 評論家

▶I don't think they will invite him to be the commentator.
我覺得他們不會請他當評論家。

com·mis·sion [kəˈmɪʃən]
Track 4445

名 委任狀、委託、佣金 動 委託做某事

▶名 The tour guide can get a commission if the tourists shop at this store.
如果遊客在這間店購物，導遊就可以抽取傭金。

▶動 Do you mind telling me who you will commission to sell your house?
你介意告訴我你會委託誰來賣你的房子嗎？

文法字詞解析
在這個網路發達的時代，要在網路上「委託」事情也越來越容易。例如若你忽然很想要掛一張犀牛在滑雪的圖在牆上，但自己畫不出來，就可以上網「委託」會畫畫的人幫忙。這類的情形越來越普遍，也稱為 commission。

com·mod·i·ty [kəˈmɑdətɪ]
Track 4446

名 商品、物產 同 product 產品

▶On one hand, the prices of commodities are stable this year, but on the other hand, the wages are relatively（相對地）low.
一方面，今年的物價穩定，但是另一方面工資卻相對偏低。

com·mon·place [ˈkɑmənˌples]
Track 4447

名 平凡的事 形 平凡的 同 general 一般的

▶名 Jet travel is now a commonplace.
搭乘噴射機旅行已經是平凡不過的事了。

▶形 Such agents will be commonplace in the next decades even if it's not so popular now. 儘管這樣的代理商現在不是很流行，但是未來幾十年裡就會很普遍了。

com·mu·nism [ˈkɑmjʊˌnɪzəm]
Track 4448

名 共產主義

▶Communism is the opposite of capitalism.
共產主義和資本主義是相對的。

com·mu·nist [ˈkɑmjʊˌnɪst]　◀≪ Track 4449

名 共產黨員 形 共產黨的

▶名 Many communists gave their lives for the revolutionary cause in the past.
過去眾多的共產黨人為革命事業獻出了自己的生命。

▶形 There are several books about communist theory on my desk.
我的書桌上有幾本關於共產主義理論的書。

Level 1

com·mute [kəˈmjut]　◀≪ Track 4450

動 變換、折合、通勤 同 shuttle 往返

▶He has to commute five miles to work every day.
他每天都要通勤五英里路去工作。

Level 2

com·mut·er [kəˈmjutɚ]　◀≪ Track 4451

名 通勤者

▶The train is crowded with commuters during rush hours.
在尖峰時刻，火車塞滿了乘客。

Level 3

文法字詞解析
通勤者天天都要搭車很辛苦，所以有了 commuter pass（通勤者專用票卡），為他們省下一些交通費。

com·pact [ˈkɑmpækt]/[kəmˈpækt]　◀≪ Track 4452

名 契約 形 緊密的、堅實的

▶名 We agreed to make a compact with your country so that we can maintain the peace between us.
我們同意和貴國訂約，以此來保持彼此之間的和平。

▶形 Please help me stamp the soil down so that it's compact.
請幫我把泥土踩結實。

Level 4

com·pass [ˈkʌmpəs]　◀≪ Track 4453

名 羅盤 動 包圍

▶名 The geographic scientist oriented himself with a compass.
地理科學家用羅盤導向。

▶動 Suddenly enemies compassed them on all sides, and it was difficult for them to break through.
敵人突然從四面八方將他們包圍，使得他們很難突圍。

Level 5

文法字詞解析
有人認為我們心中也有個「羅盤」，為我們指出自己所作的一切究竟是對是錯。這個東西英文叫做 moral compass，其實也就是我們的良心啦。如果説一個人 has no moral compass，即「他沒有道德羅盤」，也就是毫無道德觀念，不會因為做錯事而良心不安。

com·pas·sion [kəmˈpæʃən]　◀≪ Track 4454

名 同情、憐憫 同 sympathy 同情

▶It is quite clear that he showed no compassion for the patient.
很顯然他對病人毫無同情心。

com·pas·sion·ate [kəmˈpæʃənɪt]　◀≪ Track 4455

形 憐憫的 反 cruel 殘忍的

▶I wish the compassionate judge could give him a light sentence.
我希望仁慈的法官能從輕判決他。

com·pel [kəmˈpɛl]　◀≪ Track 4456

動 驅使、迫使、逼迫 同 force 迫使

▶The prisoners were compelled to stand in line.
囚犯被強迫要站成一排。

Level 6

突飛猛進、程度大進擊──擴增實力5400單字

com·pli·ment [ˋkɑmpləmənt] ◀≣ Track 4457

名 恭維 反 insult 侮辱
▶Doesn't the man deserve the compliment?
　難道這個人不應當受到這樣的讚揚嗎？

com·pound ◀≣ Track 4458

[ˋkɑmpaʊnd]/[kɑmˋpaʊnd]
名 合成物、混合物 動 使混合、達成協定
同 mix 混合
▶名 Let's start our new lesson: air is a mixture, not a compound of gases.
　我們開始新的課程：空氣是混合物，不是氣體的化合物。
▶動 We compounded several natural ingredient in our homemade detergent.
　我們混和幾種自然成分，做出自製清潔劑。

com·pre·hend [ˏkɑmprɪˋhɛnd] ◀≣ Track 4459

動 領悟、理解
▶Not all people around her can comprehend what she said.
　不是她身邊的每個都能理解她說過的話。

com·pre·hen·sion ◀≣ Track 4460

[ˏkɑmprɪˋhɛnʃən]
名 理解
▶How about giving the class a comprehension test today?
　今天給全班進行一次理解力測驗如何？

com·pro·mise [ˋkɑmprəˏmaɪz] ◀≣ Track 4461

名 和解 動 妥協 同 concession 讓步
▶名 A good negotiator（談判者）knows when to make a compromise.
　一個好的談判者知道何時該妥協。
▶動 The kid compromised and took the medicine reluctantly.
　小孩妥協，不情願地吞下藥物。

com·pute [kəmˋpjut] ◀≣ Track 4462

動 計算 同 calculate 計算
▶Can you compute the distance from the moon to the earth?
　你能計算出從地球到月球的距離嗎？

com·pu·ter·ize [kəmˋpjutəˏraɪz] ◀≣ Track 4463

動 用電腦處理
▶Let's work out a scheme to computerize the library service.
　我們來制定一個使圖書館服務電腦化的方案吧。

com·rade [ˋkɑmræd] ◀≣ Track 4464

名 同伴、夥伴 同 partner 夥伴
▶He shows patience and compassion for his comrades.
　他對同伴表現出耐心和憐憫。

萬用延伸句型

beyond comprehension 無法理解
例　如：No matter how hard he tries to explain, the subject is still beyond comprehension to me.
無論他多努力解釋，我還是無法理解這個主題。

con·ceal [kən'sil]
🔊 *Track 4465*

動 隱藏、隱匿 同 hide 隱藏

▶I think you should conceal your feelings before these serious people. 我覺得你應該在這些嚴肅的人面前隱藏你的感情。

con·ceive [kən'siv]
🔊 *Track 4466*

動 構想、構思

▶The kid conceived an interesting scrip for the stage play. 小孩為舞台劇想出一個有趣劇本。

文法字詞解析
conceive 除了有構想的意思，也可以做「受孕」解釋，如：
conceive a child = 懷了一個孩子。

con·demn [kən'dɛm]
🔊 *Track 4467*

動 譴責、非難、判刑 同 denounce 譴責

▶There is no doubt that the prisoner will be condemned. 毫無疑問這名罪犯將會被判刑。

con·duct ['kɑndʌkt]/[kən'dʌkt]
🔊 *Track 4468*

名 行為、舉止 動 指揮、處理

▶名 He is famous for his good conduct. 他因善行而遠近聞名。

▶動 The experiment was conducted with the consent of the participants. 實驗是在受試者同意下進行的。

con·fes·sion [kən'fɛʃən]
🔊 *Track 4469*

名 承認、招供

▶The little boy made a confession that he broke the window. 小男孩承認他打破了窗戶。

con·front [kən'frʌnt]
🔊 *Track 4470*

動 面對、面臨 同 encounter 遭遇

▶I wish I could confront my accuser（原告）in a court of law. 我希望我能和控告我的人當庭對質。

con·sent [kən'sɛnt]
🔊 *Track 4471*

名 贊同 動 同意、應允 同 agree 同意

▶名 There is but a faint hope that my father will give his consent to our marriage. 父親同意我們結婚的希望渺茫。

▶動 There is a possibility that he will consent to your plan. 他有可能會同意你的計畫。

文法字詞解析
age of consent 即能夠在法律上有效表示同意（進行性行為、結婚等）的年齡。

con·serve [kən'sɝv]
🔊 *Track 4472*

動 保存、保護 同 preserve 保護

▶Not every man will do his best to conserve water. 不是每個人都會盡自己的所能去節約用水。

con·sid·er·ate [kən'sɪdərɪt]
🔊 *Track 4473*

形 體貼的

▶I think that he is more considerate than any others I have met. 我認為他比我碰到的其他人更能體諒人。

Level 1

Level 2

Level 3

Level 4

Level 5

突飛猛進、程度大進擊──擴增實力5400單字

Level 6

con·sole [ˈkansol]/[kənˈsol] ◀ Track 4474

名 操作控制台 動 安慰、慰問 同 comfort 安慰

▶名 Neither of us know how to exit the console.
我們都搞不清楚怎麼退出控制台。

▶動 We tried to console her, but she was overwhelmed by sorrow.
我們試圖安慰她，但她似乎已經被悲傷擊倒。

文法字詞解析
玩電動遊戲用的操作機台就可以稱為 gaming console，像 PlayStation、Xbox、Wii 這類的都是。

con·sti·tu·tion·al ◀ Track 4475
[ˌkanstəˈtjuʃənl]

名 保健運動 形 有益健康的、憲法的 同 healthful 有益健康的

▶名 She's out on her daily constitutional.
她在外頭進行她每天的健身運動。

▶形 Will you tell me what happened at the Constitutional Convention?
你能告訴我制憲會議上發生什麼事了嗎？

con·ta·gious [kənˈtedʒəs] ◀ Track 4476

形 傳染的 同 infectious 傳染的

▶Chicken pox（水痘）is a contagious disease.
水痘是一種透過接觸而傳染的疾病。

con·tam·i·nate [kənˈtæməˌnet] ◀ Track 4477

動 污染 同 pollute 污染

▶The pigment was contaminated, and the color was murky.
顏料已經被汙染，顏色都濁濁的。

文法字詞解析
這個字加上「-d」就變形容詞「contaminated（受到汙染的）」；還有加上「-tion」的 contamination（汙染、致汙物）也是語出同源。

con·tem·plate [ˈkantɛmˌplet] ◀ Track 4478

動 凝視、苦思

▶He contemplated the problem all day but still couldn't solve it.
他苦思了一整天依然解決不了那個問題。

con·tem·po·rar·y ◀ Track 4479
[kənˈtɛmpəˌrɛrɪ]

名 同時代的人 形 同時期的、當代的

▶名 Not all people know that the writer once was looked down upon by his contemporaries.
不是所有人都知道這位作家曾被他同時代的人瞧不起。

▶形 Contemporary artists don't interest me.
我對當代藝術家沒有興趣。

con·tempt [kənˈtɛmpt] ◀ Track 4480

名 輕蔑、鄙視 同 scorn 輕蔑

▶There is no reply as sharp as silent contempt.
無言的輕蔑是最強而有力的回擊。

con·tend [kənˈtɛnd] ◀ Track 4481

動 抗爭、奮鬥

▶The company is too small to contend against large companies.
這家公司太小，無法與大公司競爭。

con·ti·nen·tal [ˌkɑntəˈnɛntl] 🔊 *Track 4482*

形 大陸的、洲的
▶Collisions of continental crusts often cause earthquakes.
大陸板塊撞擊可能導致地震。

con·ti·nu·i·ty [ˌkɑntəˈnjuətɪ] 🔊 *Track 4483*

名 連續的狀態
▶Don't you think the three parts of the book lack continuity?
你不覺得這本書裡的這三個部分缺乏連貫性嗎？

con·vert [kənˈvɝt] 🔊 *Track 4484*

動 變換、轉換 同 change 改變
▶Will you tell me at what rate the dollar converts into pounds?
你能告訴我美元兌換成英鎊的匯率嗎？

文法字詞解析
轉換格式（如將音檔轉換成 mp3 格式、
將文件轉換成 pdf）也用 convert 這個字。

con·vict [ˈkɑnvɪkt]/[kənˈvɪkt] 🔊 *Track 4485*

名 被判罪的人 動 判定有罪
▶名 The convince was sent to prison after the judgement was made. 罪犯在判決後不久，就被送進監獄。
▶動 We have enough evidence to convict this young man now.
我們現在有足夠的證據來給這個年輕人定罪。

cop·y·right [ˈkɑpɪˌraɪt] 🔊 *Track 4486*

名 版權、著作權 動 為……取得版權
▶名 It is obvious that the book is protected by copyright.
顯然該書受版權的保護。
▶動 This book is copyrighted in your father's name.
這本書的版權歸屬於你父親的名下。

cor·al [ˈkorəl] 🔊 *Track 4487*

名 珊瑚 形 珊瑚製的
▶名 Coral is often used for making jewelry.
珊瑚常被用來製作首飾。
▶形 The largest coral reef system of the world is in Australia.
世界上最大的珊瑚礁系在澳洲。

文法字詞解析
coral 也可拿來表達一種顏色「珊瑚色」。
可是珊瑚不是有很多顏色嗎？通常這個
字用來表示一種介於深粉紅與橘紅色之
間的色調。

cor·po·ra·tion [ˌkɔrpəˈreʃən] 🔊 *Track 4488*

名 公司、企業 同 company 公司
▶What do you think of working at a nonprofit（非營利的）corporation? 你覺得到一家非營利公司工作怎麼樣？

cor·re·spon·dence 🔊 *Track 4489*
[ˌkɔrəˈspɑndəns]

名 符合、相似之處 同 accordance 符合
▶The correspondence between the two articles raised suspicion of plagiarism. 這兩篇文章如此相似，懷疑是剽竊。

cor·ri·dor [ˈkɔrədɚ] 🔊 *Track 4490*

名 走廊、通道
▶Will you tell me why he is walking back and forth along the corridor? 你能告訴我他為什麼要在走廊上走來走去嗎？

Level 1
Level 2
Level 3
Level 4
Level 5
Level 6

擴增實力5400單字

突飛猛進、程度大進擊

cor·rupt [kəˋrʌpt]

◀€ *Track 4491*

動 使墮落 **形** 腐敗的 **同** rotten 腐敗的

▶**動** Her mind was corrupted by her older brothers and sisters.
她的心靈在她兄姊的影響下變得墮落了。

▶**形** The file is corrupt; I can't get it to open.
檔案已損壞，我打不開了。

coun·sel [ˋkaʊnsḷ]

◀€ *Track 4492*

名 忠告、法律顧問 **動** 勸告、建議 **同** advise 勸告

▶**名** I listened to my mentor's counsel and majored in computer science.
我聽從我導師的建議主修電腦科學。

▶**動** I would counsel you to say nothing about the affair.
關於這件事情我勸你什麼也別說了。

coun·sel·or [ˋkaʊnslɚ]

◀€ *Track 4493*

名 顧問、參事

▶I think you'd better go to the marriage counselor. Maybe things will change for the better.
我覺得你們最好去諮詢一下婚姻顧問。也許事情還會有轉機。

coun·ter·clock·wise [ˋkaʊntɚ ˋklɑkˌwaɪz]

◀€ *Track 4494*

形 反時針方向的 **副** 反時針方向地

▶**形** Can you count these numbers for me in a counterclockwise direction?
你能按照逆時針的方向來數這些數字嗎？

▶**副** Should I turn the knob counterclockwise?
我應該用逆時針方向旋轉這個門把嗎？

文法字詞解析
還有另外一個字也是「逆時針」的意思，就是「anticlockwise」。從字首「counter-」和「anti-」都可以看到「對抗」、「反」的含義。

cou·pon [ˋkupɑn]

◀€ *Track 4495*

名 優待券

▶The housewife collected some coupons to exchange for groceries.
家庭主婦收集了一些可以換雜貨的兌換卷。

court·yard [ˋkortˌjɑrd]

◀€ *Track 4496*

名 庭院、天井

▶How often does your mother sweep the courtyard?
你媽媽多久打掃一次庭院？

cow·ard·ly [ˋkaʊɚdlɪ]

◀€ *Track 4497*

形 怯懦的 **反** heroic 英勇的

▶He is a cowardly boy who runs away as soon as there is trouble.
他是個怯懦的孩子，一有了麻煩就會馬上跑掉。

萬用延伸句型
as soon as... 一……就立刻……

co·zy [ˋkozɪ]

◀€ *Track 4498*

形 溫暖而舒適的

▶The cat rested at the cozy corner of the living room.
貓咪在客廳的一個舒適角落休息。

crack·er [ˈkrækɚ]
🔊 Track 4499

名 薄脆餅乾
▶ Would you like some crackers? If so, I will buy some for you on my way home. 你要不要吃脆餅呢？如果要的話，我回來的時候就給你買一些。

cra·ter [ˈkretɚ]
🔊 Track 4500

名 火山口 動 噴火、使成坑
▶ 名 Images of the crater were taken with a aerial drone camera.
火山口的相機是無人空拍機拍下的。
▶ 動 Artillery（大炮）cratered the road, making it hard to walk on. 大炮把路面轟得凹凸不平，變得很難走。

creak [krik]
🔊 Track 4501

名 輾軋聲 動 發出輾軋聲
▶ 名 The door opened with a creak as soon as he knocked at the door.
他一敲門，門就「呀」地一聲開了。
▶ 動 The bridge creaked when I walked on it.
我過橋時，橋嘎吱嘎吱地響。

creek [krik]
🔊 Track 4502

名 小灣、小溪
▶ We often swim in the creek behind the house.
我們常在房子後面的小溪裡面游泳。

crib [krɪb]
🔊 Track 4503

名 糧倉、木屋 動 放進糧倉、作弊
▶ 名 Why is the baby not in his crib?
寶寶怎麼沒有在嬰兒床上？
▶ 動 He cribbed from Mike in the exam.
他在考試的時候抄了麥克的答案。

croc·o·dile [ˈkrɑkəˌdaɪl]
🔊 Track 4504

名 鱷魚
▶ The crocodiles shared the habitat with the hippos.
鱷魚和河馬有一個共同的棲息地。

cross·ing [ˈkrɔsɪŋ]
🔊 Track 4505

名 橫越、橫渡
▶ They had a rough crossing from Japan to China.
它們頂著險風惡浪從日本橫渡到了中國。

crouch [kraʊtʃ]
🔊 Track 4506

名 蹲伏、屈膝姿勢 動 蹲踞 同 squat 蹲
▶ 名 He waited there in a crouch.
他以蹲姿在那邊等著。
▶ 動 There is a cat crouching in the corner. Do you see it?
角落裡蜷縮著一隻貓。你看見了嗎？

文法字詞解析
如果要用形容詞描述某物「會發出輾軋聲」呢？可以用 creaky 這個形容詞。例如會發出輾軋聲的樓梯就可以說是 creaky staircase。

Level 1
Level 2
Level 3
Level 4
Level 5
擴增實力5400單字 突飛猛進、程度大進擊──
Level 6

crunch [krʌntʃ] ◀｝ *Track 4507*

名 嘎吱的聲音、危機、關鍵時刻、踩碎、咬碎、財政困難

動 嘎吱嘎吱地碾或踩、壓過、喀嚓喀嚓地咬嚼

▶名 When it comes to the crunch, you can ask for us for help.
如果遇到困難，可以向我們求助。

▶動 The shells crunched under our feet.
那些貝殼在我們腳下發出脆脆的聲音。

crys·tal [ˈkrɪstl] ◀｝ *Track 4508*

名 結晶、水晶 形 清澈的、透明的

▶名 These fine wine glasses are made of crystal.
這些漂亮的酒杯是用水晶做的。

▶形 The cabin stands by a crystal stream.
那個小木屋坐落在清澈的小溪旁邊。

cui·sine [kwɪˈzin] ◀｝ *Track 4509*

名 烹調、烹飪、菜餚

▶Would you like to try some real Sichuan cuisine in this restaurant? 你想不想到這間餐廳吃點真正的四川菜呢？

curb [kɝb] ◀｝ *Track 4510*

名 抑制器 動 遏止、抑制 同 restraint 抑制

▶名 The reason why they place a curb on expenditures（經費）is that they are in want of funds.
他們限制經費的原因是他們現在資金匱乏。

▶動 The player curbed his anger despite being physically attacked by his opponent.
球員被對手肢體攻擊，但還是抑制他的怒氣。

cur·ren·cy [ˈkɝənsɪ] ◀｝ *Track 4511*

名 貨幣、流通的紙幣

▶Will you tell me what a commodity currency is?
你能告訴我什麼是商品貨幣嗎？

cur·ric·u·lum [kəˈrɪkjələm] ◀｝ *Track 4512*

名 課程

▶Life itself is a classroom, and the curriculum is patience.
生活本身就是教室，而耐心便是課程。

cur·ry [ˈkɝɪ] ◀｝ *Track 4513*

名 咖哩粉 動 用咖哩粉調味

▶名 How much chilli（辣椒）did you put in the curry?
你在咖哩裡放了多少辣椒啊？

▶動 Do you know how to cook curried chicken?
你知道如何煮咖哩雞嗎？

cus·toms [ˈkʌstəmz] ◀｝ *Track 4514*

名 海關

▶Passengers had their luggage checked at the customs.
旅客拿行李通過海關檢查。

萬用延伸句型

crystal clear 如水晶般清澈透明，也可用來表示一件事已經說得很清楚，能讓聽者完全瞭解。

例如：I thought I already made it crystal clear that I'm not interested.

我還以為我已經表達得很清楚了，我沒有興趣。

萬用延伸句型

curry favor with sb. 獲得（某人）的好感

例如：There's no point in trying to curry favor with the boss. He doesn't care about things like that.

刻意想獲得老闆好感是沒用的。他對那種事毫不關心。

[Dd]

dart [dɑrt] ◀≣ *Track 4515*

名 鏢、鏢槍 動 投擲、發射、猛衝 同 throw 投、丟
▶ 名 I'm terrible at throwing darts.
　　我超不會射飛鏢的。
▶ 動 She screamed and darted out of the room.
　　她尖叫一聲，衝出房間。

daz·zle [ˋdæzl̩] ◀≣ *Track 4516*

名 恍然耀眼的光 動 眩目、眼花撩亂
▶ 名 It is clear that the dazzle of the spotlights made him ill at ease. 顯然聚光燈的耀眼強光使他侷促不安。
▶ 動 The chandelier in the room dazzled her eyes.
　　房裡的水晶吊燈閃到她眼睛睜不開。

文法字詞解析
想要說「被弄得眼花繚亂」，可以用「bedazzled」這個相關形容詞。

de·cay [dɪˋke] ◀≣ *Track 4517*

名 腐爛的物質 動 腐壞、腐爛 同 rot 腐爛
▶ 名 It is reported that they are trying to stop the decay of the ancient building.
　　據報導他們正想辦法試圖阻止這個古老建築朽壞。
▶ 動 It is said that the Turkish Empire decayed in the nineteenth century. 據說土耳其帝國是在十九世紀時衰落的。

de·ceive [dɪˋsiv] ◀≣ *Track 4518*

動 欺詐、詐騙 同 cheat 欺騙
▶ It is immoral for you to deceive the elderly citizens.
　　你欺騙老人是不道德的。

dec·la·ra·tion [͵dɛkləˋreʃən] ◀≣ *Track 4519*

名 正式宣告
▶ These events led to the declaration of war.
　　是這些事件導致了宣戰。

文法字詞解析
這個字也可以表示寫在紙本上的「宣言」
例如：Declaration of Independence（美國獨立宣言）；還有向海關申報物品也叫作declaration，而「申報」的動作則是用動詞declare。

del·e·gate [ˋdɛlə͵gɪt]/[ˋdɛlə͵get] ◀≣ *Track 4520*

名 代表、使節 動 派遣 同 assign 指派
▶ 名 The delegates from our ally showed respect to our local custom. 我們盟國的代表團對我國文化表示尊敬。
▶ 動 I think a boss must know how to delegate.
　　我認為當老闆的要知人善任。

del·e·ga·tion [͵dɛləˋgeʃən] ◀≣ *Track 4521*

名 委派、派遣、代表團
▶ Our cultural delegation met with a hearty welcome.
　　我們的文化代表團受到了熱烈歡迎。

dem·o·crat [ˋdɛmə͵kræt] ◀≣ *Track 4522*

名 民主主義者
▶ As a democrat, my father support freedom of speech.
　　作為民主人士，我父親支持言論自由。

Level 1
Level 2
Level 3
Level 4
Level 5
擴增實力5400單字 突飛猛進、程度大進擊——
Level 6

de·ni·al [dɪˋnaɪəl]　◀✦ Track 4523

图 否定、否認
▶He's still in denial and won't believe that his girlfriend is dead.
他還是拒絕承認、面對他女友已死的事實。

de·scrip·tive [dɪˋskrɪptɪv]　◀✦ Track 4524

形 描寫的、說明的
▶The writer was known for his descriptive language.
作者以善於描述的語言聞名。

de·spair [dɪˋspɛr]　◀✦ Track 4525

图 絕望 動 絕望 反 hope 希望
▶图 The boss rejected his project ten times and he finally gave up in despair.
老闆駁回他的計畫十次了，他在絕望之下就放棄了。
▶動 I despaired of them ever arriving.
我已經放棄他們會過來的希望了。

de·spise [dɪˋspaɪz]　◀✦ Track 4526

動 鄙視、輕視 同 scorn 輕視
▶Despise and misunderstanding are the major cause of divorce.
輕視和誤解是離婚的主因。

des·ti·na·tion [ˌdɛstəˋneʃən]　◀✦ Track 4527

图 目的地、終點 反 threshold 起點
▶How long will it take for my mail to reach its destination?
我的信件到達目的地要多久？

des·ti·ny [ˋdɛstənɪ]　◀✦ Track 4528

图 命運、宿命 同 fate 命運
▶It is a pity that it was his destiny never to see her again.
命運註定他再也見不到她，真是遺憾。

de·struc·tive [dɪˋstrʌktɪv]　◀✦ Track 4529

形 有害的 反 constructive 有建設性的、有益的
▶Does the country own any destructive weapons?
那個國家擁有哪些毀滅性的武器嗎？

de·ter·gent [dɪˋtɝdʒənt]　◀✦ Track 4530

图 清潔劑
▶I got a new brand of detergent to use in my bathroom.
我買了一種新品牌的清潔劑在浴室使用。

de·vo·tion [dɪˋvoʃən]　◀✦ Track 4531

图 摯愛、熱愛、奉獻
▶Her devotion to painting made her life after retirement colorful.
她對繪畫的投入使退休生活變得多采多姿。

de·vour [dɪˋvaur]　◀✦ Track 4532

動 吞食、吃光 同 swallow 吞嚥
▶It was only minutes before the big fire devoured the entire building. 僅僅幾分鐘的時間大火就吞沒了整棟大樓。

文法字詞解析
在搭飛機的時候，飛機上可能會貼心地為你列出「time to destination」（還有多久到目的地）、或「local time at destination」（目的地當地時間）等等。

di·a·lect [ˈdaɪəlɛkt]　　◀ Track 4533

名 方言
▶Dialects in this tribe may be unintelligible to people in other areas. 這個村落的方言可能對其他地區來說相當難懂。

dis·be·lief [ˌdɪsbəˈlif]　　◀ Track 4534

名 不信、懷疑　反 belief 相信
▶A look of disbelief replaced the smile on his face.
他原本微笑的臉上出現了一種不信任的表情。

dis·card [dɪsˈkɑrd]　　◀ Track 4535

名 被拋棄的人　動 拋棄、丟掉
▶名 Collect all the discards in a pile and shuffle them.
　　把拋棄掉的牌收集成一疊洗一洗牌。
▶動 It is wise to discard the obsolete cliché.
　　俙棄這種過時想法是明智的。

dis·ci·ple [dɪˈsaɪpl]　　◀ Track 4536

名 信徒、門徒　同 follower 跟隨者
▶Judas was one of the twelve disciples of Jesus.
猶大是耶穌的十二門徒之一。

dis·crim·i·nate [dɪˈskrɪməˌnet]　　◀ Track 4537

動 辨別、差別對待　同 distinguish 區別
▶It is important for parents to teach their children to discriminate between right and wrong.
對於父母來說教育他們的小孩分辨是非很重要。

dis·pense [dɪˈspɛns]　　◀ Track 4538

動 分送、分配、免除　同 distribute 分配
▶Press this button and hand sanitizer（清潔劑）will be dispensed.
按這個按鈕，手部清潔劑就會跑出來。

dis·pose [dɪˈspoz]　　◀ Track 4539

動 佈置、處理　同 arrange 安排、佈置
▶The nuclear waste was disposed in the deserted island.
核廢料被丟棄在無人島上。

dis·tinc·tion [dɪˈstɪŋkʃən]　　◀ Track 4540

名 區別、辨別　同 discrimination 區別
▶I don't see the distinction between this book cover and that one.
我看不出這兩本書的封面有什麼差別。

dis·tinc·tive [dɪˈstɪŋktɪv]　　◀ Track 4541

形 區別的
▶I think she has a very distinctive way of dressing.
我覺得她穿衣服很有特色。

萬用延伸句型

in disbelief 難以置信、懷疑的
例如：He stared at his phone in disbelief after receiving the message.
收到那條訊息後，他難以置信地盯著自己的手機。

文法字詞解析

能夠「分送」某物的東西就可以稱為dispenser。例如按它一下就會跑出肥皂泡泡沫的機器，就可以稱為 soap dispenser。

Level 1

Level 2

Level 3

Level 4

Level 5

Level 6

突飛猛進、程度大進擊——

擴增實力5400單字

dis·tress [dɪˈstrɛs]　　🔊 *Track 4542*

名 憂傷、苦惱　動 使悲痛

▶名 HShe was in distress after losing her house to the natural disaster. 她在天災中失去家園後，感到沮喪。

▶動 Mary's illness distressed her greatly.
瑪莉生病的事使她非常憂傷。

doc·u·ment [ˈdɑkjəmənt]　　🔊 *Track 4543*

名 文件、公文　動 提供文件

▶名 Would you please give me a copy of this document?
請您給我一份這個文件的副本好嗎？

▶動 Will you please document the case for me?
可以請你幫我把這個案件建檔嗎？

door·step [ˈdorˌstɛp]　　🔊 *Track 4544*

名 門階

▶There is a puppy sitting on our doorstep.
有隻小狗坐在我們家門口。

door·way [ˈdorˌwe]　　🔊 *Track 4545*

名 門口、出入口

▶Don't stand in the doorway. Other people can't get out.
不要站在門口，這樣別人都不能出去了。

dor·mi·to·ry [ˈdɔrməˌtorɪ]　　🔊 *Track 4546*

名 學校宿舍

▶The school dormitory can house 300 students at its maximum capacity. 學校宿舍最多可以容納三百位學生。

文法字詞解析
dormitory 也可以簡稱 dorm。

dough [do]　　🔊 *Track 4547*

名 生麵團

▶Could you tell me how to make dough from wheat powder?
你能告訴我如何用麵粉做麵團嗎？

down·ward [ˈdaʊnwəd]　　🔊 *Track 4548*

副 下降地、向下地　反 upward 上升地

▶The girl dared no look downwards when crossing the suspension bridge. 女孩過吊橋時，不敢往下看。

down·wards [ˈdaʊnwədz]　　🔊 *Track 4549*

副 下降地、向下地

▶There are several monkeys hanging head downwards from the branch.
有幾隻猴子頭朝下倒掛在樹枝上。

drape [drep]　　🔊 *Track 4550*

名 幔、窗簾　動 覆蓋、裝飾　同 curtain 窗簾

▶名 It's getting dark. Let's draw the drapes, shall we?
天快黑了。我們拉上窗簾好嗎？

▶動 The little girl draped herself all over her daddy.
那個小女孩整個人攤在她爸爸身上。

延伸萬用句型
Let's ..., shall we?（我們）這樣做好嗎？
這裡用到祈使句的附加問句，用來提議做某件事情。

dread·ful [`drɛdfəl`]

🔊 *Track 4551*

形 可怕的、恐怖的 同 fearful 可怕的
▶The dreadful scene of the accident frightened the witnesses.
這個車禍的可怕景象嚇到了目擊者。

dress·er [`drɛsɚ`]

🔊 *Track 4552*

名 梳妝臺、鏡臺
▶Did you leave the watch on your dresser?
你是把手錶放在梳妝台上了嗎？

dress·ing [`drɛsɪŋ`]

🔊 *Track 4553*

名 藥膏、服飾、裝飾
▶You'd better put the dressing table on the left.
你最好把梳粧台放在左邊。

drive·way [`draɪˌwe`]

🔊 *Track 4554*

名 私用車道、車道
▶The truck entered the driveway and drove up towards that house.
那輛卡車進入車道後向那間房屋開過去了。

du·ra·tion [djʊ`reʃən`]

🔊 *Track 4555*

名 持久、持續
▶I don't think that the duration of their marriage will be very long.
我認為他們的婚姻不會持續太久。

dusk [dʌsk]

🔊 *Track 4556*

名 黃昏、幽暗 同 twilight 微光、朦朧
▶It's already dusk; I don't think you should let the children play outside.
都黃昏了，我覺得你不應該讓小孩在外面玩。

dwarf [dwɔrf]

🔊 *Track 4557*

名 矮子、矮小動物 動 萎縮、使矮小 反 giant 巨人
▶名 The dwarfs are the leading characters in this movie.
這部電影的主角是小矮人。
▶動 The new building dwarves all the other buildings in the town.
有一棟新大樓使城裡所有其他建築物都顯得矮小了。

dwell [dwɛl]

🔊 *Track 4558*

動 住、居住、詳述
▶Not all his friends know that he'd dwelled in London for two years. 不是他的所有朋友都知道他曾在倫敦住了兩年。

dwell·ing [`dwɛlɪŋ`]

🔊 *Track 4559*

名 住宅、住處 同 residence 住宅
▶He changed his dwelling recently because the original place is too noisy.
他最近搬了家，因為他原來住的地方太吵了。

文法字詞解析
沙拉上面灑的沙拉「醬」也可以稱為 dressing，畢竟對沙拉來說沙拉醬就有如穿在身上的衣服一樣有覆蓋、增添色彩的效果吧。

文法字詞解析
由於 dwell 指「在某地長住」，因此這個字也能用來表示對某事執著很長一段時間（彷彿你的心長住在此一般）。例如若你的朋友整天想著被甩的事情想個不停，已經想了好幾個月了，你就可以跟他說：Stop dwelling on it!（不要一直這麼執著）。

Level **1**

Level **2**

Level **3**

Level **4**

Level **5**

突飛猛進、程度大進擊——擴增實力5400單字

Level **6**

[Ee]

e·clipse [ɪˋklɪps]　◀≾ *Track 4560*

名 蝕（月蝕等）　動 遮蔽　同 cover 遮蓋

▶名 Have you ever seen an eclipse before?
你有看過日蝕嗎？

▶動 The moon eclipsed the sun so we can only see half of it.
月亮遮住了太陽，我們只看得到半個太陽。

eel [il]　◀≾ *Track 4561*

名 鰻魚

▶How about asking Mom to buy some eels for dinner today?
叫媽媽今天買些鰻魚做晚餐怎麼樣？

e·go [ˋigo]　◀≾ *Track 4562*

名 自我、我　同 self 自我

▶A bruised ego may cause emotional problems.
自尊心受損可能導致情緒問題。

文法字詞解析

「ego」可以當作字首使用，因此從 ego 延伸出來的字有很多，例如要說一個人非常地「自我」可以稱他為 egoistic（自我的），要說一個人「自我到非常誇張、簡直有病的程度」，可以稱他為 egomaniac。

e·lab·o·rate [ɪˋlæbərɪt]/[ɪˋlæbəˌret]　◀≾ *Track 4563*

形 精心的　動 精心製作、詳述　反 simple 簡樸的

▶形 I hear that you have made an elaborate plan of attack.
聽說你制定了一個精心的攻擊計畫。

▶動 Do you mind elaborating your ideas before these leaders?
你介意在這些領導人面前詳述你的想法嗎？

el·e·vate [ˋɛləˌvet]　◀≾ *Track 4564*

動 舉起　同 lift 舉起

▶I can't elevate the bucket full of water unless someone helps me. 除非有人幫我，要不然我吊不起這個裝滿了水的水桶。

em·brace [ɪmˋbres]　◀≾ *Track 4565*

動 包圍、擁抱、接受　名 擁抱

▶動 They embraced the idea of democracy.
他們接受了民主的想法。

▶名 They gave each other an awkward embrace.
他們尷尬地擁抱了對方。

en·deav·or [ɪnˋdɛvɚ]　◀≾ *Track 4566*

名 努力　動 盡力　同 strive 努力

▶名 It is obvious that they have made every endeavor to satisfy their customers. 顯然他們已經盡全力來使顧客滿意。

▶動 His father endeavored to persuade him to work hard.
他的父親在努力設法去說服他努力工作。

en·roll [ɪnˋrol]　◀≾ *Track 4567*

動 登記、註冊　同 register 註冊

▶They enrolled in the taekwondo class.
他們註冊參加跆拳道課程。

en·roll·ment [ɪnˋrolmənt] ◀Track 4568

名 登記、註冊

▶It is a pity that the enrollment period has already passed.
很遺憾註冊時間已經截止了。

en·sure/in·sure [ɪnˋʃʊr]/[ɪnˋʃʊr] ◀Track 4569

動 確保、保證

▶The recommendation letter may ensure you the admission to the university. 這封推薦信可以確保你錄取那間大學。

en·ter·prise [ˋɛntəˏpraɪz] ◀Track 4570

名 企業

▶The enterprise must make profits soon, or it will go bankrupt sooner or later.
這個企業必須很快獲利，否則它遲早會破產的。

en·thu·si·as·tic [ɪnˏθjuzɪˋæstɪk] ◀Track 4571

形 熱心的

▶My brother is very enthusiastic about singing.
我弟弟很喜歡唱歌。

en·ti·tle [ɪnˋtaɪtl] ◀Track 4572

動 定名、賦予權力 反 deprive 剝奪

▶He is not entitled to access the data.
他未經授權，無法取用這個資料。

e·quate [ɪˋkwet] ◀Track 4573

動 使相等

▶You can't equate being rich to being happy.
你不能說有錢和快樂是相等的。

e·rect [ɪˋrɛkt] ◀Track 4574

動 豎立 形 直立的 同 upright 直立的

▶動 He plans to erect a monument in the town.
他計畫在鎮上建一座紀念碑。

▶形 There is an erect pine on the hill in front of our yard.
我們家院子前面的山上有一棵挺拔的松樹。

e·rupt [ɪˋrʌpt] ◀Track 4575

動 爆發

▶Don't you believe the volcano may erupt at any time?
你不相信這座火山隨時可能會爆發嗎？

es·cort [ɛsˋkɔrt]/[ˋɛskɔrt] ◀Track 4576

動 護衛、護送 名 護衛者

▶動 The bodyguards escorted the politician to the venue of the summit.
保鑣護衛這名政客到高峰會的會場。

▶名 He offered to be her escort, but she declined.
他主動說要護送她，但她謝絕了。

文法字詞解析
enthusiastic 的名詞形式為 enthusiasm。

萬用延伸句型
erupt into cheers 突然爆出喝彩聲
例如：When the singer walked onto the stage, the crowd erupted into cheers.
歌手走上台時，觀眾們大聲喝采起來。

Level 1
Level 2
Level 3
Level 4
Level 5
突飛猛進、程度大進擊──擴增實力5400單字
Level 6

es·tate [ə'stet]
◀ Track 4577

名 財產 同 property 財產

▶Real estate is really expensive these days.
最近房地產真的很貴。

es·teem [əs'tim]
◀ Track 4578

名 尊重 動 尊敬

▶名 The former mayor is held in high esteem among local people.
前市長在人名心中聲望很高。

▶動 The lady was greatly loved and esteemed there.
這位太太在那裡備受愛戴和尊敬。

e·ter·nal [ɪ'tɝnl]
◀ Track 4579

形 永恆的 同 permanent 永恆的

▶Isn't a wedding ring a symbol of eternal love between them?
結婚戒指難道不是他們之間永恆的愛的一種象徵嗎？

eth·ics ['ɛθɪks]
◀ Track 4580

名 倫理（學）

▶Ethics deals with moral conduct.
倫理學研討的是道德行為。

ev·er·green ['ɛvəˌgrin]
◀ Track 4581

名 常綠樹 形 常綠的

▶名 There are many evergreens on both sides of the road.
道路兩旁有很多萬年青。

▶形 There is a small evergreen shrub（灌木）in the park.
公園裡有一小塊常綠灌木叢。

ex·ag·ger·a·tion
[ɪgˌzædʒə'reʃən]
◀ Track 4582

名 誇張、誇大

▶The news was presented in exaggeration.
這則新聞被誇大報導。

ex·ceed [ɪk'sid]
◀ Track 4583

動 超過 同 surpass 勝過

▶The demand for vegetables exceeds the supply.
蔬菜供不應求。

ex·cel [ɪk'sɛl]
◀ Track 4584

動 勝過 同 outdo 勝過

▶He excels in many different things.
他擅長許多事情。

ex·cep·tion·al [ɪk'sɛpʃənl]
◀ Track 4585

形 優秀的

▶The kid has exceptional talent in music.
這小孩在音樂上有傑出的才華。

文法字詞解析

這個字加上形容詞字尾「-al」就變成「ethical」，意思是「論理的、道德的」，例如：ethical issues 倫理議題。

ex·cess [ɪkˋsɛs]
🔊 *Track 4586*

名 超過 形 過量的

▶名 Anything in excess is a bad thing.
任何事一旦過了頭就不太好了。

▶形 They said we should boil the excess liquid away.
他們說我們應該把多餘的液體煮掉。

ex·claim [ɪkˋsklem]
🔊 *Track 4587*

動 驚叫

▶She exclaimed when the robber took her purse.
搶匪拿走她的皮夾時,她大聲尖叫。

ex·clude [ɪkˋsklud]
🔊 *Track 4588*

動 拒絕、不包含 反 include 包含

▶All of us are here excluding Jenny.
除了珍妮以外,我們大家都在這邊。

ex·e·cute [ˋɛksɪ͵kjut]
🔊 *Track 4589*

動 實行 同 perform 實行

▶I don't agree with how he executes decisions.
我不喜歡他實施決策的方式。

ex·ec·u·tive [ɪgˋzɛkjʊtɪv]
🔊 *Track 4590*

名 執行者、管理者 形 執行的

▶名 The executive is cautious about distributing temporary pass.
行政人員對於發給暫時通行證相當謹慎。

▶形 He is a man of executive ability. 他是一個有執行能力的人。

ex·ile [ˋɛksaɪl]
🔊 *Track 4591*

名 流亡 動 放逐

▶名 Will you tell me why they sent Napoleon into exile?
你能告訴我他們為什麼要把拿破崙流放嗎?

▶動 Why was the famous writer exiled from his country?
這個著名的作家為何被流放到國外去了呢?

ex·ten·sion [ɪkˋstɛnʃən]
🔊 *Track 4592*

名 擴大、延長 同 expansion 擴張

▶It is obvious that the students dislike the extension of the term.
顯然學生們不願延長學期。

ex·ten·sive [ɪkˋstɛnsɪv]
🔊 *Track 4593*

形 廣泛的、廣大的 同 spacious 廣闊的

▶He benefited a lot from extensive reading.
他從廣泛的閱讀中受益匪淺。

ex·te·ri·or [ɪkˋstɪrɪɚ]
🔊 *Track 4594*

名 外面 形 外部的 反 interior 內部的

▶名 It is very difficult for us to judge a person by his exterior.
依據外表我們很難評判一個人。

▶形 Tiles fell off from the exterior walls of the building.
磁磚由大樓的外牆剝落。

文法字詞解析
字首「ex-」常有「外、除外」的意思,而相反的字首「in-」則常有「裡、內」的意思。因此 exclude 是「不包含、排除」的意思,而字根相同字首不同的「include」則是「包含」的意思。

文法字詞解析
extension 有「在原本的東西上再『附加』東西」的意思,因此我們常用的網頁瀏覽器添加的附加功能(例如擋廣告的功能等)就可以稱為 extension。

Level 1

Level 2

Level 3

Level 4

Level 5

突飛猛進、程度大進擊——擴增實力5400單字

Level 6

ex·ter·nal [ɪkˈstɝnl] 🔊 *Track 4595*

名 外表 形 外在的 反 internal 內在的

▶名 It is unwise（不明智的）to judge people by externals.
以貌取人是不明智的。

▶形 Don't you think the external features of the building are very attractive?
難道你不認為這棟建築物的外觀很吸引人嗎？

ex·tinct [ɪkˈstɪŋkt] 🔊 *Track 4596*

形 滅絕的 同 dead 死的

▶The Dodo has been extinct for a long time.
這種古代巨鳥已經絕種很久了。

ex·tra·or·di·nar·y 🔊 *Track 4597*
[ɪkˈstrɔrdnˌɛrɪ]

形 特別的 反 normal 正規的

▶What an extraordinary hat! How much does it cost?
多麼奇特的帽子呀！它多少錢？

eye·lash/lash [ˈaɪˌlæʃ]/[læʃ] 🔊 *Track 4598*

名 睫毛

▶He has very long eyelashes that keep getting stuck in his eyes.
他的睫毛很長，常倒插在眼睛裡。

eye·lid [ˈaɪˌlɪd] 🔊 *Track 4599*

名 眼皮

▶My eyelids feel heavy after a long day.
在漫長的一天過後，我的眼皮非常沉重。

[Ff]

fab·ric [ˈfæbrɪk] 🔊 *Track 4600*

名 紡織品、布料 同 cloth 布料

▶The fabric can be dyed within minutes with the machine.
用這種機器，布料可以在幾分鐘內就完成染色。

fad [fæd] 🔊 *Track 4601*

名 一時的流行 同 fashion 流行

▶Learning English is much more than a fad, it is really a must!
學英文不僅只是一個流行而已，而是一件必須要做的事！

Fahr·en·heit [ˈfærənˌhaɪt] 🔊 *Track 4602*

名 華氏、華氏溫度計

▶Water freezes at 32 degrees Fahrenheit (32˚F).
水在華氏三十二度時結冰。

文法字詞解析

extinct 除了表示物種滅絕外，也能拿來表示隨著時代演進，某些事情已經不會有人再做了。舉例來說，你可以說 People who still listen to music on cassette tapes are pretty much extinct now.（現在還在聽錄音帶的人已經差不多絕種了。）

萬用延伸句型

be more thanr... 不只是……

fal·ter [ˈfɔltɚ]
🔊 Track 4603

動 支吾、結巴地說、猶豫　同 stutter 結巴地說

▶He faltered for a while and was still unable to make a decision.
他猶豫了一陣子還是無法做決定。

fas·ci·nate [ˈfæsˌnet]
🔊 Track 4604

動 迷惑、使迷惑

▶The viewers were fascinated by the fountain show.
觀眾對這個噴泉表演著迷。

fa·tigue [fəˈtig]
🔊 Track 4605

名 疲勞、破碎　動 衰弱、疲勞

▶名 It is a treat to have a drink after the fatigue of the day.
累了一天之後喝杯酒可說是其樂無窮。

▶動 Sarah often complains she fatigues easily. Don't you think there's something wrong with her?
莎拉常訴說自己容易疲勞。難道你不覺得她身體有問題嗎？

fed·er·al [ˈfɛdərəl]
🔊 Track 4606

形 同盟的、聯邦（制）的

▶It is the federal government that decides U.S. foreign policy.
美國的外交政策是由聯邦政府來決定的。

fee·ble [ˈfibl]
🔊 Track 4607

形 虛弱的、無力的　同 weak 虛弱的

▶The feeble-minded employer was despised by his colleague.
這個頭腦不好的員工被他的同事輕視。

fem·i·nine [ˈfɛmənɪn]
🔊 Track 4608

名 女性　形 婦女的、溫柔的　反 masculine 男性、男子氣概的

▶名 The masculine nouns are used differently from the feminine in German.
在德文中，陽性名詞和陰性用法不同。

▶形 He is very feminine and gentle.
他是個女性化、溫柔的人。

fer·ti·liz·er [ˈfɝtlˌaɪzɚ]
🔊 Track 4609

名 肥料、化學肥料

▶It is obvious that fertilizer will accelerate（加快）the growth of these tomato plants. 顯然肥料將促進這些番茄樹的生長。

fi·an·ce/fi·an·cee [ˌfiənˈse]
🔊 Track 4610

名 未婚夫／未婚妻

▶His fiancee is a young dancer with a bright future.
他的未婚妻是個有前途的年輕舞蹈家。

fi·ber [ˈfaɪbɚ]
🔊 Track 4611

名 纖維、纖維質

▶It is no wonder that the doctor recommended more fiber in his diet. 難怪醫生建議他多吃一些纖維性的食物。

文法字詞解析

長期疲勞的狀態可稱為 chronic fatigue。

萬用延伸句型

with every fiber of sb.'s being 直翻就是「全身上下的每一根纖維」，也就是表示這個人「以渾身的力量」感受某件事。例如 want something with every fiber of sb.'s being 即「非常非常想要某事物」，而 hate something with every fiber of sb.'s being 則是「非常非常討厭某事物」。

Level 1

Level 2

Level 3

Level 4

Level 5

突飛猛進、程度大進擊──擴增實力5400單字

Level 6

fid·dle [ˈfɪdl̩]　　🔊 *Track 4612*

名 小提琴 動 拉提琴、遊蕩 同 violin 小提琴

▶名 Why don't you let your daughter learn to play the fiddle?
為什麼不讓你的女兒學拉小提琴呢？

▶動 Stop fiddling around and go do something useful.
別再到處閒晃了，去做點有用的事。

fil·ter [ˈfɪltɚ]　　🔊 *Track 4613*

名 過濾器 動 過濾、滲透

▶名 The coffee filter is a common coffee brewing utensil.
咖啡過濾器是一個常見的煮咖啡用具。

▶動 I think we need to filter the drinking water first.
我們需要把飲用水先過濾一下。

文法字詞解析

現代人常用手機拍照，而手機的相機中都會內建濾鏡功能，這個功能在英文就叫做「filter」。

fin [fɪn]　　🔊 *Track 4614*

名 鰭、手、魚翅

▶I see a shark's fin in the distance. 我看到遠方有個鯊魚鰭。

fish·er·y [ˈfɪʃərɪ]　　🔊 *Track 4615*

名 漁業、水產業、養魚場

▶It is clear that the fishery is confronted with a financial crisis now. 顯然這個養魚場正面臨財務危機。

flake [flek]　　🔊 *Track 4616*

名 雪花、薄片 動 剝、片片降落、使成薄片 同 peel 剝

▶名 Have some flakes! It's my favorite kind of breakfast.
吃點穀片吧！這是我最喜歡的早餐。

▶動 I'm afraid that the paint is going to flake off the walls.
恐怕油漆要從牆上剝落下來了。

flap [flæp]　　🔊 *Track 4617*

名 興奮狀態、鼓翼 動 拍打、拍動、空談

▶名 Even though they apologized to the hosts, it did cause a bit of flap.
儘管他們向主人道了歉，但還是引起了一點兒小騷動。

▶動 The bird flapped its wings and flew away.
那隻鳥拍拍翅膀飛走了。

flaw [flɔ]　　🔊 *Track 4618*

名 瑕疵、缺陷 動 弄破、破裂、糟蹋 同 defect 缺陷

▶名 The prosecutor found a flaw in the defendants' confession.
檢察官發現被告說詞的瑕疵

▶動 I am afraid the story is a bit flawed because its ending is so weak. 恐怕這故事有點缺陷，結尾寫得太沒力了。

flick [flɪk]　　🔊 *Track 4619*

名 輕打聲、彈開 動 輕打、輕拍 同 pat 輕拍

▶名 He gave a flick of the whip his father gave him.
他輕抽他父親送給他的鞭子。

▶動 The snake's tongue was flicking from side to side.
那條蛇忽左忽右地吐著舌頭。

文法字詞解析

近年來 flick 在口語中也能夠引申為「電影」的意思。

flip [flɪp] 🔊 *Track 4620*

名 跳動、拍打　動 輕拍、翻轉

▶名 The boat is too small. It is no wonder that a flip of the whale's tail upset it.
那條船太小了。難怪鯨魚的尾巴輕輕一拍就把它打翻了。

▶動 The dolphin flipped in the air.
那隻海豚在空中翻轉。

文法字詞解析
夏天在海灘常穿的「flip-flops（夾腳拖鞋）」就是從這個字延伸而來。

flour·ish [ˈflɝɪʃ] 🔊 *Track 4621*

名 繁榮、炫耀、華麗的詞藻　動 誇耀、繁盛　反 decline 衰退

▶名 She finished her speech with flourish.
她華麗地結束了演講。

▶動 Tourism in this country is flourishing.
這個國家的旅遊業正興盛。

flu·en·cy [ˈfluənsɪ] 🔊 *Track 4622*

名 流暢、流利

▶Fluency in English will be an added advantage.
流利的英語將是另一個優勢。

foe [fo] 🔊 *Track 4623*

名 敵人、仇人、敵軍　同 enemy 敵人

▶I'm afraid that this is the most serious challenge from his political foe. 恐怕這是來自他政敵的最嚴重挑戰。

foil [fɔɪl] 🔊 *Track 4624*

名 箔片、箔、薄金屬片

▶Can you wrap this in foil for me? 幫我用鋁箔包好好不好？

folk·lore [ˈfokˌlor] 🔊 *Track 4625*

名 沒有隔閡、平民作風、民間傳說、民俗

▶Would you please tell us some tales from folklore?
請您為我們講一些民間故事好嗎？

for·get·ful [fɚˈɡɛtfəl] 🔊 *Track 4626*

形 忘掉的、易忘的、忽略的、健忘的

▶Old people are sometimes forgetful. 老人有時很健忘。

for·mat [ˈfɔrmæt] 🔊 *Track 4627*

名 格式、版式　動 格式化

▶名 The file format would only be edited in the Macintosh computer. 這種檔案格式只能在麥金塔電腦上編輯。

▶動 Are you trying to format this floppy disc?
你是打算要將這張軟碟格式化嗎？

foul [faʊl] 🔊 *Track 4628*

動 使污穢、弄髒、使堵塞　形 險惡的、污濁的　反 clean 清潔的

▶動 Grease has fouled this drain.
油污使這條下水道塞住了。

▶形 Why don't you open the window to let out the foul air?
為什麼不打開窗戶以排放出汙濁的空氣呢？

文法字詞解析
運動比賽或遊戲中的「犯規」也可稱為 foul。

Level 1

Level 2

Level 3

Level 4

Level 5

突飛猛進、程度大進擊——
擴增實力5400單字

Level 6

fowl [faʊl]

◀ Track 4629

名 鳥、野禽 同 bird 鳥

▶What do you think of having roast fowl for dinner?
你們覺得我們晚餐吃烤雞怎麼樣？

frac·tion [ˈfrækʃən]

◀ Track 4630

名 分數、片斷、小部份 同 segment 部分

▶Only a fraction of the remains of the airplane was found.
只有一小部分的飛機殘骸被找到。

frame·work [ˈfremˌwɜk]

◀ Track 4631

名 架構、骨架、體制 同 structure 結構

▶You'd better adhere（堅持）to a basic framework when
writing the paper.
你最好照一個基本的結構來寫這篇論文。

fran·tic [ˈfræntɪk]

◀ Track 4632

形 狂暴的、發狂的

▶That noise is driving me frantic. Would you mind turning off
the music?
那種噪音真要把我弄瘋了。你介意關掉音樂嗎？

freight [fret]

◀ Track 4633

名 貨物運輸 動 運輸

▶名 It's more expensive to mail the box by express than by
freight.
用快遞運送這個箱子比普通貨運要貴很多。

▶動 It is less costly to freight these products than to mail it.
貨運這些產品比郵寄更省錢。

fron·tier [frʌnˈtɪr]

◀ Track 4634

名 邊境、國境、新領域 同 border 邊境

▶I'm afraid that we have not had any more news from the
frontier.
恐怕我們還沒有得到來自邊境的進一步消息。

萬用延伸句型
I'm afraid that... 恐怕……

fume [fjum]

◀ Track 4635

名 蒸汽、香氣、煙 動 激怒、冒出（煙、蒸汽等）
同 vapor 蒸汽

▶名 Tobacco fumes filled the air in the room.
室內的空氣中充滿了香菸的煙霧。

▶動 He was fumed for his son's rude words.
他被他兒子無禮的話氣到。

fu·ry [ˈfjʊrɪ]

◀ Track 4636

名 憤怒、狂怒 同 rage 狂怒

▶Would you like to tell me why he is white with fury? What
happened?
你能告訴我他為什麼會氣得臉色發白嗎？發生什麼事了？

fuse [fjuz] 🔊 *Track 4637*
名 引信、保險絲 動 熔合、裝引信
▶名 I don't know how to mend a fuse. 我不會修保險絲。
▶動 Could you instruct us how to fuse the pipes?
您能指導我們怎樣焊接管子嗎？

fuss [fʌs] 🔊 *Track 4638*
名 大驚小怪 動 焦急、使焦急、小題大作、過分講究
▶名 There's nothing to make a fuss over. 沒什麼好大驚小怪的。
▶動 She fussed over trivial things, which annoyed her colleagues.
她為了小事大做文章，讓同事困擾。

萬用延伸句型
kick up a fuss 大鬧、小題大作
例如：The restaurant had to tell the old man who kicked up a fuss to leave.
這家餐廳不得不請那位大吵大鬧的奧客老先生離開。

[Gg]

gal·lop [ˈɡæləp] 🔊 *Track 4639*
名 疾馳、飛奔 動 使疾馳、飛奔 同 run 跑
▶名 He rode off at a gallop as soon as he got the news.
他一聽到消息就騎馬疾馳而去。
▶動 The horse galloped away into the sunset.
那匹馬朝著夕陽奔去。

gar·ment [ˈɡɑrmənt] 🔊 *Track 4640*
名 衣服
▶There are many shops selling all kinds of garments in the mall. 購物中心有很多商店出售各種衣服。

gasp [ɡæsp] 🔊 *Track 4641*
名 喘息、喘 動 喘氣說、喘著氣息
▶名 The patient is nearly at his last gasp.
那位病人幾乎是奄奄一息了。
▶動 The man sits there gasping desperately for breath.
那個男人坐在那裡拚命喘氣。

gath·er·ing [ˈɡæðərɪŋ] 🔊 *Track 4642*
名 集會、聚集
▶We are not assembling; we are having a small social gathering.
我們不是在集會；我們是一個小型社交聚會。

萬用延伸句型
be gathering dust 收集灰塵，也就是放了很久都沒有使用的意思。
例 如：The computer doesn't work anymore, so it's just sitting there gathering dust.
這台電腦已經不能用了，於是它就一直待在那裡收集灰塵。

gay [ɡe] 🔊 *Track 4643*
名 同性戀的 形 快樂的、快活的 反 sad 悲傷的
▶名 I didn't realize that Joey was a gay.
我沒發覺喬伊是同性戀。
▶形 I have lots of gay friends. 我有很多同性戀朋友。

gen·der [ˈdʒɛndɚ] 🔊 *Track 4644*
名 性別 同 sex 性別
▶Don't you think some majors have a gender bias（偏見）？
難道你不覺得某些主修科目存在性別偏見嗎？

Level 1
Level 2
Level 3
Level 4
Level 5
擴增實力5400單字 突飛猛進、程度大進擊
Level 6

ge·o·graph·i·cal [ˌdʒiə` græfɪkļ] ◀ Track 4645

形 地理學的、地理的
▶People can know each other quickly（很快地）even if they are in different geographical regions.
儘管人們處在不同的地理區域，但是他們也能很快的知道彼此的事情。

ge·om·e·try [dʒɪ`ɑmətrɪ] ◀ Track 4646

名 幾何學
▶Geometry and algebra are quite difficult to me.
幾何學和代數對我來說很難。

gla·cier [`gleʃɚ] ◀ Track 4647

名 冰河
▶A glacier is a moving mass of snow and ice.
冰河是一大片會移動的雪和冰。

glare [glɛr] ◀ Track 4648

名 怒視、瞪眼 動 怒視瞪眼
▶名 Susan looked at him with an angry glare.
蘇珊生氣地瞪著他。
▶動 I saw my sister glaring at my father.
我看見妹妹正瞪著爸爸。

gleam [glim] ◀ Track 4649

名 一絲光線 動 閃現、閃爍
▶名 Don't you see the gleam of a lamp ahead? Maybe we can find someone there. 難道你沒看到前面的燈光嗎？也許我們可以在那裡找到人。
▶動 The lights of the little town are gleaming in the distance.
遠處小鎮有燈光在閃爍。

文法字詞解析
gleam 和 glitter 雖然都有「光」的意思，但用法卻不太相同，gleam 通常是平滑表面上發光的樣子（例如：gleaming white teeth），glitter 則是大量小光點構成閃閃發光的樣子（the glittering frost）。

glee [gli] ◀ Track 4650

名 喜悅、高興 同 joy 高興
▶The little girl clapped her hands in glee. 小女孩喜悅地拍著手。

glit·ter [`glɪtɚ] ◀ Track 4651

名 光輝、閃光、華麗 動 閃爍、閃亮 同 sparkle 閃爍
▶名 It won't be long before she sees through the gloss（虛假的表面）and glitter of Hollywood.
不久她就會看透好萊塢的虛榮與繁華。
▶動 The diamond ring is glittering on her finger.
鑽戒在她的手指上閃閃發亮。

文法字詞解析
小朋友做美勞很喜歡用的那種很難洗掉的「亮粉」也稱為 glitter。

gloom [glum] ◀ Track 4652

名 陰暗、昏暗 動 幽暗、憂鬱 同 shadow 陰暗處
▶名 It was difficult for me to see anything distinctly（清楚地）in the gloom. 我在昏暗之中什麼東西都看不清。
▶動 His life is filled with gloom since he lost his job.
自從失業之後，他的生活就充滿悲傷。

gnaw [nɔ]
🔊 Track 4653

動 咬、噬 同 bite 咬
▶The cheese has been gnawed by a mouse.
這乳酪已被老鼠咬過了。

gob·ble [ˈgɑbl̩]
🔊 Track 4654

動 大口猛吃、狼吞虎嚥 同 devour 狼吞虎嚥
▶The vagrant gobbled up the food he received by a passer-by.
流浪漢大口吞下行人給他的食物。

gorge [gɔrdʒ]
🔊 Track 4655

名 岩崖、山峽、隘道 動 狼吞虎嚥
▶名 There is a deep gorge separating the two halves of the city.
有一道深谷把這座城市分成了兩部分。
▶動 The hungry boy gorged on turkey.
那個餓壞了的男孩大吃火雞。

gor·geous [ˈgɔrdʒəs]
🔊 Track 4656

形 炫麗的、華麗的、極好的 同 splendid 壯麗的
▶What a gorgeous day it is today! Why don't we have a picnic?
今天天氣多好啊！為什麼不去野餐呢？

go·ril·la [gəˈrɪlə]
🔊 Track 4657

名 大猩猩
▶How can a monkey be more powerful than a gorilla?
猴子怎麼可能比猩猩更強大呢？

gos·pel [ˈgɑspl̩]
🔊 Track 4658

名 福音、信條
▶I don't think you should take his words as gospel.
我認為你不該把他的話當作信條。

萬用延伸句型
the gospel truth 千真萬確的事實
例如：You shouldn't just accept whatever
your professor says as the gospel truth.
你不能把你教授講過的話都當作無法推
翻的事實。

grant [grænt]
🔊 Track 4659

名 許可、授與 動 答應、允許、轉讓（財產） 同 permit 允許
▶名 Will you tell me when we can get the grant from the government?
請你告訴我，我們何時可以得到政府的許可？
▶動 He was granted with a chance to join the delegation.
他被賦予參加代表團的機會。

grav·i·ty [ˈgrævətɪ]
🔊 Track 4660

名 重力、嚴重性
▶The reason why you can't walk on the moon is that it lacks gravity. 你無法在月球行走的原因是它的引力不夠。

graze [grez]
🔊 Track 4661

動 吃草、畜牧
▶The sheep were grazing in the meadow, while a shepherd dog watched them.
羊群在草原上吃草，有隻牧羊犬看著他們。

Level 1
Level 2
Level 3
Level 4
Level 5
擴增實力5400單字 突飛猛進、程度大進擊
Level 6

grease [gris]　◀ Track 4662

名 油脂、獸脂　動 討好、塗脂、用油脂潤滑

▶名 You won't get the grease off the plates even if you use this soap. 即使你用這個肥皂，你也洗不掉盤子上的油膩。

▶動 He greases the machine very carefully（仔細地）every day even though they don't ask him to.
即使他們沒叫他做，他也會每天都很仔細地為機器加潤滑油。

greed [grid]　◀ Track 4663

名 貪心、貪婪

▶The official was involved in the bribery case out of greed.
這名官員因為貪心而涉入賄絡案。

grim [grɪm]　◀ Track 4664

形 嚴格的、糟糕的　同 stern 嚴格的

▶It is obvious that the climate here can be pretty grim in winter.
顯然這裡的冬天相當寒冷。

grip [grɪp]　◀ Track 4665

名 緊握、抓住　動 緊握、扣住　反 release 鬆開

▶名 He never loosened his grip on the rope.
他一直緊握著繩子沒有放開。

▶動 She gripped his hand when she heard the strange sound.
她聽到那奇怪的聲音時緊緊抓住了他的手。

groan [gron]　◀ Track 4666

名 哼著說、呻吟　動 呻吟、哼聲　同 moan 呻吟

▶名 You can hear the man's groans from here.
你從這裡都能聽到那個男人的呻吟聲。

▶動 The sick woman groaned all day long.
那個生病的女子呻吟了一整天。

gross [gros]　◀ Track 4667

名 總體　動 獲得……總收入　形 粗略的、臃腫的　同 total 總數

▶名 The manager says that the goods are to be sold only by the gross.
經理說這些貨物只能成批出售。

▶動 The firm grossed $5 million last year.
該公司去年獲得五百萬美元毛利。

▶形 The gross income of the company has been increasing steadily.
公司的收入快速增加。

growl [graʊl]　◀ Track 4668

名 咆哮聲、吠聲　動 咆哮著說、咆哮　同 snarl 咆哮

▶名 Didn't you hear the growl? You'd better leave the dog alone.
你沒聽見狗吠聲嗎？你最好別惹這條狗。

▶動 The man growled at his wife.
那個男人對他太太咆哮。

文法字詞解析

兩句例句分別用了 even if 與 even though 兩個句型。兩者都是「即使」的意思，但它們之間還是有差別喔！even if 帶有假設的含意，even though 則沒有假設的含意。舉例來說，如果說「I wouldn't say yes even if he cried」，就表示「就算他哭，我也不會同意」（他其實沒哭，說話者只是假設這個情境）；「I didn't say yes even though he cried」則是「雖然他哭了，我還是沒同意」（他真的有哭）。

文法字詞解析

此外，gross 也有「噁心的」的意思。如果你朋友忽然沒事放了一個很多汁的屁，就可以跟他說一句「gross!」。

grum·ble [ˈɡrʌmbl̩] 🔊 *Track 4669*

名 牢騷、不高興 動 抱怨、發牢騷 同 complain 抱怨

▶名 Tell me all your grumbles. I'm a good listener.
把你的滿腹牢騷都跟我說吧，我是個很好的傾聽者。

▶動 She grumbled about the casual attitude of the clerks.
她抱怨店員愛理不理的態度。

guide·line [ˈɡaɪd͵laɪn] 🔊 *Track 4670*

名 指導方針、指標

▶Nothing is more effective than this guideline.
沒有東西比這個指導方針更有效的了。

gulp [ɡʌlp] 🔊 *Track 4671*

名 滿滿一口 動 牛飲、吞飲

▶名 I took a gulp of the milk.
我喝了滿滿一口牛奶。

▶動 The boy was gulping for air after holding his breath for two minutes.
那個男孩在憋氣兩分鐘後大口地吸著氣。

gust [ɡʌst] 🔊 *Track 4672*

名 一陣狂風 動 吹狂風 同 blast 疾風

▶名 A gust of wind blew the door shut just now.
剛才一陣大風吹來，把門給關上了。

▶動 The wind will gust up to 35 miles an hour.
風速即將達每小時三十五英里。

gut(s) [ɡʌt(s)] 🔊 *Track 4673*

名 內臟、腸

▶He vomited his guts out after riding the roller coaster.
他在坐雲霄飛車後，吐得快把腸子都吐出來了。

gyp·sy [ˈdʒɪpsɪ] 🔊 *Track 4674*

名 吉普賽人 形 吉普賽人的

▶名 I had a gypsy predict my future.
我請一個吉普賽人幫我算命。

▶形 He'd always wanted to live a gypsy life.
他總是夢想著過著吉普賽式的生活。

[Hh]

hail [hel] 🔊 *Track 4675*

名 歡呼、雹 動 歡呼 同 cheer 歡呼

▶名 The hail damaged several houses.
那陣冰雹毀損了不少房子。

▶動 A crowd of supporters hailed for the candidate.
一群支持者為候選人歡呼。

萬用延伸句型
gulp sth. down 大口吞下（某物）
例如：He ran in, gulped down his soda, and ran out again.
他跑進來，大口喝下汽水，然後又跑了出去。

Level 1
Level 2
Level 3
Level 4
Level 5
Level 6

突飛猛進、程度大進擊——擴增實力5400單字

hair·style/hair·do

Track 4676

[ˋhɛrˌstaɪl]/[ˋhɛrˌdu]

名 髮型

▶What do you think of my new hairstyle?
你覺得我的新髮型怎麼樣？

hand·i·cap [ˋhændɪˌkæp]

Track 4677

名 障礙、吃虧 動 妨礙、吃虧、使不利

▶名 Being short is a handicap in a crowd like this.
在這樣一群人中，個子小很吃虧。

▶動 He was handicapped with his humble background.
他因為出生貧微而發展受阻。

hand·i·craft [ˋhændɪˌkræft]

Track 4678

名 手工藝品 同 craft 工藝

▶It's hard for me to pick between the two handicraft articles.
我很難從這兩件工藝品中挑選一個。

har·dy [ˋhardɪ]

Track 4679

形 強健的、能吃苦耐勞的 同 sturdy 強健的

▶Both their children are quite hardy.
他們的兩個孩子都非常能吃苦耐勞。

har·ness [ˋharnɪs]

Track 4680

名 馬具 動 裝上馬具、利用、治理

▶名 A bridle is a kind of harness.
馬勒是一種馬具。

▶動 I am afraid it will take several years to harness that river.
恐怕治理那條河流要花好幾年的時間。

haul [hɔl]

Track 4681

名 用力拖拉、一次獲得的量 動 拖、使勁拉
同 drag 拖、拉

▶名 We brought back a big haul of fish.
我們捕了一大網魚回來。

▶動 Fine, let's just haul out our swords and start fighting.
好，讓我們都拔出劍來開始戰鬥吧！

haunt [hɔnt]

Track 4682

名 常到的場所 動 出現、常到（某地）

▶名 This coffee shop is one of his haunts.
這家咖啡館是他經常出入的地方。

▶動 It is said that the deserted house was haunted by evil spirits.
據說廢棄的房子裡有鬧鬼。

heart·y [ˋhartɪ]

Track 4683

形 親切的、熱心的 反 cold 冷淡的

▶Would you please accept my hearty congratulations on your wedding?
請接受我對你們婚禮的最熱烈祝賀好嗎？

文法字詞解析

hairstyle 和 hairdo 的不同點在於，就算你什麼都不做也可以稱為 hairstyle（畢竟把長髮放下來不綁也是一種「髮型」）；而需要在頭髮上動手腳（綁起來、夾起來、噴髮膠等）才能稱為 hairdo。

萬用延伸句型

take several years to... 花好幾年（做某事）

heav·en·ly [ˈhɛvənlɪ]　🔊 *Track 4684*

形 天空的、天國的

▶It is definitely a heavenly place of rest and tranquility（寧靜）.
　那的確是一個寧靜的天堂，是個休息的好地方。

hedge [hɛdʒ]　🔊 *Track 4685*

名 樹籬、籬笆　動 制定界線、圍住

▶名 There is an opening in the hedge.
　那個籬笆上有個洞。

▶動 There are low hills hedging the town.
　這座城鎮的四周圍有低山環繞。

heed [hid]　🔊 *Track 4686*

名 留心、注意　動 留心、注意　同 notice 注意

▶名 It is obvious that a good leader should always pay heed to the voice of the masses.
　顯然一位好領導應該經常注意傾聽群眾的聲音。

▶動 Residents are advised to heed the evacuation order.
　居民應該要聽從撤離的命令。

height·en [ˈhaɪtn̩]　🔊 *Track 4687*

動 增高、加高　反 lower 放低

▶As she waited, her excitement heightened. 她越等就越興奮。

heir [ɛr]　🔊 *Track 4688*

名 繼承人

▶It is said that he is the only legal heir of the rich man.
　據說他是這位富翁的唯一法定繼承人。

hence [hɛns]　🔊 *Track 4689*

副 因此　同 therefore 因此

▶She is a musician, hence her interest in the details of the concert.
　她是個音樂家，所以她才會對那場音樂會的細節這麼有興趣。

文法字詞解析
除了 hence 之外，在寫作中也可以用「therefore」、「thus」等字來表達因果關係。

her·ald [ˈhɛrəld]　🔊 *Track 4690*

名 通報者、使者　動 宣示、公告　同 messenger 使者

▶名 In England the cuckoo（杜鵑鳥）is the herald of spring.
　在英國，杜鵑鳥預示春天的來臨。

▶動 In any event, they will herald the final result.
　在任何情況下，他們都將公告最終結果。

萬用延伸句型
in any event... 無論如何……

herb [ɝb]　🔊 *Track 4691*

名 草本植物

▶There are many herbs that are used in traditional Chinese medicine. 傳統中醫裡會使用很多種草藥。

her·mit [ˈhɝmɪt]　🔊 *Track 4692*

名 隱士、隱居者

▶The hermit concealed his real identity and isolated himself.
　隱士隱藏身分並且孤立自己。

Level 1
Level 2
Level 3
Level 4
Level 5
突飛猛進、程度大進擊──擴增實力5400單字
Level 6

he·ro·ic [hɪˈroɪk]
🔊 *Track 4693*

名 史詩 形 英雄的、勇士的 反 cowardly 懦弱的

▶名 The heroics he wrote became very popular after his death.
他過世後,他寫的史詩變得很受歡迎。

▶形 His heroic deeds was applauded by his supervisor.
他的英雄行為受到主管的讚賞。

het·er·o·sex·u·al [ˌhɛtərəˈsɛkʃʊəl]
🔊 *Track 4694*

名 異性戀者 形 異性戀的 反 homosexual 同性戀

▶名 I don't think that the heterosexuals should discriminate against the homosexuals.
我認為異性戀者不應該歧視同性戀者。

▶形 The heterosexual girl was sad because she fell in love with a gay boy.
那個異性戀的女孩因為愛上了同性戀的男孩而傷心。

hi-fi/high fi·del·i·ty [ˈhaɪˈfaɪ]/[ˈhaɪ fɪˈdɛlətɪ]
🔊 *Track 4695*

名 高傳真(靈敏度)音響

▶I' m thinking of buying a hi-fi unit. Any recommendations?
我正在考慮買一套高靈敏度的音響設備。你有推薦的嗎?

文法字詞解析
unit 在這裡不是「單位」的意思,而是指「一套設備」。

hi·jack [ˈhaɪˌdʒæk]
🔊 *Track 4696*

名 搶劫、劫機 動 劫奪

▶名 I'm afraid that the hijack might be organized by a group of terrorists. 這次劫持事件恐怕是由恐怖組織規劃的。

▶動 They are planning to hijack an airliner.
他們正在計畫劫持班機。

hiss [hɪs]
🔊 *Track 4697*

名 噓聲 動 發噓聲

▶名 He rushed in and turned the gas off as soon as he heard the hiss. 一聽到瓦斯外洩的噓噓聲,他就衝進來把它關掉了。

▶動 The snake hissed at the rat. 那條蛇向那隻老鼠發出噓噓聲。

hoarse [hors]
🔊 *Track 4698*

形 (嗓音)刺耳的、沙啞的

▶His voice got hoarse because of smoking.
他的聲音因為抽菸而變得沙啞。

文法字詞解析
cough oneself hoarse 是「咳到自己都沙啞了」的意思;以此類推,「yell oneself hoarse」、「shout oneself hoarse」是「喊到自己都沙啞了」的意思。

hock·ey [ˈhɑkɪ]
🔊 *Track 4699*

名 曲棍球

▶They got the silver medal in women's field hockey.
她們奪得了一面女子曲棍球銀牌。

ho·mo·sex·u·al [ˌhoməˈsɛkʃʊəl]
🔊 *Track 4700*

名 同性戀者 形 同性戀的

▶名 Two out of three of my cousins are homosexuals.
我的三個堂哥中有兩個是同性戀。

▶形 What do you think about the discrimination against homosexual people? 你如何看待對同性戀者的歧視?

honk [hɔŋk]
🔊 *Track 4701*

名 雁鳴、汽車喇叭聲 動 雁鳴叫、發出汽車喇叭聲

▶名 He woke us with a honk of his car horn.
他按一下汽車的喇叭把我們叫醒。

▶動 The bus driver honked the horn at the pedestrian.
公車司機對行人按喇叭。

hood [hʊd]
🔊 *Track 4702*

名 罩、蓋 動 掩蔽、覆蓋 反 uncover 揭露

▶名 Let's lift the engine hood and take a look.
我們把引擎蓋打開來檢查一下吧。

▶動 The man was hooded and therefore I couldn't see his face.
那個男人遮著臉，我看不到他的臉。

hoof [huf]
🔊 *Track 4703*

名 蹄 動 用蹄踢、步行

▶名 I'm afraid that there's something wrong with the horse's hooves.
恐怕這匹馬的蹄出了什麼毛病。

▶動 I'm afraid that the last bus had gone so we had to hoof it home.
末班公車恐怕已經開走了，我們只好走路回家了。

文法字詞解析
hoof 的複數為 hooves。

hor·i·zon·tal [ˌhɑrəˈzɑntl̩]
🔊 *Track 4704*

名 水平線 形 水準線、水平面、地平線的 反 vertical 垂直的

▶名 I drew a vertical line and he drew a horizontal.
我畫了一條垂直的線，他畫了一條水平線。

▶形 Do you see the horizontal line on your book? Now draw another one above it.
你有看到書上這條水平的線嗎？現在請你在它上方再畫一條線。

hos·tage [ˈhɑstɪdʒ]
🔊 *Track 4705*

名 人質 同 captive 俘虜

▶More than 60 foreigners have been taken hostage in recent months in Iraq.
最近幾個月來，超過六十名外國人在伊拉克遭到挾持成為人質。

hos·tile [ˈhɑstɪl]
🔊 *Track 4706*

形 敵方的、不友善的

▶Avoid hostile language when negotiating with others.
和別人協商時，要避免刻薄的言語。。

hound [haʊnd]
🔊 *Track 4707*

名 獵犬、有癮的人 動 追逐、追獵 同 hunt 打獵

▶名 My sister is a crazy movie hound.
我妹妹是個瘋狂的影迷。

▶動 He has been hounded by his creditors（債主）in the past few months.
近幾個月來，他一直被債主追債。

文法字詞解析
非常希望得到矚目、為了得到注目而刻意做很多誇張事情的人可稱為 publicity hound。

Level 1

Level 2

Level 3

Level 4

Level 5

Level 6

擴增實力5400單字 突飛猛進、程度大進擊

hous·ing [ˈhaʊzɪŋ]
Track 4708

名 住宅的供給、住宅
▶There are hundreds of people who need new housing.
有許多人需要新的住宅。

hov·er [ˈhʌvɚ]
Track 4709

名 徘徊、翱翔 動 翱翔、盤旋
▶名 A helicopter is in hover above the house. No wonder there's so much noise!
有一架直昇機在房子上方盤旋。難怪那麼吵！
▶動 The jet plane hovered around the airport before it could be allowed to land.
飛機被准許降落前，在機場上空盤旋。

howl [haʊl]
Track 4710

名 吠聲、怒號 動 吼叫、怒號 同 shout 喊叫
▶名 The little girl let out a howl all of a sudden.
那個小女孩突然嚎啕大哭。
▶動 The dog was howling over its master's dead body.
那隻狗對著主人的屍體哀嚎。

hurl [hɝl]
Track 4711

名 投 動 投擲 同 fling 丟、擲
▶名 It is said that his perfect hurl got him the championship.
據說是他完美的投擲使他得了冠軍。
▶動 It is said that the best way to forget your sadness is to hurl yourself into your work.
據說忘掉悲傷最好的方法是讓自己投入工作之中。

hymn [hɪm]
Track 4712

名 讚美詩 動 唱讚美詩讚美 同 carol 讚美詩
▶名 I can hear the hymn from the nearby church.
我能聽到從附近的教堂傳來的聖歌。
▶動 The old ladies are hymning together.
那些老太太正在一起唱聖歌。

[Ii]

id·i·ot [ˈɪdɪət]
Track 4713

名 傻瓜、笨蛋 同 fool 傻瓜
▶Are you an idiot? Cats don't grow on trees!
你是白癡嗎？貓才不是長在樹上！

im·mense [ɪˈmɛns]
Track 4714

形 巨大的、極大的 反 tiny 極小的
▶With immense relief, I stopped peaking out of the window.
因為大大地鬆了一口氣，我就不再望窗外看。

文法字詞解析
在某人的背後不斷晃來晃去（通常要偷看他在幹嘛）的這個動作可稱為 hover behind sb.。

文法字詞解析
如果說某個東西是「idiot-proof」的，就表示那個東西操作起來非常簡單，不管再怎麼傻的人都會。
例如：This cell phone comes with idiot-proof instructions, so it's very easy to use.
這支手機附有讓傻瓜也能懂的指示，所以使用起來非常簡單。

im·pe·ri·al [ɪm`pɪrɪəl]
🔊 *Track 4715*

形 帝國的、至高的 同 supreme 至高的

▶There are many ways for you to get to the Imperial Theater.
到帝國戲院有很多條路。

im·pose [ɪm`poz]
🔊 *Track 4716*

動 徵收、佔便宜、欺騙

▶The authorities imposed a ban on smoking in public places.
當局實施公共場所全面禁菸。

im·pulse [`ɪmpʌls]
🔊 *Track 4717*

名 衝動

▶Don't you think my uncle bought the house on an impulse?
難道你不覺得我叔叔是一時衝動才買下了那間房子嗎？

文法字詞解析
能夠控制自己衝動的「控制力」叫做
impulse control。

in·cense [`ɪnsɛns]
🔊 *Track 4718*

名 芳香、香 動 激怒、焚香 同 provoke 激怒

▶名 I smelled incense as soon as I entered the shrine.
我一進到神社裡，就聞到香的味道。

▶動 Why was she incensed at his behavior yesterday?
她昨天為什麼對他的行為感到很憤怒？

in·dex [`ɪndɛks]
🔊 *Track 4719*

名 指數、索引 動 編索引

▶名 I am afraid that the new colleague knows nothing about the Dow Jones Index.
新來的那個同事恐怕對道瓊指數一點都不瞭解。

▶動 I don't think the places mentioned are carefully indexed.
我覺得被提到的地名並沒有被仔細地編入索引中。

in·dif·fer·ence [ɪn`dɪfərəns]
🔊 *Track 4720*

名 不關心、不在乎
反 concern 關心

▶Not everyone present can feel his indifference at the party.
不是每個在場的人都能感覺到他在宴會上的冷淡。

in·dif·fer·ent [ɪn`dɪfərənt]
🔊 *Track 4721*

形 中立的、不關心的

▶How can you be so indifferent to what is going on in the surroundings? 你怎麼能對周遭的事物如此的冷漠？

in·dig·nant [ɪn`dɪgnənt]
🔊 *Track 4722*

形 憤怒的

▶He was indignant when his mom accused him of lying.
他媽媽說他說謊時，他非常惱怒。

in·dis·pen·sa·ble
🔊 *Track 4723*

[ˌɪndɪ`spɛnsəbl]

形 不可缺少的 同 essential 不可缺少的

▶Our textbook is an indispensable reference for the report.
我們的教科書是這篇報告不可或缺的參考資料。

文法字詞解析
相反地，拿掉表示「不、無」的字首
「in-」，變成 dispensable，意思就變成
「可以丟棄的」、「不重要的」。

Level 1
Level 2
Level 3
Level 4
Level 5

擴增實力5400單字 突飛猛進、程度大進擊

Level 6

in·duce [ɪnˋdjus]
🔊 *Track 4724*

動 引誘、引起
▶Nothing in the world will induce me to do that.
什麼都不能引誘我做那種事。

in·dulge [ɪnˋdʌldʒ]
🔊 *Track 4725*

動 沉溺、放縱、遷就
▶I love sweets, but I don't often indulge myself.
我喜歡甜食，但是不會過度放縱。

in·fi·nite [ˋɪnfənɪt]
🔊 *Track 4726*

形 無限的
▶It was the war that brought infinite harm to the nation.
正是這場戰爭給這個國家帶來了無窮的災難。

in·her·it [ɪnˋhɛrɪt]
🔊 *Track 4727*

動 繼承、接受
▶It doesn't matter if you can't inherit a fortune from your parents. You can earn a lot by yourself. 你無法從父母那繼承到財產也沒什麼大不了。你可以靠自己賺很多錢。

萬用延伸句型
It doesn't matter if... 就算……也沒關係

i·ni·ti·ate [ɪˋnɪʃɪɪt]/[ɪˋnɪʃɪet]
🔊 *Track 4728*

名 初學者 動 開始、創始 形 新加入的 同 begin 開始
▶名 He's an initiate into the world of politics.
他是個剛進入世界政壇的人。
▶動 He initiated a conversation with the magnate on the lencheon. 他在午餐會上，向一位商業巨擘搭話。
▶形 The initiate member of the team is still young.
隊伍新加入的成員還很年輕。

in·land [ˋɪnlənd]
🔊 *Track 4729*

名 內陸 副 在內陸 形 內陸的
▶名 The population of the inland is growing faster than we imagined. 內陸人口增長得比我們想像中的快。
▶副 Will you travel inland with me? 你願意和我一起去內地旅行嗎？
▶形 The economy of the inland areas has developed faster than that of coastal（沿海的）areas these years.
近幾年內地經濟發展得比沿海要快。

in·nu·mer·a·ble [ɪnˋnjumərəbl̩]
🔊 *Track 4730*

形 數不盡的
▶I hope this technological innovation（創新）would bring innumerable benefits to us.
我希望這項技術創新能給我們帶來無窮的好處。

in·quire [ɪnˋkwaɪr]
🔊 *Track 4731*

動 詢問、調查
▶Our client called to inquire when the products would be delivered.
我們的顧客打電話來問，產品何時會寄出。

萬用延伸句型
本句後半是間接問句 "when + S + V"，作為 inquire 的受詞。

in·sti·tute [ˈɪnstətjut]
🔊 *Track 4732*

名 協會、機構 動 設立、授職 同 organization 機構

▶名 The institute obtain its fund from donations of local enterprises.
這家公司由一家本地企業的捐款獲得資金。

▶動 There is a necessity for us to institute a rational（合理的）welfare system.
我們有必要設立一個合理的福利制度。

in·sure [ɪnˈʃʊr]
🔊 *Track 4733*

動 投保、確保

▶I prefer to insure with this company instead of putting my money in the bank.
我寧願向這家公司投保，也不願意把錢放在銀行。

in·tent [ɪnˈtɛnt]
🔊 *Track 4734*

名 意圖、意思 形 熱心的、急切的、專心致志的

▶名 The terrorist carried a homemade bomb with intent to endanger life.
恐怖分子在背包裡裝著炸彈，意圖危害人命。

▶形 The merchant was intent on making money.
那名商人非常專注於賺錢。

in·ter·fer·ence [ˌɪntɚˈfɪrəns]
🔊 *Track 4735*

名 妨礙、干擾

▶There is so much interference that I can't listen to the radio.
干擾太大以致於我無法聽收音機。

in·te·ri·or [ɪnˈtɪrɪɚ]
🔊 *Track 4736*

名 內部、內務 形 內部的 反 exterior 外部

▶名 It is the first time that we have found water in the interior of the cave. 我們還是第一次發現山洞的內部有水。

▶形 The website displays the exterior of the house rather than the interior look.
這個網站展示房子的外觀而不是裡面的布置。

文法字詞解析
Interior 還有一個延伸出來的字義，就是跟國家內部有關的事務。所以 Department of the Interior 就是一個國家的「內政部」。

in·ter·pre·ta·tion
🔊 *Track 4737*
[ɪnˌtɝprɪˈteʃən]

名 解釋、說明 同 explanation 解釋

▶What do you think about his interpretation of this passage?
對於他對這段文章的解釋，你認為如何呢？

in·ter·pret·er [ɪnˈtɝprɪtɚ]
🔊 *Track 4738*

名 解釋者、翻譯員

▶Would you like me to arrange for an interpreter to be present, sir? 先生，要不要我幫你安排一位口譯員在場呢？

in·tu·i·tion [ˌɪntjuˈɪʃən]
🔊 *Track 4739*

名 直覺 同 hunch 直覺

▶I have an intuition that she was involved in this bribery case.
我有個直覺，她有涉入這個賄賂案中。

Level 1

Level 2

Level 3

Level 4

Level 5

突飛猛進、程度大進擊——擴增實力5400單字

Level 6

in·ward [`ɪnwəd]
🔊 *Track 4740*

形 裡面的 副 向內、內心裡 反 outward 向外

▶形 The fence tilted in an inward direction.
圍牆往內傾斜。

▶副 The door opens inward into the room. 門是朝房間裡面開的。

in·wards [`ɪnwədz]
🔊 *Track 4741*

副 向內

▶Will you tell me whether the windows in our new house open inwards or outwards?
你能告訴我我們新房子裡的窗戶是朝裡開還是朝外開的嗎？

isle [aɪl]
🔊 *Track 4742*

名 島 同 island 島

▶It doesn't matter if you don't know the locations of the British Isles. 你不知道不列顛群島的位置也沒關係。

is·sue [`ɪʃjʊ]
🔊 *Track 4743*

名 議題 動 發出、發行

▶名 Do you accept the professor's views on the environmental issues? 你接受教授在環境議題上的那些觀點嗎？

▶動 Will you tell me when the post office will issue the stamps? 你能告訴我郵局何時將發行這些郵票嗎？

i·vy [`aɪvɪ]
🔊 *Track 4744*

名 常春藤

▶Ivy covered the exterior wall of the deserted house.
常春藤覆蓋住這廢棄房屋的外牆。

文法字詞解析
眾所周知的常春藤名校就稱為 Ivy League。

[Jj]

jack [dʒæk]
🔊 *Track 4745*

名 起重機、千斤頂 動 用起重機舉起

▶名 I'm afraid that you need an automobile jack to lift the car before repairing it.
恐怕在修汽車前你得用千斤頂把汽車抬起來。

▶動 Help me jack up this huge machine.
幫我把這個大型機器用起重機吊起來。

jade [dʒed]
🔊 *Track 4746*

名 玉、玉石

▶The bracelet is made of jade. 這個手環是玉做的。

jan·i·tor [`dʒænɪtə]
🔊 *Track 4747*

名 管門者、看門者

▶The school janitor pointed the direction to the principal's office for me.
學校的管理員幫我指向校長的辦公室。

jas·mine [ˈdʒæsmɪn]　🔊 Track 4748

名 茉莉

▶Would you like to try the jasmine tea? It tastes good.
你想試試茉莉花茶嗎？它味道還不錯。

jay·walk [ˈdʒeˌwɔk]　🔊 Track 4749

動 不守交通規則穿越街道

▶It's possible that you may get a ticket for jaywalking.
你可能會因為隨意穿越馬路而吃上罰單。

jeer [dʒɪr]　🔊 Track 4750

動 戲弄、嘲笑　同 mock 嘲笑

▶It's very unkind of you to jeer at the person who came last in the race. 你嘲笑賽跑中跑在最後的人是很不友善的。

jin·gle [ˈdʒɪŋgl̩]　🔊 Track 4751

名 叮鈴聲、節拍十分規則的簡單詩歌　動 使發出鈴聲

▶名 The bells made a jingle when I opened the door.
開門時，鈴鐺發出了叮噹聲。

▶動 Would you please stop jingling your keys like that?
請你不要把鑰匙弄得叮噹亂響好嗎？

> **萬用延伸句型**
> Would you please stop + V-ing? 可以請你不要……嗎？

jol·ly [ˈdʒɑlɪ]　🔊 Track 4752

動 開玩笑、慫恿　形 幽默的、快活的、興高采烈的　副 非常地
反 melancholy 憂鬱的

▶動 Let's jolly her into going with us, shall we?
我們慫恿她跟我們一起去吧，怎麼樣？

▶形 The hostess greeted the visitors with a jolly smile.
女主人帶著微笑招呼客人。

▶副 He's going to be a jolly tough candidate to beat.
他會是個很難擊敗的選手。

jour·nal·ism [ˈdʒɝnl̩ˌɪzəm]　🔊 Track 4753

名 新聞學、新聞業

▶After he left school, he took up journalism.
他畢業離校後從事了新聞業。

jour·nal·ist [ˈdʒɝnl̩ɪst]　🔊 Track 4754

名 新聞工作者

▶A freelance political journalist shared her adventurous stories with me. 有位自由政治記者和我分享他的冒險故事。

jug [dʒʌg]　🔊 Track 4755

名 帶柄的水壺

▶He poured the milk into a jug.
他把牛奶灌進了壺裡。

> **文法字詞解析**
> jug 通常是指大小比較大的水壺，可以用來裝水、牛奶、果汁等。一般喝熱茶用的比較小的茶壺則不會稱為 jug。

ju·ry [ˈdʒʊrɪ]　🔊 Track 4756

名 陪審團

▶It is a surprise that the jury found the prisoner not guilty.
陪審團判定囚犯無罪，這真令人驚訝。

Level 1
Level 2
Level 3
Level 4
Level 5
Level 6

突飛猛進、程度大進擊──擴增實力5400單字

jus·ti·fy [ˈdʒʌstəˌfaɪ] ◀≡ *Track 4757*

動 證明……有理
▶She thinks that she justifies taking another day off work.
她認為她再休一天假是合理的。

ju·ve·nile [ˈdʒuvənḷ] ◀≡ *Track 4758*

名 青少年、孩子 形 青少年的、孩子氣的
▶名 How to sentence juveniles has always been a controversial topic in law.
如何判決青少年一直是法律上一個有爭議的問題。
▶形 I'm afraid that he'll ultimately（最終）become a juvenile delinquent（行為不良的人）.
恐怕他最終會成為一名青少年罪犯。

joy·ous [ˈdʒɔɪəs] ◀≡ *Track 4759*

形 歡喜的、高興的
▶Why don't we convey the joyous news to her as soon as possible?
為什麼不儘快告訴她這一個令人歡喜的消息呢？

#

kin [kɪn] ◀≡ *Track 4760*

名 親族、親戚 形 有親戚關係的 同 relative 親戚
▶名 We informed his next of kin about his injury.
我們通知他的親屬有關他的傷勢的情形。
▶形 He is kin to me, so we cannot marry.
他是我的親戚，所以我們無法結婚。

文法字詞解析
你的 next of kin 即與你血緣關係最近、且目前在世的親屬。

kin·dle [ˈkɪndḷ] ◀≡ *Track 4761*

動 生火、起火
▶Do you know how to kindle a fire? 你知道怎麼點火嗎？

knowl·edge·a·ble [ˈnɑlɪdʒəbḷ] ◀≡ *Track 4762*

形 博學的
▶My teacher majored in music at college. It is no wonder that he is very knowledgeable about music. 我的老師大學時學的是音樂。怪不得他在音樂方面的知識很豐富。

[Ll]

lad [læd] ◀≡ *Track 4763*

名 少年、老友
▶A group of young lads gathered in front of the police office.
有一群少年聚集在警察局外面。

lame [lem]
🔊 *Track 4764*

形 跛的、站不住腳的

▶That is a lame excuse. You could do better.
那不是一個充分的藉口，你還可以想一個更好的藉口。

land·la·dy [ˈlændˌledɪ]
🔊 *Track 4765*

名 女房東

▶I'm afraid my landlady wouldn't allow us to do that.
恐怕我的房東太太不會允許我們那麼做的。

land·lord [ˈlændˌlɔrd]
🔊 *Track 4766*

名 房東、主人、老闆

▶The landlord wouldn't let me keep a cat.
房東不讓我養貓。

la·ser [ˈlezɚ]
🔊 *Track 4767*

名 雷射

▶The laser beam can help you get rid of nearsightedness painlessly. 雷射光可以幫你無痛治療近視。

文法字詞解析

laser 其實是 light amplification by stimulated emission of radiation（通過受激輻射產生的光放大）的縮寫。

lat·i·tude [ˈlætəˌtjud]
🔊 *Track 4768*

名 緯度 反 longitude 經度

▶It is obvious that the two cities are at approximately（大約）the same latitude.
顯然這兩個城市差不多位於同一緯度上。

law·mak·er [ˈlɔˌmekɚ]
🔊 *Track 4769*

名 立法者

▶We need to bring this issue to the lawmakers' attention.
我們得讓立法者注意到這件事。

lay·er [ˈleɚ]
🔊 *Track 4770*

名 層 動 分層

▶名 The pollution had affected the ozone layer.
污染影響了臭氧層。

▶動 The chef layered the pasta with slices of potatoes and onions. 主廚用番茄和洋蔥層層疊在麵團上。

league [lig]
🔊 *Track 4771*

名 聯盟 動 同盟 同 union 聯盟

▶名 Those nations formed a defense league to fight against their common enemy.
那些國家結成了防禦聯盟，要對付共同的敵人。

▶動 Those four countries leagued together for this battle.
那四個國家在這場戰爭中結成同盟。

萬用延伸句型

out of sb.'s league 高攀不上

例如：Are you kidding me? I can't date the president's daughter! She's totally out of my league.

你在開玩笑吧？我怎麼可能跟總統的女兒約會，我高攀不上的。

leg·is·la·tion [ˌlɛdʒɪsˈleʃən]
🔊 *Track 4772*

名 立法

▶The government has introduced legislation to limit wastewater emissions from factories. 政府立法規範工廠排放廢水。

Level **1**

Level **2**

Level **3**

Level **4**

Level **5**

突飛猛進、程度大進擊
擴增實力5400單字

Level **6**

less·en [ˈlɛsn̩]
Track 4773

動 減少 **同** decrease 減少

▶Would you tell me what we can do to lessen your vexation（煩惱）？ 你能告訴我們做些什麼才能減輕你的煩惱嗎？

lest [lɛst]
Track 4774

連 以免

▶They prepared the first aid kit lest participants in the marathon would get hurt.
他們準備急救箱，以防馬拉松跑者受傷。

lieu·ten·ant [luˈtɛnənt]
Track 4775

名 海軍上尉、陸軍中尉

▶It is a surprise that he was promoted to lieutenant so soon.
他那麼快就被提升為海軍上尉，這真令人驚訝。

> **萬用延伸句型**
> It is a surprise that... 令人驚訝地……

life·long [ˈlaɪfˈlɔŋ]
Track 4776

形 終身的

▶They've become lifelong friends.
他們成了終身的朋友。

like·li·hood [ˈlaɪklɪˌhʊd]
Track 4777

名 可能性、可能的事物 **同** possibility 可能性

▶There is a strong likelihood that the matter will soon be settled.
事情極可能不久就會獲得解決。

> **萬用延伸句型**
> There is a strong likelihood that...
> 有很大的可能性……

lime [laɪm]
Track 4778

名 萊姆（樹）、石灰 **動** 灑石灰

▶**名** This drink is made of lime.
這飲料是萊姆做的。

▶**動** Is it that careless worker who limed our backyard?
就是那個粗心的工人把石灰灑在我們的後院嗎？

limp [lɪmp]
Track 4779

動 跛行

▶The runner sprained her ankle halfway and limped toward the goal of the race.
跑者在半途扭傷腳踝，跛腳走完全程。

lin·ger [ˈlɪŋgɚ]
Track 4780

動 留戀、徘徊 **同** stay 停留、逗留

▶He lingered outside the school after everybody else had gone home.
其他人都回家後，他仍在學校外面徘徊。

live·stock [ˈlaɪvˌstɑk]
Track 4781

名 家畜

▶It is reported that the heavy rain and flood killed scores of livestock.
據報導大雨和洪水淹死了很多家畜。

liz·ard [ˋlɪzɚd]
◀ *Track 4782*

名 蜥蜴
▶This kind of small lizards originally live in Madagascar.
這種小型蜥蜴源自馬達加斯加島。

lo·co·mo·tive [ˏlokəˋmotɪv]
◀ *Track 4783*

名 火車頭 形 推動的、運動的
▶名 Can you tell me how many coaches that locomotive can pull?
你能告訴我那個火車頭能拉多少節車廂嗎？
▶形 What other locomotive organs do we have besides arms and legs?
除了手和腳，我們還有哪些其他的運動器官？

lo·cust [ˋlokəst]
◀ *Track 4784*

名 蝗蟲
▶It is a pity that the locusts have destroyed all the crops and vegetables. 真遺憾蝗蟲群已經毀壞了所有的穀物和蔬菜。

lodge [lɑdʒ]
◀ *Track 4785*

名 小屋 動 寄宿
▶名 The U.S. has lodged a protest against the arrest of the political refugee. 美國對逮捕政治庇護者的行為表示抗議。
▶動 Would you please lodge us for the night in your house?
您能讓我們在您家暫住一晚嗎？

loft·y [ˋlɔftɪ]
◀ *Track 4786*

形 非常高的、高聳的
▶I don't like her lofty treatment of her visitors.
我不喜歡她對來訪者的高傲態度。

log·o [ˋlogo]
◀ *Track 4787*

名 商標、標誌
▶I don't know what the Olympics logo means.
我不知道奧運會的標誌代表什麼。

lone·some [ˋlonsəm]
◀ *Track 4788*

形 孤獨的 同 lonely 孤獨的
▶I felt lonesome at home alone last night.
我昨天獨自在家裡度過了一個寂寞的夜晚。

lon·gi·tude [ˋlɑndʒəˏtjud]
◀ *Track 4789*

名 經度 反 latitude 緯度
▶Each point on earth is specified by latitude and longitude.
地球上的每個點都可以用緯度和經度來定位。

lo·tus [ˋlotəs]
◀ *Track 4790*

名 睡蓮
▶Lotus Cars is a British automotive company that manufactures sports cars and racing cars.
蓮花公司是一家製造跑車和賽車的汽車公司。

文法字詞解析

coach 在這裡是「車廂」的意思，或者也可以說「car」；另外，在國外旅行的時候免不了選擇搭長途巴士移動以節省開支，而長途巴士的講法也是「coach」。

萬用延伸句型

Would you please...? 您可不可以……？

Level 1
Level 2
Level 3
Level 4
Level 5
突飛猛進、程度大進擊—擴增實力5400單字
Level 6

lot·ter·y [ˈlɑtərɪ]   ◀≋ *Track 4791*

名 彩券、樂透
▶Dave, let's go buy some lottery tickets.
大衛，我們去買彩券吧。

lum·ber [ˈlʌmbɚ]   ◀≋ *Track 4792*

名 木材 動 採伐 同 timber 木材
▶名 The lumber was transported down to the town through a local stream. 木材透過河流被輸送到城鎮裡。
▶動 This valley was lumbered hard during the past decade.
在過去十年裡，這個山谷的林木被大肆採伐。

lump [lʌmp]   ◀≋ *Track 4793*

名 塊 動 結塊、笨重地移動 同 chunk 大塊
▶名 There is a lump on his head where he was beaten.
他頭上被別人毆打的地方有個腫塊。
▶動 We lumped all the dirty clothes in a pile.
我們把髒衣服都成團疊成一疊。

[Mm]

mag·ni·fy [ˈmægnəˌfaɪ]   ◀≋ *Track 4794*

動 擴大 同 enlarge 擴大
▶When the skin is magnified, we can observe the bumps and holes in it.
當皮膚被放大來看，就可以觀察到隆起和凹洞處。

maid·en [ˈmedn̩]   ◀≋ *Track 4795*

名 處女、少女 形 少女的、未婚的、處女的
▶名 The fair young maiden is the envy of many.
那位年輕美麗的少女是許多人嫉妒的對象。
▶形 When will the ship's maiden voyage start?
這艘船的處女航何時要開始？

main·land [ˈmenˌlænd]   ◀≋ *Track 4796*

名 大陸
▶The company's investment in mainland China has increased.
這家企業在中國大陸的投資增加了。

main·stream [ˈmenˌstrim]   ◀≋ *Track 4797*

名 思潮、主流
▶He never listens to mainstream music.
他從來不聽主流音樂。

main·te·nance [ˈmentənəns]   ◀≋ *Track 4798*

名 保持
▶The maintenance checks of the plane may take about an hour.
飛機維修檢查約需一個小時。

萬用延伸句型

have a lump in sb.'s throat 感覺喉嚨裡有什麼卡著，即快哭出來的感覺。
例如：He had a lump in his throat as he took his baby sister to her first day at kindergarten.
他帶著小妹妹去上幼稚園的第一天，感覺自己快哭出來了。

文法字詞解析

女性尚未結婚前的姓氏（即娘家姓）稱為 maiden name。

ma·jes·tic [məˈdʒɛstɪk]　　🔊 *Track 4799*

形 莊嚴的　同 grand 雄偉的

▶The king looks really majestic when he isn't smiling.
那個國王在不笑的時候看起來非常莊嚴。

maj·es·ty [ˈmædʒɪstɪ]　　🔊 *Track 4800*

名 威嚴

▶The majesty of the sunset was appropriately displayed in this photo. 壯觀的日落景象在相片中完美地呈現。

文法字詞解析
身為市井小民,面對皇帝、國王這類的人當然是不能用「you」來稱呼的,因此在英文中我們可以尊稱它們為「Your Majesty」。

mam·mal [ˈmæml̩]　　🔊 *Track 4801*

名 哺乳動物

▶Not everyone knows that whales are mammals that live in the sea. 不是每個人都知道鯨魚是生活在海洋中的哺乳動物。

man·i·fest [ˈmænəˌfɛst]　　🔊 *Track 4802*

動 顯示　形 明顯的　同 apparent 明顯的

▶動 He was the kind of person who always manifested a lot of emotion.
他是那種總是表現出很多情緒的人。

▶形 Fear was manifest on his face when he ran into the bear.
他遇到那頭熊時,臉上明顯地表現出恐懼。

文法字詞解析
這個字加上字尾「-tion」就變成名詞「manifestation」,除了有「顯示」的意思之外,還有「示威運動」的意思,畢竟示威就是要讓自己的彰顯自己的想法和不滿嘛。

man·sion [ˈmænʃən]　　🔊 *Track 4803*

名 宅邸、大廈

▶Will you tell me when the old mansion was built?
你能告訴我這座古宅是什麼時候建造的嗎?

ma·ple [ˈmepl̩]　　🔊 *Track 4804*

名 楓樹、槭樹

▶There are many maples in the park you mentioned yesterday.
你昨天提到的那個公園裡有好多楓樹。

mar·gin·al [ˈmɑrdʒɪnl̩]　　🔊 *Track 4805*

形 邊緣的

▶There is only a marginal increase in the wages of the local laborers. 本地勞工的薪水只有些微的增加。

ma·rine [məˈrin]　　🔊 *Track 4806*

名 海軍　形 海洋的

▶名 He is a U.S. marine, and therefore rarely at home.
他是一名美國海軍陸戰隊士兵,因此不常在家裡。

▶形 The harbor was closed to all marine traffic due to the severer weather condition.
港口因為嚴峻的氣候狀況而不開放任何海洋運輸。

mar·shal [ˈmɑrʃəl]　　🔊 *Track 4807*

名 元帥、司儀

▶I don't think the general will be appointed (任命) marshal of the armies. 我覺得這名將軍不會被任命為軍隊的元帥。

Level **1**

Level **2**

Level **3**

Level **4**

Level **5**

擴增實力5400單字　突飛猛進、程度大進擊

Level **6**

mar·tial [ˈmɑrʃəl] 　　🔊 Track 4808

形 軍事的　同 military 軍事的

▶The war criminal will be tried by the martial court.
這名戰犯將被軍事法庭審判。

mar·vel [ˈmɑrvl] 　　🔊 Track 4809

名 令人驚奇的事物、奇蹟　動 驚異　同 miracle 奇蹟

▶名 The robotic household helper is the latest technological marvel from Japan. 家用機械助手是日本的另一項科技傳奇。

▶動 I marveled at her singing skills.
我對於她的歌唱技巧感到驚奇。

mas·cu·line [ˈmæskjəlɪn] 　　🔊 Track 4810

名 男性　形 男性的　反 feminine 女性

▶名 "Host" is the masculine noun for "hostess".
host 是與 hostess 相對應的陽性名詞。

▶形 The lady has a very masculine voice.
這名太太有個很陽剛的聲音。

mash [mæʃ] 　　🔊 Track 4811

名 麥芽漿　動 搗碎

▶名 Would you please put the mash in the bottle?
請你把麥芽漿放在這個瓶子裡好嗎？

▶動 I love eating mashed potatoes. 我好喜歡吃馬鈴薯泥。

文法字詞解析
mashed 是「被搗碎成泥的」的意思，後面可以加上不同的食物。例如：mashed potatoes（馬鈴薯泥）、mashed apples（蘋果泥）、mashed pumpkin（南瓜泥）。

mas·sage [məˈsɑʒ] 　　🔊 Track 4812

名 按摩　動 按摩

▶名 I wish someone would give me a massage when I'm tired.
我希望在我疲憊的時候，能有人幫我按摩。

▶動 Would you massage my shoulders?
你可以幫我按摩肩膀嗎？

文法字詞解析
massage（按摩）和 message（訊息）長得很像，但除了意思不一樣之外，唸法也完全不一樣喔。massage 的重音是在第二個音節。

mas·sive [ˈmæsɪv] 　　🔊 Track 4813

形 笨重的、大量的、巨大的　同 heavy 重的

▶There is a massive monument in the square.
廣場上有一座巨大的紀念碑。

mas·ter·piece [ˈmæstɚˌpis] 　　🔊 Track 4814

名 傑作、名著

▶It took the artist ten years to finish this great masterpiece.
這名藝術家花了十年的時間才完成了這個偉大的傑作。

may·on·naise [ˌmeəˈnez] 　　🔊 Track 4815

名 橄欖油、蛋黃醬、美乃滋

▶I don't like mayonnaise in my sandwiches.
我不喜歡三明治裡面有美乃滋。

mean·time [ˈminˌtaɪm] 　　🔊 Track 4816

名 期間、同時　副 同時

▶名 The power supply will be restored, but in the meantime, we can light the house with candles. 電力很快就會恢復，在此同時，我們可以用蠟燭照亮屋內。

▶ 副 There are some students playing football. Meantime, some are playing games.
有些學生在踢足球。同時，有些學生在玩遊戲。

me·chan·ics [məˈkænɪks]　　Track 4817
名 機械學、力學
▶ Can you explain the mechanics of this to me?
你可以跟我解釋一下這個東西的運作方式嗎？

me·di·ate [ˈmidɪˌet]　　Track 4818
動 調解
▶ A broker was sent to mediate between the two parties.
有位中先人被派來為兩方居中協調。

men·ace [ˈmɛnɪs]　　Track 4819
名 威脅 動 脅迫 同 threat 威脅
▶ 名 In dry weather, forest fires are a great menace to people.
在乾燥的天氣裡，森林起火對人們構成了很大的威脅。
▶ 動 The poor country is menaced by war.
這個可憐的國家受到了戰爭威脅。

mer·maid [ˈmɝˌmed]　　Track 4820
名 美人魚
▶ Have you read the story about the little mermaid?
你讀過小美人魚的故事嗎？

midst [mɪdst]　　Track 4821
名 中央、中間 介 在……之中
▶ 名 Don't you believe there is a thief in our midst?
你不相信我們當中有小偷嗎？
▶ 介 The summit（峰頂）of the mountain can be seen midst the clouds. 可以在雲朵間看到山頂。

mi·grant [ˈmaɪɡrənt]　　Track 4822
名 候鳥、移民 形 遷移的
▶ 名 These birds are winter migrants from the North eastern Asia.
鳥類在冬天從東北亞遷徙過來。
▶ 形 A lot of factory work is done by migrant workers.
大量的工廠工作是由外藉勞工們來做的。

mile·age [ˈmaɪlɪdʒ]　　Track 4823
名 里數
▶ We can see the mileage of the car on the digital dashboard.
我們可以由數位儀表板上看到這輛車的里程數。

mile·stone [ˈmaɪlˌston]　　Track 4824
名 里程碑
▶ The year 2008 marked an important milestone in the diplomatic（外交上的）history of the two countries.
2008 年是兩國外交史上的一個重要里程碑。

文法字詞解析
相對於 mermaid，有人將男性的人魚稱為 merman，也有人直接以 mermaid 通稱所有性別的人魚。另外還有一種住在海裡的叫做 siren，是會唱歌誘惑人類並將其殺害的海妖。

Level 1
Level 2
Level 3
Level 4
Level 5
突飛猛進、程度大進擊——擴增實力5400單字
Level 6

min·gle [ˈmɪŋgl̩]
🔊 Track 4825

動 混合 同 blend 混合

▶The excitement of exploring a new environment is often mingled with uncertainty.
探索新環境的興奮，常是混合著不確定性。

min·i·mal [ˈmɪnɪml̩]
🔊 Track 4826

形 最小的

▶There is a minimal quantity of imperfection（瑕疵）in these goods. 這批貨物的瑕疵品極少。

mint [mɪnt]
🔊 Track 4827

名 薄荷

▶These candies he bought taste of mint.
他買的這些糖果有薄荷味。

文法字詞解析
這個單字也可用來表達「薄荷綠」的顏色（就是薄荷巧克力冰淇淋的那種顏色）。

mi·ser [ˈmaɪzɚ]
🔊 Track 4828

名 小氣鬼

▶The miser doesn't like to part with his money.
那個小氣鬼不喜歡與他的錢分開。

mis·tress [ˈmɪstrɪs]
🔊 Track 4829

名 女主人

▶The paparazzi took a photo of the politician and his mistress.
狗仔隊拍到政客和情婦的照片。

moan [mon]
🔊 Track 4830

名 呻吟聲、悲嘆 動 呻吟 同 groan 呻吟

▶名 I can hear his moans from over here.
我在這裡都能聽到他在呻吟。

▶動 My colleague always moans about all the work he has to do. 我同事總是抱怨他有很多的工作要做。

mock [mɑk]
🔊 Track 4831

名 嘲弄、笑柄 動 嘲笑 形 模仿的

▶名 The boy has become the mock of the class.
那個男孩成了班上的笑柄。

▶動 She mocked him for having a giant belly.
她嘲笑他肚子很大。

▶形 I didn't do that well in the mock test.
我模擬考考得不好。

文法字詞解析
知更鳥能夠模仿其他鳥類的叫聲，因此牠們的英文名字是 mockingbird。

mode [mod]
🔊 Track 4832

名 款式、方法 同 manner 方法

▶They should have told us the mode of payment first.
他們本來應該先告訴我們支付方式的。

mod·ern·ize [ˈmɑdɚˌnaɪz]
🔊 Track 4833

動 現代化

▶Much of the infrastructure of the city has been modernized.
城市中許多建設都已經現代化。

mod·i·fy [ˈmɑdəˌfaɪ]　◀ᵉ *Track 4834*

動 修改
▶The mischievous kids were told to modify their behaviors.
　頑皮的小孩被要求要修正他們的行為。

mold [mold]　◀ᵉ *Track 4835*

名 模型　動 塑造、磨練
▶名 Can you lend me a pastry（糕點）mold?
　你可以借我一個糕點模子嗎？
▶動 He's teaching these children to mold figures out of clay.
　你在教這些孩子們用黏土來製造人像。

mol·e·cule [ˈmɑləˌkjul]　◀ᵉ *Track 4836*

名 分子
▶We're all formed by countless molecules.
　我們都是無數分子組成的。

mon·arch [ˈmɑnɚk]　◀ᵉ *Track 4837*

名 君主、大王　同 king 君主
▶They attempted to overthrow the monarch.
　他們企圖要推翻這個國王。

mon·strous [ˈmɑnstrəs]　◀ᵉ *Track 4838*

形 奇怪的、巨大的　同 bulky 龐大的
▶Did you see that horse? It's monstrous!
　你有看到那匹馬嗎？牠超大一隻的啊！

mor·tal [ˈmɔrtl]　◀ᵉ *Track 4839*

名 凡人　形 死亡的、致命的　同 deadly 致命的
▶名 We're all mortals, with our human faults and weaknesses（弱點）.
　我們都是凡人，自然都有過錯和弱點。
▶形 Human beings are mortal; an eternal life would be impossible.
　人類生命有限：永生是不可能的。

> **文法字詞解析**
> 相反地，不是凡人、可以永遠活在世上的神仙則稱為 immortal。

moss [mɔs]　◀ᵉ *Track 4840*

名 苔蘚、用苔覆蓋
▶Be careful not to slip on the moss.
　小心別在青苔上滑倒了。

moth·er·hood [ˈmʌðɚˌhʊd]　◀ᵉ *Track 4841*

名 母性
▶Not every mother has time to appreciate every moment of motherhood.
　不是每個母親都能有時間細細品味當母親的點滴時刻。

> **文法字詞解析**
> 名詞字尾「-hood」是用來表示一段時期或是某個狀態，例如：childhood（孩童時期）、fatherhood（父親的身分）。

mo·tive [ˈmotɪv]　◀ᵉ *Track 4842*

名 動機　同 cause 動機
▶You should examine her motive in offering to lend you the money.
　你應該檢視她借錢給你的動機。

Level 1
Level 2
Level 3
Level 4
Level 5
Level 6

突飛猛進、程度大進擊——擴增實力5400單字

mound [maʊnd]　◀€ Track 4843
名 丘陵、堆積、築堤
▶There is a mound of papers on my father's desk every day.
我爸爸的辦公桌上每天都有一大堆文件。

mount [maʊnt]　◀€ Track 4844
名 山　動 攀登　同 climb 攀爬
▶名 Have you been to Mount Everest? 你去過聖母峰嗎？
▶動 The higher the climbers（登山者）mount, the more views they can enjoy.
登山者爬得越高，他們欣賞到的景色就越多。

文法字詞解析
在當作山的名稱時可縮寫為 Mt.，如 Mount Everest 就可以縮寫為 Mt. Everest。

mow·er [ˈmoɚ]　◀€ Track 4845
名 割草者（機）
▶I have to borrow a lawn mower for my father.
我得幫父親借一台割草機來。

mum·ble [ˈmʌmbl̩]　◀€ Track 4846
名 含糊不清的話　動 含糊地說　同 mutter 含糊地說
▶名 I heard a mumble from someone in the crowd.
我聽到人群中有人含糊不清地說話。
▶動 Stop mumbling and speak up!
不要講得這麼含糊，講大聲點！

mus·cu·lar [ˈmʌskjəlɚ]　◀€ Track 4847
形 肌肉的
▶The player is tall and muscular. 那名運動員身高力大。

muse [mjuz]　◀€ Track 4848
名 靈感來源
▶I started to muse about the composition of my painting.
我開始構思我畫作的構圖。

萬用延伸句型
muse over sth. 仔細思考某事
例如：I mused over his words for a long time but still couldn't figure out what he meant.
我仔細思考了他所說的話好一陣子，但還是想不出他的意思。

mus·tard [ˈmʌstɚd]　◀€ Track 4849
名 芥末
▶This meat should be seasoned with salt and mustard.
這肉裡面應該加點鹽和芥末。

mut·ter [ˈmʌtɚ]　◀€ Track 4850
名 抱怨　動 低語、含糊地說　同 complain 抱怨
▶名 I heard a mutter of discontent（不滿）, but I have no idea who from.
我聽到有人竊竊私語表示不滿，但不知道是誰。
▶動 The depressed man kept muttering to himself.
沮喪的男人一直自言自語。

mut·ton [ˈmʌtn̩]　◀€ Track 4851
名 羊肉
▶Not all people like to have mutton in the winter.
不是所有人都喜歡在冬天吃羊肉。

myth [mɪθ]
🔊 Track 4852

名 神話、傳說 同 tale 傳說
▶ I enjoy reading Greek myths.
　我喜歡讀希臘神話。

[Nn]

nag [næg]
🔊 Track 4853

名 嘮叨的人 動 使煩惱、嘮叨 同 annoy 使煩惱
▶ 名 I don't want to be a nag, but you really should start getting dressed.
　我不想做一個嘮叨的人，但你真的應該開始穿衣服了。
▶ 動 She is nagging me about my diet.
　她一直嘮叨我飲食習慣。

文法字詞解析
nagging 是 nag 的形容詞，表示「嘮叨的、挑剔的」，而名詞 nagger 則是「愛嘮叨的人」，書寫時要注意字尾必須重複。

na·ive [nɑˋiv]
🔊 Track 4854

形 天真、幼稚 反 sophisticated 世故的
▶ She's a naïve little girl that believes everything others tell her.
　她是個天真的小女孩，別人跟她說什麼她都信。

文法字詞解析
naive 這個字是從法文來的，所以它的唸法比較特別，重音在第二個音節。

nas·ty [ˋnæstɪ]
🔊 Track 4855

形 汙穢的、惡意的
▶ Did you just eat a booger（鼻屎）? That's just nasty!
　你剛吃鼻屎喔？有夠髒的！

nav·i·gate [ˋnævəˌget]
🔊 Track 4856

動 控制航向 同 steer 掌舵
▶ She studies how animals navigate during long-distance migration. 她研究動物如何在長途遷徙中導航。

news·cast [ˋnjuzˌkæst]
🔊 Track 4857

名 新聞報導
▶ Did you see her on the evening newscast?
　你有看到她主持晚間新聞嗎？

nib·ble [ˋnɪbl̩]
🔊 Track 4858

名 小撮食物 動 連續地輕咬
▶ 名 This chocolate is great. Would you like a nibble?
　這巧克力好好吃，你想吃一點嗎？
▶ 動 I could feel a fish nibbling at the bait.
　我能感覺到有條魚在輕咬魚餌。

文法字詞解析
nibble 指的是「小口咬」，而且限定是用門牙咬，想當然就不可能咬太大口（因為門牙會痛）。老鼠、兔子一類愛用門牙啃東西的小動物就常搭配這個字出現。

nick·el [ˋnɪkl̩]
🔊 Track 4859

名 鎳 動 覆以鎳……
▶ 名 Would you allow me to put in two nickels instead of a dime?
　您允許我放兩個五美分鎳幣來代替一個十美分硬幣嗎？
▶ 動 Can you help me nickel the wire?
　您能不能幫我在這條金屬線上鍍鎳？

Level 1
Level 2
Level 3
Level 4
Level 5
突飛猛進、程度大進擊──擴增實力5400單字
Level 6

night·in·gale [ˈnaɪtn̩ˌgel] 🔊 *Track 4860*

名 夜鶯、歌聲美妙的歌手
▶I've never actually heard a nightingale sing.
我從來沒真的聽過夜鶯唱歌。

nom·i·nate [ˈnɑməˌnet] 🔊 *Track 4861*

動 提名、指定 同 propose 提名
▶Nicolle Kidman was nominated for the best actress of the Academy Award.
妮可‧基曼被提名為奧斯卡獎最佳女主角。

文法字詞解析
nominate a candidate = 提名一個候選人

none·the·less [ˌnʌnðəˈlɛs] 🔊 *Track 4862*

副 儘管如此、然而
▶He is young, but I respect him nonetheless.
儘管他年輕，我並不因此而減少對他的尊重。

non·vi·o·lent [nɑnˈvaɪələnt] 🔊 *Track 4863*

形 非暴力的 反 violent 暴力的
▶It is obvious that Martin Luther King made many enemies in his nonviolent quest for equality at that time.
顯然當時馬丁‧路德‧金在以非暴力手段尋求平等的過程中，樹立了許多敵人。

nos·tril [ˈnɑstrəl] 🔊 *Track 4864*

名 鼻孔
▶He would be good-looking if his nostrils weren't so big.
如果他的鼻孔沒那麼大，那他一定很帥。

no·ta·ble [ˈnotəbl̩] 🔊 *Track 4865*

名 名人、出眾的人 形 出色的、著名的 同 famous 著名的
▶名 There are many notables attending the reception.
有許多著名人士參加了那個招待會。
▶形 Ad. The old man has a notable collection of antiques.
老人有批很值得注意的骨董收藏。

no·tice·a·ble [ˈnotɪsəbl̩] 🔊 *Track 4866*

形 顯著的、顯眼的
▶There was a noticeable transformation in her appearance.
她的容貌有了明顯的變化。

no·ti·fy [ˈnotəˌfaɪ] 🔊 *Track 4867*

動 通知、報告 同 inform 通知
▶Would you please notify us if there is any change of the address?
地址如有變動，請通知我們好嗎？

文法字詞解析
notify 相對的名詞是 notification，大家的手機上常會跳出來的通知就是 notification 喔！

no·tion [ˈnoʃən] 🔊 *Track 4868*

名 觀念、意見 同 opinion 意見
▶I only have a vague notion of what he plans to show the client.
我對他計畫要給顧客看什麼，只有約略的概念。

nov·ice [`nɑvɪs]

🔊 *Track 4869*

名 初學者
▶Whether novice or master, they should be treated equally.
我認為不管是新手還是達人都應該一視同仁。

no·where [`no͵hwɛr]

🔊 *Track 4870*

副 無處地 名 不為人知的地方
▶副 The young girl would go nowhere without her bodyguards.
難怪那個年輕女孩去任何地方都有保鑣跟著。
▶名 He says that nowhere is more beautiful than his hometown.
他說他的家鄉是最美麗的地方。

nu·cle·us [`njuklɪəs]

🔊 *Track 4871*

名 核心、中心、原子核 同 core 核心
▶The students observed the nucleus of a cell with a microscope.
學生用顯微鏡觀察細胞核。

nude [njud]

🔊 *Track 4872*

名 裸體、裸體畫 形 裸的 同 naked 裸的
▶名 What do you think of that nude he painted?
你覺得他畫的那幅裸體畫怎麼樣呢？
▶形 The nude lady walked right past us.
那個裸體的小姐就這樣從我們身邊走了過去。

[Oo]

oar [or]

🔊 *Track 4873*

名 槳、櫓
▶He lost the oars so had nothing to row the boat with.
他把槳弄丟了，沒有東西可以用來划船。

萬用延伸句型
stick sb.'s oar into sth. 直翻就是「將某人的槳插入某事」，即「多管別人閒事」的意思。
例如：I told her to stop sticking her oar into her neighbors' affairs, but she wouldn't listen.
我叫她不要多管鄰居的閒事，但她就是不聽。

o·a·sis [o`esɪs]

🔊 *Track 4874*

名 綠洲
▶It took us half a day to reach the oasis at sunset（日落）.
我們花了半天時間才在日落時到達了這片綠洲。

oath [oθ]

🔊 *Track 4875*

名 誓約、盟誓 同 vow 誓約
▶The president-elect took oath of office.
總統當選人宣誓就職。

oat·meal [`ot͵mil]

🔊 *Track 4876*

名 燕麥片
▶Would you like to have oatmeal and toast for breakfast?
你想吃麥片和吐司當早餐嗎？

萬用延伸句型
Would you like tor...? 你想要……嗎？

Level 1

Level 2

Level 3

Level 4

Level 5

突飛猛進、程度大進擊──
擴增實力5400單字

Level 6

ob·long [ˋɑblɔŋ]　　◀≼ *Track 4877*
名 長方形 形 長方形的
▶名 I told him to draw a circle but he drew an oblong.
　我叫他畫圓，他卻畫了一個長方形。
▶形 I bought an oblong table, not a square one.
　我買了一張長方形的桌子，而不是正方形的。

ob·serv·er [əbˋzɝvɚ]　　◀≼ *Track 4878*
名 觀察者、觀察員 反 performer 表演者、執行者
▶Observers of the UN are monitoring the ceasefire.
　聯合國的觀察者監控這個停火協定。

ob·sti·nate [ˋɑbstənɪt]　　◀≼ *Track 4879*
形 執拗的、頑固的 反 obedient 順從的
▶My elder sister is too obstinate to let anyone help her.
　我姐姐太倔強了，她是不會讓任何人幫她的。

oc·cur·rence [əˋkɝəns]　　◀≼ *Track 4880*
名 出現、發生
▶I am afraid that the occurrence of storms will delay our trip.
　我擔心暴風雨會延誤我們的旅行。

oc·to·pus [ˋɑktəpəs]　　◀≼ *Track 4881*
名 章魚
▶We saw a giant octopus in the sea.
　我們在海裡看到了一隻巨大的章魚。

odds [ɑds]　　◀≼ *Track 4882*
名 勝算、差別
▶If you invest in the stock market, the odds are that you may lose money sometime.
　如果你投資股票，就有機會賠錢。

o·dor [ˋodɚ]　　◀≼ *Track 4883*
名 氣味 同 smell 氣味
▶What's that strange odor coming from outside?
　外面飄來那個奇怪的氣味是什麼？

ol·ive [ˋɑlɪv]　　◀≼ *Track 4884*
名 橄欖 形 橄欖的、橄欖色的
▶名 Have you ever eaten olives before? What do they taste like?你吃過橄欖嗎？吃起來如何呢？
▶形 She has rich lips and olive eyes.
　她有著豐厚的嘴唇和橄欖色的雙眼。

op·po·nent [əˋponənt]　　◀≼ *Track 4885*
名 對手、反對者 反 alliance 同盟
▶The tennis player could observe her opponent's techniques and reacted strategically.
　網球選手可以觀察她對手的技術，策略性地回應。

文法字詞解析
字首「oct-」是「八」的意思，所以「octopus」是「八爪魚」，也就是「章魚」；「octagon」是「八邊形」。不過「October」卻不是「八月」而是「十月」，是因為羅馬的統治者凱薩和奧古斯都分別都以自己的名字為七月和八月命名，而原本的八月就被順延兩個月成為十月了。

op·ti·mism [ˈɑptəmɪzəm]
Track 4886

名 樂觀主義 反 pessimism 悲觀主義
▶Her eternal optimism can get kind of annoying.
她永遠都這麼樂觀，有時候真的有點討厭。

or·chard [ˈɔrtʃəd]
Track 4887

名 果園
▶My family decided to expand the orchard.
我們家決定要擴大果園。

or·gan·i·zer [ˈɔrgənˌaɪzə]
Track 4888

名 組織者
▶Community organizers help to make the environment of the neighborhood better.
社區組織者幫助使社區的環境變得更好。

o·ri·ent [ˈorɪənt]
Track 4889

名 東方、東方諸國 動 使適應、定位 同 adapt 使適應
▶名 They import perfumes and spices from the Orient.
他們從東方進口香水和香料。
▶動 I oriented myself by looking at the road signs.
我藉由看路牌找到自己的位置。

o·ri·en·tal [ˌorɪˈɛntl̩]
Track 4890

名 東方人 形 東方諸國的
▶名 There are a great many Orientals living in this city.
在這個城市中住有很多的東方人。
▶形 There are more than 300 kinds of oriental cherries in all in our world. 世界上一共有三百多種東方櫻花。

or·na·ment [ˈɔrnəmənt]
Track 4891

名 裝飾（品） 動 以裝飾品點綴 同 decoration 裝飾品
▶名 Tom wanted to have a fountain as the garden ornament.
湯姆想要個噴泉作為花園的裝飾。
▶動 She ornamented the room with flowers.
她用花來裝飾房間。

or·phan·age [ˈɔrfənɪdʒ]
Track 4892

名 孤兒、孤兒院
▶The boy used to live in an orphanage before he was adopted.
那個男孩在被收養前住在孤兒院裡。

os·trich [ˈɔstrɪtʃ]
Track 4893

名 鴕鳥
▶The ostrich is the fastest animal on two legs in the world.
鴕鳥是世界上跑得最快的兩條腿動物。

ounce [aʊns]
Track 4894

名 盎司
▶I put too many ounces of sugar in the juice.
我在果汁裡加太多盎司的糖了。

文法字詞解析
organizer 除了指組織某事的「人」以外，也可以指幫助你組織行程的工具，例如行程表、筆記本、APP 等。

文法字詞解析
住在 orphanage 裡的孤兒叫做 orphan。

Level 1

Level 2

Level 3

Level 4

Level 5

突飛猛進、程度大進擊——擴增實力5400單字

Level 6

out·do [ˌaʊtˋdu]
動 勝過、凌駕　**同** surpass 勝過
▶He tried to outdo his sister in terms of academic performance.
他試圖在學業表現上超過他的姊姊。

Track 4895

outdo 的動詞變化：outdo, outdid, outdone

out·go·ing [ˋaʊtˌgoɪŋ]
形 擅於社交的、外向的
▶Not all people in the office think he is an outgoing person.
不是辦公室所有的人都認為他是一個外向的人。

Track 4896

out·put [ˋaʊtˌpʊt]
名 生產、輸出　**動** 生產、大量製造、輸出　**同** input 輸入
▶**名** The country ranks last in industrial output.
這個國家的工業生產排名最後。
▶**動** This program can output the file into another file.
這個程式能將一個文件輸出成為另一個文件。

Track 4897

out·sid·er [ˌaʊtˋsaɪdɚ]
名 門外漢、局外人
▶It is not easy for an outsider to understand his logic.
要瞭解一個門外漢的邏輯是很難的。

Track 4898

萬用延伸句型
It is not easy for sb. to r... 對（某人）來
說，（做到某事）很不容易

out·skirts [ˋaʊtˌskɝts]
名 郊區　**同** suburb 郊區
▶It has been a week since I got back to the outskirts of London.
我回到倫敦郊區已經一週了。

Track 4899

out·ward(s) [ˋaʊtwɚd(z)]
形 向外的、外面的　**副** 向外　**反** inward 向內
▶**形** Her outward appearance is calm but she is seething（生氣的）inside.
她外表很鎮定，但她內心可是火大無比。
▶**副** It's better to direct your emotions outwards rather than conceal your feelings.
讓你的情緒向外發洩，比影藏自己的感受好。

Track 4900

o·ver·all [ˋovɚˌɔl]
名 罩衫、吊帶褲　**形** 全部的　**副** 整體而言　**同** whole 全部的
▶**名** These overalls are too big for me.
這吊帶褲對我來說太大了。
▶**形** How long will it take for you to finish the overall renovating（重新裝潢）？
你完成所有的重新裝潢要多久？
▶**副** Prices are still rising overall at this moment.
現在總體來看物價仍在上漲。

Track 4901

o·ver·do [ˌovɚˋdu]
動 做得過火　**同** exaggerate 誇張
▶You should work hard, but don't overdo it, or you will make yourself ill. 你應該努力工作，但也不能過頭，否則你會把自己累出病來的。

Track 4902

overdo 的動詞變化：overdo, overdid, overdone

over·eat [`ovə`it]

🔊 *Track 4903*

[動] 吃得過多

▶Having some chocolate may being some delight, but don't overeat it.
吃些巧克力可以讓人開心，但不要吃過量。

o·ver·flow [ˌovə`flo]

🔊 *Track 4904*

[名] 滿溢 [動] 氾濫、溢出、淹沒 [同] flood 淹沒

▶[名] We can't stop the overflow from the toilet.
我們都無法止住馬桶裡的水溢出。

▶[動] The water in the bathtub is overflowing.
澡盆裡的水都溢出來了。

o·ver·hear [ˌovə`hɪr]

🔊 *Track 4905*

[動] 無意中聽到

▶Kevin overheard the directors' conversation and found a trade secret.
凱文間接聽到部長們的對話，發現一個貿易的機密。

文法字詞解析
overhear 的動詞變化：overhear, overheard, overheard

o·ver·sleep [`ovə`slip]

🔊 *Track 4906*

[動] 睡過頭

▶I'm afraid he overslept this morning and has already missed his usual bus.
恐怕他今天早上睡過頭了，而且錯過了他平常坐的那班公車。

o·ver·whelm [ˌovə`hwɛlm]

🔊 *Track 4907*

[動] 淹沒、征服、壓倒

▶A great wave overwhelmed the boat.
一個巨浪吞沒了那艘小船。

文法字詞解析
如果加上「-ing」就會變成形容詞「overwhelming（壓倒性的）」。
例如：An overwhelming majority 壓倒性的大多數。

o·ver·work [`ovə`wɝk]

🔊 *Track 4908*

[名] 過度工作 [動] 過度工作

▶[名] My uncle got ill because of overwork. I wish he could recover soon.
我叔叔因為工作過度而病倒了。我希望他能很快恢復健康。

▶[動] I hope the boss did not overwork that poor boy.
我希望老闆沒有使那個可憐的男孩過度工作。

oys·ter [`ɔɪstə]

🔊 *Track 4909*

[名] 牡蠣、蠔

▶Helen thinks that the oysters have an unpleasant smell.
海倫認為牡蠣有一種腥味。

o·zone [`ozon]

🔊 *Track 4910*

[名] 臭氧

▶Scientists are concerned over the current state of our ozone layer.
科學家對於我們的臭氧層目前的狀況很擔憂。

Level 1

Level 2

Level 3

Level 4

Level 5

Level 6

突飛猛進、程度大進擊——擴增實力5400單字

[Pp]

pa·cif·ic [pə'sɪfɪk]
🔊 Track 4911

名 太平洋（首字大寫） 形 平靜的

▶名 The Pacific Ocean is much larger than the Atlantic Ocean.
太平洋比大西洋大得多。

▶形 The two countries negotiated to reach a pacific agreement.
兩國協商，達成和平協定。

pack·et ['pækɪt]
🔊 Track 4912

名 小包 同 package 包裹

▶Would you please deliver the packet to my hometown for me?
請您幫我把這個包裹寄送到我的家鄉好嗎？

pad·dle ['pædl]
🔊 Track 4913

名 槳、踏板 動 以槳划動、戲水 同 oar 槳

▶名 Can you hand me a paddle? I'll row us to the shore.
拿根槳給我好嗎？我來把我們的船划上岸。

▶動 The children were paddling in the water. 孩子們在水裡玩。

pane [pen]
🔊 Track 4914

名 方框

▶Someone broke the window pane. 有人打破了窗框。

par·a·dox ['pærədɑks]
🔊 Track 4915

名 似是而非的言論、矛盾的事

▶It is a curious paradox that drinking too much water may
make you feel thirsty.
喝太多水反而會變口渴，這是一個自相矛盾的理論。

par·al·lel ['pærəlɛl]
🔊 Track 4916

名 平行線 動 平行 形 平行的、類似的

▶名 She is an excellent singer, without parallel in the country.
她是個非常厲害的歌手，國內沒有人能達到她的水準。

▶動 Her story closely parallels what he told me.
她的說法跟他告訴我的情況極為相似。

▶形 Linda and her friends have parallel likes and dislikes.
琳達和她的朋友喜好相同。

par·lor ['pɑrlə]
🔊 Track 4917

名 客廳、起居室

▶I'm afraid that you have no chioce but to invite him into the
parlor. 恐怕你除了邀請他進客廳外別無選擇。

par·tic·i·pant [pɑr'tɪsəpənt]
🔊 Track 4918

名 參與者

▶Participants of the marathon can get a T-shirt, a bottled water,
and a cap.
馬拉松的參賽者可以得到T恤、瓶裝水、和一個杯子。

文法字詞解析

字首「para-」有「超越」的意思，而
「-dox」表示「意見、信仰」；兩者合在
一起就成了「paradox」。另外，還可以
在加上「-ical」變成形容詞「paradoxical
（似是而非的、自相矛盾的）」。

萬用延伸句型

have no choice but to... 別無選擇，只好……

par·ti·cle [ˈpɑrtɪk!]
🔊 *Track 4919*

名 微粒、極少量
▶There wasn't a particle of truth in what he said.
他說的沒有半點真話。

part·ly [ˈpɑrtlɪ]
🔊 *Track 4920*

副 部分地
▶It is obvious that his ideas were shaped partly by his early experiences.
顯然他的一些想法在一定程度上是由他早期的經歷所形成的。

pas·sion·ate [ˈpæʃənɪt]
🔊 *Track 4921*

形 熱情的
▶The kids are passionate about Go.
小孩對圍棋很有熱情。

pas·time [ˈpæsˌtaɪm]
🔊 *Track 4922*

名 消遣 同 recreation 消遣
▶Gardening is a very rewarding pastime. Don't you think so?
園藝是非常有益的消遣。你不這樣認為嗎？

pas·try [ˈpestrɪ]
🔊 *Track 4923*

名 糕餅
▶What's your favorite kind of pastry? 你最喜歡哪種糕餅？

patch [pætʃ]
🔊 *Track 4924*

名 補丁 動 補綴、修補 同 mend 縫補
▶名 I am afraid that it will take me some time to remove all the patches on the child's jeans.
恐怕我得花些時間拆掉這孩子的牛仔褲上所有的補丁。
▶動 Is there any way to patch things up between us?
我們之間的關係還有得挽救嗎？

pat·ent [ˈpetn̩t]
🔊 *Track 4925*

名 專利權 形 公開、專利的 同 copyright 著作權
▶名 She handles cases of patent and trademark infringement (侵權). 她負責受理專利和商標侵權的案件。
▶形 Would you like to try some of this new patent medicine?
你想不想試試這種新的專利藥物？

pa·tri·ot [ˈpetrɪət]
🔊 *Track 4926*

名 愛國者
▶The nationalist wanted to educate his kids to be patriots.
這名國家主義者想把小孩都教育成愛國的人。

pa·trol [pəˈtrol]
🔊 *Track 4927*

名 巡邏者 動 巡邏
▶名 I'm afraid that we will have to chance meeting an enemy patrol. 恐怕我們不得不去冒可能遇上敵人巡邏兵的危險了。
▶動 There will be many police patrolling the streets.
會有很多警察在街上巡邏。

文法字詞解析
字首「patri-」是「父親、組國」的意思，「-ot」是名詞字尾，表示「人」，合在一起就變成「patriot」。

Level 1

Level 2

Level 3

Level 4

Level 5

突飛猛進、程度大進擊
擴增實力5400單字

Level 6

pa·tron [ˈpetrən]

Track 4928

名 保護者、贊助人

▶ It is said that modern artists have difficulty in finding patrons.
據說現代藝術家們很難找到贊助人。

萬用延伸句型
have difficulty in... 在（某領域）上有困難

pea·cock [ˈpiˌkɑk]

Track 4929

名 孔雀

▶ These children have never seen a peacock before.
這些孩子從來都沒看過孔雀長什麼樣子。

peas·ant [ˈpɛznt]

Track 4930

名 佃農 同 farmer 農夫

▶ The peasants all bowed down to the king.
那些佃農都在國王面前跪下了。

peck [pɛk]

Track 4931

名 啄、啄痕、輕吻 動 啄食

▶名 She gave him a peck on the cheek.
她在他臉頰上輕輕地吻了一下。

▶動 The pigeons（鴿子）are pecking around on the ground.
那些鴿子在地上到處啄食。

ped·dler [ˈpɛdlɚ]

Track 4932

名 小販

▶ The peddler of illegal drugs was finally arrested.
非法藥品的兜售者終於被逮捕。

文法字詞解析
去掉字尾的「(e)r」後，就變成動詞 peddle，意思是叫賣、兜售，但這個字長得跟 paddle（船槳）很像，寫的時候要注意。

peek [pik]

Track 4933

名 偷看 動 窺視

▶名 Let's just take a peek at the list, shall we?
我們很快地看一下名單吧，好嗎？

▶動 It looks like there is someone peeking in through the keyhole（鑰匙孔）.
好像有個人從鑰匙孔往裡面偷看。

peg [pɛg]

Track 4934

名 釘子 動 釘牢

▶名 Would you please help me hang the coat on the peg?
請你幫我把這件上衣掛在釘子上好嗎？

▶動 The boss pegged the photo to the board.
老闆把那張照片釘在板子上。

pen·e·trate [ˈpɛnəˌtret]

Track 4935

動 刺入 同 pierce 刺穿

▶ The eyes of owls can penetrate the dark.
貓頭鷹的眼睛可透視黑暗。

per·ceive [pɚˈsiv]

Track 4936

動 察覺 同 detect 察覺

▶ The host of the talk show was perceived to be politically biased.
脫口秀主持人被認為在政治上立場偏頗。

perch [pɜtʃ]
🔊 *Track 4937*

名 鱸魚 動 棲息

▶名 I like fishing for perch. 我喜歡釣鱸魚。

▶動 The stone buildings perch on a hill crest（頂部）.
那些石頭房子坐落在山頂上。

per·form·er [pə'fɔrmə]
🔊 *Track 4938*

名 執行者、演出者

▶At the end of the stage play, performers bowed together to thank the audience.
在舞台劇結束時，表演者向觀眾鞠躬道謝。

per·il ['pɛrəl]
🔊 *Track 4939*

名 危險 動 冒險 同 danger 危險

▶名 The hero saved the old man in peril.
那名英雄救了那個有危險的老人。

▶動 He periled himself by heading into the haunted house.
他冒險走進鬼屋。

per·ish ['pɛrɪʃ]
🔊 *Track 4940*

動 滅亡 同 die 死亡

▶Almost a hundred people perished in the hotel fire last night.
昨夜有近百人在旅館的大火中喪生。

per·mis·si·ble [pə'mɪsəbl̩]
🔊 *Track 4941*

形 可允許的

▶The Environmental Protection Bureau announced a permissible level of vehicle exhaust emissions.
環保署宣布了車輛排放廢氣的可容許標準。

per·sist [pə'sɪst]
🔊 *Track 4942*

動 堅持 同 insist 堅持

▶It is reported that the cold weather will persist for the rest of the week. 根據報導，這樣寒冷的天氣將會持續到本週末。

per·son·nel [ˌpɜsn̩'ɛl]
🔊 *Track 4943*

名 人員、人事部門 同 staff 工作人員

▶Could you let me know how to contact the related personnel in this case?
你能告訴我該如何連繫這件案子的相關人員嗎？

pes·si·mism ['pɛsəˌmɪzəm]
🔊 *Track 4944*

名 悲觀、悲觀主義

▶I'm afraid that he has a tendency towards pessimism.
我擔心他有悲觀主義的傾向。

pier [pɪr]
🔊 *Track 4945*

名 碼頭 同 wharf 碼頭

▶It took him ten minutes to walk along the pier and climb down into the boat.
他花了十分鐘的時間沿著碼頭走過去，並爬進了小船。

文法字詞解析

performer 是動詞「perform（表演）」加上名詞字尾「-er」形成的，perform 後面還可以加上另一個名詞字尾「-ance」變成「performance」來表示「演出」。

Level 1

Level 2

Level 3

Level 4

Level 5

Level 6

擴增實力5400單字
突飛猛進、程度大進擊

pil·grim [ˈpɪlɡrɪm]　🔊 Track 4946
名 朝聖者
▶Thousands of pilgrims gathered in the plaza in front of the mosque. 數千名朝聖者聚集在清真寺前的廣場。

pil·lar [ˈpɪlɚ]　🔊 Track 4947
名 樑柱
▶The young people will be the pillar of society.
年輕一代將會成為社會的棟樑。

pim·ple [ˈpɪmpl̩]　🔊 Track 4948
名 面皰
▶Jane doesn't want anyone to see the pimple on her nose.
珍妮不想要別人看到她鼻子上的痘子。

pinch [pɪntʃ]　🔊 Track 4949
名 招、少量 動 招痛、捏 同 squeeze 擠、擰
▶名 He gave the little girl an affectionate（親暱的）pinch on the face. 他親暱地擰了那個小女孩的臉一下。
▶動 This pair of shoes pinched my toes.
這雙鞋夾得我的腳趾很痛。

piss [pɪs]　🔊 Track 4950
名 小便 動 尿液、激怒
▶名 He took a piss by the street. 他在路邊尿尿了。
▶動 I'm afraid that your secretary has pissed my boss off on the meeting yesterday.
恐怕你的秘書在昨天的會議上激怒了我的老闆。

萬用延伸句型
nearly piss oneself laughing 笑到快尿出來
例如：His joke was so funny we nearly pissed ourselves laughing.
他講的笑話太好笑了，我們笑到快尿出來。

pis·tol [ˈpɪstl̩]　🔊 Track 4951
名 手槍 動 以槍擊傷 同 gun 槍
▶名 The villain showed a loaded pistol and threatened to hurt the hostage. 壞人拿出上膛的手槍，威脅要傷害人質。
▶動 It sounded like he was threatening to pistol her at that time.
聽起來像是那時他在威脅她要用手槍射擊她。

plague [pleɡ]　🔊 Track 4952
名 瘟疫
▶He's been avoiding me like the plague since our quarrel.
我們吵架以後，他一直像瘟疫似的躲著我。

plan·ta·tion [plænˈteʃən]　🔊 Track 4953
名 農場 同 farm 農場
▶There were hundreds of slaves in the plantation.
這個農場裡有數百名的奴隸。

play·wright [ˈpleˌraɪt]　🔊 Track 4954
名 劇作家
▶It is obvious that Bernard Shaw was the foremost（首要的）playwright of his time.
蕭伯納顯然是他那個時代最重要的戲劇作家。

plea [pli] Track 4955

名 藉口、懇求 同 excuse 藉口
▶The victims of floods made a plea for mercy.
洪水的受害者請求幫助。

plead [plid] Track 4956

動 懇求、為……辯護 同 appeal 懇求
▶The girl who was charged with murder was mad and unable to plead for herself in the court.
那個被指控謀殺的女孩是瘋子，無法在法庭上為自己辯護。

pledge [plɛdʒ] Track 4957

名 誓約 動 立誓 同 vow 誓約
▶名 Please take this ring as a pledge of our friendship.
請收下這個戒指作為我們友誼的信物。
▶動 He pledged to be faithful to her forever.
他發誓對她永遠忠誠。

plow [plaʊ] Track 4958

名 犁 動 耕作 同 cultivate 耕作
▶名 You had better not put the plow before the oxen（牛）.
你最好不要把犁放到牛面前（本末倒置）。
▶動 He plowed his way through the crowd to look for his friends.
他用力從人群中擠過去，找尋他的朋友。

pluck [plʌk] Track 4959

名 勇氣 動 摘、拔、扯
▶名 She showed a lot of pluck in dealing with the intruders（闖入者）.她對付那些闖入的歹徒時表現得十分勇敢。
▶動 He pluck the document from my hand and started to read it. 他把我手中的文件搶走，拿去開始讀。

plunge [plʌndʒ] Track 4960

名 陷入、急降 動 插入
▶名 The price of cooking oil has started to go on a downward plunge.
食用油的價格開始狂跌了。
▶動 You had better not plunge your hand into hot water directly.
你最好不要直接將手伸進熱水裡。

poc·ket·book [ˋpɑkɪtˏbʊk] Track 4961

名 錢包、口袋書
▶Would you please hand me my pocketbook, Evan?
伊凡，麻煩你把我的錢包拿給我好嗎？

po·et·ic [poˋɛtɪk] Track 4962

形 詩意的
▶The love letter was written in richly poetic language.
這封情書用充滿詩意的話語寫成。

文法字詞解析
此句中的「mad」並非「生氣的」的意思，而是「瘋的」，意同 crazy。

萬用延伸句型
take the plunge 下定決心投入某事
例 如：After ten years, they finally took the plunge and got married.
經過十年，他們終於決定結婚了。

Level 1

Level 2

Level 3

Level 4

Level 5

突飛猛進、程度大進擊
擴增實力5400單字

Level 6

poke [pok]　◀€ *Track 4963*

名 戳 動 戳、刺、刺探
▶名 He gave the sleeping dog a poke.
　　他戳了那隻在睡覺的狗一下。
▶動 He poked his head into the room to say hi.
　　他探頭進房間打個招呼。

po·lar [ˋpolɚ]　◀€ *Track 4964*

形 極地的 同 arctic 北極的
▶Are there any animals living in the polar circles?
　南極圈和北極圈內有動物居住嗎？

porch [portʃ]　◀€ *Track 4965*

名 玄關
▶Let's wait on the porch until it stops raining.
　我們在玄關處等到雨停吧。

po·ten·tial [pəˋtɛnʃəl]　◀€ *Track 4966*

名 潛力 形 潛在的
▶名 I don't think she has any performing potential.
　　我覺得她完全沒有表演潛力。
▶形 We sent the catalogue of our latest products to potential buyers.
　　我們寄了商品型錄給潛在客戶。

poul·try [ˋpoltrɪ]　◀€ *Track 4967*

名 家禽 同 fowl 家禽
▶Poultry is rather cheap now. Don't you think so?
　現在的家禽肉類相當便宜。你不覺得嗎？

prai·rie [ˋprɛrɪ]　◀€ *Track 4968*

名 牧場、大草原
▶On the one hand, the vast Kansas prairie is beautiful; on the other hand, it holds hidden dangers.
　廣大無垠的堪薩斯草原一方面很美麗；另一方面也隱藏著無法預知的危險。

> **萬用延伸句型**
> On the one hand... on the other hand...
> 一方面……，一方面……

preach [pritʃ]　◀€ *Track 4969*

動 傳教、說教、鼓吹
▶It is said that the man devoted all his life to preaching peace.
　據說這個男人將一生奉獻於鼓吹和平。

pre·cau·tion [prɪˋkɔʃən]　◀€ *Track 4970*

名 警惕、預防
▶I think we need to take precautions against fire.
　我認為我們有必要採取防火措施。

pref·er·ence [ˋprɛfərəns]　◀€ *Track 4971*

名 偏好 同 favor 偏愛
▶She showed preference to keep a simple and humble lifestyle.
　她比較喜歡簡樸的生活方式。

pre·hi·stor·ic [ˌprihɪsˈtɔrɪk]   ◀€ *Track 4972*

形 史前的
▶How about visiting the prehistoric burial grounds discovered last year?
我們去參觀去年發現的史前墓地怎麼樣？

pre·vail [prɪˈvel]   ◀€ *Track 4973*

動 戰勝、普及 同 win 贏
▶Virtue will prevail against evil.
美德必將戰勝邪惡。

pre·view [ˈpriˌvju]   ◀€ *Track 4974*

名 預演、預習 動 預演、預習、預視
▶名 Have you seen the preview of the movie yet?
你有看那部電影的預告嗎？
▶動 Could you tell me how to preview and publish my online article?
能請您告訴我如何預覽和發佈我的網路文章嗎？

文法字詞解析
就像我們學過的，「-view」是「觀看」的意思，所以加上「pre-(預先)」就會變「預習」，如果加上「re-(重複)」就是「review (複習)」。

prey [pre]   ◀€ *Track 4975*

名 犧牲品 動 捕食 同 hunt 獵食
▶名 The leopard crunched and waited for proper moment to swoop on its prey.
獵豹蹲低，等待適合捕捉獵物的時機。
▶動 Don't you know that strong animals prey upon weaker ones?
弱肉強食的道理你不懂嗎？

price·less [ˈpraɪslɪs]   ◀€ *Track 4976*

形 貴重的、無價的 同 invaluable 無價的
▶I believe that knowledge is priceless.
我認為知識是無價的。

prick [prɪk]   ◀€ *Track 4977*

名 刺痛 動 紮、刺、豎起 同 sting 刺
▶名 He felt a sharp prick when he stepped on an upturned（朝上的）nail.
他一腳踩在一枚尖頭朝上的釘子，感到一陣劇痛。
▶動 She pricked her finger with a needle.
她不小心用針紮到了手指。

文法字詞解析
這個單字也可用來罵人是個混帳。

pri·or [ˈpraɪɚ]   ◀€ *Track 4978*

形 在前的、優先的 副 居先、先前
▶形 We could not attend the banquet due to a prior engagement.
我們因為事先有安排，無法出席晚宴。
▶副 Would you tell me what happened prior to her departure?
您能不能告訴我在她走之前發生了什麼事？

pri·or·i·ty [praɪˈɔrətɪ]   ◀€ *Track 4979*

名 優先權
▶You should really learn to manage your priorities.
你真的應該學著搞清楚事情的輕重緩急。

Level 1
Level 2
Level 3
Level 4
Level 5
Level 6

突飛猛進、程度大進擊——擴增實力5400單字

pro·ces·sion [prəˋsɛʃən] ◀ᚃ *Track 4980*

名 進行、行列
▶Thousands of people joined the funeral procession.
　有上千人參加了送葬的行列。

pro·file [ˋprofaɪl] ◀ᚃ *Track 4981*

名 側面 動 畫側面像、顯出輪廓
▶名 She is prettier in profile than from the front in my opinion.
　在我看來，她的側面比正面好看。
▶動 The editor would profile a different novelist in this column
　each week.
　編輯每周都會在這個專欄側寫一位小說家。

pro·long [prəˋlɔŋ] ◀ᚃ *Track 4982*

動 延長 反 shorten 縮短
▶Scientists are working on prolonging human life.
　科學家們在努力設法延長人類的生命。

prop [prɑp] ◀ᚃ *Track 4983*

名 支撐 動 支持
▶名 The worker put a prop against the wall of the tunnel to
　keep it from falling down.
　那名工人用東西支撐住隧道的牆壁，以使它不會倒塌。
▶動 She propped the ladder against the wall.
　她把梯子靠在牆邊。

> **文法字詞解析**
> 或許是因為道具是「支撐」著整場表演的幕後功臣，演戲或表演魔術用的道具也稱做「props」。

proph·et [ˋprɑfɪt] ◀ᚃ *Track 4984*

名 先知
▶It was said that the prophet foretold a glorious future for the
　young ruler.
　據說那位先知預言這位年輕的統治者會有輝煌的前程。

pro·por·tion [prəˋporʃən] ◀ᚃ *Track 4985*

名 比例 動 使成比例 同 ratio 比例
▶名 A large proportion of their income came from the father's
　monthly wage. 有一大部分的收入，都是靠父親的月薪。
▶動 It is clear that the punishment should be proportioned to
　the crime. 顯然罪罰應該相當。

pros·pect [ˋprɑspɛkt] ◀ᚃ *Track 4986*

名 期望、前景 動 探勘 同 anticipation 期望
▶名 The prospects of this venture（投資）aren't looking good.
　這次投資的前景似乎不是很好。
▶動 They are prospecting the region for oil.
　他們正在該區勘察油礦。

> **文法字詞解析**
> future prospect = 為來的前景

prov·ince [ˋprɑvɪns] ◀ᚃ *Track 4987*

名 省（行政單位）
▶Do you know what Ireland's westernmost province is?
　你知道愛爾蘭最西邊的省分是什麼嗎？

prune [prun]
🔊 *Track 4988*

名 乾梅子 動 修剪

▶名 The little girl was eating prunes as she read a book.
那個小女孩一邊看書一邊吃梅乾。

▶動 I'm trying to prune the bushes. 我正試著修剪樹叢。

pub·li·cize [ˈpʌblɪˌsaɪz]
🔊 *Track 4989*

動 公佈、宣傳、廣告

▶She did not make efforts to publicize her works.
她沒有花力氣去宣傳自己的作品。

puff [pʌf]
🔊 *Track 4990*

名 噴煙、吹 動 噴出、吹熄

▶名 The doctor claimed that she could know my symptoms by checking my pulse.
醫生宣稱她可以測量脈搏就知道我的症狀。

▶動 He is not willing to go outside and puff out the kerosene（煤油）lamp. 他不願意出去吹滅那盞煤油燈。

pulse [pʌls]
🔊 *Track 4991*

名 脈搏 動 脈搏、跳動

▶名 He asked a doctor to take her pulse at once.
他請醫生立刻幫她量脈搏。

▶動 I can literally feel blood pulsing through my veins（血管）because of how mad I was.
我氣到都可以感覺到熱血在血管中搏動了。

pur·chase [ˈpɝtʃəs]
🔊 *Track 4992*

名 購買 動 購買
同 buy 買

▶名 How about making several purchases in the dress shop?
我們去服裝店裡買幾件衣服怎麼樣？

▶動 He purchased cheap fruniture at an auction.
他在拍賣會買了便宜的傢俱。

pyr·a·mid [ˈpɪrəmɪd]
🔊 *Track 4993*

名 金字塔、角錐

▶The acrobats stood on each other's shoulders and formed a pyramid. 雜技演員站在彼此的肩膀上，形成金字塔。

[Qq]

quack [kwæk]
🔊 *Track 4994*

名 嘎嘎的叫聲 動 嘎嘎叫

▶名 Not everyone noticed the duck's peculiar quack.
不是每個人都注意到了這隻鴨子的獨特叫聲。

▶動 Can you hear wild ducks quacking on the river?
你有聽到野鴨子在河上呱呱叫叫嗎？

文法字詞解析
這個字加上名詞字尾「-(e)r」就變成了「purchaser」，purchaser 不只有「買家、買主」的意思，也可以是一個工作的職位，例如：I work as a purchaser in my company. 我在公司擔任採購的職務。

Level 1
Level 2
Level 3
Level 4
Level 5
Level 6

突飛猛進、程度大進擊——擴增實力5400單字

qual·i·fy [ˈkwɑləˌfaɪ]　🔊 *Track 4995*

[動] 使合格
▶She will qualify as a lawyer after passing the certification exam.
她通過認證考試之後，就會成為合格的律師。

quart [kwɔrt]　🔊 *Track 4996*

[名] 夸脫（容量單位）
▶There is a quart of milk left in the pail.
桶子裡還剩下一夸脫牛奶。

quest [kwɛst]　🔊 *Track 4997*

[名] 探索、探求
▶Man will suffer many disappointments in his quest for truth.
人類在探索真理的過程中必然會遭受挫折。

quiver [ˈkwɪvɚ]　🔊 *Track 4998*

[名] / [動] 顫抖
▶[名] There is a slight quiver in his voice as he speaks.
他說話時聲音有些顫抖。
▶[動] He quivered all over with rage.
他氣得渾身發抖。

[Rr]

rack [ræk]　🔊 *Track 4999*

[名] 架子、折磨　[動] 折磨、盡力使用　[同] shelf 架子
▶[名] Would you please put my bag on the luggage rack?
請把我的包放在行李架上好嗎？
▶[動] I couldn't think of a single example after racking my brain. Would you please help me? 就算絞盡腦汁我還是連一個例子也想不出來。你能幫幫我嗎？

rad·ish [ˈrædɪʃ]　🔊 *Track 5000*

[名] 蘿蔔
▶The dried radish was used as an ingredient in this dish.
風乾的蘿蔔被用在這道菜中作佐料。

ra·di·us [ˈredɪəs]　🔊 *Track 5001*

[名] 半徑
▶We can calculate the circular area if we know the radius.
如果我們知道半徑多少，就能計算出圓的面積。

rag·ged [ˈrægɪd]　🔊 *Track 5002*

[形] 破爛的　[同] shabby 破爛的
▶Children in the war-torn zone were wearing dirty, ragged clothes.
在戰區的小孩，穿著骯髒、破爛的衣服。

文法字詞解析

qualifying exams 資格考
例如：You need to pass the qualifying exams before graduating.
畢業前必須先考過資格考才行。
certification exam 認證考試

萬用延伸句型

be on the rack 非常緊張焦慮
例如：I was on the rack waiting for the results of the exam.
我非常緊張地等待著測驗結果出來。

rail [rel]　　　🔊 Track 5003

名 橫杆、鐵軌

▶I think it's cheaper to ship goods by road than by rail.
我覺得公路運輸比鐵路運輸更便宜。

ral·ly [ˈrælɪ]　　　🔊 Track 5004

名 集合、集會　動 召集　同 gathering 聚集

▶名 More than three thousand people held an anti-nuclear rally.
超過三千人舉辦了反核集會。

▶動 It is time for us to rally our own defense force.
我們是時候組織自己的防衛隊了。

ranch [ræntʃ]　　　🔊 Track 5005

名 大農場　動 經營大農場　同 plantation 大農場

▶名 It takes me about 10 minutes from here to my ranch on foot. 從這兒到我的農場步行約十分鐘就到了。

▶動 He spent almost all his life ranching the large farm.
他幾乎花了他一生的時間經營那個大農場。

ras·cal [ˈræskl̩]　　　🔊 Track 5006

名 流氓

▶It is said that the rascal who beat the little boy was arrested this morning.
據說那個毆打小男孩的流氓今天上午被抓起來了。

ra·tio [ˈreʃo]　　　🔊 Track 5007

名 比率、比例　同 proportion 比率、比例

▶Would you please tell me what the ratio of boys to girls in your class is?
請告訴我你們班上男女生的比例是多少好嗎？

rat·tle [ˈrætl̩]　　　🔊 Track 5008

名 嘎嘎聲　動 發出嘎嘎聲、喋喋不休地講話

▶名 The baby was scared by the rattle in the wind.
小寶寶被風聲嚇到了。

▶動 He rattled on about his job, not noticing how bored she was. 他只顧喋喋不休地說自己工作上的事，沒注意到她有多無聊。

realm [rɛlm]　　　🔊 Track 5009

名 王國、領域

▶He made outstanding contributions in the realm of foreign affairs.
他在外交領域中有卓越的成績。

reap [rip]　　　🔊 Track 5010

動 收割

▶The peasants reap the corn from what they planted in spring.
農民們在收割他們春季播種的玉米。

文法字詞解析
「欄杆」的另一個說法是 railings，例如若你在陽台上靠著欄杆，可能就會有人叫你不要 lean on the railings，那是很危險的。

文法字詞解析
這裡用形容詞子句「who beat the little boy」來修飾前面的名詞「the rascal」。

Level
1

Level
2

Level
3

Level
4

Level
5

突飛猛進、程度大進擊——
擴增實力5400單字

Level
6

rear [rɪr]
🔊 *Track 5011*

名 後面 形 後面的 同 front 前面

▶名 There's something stuck at the rear of the car.
車子後面有東西黏住了。

▶形 The boys and girls were singing loudly in the rear of the bus.
這些男孩和女孩在公車後面大聲唱歌。

reck·less [ˈrɛklɪs]
🔊 *Track 5012*

形 魯莽的 同 rash 魯莽的

▶The reckless boy was playing in the river even though he was told not to.
雖然那個魯莽的男孩不被允許在河裡玩，他還是去河裡玩了。

reck·on [ˈrɛkən]
🔊 *Track 5013*

動 計算、依賴 同 count 計算

▶I reckon that she said something nice just to be polite.
我想她只是出於禮貌，才會說些好話。

rec·om·mend [ˌrɛkəˈmɛnd]
🔊 *Track 5014*

動 推薦、託付

▶Would you please recommend a good dictionary to me?
你能為我推薦一本好字典嗎？

reef [rif]
🔊 *Track 5015*

名 暗礁

▶It is reported that the ship struck a hidden reef and went down.
據報導，那艘船撞上暗礁沉沒了。

reel [ril]
🔊 *Track 5016*

名 捲軸 動 捲線、搖擺

▶名 A reel of the movie is missing. Would you help me look for it?
那部電影的一捲片子不見了。請幫我找找好嗎？

▶動 The man quickly reeled the fish in.
那個男人很快地把魚捲上岸。

ref·e·ree/um·pire
🔊 *Track 5017*

[ˌrɛfəˈri]/[ˈʌmpaɪr]

名 裁判者 動 裁判、調停

▶名 The referee was so unfair.
這裁判真的很不公正。

▶動 My dad's job is to referee matches.
我爸爸的工作是當球賽的裁判。

ref·uge/sanc·tu·ar·y
🔊 *Track 5018*

[ˈrɛfjudʒ]/[ˈsæŋktʃuˌɛrɪ]

名 避難（所）

▶The journalist was seeking refuge from political persecution.
記者尋求政治迫害的庇護。

萬用延伸句型
Do you reckon...? 你認為⋯⋯嗎？

文法字詞解析
「reel...in」這個片語除了用在魚身上，表示釣魚時把魚拉上岸以外，也可以拿在人身上，表示把某人捲入某個計畫、活動中。

re·fute [rɪˋfjut] ◀ Track 5019

動 反駁 同 oppose 反對

▶"You can't tell me not to watch TV when you yourself watch it all day," she refuted. 「你不能叫我不要看電視啊，你自己還不是整天看，」她反駁道。

reign [ren] ◀ Track 5020

名 主權 動 統治 同 rule 統治

▶名 The reign of Queen Victoria lasted more than sixty years. 維多利亞女王的統治持續了六十多年。

▶動 Horror and anxiety reigned over the city during the war. 戰爭時，恐懼和焦慮籠罩全市。

文法字詞解析
若某人統治的時期做了很多可怕的事、讓人民苦不堪言，則可稱為 a reign of terror。

re·joice [rɪˋdʒɔɪs] ◀ Track 5021

動 歡喜 反 lament 悲痛

▶Let us rejoice together on your success. 讓我們一起歡慶你的成功吧。

rel·ic [ˋrɛlɪk] ◀ Track 5022

名 遺物

▶Not everybody knows that this custom is a relic of ancient times. 不是每個人都知道這個習俗是古代的遺風。

re·mind·er [rɪˋmaɪndɚ] ◀ Track 5023

名 提醒者

▶Send me a reminder to buy milk on my way home. 請提醒我回家路上要買牛奶。

re·pay [rɪˋpe] ◀ Track 5024

動 償還、報答 同 reward 報答

▶I wish I could repay you somehow for your kindness. 但願對你的好意我能有所報答。

re·pro·duce [͵riprəˋdjus] ◀ Track 5025

動 複製、再生

▶Most fish reproduce by laying eggs. 大多數的魚透過產卵來繁殖。

rep·tile [ˋrɛptaɪl] ◀ Track 5026

名 爬蟲類 形 爬行的

▶名 What is the difference between amphibian and reptile? 兩棲類和爬蟲類有什麼不同？

▶形 The land is teeming（充滿）with reptile life. 這片土地上有很多爬行動物。

re·pub·li·can [rɪˋpʌblɪkən] ◀ Track 5027

名 共和主義者 形 共和主義的 反 democratic 民主主義的

▶名 Richard is a dyed-in-the-wool（徹頭徹尾的）Republican. Don't you think so? 理查是個徹頭徹尾的共和主義者。難道不是嗎？

▶形 This is a very difficult moment for the Republican Party. 這對共和黨來說是非常艱難的時刻。

文法字詞解析
dyed-in-the-wool 直接翻譯就是「染在羊毛中的」，可想而知，染在羊毛上的顏色非常難洗掉，就如同理查的共和主義色彩很難洗掉一樣，因此才會說他是「徹頭徹尾的」共和主義者。

Level 1
Level 2
Level 3
Level 4
Level 5
擴增實力5400單字 突飛猛進、程度大進擊
Level 6

re·sent [rɪˋzɛnt] 🔊 *Track 5028*

動 憤恨
▶ I resent having to get his permission for everything I do.
我討厭做每件事都要得到他的許可。

re·sent·ment [rɪˋzɛntmənt] 🔊 *Track 5029*

名 憤慨 同 irritation 惱怒
▶ There is some resentment toward the new policy on dress code.
人們對於新的穿衣規則有些怨懟。

re·side [rɪˋzaɪd] 🔊 *Track 5030*

動 居住 同 dwell 居住
▶ This family has resided in this city for more than 60 years.
這個家族住在這座城已有六十多年了。

res·i·dence [ˋrɛzədəns] 🔊 *Track 5031*

名 住家
▶ It was said that he married an English woman and took up his residence in London.
據說他與一名英國女子結婚並且定居在倫敦。

res·i·dent [ˋrɛzədənt] 🔊 *Track 5032*

名 居民 形 居留的、住校的
▶ 名 Many local residents took part in that activity.
很多當地居民參加了那個活動。
▶ 形 There are many resident students in my class.
我們班上有很多住宿生。

文法字詞解析
負責某所醫院的住院醫師也稱為 resident。

re·sort [rɪˋzɔrt] 🔊 *Track 5033*

名 休閒勝地 動 依靠、訴諸
▶ 名 The place has become a famous summer resort.
這個地方已經成為一個避暑勝地。
▶ 動 He resorted to force after repeated failures.
多次失敗之後,他就訴諸於暴力解決了。

re·strain [rɪˋstren] 🔊 *Track 5034*

動 抑制
▶ She couldn't restrain her anger and shouted at her neighbor.
她無法抑制怒氣,對鄰居大吼。

re·sume [ˋrɛzʌme]/[rɪˋzjum] 🔊 *Track 5035*

名 摘要、履歷表 動 再開始
▶ 名 Would you please send a detailed resume to our company?
請寄給我們公司一份詳細的履歷表好嗎?
▶ 動 Would you please resume your job as a general manager?
您能重新做總經理的工作嗎?

文法字詞解析
要注意喔!這個單字有兩個唸法,一個指「履歷表」,重音在第一個音節;另一個意指「再開始」,重音在第二個音節。

re·tort [rɪˋtɔrt] 🔊 *Track 5036*

名 反駁 動 反駁、回嘴
▶ 名 Luckily the boss didn't hear his retort.
幸好他老闆沒聽到他反駁的話。

▶ 動 "You're no better than I am," he retorted.
「你也沒有比我好啊，」他反駁道。

re·verse [rɪˋvɝs] ◀ Track 5037

名 顛倒 動 反轉 形 相反的

▶ 名 I am afraid that the truth is just the reverse.
恐怕真實情況恰好相反吧。

▶ 動 She appealed to the supreme court, hoping to reverse the judgement.
她向最高法院上訴，希望逆轉判決。

▶ 形 The man drove in the reverse direction.
這個男人朝著相反的方向開車。

re·vive [rɪˋvaɪv] ◀ Track 5038

動 復甦、復原 同 restore 復原

▶ They were unable to revive the drowned boy.
他們無法讓那個溺水的男孩復甦。

re·volt [rɪˋvolt] ◀ Track 5039

名 叛亂 動 叛變、嫌惡 同 rebel 叛亂

▶ 名 It was the revolt of the British North American colonies that resulted in the establishment of the US. 是英國的北美殖民地人民的反抗鬥爭，導致了美國的建國。

▶ 動 They revolted the authorities and established another set of rules for the locals. 他們推翻有關當局的決定，建立另一套適用當地人的規則。

re·volve [rɪˋvɑlv] ◀ Track 5040

動 旋轉、循環

▶ It is obvious that their troubles revolve around money management. 顯然他們的麻煩圍繞在對金錢的處理上。

rhi·noce·r·os/rhi·no ◀ Track 5041
[raɪˋnɑsərəs]/[ˋraɪno]

名 犀牛

▶ Have you ever seen a rhinoceros? What does it look like?
你見過犀牛嗎？牠長什麼樣子？

rib [rɪb] ◀ Track 5042

名 肋骨 動 支撐、嘲弄

▶ 名 I don't know how many ribs a person has.
我不知道人有多少根肋骨。

▶ 動 They ribbed him for wearing mismatching（不成對的）socks. 他們嘲笑他穿了不成對的襪子。

ridge [rɪdʒ] ◀ Track 5043

名 背脊、山脊 動 （使）成脊狀

▶ 名 Two cats were sitting on the ridge of the house, enjoying the sun. 有兩隻貓坐在屋脊上享受陽光。

▶ 動 The ocean floor of the Atlantic ridges in the middle from north to south.
大西洋海底在中部形成一道由北向南的海脊。

文法字詞解析
第一個例句用了分裂句句型「It was... that...」來強調「revolt」。

Level 1

Level 2

Level 3

Level 4

Level 5

突飛猛進、程度大進擊──擴增實力5400單字

Level 6

ri·dic·u·lous [rɪˈdɪkjələs] ◀≣ *Track 5044*

形 荒謬的
▶What a ridiculous suggestion! Don't you think so?
多麼荒唐的建議！你不這樣認為嗎？

----

ri·fle [ˈraɪfl] ◀≣ *Track 5045*

名 來福槍、步兵 動 掠奪
▶名 It is said that he has been appointed captain of a company of rifles. 據說他已經被任命為步兵連連長了。
▶動 The thief rifled every drawer in the room.
竊賊洗劫了房內所有抽屜裡的東西。

----

rig·id [ˈrɪdʒɪd] ◀≣ *Track 5046*

形 嚴格的
▶The professor was rigid with the format of reports.
教授對於報告格式很嚴苛。

----

rim [rɪm] ◀≣ *Track 5047*

名 邊緣 動 加邊於
▶名 There is a red flower on the rim of the girl's hat.
那個女孩的帽子邊上有一朵紅花。
▶動 Lots of trees rimmed the cemetery（公墓）.
有很多樹木環繞在公墓四周。

----

rip [rɪp] ◀≣ *Track 5048*

名 裂口 動 扯裂
▶名 She sewed up the rip in his sleeve very fast.
她很快就縫好了他衣袖上的裂口。
▶動 The poster was ripped to pieces. 那張海報被撕得粉碎。

rip·ple [ˈrɪpl] ◀≣ *Track 5049*

名 波動 動 起連漪
▶名 I wish I could lie on the bank and listen to the ripple of the stream. 我希望能躺在河岸上傾聽小河的潺潺流水聲。
▶動 The kid threw a pebble, causing ripples in the lake.
小孩丟石頭，導致湖面產生連漪。

----

ri·val [ˈraɪvl] ◀≣ *Track 5050*

名 對手 動 競爭 同 compete 競爭
▶名 I don't believe that they are rivals for the same position.
我不相信他們是爭奪同一個職位的敵手。
▶動 I don't think that anyone could rival him in this respect.
我認為在這方面沒有人能勝過他。

----

roam [rom] ◀≣ *Track 5051*

名 漫步 動 徘徊、流浪 同 wander 徘徊
▶名 Let's take a roam in the beautiful park.
我們在這個美麗的公園漫步吧。
▶動 He has roamed the city for years.
他在這個城市流浪了很多年。

萬用延伸句型
rip sth. up 將某物撕裂
Oh, no! My dog ripped my homework up.
糟糕！我的狗把我的功課撕掉了。

文法字詞解析
出國可能會用到的「手機國際漫遊」也和「roam」這個字相關。

rob·in [ˈrɑbɪn]　　🔊 *Track 5052*

名 知更鳥
▶ If you see a robin, it means that spring is coming soon.
　一旦你看見了一隻知更鳥，就表示春天就要到了。

ro·bust [roˈbʌst]　　🔊 *Track 5053*

形 強健的　反 weak 虛弱的
▶ You need a robust pair of walking boots for the hike.
　你需要一雙耐用的鞋去健行。

rod [rɑd]　　🔊 *Track 5054*

名 竿、棒、教鞭　同 stick 棒
▶ Can you grab that fishing rod for me?
　幫我拿一下那根釣竿好不好？

> 文法字詞解析
> 避雷針稱為 lightning rod。

rub·bish [ˈrʌbɪʃ]　　🔊 *Track 5055*

名 垃圾　同 garbage 垃圾
▶ How to get rid of rubbish is a big problem.
　如何處理垃圾是個大問題。

rug·ged [ˈrʌgɪd]　　🔊 *Track 5056*

形 粗糙的　反 smooth 柔順的
▶ Would you please forgive my husband's rugged manners?
　請原諒我丈夫粗魯的態度好嗎？

rum·ble [ˈrʌmbl]　　🔊 *Track 5057*

名 隆隆聲　動 發出隆隆聲
▶ 名 We heard the occasional rumble of a passing truck.
　我們偶爾聽到卡車駛過的隆隆聲。
▶ 動 My stomach was rumbling for I was really hungry.
　我肚子太餓，才會隆隆作響。

> 文法字詞解析
> rumble 也有打架（尤指街頭幫派）的意思。

rus·tle [ˈrʌsl]　　🔊 *Track 5058*

名 沙沙響　動 沙沙作響
▶ 名 I heard a rustle from a snake in the bushes.
　我聽到了灌木叢中的蛇所發出的聲響。
▶ 動 Did you hear something rustling in the trees?
　你有聽到有東西在樹上沙沙作響嗎？

[Ss]

sa·cred [ˈsekrɪd]　　🔊 *Track 5059*

形 神聖的　同 holy 神聖的
▶ Oxen are sacred in Hinduism.
　牛在印度教中是神聖的。

Level 1
Level 2
Level 3
Level 4
Level 5
Level 6

突飛猛進、程度大進擊──
擴增實力5400單字

sad·dle [ˋsædḷ]   🔊 *Track 5060*

名 鞍 動 套以馬鞍

▶名 Will you please give me a lift onto the saddle, Tom?
湯姆，請你扶我上馬鞍好嗎？

▶動 Can you tell me how I should saddle up a horse?
你能告訴我該如何為馬套上鞍嗎？

saint [sent]   🔊 *Track 5061*

名 聖、聖人 動 列為聖徒

▶名 The nurse must be a real saint for she had immense patience for her patients.
這位護士對病人有極大的耐心，她一定是位聖人。

▶動 Do you think he will be sainted one day?
你認為他有一天會被列為聖徒嗎？

salm·on [ˋsæmən]   🔊 *Track 5062*

名 鮭 形 鮭肉色的、淺橙色的

▶名 Smoked salmon can be a very good side dish.
煙燻鮭魚會是很好的配菜。

▶形 What you described is not the salmon pink which we want.
你描述的並不是我們所需要的淺橙色。

> **文法字詞解析**
> 在第二個例句中，「what you described」做為整句的主詞，其中的「what」用來代替不確定的事物。

sa·lute [səˋlut]   🔊 *Track 5063*

名 招呼、敬禮 動 致意、致敬 同 greeting 招呼

▶名 The soldiers exchange salutes as soon as they meet each other.士兵們一遇到彼此就會互相敬禮。

▶動 The teacher asked his students to salute the flag.
那位老師要求他的學生們向國旗致敬。

san·dal [ˋsændḷ]   🔊 *Track 5064*

名 涼鞋、便鞋

▶ The girls are all wearing cute sandals.
女孩們都穿了可愛的涼鞋。

> **文法字詞解析**
> 此外，有一種木材也和 sandal 有關，叫作 sandalwood，是「檀香」的意思。

sav·age [ˋsævɪdʒ]   🔊 *Track 5065*

名 野蠻人 形 荒野的、野性的 同 fierce 兇猛的

▶名 There is an island on the sea over there inhabited（居住）by savages.
在那邊的海上有個野蠻人居住的島嶼。

▶形 It is said that there is a savage lion in the forest.
據說森林裡有頭猛獅。

scan [skæn]   🔊 *Track 5066*

名 掃描 動 掃描、審視

▶名 I scanned through the book to look for the reference I needed.
我掃描整本書，尋找我需要的參考資料。

▶動 Use this machine to scan the materials. It'll be quicker.
用這台機器掃描一下這些檔案，會更快一點。

scan·dal [ˈskændl̩]   🔊 *Track 5067*

名 醜聞、恥辱 同 disgrace 恥辱

▶By the time he was taken away by the police, all people knew about the scandal.
到他被警察抓走的時候，所有人就都知道了這件醜事。

scar [skɑr]   🔊 *Track 5068*

名 傷痕、疤痕 動 使留下疤痕

▶名 Would you tell me whether the cut will leave a scar on my face?
你能告訴我這個傷口會不會在我的臉上留下疤痕嗎？

▶動 Can you tell me when and how he scarred his face?
能請你告訴我他是何時、如何在臉上弄出傷疤嗎？

文法字詞解析
除了「真正的」疤痕外，scar 也可以拿來表示心理上的創傷、疤痕。例如若有人給你看了一個讓你一輩子難忘的恐怖影片，你就可以說：「It scarred me for life.」（這讓我留下一輩子的創傷。）

scent [sɛnt]   🔊 *Track 5069*

名 氣味、痕跡 動 聞、嗅 同 smell 氣味

▶名 The scents of flowers fill the grove（樹林）now.
現在花香充滿了小樹林。

▶動 I scent a whiff（些微的氣味）of fragrance in the house.
我在房子裡聞到了一股香味。

scheme [skim]   🔊 *Track 5070*

名 計畫、陰謀 動 計畫、密謀、擬訂

▶名 There is a new scheme in the town to encourage carpooling.
這個城裡有個鼓勵共乘的新計畫。

▶動 Why don't we scheme out a new method?
為什麼不擬訂一種新的辦法？

scorn [skɔrn]   🔊 *Track 5071*

名 輕蔑、蔑視 動 不屑做、鄙視 同 contempt 輕蔑

▶名 They all look at the boy with scorn.
他們都以蔑視的眼光看著這個男孩。

▶動 No one has the right to scorn this poor girl.
這裡的每一個人都無權鄙視這個貧窮的女孩。

scram·ble [ˈskræmbl̩]   🔊 *Track 5072*

名 攀爬、爭奪 動 爭奪、湊合

▶名 It was a long scramble to the top of the hill.
我們爬了一段長路到山頂。

▶動 It took him half a day to scramble some data for his company.
他花了半天時間才為公司收集到了一些資料。

文法字詞解析
炒蛋稱為 scrambled eggs。

scrap [skræp]   🔊 *Track 5073*

名 小片、少許 動 丟棄、爭吵 同 quarrel 爭吵

▶名 I don't think there's a scrap of truth in the claim.
我認為這種說法毫無真實性。

▶動 We scrapped out plan in for the trip to Scandinavia.
我們取消去北歐旅行的計畫。

Level
1

Level
2

Level
3

Level
4

Level
5
突飛猛進、程度大進擊
擴增實力5400單字

Level
6

scrape [skrep] 🔊 *Track 5074*

名 磨擦聲、擦掉 動 磨擦、擦刮 同 rub 磨擦

▶名 She fell off the bike and got a scrape on her knee.
她從自行車上摔下來，擦破了膝蓋。

▶動 Can you help me scrape the ashes from the furnace（火爐），Bill?
比爾，請你幫我把爐灰刮乾淨好嗎？

scroll [skrol] 🔊 *Track 5075*

名 卷軸 動 把……寫在捲軸上、（電腦術語）捲頁

▶名 Several scrolls of calligraphic paintings were hung on the wall. 有幾幅水墨畫卷軸掛在牆上。

▶動 My mouse was broken and I couldn't scroll down.
我的滑鼠壞掉了，我都沒辦法往下捲頁了。

sculp·tor [ˈskʌlptə] 🔊 *Track 5076*

名 雕刻家、雕刻師

▶In my opinion, the sculptor is greater than anyone else in his time.
在我看來，這名雕刻家比他同時代的任何其他人都要偉大。

se·cure [sɪˈkjʊr] 🔊 *Track 5077*

動 保護 形 安心的、安全的 同 safe 安全的

▶動 This national hero secured the nation against attack.
這個民族英雄使得國家免於受到攻擊。

▶形 The contract shall be kept in a secure place.
這份合約要保管在安全的地方。

seg·ment [ˈsɛgmənt] 🔊 *Track 5078*

名 部分、段 動 分割、劃分 同 section 部分

▶名 We researched the popularity of our product at a specific market segment.
我們研究產品在特定市場區塊的受歡迎程度。

▶動 The show was segmented so that it wouldn't be too long and boring. 這個節目分了好幾段，才不會又長又無聊。

sen·sa·tion [sɛnˈseʃən] 🔊 *Track 5079*

名 感覺、知覺 同 feeling 感覺

▶Don't you just love the sensation of warmth when you slip into a hot bath? 你不覺得滑進熱水澡中的感覺很棒嗎？

sen·si·tiv·i·ty [ˌsɛnsəˈtɪvətɪ] 🔊 *Track 5080*

名 敏感度、靈敏度

▶It is her sensitivity that enabled her to create so many touching stories.
正是她的多愁善感使她能寫出這麼多感人的故事。

sen·ti·ment [ˈsɛntəmənt] 🔊 *Track 5081*

名 情緒

▶The crowd shared the sentiments as the national player strived to win in the game.
人群情感上支持那個努力贏得比賽的球員。

萬用延伸句型

scrape by 指千鈞一髮地達成所需目標。舉例來說，如果在比賽中必須獲得至少 60 分才能晉級下一輪，而你得了 61 分，這就是 scrape by 了。

文法字詞解析

引起轟動、非常受到歡迎的偶像也稱為 sensation。

ser·geant [ˈsɑrdʒənt] 🔊 *Track 5082*
名 士官
▶It has been two years since my elder brother became a sergeant. 我哥哥當士官已經兩年了。

se·ries [ˈsɪriz] 🔊 *Track 5083*
名 連續 同 succession 連續
▶It was reported that a series of deadly attacks happened in India. 據報導，在印度發生了一系列的致命襲擊。

ser·mon [ˈsɝmən] 🔊 *Track 5084*
名 佈道、講道 同 detect 察覺
▶Today's sermon was on the importance of kinship. 今天的佈道主題是親屬關係的重要。

serv·er [ˈsɝvɚ] 🔊 *Track 5085*
名 侍者、服役者 同 waiter 侍者
▶Will you let a server here introduce the pub to us? 你能讓這裡的一名服務生為給我們介紹一下這家酒店嗎？

set·ting [ˈsɛtɪŋ] 🔊 *Track 5086*
名 安置的地點、背景
▶It was said that the setting of the story is a hotel in London. 據說故事的背景在倫敦的一家旅館裡。

shab·by [ˈʃæbɪ] 🔊 *Track 5087*
形 衣衫襤褸的 反 decent 體面的
▶The tramp（流浪漢） looked rather shabby in those clothes on the busy street. 這個流浪漢在繁華的街道上顯得衣著相當寒酸。

sharp·en [ˈʃɑrpn̩] 🔊 *Track 5088*
動 使銳利、使尖銳
▶My pencil is blunt（鈍的）. Will you lend me a knife to sharpen it, Mike? 我的鉛筆鈍了。麥克，你能借我把刀子削一削嗎？

shat·ter [ˈʃætɚ] 🔊 *Track 5089*
動 粉碎、砸破 同 break 砸破
▶The rumble of the thunder shattered the peace in the tranquil afternoon. 打雷聲劃破了寧靜下午的和平氣氛。

sher·iff [ˈʃɛrɪf] 🔊 *Track 5090*
名 警長
▶There is a sheriff in town that none of the kids and adults like. 鎮上有個大人小孩們都討厭的警長。

shield [ʃild] 🔊 *Track 5091*
名 盾 動 遮蔽
▶名 The shield was solid enough to protect him from the blows of his enemy. 這盾牌很堅固，足以保護他免受敵人的打擊。
▶動 These trees are not big enough to shield us from strong winds. 這些樹還不夠大，所以還不能替我們擋住強風。

文法字詞解析
除了表達衣衫破舊之外，shabby 也可以拿來描述衣物以外的東西「不體面」。相反地，如果你覺得某物還算體面，也可以反過來說：「Not too shabby, isn't it?」（還算夠體面吧？）

Level 1
Level 2
Level 3
Level 4
Level 5
Level 6

突飛猛進、程度大進擊──擴增實力5400單字

shiv·er [ˈʃɪvɚ]
🔊 *Track 5092*

名 顫抖　動 冷得發抖　同 quake 顫抖

▶名 She gave a tiny shiver.
她輕輕顫抖了一下。

▶動 The dog was shivering in the cold windy night.
這隻狗在風大的夜晚發抖著。

short·age [ˈʃɔrtɪdʒ]
🔊 *Track 5093*

名 不足、短缺　同 deficiency 不足

▶The bad harvest led to severe food shortage.
欠收引起食物嚴重短缺。

short·com·ing [ˈʃɔrtˌkʌmɪŋ]
🔊 *Track 5094*

名 短處、缺點　同 deficiency 不足

▶She likes telling people about her husband's shortcomings.
她喜歡到處跟人家說她丈夫的缺點。

shove [ʃʌv]
🔊 *Track 5095*

名 推　動 推、推動

▶名 He gave her a shove when she was standing by the lake.
她站在湖邊的時候,他推了她一把。

▶動 It's impolite for you to shove old people like that.
你那樣推老人很不禮貌哦。

萬用延伸句型
if push comes to shove 如果非不得已……
例如:I'm not good at dancing, but if push comes to shove, I'll still manage.
我不是很會跳舞,但如果非不得已,我趕鴨子上架還是能跳的。

shred [ʃrɛd]
🔊 *Track 5096*

名 細長的片段　動 撕成碎布

▶名 Susan, will you peel the carrots and cut them into shreds?
蘇珊,妳能將紅蘿蔔削皮切成絲嗎?

▶動 The important document had been shredded before the inspectors came.
這份重要文件在檢查原來之前,被剪碎了。

shriek [ʃrik]
🔊 *Track 5097*

名 尖叫　動 尖叫、叫喊　同 scream 尖叫

▶名 All of a sudden he let out a piercing（尖銳的）shriek.
他突然發出一聲尖叫。

▶動 She shrieked, but not all people on the street heard it.
她尖叫了一聲,但卻不是街上所有的人都聽了。

shrine [ʃraɪn]
🔊 *Track 5098*

名 廟、祠

▶How often does your grandma go to pray at the shrine every month?
你奶奶每月去廟裡拜拜幾次啊?

萬用延伸句型
How often...? 多常……?

shrub [ʃrʌb]
🔊 *Track 5099*

名 灌木　同 bush 灌木

▶Shrubs are much like trees, but they are much smaller than trees.灌木很像樹,但又比樹小得多。

shud·der [ˈʃʌdɚ] 🔊 *Track 5100*

名 發抖、顫抖 動 顫抖、戰慄 同 tremble 顫抖
- ▶名 A shudder of fear ran through him when the police came.
  警察到的時候他被嚇得渾身直發抖。
- ▶動 He shuddered at the thought of the scenes at war.
  他一想到戰爭場景就不寒而慄。

shut·ter [ˈʃʌtɚ] 🔊 *Track 5101*

名 百葉窗 動 關上窗
- ▶名 Will you open the shutter and let some fresh air in?
  你能把百葉窗打開，好讓一些新鮮空氣流進來嗎？
- ▶動 Will you make sure all the windows are shuttered before you leave?
  能請你離開前確保所有窗戶都關上了嗎？

silk·worm [ˈsɪlkwɝm] 🔊 *Track 5102*

名 蠶
- ▶There are not enough people to raise silkworms in the village.
  村裡養蠶的人不是很夠。

sim·mer [ˈsɪmɚ] 🔊 *Track 5103*

名 沸騰的狀態 動 煲、怒氣爆發 同 stew 燉、燜
- ▶名 I don't think you can bring water to a simmer in such a way.
  我覺得你用這樣的方法是無法將水慢慢燒開的。
- ▶動 I don't think the soup will be delicious if we simmer it too long. 我覺得這湯如果燉太久會不好喝。

skel·e·ton [ˈskɛlətn̩] 🔊 *Track 5104*

名 骨骼、骨架 同 bone 骨骼
- ▶The sick kid was reduced almost to a skeleton.
  那個生病的孩子現在幾乎是皮包骨了。

skull [skʌl] 🔊 *Track 5105*

名 頭蓋骨
- ▶I hope the scientists can find the lost crystal skull as soon as possible.
  我希望科學家們能盡快找到遺失的那個水晶頭蓋骨。

slam [slæm] 🔊 *Track 5106*

名 砰然聲 動 砰地關上
- ▶名 He threw his books down with a slam angrily.
  他生氣地砰然一聲把書摔在桌上。
- ▶動 He slammed the door in a rage.
  他盛怒下甩了門。

slap [slæp] 🔊 *Track 5107*

名 掌擊 動 用掌拍擊
- ▶名 It hit him like a cold slap in the face.
  這件事對他來說簡直就是晴天霹靂。
- ▶動 He slapped her across the face and made her cry.
  他摑了她一記耳光，讓她哭了。

萬用延伸句型
not enough... to... 沒有足夠的……能夠做……

Level 1

Level 2

Level 3

Level 4

Level 5

擴增實力5400單字——突飛猛進、程度大進擊

Level 6

slaugh·ter [ˈslɔtɚ]
🔊 *Track 5108*

名 屠宰　動 屠宰

▶名 Ancient people believe that ritual slaughter of animals can being blessings to people.
古代人相信獻祭宰殺牲畜，能為人祈福。

▶動 Millions of cattle are slaughtered every day in this country.
這個國家每天都有數百萬頭牛被屠宰。

slay [sle]
🔊 *Track 5109*

名 殺害、殺　同 kill 殺

▶It is illegal（違法的）for people to slay the cattle in most of India. 殺牛在印度大部分地區都是違法的。

slop·py [ˈslɑpɪ]
🔊 *Track 5110*

形 不整潔的、邋遢的　同 neat 整潔的

▶Why is your handwriting so sloppy?
為什麼你寫的字這麼不整齊？

slump [slʌmp]
🔊 *Track 5111*

名 下跌　動 暴跌

▶名 There was a serious slump in the rice market.
稻米市場呈現出嚴重衰退的趨勢。

▶動 Sales have slumped badly recently, and many companies went bankrupt. 最近銷售量銳減，很多企業正面臨倒閉。

sly [slaɪ]
🔊 *Track 5112*

形 狡猾的、陰險的　反 frank 坦白的

▶The sly fox tricked the rabbit. 那隻狡猾的狐狸騙了兔子。

smash [smæʃ]
🔊 *Track 5113*

名 激烈的碰撞　動 粉碎、碰撞　同 shatter 粉碎

▶名 The dog ran into the door with a smash.
那隻狗狠狠地撞上了門。

▶動 They not only robbed him but also smashed all the furniture in the house.
他們不僅搶劫他，而且還砸壞了家裡所有的傢俱。

snarl [snɑrl]
🔊 *Track 5114*

名 漫罵、爭吵　動 吼叫著說、糾結

▶名 I don't think the snarls we heard last night were from their home. 我覺得昨天晚上我們聽到的咆哮聲不是從他們家傳出來的。

▶動 The dog snarled as the toddler tried to reach its bowl.
小孩伸手拿狗的碗，狗就低鳴警告。

snatch [snætʃ]
🔊 *Track 5115*

名 片段　動 奪取、抓住　同 grab 抓取

▶名 He had a snatch of sleep sitting in this chair.
他坐在這張椅子上小睡了一會。

▶動 He snatched the notebook away from her.
他從她手中搶走了筆記本。

文法字詞解析

就像我們中文也可能會以「很殺」當作稱讚來描述某人很厲害、氣勢很強一樣，英文也可以用「slay」來表達稱讚之意，說某人或某事物非常厲害、令人折服。

文法字詞解析

在用電腦聊天，想表達自己激動情緒時常會在鍵盤上激烈地一陣亂按，打出 asdhakghladhgadfg 之類的字樣，這樣的情況就叫做 keysmash。

sneak [snik]
◀€ Track 5116

動 潛行、偷偷地走

▶No one noticed him sneaking up behind Mike.
沒有人注意到他從麥克的後面偷偷溜了上來。

sneak·er(s) [ˈsnikɚ(s)]
◀€ Track 5117

名 慢跑鞋

▶It is hard for us to find a pair of comfortable and durable（耐用的）sneakers. 我們很難找到既舒服又耐穿的運動鞋。

sniff [snɪf]
◀€ Track 5118

名 吸氣 動 用鼻吸、嗅、聞 同 scent 嗅、聞

▶名 One sniff of this is enough to kill you. Don't you believe that? 聞一聞這個東西就足以致命。你不信嗎？

▶動 I sniffed at the glass of wine before tasting it.
我在品酒之前，先聞了酒香。

snore [snor]
◀€ Track 5119

名 鼾聲 動 打鼾

▶名 Her husband's snores are so loud that she often has to take some sleeping pills before sleeping.
她老公的鼾聲很大以致於她睡前得吃些安眠藥才行。

▶動 When her husband snored, she threw a pillow at him.
她丈夫一打鼾，她就拿枕頭丟他。

snort [snɔrt]
◀€ Track 5120

名 鼻息、哼氣 動 哼著鼻子說

▶名 He gave a snort when he heard her comment.
他聽到她的評語，就哼了一聲。

▶動 She snorted when she heard him boasting about himself.
她聽到他自吹自擂時，哼了一聲。

soak [sok]
◀€ Track 5121

名 浸泡 動 浸、滲入

▶名 Let's give these clothes a long soak before washing.
洗衣服之前我們先將這些衣服多泡久一點。

▶動 You have to use paper towels to soak up the cooking oil.
你應該用紙巾把油吸乾。

so·ber [ˈsobɚ]
◀€ Track 5122

動 使清醒 形 節制的、清醒的

▶動 A cup of strong tea can sober up a drunk person.
一杯濃茶可以讓酒醉的人清醒過來。

▶形 The man claimed that he was sober enough to drive after drinking a can of beer.
這人宣稱他喝完啤酒後，還是夠清醒，可以開車。

soft·en [ˈsɔfən]
◀€ Track 5123

動 使柔軟 反 harden 使變硬

▶Why don't you buy this special cream? It will help to soften up your skin. 為什麼不買這種特殊的護膚霜呢？它有助於使你的皮膚變得柔軟。

文法字詞解析
電影、書籍等還未推出時可能會有個預告讓你「搶先看」，可稱為 sneak preview 或 sneak peek。

文法字詞解析
遇到下雨，人在外面，又沒有帶傘，全身溼透的情況也可叫做 soaked。

Level 1

Level 2

Level 3

Level 4

Level 5

擴增實力5400單字 突飛猛進、程度大進擊──

Level 6

sole [sol] 　　　　　　🔊 *Track 5124*

形 唯一的、單一的

▶Farming is not their sole livelihood（謀生）.
務農是他們的唯一謀生之道。

文法字詞解析
sole 也可當作名詞表示「鞋底」的意思。

sol·emn [`saləm] 　　　　　🔊 *Track 5125*

形 鄭重的、莊嚴的 同 serious 莊嚴的

▶Everyone looked very solemn at the religious ritual.
每個人在這個宗教儀式中看起來都很莊嚴。

sol·i·tar·y [`salə,tɛrɪ] 　　　🔊 *Track 5126*

名 隱士、獨居者 形 單獨的 同 single 單獨的

▶名 This solitary lives far away from people.
那位隱士住得離人們很遠。

▶形 Emily led a very solitary life most of the time.
艾蜜莉大部分時間都一直過著非常孤獨的生活。

so·lo [`solo] 　　　　　　🔊 *Track 5127*

名 獨唱、獨奏、單獨表演 形 單獨的

▶名 In this concert, there will be two piano solos. I am sure you will like them very much.
在這次的音樂會上，有兩首鋼琴獨奏曲。我保證你會很喜歡聽的。

▶形 He made his first solo flight in 1988.
他在 1988 年第一次做了單人飛行。

sov·er·eign [`savrɪn] 　　　🔊 *Track 5128*

名 最高統治、獨立國家 形 自決的、獨立的

▶名 No sovereign can do what he pleases, or he will be overthrown by his people. 沒有哪個君主可以為所欲為，否則他就會被他的人民推翻。

▶形 In a democratic country, sovereign power should be lying with the citizens.
在這個民主國家，統治權是在人民手中。

sow [so] 　　　　　　　🔊 *Track 5129*

動 播、播種

▶It is too early for the farmers of this country to sow yet.
現在還不到該國農民們播種的時候。

space·craft/space·ship 🔊 *Track 5130*
[`spes,kræft]/[`spes,ʃɪp]

名 太空船

▶The spaceship makes it possible to travel to the moon.
太空船的出現使得去月球旅行成為可能。

萬用延伸句型
make it possible to...
使……成為可能的事

spe·cial·ist [`spɛʃəlɪst] 　　🔊 *Track 5131*

名 專家 同 expert 專家

▶They said that your elder brother is a specialist in cell phone chips（晶片）.
他們說你哥哥是一位手機晶片的專家。

spec·i·men [ˈspɛsəmən]
Track 5132

名 樣本、樣品 同 sample 樣本
▶He has a collection of butterfly specimens.
他收藏許多蝴蝶標本。

spec·ta·cle [ˈspɛktəkl̩]
Track 5133

名 奇觀
▶What a spectacle! I will suggest my friends to visit here one day.
多麼壯麗的景色呀！我要建議我的朋友們有時間也來這看看。

spec·ta·tor [ˈspɛktetɚ]
Track 5134

名 觀眾、旁觀者
▶There are a great many spectators watching the football game.
很多觀眾都在觀看這場足球比賽。

spine [spaɪn]
Track 5135

名 脊柱、脊骨
▶It is so cold outside that I feel a chill go down my spine.
外面太冷了，以致我覺得有一股寒氣順著我的脊骨往下竄。

splen·dor [ˈsplɛndɚ]
Track 5136

名 燦爛、光輝
▶All the splendor in the world is not worth a good friend.
人世間所有的榮華富貴都不如有一個好朋友。

sponge [spʌndʒ]
Track 5137

名 海綿 動 依賴、（用海綿）擦拭
▶名 Why don't you use a clean sponge to wipe the surface?
為何不用乾淨的海綿來擦拭表面呢？
▶動 The stains on the fruit will come off if you sponge it lightly.
水果表皮的髒污可以用海綿清理掉。

spot·light [ˈspɑtˌlaɪt]
Track 5138

名 聚光燈 動 用聚光燈照明
▶名 The stage was lit by several spotlights.
舞臺被幾盞聚光燈照亮。
▶動 I don't think that the pictures should be spotlighted from below.
我認為這些畫不該用下面的聚光燈來照明。

sprint [sprɪnt]
Track 5139

名 短距離賽跑 動 衝刺、全力奔跑 同 speed 迅速前進
▶名 He made a sprint for shelter so that he wouldn't be wounded by the bomb.
為了不被炸彈傷到，他全速奔向躲避處。
▶動 I think you have to sprint so that you can catch the early bus.
我覺得你得用盡全力來奔跑才能趕上早班車。

文法字詞解析
眼鏡也可叫 spectacles（記得和 glasses 一樣是複數喔！）

萬用延伸句型
be in the spotlight 受到注目
例　如：He hates being in the spotlight, but people still stare a lot because he's so tall.
他不喜歡受到注目，但因為長得很高，還是常被人盯著看。

Level 1
Level 2
Level 3
Level 4
Level 5
Level 6

突飛猛進、程度大進擊——
擴增實力5400單字

spur [spɜ]
◀ Track 5140

名 馬刺 動 策馬、飛奔

▶名 Shoppers sometimes make an impulsive purchase on the spur of the moment.
購物這有時候會因為一時衝動而購買東西。

▶動 You shouldn't spur this poor horse on.
你不該驅策這匹可憐的馬。

squash [skwɑʃ]
◀ Track 5141

名 擠壓的聲音 動 壓扁、壓爛

▶名 Many people heard the squash.
很多人都聽到了那個擠壓的聲音。

▶動 He sat on the cake and squashed it.
他坐在蛋糕上,把它壓扁了。

squat [skwɑt]
◀ Track 5142

名 蹲下的姿勢 動 蹲下、蹲 形 蹲著的

▶名 The boy is under the table in a squat. 那個男孩蹲在桌下。

▶動 Come over here and squat down, or you'll be seen.
過來這裡,蹲下來,不然你會被看到喔。

▶形 You've been working in a squat position for a long time.
你已經蹲著工作很久了。

stack [stæk]
◀ Track 5143

名 堆、堆疊 動 堆疊 同 heap 堆

▶名 It took him twenty minutes to find his document from a stack of papers. 他花了二十分鐘才從一堆紙中找到了自己的檔案。

▶動 It took me just five minutes to stack up the plates and bowls. 我才花五分鐘就把碟子和碗疊起來了。

stag·ger [ˈstægɚ]
◀ Track 5144

名 搖晃、蹣跚 動 蹣跚 同 sway 搖動

▶名 He was so shocked on hearing the news that he gave a stagger. 他聽到這消息時很震驚,所以連步伐都變得搖晃了。

▶動 My father was tired but he still staggered to his feet.
我父親很累,但他還是搖搖晃晃地站了起來。

stain [sten]
◀ Track 5145

動 弄髒、汙染 名 汙點 同 spot 汙點

▶動 Once your shirt is stained with tomato sauce, you may have a hard time getting rid of it.
你襯衫一旦沾到番茄汁,就會很難把它清理掉。

▶名 You can't remove the stain on the table cloth if you don't use this liquid. 不用這種液體的話,你無法去掉桌布上的汙漬。

stake [stek]
◀ Track 5146

名 樁 動 把……綁在樁上、以……作為賭注

▶名 Will you put up a stake to support the newly planted tree?
你能豎一根樁來支撐新種的樹嗎?

▶動 Would you please not stake all your money on the risky business?
能不能請你別把所有的錢都賭在這充滿風險的生意上?

萬用延伸句型

the cards are stacked against sth./sb. 一切情況都對某人／某事不利

例 如:Even though the cards were stacked against their team, they still managed to win the game.
雖然一切情況都對他們的球隊不利,他們還是成功贏了比賽。

stalk [stɔk]
🔊 *Track 5147*

名 莖　同 stem 莖

▶She trimmed the stalks of the cauliflower before cooking it.
她把花椰菜的莖去掉，再烹煮。

stall [stɔl]
🔊 *Track 5148*

名 商品陳列台、攤位

▶How about buying some food from the market stall over there?
到那邊的小攤上買些吃的怎麼樣？

stan·za [ˋstænzə]
🔊 *Track 5149*

名 節、段

▶What do you think of the first stanza in the poem, Bob?
鮑勃，你覺得這首詩的第一節怎麼樣？

star·tle [ˋstɑrtl̩]
🔊 *Track 5150*

動 使驚跳　同 surprise 使吃驚

▶I was startled when the cat suddenly jumped onto the table.
那隻貓突然跳到桌上，嚇了我一跳。

states·man [ˋstetsmən]
🔊 *Track 5151*

名 政治家

▶This man is not only an excellent statesman, but also a famous poet.
這個人不僅是一位出色的政治家，還是一位著名的詩人。

sta·tis·tic(s) [stəˋtɪstɪk(s)]
🔊 *Track 5152*

名 統計值、統計量

▶It is a pity that they didn't add an explanatory（說明的）note to the list of statistics.
他們沒有在統計表前加上一段說明文字真可惜。

萬用延伸句型
It is a pity that... 很可惜……

sta·tis·ti·cal [stəˋtɪstɪkl̩]
🔊 *Track 5153*

形 統計的、統計學的

▶The statistical data we have at hand isn't quite enough.
我們手邊的統計資料實在不太夠。

steam·er [ˋstimɚ]
🔊 *Track 5154*

名 汽船、輪船

▶Gina brought a rice steamer with her when she studied abroad.
吉娜去國外念書時，帶了一個電鍋。

steer [stɪr]
🔊 *Track 5155*

名 忠告、建議　動 駕駛、掌舵

▶名 He gave me a bum steer before I got into the car.
在我上車前，他給了我一些忠告。

▶動 Can you steer the boat towards the island for me?
你能幫我把船開往那座島嗎？

文法字詞解析
除了用於開船時的「掌舵」以外，steer 也可以用在掌控話題的方向，例如說「steer the topic into another direction」即「巧妙地把話題轉到另一個方向」。畢竟改變話題和掌舵都和「轉向」有關啊。

Level 1

Level 2

Level 3

Level 4

Level 5
突飛猛進、程度大進擊──擴增實力5400單字

Level 6

ster·e·o·type [ˈstɛrɪəˌtaɪp]
🔊 Track 5156

名 鉛版、刻板印象 動 把……澆成鉛版、定型

▶名 He doesn't conform（符合）to the usual businessman stereotype.
你很容易就會發現他不像典型的商人。

▶動 It's wrong to stereotype people, I know, but I still do it.
我知道用刻板印象看人是不對的，可是我還是會這樣做。

stern [stɜn]
🔊 Track 5157

形 嚴格的 同 severe 嚴格的

▶She received a stern rebuke（責難）from her superior yesterday.
她昨天受到上司的嚴厲斥責。

stew [stju]
🔊 Track 5158

名 燉菜 動 燉煮、燉

▶名 Why don't you have some more stew? It is the specialty（特色菜）here.
為什麼不再吃點燉菜呢？它可是這裡的特色菜哦。

▶動 She prepared a hearty and delicious stew made with pork.
她準備了一道豐盛的燉豬肉。

stew·ard/stew·ard·ess/ at·tend·ant [ˈstjuwəd]/[ˈstjuwədɪs]/[əˈtɛndənt]
🔊 Track 5159

名 服務生、空服員

▶A steward will arrive instantly（馬上）as soon as you press the buzzer（呼叫器）in the room.
你一按房間裡的呼叫器，服務生就會馬上過來。

stink [stɪŋk]
🔊 Track 5160

名 惡臭、臭 動 弄臭 反 perfume 弄香

▶名 What a stink! I think you should clean your house as soon as possible.
真臭！我想你該盡快打掃你的房子了。

▶動 What did you just eat? It stinks!
你剛剛吃了什麼？很臭耶！

stock [stɑk]
🔊 Track 5161

名 庫存、紫羅蘭、股票

▶This store keeps a large stock of toys.
這家商店備有大量玩具。

stoop [stup]
🔊 Track 5162

名 駝背 動 自貶、使屈服

▶名 I don't believe that he is the man walking with a slight stoop in the movie.
我不相信他就是電影裡頭那個弓著背行走的人。

▶動 We stooped to go through the doorway.
我們經過門廊時彎下身來。

文法字詞解析

stink 可以加上不同的形容詞字尾來表達不同的含義，例如：加上「-ing」變成「stinking」就是「散發惡臭的」；加上「-y」變成「stinky」就是「臭的」。另外，stinky 也可以用 smelly 來表示，是一樣的意思。

stor·age [ˋstorɪdʒ]
◀€ *Track 5163*

名 儲存、倉庫 同 warehouse 倉庫
▶Don't you think these fish should be kept in cold storage?
你不覺得這些魚應該冷藏起來嗎？

stout [staʊt]
◀€ *Track 5164*

形 強壯的、堅固的 反 feeble 虛弱的
▶He bought a pair of stout boots from the store nearby.
他從附近的商店買了雙結實的靴子。

straight·en [ˋstretn̩]
◀€ *Track 5165*

動 弄直、整頓
▶This big room is a mess. Let's straighten it up.
這個大屋子一團亂。我們來整理一下吧。

文法字詞解析
把頭髮弄直的離子夾稱為 hair straightener.

straight·for·ward
[ˋstretˋfɔrwəd]
◀€ *Track 5166*

形 直接的、正直的 同 straight 正直的
▶Why don't you just give me a straightforward answer?
你為什麼不給我一個直截了當的回答？

strain [stren]
◀€ *Track 5167*

名 緊張 動 拉緊、強逼、盡全力 反 relax 放鬆
▶名 The wind put such a strain on the suspension bridge that it collapsed.
風吹、拉鋸的力量如此強大，以至於吊橋坍塌。
▶動 Don't strain the rope too hard, or it may break.
不要把繩子拉得太緊，要不然會斷的。

strait [stret]
◀€ *Track 5168*

名 海峽
▶It is quite dangerous to cross the strait in such terrible weather.
在這樣糟糕的天氣渡過海峽是非常危險的。

strand [strænd]
◀€ *Track 5169*

名 濱 動 擱淺、處於困境
▶名 There are many people walking along the strand.
有很多人沿著海灘散步。
▶動 He said that he was stranded in a strange town.
他說他被困在一個陌生的城市。

文法字詞解析
一「綹」頭髮稱為 a strand of hair。

strap [stræp]
◀€ *Track 5170*

名 皮帶 動 約束、用帶子捆 同 bind 捆、綁
▶名 Will you buy a new strap for me? This one is broken.
能給我買條新皮帶嗎？這條破了。
▶動 He strapped his luggage to his bike and started cycling around the island.
他把行李綁在腳踏車上，開始單車環島。

stray [stre]
◀€ *Track 5171*

名 漂泊者 動 迷路、漂泊 形 迷途的

Level 1
Level 2
Level 3
Level 4
Level 5
Level 6

突飛猛進、程度大進擊 擴增實力5400單字

▶名 The cat used to be a stray.
這隻貓以前是流浪貓。

▶動 It has been five days since the boy strayed away from home.
男孩離家走失已經五天了。

▶形 I like to feed stray dogs.
我喜歡餵流浪狗。

streak [strik] ◀ Track 5172

動 加條紋 名 條紋 同 stripe 條紋

▶動 I dyed my hair to hide my gray streaks.
我染頭髮以遮蓋白髮。

▶名 The man ran away like a streak of lightning.
那個男人快如閃電般地跑掉了。

stride [straɪd] ◀ Track 5173

名 跨步、大步 動 邁過、跨過 同 step 步伐

▶名 Everyone does things with their own stride and pace.
每個人做事都有自己的步伐和節奏。

▶動 He strode into the boss' office angrily.
他生氣地大步走進了老闆的辦公室。

stripe [straɪp] ◀ Track 5174

名 斑紋、條紋

▶Do you want stripes on your skirt?
你想要有條紋的裙子嗎？

stroll [strol] ◀ Track 5175

名 漫步、閒逛 動 漫步

▶名 How about taking a stroll in the garden with your father?
和你的父親一起到花園散步怎麼樣？

▶動 We strolled down the boulevard and enjoyed the street view.
我們沿著街道走，欣賞街景。

struc·tur·al [ˈstrʌktʃərəl] ◀ Track 5176

形 構造的、結構上的

▶It is a surprise that the earthquake should cause no structural damage.
地震居然沒有對建築結構造成破壞，這真令人驚訝。

stum·ble [ˈstʌmbl̩] ◀ Track 5177

名 絆倒 動 跌倒、偶然發現

▶名 It was just a stumble; no big deal.
稍微絆倒一下而已，沒什麼大不了的。

▶動 He stumbled into teaching English after he got a master's degree.
他在拿到碩士學位後，誤打誤撞開始教英文。

stump [stʌmp] ◀ Track 5178

名 （樹的）殘株、殘餘部分 動 遊說、難倒

同 remainder 殘餘物

文法字詞解析

stride 的動詞變化：stride, strode, stridden

萬用延伸句型

stumble upon sth. 不小心發現、看見某事

例如：She stumbled upon her two best friends kissing in the kitchen.
她不小心撞見了她的兩個好友在廚房擁吻。

▶名 It is very clever of you to use the stump as a table.
把樹樁當桌子來用，你真聰明。

▶動 The question got me stumped; it was too complicated for me to understand.
這問題難倒我了。它太過複雜，所以我無法理解。

stun [stʌn]　🔊 Track 5179

動 嚇呆
▶News of the natural disaster stunned people throughout the world.
自然災害的新聞令全球觀眾震驚。

文法字詞解析
電擊棒／電擊槍在英文中可稱為 stun gun。

sturd·y [ˋstɝdɪ]　🔊 Track 5180

形 強健的、穩固的 同 strong 強壯的
▶The chair in my study is not sturdy enough to hold an adult.
我書房裡的椅子不夠堅固，承受不了一個大人的重量。

stut·ter [ˋstʌtɚ]　🔊 Track 5181

名 結巴 動 結結巴巴地說 同 stammer 結結巴巴地說
▶名 He has a slight stutter, but it doesn't affect him much.
他有點口吃，但對他來說沒什麼影響。

▶動 He stutters a lot in front of the boss.
他常在老闆面前結結巴巴。

styl·ish [ˋstaɪlɪʃ]　🔊 Track 5182

形 時髦的、漂亮的 同 fashionable 時髦的
▶You had better wear stylish clothes to the party.
你最好穿上時髦的衣服去派對。

sub·mit [səbˋmɪt]　🔊 Track 5183

動 屈服、提交
▶Let's not submit our proposal to the manager today.
我們今天還是先別把提案交給經理吧。

sub·stan·tial [səbˋstænʃəl]　🔊 Track 5184

形 實際的、重大的 同 actual 實際的
▶We have no need to buy a substantial number of weapons unless we're facing a war.
除非戰爭來臨，否則我們沒有必要購買大量武器。

萬用延伸句型
have no need to... 不需要……

sub·sti·tute [ˋsʌbstətjut]　🔊 Track 5185

名 代替者 動 代替 同 replace 代替
▶名 There's no substitute for experience.
沒有什麼能夠取代經驗。

▶動 You can substitute carrots for potatoes in this recipe.
你可以將食譜中的馬鈴薯換成紅蘿蔔。

suit·case [ˋsutˏkes]　🔊 Track 5186

名 手提箱
▶Don't worry. He will have your suitcases sent forward to the hotel. 別擔心。他會叫人先把你的行李箱送到旅館去的。

Level 1

Level 2

Level 3

Level 4

Level 5

突飛猛進、程度大進擊──
擴增實力5400單字

Level 6

sul·fur [ˈsʌlfɚ] 🔊 *Track 5187*

名 硫磺

▶ Sulfur can be used to make gunpowder（火藥）.
硫磺可以被人們用來製造火藥。

sum·mon [ˈsʌmən] 🔊 *Track 5188*

動 召集

▶ We were summoned to the principal's office.
我們被召喚去校長的辦公室。

文法字詞解析
除了用在召集「人」以外，文學作品中 summon 這個字也常用於召喚怪物、惡魔、動物、鬼魂等。

su·per·fi·cial [ˈsupɚˈfɪʃəl] 🔊 *Track 5189*

形 表面的、外表的 反 essential 本質的

▶ Maybe we are too superficial to appreciate great literature like this. 也許我們都太膚淺，無法欣賞這類文學巨著。

su·per·sti·tion [ˌsupɚˈstɪʃən] 🔊 *Track 5190*

名 迷信

▶ The more you know, the less likely you are to believe in superstitions.
你知道的越多，你就越不會相信迷信。

su·per·vise [ˈsupɚvaɪz] 🔊 *Track 5191*

動 監督、管理 同 administer 管理

▶ Do you mind if I ask him to supervise the workers loading the lorry（卡車）?
你介意我叫他去監督工人把貨物裝上卡車嗎？

萬用延伸句型
Do you mind if...? 你介意……嗎？

su·per·vi·sor [ˌsupɚˈvaɪzɚ] 🔊 *Track 5192*

名 監督者、管理人 同 administrator 管理人

▶ I don't believe that such a devious（不坦誠的）man can become a good supervisor.
我不相信這樣一個不坦誠的人能成為一個好主管。

sup·press [səˈprɛs] 🔊 *Track 5193*

動 壓抑、制止 同 restrain 抑制

▶ It is quite clear that they are trying in every way to suppress the truth. 他們很明顯是在千方百計地掩蓋事實的真相。

su·preme [səˈprim] 🔊 *Track 5194*

形 至高無上的

▶ She showed supreme bravery when protecting her child from being harmed by the villain.
她保護小孩不受壞人傷害時，表現高度勇氣。

surge [sɝdʒ] 🔊 *Track 5195*

名 大浪 動 洶湧

▶ 名 A surge of shoppers（顧客）poured into the store.
有一批顧客湧入商店中。

▶ 動 A great wave surged over the ship.
巨浪沖打著船。

sus·pend [sə'spɛnd]
🔊 *Track 5196*

動 懸掛、暫停 同 hang 懸掛

▶The boy has been suspended from school many times.
那個男孩已經被勒令停學很多次了。

sus·tain [sə'sten]
🔊 *Track 5197*

動 支持、支撐 同 support 支持

▶He had trouble sustaining long-term relationship with women.
他無法和女性長久交往。

swamp [swɑmp]
🔊 *Track 5198*

名 沼澤 動 陷入泥沼 同 bog 沼澤

▶名 The heavy rain has turned not only my garden but also my neighbor's into swamps.
大雨把我和鄰居的花園都變成了沼澤地。

▶動 Not only the horse but also the carriage were swamped in the mud.
馬和馬車都陷在泥沼中了。

swarm [swɔrm]
🔊 *Track 5199*

名 群、群集 動 聚集、一塊 同 cluster 群、組

▶名 There is a swarm of bees in the tree at the back of our house.
我家屋後的樹上有一窩蜜蜂。

▶動 Lots of people swarmed into the cinema tonight because of this new film.
因為這部新片的緣故，今晚有很多人湧進電影院。

sym·pa·thize ['sɪmpə,θaɪz]
🔊 *Track 5200*

動 同情、有同感 同 pity 同情

▶It's hard for us to sympathize with his political opinions.
我們難以贊同他的政治觀點。

[Tt]

tack·le ['tækl̩]
🔊 *Track 5201*

動 著手處理、捉住 同 undertake 著手處理

▶Can you suggest us how to tackle this big problem?
我們該如何處理這個大難題呢？你能給個建議嗎？

tan [tæn]
🔊 *Track 5202*

名 日曬後的顏色 形 棕褐色的

▶名 His arms and legs had a dark tan from working outside all day long.
他的手臂和腿曬得黑黑的，因為他整天都在室外工作。

▶形 The healthily tan girl had a heartwarming smile.
膚色健康的女孩有溫暖人心的笑容。

文法字詞解析
要描述事情多到不行，有如身陷泥沼無法抽身時，也可以說 I'm swamped。

Level 1

Level 2

Level 3

Level 4

Level 5

突飛猛進、程度大進擊──擴增實力5400單字

Level 6

tan·gle [ˈtæŋgl̩]   🔊 *Track 5203*

名 混亂、糾結 動 使混亂、使糾結

▶名 The dog's fur is in tangles.
她那隻狗的毛都糾結起來了。

▶動 The wires tangled, which made it difficult for me to repair the machine.
電線打結，讓我很難去修理這台機器。

tar [tɑr]   🔊 *Track 5204*

名 焦油、柏油 動 塗焦油於

▶名 This road is uneven. Why not cover it with tar?
這條路很不平。何不在上面鋪柏油呢？

▶動 The street has already been tarred.
那條街道已經鋪上了柏油。

tart [ˈtɑrt]   🔊 *Track 5205*

形 酸的、尖酸的 同 sour 酸的

▶I wish you hadn't given him such a tart answer.
我真希望你沒給過他如此尖酸的回答。

taunt [tɔnt]   🔊 *Track 5206*

名 辱罵 動 嘲弄

▶名 The little girl had to endure the taunts from her classmates.
那個小女孩不得不忍受同學們的奚落。

▶動 We shouldn't taunt others for their shortcomings.
我們不該嘲笑其他人的缺點。

tav·ern [ˈtævən]   🔊 *Track 5207*

名 酒店、酒館

▶How about finding a tavern to have a drink?
我們去找間酒館喝一杯怎麼樣？

tell·er [ˈtɛlə]   🔊 *Track 5208*

名 講話者、敘述者、出納員

▶As soon as I complete my training, I am going to become a bank teller. 一旦我結束訓練，我就將成為一名銀行出納員。

tem·po [ˈtɛmpo]   🔊 *Track 5209*

名 速度、拍子 同 rhythm 節拍

▶A change in tempo occurred halfway through the song.
歌曲播到一半，節奏突然改變。

tempt [tɛmpt]   🔊 *Track 5210*

動 誘惑、慫恿

▶Nothing could tempt him to do such a terrible thing.
什麼都不能誘使他做出這麼糟的事。

temp·ta·tion [tɛmpˈteʃən]   🔊 *Track 5211*

名 誘惑

▶It is a pity that he couldn't resist the temptation of drugs in the end. 很遺憾他最終還是沒能抵擋住毒品的誘惑。

萬用延伸句型
I wish you hadn't... 我真希望你沒有（做某事）（用於對方已經做了某事，無法改變此情形時）

ten·ant [ˈtɛnənt]
◀ Track 5212

名 承租人 動 租賃 同 landlord 房東

▶名 I am afraid that it's difficult for you to sell a house with a tenant still living in it.
恐怕你很難賣出還住著房客的房子。

▶動 That old house has not been tenanted for many years.
那幢老房子已經多年無人居住了。

ten·ta·tive [ˈtɛntətɪv]
◀ Track 5213

形 暫時的

▶ I think we can draw up a tentative plan now.
我認為現在可以先草擬一個臨時方案。

ter·mi·nal [ˈtɜmənl]
◀ Track 5214

名 終點、終站 形 終點的

▶名 Let's put the data into the computer terminal.
我們把這些資料輸入電腦終端吧。

▶形 The patient suffering from terminal cancer decided to pursue his bucket list.
患有末期癌症的病患，決定要追求人生目標清單。

文法字詞解析
火車、電車等的「終點站」即為 terminal station。

---

ter·race [ˈtɛrəs]
◀ Track 5215

名 房屋的平頂、陽臺 動 使成梯形地

▶名 This open-air terrace is really spacious. Don't you think so?這個陽臺很寬敞，你不覺得嗎？

▶動 Terraced fields can be seen everywhere in this area.
這一地區梯田到處可見。

thigh [θaɪ]
◀ Track 5216

名 大腿

▶ The water is already up to my thighs.
水已經淹到了我的大腿。

萬用延伸句型
thorn in sb.'s side 直譯為「（某人）身上的一根刺」，指的就是「讓人覺得很煩的人、事、物」。
例如：His considers his elderly neighbor a thorn in his side. She's always knocking on his door and wanting to chat.
他覺得他年邁的鄰居非常煩人，她老是跑來敲他的門、想跟他聊天。

---

thorn [θɔrn]
◀ Track 5217

名 刺、荊棘

▶ Be careful not to be pricked by thorns when picking the flowers.
採花的時候請小心不要被荊棘刺到。

thrill [θrɪl]
◀ Track 5218

名 戰慄 動 使激動 同 excite 使激動

▶名 It gave me a real thrill to accomplish the project on my own. 獨自完成這項計畫，讓我非常開心。

▶動 He was thrilled to hear the good news.
他聽到這個好消息非常興奮。

thrill·er [ˈθrɪlɚ]
◀ Track 5219

名 恐怖小說、令人震顫的人事物

▶ There's a new American thriller on. Would you like to go to see it?
有一部新的美國驚悚片正在上映。你想不想去看呢？

突飛猛進、程度大進擊—擴增實力5400單字

throne [θron]
🔊 *Track 5220*

名 王位、寶座

▶The prince ascended to his throne. 王子登上了王位。

throng [θrɔŋ]
🔊 *Track 5221*

名 群眾 動 擠入

▶名 She pushed through the throng of people on the street.
她從街上的人群中推擠著過去。

▶動 There are many passengers thronging the station waiting
for their trains. 火車站擠滿了等車的乘客。

thrust [θrʌst]
🔊 *Track 5222*

名 用力推 動 猛推 同 shove 推

▶名 They finally opened the door with a thrust.
他們用力地一推，終於推開了門。

▶動 The protester thrust past the policemen to get to the politician.
抗議者一路擠開警察，走道政客面前。

tick [tɪk]
🔊 *Track 5223*

名 滴答聲 動 發出滴答聲、標上記號

▶名 Even the ticks of the clock are too noisy for me.
就連時鐘的滴答聲都太吵了。

▶動 The clock ticked too loudly for me to sleep.
時鐘發出的滴答聲太大，以致於我睡不著。

tile [taɪl]
🔊 *Track 5224*

名 瓷磚 動 用瓦蓋 同 slope 傾斜

▶名 Would you please help me collect some tiles?
你能幫我收集一些瓷磚嗎？

▶動 Would you please tile a little house for our pet dog?
你能不能用磚瓦為我們的寵物狗蓋個小房子呢？

tilt [tɪlt]
🔊 *Track 5225*

動 傾斜、刺擊 同 pierce 刺穿

▶I felt like the ground is tilting. 我感覺地板好像要歪斜了一樣。

tin [tɪn]
🔊 *Track 5226*

名 錫 動 鍍錫

▶名 I fed the cat with food from a tin can.
我從錫罐拿出貓食餵了貓。

▶動 The expiration date of tinned beans has passed.
罐裝豆子的保存期限過了。

tip·toe [ˈtɪpˌto]
🔊 *Track 5227*

名 腳尖 動 用腳尖走路 副 以腳尖著地

▶名 I'm afraid that I can only reach the shelf if I stand on tiptoe.
我恐怕得踮著腳才剛能碰得到架子。

▶動 You have to tiptoe quietly up the stairs, for everyone has
fallen asleep.
你得踮著腳輕輕走上樓梯，因為大家都已經睡了。

▶副 He stood tiptoe on a chair to see the stage.
他踮著腳站在一把椅子上，才能看到舞台。

文法字詞解析

除了用於真的有皇室身分的人坐的「王座」之外，throne 也可以單純指在某領域、某比賽第一名的人所擁有的「冠軍寶座」。

文法字詞解析

「歪頭」的動作稱為 head tilt。

toad [tod] 🔊 *Track 5228*
名 癩蛤蟆
▶Even though toads have an ugly appearance, they are useful.
儘管蟾蜍外表醜陋，但牠們很有用。

toil [tɔɪl] 🔊 *Track 5229*
名 辛勞 動 辛勞 反 leisure 悠閒
▶名 It is obvious that he is quite exhausted with the toil.
顯然他因那件辛苦的工作而感到十分疲憊。
▶動 Tina had a feast after toiling at work for all week.
辛苦工作一整週之後，蒂娜去吃了大餐。

to·ken [ˈtokən] 🔊 *Track 5230*
名 表徵、代幣 同 sign 象徵
▶Would you please accept this token of our appreciation?
請接受這一禮物好嗎？這象徵著我們對您的謝意。

torch [tɔrtʃ] 🔊 *Track 5231*
名 火炬、引火燃燒、手電筒
▶Why don't you light the torch? I can't see the path.
為什麼不打開手電筒呢？我看不見路了。

tor·ment [ˈtɔrˌmɛnt] 🔊 *Track 5232*
名 苦惱 動 使受苦、煩擾 同 comfort 安慰
▶名 What a little torment that child is!
這孩子真煩人！
▶動 She always torments everyone with silly questions.
她總是用很多無聊的問題來煩擾大家。

tor·rent [ˈtɔrənt] 🔊 *Track 5233*
名 洪流、急流
▶The torrent of water turned our little boat over.
急流將我們的小船掀翻了。

tor·ture [ˈtɔrtʃɚ] 🔊 *Track 5234*
名 折磨、拷打 動 使……受折磨
▶名 There are a lot of scenes of torture in the movie.
那個電影裡有很多折磨人的畫面。
▶動 She was tortured by the negative thoughts.
她被負面想法折磨。

tour·na·ment [ˈtɝnəmənt] 🔊 *Track 5235*
名 競賽、比賽 同 contest 競賽
▶The tournament is open to not only the professionals but also the amateurs. 這次比賽不僅職業運動員可以參加，而且業餘運動員也可以參加。

tox·ic [ˈtaksɪk] 🔊 *Track 5236*
形 有毒的 同 poisonous 有毒的
▶You'd better be careful when you handle the toxic chemicals.
你最好小心處理有毒的化學藥品。

文法字詞解析
torch 後來也延伸成能夠當作動詞，表示「用火炬放火燒某處」的行為。例如「torch a store」就是「放火去燒一家店」。

文法字詞解析
若有人充滿負能量，跟他在一起時盡聽他抱怨別人的事，即可形容這樣的人為 toxic。

Level 1
Level 2
Level 3
Level 4
Level 5
突飛猛進、程度大進擊——擴增實力5400單字
Level 6

trade·mark [`tred͵mɑrk］ ◀𝄈 *Track 5237*

图 標記、商標 同 brand 商標

▶The trademark license contract shall be submitted to the Trademark Office for record.
商標使用許可合約應當呈報商標局備案。

trai·tor [`tretɚ] ◀𝄈 *Track 5238*

图 叛徒

▶He was denounced as a traitor to his country.
他被指責為賣國賊。

tramp [træmp] ◀𝄈 *Track 5239*

图 不定期貨船、長途跋涉、徒步旅行 動 踐踏、長途跋涉

▶图 I want to go for a tramp in the country. Would you like to go with me?
我想在鄉下徒步旅行。你想不想跟我一起去呢？

▶動 We have already tramped through the wood.
我們已經吃力地走過樹林了。

tram·ple [`træmpl] ◀𝄈 *Track 5240*

動 踐踏 图 踐踏、踐踏聲

▶動 You'd better not trample on the grass.
你最好不要踐踏草地。

▶图 I heard the trample of many feet.
我聽到許多人的腳步聲。

trans·par·ent [træns`pɛrənt] ◀𝄈 *Track 5241*

形 透明的

▶The woman's blouse was practically transparent!
這個女生的襯衫幾乎是透明的！

trea·sur·y [`trɛʒərɪ] ◀𝄈 *Track 5242*

图 寶庫、金庫、財政部

▶The authorities believe that there is a mole in the Treasury Department.
當局認為財政部裡有內奸。

trea·ty [`tritɪ] ◀𝄈 *Track 5243*

图 協議、條約 同 contract 合約

▶The treaty gave fresh impetus（推動）to trade.
這條約使貿易又前進了一步。

trench [trɛntʃ] ◀𝄈 *Track 5244*

图 溝、渠 動 挖溝渠 同 ditch 渠

▶图 The farmer dug several trenches so that he can irrigate the rice fields.
這個農民挖了好幾條溝以便灌溉稻田。

▶動 They were busy trenching the fields so that they can drain the water.
他們正忙著在田裡挖溝渠以便能夠排水。

trib·ute [ˈtrɪbjut]   🔊 Track 5245

名 致敬、進貢
▶People around the country paid tribute to late president.
全國人民向已故總統致敬。

tri·fle [ˈtraɪfḷ]   🔊 Track 5246

名 瑣事 動 疏忽、輕忽、戲弄
▶名 I think it's not wise of you to trouble yourself with such a trifle.
我覺得你因為這樣的小事而煩惱是不明智的。
▶動 It's immoral（不道德的）of you to just trifle with her affections. 你只是在玩弄她的感情，這是不道德的。

trim [trɪm]   🔊 Track 5247

名 齊備狀態、整齊、整潔 動 整理、修剪、削減
形 整齊的、整潔的、苗條的 同 shave 修剪
▶名 Your hair needs a good trim.
你的頭髮需要好好修剪一下了。
▶動 I hope the school budgets won't be trimmed back.
我希望學校預算不會被削減。
▶形 I wish I could have a trim figure.
我希望能有勻稱漂亮的身材。

tri·ple [ˈtrɪpḷ]   🔊 Track 5248

名 三倍的數量 動 變成三倍 形 三倍的
▶名 It is obvious that fifteen is the triple of five.
顯然十五是五的三倍數。
▶動 In the past five years, the company has tripled its sales.
在過去五年中，該公司銷售量增加至三倍。
▶形 He received triple pay because of his extra work.
他得到三倍的報酬，是因為超額工作。

trot [trɑt]   🔊 Track 5249

動 使小跑步 名 小跑步
▶動 The horses trotted down the road happily.
馬兒們開心地沿著路小跑步。
▶名 The horses in the parade proceeded at a relaxed trot.
遊行中的馬兒踩著輕鬆步伐前進。

trout [traʊt]   🔊 Track 5250

名 鱒魚
▶I caught seven trout in fifteen minutes.
我十五分鐘內捉到七條鱒魚。

tuck [tʌk]   🔊 Track 5251

名 縫褶 動 打褶
▶名 Mom put a tuck in the dress because it was too big.
由於衣服太大了，所以媽媽在裡面打了褶。
▶動 The lady tucked her son into bed.
那個太太幫她兒子把毯子蓋好。

文法字詞解析
和這個字長得很像的一個單字是「triplets」，是「三胞胎」的意思。

Level 1

Level 2

Level 3

Level 4

Level 5

擴增實力5400單字 突飛猛進、程度大進擊

Level 6

tu·i·tion [tjuˈɪʃən]　◀≋ *Track 5252*

图 教學、講授、學費　同 instruction 教學
▶The students received tuition in literature and mathematics.
　學生收到文學課和數學課的學費單。

tu·na [ˈtunə]　◀≋ *Track 5253*

图 鮪魚
▶My cat loves tinned tuna fish.
　我的貓很愛鮪魚罐頭。

ty·rant [ˈtaɪrənt]　◀≋ *Track 5254*

图 暴君、獨裁者
▶Mr. Smith is a tyrant in his office.
　史密斯先生在他辦公室裡是個獨裁者。

[Uu]

um·pire [ˈʌmpaɪr]　◀≋ *Track 5255*

图 仲裁者、裁判員　動 擔任裁判　同 judge 裁判員
▶图 Will you tell me why they refuse to accept the umpire's decision?
　你能告訴我他們為什麼拒絕接受裁判的判決嗎？
▶動 Can you umpire the cricket match for us next week?
　請你下週來擔任我們板球比賽的裁判好嗎？

un·der·grad·u·ate　◀≋ *Track 5256*
[ˌʌndəˈgrædʒʊɪt]

图 大學生
▶The segment of the self-study room was reserved for the undergraduate students.
　自習室的這一區是留給大學部學生用的。

un·der·line [ˌʌndəˈlaɪn]　◀≋ *Track 5257*

图 底線　動 畫底線
▶图 Please highlight（使突出）the underlines in the article so that I can notice them.
　請突出文中的底線，以便我能注意到它們。
▶動 Please underline those important sentences so that you can easily find them later.
　請在重要的句子下面畫線，以便你以後能輕易地找到它們。

un·der·neath [ˌʌndəˈniθ]　◀≋ *Track 5258*

介 在下面　同 below 在下面
▶The ball has rolled underneath the desk. Will you help me pick it up?
　球滾到了桌下。你能幫我把它撿起來嗎？

un·der·stand·a·ble [ˌʌndɚˈstændəbḷ]
🔊 *Track 5259*

形 可理解的
▶Her reluctance（不願意）to agree is understandable to me.
她不願同意，我可以理解。

un·doubt·ed·ly [ʌnˈdaʊtɪdlɪ]
🔊 *Track 5260*

副 無庸置疑地
▶Undoubtedly, the point you made does hold water.
毫無疑問地，你提的論點確實是站得住腳的。

up·date [ʌpˈdet]
🔊 *Track 5261*

名 最新資訊 動 更新
▶名 It is time for us to explain the fake news update to our audience. 我們該向觀眾們解釋這條造假的新聞了。
▶動 An updated version of the software is available on the official website of the company.
這種軟體的更新版本可以在官方網站下載。

up·right [ˈʌpˌraɪt]
🔊 *Track 5262*

名 直立的姿勢 形 直立的 副 直立地 同 erect 直立的
▶名 If I put it upright, would it look better?
我把它直著放會不會比較好看？
▶形 What do you think of moving the upright post there?
把這根直立的柱子移到那去怎麼樣？
▶副 The sack is empty, and therefore cannot stand upright.
那個袋子是空的，所以站不直。

up·ward(s) [ˈʌpwəd(z)]
🔊 *Track 5263*

形 向上的 副 向上地 同 downward 向下
▶形 It doesn't matter if you encounter an upward current at high altitudes. 你要是在高空中遇到了上升氣流也沒什麼關係。
▶副 It doesn't matter what they do, sales won't move upwards any more. 不管他們怎麼做，銷售額都不會再好轉了。

ut·ter [ˈʌtɚ]
🔊 *Track 5264*

形 完全的 動 發言、發出 同 complete 完全的
▶形 I was so shocked that I was at an utter loss what to do.
我震驚到完全不知道該怎樣做才好。
▶動 All words we utter should be chosen with care.
我們所說的話，都要小心思考。

[Vv]

va·can·cy [ˈvekənsɪ]
🔊 *Track 5265*

名 空缺、空白
▶George is the best person to fill this vacancy.
喬治是填補這一個空缺的最佳人選。

文法字詞解析
和 undoubtedly 意思差不多的一個字是 doubtlessly（毫無疑問的），兩個都有 doubt 這個字根，一個在前面加上表示「不、無」的字首「un-」，一個在後面加上表示「沒有」的字尾「-less」。

萬用延伸句型
It doesn't matter... ……都沒關係

Level 1
Level 2
Level 3
Level 4
Level 5
擴增實力5400單字 突飛猛進、程度大進擊
Level 6

vac·u·um [ˈvækjʊəm]　🔊 *Track 5266*

名 真空、空虛　動 以真空吸塵器打掃

▶ 名 No artist works in a vacuum—we have to get inspiration from life experience. 沒有藝術家能憑空創作—我們必須由生活經驗中得到啟發。

▶ 動 It is clear that it was Mom who vacuumed my room yesterday. 顯然昨天是媽媽用吸塵器清掃了我的房間。

vague [veg]　🔊 *Track 5267*

名 不明確的、模糊的　反 explicit 明確的

▶ If you want me to go, why not say so in plain English instead of making vague hints?
如果你想叫我走，為什麼要拐彎抹角而不直說？

van·i·ty [ˈvænətɪ]　🔊 *Track 5268*

名 虛榮心、自負　同 conceit 自負

▶ Would you please not buy things just to gratify your vanity?
能不能請你別為了滿足自己的虛榮心而買東西？

va·por [ˈvepɚ]　🔊 *Track 5269*

名 蒸發的氣體　同 mist 水氣

▶ A cloud is a mass of vapor. 雲是天空中的水氣形成的團塊。

veg·e·ta·tion [ˌvɛdʒəˈteʃən]　🔊 *Track 5270*

名 草木、植物　同 plant 植物

▶ There is luxuriant tropical vegetation in our country.
我們國家有很多繁茂的熱帶植物。

veil [vel]　🔊 *Track 5271*

名 面紗　動 掩蓋、遮蓋　同 cover 遮蓋

▶ 名 The widow wore a black veil to cover her swollen eyelids.
寡婦戴著黑色面紗，掩飾她哭紅的雙眼。

▶ 動 He tried to veil his contempt at my ignorance.
他試圖掩飾對我的無知的蔑視。

vein [ven]　🔊 *Track 5272*

名 靜脈　反 artery 動脈

▶ She is so skinny you can practically see veins under her skin.
她瘦到你都能看見她皮膚之下的靜脈了。

vel·vet [ˈvɛlvɪt]　🔊 *Track 5273*

名 天鵝絨　形 柔軟的、平滑的、天鵝絨製的　同 soft 柔軟的

▶ 名 The lawn looks like green velvet.
那草坪看上去就像綠色的天鵝絨。

▶ 形 What do you think about buying that velvet dress?
你覺得買那件天鵝絨製的洋裝怎麼樣？

ven·ture [ˈvɛntʃɚ]　🔊 *Track 5274*

名 冒險　動 以……為賭注、冒險

▶ 名 Not everyone can take a costly venture like this.
不是每個人都能夠冒代價如此高的風險。

文法字詞解析
專門裝化妝用品類的小化妝包稱為 vanity case。

▶ 動 He ventured into the burning house to look for his pet.
他冒險進入燃燒著的房子裡找尋他的寵物。

ver·bal [ˈvɝbl̩] ◀€ *Track 5275*

形 言詞上的、口頭的 同 oral 口頭的

▶ Verbal agreement would not take legal effect, so you'd better sign a contract.
口頭同意不會有法律效力,所以你還是簽約比較好。

ver·sus [ˈvɝsəs] ◀€ *Track 5276*

介 ……對……(縮寫為vs.)

▶ I'm afraid that this election is about the new generation versus the old generation.
恐怕這個選舉是新世代和舊世代之間的鬥爭。

ver·ti·cal [ˈvɝtɪkl̩] ◀€ *Track 5277*

名 垂直線、垂直面 形 垂直的、豎的

▶ 名 The so-called vertical has inclined.
那條所謂的垂直線已經傾斜了。

▶ 形 It is obvious that the northern side of the mountain is almost vertical.
顯然這座山的北側幾乎是垂直的。

> **文法字詞解析**
> 相對地,「水平的」則是 horizontal,而「斜的」則是 diagonal。

ve·to [ˈvito] ◀€ *Track 5278*

名 否決 動 否決 同 deny 否定

▶ 名 It is said that the president threatened to use his veto over the bill. 據說總統威脅要對這個議案行使否決權。

▶ 動 The president has the power to veto any bill.
總統有權否決任何法案。

vi·a [ˈvaɪə] ◀€ *Track 5279*

介 經由 同 through 經由

▶ Let's keep in contact via email, shall we?
讓我們以後透過電子郵件來保持聯繫,好嗎?

vi·brate [ˈvaɪbret] ◀€ *Track 5280*

動 震動

▶ Your phone is vibrating. 你的手機在震動喔。

> **文法字詞解析**
> vibrate 多半用於機械方面或地殼震動等比較固定形式的震動,人類或動物發抖時不會用這個字來表示。

video·tape [ˈvɪdɪoˌtep] ◀€ *Track 5281*

名 錄影帶 動 錄影

▶ 名 People don't use videotapes anymore.
人們現在不使用錄影帶了。

▶ 動 Would you like to videotape this program for us?
你能幫我們把這個節目錄到帶子裡嗎?

view·er [ˈvjuɚ] ◀€ *Track 5282*

名 觀看者、電視觀眾 同 spectator 旁觀者

▶ Viewers cheered for the acrobats as they performed the difficult trick.
觀眾在雜耍表演者做出困難動作時歡呼。

Level
1

Level
2

Level
3

Level
4

Level
5

擴增實力5400單字

突飛猛進、程度大進擊──

Level
6

vig·or [ˈvɪgɚ]
Track 5283

名 精力、活力 同 energy 精力

▶ It is obvious that the leader of the expedition must be a man of great vigor.
顯然探險隊的負責人必須是個精力充沛的人。

vig·or·ous [ˈvɪgərəs]
Track 5284

形 有活力的 同 energetic 有活力的

▶ There are three vigorous young birds in the nest.
這鳥巢裡有三隻活潑的小鳥。

vil·lain [ˈvɪlən]
Track 5285

名 惡棍 同 rascal 惡棍

▶ I don't think the guy is a villain.
我認為這個傢伙不是個壞人。

vine [vaɪn]
Track 5286

名 葡萄樹、藤蔓

▶ Grape vines covered our fence in the yard.
葡萄藤覆蓋住我們庭院的圍牆。

vi·o·lin·ist [ˌvaɪəˈlɪnɪst]
Track 5287

名 小提琴手

▶ I wish I could become a famous violinist one day.
我希望有朝一日能成為一位著名的小提琴家。

vi·sa [ˈvizə]
Track 5288

名 簽證

▶ I'm afraid that we have to cut a few corners to get your visa ready in time. 恐怕我們得簡化手續才能把你的簽證及時辦妥。

vow [vaʊ]
Track 5289

名 誓約、誓言 動 立誓、發誓 同 swear 發誓

▶ 名 Once he took the vow, his loyalty never wavered（動搖）.
他一旦宣了誓，就會一直忠貞不渝。

▶ 動 Once she vowed that she would take the matter to court, it will be more difficult for us to handle this.
一旦她誓要把這件事訴諸法律，那麼我們就更難處理了。

[Ww]

wade [wed]
Track 5290

名 涉水、跋涉 動 艱辛地進行、跋涉

▶ 名 They went for a wade in the shallows.
他們由水淺的地方涉水過去。

▶ 動 The soldiers had to wade through a swamp.
軍人必須涉水渡過一個沼澤。

萬用延伸句型
It is obvious that... 顯然地……

文法字詞解析
句中的 woven 是 weave（織）的完成式形態，weave 的動詞三態是 weave, wove, woven。

wail [wel] *Track 5291*

名 哀泣 動 哭泣

▶名 The child burst into loud wails.
那個小孩突然大哭起來。

▶動 The girl wailed when the dog barked at her.
那隻狗對那個小女孩吠時，她大哭起來。

ward [wɔrd] *Track 5292*

名 行政區、守護、病房 動 守護、避開 同 avoid 避開

▶名 The patient has been confined to the ward for months.
病人已經限制在病房裡好幾個月了。

▶動 He reacted quickly and warded off the blow.
他反應很快，避開了這一擊。

ware [wɛr] *Track 5293*

名 製品、貨品

▶The shop sells a great variety of porcelain（瓷器）ware.
這家店鋪出售種類繁多的瓷器。

ware·house [ˈwɛrˌhaʊs] *Track 5294*

名 倉庫、貨棧 動 將貨物存放於倉庫中

▶名 Don't you think the warehouse full of paper is a fire hazard
（危險）?
你不覺得裝滿紙張的倉庫有引發火災的危險嗎？

▶動 We should warehouse these goods as quickly as we can.
我們應該儘快把這批貨物存放到倉庫中。

war·rior [ˈwɔrɪɚ] *Track 5295*

名 武士、戰士 同 fighter 戰士

▶I am fond of reading the stories of ancient warriors. What
about you?
我很喜歡讀有關古代武士的故事。你呢？

war·y [ˈwɛrɪ] *Track 5296*

形 注意的、小心的 同 cautious 小心的

▶You'd better keep a wary eye on the weather before you go
out for a long journey.
你出門長途旅行前最好密切注意一下天氣。

萬用延伸句型
be wary of sb./sth. 小心（某人或某事）
例如：You need to be wary of strangers
on the street.
要小心路上的陌生人。

wea·ry [ˈwɪrɪ] *Track 5297*

形 疲倦的 動 使疲倦

▶形 Why not sit on the bench in the park and rest your weary
limbs? 為什麼不到公園的長凳上坐坐，讓你疲倦的腿休息
一下呢？

▶動 She was a little weary after a long flight.
長途飛行後，她有點疲倦。

weird [wɪrd] *Track 5298*

形 怪異的、不可思議的 同 strange 奇怪的

▶My brother likes to wear really weird clothes.
我弟弟喜歡穿很奇怪的衣服。

Level
1

Level
2

Level
3

Level
4

Level
5

擴增實力5400單字 突飛猛進、程度大進擊──

Level
6

wharf [hwɔrf] 🔊 Track 5299

名 碼頭 同 pier 碼頭

▶Let's wait for others on the small wharf, shall we?
我們到那個小碼頭上等其他人吧，可以嗎？

where·a·bouts [ˋhwɛrəˋbaʊts] 🔊 Track 5300

名 所在的地方 副 在何處 同 location 位置、所在地

▶名 The Google map may show his exact whereabouts.
Google地圖會顯示他的所在位置。

▶副 Whereabouts on earth did you leave your bag?
你到底把包包放在哪了啊？

文法字詞解析
句中的「on earth」並非真的想問「在地
球上的哪裡」，純粹是一個強調用的慣用
語。也可以問「where on earth...」、「why
on earth...」、「what on earth...」等等
變化形式。

where·as [hwɛrˋæz] 🔊 Track 5301

連 雖然、卻、然而

▶Some people like the cold weather, whereas some hate it.
有些人喜歡冷天氣，然而有些人卻很討厭。

whine [hwaɪn] 🔊 Track 5302

名 哀泣聲、嘎嘎聲 動 發牢騷、怨聲載道

▶名 Do you hear the whines of the dog?
你聽見了那隻狗的哀鳴聲嗎？

▶動 The dog was whining outside the door last night.
昨晚那隻狗在門外哀叫。

whirl [hwɜl] 🔊 Track 5303

名 迴轉 動 旋轉 同 turn 旋轉

▶名 Put the fruits into the blender and give them a whirl.
把水果放到果汁機裡面讓它轉一下吧。

▶動 The leaves whirled beautifully as they fell.
樹葉美麗地旋轉飄落。

文法字詞解析
漩渦就是水在池中「旋轉」，所以叫做
whirlpool。

whisk [hwɪsk] 🔊 Track 5304

名 小掃帚 動 掃、揮 同 sweep 掃

▶名 Will you borrow a whisk from the neighbors?
你能從鄰居那借把掃帚來嗎？

▶動 The lady whisked the kids out of the room.
那個女士迅速把孩子們掃出門外。

whis·key/whis·ky [ˋhwɪskɪ] 🔊 Track 5305

名 威士忌

▶Whisky is stronger than beer. 威士忌比啤酒還要烈。

whole·sale [ˋholˏsel] 🔊 Track 5306

名 批發 動 批發賣出 形 批發的

▶名 Would you like to tell me how we can buy these goods at
wholesale? 你能告訴我，我們如何才能整批買進這批貨嗎？

▶動 They wholesale these shirts at $6 each.
他們以每件六美元的價格批發出售這些襯衫。

▶形 Mr. Wang is a local wholesale supplier.
王先生是本地的批發供應商。

whole·some [ˈholsəm]　　🔊 *Track 5307*

形 有益健康的　反 harmful 有害的
▶The food we cook is really wholesome.
我們煮的菜都很有益健康。

wide·spread [ˈwaɪdˌsprɛd]　　🔊 *Track 5308*

形 流傳很廣的、廣泛的　同 extensive 廣泛的
▶There are reports of widespread flooding after the typhoon hit this island. 颱風襲擊本島後，特地都有淹水情況。

wid·ow/wid·ow·er　　🔊 *Track 5309*
[ˈwɪdo]/[ˈwɪdəwɚ]

名 寡婦 / 鰥夫
▶It was the widow who brought him up.
正是這個寡婦把他扶養長大。

wig [wɪg]　　🔊 *Track 5310*

名 假髮
▶His wig was blown away by the strong wind.
他的假髮被強風吹走了。

wil·der·ness [ˈwɪldənɪs]　　🔊 *Track 5311*

名 荒野
▶The man got lost in the Canadian wilderness.
那個男人在加拿大的荒野迷路了。

wild·life [ˈwaɪldˌlaɪf]　　🔊 *Track 5312*

名 野生生物
▶We must protect wildlife and their habitats（棲息地）by all means.
我們該盡一切辦法來保護野生生物以及它們的棲息地。

with·er [ˈwɪðɚ]　　🔊 *Track 5313*

動 枯萎、凋謝　同 fade 枯萎、凋謝
▶The reason why the flower withered was that there was no water. 這朵花枯萎的原因是缺水。

woe [wo]　　🔊 *Track 5314*

名 悲哀、悲痛　同 sorrow 悲痛
▶The typhoon and earthquake added to the country's woes.
颱風和地震為這個國家帶來更多苦難。

wood·peck·er [ˈwʊdˌpɛkɚ]　　🔊 *Track 5315*

名 啄木鳥
▶How long will it take for a woodpecker to peck a hole in a tree? 啄木鳥在樹上啄個洞要花多久的時間？

work·shop [ˈwɝkˌʃɑp]　　🔊 *Track 5316*

名 小工廠、研討會
▶There are more than sixty workers in a workshop here.
這裡的一間小工廠裡有六十多個工人。

文法字詞解析

若假髮被人家 snatch（一把拿走、抓走），肯定會覺得非常驚訝。因此 snatch sb.'s wig 即表示做了某件令人非常驚訝的事，而 sb.'s wig be snatched 則描述某人被狠狠嚇了一跳（帶點讚賞的意味）。
例如：The artist's new MV was amazing. My wig was snatched.
這位歌手的新 MV 超讚的。我驚訝得假髮都掉了。

萬用延伸句型

Woe is me! 我真是悲慘！（用於自我怨嘆的時候）
例如：Woe is me! All the plants I keep are dead!
我真是太慘了！我種的植物都死光了！

Level 1
Level 2
Level 3
Level 4
Level 5
擴增實力5400單字 突飛猛進、程度大進擊
Level 6

wor·ship [ˈwɝʃɪp]
Track 5317

名 禮拜 動 做禮拜

▶名 My father asked us to attend worship by ourselves this morning.
爸爸早上叫我們自己去做禮拜。

▶動 People are busy with their work now. It is no wonder that they have little time to worship.
人們現在都忙於工作。難怪他們很少有時間去做禮拜了。

worth·while [ˈwɝθˈhwaɪl]
Track 5318

形 值得的 同 worthy 值得的

▶The investment will be financially worthwhile.
這項投資在金融來說很值得。

wor·thy [ˈwɝðɪ]
Track 5319

形 有價值的、值得的

▶This book is worthy of reading.
這本書很值得一讀。

wreath [riθ]
Track 5320

名 花環、花圈

▶They hung a wreath above the door.
他們在門上掛了一個花圈。

wring [rɪŋ]
Track 5321

名 絞、絞扭 動 握緊、絞 同 twist 絞、扭

▶名 Give those clothes a wring, so that they'll dry faster.
把那些衣服擰一擰,這樣比較快乾。

▶動 The girl was wringing her hands as she cried.
那個小女孩邊哭邊絞著手。

[Yy]

yacht [jɑt]
Track 5322

名 遊艇 動 駕駛遊艇、乘遊艇

▶名 The wealthy man can afford a yacht.
有錢人可以買得起遊艇。

▶動 I have time to go yachting with you this weekend.
我這週末有時間來陪你去坐遊艇。

yarn [jɑrn]
Track 5323

名 冒險故事、紗 動 講故事

▶名 How long will it take for you to wind the yarn into a ball?
你把毛線纏成一個球要多久?

▶動 How long did the old mariner（水手）yarn about his sea adventures?
老水手講他的海上奇遇講了多久?

萬用延伸句型

worship the ground sb. walks on 直譯就是「趴在某人走過的地上做禮拜」,也就是「非常崇拜、喜愛某人」的意思。
例如:You can tell he loves his wife a lot. He practically worships the ground she walks on.
看得出來他非常愛他太太,甚至連她走過的地面都令他想要膜拜。

文法字詞解析

比起 yacht 大得多的「遊輪」則叫做 cruise。

yeast [jist]

〔名〕酵母、發酵粉
▶Don't you know yeast can be used in making beer and bread?
你不知道嗎？酵母可用於釀啤酒和發酵麵包。

yield [jild]

〔名〕產出 〔動〕生產、讓出 〔同〕produce 生產
▶〔名〕The weather was favorable this year. It is no wonder that these trees give a high yield of fruit.
今年風調雨順。怪不得這些果樹獲得了大豐收。
▶〔動〕The experiment yielded an unexpected result.
這個實驗產生出意料之外的結果。

Track 5325

yo·ga [ˈjogə]

〔名〕瑜伽
▶I am so busy everyday that I have no time to go to yoga lessons. 我每天都很忙，以致於我都沒時間去上瑜伽課。

Track 5326

[Zz]

zinc [zɪŋk]

〔名〕鋅 〔動〕鍍鋅
▶〔名〕Zinc can be used to cover other metals to keep them from rusting. 鋅可塗在其他金屬表面上用來防銹。
▶〔動〕I heard that he can zinc on the container.
我聽說他能在那個容器上鍍鋅。

Track 5327

zip [zɪp]

〔名〕尖嘯聲、拉鍊 〔動〕呼嘯而過、拉開或拉上拉鍊
▶〔名〕The car passed by in a zip.
那台車呼嘯而過。
▶〔動〕The dress zips at the back.
洋裝的拉鍊在背後。

Track 5328

ZIP [zɪp]

〔名〕郵遞區號
▶Would you please tell me your complete address and ZIP code, Mr. Kelly?
凱利先生，您能告訴我您的完整地址及郵遞區號嗎？

Track 5329

zoom [zum]

〔動〕調整焦距使物體放大或縮小
▶Do you know how to use the "zoom in" function of the copier （影印機）？
你知道怎麼把影印機設定成放大模式嗎？

Track 5330

萬用延伸句型
zip past sb. 從（某人）身旁快速跑過
例　如：What happened? Why did a group of people just zip past me?
發生什麼事？為什麼有一群人忽然從我身邊衝過去？

Level 1

Level 2

Level 3

Level 4

Level 5

擴增實力5400單字 突飛猛進、程度大進擊

Level 6

下面有五篇文章，全是根據 Level1-5 的單字寫出來的，文章中超出 level5 的單字，有註記在一旁。

請先不要看全文的中文翻譯，試著讀讀看這五篇文章，若能全盤了解意思，代表你對 Level5 單字已經駕輕就熟，可以升級到 Level6 囉！快來自我挑戰看看吧！

Reading Practice 1

Many countries around the world celebrate Earth Day. It is a day that is meant to raise awareness and appreciation about the Earth's natural environment.

The first Earth Day was held in the USA. It was founded by United States Senator (參議員) Gaylord Nelson as an environmental protection campaign – a sort of general educational forum or conference. That was on April 22, 1970. While this first Earth Day was focused on the United States, an organization launched by Denis Hayes, the original organizer of the Earth Day at national level, took in international in 1990. Then, events for the Earth Day were held in 141 nations.

Earth Day is now coordinated (協調) globally by the Earth Day Network, and is celebrated in more than 175 countries every year. Numerous communities celebrate Earth Week, an entire week of activities focused on environmental issues. In 2009, the United Nations designated (指定) April 22 International Mother Earth Day.

Reading Practice 2

The Academy Awards, informally known as The Oscars, are a set of awards given annually for excellence of cinematic achievements. The award is organized and supervised by the Academy of Motion Picture Arts and Sciences (AMPAS), and the awards are given each year at a formal ceremony. As one of the most prominent award ceremonies in the world, the Academy Awards ceremony is live broadcast on TV in more than 100 countries annually.

The awards were first given in 1929, at the Hotel Roosevelt in Hollywood. Over the years, the awards have been given, the categories presented have changed. Currently, Oscars are given in more than a dozen categories, including films of various types.

The Oscar statuette is officially named the Academy Award of Merit. When it is under the ownership of the recipient (受獎者), it is essentially not on the open market. Since 1950, there has been an agreement that neither winners nor their heirs could sell that statuettes (小雕像) without fist offering to sell them back to the Academy for US$1. However, some of the awards have been sold in public auctions and private deals for six-figure sums.

Reading Practice 3

The sportswear Nike has announced it would use America football player Colin Kaepernick in its advertising campaign to celebrate its "Just Do It" 30th anniversary. Mr. Kaepernick has initiated controversy in 2016 while as quarterback for his team the San Francisco. He refused to stand for the national anthembutknelt down on one knee as a protest against racial injustice and social issues. This started a trend of other players "taking the knee" in support of the Black Lives Matter Movement.

Kaepernick's actions caused heated debate. In September 2017, president Donald Trump tweeted that NFL players should be either fired of suspended if they failed to stand up for the national anthem.

A close-up image of Kaepernick's face would be used in Nike's new ad with the caption (標語) "Believe in something. Even if it means sacrificing everything." Nike knows that it will receive a drawback (衰退) for using Mr. Kaepernick in its ads. However, it still applauded Mr. Kaepernick's actions, saying: "We believe Colin is one of the most inspiring athletes of the generation, who has leveraged the power of sport to help move the world forward."

Reading Practice 4

The Great Wall of China, one of the greatest marvels of the world, was first built between 220 – 206 B.C. At first, it was initially established to as independent walls for different provinces for the purpose of defending against barbarians from the north. It did not become the "Great Wall" until the Qin Dynasty. Emperor Qin Shihuang succeeded in his efforts to have the walls joined together. Then, it was a complete fortification(防禦)to protect the northern borders of the Chinese Empire from invasion. Afterwards, it was rebuilt and maintained over the years, between 5th century BC and the 16th century.

One of the myths associated with Great Wall of China is that it is the only man-made structure that can be seen from the moon with the naked eye. However, the assumption contradicted with astronauts' words. Actually, Great Wall can be visible from a low orbit of the earth, which is not unique in this regard, for many artificial structures can be seen from that height.

Reading Practice 5

Since 2015, an immense number of refugees came into Germany, which has made some people uneasy. About one million migrants flooded in the country. Residential shelters were built to house the immigrants, and the newcomers sought for chances to be employed.

Some citizens thought the outsiders may pose threat to their safety. In Chemnitz, Germany, thousands of far-right protestants gathered in response to the case that a German citizen got killed by Syrian and Iraqi migrants. Many members of the party called "Alternative for Germany" wore all black clothing at the "mourning march."

Police had to intervene (介入) when the event became violent, and they made an attempt to keep protesters away from counter-demonstrators. At that time, about thousands of people went on a separate protest in support of foreign sentiment. The authorities have to consider the welfare of both the local people and the immigrants.

Level
1

Level
2

Level
3

Level
4

Level
5

Level
6

Reading Practice1 中譯

　　世界上許多國家有慶祝「地球日」。這是一個希望引起人們注意地球自然環境的日子。

　　第一屆地球日是在美國舉辦的。這是由一位美國的參議員蓋洛 · 尼爾森發起的環保運動——一種一般的教育論壇或研討會。當時是在 1970 年 4 月 22 日。第一屆的地球日主要是在美國舉行，然而，在 1990 年，早期參與計畫美國國內地球日活動的丹尼斯 · 海因斯，發起了國際的活動。接著，地球日的活動遍及到 141 個國家。

　　地球日現在是由〈地球日聯合網〉這個單位在全球舉辦，每年有超過 175 個國家參與這項活動。許多社區還會舉辦地球週，有一整周的活動在探討環保議題。在 2009 年，聯合國指定 4 月 22 日作為〈國際地球日〉。

Reading Practice2 中譯

　　奧斯卡金像獎，又被稱為奧斯卡獎，是每年一度頒發給在傑出電影作品的獎項。這個獎項是由美國電影藝術與科學學會所舉辦與監督的，這個獎項每年會於正式典禮上頒發。奧斯卡是世界上最著名的頒獎典禮之一，每年都有超過 100 個國家，電視實況轉播這個頒獎典禮。

　　這個獎項最早是在 1929 年，在好萊塢的羅斯福酒店頒發的。多年以後，頒發的獎項、以及獎項的種類都有些改變。目前，奧斯卡有超過十二種類的獎項，包括各種電影類型。

　　奧斯卡小金人正式的名稱是〈學院功績獎〉。頒發給受獎者之後，它就不應該被公開販售。從 1950 年開始，就有不成文的規定説，受獎者本人或者後代子孫想要變賣獎座時，需要以 1 美元的價格賣回去給電影學院。然而，有些獎座已經在公開拍賣或私下交易中，賣到六位數以上的價格了。

Reading Practice3 中譯

　　運動用品 Nike 宣布美國足球選手柯林 · 卡佩尼克會登上該公司慶祝「放手一搏吧！」這句標語三十週年的廣告上。卡佩尼克在 2016 年作為隊上的四分衛在舊金山比賽時，曾引發爭議。他拒絕以肅立表示對國歌的敬意，而是單膝下跪，以表達抗議種族不公義以及其他社會議題。於是，其他選手也開始「下跪」，支持「黑人也是命」的活動。卡佩尼克的行動引發議論。在

2017 年九月，川普總統在推特發文表示，國家美式橄欖球聯盟 (NFL) 的球員如果不肅立對國歌表示敬意，就應該被開除。

Nike 新的廣告中呈現卡佩尼克的臉部特寫，旁邊有標語寫著「堅持信念。即使那代表失去一切。」Nike 知道讓卡佩尼克作為廣告代言人，會讓生意變差。但是，該公司還是讚賞卡佩尼克的作為，並且表示「我們相信柯林是當代最啟發人心的球員之一，他利用運動的力量，讓世界更好。」

Reading Practice4 中譯

長城是世界最著名的奇觀之一，最早是在西元前 220 至 206 年之間。一開始，它是每個省獨立建造起來，要防禦北方野蠻人入侵的城牆。一直到秦代，它才成為一座「長城」。秦始皇成功地將這些城牆連在一起。接著，它就成為保護中國北面邊界不受侵略的堡壘。之後，它又在西元前五世紀到西元 16 世紀這段期間，不斷被重建與維修。

其中一個和中國長城有關的迷思是，它是地表上唯一可以從月球用肉眼就看得見的人造建築。然而，這個假設和太空人的描述不符合。事實上，從離地球較近的軌道上，才能看見長城。就這方面來說，長城不是獨一無二的。在同樣的高度，還可以看到許多其他人造建築物。

Reading Practice5 中譯

從 2015 年開始，有大量的難民來到德國，讓一些居民感到不安。大約有一百萬遷徙湧入這個國家。他們蓋了收容所所來容納這些難民，而新來的成員希望能在當地找工作。

有些人民認為這些外來者會威脅他們的安全。在德國的肯次尼城，數千名極右派抗爭者聚集，針對一個德國人民被敘利亞和伊拉克移民殺害的案件表達抗議。許多「德國另類選擇黨」穿黑色衣服來參加這個「哀悼的遊行」。事件變得比較嚴重時，警察必須介入，他們將黑衣人和另外一群抗爭者分隔開來。當時，數千人去參加另一場支持外國人的遊行。有關當局必須同時考慮當地人和移民者的福祉才行。

NOTE

Level
1

Level
2

Level
3

Level
4

Level
5

突飛猛進、程度大進擊──
擴增實力5400單字

Level
6

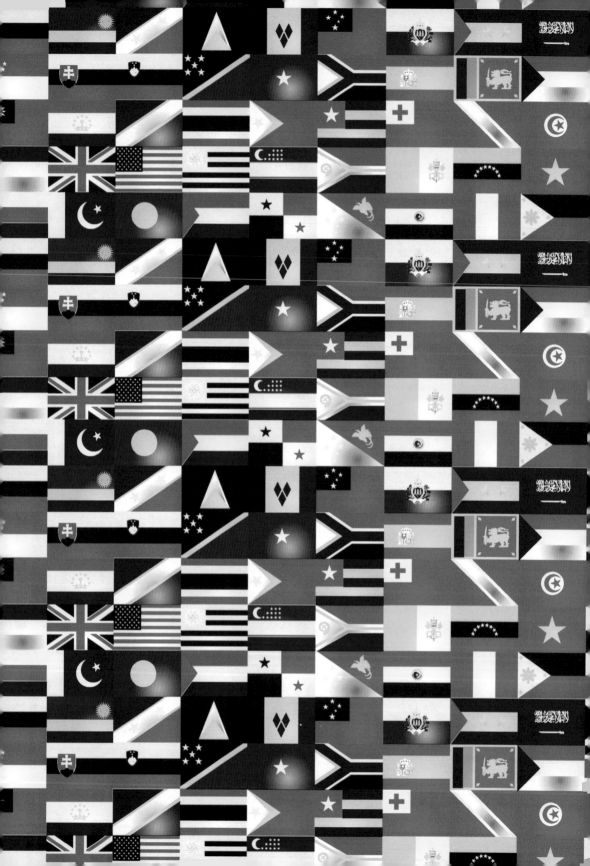

Level 6

精進自我、聽說讀寫通——
突破瓶頸7000單字

Level 6　精進自我、聽說讀寫通——
突破瓶頸7000單字

[Aa]

ab·bre·vi·ate [əˋbrivɪˌet]　◀ Track 5331

動 將……縮寫成　同 shorten 縮短
▶There is a glossary of abbreviated terms in the book.
　這本書有縮寫字的字表。

ab·bre·vi·a·tion [əˌbrivɪˋeʃən]　◀ Track 5332

名 縮寫
▶Not everyone knows that "Mr." is the abbreviation of "Mister".
　不是每個人都知道「Mr.」是「Mister」的縮寫。

ab·nor·mal [æbˋnɔrml]　◀ Track 5333

形 反常的
▶I'm afraid that it's abnormal for the boy to eat so much.
　這個男孩吃這麼多恐怕不太正常吧。

> **萬用延伸句型**
> It's abnormal for sb. to... 對某人來說做某事很不正常

ab·o·rig·i·nal [ˌæbəˋrɪdʒənl̩]　◀ Track 5334

名 土著、原住民　形 土著的、原始的
▶名 It seems that all the aboriginals there are very good at singing and dancing.
　那裡的土著似乎都非常擅長唱歌和跳舞。
▶形 It seems that more and more people are beginning to appreciate the beauty of aboriginal works of art.
　似乎越來越多的人開始欣賞當地土著居民的工藝之美。

ab·o·rig·i·ne [ˌæbəˋrɪdʒəni]　◀ Track 5335

名 原住民
▶There are many aborigines living in this mountain.
　有很多原住民住在這座山裡。

a·bound [əˋbaʊnd]　◀ Track 5336

動 充滿　同 overflow 充滿
▶Theories abound why the climate changes become more obvious.
　關於氣候變遷為何變明顯，有很多理論可說明。

ab·sent·mind·ed [ˋæbsəntˋmaɪndɪd]　◀ Track 5337

形 茫然的
▶It is no wonder that the absent-minded boy always loses his books.
　難怪這個心不在焉的男孩總是把書弄丟。

> **萬用延伸句型**
> It is no wonder that... 難怪……

ab·strac·tion [æb`strækʃən] 🔊 Track 5338

名 抽象、出神
▶It's hard to describe this idea to you in abstraction.
用抽象的方式解釋這個概念給你聽是很困難的。

a·bun·dance [ə`bʌndəns] 🔊 Track 5339

名 充裕、富足
▶There is an abundance of information on this search engine.
這個搜尋網站上有很多資訊。

a·buse [ə`bjuz] 🔊 Track 5340

名 濫用、虐待 動 濫用、虐待、傷害 同 injure 傷害
▶名 There are many child abuse cases in that country.
那個國家有很多孩童受虐的案例。
▶動 The man abused his children when he got drunk.
這個男人喝醉時就會虐待小孩。

ac·cel·er·ate [æk`sɛləˌret] 🔊 Track 5341

動 促進、加速進行
▶Let's accelerate the speed of our community construction.
讓我們加快我們社區建設的速度吧。

> **文法字詞解析**
> 加速器為 accelerator。

ac·cel·er·a·tion [ækˌsɛlə`reʃən] 🔊 Track 5342

名 加速、促進
▶It is said that this type of car has good acceleration.
據說這種車的加速性能很好。

ac·ces·si·ble [æk`sɛsəbl] 🔊 Track 5343

形 可親的、容易接近的
▶I'm afraid that this database is only accessible for the authorized manager.
恐怕只有授權的管理員才可以使用此資料庫。

ac·ces·so·ry [æk`sɛsərɪ] 🔊 Track 5344

名 附件、零件 形 附屬的
▶名 Would you please ask him to buy some car accessories for me? 請你叫他幫我買些汽車零件好嗎？
▶形 The watch is a valuable accessory item.
這支手錶是很有價值的配件。

> **文法字詞解析**
> 知情不報幫助罪犯（但自己本身沒有做犯罪舉動）的人也可稱為 accessory。

ac·com·mo·date [ə`kɑməˌdet] 🔊 Track 5345

動 使……適應、提供 同 conform 適應
▶The athletes may accommodate in the Olympic Village.
運動員住在奧運選手村。

ac·com·mo·da·tion 🔊 Track 5346
[əˌkɑmə`deʃən]

名 便利、適應
▶I'm afraid that the accommodation is rather rough and ready.
恐怕這個住處還算差強人意。

Level 1
Level 2
Level 3
Level 4
Level 5
Level 6

突破瓶頸7000單字

精進自我、聽說讀寫通

ac·cord [əˈkɔrd]
Track 5347

名 一致、和諧 動 和……一致
▶名 His words are in accord with his actions.
他做的跟說的如出一轍。
▶動 I'll try to accord the controversy over the housing scheme.
我會試著調解在住房建築規劃方面的爭議。

ac·cor·dance [əˈkɔrdns]
Track 5348

名 給予、根據、依照
▶We proceeded with the plan in accordance with her wish.
我們依照她的希望繼續進行這個計畫。

ac·cord·ing·ly [əˈkɔrdɪŋlɪ]
Track 5349

副 因此、於是、相應地
▶I have told you the circumstances, and you are supposed to act accordingly.
我已將情況告訴你了，你應該酌情處理。

ac·count·a·ble [əˈkaʊntəbl̩]
Track 5350

形 應負責的、有責任的、可說明的 同 responsible 有責任的
▶We should both be accountable for this.
我們兩人都該為這件事負責。

ac·count·ing [əˈkaʊntɪŋ]
Track 5351

名 會計、會計學
▶I don't think he is quite fit for accounting work.
我覺得他不是很適合這份會計工作。

ac·cu·mu·late [əˈkjumjəˌlet]
Track 5352

動 累積、積蓄 同 gather 聚集
▶Rubbish has been accumulating in the front yard.
垃圾在前院裡堆積。

ac·cu·mu·la·tion
[əˌkjumjəˈleʃən]
Track 5353

名 累積
▶Would you please be quick? An accumulation of work is waiting to be done.
請你快點好嗎？一堆工作等著要做呢。

ac·cu·sa·tion [ˌækjəˈzeʃən]
Track 5354

名 控告、罪名
▶You can't make such baseless accusation at your colleagues.
你不能毫無根據地指控你的同事。

ac·qui·si·tion [ˌækwəˈzɪʃən]
Track 5355

名 獲得
▶The man devoted his life to the acquisition of knowledge.
那個男人把一生的時間都用在獲取知識上。

萬用延伸句型
hold sb. accountable 認為（某人）應為某事負責
例如：His parents held him accountable for his little sister's safety.
他父母要他為他妹妹的安全負責。

ac·tiv·ist [ˈæktɪvɪst]
🔊 *Track 5356*

名 行動者
▶What if all these activists complain about the decision?
如果把這些積極分子都抗議這個決策呢？

a·cute [əˈkjut]
🔊 *Track 5357*

形 敏銳的、激烈的 同 keen 敏銳的
▶She felt acute embarrassment when she forgot her lines.
她在台上忘詞，突然一陣尷尬。

ad·ap·ta·tion [ˌædəpˈteʃən]
🔊 *Track 5358*

名 適應、順應
▶It is said that this play is an adaptation of a novel.
據說這一個劇本是由小說改編而成的。

ad·dict [ˈædɪkt]/[əˈdɪkt]
🔊 *Track 5359*

名 有毒癮的人 動 對……有癮、使入迷
▶名 There are no lengths to which an addict will not go to obtain his drugs. 癮君子為了得到毒品什麼事都做得出來。
▶動 It is no wonder that she is addicted to television.
難怪她對電視入了迷。

ad·dic·tion [əˈdɪkʃən]
🔊 *Track 5360*

名 熱衷、上癮
▶It was his addiction to drugs that propelled him towards a life of crime. 吸毒成癮使他走上了犯罪的道路。

ad·min·is·ter/ ad·min·is·trate [ədˈmɪnəstə]/[ədˈmɪnəˌstret]
🔊 *Track 5361*

動 管理、照料
▶It takes brains to administer a large corporation.
管理大公司要有頭腦。

ad·min·is·tra·tion [ədˌmɪnəˈstreʃən]
🔊 *Track 5362*

名 經營、管理、政府 同 government 管理
▶Her work involved more than administration of first aid to the wounded. She also has to assist other doctors.
她的工作不僅僅是對傷者的急救，她還得協助其他的醫生。

ad·min·is·tra·tive [ədˈmɪnəˌstretɪv]
🔊 *Track 5363*

形 行政上的、管理上的
▶The administrative procedure may take months.
行政的流程可能要花好幾個月。

ad·min·is·tra·tor [ədˈmɪnəˌstretə]
🔊 *Track 5364*

名 管理者
▶You had better not underestimate（低估）an administrator's resolutions! 你最好不要低估管理者的決心！

文法字詞解析
acute triangle 即銳角三角形。

文法字詞解析
電腦的系統管理員也稱為 administrator，因此每當電腦出問題時就常會看到叫你去找 administrator 的訊息。

Level 1
Level 2
Level 3
Level 4
Level 5
Level 6

突破瓶頸7000單字 精進自我、聽說讀寫通

ad·vo·cate [ˈædvəkɪt]/[ˈædvəˌket]　🔊 *Track 5365*

名 提倡者 動 提倡、主張 同 support 擁護

▶名 I don't think that they are advocates of free trade.
我不認他們是自由貿易的宣導者。

▶動 I don't believe that he really advocates reforming the prison system. 我不相信他是真的主張改良監獄制度。

af·fec·tion·ate [əˈfɛkʃənɪt]　🔊 *Track 5366*

形 摯愛的

▶He gave his wife an affectionate kiss.
他給他太太深情的一吻。

af·firm [əˈfɝm]　🔊 *Track 5367*

動 斷言、證實 同 declare 斷言

▶I can affirm that the girl did quite a bit of reading.
我能證實這個女孩子讀了不少書。

ag·gres·sion [əˈgrɛʃən]　🔊 *Track 5368*

名 進攻、侵略

▶It is obvious that such an action constitutes an aggression upon women's rights.
顯然這種行為是對婦女權利的侵犯。

al·co·hol·ic [ˌælkəˈhɔlɪk]　🔊 *Track 5369*

名 酗酒者 形 含酒精的

▶名 She has had enough of her alcoholic husband.
她對酒鬼丈夫再也無法容忍了。

▶形 She never has alcoholic beverages because she is allergic.
她從來不喝含酒精的飲料，因為她對酒精過敏。

a·li·en·ate [ˈeljənˌet]　🔊 *Track 5370*

動 使感情疏遠 同 separate 使疏遠

▶You'd better not alienate yourself from your colleagues.
你最好還是不要與同事們疏遠。

al·li·ance [əˈlaɪəns]　🔊 *Track 5371*

名 聯盟、同盟

▶They formed an alliance against the common enemy.
他們聯合起來抵禦共同的敵人。

al·lo·cate [ˈæləˌket]　🔊 *Track 5372*

動 分配 同 distribute 分配

▶The supervisor allocated the tasks to people.
主管分派任務給同事們。

a·long·side [əˈlɔŋsaɪd]　🔊 *Track 5373*

副 沿著、並排地 介 在……旁邊

▶副 The police car pulled up alongside all of a sudden.
那輛警車突然在旁邊停下了。

▶介 The boat stopped alongside the dock so that the passenger can get off. 那條船停靠在碼頭旁，好讓那名乘客可以下船。

文法字詞解析

alien 有「外星人」的意思，加上帶有「使變成……」意思的動詞字尾，alienate 就成了「使變成外星人」的意思。讓某人「變成外星人」，大家當然就不敢親近他，也難怪這個單字的意思會是「使感情疏遠」了。

al·ter·na·tive [ɔl`tɝnətɪv] 🔊 *Track 5374*

名 二選一、供選擇的東西 形 二選一的 同 substitute 代替

▶名 It seems that there is no alternative.
  似乎沒有別的選擇了。

▶形 Can we take an alternative route instead?
  我們改走別條路好不好？

文法字詞解析
除了常見的 rock、pop 外，alternative 也是一種音樂的分類，指的是地下獨立製作的另類音樂風格。

am·bi·gu·i·ty [æmbɪ`gjuətɪ] 🔊 *Track 5375*

名 曖昧、模稜兩可

▶I'm afraid that the dispute resulted from ambiguities in the contract.
  恐怕爭議是由合約中模稜兩可的詞句引起的。

am·big·u·ous [æm`bɪgjuəs] 🔊 *Track 5376*

形 曖昧的 同 doubtful 含糊的

▶The authorities held an ambiguous stance.
  當局採取模稜兩可的立場。

am·bu·lance [`æmbjələns] 🔊 *Track 5377*

名 救護車

▶He's in a pretty bad way. You'd better get an ambulance.
  他的狀況很不好。你最好叫輛救護車。

am·bush [`æmbuʃ] 🔊 *Track 5378*

名 埋伏、伏兵 動 埋伏並突擊 同 trap 陷阱

▶名 We fell into the enemy's ambush.
  我們中了敵人的埋伏。

▶動 They ambushed the enemy the very next day.
  他們第二天就突襲了敵軍。

a·mi·a·ble [`emɪəbl] 🔊 *Track 5379*

形 友善的、可親的

▶The next-door neighbors are amiable people.
  隔壁鄰居們都是和藹可親的人。

am·pli·fy [`æmpləˌfaɪ] 🔊 *Track 5380*

動 擴大、放大

▶The host's words amplified the sense of guilt of the suspect.
  主持人的話讓嫌疑犯的罪惡感擴大了。

文法字詞解析
能夠把聲音「放大」的揚聲器就稱為 amplifier。

an·a·lects [`ænəˌlɛkts] 🔊 *Track 5381*

名 語錄、選集 同 collection 收集品

▶There are some errors in the annotation（注解）of the Analects.
  這本《論語》中有不少釋義不當的地方。

文法字詞解析
Analects 字首大寫時專門指《論語》。

a·nal·o·gy [ə`nælədʒɪ] 🔊 *Track 5382*

名 類似

▶I don't think that it is always reliable to argue by analogy.
  我認為用類推法論證並不總是可靠的。

Level 1
Level 2
Level 3
Level 4
Level 5
Level 6

突破瓶頸7000單字 精進自我、聽說讀寫通

an·a·lyst [ˈænəlɪst]　　🔊 Track 5383
名 分解者、分析者
▶I hope I could become a highly trained and practiced（熟練的）system analyst.
我希望我能成為一位受過嚴格訓練、經驗豐富的系統分析員。

an·a·lyt·i·cal [ˌænəˈlɪtɪk!]　　🔊 Track 5384
形 分析的
▶She employed an analytical method in this investigation.
她用分析式的研究方法來做調查。

> **文法字詞解析**
> analytical 也能用來描述一個人的個性，說這個人「擅長分析」、「喜歡分析」。

an·ec·dote [ˈænɪkˌdot]　　🔊 Track 5385
名 趣聞
▶Would you tell me some anecdotes about that famous actor?
你能為我講幾個關於那位名演員的趣聞嗎？

an·i·mate [ˈænəˌmet]　　🔊 Track 5386
動 賦予……生命 形 活的 同 encourage 激發、助長
▶動 It is obvious that Jim's arrival served to animate the whole party.
顯然吉姆的到來使聚會的整個氣氛活躍了起來。
▶形 There are so many beautiful things in animate nature.
充滿生命力的大自然中有許多美麗的事物。

> **文法字詞解析**
> 這個字後面加上名詞字尾「-tion」就變成了「animation」，而這個字不僅有「生氣、活潑」的意思，還可以表示「動畫片」，因為動畫片賦予了所有的卡通人物生命嘛。

an·noy·ance [əˈnɔɪəns]　　🔊 Track 5387
名 煩惱、困擾
▶The man slammed the door in annoyance.
那個男人不高興地甩上了門。

a·non·y·mous [əˈnɑnəməs]　　🔊 Track 5388
形 匿名的
▶The donation was from an anonymous benefactor.
這筆捐款是來自不具名的捐贈者。

Ant·arc·tic/ant·arc·tic [ænˈtɑrktɪk]　　🔊 Track 5389
名 南極洲 形 南極的
▶名 It is reported that the scientist has spent three months in the solitude of the Antarctic.
據報導這位科學家已經在人跡罕至的南極待了三個月了。
▶形 It is said that the Antarctic Peninsula hasn't been polluted yet.
據說南極半島尚未受到污染。

an·ten·na [ænˈtɛnə]　　🔊 Track 5390
名 觸角、觸鬚、天線
▶There is a TV antenna upon the roof.
屋頂上有一根電視天線。

an·ti·bi·ot·ic [ˌæntɪbaɪˋɑtɪk] ◀╎ *Track 5391*

名 抗生素、盤尼西林 形 抗生的、抗菌的 同 medicine 藥物

▶名 Antibiotics can be used against infection.
　抗生素可以用來防止感染。

▶形 It is said that earthworms（蚯蚓）can produce antibiotic substances.
　據說蚯蚓可以產生抗菌物質。

文法字詞解析
antibiotic 這個字當作名詞時，較常以複數形式（antibiotics）出現。

an·ti·bod·y [ˋæntɪˌbɑdɪ] ◀╎ *Track 5392*

名 抗體

▶Infants can get some important antibodies from breast milk.
　嬰兒可以從母乳中得到重要的抗體。

an·tic·i·pate [ænˋtɪsəˌpet] ◀╎ *Track 5393*

動 預期、提前支用 同 expect 預期

▶He didn't anticipate being chosen for the show.
　他沒預期到他會被選上去上節目。

an·tic·i·pa·tion [ænˌtɪsəˋpeʃən] ◀╎ *Track 5394*

名 預期、預料

▶The girl paced around the room in anticipation.
　女孩期待地在房間裡走來走去。

an·to·nym [ˋæntəˌnɪm] ◀╎ *Track 5395*

名 反義字

▶It is quite clear that "long" is the antonym of "short".
　很顯然「長」是「短」的反義詞。

文法字詞解析
字首「ant-」是「anti-」的變形，也就是「相反」的意思，字尾「-nym」的意思則是「字、名字」，所以兩者合在一起就是「相反的字」，也就變成「反義字」了。那「同義字」又要怎麼說呢？就是「synonym」。「syn-」有「將分開的東西結合在一起」的意思。

ap·pli·ca·ble [ˋæplɪkəbl] ◀╎ *Track 5396*

形 適用的、適當的 同 appropriate 適當的

▶I don't think that the regulation is applicable to this case.
　我認為那條規定不適用於這一情況。

ap·pren·tice [əˋprɛntɪs] ◀╎ *Track 5397*

名 學徒 動 使……做學徒 同 beginner 新手

▶名 The apprentice was sent on errands by the chef.
　大廚叫學徒去跑腿打雜。

▶動 Not all parents in that village want to apprentice their children to a carpenter.
　那個村子裡不是所有的家長都想讓他們的孩子去當木匠的學徒。

ap·prox·i·mate [əˋprɑksəmɪt] ◀╎ *Track 5398*

動 相近 形 近似的、大致準確的

▶動 The distance was approximated as three kilometers.
　估計這段距離大約為三公里。

▶形 Would you please give me an approximate figure of the budget?
　您能不能給我一個關於預算的大概數據呢？

Level
1

Level
2

Level
3

Level
4

Level
5

Level
6

精進自我、聽說讀寫通
突破瓶頸7000單字

ap·ti·tude [ˈæptəˌtjud]
🔊 Track 5399

名 才能、資質 同 ability 才能
▶It is obvious that the little girl has an aptitude for languages.
顯然這個小女孩具有學習語言的才能。

Arc·tic/arc·tic [ˈɑrktɪk]
🔊 Track 5400

名 北極地區 形 北極的
▶名 The Arctic is much colder than the place we live.
北極地區比我們住的地方冷多了。
▶形 I guess there are much less people in the Arctic regions than here. 我想北極地區的人要比這裡的少得多。

ar·ro·gant [ˈærəgənt]
🔊 Track 5401

形 自大的、傲慢的 反 humble 謙虛的
▶The authorized inspector had an arrogated attitude.
官方授權的檢查員有傲慢的態度。

ar·ter·y [ˈɑrtərɪ]
🔊 Track 5402

名 動脈、主要道路
▶Now, how am I supposed to get around that artery?
現在，我要如何繞過那條主要道路？

ar·tic·u·late [ɑrˈtɪkjəˌlet]/[ɑrˈtɪkjəlɪt] 🔊 Track 5403

動 清晰地發音 形 清晰的
▶動 Would you please articulate your words carefully? I don't quite follow you.
請把話仔細地說清楚好嗎？我聽不太明白。
▶形 He can't come up with an articulate argument.
他想不出一個清楚有力的論點。

延伸萬用句型
I don't quite follow you. 我聽不太懂你的意思。

ar·ti·fact [ˈɑrtɪˌfækt]
🔊 Track 5404

名 加工品
▶I feel that the ancient Egypt artifacts in the exhibition are gorgeous. 我覺得展覽中的古埃及手工藝品真是美極了。

as·sas·si·nate [əˈsæsṇˌet]
🔊 Track 5405

動 行刺 同 kill 殺死
▶It is reported that the police has uncovered a plot to assassinate the president.
據說警察已破獲一起暗殺總統的陰謀。

as·sert [əˈsɝt]
🔊 Track 5406

動 斷言、主張
▶The speaker asserts that human labor will be replaced by AI.
講者肯定地說，人力會被人工智慧取代。

as·sess [əˈsɛs]
🔊 Track 5407

動 估計價值、課稅
▶It is too early to assess the effects of the new legislation.
現在來評價新法規的效果還為時過早。

萬用延伸句型
It is too early to... 要（做某事）還太早

as·sess·ment [əˈsɛsmənt]
🔊 *Track 5408*

名 評估、稅額
▶The purpose of the assessment was unknown.
這個測驗的目的不明。

as·sump·tion [əˈsʌmpʃən]
🔊 *Track 5409*

名 前提、假設、假定 反 conclusion 結論
▶My assumption is that the man and the girl are probably father and daughter.
我猜測這個男人和那個女孩大概是父女。

asth·ma [ˈæzmə]
🔊 *Track 5410*

名 【醫】氣喘
▶Secondhand smoke has been proven over and over again to be a major trigger of asthma attacks.
二手菸一再被證實是引發氣喘的主要原因之一。

a·sy·lum [əˈsaɪləm]
🔊 *Track 5411*

名 收容所
▶He was soon committed to an insane asylum.
不久他就被送進了精神病院。

at·tain [əˈten]
🔊 *Track 5412*

動 達成 反 fail 失敗
▶I finally attained a diploma at the university.
我終於在大學取得了文憑。

at·tain·ment [əˈtenmənt]
🔊 *Track 5413*

名 到達
▶He's a man of great attainments in several fields.
他在幾個領域中都有很高造詣，這令人驚訝。

at·ten·dant [əˈtɛndənt]
🔊 *Track 5414*

名 侍者、隨從 形 陪從的
▶名 Being a good flight attendant means making your passengers feel relaxed.
當一個好的空服員就是要讓乘客們感到旅途輕鬆愉快。
▶形 What do you think about hiring an attendant nurse to take care of her? 你覺得請一位隨行護士來照顧她怎麼樣？

at·tic [ˈætɪk]
🔊 *Track 5415*

名 閣樓、頂樓
▶I stored some photo albums in the attic.
我將一些相簿收在閣樓裡。

auc·tion [ˈɔkʃən]
🔊 *Track 5416*

名 拍賣 動 拍賣 同 sale 拍賣
▶名 They sold the villa by auction.
他們拍賣了那棟別墅。
▶動 It is said that they are going to auction the pictures at the end of the month. 據說他們將在月底拍賣這些畫。

萬用延伸句型
make assumptions about sth. 做出關於某件事的假設
例如：You shouldn't make assumptions about other people's intentions.
不要隨意臆測別人的動機。

Level 1

Level 2

Level 3

Level 4

Level 5

Level 6
突破瓶頸7000單字
精進自我、聽說讀寫通

萬用延伸句型
auction sth. off 將（某物）拍賣掉
例如：Grandma managed to auction the antique vase off.
奶奶成功把古董花瓶拍賣掉了。

au·then·tic [ɔˈθɛntɪk]　◀ Track 5417

形 真實的、可靠的

▶His words were the only authentic account for the accident.
他的話是那場意外唯一可信的證詞。

文法字詞解析
authentic 也可以解釋為「道地的」，如：
authentic food = 道地的菜餚
authentic material = 道地的學習資料

au·thor·ize [ˈɔθəˌraɪz]　◀ Track 5418

動 委託、授權、委任

▶It is really a joy that I've been authorized by the court to repossess（重新擁有）this property.
我得到法庭認可重新擁有這筆財產，這真是件樂事。

au·to·graph/ sig·na·ture [ˈɔtəˌɡræf]/[ˈsɪɡnətʃɚ]　◀ Track 5419

名 親筆簽名　動 親筆寫於……　同 sign 簽名

▶名 Would you please give me your autograph? You are my idol! 您能幫我簽個名嗎？您是我的偶像！

▶動 Would you please autograph my T-shirt?
您能把名字簽在我的 T 恤上嗎？

au·ton·o·my [ɔˈtɑnəmɪ]　◀ Track 5420

名 自治、自治權

▶Not everyone in this city think that it's necessary to strive for autonomy.
這城市裡不是每個人都認為有必要爭取自治權。

a·vi·a·tion [ˌevɪˈeʃən]　◀ Track 5421

名 航空、飛行　同 flight 飛行

▶Both his father and he devoted all their lives to aviation.
他和他的父親都把自己的一生奉獻給了航空事業。

awe·some [ˈɔsəm]　◀ Track 5422

形 有威嚴的

▶The awesome scenery made the visitors speechless.
極佳的風景讓遊客無從形容。

文法字詞解析
awesome 這個單字一開始是「有威嚴的」的意思，後來在口語中逐漸轉化成了「很棒」的稱讚意味，而這個新的意思已經逐漸取代了這個單字的原意，因此如果聽到有人稱讚你做的某事很 awesome，他有很大的機率不是在說你有威嚴，純粹覺得你很棒而已。

[Bb]

ba·rom·e·ter [bəˈramətɚ]　◀ Track 5423

名 氣壓計、晴雨錶

▶The stock market is a barometer for business, isn't it?
股票市場是商業的晴雨錶，不是嗎？

beck·on [ˈbɛkn̩]　◀ Track 5424

動 點頭示意、招手

▶Do you mind telling me why he beckoned me to come nearer?
麻煩你告訴我他為什麼招手叫我過去？

be·siege [bɪˋsidʒ]
◀ *Track 5425*

動 包圍、圍攻　反 release 釋放

▶The enemy has been besieged by us since last month.
自從上個月起，敵軍就被我們包圍了。

be·tray [bɪˋtre]
◀ *Track 5426*

動 出賣、背叛　同 deceive 欺騙

▶He betrayed his company by transferring to the rival company.
他背叛公司，轉任至對手的公司。

bev·er·age [ˋbɛvrɪdʒ]
◀ *Track 5427*

名 飲料

▶This beverage is in a new flavor. Would you like to have a drink?
這種飲料是新口味的。你要不要喝喝看？

bi·as [ˋbaɪəs]
◀ *Track 5428*

名 偏心、偏袒　動 使存偏見

▶名 You must deal with the matter without bias.
你必須無偏見地解決這件事情。

▶動 Don't you know that he is biased against the plan from the beginning?
難道你不知道他從一開始就對這個計畫心存偏見嗎？

文法字詞解析
在一個偶像團體中，你最喜歡的成員就是你的 bias。

bin·oc·u·lars [baɪˋnɑkjələz]
◀ *Track 5429*

名 雙筒望遠鏡

▶How about buying a pair of binoculars for your son as his birthday present?
買一副雙筒望遠鏡給你兒子作為他的生日禮物怎麼樣？

bi·o·chem·i·stry [͵baɪoˋkɛmɪstrɪ]
◀ *Track 5430*

名 生物化學

▶He does better in biochemistry than anyone else in his class.
他生物化學這科，學得比班上其他人都要好。

bi·o·log·i·cal [͵baɪoˋlɑdʒɪkl̩]
◀ *Track 5431*

形 生物學的、有關生物學的

▶The advice has a solid biological basis; don't you think so?
這個建議具有堅固的生物學基礎，你不覺得嗎？

文法字詞解析
biological clock 即「生物時鐘」。

bi·zarre [bɪˋzɑr]
◀ *Track 5432*

形 古怪的、奇異的

▶He was stunned by the bizarre situation.
他被這個奇異的景象嚇到。

bleak [blik]
◀ *Track 5433*

形 淒涼的、暗淡的

▶I am afraid that our company's prospects will look rather bleak because of the financial crisis.
恐怕我們公司將會因為這次的金融危機而顯得前景異常暗淡。

Level 1
Level 2
Level 3
Level 4
Level 5
Level 6

突破瓶頸7000單字　精進自我、聽說讀寫通

blun·der [ˈblʌndɚ]
🔊 *Track 5434*

名 大錯 動 犯錯

▶名 I made a blunder by mistaking the two documents.
我犯了錯誤，把兩個文件搞混了。

▶動 Even the best worksman（工匠）sometimes blunders, so there is no need to blame yourself.
即使是最厲害的工匠也難免犯錯，因此你沒必要自責。

blunt [blʌnt]
🔊 *Track 5435*

動 使遲鈍 形 遲鈍的 反 sharp 敏銳的

▶動 The drug blunted his senses, so it is too hard for him to keep awake.
藥使得他的感覺遲鈍了，因此他很難保持清醒。

▶形 The axe you gave me is too blunt to cut down the tree.
你給我的那把斧頭太鈍，砍不倒這棵樹。

文法字詞解析
講話極為直接、不顧聽者心情，也可用 blunt 來描述。例如當你想要直話直說時，就可以先以「forgive me for being blunt...」（請原諒我直說……）當作開場白。

bom·bard [bɑmˈbɑrd]
🔊 *Track 5436*

動 砲轟、轟擊

▶The man bombarded us with questions.
那個男人連珠砲似地問了我們一大堆問題。

bond·age [ˈbɑndɪdʒ]
🔊 *Track 5437*

名 奴役、囚禁

▶It is easy for a man to fall under the bondage of gold.
人很容易被金錢所奴役。

boost [bust]
🔊 *Track 5438*

名 幫助、促進 動 推動、增強、提高 同 increase 增加

▶名 They really need a boost to their morale.
他們非常需要激勵一下士氣。

▶動 This method should help boost sales.
這個策略應該能夠幫助促進銷售。

文法字詞解析
兒童的身高比較矮，而有墊高效果、「幫助」他們「增高」的輔助座椅可稱為 booster、booster seat。

bout [baʊt]
🔊 *Track 5439*

名 競賽的一回合

▶Will you tell me how many rounds there are in a bout?
你能告訴我一場比賽有幾局嗎？

boy·cott [ˈbɔɪkɑt]
🔊 *Track 5440*

名 杯葛、排斥 動 杯葛、聯合抵制

▶名 The law has harmed their interests. It is no wonder that they want to put it under a boycott. 該法律已侵害到了他們的利益。怪不得他們想聯合抵制它。

▶動 People boycotted the produce of the farm which mistreated animals.
那間農場會虐待動物，人們拒絕購買他們的產品。'

break·down [ˈbrekˌdaʊn]
🔊 *Track 5441*

名 故障、崩潰

▶The man had a nervous breakdown at the hospital.
那名男子在醫院情緒崩潰了。

break·through [ˈbrekˌθru]
名 突破
▶I hope the scientists could make a breakthrough in the treatment of that disease.
我希望科學家們能在治療那種疾病方面獲得突破。

Track 5442

break·up [ˈbrekˌʌp]
名 分散、瓦解
▶It was a sequence of incidents that led to the couple's breakup. 正是這一連串的事件導致了這對情侶的分手。

Track 5443

brew [bru]
名 釀製物 動 釀製
▶名 I know what his favorite brew of beer is.
我知道他愛喝什麼樣的啤酒。
▶動 He brewed coffee for his guests.
他為客人煮咖啡。

Track 5444

brink [brɪŋk]
名 陡峭邊緣
▶The company is on the brink of bankruptcy（破產）because of poor management.
這家公司已瀕臨破產的邊緣，因為它的管理不善。

Track 5445

brisk [brɪsk]
形 活潑的、輕快的
▶The old lady is a brisk walker. 這名老太太走路很快。

Track 5446

bro·chure [broˈʃʊr]
名 小冊子 同 pamphlet 小冊子
▶Would you please send me a brochure about your company?
請寄給我你們公司的簡介手冊好嗎？

Track 5447

brute [brut]
名 殘暴的人 形 粗暴的
▶名 He is an unfeeling（無情的）brute. You'd better stay away from him. 他是個無情的畜生。你最好離他遠一點。
▶形 He opened the door by brute force.
他以暴力將門打開。

Track 5448

buck·le [ˈbʌkl]
名 皮帶扣環 動 用扣環扣住 同 fasten 扣緊
▶名 The seatbelt buckle seems to be broken.
這安全帶扣環好像壞掉了。
▶動 Buckle up, or you might get fined.
要繫安全帶，不然你可能會被罰錢喔。

Track 5449

bulk·y [ˈbʌlkɪ]
形 龐大的
▶The soldier left his bulky equipment behind.
軍人丟棄了笨重的裝備。

Track 5450

文法字詞解析
breakup 為名詞，如要表示動詞，則必須將 break 與 up 分開，變成片語。例如：They decided to break up after dating for a month.
他們在一起一個月後，決定要分手。

萬用延伸句型
buckle down and 原 V：（在一陣子不努力之後）開始努力做某事
例 如：You really need to buckle down and start studying! Do you want to flunk the class?
你真的得開始努力唸書了！不然你想被當嗎？

Level 1 / Level 2 / Level 3 / Level 4 / Level 5 / Level 6 精進自我、聽說讀寫通 突破瓶頸7000單字

bu·reau·cra·cy [bjuˈrɑkrəsɪ]　◀≷ *Track 5451*

名 官僚政治
▶It is impossible（不可能的）for us to understand the workings（運轉）of such a huge bureaucracy.
想瞭解這樣龐大的官僚體系的運作情況，對我們而言是不可能的。

bur·i·al [ˈbɛrɪəl]　◀≷ *Track 5452*

名 埋葬、下葬　同 funeral 葬儀、出殯
▶All family members gathered for the burial of my uncle.
所有家族成員都聚集在叔叔的喪禮上。

byte [baɪt]　◀≷ *Track 5453*

名【電算】位元組
▶How many megabytes can this computer hold?
這台電腦可以裝得下幾百萬位元的東西？

[Cc]

caf·feine [ˈkæfiɪn]　◀≷ *Track 5454*

名 咖啡因
▶There is a large amount of caffeine in this kind of coffee.
在這種咖啡裡有大量的咖啡因。

cal·ci·um [ˈkælsɪəm]　◀≷ *Track 5455*

名 鈣
▶It is obvious that calcium is beneficial to our bones.
顯然鈣對我們的骨骼有益。

can·vass [ˈkænvəs]　◀≷ *Track 5456*

名 審視、討論　動 詳細調查
▶名 There will be a canvass in the neighborhood next month.
下個月在鄰近地區有一次募捐活動。
▶動 It seems that the city council has canvassed the plan thoroughly.
市議會似乎已經詳細討論了那個計畫。

ca·pa·bil·i·ty [ˌkepəˈbɪlətɪ]　◀≷ *Track 5457*

名 能力
▶The algebra question is beyond the kid's capability.
代數問題已經超出小孩的能力。

cap·sule [ˈkæpsḷ]　◀≷ *Track 5458*

名 膠囊
▶Would you please tell me how many capsules I should take per day?
可以請你告訴我每天該吃幾顆膠囊嗎？

文法字詞解析
沒有咖啡因的咖啡可以稱為「decaf」，在這裡字首「de-」有「去除、沒有」的意思。

cap·tion [ˈkæpʃən]　🔊 *Track 5459*

名 標題、簡短說明　動 加標題

▶名 I am sure you can understand the meaning of this picture, because there is a caption under it.
我保證你能了瞭這幅圖片的意思，因為圖片下面附有說明。

▶動 I forgot to caption this article.
我忘了幫這篇文章加標題了。

cap·tive [ˈkæptɪv]　🔊 *Track 5460*

名 俘虜　形 被俘的　同 hostage 人質

▶名 The captives were abused by the prison warden.
囚犯被獄卒虐待。

▶形 John was taken captive for almost 10 days by the enemy.
約翰被敵軍俘虜了將近十天。

cap·tiv·i·ty [kæpˈtɪvətɪ]　🔊 *Track 5461*

名 監禁、囚禁

▶It is said that he has been released from his long captivity.
據說他已經從長期被囚禁的生活中被釋放了。

car·bo·hy·drate　🔊 *Track 5462*
[ˌkɑrboˈhaɪdret]

名 碳水化合物、醣

▶You'd better not have too much carbohydrates in your diet.
在日常飲食中你最好不要吃過多的碳水化合物。

ca·ress [kəˈrɛs]　🔊 *Track 5463*

名 愛撫　動 撫觸　同 touch 碰觸

▶名 The lonely child is longing for the caress of his mother.
這個孤獨的孩子渴望母親的擁抱。

▶動 The young lady caressed that baby lovingly.
那位年輕的小姐疼愛地撫摸那個嬰兒。

car·ol [ˈkærəl]　🔊 *Track 5464*

名 頌歌、讚美詞

▶Children go caroling during the week before Christmas in lots of western countries.
在西方許多國家，耶誕節前一週孩子們會到各家各戶去報佳音。

cash·ier [kæˈʃɪr]　🔊 *Track 5465*

名 出納員

▶The cashier remined the shoppers to queue.
收銀員提醒購物者要排隊。

cas·u·al·ty [ˈkæʒʊəltɪ]　🔊 *Track 5466*

名 意外事故、橫禍　同 accident 事故、災禍

▶There were dozens of casualties in the train crash.
在那次火車撞擊事故中有數十人傷亡。

文法字詞解析
單字裡的「carbo-」就是從「carbon（碳）」而來，「hydrate-」則是「水合物」的意思，兩者合併一起看，是不是就能猜到「碳水化合物」了呢？

Level 1
Level 2
Level 3
Level 4
Level 5
Level 6

突破瓶頸7000單字　精進自我、聽說讀寫通

ca·tas·tro·phe [kəˈtæstrəfɪ] ◀ Track 5467
名 大災難
▶This catastrophe killed over 16000 people, injuring more than 20000 people.
這場災難導致超過 16000 人死亡，以及 20000 人以上受傷。

ca·ter [ˈketɚ] ◀ Track 5468
動 提供食物、提供娛樂
▶What songs will be catering at the wedding reception?
什麼歌適合在婚宴上面播放？

文法字詞解析
如果 cater 加上了字尾「-ing」就變成了名詞「提供食物」，也就是「外燴、承辦酒席」的意思。

cav·al·ry [ˈkævl̩rɪ] ◀ Track 5469
名 騎兵隊、騎兵
▶Not all his neighbors know that he was an officer in the cavalry when he was young.
不是他所有的鄰居都知道他年輕時曾是騎兵軍官。

cav·i·ty [ˈkævətɪ] ◀ Track 5470
名 洞、穴
▶I am afraid that the cavity is not wide enough for me to get in.
洞口太窄了，我怕我會進不去。

文法字詞解析
因為蛀牙也是在牙齒中蛀出一個「洞穴」來，因此蛀牙也可以稱為 cavity。

cem·e·ter·y [ˈsɛmə͵tɛrɪ] ◀ Track 5471
名 公墓
▶It is said that his remains were shipped back and laid down in a cemetery. 據說他的遺體被運回並埋葬在一個公墓裡。

cer·tain·ty [ˈsɝtn̩tɪ] ◀ Track 5472
名 事實、確定的情況
▶I'm afraid that I have no certainty of success.
我恐怕沒有成功的把握。

cer·ti·fy [ˈsɝtə͵faɪ] ◀ Track 5473
動 證明
▶You should ask the bank manager to certify this check.
你應該請銀行經理來簽署證明這張支票。

cham·pagne [ʃæmˈpen] ◀ Track 5474
名 白葡萄酒、香檳
▶The champagne fizzed as waiter poured it into my glass.
服務生倒香檳倒杯子裡時，發出滋滋聲響。

文法字詞解析
champagne 這個單字是從法國來的，因此它的發音也比較特別。注意一下開頭的 ch 和我們常說的 chair 的 ch 發音方法不一樣喔！

cha·os [ˈkeɑs] ◀ Track 5475
名 無秩序、大混亂 同 confusion 混亂
▶There was chaos in the town after the hurricane had struck.
颶風過後，城裡一片混亂。

char·ac·ter·ize [ˈkærɪktə͵raɪz] ◀ Track 5476
動 描述……的性質、具有……特徵
▶This kind of dog is characterized by its curly fur.
這種狗的特徵是捲捲的毛。

char·coal [ˈtʃɑrˌkol]　🔊 Track 5477

名 炭、木炭

▶Would you please help me move the charcoal to the trunk?
可以請你幫我把木炭搬到後車廂裡嗎？

char·i·ot [ˈtʃærɪət]　🔊 Track 5478

名 戰車、駕駛戰車

▶The duke steered his chariot through the streets.
公爵自己駕著馬車通過街道。

char·i·ta·ble [ˈtʃærətəbl̩]　🔊 Track 5479

形 溫和的、仁慈的

▶He enjoys doing charitable work.
他是個樂善好施的人。

cho·les·ter·ol [kəˈlɛstəˌrol]　🔊 Track 5480

名 膽固醇

▶His high cholesterol levels are a huge worry for his family.
他的高膽固醇對於他的家人造成很大的煩惱。

chron·ic [ˈkrɑnɪk]　🔊 Track 5481

形 長期的、持續的　同 constant 持續的

▶There is a chronic unemployment problem in America.
美國存在著長期失業的問題。

chuck·le [ˈtʃʌkl̩]　🔊 Track 5482

名 滿足的輕笑　動 輕輕地笑

▶名 She let out a small chuckle when she saw the picture in the magazine.
她看到雜誌裡那張圖時輕輕笑了一下。

▶動 The boys were chuckling over the photograph.
那些男孩們看著照片咯咯地笑了起來。

chunk [tʃʌnk]　🔊 Track 5483

名 厚塊、厚片

▶A good chunk of my time was spent on correcting your mistakes.
我大部分的時間都花在修正你的錯誤上。

civ·i·lize [ˈsɪvəˌlaɪz]　🔊 Track 5484

動 啟發、使開化　同 educate 教育

▶David did a good job civilizing his younger brother.
大衛對於教化他的小弟有功勞。

clamp [klæmp]　🔊 Track 5485

名 夾子、鉗子　動 以鉗子轉緊

▶名 He had to hold the hooks together with a clamp.
他得用一個夾子把那些勾子夾在一起。

▶動 Why don't you clamp these two pieces of wood together?
為什麼不把兩根木頭鉗緊呢？

文法字詞解析

charcoal 也可以當作一種「顏色」（即指木炭的顏色）。

萬用延伸句型

blow chunks 嘔吐
例如：He blew chunks after drinking two glasses.
他喝了兩杯後就吐了。

Level
1

Level
2

Level
3

Level
4

Level
5

Level
6

突破瓶頸7000單字

精進自我、聽說讀寫通

cla·r·ity [ˈklærətɪ]
Track 5486

名 清澈透明

▶He speaks with clarity and grace.
他說話的方式清楚而優雅。

cleanse [klɛnz]
Track 5487

動 淨化、弄清潔

▶Before you bandage the wound, cleanse it thoroughly.
在你包扎傷口前,要仔細清理傷口。

文法字詞解析
除了生理上清潔某物,「淨化心靈」也可稱為 cleanse。例如看了某些兒童不宜的內容後,就可以說 I need to cleanse my soul(我的心靈需要淨化一下了)。

clear·ance [ˈklɪrəns]
Track 5488

名 清潔、清掃

▶All these clothes are labeled for clearance.
這些衣服都標示要出清。

clench [klɛntʃ]
Track 5489

名 緊握 動 握緊、咬緊

▶名 I felt the clench of someone's hand on my arm.
我感覺到有個人的手牢牢地抓住我的手臂。

▶動 He clenched his teeth and refused to tell anything.
他咬緊牙關什麼也不肯說。

clin·i·cal [ˈklɪnɪk!]
Track 5490

形 門診的

▶It seemed that this new therapy hasn't passed the clinical trial(試驗) yet.
這個新療法似乎尚未通過臨床試驗。

clone [klon]
Track 5491

名 無性繁殖、複製 同 copy 複製

▶I don't know why this new laptop is so popular; it is obvious that it's nothing but an IBM clone.
我不知道這台筆記型電腦為什麼這麼受歡迎,很顯然地它不過是台IBM的複製品罷了。

文法字詞解析
「複製人」也稱為 clone。

clo·sure [ˈkloʒɚ]
Track 5492

名 封閉、結尾 同 conclusion 結尾

▶The economic downturn has cause factory closures.
經濟衰退導致工廠關閉。

coffin [ˈkɔfɪn]
Track 5493

名 棺材

▶He is so tall that he can't fit in the coffin.
他高到棺材都裝不下了。

co·her·ent [koˈhɪrənt]
Track 5494

形 連貫的、有條理的

▶The lyrics he wrote were all over the place and not coherent at all.
他寫的歌詞毫無重點,完全沒有條理。

co·in·cide [koɪnˋsaɪd]
🔊 *Track 5495*

動 一致、同意　同 accord 一致

▶The thunderstorm coincided with a tornado.
雷陣雨和龍捲風同時出現。

co·in·ci·dence [koˋɪnsdəns]
🔊 *Track 5496*

名 巧合

▶I'm afraid that's the most incredible coincidence I've ever heard of!
恐怕那是我聽說過的最難以置信的巧合！

col·lec·tive [kəˋlɛktɪv]
🔊 *Track 5497*

名 集體　形 共同的、集體的

▶名 Only with organization can the wisdom of the collective be given full play.
集體智慧唯有組織後才能充份被發揮。

▶形 The collective consensus is that we really should not accept these terms.
大家的共識是我們真的不應該接受這些條件。

col·lec·tor [kəˋlɛktɚ]
🔊 *Track 5498*

名 收集的器具

▶The stamp collector had hundreds of volumes containing valuable stamps.
那位集郵迷有上百本裝著高價郵票的冊子。

col·lide [kəˋlaɪd]
🔊 *Track 5499*

動 碰撞　同 bump 碰撞

▶It is reported that the bus collided with a van when turning the corner.
根據報導這台公車在轉過街角時與小貨車相撞。

col·li·sion [kəˋlɪʒən]
🔊 *Track 5500*

名 相撞、碰撞、猛撞

▶A collision between a bus and a taxi occurred here.
公車和計程車在這裡互撞了。

col·lo·qui·al [kəˋlokwɪəl]
🔊 *Track 5501*

形 白話的、通俗的

▶It's much more useful to learn colloquial English than super formal English.
學口語英文比學超級正式的英文來得有用多了。

col·um·nist [ˋkɑləmɪst]
🔊 *Track 5502*

名 專欄作家

▶There is a very popular columnist commenting on current affairs for that newspaper.
有一位深受歡迎的專欄作家為那家報紙評論時事。

萬用延伸句型
It is reported that... 據報導……

文法字詞解析
是不是覺得這個字很眼熟呢？我們先前學過的「column」有「樑柱」和「專欄」的意思，因為報紙中的專欄都是長長一條、像柱子一樣的；而 columnist 就是在後面加上代表「專精某個領域的人」的名詞字尾「-ist」。

Level 1

Level 2

Level 3

Level 4

Level 5

Level 6

突破瓶頸7000單字　精進自我、聽說讀寫通

com·mem·o·rate
◄€ *Track 5503*

[kə`mɛməˌret]

動 祝賀、慶祝　**同** celebrate 慶祝

▶It is said that Christmas commemorates the birth of Christ.
據說耶誕節是為了紀念耶穌的誕生。

萬用延伸句型
It is said that... 據說……

com·mence [kə`mɛns]
◄€ *Track 5504*

動 開始

▶The construction of the bridge will commence soon.
這座橋的建築工程即將開始。

com·men·tar·y [`kɑmənˌtɛrɪ]
◄€ *Track 5505*

名 注釋、說明

▶I don't think that his commentary on this issue is correct.
我不認為他對這個問題的評論是正確的。

com·mit·ment [kə`mɪtmənt]
◄€ *Track 5506*

名 承諾、拘禁、託付

▶Your commitment towards your work is highly appreciated.
我們很欣賞你對工作的投入奉獻。

com·mu·ni·ca·tive
◄€ *Track 5507*

[kəˌmjunə`ketɪv]

形 愛說話的、口無遮攔的

▶Both Sara and her sister are very communicative people with positive personalities.
莎拉和她的姐姐都非常暢談，且擁有積極的個性。

com·pan·ion·ship
◄€ *Track 5508*

[kəm`pænjənˌʃɪp]

名 友誼、交往

▶The reason why I trust her so much is that we have a companionship of many years.
我之所以能如此信任她，是因為我們有多年的交情。

萬用延伸句型
enjoy sb.'s companionship 享受（某人）的陪伴
例如：We sat there in silence, enjoying each other's companionship.
我們安靜地坐在那裡，享受彼此的陪伴。

com·pa·ra·ble [`kɑmpərəbl]
◄€ *Track 5509*

形 可對照的、可比較的

▶It is obvious that their achievements are not comparable.
顯然他們的成就不能相提並論。

com·par·a·tive [kəm`pærətɪv]
◄€ *Track 5510*

形 比較上的、相對的

▶"More friendly" is the comparative of "friendly."
「更加友善」是「友善」的比較級。

com·pat·i·ble [kəm`pætəbl]
◄€ *Track 5511*

形 一致的、和諧的

▶Even though Susan and I have very different backgrounds, we are very compatible.
雖說我和蘇珊的背景很不相同，但我們非常合得來。

com·pen·sate [ˈkɑmpənˌset] 🔊 *Track 5512*
動 抵銷、彌補
▶I'm afraid that nothing can compensate for the loss of one's health. 恐怕什麼都不能補償健康的受損。

com·pen·sa·tion [ˌkɑmpənˈseʃən] 🔊 *Track 5513*
名 報酬、賠償
▶We receive a compensation of 3000 dollars for the inconvenience.
我們這次遭遇不便，收到三千元補償金。

com·pe·tence [ˈkɑmpətəns] 🔊 *Track 5514*
名 能力、才能
▶He has shown a lot of competence in the week he has been here. 他在這裡的一週來表現出來相當大的才幹。

com·pe·tent [ˈkɑmpətənt] 🔊 *Track 5515*
形 能幹的、有能力的
▶He is competent enough to fill that position in my view.
在我看來，他足以勝任那個職位。

com·pile [kəmˈpaɪl] 🔊 *Track 5516*
動 收集、資料彙編 同 collect 收集
▶It takes years of hard work to compile a good dictionary.
編一本好字典需要多年的艱苦工作。

文法字詞解析
compile 的名詞形式為 compilation。

com·ple·ment [ˈkɑmpləmənt] 🔊 *Track 5517*
名 補足物 動 補充、補足
▶名 It is obvious that homework is a necessary complement to classroom study.
顯然功課是課堂教學的必要補充。
▶動 This wine complements the food perfectly.
顯然用這種酒配這些菜餚是相得益彰。

com·plex·ion [kəmˈplɛkʃən] 🔊 *Track 5518*
名 氣色、血色
▶I'm afraid that that color doesn't suit your complexion.
恐怕那個顏色不適合你的膚色。

com·plex·i·ty [kəmˈplɛksətɪ] 🔊 *Track 5519*
名 複雜
▶The complexity surrounding the issue cause a haul on the negotiation. 複雜的環境因素造成協商停擺。

com·pli·ca·tion [ˌkɑmpləˈkeʃən] 🔊 *Track 5520*
名 複製、混亂
▶We're trying to solve all the complications that have arisen in the past two weeks.
我們正在試著解決前兩週出現的一堆新問題。

Level 1

Level 2

Level 3

Level 4

Level 5

Level 6

突破瓶頸7000單字 精進自我、聽說讀寫通

com·po·nent [kəmˈponənt]　🔊 Track 5521
名 成分、部件　形 合成的、構成的　同 part 部分
▶ 名 A computer consists of thousands of components.
　　電腦是由上千萬的零件所組成。
▶ 形 Yoga is an important component part in her life.
　　瑜伽是她生活中重要的組成部分。

com·pre·hen·sive [ˌkɑmprɪˈhɛnsɪv]　🔊 Track 5522
形 廣泛的、包羅萬象的
▶ You can receive comprehensive medical training here.
　　你可以在這裡受到全面的醫療訓練。

com·prise [kəmˈpraɪz]　🔊 Track 5523
動 由……構成
▶ The medical team comprises of three doctors and six nurses.
　　這個醫療團隊是由三位醫師和六個護士所組成的。

con·cede [kənˈsid]　🔊 Track 5524
動 承認、讓步　同 confess 承認
▶ I am afraid that you have no choice but to concede in this matter.
　　恐怕在這件事情上你只能讓步了。

萬用延伸句型
have no choice but to...
無可選擇，只能……

con·ceit [kənˈsit]　🔊 Track 5525
名 自負、自大
▶ His conceit makes him hard to approach.
　　他的自負讓他很難以接近。

con·cep·tion [kənˈsɛpʃən]　🔊 Track 5526
名 概念、計畫　同 idea 計畫、概念
▶ He has absolutely no conception of how to run a business.
　　他對於經營生意完全一點概念都沒有。

con·ces·sion [kənˈsɛʃən]　🔊 Track 5527
名 讓步、妥協
▶ I wish you could make some concession. Can you?
　　我希望你能做一些讓步。可以嗎？

con·cise [kənˈsaɪs]　🔊 Track 5528
形 簡潔的、簡明的
▶ Concise wording is expected in this report.
　　這篇報導應該要有精簡的用字。

con·dense [kənˈdɛns]　🔊 Track 5529
動 縮小、濃縮
▶ I'm afraid that you are supposed to condense your report; it's too long.
　　恐怕你應該濃縮一下你的報告，它太冗長了。

con·fer [kənˋfɝ]
🔊 *Track 5530*

動 商議、商討

▶Why don't we confer with the advisers before making a decision? 為什麼不先請教顧問然後再來做決定呢？

con·fi·den·tial [ˌkɑnfəˋdɛnʃəl]
🔊 *Track 5531*

形 可信任的、機密的 同 secret 機密的

▶The confidential files were encrypted. 機密文件都有加密處理。

con·form [kənˋfɔrm]
🔊 *Track 5532*

動 使符合、類似

▶I am afraid that if you don't start conforming to the rules, you may be kicked out of the school. 如果你不遵守校規的話，恐怕就有可能被退學。

con·fron·ta·tion
[ˌkɑnfrʌnˋteʃən]
🔊 *Track 5533*

名 對抗、對峙

▶The confrontation with him yesterday was still fresh in my mind. 昨天和他起衝突的事，我現在依然記得很清楚。

文法字詞解析
confrontation 的動詞形式為 confront。

con·gress·man/ con·gress·wom·an
[ˋkɑŋɡrəsˌmæn]/[ˋkɑŋɡrəsˌwumən]
🔊 *Track 5534*

名 眾議員 / 女眾議員

▶It is reported that the congressman was murdered. 據報導那位眾議員是被謀殺的。

con·quest [ˋkɑnkwɛst]
🔊 *Track 5535*

名 征服、獲勝 同 submit 使屈服

▶The handsome and rich man made a conquest of Mary's heart. 這個又帥又有錢的男人擄獲了瑪莉的芳心。

con·sci·en·tious [ˌkɑnʃɪˋɛnʃəs]
🔊 *Track 5536*

形 本著良心的、有原則的 同 faithful 忠誠的

▶She is the most conscientious staff member in our office. 她是我們辦公室裡最盡責的員工。

con·sen·sus [kənˋsɛnsəs]
🔊 *Track 5537*

名 一致、全體意見

▶They haven't reached a consensus on this matter. 他們還在這件事情上取得共識。

con·ser·va·tion [ˌkɑnsɚˋveʃən]
🔊 *Track 5538*

名 保存、維護

▶People need to understand the need for conservation of natural resources. 人們必須認識到保護自然資源的必要性。

文法字詞解析
這個字和 conversation（會話）很像，只是把 s 和 v 調換過來而已，但意思卻大不相同，要注意不要寫錯了。

Level 1

Level 2

Level 3

Level 4

Level 5

Level 6

突破瓶頸7000單字

精進自我、聽說讀寫通

con·so·la·tion [ˌkɑnsəˈleʃən] 🔊 *Track 5539*

名 撫恤、安慰、慰藉 反 pain 使痛苦
▶ It is obvious that her child is her only consolation.
　顯然她的孩子是她唯一的安慰。

con·spir·a·cy [kənˈspɪrəsɪ] 🔊 *Track 5540*

名 陰謀
▶ You had better be cautious about their conspiracy.
　你最好要小心他們的陰謀。

con·stit·u·ent [kənˈstɪtʃʊənt] 🔊 *Track 5541*

名 成分、組成要素 形 組成的、成分的 同 component 成分
▶ 名 The constituent of the mixture is recorded in the report.
　這種混合物的成分記載在這份報告裡。
▶ 形 Not everyone knows what the constituent parts of happiness are.
　不是每個人都知道幸福的組成要素是什麼。

con·sul·ta·tion [ˌkɑnsl̩ˈteʃən] 🔊 *Track 5542*

名 討教、諮詢
▶ The couple resolved their differences with consultation.
　那對夫妻透過諮商來解決他們之間的不愉快。

con·sump·tion [kənˈsʌmpʃən] 🔊 *Track 5543*

名 消費、消費量 同 waste 消耗
▶ I think there is too great a consumption of alcohol in China.
　我覺得酒在中國的消耗量太大了。

con·tem·pla·tion 🔊 *Track 5544*
[ˌkɑntɛmˈpleʃən]

名 注視、凝視
▶ He reached a decision after a good deal of contemplation.
　他在經過深思熟慮後才做出決定。

con·test·ant [kənˈtɛstənt] 🔊 *Track 5545*

名 競爭者
▶ Contestants on the game have to answer the questions accurately.
　參賽者必需要精準地回答這些問題。

con·trac·tor [ˈkɑntræktɚ] 🔊 *Track 5546*

名 立契約者
▶ Would you let me know who the contractor of the new motorway（高速公路）is?
　麻煩您告訴我，誰是這條新公路的承包商？

con·tra·dict [ˌkɑntrəˈdɪkt] 🔊 *Track 5547*

動 反駁、矛盾、否認
▶ It is obvious that the report contradicts what we heard yesterday.
　顯然這個報導與我們昨天聽到的有所出入。

萬用延伸句型

If it's any consolation... 如果這樣能安慰到你的話……
例如：If it's any consolation, I'm just about as clueless as you are.
如果這樣能安慰到你的話，那就是「我也跟你一樣完全不懂呢」。

文法字詞解析

contemplation 的動詞形式為 contemplate。

con·tra·dic·tion [ˌkɑntrəˈdɪkʃən] 🔊 *Track 5548*

名 否定、矛盾　同 denial 否認

▶There is a contradiction between his statement and hers.
他和她的聲明之間有矛盾之處。

con·tro·ver·sial [ˌkɑntrəˈvɜʃəl] 🔊 *Track 5549*

形 爭論的、議論的

▶The controversial issues were avoided in the conversation.
爭議的話題在對話中被避開了。

con·tro·ver·sy [ˈkɑntrəˌvɜsɪ] 🔊 *Track 5550*

名 辯論、爭論

▶There was a huge controversy over the plans for the new school.
眾人對建造新學校的計畫存有極大爭議。

con·vic·tion [kənˈvɪkʃən] 🔊 *Track 5551*

名 定罪、說服力

▶There is no conviction in your voice.
你說話的聲音中毫無決心。

co·or·di·nate 🔊 *Track 5552*
[koˈɔrdnˌet]/[koˈɔrdn̩ɪt]

動 調和、使同等　形 同等的　同 equal 同等的

▶動 Once we coordinate our efforts, we will be sure to win this game.
一旦我們同心協力，我們一定能夠打贏這場比賽。

▶形 These are coordinate clauses.
這是兩句並列句。

cor·dial [ˈkɔrdʒəl] 🔊 *Track 5553*

形 熱忱的、和善的

▶He received a cordial welcome at Cambridge.
他在劍橋受到了熱誠的歡迎。

core [kor] 🔊 *Track 5554*

名 果核、核心

▶Kinship is considered the core value in a Chinese family.
親屬關係是中國文化的核心價值。

cor·po·rate [ˈkɔrpərɪt] 🔊 *Track 5555*

形 社團的、公司的

▶The corporate spy got into deep trouble.
這位商業間諜惹了大麻煩。

corps [korps] 🔊 *Track 5556*

名 軍團、兵團

▶It is said that his father served in the medical corps during World War II.
據說在第二次大戰時，他父親在醫務部隊服過役。

文法字詞解析
上面幾個字都可以感覺到「相反、牴觸」的意思存在，因為字首「contra-、contro-」就有「相對」的意思。不過「contractor」是從「contract（合約）」在加上名詞字尾「-or（人）」而來，和其他的字是不一樣的，不要搞混了。

萬用延伸句型
rotten to the core 壞到骨子裡
例如：No use trying to reason with him. He's rotten to the core.
跟他講道理是沒用的，他壞到骨子裡了。

Level 1
Level 2
Level 3
Level 4
Level 5
Level 6

突破瓶頸7000單字
精進自我、聽說讀寫通

corpse [kɔrps] ◀€ Track 5557
名 屍體、屍首
▶The girl screamed when she saw the corpse.
那個女孩看到屍體的時候尖叫了起來。

cor·re·spon·dent ◀€ Track 5558
[ˌkɔrəˈspɑndənt]
名 通信者 同 journalist 新聞工作者
▶Jerry volunteered to be a war correspondent.
傑瑞自願當戰地記者。

cor·rup·tion [kəˈrʌpʃən] ◀€ Track 5559
名 敗壞、墮落
▶The corruption in their government isn't something that can be solved in one day.
他們政府的腐敗不是一天兩天就能解決的事情。

萬用延伸句型
...isn't something that can be solved in one day ……不是一天就能解決的事

cos·met·ic [kɑzˈmɛtɪk] ◀€ Track 5560
形 化妝用的
▶You had better solve this problem by using cosmetic cream.
你最好透過使用美容霜來解決這個問題。

cos·met·ics [kɑzˈmɛtɪks] ◀€ Track 5561
名 化妝品
▶How about buying some cosmetics for her as a Mother's Day present?
買點化妝品給她作為母親節禮物怎麼樣？

cos·mo·pol·i·tan ◀€ Track 5562
[ˌkɑzməˈpɑlətn̩]
名 世界主義者 形 世界主義的 同 international 國際的
▶名 Aaron is not only a scholar but also a rootless（無根的）cosmopolitan.
艾倫不但是個學者，還是個四海漂泊的人。
▶形 Beijing is not only the capital of China but also a cosmopolitan city.
北京不僅是中國的首都，而且是一個國際大都市。

coun·ter·part [ˈkaʊntɚˌpɑrt] ◀€ Track 5563
名 副本
▶Our manager met with the counterpart of our rival company.
我們經理去見了對手公司的經理。

cov·er·age [ˈkʌvərɪdʒ] ◀€ Track 5564
名 覆蓋範圍、保險範圍
▶We need more media coverage if we really want the whole country to know about what happened.
如果真要讓全國的人知道發生了什麼事，我們就需要更多媒體報導。

文法字詞解析
保險所涵蓋的範圍也稱為 coverage。

cov·et [ˋkʌvɪt]　◀≣ Track 5565

動 垂涎、貪圖
▶She coveted the brand-named purse but never got it.
　她很想要名牌的皮包，但無法得到。

cramp [kræmp]　◀≣ Track 5566

名 抽筋、鉗子　動 用鉗子夾緊、使抽筋
▶名 She got cramps in her leg when she was swimming.
　她游泳的時候腿抽筋了。
▶動 The room is so cramped and stuffy. Let's just leave.
　這房間太擠了、又悶，我們還是離開吧。

cred·i·bil·i·ty [ˌkrɛdəˋbɪlətɪ]　◀≣ Track 5567

名 可信度、確實性
▶The president has lost all credibility with the people.
　那名總統在人民眼中的威信已喪失。

cred·i·ble [ˋkrɛdəbḷ]　◀≣ Track 5568

形 可信的、可靠的
▶Is the evidence you found credible?
　你找到的證據可靠嗎？

cri·te·ri·on [kraɪˋtɪrɪən]　◀≣ Track 5569

名 標準、基準　同 standard 標準
▶Would you tell me what criteria you use when judging the quality of a student's work?
　您能告訴我您是用什麼標準來衡量學生的課業嗎？

文法字詞解析
這裡要注意，criterion 的複數形是 criteria。

crook [krʊk]　◀≣ Track 5570

名 彎曲、彎處　動 使彎曲
▶名 A bunch of crooks shall never win the race.
　一群烏合之眾無法贏得比賽。
▶動 He crooked his arm around the box.
　他把手臂彎著圈住了箱子。

文法字詞解析
因為惡棍的個性多半是「不正直的」，既然不直也就是「彎的」，因此惡棍也可以稱為 crook。

crooked [ˋkrʊkɪd]　◀≣ Track 5571

形 彎曲的、歪曲的
▶His back is so crooked that he cannot stand upright.
　他的背彎得都站不直了。

cru·cial [ˋkruʃəl]　◀≣ Track 5572

形 關係重大的　同 important 重大的
▶These negotiations are crucial to the future of our firm.
　這些談判對我們公司的前途非常重要。

crude [krud]　◀≣ Track 5573

形 天然的、未加工的
▶It is said that the great man was born in a crude hut.
　據說那個偉人生於一個簡陋的小屋裡。

Level 1
Level 2
Level 3
Level 4
Level 5
Level 6

精進自我、聽說讀寫通──突破瓶頸7000單字

cruise [kruz]

🔊 *Track 5574*

動 航行、巡航

▶The cruise around Mediterranean Sea would take a week.
航行地中海可能需要一個星期。

cruis·er [ˈkruzɚ]

🔊 *Track 5575*

名 遊艇

▶The cruiser fell behind the others because its controls was broken.
那艘遊艇落在其他艦隻的後面，因為它的控制盤壞掉了。

crumb [krʌm]

🔊 *Track 5576*

名 小塊、碎屑、少許

▶The birds are eating crumbs off the ground.
這些小鳥在吃地上的碎屑。

crum·ble [ˈkrʌmbl]

🔊 *Track 5577*

名 碎屑、碎片 動 弄成碎屑 同 mash 壓碎

▶名 The puppy is eating the cookie crumbles.
那隻小狗在吃餅乾碎屑。

▶動 She has a tendency to crumble her bread on the table.
她很容易把麵包碎屑弄到桌子上。

萬用延伸句型
crumble away 碎裂
例如：This wall has been standing here forever and is slowly crumbling away.
這堵牆已經在這裡很久了，它正在慢慢崩裂。

crust [krʌst]

🔊 *Track 5578*

名 麵包皮、派皮 動 覆以外皮

▶名 How about putting tomato sauce and cheese on the crust?
我們把番茄醬和起司放在派皮上怎麼樣？

▶動 The snow crusted the lake last night.
昨夜的雪使湖面結了冰。

cul·ti·vate [ˈkʌltəˌvet]

🔊 *Track 5579*

動 耕種

▶My parents work hard to cultivate the plants.
我的父母很努力培育植物。

cu·mu·la·tive [ˈkjumjəˌletɪv]

🔊 *Track 5580*

形 累增的、累加的

▶The cumulative effect of noise may cause harm to your ears.
長期累積的噪音影響可能損害聽力。

cus·tom·ar·y [ˈkʌstəmˌɛrɪ]

🔊 *Track 5581*

形 慣例的、平常的

▶It's customary for people to give others gifts on their birthdays.
有人生日時送他生日禮物是很平常的事。

萬用延伸句型
It's customary for... 對……來說是一種慣例

[Dd]

daf·fo·dil [ˈdæfədɪl] 🔊 *Track 5582*

名 黃水仙

▶Have you ever seen a daffodil? What does it look like?
你有看過黃水仙嗎？它長什麼樣子呢？

dan·druff [ˈdændrəf] 🔊 *Track 5583*

名 頭皮屑

▶The dandruff was apparent on his coat.
頭皮屑在他的外套上面很明顯。

day·break [ˈdeˌbrek] 🔊 *Track 5584*

名 破曉、黎明

▶By the time my father came back home, it was daybreak.
父親回來時天已破曉。

dead·ly [ˈdɛdlɪ] 🔊 *Track 5585*

形 致命的 副 極度地

▶形 If only the doctors could cure this deadly disease soon.
要是醫生們能很快治好這種致命的疾病，該有多好啊。

▶副 If only I could stay at home when the air was deadly cold.
在極度寒冷的時候，我要是能待在家裡就好了。

> **文法字詞解析**
> deadly disease = 致命的疾病
> deadly poison = 致命的毒藥

de·cent [ˈdisn̩t] 🔊 *Track 5586*

形 端正的、正當的 同 correct 端正的

▶It is not decent for one to laugh at a funeral, so please keep a straight face.
在葬禮時發笑是失禮的，因此請保持嚴肅。

de·ci·sive [dɪˈsaɪsɪv] 🔊 *Track 5587*

形 有決斷力的

▶She's not a very decisive person.
她這個人相當優柔寡斷。

> **文法字詞解析**
> 相反地，「沒有決斷力的」、「優柔寡斷的」則可以用 indecisive 這個字來形容。

de·cline [dɪˈklaɪn] 🔊 *Track 5588*

名 衰敗 動 下降、衰敗、婉拒

▶名 Grandpa is on the decline and may die soon.
爺爺的健康每況愈下，可能不久於人世。

▶動 His interest in oil pointing declined with time.
他對油畫的興趣隨時間流逝而降低。

ded·i·cate [ˈdɛdəˌket] 🔊 *Track 5589*

動 供奉、奉獻 同 devote 奉獻

▶He dedicated his first book to his teacher.
他把自己的第一本書獻給了自己的老師。

Level 1
Level 2
Level 3
Level 4
Level 5
Level 6

精進自我、聽說讀寫通
突破瓶頸7000單字

ded·i·ca·tion [ˌdɛdəˋkeʃən] ◀€ Track 5590

名 奉獻、供奉

▶His dedication to social welfare impressed the local people.
他對社會福利的投入感動了當地人。

deem [dim] ◀€ Track 5591

動 認為、視為　同 consider 認為

▶Not everyone deems it his / her duty to help others.
不是每個人都認為幫助他人是自己的責任。

萬用延伸句型
deem it sb.'s duty to...
認為……是自己的責任

de·fect [dɪˋfɛkt] ◀€ Track 5592

名 缺陷、缺點　動 脫逃、脫離

▶名 This product has several defects. 這個產品有許多缺陷。
▶動 The young scientist defected to another country.
這名年輕的科學家叛逃到另一國家去了。

de·fi·cien·cy [dɪˋfɪʃənsɪ] ◀€ Track 5593

名 匱乏、不足　同 shortage 短缺

▶It is obvious that there are many deficiencies in the system.
顯然這一制度存在諸多缺陷。

de·grade [dɪˋgred] ◀€ Track 5594

動 降級、降等

▶You are not supposed to degrade yourself by telling such a
lie. 你不應該說那樣的謊話來降低自己的人格。

de·lib·er·ate [dɪˋlɪbəret]/[dɪˋlɪbərɪt] ◀€ Track 5595

動 仔細考慮　形 慎重的

▶動 We still need to deliberate how the plan should be carried
out. 我們仍需慎重考慮該如何去做那件事。
▶形 He slammed the door in a deliberate manner.
他故意摔上了門。

萬用延伸句型
a deliberate lie 刻意的謊言
例 如：We can all tell that what he said
was a deliberate lie.
我們都看得出他所說的是個刻意的謊言。

de·lin·quent [dɪˋlɪŋkwənt] ◀€ Track 5596

名 違法者　形 拖欠的、違法的

▶名 She has been a delinquent in paying her taxes.
她因為逃稅而犯法。
▶形 Several years have passed since it happened and still we
had not found the delinquent party. 這件事情已經過去好幾
年了，但我們還是沒找到違法的當事人。

de·nounce [dɪˋnaʊns] ◀€ Track 5597

動 公然抨擊

▶She denounced her sister for being unfaithful to her husband.
她抨擊她妹妹對丈夫不忠。

den·si·ty [ˋdɛnsətɪ] ◀€ Track 5598

名 稠密、濃密

▶I don't like the density of population in the city.
我不喜歡城市這麼高的人口密度。

den·tal [`dɛntl̩]
🔊 *Track 5599*

形 牙齒的

▶Do you mind telling me what causes dental cavities（蛀牙）？
麻煩你告訴我蛀牙是由什麼引起的？

文法字詞解析
除了 dentist 外，牙醫也有個說法叫
dental surgeon。

de·pict [dɪ`pɪkt]
🔊 *Track 5600*

動 描述、敘述

▶The writer depicted her mother as a witch.
作者將她的母親描寫得像巫婆一樣。

de·prive [dɪ`praɪv]
🔊 *Track 5601*

動 剝奪、使……喪失

▶It is clear that the government cannot deprive its people of their basic rights.
顯然政府不能剝奪人民的基本權利。

de·rive [də`raɪv]
🔊 *Track 5602*

動 引出、源自

▶Not all people know that many English words are derived from Latin.
不是所有人都知道許多英語單字其實是源於拉丁文。

dep·u·ty [`dɛpjətɪ]
🔊 *Track 5603*

名 代表、代理人　同 agent 代理人

▶Would you like to be my deputy while I am away, Mike?
麥克，你願意在我不在的時候當我的代理人嗎？

de·scend [dɪ`sɛnd]
🔊 *Track 5604*

動 下降、突襲　同 drop 下降

▶The trail descended steeply into the valley.
小路急速往下，通往山谷。

de·scen·dant [dɪ`sɛndənt]
🔊 *Track 5605*

名 子孫、後裔

▶Suppose you were a descendant of a loyal family. What would you do for the people?
假如你是一位皇族後裔，你會為人民做些什麼呢？

萬用延伸句型
Suppose you were... 假如你是……

de·scent [dɪ`sɛnt]
🔊 *Track 5606*

名 下降

▶The descent of the plane was smooth and without trouble.
飛機下降的過程順利且毫無問題。

des·ig·nate [`dɛzɪɡˌnet]
🔊 *Track 5607*

動 指出　形 選派的

▶動 They designated Boston as the unloading（卸貨）port.
他們選擇波士頓為卸貨港。

▶形 Why don't we talk about this matter with the ambassador designate?
為何不跟大使指定人選探討一下這件事呢？

Level
1

Level
2

Level
3

Level
4

Level
5

Level
6

突破瓶頸7000單字

精進自我、聽說讀寫通

des·tined [ˋdɛstɪnd]　◀ Track 5608

形 命運註定的

▶They are destined never to see each other again.
他們命中註定再也不能相見了。

---

de·tach [dɪˋtætʃ]　◀ Track 5609

動 派遣、分開　同 separate 分開

▶The hook can be detached from the wall easily.
這個掛勾可以很容易從牆上移除。

---

de·tain [dɪˋten]　◀ Track 5610

動 阻止、妨礙

▶The bad weather has detained us for several hours.
這惡劣的天氣耽擱了我們好幾個小時。

---

de·ter [dɪˋtɝ]　◀ Track 5611

動 使停止做

▶The bad weather deterred us from going out.
壞天氣使得我們不想出門。

---

de·te·ri·o·rate [dɪˋtɪrɪəˌret]　◀ Track 5612

動 惡化、降低

▶Once the food is in contact with air, it will deteriorate rapidly.
一旦這種食物接觸到空氣，它就會迅速變壞。

---

de·val·ue [diˋvælju]　◀ Track 5613

動 降低價值

▶The country has decided to devalue the dollar to mitigate（緩和）the economic recession.
該國對美元實行貶值來減緩經濟衰退。

---

di·a·be·tes [ˌdaɪəˋbitiz]　◀ Track 5614

名 糖尿病

▶Diabetes is a chronic disease.
糖尿病是一種慢性病。

---

di·ag·nose [ˋdaɪəgnoz]　◀ Track 5615

動 診斷

▶It is rather difficult for the doctor to diagnose the rare disease.
醫生很難診斷出這種罕見的疾病。

---

di·ag·no·sis [ˌdaɪəgˋnosɪs]　◀ Track 5616

名 診斷（複數）

▶Not until the next day did I know the doctor's diagnosis of my disease.
直到第二天我才獲知醫生對我的病的診斷情況。

文法字詞解析

要說一個人的態度很「抽離」，可以用相關的形容詞 detached 來描述。

萬用延伸句型

be diagnosed with sth. 被診斷出罹患（某疾病）
例如：He was diagnosed with diabetes the day he turned fifty.
他在五十歲那天被診斷出罹患糖尿病。

di·a·gram [ˈdaɪəˌɡræm]   🔊 *Track 5617*

名 圖表、圖樣 動 圖解 同 design 圖樣

▶名 Will you help me alter the diagram today, Susan?
蘇珊，你今天能幫我修改一下圖表嗎？

▶動 Will you diagram the floor plan so that we can understand what you said better?
你能把樓面的平面圖畫出來嗎？這樣我們對於你說的話就會更明白些了。

di·am·e·ter [daɪˈæmətə]   🔊 *Track 5618*

名 直徑

▶The kids measure the diameter of the basketball hoop.
小孩量了籃框的直徑。

dic·tate [ˈdɪktet]   🔊 *Track 5619*

動 口授、聽寫

▶I don't think they are now in a position to dictate their own demands.
我不認為他們現在有提出自己的要求。

文法字詞解析
現在許多的手機也有好用的 dictate 功能，對著它說話，它就會把你所說的轉換成文字了。當然實際效果視不同手機而定。

dic·ta·tion [dɪkˈteʃən]   🔊 *Track 5620*

名 口述、口授

▶He asked the secretary to take down his dictation at once.
他叫秘書立刻將他口述的寫下來。

dic·ta·tor [ˈdɪkˌtetə]   🔊 *Track 5621*

名 獨裁者、發號施令者

▶It won't be long before the people revolt against this dictator.
不久人民就會起來反抗這個獨裁者的。

dif·fer·en·ti·ate [dɪfəˈrɛnʃɪet]   🔊 *Track 5622*

動 辨別、區分

▶I can't differentiate these two pens. They look exactly the same. 我分辨不了這兩枝筆，它們長得完全一樣啊。

di·lem·ma [dəˈlɛmə]   🔊 *Track 5623*

名 左右為難、窘境

▶She faced a dilemma over whether she should give up the job offer.
她面對要不要放棄這個工作機會的兩難問題。

di·men·sion [dəˈmɛnʃən]   🔊 *Track 5624*

名 尺寸、方面 同 size 尺寸

▶We're facing a problem with alarmingly enourmous dimensions.
我們面對的這個問題大得驚人。

文法字詞解析
我們常說的 2D、3D 的 D 即是 dimension 的縮寫。

di·min·ish [dəˈmɪnɪʃ]   🔊 *Track 5625*

動 縮小、減少

▶If I were you, I would try to diminish the cost of production.
如果我是你的話，我會盡力減少生產成本。

Level 1
Level 2
Level 3
Level 4
Level 5
Level 6

突破瓶頸7000單字 精進自我、聽說讀寫通

di·plo·ma·cy [dɪˈplomǝsɪ] Track 5626
名 外交、外交手腕 同 politics 手腕
▶Her diplomacy had brought peace between the two countries.
她的外交手腕促成兩國間的和平。

dip·lo·ma·tic [ˌdɪpləˈmætɪk] Track 5627
形 外交的、外交官的
▶The two countries have broken off diplomatic relations again.
兩國再次終止了外交關係。

di·rec·to·ry [dəˈrɛktərɪ] Track 5628
名 姓名地址錄
▶Will you tell me what number I shall dial for directory enquiry?
你能告訴我查號台的電話號碼是多少嗎？

dis·a·bil·i·ty [ˌdɪsəˈbɪlətɪ] Track 5629
名 無能、無力
▶He never lets his disability bring him down.
他從來不讓自己行動不便的事影響自己。

dis·a·ble [dɪsˈebl̩] Track 5630
動 使無能力、使無作用
▶That teacher was disabled in the car accident.
那位老師在那次車禍中成了殘廢。

dis·ap·prove [ˌdɪsəˈpruv] Track 5631
動 反對、不贊成 同 oppose 反對
▶His mother disapproved of his new girlfriend.
他媽媽不喜歡他的新女友。

dis·as·trous [dɪzˈæstrəs] Track 5632
形 災害的、悲慘的 同 tragic 悲慘的
▶If you don't work harder the results could be disastrous.
如果你不更努力一點，結果會很悲慘。

dis·charge [dɪsˈtʃɑrdʒ] Track 5633
名 排出、卸下 動 卸下
▶名 Can you tell me how long the discharge of the cargo will take? 你能告訴我需要多久才能卸完貨嗎？
▶動 She had been discharged from hospital.
她已經出院了。

dis·ci·pli·nar·y [ˈdɪsəplɪnˌɛrɪ] Track 5634
形 訓練上的、訓育的
▶In cases of this kind, it is wrong for you to take disciplinary measures. 在這種情況下，給予紀律處分是不正確的。

dis·close [dɪsˈkloz] Track 5635
動 暴露、露出
▶I hope they would disclose the truth to the press one day.
我真希望有天他們能向新聞界透露真相。

文法字詞解析
「disable」這個單字在這個數位時代也非常重要喔！使用手機等電子產品時，有時會開啟各種有的沒的內建功能，你根本不想要用它們，這時就可以選擇 disable 來把它們關掉。舉例來說，如果你一不小心設了鬧鐘，就可以選擇 disable alarm 讓鬧鐘不要響。

dis·clo·sure [dɪs'kloʒɚ]
◀ Track 5636

名 暴露、揭發
▶The disclosure that he had been in jail made him lose his job.
公開他曾坐牢一事，令他丟了工作。

dis·com·fort [dɪs'kʌmfɚt]
◀ Track 5637

名 不安、不自在 動 使不安、使不自在
▶名 She felt little discomfort after the surgery.
手術後，她沒有什麼不舒服的地方。
▶動 She is so melancholy that she is often discomforted over trifles.
她是如此地憂鬱，以致她總是會為一些瑣事而苦惱。

dis·creet [dɪ'skrit]
◀ Track 5638

形 謹慎的、慎重的
▶It isn't discreet of you to ring him up at the office when he is busy.
他正在忙的時候，你打電話到他辦公室，真是太魯莽了。

萬用延伸句型
It isn't discreet of you to... 你（做某事）不謹慎

dis·crim·i·na·tion
[dɪ,skrɪmə'neʃən]
◀ Track 5639

名 辨別；歧視
▶What do you think of racial discrimination in America?
你是如何看待美國種族歧視的現象呢？

dis·grace [dɪs'gres]
◀ Track 5640

名 不名譽 動 羞辱 同 shame 羞恥
▶名 Don't you think such an act is a disgrace to your family?
你不覺得這種行為會為你全家帶來恥辱嗎？
▶動 The man has disgraced the family name.
那個男人讓他們全家丟臉了。

dis·grace·ful [dɪs'gresfəl]
◀ Track 5641

形 可恥的、不名譽的
▶She was despised for the disgraceful conduct.
她因為不光彩的行為而被輕視。

dis·man·tle [dɪs'mæntl]
◀ Track 5642

動 拆開、分解、扯下
▶Will you help me dismantle the faulty（有毛病的）machine, Bob?
鮑勃，你能幫我把這台有毛病的機器拆開嗎？

dis·may [dɪs'me]
◀ Track 5643

名 恐慌、沮喪 動 狼狽、恐慌
▶名 The little boy looked at me in dismay.
那個小男孩驚慌地望著我。
▶動 The man is dismayed to hear that the plane he is supposed to take has already taken off.
那個男人聽到他要搭的飛機已經起飛了，顯得非常困擾。

萬用延伸句型
to sb.'s dismay 讓（某人）不悅地……
例如：To his dismay, his cats had peed all over the floor.
讓他不悅的是，他的貓尿得滿地都是。

Level 1
Level 2
Level 3
Level 4
Level 5
Level 6

突破瓶頸7000單字
精進自我、聽說讀寫通

dis·patch [dɪ`spætʃ] 🔊 *Track 5644*

名 急速、快速處理 動 派遣、發送 同 send 發送

▶名 The commander's hasty dispatch of the messangers won them the battle.
指揮官迅速地派出了信差，讓他們在這次戰役中獲勝了。

▶動 Can't you dispatch the goods by sea instead of by air?
你不能用海運代替空運嗎？

dis·pens·a·ble [dɪ`spɛnsəbḷ] 🔊 *Track 5645*

形 非必要的

▶The laborers were regarded as dispensable after the machinery was introduced.
引進機器之後，勞工被認為是可以淘汰掉的。

文法字詞解析

相反地，非常必要、絕對要帶著的東西則可以用 indispensable 來描述。

dis·perse [dɪ`spɝs] 🔊 *Track 5646*

動 使散開、驅散

▶A large crowd of protesters（抗議者）has gathered in the square. I am afraid the police will come to disperse them soon. 眾多抗議者已經聚集在廣場上。恐怕警察很快就會來驅散他們了。

dis·place [dɪs`ples] 🔊 *Track 5647*

動 移置、移走

▶The war has displaced thousands of people.
這場戰爭使得成千上萬的人離鄉背井。

dis·please [dɪs`pliz] 🔊 *Track 5648*

動 得罪、使不快

▶I am afraid that your reply will displease your boss.
恐怕你的回答會令你的老闆不快。

dis·pos·a·ble [dɪ`spozəbḷ] 🔊 *Track 5649*

形 可任意使用的、免洗的

▶Gina wears daily disposable contact lenses.
吉娜戴著日拋式隱形眼鏡。

dis·pos·al [dɪ`spozḷ] 🔊 *Track 5650*

名 分佈、配置

▶You'd better discuss with you wife the disposal of the furniture in advance.
你最好事先和你的妻子討論一下如何佈置這些傢俱。

萬用延伸句型

at sb.'s disposal 隨時可幫助（某人）、隨時可為（某人）使用
例　如：If you need anything, the hotel staff will be at your disposal at all times.
如果需要什麼東西，這家旅館的工作人員隨時樂意幫助你。

dis·re·gard [ˌdɪsrɪ`gɑrd] 🔊 *Track 5651*

名 蔑視、忽視 動 不理、蔑視

▶名 He did it in disregard of my advice.
他不顧我的勸告做了這件事。

▶動 It will be very dangerous for you to disregard your father's advice.
你漠視你父親的忠告，這樣是很危險的。

dis·si·dent [ˋdɪsədənt] ◀ᴇ *Track 5652*

名 異議者 形 有異議的

▶名 The political dissidents were suppressed in various occasions.
政治異議者在許多方面受到打壓。

▶動 I've never talked to the dissident Russian novelist.
我從來沒和那位持不同意見的俄國小說家說過話。

dis·solve [dɪˋzɑlv] ◀ᴇ *Track 5653*

動 使溶解

▶The tablet dissolved in the warm water.
藥片在溫水中溶解了。

dis·suade [dɪˋswed] ◀ᴇ *Track 5654*

動 勸阻、勸止 同 discourage 勸阻

▶My teacher dissuaded me from accepting the difficult job.
老師勸我不要接受這份艱難的工作。

dis·tort [dɪsˋtɔrt] ◀ᴇ *Track 5655*

動 曲解、扭曲

▶His face was distorted with rage when he heard about their betrayal. 他聽到他們背叛的事情時，怒得臉都扭曲了。

dis·tract [dɪˋstrækt] ◀ᴇ *Track 5656*

動 分散

▶It is obvious that the noise outside distracts her from her work. 顯然外面的噪音使她無法專心工作。

dis·trac·tion [dɪˋstrækʃən] ◀ᴇ *Track 5657*

名 分心、精神渙散、心煩不安

▶There are too many distractions here for one to work properly.
這裡讓人分心的事太多，使人無法好好工作。

dis·trust [dɪsˋtrʌst] ◀ᴇ *Track 5658*

名 不信任、不信 動 不信

▶名 He looked at the man with distrust.
他用懷疑的眼光打量著那個男人。

▶動 He distrusts even his own father.
他就連自己的爸爸都不相信。

dis·tur·bance [dɪˋstɝbəns] ◀ᴇ *Track 5659*

名 擾亂、騷亂

▶Residents could not bear the disturbance of the motorbikes.
居民無法忍受摩托車的噪音打擾。

di·verse [dəˋvɝs] ◀ᴇ *Track 5660*

形 互異的、不同的 同 different 不同的

▶It is clear that the opinions of the two factions are widely diverse. 顯然這兩個派系的意見大相逕庭。

萬用延伸句型
dissolve into laughter 大笑起來
例 如：The audience dissolved into laughter at the talk show host's joke.
聽到那個脫口秀主持人的笑話，觀眾們立刻大笑起來。

文法字詞解析
disturbance 的動詞為 disturb。

Level 1
Level 2
Level 3
Level 4
Level 5
Level 6

突破瓶頸7000單字 精進自我、聽說讀寫通

di·ver·si·fy [daɪˋvɝsəˌfaɪ]
🔊 Track 5661

動 使……多樣化

▶You are supposed to diversify your investments, not to have all your eggs in one basket.
你應該多方面投資,而不該孤注一擲。

di·ver·sion [dəˋvɝʒən]
🔊 Track 5662

名 脫離、轉向、轉換

▶The board has agreed to the diversion of money to other projects.
董事會同意將資金分到其他計畫使用。

di·ver·si·ty [dəˋvɝsətɪ]
🔊 Track 5663

名 差異處、不同點、多樣性

▶Don't you think that it is important to develop a great diversity of interests?
你不覺得培養多方興趣很重要嗎?

文法字詞解析
描述某處(如國家、公司、學校等)充滿了各種人種、背景的人,也可以用 diversity 來形容。

di·vert [dəˋvɝt]
🔊 Track 5664

動 使轉向

▶I'm using iPad games to divert the kids' attention.
我在用iPad遊戲來轉移孩子們的注意力。

doc·trine [ˋdɑktrɪn]
🔊 Track 5665

名 教義

▶It is obvious that his doctrine contains nothing novel.
顯然他的學說並未包含新穎的思想。

doc·u·men·ta·ry
[ˌdɑkjəˋmɛntərɪ]
🔊 Track 5666

名 紀錄 形 文件的

▶名 Would you like to watch the documentary on the Civil War with me? 你願意和我一起去看那部關於內戰的紀錄片嗎?

▶形 Would you like to show us the documentary evidence at the court? 你願意在法庭上向我們出示書面證據嗎?

dome [dom]
🔊 Track 5667

名 拱形圓屋頂、穹窿 動 覆以圓頂、使成圓頂、拱形屋頂上的

▶名 We appreciated the domes over Byzantine churches.
我們欣賞拜占庭教堂的圓頂藝術。

▶動 The underlying (潛在的) magma (岩漿) domes the surface. 地下岩漿使地面呈圓頂形。

文法字詞解析
許多大型體育館、表演場地等都呈現拱形,這些場館也可以稱作 dome。

do·nate [ˋdonet]
🔊 Track 5668

動 贈與、捐贈 同 contribute 捐獻

▶He donated a large sum of money to this stranger.
他捐了一大筆錢給這名陌生人。

do·na·tion [ˋdoneʃən]
🔊 Track 5669

名 捐贈物、捐款

▶He made a huge donation to the orphanage.
他捐贈了一大筆錢給孤兒院。

do·nor [ˋdonɚ]
◀≣ Track 5670

名 寄贈者、捐贈人

▶It is hard for the doctors to find a blood donor for him at once because of his blood type.
由於他血型的緣故，醫生們很難立刻替他找到一個捐血的人。

doom [dum]
◀≣ Track 5671

名 命運 動 注定

▶名 They can do nothing but await their doom.
他們只能坐以待斃了。

▶動 We were doomed for repeating the same mistakes!
我們重複同樣的錯誤，死定了！

dos·age [ˋdosɪdʒ]
◀≣ Track 5672

名 藥量、劑量

▶A large dosage of this can cause death.
大劑量的這種藥物能致命。

dras·tic [ˋdræstɪk]
◀≣ Track 5673

形 激烈的、猛烈的 同 rough 劇烈的

▶I am afraid that it will require a drastic revision of the plan.
恐怕這個計畫需要進行大幅度地修改。

draw·back [ˋdrɔ͵bæk]
◀≣ Track 5674

名 缺點、弊端

▶Every one of these plans has its drawbacks.
這些計畫每個皆有不足之處。

drear·y [ˋdrɪərɪ]
◀≣ Track 5675

形 陰鬱的、淒涼的

▶The old lady's life was very dreary.
那個老太太的生活非常陰鬱。

driz·zle [ˋdrɪzl̩]
◀≣ Track 5676

名 細雨、毛毛雨 動 下毛毛雨 同 rain 雨

▶名 Why are you walking outside in the drizzle? You'll catch a cold.
你為什麼在細雨中在外面散步？你會感冒的。

▶動 The chef drizzled the shredded cheese on the dough.
主廚將起司絲撒在麵團上。

drought [draʊt]
◀≣ Track 5677

名 乾旱、久旱

▶How long do you think the drought will last this year?
你覺得今年的乾旱會持續多久呢？

du·al [ˋdjuəl]
◀≣ Track 5678

形 成雙的、雙重的 同 double 成雙的

▶I am afraid that US dollar revaluation（升值）has dual effects.
恐怕美元升值有雙重效應。

萬用延伸句型

take drastic measures 使出激烈的手段
例 如：If the cockroaches don't stop invading the kitchen, we have to take drastic measures.
如果蟑螂還是一直入侵廚房，我們就得使出激烈的手段了。

Level 1

Level 2

Level 3

Level 4

Level 5

Level 6

精進自我、聽說讀寫通

突破瓶頸7000單字

du·bi·ous [`djubɪəs]
🔊 Track 5679

形 曖昧的、含糊的

▶ What he said yesterday was dubious. 他昨天說的話很含糊。

dy·na·mite [`daɪnəˌmaɪt]
🔊 Track 5680

名 炸藥 動 爆破、炸破 同 explosive 炸藥

▶ 名 The villain hid a stick of dynamite in his backpack.
壞人在被包裡藏了一個炸藥。

▶ 動 A part of the mountain was dynamited.
山有一部份炸毀了。

[Ee]

ebb [ɛb]
🔊 Track 5681

名 退潮 動 衰落

▶ 名 I'm afraid that the scandal brought his credibility to the lowest ebb. 恐怕那件醜聞使他的信譽跌到最低點。

▶ 動 Our hope of winning began to ebb in the forth round.
比賽進入第四回合時，我們獲勝的希望就變得渺茫了。

ec·cen·tric [ɪk`sɛntrɪk]
🔊 Track 5682

名 古怪的人 形 異常的

▶ 名 The old lady is a bit of an eccentric. Can you communicate with her? 這位老太太是個有點古怪的人。你能跟她溝通嗎？

▶ 形 I wonder how to explain his eccentric behaviors.
我想知道該如何解釋他這種古怪的行為。

e·col·o·gy [ɪ`kɑlədʒɪ]
🔊 Track 5683

名 生態學

▶ I wish I could study ecology in college.
要是我能在大學裡能修生態學就好了。

ec·sta·sy [`ɛkstəsɪ]
🔊 Track 5684

名 狂喜、入迷 同 joy 歡樂

▶ He listened to the song in ecstasy. 他聽這首歌聽得入迷。

ed·i·ble [`ɛdəbl]
🔊 Track 5685

形 食用的

▶ The pancake is burnt; it's not edible.
這煎餅燒焦了；不能吃了。

ed·i·to·ri·al [ɛdə`torɪəl]
🔊 Track 5686

名 社論 形 編輯的

▶ 名 Would you like to tell me which you like better, the news or the editorial?
你能不能告訴我新聞和社論你比較喜歡看哪一個？

▶ 形 Would you like to expand the editorial staff?
你想不想擴大編輯部呢？

文法字詞解析

如果一個東西是「曖昧的、含糊的」，想當然你也不會太信任它，因此 dubious 還包含了「不可信的、可疑的」的意思。

萬用延伸句型

Would you like to...? 你想要……嗎？

e·lec·tron [ɪ'lɛktrɑn]

🔊 *Track 5687*

名 電子
▶It is said that the electron microscope can show the object as a million times its original size.
據說那架電子顯微鏡可以把物體放大一百萬倍。

el·i·gi·ble ['ɛlɪdʒəbl]

🔊 *Track 5688*

形 適當的
▶Only half of the villagers were eligible to vote.
只有一半的村民有資格投票。

e·lite [e'lit]

🔊 *Track 5689*

名 精英 形 傑出的
▶名 She has become a famous political elite.
她成了政界名人。
▶形 They trained their son from childhood so that he could become an elite pianist. 他們在兒子小的時候就訓練他，要他成為一名傑出的鋼琴家。

el·o·quence ['ɛləkwəns]

🔊 *Track 5690*

名 雄辯
▶Her eloquence is so impressive that we can't help but be convinced.
她的口才如此之好，我們都不由得被說服了。

el·o·quent ['ɛləkwənt]

🔊 *Track 5691*

形 辯才無礙的
▶She is not only eloquent but also elegant.
她不但口才好，而且還很高雅。

em·bark [ɪm'bɑrk]

🔊 *Track 5692*

動 從事、搭乘
▶I heard that he was about to embark on a new business venture.
我聽說他就要開始一項新的事業。

em·i·grant ['ɛməgrənt]

🔊 *Track 5693*

名 移民者、移出者 形 移民的、移居他國的
同 immigrant 外來移民
▶名 The emigrates left their homeland to flee from wars.
往境外的移民為了逃離戰爭而離開家鄉。
▶形 It is said that they are emigrant laborers.
據說他們是移民勞工。

em·i·grate ['ɛmə‚gret]

🔊 *Track 5694*

動 移居
▶His family emigrated from Italy to America after the war broke out in Italy.
義大利發生戰爭後，他們家從義大利移居到了美國。

萬用延伸句型
can't help but（＋原形動詞）不由得……

Level 1
Level 2
Level 3
Level 4
Level 5
Level 6

突破瓶頸7000單字
精進自我、聽說讀寫通——

em·i·gra·tion [ˌɛməˈɡreʃən] 🔊 *Track 5695*

名 移民

▶There's a wide diversity of opinions on the issue of the emigration.
關於移民這個議題存在著相當多元的意見。

em·phat·ic [ɪmˈfætɪk] 🔊 *Track 5696*

形 強調的

▶He rejected my request with an emphatic shake of his head.
他很堅決地搖頭，拒絕了我的要求。

en·act [ɪnˈækt] 🔊 *Track 5697*

動 制定

▶It is time to stop arguing and enact a measure into law.
現在該是停止爭辯把它制定為法律的時候了。

萬用延伸句型
It is time to... 是時候該……

en·act·ment [ɪnˈæktmənt] 🔊 *Track 5698*

名 法規

▶Scholars are pleading for the enactment of the bill.
學者請求執行這項法案。

en·clo·sure [ɪnˈkloʒɚ] 🔊 *Track 5699*

名 圍住

▶There are several enclosures in the envelope. You'd better keep them well.
信封內裝有幾份附件。你最好把它們收好。

en·cy·clo·pe·di·a/ en·cy·clo·pae·di·a [ɪnˌsaɪkləˈpidɪə] 🔊 *Track 5700*

名 百科全書

▶Would you please put the encyclopedia back on the shelf?
請把百科全書放回架上好嗎？

en·dur·ance [ɪnˈdjurəns] 🔊 *Track 5701*

名 耐力

▶She showed great endurance during the climb.
她在攀登過程中表現出極大的耐力。

文法字詞解析
climb 較常當作動詞，有「攀爬」的意思，在此則是當名詞，表示「攀爬的整個過程」。

en·hance [ɪnˈhæns] 🔊 *Track 5702*

動 提高、增強 同 improve 提高、增進

▶The encyclopedia enhanced my knowledge in various fields.
百科全書增進我在各領域的知識。

en·hance·ment [ɪnˈhænsmənt] 🔊 *Track 5703*

名 增進

▶Nicotine（尼古丁）is what they call a flavor enhancement.
尼古丁是他們所稱的提味劑。

en·light·en [ɪnˈlaɪtn̩]　🔊 *Track 5704*

動 啓發

▶I don't understand this paragraph that you've written. Would you enlighten me?

我讀不懂你寫的這段話。你能為我講解嗎？

en·light·en·ment [ɪnˈlaɪtn̩mənt]　🔊 *Track 5705*

名 文明

▶Would you give me some enlightenment on what is going on?

你可以好心給我點提示，現在發生什麼事嗎？

en·rich [ɪnˈrɪtʃ]　🔊 *Track 5706*

動 使富有

▶Putting spices in food can enrich the flavor.

把調味料放進食物中可以使味道更豐富。

en·rich·ment [ɪnˈrɪtʃmənt]　🔊 *Track 5707*

名 豐富

▶Good books are an enrichment of life.

好書能使人生變得充實。

ep·i·dem·ic [ˌɛpɪˈdɛmɪk]　🔊 *Track 5708*

名 傳染病　形 流行的

▶名 It is reported that a flu epidemic has raged through the school for weeks.

據報導流感已經在那所學校裡蔓延了幾個星期了。

▶形 Buying in installments has become epidemic in recent years.

近幾年來十分流行用分期付款的方式來購物。

ep·i·sode [ˈɛpəˌsod]　🔊 *Track 5709*

名 插曲

▶The latest episode of the Korean drama will be broadcasted tonight.

這個韓劇最新一集今晚會播出。

文法字詞解析
episode 也有「一齣、一集連續劇」的意思，我們常在一系列的影片的標題中看到「ep. XX」，其中「ep.」就是 episode 的縮寫。

EQ/ e·mo·tion·al quo·tient/ e·mo·tion·al in·tel·li·gence

[i kju]/[ɪˈmoʃən̩l ˈkwoʃənt]/[ɪˈmoʃən̩l ɪnˈtɛlədʒəns]　🔊 *Track 5710*

名 情緒智商

▶A good EQ helps you predict how other people feel.

高EQ能幫助你預測他人的感覺。

e·qua·tion [ɪˈkweʃən]　🔊 *Track 5711*

名 相等

▶The equation of wealth and happiness can be dangerous. Don't you think so?

把財富與幸福等同起來是很危險的。你不這樣認為嗎？

Level 1

Level 2

Level 3

Level 4

Level 5

Level 6

突破瓶頸7000單字　精進自我、聽說讀寫通

e·quiv·a·lent [ɪˋkwɪvələnt]
🔊 *Track 5712*

名 相等物 形 相當的

▶ 名 I'm afraid that some English words have no Chinese equivalents.
恐怕有些英文字在中文裡沒有相對應的詞。

▶ 形 An imperial gallon is equivalent to 4546 cubic centimeters.
英制一加侖等於4546立方公分。

e·rode [ɪˋrod]
🔊 *Track 5713*

動 蝕

▶ The sea have eroded the cliff over the years.
海水經年累月的沖刷已經侵蝕了峭壁。

e·rup·tion [ɪˋrʌpʃən]
🔊 *Track 5714*

名 爆發

▶ There have been several volcanic eruptions this year.
今年已經出現了好幾次火山爆發。

es·ca·late [ˋɛskəˌlet]
🔊 *Track 5715*

動 擴大、延長

▶ The tension between the countries soon escalated into war.
這些國家間的緊張很快地發展成了戰爭。

文法字詞解析
我們常搭的電扶梯（escalator）功能就是將你舉到比較高的地方、將你去到的範圍「延伸」，因此才會和有「擴大、延長」意味的 escalate 語出同源。

es·sence [ˋɛsn̩s]
🔊 *Track 5716*

名 本質

▶ The essence of this article is pretty interesting, but the article itself isn't written well.
這篇文章的精華內容很有趣，但文章本身卻寫得不太好。

e·ter·ni·ty [ɪˋtɝnətɪ]
🔊 *Track 5717*

名 永遠、永恆

▶ Nothing can last for an eternity.
沒有什麼是永恆的。

e·thi·cal [ˋɛθɪkl̩]
🔊 *Track 5718*

形 道德的

▶ It is obviously it's not ethical to do that.
顯然這麼做並不符合道德。

eth·nic [ˋɛθnɪk]
🔊 *Track 5719*

名 少數民族的成員 形 人種的、民族的

▶ 名 It is an enthusiastic and friendly ethnic.
那是一個充滿熱情和友好的民族。

▶ 形 China is a united country of many ethnic groups.
中國是一個統一的多民族國家。

e·vac·u·ate [ɪˋvækjuˌet]
🔊 *Track 5720*

動 撤離 同 leave 離開

▶ A typhoon is coming; you had better get everything ready to evacuate. 颱風快要來了，你最好做好一切撤離的準備。

ev·o·lu·tion [ˌɛvəˈluʃən]
◀≣ *Track 5721*

名 發展

▶Darwin's theory of evolution was once met with challenges.
達爾文的進化論曾經被挑戰過。

e·volve [ɪˈvɑlv]
◀≣ *Track 5722*

動 演化 同 develop 發展

▶The simple plan has evolved into a complicated scheme.
這個簡單的計畫已經發展成了一項複雜的規劃。

ex·cerpt [ˈɛksɝpt]/[ɪkˈsɝpt]
◀≣ *Track 5723*

名 摘錄 動 引用

▶名 I like to read the excerpt of a book before buying it.
我喜歡先讀書中摘錄的部分，然後才把那本書買下來。

▶動 She excerpted a passage from the magazine.
她從那本雜誌上摘錄了一段。

ex·ces·sive [ɪkˈsɛsɪv]
◀≣ *Track 5724*

形 過度的

▶The quality of urban living has been damaged by excessive noise.
城市生活的品質已被過度的噪音所破壞。

ex·clu·sive [ɪkˈsklusɪv]
◀≣ *Track 5725*

形 唯一的、排外的、獨家的

▶This is an exclusive interview on the famous singer.
這是這名知名歌星的獨家專訪。

文法字詞解析
exclusive 的反義詞是 inclusive。

ex·e·cu·tion [ˌɛksɪˈkjuʃən]
◀≣ *Track 5726*

名 實行

▶The execution of the project will take a long time.
執行這項計畫會花很多時間。

ex·ert [ɪgˈzɝt]
◀≣ *Track 5727*

動 運用、盡力 同 employ 利用

▶He exerted all his influence to make them accept his plan.
他用盡一切影響力使他們接受他的計畫。

萬用延伸句型
exert oneself 使勁全力做某事
例　如：You just recovered from the illness. Don't exert yourself too much today.
你病才剛好，今天不要做得太賣力了。

ex·ot·ic [ɛgˈzɑtɪk]
◀≣ *Track 5728*

形 外來的

▶The film retains much of the book's exotic flavor.
這部電影保存了原著的許多異國情調。

ex·pe·di·tion [ˌɛkspɪˈdɪʃən]
◀≣ *Track 5729*

名 探險、遠征

▶It is said that they are planning to organize a scientific expedition.
據說他們正計畫組織一次科學探險。

Level 1

Level 2

Level 3

Level 4

Level 5

Level 6

突破瓶頸7000單字　精進自我、聽說讀寫通

ex·pel [ɪk`spɛl]
◀≲ *Track 5730*

動 逐出

▶Political dissidents were expelled from the country.
政治異議者被逐出這個國家。

ex·per·tise [ˌɛkspɚ`tiz]
◀≲ *Track 5731*

名 專門知識

▶His business expertise is of help to all of us.
他的商業知識對我們大家都有助益。

ex·pi·ra·tion [ˌɛkspə`reʃən]
◀≲ *Track 5732*

名 終結

▶Would you please tell me the expiration date of your card?
請您告訴我您信用卡的期限好嗎？

ex·pire [ɪk`spaɪr]
◀≲ *Track 5733*

動 終止

▶I'm afraid your lease will expire on July 30th of this year.
不好意思，您的租約今年7月30日到期。

ex·plic·it [ɪk`splɪsɪt]
◀≲ *Track 5734*

形 明確的

▶It seems that he's avoiding giving us an explicit answer.
他似乎在避免給我們明確的回答。

文法字詞解析
「限制級、兒童不宜」的內容常稱為 explicit content，因此當看到 CD、電影光碟上有標示「explicit content」時，就知道別拿給小孩看了。

ex·ploit [ɪk`splɔɪt]
◀≲ *Track 5735*

名 功績 動 利用

▶名 His daring exploits are the talk of the company.
他大膽的行為是整個公司閒聊的話題。

▶動 The company was accused of exploiting its employees.
公司被指控剝削員工。

ex·plo·ra·tion [ˌɛksplə`reʃən]
◀≲ *Track 5736*

名 探測

▶It is obvious that the Elizabethan age was a time of exploration and discovery.
顯然英國女王伊莉莎白一世時代是探索和發現的時代。

ex·qui·site [`ɛkskwɪzɪt]
◀≲ *Track 5737*

形 精巧的

▶It is said that the hostess had exquisite taste in clothes.
據說那位女主人對衣著十分講究。

萬用延伸句型
have + adj. taste in sth. 對某事物有……的品味

ex·tract [`ɛkstrækt]/[ɪk`strækt]
◀≲ *Track 5738*

名 摘錄 動 引出、源出

▶名 Let's just read several extracts from the poem, shall we?
我們就讀從詩中摘錄的幾段吧，如何？

▶動 He tried to extract this pole from the mud.
他試著把竿子從泥中拔出來。

extra·cur·ric·u·lar　◀≲ *Track 5739*
[͵ɛkstrəkəˋrɪkjələ]
形 課外的
▶You should take part in extracurricular activities. That will help you make friends. 你應該要參加課外活動，這會幫助你交朋友。

eye·sight [ˋaɪ͵saɪt]　◀≲ *Track 5740*
名 視力
▶The enlisted soldiers had their eyesight tested.
被徵召的士兵已做了視力檢查。

文法字詞解析
視力不好可以說 poor eyesight 或 bad eyesight。

[Ff]

fa·bu·lous [ˋfæbjələs]　◀≲ *Track 5741*
形 傳說、神話中的　同 marvelous 不可思議的
▶The little boy's performance was fabulous.
那個小男孩的表演真是精彩。

fa·cil·i·tate [fəˋsɪlə͵tet]　◀≲ *Track 5742*
動 利於、使容易　同 assist 促進
▶Zip codes are used to facilitate mail service.
郵遞區號利於郵遞服務。

fac·tion [ˋfækʃən]　◀≲ *Track 5743*
名 黨派、當中之派系
▶The party has split into petty factions.
該黨分裂成了若干小派系。

fac·ul·ty [ˋfækḷtɪ]　◀≲ *Track 5744*
名 全體教員、系所
▶He applied for a job in the linguistic faculty.
他申請教語言學的職缺。

fa·mil·i·ar·i·ty [fə͵mɪlɪˋærətɪ]　◀≲ *Track 5745*
名 熟悉、親密、精通
▶His familiarity with the local languages is a great asset to us.
他對當地語言的精通對我們有很大的幫助。

fam·ine [ˋfæmɪn]　◀≲ *Track 5746*
名 饑荒、饑饉、缺乏　同 starvation 飢餓
▶Both the war and famine have made the country poverty-stricken（被貧苦所困惱的）.
戰爭和饑荒使這個國家變得貧困不堪。

文法字詞解析
stricken 是 strike（打擊）的過去分詞，此處即指這個國家「受到了貧苦的打擊」。

fas·ci·na·tion [͵fæsəˋneʃən]　◀≲ *Track 5747*
名 迷惑、魅力、魅惑
▶She has a fascination for all things astrology-related.
她對和占星相關的事情都充滿了興趣。

Level 1
Level 2
Level 3
Level 4
Level 5
Level 6

突破瓶頸7000單字
精進自我、聽說讀寫通

fea·si·ble [ˈfizəbl̩] ◀€ *Track 5748*

形 可實行的、可能的

▶It's quite clear that this is a feasible scheme.
很顯然這是一個切實可行的計畫。

fed·er·a·tion [ˌfɛdəˈreʃən] ◀€ *Track 5749*

名 聯合、同盟、聯邦政府

▶The Russian federation denied any attempt to manipulate the U.S. election.
俄國聯邦政府否認企圖影響美國大選。

feed·back [ˈfidˌbæk] ◀€ *Track 5750*

名 回饋 同 response 反應

▶The more feedback we get from the customers the better.
從顧客那兒得到的回饋越多越好。

萬用延伸句型
The more... the better 越多……越好

fer·til·i·ty [fɚˈtɪlətɪ] ◀€ *Track 5751*

名 肥沃、多產、繁殖力

▶She is taking medicine to increase her fertility, isn't she?
她為了增強生育能力而服藥，不是嗎？

fi·del·i·ty [fɪˈdɛlətɪ] ◀€ *Track 5752*

名 忠實、精準度、誠實 同 faith 誠實

▶Fidelity towards your spouse is important.
對於配偶忠誠是很重要的。

文法字詞解析
相反地，若對配偶「不忠」則可加上表示「不、無」的字首「in-」稱為 infidelity。

fire·proof [ˈfaɪrˌpruf] ◀€ *Track 5753*

形 耐火的、防火的

▶It is impossible for us to make the house completely fireproof.
我們無法使房屋完全防火。

flare [flɛr] ◀€ *Track 5754*

名 閃光、燃燒 動 搖曳、閃亮、發怒

▶名 We all saw a match flare in the darkness at that time.
我們大家當時都看到有火柴的光亮在黑暗中閃了一下。

▶動 Her temper flares up very easily.
她總是動不動就發脾氣。

fleet [flit] ◀€ *Track 5755*

名 船隊、艦隊、車隊

▶A fleet of 20 sailing ship occurred on the sea.
據說這家公司擁有一個車隊來供其員工使用。

flick·er [ˈflɪkɚ] ◀€ *Track 5756*

名 閃耀 動 飄揚、震動

▶名 I saw a flicker of interest in her eyes.
我看到她的眼中閃過了一絲感興趣的神情。

▶動 A faint hope still flickers in his heart.
一絲微弱的希望仍在他的心中閃動著。

fling [flɪŋ] ◀€ *Track 5757*

名 投、猛衝 動 投擲、踢、跳躍
▶名 He tossed the coat onto the hook with a careless fling.
他隨手一丟就把外套掛上了勾子。
▶動 The children were flinging mud everywhere.
孩子們在到處丟泥巴。

flu·id [ˈfluɪd] ◀€ *Track 5758*

名 流體 形 流質的 反 solid 固體
▶名 Plenty of fluid can be a good treatment for a fever.
補充大量流質對發燒有好的療效。
▶形 We don't have enough fluid capital to work on this project.
我們沒有足夠的流動資金來做這個計畫。

flut·ter [ˈflʌtɚ] ◀€ *Track 5759*

名 心亂、不安 動 拍翅、飄動
▶名 Did you hear a flutter of wings among the trees?
你有聽到樹林裡響起一陣飛鳥的拍翅聲？
▶動 There is a bird fluttering its wings in the cage.
有隻鳥在籠中拍著翅膀。

fore·see [forˈsi] ◀€ *Track 5760*

動 預知、看穿
▶We can't foresee what will happen in the future.
我們無法預知將來會發生什麼事。

> **文法字詞解析**
> foresee 的動詞變化：
> foresee, foresaw, foreseen

for·mi·da·ble [ˈfɔrmɪdəbl] ◀€ *Track 5761*

形 可怕的、難應付的
▶My grandma is a really formidable old lady.
我奶奶是個很難應付的老太太。

for·mu·late [ˈfɔrmjəˌlet] ◀€ *Track 5762*

動 明確地陳述、用公式表示 同 define 使明確
▶He is able to formulate his thoughts clearly.
他能夠清楚地表達自己的想法。

for·sake [fɚˈsek] ◀€ *Track 5763*

動 拋棄、放棄、捨棄 同 abandon 拋棄
▶He decided to forsake business for education.
他決定棄商轉投入教職。

> **文法字詞解析**
> 若要説「被放棄的、被拋棄的」，則可以用 forsaken 這個形容詞。

forth·com·ing [ˌforθˈkʌmɪŋ] ◀€ *Track 5764*

形 不久就要來的、下一次的
▶Will you give me a list of their forthcoming books now?
你能現在就給我一張他們即將出版的書籍的目錄嗎？

for·ti·fy [ˈfɔrtəˌfaɪ] ◀€ *Track 5765*

動 加固、強化工事
▶It's high time that this country fortified the coastal（沿海的）areas. 這個國家真該好好加強一下沿海地區的防禦了。

fos·ter [ˋfɔstɚ]

◀ㅌ *Track 5766*

動 養育、收養 **形** 收養的

▶**動** He fostered an interest in nature in his children.
他在他的孩子們心中培養起對大自然的興趣。

▶**形** She took care of his foster child after he died.
他死後，就由她來照顧他的養子。

frac·ture [ˋfræktʃɚ]

◀ㅌ *Track 5767*

名 破碎、骨折 **動** 挫傷、破碎 **同** crack 破裂

▶**名** The fracture of a crashed plane was found in the village.
墜毀飛機的碎片在小鎮中被發現。

▶**動** It was the fall that fractured his skull.
正是這一跤把他的顱骨給摔裂了。

frag·ile [ˋfrædʒəl]

◀ㅌ *Track 5768*

形 脆的、易碎的

▶These glasses look very fragile, so please handle them
carefully. 這些玻璃杯看起來很容易碎，因此請小心地拿著。

frag·ment [ˋfrægmənt]

◀ㅌ *Track 5769*

名 破片、碎片

▶I saw lots of fragments of the vase on the floor in the morning.
早上的時候我看見地板上有很多花瓶碎片。

frail [frel]

◀ㅌ *Track 5770*

形 脆弱的、虛弱的 **同** weak 虛弱的

▶My grandpa is too frail to get out of the bed himself now.
我爺爺現在太虛弱了，都無法自己下床。

fraud [frɔd]

◀ㅌ *Track 5771*

名 欺騙、詐欺

▶It's no less than a fraud; don't you think so?
這簡直是一場騙局，難道你不這樣覺得嗎？

freak [frik]

◀ㅌ *Track 5772*

名 怪胎、異想天開 **形** 怪異的

▶**名** Gary was considered a freak for his buzzer outfit.
蓋瑞因為奇異的裝扮而被視為怪胎。

▶**形** What we got in the experiment was a freak result.
我們在那次實驗中得到的是異常的結果。

fret [frɛt]

◀ㅌ *Track 5773*

動 煩躁、焦慮

▶I wish she wouldn't fret over something so unimportant.
我真希望她不要為一些小事而焦慮不安。

fric·tion [ˋfrɪkʃən]

◀ㅌ *Track 5774*

名 摩擦、衝突 **同** conflict 衝突

▶It is quite clear that family frictions will have a harmful effect
on a child. 很顯然家庭中的爭吵會對孩子產生很不好的影響。

萬用延伸句型

It is no less than... 簡直是……、根本是……

文法字詞解析

friction 不但可以用來指人與人之間的衝突、「摩擦」，也可以拿來指真正的「摩擦力」，在學物理時就常會用到這個單字。

[Gg]

gal·ax·y [ˈɡæləksɪ]　　🔊 *Track 5775*

名 星雲、星系
▶How many stars can you name in the galaxy?
整個星系中,你能說出幾個星星的名字?

gen·er·a·lize [ˈdʒɛnərəˌlaɪz]　　🔊 *Track 5776*

動 一般化
▶This principle can be generalized to various situations.
這項原則可以廣泛應用各種情境中。

gen·er·ate [ˈdʒɛnəˌret]　　🔊 *Track 5777*

動 產生、引起
▶Investments can generate higher income.
投資能帶來更高的收入。

gen·er·a·tor [ˈdʒɛnəˌretə]　　🔊 *Track 5778*

名 創始者、產生者
▶Not all of us know how to use a generator.
我們當中不是所有人都知道如何使用發電機。

ge·net·ic [dʒəˈnɛtɪk]　　🔊 *Track 5779*

形 遺傳學的
▶He chose genetic engineering to be his lifelong career.
他選擇了遺傳工程學作為終生的事業。

ge·net·ics [dʒəˈnɛtɪks]　　🔊 *Track 5780*

名 遺傳學
▶It is said that professors at the University of Edinburgh think that genetics play an important role in modern science.
據說愛丁堡大學的教授認為遺傳學在當代科學扮演重要角色。

glam·our [ˈɡlæmə]　　🔊 *Track 5781*

名 魅力
▶The glamour of the noble lady fascinated us.
我們被高貴女士的光彩吸引。

glass·ware [ˈɡlæsˌwɛr]　　🔊 *Track 5782*

名 玻璃製品、玻璃器皿
▶He felt he had to buy this lovely piece of glassware for his wife.
他覺得他該買下這個可愛的玻璃器皿給他太太。

glis·ten [ˈɡlɪsn̩]　　🔊 *Track 5783*

動 閃耀、閃爍
▶Her eyes glistened with tears as she ran out the door.
她跑出門外時,眼中的淚水在閃爍。

文法字詞解析
generator 不但能用來表示「產生電」的發電機,也能拿來表示產生許多其他東西的「產生者」。例如不知道自己生了孩子該取什麼名字時,就可以使用「baby name generator」(寶寶姓名產生器)來隨機為自己的寶寶「產生」一個名字。

Level 1
Level 2
Level 3
Level 4
Level 5
Level 6

突破瓶頸7000單字　精進自我、聽說讀寫通

gloom·y [ˋglumɪ]
Track 5784

形 幽暗的、暗淡的
▶He looked a little bit gloomy and troubled.
顯然他看起來有些憂愁不安。

GMO/ge·net·i·cal·ly mod·i·fied or·gan·ism
Track 5785

[dʒəˋnɛtɪklɪ ˋmɑdəˌfaɪd ˋɔrgəˌnɪzm]
名 基因改造食品
▶You really shouldn't eat GMO food, because it may have a bad impact on your health.
你最好別吃基因改造食品，因為它們有可能對健康有不良影響。

graph [græf]
Track 5786

名 曲線圖、圖表 動 圖解
▶名 Can you draw this into a graph for me?
你可以幫我把這畫成一個圖表嗎？
▶動 The professor graphed the theoretical model for his students.
教授用圖表向學生解釋這個理論模式。

graph·ic [ˋgræfɪk]
Track 5787

形 圖解的、生動的
▶The article gave a graphic description of the earthquake.
那篇文章生動地描述了地震的情況。

grill [grɪl]
Track 5788

名 烤架 動 烤 同 broil 烤
▶名 You had better clean the grill first before starting a fire.
在生火前你最好先把烤架清理乾淨。
▶動 You had better confess, or the police will keep grilling you.
你最好坦白承認，否則警察會一直對你嚴加盤問的。

gro·cer [ˋgrosɚ]
Track 5789

名 雜貨商
▶There is a grocer's at the corner of the street.
在街道轉彎處有一間食品雜貨店。

grope [grop]
Track 5790

名 摸索 動 摸索找尋
▶名 She groped for her wrist watch on the bedside table.
她在床頭桌上摸索著找她的手錶。
▶動 I'm afraid that we have to grope our way through the dark hall. 恐怕我們得摸黑走過這個走廊了。

guer·ril·la [gəˋrɪlə]
Track 5791

名 非正規的軍隊、游擊隊 同 soldier 軍人
▶The guerrilla force was in trouble and had to go into hiding.
游擊隊陷入了困境，因此只能躲了起來。

文法字詞解析
graphic novel 是一種圖像式的小說，即「視覺文學」。

[Hh]

hab·it·at [ˈhæbəˌtæt]　🔊 *Track 5792*
名 棲息地
▶The habitat of raccoons has been invaded by human.
浣熊的棲息地遭到人類入侵。

hack [hæk]　🔊 *Track 5793*
動 割、劈、砍
▶You'd better hack off the branches of that big tree.
你最好把那棵大樹的枝椏砍掉。

hack·er [ˈhækɚ]　🔊 *Track 5794*
名 駭客
▶The hacker can obtain your passwords easily.
這名駭客很容易就能取得你的密碼。

hail [hel]　🔊 *Track 5795*
名 歡呼、冰雹 動 歡呼 同 cheer 歡呼
▶名 It has hailed the whole afternoon.
　整個下午不停地下冰雹。
▶動 People hailed these famous singers as soon as they got out of the car.
　這些有名的歌手一下車，人們就開始歡呼。

ha·rass [ˈhærəs]　🔊 *Track 5796*
動 不斷地困擾 同 bother 打擾
▶It is said that the villagers have been harassed by thieves recently.
據說最近村民們常常受到小偷的騷擾。

ha·rass·ment [ˈhærəsmənt]　🔊 *Track 5797*
名 煩惱、侵擾
▶Does what just happened count as sexual harassment?
剛剛發生的事情算是性騷擾嗎？

haz·ard [ˈhæzɚd]　🔊 *Track 5798*
名 偶然、危險 動 冒險、受傷害
▶名 The hazard left the hikers trapped in the cave.
　暴風雪讓登山者被困在山洞裡。
▶動 Let me hazard a guess: you're a Virgo（處女座）, right?
　我來冒險猜一猜：你是處女座對不對？

hem·i·sphere [ˈhɛməsˌfɪr]　🔊 *Track 5799*
名 半球體、半球
▶I don't think this kind of animal is to be found only in the Northern Hemisphere.
我不相信只能在北半球找到這種動物。

萬用延伸句型
hail a taxi 叫計程車
例　如：Please hail a taxi for him. He's too drunk to walk.
請幫他叫計程車，他醉得走不動了。

文法字詞解析
在這個字的前面加上表示「生物的」的字首「bio-」就成了 biohazard，即「生化危機」的意思。

Level 1
Level 2
Level 3
Level 4
Level 5
Level 6

精進自我、聽說讀寫通
突破瓶頸7000單字

here·af·ter [ˌhɪrˋæftə] ◀≶ Track 5800

名 來世 副 隨後、從此以後

▶名 We have done our best. I guess now we can do nothing but speculate about the hereafter.
我們已經盡力了。我想我們現在只能預測未來了。

▶副 There's nothing you can do except work harder hereafter.
我猜想你今後只能用功點學習了。

her·i·tage [ˋhɛrətɪdʒ] ◀≶ Track 5801

名 遺產

▶This old theater is recognized as a cultural heritage.
舊戲院被認為是文化遺產。

he·ro·in [ˋhɛroɪn] ◀≶ Track 5802

名 海洛因

▶It is illegal for one to sell heroin.
販賣海洛因是違法的。

high·light [ˋhaɪˌlaɪt] ◀≶ Track 5803

名 精彩場面 動 使顯著、強調 同 emphasize 強調

▶名 Will you please let me show you the highlights of the event?
請允許我為您展示這個活動最精彩的部分好嗎？

▶動 I will highlight the need for educational reform at the meeting. 我會在會議上強調一下教育改革的必要性。

hon·or·ar·y [ˋɑnəˌrɛrɪ] ◀≶ Track 5804

形 榮譽的

▶The college is supposed to give the remarkable scholar an honorary degree.
學院應該授予這位出色的學者榮譽學位。

hor·mone [ˋhɔrmon] ◀≶ Track 5805

名 荷爾蒙

▶Imbalance of hormones may cause mental disturbances.
賀爾蒙失調會造成心情不穩定。

hos·pi·ta·ble [ˋhɑspɪtəbl̩] ◀≶ Track 5806

形 善於待客的 同 generous 慷慨的

▶The islanders are said to be hospitable.
住在島上的居民們很好客。

hos·pi·tal·i·ty [ˌhɑspɪˋtæləti] ◀≶ Track 5807

名 款待、好客

▶The family shows great hospitality to everyone they meet.
這家人對遇到的所有人都熱情款待。

hos·pi·tal·ize [ˋhɑspɪtəˌlaɪz] ◀≶ Track 5808

動 使入院治療

▶He is seriously ill and is hospitalized for three weeks.
他的病情嚴重，必須住院三個星期。

萬用延伸句型
It is illegal for sb. to...
對某人來說（做某事）是犯法的

萬用延伸句型
be said to be... 被說成是……

hos·til·i·ty [hɑsˋtɪlətɪ]
🔊 *Track 5809*

名 敵意
▶Don't show hostility to the newcomer so soon.
不要這麼快對新來的移民產生敵意。

hu·man·i·tar·i·an
[hjuˌmænəˋtɛrɪən]
🔊 *Track 5810*

名 人道主義者、博愛 形 人道主義的
▶名 The famous humanitarian passed away yesterday.
那位有名的人道主義者昨天過世了。
▶形 Not until he met this man did he begin to devote himself to
humanitarian causes.
直到他遇到了這個人，他才開始投身於人道主義事業。

hu·mil·i·ate [hjuˋmɪlɪˌet]
🔊 *Track 5811*

動 侮辱、羞辱
▶He felt so humiliated that he left the room immediately.
他感到很屈辱，於是立刻離開了房間。

hunch [hʌntʃ]
🔊 *Track 5812*

名 瘤 動 突出、弓起背部 同 bump 凸塊
▶名 I have a hunch that he is lying.
我的直覺告訴我他在撒謊。
▶動 She hunched up her shoulders as she sat at the desk
thinking about this problem.
她聳著肩坐在書桌前想這個問題。

萬用延伸句型
sb. has a hunch that... 某人有種預感……

hur·dle [ˋhɝdl̩]
🔊 *Track 5813*

名 障礙物、跨欄 動 跳過障礙
▶名 You should try to overcome the hurdles ahead, no matter
how difficult they are.
你應該努力克服前面的困難，不管它們有多艱難。
▶動 He hurdled the fence and jumped into her yard.
他翻過籬笆跳進她家的院子。

hy·giene [ˋhaɪdʒin]
🔊 *Track 5814*

名 衛生學、衛生
▶No matter where we go, we must pay attention to our
personal hygiene. 無論我們人在哪裡，都必須注意個人衛生。

hy·poc·ri·sy [hɪˋpɑkrəsɪ]
🔊 *Track 5815*

名 偽善、虛偽
▶Her courtesy was dismissed as hypocrisy by her rival.
她的對手認為她的禮貌只是偽裝。

hyp·o·crite [ˋhɪpəˌkrɪt]
🔊 *Track 5816*

名 偽君子
▶The old lady is a hypocrite. She talks about the importance of
kindness, yet is mean herself.
這位老太太是個偽君子。她總是在說待人善良很重要，然而她
待人卻很不好。

文法字詞解析
與 hypocrite 相關的形容詞（言行不一
的）是 hypocritical。

Level 1
Level 2
Level 3
Level 4
Level 5
Level 6

精進自我、聽說讀寫通
突破瓶頸7000單字

hys·ter·i·cal [hɪsˋtɛrɪkl̩]　◀≷ *Track 5817*

形 歇斯底里的　同 upset 心煩的

▶The victims' family members all became quite hysterical after the accident.
事故發生後受害者的家人都變得非常歇斯底里。

[Ii]

il·lu·mi·nate [ɪˋlumə͵net]　◀≷ *Track 5818*

動 照明、點亮、啓發

▶The philosopher illuminates his deciphers with witty words.
哲學家用機智的話語啓發他的弟子。

il·lu·sion [ɪˋljuʒən]　◀≷ *Track 5819*

名 錯覺、幻覺

▶He is under the illusion that his position is secure.
他誤以為他的地位很穩固。

im·mune [ɪˋmjun]　◀≷ *Track 5820*

形 免除的

▶It seemed that he was immune to criticism.
他似乎不受批評的影響。

im·per·a·tive [ɪmˋpɛrətɪv]　◀≷ *Track 5821*

名 命令　形 絕對必要的

▶名 I'm afraid that job creation has become an imperative for the government.
恐怕創造就業機會已經成為一件政府必須做的事了。

▶形 It is imperative for me to find a food source.
對我來說最首要的問題是取得食物來源。

im·ple·ment [ˋɪmpləmənt]　◀≷ *Track 5822*

名 工具　動 施行

▶名 I don't think the store supplies agricultural implements.
我不覺得這商店會供應農具。

▶動 New techniques will be implemented in this experiment.
新的技術會使用在這個實驗中。

im·pli·ca·tion [͵ɪmplɪˋkeʃən]　◀≷ *Track 5823*

名 暗示、含意

▶I didn't gather the implications of her remark.
我沒聽出她那番話的含義。

im·plic·it [ɪmˋplɪsɪt]　◀≷ *Track 5824*

形 含蓄的、不表明的　反 explicit 明確的

▶It seems that there was implicit consent in her silence.
她的沉默似乎是表示了默許。

im·pos·ing [ɪmˈpozɪŋ]
🔊 Track 5825

形 顯眼的

▶What an imposing building it is! Don't you think so?
多麼氣勢宏偉的建築物啊！你不覺得嗎？

im·pris·on [ɪmˈprɪzn̩]
🔊 Track 5826

動 禁閉

▶The convict was imprisoned for eight years.
罪犯被關了八年。

im·pris·on·ment
🔊 Track 5827
[ɪmˈprɪzn̩mənt]

名 坐牢

▶He was sentenced to life imprisonment.
他被判終身監禁。

in·cen·tive [ɪnˈsɛntɪv]
🔊 Track 5828

名 刺激、誘因 形 刺激的

▶名 Money is still a major incentive to most people.
對於大多數人來說，金錢仍是主要的誘因。

▶形 I'm afraid that my incentive payments this month will end up in smoke. 恐怕我這個月的獎金要泡湯了。

in·ci·den·tal [ˌɪnsəˈdɛntl̩]
🔊 Track 5829

形 臨時發生的

▶It is said that this couple fell in love with each other through an incidental meeting on a bus.
據說這對情侶是因公車上的邂逅而愛上彼此的。

in·cline [ɪnˈklaɪn]
🔊 Track 5830

動 傾向 名 傾斜面

▶動 I'm inclined to believe that he's innocent. How about you?
我傾向於相信他是無辜的。你呢？

▶名 The road has a very steep incline.
這條路有個非常陡的斜坡。

in·clu·sive [ɪnˈklusɪv]
🔊 Track 5831

形 包含在內的 反 exclusive 排外的

▶The inclusive nature of the club made it expand rapidly.
這個社團兼容並蓄的特質使它快速擴大。

in·dig·na·tion [ˌɪndɪgˈneʃən]
🔊 Track 5832

名 憤怒 同 anger 憤怒

▶He could scarcely keep in his indignation when he realized that he was lied to.
他發現自己受騙時，憤怒得難以自持。

in·ev·i·ta·ble [ɪnˈɛvətəbl̩]
🔊 Track 5833

形 不可避免的

▶It is inevitable for us to lose because our rival is so strong.
既然我們遇到了如此強大的對手，失敗是不可避免的。

萬用延伸句型

imprison sb. in sth. 將（某人）關在（某個地方）裡
例如：They imprisoned the hostages in a small room.
他們把人質關在小房間裡。

文法字詞解析
indignation 相對的形容詞是 indignant。

Level **1**

Level **2**

Level **3**

Level **4**

Level **5**

Level **6**

精進自我、聽說讀寫通
突破瓶頸7000單字

in·fec·tious [ɪnˈfɛkʃəs]　◀⦚ *Track 5834*

形 能傳染的
▶ Flu is an infectious disease characterized by fever, aches and pains and exhaustion（疲勞）.
　流感是一種傳染病，其特徵是發熱、全身疼痛和疲乏無力。

in·fer [ɪnˈfɚ]　◀⦚ *Track 5835*

動 推斷、推理　同 suppose 假定、猜想
▶ You can infer the writer's stance on this issue from his wording.
　你可以由作者的用詞遣字知道他對這件事情的看法。

in·fer·ence [ˈɪnfərəns]　◀⦚ *Track 5836*

名 推理
▶ Suppose he is guilty, then by inference so is she.
　假設他有罪的話，那麼可以推斷出她也有罪。

in·gen·ious [ɪnˈdʒinjəs]　◀⦚ *Track 5837*

形 巧妙的
▶ This book shows that he is an ingenious author.
　這本書表明了他是一個有創造力的作家。

in·ge·nu·i·ty [ˌɪndʒəˈnuətɪ]　◀⦚ *Track 5838*

名 發明才能
▶ She had the ingenuity to succeed when everyone else had failed. 她發揮了聰明才智而成功辦到了別人辦不到的事。

in·hab·it [ɪnˈhæbɪt]　◀⦚ *Track 5839*

動 居住
▶ It is said that there are only a few people inhabiting the island.
　據說只有少數人在這個島上居住。

文法字詞解析
inhabit 是及物動詞，所以後面直接接受詞，而不需要再加介係詞。

in·hab·it·ant [ɪnˈhæbətənt]　◀⦚ *Track 5840*

名 居民
▶ Most of the inhabitants in the town are rather nice.
　這個城裡的居民都是不錯的人。

in·her·ent [ɪnˈhɪrənt]　◀⦚ *Track 5841*

形 天生的　同 internal 固有的、本質的
▶ The inherent characteristics could not be changed easily.
　與生俱來的特質不是那麼容易改變的。

i·ni·ti·a·tive [ɪˈnɪʃətɪv]　◀⦚ *Track 5842*

名 倡導　形 率先的
▶ 名 It is hoped that the government's initiative will bring the strike to an end.
　希望政府採取的主動措施可以結束罷工。
▶ 形 The new company is hoping to bring about its initiative prosperity.
　那間新公司希望能實現初步繁榮。

in·ject [ɪnˋdʒɛkt]
🔊 Track 5843

動 注入

▶They injected him with a new drug.
他們給他注射了新的藥。

in·jec·tion [ɪnˋdʒɛkʃən]
🔊 Track 5844

名 注射

▶The doctor gave her an injection to alleviate her pain.
醫生替她注射以減輕她的疼痛。

in·jus·tice [ɪnˋdʒʌstɪs]
🔊 Track 5845

名 不公平 **反** justice 公平

▶Injustice on the political refuge caught attention from the international community.
對這位政治流亡者的不公平待遇引起國際社會的關注。

in·no·va·tion [ˌɪnəˋveʃən]
🔊 Track 5846

名 革新 **同** formation 公平

▶It seems that the innovation of air travel during this century has made the world smaller.
本世紀的空中旅行革新似乎使世界變小了。

in·no·va·tive [ˋɪnoˏvetɪv]
🔊 Track 5847

形 創新的

▶She always comes up with innovative ideas.
她總是能想出一些創新的點子。

in·quir·y [ɪnˋkwaɪrɪ]
🔊 Track 5848

名 詢問、調查 **同** research 調查

▶Would you mind filling out this inquiry form?
請您填一下這張問卷好嗎？

in·sight [ˋɪnˏsaɪt]
🔊 Track 5849

名 洞察

▶The book is filled with remarkable insights.
這本書很有真知灼見。

in·sis·tence [ɪnˋsɪstəns]
🔊 Track 5850

名 堅持

▶His insistence on trivial things annoyed the client.
他對瑣事的堅持惹惱了他的客戶。

in·stal·la·tion [ˌɪnstəˋleʃən]
🔊 Track 5851

名 就任、裝置

▶The installation of the telephone in our room will take a few hours. 我們房間的電話要花幾個小時才能安裝好。

in·stall·ment [ɪnˋstɔlmənt]
🔊 Track 5852

名 分期付款

▶I had to pay for the car in installements.
我得用分期付款的方式付這台車的錢。

萬用延伸句型

inject sth. into sth./sb. 將（某物）注射入（某物／某人）

例　如：She injected the liquid into the patient.
她將液體注射入病人體內。

Level 1

Level 2

Level 3

Level 4

Level 5

Level 6

突破瓶頸7000單字 精進自我、聽說讀寫通

文法字詞解析

我們在電腦上「安裝」軟體常用到的「安裝」這個動作就稱為「install」。

in·sti·tu·tion [ˌɪnstə'tjuʃən] 🔊 *Track 5853*
名 團體、機構、制度
▶ Marriage is an institution in most societies.
婚姻是大多數社會早已確立的制度。

in·tact [ɪn'tækt] 🔊 *Track 5854*
形 原封不動的
▶ The body of the fox remained intact in the freezing surroundings. 在冰凍的環境裡，狐狸的遺體完整保存下來。

萬用延伸句型
keep sth. intact 保持（某物）完整
例　如：Despite the bad weather, they managed to keep the garden intact.
雖然天氣很差，他們還是能夠讓花園維持完好無損。

in·te·grate [ˈɪntəˌgret] 🔊 *Track 5855*
動 整合
▶ It has been very difficult for central government to integrate all of the local agencies into the national organization. 中央政府將所有的地方機構合併為全國性的機構一直非常困難。

in·te·gra·tion [ˌɪntə'greʃən] 🔊 *Track 5856*
名 統合、完成
▶ The secret of learning lies in the integration of theory and practice. 學習的秘訣在於理論與實踐的統一。

in·teg·ri·ty [ɪn'tɛgrətɪ] 🔊 *Track 5857*
名 正直 同 honesty 正直
▶ A good man will respect a woman of integrity.
好男人都會尊敬那些正直誠實的女性。

in·tel·lect [ˈɪntl̩ˌɛkt] 🔊 *Track 5858*
名 理解力
▶ I'm afraid that you have estimated his intellect too highly.
恐怕你把他的智力評估得太高了。

in·ter·sec·tion [ˌɪntə'sɛkʃən] 🔊 *Track 5859*
名 橫斷、交叉
▶ The traffic signals at the intersection are confusing to me.
十字路口的交通號誌讓我覺得困惑。

in·ter·val [ˈɪntəvl̩] 🔊 *Track 5860*
名 間隔、休息時間 同 break 休息
▶ The interval between the game lasted for 20 minutes.
比賽中間的休息時間共有20分鐘。

in·ter·vene [ˌɪntə'vin] 🔊 *Track 5861*
動 介入
▶ You had better not intervene in the affairs of others.
你最好不要干涉別人的事務。

萬用延伸句型
intervene between sb. and sb. 介入（某人）與（某人）之間
例　如：Mom couldn't help intervening between John and his friend, who wouldn't stop fighting.
媽媽忍不住介入約翰與他朋友之間，試圖阻止他們一直吵架。

in·ter·ven·tion [ˌɪntə'vɛnʃən] 🔊 *Track 5862*
名 介入、調停
▶ It seems that it is necessary to accept a proper degree of state intervention.
似乎接受適當程度的國家干預是必要的。

in·ti·ma·cy [ˈɪntəməsɪ]
Track 5863

名 親密
▶He felt no intimacy with his children.
他對小孩一點都不親近。

in·tim·i·date [ɪnˈtɪməˌdet]
Track 5864

動 恐嚇
▶Not everyone knows how to react when he or she is intimidated. 不是每個人都知道當自己被恐嚇時該如何反應。

in·trude [ɪnˈtrud]
Track 5865

動 侵入、打擾 同 interrupt 打擾、打斷
▶This isn't your room, these people are not your friends, they're not talking about you, so you really shouldn't intrude.
這不是你的房間,這些人不是你的朋友,他們也沒在討論你,所以你真的不應該打擾。

in·trud·er [ɪnˈtrudɚ]
Track 5866

名 侵入者
▶They chased out the intruders with guns.
他們拿槍把入侵者趕出去了。

in·val·u·a·ble [ɪnˈvæljəbl]
Track 5867

形 無價的
▶A dictionary is an invaluable aid in learning a new language.
在學習一種新語言時,字典是非常貴重的工具。

in·ven·to·ry [ˈɪnvənˌtorɪ]
Track 5868

名 物品的清單 動 製作目錄
▶名 We checked our inventory before undertaking the order.
我們接受訂單之前先查看了存貨。
▶動 Could you tell me how often you inventory your store?
您能不能告訴我你多久清點一次你店裡的庫存?

文法字詞解析
在會計學中,inventory 有「存貨」的意思,例如:merchandise inventory (商品存貨)。

in·ves·ti·ga·tor [ɪnˈvɛstəˌgetɚ]
Track 5869

名 調查者、研究者
▶Investigators are searching the wreckage of the plane so that they can find the cause of the tragedy. 調查人員正在飛機殘骸中搜索,以便找出造成這一悲慘事件的原因。

IQ/in·tel·li·gence qu·o·ti·ent [ɪnˈtɛlədʒəns ˈkwoʃənt]
Track 5870

名 智商
▶Even though his IQ is high, he has almost no EQ.
儘管他的智商很高,但他的情緒智商幾乎是零。

文法字詞解析
此處提到的 EQ 則是 Emotional quotient 的意思。

i·ron·ic [aɪˈrɑnɪk]
Track 5871

形 諷刺的、愛挖苦人的
▶The boy who laughed at the cripple(殘障人士)ended up losing one leg himself. Ironic, isn't it? 那個嘲笑殘障人士的男孩自己也失去了一條腿。很諷刺,對吧?

i·ro·ny [ˈaɪrənɪ] ◀€ *Track 5872*
名 諷刺、反諷
▶The greatest irony was that he was actually not lying this time, yet no one believed him anymore.
最諷刺的是：他這次其實沒撒謊，但大家都不相信他了。

ir·ri·ta·ble [ˈɪrətəbl̩] ◀€ *Track 5873*
形 暴躁的、易怒的 同 mad 發狂
▶The old man became irritable after he was awakened from sound sleep.
老人熟睡中被叫醒，變得暴躁易怒。

ir·ri·tate [ˈɪrəˌtet] ◀€ *Track 5874*
動 使生氣
▶You had better not irritate her. She's on a short fuse today.
你最好別惹她。她今天動不動就發火。

ir·ri·ta·tion [ˌɪrəˈteʃən] ◀€ *Track 5875*
名 煩躁
▶He could not hide his irritation at his little sister.
他無法掩飾他的妹妹讓他覺得有多煩。

[Jj]

joy·ous [ˈdʒɔɪəs] ◀€ *Track 5876*
形 歡喜的、高興的 同 cheerful 高興的
▶This is really a joyous moment.
真是歡喜的時刻。

文法字詞解析
joy（名詞，歡樂的意思）加上形容詞字尾「-ous」即變成了 joyous 這個形容詞。

[Kk]

ker·nel [ˈkɚnl̩] ◀€ *Track 5877*
名 穀粒、籽、核心
▶The squirrel ate the pulp and left the kernel.
松鼠吃掉果肉、留下果核。

kid·nap [ˈkɪdnæp] ◀€ *Track 5878*
動 綁架、勒索 同 snatch 搶奪、綁架
▶Supposing the boy is kidnapped, what then?
假如那個男孩被綁架了，那怎麼辦？

文法字詞解析
要表示「綁架犯」的話，只要在 kidnap 後面加上表示「……者」的字尾「-er」，並重複尾音的 p，變成 kidnapper 即可。

[Ll]

la·ment [lə`mɛnt]　🔊 *Track 5879*
名 悲痛　動 哀悼　同 sorrow 悲痛
▶名 Her laments were ignored by most people.
　　大部分的人都忽視了她的哀嘆聲。
▶動 People often lament the passing of the good old days.
　　人們常常會惋惜美好過往的逝去。

la·va [`lɑvə]　🔊 *Track 5880*
名 熔岩
▶The lava sprawled through the area and destroyed the landscape. 岩漿蔓延到這個區域，破壞了景觀。

lay·man [`lemən]　🔊 *Track 5881*
名 普通信徒
▶The terms are difficult for a layman to understand.
　這些術語對外行人來說很難理解。

lay·out [`le͵aʊt]　🔊 *Track 5882*
名 規劃、佈局
▶Can you tell me what the layout of this house is like?
　你能告訴我房子的格局是怎麼樣的嗎？

LCD/liq·uid crys·tal dis·play [͵ɛl`si`di]/[`lɪkwɪd `krɪstl̩ dɪ`sple]　🔊 *Track 5883*
名 液晶顯示器
▶You'd better get a new LCD screen for your laptop.
　你最好為你的手提電腦換一個新的液晶螢幕。

leg·end·ar·y [`lɛdʒənd͵ɛrɪ]　🔊 *Track 5884*
形 傳說的
▶The legendary singer had a charity concert.
　這位傳奇歌手舉辦了慈善演唱會。

leg·is·la·tive [`lɛdʒɪs͵letɪv]　🔊 *Track 5885*
形 立法的
▶It's high time that the country undertook legislative reform.
　國家該開始進行立法改革了。

leg·is·la·tor [`lɛdʒɪs͵letɚ]　🔊 *Track 5886*
名 立法者
▶It is said that five legislators will be elected this time.
　據說這次將選舉出五名立法委員。

leg·is·la·ture [`lɛdʒɪs͵letʃɚ]　🔊 *Track 5887*
名 立法院
▶He is an outstanding member of the legislature.
　他是立法機關中的傑出成員。

文法字詞解析
有一種漂亮的裝飾用「岩漿電燈」稱為 lava lamp。

萬用延伸句型
It is high time that S + V（過去式）
是時候做……
要注意這個句型其實用到了與現在事實相反的假設，因為在說話的當下並還沒做那件事，所以動詞要用過去式。

Level 1
Level 2
Level 3
Level 4
Level 5
Level 6

突破瓶頸7000單字　精進自我、聽說讀寫通

le·git·i·mate
[lɪˋdʒɪtəˏmet]/[lɪˋdʒɪtəmɪt]

🔊 *Track 5888*

動 使合法 形 合法的

▶動 We're working on legitimating homosexual marriage.
我們正努力將同性戀婚姻合法化。

▶形 You have to give me a legitimate reason for being late.
你得給我一個合理的遲到理由。

length·y [ˋlɛŋθɪ]

🔊 *Track 5889*

形 漫長的

▶Her speech was lengthy and boring.
她的演講又冗長又無聊。

li·a·ble [ˋlaɪəbl]

🔊 *Track 5890*

形 可能的 同 probable 可能的

▶People are liable to make mistakes when they're tired.
人們疲勞的時候容易出錯。

lib·er·ate [ˋlɪbəˏret]

🔊 *Track 5891*

動 使自由 同 free 使自由

▶They liberated the gorillas from the zoo.
他們放生了動物園的猩猩。

lib·er·a·tion [ˏlɪbəˋreʃən]

🔊 *Track 5892*

名 解放

▶The people in that area are still struggling for liberation?
那一區的人仍然為解放運動而奮鬥。

like·wise [ˋlaɪkˏwaɪz]

🔊 *Track 5893*

副 同樣地

▶He walked straight through the door, and I did likewise.
他筆直地走進門，我也同樣這麼做。

lim·ou·sine/limo
[ˋlɪməˏzin]/[ˋlɪmo]

🔊 *Track 5894*

名 小客車

▶The wealthy man purchased a bulletproof limousine.
富豪買了一台防彈轎車。

lin·er [ˋlaɪnə]

🔊 *Track 5895*

名 定期輪船（飛機）

▶It is reported that a liner collided with an oil tanker（油輪）last night.
據報導昨晚有一艘客輪與一艘油輪相撞了。

lin·guist [ˋlɪŋgwɪst]

🔊 *Track 5896*

名 語言學家

▶I'm no linguist, so I wouldn't be able to tell you what language this is written in. 我不是語言學家，所以我可沒辦法告訴你這是用什麼語言寫成的。

萬用延伸句型
be liable to + 原 V.：容易（做某事）、很可能（做某事）
例如：Watch out! These vases are liable to break.
小心！這些花瓶很容易破。

li·ter [ˈlitɚ]
🔊 Track 5897
名 公升
▶A liter of gas has less mass than a liter of water.
一公升汽油的質量比一公升水的質量小。

lit·er·a·cy [ˈlɪtərəsɪ]
🔊 Track 5898
名 讀寫能力
▶Computer literacy is considered an essential ability for kids nowadays.
電腦能力被認為是現在小孩的必備能力。

lit·er·al [ˈlɪtərəl]
🔊 Track 5899
形 文字的
▶Do you mind telling me what the literal meaning of the word is? 麻煩你告訴我這個字的原義是什麼好嗎？

lit·er·ate [ˈlɪtərɪt]
🔊 Track 5900
名 有學識的人 形 精通文學的 同 intellectual 知識分子
▶名 The literate read the letter for the illiterate man.
那個識字的人讀了那封信給那名不識字的人聽。
▶形 He's a very literate man and everything he writes is beautiful.
他是個精通文學的男人，寫出來的作品都非常美。

文法字詞解析
在 literate 前面加上含有「不、不是」含意的字首「il-」，就變成了 illiterate（不識字的）的意思。

lon·gev·i·ty [lɑnˈdʒɛvətɪ]
🔊 Track 5901
名 長壽
▶Proper rest and enough sleep contribute to longevity. What do you think about it?
適當的休息和足夠的睡眠有益於長壽。你覺得呢？

lounge [laʊndʒ]
🔊 Track 5902
名 交誼廳 動 閒逛
▶名 The manager is in a conference, so the secretary asked me to wait in the lounge.
經理正在開會，所以秘書叫我在交誼廳等候。
▶動 The old man enjoys lounging around at home.
那個老人喜歡懶洋洋地在家裡坐著。

lu·na·tic [ˈlunəˌtɪk]
🔊 Track 5903
名 瘋子 形 瘋癲的 同 crazy 瘋的
▶名 The convict pretended to be lunatic for lighter penalty.
罪犯假裝發瘋，換取較輕的罰則。
▶形 Isn't his lunatic behavior a menace to our society?
他的瘋狂行為對我們的社會不是構成一種威脅了嗎？

lure [lʊr]
🔊 Track 5904
名 誘餌 動 誘惑 同 attract 吸引
▶名 I don't believe that your brother can resist the lure of money. 我不相信你哥哥抵擋得住金錢的誘惑。
▶動 This high price will probably not lure plenty of buyers (買家).
這個高價格大概不能夠吸引多少買家。

萬用延伸句型
lure sb./sth. in 引誘（某人／某物）
例如：We have the trap prepared so that we can lure the mice in.
我們準備好陷阱要引誘老鼠。

Level 1
Level 2
Level 3
Level 4
Level 5
Level 6
突破瓶頸7000單字 精進自我、聽說讀寫通

lush [lʌʃ]
🔊 *Track 5905*

形 青翠的
▶The pasture（牧場）is filled with lush grass.
這個牧場滿是茂盛的青草。

lyr·ic [ˈlɪrɪk]
🔊 *Track 5906*

名 抒情詩　形 抒情的
▶名 The lyrics was composed based on a poem he wrote for her. 歌詞是根據他為她寫的詩而做出的。
▶形 This is a good example of Wordsworth's lyric poetry.
這首詩是華滋華斯抒情詩的一個好範例。

[Mm]

mag·ni·tude [ˈmæɡnəˌtjud]
🔊 *Track 5907*

名 重大
▶The earthquake that just happened was magnitude 5.
剛剛發生的地震是震度5級。

ma·lar·i·a [məˈlɛrɪə]
🔊 *Track 5908*

名 瘧疾、瘴氣
▶It is said that malaria is an endemic（地方病）in many hot countries.
據說瘧疾是許多熱帶國家特有的疾病。

ma·nip·u·late [məˈnɪpjəˌlet]
🔊 *Track 5909*

動 巧妙操縱
▶He manipulated them to voting for him.
他巧妙操縱他們為他投票。

man·u·script [ˈmænjəˌskrɪpt]
🔊 *Track 5910*

名 手稿、原稿
▶The manuscript of the novel was displayed on the museum.
這個小說的手稿在博物館裡展示。

mar [mɑr]
🔊 *Track 5911*

動 毀損
▶His reputation is marred by several small scandals.
他的名聲被許多小的緋聞給毀了。

mas·sa·cre [ˈmæsəkə]
🔊 *Track 5912*

名 大屠殺　動 屠殺　同 slaughter 屠殺
▶名 Many people witnessed the horrendous（令人驚悚的）massacre.
許多人目擊那次令人不寒而慄的大屠殺。
▶動 The German fascists（法西斯主義者）massacred almost all the Jews in town.
德國法西斯分子幾乎殺光了城裡所有的猶太人。

文法字詞解析
manipulate 除了表示操縱「人心」以外，也能用來表示「操縱、改變」一些其他的東西。舉例來說，我們使用影像編輯功能來將照片修得更漂亮，就可以稱為 photo manipulation。

文法字詞解析
除了用來表示真的大屠殺之外，massacre 在口語中也可以表示在比賽中實在贏太多，對方等於「被屠殺了」一樣。例如籃球比賽以 90 比 50 贏了敵隊，就可以說「We massacred them.」（我們贏他們很多）。

mas·ter·y [ˋmæstərɪ] 🔊 Track 5913

名 優勢、精通、掌握

▶Her mastery of the violin impressed all the spectators.
她對小提琴的精通給觀眾們留下了深刻的印象。

ma·te·ri·al(ism)

[məˋtɪrɪəl]/[məˋtɪrɪəˏlɪzm] 🔊 Track 5914

名 材質、材料、唯物論

▶The hermit abandoned material pleasure for spiritual fulfillment.
隱士放棄物質的享受，追求心靈的滿足。

mat·tress [ˋmætrɪs] 🔊 Track 5915

名 墊子

▶Would you please go and buy a new mattress for my bed with me?
你能陪我去買個新床墊嗎？

mech·a·nism [ˋmɛkəˏnɪzəm] 🔊 Track 5916

名 機械裝置 同 machine 機械

▶An airplane engine is a complex mechanism.
飛機引擎是種複雜的機械裝置。

med·i·ca·tion [ˏmɛdɪˋkeʃən] 🔊 Track 5917

名 藥物治療

▶You had better not share this medication with others.
你最好不要把這種藥分給其他人使用。

me·di·e·val [ˏmɪdɪˋivəl] 🔊 Track 5918

形 中世紀的

▶It is said that this church is a classic example of medieval architecture.
據說這座教堂是中世紀建築風格的典型實例。

med·i·tate [ˋmɛdəˏtet] 🔊 Track 5919

動 沉思

▶Edward meditated over the possibility of studying abroad.
愛德華思考去國外唸書的可能性。

med·i·ta·tion [ˏmɛdəˋteʃən] 🔊 Track 5920

名 熟慮

▶He reached his decision only after much meditation.
他是在經過一番沉思後才做出了決定。

mel·an·chol·y [ˋmɛlənˏkɑlɪ] 🔊 Track 5921

名 悲傷、憂鬱 形 悲傷的 同 miserable 悲慘的

▶名 A deep melancholy runs through her poetry.
她的詩中貫穿著悲傷的情調。

▶形 He is a melancholy man who never smiles.
他是一個鬱鬱寡歡的人，從來都不笑。

Level 1

Level 2

Level 3

Level 4

Level 5

Level 6

突破瓶頸7000單字 精進自我、聽說讀寫通

萬用延伸句型
be on medication 正在服藥期間
例如：I'm not allowed to drive because I'm on medication.
我正在服藥，所以無法開車。

文法字詞解析
「憂鬱症」的英文說法也和這個字相關，可以說成 melancholia（另一個更常見的說法則是 depression）。

mel·low [`mɛlo]
🔊 *Track 5922*

動 成熟 形 成熟的、圓潤的

▶動 Age has mellowed his attitude to some things.
隨著年齡的增加，他對某些事情的看法已日趨成熟。

▶形 Her voice sounded nice and mellow.
她的嗓音聽起來很圓潤好聽。

men·tal·i·ty [mɛn`tælətɪ]
🔊 *Track 5923*

名 智力

▶Positive mentality may contribute to better effect of the treatment.
正面心態可能會對治療有幫助。

mer·chan·dise [`mɝtʃən͵daɪz]
🔊 *Track 5924*

名 商品 動 買賣 同 product 產品

▶名 It is more expensive to mail merchandise than to freight it.
郵寄商品比貨運更昂貴。

▶動 If this product is properly merchandised, it should sell better than before.
這個產品如果促銷得當，應該會銷售得比以前更好。

merge [mɝdʒ]
🔊 *Track 5925*

動 合併 同 blend 混合

▶Why didn't they merge the two firms into a big one?
他們為什麼沒把兩家公司合併成一家大公司呢？

met·a·phor [`mɛtəfə]
🔊 *Track 5926*

名 隱喻

▶In poetry the rose is often a metaphor for love.
玫瑰在詩中常被作為愛的象徵。

met·ro·pol·i·tan [͵mɛtrə`palətn̩]
🔊 *Track 5927*

名 都市人 形 大都市的 同 city 城市的

▶名 The metropolitan's behavior is different from us villagers.
那個都市人的行為方式跟我們鄉下人不一樣。

▶形 She left the small island and became famous in metropolitan France.
她離開了小島後在法國的都市地區中成名。

mi·grate [`maɪgret]
🔊 *Track 5928*

動 遷徙、移居

▶Thousands of people migrated to the south for better living environment.
數千人移民至南方追求更好的環境。

mi·gra·tion [maɪ`greʃən]
🔊 *Track 5929*

名 遷移

▶There was a huge migration of people into Europe because of the war.
因為戰爭，大量的移民湧入歐洲。

萬用延伸句型

merge into the background 融入背景
例如：In parties, I like to merge into the background and just eat.
參加派對的時候，我喜歡融入背景、專心吃東西。

mil·i·tant [ˈmɪlətənt] 🔊 *Track 5930*

名 好戰份子 形 好戰的 同 hostile 懷敵意的
▶名 He is a militant in my opinion.
　　在我看來他是個好戰份子。
▶形 It seems that nothing could foil their militant spirit.
　　似乎沒有什麼能挫傷他們的鬥志。

mill·er [ˈmɪlɚ] 🔊 *Track 5931*

名 磨坊主人
▶This miller is a rich man who never leaves his mill.
　　這個磨坊主人很有錢，從不離開自己的磨坊。

mim·ic [ˈmɪmɪk] 🔊 *Track 5932*

名 模仿者 動 模仿
▶名 One of his brothers is a wonderful mimic.
　　他的一個兄弟很善於模仿。
▶動 Wendy found the way Zoe mimic her disturbing.
　　溫蒂覺得柔伊模仿她的樣子很煩人。

> **文法字詞解析**
> mimic 在變成進行式的形式時，後面不能只加上 -ing，必須多一個 k 變成 mimicking。

min·i·a·ture [ˈmɪnɪətʃɚ] 🔊 *Track 5933*

名 縮圖、縮印 形 小型的
▶名 She is just like her mother in miniature. Don't you think so?
　　她簡直是她母親的縮影。你不覺得嗎？
▶形 The little girl has miniature furniture for her dolls.
　　那個小女孩有供洋娃娃用的迷你型傢俱。

min·i·mize [ˈmɪnəˌmaɪz] 🔊 *Track 5934*

動 減到最小
▶Minimize the window so that I can see your desktop（桌面）.
　　把視窗縮到最小，我才能看到你的桌面。

> **文法字詞解析**
> 相反於 minimize（減到最小），放到最大則是 maximize。

mi·rac·u·lous [məˈrækjələs] 🔊 *Track 5935*

形 奇蹟的
▶The miraculous healing effect of the spring amazed the villagers.
　　這個泉水的神奇療效令當地人驚奇。

mis·chie·vous [ˈmɪstʃɪvəs] 🔊 *Track 5936*

形 淘氣的、有害的
▶What if the mischievous boy keeps behaving like that?
　　如果這個淘氣的男孩繼續這樣淘氣會怎麼樣？

mis·sion·ar·y [ˈmɪʃənˌɛrɪ] 🔊 *Track 5937*

名 傳教士 形 傳教的
▶名 I wish I could go to India as a missionary one day in the future. 要是將來有一天我能以傳教士的身份去印度就好了。
▶形 The whole group understood the value of missionary work.
　　整個團體的人都瞭解傳教工作的價值。

Level 1

Level 2

Level 3

Level 4

Level 5

Level 6

突破瓶頸7000單字　精進自我、聽說讀寫通

mo·bi·lize [`mobə‚laɪz]
Track 5938

動 動員

▶Our country's in great danger; I'm afraid that we must mobilize the army. 我們國家正處於嚴重危險之中，恐怕我們必須把軍人動員起來。

mod·er·ni·za·tion [‚mɑdənə`zeʃən]
Track 5939

名 現代化

▶The modernization of the subway has been a great benefit for the commuters.
地下鐵現代化對通勤族來說好處很多。

mold [mold]
Track 5940

名 鑄模 **動** 鑄造 **同** shape 塑造

▶**名** The two children look like they came out of the same mold.
那兩個孩子看起來像是一個模子刻出來的。

▶**動** The children can mold figures out of clay.
孩子們能用黏土塑造人像。

mo·men·tum [mo`mɛntəm]
Track 5941

名 動量、動力

▶The struggle for independence is gaining momentum every day. 為獨立而鬥爭的氣勢日益增長。

mo·nop·o·ly [mə`nɑplɪ]
Track 5942

名 獨佔、壟斷

▶No one could compete with these steel monopolies.
沒有人能和這些鋼鐵壟斷企業競爭。

mo·not·o·nous [mə`nɑtənəs]
Track 5943

形 單調的

▶The monotonous lifestyle made Fiona desire to change her career path.
一成不變的生活讓費歐娜想要轉換職涯跑道。

mo·not·o·ny [mə`nɑtənɪ]
Track 5944

名 單調

▶These activities help people add color to the monotony of everyday life.
這些活動能為人們平日單調的生活增添色彩。

mo·rale [mə`ræl]
Track 5945

名 士氣

▶Our team needs to boost its morale.
我們的球隊需要恢復士氣。

mo·ral·i·ty [mɔ`rælətɪ]
Track 5946

名 道德、德行 **同** character 高尚品德

▶Mr. Huang is a man of strict morality.
黃先生是一個品行極為端正的人。

文法字詞解析
大家都玩過的大富翁遊戲也叫 Monopoly。畢竟玩大富翁的目標就是「獨占」土地嘛！

mot·to [ˈmɑto]
🔊 Track 5947

名 座右銘 同 proverb 諺語
▶My motto is "Never give up". 我的座右銘是「永不氣餒」。

mourn·ful [ˈmornfəl]
🔊 Track 5948

形 令人悲痛的
▶It is absurd to tell a joke at the mournful occasion.
在哀悼的場合講笑話很不妥。

mouth·piece [ˈmaʊθ‚pis]
🔊 Track 5949

名 樂器吹口、代言人
▶I forgot to clean the mouthpiece of the flute.
我忘記清理長笛的吹口了。

mouth·piece/ spokes·per·son/spokes·man/ spokes·wom·an
🔊 Track 5950

[ˈmaʊθ‚pis]/[ˈspoks‚pɝsn̩]/[ˈspoksmən]/[ˈspokswʊmən]
名 發言人、代言人
▶Tom is the mouthpiece of this company.
湯姆是這家公司的代言人。

mu·nic·i·pal [mjuˈnɪsəpl̩]
🔊 Track 5951

形 內政的
▶The municipal affairs of this country are very corrupt.
這個國家的內政相當腐敗。

mute [mjut]
🔊 Track 5952

名 啞巴 形 沉默的 同 silent 沉默的
▶名 It was the accident ten years ago that made him a mute.
是十年前的一次事故使他變成了啞巴。
▶形 The child has been mute since birth.
那個孩子生來就是啞巴。

my·thol·o·gy [mɪˈθɑlədʒɪ]
🔊 Track 5953

名 神話
▶Greek mythology is the required reading material for the literature course.
希臘神話是文學課的必讀資料。

[Nn]

nar·rate [næˈret]
🔊 Track 5954

動 敘述、講故事 同 report 報告
▶The writer narrated his own experiences in the book.
作家在書中講述的是他自身的經歷。

文法字詞解析
My phone is on mute. = 我的手機是靜音模式。

文法字詞解析
mythology 也可以簡稱 myth。

Level 1
Level 2
Level 3
Level 4
Level 5
Level 6

精進自我、聽說讀寫通
突破瓶頸7000單字

nar·ra·tive [ˈnærətɪv]
🔊 Track 5955

名 敘述、故事 形 敘事的

▶名 The narrative of the book was quite hard to understand.
書中的敘述很難懂。

▶形 Will you explain what this narrative poem means?
請你為我解釋一下這首敘事詩的意思好嗎？

nar·ra·tor [næˈretə]
🔊 Track 5956

名 敘述者、講述者

▶The narrator enunciated the names of the characters.
旁白清楚念出角色的名字。

na·tion·al·ism [ˈnæʃənlˌɪzəm]
🔊 Track 5957

名 民族主義、國家主義

▶It is hard for the students to understand what nationalism means.
學生們很難理解民族主義的含義。

nat·u·ral·ist [ˈnætʃərəlɪst]
🔊 Track 5958

名 自然主義者

▶It is a surprise that his theory should be so similar to that of the famous naturalist, Charles Darwin.
他的理論竟然跟著名的博物學家查爾斯・達爾文如此相似，這真令人驚訝啊。

na·val [ˈnevl̩]
🔊 Track 5959

形 有關海運的

▶It is said that the old man used to be a great naval officer in World War II.
據說這位老人曾是第二次世界大戰中的偉大海軍軍官。

na·vel [ˈnevl̩]
🔊 Track 5960

名 中心點、肚臍

▶I want to get a ring on my navel.
我想在肚臍上穿個環。

nav·i·ga·tion [ˌnævəˈgeʃən]
🔊 Track 5961

名 航海、航空

▶The navigation was conducted by the automatic system.
航行的任務由自動化系統執行。

ne·go·ti·a·tion [nɪˌgoʃɪˈeʃən]
🔊 Track 5962

名 協商、協議

▶Do you mind telling me how the negotiation is going?
能麻煩你告訴我協商進行得怎麼樣了嗎？

ne·on [ˈniˌɑn]
🔊 Track 5963

名 霓虹燈

▶You will see the colorful neon lights in the city wherever you go. 城市裡霓虹燈隨處可見。

文法字詞解析
first-person narrative = 第一人稱敘事觀點

文法字詞解析
這個字也可拿來當作形容詞，描述極為鮮艷明亮的顏色，如 neon red 就是有如紅色霓虹燈般的顏色。

neu·tral [`njutrəl] ◀ Track 5964
名 中立國 形 中立的、中立國的 同 independent 無黨派的
▶動 Was Switzerland a neutral during World War II?
瑞士在第二次大戰中是一個中立國嗎？
▶形 Suppose you were him. Would you also remain neutral during the debate?
如果你是他的話，你也會在辯論中保持中立嗎？

new·ly-wed [`njulɪ.wɛd] ◀ Track 5965
名 新婚夫婦
▶How is the newly-wed couple getting on?
這對新婚夫婦最近怎麼樣了？

文法字詞解析
「新婚夫婦」也可以直接稱「newly-weds」，後面不一定需要加上 couple。

news·cast·er/ an·chor·man/an·chor·wom·an ◀ Track 5966
[`nuzkæstə]/[`æŋkəmæn]/[`æŋkə.wumən]
名 新聞播報員
▶Do you have a favorite newscaster?
你有最喜歡的新聞播報員嗎？

nom·i·na·tion [ˌnɑmə`neʃən] ◀ Track 5967
名 提名、任命 同 selection 被挑選出的人或物
▶Nomination of the academy award was completed weeks ahead of the ceremony.
奧斯卡獎的提名在頒獎典禮前幾週就完成了。

nom·i·nee [ˌnɑmə`ni] ◀ Track 5968
名 被提名的人
▶The presidential nominee was always starting quarrels on TV.
那個總統候選人總是在電視上跟人家吵架。

norm [nɔrm] ◀ Track 5969
名 基準、規範 同 criterion 準則
▶Everyone in the nation is supposed to abide by the social norms. 國家裡的每一個人都應該遵守社會行為準則。

no·to·ri·ous [no`torɪəs] ◀ Track 5970
形 聲名狼藉的
▶Isn't Hitler a notorious dictator?
希特勒不是一個惡名昭彰的獨裁者嗎？

nour·ish [`nɝɪʃ] ◀ Track 5971
動 滋養
▶The plants were nourished by the fallen leaves.
植物受到落葉的滋養。

nour·ish·ment [`nɝɪʃmənt] ◀ Track 5972
名 營養
▶You need more nourishment. Come in and let me get you something to eat. 你還需要吃得更營養一些。進來，我弄點東西給你吃。

文法字詞解析
nourishment 指的不一定是身體上的營養喔！事實上「心靈上的養分」也可以稱做 nourishment of the mind。

Level 1
Level 2
Level 3
Level 4
Level 5
Level 6

精進自我、聽說讀寫通
突破瓶頸7000單字

nui·sance [ˈnjusn̩s] ◀ *Track 5973*

名 討厭的人、麻煩事
▶ Did the rats get in the kitchen again? What a nuisance!
老鼠們又跑進廚房了嗎？真是麻煩。

nur·ture [ˈnɝtʃɚ] ◀ *Track 5974*

名 養育、培育 動 培育、養育
▶ 名 This course is about the early nurture of the infant.
這堂課是關於嬰兒早期教養。
▶ 動 It's a mother's duty to nurture her children.
養育子女是一個母親的責任。

nu·tri·ent [ˈnjutrɪənt] ◀ *Track 5975*

名 營養物 形 有養分的、營養的
▶ 名 The plant drew minerals and other nutrients from the soil.
植物從泥土中吸收礦物質和其他養分。
▶ 形 Even though she ate so much nutrient food, she is still very slim.
即使她吃了這麼多營養的食物，她還是這麼苗條。

nu·tri·tion [njuˈtrɪʃən] ◀ *Track 5976*

名 營養物、營養 同 nourishment 營養
▶ People nowadays eat much more food, yet gain less nutrition.
現代的人吃得更多，卻得到更少的營養。

nu·tri·tious [njuˈtrɪʃəs] ◀ *Track 5977*

形 有養分的、營養的
▶ Buying all kinds of nutritious food won't make you healthier if you don't exercise.
你不運動的話，買各種營養食品也不會變得比較健康。

[Oo]

ob·li·ga·tion [ˌɑbləˈgeʃən] ◀ *Track 5978*

名 責任、義務
▶ It is our obligation to work in a satisfactory way.
令人滿意的工作成效是我們的責任。

o·blige [əˈblaɪdʒ] ◀ *Track 5979*

動 使不得不、強迫
▶ He was finally obliged to abandon that plan.
他終於不得不放棄那個計畫。

ob·scure [əbˈskjʊr] ◀ *Track 5980*

動 使陰暗 形 陰暗的
▶ 動 The clouds obscured the moon. 雲朵遮住了月亮。
▶ 形 The poem is completely obscure to me.
這首詩對我來說完全看不懂。

萬用延伸句型
feel obliged to 覺得自己不得不做某事、覺得做某事是自己的責任
例　如：Don't feel obliged to come. It's all right if you have something else scheduled.
不用覺得一定得來沒關係，你已經安排了其他的活動的話也不要緊。

of·fer·ing [ˈɔfərɪŋ]
🔊 Track 5981

名 供給
▶They ended up not only having to apologize but also offering a refund.
他們最後不但同意道歉，而且還會退款。

off·spring [ˈɔfsprɪŋ]
🔊 Track 5982

名 子孫、後裔 同 descendant 子孫、後裔
▶The old lady left a huge amount of heritage for her offspring.
老太太有一大筆遺產給後代子孫。

op·er·a·tion·al [ˌɑpəˈreʃənl]
🔊 Track 5983

形 操作的
▶Do you mind telling me what the operational hours of the restaurant are?
您介意告訴我這家餐廳營業的時間嗎？

op·po·si·tion [ˌɑpəˈzɪʃən]
🔊 Track 5984

名 反對的態度 同 disagreement 反對
▶There is a fierce opposition to the new tax program.
針對新的徵稅計畫，出現了強烈的反對意見。

op·press [əˈprɛs]
🔊 Track 5985

動 壓迫、威迫
▶A tyrannic（暴虐的）government which oppresses people will be overthrown one day.
一個壓迫人民的暴虐政府終究會被推翻的。

文法字詞解析
oppress 加上「-ed」就變成了形容詞「oppressed（受壓迫的）」。

op·pres·sion [əˈprɛʃən]
🔊 Track 5986

名 壓迫、壓制
▶It is said that the early sex anxiety and sex oppression will cause the distortion of the personality.
據說早期性焦慮與性壓抑將導致人格扭曲。

op·tion [ˈɑpʃən]
🔊 Track 5987

名 選擇、取捨 同 choice 選擇
▶We had no option but to follow her command.
我們別無選擇，只能聽從她的命令。

op·tion·al [ˈɑpʃənl]
🔊 Track 5988

形 非強制性的、可選擇的
▶Would you please tell me if the optional course is as hard as everybody says?
你能不能告訴我那門選修課真的像大家所說的那麼難嗎？

or·deal [ɔrˈdiəl]
🔊 Track 5989

名 嚴酷的考驗
▶His courage was severely tried by his ordeal.
他的勇氣在艱難困苦中經受了嚴峻的考驗。

Level 1
Level 2
Level 3
Level 4
Level 5
Level 6

精進自我、聽說讀寫通
突破瓶頸7000單字

or·der·ly [ˈɔrdəlɪ]
🔊 *Track 5990*

名 勤務兵 形 整潔的、有秩序的

▶名 The orderlies in this hospital are very professional.
這家醫院的護理人員非常專業。

▶形 He gave an orderly answer to that strict teacher.
他條理分明地回答了那個嚴格的老師的問題。

or·gan·ism [ˈɔrgənˌɪzəm]
🔊 *Track 5991*

名 有機體、生物體 同 organization 有機體

▶All the living organisms in this ecosystem rely on the river to survive. 在這個生態系統中所有的生物都靠這條河生存。

o·rig·i·nal·i·ty [əˌrɪdʒəˈnælətɪ]
🔊 *Track 5992*

名 獨創力、創舉 同 style 風格

▶Tom is distinguished for his originality and for having produced many special products.
湯姆以有創意著稱，且創造出許多特別的產品。

o·rig·i·nate [əˈrɪdʒəˌnet]
🔊 *Track 5993*

動 創造、發源

▶It is said that the style of architecture originated from the ancient Greeks. 據說這種建築風格起源於古希臘。

out·break [ˈaʊtˌbrek]
🔊 *Track 5994*

名 爆發、突然發生

▶I'm afraid that the outbreak of the war will paralyze the traffic in the city. 恐怕戰爭的爆發將使城內的交通癱瘓。

out·fit [ˈaʊtˌfɪt]
🔊 *Track 5995*

名 裝備 動 提供必需的裝備

▶名 My dad bought a new outfit for me.
我爸爸幫我買了一套新服裝。

▶動 You need to outfit yourself with the latest equipment.
你得用最新的設備把自己裝備起來。

文法字詞解析

除了「裝備」外，outfit 也可以指平常穿在身上的一整套衣服，例如「春裝」就可以稱為 spring outfit。你現在穿在身上的，從衣帽到鞋襪都是你「outfit」的一部分。

out·ing [ˈaʊtɪŋ]
🔊 *Track 5996*

名 郊遊、遠足

▶It's a pity that the weather isn't better for our outing today.
今天天氣不好所以我們不能去遠足，真遺憾。

out·law [ˈaʊtˌlɔ]
🔊 *Track 5997*

名 逃犯 動 禁止

▶名 The outlaw was found to hide in the deserted cottage.
有個亡命之徒藏匿在廢棄的小屋裡。

▶動 I hope the sale of tobacco will be outlawed someday.
要是有朝一日煙草製品被禁止銷售就好了。

out·let [ˈaʊtˌlɛt]
🔊 *Track 5998*

名 逃離的出口

▶There is a huge sales outlet for weight-losing products.
我認為瘦身產品有極大的市場。

out·look [ˋaʊtˏlʊk]
🔊 *Track 5999*

名 觀點、態度　同 attitude 態度
▶ Optimism is a healthy outlook on life.
　樂觀是一種健康的人生觀。

out·num·ber [aʊtˋnʌmbɚ]
🔊 *Track 6000*

動 數目勝過　同 exceed 超過
▶ Male workers are outnumbered by female workers in this office.
　這間辦公室裡，女性員工人數超過男性員工。

文法字詞解析
字首「out-」有「超過、越過」的意思，而既然超過了「number」（數字），也就是「數目比……大」、「數目勝過……」的意思了。

out·rage [ˋaʊtˏredʒ]
🔊 *Track 6001*

名 暴行　動 施暴
▶ 名 What an outrage! How could he do something like that?
　真是太過份了吧！他怎麼可以做這樣的事？
▶ 動 The people were outraged by the government's decision.
　大眾對政府的這一決定非常憤怒。

out·ra·geous [aʊtˋredʒəs]
🔊 *Track 6002*

形 暴力的
▶ The outrageous book created a sensation.
　那部聳人聽聞的書曾轟動一時。

out·right [ˋaʊtˏraɪt]
🔊 *Track 6003*

形 毫無保留的、全部的　副 無保留地、公然地
▶ 形 She is the outright winner without question.
　毫無疑問她是優勝者。
▶ 副 Why don't you tell him outright what you thought of him?
　為什麼不坦率地向他說出你對他的想法呢？

out·set [ˋaʊtˏsɛt]
🔊 *Track 6004*

名 開始、開頭
▶ The novel fascinates the reader from the outset.
　這本小說一開頭就把讀者迷住了。

文法字詞解析
調換一下順序的話，set out 是一個片語，意思是「出發（去某地、做某事）」的意思。例如：The kids set out to look for the dog. 孩子們出發去找狗。

o·ver·head [ˋovɚˏhɛd]
🔊 *Track 6005*

形 頭頂上的、位於上方的　副 在上方地、在頭頂上地
同 above 在上方
▶ 形 The overhead projector is not working normally.
　投影機沒有正常運作。
▶ 副 The people in the room overhead are very noisy.
　樓上那個房間的人很吵。

o·ver·lap [ovɚˋlæp]
🔊 *Track 6006*

名 重疊的部份　動 重疊
▶ 名 There is an overlap between the two courses.
　這兩門課程之間有衝堂的問題。
▶ 動 The functions of the new office overlaps the functions of the one already in existence.
　新機構的機能與現存機構的機能有部分重疊。

Level 1
Level 2
Level 3
Level 4
Level 5
Level 6

突破瓶頸7000單字

精進自我、聽說讀寫通

o·ver·turn [`ovɚ͵tɝn]/[͵ovɚ`tɝn] 🔊 *Track 6007*

名 顛覆 動 顛倒、弄翻

▶ 名 The overturn of that irresponsible government was something worth celebrating.
那個不負責任的政府垮臺,真是太值得慶祝了。

▶ 動 The tyrant was overturned by the angry people.
暴君政權被憤怒人民推翻。

[Pp]

pact [pækt] 🔊 *Track 6008*

名 契約

▶ I have no idea what the Warsaw Pact stood for.
我不知道華沙條約的意義是什麼。

pam·phlet [`pæmflɪt] 🔊 *Track 6009*

名 小冊子 同 brochure 小冊子

▶ I have no time to distribute these pamphlets.
我沒有時間分發這些小冊子了。

par·a·lyze [`pærə͵laɪz] 🔊 *Track 6010*

動 麻痺

▶ This kind of poison can quickly paralyze the fish.
這種毒素會讓魚很快麻痺。

par·lia·ment [`pɑrləmənt] 🔊 *Track 6011*

名 議會

同 congress 美國國會

▶ Several members of the parliament attended the press conference.
好幾位國會成員出席了這場記者會。

pa·thet·ic [pæ`θɛtɪk] 🔊 *Track 6012*

形 悲慘的

▶ What a pathetic performance! I am sure it is the worst I have seen.
好爛的一場表演!我敢確定這是我看過最糟糕的一場表演。

文法字詞解析
和 pathetic 相關的一個形容詞是 apathetic,意思是「無感覺的、冷淡的」。

pa·tri·ot·ic [͵petrɪ`ɑtɪk] 🔊 *Track 6013*

形 愛國的 同 loyal 忠誠的

▶ The patriotic soldier refused to surrender to the enemy.
愛國的士兵拒絕向敵人投降。

PDA [`pi`di`e] 🔊 *Track 6014*

名 個人數位秘書、掌上型電腦

▶ PDA stands for "Personal Digital Assistant".
PDA 是「個人數位助理」的縮寫。

文法字詞解析
除了表示 Personal Digital Assistant 以外,PDA 還可以代表 Public Display of Affection,即在公開場合公然表現親暱行為的意思。也就是說,如果你在圖書館,對面坐了一對情侶在卿卿我我,他們做的事就是一種 PDA。

ped·dle [ˋpɛdl̩]　◀ Track 6015

動 叫賣、兜售　**同** sell 銷售
▶His brother has been peddling from house to house for weeks.
他弟弟挨家挨戶地叫賣已經有好幾個星期了。

文法字詞解析
叫賣的小販則稱為 peddler。

pe·des·tri·an [pəˋdɛstrɪən]　◀ Track 6016

名 行人　**形** 徒步的
▶**名** Pedestrians were advised to take the zebra cross.
行人應該要走斑馬線。
▶**形** They should cross the road at the pedestrian crossing.
他們應該從行人穿越道過馬路。

pen·in·su·la [pəˋnɪnsələ]　◀ Track 6017

名 半島
▶There's a lighthouse at the end of the peninsula.
在半島的尾端有一座燈塔。

pen·sion [ˋpɛnʃən]　◀ Track 6018

名 退休金　**動** 給予退休金
同 allowance 津貼、發津貼
▶**名** The reason he claimed a pension was that he had been ill for a long time.
他之所以申請救助金是因為他長期生病。
▶**動** He is pensioned off because the company wants to replace him with a young man.
他被迫提早退休的原因，是公司想讓一位年輕人來接替他的職務。

Level
1

Level
2

Level
3

Level
4

Level
5

per·cep·tion [pɚˋsɛpʃən]　◀ Track 6019

名 感覺、察覺　**同** sense 感覺
▶He is admired for the depth of his perception.
他因為深具洞察力而受到了賞識。

per·se·ver·ance [ˌpɝsəˋvɪrəns]　◀ Track 6020

名 堅忍、堅持
▶Hard work and perseverance are what made him succeed.
努力和毅力是他成功的原因。

Level
6
突破瓶頸7000單字
精進自我、聽說讀寫通

per·se·vere [ˌpɝsəˋvɪr]　◀ Track 6021

動 堅持
▶Even if you persevere, you won't always succeed.
即使你堅持下去，最終也不見得一定會獲得成功。

萬用延伸句型
Even if... 就算⋯⋯、即使⋯⋯

per·sis·tence [pɚˋsɪstəns]　◀ Track 6022

名 固執、堅持　**同** maintenance 維持
▶His persistence in the matter is getting a bit annoying.
他一直固執在這件事上面，令人覺得有點煩。

per·sist·ent [pɚˋsɪstənt] ◀ Track 6023

形 固執的
▶His persistent phone calls made her throw her cell phone at the wall. 他堅持不懈地一直打電話給她，讓她受不了地把手機砸向牆壁。

per·spec·tive [pɚˋspɛktɪv] ◀ Track 6024

名 透視、觀點 形 透視的 同 position 立場
▶名 The novel was written form a first-person perspective. 這部小說是由第一人稱角度寫的。
▶形 This teacher taught me what perspective drawing is. 這位老師教了我透視畫的畫法。

pes·ti·cide [ˋpɛstɪˏsaɪd] ◀ Track 6025

名 農藥
▶It's time for the farmers to spread the pesticide over the rice fields. 該是農民們在稻田裡噴灑農藥的時候了。

pe·tro·le·um [pəˋtrolɪəm] ◀ Track 6026

名 石油
▶There is a shortage of petroleum recently in our nation. 最近我國的石油短缺。

pet·ty [ˋpɛtɪ] ◀ Track 6027

形 瑣碎的、小的 同 small 小的
▶Why are you fighting over such a petty matter? 你們為什麼要因為這麼小的事情而吵架？

phar·ma·cist [ˋfɑrməsɪst] ◀ Track 6028

名 藥劑師
▶I obtained my pharmacist's license last month. 我上個月拿到了藥劑師執照。

phar·ma·cy [ˋfɑrməsɪ] ◀ Track 6029

名 藥劑學、藥局
▶Would you like me to get some painkillers（止痛藥）from the pharmacy for you? 要不要我到藥局去幫你買一些止痛藥啊？

phase [fez] ◀ Track 6030

名 階段 動 分段實行 同 stage 階段
▶名 A flaw of the prototype was found at the phase of test. 測試階段發現產品雛型有個瑕疵。
▶動 Not all people believe that the U.S. army will complete the phased withdrawal（撤軍）in four months. 不是所有人都相信美軍會在四個月內完成分段撤軍。

pho·to·graph·ic [ˏfotəˋɡræfɪk] ◀ Track 6031

形 攝影的
▶I have no idea what this photographic equipment is used for. 我對這種攝影器材的用處一無所知。

萬用延伸句型

rom my perspective... 從我的角度來看……

例 如：From my perspective, what your friend said was quite sensible and you might want to take her advice.
從我的角度來看，你朋友所説的話非常有道理，你可以聽聽她的意見。

萬用延伸句型

go through a phase 經歷某個（暫時的）階段

例如：The boy went through a phase of being obsessed with robots.
那個男孩有個階段瘋狂熱愛機器人。

pic·tur·esque [ˌpɪktʃəˈrɛsk] ◀€ *Track 6032*

形 如畫的
▶I took photos of the picturesque shores beside the river.
我用相機照下景色如畫的河岸。

pierce [pɪrs] ◀€ *Track 6033*

動 刺穿
▶She got her ears pierced back in high school.
她以前高中的時候打了耳洞。

pi·e·ty [ˈpaɪətɪ] ◀€ *Track 6034*

名 虔敬
▶We consider filial piety to be the core value of Chinese culture.
我們認為孝道是中國文化的中心價值。

pi·ous [ˈpaɪəs] ◀€ *Track 6035*

形 虔誠的 同 faithful 忠誠的
▶He is a pious follower of God, like his parents.
他跟他的父母親一樣也是個虔誠的基督徒。

pipe·line [ˈpaɪpˌlaɪn] ◀€ *Track 6036*

名 管線
▶It took the workers two years to lay these oil pipelines.
工人們花了兩年的時間才把這些輸油管鋪設好。

pitch·er [ˈpɪtʃɚ] ◀€ *Track 6037*

名 投手
▶The handsome pitcher led his team to victory.
這個英俊的投手領導了他的球隊獲得勝利。

plight [plaɪt] ◀€ *Track 6038*

名 誓約、婚約
▶It seemed that the man is in a sad plight.
這個男人的處境似乎非常困難。

pneu·mo·nia [njuˈmonjə] ◀€ *Track 6039*

名 肺炎
▶A lot of people caught pneumonia in a short time.
在很短的時間內,有很多人感染肺炎。

poach [potʃ] ◀€ *Track 6040*

動 偷獵、水煮
▶Rhinos and elephants were poached by un-licensed hunters.
未經授權的獵人盜獵犀牛和大象。

poach·er [ˈpotʃɚ] ◀€ *Track 6041*

名 偷獵者
▶The poacher is fined heavily by the authorities.
偷獵者被管理機構罰了不少錢。

萬用延伸句型
pierce through sth. 刺穿(某物)
例如:He pierced through the fabric with a needle.
他用針刺穿了布料。

文法字詞解析
要注意 pneumonia 開頭的 p 是不發音的喔!

Level
1

Level
2

Level
3

Level
4

Level
5

Level
6

精進自我、聽說讀寫通
突破瓶頸7000單字

pol·lu·tant [pə`lutənt]
🔊 *Track 6042*

名 污染物 形 污染物的

▶名 We found a lot of industrial pollutants in the lake.
我們在湖中發現了很多工業污染物。

▶形 Few people pay attention to the Pollutant Standards Index.
很少有人關注空氣污染指數。

pon·der [`pɑndɚ]
🔊 *Track 6043*

動 仔細考慮 同 consider 考慮

▶Ponder over the problem before you reply.
回覆之前，先仔細思考這個問題。

pop·u·late [`pɑpjəˏlet]
🔊 *Track 6044*

動 居住

▶The city is heavily populated by immigrants.
這個城市居住著很多外來移民。

文法字詞解析
如 要 說 一 個 地 方 無 人 居 住，可 用 unpopulated 來形容。

pos·ture [`pɑstʃɚ]
🔊 *Track 6045*

名 態度、姿勢 動 擺姿勢

▶名 Good posture is very important for health.
良好的姿勢對健康很重要。

▶動 He enjoys posturing in front of people, so nobody likes him. 他很喜歡在人前裝模作樣，所以沒人喜歡他。

pre·cede [pri`sid]
🔊 *Track 6046*

動 在前 同 lead 走在最前方

▶It is obvious that this duty should precede all others.
顯然這項義務應該優先於其他一切義務。

pre·ce·dent [`prɛsədənt]
🔊 *Track 6047*

名 前例

▶She is the first queen who broke the precedent by sending her children to a public school.
她是首位破例讓自己的孩子到公立學校就讀的女王。

pre·ci·sion [pri`sɪʒən]
🔊 *Track 6048*

名 精準 同 accuracy 準確

▶The gadgets in the laboratory were made with great precision.
實驗室的器材製造過程都相當精準。

pred·e·ces·sor [ˏprɛdɪ`sɛsɚ]
🔊 *Track 6049*

名 祖先、前輩

▶The new worker is better than his predecessor.
這名新的工作人員比他的前任做得更好。

文法字詞解析
相反地，要說繼承自己位置的後輩，則可稱為 successor。

pre·dic·tion [pri`dɪkʃən]
🔊 *Track 6050*

名 預言

▶He was as surprised as anyone that his prediction came true.
他的預言成真了，連他自己都跟其他人一樣驚訝。

pref·ace [ˈprɛfɪs] 　 Track 6051

名 序言 同 introduction 序言
▶Will you find someone to translate the preface from French to English?
你能找個人將序言從法文翻譯成英文嗎？

prej·u·dice [ˈprɛdʒədɪs] 　 Track 6052

名 偏見 動 使存有偏見
▶名 Prejudice and bias would be the obstacles for mutual understanding.
偏見是互相理解的障礙。
▶動 Don't you think these facts will prejudice them in his favor?
你不覺得這些事實會使他們偏袒他嗎？

pre·lim·i·nar·y [prɪˈlɪməˌnɛrɪ] 　 Track 6053

名 初步 形 初步的
▶名 The exciting matches will begin soon now that the preliminaries are almost over.
預賽快比完了，真正刺激的比賽快要開始了。
▶形 The preliminary results are posted on the board.
佈告板上把初步的結果貼出來了。

pre·ma·ture [ˌpriməˈtjʊr] 　 Track 6054

形 過早的、未成熟的
▶It's premature to say what will happen for sure now.
現在要確定地說出會發生什麼事還太早了。

pre·mier [ˈprimɪə] 　 Track 6055

名 首長 形 首要的 同 prime 首要的
▶名 He requested the premier to meet him in secret.
他要求總理秘密接見他。
▶形 People think this is Europe's premier port.
人們都認為這裡是歐洲第一大港。

pre·scribe [prɪˈskraɪb] 　 Track 6056

動 規定、開藥方
▶The prescribed medicine can relieve you from the pain.
處方藥物可以幫你舒緩疼痛。

pre·scrip·tion [prɪˈskrɪpʃən] 　 Track 6057

名 指示、處方
▶Do you mind my leaving this prescription with you?
你介意我把這張處方留在你這兒嗎？

pre·side [prɪˈzaɪd] 　 Track 6058

動 主持
▶Until now, who is to preside over the meeting still hasn't been decided.
直到現在，這個會議要由誰來主持還未決定。

Level 1
Level 2
Level 3
Level 4
Level 5
Level 6

精進自我、聽說讀寫通
突破瓶頸7000單字

pres·i·den·cy [ˈprɛzədənsɪ]　◀≋ *Track 6059*

名 總統的職位

▶I don't think he is going to run for presidency this year.
我不覺得他今年會競選總統。

pres·i·den·tial [ˈprɛzədɛnʃəl]　◀≋ *Track 6060*

形 總統的

▶They are the front runners in the presidential elections.
這些人在總統競選中最有可能獲勝。

文法字詞解析
總統套房稱為 presidential suite。

pres·tige [prɛsˈtiʒ]　◀≋ *Track 6061*

名 聲望

▶The educational institution has gained international prestige.
這個教育機構獲得國際聲譽。

pre·sume [prɪˈzum]　◀≋ *Track 6062*

動 假設　同 guess 推測

▶You can't just presume that he will approve of the plan.
你不能就這樣假設他一定會支持這個計畫。

pre·ven·tive [prɪˈvɛntɪv]　◀≋ *Track 6063*

名 預防物　形 預防的

▶名 She took some preventives before the headache started.
她在開始頭痛前就先吃了預防的藥。

▶形 It's about time that we took preventive measures.
我們該採取預防措施了。

pro·duc·tiv·i·ty [ˌprodʌkˈtɪvətɪ]　◀≋ *Track 6064*

名 生產力

▶It is wrong for us to underestimate or overestimate（高估）
our agricultural productivity.
低估和高估我們的農業生產力都是不對的。

pro·fi·cien·cy [prəˈfɪʃənsɪ]　◀≋ *Track 6065*

名 熟練、精通

▶They were surprised at his English proficiency.
他們對於他精通英語的程度驚訝不已。

文法字詞解析
與 proficiency 相應的形容詞為 proficient。

pro·found [prəˈfaʊnd]　◀≋ *Track 6066*

形 極深的、深奧的

▶Nick's speech has a profound impact on the school kids.
尼克的演講對學童有很深遠的影響。

pro·gres·sive [prəˈgrɛsɪv]　◀≋ *Track 6067*

形 前進的

▶What do you think of the progressive party in the country? I
heard they once carried out many reforms. 你如何看待這個國
家的改革派？聽說他們曾經進行過很多改革。

pro·hi·bit [prəˈhɪbɪt]
🔊 *Track 6068*

動 制止
▶We are prohibited on feeding animals in the zoo.
我們被禁止餵食動物園裡的動物。

pro·hi·bi·tion [ˌproəˈbɪʃən]
🔊 *Track 6069*

名 禁令、禁止
▶The municipal office announced a prohibition on smoking in public. 市政府宣布禁止在公眾場合吸菸。

pro·jec·tion [prəˈdʒɛkʃən]
🔊 *Track 6070*

名 計畫、預估
▶The company has made projections of sales of 2000 aircrafts.
據說該公司已預估將銷售兩千架飛機。

文法字詞解析
投影機（projector）所映照出的「投影」也稱為 projection。

prone [pron]
🔊 *Track 6071*

形 俯臥的、易於……的
▶It seems that children of poor health are very prone to colds in winter.
健康不佳的孩子似乎容易在冬天感冒。

prop·a·gan·da [ˌprɑpəˈgændə]
🔊 *Track 6072*

名 宣傳活動 同 promotion 促銷活動
▶In recent years, there has been a lot of anti-global warming propaganda.
近年來，一直有許多抗暖化的宣導活動。

pro·pel [prəˈpɛl]
🔊 *Track 6073*

動 推動
▶He is a man propelled by ambition.
他是一個被野心所驅策的男人。

pro·pel·ler [prəˈpɛlə]
🔊 *Track 6074*

名 推進器
▶Peoples' needs are the propeller of innovation.
人們的需求是創新的推手。

prose [proz]
🔊 *Track 6075*

名 散文
▶Would you like to have a look at his latest prose?
你要不要看一下他最新的散文？

文法字詞解析
充滿華麗詞藻、沒什麼實質內容的文章即可稱為 purple prose。

pros·e·cute [ˈprɑsɪˌkjut]
🔊 *Track 6076*

動 檢舉、告發
▶Can you tell me who you want to prosecute? And for what?
您可以告訴我您要投訴誰嗎？還有，為什麼要投訴他？

pros·e·cu·tion [ˌprɑsɪˈkjuʃən]
🔊 *Track 6077*

名 告發
▶New evidence has revealed the weakness of the prosecution's case. 新的證據已顯示出原告的理由不充足。

Level 1
Level 2
Level 3
Level 4
Level 5
Level 6

精進自我、聽說讀寫通
突破瓶頸7000單字

pro·spec·tive [prəˋspɛktɪv] 🔊 *Track 6078*

形 將來的 同 future 未來的

▶They are not likely to be our prospective clients.
他們不太可能是我們潛在的顧客。

pro·vin·cial [prəˋvɪnʃəl] 🔊 *Track 6079*

名 省民 形 省的

▶名 The provincials who were left homeless by the hurricane received help from the troops sent by the government.
因颶風而無家可歸的省民受到政府派來軍隊的幫助。

▶形 Talking to smart and well-dressed people makes me feel so provincial.
和聰明、穿著體面的人講話，會讓我覺得自己很土氣。

pro·voke [prəˋvok] 🔊 *Track 6080*

動 激起

▶No matter what you do, please don't provoke the bears.
不管你做什麼，請千萬不要激怒那些熊。

prowl [praʊl] 🔊 *Track 6081*

名 徘徊 動 潛行

▶名 The mad man is still on the prowl around the streets at night. 那個瘋子深夜時還在街上徘徊。

▶動 Did you see someone prowling around among the trees?
你有沒有看見有人在樹林裡鬼鬼祟祟地走動？

punc·tu·al [ˋpʌŋktʃʊəl] 🔊 *Track 6082*

形 準時的

▶Being punctual for business occasions is essential.
準時到達商業場合是很重要的。

pu·ri·fy [ˋpjʊrəˏfaɪ] 🔊 *Track 6083*

動 淨化 同 cleanse 淨化

▶You can purify the water by distilling（蒸餾）.
你可以透過蒸餾來淨化水。

pu·ri·ty [ˋpjʊrətɪ] 🔊 *Track 6084*

名 純粹

▶The book depicts her as a woman of purity and goodness（善良）. 書中把她描寫成一個純潔善良的婦女。

[Qq]

qual·i·fi·ca·tion(s) 🔊 *Track 6085*
[ˏkwɑləfəˋkeʃən(z)]

名 賦予資格、證照 同 competence 勝任

▶Do you mind telling me what sort of qualifications I need for the job? 能麻煩您告訴我這份工作需要具備什麼樣的資格嗎？

文法字詞解析

可用「thought-provoking」形容發人深省的事物。

萬用延伸句型

on the prowl for sth. 如狩獵者般積極找尋（某事物）、
例如：I'm on the prowl for a nice place to rent in this neighborhood.
我正在這個社區裡找尋不錯的租屋房源。

quar·rel·some ['kwɔrəlsəm]　◀€ *Track 6086*

形 愛爭吵的
▶The quarrelsome woman leaves a bad impression on her neighbors. 他的兄弟們似乎都非常貪婪而且喜歡爭吵。

quench [kwɛntʃ]　◀€ *Track 6087*

動 弄熄、解渴
▶Having a can of soda is not enough to quench my thirst.
喝一罐汽水不夠我解渴。

que·ry ['kwɪrɪ]　◀€ *Track 6088*

名 問題 動 質疑 同 inquire 詢問
▶名 I have forwarded the customer's query to the relevant personnel（人員）.
我已經把那個消費者的疑問轉達給相關人員了。
▶動 "Are you sure you're not mistaken?" John queried.
「你確定你沒搞錯嗎？」約翰懷疑地問。

ques·tion·naire [.kwɛstʃən'ɛr]　◀€ *Track 6089*

名 問卷、調查表
▶They gave the passers-by some questionnaires.
他們發給路人一些問卷。

[Rr]

rac·ism ['resɪzəm]　◀€ *Track 6090*

名 種族歧視
▶It is believed that racism is an obsolete idea.
種族歧視是個過時的概念。

ra·di·ant ['redjənt]　◀€ *Track 6091*

名 發光體 形 發光的、輻射的
▶名 I heard that they saw a mysterious radiant that day.
據說他們那天看見了一個神秘的發光體。
▶形 Did something good happen? You look radiant.
發生了什麼好事嗎？你看起來滿面容光。

ra·di·ate ['redɹet]　◀€ *Track 6092*

動 放射 形 放射狀的
▶動 The sun in the sky radiates both light and heat every day. That is why things can grow on the earth. 天空中的太陽每天發出光和熱。這就是萬物能在地球上生長的原因。
▶形 There was a radiate head of the president on the coin.
那枚錢幣上畫著一個光芒四射的總統頭像。

ra·di·a·tion [.redɪ'eʃən]　◀€ *Track 6093*

名 放射、發光
▶The apparatus（儀器）emits harmful radiation.
這台儀器會放射出有害的輻射物。

文法字詞解析
要說「填」問卷的「填」這個動作，可以用 fill out 這個片語。
例如：I filled out the questionnaire and handed it back to the man.
我填完問卷就把它交回給那個先生了。

Level 1
Level 2
Level 3
Level 4
Level 5
Level 6

精進自我、聽說讀寫通
突破瓶頸7000單字

rav·age [ˈrævɪdʒ] ◀ *Track 6102*

名 毀壞 動 破壞

▶名 The ravage of inflation（通貨膨脹）led to the hardship in people's lives. 通貨膨脹的惡果使得人們生活困難。

▶動 The whole area was ravaged by forest fires last week. 上星期整個地區都被森林大火給毀滅了。

re·al·ism [ˈriəlɪzəm] ◀ *Track 6103*

名 現實主義

▶His down-to-earth realism was the reason why he abandoned the expansion plan. 他的現實的想法使他放棄擴張計畫。

文法字詞解析
「超現實主義」則是 surrealism。

re·al·i·za·tion [ˌriələˈzeʃən] ◀ *Track 6104*

名 現實、領悟

▶She was suddenly hit with the realization that he had never loved her. 她忽然領悟到，他根本從來沒愛過她。

re·bel·lion [rɪˈbɛljən] ◀ *Track 6105*

名 叛亂

▶No one knows who led or planned the rebellion. 沒有人知道到底是誰領到、計畫了這次叛亂。

re·ces·sion [rɪˈsɛʃən] ◀ *Track 6106*

名 衰退

▶Many countries suffered an economic recession this year. 很多國家今年都遭遇了經濟衰退。

re·cip·i·ent [rɪˈsɪpɪənt] ◀ *Track 6107*

名 接受者、接受的 同 receiver 接受者

▶The recipient of the Nobel Prize did not attend the award ceremony. 諾貝爾獎的得主沒有出席頒獎典禮。

rec·om·men·da·tion ◀ *Track 6108*
[ˌrɛkəmɛnˈdeʃən]

名 推薦 同 reference 推薦

▶Will you write a recommendation for me, Professor Wang? 王教授，您能替我寫一封推薦信嗎？

rec·on·cile [ˈrɛkənˌsaɪl] ◀ *Track 6109*

動 調停、和解

▶You'd better have someone reconcile the disputes among them, or it will affect the whole organization. 你最好請人去調解一下他們之間的糾紛，否則它將會影響到整個組織。

萬用延伸句型
reconcile with sb. 與（某人）和好
例 如：Two days after the fight, they finally reconciled with each other.
大吵一架兩天後，他們終於和好了。

rec·re·a·tion·al [ˌrɛkrɪˈeʃən!] ◀ *Track 6110*

形 娛樂的

▶It is said that there are running tracks built in the recreational center. 據說休閒中心建有跑道。

突破瓶頸7000單字

ra·di·a·tor [ˈredɪˌetəˈ]
Track 6094

名 發光體
▶Every room is equipped with a radiator.
　每個房間都裝有暖氣。

rad·i·cal [ˈrædɪkl̩]
Track 6095

名 根本 形 根源的
▶名 Some radicals are seeking to overthrow the social order.
　有些激進分子正企圖擾亂社會秩序。
▶形 He decided to make a radical change to the plan.
　他決定對計畫做一次徹底的修改。

raft [ræft]
Track 6096

名 筏 動 乘筏
▶名 Can you tell me how long the survivors were adrift（漂流的）on the raft?
　你能告訴我倖存者們在木筏上漂浮了多久嗎？
▶動 How long will it take for me to raft down the stream?
　我搭乘木筏順流而下要花多久的時間呢？

raid [red]
Track 6097

名 突擊 動 襲擊
▶名 I heard from a source that the police would carry out a dawn raid. 我接獲線報，聽說警方將在清晨展開突擊。
▶動 Their troops will raid the enemy camp by night.
　他們的部隊要夜襲敵營。

文法字詞解析
除了用於戰爭等較嚴肅的場合，這個單字也可用於日常生活中的「突襲」情況。例如若你妹突然跑進來翻遍你的衣櫃，就可以說她 raided my closet。

ran·dom [ˈrændəm]
Track 6098

形 隨意的、隨機的 反 deliberate 蓄意的
▶I always listen to music on random.
　我聽音樂都是隨機播放。

ran·som [ˈrænsəm]
Track 6099

名 贖金 動 贖回
▶名 The kidnapper requested a ransom of ten million dollars.
　綁匪要求一千萬贖金。
▶動 The police promise to ransom the child with 100,000 dollars.
　警察保證會用十萬美金來贖回那個孩子。

rash [ræʃ]
Track 6100

名 疹子 形 輕率的
▶名 My skin has broken out in a rash for some reason.
　我的皮膚不知道為什麼起了疹子。
▶形 I wish my colleague would keep himself from doing anything rash. 我希望我的同事不要做出任何莽撞的事來。

ra·tion·al [ˈræʃənl̩]
Track 6101

形 理性的 反 absurd 不合理的
▶I know you're worried about your child's safety, but you need to be rational now.
　我知道你很擔心孩子的安全，但你現在一定要理性點。

文法字詞解析
相反地，「不理性的」則是 irrational。

re·cruit [rɪˋkrut]
Track 6111

動 徵募 名 新兵 同 draft 徵兵

▶動 Most of the teachers in this school are recruited from abroad. 這所學校大部分的老師都是從國外聘請來的。

▶名 New recruits of the company were required to attend the orientation day.
公司的新員工被要求參加新進人員訓練。

re·cur [rɪˋkɝ]
Track 6112

動 重現

▶This kind of problem is likely to recur, so you need to be more careful. 這類問題可能還會再發生,所以你最好更小心。

re·dun·dant [rɪˋdʌndənt]
Track 6113

形 過剩的、冗長的 反 concise 簡要的

▶The manager promised there would be no question of anyone being made redundant.
經理承諾絕對不會裁掉任何人。

re·fine [rɪˋfaɪn]
Track 6114

動 精練 同 improve 改善

▶Works of taste can refine the soul.
高雅的作品能陶冶心靈。

re·fine·ment [rɪˋfaɪnmənt]
Track 6115

名 精良

▶Both good manners and correct speech are works of refinement.
彬彬有禮和談吐得體都是文雅的象徵。

re·flec·tive [rɪˋflɛktɪv]
Track 6116

形 反射的

▶The reflective surface of glass made it a substitute of a mirror.
玻璃可以反射影像,所以被拿來當作鏡子。

re·fresh·ment(s) [rɪˋfrɛʃmənt(s)]
Track 6117

名 清爽、提神之物

▶In an office where everyone's always mad, his pleasant personality is a refreshment. 在一個大家總是很容易生氣的辦公室中,他好相處的個性令人感到舒爽。

re·fund [rɪˋfʌnd]/[ˋrɪfʌnd]
Track 6118

名 償還、退款 動 償還

▶名 The store won't give me a refund for the product I bought because I have lost my receipt.
這家商店不肯為我購買的產品退款,因為我已經把發票給弄丟了。

▶動 I am afraid that the travel agency won't refund you the full cost of your fare because you didn't inform them of your cancellation immediately.
恐怕這家旅行社不會退還你全部的旅費,因為你沒有及時通知他們要取消。

文法字詞解析
總是不斷復發的症狀可稱為 recurring symptoms。

文法字詞解析
也可指茶點、飲料等令人神清氣爽的點心。

re·gard·less [rɪˋgɑrdlɪs] 🔊 *Track 6119*

形 不關心的　副 不關心地、無論如何　同 despite 儘管

▶形 He climbed the tower regardless of the dangerous weather.
他不顧危險的天氣，爬上了高塔。

▶副 Regardless of her father's advice, Jenny pursued her dream to become an idol.
珍妮不管她爸爸的勸告，追求了成為偶像的夢想。

re·gime [rɪˋʒim] 🔊 *Track 6120*

名 政權

▶It seems that many things will change under the new regime.
在新政權下似乎很多事情將會發生變化。

re·hears·al [rɪˋhɝsl] 🔊 *Track 6121*

名 排演　同 practice 練習

▶Would you like to participate in our rehearsal, Mrs. Wang?
王女士，您願意來參加我們的排練嗎？

re·hearse [rɪˋhɝs] 🔊 *Track 6122*

動 預演

▶How about rehearsing the play after the break?
休息之後來排練戲劇怎麼樣？

rein [ren] 🔊 *Track 6123*

名 箝制　動 控制

▶名 The boy pulled at the reins nervously.
那個男孩緊張地使勁拉韁繩。

▶動 He was unable to rein in his anger any longer.
他再也按捺不住他的怒氣了。

re·in·force [ˌriɪnˋfors] 🔊 *Track 6124*

動 增強　同 intensify 增強

▶The pockets of my coat were reinforced with double stitching.
我外套的口袋縫了兩道線來使它更穩固。

re·lay [ˋrɪle]/[rɪˋle] 🔊 *Track 6125*

名 接力（賽）　動 傳達

▶名 Do you know how many people took part in the torch relay?
你知道有多少人參與了這次的火把傳遞接力嗎？

▶動 Will you please relay the news to his mother in the country?
請你把這個消息轉達給他住在鄉下的母親好嗎？

rel·e·vant [ˋrɛləvənt] 🔊 *Track 6126*

形 相關的

▶You'd better send me the relevant papers on the case today.
你最好今天就把跟案件有關的檔案送過來給我。

萬用延伸句型

keep a tight rein on sth./sb. 看緊（某人／某事）

例　如：She keeps a tight rein on her husband, who tends to gamble a lot.
她看她那經常賭錢的老公看得很緊。

文法字詞解析

相反地，「不相關的、不重要的」則是 irrelevant。

Level 1
Level 2
Level 3
Level 4
Level 5
Level 6

精進自我、聽說讀寫通
突破瓶頸7000單字

743

re·li·ance [rɪˋlaɪəns] 🔊 *Track 6127*

名 信賴、依賴

▶Don't place too much reliance on what he said, or you will regret it.
對他所說的話不要過於信賴，要不然你會後悔的。

rel·ish [ˋrɛlɪʃ] 🔊 *Track 6128*

名 嗜好、美味 動 愛好、品味

▶名 I had tomato and onion relish on my burger.
我在漢堡上點綴番茄和洋蔥。

▶動 The dog relished the food we gave him.
那隻狗極享受地吃了我們給牠的食物。

萬用延伸句型
with relish 非常享受地
例如：He licked the sauce off his fingers with relish.
他非常享受地舔掉手指上的醬汁。

re·main·der [rɪˋmendə] 🔊 *Track 6129*

名 剩餘 同 remain 殘留

▶He spent the remainder of his life alone in the country.
他獨自在鄉間度過了餘生。

re·mov·al [rɪˋmuvl̩] 🔊 *Track 6130*

名 移動

▶The factory has announced its removal to another town.
這家工廠已經宣佈將遷往另一座城市。

re·nais·sance [ˌrəˋnesn̩s] 🔊 *Track 6131*

名 再生、文藝復興

▶Da Vinci was a very famous painter in the Renaissance period.
達文西是文藝復興時期非常著名的一位畫家。

ren·der [ˋrɛndə] 🔊 *Track 6132*

動 給予、讓與、表達、翻譯

▶The way he rendered the poem impressed his teacher.
他註釋這首詩的方式令老師印象深刻。

re·nowned [rɪˋnaʊnd] 🔊 *Track 6133*

形 著名的 同 famous 著名的

▶He had become a renowned landscape painter.
他後來成為一名著名的風景畫畫家。

rent·al [ˋrɛntl̩] 🔊 *Track 6134*

名 租用物

▶The yearly rental of her house is 12,000 dollars.
她這棟房子的年租金要一萬兩千美元。

re·press [rɪˋprɛs] 🔊 *Track 6135*

動 抑制

▶She could not repress a shiver whenever she thought of the cruel criminal.
每當想到這名殘暴的罪犯時，她就會忍不住顫抖。

文法字詞解析
repress 相應的名詞為 repression。

re·sem·blance [rɪˋzɛmbləns] ◀≲ *Track 6136*

名 類似 同 similarity 類似
▶There's a strong resemblance between Mike and Bob.
麥克和鮑勃長相非常類似。

res·er·voir [ˋrɛzəˏvɔr] ◀≲ *Track 6137*

名 儲水池、倉庫 同 warehouse 倉庫
▶It is reported that this new reservoir can supply water to the whole city.
根據報導，這座水庫能供應水給整座城市。

res·i·den·tial [ˏrɛzəˋdɛnʃəl] ◀≲ *Track 6138*

形 居住的
▶The residential shelter was set up to house the victims of earthquake. 居民避難所被搭建起來收容地震受災戶。

re·si·stant [rɪˋzɪstənt] ◀≲ *Track 6139*

形 抵抗的
▶A healthy diet creates a body resistant to disease.
健康的飲食有助於增強體內對疾病的抵抗力。

文法字詞解析
resistant 可用來表示「防……」的意思，如 wrinkle-resistant（防皺紋）、heat-resistant（防熱）、stain-resistant（防污漬）等。

res·o·lute [ˋrɛzəˏlut] ◀≲ *Track 6140*

形 堅決的
▶We tried to persuade him not to do it, but he was resolute.
我們有試著說服他不要做，但他很堅決。

re·spec·tive [rɪˋspɛktɪv] ◀≲ *Track 6141*

形 個別的 同 individual 個別的
▶These people all excel in their respective fields.
這些人在各自的領域裡都很出類拔萃。

res·to·ra·tion [ˏrɛstəˋreʃən] ◀≲ *Track 6142*

名 恢復
▶The restoration of the files took a surprisingly long time.
把檔案復原花了異常久的時間。

re·straint [rɪˋstrent] ◀≲ *Track 6143*

名 抑制
▶He always eats without restraint. 他吃東西總是毫不節制。

re·tail [ˋritel] ◀≲ *Track 6144*

名 零售 動 零售 形 零售的 副 零售地 反 wholesale 批發
▶名 Applicant with two years' experience in retail is preferred.
歡迎有兩年以上零售經驗的求職者。
▶動 If he intends to retail these shoes, will you order some there?
如果他打算零售這些鞋子的話，你會從那訂購一些嗎？
▶形 Can you tell me the retail prices of these slippers?
你能告訴我這些拖鞋的零售價嗎？
▶副 His method of buying wholesale and selling retail helped him gain a lot of profit.
他整批買下來之後拿去零售的作法幫他賺了不少錢。

Level 1
Level 2
Level 3
Level 4
Level 5
Level 6

突破瓶頸7000單字 精進自我、聽說讀寫通

re·tal·i·ate [rɪˋtælɪˌet]
🔈 *Track 6145*

動 報復

▶The terrorists retaliated by killing the travelers.
恐怖份子以殺害旅客作為報復。

re·trieve [rɪˋtriv]
🔈 *Track 6146*

動 取回

▶The dog retrieved the ball for me.
那隻狗幫我把球叼了回來。

rev·e·la·tion [ˌrɛvəˋleʃən]
🔈 *Track 6147*

名 揭發 同 disclosure 揭發

▶His revelation that he was actually gay wasn't much of a surprise to me.
他揭露了自己其實是同性戀的事實，我一點都不覺得驚訝。

rev·e·nue [ˋrɛvəˌnju]
🔈 *Track 6148*

名 收入

▶The revenue of our company is displayed on the annual financial report.
我們公司的營收有呈現在年度財報上。

文法字詞解析
gross annual revenue = 年度總收入
revenue 也可以代換成 income(收入)

re·viv·al [rɪˋvaɪvl̩]
🔈 *Track 6149*

名 復甦

▶There is a visible sign of a revival in the stock market.
有明顯的跡象顯示股市即將復甦。

rhet·o·ric [ˋrɛtərɪk]
🔈 *Track 6150*

名 修辭（學）

▶His rhetoric is too profound for us to understand.
他說話的方式深奧無比，我們難以理解。

rhyth·mic [ˋrɪðəmɪk]
🔈 *Track 6151*

形 有節奏的

▶A rhythmic sound has a regular movement that is repeated.
韻律的聲音有固定重複的特質。

rid·i·cule [ˋrɪdɪkjul]
🔈 *Track 6152*

名 嘲笑 動 嘲笑

▶名 To say something this ignorant is basically like inviting ridicule.
說出這麼無知的話，簡直就是在邀請別人來嘲笑你。

▶動 He ridiculed his sister's unfortunate outfit choices.
他嘲笑了他妹妹選的衣服難看。

rig·or·ous [ˋrɪgərəs]
🔈 *Track 6153*

形 嚴格的

▶The scientists are making a rigorous study of the rare plants in the area.
科學家們正在對該地的稀有植物進行縝密的研究。

ri·ot [ˈraɪət]　🔊 Track 6154

名 暴動 動 騷動、放縱

▶名 The demonstration soon went out of control and became a riot. 根據報導，示威遊行很快失控，變成了一場暴動。

▶動 It is reported that a mob（一群暴民）was rioting against the government yesterday.
根據報導，昨天有一群暴民鬧事並反對政府。

ri·te [raɪt]　🔊 Track 6155

名 儀式、典禮

▶Will you tell me how much you know about the religious rite?
能請告訴我你對這一個宗教儀式瞭解多少嗎？

文法字詞解析
funeral rites 即指「喪禮的儀式」。

rit·u·al [ˈrɪtʃʊəl]　🔊 Track 6156

名 （宗教）儀式 形 儀式的 同 ceremony 儀式

▶名 Would you like to attend my ritual of inauguration（就職）next week?
你願意來參加我下星期的就職典禮嗎？

▶形 Having some water before going to sleep is a ritual habit for him.
睡前喝點水是他每天必經的儀式。

ri·val·ry [ˈraɪvəlrɪ]　🔊 Track 6157

名 競爭

▶The rivalry among business firms is intense now.
現在公司間的競爭非常激烈。

ro·tate [roˈtet]　🔊 Track 6158

動 旋轉

▶How about rotating watches? Then we'll be less tired.
我們輪流看守如何？這樣比較不累。

ro·ta·tion [roˈteʃən]　🔊 Track 6159

名 旋轉

▶The sun appears to rise and set because of the earth's rotation.
因為地球自轉，才會看起來日昇日落的現象。

roy·al·ty [ˈrɔɪəltɪ]　🔊 Track 6160

名 貴族、王權 同 commission 職權

▶He claimed that his ancestors were royalty.
他聲稱他是皇室的後裔。

ru·by [ˈrubɪ]　🔊 Track 6161

名 紅寶石 形 紅寶石色的

▶名 Will you tell me which attracts you more, rubies or emeralds（綠寶石）？
你能告訴我紅寶石和綠寶石兩者你比較喜歡哪個嗎？

▶形 Can I have some more ruby wine? It tastes quite good.
我可以再喝一些深紅色葡萄酒嗎？它的味道相當不錯。

文法字詞解析
第一個例句中用到了「S + V + IO + DO」的句型，會使用這類句型的動詞通常是像 tell 這樣的授與動詞，而句中的名詞子句「which attracts you more」當作直接受詞，me 是間接受詞。

Level 1
Level 2
Level 3
Level 4
Level 5
Level 6

突破瓶頸7000單字
精進自我、聽說讀寫通——

[Ss]

safe·guard [ˈsefˌgɑrd] ◀⟨ *Track 6162*
名 保護者、警衛 動 保護
▶名 It is reported that the new law constitutes a safeguard against the abuse of government power.
根據報導，新法律可以防止濫用政府權力。
▶動 This agreement will safeguard the newspapers from government interference.
這一協議將保護報社不受政府干涉。

sa·loon [səˈlun] ◀⟨ *Track 6163*
名 酒店、酒吧
▶He left the saloons of New York for the green glades （林間空地） of the country.
他離開了紐約的歡樂酒店，來到鄉村綠色的林間空地。

sal·va·tion [sælˈveʃən] ◀⟨ *Track 6164*
名 救助、拯救
▶The army were viewed as salvation by the hostages.
軍隊被人質視為是他們的救星。

sanc·tion [ˈsæŋkʃən] ◀⟨ *Track 6165*
名 批准、認可 動 批准、認可 同 permit 准許
▶名 It seems that the book was translated without the sanction of the author.
這本書好像未經作者許可就翻譯了。
▶動 His old-fashioned parents did not sanction his second marriage. 他老派的父母不認可他的第二次婚姻。

sanc·tu·ar·y [ˈsæŋktʃuˌɛrɪ] ◀⟨ *Track 6166*
名 聖所、聖堂、庇護所 同 refuge 庇護所
▶The found their sanctuary on the island.
他們在這個島上找到了他們的避難所。

sane [sen] ◀⟨ *Track 6167*
形 神智穩健的
▶After being tortured for months, he was no longer sane.
被凌虐了好幾個月後，他的精神狀態已經不正常了。

文法字詞解析
與 sane 相反的「神智不清的」則為 insane。

san·i·ta·tion [ˌsænəˈteʃən] ◀⟨ *Track 6168*
名 公共衛生
▶Sanitation is the major concern when it comes to infrastructure. 衛生是基礎建設最重要的考量。

sce·nic [ˈsinɪk] ◀⟨ *Track 6169*
形 舞臺的、佈景的
▶It is said that there is a scenic route across the Alps.
據說有一條風景優美的路穿越阿爾卑斯山。

scope [skop]
🔈 *Track 6170*

名 範圍、領域 同 range 範圍

▶I'm afraid your question is beyond the scope of my understanding.
恐怕你所問的問題已超出了我的理解範圍。

script [skrɪpt]
🔈 *Track 6171*

名 原稿、劇本 動 編寫

▶名 The actress browsed through the script and decided to take the role. 女演員看過劇本之後就決定接下這個角色。

▶動 What do you think about scripting this novel in to a TV show? 你覺得把這部小說改編成電視劇本怎麼樣？

sec·tor [ˈsɛktɚ]
🔈 *Track 6172*

名 扇形

▶There are several sectors in the building that we are not allowed to enter. 這棟大樓有幾區我們不被允許進入。

se·duce [sɪˈdjus]
🔈 *Track 6173*

動 引誘、慫恿 同 tempt 引誘

▶She is trying to seduce him to bed. 她試著引誘他到床上。

se·lec·tive [səˈlɛktɪv]
🔈 *Track 6174*

形 有選擇性的

▶She is selective in people she talk to.
她只選擇性地和某些人說話。

sem·i·nar [ˈsɛmənɑr]
🔈 *Track 6175*

名 研討會、講習會

▶I'm afraid that I will not be able to attend the seminar.
我恐怕將無法參加這次的研討會。

sen·a·tor [ˈsɛnətɚ]
🔈 *Track 6176*

名 參議員、上議員

▶It is said that there are three senators who voted against the bill. 據說有三位參議員投票反對這一個議案。

sen·ti·men·tal [ˌsɛntəˈmɛntl̩]
🔈 *Track 6177*

形 受情緒影響的 同 emotional 情緒的

▶The sentimental consultant cried for her client.
多愁善感的顧問為她顧客的遭遇而哭。

se·quence [ˈsikwəns]
🔈 *Track 6178*

名 順序、連續 動 按順序排好 同 succession 連續

▶名 The test asked us to put the mixed historical facts in sequence.
這次考試要我們把混淆的歷史事件按順序排列。

▶動 You had better sequence the names right away. The manager needs the list later on.
你最好馬上按順序排列好名單。經理稍後會用到它。

文法字詞解析

sector 除了指面積上的「扇形區域」外，也可以指「區域、部門」，例如「政府部門」就可以稱為 government sector。這個部門的形狀不一定要是扇形的。

文法字詞解析

失憶時若只失去某一部份的記憶，其他記憶則維持完好，可稱為 selective memory loss（選擇性記憶喪失）。

Level 1
Level 2
Level 3
Level 4
Level 5
Level 6

突破瓶頸7000單字　精進自我、聽說讀寫通

se·rene [səˋrin]　🔊 *Track 6179*

形 寧靜的、安祥的　反 furious 狂暴的
▶The story took place on a serene summer night.
故事發生在一個寧靜的夏夜。

se·ren·i·ty [səˋrɛnətɪ]　🔊 *Track 6180*

名 晴朗、和煦、平靜　同 peace 平靜
▶You can obtain inner serenity by meditation.
你可以透過冥想找到內心寧靜。

serv·ing [ˋsɝvɪŋ]　🔊 *Track 6181*

名 服務、服侍、侍候
▶You had better let the hot pie cool off a little before serving.
你最好等熱騰騰的派涼了一些再端上桌。

ses·sion [ˋsɛʃən]　🔊 *Track 6182*

名 開庭、會議　同 conference 會議
▶Do you mind telling me when the court will be in session?
能麻煩您告訴我法庭何時開庭嗎？

文法字詞解析
除了「會議」、「法庭」等這類比較正式的場合外，其實一些比較沒那麼正式，但也是「一段固定的時間」的事情也可以用上 session 這個字。像是「一堂課的時間」可以稱為「a class session」，「一場遊戲」也可以稱為「a gaming session」。

set·back [ˋsɛtˌbæk]　🔊 *Track 6183*

名 逆流、逆轉、逆行
▶What happened just now was a huge setback to the plan.
剛剛發生的事情對於這個計畫造成很大的麻煩。

sew·er [ˋsjuɚ]　🔊 *Track 6184*

名 縫製者
▶She was the best sewer in the factory.
她是這間工廠最好的縫紉工。

shed [ʃɛd]　🔊 *Track 6185*

動 流出、發射出
▶She shed many tears over the loss of her beloved puppy.
她因失去了心愛的小狗而流了不少淚。

文法字詞解析
shed 的動詞變化：shed, shed, shed

sheer [ʃɪr]　🔊 *Track 6186*

形 垂直的、絕對的　副 完全地　動 急轉彎
▶形 The hacker broke into the municipal system out of sheer menace.
駭客基於惡意，侵入市政府系統。
▶副 The mountain rises sheer from the plain.
那座山陡峭地矗立在平原上。
▶動 The boat came close to the rocks and then sheered away.
據說那艘船靠近了礁石，然後緊接著轉向行駛。

shil·ling [ˋʃɪlɪŋ]　🔊 *Track 6187*

名 （英國幣名）先令
▶The beggar was overjoyed（欣喜若狂的）when I gave him a shilling.
當我給這個乞丐一先令時，他喜出望外。

shop·lift [`ʃɑp‚lɪft`]
◀ Track 6188

動 逛商店時行竊 同 pirate 掠奪

▶The boy was caught shoplifting.
　那個男孩在商店順手牽羊被逮到了。

shrewd [ʃrud]
◀ Track 6189

形 敏捷的、精明的

▶The man made a shrewd investment.
　這人做了一項精明的投資。

shun [ʃʌn]
◀ Track 6190

動 避開、躲避

▶The children shunned the little girl because of her ugly face.
　那些孩子們因為那個小女孩長得很醜而避開她。

siege [sidʒ]
◀ Track 6191

名 包圍、圍攻 同 surround 包圍

▶Close to one million people died as the result of the siege.
　此次圍攻造成了近百萬人死亡。

sig·ni·fy [`sɪgnə‚faɪ`]
◀ Track 6192

動 表示

▶Would you please tell me what these marks signify?
　你能告訴我這些符號代表什麼意思嗎？

sil·i·con [`sɪlɪkən`]
◀ Track 6193

名 矽

▶The Silicon Valley has become a new economic model because of its advanced science and technology.
　矽谷因先進的科技成為了一種新的經濟模式。

sim·plic·i·ty [sɪm`plɪsətɪ`]
◀ Track 6194

名 簡單、單純

▶The beauty of the plan lies in its simplicity.
　此計畫的妙處正在於它的簡潔明瞭。

sim·pli·fy [`sɪmplə‚faɪ`]
◀ Track 6195

動 使……簡易、使……單純 反 complicate 使複雜

▶The simplified tax system is easier for me to understand.
　簡化後的計稅系統對我來說比較易懂。

si·mul·ta·ne·ous [‚saɪml`tenɪəs`]
◀ Track 6196

形 同時發生的

▶My dream is to become a simultaneous interpreter in the future. What about yours?
　我的夢想是將來成為一名同步口譯員。你的夢想呢？

skep·ti·cal [`skɛptɪkl̩`]
◀ Track 6197

形 懷疑的

▶It is no wonder that many were skeptical about this solution.
　難怪許多人對這一個解決辦法表示懷疑。

文法字詞解析

在商店行竊者稱為 shoplifter。

萬用延伸句型

skeptical of sth. 對（某事）抱持懷疑態度

例如：I'm very skeptical of what he told us. I don't think he's telling the truth.
對於他所說的話，我非常懷疑。我覺得他沒說實話。

Level 1
Level 2
Level 3
Level 4
Level 5
Level 6

精進自我、聽說讀寫通

突破瓶頸7000單字

skim [skɪm]
🔊 *Track 6198*

動 掠去、去除 名 脫脂乳品

▶動 It took me a few seconds to skim the book.
我花了幾秒把這本書瀏覽了一遍。

▶名 When I drink milk, I like it skim.
我喝牛奶時喜歡喝脫脂的。

slang [slæŋ]
🔊 *Track 6199*

名 俚語 動 謾罵、說俚語

▶名 The online dictionary specifies the slangs among young people. 這個線上字典專門收錄年輕人用的俚語。

▶動 He slanged his friend with all the dirty words he knew.
他用他所知的所有髒話罵他朋友。

slash [slæʃ]
🔊 *Track 6200*

名 刀痕、裂縫 動 亂砍、鞭打 同 cut 砍

▶名 The knife made a slash across his leg.
刀在他的腿上劃出了一道傷口。

▶動 You had better not slash your horse in that cruel way.
你最好不要那麼殘忍地鞭打你的馬。

文法字詞解析
那種常有人拿著刀到處砍人的「殺人魔電影」就可以稱為 slasher film。

slav·er·y [ˈslevərɪ]
🔊 *Track 6201*

名 奴隸制度 反 liberty 自由

▶It was Abraham Lincoln who abolished slavery in the United States.
是亞伯拉罕・林肯廢除了美國的奴隸制度。

slot [slɑt]
🔊 *Track 6202*

名 狹槽、職位 動 在……開一狹槽

▶名 He replaced me in the game and took my slot.
他在此遊戲中取代我的位置。

▶動 I'll slot you for the nine a.m. appointment.
我會把你的約診安排在九點。

slum [slʌm]
🔊 *Track 6203*

名 貧民區 動 進入貧民區

▶名 The kid escaped from the slum, trying to overturn his fate.
小孩逃出貧民窟，想要改變命運。

▶動 We were forced to slum it for a few days because our house was flooded.
因為我們家淹水了，我們不得不過幾天苦日子。

文法字詞解析
要說「在貧民窟中」可以直接使用 slum 的複數，說「in the slums」。

smack [smæk]
🔊 *Track 6204*

動 拍擊、甩打 同 slap 拍擊

▶You'd better put that down, otherwise I'll smack you.
你最好把它放下來，不然我就會揍你。

small·pox [ˈsmɔl‚pɑks]
🔊 *Track 6205*

名 天花

▶Smallpox has been brought under control by the use of vaccines（疫苗）. 透過接種疫苗，使得天花已得到控制。

smoth·er [ˈsmʌðɚ]
Track 6206

動 使窒息、掩飾 名 使窒息之物

▶動 You had better not put that cloth over the baby's face, or you'll smother him! 你最好不要把那塊布蓋在嬰兒的臉上，否則你會害他窒息的！

▶名 The air has been polluted by the smother of industrial smog. 空氣已經被令人窒息的工業煙霧污染了。

smug·gle [ˈsmʌgl̩]
Track 6207

動 走私

▶The smuggled cocaine was confiscated by the custom. 走私的古柯鹼被海關沒收。

文法字詞解析
走私犯稱為 smuggler。

snare [snɛr]
Track 6208

名 陷阱、羅網 動 誘惑、捕捉

▶名 He has fallen into a snare laid by his enemy. 他已經落入了敵人所設的圈套。

▶動 The rabbit was snared by the hunter. 那隻兔子被獵人捕住了。

sneak·y [ˈsnikɪ]
Track 6209

形 鬼鬼祟祟的

▶The sneaky girl was disliked by the rest of the class. 全班都不喜歡這個賊頭賊腦的女學生。

sneer [snɪr]
Track 6210

名 冷笑 動 嘲笑地說

▶名 The man let out a sneer and took out a gun. 那個男人冷笑一聲拔出槍。

▶動 "You think you're so smart," sneered the woman. 「你以為你很聰明，」那個女子嘲諷地說道。

萬用延伸句型
spirits soar 心情變得極好
例如：Our spirits soared when we heard the good news.
聽到好消息時，我們的心情立刻都變得很好。

soar [sor]
Track 6211

動 上升、往上飛

▶The hot-air balloon soared into the sky. 那個熱汽球飛上了天空。

so·cia·ble [ˈsoʃəbl̩]
Track 6212

形 愛交際的、社交的

▶Gina's sociable character made her the focus of the conversation. 吉娜善於社交的個性，使她成為對話的焦點。

so·cial·ism [ˈsoʃəlɪzəm]
Track 6213

名 社會主義

▶My father doesn't believe in socialism. What about yours? 我爸爸不信奉社會主義，你爸爸呢？

so·cial·ist [ˈsoʃəlɪst]
Track 6214

名 社會主義者

▶It's obvious that most of the people in this country are socialists. 這個國家大多數的人顯然都是社會主義者。

Level 1
Level 2
Level 3
Level 4
Level 5
Level 6

突破瓶頸7000單字

精進自我、聽說讀寫通

so·cial·ize [ˋsoʃəlˌɪaɪz]
◀ *Track 6215*

動 使社會化 **同** civilize 使文明、使開化
▶A good salesperson needs to learn how to socialize with his or her customers.
好的業務員要學習如何和客戶交際。

文法字詞解析
除了「使社會化」外，socialize 更含有「與人社交」、「交際」的意思。

so·ci·ol·o·gy [ˌsoʃɪˋɑlədʒɪ]
◀ *Track 6216*

名 社會學
▶The number of sociology majors has been decreasing.
主修社會學的學生一直在減少。

so·di·um [ˋsodɪəm]
◀ *Track 6217*

名 鈉
▶The reason you should avoid high-sodium foods is that they may raise blood pressure.
你應該避免食用鈉含量高的食物，因為這些食物可能會使血壓升高。

sol·i·dar·i·ty [ˌsɑləˋdærətɪ]
◀ *Track 6218*

名 團結、休戚相關
▶The people showed solidarity for the unfortunate victims that lost their homes in the flood.
那些人們對在水災中失去家園的受害者表現出了一致同情的態度。

sol·i·tude [ˋsɑləˌtjud]
◀ *Track 6219*

名 獨處、獨居
▶He is searching for a place where he can live in solitude.
他正在尋找一個可以過隱居生活的地方。

soothe [suð]
◀ *Track 6220*

動 安慰、撫慰 **同** comfort 安慰
▶Why aren't you soothing the crying child?
為什麼你不去哄哄那個在哭的孩子呢？

so·phis·ti·cat·ed [səˋfɪstɪˌketɪd]
◀ *Track 6221*

形 世故的
▶Kids who learn to play Go appear more supplicated than their peers.
學習圍棋的小孩比同齡的孩子更成熟一點。

sov·er·eign·ty [ˋsɑvrɪntɪ]
◀ *Track 6222*

名 主權
▶The treaty violated and trampled on the sovereignty of the country. 這個條約是對該國主權的侵犯和踐踏。

spa·cious [ˋspeʃəs]
◀ *Track 6223*

形 寬敞的、寬廣的
▶The hotel is not only spacious but also comfortable.
這間旅館不但寬敞而且還很舒適。

文法字詞解析
這個字加上名詞字尾「-ness」就變成「spaciousness（寬敞、寬廣）」。

span [spæn]
Track 6224

名 跨距 動 橫跨、展延
- ▶名 Over a short span of three years, we've achieved a surprising success.
  在短短三年時間裡，我們已經取得了驚人的成就。
- ▶動 His research in cancer that spanned 5 years has made considerable headway.
  他對癌症持續五年的研究取得了重大進展。

spe·cial·ize [ˈspɛʃəˌlaɪz]
Track 6225

動 專長於
- ▶Tina specialize in computer science. 提娜專長在電腦科學。

spe·cial·ty [ˈspɛʃəltɪ]
Track 6226

名 專門職業、本行
- ▶What's the specialty today? 今天的特餐是什麼？

spec·i·fy [ˈspɛsəˌfaɪ]
Track 6227

動 詳述、詳載
- ▶Would you please specify when you will be at home tomorrow?
  請你確切說明你明天什麼時候會在家好嗎？

spec·tac·u·lar [spɛkˈtækjələ]
Track 6228

名 大場面 形 可觀的 同 dramatic 引人注目的
- ▶名 This movie is a real spectacular.
  這部電影真是一部很棒的影片。
- ▶形 The new play was a spectacular success.
  這部新劇獲得了巨大的成功。

spec·trum [ˈspɛktrəm]
Track 6229

名 光譜
- ▶There's a wide spectrum of opinions on this problem.
  針對這個問題的說法眾說紛紜，莫衷一是。

spec·u·late [ˈspɛkjəˌlet]
Track 6230

動 沉思；預測
- ▶The investors speculated a bear market this year.
  這位投資者預測今年市場會不景氣。

sphere [sfɪr]
Track 6231

名 球、天體
- ▶There are nine spheres in the solar system.
  在太陽系裡有九大行星。

spike [spaɪk]
Track 6232

名 長釘、釘尖 動 以尖釘刺、把烈酒攪入……
- ▶名 They forced the prisoner to sit on a chair with spikes.
  他們逼迫那名囚犯坐在上有長釘的椅子上。
- ▶動 The boys spiked the drinks, so everyone at the party got drunk.
  男孩們把烈酒攪入飲料，所以宴會中的每個人都喝醉了。

文法字詞解析
光譜的一端到另一端之間是兩個極端，因此一些其他的事情（不只是「光」）也可以使用 spectrum 來測量。舉例來說，自閉症的程度就有一個 autism spectrum，由在光譜上的位置來判斷一個人的症狀嚴重程度。

Level 1
Level 2
Level 3
Level 4
Level 5
Level 6

突破瓶頸7000單字 精進自我、聽說讀寫通

spi·ral [ˈspaɪrəl] ◀≋ *Track 6233*
名 螺旋 動 急遽上升或下降 形 螺旋的 同 twist 旋轉
▶名 The bubbles drifted in an upward spiral.
泡泡以螺旋狀向上漂移。
▶動 Their profits have begun to spiral downwards.
他們的利潤開始急遽地下降。
▶形 The snail's shell is spiral in form.
蝸牛的殼是螺旋形的。

spire [spaɪr] ◀≋ *Track 6234*
名 尖塔、尖頂 動 螺旋形上升、發芽
▶名 The church spires could be seen from the distance.
我們可以看到遠處教堂的尖塔。
▶動 It's necessary for us to sow the seeds before they spire.
我們必須在種子發芽前播種。

spokes·per·son/ spokes·man/spokes·wom·an ◀≋ *Track 6235*
[ˈspoksˌpɝsn̩]/[ˈspoksmən]/[ˈspoksˌwʊmən]
名 發言人
▶It is reported that the IOC spokesperson will investigate the incident.
根據報導，國際奧委會發言人將對此事展開調查。

spon·sor [ˈspɑnsɚ] ◀≋ *Track 6236*
名 贊助者 動 贊助、資助
▶名 I am afraid that if there are not enough sponsors, we have to give up this plan.
恐怕如果沒有足夠的贊助者，我們就得放棄這個計劃。
▶動 It is a pity that he doesn't have enough money to sponsor the project.
遺憾的是，他沒有足夠的錢來支持這項計畫。

spon·ta·ne·ous [spɑnˈtenɪəs] ◀≋ *Track 6237*
形 同時發生的
▶The spontaneous reaction of the kid amused his parents.
小孩自然的反應讓父母覺得好笑。

文法字詞解析
也可拿來形容人個性非常隨興，想到什麼就做什麼。

spouse [spaʊz] ◀≋ *Track 6238*
名 配偶、夫妻 同 mate 配偶
▶I don't think that you should compare your spouse with other people. 我認為你不應該拿你的伴侶與他人做比較。

sprawl [sprɔl] ◀≋ *Track 6239*
名 / 動 任意伸展
▶名 He is still lying on the bed in a sprawl.
他還歪歪斜斜地癱在床上。
▶動 The boy sprawled all over the sofa.
那個男孩癱在沙發上。

squad [skwɑd]
◀╴ Track 6240

名 小隊、班

▶My boyfriend is the squad leader in the army.
我的男朋友在軍中當班長。

文法字詞解析
除了真的有組織的那種小隊、小組外，「一群朋友」在口語中也可以稱為 squad。

squash [skwɑʃ]
◀╴ Track 6241

名 壓擠 動 壓擠

▶名 The squash of the glass bottle surprised the customer.
玻璃瓶摔碎的聲音嚇到顧客。

▶動 Don't sit on my hat, or you will squash it!
別坐在我的帽子上，否則你會把它壓扁的！

sta·bil·i·ty [ste`bɪlətɪ]
◀╴ Track 6242

名 穩定、穩固

▶The government has taken a measure to maintain the stability of prices. 政府已採取措施以確保物價穩定。

sta·bi·lize [`stebl͵aɪz]
◀╴ Track 6243

動 保持安定、使穩定

▶Do you know how to stabilize the price of vegetables?
你知道該如何穩定蔬菜的價格嗎？

stalk [stɔk]
◀╴ Track 6244

名 軸、莖 動 蔓延、追蹤

▶名 He poured wine into the glass with a tall stalk.
他把酒倒到那個高腳玻璃杯裡了。

▶動 He stalked her all the way home.
他一路跟蹤了她回家。

文法字詞解析
在 stalk 後面加上意為「……者」的字尾「-er」，則變成了 stalker，是「跟蹤狂」的意思。

stam·mer [`stæmɚ]
◀╴ Track 6245

名 口吃 動 結結巴巴地說

▶名 The boy is often laughed at by his classmates because of his stammer. 這個小男孩常常因為結巴而被同學嘲笑。

▶動 Gary stammered when he was asked about his occupation.
蓋瑞講到自己的職業就結結巴巴。

sta·ple [`stepl̩]
◀╴ Track 6246

名 釘書針、主要產物 動 用釘書針釘住、分類、選擇
同 attach 貼上

▶名 That song is a staple that's performed in every one of her concerts. 這首歌在她每場演唱會都會表演，已經變成固定的形式了。

▶動 The letter was stapled to the other documents in the file.
那封信與檔案夾裡的其他文件釘在一起了。

sta·pler [`steplɚ]
◀╴ Track 6247

名 釘書機

▶Would you please lend me your stapler? Mine doesn't work.
能借我用一下你的釘書機嗎？我的壞了。

Level 1

Level 2

Level 3

Level 4

Level 5

Level 6

精進自我、聽說讀寫通

突破瓶頸7000單字

starch [stɑrtʃ] ◀€ *Track 6248*

名 澱粉 動 上漿

▶名 Protein and starch are the major ingredients of the dish.
蛋白質和澱粉是這道菜的主要原料。

▶動 He wore a starched cap to the party.
他戴了一頂上漿上得筆挺的帽子去派對。

star·va·tion [stɑrˋveʃən] ◀€ *Track 6249*

名 饑餓、餓死 同 famine 饑餓

▶There are still many people living on the verge（邊緣）of starvation nowadays.
如今仍然有很多人在饑餓的邊緣掙扎。

sta·tion·ar·y [ˋsteʃənˏɛrɪ] ◀€ *Track 6250*

形 不動的

▶We were stationary for a while on the street because of the traffic. 我們因為塞車，在路上卡了一會。

sta·tion·er·y [ˋsteʃənˏɛrɪ] ◀€ *Track 6251*

名 文具

▶Excuse me, can you tell me where to find a stationery store?
不好意思，能請您告訴我哪裡有文具店嗎？

stat·ure [ˋstætʃə] ◀€ *Track 6252*

名 身高、身材

▶It is his red hair and short stature that made him easy to recognize.
正是他的一頭紅髮與五短的身材讓人一眼就能認出他來。

steam·er [ˋstimə] ◀€ *Track 6253*

名 汽船、輪船

▶There is a steamer sailing into the harbor.
有一艘汽船正開進港口。

stim·u·late [ˋstɪmjəˏlet] ◀€ *Track 6254*

動 刺激、激勵 同 motivate 刺激

▶The government stimulated economic growth by encouraging consumption.
政府用鼓勵消費的方式刺激經濟發展。

stim·u·la·tion [ˏstɪmjəˋleʃən] ◀€ *Track 6255*

名 刺激、興奮

▶No amount of stimulation could make him show any reaction.
無論怎樣刺激他，他還是一點反應也沒有。

stim·u·lus [ˋstɪmjələs] ◀€ *Track 6256*

名 刺激、激勵

▶Books with a different worldviews are a stimulus to endless imagination.
有不同世界觀的書能夠刺激無垠的想像力。

萬用延伸句型

save sb. from starvation 拯救（某人）免於餓死
例如：The kind lady saved the stray dog from starvation.
那位善良的太太拯救了那隻流浪狗，讓牠免於餓死。

萬用延伸句型

No amount of... can...
無論多少……都沒辦法……

stock [stɑk] ◀€ *Track 6257*
名 庫存 動 庫存、進貨
▶名 It is said that the store always takes stock on Monday.
據說那家商店每逢星期一都進行盤點。
▶動 That store stocks all types of fur coats.
那家商店供應各種毛皮大衣。

stran·gle [ˋstræŋgl̩] ◀€ *Track 6258*
動 勒死、絞死
▶The woman was strangled with her own scarf.
這個女士被她自己的圍巾勒斃。

stra·te·gic [strəˋtidʒɪk] ◀€ *Track 6259*
形 戰略的
▶We made a strategic withdrawal（撤退）so that we could build up our forces for another attack.
我們做了一次戰略性撤退，以便我們能積蓄力量再次進攻。

stunt [stʌnt] ◀€ *Track 6260*
名 特技、表演 動 阻礙 同 performance 表演
▶名 The stunt was supposed to draw attention to global warming.
此驚人之舉應是為了引起人們對全球氣候暖化問題的關注。
▶動 Inadequate food could stunt a child's development.
食物不足可能會影響到兒童的發育。

sub·jec·tive [səbˋdʒɛktɪv] ◀€ *Track 6261*
形 主觀的 同 internal 內心的、固有的
▶I found the cover ugly, but that's totally my subjective opinion.
我覺得那個封面很醜，但那也完全是我的主觀意見。

sub·or·di·nate [səˋbɔrdṇɪt] ◀€ *Track 6262*
名 附屬物 形 從屬的、下級的 同 secondary 從屬的
▶名 It seems that he treats his subordinates very kindly.
他似乎對待他的屬下非常和藹可親。
▶形 All the other issues are subordinate to this one.
所有其他的問題都沒有這一個問題這麼重要。

sub·scribe [səbˋskraɪb] ◀€ *Track 6263*
動 捐助、訂閱、簽署 同 contribute 捐助
▶To subscribe the service, you only have to submit application online. 要訂閱這項服務，你只需要在網路上提交申請就行了。

sub·scrip·tion [səbˋskrɪpʃən] ◀€ *Track 6264*
名 訂閱、簽署、捐款
▶It is said that the subscription of this magazine is very popular.
據說這本雜誌的訂閱相當受歡迎。

sub·se·quent [ˋsʌbsɪˎkwɛnt] ◀€ *Track 6265*
形 伴隨發生的
▶Subsequent events confirmed his suspicions.
後來發生的事實顯示他的懷疑是有道理的。

萬用延伸句型
pull a stunt 惡作劇、開玩笑
例 如：He pulled the same stunt on his teachers every year.
他每年都用同樣的惡作劇開老師玩笑。

Level 1
Level 2
Level 3
Level 4
Level 5

Level 6
精進自我、聽說讀寫通
突破瓶頸7000單字

sub·sti·tu·tion [ˌsʌbstəˈtjuʃən] 🔊 *Track 6266*
名 代理、代替 同 relief 接替
▶They are looking for a kind of medicine to be used as its substitution. 他們正在找尋一種能代替該藥品的藥品。

sub·tle [ˈsʌtl] 🔊 *Track 6267*
形 微妙的 同 delicate 微妙的
▶The subtle difference between two products was detected by the scanner. 掃瞄器可以偵測到這兩項產品的細微差別。

sub·ur·ban [səˈbɝbən] 🔊 *Track 6268*
形 郊外的、市郊的
▶There are a lot of good things about suburban life.
在郊區生活有許多優點。

suc·ces·sion [səkˈsɛʃən] 🔊 *Track 6269*
名 連續
▶She has been awarded the first prize four years in succession.
她已連續四年獲得第一名。

suc·ces·sive [səkˈsɛsɪv] 🔊 *Track 6270*
形 連續的、繼續的 同 continuous 繼續的
▶It is a pleasure that we have had three successive years of good harvest.
我們已連續三年獲得豐收，這真令人高興。

suc·ces·sor [səkˈsɛsɚ] 🔊 *Track 6271*
名 後繼者、繼承人 同 substitute 代替者
▶It is known that his son is his only successor.
大家都知道他兒子是他唯一的繼任人。

suf·fo·cate [ˈsʌfəˌket] 🔊 *Track 6272*
動 使窒息 同 choke 使窒息
▶It's suffocating in here. Do you mind if I open a few windows?
我覺得這裡很悶。你介意我打開幾扇窗戶嗎？

suite [swit] 🔊 *Track 6273*
名 隨員、套房
▶Kevin reserved a suite for his business trip.
凱文訂了出差時要住的套房。

su·perb [suˈpɝb] 🔊 *Track 6274*
形 極好的、超群的 同 excellent 出色的
▶From the summit there is a superb panorama（全景）of the Alps. 從山頂俯瞰，阿爾卑斯山壯麗的景色盡收眼底。

su·pe·ri·or·i·ty [səˌpɪriˈɔrətɪ] 🔊 *Track 6275*
名 優越、卓越
▶Your army has numerical（數字的）superiority over theirs.
與他們相比你們的軍隊佔有人數的優勢。

文法字詞解析
我們中文所說的「微妙的」含有「有點奇怪」的意思，但 subtle 沒有這個層面的意思，單純指事物「很難察覺」、「隱晦」。舉例來說，如果化妝化得很淡就可以說這妝很 subtle。

萬用延伸句型
It is a pleasure that... 很令人高興地……

文法字詞解析
特別注意這個單字的唸法，它雖然和常見的 suit 長得很像，但唸法卻比較接近 sweet 喔。聽著音檔唸唸看吧！

su·per·son·ic [ˌsupɚˈsɑnɪk] 🔊 *Track 6276*

形 超音波的、超音速的

▶Developing the supersonic jet is quite an accomplishment.
開發超音速噴射機是一項了不起的成就。

su·per·sti·tious [ˌsupɚˈstɪʃəs] 🔊 *Track 6277*

形 迷信的

▶The superstitious ideas were dismissed by the scientist.
這個迷信的想法被科學家秉棄。

su·per·vi·sion [ˌsupɚˈvɪʒən] 🔊 *Track 6278*

名 監督、管理 同 leadership 領導

▶You are not supposed to leave children to play without supervision.
你不應該讓孩子在無人照顧的情況下玩耍。

sup·ple·ment 🔊 *Track 6279*
[ˈsʌpləmənt]/[ˈsʌpləˌmɛnt]

名 副刊、補充 動 補充、增加

▶名 You'd better buy some diet supplements for your daughter.
你最好給你女兒買點飲食補品。

▶動 He had to get a part-time job to supplement the family income.
他不得不找個兼差工作以增加家庭收入。

sur·pass [sɚˈpæs] 🔊 *Track 6280*

動 超過、超越 同 exceed 超過

▶No matter what difficulties are in front of you, you should find the way to surpass them.
無論你們遇到什麼樣的困難，你們都應該想辦法克服它。

sur·plus [ˈsɚplʌs] 🔊 *Track 6281*

名 過剩、盈餘 形 過剩的、過多的 同 extra 額外的

▶名 The food surplus became an environmental issue.
多餘的食物已經成為環保問題。

▶形 We must work off the surplus goods as soon as possible.
我們必須儘快把多餘的貨物處理掉。

sus·pense [səˈspɛns] 🔊 *Track 6282*

名 懸而未決、擔心 同 concern 擔心、掛念

▶Everyone is waiting in great suspense for the doctor's diagnosis.
大家都焦急萬分地等著醫生做出診斷。

sus·pen·sion [səˈspɛnʃən] 🔊 *Track 6283*

名 暫停、懸掛

▶It is dangerous for the toddler to cross the suspension bridge alone.
那個小孩子一個人過吊橋會很危險的。

Level **1**

Level **2**

Level **3**

Level **4**

Level **5**

Level **6**

突破瓶頸7000單字 精進自我、聽說讀寫通

萬用延伸句型

keep sb. in suspense 讓（某人）擔心、不告訴（某人）事情發展
例 如：Stop keeping me in suspense. Tell me what happened next in the story!
別賣關子了，快告訴我故事中接下來發生了什麼事！

swap [swɑp]
◀‿ *Track 6284*

名 交換 動 交換 同 exchange 交換

▶名 Since you have what I want and I have what you like, would you do a swap with me? 既然你有我想要的東西，我有你喜歡的東西。那麼我們來交換好嗎？

▶動 I didn't like my drink so I swapped mine with his.
我不喜歡我的飲料，所以就把我的跟他的飲料交換了。

sym·bol·ic [sɪmˋbɑlɪk]
◀‿ *Track 6285*

形 象徵的

▶The symbolic icon of Nazi was recognized by many people.
很多人都知道象徵納粹的符號。

sym·bol·ize [ˋsɪmbəˌlaɪz]
◀‿ *Track 6286*

動 作為……象徵

▶Not everyone knows what the Olympic（奧運會的）rings symbolize. 不是每個人都明白奧運五環的象徵意義。

sym·me·try [ˋsɪmɪtrɪ]
◀‿ *Track 6287*

名 對稱、相稱 同 harmony 和諧

▶They hold that order and symmetry were important elements of beauty. 他們認為秩序和對稱是美的重要因素。

symp·tom [ˋsɪmptəm]
◀‿ *Track 6288*

名 症狀、徵兆

▶You have to tell me first when the symptoms began to appear.
你得先告訴我這種症狀是什麼時候開始的。

syn·o·nym [ˋsɪnəˌnɪm]
◀‿ *Track 6289*

名 同義字 反 antonym 反義字

▶Please don't mix up this pair of synonyms.
請別把這兩個同義詞混淆了。

syn·thet·ic [sɪnˋθɛtɪk]
◀‿ *Track 6290*

名 合成物 形 綜合性的、人造的 同 artificial 人造的

▶名 It is said that the type of synthetic sells very expensively.
據說那種合成纖維賣得非常貴。

▶形 The synthetic material was made into bottles and cups.
這種合成材料被用來做瓶子或杯子。

[Tt]

tact [tækt]
◀‿ *Track 6291*

名 圓滑 同 diplomacy 圓滑

▶Don't you think a minister of foreign affairs has to have tact?
難道你不認為作為一名外交部長，必須夠圓滑嗎？

文法字詞解析
相反地，「反義字」則是 antonym。

tac·tic(s) [ˋtæktɪk(s)]
🔊 *Track 6292*

名 戰術、策略

▶You'd better plan the tactics for the next few days' games so that we can prepare in advance.
你最好把今後幾天球賽的戰術都擬定好，以便我們可以提前做準備。

tar·iff [ˋtærɪf]
🔊 *Track 6293*

名 關稅、稅率 同 duty 稅

▶The import tariff has been increasing in the past few months.
進口關稅在過去幾個月一直增加。

te·di·ous [ˋtidɪəs]
🔊 *Track 6294*

形 沉悶的

▶His story is so tedious that I don't think anyone would like to listen to it again.
他的故事太冗長乏味了，所以我想沒有人會再願意聽了吧。

文法字詞解析
tedious 還可以加上副詞字尾「-ly」來修飾另一個形容詞，例如：tediously long 冗長的。

tem·per·a·ment [ˋtɛmprəmənt]
🔊 *Track 6295*

名 氣質、性情 同 character 性格

▶It is obvious that the two brothers differ markedly（明顯地）in temperament.
顯然這兩兄弟的氣質迥異。

tem·pest [ˋtɛmpɪst]
🔊 *Track 6296*

名 大風暴、暴風雨 同 storm 暴風雨

▶You'd better take in the sail because the tempest is approaching.
暴風雨要來了，你最好先將風帆放下。

ter·mi·nate [ˋtɝmənet]
🔊 *Track 6297*

動 終止、中斷 同 conclude 結束

▶They told me the next train terminates here.
他們告訴我這是下一班火車的終點站。

文法字詞解析
坐捷運坐到終點站時是不是常會聽到廣播說「terminal station」呢？
terminal和terminate是相關的字，意思是「終點的」，不過它也可以當作名詞，當名詞時除了「終點」之外，也可以作為機場的「航廈」。

tex·tile [ˋtɛkstaɪl]
🔊 *Track 6298*

名 織布 形 紡織成的 同 material 織物

▶名 The leading company in the textile industry will expand its business.
紡織工業的龍頭公司將會擴大事業。

▶形 I heard that til（胡麻）can be used as a textile material.
我聽說胡麻可做為紡織原料。

tex·ture [ˋtɛkstʃɚ]
🔊 *Track 6299*

名 質地、結構 動 使具有某種結構（特徵）同 structure 結構

▶名 Don't you know that each variety of melon has its individual flavor and texture?
你不知道每一種不同的瓜都有自己獨特的味道和質地嗎？

▶動 They textured the bowl with lines and dots.
他們使用線與點裝飾碗的表面。

Level 1

Level 2

Level 3

Level 4

Level 5

Level 6

突破瓶頸7000單字 精進自我、聽說讀寫通

the·at·ri·cal [θɪˋætrɪkl̩]
◀€ *Track 6300*

形 戲劇的
▶His theatrical antics（舉動）are kind of funny.
他戲劇化的表現還蠻好笑的。

theft [θɛft]
◀€ *Track 6301*

名 竊盜 同 steal 偷竊
▶The theft case was solved within a day.
偷竊案件在一天之內破案。

the·o·ret·i·cal [θiəˋrɛtɪkl̩]
◀€ *Track 6302*

形 理論上的
▶This professor is very theoretical and also very hard to understand. 這個教授很精通理論，而且說的話總是很難懂。

ther·a·pist [ˋθɛrəpɪst]
◀€ *Track 6303*

名 治療學家、物理治療師
▶You should talk to my friend, who is a therapist.
你應該和我的朋友談談，他是治療師。

文法字詞解析
therapist 除了物理方面的復健治療以外，也可以治療心理上的症狀，因此在美國找 therapist 談談是常見的事。

ther·a·py [ˋθɛrəpɪ]
◀€ *Track 6304*

名 療法、治療 同 treatment 治療
▶He receives speech therapy for his stutter.
他因為口吃而必須接受語言治療。

there·af·ter [ðɛrˋæftɚ]
◀€ *Track 6305*

副 此後、以後 同 afterward 以後
▶The meeting concluded last week, and the president signed the bill shortly thereafter.
會議於上星期結束，總統隨後立即簽署了這項議案。

there·by [ðɛrˋbaɪ]
◀€ *Track 6306*

副 藉以、因此
▶My brother hoped to travel abroad and thereby improve his English ability. 我哥哥希望藉由到國外旅行來加強英文能力。

ther·mom·e·ter [θəˋmɑmətɚ]
◀€ *Track 6307*

名 溫度計
▶The thermometer showed both the Celsius and Fahrenheit system. 溫度計顯示攝氏和華氏兩種標準。

thresh·old [ˋθrɛʃold]
◀€ *Track 6308*

名 門口、入口
▶I hope the treaty would be the threshold of lasting peace.
我希望這個條約將成為長久和平的開端。

thrift [θrɪft]
◀€ *Track 6309*

名 節約、節儉 同 economy 節約
▶It is not right to equate thrift with stinginess（吝嗇）.
把勤儉和吝嗇劃上等號是不對的。

thrift·y [ˈθrɪftɪ]
Track 6310

形 節儉的 同 economical 節約的
▶Mom is really a thirfty housekeeper, isn't she?
老媽真是個勤儉持家的人，不是嗎？

thrive [θraɪv]
Track 6311

動 繁茂
▶The crop can thrive even in harsh conditions.
這種作物在艱困環境下也能生存的很好。

throb [θrɑb]
Track 6312

名 脈搏、抽痛 動 悸動、跳動 同 beat 跳動
▶名 A throb of pain ran through my back.
一陣抽痛貫穿了我的背部。
▶動 His good looks made my heart throb.
他帥得讓我小鹿亂撞。

文法字詞解析
迷人得令人心臟抽痛的人物（如受歡迎的偶像等）即可稱為 heartthrob（通常是用來描述男性）。

toll [tol]
Track 6313

名 裝貨、費用、通行稅 動 徵收、繳費 同 fare 車費
▶名 It is the only bridge that everyone should pay a toll on when crossing.
這是唯一一座要收過路費的橋。
▶動 The officials decided to toll the road into this city.
這些官員決定要對進城的那條路收費。

top·ple [ˈtɑpl]
Track 6314

動 推倒、推翻 同 tumble 顛覆
▶It seems that the building is going to topple down.
那棟建築物似乎搖搖欲墜了。

萬用延伸句型
topple over 倒下
例如：My son's stack of blocks toppled down when I walked by.
我經過的時候，我兒子的積木堆倒下了。

tor·na·do [tɔrˈnedo]
Track 6315

名 龍捲風
▶The entire village was destroyed by the tornado.
整個村莊都被龍捲風摧毀了。

trait [tret]
Track 6316

名 特色、特性 同 characteristic 特性
▶Her personality traits made her the most popular worker in the office.
她的人格特質使她成為辦公室裡最受歡迎的員工。

tran·quil [ˈtræŋkwɪl]
Track 6317

形 安靜的、寧靜的 同 peaceful 寧靜的
▶I wish one day I could live a tranquil life in the countryside.
我希望有天能去鄉下過寧靜的生活。

tran·quil·iz·er [ˈtræŋkwɪˌlaɪzɚ]
Track 6318

名 鎮靜劑
▶Laughter is a tranquilizer with no side effects.
笑聲是一種沒有副作用的鎮靜劑。

Level 1
Level 2
Level 3
Level 4
Level 5
Level 6

突破瓶頸7000單字 精進自我、聽說讀寫通

trans·ac·tion [træn`sækʃən]
🔊 *Track 6319*

名 處理、辦理、交易 同 deal 交易

▶You are not supposed to lend yourself to such a transaction.
It is illegal. 你不應該參與這種交易。它是違法的。

tran·script [`træn͵skrɪpt]
🔊 *Track 6320*

名 抄本、副本

▶I am afraid that I can't vouch（擔保）for the correctness of
the transcript of proceeding.
恐怕我不能擔保訴訟的官方記錄是正確的。

trans·for·ma·tion
🔊 *Track 6321*

[͵trænsfɚ`meʃən]

名 變形、轉變

▶The transformation of the village into a city took decades.
這個小村莊經過幾十年變成大城市。

tran·sis·tor [træn`zɪstɚ]
🔊 *Track 6322*

名 電晶體

▶Many old men always carry about transistors with themselves.
好多老人家總是會隨身攜帶一台電晶體收音機。

tran·sit [`trænsɪt]
🔊 *Track 6323*

名 通過、過境 動 通過

▶名 It is quite clear that the damage was caused during transit.
很顯然這批貨的損壞是在運輸途中造成的。

▶動 This is an aircraft transiting the United States and Canada.
這是一架飛越美國和加拿大的飛機。

萬用延伸句型
It is quite clear that... 很明顯地⋯⋯

tran·si·tion [træn`zɪʃən]
🔊 *Track 6324*

名 轉移、變遷

▶The transition of her mood from good to bad went by unnoticed.
沒人注意到她的好心情轉變成壞心情。

trans·mis·sion [træns`mɪʃən]
🔊 *Track 6325*

名 傳達

▶The transmission of signals may be completed within
seconds. 訊息的傳遞可以在幾秒內就完成。

trans·mit [træns`mɪt]
🔊 *Track 6326*

動 寄送、傳播 同 forward 發送

▶Will you tell me why wood has a poor ability to transmit heat?
能請你告訴我為什麼木頭的導熱性很差嗎？

trans·plant
🔊 *Track 6327*

[`trænsplænt]/[træns`plænt]

名 移植手術 動 移植

▶名 It was the first time that the patient had received a heart
transplant. 這是該病人第一次接受心臟移植手術。

▶動 I have transplanted the flowers to the garden.
我把這些花移植到花園裡。

萬用延伸句型
It was the first time that...
是（某人）第一次⋯⋯

trau·ma [`trɔmə]
◀≒ Track 6328
名 外傷、損傷、心理創傷
▶Don't you think minor accidents may cause a lot of trauma?
你不覺得小小的事故就可能引發很大的創傷嗎？

文法字詞解析
讓人留下心理創傷的事情則可形容為
traumatic、traumatizing。

tread [trɛd]
◀≒ Track 6329
名 腳步 動 踩、踏、走 同 walk 走
▶名 The tread on the stairs could be heard from upstairs.
從樓上就可以聽到踏上樓梯的聲音。
▶動 He asked me not to tread on the crops.
他叫我不要踩到穀物。

trea·son [`trizn̩]
◀≒ Track 6330
名 叛逆、謀反 同 betray 背叛
▶It was said that the spy was executed for treason.
據說這名間諜因叛國罪被處死。

trek [trɛk]
◀≒ Track 6331
名 移居 動 長途跋涉
▶名 No matter what he said, I was determined to set off on this long trek.
不管他說什麼，我都決心開始這次的長途旅行。
▶動 You can trek down to the store and buy whatever you like.
你可以慢慢地走到那家商店，買你喜歡的任何東西。

trem·or [`trɛmɚ]
◀≒ Track 6332
名 震動 同 shake 震動
▶The story my grandpa told was so scary that it sent tremors down my spine.
爺爺講的故事太可怕了，它使我不寒而慄。

tres·pass [`trɛspəs]
◀≒ Track 6333
名 犯罪、非法侵入 動 踰越、侵害
▶名 You should sue the man for his trespass.
你應該控告那個人非法侵入。
▶動 There was a sign saying no trespassing, but people ignored it most of the time. 有張「禁止進入」的牌子，但大家大部分的時候都沒在管它。

trig·ger [`trɪgɚ]
◀≒ Track 6334
名 扳機 動 觸發
▶名 The gun went off as soon as I pulled the trigger.
我一扣扳機，槍就響了。
▶動 His interest in art was triggered by a movie.
他對藝術的興趣是受到一部電影觸發。

文法字詞解析
如果你一旦聽到某件事就會感覺有如心中某個機關被「觸發」了一樣渾身不舒服，就可以將這件事稱為你的「trigger」。例如有的人不喜歡被說胖，聽到任何人講到胖這個字都會不開心，這時「胖」就是他的「trigger」。

tri·um·phant [traɪˋʌmfənt]
◀≒ Track 6335
形 勝利的、成功的 同 successful 成功的
▶There are some defeats more triumphant than victories.
有些戰敗比勝利更值得慶祝。

Level 1
Level 2
Level 3
Level 4
Level 5
Level 6

突破瓶頸7000單字 精進自我、聽說讀寫通

triv·i·al [ˈtrɪvɪəl]　🔊 *Track 6336*

形 平凡的、淺薄的 同 superficial 淺薄的

▶Will you tell me why she got angry over such trivial matters?
你能告訴我她為什麼要為這種瑣事生氣嗎？

tro·phy [ˈtrofɪ]　🔊 *Track 6337*

名 戰利品、獎品

▶She won't win a trophy for shooting（射擊）unless she keeps practicing every day.
除非她每天持續訓練，否則她在射擊比賽中將得不到獎。

trop·ic [ˈtrɑpɪk]　🔊 *Track 6338*

名 回歸線 形 熱帶的

▶名 The botanist spent several months doing research in the tropics.
植物學家花了好幾個月在熱帶地區做研究。

▶形 He has been to many tropic countries these years.
這幾年他去過很多熱帶國家。

> **文法字詞解析**
> Tropic of Cancer 是北回歸線，而相反地南回歸線則是 Tropic of Capricorn。

tru·ant [ˈtruənt]　🔊 *Track 6339*

名 蹺課者 形 曠課的、蹺課的 同 absent 缺席的

▶名 You are not supposed to play truant.
你不應該蹺課的。

▶形 These children are likely to be truant.
這些孩子很可能蹺課。

truce [trus]　🔊 *Track 6340*

名 停戰、休戰、暫停 同 pause 暫停

▶Not all people were in favor of the declaration of a truce at that time. 那時並不是所有人都贊成宣佈停戰。

tu·ber·cu·lo·sis [tjʊˌbɝkjəˈlosɪs]　🔊 *Track 6341*

名 肺結核

▶His tuberculosis is so serious that he can't be cured at all.
他的肺病已嚴重到無法治療的地步了。

tu·mor [ˈtjumɚ]　🔊 *Track 6342*

名 腫瘤、瘤

▶A surgery will be performed to remove the brain tumor of the patient. 有一場手術會被進行，幫病人切除腫瘤。

tur·moil [ˈtɝmɔɪl]　🔊 *Track 6343*

名 騷擾、騷動 同 noise 喧鬧

▶It is reported that the town is in turmoil during this election.
根據報導，該城鎮在選舉期間陷入了混亂。

twi·light [ˈtwaɪˌlaɪt]　🔊 *Track 6344*

名 黎明、黃昏 同 dusk 黃昏

▶It's twilight already, so we'd better go home.
黃昏了，我們還是回家吧。

tyr·an·ny [ˈtɪrənɪ]　🔊 Track 6345

名 殘暴、專橫
▶They fight against the tyranny together in order to attain freedom. 為了獲取自由，他們共同一起對抗專政。

[Uu]

ul·cer [ˈʌlsɚ]　🔊 Track 6346

名 潰瘍、弊病
▶His stomach ulcer caused great pain.
他胃潰瘍，很痛。

ul·ti·mate [ˈʌltəmɪt]　🔊 Track 6347

名 基本原則 形 最後的、最終的 同 final 最後的
▶名 To me, that song was the ultimate. No other song could ever beat it. 對我來說，那首歌是最終極的好歌，沒有哪首歌能贏得過它。
▶形 Even though we suffered many defeats, we won the ultimate victory in the end.
儘管遭受了多次失敗，我們最終還是取得了勝利。

u·nan·i·mous [juˈnænəməs]　🔊 Track 6348

形 一致的、和諧的
▶She was elected by a unanimous vote.
她獲得一致同意而當選。

文法字詞解析
要特別注意這個字的發音喔！它的 un- 和其他 un- 開頭的單字發音完全不一樣。

un·cov·er [ʌnˈkʌvɚ]　🔊 Track 6349

動 掀開、揭露 同 expose 揭露
▶It was the two young reporters who uncovered the whole plot.
是這兩名年輕記者揭露了整樁陰謀。

un·der·es·ti·mate　🔊 Track 6350

[ˈʌndɚˈɛstəmɪt]/[ˈʌndɚˈɛstəmet]
動 低估
▶I underestimated the time we needed to finish the task.
我低估了要完成這項任務所需的時間。

un·der·go [ˌʌndɚˈgo]　🔊 Track 6351

動 度過、經歷
▶It is said that this city underwent great changes.
據說這座城市經歷了巨大的變化。

文法字詞解析
undergo 的動詞變化：
undergo, underwent, undergone

un·der·mine [ˌʌndɚˈmaɪn]　🔊 Track 6352

動 削弱基礎 同 destroy 破壞
▶It is obvious that the bad cold had undermined her health.
顯然重感冒損傷了她的健康。

Level 1
Level 2
Level 3
Level 4
Level 5
Level 6

突破瓶頸7000單字　精進自我、聽說讀寫通

un·der·take [ˌʌndɚˈtek] 🔊 *Track 6353*
動 承擔、擔保、試圖　**同** attempt 試圖
▶The work was undertaken by members of the committee.
這項工作由委員會成員承擔。

un·do [ʌnˈdu] 🔊 *Track 6354*
動 消除、取消、解開　**反** bind 捆綁
▶The knot was fastened too tightly to undo.
這個結繫得太緊了，根本解不開。

文法字詞解析
undo 的動詞變化：undo, undid, undone

un·em·ploy·ment [ˌʌnɪmˈplɔɪmənt] 🔊 *Track 6355*
名 失業、失業率
▶The unemployment rate remained high after the new president took the office.
失業率在新總統上任後還是很高。

un·fold [ʌnˈfold] 🔊 *Track 6356*
動 攤開、打開　**同** reveal 揭示
▶Why don't we unfold the letter and read it before making a decision?
我們為什麼不拆開信讀一讀然後再做決定呢？

u·ni·fy [ˈjunəˌfaɪ] 🔊 *Track 6357*
動 使一致、聯合　**同** combine 聯合
▶It's almost impossible for us to be unified against the enemy.
我們幾乎不可能聯合起來對抗敵人。

un·lock [ʌnˈlɑk] 🔊 *Track 6358*
動 開鎖、揭開
▶It is obvious that we can't unlock the door because we don't have the key.
很顯然我們無法打開門鎖，因為沒有鑰匙。

un·pack [ʌnˈpæk] 🔊 *Track 6359*
動 解開、卸下　**同** discharge 卸下
▶Let's unpack before we go into the house, shall we?
我們卸下行李後再進房子去吧，好嗎？

文法字詞解析
上面幾個單字都可以看到字首「-un」，相信看了這麼多例子後都能猜出它的意思了：「-un」的意思就是「相反」，所以前面加上「-un」的字，就是和那個單字原本的意思相反。

up·bring·ing [ˈʌpˌbrɪŋɪŋ] 🔊 *Track 6360*
名 養育、教養
▶Her aptitude and upbringing led her to become a professional pianist.
她的性向和教養背景使她成為專業的鋼琴手。

up·grade [ˈʌpˌgred]/[ˌʌpˈgred] 🔊 *Track 6361*
名 增加、向上、升級　**動** 改進、提高、升級　**同** promote 升級
▶**名** I'm afraid that this computer requires an upgrade.
恐怕這台電腦需要升級了。
▶**動** I think you have to upgrade your computer software.
我覺得你得幫你的電腦軟體升級了。

up·hold [ʌpˋhold]

Track 6362

動 支持、支撐

▶It is obvious that I cannot uphold such conduct.
我當然不能贊成這種行為。

文法字詞解析
uphold 的動詞變化：
uphold, upheld, upheld

u·ra·ni·um [juˋrenɪəm]

Track 6363

名 鈾

▶It is illegal for people to trade uranium in some countries.
在某些國家買賣鈾是非法的。

ur·gen·cy [ˋɝdʒənsɪ]

Track 6364

名 迫切、急迫

▶The urgency alarm sound astonished the passengers.
緊急鈴聲嚇到乘客。

u·rine [ˋjʊrɪn]

Track 6365

名 尿、小便

▶Did you have a urine test yet?
你驗尿了沒？

ush·er [ˋʌʃɚ]

Track 6366

名 引導員 動 招待、護送

▶名 Why don't you let the usher seat them in the front row?
為什麼不讓帶位的人帶領他們去前排就座呢？

▶動 He quickly ushered us into the room.
他很快地把我們招入進房間裡。

u·ten·sil [juˋtɛnsḷ]

Track 6367

名 用具、器皿 同 implement 用具

▶I'm afraid that I have to buy new cooking utensils, because these are too shabby.
恐怕我得去買些新的器皿了，因為這些太破舊了。

u·til·i·ty [juˋtɪlətɪ]

Track 6368

名 效用、有用

▶It looks like their research project has limited practical utility.
看來他們研究的實際效用很有限。

文法字詞解析
多功能的小刀即可稱為 utility knife。

u·ti·lize [ˋjutḷͺaɪz]

Track 6369

動 利用、派上用場

▶She tried several ways to utilize the geothermal energy.
她試了好幾個可以利用地熱能源的方式。

ut·most [ˋʌtͺmost]

Track 6370

名 最大可能、極度 形 極端的 同 extreme 極端的

▶名 They have done their utmost to learn the techniques of production. 他們盡了最大努力去學習生產技術。

▶形 Conservation of natural resources is of the utmost importance.
保護自然資源顯然是至關重要的。

Level 1
Level 2
Level 3
Level 4
Level 5
Level 6

突破瓶頸7000單字 精進自我、聽說讀寫通

[Vv]

vac·cine [ˋvæksɪn]　　🔊 Track 6371
名 疫苗
▶Will you tell me how much polio（小兒麻痺症）vaccines cost?
　請告訴我小兒麻痺疫苗的費用是多少好嗎？

val·iant [ˋvæljənt]　　🔊 Track 6372
形 勇敢的　同 brave 勇敢的
▶She made a valiant attempt to rescue the drowned children.
　她英勇地嘗試去救溺水的小孩。

val·id [ˋvælɪd]　　🔊 Track 6373
形 有根據的、有效的
▶Is this contract still valid?
　這合約還有效嗎？

文法字詞解析
相反地，「無效的」、「已經沒效的」則可以說 invalid。

va·lid·i·ty [vəˋlɪdətɪ]　　🔊 Track 6374
名 正當、正確　同 justice 正義
▶What he said had no validity at all.
　他說的話毫無可信度。

va·ni·lla [vəˋnɪlə]　　🔊 Track 6375
名 香草
▶Would you like to add a teaspoon（茶匙）of vanilla extract to the tea?
　你要不要在茶裡加一茶匙的香草香精呢？

var·i·a·ble [ˋvɛrɪəbl]　　🔊 Track 6376
形 不定的、易變的
▶Prices are variable according to the rate of exchange in most countries.
　大部分國家的物價都是隨匯率而變動的。

文法字詞解析
做實驗時會用到的「變因」也可以稱為 variable。

var·i·a·tion [ˏvɛrɪˋeʃən]　　🔊 Track 6377
名 變動
▶There are variations in prices of tickets to the exhibition.
　這個展覽的票價在各通路不一樣。

vend [vɛnd]　　🔊 Track 6378
動 叫賣、販賣
▶Would you please buy me a Coke from that vending machine?
　你能幫我到那台販賣機買一罐可樂嗎？

ven·dor [ˋvɛndɚ]　　🔊 Track 6379
名 攤販、小販
▶Let's buy some newspaper copies from the vendor across the street.
　我們到對街的攤販那裡買幾份報紙吧。

verge [vɝdʒ]　　🔊 Track 6380

名 邊際、邊　動 接近、逼近　同 edge 邊緣
▶名 It is said that the firm is on the verge of bankruptcy.
據說這家公司正瀕臨破產。
▶動 He's verging on a nervous breakdown.
他正瀕臨精神崩潰。

ver·sa·tile [ˈvɝsətl]　　🔊 Track 6381

形 多才的、多用途的　同 competent 能幹的
▶The versatile actor had taken both benevolent roles and villains.
多才多藝的演員曾演過好人角色、也演過壞人。

ver·sion [ˈvɝʒən]　　🔊 Track 6382

名 說法、版本　同 edition 版本
▶You'd better read its English version. It would be more helpful to you.
你最好讀一下它的英文版。這樣對你會更有幫助。

vet·er·an [ˈvɛtərən]　　🔊 Track 6383

名 老手、老練者　同 specialist 專家
▶You have to consult a veteran doctor about your illness, or it will get worse.
你得找一位經驗老到的醫生幫你看病，要不然你的病情會加重的。

vet·er·i·nar·i·an / vet　　🔊 Track 6384
[ˌvɛtərəˈnɛrɪən]/[vɛt]

名 獸醫
▶I've tried every treatment the vet suggested.
獸醫建議的每一種治療方法我都試過了。

vi·bra·tion [vaɪˈbreʃən]　　🔊 Track 6385

名 震動
▶Fish and amphibians can sense subtle vibration of the ground.
魚和兩棲動物對於地面震動很敏感。

vice [vaɪs]　　🔊 Track 6386

名 不道德的行為　反 virtue 美德
▶Despite all his vices, he's quite a nice person.
雖然他做過一些壞事，他還是個不錯的人。

vi·cious [ˈvɪʃəs]　　🔊 Track 6387

形 邪惡的、不道德的
▶The vicious animal attacked the children.
那隻兇惡的動物攻擊了孩子們。

文法字詞解析
有個和 vicious 長得很像的形容詞 viscous，是「有黏性的」、「黏滑的」的意思，別搞混了。

vic·tim·ize [ˈvɪktɪmˌaɪz]　　🔊 Track 6388

動 使受騙、使受苦
▶He victimized me by stealing my money.
他騙了我，偷了我的錢。

Level 1
Level 2
Level 3
Level 4
Level 5
Level 6

突破瓶頸7000單字　精進自我、聽說讀寫通

vic·tor [ˈvɪktɚ]
🔊 Track 6389

名 勝利者、戰勝者 同 winner 勝利者
▶The victor of the match will advance to the next round.
這場比賽的獲勝者會晉級到下一輪。

vic·to·ri·ous [vɪkˈtorɪəs]
🔊 Track 6390

形 得勝的、凱旋的
▶He gave me a victorious look after winning the bet.
他打賭贏了，給我一個勝利的眼神。

vil·la [ˈvɪlə]
🔊 Track 6391

名 別墅
▶It is said that the villa is famous for its style.
據說這所別墅以其風格而著名。

vine·yard [ˈvɪnjɚd]
🔊 Track 6392

名 葡萄園
▶It seems they are planning to arrange a visit to the local vineyards.
他們似乎正在計畫安排去當地葡萄園參觀的事情。

vir·tu·al [ˈvɝtʃʊəl]
🔊 Track 6393

形 事實上的、實質上的 同 actual 事實上的
▶It is said that the virtual ruler of this country is the president's wife. 據說這個國家實質上的統治者是總統的妻子。

vi·su·al·ize [ˈvɪʒʊəˌlaɪz]
🔊 Track 6394

動 使可見、使具形象 同 fancy 想像
▶It is hard for me to visualize how the place might have looked in the past.
我很難想像這個地方過去會是什麼樣子。

vi·tal·i·ty [vaɪˈtælətɪ]
🔊 Track 6395

名 生命力、活力
▶The vitality of the woman who is in her seventies surprised us.
這位七十多歲的女士相當有精神，讓我們很驚訝。

vo·cal [ˈvokl̩]
🔊 Track 6396

名 母音 形 聲音的
▶名 He not only plays the guitar in his band but also does vocals. 他在他的樂團裡不但彈吉他，也唱歌。
▶形 I wish you weren't so vocal about some things.
我真希望你對於某些事不要這麼急於發表意見。

vo·ca·tion [voˈkeʃən]
🔊 Track 6397

名 職業 同 occupation 職業
▶Nursing is a vocation as well as a responsibility.
護理工作既是職業又是責任。

文法字詞解析
大家所說的 VR（虛擬實境）科技就是 virtual reality。

vo·ca·tion·al [voˈkeʃənl̩]　◀≣ Track 6398
形 職業上的、業務的　同 professional 專業的、職業上的
▶Not everyone thinks vocational training will help them find a good job.
不是每個人都認為職業培訓能使他們找到一份好的工作。

vogue [vog]　◀≣ Track 6399
名 時尚、流行物　同 fashion 時尚
▶The vague image made it impossible for use to tell the identity of the culprit.
這模糊的影像讓我們沒辦法判斷真兇的身分。

vom·it [ˈvɑmɪt]　◀≣ Track 6400
名 嘔吐、催嘔藥　動 嘔吐、噴出
▶名 She saw his vomit on the bus and threw up too.
她在公車上看見了他的嘔吐物，結果也吐了。
▶動 She got ill and vomited all the food she ate.
她生病了，把所有她吃的食物都吐出來了。

vul·gar [ˈvʌlgɚ]　◀≣ Track 6401
形 粗糙的、一般的　反 decent 體面的
▶The story was vulgar but very popular.
這故事很不雅，但很受歡迎。

vul·ner·a·ble [ˈvʌlnərəbl̩]　◀≣ Track 6402
形 易受傷害的、脆弱的　同 sensitive 易受傷害的
▶The child was still young and vulnerable.
那個孩子還很小、很脆弱。

[Ww]

ward·robe [ˈwɔrdˌrob]　◀≣ Track 6403
名 衣櫃、衣櫥　同 closet 衣櫥
▶I'm afraid that the wardrobe takes up too much space.
恐怕這個衣櫥太佔空間了。

war·fare [ˈwɔrˌfɛr]　◀≣ Track 6404
名 戰爭、競爭
▶She works hard for the welfare of the poor.
她努力爭取窮人的福利。

war·ran·ty [ˈwɔrəntɪ]　◀≣ Track 6405
名 依據、正當的理由
▶Do you mind telling me how long the warranty period is?
能麻煩您告訴我保固期是多久嗎？

文法字詞解析
除了 vomit 外，throw up、puke 都可以表達「嘔吐」的意思。

Level 1
Level 2
Level 3
Level 4
Level 5
Level 6

突破瓶頸7000單字　精進自我、聽說讀寫通

wa·ter·proof/ wa·ter·tight [`wɔtɚ`pruf]/[`wɔtɚ`taɪt]
🔲形 防水的 🔲同 resistant 防……的
▶I want to buy a waterproof watch.
　我想買一隻防水手錶。
◀≤ *Track 6406*

what·so·ev·er [͵hwɑtso`ɛvɚ]
🔲形 任何的 🔲代 不論什麼 🔲同 however 無論如何
▶🔲形 You can take whatsoever options you like.
　　你可以照你的意思，做出任何選擇。
▶🔲代 Don't worry. She would not miss the grand finale whatsoever.
　　不用擔心。她無論如何會來看壓軸表演的。
◀≤ *Track 6407*

wind·shield [`wɪnd͵ʃild]
🔲名 擋風玻璃
▶It is dangerous for you to drive with a dirty windshield.
　你開一輛擋風玻璃髒了的車子是很危險的。
◀≤ *Track 6408*

文法字詞解析
用來擦擋風玻璃的雨刷稱為 windshield wiper。

with·stand [wɪθ`stænd]
🔲動 耐得住、經得起 🔲同 resist 忍耐
▶I don't think that I could withstand the heat.
　我覺得我受不了那樣的溫度。
◀≤ *Track 6409*

wit·ty [`wɪtɪ]
🔲形 機智的、詼諧的 🔲同 clever 機敏的
▶I like the witty host in the program very much.
　我非常喜歡這個節目中風趣的主持人。
◀≤ *Track 6410*

woo [wu]
🔲動 求婚、求愛、爭取……的支持
▶Politicians try to woo the voters before an election.
　政治家們在選前力爭選民的支持。
◀≤ *Track 6411*

wrench [rɛntʃ]
🔲名 扭轉 🔲動 猛扭 🔲同 wring 擰、扭斷
▶🔲名 I used a wrench to fix the broken door.
　　我用扳手修好了壞掉的門。
▶🔲動 He wrenched his ankle during the training on the field.
　　他在場上受訓時扭傷腳踝。
◀≤ *Track 6412*

wres·tle [`rɛsl̩]
🔲動 角力、搏鬥 🔲同 struggle 奮鬥
▶I love watching wrestling matches.
　我很愛看摔角比賽。
◀≤ *Track 6413*

[Xx]

Xe·rox/xe·rox [`zɪrɑks]

◀≀ *Track 6414*

名 全錄影印 動 以全錄影印法影印

▶名 Will you help get a Xerox of the material on the desk for me?
　　請你幫忙把辦公桌上的那些資料複印給我好嗎？

▶動 Can you please Xerox the two letters for me, Susan?
　　蘇珊，請妳把這兩封信各複印一份給我好嗎？

文法字詞解析
注意這個字的唸法，它的第一個子音比較接近「z」的發音喔！

[Yy]

yearn [jɜn]

◀≀ *Track 6415*

動 懷念、想念、渴望

▶She yearned to visit the hometown of Shakespeare.
　她渴望去探訪莎士比亞的故鄉。

[Zz]

zeal [zil]

◀≀ *Track 6416*

名 熱誠、熱忱

▶He had great zeal for basketball-related activities.
　他對於和籃球相關的活動都超有熱忱。

Level 1

Level 2

Level 3

Level 4

Level 5

Level 6

精進自我、聽說讀寫通——突破瓶頸7000單字

Level 6 程度檢測閱讀練習

下面有五篇文章,全是根據Level1-6的單字寫出來的,文章中超出level6的單字,有註記在一旁。

請先不要看全文的中文翻譯,試著讀讀看這兩篇文章,若能全盤了解意思,代表你對 Level6 單字已經駕輕就熟囉!快來自我挑戰看看吧!

Reading Practice 1

Productivity, in economics, measures output per unit of input, such as labor, capital, or any other resource. It is typically calculated for the economy as a whole, as a ratio of gross domestic product (GDP) to hours worked. Labor productivity may be further broken down by sector to examine trends in labor growth, wage levels and technological improvement. Corporate profits and shareholder returns are directly linked to productivity growth.

At the corporate level, productivity is a measure of the efficiency of a company's production process. From this perspective, it is calculated by measuring the number of units produced relative to employee labor hours. It can also be calculated by measuring a company's net sales relative to employee labor hours. The statistics may be helpful for the executive officers when they adjust operational strategies.

Reading Practice 2

Screenwriter, Rowan Sebastian Atkinson, was born on 6 January 1955 in a small town in England. He is best known for his work on the TV series Mr. Bean and Blackadder. Atkinson has been listed in The Observer as one of the 50 most amusing actors in British comedy. He was also ranked among the top 50 comedians ever in a 2005 poll of contemporary comedians.

Atkinson got a master's degree in Electrical Engineering at the Queen's College, Oxford. While studying there, he started performing his first sketches. Later, he started performing in theater. He reached success in TV performances such as Not the Nine O'clock News (1979-82), Blackadder (1983-89), and the Thin Blue line (1995-96). Atkinson became world renowned by writing scripts and starring the TV sitcom Mt. Bean (1990-95). The series of Mr. Bean has enabled his character to secure a place in the popular culture of several countries. Many people even pay tribute to him by making videos mimicking his performance.

Reading Practice 3

Comprehensive lifestyle changes, including a better diet and more exercise, can lead not only to a better physical condition, but also to swift and dramatic changes at the genetic level.

U.S. researchers published a study to support this theory. They tracked 30 men with low-risk cancer who decided against conventional medical treatment such as surgery, radiation, or hormone therapy. They underwent three months of major lifestyle changes as they changed their diet, did moderate exercise, and employed daily stress management methods like meditation. Researchers compared prostate biopsies taken before and after the lifestyle was adjusted and found profound changes. According to the comparison, the activity of disease-preventing genes increased, while the disease-promoting genes were shut down.

The researcher was led by Dr. Dean Ornish, head of the preventive Medicine Research Institute in Sausalito, California, and a well-know author advocating lifestyle changes. He reminded the public of the implication of the study: the benefits of healthy lifestyle are not limited to cancer patients; it may be generalized to everyone.

Reading Practice 4

The food a person purchases is usually inside a box or other container which includes a food label printed on the outside. A food label is used to show the buyer the nutrients, vitamins, and other minerals found in the ingredients of the food. Food labels are also referred to as nutrition labels.

The labels show what everyone needs to know, including the serving size, calories, nutrients and their daily values in a diet. The ingredients and number of servings inside the package is also manifested on the label.

There are basically six groups of nutrients that work together to keep a person's body healthy, including carbohydrates, fats, proteins, vitamins, mineral,

Level 1

Level 2

Level 3

Level 4

Level 5

Level 6

突破瓶頸7000單字 精進自我、聽說讀寫通

and water. Nutrients listed on the label include total fat, saturated(飽 和) fat, cholesterol and sodium. Other nutrients that people need may include fiber, vitamin A and C, calcium, and iron. A person should try to eat 100% of these nutrients each day.

Reading Practice 5

Hypertension, also called high blood pressure, is a chronic medical condition in which the blood pressure in the arteries is persistently elevated. High blood pressure usually does not cause symptoms. Long-term high pressure, however, is a major risk for many illnesses such as coronary artery disease, stroke, heart failure, peripheral (周邊) vascular(動脈) disease, vision loss, and dementia(老 年痴呆).

There are two major types of hypertension: primary (essential) high blood pressure and secondary high blood pressure. According to statistics, about 90-95% of cases are primary hypertension, which is related to certain lifestyle such as excess salt in diet, smoking, and alcohol use. The remaining 5-10% of cases belong to the secondary high blood pressure. The causes are not specified, but it may be related to chronic kidney disease, narrowing of the kidney arteries, and hormone disorder.

Blood pressure is expressed by two measurements, the systolic and diastolic pressures, which are the maximum and minimum pressure respectively. When an adult's resting blood pressure is persistently at or above 130/90 mmHg, hypertension is present. Then, lifestyle changes such as decreased salt consumption and physical exercise, along with treatment of moderately high arterial blood pressure would be necessary to improve life longevity.

Level
1

Level
2

Level
3

Level
4

Level
5

Level
6

Reading Practice1 中譯

在經濟學中，生產力測量的是，每個輸入的單位，像是勞力、資金、或是其他任何類型的資源，可以達成多少個輸出單位。通常，生產力是以整個經濟體為單位，像是國內生產總值 (GDP) 對應所有工作時數的比率。勞動生產力可以再根據產業類型細分，以檢視勞動力成長、薪資等級、以及科技進步的趨勢。企業的利潤以及股東的分紅，都和生產力能否成長息息相關。

就企業角度來看，生產力就是測量一個公司生產過程的效率。從這個角度來看，生產力就是算出每個員工在上班時每小時可以產出多少的成果。它也用公司總營收除以員工的工作總時數的結果來看。這個數據可以幫助公司執行長們思考如何調整營運策略。

Reading Practice2 中譯

劇作家羅溫 ‧ 賽巴斯汀 ‧ 艾金森，1955 年 1 月 6 日出生於英格蘭的一個小鎮。他最有名的作品是電視節目〈豆豆先生〉以及〈黑爵士〉。艾金森被《觀察》雜誌譽為在英國喜劇中最有趣的演員。他在 2005 年一項針對當代所有喜劇演員的調查中，也是排在前五十名的喜劇演員。

艾金森在牛津大學皇后校區取得了電子工程學位。在念書時，他開始表演一些橋段。之後，他進入劇場表演。他後來成功在影視界發展，代表作有〈非九點新聞〉(1979-82)、〈黑爵士〉(1983-89)、〈細細的藍線〉(1995-96) 等。艾金森開始寫腳本以及主演電視連續劇〈豆豆先生〉(1990-95)，變得全球知名。豆豆先生這個角色在好幾個國家文化中都佔有一席之地。許多人甚至會錄製模仿豆豆先生的影片向艾金森致敬。

Reading Practice3 中譯

全面改變生活方式，包括注意飲食以及更常運動，不僅可以帶來更好的體能狀態，還能以快速、大幅地改善基因的狀態。

美國有研究者發布一篇研究支持這個論點。他們追蹤三十位病情風險較低的癌症病患，他們不想接受傳統的手術、輻射或賀爾蒙療程。這些病患花三個月的時間，大幅改變生活型態，包括改變飲食、適當運動、並且每天進行減壓冥想。研究者將患者在改變生活型態之前和之後的患者細胞切片做比較。根據比較的結果，預防疾病的基因變得比較活躍了，而導致癌症的基因則被關閉了。

這項研究是由加州索薩利托預防醫學研究中心主任、同時也推廣改變生活方式的作家，狄恩 · 歐尼西所主導。他提醒社會大眾這項研究的啟示：改變生活方式不僅在癌症病患身上效果顯著；這個結果可以適用在每個人身上。

Reading Practice4 中譯

我們購買的食物通常是裝在盒子或者其他的容器裡，上面會貼一個標籤。食物標籤目的在讓購買者知道食物成分中有那些營養素、維他命、以及其他礦物質。食物標籤也可以被稱做是營養標籤。

食物標籤會呈現必要的資訊，包括食品分量、熱量、營養素，以及每日建議食用量。包裝中的食物成分及份量也會清楚呈現在標籤上。

一個人維持生體健康所需的營養素基本上有六類：碳水化合物、脂肪、蛋白質、維他命、礦物質、和水。會列在食物標籤上的營養素包括總脂肪量、飽和脂肪、膽固醇，以及鈉。其他人體所需要的營養素還有纖維質、維他命 A 和 C、鈣質、鐵質。每個人每天都應該攝取上述所有的營養素。

Reading Practice5 中譯

高血壓是一種慢性的疾病，患者動脈中的血壓會持續上升。高血壓通常沒有症狀。但是，長期罹患高血壓會造成冠狀動脈疾病、中風、心臟衰竭、周邊動脈疾病、視力模糊、以及老年癡呆的風險。

高血壓大致分為兩種：原發性高血壓與次發性高血壓。數據顯示，百分之 90-95 的病例是原發性高血壓，常和特定的生活方式，如攝取過量鹽分、抽菸、喝酒有關。剩下的百分之 5-10 病例，屬於次發性高血壓。原因還未被釐清，但可能與慢性腎臟病、腎臟動脈窄化、以及賀爾蒙失調有關。

血壓有兩種測量方式，包括收縮壓與舒張壓，各自有最大值與最小值。當一個成人休息狀態下的血壓高於 130/90 毫米汞柱，就是有高血壓。那麼，生活型態改變，像是減少攝取鹽分以及運動，同時針對稍高的動脈血壓接受治療，就會是必要的，可以幫助延長壽命。

NOTE

Level
1

Level
2

Level
3

Level
4

Level
5

Level
6

精進自我、聽說讀寫通──
突破瓶頸7000單字

英語學習 系列 016

全方面破解英文**7000單字**：
萬用例句╳補充句型╳文法解析的必勝三「步」曲

一字多用事半功倍，紅字膠片幫助記憶！

作　　者	張慈庭英語教學團隊
顧　　問	曾文旭
社　　長	王毓芳
編輯統籌	耿文國、黃璽宇
主　　編	吳靜宜
執行主編	潘妍潔
執行編輯	吳芸蓁、范筱翎
美術編輯	王桂芳、張嘉容
行銷企劃	吳欣蓉
封面設計	阿作
法律顧問	北辰著作權事務所　蕭雄淋律師、幸秋妙律師

初　　版	2021年01月初版1刷 2022年初版9刷
出　　版	捷徑文化出版事業有限公司──資料夾文化出版
電　　話	（02）2752-5618
傳　　真	（02）2752-5619

定　　價	新台幣420元／港幣140元
產品內容	1書＋單字記憶紅膠片

總 經 銷	知遠文化事業有限公司
地　　址	222新北市深坑區北深路3段155巷25號5樓
電　　話	（02）2664-8800
傳　　真	（02）2664-8801

港澳地區總經銷	和平圖書有限公司
地　　址	香港柴灣嘉業街12號百樂門大廈17樓
電　　話	（852）2804-6687
傳　　真	（852）2804-6409

▲本書部分圖片由 Shutterstock、123RF提供。

▶ 捷徑 Book站

現在就上臉書（FACEBOOK）「捷徑BOOK站」並按讚加入粉絲團，
就可享每月不定期新書資訊和粉絲專享小禮物喔！

http://www.facebook.com/royalroadbooks
讀者來函：royalroadbooks@gmail.com

國家圖書館出版品預行編目資料

全方面破解英文7000單字：萬用例句╳補充
句型╳文法解析的必勝三「步」曲／張慈庭英
語教學團隊著. -- 初版. -- 臺北市：資料夾文化,
2021.01
　　面；　公分（英語學習：016）
ISBN 978-986-5507-52-7(平裝)
1. 英語　2. 讀本
805.12　　　　　　　　　　　　　109021023